FREE

"The Lark and the Wren . . . [has] a world distinctly different from that of the Heralds of Valdemar. The political intrigues are more complex . . . and there's a subtle weaving of very old Celtic material on the musical side of the plot. . . . It's a good read. . . .
—*Dragon*

"[The Robin and the Kestrel] is a great story; lots of action, mystery, a little romance, and a ghost. . . . All collections should own this book. . . ." —*VOYA*

"[The prose in *The Robin and the Kestrel* is] deft and readable. . . . as lively as one might wish, and the reappearances of the Skull Hill Ghost from *The Lark and the Wren* are especially well-rendered."—
Dragon

"Mercedes Lackey returns to her tales of Free Bards with *The Robin and the Kestrel*. . . . They have to face both a music loving ghost and a town gone gaga over religion in this fun tale."
—*Philadelphia Weekly Press*

"Gypsy encounters and magic permeate a fast-paced fantasy well laced with romance." —*The Bookwatch*

". . . . interesting, well-told, and complete. . . . a fun read and a fix for Lackey fans who have been looking forward to reading further about the Free Bards."
—*ConNotations*

BAEN BOOKS by MERCEDES LACKEY

BARDIC VOICES
The Lark & the Wren
The Robin & the Kestrel
The Eagle & the Nightingales
The Free Bards
Four & Twenty Blackbirds
Bardic Choices: A Cast of Corbies
(with Josepha Sherman)

The Fire Rose
The Ship Who Searched
(with Anne McCaffrey)
Wing Commander: Freedom Flight
(with Ellen Guon)
If I Pay Thee Not in Gold
(with Piers Anthony)

URBAN FANTASIES
Bedlam's Bard (with Ellen Guon)
Beyond World's End (with Rosemary Edghill)

The SERRAted Edge:
Born to Run (with Larry Dixon)
Wheels of Fire (with Mark Shepherd)
The Chrome Borne (with Larry Dixon)
The Otherworld (with Mark Shepherd & Holly Lisle)

THE BARD'S TALE NOVELS
Castle of Deception
(with Josepha Sherman)
Fortress of Frost & Fire
(with Ru Emerson)
Prison of Souls
(with Mark Shepherd)

THE
FREE BARDS

MERCEDES LACKEY

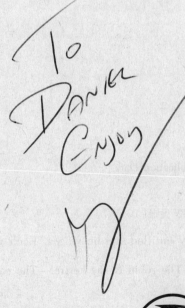

To
Daniel
Enjoy

THE FREE BARDS

This is a work of fiction. All the characters and events portrayed in this book are fictional, and any resemblance to real people or incidents is purely coincidental.

The Free Bards has been published in three parts as *Bardic Voices: The Lark & the Wren* © 1992, *The Robin and the Kestrel* © 1993, and *The Eagle and the Nightingales* © 1995, all by Mercedes Lackey.

All rights reserved, including the right to reproduce this book or portions thereof in any form.

A Baen Books Original

Baen Publishing Enterprises
P.O. Box 1403
Riverdale, NY 10471
www.baen.com

ISBN: 0-671-87778-X

Cover art by Darrell K. Sweet

First printing, May 1997
Second printing, October 2000

Distributed by Simon & Schuster
1230 Avenue of the Americas
New York, NY 10020

Library of Congress Cataloging-in-Publication Data

Lackey, Mercedes.
  The free bards / Mercedes Lackey.
    p. cm.
  Originally published as a trilogy entitled Bardic voices. Each vol.
    published separately.
  Contents: The lark & the wren—The robin & the kestrel—The eagle
    & the nightingales.
  ISBN 0-671-87778-X (trade pb)
  1. Bards and bardism—Fiction. 2. Fantastic fiction, American. I. Title.
PS3562.A246F7   1997
813'.54—dc21
                                                              97-637
                                                                CIP

Printed in the United States of America

CONTENTS

Book I
~The~
Lark and
the Wren

Dedicated to
Ellen Guon:
writer, musician, and lady of quality
And to those who dream, then work to make
their dream a reality

CHAPTER ONE

The attic cubicle was dark and stuffy, two conditions the tiny window under the eaves did little to alleviate. Rune reached up to the shelf over her pallet for her fiddle case, and froze with her hand less than an inch away. Her mother's nasal whine echoed up the stairs from the tavern sleeping rooms below.

"Rune? Rune!"

Rune sighed, and her hand dropped to her side. "Yes, Mother?" she called over her shoulder. She'd hoped to get a little practice in before the evening customers began to file in.

"Have you swept the tavern and scrubbed the tables?" When Stara said "the tavern," she meant the common room. The kitchen was not in Rune's purview. The cook, Annie, who was also the stableman's wife, reigned supreme there, and permitted no one within her little kingdom but herself and her aged helper, known only as Granny.

"No, Mother," Rune called down, resignedly. "I thought Maeve—"

"Maeve's doing the rooms. Get your behind down there. The sooner you get it over with, the sooner you can get on with that foolish scraping of yours." Then, as an afterthought, as Rune reached the top step, "And don't call me 'Mother.'"

"Yes M—Stara." Stifling another sigh, Rune plodded down the steep, dark attic stairs, hardly more than a ladder down the back wall. As she passed the open doors, she heard Maeve's tuneless humming and the slow scrape of a broom coming from the one on her right. From the bottom, she crossed the hall to the real stairs taking them two at a time down into the common room.

The shutters on the windows on two sides of the room had been flung wide to the brisk spring air; a light breeze slowly cleared out the last of the beer fumes. A half-worn broom leaned against the bar at the back of the room, where Maeve had undoubtedly left it when Stara ordered her upstairs. Rune took it; her first glance around had told her that nothing more had been accomplished except to open the shutters. The benches were still stacked atop the tables, and the latter pushed against the walls; the fireplace was still full of last night's ashes. Nothing had been cleaned or put into order, and the only sign that the tavern was opening for business was the open shutters. Probably because that was all anyone had thought to tell Maeve to do.

Rune went to the farthest corner of the room and started sweeping, digging the worn bristles of the broom firmly against the floorboards. The late Rose, wife of Innkeeper Jeoff, had called Maeve "an innocent." Annie said she was "a little simple."

What Stara called her was "a great lump."

Poor Maeve was all of those, Rune reflected. She lived in a world all her own, that was certain. She could—and did, if left to her own devices—stand in a window for hours, humming softly with no discernible tune, staring at nothing. But if you gave her clear orders, she would follow them to the exact letter. Told to sweep out a room, she would do so. That room, and no more, leaving a huge pile of dirt on the threshold. Told to wash the dishes, she would wash the dishes all right, but not the pots, nor the silverware, and she wouldn't rinse them afterwards. Of course, if anyone interrupted her in the middle of her task, she would drop what she was doing, follow the new instructions, and never return to the original job.

Still, without her help, Rune would have a lot more to do. She'd never have time to practice her fiddling.

Rune attacked the dirt of the floor with short, angry strokes, wishing she could sweep the troubles of her life out as easily. Not that life here was bad, precisely—

"Rune?" Stara called down the stairs. "Are you sweeping? I can't hear you."

"Yes M—Stara," Rune replied. The worn bristles were too soft to scrape the floor the way Maeve's broom was doing, but it was pointless to say anything about it.

So Stara didn't want to be called "Mother" anymore. Rune bit her lip in vexation. Did she really think that if Rune stopped referring to her as "Mother" people would forget their relationship?

Not here, Rune told herself sourly. *Not when my existence is such a pointed example of why good girls don't do That without wedding banns being posted.*

Even though Stara was from a village far from here—even though she wore the braids of a married woman and claimed that Rune's father had been a journeyman muleteer killed by bandits—most of the village guessed the real truth. That Stara was no lawfully wedded widow; that Rune was a bastard.

Stara had been a serving wench in the home of a master silversmith, and had let the blandishments of a peddler with a glib tongue and ready money lure her into his bed. The immediate result had been a silver locket and scarlet ribbons from his pack. The long-term result was a growing belly, and the loss of her place.

Stara lived on the charity of the Church for a time, but no longer than she had to. After Rune had been born, Stara had packed up her belongings and her meager savings, and set out on foot as far as her money would take her, hoping to find some place where her charm, her ability to wheedle, and her soft blond prettiness would win her sympathy, protection, and a new and better place.

Rune suspected that she had soon discovered—much to her shock—that while her looks, as always, won her the sympathy of the males of the households she sought employment with, she got no favor from the females. Certainly on the rare occasions when she talked to her daughter about those long-ago days, she had railed against the "jealous old bitches" who had turned her out again after they discovered what their spouses had hired.

And so would I have, Rune thought wryly, as the pile of dirt in front of her broom grew to the size of her closed fist. The girl Stara had been was all too likely to have a big belly again as soon as she'd wormed her way into the household. And this time, the result would have been sure to favor the looks of the master of the house. She had no credentials, no references—instead of applying properly to the women of the household, she went straight to the men. *Stupid, Mother. But then, you never have paid any attention to women when there were men around.*

But finally Stara had wound up here, at the "Hungry Bear." The innkeeper's wife, Rose, was of a credulous, generous and forgiving nature; Innkeeper Jeoff a pious Churchman, and charitable. That alone might not have earned her the place as the serving-maid in the tavern. But luck had been with her this time; their pot-boy had signed with the army and gone off to the city and there was no one in the village willing or able to take his place. Stara's arrival, even encumbered as she was, must have seemed like a gift from God, and they had needed her desperately enough to take her story at face value.

Although the villagers guessed most of the tale easily enough, they too were obliged to accept the false story, (outwardly, at least) since Jeoff and Rose did. But Rune was never allowed to forget the truth. Stara threw it in Rune's face every time she was angry about anything—and the village children had lost no opportunity to imply she was a bastard for as long as she could remember.

They only said openly what their parents thought. Stara didn't seem to care, wearing low-cut blouses and kilted-up skirts when she went into the village on errands, flirting with the men and ignoring the sneers of the women. Back in the tavern, under Rose's eye, however, she had pulled the drawstrings of her blouses tight and let her skirts down, acting demure and briskly businesslike in all her dealings with males. Rune had more than once heard Rose defending her foundling to her friends among the villagers, telling Jeoff afterwards that they were just envious because of Stara's youth and attractiveness.

And that much was certainly true. The village women *were* jealous. Stara was enough to excite any woman's jealousy, other than a tolerant, easy-going lady like Rose, with her long, blond hair, her plump prettiness, her generous breasts and her willingness to display her charms to any eye that cared to look. Of course, none of this did any good at all for her reputation in the village, but Stara didn't seem to concern herself over trifles like what the villagers thought.

It was left to Rune to bear the brunt of her mother's reputation, to try to ignore the taunts and the veiled glances. Stara didn't care about that, either. So long as nothing touched or inconvenienced her directly, Stara was relatively content.

Only relatively, since Stara was not happy with her life as it was, and frequently voiced her complaints in long, after-hours monologues to her daughter, with little regard for whether or not Rune was going to suffer from loss of sleep the next day.

Last night had been one of those nights, and Rune yawned hugely as she swept.

Rune wasn't precisely certain what her mother wanted—besides a life of complete leisure. Just what Stara had done to deserve such a life eluded Rune—but Stara seemed to feel quite strongly that she deserved it. And had gone on at aggrieved and shrill length about it last night. . . .

Rune yawned again, and swept the last of the night's trod-in dirt out into the road. It would, of course, find its way right back inside tonight; only in the great cities were the streets paved and kept clean. It was enough that the road through the village was graveled and graded, from one end to the other. It kept down the mud, and kept ruts to a minimum.

As well wish for Stara to become a pious churchgoer as to wish for a paved road. The second was likelier to occur than the first.

Rune propped the broom in a corner by the fireplace and emptied the ashes and clinkers into the ash-pit beneath the fireplace floor. Every few months the candle-maker came to collect them from the cellar; once a year the inn got a half-dozen bars of scented soap in exchange. A lot of the inn's supplies came from exchange; strawberries for manure, hay and straw for use of the donkey and pony, help for room and board and clothing.

There were four folk working under that exchange right now; of the six employees only two, Annie Cook and Tarn Hostler, received wages. The rest got only their rooms, two suits of clothing each year, and all they could eat. While Rune had been too young to be of much help, she'd had to share her mother's room, but now that she was pulling her share of her load, she had a room to herself. There wasn't a door, just a curtain, and there was no furniture but the pallet she slept on, but it was hers alone, and she was glad of the privacy. Not that Stara ever brought men up to her room—she wouldn't have dared; even the easy-going Rose would not have put up with that—but it was nice to be able to pull the curtain and pretend the outside world didn't exist.

Provided, of course, Stara didn't whine all night. There was no escaping that.

With the fireplace swept and logs laid ready to light, Rune fetched a pail of water, a bit of coarse brown soap, and a rag from the kitchen, with a nod to Granny, who sat in the corner peeling roots. Annie Cook was nowhere in sight; she was probably down in the cellar. From the brick ovens in the rear wall came a wave of heat and the mouth-watering smell of baking bread. Rune swallowed hard as her stomach growled. Breakfast had been a long time ago, and dinner too far away. She was always hungry these days, probably because she was growing like a sapling—the too-short cuffs of her shirt and breeches gave ample evidence of that.

If I hurry up, maybe I can get Granny to give me a bit of cheese and one of yesterday's loaf-ends before Annie makes them all into bread pudding.

With that impetus in mind, Rune quickly hauled the tables and benches away from the walls, got the benches down in place, and went to work on the tabletops, scouring with a will. Fortunately there weren't any bad stains this time; she got them done faster than she'd expected, and used the last of the soapy water to clean herself up before tossing the bucketful out the door.

But when she returned the bucket to the kitchen, Annie was back up from her journey below.

Her stomach growled audibly as she set the bucket down, and Annie looked up sharply, her round face red with the heat from the oven. "What?" she said, her hair coming loose from its pins and braids, and wisping damply about her head. "You can't be hungry *already*?"

Rune nodded mutely, and tried to look thin and pathetic.

She must have succeeded, for Annie shook her head, shrugged, and pointed her round chin towards the pile of ingredients awaiting her attention. "Two carrots, one loaf-end, and a piece of cheese, and get yerself out of here," the cook said firmly. "More than that can't be spared. And mind that piece is no bigger than your hand."

"Yes, Cook," Rune said meekly—and snatched her prizes before Annie changed her mind. But the cook just chuckled as she cut the cheese. "I should ha' known from yer breeches, darlin', yer into yer growth. Come back later if yer still hungry, an' I'll see if sommat got burnt too much fer the custom."

She thanked Annie with an awkward bob of her head, took her food out into the common room, and devoured it down to the last crumb, waiting all the while for another summons by her mother. But no call came, only the sound of Stara scolding Maeve, and Maeve's humming. Rune sighed with relief; Maeve never paid any attention to anything that wasn't a direct order. Let Stara wear her tongue out on the girl; the scolding would roll right off the poor thing's back—and maybe Stara would leave her own daughter alone, for once.

Rune stuffed that last bite of bread and cheese in her mouth and stole softly up the stairs. If she could just get past the sleeping rooms to get her fiddle—once she began practicing, Stara would probably leave her alone.

After all, she'd done her duty for the day. Sweeping and cleaning the common room was surely enough, especially after all the cleaning she'd done in the kitchen this morning. Sometimes she was afraid that her hands would stiffen from all the scrubbing she had to do. She massaged them with the lotion the farmers used on cow's udders, reckoning that would help, and it seemed to—but she still worried.

From the sound of things in the far room, Stara had decided to turn it out completely. She must have set Maeve to beating the straw tick; that monotonous thumping was definitely following the rhythm of Maeve's humming, and it was a safe enough task for even Maeve to manage. This time she got to her fiddle, and slipped down the stairs without being caught.

She settled herself into a bench in the corner of the room, out of direct line-of-sight of the stairs. It hadn't always been this hard to get her practice in. When Rose was alive, the afternoons had always been her own. Yes, and the evenings, too. As long as Rune helped, Rose had made it very clear that she was to be considered as full an employee as Stara—and Rose had counted entertainment as "helping."

Rose had forbidden Stara—or anyone else—to beat Rune, after the one time Rose had caught her mother taking a stick to her for some trifle.

Rune carefully undid the old clasps on the black leather-and-wood case. They were stiff with age, and hard to get open, but better too stiff than too loose. Rose had taken a special interest in Rune, for some reason. Maybe because Rose had no children of her own. But when Rose died of the cough last winter, everything changed.

At first it hadn't been bad, really; it made sense for Rune to take over some of Stara's duties, since Stara was doing what Rose had done. And work in the winter wasn't that difficult. Hardly anyone came in for mid-meal, there were very few travelers to mess up the rooms, and people came for their beer and a bit of entertainment, but didn't stay late. There wasn't any dirt or mud to be tracked in, just melting snow, which soaked into the old worn floorboards fairly easily. Really, winter work was the lightest of the four seasons, and Rune had assumed that once the initial confusion following Rose's death resolved itself, Jeoff would hire someone else to help. Another boy, perhaps; a boy would be just as useful inside the inn as a girl, and stronger, too. There had even been a couple of boys passing through earlier this month on the way to the hiring fairs who'd looked likely. They'd put in a good day's work for their meal and corner by the fire—and they'd even asked Rune if she thought Jeoff would be interested in hiring them on permanently. But Jeoff always found some excuse not to take them on—and Rune kept losing a little more of her free time with every day that passed.

Now she not only found herself scrubbing and cleaning, she was serving in the common room at night, something she hadn't had to do since she was a good enough fiddler to have people ask her to play. That was one of the reasons the Hungry Bear was so popular; even when there weren't any traveling musicians passing through, people could always count on Rune to give 'em a tune to sing or dance to. Why, people sometimes came from as far away as the next village of Beeford because of her.

But now—she was allowed to play only when the crowds asked Jeoff for her music. If they forgot to ask, if there was no one willing to speak up—then she waited on them just like silly Maeve, while Stara presided in Rose's place over the beer barrels, and Jeoff tended, as always, to the cashbox.

Rune bit her lip, beginning to see a pattern in all this. There were more changes, and they were even more disturbing. There was no doubt in Rune's mind that her mother had set her sights on Jeoff. Aiming, no doubt, for matrimony.

When Rose was alive, Stara had kept herself quietly out of sight, her hair tightly braided and hidden under kerchiefs, wearing her blouse-strings pulled tight, her skirts covering her feet, and keeping her eyes down. Rune knew why, too—Stara flung it in her face often enough. Stara had one bastard; she was not minded to attract the master's eye, only to find herself in his bed and saddled with another bastard.

But since Jeoff put off his mourning bands, Stara had transformed from a drab little sparrow to a bird of a different feather entirely. She was rinsing her hair with herbs every night, to make it yellow as new-minted gold and smell sweet. She had laced the waist of her skirts tight, kilted them up to show ankles and even knees, and pulled her blouses low. And she was painting her face, when she thought no one could see her; red on the lips and cheeks, blackening her lashes with soot, trying to make herself look younger. Where she got the stuff, Rune had no idea. Possibly a peddler, though there hadn't been any with things like that through here since before winter.

Stara didn't like being reminded that she had a fourteen-year-old daughter, and she certainly didn't want Jeoff reminded of the fact. It helped that Rune looked nothing like her mother; Rune was tall, thin, with light brown, curly hair, and deep brown eyes. She could—and occasionally did—pass for a boy in the crowded common-room. She was nothing at all like soft, round, doll-pretty Stara. Which was exactly as Stara wanted things, Rune was sure of it.

For there was a race on to see who'd snare Jeoff. Maeve was no competition; the girl was plain as well as simple—although it was a good thing she *was* plain, or she would have been fair game for any fellow bent on lifting a skirt. Rune wasn't interested—and half the time Jeoff absentmindedly called her "lad" anyway.

Stara's only competition would come from the village. There were a couple of young women down there in Westhaven of marriageable age, whose fathers saw nothing wrong with running a good, clean inn. Fathers who would not be averse to seeing their daughters settled in as the innkeeper's wife. None were as pretty as Stara—but they all had dowers, which she did not. And they *were* younger, with plenty of childbearing years ahead of them.

Much younger, some of them. One of the possible prospects was only sixteen. Not that much older than Stara's daughter. No wonder Stara wanted to be thought younger than she was.

Rune got out her fiddle and began tuning it. It was a little too cold to be playing outside—but Jeoff liked hearing the music, and once she started playing it was unlikely that Stara would order her to do something else.

The gift of the fiddle had been Rose's idea. She'd watched as Rune begged to play with traveling minstrels' instruments—and had begun to coax something like music out of them right away—she'd seen Rune trying to get a good tune out of a reed whistle, a blade of grass, and anything else that made a noise. Perhaps she had guessed what Rune might do with a musical instrument of her own. For whatever reason, when Rune was about six, a peddler had run off without paying, leaving behind a pack filled with trash he hadn't been able to sell. One of the few things in it worth anything was the fiddle, given immediately to Rune, which Rune had named "Lady Rose" in honor of her patron.

It had taken many months of squealing and scraping out in the stable where she wouldn't offend any ears but the animals' before she was able to play much. But by the time she was eight, minstrels were going out of their way to give her a lesson or two, or teach her a new song. By the time she was ten, she was a regular draw.

Rune was smart enough to remember what the common room had

looked like on any day other than a market-day before she had started to play regularly—and she knew what it was like now. Rose's "investment" had paid off handsomely over the years—gaining in new business several times over the worth of the old fiddle.

But Stara—and there was no doubt in Rune's mind who was behind all the changes—evidently didn't see things that way, or thought that now that the extra custom was here, it would stay here. Rose could have told her differently, told her how it wasn't likely the Hungry Bear would hold anyone who didn't actually belong in Westhaven if there wasn't something beyond the beer to offer them. But Rose wasn't here, and Jeoff was not the kind to worry about tomorrow until it arrived.

On the other hand, although Stara was behind the changes, Jeoff was behind the cashbox. If Rune pointed out to him that he was losing money right now, that people weren't coming from outside the village bounds, and that those within the village weren't staying as long of an evening because she wasn't playing, well, maybe he'd put a stop to this, and hire on a good strong boy to do some of the work.

She thought again about going outside to practice, but the breeze coming in the window decided her against the idea. It was really too cold out there; her fingers would stiffen in no time.

She tuned the fiddle with care for its old strings; she wanted to replace them, but strings were hard to come by in this part of the world. If she was lucky, maybe a peddler would have a set. Until then, she'd just have to make sure she didn't snap one.

She closed her eyes for a moment, and let her fingers select the first couple of notes. The tune wandered a bit, before it settled on a jig, a good finger-warmer, and one of the earliest melodies she'd learned. "Heart for the Ladies," it was called, and folks around here usually called for it twice or three times a night when they were in the mood for dancing.

Rune closed her eyes again; she remembered the woman who had taught it to her as clearly as something that had happened yesterday.

Linnet had been her name, so she said; odd, how many of the traveling players had bird-names. Or maybe they just assumed bird-names when they started playing. Linnet had been one of a trio of traveling minstrels doing the Faire circuit, a mandolin player, herself on flute, and a drummer. Linnet was a tiny thing, always smiling, and ready with a kind word for a child. She had more hair than Rune had ever seen let down on a woman; she didn't wear it in a wife's braids, nor loose under a coif like a maid. The coppery-brown tresses were twined with flowers and piled in loose coils about her head when Rune first saw her, and later, it was tied in two long tails bound around with leather and thongs for traveling. When she let it down, it reached past her knees.

She had been as ready with her help as her smiles. When Rune brought out her fiddle, and attempted to follow their tunes silently, fingering but not bowing, she had taken the girl aside and played "Heart for the Ladies" over and over until Rune had gotten it in her head, then helped her to find the fingerings for it on the fiddle.

And then, the next day, when the trio had gone their way, Rune had practiced the piece for hours until she got it right. She'd waited until someone in the crowd that night saw her and called out, "Well, little Rune, and have ye got a new piece for us to hear?" the way some of them used to, half in earnest, half to tease her. This time, she'd answered "yes," and brought out her fiddle.

She'd surprised them all with the jig, so much so that they'd made her play it again and again—and then, several times more, so that they all could dance to it.

That night had brought her a pair of copper bits, the first time she'd been paid for her fiddling. It had been a heady moment, made all the headier by the first money she had ever owned.

She played the jig over twice more, until her fingers felt flexible and strong, ready for anything she might ask of them.

But what she asked of them next was the very latest piece she had learned, a slow, languorous love song. The lilting melody was the kind of song popular at weddings, but mostly not in the tavern.

A real fiddler had taught her this one; this and near two dozen more.

She smiled to think of him. Oh, he was a villainous-looking lad, with a patch over one eye, and all in gypsy-colors, half a brigand by his looks. But he had played like an angel, he had. And he'd stayed several days the first time he'd stopped at the Bear—because of the bad weather for traveling, so he'd said, and indeed, it had been raining heavily during all that time. But he'd had a horse—a pony, rather—a sturdy beast that was probably quite capable of taking him through rain and snow and anything else he might ask of it. It wasn't weather that had kept him, but his own will.

The rains pounded the area for a week, providing him ample excuse. So he stayed, and enlivened the tavern by night, bringing folks in from all over, despite the weather. And he'd schooled Rune by day.

Quite properly, despite her early fears as to his behavior. Fears—well, that wasn't quite true, it was half hope, actually, for despite his rascally appearance, or even because of it, she'd wondered if he'd pay court to her. . . .

She certainly knew at thirteen what went on between man and maid, male and female. She had taken some thought to it, though she wasn't certain what it was she wanted. The ballads were full of sweet courtings, wild ones, and no courtings at all—

But he was as correct with her as he had been bawdy with the men in the tavern the night before. He'd stopped her on her way to some trivial errand, as he was eating his luncheon in the otherwise empty common room.

"I hear you play the fiddle, young Rune," he'd said. She had nodded, suddenly shy, feeling as awkward as a young calf.

"Well?" he'd said then, a twinkle in the one eye not covered with a patch. "Are you going to go fetch it, or must I beg you?"

She had run to fetch it, and he'd begun her lesson, the first of four, and he had made her work, too. She worked as hard at her fiddling under his critical eye as she'd ever worked at any task in the tavern.

He saved the love songs until the last day—"A reward," he'd said, "for being a good student"—for they were the easiest of the lot.

If he'd introduced them at the beginning of the lessons, she might have suspected them of being a kind of overture. But he'd waited until the last day of his stay, when he'd already told her that he was leaving the following morning. So the songs came instead as a kind of gift from a friend, for a friend was what Raven had come to be. And she treasured them as completely as she would have treasured any material gift.

He'd returned over the winter, and again the next summer, and this winter again. That was when he had taught her this melody, "Fortune, My Foe." He should be coming through again, once the weather warmed. She was looking forward to seeing him again, and learning more things from him. Not just songs—though courting was not on her mind, either. There was so much she needed to learn, about music, about reading it and writing it. There were songs in her head, words as well as music, but she couldn't begin to get them out. She didn't know how to write the tunes down, and she didn't have enough reading and writing of words to get her own down properly so that another could read them. She had barely enough of writing to puzzle out bits of the Holy Book, just like every other child of the village, and there was no learned Scholar-Priest here to teach her more. There must be more . . . there must be a way to write music the way words were written, and there must be more words than she knew. She needed all of that, needed to learn it, and if anyone would know the way of such things, Raven would, she sensed it in her bones.

Raven was weeks away, though. And she would have to be patient and wait, as the Holy Book said women must be patient.

Even though she was almighty tired of being patient.

Oh, enough of such lazy tunes.

The trill of an early songbird woke another melody in her fingers, and that led to many more. All reels this time, and all learned from a rough-faced, bearded piper just a few weeks ago. He'd come to play for the wedding of some distant relations, and though he had not made any formal attempt at giving her lessons, when he watched her frowning and following his music silently, he'd played everything at least three times over until she smiled and nodded by way of a signal that she'd got the tune straight in her head.

He'd gone before nightfall, not staying—he couldn't have played at the tavern anyway; the pipes were *not* an instrument for indoors.

But this winter, after her fiddler had come and gone, there had been a harper who had stayed for nearly two weeks. He was a Guild Minstrel, and was taking a position at the court of the Sire. He was ahead of time, having come much faster than anyone would have ever expected because of a break in the weather, and had taken the opportunity to rest a bit before taking the last leg of the journey.

He was an old man, his hair half silver, and he had been very kind to her. He'd taught her many of the songs popular at the courts, and she had painstakingly adapted them for fiddle. He hadn't had much patience, but fortunately the melodies were all simple ones, easy to remember, and easy to follow.

But from those simple songs, her fingers slowed, and strayed into a series of laments, learned from another harpist, a real Gypsy, who would not come into the village at all. Rune had found her with her fellows, camped beyond the bridge as she had returned from an errand. Unaccountably, eerily, the girl had known who she was, and what instrument she played. It still gave Rune a chill to think of her, and wonder how it was the other musician had known all about her.

She'd stopped Rune as the girl lingered, watching the Gypsies with burning curiosity. "I am Nightingale. Bring your fiddle," she'd said abruptly, with no preamble. "I shall teach you songs such as you have never heard before."

With a thrill of awe and a little fear, Rune had obeyed. It had been uncanny then, and it was uncanny now. How had Nightingale known who she was, and what she did? No one in the village would have told her—surely.

And indeed, Nightingale had taught her music the like of which she had never heard before. The strange, compelling dance music was too complicated to learn in a single afternoon—but the laments stuck in her mind, and seemed to make her fingers move of their own accord. . . .

"Rune!"

She started, and opened her eyes. Stara had a mug in one hand, and most of the rest up on their pegs, above the beer barrels, and she had turned to stare at Rune with a strange, uneasy expression on her face. Rune got ready for a tongue-lashing; whenever Stara was unhappy or uneasy, she took it out on someone. And Maeve wasn't within reach right now.

"Haven't you practiced enough for one day?" Stara snapped crossly. "You give me the chills with that Gypsy howling. It sounds like lost souls, wailing for the dead."

Well, that was what it was supposed to sound like—

"—or cats in heat," Stara concluded, crudely. "Haven't you got anything better to do than to torture our ears with that?"

"I—" she began.

A cough interrupted her, and she glanced over at the door to the kitchen. Jeoff stood there, with a keg of the dark ale on one shoulder.

"We're going to be working in here for a while, Rune," he said. "I don't want to sound mean, but—that music bothers me. It's like you're calling something I'd rather not see."

Meaning he's feeling superstitious, Rune thought cynically.

"Don't you think Jib could use your help in the stables?" he said—but it sounded like an order.

"Yes, sir," she said, trying not to sound surly. *Just when I was really getting warmed up. It figures.* "I'll see to it, Master Jeoff."

But as she put her fiddle away, she couldn't help watching Jeoff and her mother out of the corner of her eye. There was something going on there, and it had nothing to do with the music.

It looked like Stara's ploys were working.

The only question was—where did that leave Rune?

CHAPTER TWO

With her fiddle safely stowed away, Rune made her reluctant way to the stable-yard—such as it was. This little road wasn't used by too many people, certainly not the kind of people who would be riding high-bred horses that required expensive stabling. When the Sire traveled, he took the roads patrolled and guarded by the Duke's Men. And when someone was sent to collect taxes and take the man-count, it was never anyone important, just a bailiff. This village never gave any trouble, always paid its taxes with a minimum of cheating, and in general was easy to administer to. There were robbers, occasionally, but when robbers cropped up, a quick foray into the woods by the local men usually took care of them. There were places said to be dangerous, because of magic or supernatural menaces, but the road bypassed them. People who traveled between here and Beeford were simple people, without much in the way of valuables.

So the stable was a bare place, nothing more than four walls and a roof, with a loft and a dirt floor. Half of it was the storage place for hay and straw—no grain; the inn pony and donkey were sturdy enough to live on thistles if they had to, hay and grass suited them very well. The other half had been partitioned into rough stalls. There was a paddock, where beasts could be turned loose if their owners couldn't afford stable-fees, or the inn beasts could be put if their stalls were needed for paying tenants. That had never happened in Rune's experience, though they had come near to it in Faire season. The loft stood over the half where hay was stored, and that was where Jib slept, hemmed in and protected by bales of hay, and generally fairly snug. Tarn Hostler, the stable-master, slept with his wife Annie Cook in her room next to the kitchen. In the winter, Jib slept next to the kitchen fire with Granny.

Rune hoped, as she took herself out the kitchen door, that Jib wouldn't try to court her again today. He was her best friend—in point of fact, he was her only friend—but he was the last person she wanted courting her.

She'd been trying to discourage him; teasing him, ignoring his clumsy attempts at gallantry, laughing at his compliments. She could understand why he had the silly idea that he was in love with her, and it had nothing to do with her looks or her desirability. There were two available women here at the Bear, for Jib was too lowly ever to be able to pay court to one of the village girls. And of the two of them, even a blind man would admit she was preferable to Maeve.

Jib was fine as a friend—but nothing more. For one thing, he was at least a year younger than Rune. For another—he just wasn't very bright. He didn't understand half of what she said to him, sometimes. He wasn't at all ambitious, either; when Rune asked him once what he wanted to

12

be when he was a man, he'd looked at her as if she was crazed. He was perfectly happy being the stableboy, and didn't see any reason for that to change. He didn't want to leave the village or see anything of the outside world but the Faire at Beeford. The only wish he'd ever expressed to her was to become a local horse-trader, selling the locally bred, sturdy little ponies and cobs to bigger traders who would take them to the enormous City Faires. He didn't even want to take the horses there himself.

And—to be honest—when a girl dreamed of a lover, she didn't dream of a boy with coarse, black hair, buck teeth, ears like a pair of jug handles, a big round potato of a nose, and spots. Of course, he'd probably grow out of the spots, but the rest was there to stay.

All in all, she wished he'd decide to settle for Maeve. They'd probably suit one another very well as long as he told her exactly what to do. . . .

The yard was deserted, and Tarn Hostler was grooming the two beasts in the paddock, alone, but Rune heard straw rustling and knew where she'd find Jib. And sure enough, when she entered the stable, there he was, forking straw into a pair of stalls.

She grabbed a pitchfork and went to help him, filling the mangers with fresh hay, and rinsing and filling the water buckets at the paddock pump. The pony, Dumpling (brown and round as one of Cook's best dumplings), and the donkey, Stupid (which he was not), watched her with half-closed eyes as old Tarn gave them a carefully currycombing, brushing out clouds of winter hair. They knew the schedule as well as anyone. Bring back loads of wood for the ovens on Monday, haul food for the inn on Tuesday, wood again on Wednesday (but this time for the baker in the village), be hitched to the grindstone on Thursday, since the village had no water-mill, wood again on Friday for the woodcutter himself, odd jobs on Saturday, and be hitched to the wagon to take everyone to Church on Sunday. They'd done their duty for the day. Now they could laze about the yard and be groomed, then put in their stalls for the night, once Jib and Rune finished cleaning them.

"Hey, Rune," Jib said, after trying to get her attention by clearing his throat several times.

"You ought to see Annie about that cough you've got," she interrupted him. "It sounds really bad."

"My cough?" he replied, puzzled. "I don't have a cough."

"You've been hemming and hacking like a wheezy old man ever since I got out here," she replied sharply. "Of course you have a cough. You ought to take care of it. Get Annie to dose you. I'll tell her about it—"

"Uh, no, please," he said, looking alarmed, as well he might. Annie's doses were fearsome things that took the skin off a person's tongue and left a nasty, lingering taste in the back of the throat for days afterwards. "I'm fine, really I am, please, don't tell Annie I'm sick—"

He babbled on about how healthy he was for some time; Rune paid scant attention, simply pleased that she'd managed to elude whatever he'd planned to ask her. With that much nervousness showing, it had to be romantic in nature, at least by Jib's primitive standards of romance.

Which were at best, one step above Dumpling's.

She looked about for something else to distract him when he finally wound down, but fate took a hand for her—for his babble was interrupted by the sounds of hooves on the hard-packed dirt outside, and a strange voice.

They both ran to see who it was, just as they had when they were children, Rune reaching the stable door a little before Jib.

At first glance, the newcomer looked to be a peddler; his pony had two largish packs on its back, and he was covered from head to knee in a dust-colored cloak. But then he pulled the cloak off, and shook it, and Rune saw he was dressed in a linen shirt with knots of multicolored ribbon on the sleeves, a bright blue vest, and fawn-colored breeches. Only one kind of traveler would dress like that, and her guess was confirmed when he pulled a lute in its case out of one of the packs.

He was very tall, taller than Rune, and lanky, with dust-colored hair, and wonderfully gentle brown eyes. The stable-master saw them both gawking from the shelter of the doorway, and waved them over abruptly.

They obeyed at once; Tarn told them to groom the minstrel's pony and put it in one of the prepared stalls, then come fetch the inn beasts when a third stall was ready. He himself took the stranger's packs, leading him into the inn as if he owned it.

Jib and Rune eyed each other over the empty pack-saddle. "Flip you for it," Rune said. Jib nodded wordlessly, and Rune bent down long enough to fetch a pebble from the dust at her feet. She spat on it, and tossed it into the air, calling out, "Wet!" as it fell.

It landed wet side up, and Jib shrugged philosophically.

She led the visitor's pony into one of the stalls, unsaddled him and hung his tack over the wall of his stall, and gave him a brisk grooming. He seemed to enjoy it, leaning into the strokes of the currycomb with an expression of bliss on his round little face.

When she had finished, Jib was still forking in hay for the new stall. She turned the pony loose in this temporary home, made sure that the door was secure (some ponies were wizards at finding ways to escape), and took herself back into the inn.

She was met at the inner door by her mother, who barred the way with her arm across the doorway. "His name is Master Heron and he's on his way to the Lycombe Faire," she said, as Rune fidgeted. "He promised Jeoff he'd play tonight, and that means that you serve."

"Yes, M—Stara," she replied, catching herself at the last minute before saying the forbidden word.

"Jeoff wants you to go down to the village and make the rounds of all the Guildsmen," Stara continued. "He wants you to tell them all that Master Heron will be entertaining tonight; from them it will spread to everyone else in Westhaven."

"Yes, Stara," Rune said, curbing her impatience.

"He has to be on his way first thing in the morning if he's going to make the Faire in time," Stara finished, dashing Rune's hopes for a lesson. "And you'd better be on your way now, if we're going to have the extra custom tonight."

Rune sighed, but said nothing more. If she got down to the village before the men went home to their suppers, they'd likely eat lightly or not at all, those who could afford to. Then they'd come here, and eat plates of salt-laden sausage rolls and sharp cheese while they listened to the minstrel, making themselves thirsty. They'd drink plenty of beer tonight to drown the salty sausages. Jeoff was probably already hauling up extra kegs and putting them behind the bar. It would be a good night for the inn.

And at least Rune would hear some new songs. If she was lucky, the minstrel would repeat them enough for her to learn one or two.

She turned and started down the path to the village, hoping to get back quickly enough not to miss anything.

The village of Westhaven was set back from the road, because there wasn't enough flat land for more than the inn right up beside it. Those who had business in Westhaven itself—not many—took the path up the valley to find the village. Rune usually enjoyed the walk, although it was a bit long, and a little frightening after the sun went down. But today, halfway between the inn and the first buildings of the village itself, she stopped; the path was blocked by two of Westhaven's girls, Joyse and Amanda, gossiping in the middle of the path and making no effort to move out of the way.

They knew she was coming; they could hardly miss her. But they pretended not to notice her, clutching baskets of early flowers and keeping their heads close together. Joyse, as blond as Stara, but thin, was the baker's daughter; Amanda, as round and brown as Dumpling, but without the pony's easy-going nature, was the offspring of one of the local farmers. Joyse, with her hair neatly confined under a pretty red scarf that matched her brand new kirtle, was betrothed already to another farmer's son. Amanda, in a blue dress that looked almost as new, but was already straining at the seams around her middle, was one of the contenders to replace Rose. From the way it looked, one or the other had been up to the inn, possibly to spy on Rune, Stara, or both. Rune had the feeling that Amanda would do just about anything to become the innkeeper's new wife, except surrendering her virginity before taking wedding vows.

Both girls looked down their noses at Rune as she approached slowly. "Well, I wish *I* had time to play games in the hay and flirt with boys," Amanda said nastily. "Of course, some people have lots of time. Some people have all the time they want, not just to play games, but to pretend they're minstrels."

Joyse laughed shrilly, showing buckteeth, and looking uncannily like a skinny old mare whinnying.

"And *some* people are so lazy, they pretend to be working, when all they really do is stand around and make up stories because the truth is too dull," Rune said aloud, to a squirrel in one of the trees beside her. It chattered, as if it was responding to her. "And *some* people are so fat they block the path, so people with work to do can't travel it. And of course, *some* people are so bad-tempered that no one will have them for a wife, not even with a big dower."

Amanda squealed with rage, turning to face her directly, and Rune pretended to notice her for the first time. "Why Amanda, I didn't see you there. I thought it was a pony blocking the path."

Amanda's round face turned bright red, and her hands balled into fists beside her skirt. "You, little bastard-brat—were you talking about me?"

"Talking about you?" Rune shrugged, and pretended surprise. "Why would I bother? There's nothing at all interesting about you. I'd put myself and that squirrel to sleep talking about you. Besides, you know what Father Jacob says about gossiping. He says that women who spend their time in idle gossip spend three hundred years in hell when they die, with their lips sewn shut." She shuddered artistically. "I'd never want to end up like that."

"I'll show *you* how you'll end up," Amanda hissed, taking a step forward.

But Joyse grabbed her shoulder, bent to her ear, and whispered something fiercely to her, stopping her. Rune had a fairly good idea what the general gist of the advice was, because the last time any of the Westhaven youngsters had tried to turn a confrontation with Rune into something physical, it had ended with the girl getting her hair rubbed full of mud while Rune sat on her back. Not even the boys wanted to risk a physical fight with her; she was taller and stronger than most of them, and knew some tricks of dirty fighting Tarn had taught both her and Jib (though Jib never kept his head long enough to use them) that they didn't.

Rune took one deliberate step forward, then a second. Joyse whispered something else, her eyes round with urgency, and Amanda backed up—then turned, and the two of them flounced their way up the path. Rune watched them go, seething inwardly, but refusing to show it.

She'd won—sort of. In most ways, though, it had been a draw. They could continue to pick on her verbally, and she could do nothing, and they all three knew it. Most of the time she couldn't even get her own hits in when it was a verbal confrontation. It wasn't fair.

She waited a few more minutes for them to get far enough ahead of her that she shouldn't have to encounter them again, then continued on her way. Slower, this time, trying to get her temper to cool by listening to the blackbirds singing their hearts out in the trees around her, trying to win themselves mates.

There was this much satisfaction; at least this time she'd been able to give as good as she got. And none of them would try to touch even Jib, these days, not even in a group. Everyone knew she was Jib's protector. She wasn't averse to using teeth and feet as well as fists when she was cornered, either. They *had* to keep their abuse verbal.

One of these days I'm going to write a song about them, she thought angrily. *About Amanda, Joyse, all of them. All of them pretending to be so much better than me . . . but Amanda steals her mother's egg-money, and Joyse only got Thom because her father promised to help his father cheat on his taxes. And they don't know I know about it. That'd serve them right, to go to a Faire and hear some strange minstrel singing a song mocking them.*

Not a one of them ever missed a chance to tell her that she was scum. It would be nice to watch their faces as someone told *them* exactly what they were. And why not? When Raven came, maybe she could get him to help her with that song. With his help, surely it would be picked up by other singers.

Savoring that sweet thought, she picked up her pace a little. The first stop was going to be the chandler's shop.

Maybe with luck she'd get through this without having any more little "encounters."

After the chandler, she left her message at the tannery and the baker's, wishing she could stay longer and savor the wonderful aromas there. The baker said nothing about her little encounter with his daughter; she hadn't really expected that he would. If he knew about it, he'd likely just chalk it up to the "bastard-brat's" bad breeding. But since Rune had gotten the better of that exchange, and in fact had not said a single thing that—taken literally—could be called an insult, she doubted either girl would even mention it to a parent.

In fact, she thought, as she crossed the lane to the smithy, she'd handled it rather well. She'd simply said that some people were fat, were gossips, and couldn't get a husband because they had such terrible tempers. She'd only repeated what the Westhaven priest—shared with Beeford—had told all of them about the fate of gossiping women. She hadn't once said that either Amanda or Joyse were anything other than dull. And while that was an insult, it was hardly one that was anything other than laughable.

The smithy was full; Hob and his two older apprentices, hard at work on sharpening farm tools gone rusty after a winter's storage. They stopped work long enough to hear what she had to say; she spoke her piece quickly, for the forge was hot as a midsummer day, and plain took her breath away. All three men paid her little heed until they heard her news. Then they reacted with considerably more enthusiasm; it had been several weeks since the last real minstrel had been through, after all, and spring had brought with the new growth a predictable restlessness on everyone's part. Tonight's entertainment would give them a welcome outlet for some of that restlessness.

The next stop on Rune's mental list, as she passed behind the smithy and the blacksmith resumed his noisy work, was the carpenter—she'd take this shortcut behind the smithy, between it and its storage sheds, for the smithy and the carpenter's shop lay a little to one side of Westhaven proper, on the other side of the tiny village pond, out where their pounding wouldn't disturb anyone, and where, if the smithy caught fire, there'd be no danger of houses taking flame.

"Well, look what jest wandered inta town." The blacksmith's son Jon stepped out from the side of the shop, blocking her path.

She stopped; he grinned, showing a mouth with half the teeth missing, and rubbed his nose on the back of his hand, sniffing noisily. His manners hadn't improved over the winter. "You lookin' fer me, girl?" he drawled.

She didn't answer, and she didn't acknowledge him. Instead, she turned slowly, figuring that it would be better—much better—if she simply pretended to ignore him. He'd grown over the winter. Quite a bit, in fact. Suddenly, her feeling of superiority to the rest of the village youngsters began to evaporate.

As Hill and Warran, two of the farm boys, moved out from the other side of the blacksmith shop to block her escape, the last of her assumption of superiority vanished. They'd grown over the winter, too. All three of them were taller than she was, and Jon had huge muscles in his arms and shoulders that matched his father's. Becoming his father's apprentice on his fifteenth birthday had developed his body beyond anything she would have anticipated.

It hadn't done much for his mind, though. She whirled at a sound behind her, and saw that he had already moved several paces closer.

"What do you want, Jon?" she asked, trying to sound bored. "I'm busy. I'm supposed to be delivering messages from Master Jeoff. I left one with your *father*," she concluded pointedly.

"What's the matter?" he asked, scratching his behind with one sooty hand, and grinning still wider. "You in a big hurry t' get back t' yer lo-o-over?" He laughed. "What's Jib got, huh? Nothin', that's what."

So, now it was out in the open, instead of being sniggered about, hinted at. Someone had finally said to her face what everyone in Westhaven had been telling each other for a year.

"He's not my lover," she said as calmly as she could. "I don't have any *lover*."

"Then maybe it's time you got one," said Hill, snickering. "Little lovin' might do you some good, string bean. Teach you what a woman's for."

"Aww, Hill, she just means she ain't got a *real* lover," Jon said genially, flexing the muscles of his shoulders, presumably for her benefit. "She just means she wants one, eh?"

"I meant what I said," she told him defiantly.

"Ah, don't fool around, Rune. We know your Mam's been in ol' Jeoff's bed since Rose died. An' we know 'bout you. Your Mam wasn't any more married than m' Dad's anvil." He advanced, and she backed up—into Hill's and Warran's hands. She suppressed a yelp as they grabbed her. "You got no call pretendin' that you're all goody-good." She struggled in the farm boys' hands; they simply tightened their grips.

She stopped fighting, holding very, very still, part of her mind planning every second of the next few minutes, the rest of her too scared to squeak. "Let me go," she said, slowly, clearly, and sounding amazingly calm even to herself.

"Yer Mam's a whore," Jon said, his grin turning cruel, as he reached out for her. "Yer Mam's a whore, an' yer a whore's daughter, an' if yer not a whore now, ye will be—"

He grabbed her breast, crushing it in his hand and hurting her, as he slammed his foul mouth down on hers, trying to force her lips open with his tongue.

She opened her mouth and let his tongue probe forward—and bit down on it, quick, and as hard as she could, tasting blood briefly.

At the same time, she slammed her knee up into his crotch.

As Jon screamed and fell away from her, she brought her heel down hard on Hill's instep, and slammed her head back against his teeth. That hurt, and she reckoned she'd cut her scalp a bit, but it surely hurt him worse.

Hill let out a hoarse cry and let go of her immediately, and bumbled into Warran. She pivoted as much as she could with Warran still holding onto her, and kicked Hill in the knee, toppling him; he went down, taking Warran with him. As Warran fell, she managed to pull free of the last boy's grip—and she pelted away as fast as her legs would carry her, never once looking back to see if she'd hurt them seriously or not.

She ran all the way out of the village, her side aching, her head hurting, half blinded with fright. No matter who might have been following her, she still had longer legs and better wind than any of them. When she slowed and finally paused, near where she'd been stopped by the girls earlier, she couldn't hear any pursuit.

That was when she started to shake.

She started to drop to her knees beside the path, then thought better of the idea. What if there was someone following? What if the boys recovered and decided to come after her?

But she had one place of shelter, one they wouldn't know about—one that was completely defensible.

She got off the path somehow, and fought her way through the brush some twenty or thirty feet into the forest. And there was her shelter, the biggest oak tree for miles around. She forced her shaking legs to carry her up the side of the forest giant, and into the huge fork, completely hidden from below by the new young leaves of lesser trees. There she curled up, and let her mind go blank, while she shook with reaction.

After a while, her heart stopped pounding in her ears, and she stopped feeling sick to her stomach. Mostly, anyway.

Her mind began to work again, if slowly.

She put her hand to the back of her head, but surprisingly, didn't come away with any blood on it, though she felt the hard lump of a rising goose egg back there. That, and a torn and dirty shirt were the worst she'd taken out of the encounter.

This time.

She chewed some young leaves to get the nasty taste of Jon out of her mouth, but she couldn't get the nasty feel of him out of her mind.

One thing was certain; her immunity had vanished with the snows of winter. The girls might leave her alone, but she was completely at the mercy of the boys, even in daylight. The girls might even have set their brothers on her; that would certainly fit Amanda and Joyse's personalities. And that this attack had taken place in daylight meant that they were not particularly worried about hiding their actions from their parents.

That meant their parents didn't care what they were doing to her. If anything happened to her, nothing would be done to punish her attackers. That had always been true—but the threat of attack had never included rape before.

The boys had said it all; her mother was a whore, she was the daughter of a whore, therefore she was a whore. No one would believe anything else. Anything that happened to her would be her own fault, brought on her own actions, or simply by being born of bad blood.

Not even the Priest would help, unless she took holy vows. And even then—he might not believe that she was an innocent, and he might refuse her the protection of the Church. She had nowhere to turn to for help, and no one to depend on but herself.

How long was it going to be before she was cornered by a gang she *couldn't* escape? It was only the purest luck, and the fact that they hadn't expected her to fight back, that had let her get away this time.

Next time she might not be so lucky.

Next time, they might win.

The realization made her start to shake all over again.

It felt like hours later that she managed to get herself under control, and climb down out of the tree—but when she made her way back to the inn, no one seemed to have missed her. At least, no one seemed to think she had taken an extraordinary amount of time to deliver her messages.

After much thought, she had decided to keep quiet about the attack; after all, what good would complaining about it do? None of this would have happened if the boys hadn't been sure they were safe from punishment. Jeoff wouldn't do anything to risk the anger of his customers, Stara and Annie Cook would be certain she'd brought it on herself, and Jib would only get himself into fights he couldn't hope to win. No one would care, at least, not enough to help protect her.

But she could protect herself, in clever ways. She could refuse to go into the village alone, or better still, she could send Jib to run errands for her, trading chore for chore. Even if it meant more of the kind of work that might stiffen her hands. . . .

Better that, than the little entertainments Jon and his friends had planned.

But she didn't have long to brood on her troubles, for despite the fact that she hadn't been able to deliver more than half her messages, word of the new minstrel had traveled all through the village, and the men and their wives were already beginning to take their places behind the rough wooden tables. There were three couples there already; the baker and his wife, and a couple of the nearer farmers and their spouses. The place would be full tonight, for certain.

She dashed upstairs to change her torn shirt for a clean, older one—a loose and baggy one that didn't show anything of her figure—making sure no one saw her to ask about what had happened to the first shirt.

She stripped off the shirt and frowned—more in anger now, than fear—at the bruises on her breast. She touched it gingerly; it was going to hurt more later than it did now, and it hurt bad enough now that she waited long enough to wrap her chest in a supporting and protecting—and concealing—band of cloth. She slipped the new shirt over her head, pledging herself that she'd find a way to make Jon hurt as much as he'd hurt her.

If he didn't already. She hoped, devoutly, that he did. He'd surely have a hard time explaining away his bitten and swollen tongue. She was quite sure she'd drawn blood, for there'd been blood on the back of her hand when she'd wiped it across her mouth. With any luck it would be so bad he'd have to drink his meals tonight and tomorrow. And she had a notion his privates ached more than her breast did right now.

The thought made her a little more cheerful.

She scraped her hair back and tied it into a severe knot at the nape of her neck. There had been no sign from any of the adults today that they thought the way the boys did, but she had no intention of finding out the hard way. When she made herself look like a boy this way, most of them actually forgot she was a girl. And she didn't want to start anything among the beer-happy men—she knew for a fact that she wouldn't be able to defend herself from a grown man. Stara was safe enough behind the bar, but she was going to be out in the open.

A few months ago, with Rose in charge, anyone bothering "the wenches" would have found himself getting a rap on the head or hand with a spoon—or invited to leave and not return, which could be quite a punishment in a village with only one inn. Rune hadn't ever thought that the situation might change—

Until this afternoon. That changed everything.

Now, she wasn't taking any chances.

For a moment she hesitated at the foot of the stairs, afraid to face the crowd, afraid that she might see knowing looks in their faces, afraid of what they might be thinking—

But Annie Cook seized her as soon as the red-faced woman spotted her, and shoved a tray of sausage rolls into her hands, not giving her a chance to think about anything else.

The young minstrel was in the common room, tuning his instrument, as she delivered the salty sausage rolls to the customers. He glanced up at her as she passed, and smiled, the setting sun coming in through the inn windows and touching his hair and face with a gentle golden light. It was a plain, friendly smile, unlike the leers of Jon and his companions, and it warmed a place within her that had been cold all afternoon.

The next time she passed, this time with a tray full of beer mugs, he stopped her, on the pretense of getting a mugful of beer himself.

"I understand you're a fiddler," he said, quietly, taking his time about choosing a mug. "Will you be playing tonight? Do you think you'd like to try a duet?"

If only I could— But Stara had given her direct orders. She shook her head, not trusting her voice.

"That's too bad," he answered, making it sound as if he really *was* disappointed that she wouldn't be fiddling. "I was hoping to hear you; well, let me know if I do anything new to you, all right? I'll make sure to try and repeat the new songs so you can pick them up."

Speechless now with gratitude, she nodded emphatically, and he took his mug and let her go.

As the evening passed—and the women left—the atmosphere in the room changed. Some of the men from the village, who a month ago would never have dreamed of taking liberties, were pinching and touching Maeve, their hands lingering on her arm or shoulder—or, when they thought no one was watching, her breasts. Maeve seemed oblivious as usual. And neither Jeoff nor Stara were doing anything about it. Now, more than ever, Rune was glad she'd made herself less of a target. As she'd hoped, some of the men, with several mugs of dark beer in them, were calling her "boy." As long as they thought her a boy, she'd probably be safe enough.

True to his promise, Master Heron watched her closely at the conclusion of every tune he played. If she nodded, she could be sure he'd play that song later in the evening, and as the crowd grew more intoxicated, he could repeat the songs a little more often. His hat, left at his feet, was quite full of copper by now. There was even a silver piece or two among the copper. Rune didn't know for certain what he was used to, but by the standards of Westhaven he was doing very well indeed.

Finally he pled the need to take a break, and as Rune brought him more beer and a bit of bread and cheese and an apple, the villagers gathered closer to ask him questions. She ran into the kitchen and out again, not wanting to miss a single word.

"Lad, you're the best these parts have heard in a long while. Are you a Guild Bard?" the mayor wanted to know.

Of course he'd ask that, Rune thought cynically. *It's always better if it comes from a Guildsman. As if the music cared who plays it!*

"No, that I'm not," he replied, easily. "Look you, Guildsmen always wear purple ribbon on their sleeves, purple and gold for Bards, purple and silver for Minstrels. I doubt you'd ever see a Guildsman through here, though; they're not for the likes of you and me. They play for no less than Sires, and sure they'll tell you so, quick enough!"

He said it so lightly that no one took offense, not even the mayor, who looked a bit disappointed, but not angered.

"No, now I'm just a rover, a Free Bard, seeing that everyone gets to hear a bit of a tune now and again," he continued. "Though after the Faire, I'll admit to you I've been asked to play for the Sire."

That put the mayor in a better humor. "So what's the difference, lad?" he asked genially. "Besides a bit of ribbon, that is."

"Ah, now that *is* the question," he replied, with his eyebrows raised as high as they could go. "And the answer to it is more than you might think. It's not enough to be able to play, d'ye see. The Bardic Guild seems to think that's only part of what a man needs to get into it. You've all heard of the great Midsummer Faire at Kingsford, right by Traen, have you not?"

All heads nodded; who hadn't heard of the King's Faire? It was the greatest Faire in the land, and one or two of the crowd, the mayor being chiefest, had actually been there once. So great a Faire it was, it couldn't be held inside the capital city of Traen, but had to be set up in its own, temporary city of tents, at Kingsford nearby. It lasted for six weeks, three weeks on either side of Midsummer's Day, with a High Holy Mass celebrated on the day itself, adding the Church's blessing to the proceedings.

"Well," Master Heron said, leaning back against the hearth, so that the firelight caught all the angles of his face, "it's like this. On the second week of Kingsford Midsummer Faire, the Guild comes and sets up a big tent, hard by the cathedral-tent. That's where they hold trials, and they go on for three days. Anyone who wants can sign up for the trials, but there aren't many that make it to the third day."

"You didn't make it, then?" said Ralf, the candle-maker, insolently.

But Master Heron only laughed. "I never tried," he said, "I'm too great a coward to face an audience all of musicians!"

The others laughed with him, and Ralf had the grace to flush.

"So, here's what happens," the minstrel continued. "The first day, you sing and play your best instrument, and you can choose whatever song you wish. There's just one catch—as you play, the judges call out a kind of tune, jig, reel, lament—and you have to play that song in that style, and improvise on it. The second day, you sing and play your *second* instrument, but you have to choose from a list of songs *they* pick, then you drum for the next to play. And the third day, you go back to your first instrument, or on to your third, if you have one, and you play and sing a song you have made. And each day, the list of those that get to go on gets shorter by half." He laughed. "Do you see now why I hadn't the courage to try? 'Tis enough to rattle your nerves to pieces, just thinking on it!"

The mayor whistled, and shook his head as the crowd fell silent. "Well, that's a poser. And all that just to get in as an *apprentice*?"

"Aye," Master Heron replied. "When I was young enough, I didn't have the courage, and now—" he spread his hands. "Wouldn't I look foolish now, as an apprentice?"

The men nodded agreement, as Rune went back to the kitchen, aflame with ambition, but half-crushed as well. She could compose, all right— yes, and she played her fiddle well enough, and drummed too, and sang—

But he'd said quite distinctly that you had to have *two* instruments, or even a third, and be proficient on all of them.

Even if she could find someone with a lute or mandolin to sell, she could never afford it. She could never afford the lessons to learn to play it, either—and that was assuming she could find a teacher. And if she waited for minstrels to come along to teach her, the way she'd learned fiddle, she'd be an old woman of eighteen or twenty by the time she was ready to go to the Midsummer Faire and the trials.

Well, she *could* play the shepherd's flute, and even she could make one of those—

No. That was no kind of instrument for the trials before the Guild. These were people who played before princes and kings; they'd hardly be impressed by someone tootling simple shepherd's jigs on a two-octave pipe.

Then the mayor put the crowning touch on her ambitions, placing it out of the realm of "want" and into "need." For what he told the rest, told *her* that this was the way out of all her problems. Apprenticeship to the Guild would not only get her out of this village, out of danger, but it would place her in a position where no one would ever threaten her again.

"I heard that no one touches a Guild Bard or a Guild Minstrel, am I right, Master Heron?" he asked.

The minstrel nodded, though his face was in shadow now, and Rune couldn't read his expression. His voice held no inflection at all. "That's the truth, sir," he replied. "Only the Church has a right to bring them to trial, and if anyone harms a Guild musician, the Church will see to it that they're found and punished. I'm told that's because a good half of the Guild apprentices go into the Church eventually—and because musicians go everywhere, sometimes into dangerous situations."

No one could ever harm her again. She was so involved in her own thoughts that she hardly noticed when Master Heron resumed playing, and had to forcibly drag her attention back to the music.

There had to be a way to get that second instrument, to get to the trials. There *had* to be!

CHAPTER THREE

The customers stayed later than usual, and only left when Master Heron began pointedly to put his instrument away for travel. By the time the evening was over, Rune was exhausted, too tired to think very clearly, arms aching from all the heavy trays and pitchers she had carried all night, legs aching from the miles she'd traveled between kitchen and tables, bar and tables, and back again. From the look of him, Master Heron wasn't in much better shape. There were hundreds of things she wanted to ask him about getting into the Bardic Guild, but she knew from experience how *his* arms must feel after a night of non-stop playing, and how his tongue was tripping over the simplest of words if they weren't in a song.

So she left him alone as she carried the heaps of dirty plates and mugs into the kitchen again—and predictably, was recruited as dish-dryer and stacker, for Granny couldn't cope with putting the plates away. So she walked several more miles returning mugs to the bar and dishes to the cupboard. By the time she was able to leave the kitchen, he'd gone up to his room and his well-earned rest.

The common room was empty at last, fire dying, benches stacked atop tables, and both pushed against the walls, shutters closed and latched against the night. She didn't see her mother anywhere about, which in itself was predictable enough. Stara did not much care for kitchen and clean-up work, and never performed either if she had a way out of doing so. Rune expected to find Stara up in her own attic cubicle next to her daughter's.

But when Rune reached the top of the attic stairs, the moonlight shining through the attic window betrayed the fact that Stara's bed was empty.

Odd. But she'd probably gone to visit the privy before turning in. Rune stripped off her shirt and breeches, and slipped into an old, outworn shift of Rose's, cut down to make a night-shift just before Rose had taken sick, expecting to hear her mother coming up the stairs at any moment, and hoping this wasn't going to be another night of complaint.

But as Rune crawled under the coarse sheet of her pallet, she froze at the sound of murmuring voices in the hall outside Jeoff's rooms below.

One was certainly Jeoff. And the other, just as certainly, was her mother.

Suddenly Rune was wide-eyed; no longer the least bit sleepy.

She had only time to register shock before the closing door below cut off the last sound of whispers.

Stara—and Jeoff. There was no doubt in Rune's mind what was going on. Stara had been unable to get Jeoff to marry her by simply tempting him, but remaining just out of reach. So for some reason, tonight she had decided to give the man what he wanted to see if that would bring him before the altar.

She must be desperate, Rune thought, numbly. *She'd never have gone to him otherwise. She must think that if she lets him sleep with her, guilt will make him want to make an honest wife of her in the morning. Or else she thinks she can seduce him into marrying her, because she's such a fabulous lover. Or both.*

Whatever was going on in Stara's mind, there were a number of possible outcomes for this encounter, and they didn't auger well for Rune.

The worst threat was that her mother would slip and become pregnant. In all the time Rune had been paying any attention, Stara had never once calculated anything correctly if it involved numbers greater than three. That made a pregnancy horribly likely—if not this time, then the next.

Rune stared up blankly at the darkness of the roof above her. If Stara became pregnant, married or not, it would mean the end of Rune's free time. She'd have to take all of Stara's work as well as her own for months before the birth, and after—

And doubtless the added expense of a non-productive mouth to feed would convince Jeoff there was no money to hire any more help.

And Rune would have to help with the baby, when it came. As if she hadn't already more than enough to do! There would be no time for anything but work, dawn to dusk and past it. There would be no time to even practice her fiddling, much less learn new music, or work out songs of her own.

No time for herself at all . . . things were bad enough now, but with Stara pregnant, or caring for another child, they'd be infinitely worse.

Her eyes stung and she swallowed a lump in her throat as big as an egg. It wasn't fair! Stara had a perfectly good situation here, she didn't need to do this! She wasn't thinking—or rather, she wasn't thinking of anyone except herself. . . .

Rune turned on her side as despair threatened to smother her, choking her breath in her throat, like a hand about it. *At least I'll have a roof over my head,* she thought bleakly. *There's plenty that can't even say that. And food; I never go hungry around here.*

But that wasn't the worst possible situation. Supposing Stara's ploy didn't work? Suppose she couldn't get Jeoff to marry her—and got with child anyway? Jeoff probably wouldn't throw them out of his own accord, but there were plenty of people in the village who'd pressure him to do so, especially those with unmarried daughters. He was a member of the Church, a deacon, he had a reputation of his own to maintain; he could decide to lie, and say that Stara had been sleeping with the customers behind his back, so as to save that reputation. Then, out she'd go, told to leave the village and not return. Just like the last time she'd gotten herself with child.

Oh yes, and what would happen to Rune *then*?

She might well be tossed out with her mother—but likelier, far likelier, was that Jeoff would get rid of Stara, but keep her daughter. After all, the daughter was a proven hard worker, with nothing against her save that she was a light-skirt's daughter, and possibly a bastard herself.

That wasn't her fault, but it should give Rune all the more reason that she should be grateful for a place and someone willing to employ her.

And what would that mean, but the same result as if he married Stara?

Rune could predict the outcome of that, easily enough. She'd wind up doing all her work and Stara's too.

Eventually Jeoff would marry some girl from the village, like Amanda, who'd lord it over Rune and pile more work on her, and probably verbal abuse as well, if not physical abuse. It would depend on just how much Jeoff would be willing to indulge his wife, how much he'd support her against the "hired help."

And when the new wife got pregnant, there'd be all the work tending to *her* precious brat. Or rather, brats; there'd be one a year, sure as the spring coming, for that was the way the village girls conducted their lives. It was proper for a wife to do her duty by her husband, and make as many babies as possible.

No time for fiddling, then, for certain sure. No time for anything. At least Stara was old enough that there likely wouldn't be another child after the first. With a new, young wife, there'd be as many as she could spawn, with Rune playing nursemaid to all of them.

Unless Rune told them all that she wasn't having any of that, and went off on her own, to try her hand at making a living with her fiddle.

And for a moment, that seemed a tempting prospect, until cold reality intruded.

Oh, surely, she told herself cynically. *A fine living I'd make at it, too. I'm not as good as the worst of the minstrels who've been here—and surely they aren't as good as the Guild Musicians, or the folk who make the circuits of the great Faires. Which means, what? That I'd starve, most like.*

What would be better—or worse? Starvation, or the loss of music, of a life of her own? A dangerous life alone on the open road, living hand-to-mouth, or a life of endless drudgery?

She sniffed, and stifled a sob. There didn't seem to be much of a choice, no matter which way she turned—both lives were equally bleak.

And what about Stara herself? Stara was her mother; how much did Rune owe her?

If she did get with child, and Jeoff did throw her out, Stara would be in an even worse plight than Rune faced. She would be pregnant, out of work, nowhere to go, and no longer young enough to charm her way, however briefly, into someone's household.

For a moment, Rune suffered a pang of guilt and worry. *But no one forced her into Jeoff's bed,* she told herself after a moment. *No one told her to go chasing after her master, hoping for a wedding ring. She's the one that made the decision, to risk her future without even a thought for what might happen to me as well as her!*

That killed any feelings of guilt. If Stara got herself into trouble, it was *her* problem, and she could get herself right back out again. *Why should*

I suffer because my mother's a damn fool? She doesn't even want me to call her "Mother" any more.

But that brought up still another possibility.

There was no doubt of it that Stara didn't like having a fourteen-year-old daughter; that she thought it made her look old. If she decided that Rune was a liability in her plan to capture Jeoff and become his wife, she might well do something to drive Rune away herself.

It wouldn't even be hard to find an excuse. All Stara would have to do would be to tell him that Rune was sleeping with Jib or any of the boys from the village—or, most likely of all, with the musicians that had been passing through. The villagers would be glad to believe such tales, and might even make up a few of their own.

And Jeoff was like any other man; he was fallible and flawed, and subject to making some irrational decisions. Even though he was enjoying himself with Stara—or perhaps, because he was enjoying himself with Stara—he would never tolerate openly loose morals on his premises on the part of anyone else.

While the large inns—so Rune had heard, from the female musicians—were tolerant of such things, Jeoff never had been. He could get away with forbidding prostitutes to use his inn because most of his custom was local. Larger inns couldn't afford such niceties, and in fact, larger inns often kept whores to supply their clients. But the folk needing rooms out here, off the main roads, most often traveled alone, or with a long-time partner. In a case like that, if the partner was a female, and the male of the pair said they were married, then they might as well have posted the banns, so Jeoff didn't enforce his rule. There was no inn nearer than Beeford, and that gave him something of a monopoly on trade. Those who needed Jeoff's rooms had no choice—and the locals would come to drink his beer whether or not he allowed loose women about.

In fact, Jeoff and Rose had been considered pillars of the community for their godly ways. That was part of what made Jeoff such a good marital prospect now.

And that was precisely what made it likely that he'd dismiss her at the first complaint of looseness, particularly if it came from her mother.

Maybe I just ought to turn whore, she thought with another stifled sob. *At least then I'd have something in the way of a trade. . . .*

Despite Jeoff's strictness, she wasn't entirely innocent of the ways of light-skirts. Some few of the travelers, men with gold and silver in their purses rather than copper and silver, had brought with them their own, brazen, hard-eyed women. And once or twice, other travelers in Faire season had met such a woman here, each departing in another direction after a single shared night. Jeoff had never turned these men away; they paid well, they often carried weapons or acted haughtily, and as if they were either dangerous or important. But he had served them himself, not permitting either Stara or Rune anywhere near them, and Rose had always worn a frown the entire time such women were under her roof.

Then there was the fellow who came through at Faire-time with his own tents and wagons, and a collection of freaks and "dancing maidens." His "maidens" were nothing of the sort, whatever his freaks were. There

were always a lot of male visitors from the village to his tents after dark
when the Faire closed. . . .

She turned on her back again, biting her lip in remembrance. That
man—he'd made her feel so filthy, just by the way he acted, that she'd
wanted to bathe every time she had to be anywhere near him. . . .

He'd hired Rune once, when his own musician took sick, having her
play for the performances given during the day. Rose, innocent of what
those performances were like, had judged she was unlikely to come to
any harm during the daylight hours and had given her leave.

The dancers hadn't danced, much. Their costumes seemed to consist
of skirts and bodices made entirely of layers and layers of veils. Their
movement was minimal, and consisted of removing one veil after another,
while wiggling in a kind of bored pantomime of desire to the drumbeats.
It wasn't even particularly graceful.

Rune hadn't said anything to anyone; if Jeoff knew what was going on,
he didn't bother to enlighten Rose, and Rune doubted anyone else would
tell her. There wasn't any reason to; Rune sat behind a screen to play for
the "dancers," and no one in the audience had any notion who the musician back there was. She'd needed the money rather badly, for strings
and a new bow, the old one having cracked to the point that Rune was
afraid to subject it to too much stress—and she'd given her word that
she'd take the job, and felt as if she couldn't walk out on it once she'd
agreed. But she'd been horribly uncomfortable, embarrassed beyond
words, and feeling vaguely sickened by what she saw from her hiding
place. She'd been glad when the regular musician recovered from his
illness after two days and resumed his place.

It hadn't been the taking off of clothes that had bothered her, it was
the way the women had done it. Even at thirteen, she'd known there was
something wrong with what was going on.

The Church said displays like that, of a woman's body, were forbidden,
and a sin. Rune had never quite reasoned out why that should be so—for
the Holy Book said other things, entirely, about taking joy in the way of a
man and a maid, and celebrating the body and the spirit. But the dancers
certainly seemed to feel the same way as the Church—yet they kept dancing,
as if they reveled in doing the forbidden. And the men who came to watch
them gave Rune the same feeling. There was something slimy about it all,
tawdry and cheap, like the way Jon had made her feel this afternoon.

The man who ran the show was horrible, able to make almost anything
sound like an innuendo. He was *using* those women, using them with
the same callousness that Kerd the Butcher displayed with the animals
he slaughtered.

But they, in turn, were using their audience, promising something they
wouldn't deliver, not without a further price attached. Promising something they probably *couldn't* give—promising gold, and delivering cheap
gilded lead.

And the men in the audience were part of the conspiracy. *They* certainly
didn't care about the women they ogled, or later bedded. They cared only
for the moment's pleasure, sating themselves without regard for the women,
using them as if they were soulless puppets. Things, not human beings.

No, she couldn't do that . . . couldn't reduce herself to a creature. There was something wrong about that. And not the Church's notion of right and wrong, either. No matter what happened, she could not put herself in the position of used and user. . . .

And yet, that's exactly the position that Stara put herself in. She was no different from any of those hard-eyed women who stayed only the night, from the "dancers" at the Faire. She had determined on a price for herself, and she was using Jeoff to get it, with never any thought of love or joy involved.

And Jeoff was most definitely using Stara, for he was taking advantage of her by demanding what he wanted without "paying" for it first, forcing Stara to put herself in the position of begging for that price.

It would be a different story if they had come together with care for one another.

Not that it mattered, in the end. Whatever came of this, it would probably spell trouble for Rune.

And with that comforting thought, exhaustion finally got the better of her, and she slept.

". . . and when I got out of the kitchen, he was already gone," she lamented to Jib, as they raked the area in front of the stable clean of droppings, and scattered water over the pounded dirt to keep the dust down. "I picked up a few songs from him, but he really was awfully good, and he knew more about the Bardic Guild than anyone I ever talked to before. There was so much I wanted to ask him about! I wish I hadn't had to work so hard—I could have gotten a lesson from him—"

"It don't seem fair to me," Jib said slowly. "I know Stara wasn't doin' anythin'. She was just foolin' around the common room, actin' like she was cleanin' mugs and whatall, but she weren't doin' nothin' but fill pitchers now an' again. Them mugs was still dirty when she was done. Cook was talkin' about it this mornin' t' Tarn."

"I shouldn't have had to play server," she complained bitterly, swinging the watering can back and forth to cover as much ground as possible. "They should've let me fiddle, like they used to. You can't have a whole evening of music with just one musician, not if you don't want him to wish he'd never walked in before the night's over. Master Heron was tired, really tired, by the time he was done. If they'd let me play, I could've let him take a good long break or two. And he *wanted* me to play, he said so, he wanted to know if I would play a duet with him. He could have helped me, taught me songs right—"

"Well, heckfire, Rune," Jib replied, sounding, for the first time in weeks, like her old friend instead of the odd, awkward stranger who wanted to court her. "I dunno what t' say. Seems t' me pretty rotten unfair. Ye know? Looks t' me like your Mam is gettin' what she wants, an' ol' Jeoff is gettin' what he wants, an' all you're gettin' is hind teat. Ev'body here is doin' all right but you, and ye're th' one pickin' up the slack."

Rune nodded unhappily, as they walked back to the stable to put the watering cans away under the shelves by the stable door. "Nobody ever asks me what I want," she said bitterly. "Anything that needs done, they throw on me, without ever asking if I've got the time. They all seem to think they can do whatever they want with me, because I'm not important. I'm just a girl, just Stara's brat, and I don't count. I'm whatever they want me to be, with no say in it."

And that includes Jon and his friends.

"Well, ye got a roof, an' plenty t' eat," Jib began, echoing her pessimistic thoughts of last night. "This ain't a bad life, really—"

"It's not enough," she continued, angry now. "I hate this place, and I hate most of the people in it! I don't *want* to be stuck here the rest of my life, in this little hole back of beyond, where everybody knows everything about everybody else, or they think they do. And they think that they're so good, God's keeping a special place in heaven for them! I can't get anywhere here, because no matter what I did, I'd never be good enough for *them* to even be civil to."

Jib's brow puckered, as if he had never once thought that someone might want something other than the life they now shared. That Rune would want the freedom to play her fiddle, he should have understood—she'd dinned it into his head often enough. But that she'd want to leave was probably incomprehensible. He certainly looked surprised—and puzzled—by her outburst. "Well," he said slowly, "What do you want, then?"

Rune flung her arms wide. "I want the world!" she cried extravagantly. "I want all of it! I want—I want kings and queens at my feet, I want wealth and power and—"

"Na, na, Rune," Jib interrupted, laughing at her in a conciliating tone. "That's not sensible, lass. Nobody can have that, outside of a tale. Leastwise, no musicker. What is it ye really want?"

"Well, if I have to be sensible . . ." She paused a moment, thought about what it was that was making her so unhappy. It wasn't the drudgery so much, as the loss of hope that there'd ever be anything else. And the confinement in a corner of the world where nothing ever happened, and nothing ever changed, and she'd always be looked down on and taken advantage of. "Jib, I want to get out of here. The people here think I'm scum, you know that. Even if the High King rode up here tomorrow and claimed me as his long-lost daughter, they'd look down their noses at me and say, 'Eh, well, and she's a bastard after all, like we thought.' "

Jib nodded agreement, and sighed. He leaned up against the doorpost of the stable and selected a straw to chew on from one of the bales stacked there.

"So?" he said, scratching his head, and squinting into the late afternoon sunlight. "If ye could go, how'd ye do it? Where'd ye go, then?"

"I'd want some money," she said, slowly. "Enough to buy another instrument, a guitar, or a lute, or even a mandolin. And enough to keep me fed and under shelter, and pay for the lessons I'd need. I couldn't do that here, it would have to be in a real city. Even if I had the money, and the instrument, I can't keep going on like I have been, begging for time to play, and making do with lessons snatched from other minstrels. I need to learn to read and write better, and read and write music, too."

"All right," Jib responded, pushing away from the doorpost. "Say you've got all that. What then?" He led the way towards the door on the other side of the stable-yard, where they both had chores awaiting them—her to clean the common room, him to scrub pots for the cook.

"Then—" She paused just outside the inn door and looked off down the road with longing. "Then—I'd go to the big Midsummer Faire at Kingsford. I'd march straight in there, and I'd sign right up for the trials for the Bardic Guild. And I'd win them, too, see if I wouldn't. I'd win a place in the Guild, and a Master, and then just see what I'd do!" She turned to Jib with such a fierce passion that he took an involuntary step back. "You said nobody had money and power and kings and queens at their feet outside of a tale? Well, the Guild Bards have all that! All that and more! And when I was a Guild Bard there'd be nobles come wanting me to serve them, begging me to serve them, right up to kings and even the High King himself! I could come riding back in here with a baggage train a half dozen horses long, and servants bowing to me and calling me 'My Lady,' and a laurel and a noble title of my own. And *then* these backwater blowhards would see—"

"Oh, would we now?" asked Kaylan Potter mockingly, behind her.

She whirled, already on the defensive. Kaylan and three of his friends lounged idly against the door to the common room. Kaylan and his friends were almost fully adult; journeymen, not 'prentices, tall and strong. They looked enough alike to be from the same family, and indeed, they were all distant cousins, rawboned, muscular and swarthy, in well-worn smocks and leather vests and breeches. She wondered, frantically, if she was in for another attempt like the one Jon and his friends had made. Her heart raced with sudden fear. Surely not right here, where she'd thought she was safe—

No. Her heart slowed, as the young men made no move towards her. No, they were older and smarter than Jon. They wouldn't risk their tavern-privileges by trying to force her on the doorstep in broadest daylight. Elsewhere, perhaps, they might have made some sort of move—but not here and now.

But they were not particularly amused at her description of them—by implication—nor her assessment of their parents and neighbors.

"We'd see, would we?" Kaylan repeated, looking down his snub nose at her. "And just what would we see? We'd see a braggart, foolish girl-child with her head full of foolish fancies getting her comeuppance, I'm thinking. We'd see a chit with a head too big for her hat learning just what a little fish she is. We'd see a brat who never was able to win even a village Faire fiddling contest learning what it means to brag and fall. That's what I think we'd be seeing, eh, lads?"

The other three nodded solemnly, superior smirks on their dark faces. Her heart squeezed in her chest; she felt her face grow hot, then cold.

"Oh, aye," said Thom Beeson, his hair falling into his eyes as he nodded. "Aye that I'd say, seein' as the wee chit couldn't even win the Harvest Faire fiddlin' contest four years agone, and her only competition a couple of old men, a lad claimin' t' be a Guild 'prentice, and a toy-maker."

She gathered all her dignity about her and strode past them, into the tavern. There wasn't anyone in the common room but Maeve, who was sweeping the floor with a care that would have been meticulous in anyone but her. The four young men followed her inside and threw themselves down on a bench, their attitude betraying the fact that they figured they had her cowed. "Now, how about beer and a bit of bread and cheese for some hard workin' men, wench," said Kaylan carelessly. "You can be a first-rate servin' wench even if you're only a second-rate fiddler."

She held her temper so as not to provoke them, but it was a struggle. She wanted to hit them—she wanted to throw their damned beer in their smug faces. And she didn't dare do any of it. Thom was right, damn him. She *had* lost the Harvest Faire fiddling contest four years ago, and it had been the last contest their little village Faire had held. She'd never had another chance to compete. And they all remembered her failure. So did she; the remembrance was a bitter taste in her mouth as she filled their mugs from the tap and took them to the table.

She thudded the filled mugs down in front of them, so that they foamed over, and turned on her heel.

"So, what else were you going to show us, wench?" Kaylan asked lazily. "Is it true that you're takin' after your mother that way?"

Someone else had been spreading tales, it seemed. Already she was judged—

"Or are we gonna hear more boastin'?" Thom drawled. "Empty air don't mean a thing, wench. If ye could fiddle as well as ye can yarn, ye might be worth listenin' to."

She lost the tenuous hold she had on her temper.

She spun, let the words fly without thinking about the consequences. They had challenged her too far, in a way she couldn't shrug off.

"What am I going to show you?" she hissed, her hands crooked into claws, her heart near bursting. "I'll tell you! I'll do more than *show* you! I'll prove to you I'm the best fiddler these parts have ever seen, and too good for the likes of *you*! I'll go fiddle for—for—"

"For who, wench?" Thom laughed, snapping his fingers at her. "For the Sire?"

"For the Skull Hill Ghost!" she snarled without thinking. "I reckon he'd know a good fiddler when he heard one, even if a lout like you doesn't!"

Thom threw back his head and laughed. "From braggart t' liar in one breath!" he said derisively. "You? Fiddle for the Ghost? Ye'd never dare set foot on Skull Hill in daylight, much less by night! Why, ye never even step outside th' building oncet the sun goes down! I bet ye're so 'fraid of the dark, ye hide yer head under the covers so's th' goblins don' git ye!"

"Liar, liar," taunted Kaylan, wagging his finger at her. "Little girls shouldn't lie t' their betters. Little girls should know their place. Specially when they're old 'nuff t' be big girls." He grinned, insinuatingly. "Specially when there's big boys as can give 'em things, an' do nice things for 'em, if they've got the wit t' be nice back."

If she'd had any notion of backing down, those words put the idea right out of her head.

"I'll show you who's a liar!" she shouted, too angry to keep her voice down. "I'll show you who's the better around here! I'll go tonight! Right now! Then we'll see who's the coward and who isn't!"

She dashed for the stairs, and took them two at a time, grabbed her fiddle from the shelf, and pelted down the stairs again as fast as her feet could take her without breaking her neck. She burst into the common room to see Jeoff just entering from the kitchen, alerted by the shouting. He turned around to see her hitting the bottom landing with a *thud*.

"Rune!" he called, holding out a cautionary hand. "Rune, what's a-goin' on?"

"*You* tell him," she spat at Kaylan, as she headed out the door, fiddle in hand, at a fast, angry walk. "You started this, you bully—*you* tell him."

By then she was out the door, and the walk had become a run, and no one of Jeoff's girth was going to be able to catch up with her. She pelted down the dirt road as hard as she could run, her fiddle case bumping against her back where she'd slung it, her heart burning within her and driving her to run even faster, as if she could outdistance the cruel taunts.

At least her parting sally should get Kaylan and his friends into a situation they'd have a hard time explaining themselves out of. Jeoff wasn't going to like losing his help for the night.

She took the road away from the village, deeper into the forested hills, slowing to a walk once she was out of sight of the inn and it looked as if there wouldn't be any immediate pursuit.

By then, her side hurt and she was winded and sticky with sweat and road dust. And by the time she reached the place where the Old Road joined the new one, she'd had ample chance to cool down and think about just how stupid she'd been.

The Old Road represented a more direct path through the hills—but one that was never taken after dark. And, more often than not, local travelers avoided it even in daylight. Hence the overgrown condition of the Old Road, the grasses sprouting in the eroded ruts, the bushes creeping up onto it a little more every year. Even though the Old Road would save the weary traveler several miles, no one took it who had the slightest chance of being on it after the sun went down.

For there *was* a ghost that haunted the place, a vengeful, angry ghost; one that inhabited the Skull Hill Pass. It was no legend; it had been seen reliably by the few very fortunate souls who had managed to elude his grasp by fleeing his pursuit past the running water of the stream at the foot of the hill. The new road had been built fifty years ago, or so Rune had been told, after Father Donlin went up on the hill to exorcise the Ghost, and was found up there in the morning, stone cold dead, with a look of utter terror on his face.

That, in fact, was how most of the victims were found; and no one who ever went up there at night returned alive. Those few who had escaped death had been going down the hill when the sun set, having miscalculated or suffered some mishap on the road that had delayed them past the safe hour. There had been five victims besides the Father that Rune herself knew about, and stories spoke of dozens. . . .

No one knew how long the ghost had been there, nor why he haunted and killed. Granny Beeson, Thom's grandmother, and the oldest person in the village, said he'd been there as long as she remembered.

And now Rune was walking straight up the haunted hill, into the Ghost's power. Deliberately. Seeking the Ghost out, a spirit that had killed a holy priest, as if her music had a chance of appeasing it.

With more than enough time, as she climbed the uneven, root-ridged track, to regret her impulse.

She squinted through the trees at the setting sun; she reckoned by the angle that once she reached the top of the pass, she'd have a little more than half an hour to settle herself and wait for her—host. There seemed fewer birds on this track than the other, and they all seemed to be birds of ill-omen: ravens, corbies, blackbirds, black boat-tails.

She tried to think if any of the ghost's other victims had been female. Maybe he only went after men—

But, no. Granny Beeson had said that two of the dead had been lovers running off to get married against the girls' parental wishes, so the thing killed women too.

Stupid, stupid, stupid, she berated herself. *If I live through this, I am never going to let my temper get me into this kind of mess again. Not ever. I swear.*

But first, she was going to have to survive the rest of the night.

CHAPTER FOUR

As sunset neared, the few birds that had been about made themselves vanish into the brush, and Rune was left alone on Skull Hill without even a raven for company. It might have been her imagination, but the trees seemed a little starved up here, a strange, skeletal growth, with limbs like bony hands clawing the sky. It seemed colder up here as well—and the wind was certainly stronger, moaning softly through the trees in a way that sounded uncannily human, and doing nothing for her confidence level.

She looked around at the unpromising landscape and chose a rock, finding one with a little hollow. She spent some time pulling up some of the dry grass of last year's growth, giving the rock a kind of cushion to keep the cold away, and sat down to wait. As the crimson sun touched the top of Beacon Hill opposite her perch, and crept all-too-quickly behind it, she began to shiver, half with cold, and half with the fear she had no difficulty in admitting now that she was alone.

Of all the stupid things I've ever done, this was one of the stupidest.

It was not a particularly spectacular sunset; no clouds to catch and hold the sun's last rays. Just the red disk sinking towards and then behind the hill, the pale sky growing darker—deepening from blue to black, and all too soon; the stars coming out, brightest first, pinpoints of cold blue-white light.

The wind died to nothing just at sunset, then picked up again after the last stars appeared. Rune took out her fiddle with benumbed fingers, and tuned it by feel, then sat on her rock and fingered every tune she knew without actually playing, to keep her fingers limber. And still nothing happened.

She was tired, cold, and her fear was fading. Her bones began to ache with the cold. It would be so easy to pack up, creep down the hill, and return to the inn claiming that she'd fiddled for the Ghost and gotten away.

The idea was very tempting.

But—that would be a lie and a cheat. She swore she'd do this; she pledged her word, and even if the villagers thought her word was worthless, that didn't make it so. If she broke her word, if she lied about what she'd done, what would that make her? As worthless as the villagers claimed she was.

Besides, they probably wouldn't believe me anyway.

The moon appeared, its cold silver light flooding over the hills and making them look as if they'd been touched with frost. She marked time while it climbed, keeping her fingers warm by tucking them in her armpits, and taking out the fiddle now and again to make sure it was still in tune. There was a great deal more life around here than there had been in the daylight—unless her presence had frightened everything away until she stopped moving. Owls hooted off in the distance, and a few early crickets sang nearby. Frogs croaked in the stream below her as bats and a nighthawk swooped through the pass, looking for flying insects. And once, a great hare loped lazily down the road, pausing in surprise at the sight of her, and standing up on his haunches to take a better look, for all the world like a white stone garden statue of the kind the Sire had in his pleasure-garden.

At the sight of him, she lost the last of her fear. He was so quizzical, so comical—it was impossible to be afraid of a place that held an animal like this.

She chuckled at him, and he took fright at the sound, whirling on his hind feet and leaping into the underbrush in a breath.

She shook her head, relaxing a little in spite of the chill. There was no Ghost, most likely, and perhaps there never had been. Perhaps the "ghost" had been no more than a particularly resourceful bandit. Perhaps—

The moon touched the highest part of her arc, marking the hour as midnight, just as the thought occurred to her. And at that moment, absolute silence descended on the hill, as if everything within hearing had been frightened into frozen immobility.

The crickets stopped chirping altogether; the owl hoots cut off. Even the wind died, leaving the midnight air filled only with a stillness that made the ears ache as they sought after the vanished sounds.

Then the wind returned with a howl and a rush, blowing her shirt flat to her body, chilling her to the bone and turning the blood in her veins to ice. It moaned, like something in pain, something dying by inches.

Then it changed, and whipped around her, twisting her garments into confusion. It swirled around her, picking up dead leaves and pelting her with them, the center of a tiny, yet angry cyclone that was somehow more frightening than the pounding lightning of the worst thunderstorm.

It lashed her with her own hair, blinded her with dust. Then it whisked away to spin on the road in front of her, twisting the leaves in a miniature whirlwind less than ten paces from her.

Her skin crawled, as if there were something watching her from the center of the wind. Malignant; that was what it felt like. As if this wind was a living thing, and it hated every creature it saw. . . .

She shook her hair out of her eyes, hugged her arms to her body and shook with cold and the prickling premonition of danger. She couldn't take her eyes off the whirlwind and the swirling leaves caught in it. The leaves—it was so strange, she could see every vein of them—

A claw of ice ran down her spine, as she realized that she could see every vein of them—because they were glowing.

She'd seen foxfire—what country child hadn't—but this was different. Each leaf glowed a distinct and leprous shade of greenish-white. And they were drawing closer together into a column in the center of the whirlwind, forming a solid, slightly irregular shape, thicker at the bottom than at the top, with a kind of cowl-like formation at the very top.

Kind of? It *was* a cowl; the leaves had merged into a cowled and robed figure, like a monk. But the shape beneath the robe suggested nothing remotely human, and she knew with dread that she didn't want to see the face hidden within that cowl. . . . The wind swirled the apparition's robes as it had swirled the leaves, but disturbed it not at all.

Then, suddenly, the wind died; the last of the leaves drifted to pile around the apparition's feet . . . if it had feet, and not some other appendages. The cowl turned in Rune's direction, and there was a suggestion of glowing eyes within the shadows of the hood.

A voice, an icy, whispering voice, came out of the darkness from all around her; from everywhere, yet nowhere. It could have been born of her imagination, yet Rune knew the voice was the Ghost's, and that to run was to die. Instantly, but in terror that would make dying seem to last an eternity.

"Why have you come here, stupid child?" it murmured, as fear urged her to run anyway. "Why were you waiting here? For me? Foolish child, do you not know what I am? What I could do to you?"

At least it decided to talk to me first. . . .

Rune had to swallow twice before she could speak, and even then her voice cracked and squeaked with fear.

"I've come to fiddle for you—sir?" she said, gasping for breath between each word, trying to keep her teeth from chattering.

And it's a good thing I'm not here to sing. . . .

She held out Lady Rose and her bow. "Fiddle?" the Ghost breathed, as if it couldn't believe what it had heard. "You have come to *fiddle*? To play mortal music? For me?"

For the first time since it had appeared, Rune began to hope she might survive this encounter. At least she'd surprised this thing. "Uh—yes. Sir? I did."

The glow beneath the hood increased, she was not imagining it. And the voice strengthened. "Why, mortal child? Why did you come here to— fiddle for me?"

She toyed with the notion of telling it that she'd done so for some noble reason, because she felt sorry for it, or that she wanted to bring it some pleasure—

But she had the feeling that it would know if she lied to it. She also had the feeling that if she lied to it, it would not be amused.

And since her life depended on keeping it amused—

So she told it the truth.

"It was on a dare, sir," she stammered. "There's these boys in the town, and they told me I was a second-rater, and—I swore I'd come up here and fiddle for you, and let you judge if I was a second-rater or a wizard with m' bow."

The cowl moved slightly, as if the creature were cocking its head a little sideways. "And why would they call you second-rate?"

"Because—because they want me to be, sir," she blurted. "If I'm second-rate they can look down on me, an'—do what they want to me—"

For some reason, the longer she spoke, the easier it became to do so, to pour out all her anger, her fear, all the bottled emotions she couldn't have told anyone before this. The spirit stayed silent, attentive through all of it, keeping its attitude of listening with interest, even sympathy. This was, by far, the most even-handed hearing she'd had from anyone. It was even easy to speak of the attack Jon and his friends had made, tears of rage and outrage stinging her eyes as she did.

Finally, her anger ran out, and with it, the words. She spread her hands, bow in one, fiddle in the other. "So that's it, sir. That's why I'm here."

"You and I have something in common, I think." Did she really hear those barely whispered words, or only imagine them?

She certainly didn't imagine the next ones.

"So you have come to fiddle for me, to prove to these ignorant dirt-grubbers that you are their—equal." The Ghost laughed, a sound with no humor in it, the kind of laugh that called up empty wastelands and icy peaks. "Well, then, girl. Fiddle, then. And pray to that Sacrificed God of yours that you fiddle well, very well. If you please me, if you continue to entertain me until dawn, I shall let you live, a favor I have never granted any other, and that should prove you are not only their paltry equal, but their better. But I warn you—the moment my attention lags, little girl—you'll die like all the others, and you will join all the others in my own, private little Hell." It chuckled again, cruelly. "Or, you may choose to attempt to run away, to outrun me to the stream at the bottom of the hill. Please notice that I did say *attempt*. It is an *attempt* that others have made and failed."

She thought for a moment that she couldn't do it. Her hands shook too much; she couldn't remember anything—not a single song, not so much as a lullabye.

Running was no choice either; she knew that.

So she tucked her fiddle under her chin anyway, and set the bow on the strings. . . .

And played one single, trembling note. And that note somehow called forth another and another followed that, until she was playing a stream, a cascade of bright and lively melody—

And then she realized she was playing "Guard's Farewell," one of her early tunes, and since it was a slip-jig, it led naturally to "Jenny's Fancy," and that in its turn to "Summer Cider"—

By then she had her momentum, and the tunes continued to come, one after another, as easily and purely as if she were practicing all by herself. She even began to enjoy herself, a little; to relax at least, since the Ghost hadn't killed her yet. This might work. She just might survive the night.

The Ghost stood in that "listening" stance; she closed her eyes to concentrate better as she often did when practicing, letting the tunes bring back bright memories of warm summer days or nights by the fire as she had learned them. The memories invoked other tunes, and more memories, and the friendships shared with musicians who called themselves by the names of birds: Linnet, Heron, Nightingale, and Raven; Robin, Jay and Thrush. When only parts of tunes came, half-remembered bits of things other musicians had played that she hadn't quite caught, she made up the rest. She cobbled together children's game-rhymes into reels and jigs. She played cradle-songs, hymns, anything and everything she had ever heard or half-heard the melody to.

When she feared she was going to run dry, she played a random run, improvised on that, and turned it into a melody of her very own.

It happened with an ease that amazed her, somewhere in the back of her mind. She'd wanted to write songs, she'd had them living in the back of her mind for so long, and yet she'd never more than half-believed that she was going to get them to come out. It was a marvel, a wonder, and she would have liked to try the tune over a second and third time. But the Ghost was still waiting, and she dared not stop.

Hours passed, longer than she had ever played without stopping before. Gradually the non-stop playing began to take its toll, as she had known would happen. Her upper bow-arm ached, then cramped; then her fingering hand got a cramp along the outside edge. The spot below her chin in her collarbone felt as if she was driving a spike into her neck.

Then her fingering arm burned and cramped, and her back started to hurt, spreading agony down her spine into her legs. She fiddled with tears of pain in her eyes, while her fingers somehow produced rollicking dance music completely divorced from the reality of her aching limbs.

Her fingers were numb; she was grateful for that, for she was entirely certain that there were blisters forming on her fingertips under the calluses, and that if she ever stopped, she'd feel them.

Finally, she played "Fields of Barley," and knew a moment of complete panic as her mind went blank. There was nothing there to play. She'd played everything she knew, and she somehow had the feeling that the Ghost wouldn't be amused by repeating music.

And there was no sign of dawn. She was going to die after all.

But her fingers were wiser than she was, for they moved on their own, and from beneath them came the wild, sad, wailing notes of the laments that the Gypsy Nightingale had played for her. . . .

Now, for the first time, the Ghost stirred and spoke, and she opened her eyes in startlement.

"More—" it breathed. "More—"

Rune closed her eyes again, and played every note she remembered, and some she hadn't known she'd remembered. And the air warmed about

her, losing its chill; her arms slowly grew lighter, the aches flowed out of
them, until she felt as fresh as she'd been when first she started this. Free
from pain, she gave herself up to the music, playing in a kind of trance
in which there was nothing but the music.

At last she came as far as she could. There was no music left, her own,
or anyone else's. She played the last sobbing notes of the Gypsy song
Nightingale had told her was a lament for her own long-lost home, holding
them out as long as she could.

But they flowed out and away, and finally, ended.

She opened her eyes.

The first rays of dawn lightened the horizon, bringing a flush of pink
to the silver-blue sky. The stars had already faded in the east and were
winking out overhead, and somewhere off in the distance, a cock crowed
and a chorus of birdcalls drifted across the hills.

There was nothing standing before her now. The Ghost was gone—but
he had left something behind.

Where he had stood, where there had once been a heap of leaves,
there was now a pile of shining silver coins. More than enough to pay for
that second instrument, the lessons for it, and part of her keep while she
mastered it.

As she stared at the money in utter disbelief, a whisper came from
around her, like a breath of the cool dawn wind coming up off the hills.

"Go, child. Take your reward, and go. And do not look back." A laugh,
a kindly one this time. "You deserved gold, but you would never have
convinced anyone you came by it honestly."

Then, nothing, but the bird song.

She put her fiddle away first, with hands that shook with exhaustion,
but were otherwise unmarred, by blisters or any other sign of the abuse
she'd heaped on them.

Then, and only then, did she gather up the coins, one at a time, each
one of them proving to be solid, and as real as her own hand. One
handful; then two—so many she finally had to tear off the tail of her shift
for a makeshift pouch. Coins so old and worn they had no writing left,
and only a vague suggestion of a face. Coins from places she'd never
heard of. Coins with non-human faces on them, and coins minted by the
Sire's own treasury. More money than she had ever seen in her life.

And all of it hers.

She stopped at the stream at the foot of the hill, the place that traditionally marked the spot where the Ghost's power ended. She couldn't help
but stop; she was exhausted and exhilarated, and her legs wouldn't hold
her anymore. She sank down beside the stream and splashed cold water
in her face, feeling as if she would laugh, cry, or both in the next instant.

The money in a makeshift pouch cut from the tail of her shift weighed
heavily at her belt, and lightly in her heart.

Freedom. That was what the Ghost had given her—and from its final
words, she knew that the spirit had been well aware of the gift it had
granted.

Go and don't look back. . . .

It had given her freedom, but only if she chose to grasp it—if she did go, and didn't look back, leaving everything behind. Her mother, Jib, the tavern . . .

Could she do that? It had taken a certain kind of courage to dare the Ghost, but it would take another, colder kind of emotion to abandon everything and everyone she'd always known. No matter what they had done to her, could she leave them for the unknown?

Her elation faded, leaving the weariness. She picked herself up and started for home, at a slower pace, sure only of her uncertainty.

Go—or stay? Each step asked the same question. And none of the echoes brought back an answer. The road was empty this time of the morning, with no one sharing it but her and the occasional squirrel. A cool, damp breeze brought the scent of fresh earth, and growing things from the forest on either hand. It was a shame to reach the edge of the village, and see where the hand of man had fallen heavily.

The inn, with its worn wooden siding and faded sign, seemed shabby and much, much smaller than it had been when she left yesterday. Dust from the road coated everything, and there wasn't even a bench outside for a weary traveler to sit on, nor a pump for watering himself and his beast. These were courtesies, yes, but they cost nothing and their absence bespoke a certain niggardliness of hospitality. She found herself eyeing her home with disfavor, if not dislike, and approached it with reluctance.

Prompted by a caution she didn't understand, she left the road and came up to the inn from the side, where she wouldn't be seen from the open door. She walked softly, making no noise, when she heard the vague mumble of voices from inside the common room through the still-shuttered windows.

She paused just outside the open door and still hidden from view, as the voices drifted out through the cracks in the shutters.

". . . her bed wasn't slept in," Stara said, and Rune wondered why she had never noticed the nasal, petulant whine in her mother's voice before. "But the fiddle's gone. I think she ran away, Jeoff. She didn't have the guts to admit she couldn't take the dare, and she ran away." Stara sounded both aggrieved and triumphant, as if she felt Rune had done this purely to make her mother miserable, and as if she felt she had been vindicated in some way.

Maybe she's been telling tales to Jeoff herself, the way I figured.

"Oh aye, that I'm sure of," Kaylan drawled with righteous self-importance. "Young Jon said she been a-flirtin' wi' him day agone, and she took it badly when he gave her the pass."

So that was how he explained it, she thought, seething with sudden anger despite her weariness. *But how did he explain his swollen tongue and bruised crotch? That I hit him when he wouldn't lay with me?*

"Anyways, she's been causin' trouble down to village, insultin' the girls and mockin' the boys. Think she got too big fer her hat and couldn't take it t' have her bluff called." Kaylan yawned hugely. "I think ye're well rid of her, Mistress Stara. Could be it was nobbut spring, but could be the girl's gone bad."

"I don't know—" Jeoff said uncertainly. "We need the help, and there's no denying it. If we can find her and get her back, maybe we ought to. A good hiding—"

I'd turn the stick on you, first! she thought angrily.

"Well, as to that," Kaylan said readily. "Me da's got a cousin down Reedben way with too many kids and too little land—happen that he could send ye the twins to help out. Likely ye're goin' to want the extra help, what with summer comin' on. Boy and girl, and 'bout twelve. Old 'nough to work, young 'nough not to cause no trouble.'"

"If they were willing to come for what Rune got," Jeoff said with eagerness and reluctance mixed. "Room, board and two suits 'f clothes in the year . . . haven't got much to spare, not even t' take a new wife, unless things get better."

Rune looked down at the bag of silver coins at her belt, hearing a note in Jeoff's voice she'd never noticed before. A note of complaint, and a tight-fisted whine similar to the one in Stara's voice. And as if she had been gifted with the Sight of things to come, she knew what would happen if she went into that doorway.

No one would ever believe that she had dared Skull Hill and its deadly Ghost, not even with this double-handful of coins to prove it. They'd think she'd found it, or—more likely—that she had stolen it. Jeoff would doubtless take it away from her, and possibly lock her in her room if suspicion ran high enough against her, at least until she could prove that she'd stolen nothing.

Then when no one complained of robbery, they would let her go, but she'd bet they still wouldn't return her hard-earned reward to her. They'd figure she had found a cache of coins along the Old Road, dug it up in the ruins in the Skull Hill Pass, or had found a newly dead victim of the Ghost and had robbed the dead.

And with that as justification, and because she was "just a child," Stara and Jeoff would take it all "to keep it safe for her."

That would surely be the last she would see of it, for Stara would see to it that it was "properly disposed of." She would probably spend a long night closeted with Jeoff, and when it was over, the money would be in *his* coffers. She'd promise it all to him as her "dower," if he agreed to marry her; and since there wasn't a girl in the village who could boast a double handful of silver as her dower, he'd probably agree like a lightning strike. Stara would tell herself, no doubt, that since this ensured Rune a home and a father, it was in her "best interest." Never mind that Rune would be no better off than before—still an unpaid drudge and still without the means to become a Guild Bard.

Jeoff would hide the money away wherever it was he kept the profits of the inn. Rune would *never* get her lessons, her second instrument. She would always be, at best, the local tavern-musician. She would still lack the respect of the locals, although Jeoff as her stepfather would provide some protection from the kind of things Jon had tried. She'd live and die here, never seeing anything but this little village and whoever happened to be passing through.

If she was very lucky, Jib might marry her. In fact, Jeoff would probably encourage that idea. It would mean that he would not have to part with

any of the Ghost's silver for Rune's dower—assuming she could induce any
of the local boys to the wedding altar—and he would then have Jib as an
unpaid drudge forever, as well as Rune and her mother. He would do
well all the way around.

She would still have the reputation of the tavern wench's bastard. She
would still have trouble from the local girls and their mothers, if not the
local boys. And there might come a time when beer or temper overcame
someone's good sense—and she still might find herself fighting off a
would-be rapist. There would be plenty of opportunities over the next
few years for just that kind of "accident." And the boy could always pledge
she'd lied or led him on, and who would the Sire's magistrate believe?
Not Rune.

That was what was in store for her if she stayed. But if she followed
the Ghost's advice, to go, and not look back—

What about Mother? part of her asked.

A colder part had the answer already. Stara could take care of herself.
If she couldn't, that wasn't Rune's problem.

*Besides, I've been standing here for the past few minutes listening to
my own mother slash what little reputation I had to ragged ribbons. She's
not exactly overflowing with maternal protection and love.*

Her jaw clenched; her resolve hardened. No, Stara could damned well
take care of herself. Rune wasn't about to help her.

But what about Jib?

That stopped her cold for a moment. Jib had been as much prey to
the village youngsters as she had, and she'd protected him for a long
time now. What would they do when they found out he didn't have that
protection anymore?

How could she just leave him without a word?

She moved into the shelter of some bushes around the forested side of
the inn, leaned up against a tree, and shut her eyes for a moment, trying
to think.

He didn't need to worry about rape. No one was going to try and force
him because his mother had the word of being a slut. His problems had
always stemmed from the bigger, stronger boys seeing him as an easy
target, someone they could beat up with impunity.

But the bigger, stronger boys had other things to occupy them now.
They'd all either been apprenticed, or they'd taken their places in the
fields with their farmer-fathers. They had very little time to go looking
for mischief, and there'd be no excuse for them giving Jib a hiding if he'd
been sent to the village on an errand.

Nor did Jib have to worry about the girls' wagging tongues. They didn't
care one way or another about him—except, perhaps, as to whether or
not he'd been tupping Rune. That might even earn him a little grudging
admiration, if he refused to tell them, or denied it altogether. They'd be
certain to think that he had, then.

Besides, one way or another, he was going to have to learn to fend for
himself eventually. It might as well be now.

Sorry, Jib. You'll be all right.

She worked her way through the bushes, farther along the side of the inn, to stand below the eaves.

There was one way into her room that she hadn't bothered to take for years, not since she and Jib had gone swimming at night and hunting owls.

She looked up, peering through the leaves of the big oak that grew beside the inn, and saw that, sure enough, the shutters were open on the window to her room. Stara hadn't bothered to close them.

Very well, then. She'd make the truth out of part of the lie. Carefully, she put the fiddle down beside the trunk and pulled the pouch of coins from her belt, tucking it into her shirt. It was safer there than anywhere else while she climbed.

She jumped up and caught the lowest limb of the oak she'd been leaning against, pulling herself up onto it, and calling up an ache in her arms. It was a lot harder to climb the tree than she remembered—but not as hard as fiddling all night.

From that limb she found hand- and toe-holds up the trunk to the next branch. This one went all the way to her attic window, slanting above the roof and sometimes scraping against it when high winds blew.

She eased her way belly-down along the branch, with the pouch of silver resting against her stomach above her belt. She crept along it like a big cat, not wanting to sling herself underneath the way she had when she was a kid. It was easier to climb that way, but also easier to be seen. The branch was still strong enough to take her weight, though it groaned a little as she neared the roof.

When she got to the rooftop, she eased herself over, hanging onto the branch with both hands and arms, feeling with her toes for the windowsill. This part was easier now that she was older; it wasn't as far to reach.

It was a matter of minutes to pack her few belongings in a roll made from her bedding: shirts, breeches, a winter cloak that was a castoff from Rose, a single skirt, and a couple of bodices and vests. Some underclothing. A knife, a fork; a wooden dish and a mug. Two hats, both battered. Stockings, a pair of sandals, and a pair of shoes. Rosin for the bow, and a string of glass beads. An old hunting knife.

She hesitated about taking the bedding, but remembered all the work she'd done, and lost her hesitation. Jeoff owed her a couple of sheets and blankets at least, she figured, for all the work she'd done for him without pay.

Then she tossed the bundle into the brush where she'd left her fiddle, and eased herself down over the sill, catching the branch above and reversing her route to the ground.

Bedroll on her back, fiddle in her hand, and silver in her shirt, she headed down the road to Beeford and beyond, without a single glance behind her.

CHAPTER FIVE

Rune paused for a moment, at the top of what passed for a hill hereabouts, and looked down on the city of Nolton. She forgot her aching feet, and the dry road-dust tickle at the back of her throat no amount of water would ease. She had been anticipating something large, but she was taken a bit aback; she hadn't expected anything this big. The city spread across the green fields in a dull red-brown swath, up and down the river, and so far as she could see, there was no end to it. A trade-city, a city that had never been under attack, Nolton had no walls to keep anyone out. Nolton wanted all comers *inside,* spending their coin, making the city prosper.

The strategy must be working, for it surely looked prosperous. Houses of two and even three stories were common; in the center, there were buildings that towered a dizzying ten or eleven stories tall. The cathedral was one; it loomed over everything else, overshadowing the town as the Church overshadowed the lives of the townsfolk.

She had also been expecting noise, but not this far away from the city itself. But already there was no doubt that she heard sounds that could only come from Nolton; even at this distance, the city hummed, a kind of monotonous chant, in which the individual voices blended until there was no telling what were the parts that comprised it.

She had anticipated crowds; well, she'd gotten them in abundance. There had been some warning in the numbers of travelers for the past day and more on the road.

Although there were throngs of people, until today she hadn't been as apprehensive as she might have been. After all, the whole way here, she had made her way with her fiddle and her songs—

It hadn't been easy, drumming up the courage to approach that first innkeeper, trying to appear nonchalant and experienced at life on the road. She'd taken heart, at first, from the heavy belt of silver coins beneath her shirt. The Ghost had thought her worth listening to, and worth rewarding, for that matter. The memory gave her courage; courage to stride up to inns with all the assurance of the minstrels that had been her teachers, and present herself with an offer of entertainment in exchange for room and board.

It got a little easier with each approach, especially when the innkeepers stayed civil at the very least, and most were cordial even in their rejection.

Not that she had tried great inns; the inns where the Guildsmen and lesser nobles stayed. She didn't even try for the traders' inns, the kind where every traveler had at least a two-horse string. No, she had stuck to common enough inns, the sort simple peddlers and foot-travelers used.

Inns like the one she had grown up in, where she figured she knew the custom and the kind of music they'd prefer. She'd been right, for they welcomed her; always, when they had no other musicians present, and sometimes even when they did, if the other musician was a local or indicated a willingness to share out the proceeds.

No one ever complained about her playing—although she dared not try her luck too far. She didn't want to run afoul of a Guild Minstrel, so she kept her ambitions modest, collected her pennies, and didn't trespass where she had any reason to doubt her welcome. There would be time enough to play for silver or even gold, later; time enough for the fine clothing and the handsome pony to ride. Time enough, when *she* was a Guild Bard. She didn't want to give *any* Guildsman reason to protest her admittance.

So for now, she pleased the peddlers, the farmers, and the herdsmen well enough. She took her dinner, her spot by the hearth-fire, and her bread and cheese in the morning with no complaint. She collected the occasional penny with a blessing and a special song for the giver. Every copper saved on this journey was one she could use to buy lessons and that precious instrument when she reached Nolton.

And when there was no dinner, no spot on the hearth—she slept in barns, in haystacks, or even up a tree—and she ate whatever she had husbanded from the last inn, or doled out a grudging coin or two for the cheapest possible meal, or a bit of bread or a turnip from a market-stall. Twice, when the inns failed her, she was able to avail herself of a travelers' shelter operated by the Church. For the price of a half loaf, she was able to get not only a pallet in a dormitory with other woman travelers, but a bath and two meals. Dinner was a bowl full of thick pease-porridge and a slice of oat bread, and breakfast was more of the bread, toasted this time, with a bit of butter and a trickle of honey. More copper, or silver, produced better food and accommodations, but she saw no reason to waste her coins.

The hidden price of this largess was that she also had to listen to sermons and scripture at both meals, and attend holy services before and after dinner and dawn prayers in the morning.

She had been left alone, other than that, though any females with a look of prosperity about them were singled out for special attentions. Those who were single, and well-dressed, but not Guild members, were urged to consider the novitiate—those who were married or in a trade were reminded that the Church favored those daughters who showed their faith in material ways.

Those two rest stops were enlightening, a bit amusing, and a bit disturbing. She had never quite realized the extent to which the Church's representatives worked to build and keep a hold on people. It was true that the Church did a great deal of good—but after years of living in an inn, Rune had a fair notion of how much things cost. Oat bread was the cheapest type there was; pease-porridge just as inexpensive. The Hungry Bear had never served either, except in the dead of winter when there were no customers at all and only the staff to feed. Granted, both meals at the hostel were well-made and food was given out unstintingly. But the labor involved was free; as was the labor involved in keeping the travelers' dormitory and bathhouse clean. That was provided by the novices—the lower-class novices, or so Rune suspected; she doubted those of gentler birth would be asked to scrub and cook. The Church was probably not making enough just from the meals and the price of lodging to make the kind of profit a real inn would—but there was another factor involved here, the donations coaxed from the purses of the well-off. The Church got more than enough to make a tidy profit in "free-will offerings"—at least on the two occasions Rune observed. So the lodging was a pretense for extracting more donations. For all the prating about the poverty of the Church, for all that what she saw was as bare and sparse as the clergy claimed, the money had to be going somewhere.

She couldn't help wondering as she walked away that second morning; what happened to all that money?

Was there something beyond those stark, severe walls, in the places where the layman was not allowed to walk?

It was a good question, but one she didn't dwell on for long. She had her own agenda, and it had nothing to do with the Church's. She simply resolved to keep a wary eye on dealings that involved the clergy from here on. So long as they left her alone, she'd hold her peace about their profits.

Nolton had become her goal very soon after leaving the Hungry Bear, once she'd had a chance to talk to other travelers. For all that she'd never been outside the bounds of her own village, she knew what she needed out of a town. Nolton was the nearest city with enough musicians to give her a choice in teachers—dozens of inns and taverns, she'd been told, with all manner of entertainers.

Musicians could make a good living in Nolton. The rich had their own, family musicians as retainers—there were several Guild Halls which often hired singers and players, even whole ensembles. There were even instrument-makers in Nolton, enough of them that they had their own section in the weekly market. It was *not* in the direction of the Midsummer Faire, but she wouldn't be ready for the trials for at least a year, maybe two. So direction didn't much matter at the moment. What did matter was finding a good teacher, quickly.

She hadn't once considered how big a city would have to be in order to provide work for that many musicians. The number of ordinary folk that meant simply hadn't entered her mind; she'd simply pictured, in a vague sort of way, a place like her own village, multiplied a few times over.

Now she found herself standing on the edge of the road, looking down on a place that contained more people than she had ever imagined lived in the whole world, and suddenly found herself reluctant to enter it.

With all those people—the abundance of musicians abruptly became more than just a wide choice of teachers. It had just occurred to her that all those teachers were also *competition*. Suddenly her plan of augmenting her savings with her fiddling seemed a lot riskier. What if she wasn't good enough?

But the Ghost thought I was. The weight of the coins she'd sewn into the linen belt she wore under her shirt served as a reminder of that.

Still—she was good in a little village, she was passable in the country inns; but here she was likely to be just one more backwater fiddler. The tunes she knew could be hopelessly outdated, or too countrified to suit townsfolk. And she'd heard that everything was more expensive in cities; her hoard of coins might not be enough to keep her for any length of time. Apprehension dried her mouth as she stared at the faraway roofs. Maybe she just ought to forget the whole idea; turn back, and keep on as she had been, fiddling for food and a place to sleep in little wayside inns, traveling about, picking up a few coppers at weddings and Faires.

Tempting; it was the easy way out. It was the way her mother would have counseled. *Stick with the sure thing.*

But the thought of Stara's counsel made her stiffen her back. Maybe she should—but no. That wasn't what she *wanted* to do. It wasn't enough. And look where Stara's counsel had gotten *her.*

She gave herself a mental shake, and squared her shoulders under her pack. It wasn't enough—and besides, practically speaking, this fiddling about was a fine life in the middle of summer, but when winter came, she'd be leading a pretty miserable existence. Many inns closed entirely in the winter, and it would be much harder to travel then. Her pace would be cut to half, or a third, of what it was now. She'd be spending a lot of time begging shelter from farmers along the road. Some of them were friendly; some weren't. Then there were robbers, highwaymen, bandits—she hadn't run afoul of any of them yet, but that had been because she was lucky and didn't look worth robbing. In winter, anything was worth robbing.

No, there was no hope for it. The original plan was the best.

She took a deep breath, remembered the Ghost—with a bit of a chuckle to think that she was finding comfort in the memory of *that* creature— and joined the stream of humanity heading into the city.

She kept her eyes on the road and the back of the cart in front of her, watching to make sure she didn't step in anything. The pace slowed as people crowded closer and closer together, finally dropping to a crawl as the road reached the outskirts of the city. There was no wall, but there *was* a guard of some kind on the roadway, and everyone had to stop and talk to him for a moment. Rune was behind a man with an ox cart full of sacks of new potatoes, so she didn't hear what the guard asked before she reached him herself.

A wooden barrier dropped down in front of her, startling her into jumping back. The guard, a middle-aged, paunchy fellow, yawned and examined her with a bored squint, picking his teeth with his fingernail. She waited, stifling a cough, as he picked up a piece of board with paper fastened to it; a list of some kind. He studied it, then her, then it again.

"Name?" he said, finally.

"Rune," she replied, wishing her nose didn't itch. She was afraid to scratch it, lest he decide she meant something rude by the gesture. He scribbled a few things on the list in his hand.

"Free, indentured or Guild?" came the next question. She wrinkled her forehead for a moment, puzzled by that middle term. He looked at her impatiently, and swatted at a horsefly that was buzzing around his ears.

"What's matter, boy?" he barked. "Deaf? Or dumb?"

For a moment she was confused, until she remembered that she had decided to wear her loose shirt, vest, and breeches rather than attract unwelcome attention. "Boy," was her. But what on Earth was he asking her? Well, she wasn't Guild, and if she didn't know what "indentured" was, she probably wasn't that, either. "No, sir," she said, hesitantly. "I—uh—"

"Then answer the question! Free, indentured or Guild?" He swatted at the fly again.

"Free, sir." She was relieved to see him make another note. He didn't seem angry with *her,* just tired and impatient. Well, she was pretty hot and tired herself; she felt a trickle of sweat running down the back of her neck, and her feet hurt.

"From Westhaven, sir," she added. "My mother is Stara at the Hungry Bear."

He noted that, too.

"Profession?" That at least she could answer. She touched the strap of Lady Rose and replied with more confidence.

"Fiddler, sir. Musician, sir, but not Guild."

He gave her another one of those sharp glances. "Passing through, planning to stay a while?"

She shook her head. "Going to stay, sir. Through winter, anyway."

He snorted. "Right. They all are. All right, boy. You bein' not Guild, you can busk in the street, or you can take up with a common inn or a pleasure-house, but you *can't* take no gentry inns an' no gentry jobs 'less you get Guild permission, an' you stay outa the parks—an' you got a three-day to get a permit. After that, if you be caught street-buskin', you get fined, maybe thrown in gaol. Here." He shoved a chip of colored wood at her with a string around it. She took it, bewildered. "That shows what day ye come in. Show it when yer buskin' or when innkeeper asks fer it, till ye get yer permit. Mind what I said. Get that permit." He raised the barrier, and she stepped gingerly past him and into the town.

"An' don't think t' come back through an' get another chit!" he shouted after her. "Yer down on the list! Constables will know!"

Constables? What on Earth is a constable? She nodded as if she understood, and got out of the way of a man leading a donkey who showed the guard a piece of paper and was waved through. The fellow with the ox cart had disappeared into the warren of streets that led from the guardpost, and she moved off to the side of the road and the shade of some kind of storage building to study the situation.

She stood at the edge of a semicircular area paved with flat stones, similar to streets she had seen in some of the larger villages and in the courtyards of the Church hostels. That only made sense; with all these people, a dirt street would be mud at the first bit of rain, and dust the rest of the time. Storage buildings, padlocked and closed up, made a kind of barricade between the open fields and the edge of town. The streets led between more of these buildings, with no sign of houses or those inns the guard spoke of.

She watched the steady stream of travelers carefully as she rubbed her nose, looking for a system in the way people who seemed to know what they were doing selected one of the streets leading from this crossing.

She took off her hat and fanned herself with it, the sweat she had worked up cooling in the shade of the building. No one seemed inclined to make her move on, which was a relief. Finally she thought she had a pattern worked out. There weren't so many streets as she had thought; just a half dozen or so. The people with the bits of paper, the ones with beasts laden with foodstuffs, were taking the street farthest left.

That probably leads to a market. There won't be any inns there; too noisy and too smelly.

The three streets on the right were being followed by folks who were plainly Church, Guild or noble; mounted and well-dressed. The street directly before her was taken only by commoner folk, or by guards, they were all people who'd been waved through without being stopped, so it probably led to homes. A wide assortment of folks, the kind questioned by the guard before he let them in, were taking the market-street or the one next to it. After a moment, she decided to take the latter.

She made her way across the fan-shaped crossing-area, darting under the noses of placid oxen, following in the wake of a peddler leading a donkey loaded with what looked like rolls of cloth. As she had hoped, he took that second street, and she continued to follow him, being jostled at every turn before she got the knack of avoiding people. It was a little like a dance; you had to watch what they were going to do, but there was a kind of rhythm to it, although she lost her guide before she figured it all out. After a few moments, she settled into the pace, a kind of bobbing walk in which she took steps far shorter than she was used to, and began looking around her with interest.

All the buildings here were of wood with slate roofs, two or three stories tall; the upper stories overhung the street, and some were near enough to each other that folk sat in their open windows and gossiped above the heads of the the crowd like neighbors over a fence. For the most part there was scarcely enough room for a dog to squeeze between the buildings, and the street itself was several degrees darker for being overshadowed. A gutter ran down the center of the street, and she assumed at first that it was for the dung of the beasts—but a moment later, she saw a little old man with a barrow and a shovel, adroitly skipping about his side of the street and scooping up every fragrant horse-apple in sight, often before anyone had a chance to tread on it.

He acted as if he was collecting something valuable; he certainly didn't miss much. And what he didn't get, the sparrows lining the rooftops swooped down on, scattered it, and picked it over, looking for undigested grain.

Behind the fellow with the barrow came another, with a dog cart drawn by a huge mongrel, holding a barrel with boards bulging and sprung so that it leaked water in every direction. Rune stared at it, aghast at what she thought was his loss through foolishness or senility—and then realized it was on purpose. The water washed whatever the dung-collector had missed into the gutter, where it ran away, somewhere.

It wasn't the arrangement itself that caught her by surprise, it was what it implied. Here were people who spent all day, every day, presumably making a living—*keeping the streets clean.* The very idea would have made someone from her own village stare and question the sanity of anyone who proposed such an outlandish notion. This was not just a new world she'd jumped into, it was one that entertained things she'd never even dreamed of as commonplaces.

She felt dizzy, rootless—and terribly alone. How could she have enough in common with these townsfolk to even begin to entertain them?

But the next moment she heard the familiar sounds of a jig she knew well—"Half a Penny"—played on some kind of fife or pipe. She craned her neck to try and spot the player, waiting impatiently for the flow of the traffic to take her close enough to see him. Finally she spotted him, wedged in a little nook under the overhanging second story of one of the houses, with his hat on the stones in front of him, and a bit of paper pinned to his hat. He was surrounded by a mix of people, none very well-born, but of all ages and trades, clapping in time to his piping.

She focused on that brightly colored bit of paper. *That must be the permit the guard told me I had to get—*

She tried to get over to him, to ask him where he'd gotten it, but the crowd carried her past and she wasn't sure enough of her way to try and fight her way back. Still, his hat had held a fair amount of coin—which meant that *someone* thought country jigs were good enough entertainment. . . .

The houses began to hold shops on the lower level, with young 'prentices outside, crying the contents. The street widened a bit as well, and she began to spot roving peddlers of the sort that walked the Faires, trays of goods carried about their necks. The peddlers seemed mostly to be crying foodstuffs: meat pies, roast turnips, nuts; bread-and-cheese, muffins, and sweets. One of them passed near enough to her that she got a good whiff of his meat-pies, and the aroma made her stomach growl and her mouth water. It had been a long time since noon and her hoarded turnip.

But it wasn't only caution that kept her from reaching for her purse of coppers; it was common sense. No use in letting any thief know where her money was; she'd felt ghostly fingers plucking at her outer sash-belt a number of times, and at her pack, but the clever knots she'd tied the pack with foiled them, and the pouch, lean as it was, she had tucked inside her belt. If she let pickpockets see where that pouch was, she had a shrewd idea it wouldn't stay there long. She mentally blessed Raven for warning her to make a cloth belt to wear inside her clothes for most of any money she had, once she was on the road.

"*It won't keep you safe from true robbers,*" he'd said, "*Not the kind that hit you over the head and strip you—but it'll save you from cut-purses.*"

There was more advice he'd given her, and now that she was a little more used to the city, some of it was coming back, though she hadn't paid a lot of attention to it originally. The lessons in music had seemed a lot more important.

"*Never ask for directions except from somebody wearing a uniform or from an innkeeper. If you find yourself on a street that's growing deserted, turn around and retrace your steps quickly, especially if the street seems very dirty and dark, with the buildings closed up or in bad repair. If a friendly passerby comes up out of nowhere and offers to help you, ignore him; walk away from him or get by him before he can touch you. Never do anything that marks you as a stranger, especially as a stranger from the country. That'll show you as an easy mark for robbers or worse.*"

All right then, exactly how was she going to find an inn, and a place where she might be able to set herself up as the resident musician?

This was a street of shops—but sooner or later there had to be an inn, didn't there?

Maybe. Then again, maybe not. There were other streets branching off this one; maybe the inns were on these side streets. She'd never know—

She spotted a dusty hat just ahead of her; a hat that had once been bright red, but had faded to a soft rose under sun and rain. Something about the set of the rooster feathers in it seemed familiar; when the crowd parted a little, she realized that it belonged to one of the journeymen who had been in the same inn she'd played at last night, and had tossed her a copper when she played the tune he'd requested.

She'd overheard him talking quite a bit to a fellow in the Apothecary's Guild. She remembered now that he had said he wasn't from Nolton himself, but he was familiar with the city, and had recommended a number of inns and had given directions to the other man. She hadn't paid attention then—the more fool her—she'd thought she would have no trouble, as an inn-brat herself, in finding plenty of places.

But he bobbed along in the crowd with a purposeful stride; he obviously knew exactly where he was going. An inn? It was very likely, given the time of day. And any inn he frequented would likely be the sort where her playing would be welcome.

She darted between two goodwives with shopping baskets over their arms, and scraped along a shop front past a clutch of slower-paced old men who frowned at her as she scooted by. The feathers bounced in the breeze just ahead of her, tantalizingly near, yet far enough away that she could all too easily lose their owner in the press. She found herself stuck behind a brown-clad, overweight nursemaid with a gaggle of chattering children on their way home from the Church school. The two eldest, both girls, one in scarlet and one in blue, and both wearing clothing that cost more than every item she'd ever owned in her life bundled together, looked down their noses at her in a vaguely threatening fashion when she made as if to get past them. She decided not to try to push her way by. They might think she was a thief, and get a guard or something. In fact, they might do it just to be spiteful; the pinched look about their eyes put her in mind of some of the more disagreeable village girls. She loitered behind them, and fumed.

But they were moving awfully slow, as the nursemaid called back the littler ones from darting explorations of store fronts, time and time again. The rooster feathers were bobbing away, getting ahead of her, their owner making a faster pace than she dared.

Then, suddenly, as she strained her neck and her eyes, trying to keep them in sight, Red-Hat turned into a side street, the rooster feathers swishing jauntily as he ducked his head to cut across the flow of traffic. Then hat and feathers and all disappeared behind a building.

Oh, no— Heedless now of what the unfriendly girls might say or do, Rune dashed between them at the first break, ignoring their gasps of outrage as she wormed her way through the crowd to the place where Red-Hat had vanished. She used her elbows and thin body to advantage, ignoring the protests of those whose feet she stepped on or who got an elbow in the ribs, taking care only to protect Lady Rose and her pack.

She broke out of the crowd directly under the nose of a coach horse. It snorted in surprise, and came to a hoof-clattering halt. She flung herself against the wall, plastering herself against the brick to let the coach pass. The driver cursed her and the other foot-travelers roundly, but the well-trained, placid horse simply snorted again at her, as if to register his surprise when she had appeared under his nose, and ignored her once she was out of his way. The wheels of the coach rumbled by her feet, missing them by scant inches, the driver now too busy cursing at the other folk in his way to pay any more attention to her.

She sighed, and wiped her sweating brow when he had passed. That was a lot closer than she cared to come to getting run over, and if the horse hadn't been a particularly stolid beast, she could have gotten trampled or started a runaway. But now that the coach was gone, she saw that this street carried a lot less traffic than the main street; it should be easy to find Red-Hat.

She peered down the cobblestone street, but the conspicuous hat was nowhere to be seen. For a moment her heart sank, but then she raised her eyes a little, and couldn't help but grin. There, not twenty feet from her, swung a big, hand-painted sign proclaiming the "Crowned Corn Public House, Drink & Vittles," superimposed over a garish yellow painting of a barley-sheaf with a crown holding the straws in place. Beside it swung a huge wooden mug with carved and white-painted foam spilling over the sides, for the benefit of the illiterate. Whether or not Red Hat was in there, the presence of the beer mug meant that it was a "common" place, and its clientele shouldn't be too different from the travelers she'd been entertaining. If she couldn't strike up a bargain here, she could probably get directions to a place that could use a musician. If the owner proved unfriendly, at least now she knew that the inns *were* on the side streets.

I can retrace my steps if I have to, and find another. She trotted the remaining few steps to the door, and pushed it open.

She blinked, trying to get her eyes to adjust quickly to the dark, smoky interior. The aroma that hit her, of smoke, baking bread and bacon, of stew and beer, was so like the way the Hungry Bear smelled that she could have been there instead of here. But the crowds! This place was packed full, with more people than the Bear ever saw except at the height of Harvest Faire. There were five or six girls in bright, cheap skirts and tight-laced bodices, and young men in leather aprons, breeches, and no-color shirts scurrying about the room, tending to the customers. She despaired of being able to catch anyone's eye to ask directions to the owner, but one of the girls must have caught the flicker of movement at the door, for she bustled over as soon as she'd finished gathering the last of the mugs from an empty table.

She appraised Rune with a knowing eye, a little disappointed that it wasn't a paying customer, but willing to see what Rune wanted. "Ye be a musicker, boy?" she asked, and Rune nodded. "Come wi' me, then," she said, and turned on her heel to lead the way through the crowd, her striped skirts swishing jauntily with every step. There evidently wasn't any prohibition *here* about fondling the help, and the many pats and pinches the girl got made Rune very glad for her boy's garb.

She pushed past two swinging half-doors into what could only be the kitchen; it was hot as the inside of a bake-oven and overcrowded with people. On the wall nearest the door stood a pair of dish-tubs on a tall bench or narrow table, with a draggle-haired girl standing beside it and working her way through a mountain of mugs and bowls. Rune's guide heaved her own double-handful of wooden mugs up onto the table with a clatter, then turned to the rest of the room. It was dominated by the bake-ovens at the far end, all of them going full blast; three huge windows and the door open to the yard did little to ease the burden of heat the roaring fires beneath the ovens emitted. There was a big table in front of the ovens, with a man and a woman rolling out crust for a series of pies at one end, and cooling loaves stacked at the other. Another table, next to that, held a man cutting up raw chickens; beside him was another woman slicing some kind of large joint of cooked meat. A third table held six small children cleaning and chopping vegetables. There were other folks darting in and out with food or the dirty dishes, and a knot of people at the oven end.

"Mathe!" the serving girl shouted over the din. "Mathe! Sommut t' see ye!"

A short, round, red-faced man in a flour-covered apron detached himself from the clump of workers beside the ovens, and peered across the expanse of the kitchen toward them. His bald head, shiny with sweat, looked like a ripening tomato.

"What is it?" he yelled back, wiping his brow with a towel he tucked back into his waistband.

"Musicker!" the girl called, a bit impatiently. "Wants a job!"

Mathe edged around the end of the table by the oven, then squeezed in between the wall with the windows and the children cleaning vegetables to make his way towards them. Rune waited for him, trying not to show any anxiety. The serving girl watched them both with avid curiosity as Mathe stopped a few feet away.

The owner planted both fists on his hips and stood slightly straddle-legged, looking her up and down with bright black eyes. As keen as his eyes seemed to be, however, she got the feeling he didn't realize she wasn't a boy. Plenty of young men wore their hair longer than hers, and her thin face and stick-straight body wasn't going to set any hearts aflame even when she was in skirts. Certainly the serving girl had made the same mistake that the gate-guard had made, and she wasn't going to correct any of them.

"Musicker, eh?" Mathe said at last. "Guild?"

She shook her head, wondering if she had doomed herself from the start. What had the gate-guard said about jobs she could take? There had been something about inns—

"Good," Mathe said in satisfaction. "We can't afford Guild fees. From country, are ye? Singer or player?"

"From down near Beeford. I'm a player, sir," she replied. "Fiddle, sir."

"Got permit? When ye come in?" he asked, "Where's yer chit?" These city-folk spoke so fast she had to listen carefully to make out what they were saying.

Wordlessly she showed him her scrap of wood. He took a quick glance at it.

"Today, hmm?" He examined her a moment more. "You know 'Heart to the Ladies'?" he asked, and at her nod, said, "Unlimber that bit'a wood and play it."

She dropped her pack on the flagstone floor and took Lady Rose out of her traveling bag, tuning her hastily, with a wince for her in this overheated room. She set the bow to the strings, and played—not her best, but not her worst—though it was hard to make the music heard in the noisy kitchen. Still, the serving girl's foot was tapping when Mathe stopped her at the second chorus.

"Ye'll do," he said. "If we c'n agree, ye got a one-day job. Here's how it is. We got a reg'lar musicker, but he took a job at a weddin'. We was gonna do wi'out t'night, but music makes the beer flow better, an since here ye be, I don't go lookin' a gift musicker i' the mouth."

He chuckled, and so did Rune, though she didn't get the joke, whatever it was.

"Now, here's the bargain," Mathe continued, wiping the back of his neck with his towel. It was a good thing he was mostly bald, or his hair would have been in the same greasy tangles as the dishwasher girl's. "I feeds ye now; ye plays till closin'. Ye gets a place by th' fire t' sleep—this ain't no inn, an' I'm not s'pposed t' be puttin' people up, but you bein' on yer three-day chit th' law'll look 'tother way. Ye put out yer hat, I get two coins outa every three."

That wasn't as good a bargain as she'd been getting on the road, but it sounded like he was waiting for her to make a counteroffer. She shook her head. "Half, and I get bread and stew in the morning."

"Half, an' ye get bread'n dripping," he countered. "Take it or leave it, it's m'last offer."

Bread and butter, or bread and honey, would have been better—but butter and honey could be a lot more expensive in the city, where there were neither cows nor bees. "Done," she said, putting out her hand. They shook on it, solemnly.

"All right, then," he said, rubbing his hands together in satisfaction. "Beth there'll show ye where t'set up, and gi' ye the lay'a the land, an' she'll see to yer feedin'. Don' touch th' girls 'less they invite it, or m'bar-keep'll have yer hand broke. Oh, one other thing. I don' let me musickers get dry, but I don' let 'em get drunk, neither. Small beer or cider?"

"Cider," Rune said quickly. The last thing she needed was to get muddle-headed in a strange eating-house in a strange city, and although small beer didn't have a lot of punch to it, drinking too much could still put you under the table, and if it was this hot all night, she'd be resorting to her mug fairly often.

Mathe had given her an interesting piece of information. So inns didn't necessarily take sleepers here? That was worth noting. She reckoned that would suit Stara just fine—it would mean less than half the work . . . but this place wasn't called an "inn," it was something called a "public house." They must be two different things—

"Good lad," Mathe replied with satisfaction. "Don't talk much, sensible, and ye drive a good bargain. Ye'll do. Now get 'long wi' ye, I got my work t' tend."

Beth laughed and wrinkled her nose at him, and Rune picked up her pack and followed the serving girl out. Her hips waggled saucily, and Rune wondered just what constituted an "invitation." Certainly the girl was trying to see if this new musician could be tempted.

Too bad for her I'm not a boy. I'm afraid I'm going to disappoint her if she wants a sweaty-palm reaction.

There was just enough of a clear path behind the benches and tables to walk without bumping into the customers. They edged around the wall until they came to a corner with a stool and a shelf very near the bar, and the massive bartender presiding over the barrels of beer and ale; his expression impassive, statue-like.

"Here," Beth said, gesturing at the stool, flipping her dark hair over her shoulder. If she was disappointed that Rune hadn't answered her flirtations, she didn't show it. Maybe she was completely unaware she'd been flirtatious. Manners could be a lot different here than what Rune was used to. "This be where ye set up an' play. We likes country-tunes here, an' keep it lively. If they gets t' clappin', they gets t' drinkin'."

Rune nodded, and tucked her pack behind the stool. Lady Rose was still in her hand, and she set the fiddle down on top of the pack gently, so that the instrument was cradled by the worn fabric of the pack and the clothing it contained.

"Look sharp here, boy," Beth said, and Rune looked up. "Ye see how close ye are t' the bar?" She pointed with her chin at the massive barrier of wood that stood between the customers and the barrels of beer and wine.

Rune nodded again, and Beth grinned. "There's a reason why we put th' musicker here. Most of ye ain't big 'nuff t' take care'a yerselves if it comes t' fightin'. Now, mostly things is quiet, but sometimes a ruckus comes up. If there's a ruckus, ye get yer tail down behin' that bar, hear? Ain't yer job t' stop a ruckus. Tha's Boony's job, an' he be right good at it."

Beth tossed her curly tangle of hair over her shoulder again, and pointed at a shadowy figure across the room, in a little alcove near the door. She hadn't noticed it when she first came in, because her back had been to it, and the occupant hadn't moved to attract her attention. Rune squinted, then started. Surely she hadn't seen what she thought she'd seen—

Beth laughed, showing that she still had most of her teeth, and that they were in good shape. "Ain't never seen no Mintak, eh, fiddler? Well, Boony's a Mintak, an' right good at keepin' the peace. So mind what I said an' let him do what he's good at, 'f it come to it."

Rune blinked, and nodded. She wanted to stare at the creature across the room, but she had the vague feeling that too many people already stared at Boony, openly or covertly, and she wasn't going to add to their rudeness.

A Mintak . . . she'd heard about the isolated pockets of strange creatures that were scattered across the face of Alanda, but no one in her village had ever seen so much as an elven forester, much less a Mintak. They were supposed to have bodies like huge humans, but the heads of horses. The brief glimpse she'd gotten didn't make her think of a horse so much as a dog, except that the teeth hadn't been the sharp, pointed rending teeth of a canine, but the flat teeth of an herbivore. And the eyes had been set on the front of the head, not the sides. But the Mintak loomed a good head-and-a-half above the bartender, and that worthy was one of the tallest men Rune had ever seen.

Beth came bustling back with a bowl of stew, a mug, and a thick slice of bread covered in bacon drippings in one hand, and a pitcher with water beading the sides in the other. "Take this, there's a good lad." She'd evidently decided that Rune was terribly young, too young and girl-shy to be attracted, and had taken a big-sisterly approach to dealing with her. "You get dry an' look to run short, you nod at me or one'a th' other girls. Ol' Mathe, he don't like his musickers goin' dry; you heard him sayin' that, an' he meant it."

She put the pitcher on the floor beside the stool, shoved the rest into Rune's hands, and scampered off, with a squeal as one of the customers' pinches got a little closer to certain portions of her anatomy than she liked. She slapped the hand back and huffed away; the customer started to rise to follow—

And Boony stepped forward into the light. Now Rune saw him clearly; he wore a pair of breeches and a vest, and nothing else. He carried a cudgel, and he was a uniform dark brown all over, like a horse, and he had the shaggy hair of a horse on his face and what could be seen of his body. His eyes seemed small for his head; he had pointed ears on the top of his head, peeking up through longer, darker hair than was on his face, and that hair continued down the back of his neck like a mane. He looked straight at the offending customer, who immediately sat down again.

So Boony kept the peace. *It looks like he does a good job,* Rune mused.

But there was dinner waiting, and beyond that, a room full of people to entertain. She wolfed down her food, taking care not to get any grease on her fingers that might cause problems with the strings of her fiddle. The sooner she started, the sooner she could collect a few coins.

And hopefully, tonight Boony's services wouldn't be needed. Nothing cooled a crowd like a fight, and nothing dried up money faster.

She put out her hat, wedging it between her feet with one foot on the brim to keep it from being "accidentally" kicked out into the room, and retuned Lady Rose.

Cider or no, with all these people and only herself to entertain them, it was going to be a long night.

"Seventeen, eighteen, nineteen," Rune counted out the coins on the table under Mathe's careful eye. "That's the whole of it, sir. Nineteen coppers." The candle between them shone softly on the worn copper coins, and Mathe took a sip of his beer before replying.

"Not bad," Mathe said, taking nine and leaving her ten, scooping his coins off the table and into a little leather pouch. "In case ye were won-derin' lad. That's not at all bad for a night that ain't a feast nor Faire-day. Harse don' do much better nor that."

He set a bowl down in front of her, and a plate and filled mug. "Ye did well 'nough for another meal, boy. So, eat whiles I have my beer, an' we'll talk."

This time the stew had meat in it, and the bread had a thin slice of cheese on top. Getting an extra meal like that meant that she'd done more than "all right." She could use it, too; she was starving.

The public house was very quiet; Beth and the other girls had gone off somewhere. Whether they had lodgings upstairs or elsewhere, Rune had no idea, for they'd left while Rune was packing up, going out the back way through the kitchen. Presumably, they'd gotten their meals from the leftovers on their way through. Boony slept upstairs; she knew that for certain. So did Mathe and one of the cooks and all of the children, who turned out to be his wife and offspring.

Right now, she was was thinking about how this would have meant a month's take in Faire-season at home. She shook her head. "It seems like a lot—" she said, tentatively, "—but people keep telling me how much more expensive it is to live in the city."

Mathe sipped his own beer. "It is, and this'd keep ye for 'bout a day; but it's 'cause'a the rules, the taxes, an' the Priests," he said. "Ye gotta tithe, ye gotta pay yer tax, an' ye gotta live where they say. Here—lemme show ye—"

He stretched out his finger and extracted two coppers, and moving them to the side. "That's yer tithe—ye gotta pay tithe an' tax on what ye made, *b'fore* I took my share." He moved two more. "That's yer tax. Now, ye got six pence left. Rules say ye gotta live in res'dential distrik, 'less yer a relative or a special kinda hireling, like the cooks an' the kids and Boony is. Musickers don' count. So—there's fourpence a day fer a place w' decent folks in it, where ye c'n leave things an' know they ain't gonna make legs an' walk while ye're gone. That leaves ye tuppence fer food."

Rune blinked, caught off guard by the way four pennies evaporated—close to half her income for the day. "Tax?" she said stupidly. "Tithe?" Fourpence, gone—and for what?

Mathe shook his head. "Church *is* the law round 'bout towns," he told her, a hint of scolding in his voice. "Ye *tithe*, lad, an' ye base it on what ye took in. Same fer taxes. If ye don' pay, sooner 'r later they cotch up wi' ye, or sommut turns ye in, an' then they fine ye. They fine ye *ten times* what they figger ye owe."

"But how would they know what I owe them?" she asked, still confused. " 'Specially if I work the street—"

"They know 'bout what a musicker like you should make in a night, barrin' windfalls," he replied. "Twenny pence. That's two fer Church an' two fer tax. An' if ye get them windfalls, the lad as drops bit'a gold in yer hat an' the like, ye best r'port 'em too. Could be sommut saw it go in yer hat, an's gone t' snitch on ye. Could be 'tis a Priest in disguise, belike, testin' ye."

This all seemed terribly sinister. "But what happens if I couldn't pay?"

she asked. "I mean, what if I'd been holding back for a year—" *Ten times*
tuppence times—how many days in a year? The figures made her head
swim. It was more than she'd ever seen in her life, except for the windfall
of the silver. And she panicked over that for a moment, until she realized
that no one knew about it but her—nor ever would, if she kept her
mouth shut.

"Happened to a girl'a mine," Mathe said warningly. "She owed 'em fer
'bout three year back; spent it all, a' course, stupid cow. Couldn't pay.
She got indentured t' pay the bill."

Indentured? There was that word again. "What's 'indentured,' Mathe?"
she asked.

"Worse than slavery," boomed a voice over her head, so that she
jumped. "Worse than being chattel."

"Ol' Boony, he's got hard feelin's 'bout bein' indentured," Mathe
offered, as Boony moved around to the other side of the table and sat
down on the bench, making it creak under his weight.

"There are laws to keep a slave from being beaten," Boony rumbled.
"There are laws saying he must be fed so much a day, he must have
decent clothing and shelter. The Church sees to these laws, and fines the
men who break them. There are no such laws for the indentured."

The Mintak nodded his massive head with each word. Now that he was
so close, he looked less animal-like and more—well, human wasn't the
word, but there was ready intelligence in his face; he had expressions
Rune was able to read. His face was flatter than a horse's, and his mouth
and lips were mobile enough to form human speech without difficulty.
His hands only had three broad fingers, though, and the fingers had one
less joint than a human's, though the joints seemed much more flexible.

"Boony didn' know 'bout tithin' an taxes when he come here," Mathe
said, as Boony took a turnip from the bowl at the end of the table and
began stolidly chewing it. "He got indentured t' pay 'em. An' he's right,
the way indenturin' works is that ye work fer yer wage. But yer wage goes
first t' yer master, t' pay off yer debt, an' there ain't no law saying how
much he c'n take, so long as he leaves ye a penny a day."

And a penny, as she had just learned, wouldn't go far in this city.

"I was bought by a greedy man who used my strength in his warehouse,
took all, and left me with nothing," Boony said. "He thought I was stupid."
A dark light in his eyes told her he'd somehow managed to turn the tables
on his greedy owner, and was waiting for her to ask how he'd done it.

"What did you do?" she asked, obediently.

Boony chewed up the last of the turnip, top and all, confirming her
notion that he was herbivorous. He laughed, a slow, deep laugh that
sounded like stones rolling down a hill. "I was so *very* stupid that I did
not know my own strength," the Mintak said, smiling. "I began to break
things. And when he ordered me beaten, I would catch the hand of the
overseer, and ask him, ever so mildly, why he did this to me. Soon I was
costing the scum much, and there was no one in his employ willing to
face me, much less beat me."

"That's when I bought 'im out," Mathe said. "I've had a Mintak cus-
t'mer or twain here, an' I knew th' breed, d'ye see. He earned back 'is

fine a long time agone, but he reckoned on stayin' wi' me, so we've got 'im listed as adopted so's he c'n live here." He and the Mintak exchanged backslaps, the Mintak delivering one that looked like a fly-swat and staggered his employer. "He'll run th' place fer the wife when I'm gone, won't you, old horse?"

"May God grant that never come to be," the Mintak said piously. "But admit it—you are the exception with indentures."

Mathe shrugged. "Sad, but Boony's got the right 'f it. And 'member, boy—if ye get indentured, the law says ye work at whatever yer bond-holder says ye do. That means 'f he runs a boy-brothel. . . ."

"Which is where a-many young men and women go," Boony rumbled. "Into shame. The law says nothing about that. Nor the Church."

Mathe made a shushing motion. "Best not t' get inta *that*. Best t' jest finish warnin' the young'un here." He took another pull on his beer, and Boony chomped up a couple of carrots and a head of lettuce, jaws moving stolidly. She took the opportunity to finish her food.

"All right," Mathe said after a moment of silence. "Tonight, ye sleep on that straw mat by th' fire—which's what payin' customers'd get if I took any—an' in the mornin' I feeds ye, an' yer on yer way. Now, ye know where ye go first?"

"To get a permit?" she ventured. He shook his head.

"Not 'less ye got a silver penny on ye; that's th' cost 'f a street-buskin' permit. No, ye go straight t' Church-box on t'end 'a this street, an ye pay yer tithe an' tax from today. Church clerk'll put down yer name, an' that goes in at end 'f day t' Church Priest-house w' th' rest on the records. *Then* ye busk on street, outside Church-box. By end'a day, ye'll have th' silver penny, ye' get the permit. Go get *that* fr'm same place; Church-box. Then ye busk where the pleasure-houses be, thas on Flower Street, 'till ye can't stay awake no more. That'd be dawn, an' ye'll have 'nough for tithe an' tax from t'day."

"This is the one time you may safely skim a little, to pay for the permit, in all the time you may be here," the Mintak rumbled. "They will not expect you to play enough to earn double wages."

She nodded. "But—" she began, then hesitated.

"So?" Mathe said, as his wife shooed her children up the stairs behind them to their living quarters.

"Don' be t' long, eh sweeting?" she called. "Boy's a good'un, but ye both needs sleep."

Mathe waved at her, his eyes fixed on Rune. She dropped her eyes to her hands. "What I—really came here for, to Nolton, I mean, was lessons. I—want to join the Guild."

"I told you," Boony said, booming with satisfaction. "Did I not tell you he knew more than to be simple busker?"

"Ye did, ye did, I heerd ye," Mathe replied. "Ye won yer bet, old horse. Now, boy, lemmee think." He rubbed his bare chin and pursed his lips. "There's places t' get secondhand instruments, an' places t' get lessons. Sometimes, they be th' same place. Tell ye what, I gi' ye a map i' th' mornin'. Tell ye what else, sommut 'em gonna know where there's places lookin' fer musickers. If ye got a place, ye don' need no permit—or ye c'an git one, an' play double, by day fer pennies i' th' street, an' by night fer yer keep."

Rune could hardly restrain herself. This was far more than she'd expected in the way of help. "I don't know how to thank you, sir," she said, awkwardly. "I mean—"

"Hush," Mathe said. "Thank yon Beth an' Boony. 'Twas she brought ye back; 'twas he tol' me I'd best sit ye down an' 'splain how things is 'round here, afore ye got yersel' in a mess."

"I've already thanked Beth, sir," she said, truthfully, for she'd asked the girl what her favorite tunes were, and had played them all. "It was kindness to take me back to you and not show me the street."

"Well, she said ye had th' look'a sommut that knew his way about an inn," Mathe replied, blushing a little. "I figgered if ye did, ye knew what t' play t' please m' custom. An' ye did; sold a good bit'a beer t'night. Ye done good by me."

"I'm glad," she replied sincerely. "And thank *you*, sir," she said, turning to Boony. "Although I'm sure I know your reasons—that you didn't want to see a weaker creature put in the same position you'd been in. I've heard many good things about the Mintak; I will be glad to say in the future that they are all true."

Boony laughed out loud. "And I will say that it is true that Bards have silver tongues and the gift of making magic with word and song," he replied. "For I am sure you will be a Bard one day. It pleases me to have saved a future Bard from an unpleasant fate. And now—" he looked significantly at Mathe.

The man laughed. "All right, old horse. It's off t' bed for all of us, or m'wife 'll have Boony carry me up. G'night, young Rune."

He and Boony clumped up the stairs, taking the candle, but leaving the fire lit so she could see to spread her blankets out on the sack of clean straw they'd given her to sleep on.

She had thought that she'd be too excited to sleep, but she was wrong. She was asleep as soon as she'd found a comfortable position on the straw sack, and she slept deeply and dreamlessly.

CHAPTER SIX

Breakfast, dished up by Mathe's wife after the morning cleaning crew rousted her out of her bed, was not bread and drippings nor leftover stew; it was oat-porridge with honey and a big mug of fresh milk. When Rune looked at her with a lifted eyebrow, she shrugged, and cast a half-scornful look at Mathe's back.

" 'Tis what my younglings get," she said, "Ye need a healthy morning meal, ye do. And I told Mathe, I did, that you're not much bigger nor they. Bread and drippings, indeed, for a growing boy! Ye'd think the man had no childer of his own!" And she sniffed with disdain.

Rune knew when to leave well enough alone, and she finished the porridge with appreciation. She gathered up her things, slung her pack and Lady Rose over her back, and headed for the outer door. She found the owner there, as if he was waiting for her, and somehow she wasn't surprised when Mathe slipped a packet into her hand as she bade him farewell. The cooks from last night were already hard at work in the kitchen; the serving-boys were scrubbing down tables, benches and floor, while the girls swept the fireplaces and cleaned beer mugs. Mathe took her outside, and stood on the door-sill, closing the door behind them.

The street before them had a few carts on it, but not many. By the angle of the sunlight it was about an hour past dawn. In the country, folks would already be out in their fields, working; here in the city, it seemed that most people weren't even awake yet. Since Rune had always preferred lying late abed, she had the feeling she was going to like being a city person.

"Ye go straight down this street, east," Mathe said, waving his hand down the quiet, sunlit lane. Dust-motes danced in the shaft of light that ran between the overhanging buildings. "At second crossing, there be a little black stall. That be Church-box; there be priest inside, ye gi' him yer tithe an' tax, an make sure ye gi' him separate. Elsewise, he'll write all fourpence down as tithe, an' leave ye owin' fourpence tax."

And I wonder how many people that's happened to? I bet the Church wouldn't give it back, either, even if you could get them to admit that a mistake was made.

She nodded, slipping the packet into the pocket in her vest. It felt like bread; maybe even bread and cheese. That would be welcome, in a few hours. It meant something more she wouldn't have to buy.

And courtesy of Mathe's wife, too, she had no doubt. That was a good woman, and very like Rose.

Mathe continued with his directions and instructions. "Now, then ye go 'cross street; there be couple stalls sells vittles. Play there. There's always a crowd there—ye got the people as come t' pay tax an' tithe, ye got people as wants a bit t'eat. It's a bit too noisy fer a singer, but ye'll do fine. Nobody got that as set yet, that I heerd of. Here's bit'a map." He handed her a folded paper, and watched as she unfolded it; the maze of lines was incomprehensible at first, until she resolved it into streets, and even found the one the public house stood on, the gate she'd come in by, and the street she had followed. "See, this here, this's where we be. These little red dots, thas some'a them teachers an' instr'ment makers. See if any on 'em'll do ye." He nodded as she folded it up and stowed it in her belt-pouch, where the ten pennies from her evening's labor chinked. "Now, if I was in yer shoes, I'd play till after nuncheon, thas midmeal, when people stop buyin' things at stall, an then I'd go look up some'a them teachers and the like. But thas me. Think ye'll do?"

"You've done more for me than I ever hoped, sir," she replied honestly. "I can't begin to thank you."

And I don't know why you've done it, either. I'm glad you did, but I wish I knew why. . . .

He flushed a little with embarrassment. "Ah, musickers done me a good turn or twain, figger this helps pay back. When I was jest startin' this place, musickers came round t' play jest fer the set-out, 'till I could afford t' feed 'em. Then I got my reg'lar man, an' he bain't failed me. So—I gi' ye a hand, ye gi' sommut else one 'f it's needed—"

Someone inside called him, urgently, and he turned. "Can't be away a breath an' they need me. God be wi' ye, youngling. Watch yerself."

And he dashed back inside, shouting, "All right! All right! I'm gettin' there fast as I can!"

Rune headed up the street, in the same direction Mathe had pointed. It was considerably quieter in the early hours of the morning. Shops were just opening, merchants taking down massive wooden shutters, and laying displays in the windows behind thinner wooden grates to foil theft.

The shops here seemed to tend to clothing; materials, or clothing ready-made. She passed a shop full of stockings, hats and gloves, a shoemaker, and several shops that appeared to be dressmakers and tailors. The Crowned Corn seemed to be the only inn or public house on this street, although there were vendors of foodstuffs already out with their trays about their necks. They weren't crying their wares, though; the streets weren't so full that customers couldn't see them. They ignored Rune for the most part, as being unlikely to have enough spare coin to buy their goods.

A cart passed, and Rune noticed another odd contrivance, just under the horse's clubbed tail. This was a kind of scoop rigged to the cart that caught any droppings. A good notion, given the number of animals here. That would mean only those carts without the scoop and horses being ridden would be leaving refuse. The city, while not exactly sweet-smelling, would be a lot worse without the care taken to keep it clean.

The merchants were doing their part, too; there were folks out scrubbing their doorsteps, and the street immediately in front of the shop, right up to the gutter-line. How the folk back in the village would stare!

Not even the late Rose was that fanatical about cleanliness.

On the other hand, there weren't that many people in the village. With all these people, all these animals, there would have to be extra precautions against the illnesses that came from dirt and contaminated water.

The little black stall that Mathe had called the "Church-box" was plainly visible as soon as she crossed the first street. It had an awning above it, supported by carved wooden angels instead of simple props. And without a doubt, the awning was decorated with painted saints distributing alms, to remind the pious and impious alike where their tithes were going.

In all probability, the stall was the last business to close at night, and the first to open in the morning. The Church never lost an opportunity to take gifts from her children.

There was a grill-covered window in the front of the stall, and beneath it, a slot. Behind the window sat a bored young novice-Priest in his plain, black robes, yawning and making no attempt to cover his indifference to his surroundings. He blinked at her without interest, and reached for a pen when he saw she was going to stop and give him something to do. Or rather, force him to do something.

"Name?" he mumbled. She gave it; likewise her occupation, and that she was beginning her second day in Nolton. He noted all of it down, and warned her, in a perfunctory manner, that she would have to purchase her permit to busk before the fourth day. From him, of course. And that it would be a silver penny. He did *not* issue any of the warnings Mathe had, about what it would mean if she neglected to do so.

"Here's my two-pence tithe for yesterday, sir," she said, pushing the pennies across the counter to him, through the slit. He took it, with a slightly wrinkled nose, as if in disdain for the tiny amount, but he took it, nevertheless. She noted that he seemed well-fed; very well-fed in fact, round-cheeked and healthier than most. His hands were soft, and white where the ink of his occupation hadn't stained them. He dropped the two coins into something beneath the counter, just out of sight, and made a notation after her name. "And here's my two-pence tax," she said, shoving those coins across when she knew he'd made his first notation and couldn't change it.

He frowned at her as he took the two coins. "You could have given it to me all at once," he grumbled, making a second notation. She blinked, and contrived to look stupid, and he muttered something under his breath, about fools and music, and waved her off.

She turned away from the window. Well, that was that; fourpence lighter, and nothing to show for it. Could have been worse, she supposed. If she hadn't been warned, sooner or later the Church would have caught up with her. . . . Boony's description of his treatment as a bondservant hadn't been inviting.

Although the idea of seeing a bondholder's face when he realized that the boy he'd thought he'd bought off was a girl was amusing, she didn't care to think about what would have followed that discovery. Probably something very unpleasant.

Across the street were the two food-stalls Mathe had described for her, with a bit of space in between for a tall counter where folk could eat standing up; one was red-painted, and one was blue. She crossed the street under the disdainful gaze of the novice-Priest and approached the first stall-holder.

"Would you mind if I put out my hat here, sir?" she asked politely of the thin fellow frying sausage rolls in deep skillets of lard. He glanced up at her, and shook his head.

"So long as ye don' drive th' custom away, 'tis nobbut t' me," he replied absently. Encouraged, she repeated her question at the second stall, which sold drink, and got the same answer.

So she found a place where she wasn't going to be in the way of people buying or eating, and set her hat at her feet, with her pack to hold it down. She took the fiddle from her carrying bag, gave Lady Rose a quick tuning, and began playing, choosing a simple jig, bright and lively.

Although she quickly attracted a small crowd, they were mostly children and people who didn't look to have much more money than she. Still, they enjoyed her music, and one or two even bought something at the stalls on either side of her, so she was accomplishing that much. And as long as her listeners bought something, she wasn't likely to be chased away.

By noon bell, she'd acquired a grand total of three pennies, a marble dropped in by a solemn-faced child, a little bag of barley-sugar candy added by a young girl, a bit of yellow ribbon, and at least a dozen pins. She'd never collected pins before, but any contribution was better than nothing. Once she'd straightened and cleaned them, pins were worth a penny the dozen, so that wasn't so bad, really.

The bad part was that she'd fiddled most of the morning and not even gained half what she'd gotten in the public house last night. She was a long way from the silver penny that permit would cost her. She took a moment for a breather, to look over the traffic on the street.

Early days yet, she told herself, as the crowds thickened, the street filling with folk looking for a bit to eat. The first noon bell seemed to signal a common hour for nuncheon, which the people back home called midmeal. She took her eyes off her hat and fixed them on the faces about her, smiling as if she hadn't a care in the world. *When you're fiddling, think about music,* Raven had admonished her. *Don't think about your dinner, or where you're going to sleep tonight. Tell yourself you're happy, and put that happiness into the way you're playing. Make people feel that happiness. . . .*

The faces of those about her changed as they got within earshot of the fiddle. They generally looked surprised first, then intrigued. Their eyes searched the edge of the crowd for the source of the music, then, when they found it, a smile would creep onto their lips. And, most times, they'd stop for a moment to listen. She found herself looking for those smiles, trying to coax them onto otherwise sour faces; playing light, cheerful tunes, tunes meant to set feet tapping.

Her efforts began to pay off, now that she was looking to those smiles for her reward and not the money in the hat. A couple of children broke into an impromptu jig at her feet once; and a young couple with the look of the infatuated did an entire dance-set beside her until the glare and a word from a passing Priest sent them laughing away.

She played a mocking run on her fiddle to follow the fat, bitter man, and thought then how odd it was that the Church seemed to frown upon everything that was less than serious—

But frivolity puts no coins in their coffers, she reminded herself—and realized that the crowds had thinned again; the second noon-bell had rung, and the stall-keepers on either side of her were cleaning their counters instead of cooking or serving customers. She finished the piece, then looked down at her hat, and saw that the three pennies had multiplied to nine, there was a second bag of sweets beside the first, and a veritable rain of pins covered the bottom of the hat.

"Eh, lad," said the second stall-keeper, leaning out to examine the contents of her hat with interest. " 'F ye got no plans fer them pins, I trade 'em fer ye. Fifteen pins fer a mug'a cider, an' don' matter what shape they be in, I'll swap. Wife c'n allus use pins."

"Same here," said the sausage-roll vendor. "Fifteen pins fer a roll."

Well, that would take care of her nuncheon with nothing out of her pocket, and she'd be saved the trouble of straightening the pins herself. And dealing with them; she hadn't a paper to stick them in, and she didn't relish the idea of lining them up in rows on her hat. She'd probably forget they were there and put her hand on them. "Done, to both of you," she replied, "and grateful, too."

"Good enough," said the sausage vendor. And when a count proved her to have forty-three, offered her two rolls for what was left when she got her cider. She stowed the rest of her take in her pouch and pack, put away Lady Rose, drank her cider, and considered what to do with the rest of her day, devouring her rolls while she thought.

It really wasn't worth playing her fingers off for only three pennies, not when she needed to find a place to live, a teacher, and a second instrument, in that order. So, with a wave of farewell to the two vendors, she packed herself up, and took out her map.

After a few times of getting turned around, she learned the trick of following it. It was too bad that none of the places Mathe had marked were terribly nearby, but there were three that were kind of in a row, and she headed in their direction.

The first shop was in the middle of a neighborhood where her shabby clothing drew dubious looks; nearly everyone she saw on the street wore clothing like the wealthier farmers' sons and daughters wore to Church services back home. One look in the shop window convinced her that this was no place for her. The instruments hung on the wall were polished and ornamented with carving and inlay work; they might well be second-hand, but they were still beyond her reach, and so, likely, was the teaching to be had.

The second place was much like the first, and she caught sight of some of the students waiting their turns. They were very well dressed, hardly a patch or a darn or let-down hem to be seen, and most of them were much younger than she. From the bored expressions they wore, she had the notion that the only reason they were taking music lessons at all was because it was genteel to do so.

She left the brightly painted shops behind, passed through a street of nothing but wrought-iron gates set into brick walls a story tall, gates giving onto small, luxurious gardens. The gardens were beautiful, but she didn't linger to admire them. Some of those gates had men in livery behind them, and those men wore weapons, openly. No point in giving them a reason to think she was here by anything other than accident.

That street became a street of shops; food shops this time, Vegetables, fruit, wooden replicas of meat and fish and poultry, all displayed enticingly inside open windows, with the real meat and dairy products lying on counters inside, or hanging from the rafters and hooks on the walls. Here, the clothing of the folk in the street had a kind of uniform feel to it; all sober colors, with white aprons and caps or dark hats. *Servants,* she decided. Sent from those houses behind her to buy the goods for dinner. How strange to have a servant to send out—what a thought! To wait, doing whatever it was that rich folk did, until dinner appeared like magic, without ever having to raise a finger to make it all happen! And then to go up to a room, and find a bath hot and waiting, and a bed warmed and ready—a book, perhaps, beside it. And in the morning, to find clean clothing set out, breakfast prepared. . . .

She daydreamed about this as she wormed her way down street after street, each one getting progressively narrower, and gradually shabbier. Finally she found herself on a street much too narrow for a cart, unless it was one of the dog carts; a street that even a ridden horse would probably find uncomfortably confining.

There was only one shop in the street that had three instruments hanging in the window, although it had other things there as well; cheap copper jewelry, religious statues, cards of lace and tarnished trim that showed bits of thread on the edge where it had been picked off a garment, knives and a sword, a tarnished silver christening-goblet. . . .

A small sign in the window said "We Buy and Sell" and "Loans Made." Another sign beneath it showed two pairs of hands; one offering a knife, the other a silver coin. A third, smaller sign said "Music Lessons."

She looked back up at the instruments, a lute, a harp, and a guitar; they were old, plain, but well-cared-for. There wasn't a speck of dust on them anywhere. The strings looked a little loose, which meant they weren't kept tuned—something that would warp an instrument's neck if it wasn't taken down and played often. Whoever had hung them there knew what he was doing.

The street itself was quiet; one of those "residential" areas Mathe had spoken of. There was another food-shop on the corner, but otherwise, this seemed to be the only store in this block of buildings. The rest were all wooden, two-storied, with slate roofs; they had single doors and a window on either side of the door, with more windows in the overhanging second story. A rat might have been able to scurry in the spaces between them, but nothing larger.

The buildings themselves were old, in need of a new coat of paint, and leaned a little. They reminded Rune of a group of old granddams and grandsires, shabby, worn, but always thinking of the days when they had been young.

Instruments and lessons—and a place where she might find somewhere to live. This was the most promising area, at least insofar as her purse was concerned, that she had encountered yet. She opened the door and went inside.

The interior of the shop was darker than the public house had been, and smelled of mildew and dust. When she closed the door behind her, a bell jangled over it, and a voice from the back of the store said, "Be patient a moment, please! I'm up on a ladder!" The voice matched the store; a little tired, old, but with a hint that it had been richer long ago.

Rune waited, letting her eyes adjust to the darkness of the shop. The place was crowded with all sorts of oddments, even more so than the tiny window. Behind and in front of her were floor-to-ceiling shelves; on them were books, stuffed animals, neatly folded clothing, statues of all sorts, not just religious, one or two of which made her avert her eyes in flushed embarrassment. There were dusty crystals, strange implements of glass and metal, lanterns, and cutlery. All of it was used, much of it was old, and some of it looked as if it had sat there for centuries. Every object had a little paper tag on it; she couldn't imagine why.

Suspended from the rafters were cloaks and coats, each with moth-bane festooning the hems. The shop itself was barely large enough for Rune, the shelves, and the tiny counter at the rear of the shop.

After a moment, an old man dressed in a dust-colored shirt and breeches pushed aside the curtain behind the counter and peered at her, then shook his gray, shaggy head.

"I'm sorry, lad," he said regretfully. "I'm not buying today—"

"And I'm not selling, sir," she interrupted, approaching the counter so he could get a better look at her.

He blinked, looked again, and chuckled; a rich, humor-filled sound that made her want to like him. He reminded her of Raven, a little. And a little of that Guild Minstrel. "And you're no lad, either. Forgive me, lass. What can I do for you?"

A little surprised, since no one else had seen her true sex through her purposefully sexless clothing, she took another step forward. "My name is Rune. I'm a player, sir," she said, hesitantly. "I was told that I could find an instrument and lessons here."

"That's true," the old man said, his sharp black eyes watching her so closely she felt as if her skin were off. "You can, as you know if you saw the signs in the windows. But there's more to it than that—the things that brought you to this shop in this city. Now, I like a good tale as well as any man, and it's late and near time to close up. If you'd care to share a cup of tea with me—and tell me your tale?"

Part of her said not to trust this man—here he was a stranger, and offering to share his hospitality with another stranger—

But the rest of her thought—what could he possibly *do* to her? He was old, he moved slowly; he couldn't possibly out-wrestle her in a bad situation. Where was the harm in indulging him?

And there was more of Raven's advice. *If you find yourself with some-one who cares for his instruments, no matter how old, or how plain—or even how cheap—you can trust him. He's a man who knows that all value isn't on the surface. And he may have some of that hidden value himself.*

"I'd like that, sir," she said, finally. But he had already raised his tiny counter on the hinges at one side, and was motioning her through as if he had never expected she would do anything other than accept. She pushed the curtains aside, hesitantly, and found herself in another narrow room, with a staircase at the farther end leading up to a loft. This room was just as crowded as the shop. There was a stove with a tiny fire in it, with a kettle atop; a broken-down bed that seemed to be in use as seating, since it was covered with worn-out cushions in a rainbow of faded materials. There seemed to be more furniture up in the loft, but the shadows up there were so thick that it was hard to see.

Besides the bed, there was a basin and ewer on a stand, a couple of tables piled with books, two chairs, and a kitchen-cupboard next to the stove. Everything stood within inches of the furniture beside it. There wasn't any possible way one more piece of furniture could have been crammed in here.

Rune took a seat on one of the chairs, placing her pack and Lady Rose at her feet. The only light came from a window at the rear of the room, below the loft, covered in oiled paper; and from a lantern on the table beside her.

There was a *thump*, as of heavy shutters closing, the door-bell jangled, and then a scraping sound of wood on wood came to her ears as the old man pushed the bar into place across his shutters. A moment later, he pushed aside the curtains and limped into the room.

Instead of speaking, he went straight to the stove at the rear and took a kettle off the top, pouring hot water into a cracked teapot that was missing its lid and stood on the shelf of the kitchen-cupboard beside him. He brought the pot and a pair of mugs with him, on a tarnished tray, which he sat down on the table beside her, next to the lamp, pushing the books onto the floor to make room for the tray.

"Now," he said, taking the other chair, "My name's Tonno. Yours, you said, is Rune, as I believe. While we wait for the herbs to steep, why don't you tell me about yourself? You're obviously not from Nolton, and your accent sounds as if you're from—hmm—Beeford, or thereabouts?"

She nodded, startled.

He chuckled and smiled, a smile that turned his face into a spiderweb of tiny lines, yet made him look immensely cheerful. "So, how is it that a young lady like you finds herself so far from home, and alone?"

She found herself telling him everything, for somehow his questions coaxed it all out of her; from the bare facts, to how she had managed to come here, to her desire for a place in the Guild. As the light beyond the oiled paper dimmed, and her confidence in him grew, she even told him about the Ghost, and her secret hoard of coins. Somehow she felt she could trust him even with that, and he wouldn't betray her trust.

He pursed his lips over that. "Have you told anyone else about this?" he asked sternly. She shook her head. "Good. Don't. The Church would either take a lion's share, or confiscate it all as coming from demons. I'll give you a choice; either you can keep them hidden and safe, or you can give them to me, and I'll provide you with that instrument you want and a year's worth of lessons—and give you whatever's left over, but I'll have it all changed into smaller coins. Smaller coins won't call attention to you the way silver would. I can probably manage that just on what I've saved."

She thought about that; thought about how easy it would be for the money to just trickle away, without her ever getting the lessons or the instrument. If she paid him now—

"This won't be just lessons in learning tunes, mind," Tonno said abruptly. "I'll teach you reading music, and writing it—you'll have the freedom to read any book in this shop, and I'll expect you to read one a week. I'm a hard teacher, but a fair one."

She nodded; this was more than she had expected.

"Can you play me a tune on that little fiddle of yours?" he asked—and once again, Rune took her lady from her case, and tuned her. This time, with care—for Tonno was a fellow musician, and she wanted to give him her very best.

She played him three pieces; a love song, a jig, and one of the strange Gypsy tunes that Nightingale had taught her. The last seemed to fill the shadows of the room with life, and turn them into things not properly of the waking world. It wasn't frightening, but it was certainly uncanny. She finished it with gooseflesh crawling up her arms, despite the fact that she had played the tune herself.

When she'd finished, Tonno sighed, and his eyes were a little melancholy. "I'll tell you something else," the old man said, slowly, "and I'm not ashamed to admit it, not after listening to you. I'm no better than a talented amateur. I knew better than to try and make a living at music, but I promise you that I know how to play every instrument in this shop, and I'm quite good enough to give you basic lessons. And believe me, child, if you've learned this much on your own, basic lessons in a new instrument, the ways of reading and writing the tunes you surely have in your head, and all the education you'll get from reading whatever you can get your hands on for the next year will be all that you need." He shook his head again. "After that you'll need more expert help than that, and I can probably find someone to give it to you. But I don't think that you'll need it for at least a year, and tell the truth, I wonder if some people who heard you now might not hold you back out of jealousy to keep you from outstripping them. When you get beyond me, I can send you out to others for special lessons, but until then—"

She let out the breath she'd been holding in a sigh.

"Can we chose an instrument now, sir?" she asked. "I'd like to make this a firm bargain."

They picked out a delicate little lute for her; she fell in love with its tone, and decided against the harp that Tonno thought might suit her voice better. Besides, the lute only had four strings; it would be easier to tune and keep tuned in the uncertain climes a traveling musician was likely to encounter. They agreed on a price for it and the year of lessons, and Rune retired behind a screen to take off her belt of silver coins. She knew she had spent a lot getting to Nolton; even augmenting her cash with playing on the road, the coins had been spent a lot faster than she'd liked. There was some left when they got through reckoning up how much three hours of lessons every day for a year would cost. Not much, but some. She could go ahead and buy her permit; and she would have a hedge against a lean spell.

When the commercial exchange had been accomplished, an awkward silence sprang up between them. She coughed a little, and bit her lip, wondering what to say next.

"I probably should go," she said, finally. "It's getting darker, and I've taken up too much of your time as it is. I'll come about the same time tomorrow for my first lesson—"

"Now what are your plans?" he asked, interrupting her. "Never mind what you're going to do tomorrow, what are you planning on doing tonight? You don't know the city—you could get yourself in a bad area, wandering about."

"I need a place to live," she said, now uncertain. Daylight was long spent, and she wasn't certain if those who took in lodgers would open their doors to a stranger after dark.

"What about a place to earn your keep?" he asked. "Or part of it, anyway—I—know someone looking for a musician. She could offer you a good room in exchange for playing part of the night. Possibly even a meal as well."

There was something about his manner that made her think there was a great deal more about the place than he was telling her, and she said as much.

He nodded, reluctantly. "It's a public house—a real one, but a small one. In part. And—well, the rest I'd rather Amber told you herself. If you want to go talk to her."

Tonno's diffident manner convinced her that there was something odd going on, but she couldn't put her finger on what it was. She frowned a little.

He shrugged, helplessly. "It's only a few blocks away," he said. "And it's in the area where there are a lot of—places of entertainment. If you don't like Amber, or she doesn't like you, you can try somewhere else. *That* area is safe enough you could even busk on the street-corner and *buy* yourself a room when you have the two pence." He smiled apologetically. "I often go there for my dinner. I would be happy to walk you there, and introduce you to Amber."

She thought about it; thought about it a long time. In the end, what decided her was Tonno's expression. It wasn't that of a man who was planning anything, or even that of a man who was trying to keep his plans hidden. It was the anxious look of someone who has a friend of dubious character that he likes very much—and wants his new friend to like as well.

Rune was well enough acquainted with the way the world wagged to guess what Tonno's friend Amber was. A public house—"of sorts," hmm? A small one? That might be what it was below-stairs, but above . . .

Amber probably has pretty girls who serve more than just beer and wine, I'd reckon.

On the other hand, it couldn't hurt to go look. People who came to a whorehouse had money, and were ready to spend it. They might be willing to toss a little of it in the direction of a player. As long as Amber knew she was paying for the music, and not the musician.

Besides, if there was one thing the Church Priests preached against, it was the sins of the flesh. It would ease the burden of having to pay the Priests their damned tithe knowing that the money came from something they so violently disapproved of.

"All right," she said, standing up and catching Tonno by surprise. "I'll see this friend of yours. Let's go."

And I can always say no, once I've met her.

CHAPTER SEVEN

In the streets of Nolton darkness was total, and at first the only light they had to show them their footing were the torches at the crossroads, and the occasional candle or rushlight in a window at street level. Tonno kept a brisk pace for such an old man; Rune had to admire him. It helped that he knew the way, of course, and she didn't. He kept pointing out landmarks as they passed—a building that dated back several hundred years, a place where some significant event in the history of the city had occurred, or the site of someone's birth or death. She would strain her eyes, and still see only one more shapeless bulk of a building, with a furtive light or two in the windows. Finally she gave up trying to see anything; she just nodded (foolish, since he wouldn't be able to see the nod), and made an appreciative grunt or a brief comment.

The street Tonno led her to was not one she would have found on her own; it was reached only by passing through several other side streets, and the street itself was about a dozen houses long, and came to a dead end, culminating in a little circle with an ornamental fountain in the center of it. It was, however, very well lit, surprisingly so after the darkness of the streets around it; torches outside every door, and lanterns hanging in the windows of the first and second stories saw to that. There was an entire group of musicians and a dancer busking beside the fountain, and from the look of the money they'd collected on the little carpet in front of the drummer, the pickings were pretty good here. The fountain wasn't one of the noisy variety; it would be easy enough even for a single singer to be heard over it. A good place to put out a hat, it would seem.

The musicians looked familiar, in the generic sense; finally she realized that they were dressed in the same gaudy fashion as the Gypsies the harpist Nightingale traveled with. If this "Amber" didn't prove out, perhaps she'd see if they'd let her join them. They didn't have a fiddler, and they might recognize Nightingale's name or description, and be willing to let her join them on the basis of a shared acquaintance.

Most of the places on the circle itself were large, with three stories and lights in every window, sometimes strings of lanterns festooning the balconies on the second and third stories, as if it were a festival. There were people coming and going from them in a steady stream; men, mostly. And, mostly well-dressed. Whenever a door opened, Rune heard laughter and music for a moment, mingling with the music of the quartet by the fountain. There were women leaning over the balconies and out of the windows; most disheveled, most wearing only the briefest of clothing, tight-laced bodices and sleeveless under-shifts that fluttered like the drapes of the Ghost—

71

She shivered for a moment with a chill, then resolutely put the memory out of her mind. There was no Ghost here—and anyway, he'd favored her, he hadn't harmed her.

Sheer luck, whispered the voice of caution. She turned her attention stubbornly to her surroundings. Here was warmth and light and laughter, however artificial. There were no ghosts here.

All of the women, she had to admit, were very attractive—at least from this distance. They flirted with fans, combed their hair with languid fingers, or sometimes called out to the men below with ribald jokes.

She'd have to be a simpleton not to recognize what kind of a district this was. It might even be the same street Mathe had mentioned as a good place to busk at night. Her guise of a boy would probably keep her safely unmolested here—she'd seen no signs that these brothels catered to those whose tastes ran to anything other than women.

But Tonno took her to a tiny place, just two stories tall, tucked in beneath the wings of the biggest building on the circle. There were lights in the windows, but no women hanging out of them, and no balcony at all, much less one festooned with willing ladies. The sign above the door said only, "Amber's." And when Tonno opened the door, there was no rush of light and sound. He invited Rune in with a wave of his hand, and she preceded him inside while he shut the door behind them.

The very first thing she noticed were the lanterns; there was one on every table—and every table seemed to have at least one customer. So whatever this place was or did, it wasn't suffering from lack of business. The common room was half the size of the Bear's, but the difference was in more than size. Here, there were no backless benches, no trestle tables. Each square table was made of some kind of dark wood, and surrounding it were padded chairs, and there were padded booths with tables in them along the walls. The customers were eating real meals from real plates, with pewter mugs and forks to match. And the whiff Rune got of beef-gravy and savory was enough to make her stomach growl. She told it sternly to be quiet, promising it the bread and cheese still tucked into her pack. No matter what came of this meeting, she had a meal and the price of a room on her—and tomorrow would be another day to try her luck.

She'd certainly been lucky today, so far. It was enough to make her believe in guardian spirits.

Across the room, a woman presiding over a small desk beside a staircase saw them, smiled, and rose to greet them. She was middle-aged; probably a little older than Stara, and Rune couldn't help thinking that *this* was what Stara was trying to achieve with her paints and her low-cut bodices, and failing. Her tumbling russet curls were bound back in a style that looked careless, and probably took half an hour to achieve. Her heart-shaped face, with a wide, generous mouth, and huge eyes, seemed utterly ageless—but content with whatever age it happened to be, rather than being the face of a woman trying to hold off the years at any cost. The coloring of her complexion was so carelessly perfect that if Rune hadn't been looking for the signs, and seen the artfully painted shadows on lids and the perfect rose of the cheeks, she'd never have guessed the woman used cosmetics. Her dress, of a warm, rich brown, was of modest cut—

but clung to her figure as if it had been molded to it, before falling in graceful folds to the floor.

Any woman, presented with Stara and this woman Amber, when asked to pick out the trollop, would point without hesitation to Stara, ignoring the other entirely. And Rune sensed instinctively that any man, when asked which was the youngest, most nubile, attractive, would select Amber every time. The first impression of Amber was of generosity and happiness; the first impression of Stara was of discontent, petulance, and bitterness.

She found herself smiling in spite of herself, and in spite of her determination not to let herself be charmed into something she would regret later.

"Tonno!" Amber said, holding out both hands to him, as if he was the most important person in the world. He clasped them both, with a pleased smile on his lips, and she held them tightly. "I had given up on seeing you tonight! I am *so* pleased you decided to come after all! And who is this young lad?"

She turned an inquiring smile on Rune that would likely have dazzled any real "lad," and yet was entirely free of artifice. It didn't seem designed to dazzle; rather, that the ability to dazzle was simply a part of Amber's personality.

"Amber, this *lass* is my new pupil, Rune. And, I hope, is the musician you've been asking me to find." Tonno beamed at both of them, but the smile that he turned to Rune held a hint of desperation in it, as if he was begging Rune to like this woman.

We'll see how she reacts to being told I'm a girl, first—if all she's interested in is what she can get out of someone, and she knows that as a woman I'm not as likely to be manipulated—

"A lass!" Amber's smile didn't lose a bit of its brightness. In fact, if anything, it warmed a trifle. "Forgive me, Rune—I hope you'll take my mistake as a compliment to your disguise. It really is very effective! Was this a way to avoid trouble in public? If it is, I think you chose very well."

Rune found herself blushing. "It seemed the safest way to travel," she temporized. "I never wore skirts except when I planned to stay at a hostel."

"Clever," Amber replied with approval. "Very clever. Now what was this about your being a musician? I take it you have no place yet? Tonno, I thought you said she was your student—" She interrupted herself with a shake of her head. "Never mind. Let's discuss all this over food and drink, shall we?"

Rune glanced sideways at the customer nearest her. She knew what *she* could afford—and she didn't think that this place served meals for a penny.

She thought she'd been fairly unobtrusive, but Amber obviously caught that quick sideways glance. And had guessed what it meant—though that could have been intuited from the threadbare state of Rune's wardrobe. "Business before pleasure, might be better, perhaps. If you'd feel more comfortable about it, we can discuss this now, in my office, and Tonno can take his usual table. Would that be more to your liking?"

Rune nodded, and Amber left her for a moment, escorting Tonno to a small table near the door, then returning with a faint swish of skirts. Rune sighed a little with envy; the woman moved so gracefully she turned the mere act of walking into a dance.

"Come into my office will you?" she said, and signaled to one of the serving girls to take care of Tonno's table. Obediently, Rune followed her, feeling like an awkward little donkey loaded down with packs, carrying as she was her worldly goods and the fiddle and lute cases.

The office was just inside the door to the staircase, and held only a desk and two chairs. Amber took the first, and Rune the other, for the second time that day dropping her packs down beside her. Amber studied her for a moment, but there was lively interest in the woman's eyes, as if she found Rune quite intriguing.

"Tonno is a very good friend, and has advised me on any number of things to my profit," she said at last. "He's very seldom wrong about anything, and about music, never. So perhaps you can explain how you can be both his student and the musician I've needed here?"

"I'm self-taught, milady," Rune replied with care. "Last night, my first in the city, the owner of the Crowned Corn said I was good enough to expect the same profit as anyone else who isn't a Guild musician. But that's on the fiddle—and I can't read nor write music, can't read much better than to puzzle out a few things in the Holy Book. So that's how I'm Tonno's student, you see—on the lute, and with things that'll make me ready for the Guild trials."

Amber nodded, her lips pursed. "So you've ambitions, then. I can't blame you; the life of a common minstrel is not an easy one, and the life of a Guild musician is comfortable and assured."

Rune shrugged; there was more to it than that, much more, but perhaps Amber wouldn't understand the other desires that fired her—the need to find the company of others like herself, the thirst to learn more, much more, about the power she sensed in music—and most especially, the drive to leave something of herself in the world, if only one song. As she knew the names of the Bards who had composed nearly every song in her repertory except the Gypsy ballads, so she wanted to know that in some far-off day some other young musician would learn a piece of hers, and find it worth repeating. Perhaps even—find it beautiful.

No, she'd never understand that.

"I will be willing to take Tonno's assessment of your ability as a given. This is what I can offer: a room and one meal a day of your choice. This is what your duty would be: to play here in the common room from sundown until midnight bell. I should warn you that you can expect little in the way of tips here; as you have probably guessed already, this is not an inn as such."

"It's a—pleasure-house, isn't it?" She had to think for a moment before she could come up with a phrase that wouldn't offend.

Amber nodded. "Yes, it is—and although many clients come here only for the food, the food is not where the profit is; it is merely a sideline. It serves to attract customers, to give them something to do while they wait their turn. Your capacity would be exactly the same. You would *not* be expected to serve above-stairs, is that clear?"

The relief must have been so obvious in spite of Rune's effort not to show it that Amber laughed. "My dear Rune—you are a very pleasant girl, but a *girl* is all you are, no matter how talented you might be in other areas. This house serves a very specific set of clients, by appointment only. And let me tell you that the four young ladies entertaining above are quite a peg beyond being either girls or merely pleasant. Beside them, I am a withered old hag indeed, and their talents and skills far outstrip mine!"

Irrationally, Rune felt a little put out at being called a "pleasant young girl"—but good sense got the better of her, and she contemplated the offer seriously for the first time since Tonno had brought the possibility up.

This meant one sure meal a day, a particularly good meal at that, and a room. She need only play until midnight bell; she would have the morning and noon and part of the afternoon to busk before her lessons with Tonno. Not a bad arrangement, really. It would let her save a few pennies, and in the winter when it was too cold to busk, she could stay inside, in a building that would, by necessity, be warmly heated. Still, this was a whorehouse . . . there were certain assumptions that would be made by the clients, no matter what Amber claimed. If Amber wanted her to dress as a female, there could be trouble.

"No one will bother you," Amber said firmly, answering the unspoken question. "If you like, you can keep to that boy's garb you've taken, although I would prefer it if you could obtain something a little less—worn."

Rune looked down reflexively at her no-color shirt, gray-brown vest and much-patched breeches, all of which had been slept in for the past three days, and flushed.

"Tonno can help you find something appropriate, I'm sure," Amber continued, with a dimpling smile. "I swear, I think the man knows where every second-hand vendor in the city is! As for the clients and your own safety—I have two serving girls and two serving boys below-stairs; you may ask them if they have ever been troubled by the clients. The ladies do not serve meals; the below-stairs folk do not serve the clients. Everyone who comes here knows that."

Rune licked her dry lips, took a deep breath, and nodded. "I'd like to try it then, Lady Amber."

"Good." Amber nodded. "Then let's make your meal for the day a bit of dinner with Tonno, and we can call tonight's effort your tryout. If you suit us, then you have a place; if not—I'll let you have the room for the rest of the night, and then we'll see you on your way in the morning."

A short trial-period, as these things went, and on generous terms. But she had nothing to lose, and if nothing else, she'd gain a dinner and a place to sleep for the night. She followed Amber back out into the common room, where she sat at Tonno's table, ate one of the best beef dinners she had ever had in her life, and listened while Amber and Tonno talked of books. The only time she'd ever eaten better was when the Sire had sent a bullock to the village to supply a feast in celebration of his own wedding, and Rune had, quite by accident she was sure, been given a slice of the tenderloin. The beef she'd normally eaten was generally old, tough, and stewed or in soup.

During that time, she saw several men leave by the stairs, and several more ascend when summoned by a little old man, so bent and wizened he seemed to be a thousand years old. They were all dressed well, if quietly, but for the rest, they seemed to fit to no particular mold.

As soon as she'd finished, she excused herself, and returned to Amber's office for Lady Rose, figuring that the office was the safest place to leave her gear for the moment. Fiddle in hand, she came back to the table, and waited for a break in the conversation.

"Lady Amber, if you please, where would you like me to sit, and what would you prefer I played?" she asked, when Amber made a point that caused Tonno to turn up his hands and acknowledge defeat in whatever they were discussing. They both turned to her as if they had forgotten she was there. Tonno smiled to see her ready to play, and Amber nodded a little in approval.

Amber's brows creased for a moment. "I think—over there by the fireplace, if you would, Rune," she said, after a moment of glancing around the room for the best place. "And I would prefer no dance tunes, and no heart-rending laments. Anything else would be perfectly suitable. Try to be unobtrusive—" She smiled, mischievously. "Seduce them with your music, instead of seizing them, if you will. I would like the clients relaxed, and in a good mood; sometimes they get impatient when they are waiting, and if you can make the wait enjoyable instead of tedious, that would be perfect."

Rune made her way around the edge of the room, avoiding the occupied tables, a little conscious of Amber's assessing eyes and Tonno's anxious ones. That was an interesting choice of music, for normally innkeepers wanted something lively, to heat the blood and make people drink faster. Evidently the "inn" was not in the business of selling liquor, either. It must be as Amber had said, that their primary income came from the rooms above. Rune would have thought, though, that an intoxicated client would be easier to handle.

On the other hand, maybe you wouldn't want the clients drunk; they might be belligerent; might cause trouble or start fights if they thought they'd waited longer than they should. So—must be that I'm supposed to keep 'em soothed. Soothing it is.

She found a comfortable place to sit in the chimney-corner, on a little padded bench beside the dark fireplace. She set her bow to her strings, and began to play an old, old love song.

This was a very different sort of playing from everything she'd done in inns up to this moment. There she had been striving to be the center of attention; here she was supposed to be invisible. After a moment, she began to enjoy it; it was a nice change.

She played things she hadn't had a chance to play in a while; all the romantic pieces that she normally saved for the odd wedding or two she'd performed at. Keeping the volume low, just loud enough to be heard without calling attention to the fact that there was a musician present, she watched her audience for a while until she became more interested in what she was playing than the silent faces at the tables. The serving-girls and men gave her an appreciative smile as they passed, but that was all the reward she got for her efforts. It was as if the men out there actually took her playing for granted.

Then it dawned on her that this was exactly the case; these were all men of some means, and no doubt many of them had household musicians from the Bardic Guild whose only duty was to entertain and fill the long hours of the evening with melody. That was why Amber had warned her she should expect little in the way of remuneration. Men like these didn't toss coins into a minstrel's hat—they fed him, clothed him, housed him, saw to his every need. And on occasion, when he had performed beyond expectation or when they were feeling generous, they rewarded him. But that only happened on great occasions, and in front of others, so that their generosity would be noted by others. They never rewarded someone for doing what she was doing now; providing a relaxing background.

Ah well. If I become a Guild musician, this may well be my lot. No harm in getting used to it.

After a while, she lost herself in the music—in the music itself, and not the memories it recalled for her. She began to play variations on some of the pieces, doing some improvisational work and getting caught up in the intricacies of the melody she was creating. She closed her eyes without realizing she'd done so, and played until her arm began to ache—

She opened her eyes, then, finished off the tune she'd been working on, and realized that she must have been playing for at least an hour by the way her arms and shoulders felt. The customers had changed completely; Tonno was gone, and Amber was nowhere to be seen. One of the serving-girls glided over with a mug of hot spiced cider; Rune took it gratefully. They exchanged smiles; Rune found herself hoping she'd be able to stay. Everything so far indicated that all Amber had claimed was true. She hadn't seen the serving-girls so much as touched. And both the girls, pretty in their brown skirts and bodices, one dark-haired and one light, had been friendly to her. They acted as if they were glad to have her there, in fact. Perhaps the clients were making fewer demands on them with Rune's playing to occupy their thoughts.

When she had shaken the cramps out, and had massaged her fingers a bit, she felt ready to play again. This time she didn't lose herself in the spell of the music; she watched the customers to see what their reaction was to her playing.

A head or two nodded in time to the music. There were two tables where there were pairs of men involved in some kind of game; it wasn't the draughts she was used to, for the pieces were much more elaborate. Those four ignored her entirely. There were another three involved in some kind of intense conversation who didn't seem to be paying any attention either. Then she noticed one richly dressed, very young man— hardly more than a boy—in the company of two older men. The boy looked nervous; as an experiment, she set out deliberately to soothe *him*. She played, not love songs, but old lullabies; then, as he began to relax, she switched back to love songs, but this time instead of ballads, she chose songs of seduction, the kind a young man would use to lure a girl into the night and (hopefully, at least from his point of view) into his bed.

The young man relaxed still further, and began to smile, as if he envisioned himself as that successful lover. He sat up straighter; he began to sip at his drink instead of clutch it, and even to nibble at some of the

little snacks his companions had ordered for their table. By the time the
wizened man summoned them, he was showing a new self-assurance, and
swaggered a bit as he followed the old man up the stairs. His two companions chuckled, and sat back to enjoy their drink and food; one summoned
one of the serving-boys, and a moment later, they, too, were embroiled
in one of those games.

At first Rune was amused. But then, as she started another languid
ballad, she felt a twinge of conscience. If the boy had actually responded
to what she'd been doing, rather than simply calming normally, then she
had manipulated him. She'd had her own belly full of manipulation; was
it fair to do that to someone else, even with the best of intentions?

*Did I do that, or was it just the liquor? And if it was me, what gave
me the right?*

She wondered even more now about these invisible "women" Amber
employed. Did they enjoy what they were doing? Were they doing it by
choice, or because of some kind of constraint Amber had on them? Were
they pampered and protected, or prisoners? Just what kind of place was
this, exactly?

She had finished her second mug of cider and was well into her third
set, when the midnight bell rang, signaling the end of her stint. There
was no sign that the custom had abated any, though; the tables were just
as full as before. While she wondered exactly what she should do, Amber
herself glided down the stairs and into the room, and nodded to her. She
finished the song, slid Lady Rose into her carrying bag, and stood up, a
little surprised at how stiff she felt. She edged past the fireplace to
Amber's side, without disturbing anyone that she could tell. Amber drew
her into the hall of the staircase, and motioned that she should go up.

"At this point, the gentlemen waiting are in no hurry," she said. "At
this late hour, the gentlemen have usually exhausted their high spirits and
are prepared to relax; past midnight I probably won't ever need your
services to keep them occupied."

They got to the top of the stairs, where there was a hall carpeted in
something thick and plushly scarlet, paneled in rich wood, and illuminated
by scented candles in sconces set into the walls. She started to turn
automatically down the candlelit hallway, but Amber stopped her before
she'd gone a single pace. "Watch this carefully," the woman said, ignoring
the muffled little sounds of pleasure that penetrated into the hall and
made Rune blush to the hair. "You'll have to know how to do this for
yourself from now on."

She tried to ignore the sounds herself, and watched as Amber turned
to the shelves that stood where another hall might have been. She reached
into the second set of shelves, grasped a brass dog that looked like a
simple ornament, and turned it. There was a *click,* and a door, upon
which the set of shelves had been mounted, swung open, revealing another
hall. Amber waved Rune through and shut the door behind them.

This was a much plainer hallway; lit by two lanterns, and with an ordinary wooden floor and white-painted walls. "This subterfuge is so that the
customers don't 'lose their way,' and blunder into our private quarters,"
Amber said, in a conversational voice. "I never could imagine why, but

some people seem to think that anything ordinary in a pleasure-house must conceal something extraordinary. The serving-girls got very tired of having clients pester them, so I had the shelves built to hide the other hall. I took the liberty of having old Parro bring your things up to your new room so you wouldn't have to; I imagine that you're quite fatigued with all your walking about the streets today."

Rune tried to imagine that poor, wizened little man hauling her pack about, and failed. "He really didn't have to," she protested. "He—he doesn't—"

"Oh, don't make the mistake of thinking that because he's small and a bit crippled that he's weak," Amber said. "He wouldn't thank you for that. He's quite fiercely proud of his strength, and I have him as my summoner for a good reason. He can—and has—brought strong guardsmen to their knees, and men constantly underestimate him because of the way he looks."

"Oh," Rune said weakly.

"You'll meet everyone tomorrow; I thought you'd rather get to sleep early tonight," Amber continued, holding open a door for her. "This is your room, by the way. You did very well, just as well as Tonno said you would. I'm happy to welcome you to my little family, Rune."

Rune stepped into the room before the last remark penetrated her fatigue. "You are?" she said, a little stupidly.

Amber nodded, and lit a candle at the lantern outside the door, placing it in a holder on a little table just inside. "The bathroom is at the end of the hall, and there should be hot water in the copper if you want to wash before you go to bed. In the morning, simply come downstairs when you're ready, and either Parro or I will introduce you. Goodnight, Rune."

She had closed the door before Rune had a chance to say anything. But what could she say, really? "Wait, I'm not sure I should be doing this?" That wasn't terribly bright. "Just what is going on around here?" She *knew* what was going on. This was a whorehouse. She was going to entertain here. The madam was a gracious lady, of impeccable manners and taste, but it was still a house of pleasure—

But this was certainly the oddest bawdy-house she'd ever heard of.

She looked around at her room—*her* room, and what an odd sound that had! There wasn't much: a tiny table, a chair, a chest for clothing, and the bed. But it was a real bed, not a pallet on the floor like she'd had all her life. And it was much too narrow for two, which in a way, was reassuring.

There's no way anyone would pay to share that with Amber, much less with me.

The frame was the same plain wood as the rest of the furniture; the mattress seemed to be stuffed with something other than straw. Not feathers, but certainly something softer than she was used to; she bounced on it, experimentally, and found herself grinning from ear to ear.

There were clean, fresh sheets on the bed, and blankets hung over the footboard, with clean towels atop them. The plain wooden floor was scrubbed spotless, as were the white-painted walls. There was one window with the curtains already shut; she went to it and peeked out. Less than an arm's length away loomed the wooden side of the house next door; there were windows in it, but they were set so that they didn't look into any windows in this building, thus ensuring a bit of privacy. Not much of a view, but the window would probably let in some air in the summer, as soon as the warmer weather really arrived. It was better than being in the attic, where the sun beating down on the roof would make an oven of the place in summer, and the wind whistling under the eaves would turn it into the opposite in winter.

Her room. *Her* room, with a latch on the inside of the door, so she could lock it if she chose. Her room, where no one could bother her, a room she didn't have to share with anyone. Maybe it was the size of a rich man's closet, but it was all hers, and the thrill of privacy was heady indeed.

She looked longingly at the bed—but she knew she was filthy; she hadn't had a bath in several days, and to lie down in the clean sheets unwashed seemed like a desecration. It also wouldn't give Amber a very good impression of her cleanliness; after all, the woman had gone out of her way to mention that there was water ready for washing even at this late hour. That could have been a hint—in fact, it probably was.

She took the towels and went to the end of the hall to find the promised bathroom. And indeed, it was there, and included the indoor privies she had seen in the Church hostels, which could be flushed clean by pulling a chain that sluiced down a measured amount of water from a reservoir on the roof. There were two privies in stalls, and two bath-basins behind tall screens. One was big enough to soak in, but the other wouldn't take as long to fill, and she was awfully tired. Both the baths were fixed to the floor, with permanent drains in their bottoms.

She filled the shallow bath with equal measures of hot and cold water, dipped from the copper and a jar, both of which were also fed by the roof-reservoir. As she dipped the steaming water out of the top of the cauldron, she longed more than ever to be able to take a good long soak—

But that could wait until she had a half-penny to spare for the public baths and steam-house. Then she could soak in the hot pools, swim in the cold, and go back to soak in the hot pools until every pore was cleansed. She could take an afternoon from busking, perhaps the Seventh-Day, when people would be going to Church in the morning and spending the afternoon at home. That would mean there'd be fewer of them in the streets, and her take wouldn't be that much anyway; it wouldn't hurt her income as much to spend the afternoon in the bath-house.

But for now, at least, she could go to bed clean.

She scrubbed herself hastily, rinsed with a little more cold water, and toweled herself down, feeling as if she were a paying patron. And if *this* was the treatment that the help got, how *were* the patrons treated?

With that thought in mind, she returned to her room, locked herself in for the night, and dug out her poor, maltreated bread and cheese. It was squashed, but still edible, and she found herself hungry enough to devour the last crumb.

And with the last of her needs satisfied, she blew out the candle and felt her way to her bed, to dream of dancing lutes dressed in Gypsy ribbons, and fiddles that ran fiddle-brothels where richly dressed men came to caress their strings and play children's lullabies, and strange, wizened old men who lifted houses off their foundations and placed them back down, wrong-way about.

She woke much later than she had intended, much to her chagrin. She hurried into the only clean set of clothing she had—a shirt and breeches that had seen much better days—and resolved to find herself more clothing before Amber had a chance to comment on the state of her dress.

When she found her way down to the common room, she discovered the exterior doors locked tight, and a half-dozen people eating what looked like breakfast porridge, and talking.

One of those was the most stunning young woman Rune had ever seen. Even in a simple shift with her hair combed back from her face, she looked like—

An angel, Rune thought wonderingly. She was inhumanly lovely. No one should look that lovely. No one *could,* outside of a ballad.

The girl was so beautiful it was impossible to feel jealousy; Rune could only admire her, the way she would admire a rainbow, a butterfly, or a flower.

Her hair was a straight fall of gold, and dropped down past her waist to an inch or two above the floor; her eyes were the perfect blue of a summer sky after a rain. Her complexion was roses and cream, her teeth perfect and even, her face round as a child's and with a child's innocence. Her figure, slight and lissome, was as delicate as a porcelain figure of an idealized shepherdess.

Her perfect rosebud mouth made a little "o" as she saw Rune, and the person sitting with her, who Rune hadn't even noticed at that moment, turned. It was Amber.

"Ah, Rune," she said, smiling. "Come here, child. I'd like you to meet Sapphire. She is one of the ladies I told you about last night."

Rune blinked, and made her way carefully to the table. *Anyone with that much beauty can't be human. She probably has the brains of a pea—*

"Hello, Rune," Sapphire said, with a smile that eclipsed Amber's. "That isn't my real name, of course—Amber insisted we all take the names of jewels so when I leave here and retire, I can leave 'Sapphire' behind and just be myself."

Amber nodded. "It will happen, of course. This is not a profession one can remain in for long."

"Oh," Rune said, awkwardly. "Then—"

"Amber is not my real name, either—at least, it isn't the one I was born with," Amber said easily.

"I'll probably become 'Amber' when I take over as Madam," Sapphire continued. "Since there's always been an 'Amber' in charge here. This Amber decided to take me as her 'prentice, so to speak. I already help with the bookkeeping, but I'm going to need a lot more schooling in handling people, that much I know."

Rune nearly swallowed her tongue; *this* delicate, brainless-looking creature was doing—bookkeeping?

Sapphire laughed at the look on her face; Rune felt like a fool. "You're not the first person who's been surprised by Sapphire," Amber said indulgently. "I told you the ladies were all something very special."

"So are you, love," Sapphire replied warmly. "Without you, we'd all be—"

"Elsewhere," Amber interrupted. "And probably just as successful. All four of you have brains and ambition; you'd probably be very influential courtesans and mistresses."

"But not wives," Sapphire replied, and her tone was so bitter that Rune started.

"No," Amber said softly. "Never wives. That's the fate of a lovely woman with no lineage and no money. The prince doesn't fall in love with you, woo you gently, carry you away on his white horse and marry you over his father's objections."

"No, the prince seduces you—if you're lucky. More often than not he carries you off, all right, screaming for your father who doesn't dare interfere. Then he rapes you—and abandons you once he knows you're with child," Sapphire said grimly, her mouth set in a thin, hard line.

"And that is the prerogative of princes," Amber concluded with equal bitterness. "Merchant princes, princes of the trades, or princes by birth."

They both seemed to have forgotten she was there; she felt very uncomfortable. This was not the sort of thing one heard in ballads. . . .

Well, yes and no. There were plenty of ballads where beautiful women *were* seduced, or taken against their will. But in those ballads, they died tragically, often murdered, and their spirits pursued their ravagers and brought them to otherworldly justice. Or else they retired to a life in a convent, and only saw their erstwhile despoilers when the villains were at death's door, brought there by some other rash action.

Apparently, it wasn't considered to be in good taste to survive one's despoiling as anything other than a nun.

"Well, I'm not going to let one damn fool turn me into a bitter old hag," Sapphire said with a sigh, and stretched, turning from bitter to sunny in a single instant. "That's over and done with. In a way, he did me a favor," she said, half to Rune, half to Amber. "If he hadn't carried me off and abandoned me here, I probably would have married Bert, raised pigs, and died in childbed three years ago."

Amber nodded, thoughtfully. "And I would have pined myself over Tham wedding Jakie until I talked myself into the convent."

Sapphire laughed, and raised a glass of apple juice. A shaft of sunlight lancing through the cracks in the shutters pierced it, turning it into liquid gold

"Then here's to feckless young men, spoiled and ruthless!" she said gaily. "And to women who refuse to be ruined by them!"

Amber solemnly clinked glasses with her, poured a third glass for Rune without waiting for her to ask, and they drank the toast together.

"So, Rune, how is it that you come here," Sapphire asked, "with your accent from my own hills, and your gift of soothing the fears out of frightened young men?"

Rune's jaw dropped, and Amber and Sapphire both laughed. "You thought I hadn't noticed?" Amber said. "That was the moment when I knew you were for us. If you can soothe the fears out of a young man, you may well soothe the violence out of an older one. That is a hazard of our profession. Oh, our old and steady clients know that to come here means that one of the ladies will be kind and flattering, will listen without censure, and will make him feel like the most virile and clever man on Earth—but there are always new clients, and many of them come to a whore only because they hate women so much they cannot bear any other relationship."

"Then—I did right?" Rune asked, wondering a little that she brought a question of morality to a whore—but unable to believe that these two women were anything but moral. "I thought—it seemed so calculating, to try and calm him down—"

"The men who come here, come to feel better," Amber said firmly. "That is why I told you we serve a very special need. We hear secrets they won't even tell their Priests, and fears they wouldn't tell their wives or best friends. If all they wanted was lovemaking, they could go to any of the houses on the street—"

"Unskilled sex, perhaps," Sapphire commented acidly, with a candor that held Rune speechless. "Not lovemaking. That takes ability and practice."

"Point taken," Amber replied. "Well enough. Our clients come to us for more than that. Sapphire, Topaz, Ruby, and Pearl are more than whores, Rune."

"I'm—" she said, and coughed to clear her throat. "I'm, uh—beginning to see that."

"So how *did* you come here, Rune?" Sapphire persisted. "When I heard you speak, I swear, you carried me right back to my village!"

Once again, Rune gave a carefully edited version of her travels and travails—though she made light of the latter, sensing from Sapphire's earlier comments that *her* experiences had been a great deal more harrowing than Rune's. She also left out the Skull Hill Ghost; time enough to talk about him when she'd made a song out of him and there'd be no reason to suspect that the adventure was anything more than a song.

Sapphire sat entranced through all of it, though Rune suspected that half of her "entrancement" was another skill she had acquired; the ability to listen and appear fascinated by practically anything.

When Rune finished, Sapphire raised her glass again. "And here's to a young lady who refused to keep to her place as decreed by men and God," she said. "And had the gumption to pack up and set out on her own."

"Thank you," Rune said, flattered. "But I've a long way to go before I'm a Guild apprentice. Right now I intend to concentrate on keeping myself fed and out of trouble until I master my second instrument."

"Good." Amber turned a critical eye on her clothing, and Rune flushed again. "Please talk to Tonno about finding you some costumes, would you?"

That was a clear dismissal if ever Rune had heard one. And since she had decided to take advantage of her promised meal by making it supper—especially if she was going to dine like she had last night—she took her leave.

But she took to the streets in search of a busking-corner with her head spinning. Nothing around here was the way she had thought it would be. The folk who should have been honest and helpful—the Church—were taking in money and attempting to cheat over it at every turn. And the folk who should have been the ones to avoid—Amber and her "ladies"— had gone out of their way to give her a place. Of course, she was going to have to work for that place, but still, that didn't make things any less than remarkable. Amber was about as different from the fellow who set up at the Faires as could be imagined—and the ladies, at least Sapphire, as different from his hard-eyed dancers. They seemed to think of themselves as providing a service, even if it was one that was frowned upon by the Church.

Then again, it was the Church who frowned upon anything that didn't bring money to its coffers and servants to its hands. Doubtless the Church had found no way for the congress between men and women to bring profit to them—so they chose instead to make it, if not forbidden, then certainly not encouraged.

Rune shook her head and stepped out into the sunlight surrounding the fountain. It was all too much for her. Those were the worries of the high and mighty. *She* had other things to attend to—to find breakfast, pay her tax and tithe, buy her permit, and set up for busking until it was time for her lessons.

And that was enough for any girl to worry about on a bright early summer morning.

CHAPTER EIGHT

Midmorning found her back on the corner between the drink-stall and the sausage-stall, and both owners were happy to see her; happier still to see the badge of her permit pinned to the front of her vest. She set herself up with a peculiar feeling of permanence, and the sausage roll vendor confirmed that when he asked her if she planned to make this her regular station. She didn't have a chance to answer him then, but once the nuncheon rush was over and he had time again to talk, he brought it up again.

She considered that idea for a moment, nibbling at her lip. This wasn't a bad place; not terribly profitable, but not bad. There was a good deal of traffic here, although the only folks that passed by that appeared to have any money at all were the Church functionaries. Still, better spots probably already had "residents." This one might even have a regular player later in the day, when folk were off work and more inclined to stop and listen.

"I don't know," she said truthfully. "Why?"

"Because if ye do, me'n Jak there'll save it for ye," the sausage-man told her, as she exchanged part of her collection of pins for her lunch.

"There's a juggler what has it at night, but we c'n save it fer ye by day. Th' wife knows a seamstress; th' seamstress allus needs pins." He leaned forward a bit, earnestly, his thin face alive with the effort of convincing her. "Barter's no bad way t'go, fer a meal or twain. An 'f ye get known fer bein' here, could be ye'll get people comin' here t' hear ye a-purpose."

"An we'll get th' custom," the cider-vendor said with a grin, leaning over his own counter to join the conversation. "Ain't bad fer ev'body."

Now that was certainly true; she nodded in half-agreement.

"Ye get good 'nough, so ye bring more custom, tell ye what we'll do," the cider-vendor Jak said, leaning forward even farther, and half-whispering confidentially. "We'll feed ye fer free. Nuncheon, anyway. But ye'll have t' bring us more custom nor we'd had already."

After a moment of thought, the sausage-vendor nodded. "Aye, we c'n do that, if ye bring us more custom. 'Nough t' pay th' penny fer yer share, anyway," he said. "That'll do, I reckon."

His caution amused her, even while she felt a shade of annoyance at their penny-pinching. Surely one sausage roll and a mug of cider wasn't going to ruin their profits in a day! "How would I know?" Rune asked with a touch of irony. "I mean, I'd only have your word that I hadn't already done that."

"Well now, ye'd just haveta trust us, eh?" Jak said with a grin, and she found herself wondering what the juggler thought of these two rogues. "What can ye lose? Good corners are hard t' find. A' when ye find one, mebbe sommut's already there. An' ye *know* ye can trade off yer pins here, even if we says ye hain't brought in 'nough new business t' feed ye free. Not ev'body takes pins. Ask that blamed Church vulture t'take pins, he'll laugh in yer face."

That was true enough. She looked the corner over with a critical eye. It seemed to be adequately sheltered from everything but rain. The wind wouldn't whip through here the way it might a more open venue. Sure, it was summer now, but there could be cold storms even in summer, and winter was coming; she was going to have to think ahead to the next season. She still had to eat, pay her tax and tithe on the trade-value of what she was getting from Amber, and enlarge her wardrobe. Right now she had no winter clothes, and none suitable for the truly hot days of summer. She'd have to take care of that, as well.

" 'F it rains, ye come in here," Jak said, suddenly. "I reckon Lars'd offer, but he's got that hot fat back there, an' I dunno how good that'd be fer th' fiddle there. Come winter, Lars peddles same, I peddle hot cider wi' spices. Ye can come in here t'get yer fingers an' toes warm whene'er ye get chilled."

That settled it. "Done," Rune replied instantly. It wasn't often a street-busker got an offer of shelter from a storm. That could make the difference between a good day's take and a poor one—shelter meant she could play until the last moment before a storm broke, then duck inside and be right back out when the weather cleared. And a place out of the cold meant extra hours she could be busking. That alone was worth staying for. These men might be miserly about their stock, but they were ready enough to offer her what someone else might not.

She left the corner for the day feeling quite lighthearted. On the whole, her day so far had been pretty pleasant, including the otherwise unpleasant duty of paying the Church. She'd been able to annoy the priest at the Church-box quite successfully; playing dunce and passing over first her tithe, counted out in half-penny and quarter-pennies, then her tax, counted out likewise, and then, after he'd closed the ledger, assuming she was going to move on, her permit-fee, ten copper pennies which were the equivalent of one silver. She'd done so slowly, passing them in to him one at a time, much to the amusement of a couple of other buskers waiting to pay their own tithes and taxes. *They* knew she was playing the fool, but he didn't. It almost made it worth the loss of the money. He had cursed her under his breath for being such a witling, and she'd asked humbly when she finished for his blessing—he'd had to give it to her— and he'd been so annoyed his face had been poppy-red. The other buskers had to go around the corner to stifle their giggles.

Now it was time to go find Tonno's shop—she needed at least one "new" outfit to satisfy Amber's requirements, and Tonno knew where she was going to be able to find the cheapest clothes. That expenditure wasn't something she was looking forward to, for the money for new clothing would come out of her slender reserve, but she had no choice in the matter. Amber's request had the force of a command, if she wanted to keep her new place, and even when she'd gotten her old clothing clean, it hadn't weathered the journey well enough to be presentable "downstairs." It would do for busking in the street, where a little poverty often invited another coin or two, but not for Amber's establishment.

On the other hand, the money for her lodging was *not* coming out of her reserves, and that was a plus in her favor. And she did need new clothes, no matter what.

When she pushed open the door, she saw that Tonno had a customer. He was going over a tall stack of books with a man in the long robes of a University Scholar, probably one of the teachers there. She hung back near the door of the shop until she caught his eye, then waited patiently until the Scholar was engrossed in a book and raised her eyebrows in entreaty. He excused himself for a moment; once she whispered what she needed, he took Lady Rose and her lute from her to stow safely behind the counter until lesson time, then gave her directions to Patch Street, where many of the old clothes sellers either had shops or barrows. She excused herself quickly and quietly—a little disappointed that he wouldn't be able to come with her. She had the feeling that he'd be able to get her bargains she hadn't a chance for, alone.

It was a good thing that she'd started out with a couple of hours to spend before her first lesson. Patch Street was not that far away, but the number of vendors squeezed into a two-block area was nothing less than astonishing. The street itself was thick with buyers and sellers, all shouting their wares or arguing price at the tops of their lungs. The cacophony deafened her, and she began to feel a little short of breath from the press of people the moment she entered the affray. The sun beat down between the buildings on all of them impartially, and she was soon limp with heat as well as pummeled by noise and prodded by elbows.

She now was grateful she had left Lady Rose with Tonno; there was scarcely room on this street to squeeze by. She tried to keep her mind on what she needed—good, servicable clothing, not too worn—but there were thousands of distractions. The woman in her yearned for some of the bright silks and velvets, worn and obviously second-hand as most of them were, and the showman for some of the gaudier costumes, like the ones the Gypsies had worn—huge multicolored skirts, bright scarlet sashes, embroidered vests and bodices—

She disciplined herself firmly. *Under-things first. One pair of breeches; something strong and soft. Two new shirts, as lightweight as I can get them. One vest. Nothing bright, nothing to cry out for attention. I'm supposed to be inconspicuous. And nothing too feminine.*

The under-things she found in a barrow tended by a little old woman who might have been Parro's wizened twin. She suspected that the garments came from some of the houses of pleasure, too; although the lace had been removed from them, they were under-things meant to be seen— or rather, they had been, before they'd been torn. Aside from the tears, they looked hardly used at all.

She picked up a pair of underdrawers; they were very lightweight, but they were also soft—not silk, but something comfortable and easy on the skin. Quite a change from the harsh linen and wool things she was used to wearing. The tears would be simple enough to mend, though they would be very obvious. . . .

Then again, Rune wasn't likely to be in a position where anyone was going to notice her mended underwear. The original owners though—it probably wasn't good for business for a whore to be seen in under-things with mends and patches.

It was odd, though; the tears were all in places like shoulder-seams, or along the sides—where the seams themselves had held but the fabric hadn't. As if the garments had been torn from their wearers.

Maybe they had been. Either a-purpose or by chance.

Perhaps the life of a whore wasn't all that easy. . . .

Her next acquisition must be a pair of shirts, and it was a little hard to find what she was looking for here. Most shirts in these stalls and barrows were either ready to be turned into rags, or had plainly been divested of expensive embroidery. The places where bands of ornamentation had been picked off on the sleeves and collars were distressingly obvious, especially for someone whose hands and arms were going to be the most visible parts of her. Although Rune wasn't the most expert seamstress in the world, it looked to her as if the fine weave of the fabrics would never close up around the seam-line. It would always be very clear that the shirt was second-hand, and that wouldn't do for Amber's. As she turned over garment after garment, she wondered if she was going to be able to find *anything* worth buying. Or if she was going to have to dig even deeper into her resources and buy new shirts. She bit her lip anxiously, and went back to the first barrow, hoping against hope to find *something* that might do—

" 'Scuse me, dearie." A hand on her arm and a rich, alto voice interrupted her fruitless search. Rune looked up into the eyes of a middle-aged, red-haired woman; a lady with a busking-permit pinned to the front of *her* bodice, and a look of understanding in her warm green-brown eyes. "I think mebbe I c'n help ye."

She licked her lips, and nodded.

"Lissen, boy," the woman continued, when she saw she'd gotten Rune's attention, leaning towards Rune's ear to shout at her. "Can ye sew at all? A straight seam, like? An' patch?"

What an odd question. "Uh—yes," Rune answered, before she had time to consider her words. "Yes, I can. But I can't do any more than that—"

"Good," the woman said in satisfaction. "Look, here—" She held up two of the shirts Rune had rejected, a faded blue, and a stained white, both of lovely light material, and both useless because the places where bands of ornament had been picked off or cut away were all too obvious. "Buy these."

Rune shook her head; the woman persisted, "Nay, hear me out. Ye go over t' *that* lass, th' one w' th' ribbons." She pointed over the heads of the crowd at a girl with a shoulder-tray full of ribbons of various bright colors. "Ye buy 'nough plain ribbon t' cover th' places where the 'broidery was picked out, an' wider than' the 'broidery was. Look, see, like I done wi' mine."

She held up her own arm and indicated the sleeve. Where a band of embroidery would have been at the cuff, there was a wide ribbon; where a bit of lace would have been at the top of the sleeve, she'd put a knot of multicolored ribbons. The effect was quite striking, and Rune had to admit that the shirt did not look as if it had come from the rag-bin like these.

The woman held up the white one. "This 'un's only stained at back an' near th' waist, ye see?" she said, pointing out the location of the light-brown stains. "Sleeves 'r still good. So's top. Get a good vest, sew bit'a ribbon on, an nobbut'll know 'tis stained."

Rune blinked, and looked at the shirts in the woman's hands in the light of her suggestions. It would work; it would certainly work. The stained shirt could even be made ready by the time Rune needed to take up her station at Amber's tonight.

"Thank you!" she shouted back, taking the shirts from the woman's hands, and turning to pay the vendor for them. "Thank you very much!"

"Think nowt on't," the woman shouted back, with a grin. "'Tis one musicker to 'nother. Ye do sommut else the turn one day. 'Sides, me niece's th' one w' the ribbon!"

She bought the shirts—dearer than she'd hoped, but not as bad as she'd feared—and wormed her way to the ribbon vendor's side. A length of dark blue quite transformed the faded blue shirt into something with dignity, and a length of faded rose—obviously also picked off something else—worked nicely on the stained white. And who knew? Maybe someone at Amber's would know how to take the stains out; they looked like spilled wine, and there was undoubtably a lot of spilled wine around a brothel.

Now for the rest; she had better luck there, thankful for her slight frame. She was thin for a boy, though tall—her normal height being similar to the point where a lad really started shooting up and outgrowing clothing at a dreadful rate. Soon she had a pair of fawn-colored corduroy breeches, with the inside rubbed bare, probably from riding, but that wouldn't show where she was sitting—and a slightly darker vest of lined leather that laced tight and could pass for a bodice when she wore her skirts. The seams on the vest had popped and had not been mended; it would be simplicity to sew them up again. With the light-colored shirt, the breeches, and the new vest, she'd be fit for duty this evening, and meanwhile she could wash and dry her blue breeches and skirt, and her other three shirts. Once they were clean, she could see how salvageable they were for night-duty. If they were of no use, she could come back here, and get a bit more clothing. And they'd be good enough for street-busking; it didn't pay to look too prosperous on the street. People felt sorry for you if you looked a bit tattered, and she didn't want that nosy Church-clerk to think she was doing too well.

She wormed her way out of the crowd to find that two hours had gone by—as well as five pennies—and it was time to return to Tonno.

Rune's head pounded, and her hands hurt worse than they had in years. *Blessed God.* She squinted and tried to ignore the pain between her eyebrows, without success. Her fingers and her head both hurt; she was more than happy to take a break from the lesson when Tonno ran his hand through his thick shock of gray hair and suggested that she had quite enough to think about for the moment. She had always known that the lute was a very different instrument from the fiddle, but she hadn't realized just how different it was. She shook her left hand hard to try and free it from the cramps, and licked and blew on the fingertips of her right to cool them. There wouldn't be any blisters, but that was only because Tonno was merciful to his newest pupil.

Playing the lute was like playing something as wildly different from the fiddle as—a shepherd's pipe. The grip, and the action, for instance; it was noticably harder to hold down the lute's strings than the fiddle's. And now she was required to *do* something with her right hand—bowing required control of course, but all of her fingers worked together. Now she was having to pick in patterns as complicated as fingering . . . more so, even. She was sweating by the time Tonno called the break and offered tea, and quite convinced that Tonno was earning his lesson money.

It didn't much help that she was also learning to read music—the notes on a page—at the same time she was learning to play her second instrument. It was hard enough to keep notes and fingerings matched now, with simple melodies—but she'd seen some music sheets that featured multiple notes meant to be played simultaneously, and she wasn't sure she'd *ever* be ready for those.

"So, child, am I earning my fee?" Tonno asked genially.

She nodded, and shook her hair to cool her head. She was sweating like a horse with her effort; at this rate, she'd have to wash really well before she went on duty tonight. "You're earning it, sir, but I'm not sure I'm ever going to master this stuff."

"You're learning a new pair of languages, dear," he cautioned, understanding in his eyes. "Don't be discouraged. It will come, and much more quickly than you think. Trust me."

"If you say so." She put the lute back in its carrying case, and looked about at the shop. There were at least a dozen different types of instruments hanging on the wall, not counting drums. There were a couple of fiddles, another lute, a guitar, a shepherd's pipe and a flute, a mandolin, a hurdy-gurdy, a trumpet and a horn, three harps of various sizes, plus several things she couldn't identify. "I can't imagine how you ever learned to play all these things. It seems impossible."

"Partially out of curiosity, partially out of necessity," Tonno told her, following her gaze, and smiling reminiscently. "I inherited this shop from my father; and it helps a great deal to have a way to bring in extra money. But when he still owned it and I was a child, he had no way of telling if the instruments he acquired were any good, so when I showed some aptitude for music, he had me learn everything so that I could tell him when something wasn't worth buying."

"But why didn't you—" Rune stopped herself from asking why he hadn't become a Guild musician. Tonno smiled at her tolerantly and answered the question anyway.

"I didn't even try to enter the Guild, because I have no real talent for music," he said. "I have a knack for picking up the basics, but there my abilities end. I'm very good at *teaching* the basics, but other than that, I am simply a gifted amateur. Oh—and I can tell when a musician has potential. I am good enough to know that I am not good enough, you see."

Rune felt inexplicably saddened by his words. She couldn't imagine not pursuing music, at least, not now. Yet to offer sympathy seemed rude at the least. She kept her own counsel and held her tongue, unsure of what she could say safely.

"So," Tonno said, breaking the awkward silence, "It's time for your other lessons. What do you think you'd like to read? Histories? Collected poems and ballads? Old tales?"

Reading! She'd forgotten that was to be part of her lessoning. Her head swam at the idea of something more to learn.

"Is there anything easy?" she asked desperately. "I can't read very well, just enough to spell things out in the Holy Book."

Tonno got up, and walked over to the laden shelves without answering, scrutinizing some of the books stacked there for a moment.

"Easy, hmm?" he said, after a moment or two. "Yes, I think we can manage that. Here—"

He pulled a book out from between two more, and blew the dust from its well-worn cover. "This should suit you," he told her, bringing the book back to where she sat with her lute case in her lap. "It's a book of songs and ballads, and I'm sure you'll recognize at least half of them. That should give you familiar ground to steady you as you plunge into the new material. Here—" He thrust it at her, so that she was forced to take it before he dropped it on her lute. "Bring it back when you've finished, and I'll give you something new to read. Once you're reading easily, I'll start picking other books for you. It isn't possible for a minstrel to be too widely read."

"Yes, sir," she said hastily. "I mean, no, sir."

"Now, run along back to Amber's," he said, making a shooing motion with his hands. "I'm sure you'll have to do something with those new clothes of yours to make them fit to wear. I'll see you tomorrow."

How he had known that, she had no idea, but she was grateful to be let off. Right now her fingers stung, and she wanted a chance to rest them before the evening—and she did, indeed, have quite a bit of mending and trimming to do before her garments were fit for Amber's common room.

The first evening-bell rang, marking the time when most shops shut their doors and the farmer's market was officially closed. She hurried back through the quiet streets, empty of most traffic in this quarter, reaching Amber's and Flower Street in good time.

None of the houses on the court were open except Amber's, and Rune had the feeling that it was only the "downstairs" portion that was truly ready for business. There were a handful of men, and even one woman sitting in the common room, enjoying a meal. As Rune entered the common room, her stomach reminded her sharply that it would be no bad thing to perform with a good meal inside her. As she hesitated in the stairway, one of the serving-girls, the cheerful one who had smiled at her last night, stopped on her way to a table.

"If you'd like your meal in your room," she said, quietly, "go to the end of the corridor, just beyond the bathroom. There's a little staircase in a closet there that leads straight down into the kitchen. You can get a tray there and take it up, or you can eat in the kitchen—but Lana is usually awfully busy, so it's hard to find a quiet corner to eat in. This time of night, she's got every flat space filled up with things she's cooking."

"Thanks," Rune whispered back; the girl grinned in a conspiratorial manner, and hurried on to her table.

Rune followed her instructions and shortly was ensconced in her own room with a steaming plate of chicken and noodles, a basket of bread and sliced cheese, and a winter apple still sound, though wrinkled from storage. Although she was no seamstress, she made a fairly quick job of mending the vest and trimming the light shirt, taking a stitch between each couple of bites of her supper. The food was gone long before the mending was done, of course; she was working by the light of her candle when a tap at her door made her jump with startlement.

"Y-yes?" she stuttered, trying to get her heart down out of her throat.

"It's Maddie," said a muffled voice. "Lana sent me after your dishes."

"Oh—come in," she said, standing up in confusion, as the door opened, revealing the serving-girl who'd told her the way to the kitchen. With her neat brown skirt and bodice and apron over all, she looked as tidy as Rune felt untidy. Rune flushed. "I'm sorry, I meant to take them down— I didn't mean to be any trouble—"

The girl laughed, and shook her head until her light brown hair started to come loose from the knot at the back of her neck. "It's no bother," she replied. "Really. There's hardly anyone downstairs yet, and I wanted a chance to give you a proper hello. You're Rune, right? The new musician? Carly thought you were a boy—she is going to be so mad!"

Rune nodded apprehensively. The girl seemed friendly enough—she had a wonderful smile and a host of freckles sprinkled across her nose that made her look like a freckled kitten. She looked as if she could have been one of the village girls from home.

Which was the root of Rune's apprehension. Those girls from home hadn't ever been exactly friendly. And now this girl had been put out of her way to come get the dishes, and had informed her that the other serving-girl was going to be annoyed when she discovered the musician wasn't the male she had thought.

"Well, I'm Maddie," the girl said comfortably, picking up the tray, but seeming in no great hurry to leave with it. "I expect we'll probably be pretty good friends—and I expect that Carly will probably hate you. She's the other server, the blond, the one as has the sharp eyes and nose. She hates everyone—every girl, anyway. But she's Parro's daughter, so Lady Amber puts up with her."

"What's Carly's problem?" Rune asked, putting her sewing down.

"She wants to work upstairs," Maddie said with a twist of her mouth. "And there's no way. She's not nowhere good enough. Or nice enough." Maddie shrugged, at least as much as the tray in her arms permitted. "She'll probably either marry some fool and nag him to death, or end up down the street at the Stallion or the Velvet Rope. There's men enough around that'll pay to be punished that she'd be right at home."

Rune found her mouth sagging open at Maddie's matter-of-fact assessment of the situation. And at what she'd hinted. Back at home—

Well, she wasn't back at home.

She found herself blushing, and Maddie giggled. "Best learn the truth, Rune, and learn to live with it. We're on Flower Street, and that's the whore's district. There's men that'll pay for whores to do weirder things than just nag or beat 'em, but that doesn't happen here. But this's a whorehouse, whatever else them 'nice' people call it; the ladies upstairs belong to the Whore's Guild, and they got the right to make a living like any other Guild. Got Crown protection and all."

Rune's mouth sagged open further. "They—do?" she managed.

"Surely," Maddie said, with a firm nod. "I know, 'tis a bit much at first. Me, my momma was a laundry-woman down at Knife's Edge, so I seen plenty growing up. . . . and let me tell you, I was right glad to get a job *here* instead of there! But young Shawm, he's straight from the country like you, and Carly made his life a pure misery until me and Arden and Lana took him in hand and got him used to the way things is. Like we're gonna do with you."

Rune managed a smile. "Thanks, Maddie," she said weakly, still a little in shock at the girl's frankness. "I probably seem like a real country-cousin to you—"

Maddie shook her head cheerfully. "Nay. Most of the people here in town think just like you—fact is, Amber's had a bit of a problem getting a good musicker because of that. Whoring is a job, lass, like any other. Whore sells something she can *do,* just like a cook or a musicker. Try thinking on it that way, and things'll come easier." She tilted her head to one side, as Rune tried not to feel too much a fool. At the moment, she felt as naive as a tiny child, and Maddie, though she probably wasn't more than a year older, seemed worlds more experienced.

"I got to go," the other girl said, hefting the tray a little higher. "Tell you what, though, if you got clothes what need washing, you can give 'em to me and I'll take 'em to Momma with Lana and Shawm's and mine tonight. 'Twon't cost you nothing; Momma does it 'cause Lana gives her what's left over. Lady Amber don't allow no leftovers being given to our custom."

"Oh—thank you!" Rune said, taken quite aback. "But are you sure?"

Maddie nodded. "Sure as sure—and sure I won't *never* do the same for Carly!" She winked, and Rune stifled a giggle, feeling a sudden kinship with the girl. "I'll come by in the morning and you can help me carry it all down to Momma, eh?"

Rune laughed. "Oh, I see! This way you get somebody to help you carry things!"

Maddie grinned. "Sure thing, and I don't want to ask Shawm. I got other things I'd druther ask him to do."

Rune grinned a little wider—and dared to tease her a little. "Maddie, are you sweet on Shawm?"

To her surprise, the girl blushed a brilliant scarlet, and mumbled something that sounded like an affirmative.

Rune could hardly believe Maddie's sudden shyness—this from the girl who had just spoke about being brought up in a whorehouse with the same matter-of-factness that Rune would have used in talking about her childhood at the Hungry Bear. "Well, don't worry," she said impulsively, "I won't tell him *or* Carly. If that's what you want."

Maddie grinned gratefully, still scarlet. "Thanks. I knew you were a good'un," she said. "Now I really *do* have to go. The custom's gonna start coming in right soon, and Shawm's down there by himself."

"I'll see you down there in a little bit," Rune replied. "And if you can think of anything you'd like to hear, let me know. If I don't know it, I bet Tonno does, and I can learn it from him."

"Thanks!" Maddie said with obvious surprise. "Hey—you know, 'Rat-catcher'? I really like that song, and I don't get to hear it very often."

"I sure do!" Rune replied, happy to be able to do something for Maddie right away in return for the girl's kindness. "I'll play it a couple times tonight, and if you think of anything else, tell me."

"Right-oh!" Maddie said, and turned to go. Rune held the door open for her, then trotted down to the end of the hall to hold open the door to the stairway as well.

She returned to put the last touches on her costume for tonight and get Lady Rose in tune, feeling more than a little happy about the outcome of the day so far. She'd gotten her first lesson, a permanent busking site with some extra benefits, acquired the first "new" clothing she'd had in a while, been warned about an enemy—

And found a friend. That was the most surprising, and perhaps the best part of the day. She'd been half expecting animosity from the other girls—but she was used to that. She'd never expected to find one of them an ally.

She slipped into her new garb and laced the vest tight, flattening her chest—what there was of it—and looking down at herself critically. Neat, well-dressed—and not even remotely feminine looking. That would do.

Time to go earn her keep. She grinned at the thought. _Time to go earn my keep. At a house of pleasure. With my fiddle. And my teacher thinks I'm going to be good. Go stick that in your cup and drink it, Westhaven._

And she descended the front stairs with a heady feeling of accomplishment.

CHAPTER NINE

"I can't imagine what Lady Amber thinks she's doing, hiring that scruffy little catgut-scraper," Carly said irritably—and very audibly—to one of the customers, just as Rune finished a song. "I should think she'd drive people away. She gives _me_ a headache."

Rune bit her tongue and held her peace, and simply smiled at Carly as if she hadn't been meant to overhear that last, then flexed her fingers to loosen them.

Bitch. She'd fit right in at Westhaven. Right alongside those other sanctimonious idiots.

"I think it's very pleasant," the young man said in mild surprise. He looked over to Rune's corner and lifted a finger. "Lass, you wouldn't know 'Song of the Swan,' would you?"

"I surely would, my lord," she said quickly, and began the piece before Carly could react, keeping her own expression absolutely neutral. No point in giving the scold any more ammunition than she already had. Rune got along fine with everyone else in the house; it was only Carly who was intent on plaguing her life. Why, she didn't know, but it was no use taking tales to Lady Amber; Amber would simply fix her with a chiding look, and ask her if it was _really_ so difficult to get along with one girl.

The young man looked gratified at being called "my lord"; Amber had told her to always call men "my lord" and the few women who frequented the place "my lady." "It does no harm," Amber had said with a lifted eyebrow, "and if it makes someone feel better to be taken for noble, then it does some good."

That seemed to be the theme of a great many things that Amber said. She even attempted to make the sour-tempered Carly feel more contented. Of course, the girl _did_ do her work, quickly, efficiently, and expertly—she could serve more tables than Shawm, Maddie, or Arden. That was probably one of the things that saved her from getting the sack, Rune reflected. If she'd shirked her work, there would be no way that even Amber would put up with her temper.

Now that summer was gone, and autumn nearly over as well, Rune was a standard fixture at Amber's and felt secure enough there that she had dropped the boy disguise, even when she wore her breeches instead of skirts. The customers never even hinted at services other than music, for she, along with the rest of the downstairs help, did *not* sport the badge of the Whore's Guild. And that made her absolutely off-limits, at least in Amber's. In one of the other houses on the street, that might not be true, but here she was safe.

She knew most of the regular customers by sight now, and some by name as well. Tonno's friends she all knew well enough even to tease them a bit between sets—and they frequently bought her a bit of drink a little stronger than the cider she was allowed as part of her keep. A nice glass of brandy-wine did go down very well, making her tired fingers a little less tired, and putting a bit more life in her hands at the end of a long night. That was the good part; the bad part was that her income had fallen off. There were fewer people on the street seeking nuncheon during the day, the days themselves were shorter, and winter was coming on very early this year. Jak and his fellow vendor had been looking askance at the weather, and Jak had confessed that he thought they might have to close down during the bitterest months this year, shutting up the stalls and instead taking their goods to those public houses that didn't serve much in the way of food.

If that happened, Rune would still have her corner, but no shelter. Already she had lost several days to rotten weather; rains that went on all day, soaking everything in sight, and so cold and miserable that even Amber's had been shy of custom come the evening hours.

The winter did not look to be a good one, so far as keeping ahead of expenses went. The best thing she could say for it was that at least she had a warm place to live, and one good, solid meal every day—she still had her teacher, and a small store of coin laid up that might carry her through until spring. If only she didn't have the damned tax and tithe to pay. . . .

No one made any further suggestions, so Rune let her wandering mind and fingers pick their own tunes. Today had been another of those miserable days; gray and overcast, and threatening rain though it never materialized. The result was that her take was half her norm: five pennies in half and quarter pence and pins, and out of that was taken three pence for tithes and taxes. The only saving grace was that since her corner was right across from the Church-box, the Priest could see for himself how ill she was doing and didn't contest her now that she was paying less. Nor, thank God, had he contested her appraisal of her food and lodging as five pennies. She hadn't told him where it was, or she suspected he'd have levied it higher. She'd seen the clients paying over their bills, and the meal alone was generally five copper pennies.

It's a good thing I've already got my winter clothes. I'd never be able to afford them now. The local musicians had a kind of unofficial uniform, an echo of what the Guild musicians wore. Where Guildsmen always wore billowy-sleeved shirts with knots of purple and gold or silver ribbons on the shoulders of the sleeves, the non-Guild Minstrels wore knots of multi-colored ribbons instead. Rune had modified all her shirts to match; and since no one but a musician ever sported that particular ornament, she was known for what she was wherever she went. During the summer she'd even picked up an odd coin now and again because of that, being stopped on the street by someone who wanted music at his party, or by an impromptu gathering on a warm summer night that wanted to dance.

But that had been this summer—

A blast of cold wind hit the shutters, shaking them, and making the flames on all the lanterns waver. Rune was very glad of her proximity to the fireplace; it was relatively cozy over here. Maddie and Carly wore shawls while they worked, tucking them into their skirt bands to keep their hands free. She couldn't wear a shawl; she had to keep hands and arms completely free. If she hadn't been in this corner, she'd be freezing by now, even though fiddling was a good way to keep warm.

The winter's going to be a bad one. All the signs pointed in that direction. For that matter, all the signs pointed to tomorrow being pretty miserable. *Maybe I ought to just stay here tomorrow. . . .*

Carly passed by, scowling. Just to tweak the girl's temper, Rune modulated into "I've A Wife." Since it was quite unlikely that Carly would ever attain the married state, it was an unmistakable taunt in her direction. Assuming the girl was bright enough to recognize it as such.

On the other hand, staying here tomorrow means I'd have to put up with her during the day. I can't stay in bed all day reading, and it's too cold to stay up there the whole day. It's not worth it.

Maybe Tonno could use some help in his shop. . . .

She changed the tune again, to "Winter Winds," as another blast hit the shutters and rattled them. She told herself again that it could be worse. She could be on the road right now. She could be back in Westhaven. There were a hundred places she *could* be; instead she was here, with a certain amount of her keep assured.

Sapphire drifted down the stairs, dressed in a lovely, soft kirtle of her signature blue. That was a rarity, the ladies didn't usually come downstairs after dark. Rune was a little surprised; but then she saw why Sapphire had come down. While luxurious, the lady's rooms were meant for one thing only—besides sleep. And then, it got very crowded with more than two. If clients wanted simple company, and in a group rather than alone, well, the common room was the best place for that. There were four older gentlemen waiting eagerly for Sapphire at their table, a pentangle board set up and ready for play.

If all they wanted was to play pentangle with a beautiful woman who would tease and flatter all of them until they went home—or one or more of them mustered the juice to take advantage of the other services here— then Amber's would gladly provide that service. And now Rune knew why Carly was especially sour tonight. Bad enough that *she* wasn't good enough to take her place upstairs. Worse that one of the ladies came down here, into her sphere, to attract all eyes and remind her of the fact. For truly, there wasn't an eye in the place that wasn't fastened on Sapphire, and well she knew it. Though Carly was out-of-bounds, she liked having the men look at her; now no one would give her any more attention than the lantern on the table.

Sapphire winked broadly at Rune, who raised her eyebrows and played her a special little flourish as she sat down. Rune knew all the ladies now, and to her immense surprise, she found that she liked all of them. And never mind that one of them wasn't human. . . .

That was Topaz; a lady she had met only after Maddie had taken her aside and warned her not to show surprise if she could help it. What Topaz was, Rune had never had the temerity to ask. Another one of those creatures who, like Boony, came from—elsewhere. Only Topaz was nothing like Boony; she was thin and wiry and com- pletely hairless, from her toe and finger-claws to the top of her head. Her golden eyes were set slantwise in her flat face, which could have been catlike; but she gave an impression less like a cat and far more like a lizard with her sinuosity and her curious stillness. Her skin was as gold as her eyes, a curious, metallic gold, and Rune often had the feeling that if she looked closely enough, she'd find that in place of skin Topaz really had a hide covered in tiny scales, the size of grains of dust. . . .

But whatever else she looked like, Topaz was close enough to human to be very popular at Amber's. Or else—

But Rune didn't want to speculate on that. She was still capable of being flustered by some of the things that went on here.

Her fingers wandered into "That Wild Ocean"—which made her think of Pearl, not because Pearl was wild, but because she reminded Rune of the way the melody twisted and twined in complicated figures, for all that it was a slow piece. Pearl was human, altogether human, though of a different race than anyone Rune had ever seen. She was tiny and very pale, with skin as colorless as white quartz, long black hair that fell unfettered right down to the floor, and black, obliquely slanted eyes. She and Topaz spent a great deal of their free time together; Rune suspected that there were more of Topaz's kind where Pearl came from, although neither of them had ever said anything to prove or disprove that. Occasionally Rune would catch them whispering together in what sounded like a language composed entirely of sibilants, but when Rune had asked Pearl if that was her native tongue, the tiny woman had shaken her head and responded with a string of liquid syllables utterly unlike the hissing she had shared with Topaz.

But for all their strangeness, Pearl and Topaz were very friendly, both to her and to Maddie, Shawm, and Arden. Maddie frankly adored Pearl, and would gladly run any errand the woman asked of her. Shawm, white-blond and bashful, with too-large hands and feet, was totally in awe of all the ladies, and couldn't even get a word out straight when they were around. Arden, tall and dark, like Rune, teased them all like a younger brother, and took great pleasure in being teased back. He was never at a loss for words with any of them—

Except for one; the fourth lady, Ruby, who was the perfect compliment to Sapphire. Her eyes were a bright, challenging green, in contrast to Sapphire's dreamy blue. Her hair was a brilliant red, cut shorter than Rune's. Her figure was athletic and muscular, and she kept it that way by running every morning when she rose, and following that by two hours of gymnastic exercises. Where Sapphire was soft and lush, she was muscle and whipcord. Where Sapphire was gentle, she was wild. Where Sapphire was languid, she was quicksilver; Sapphire's even temper was matched by her fiery changeability.

Predictably enough, *they* were best friends.

And where Arden could tease Sapphire until she collapsed in a fit of giggles, he became tongue-tied and silent in the presence of Ruby.

And Carly *hated* that.

Well, fortunately Ruby was fully occupied at the moment—so Arden could tease Sapphire as she teased the old gentlemen at her table, and Carly only glowered, she didn't fume.

All four of them, plus Maddie, were the first female friends Rune had ever had. She found herself smiling a little at that, and smiled a bit more when she realized that her fingers had started "Home, Home, Home." Well, this *was* the closest thing she'd ever had to a home. . . .

One by one, the four ladies had introduced themselves over the course of her first few weeks at Amber's, and gradually Rune had pieced together their stories. Topaz's history was the most straightforward. Topaz, like Boony, had been a bondling, and had been taken up for the same reason; failure to pay tax and tithe. She had been a small merchant-trader until that moment. Amber had bought her contract from one of the other houses at Pearl's hysterical insistence when the tiny creature learned that Topaz was in thrall there.

"And just as well," Topaz had said, once. "One more night there, and . . . something would have been dead. It might have been a client. It might have been me. I cannot say."

Looking at her strange, golden eyes, and the wildness lurking in them, Rune could believe it. It was not that Topaz had objected to performing what she called "concubine duties." Evidently that was a trade with no stigma attached in her (and Pearl's) country. It was some of the other things the house had demanded she perform. . . .

Her eyes had darkened and the pupils had widened until they were all that was to be seen when she'd said that. Rune had not asked any further questions.

Pearl had come as a concubine in the train of a foreign trader; when he had died, she had been left with nowhere to go. By the laws of her land, she was property—and should have been sent back with the rest of his belongings. But by the laws of Nolton, even a bondling was freed by the death of his bondholder, and no one was willing to part with the expense of transporting her home again.

But she had learned of Flower Street and of Amber's from her now-dead master, and had come looking for a place. Originally she had intended to stay only long enough to earn the money to return home, but she found that she liked it here, and so stayed on, amassing savings enough to one day retire to a place of her own, and devote herself to her other avocation, the painting of tiny pictures on eggshells. As curiosities, her work fetched good prices, and would be enough to supplement her savings.

Sapphire's story was the one she had obliquely referred to that first morning when Rune had met her; carried off and despoiled by a rich

young merchant's son, she had been abandoned when her pregnancy first
became apparent. She had been befriended by Tonno, who had found
her fainting on his doorstep, and taken to Amber. What became of the
child, Rune did not know, though she suspected that Amber had either
rid the girl of it or she had miscarried naturally. Amber had seen the
haggard remains of Sapphire's great beauty, and had set herself to bringing
it back to full bloom again. And had succeeded. . . .

Then there was Ruby, who had been a wild child, willful, and determined to be everything her parents hated and feared. Possibly because
they had been *so* determined that she become a good little daughter of
the Church—perhaps even a cleric-Priest or a nun. She had run away
from the convent, got herself deflowered by the first man she ran across
(a minstrel, she had confided to Rune, "And I don't know who was the
more amazed, him or me") and discovered that she not only had a talent
for the games of man and maid, she *craved* the contact. So she had come
to Nolton ("Working my way"), examined each of the brothels on Flower
Street, then came straight to Amber, demanding a place upstairs.

Amber, much amused by her audacity and impressed by her looks, had
agreed to a compromise—a week of trial, under the name "Garnet," promising her a promotion to "Ruby" and full house status if she did well.

She was "Ruby" within two days.

Ruby was the latest of the ladies, a fact that galled Carly no end. Carly
had petitioned Amber for a trial so many times that the lady had forbidden
her to speak of it ever again. She could not understand *why* Ruby had
succeeded where she had failed.

Sapphire left the gentlemen for a moment and drifted over to Rune's
corner. Seeing where she was headed, Rune brought her current song to
an end, finishing it just as Sapphire reached the fireplace. The young
gentleman who had earlier requested a song hardly breathed as he
watched her move, his eyes wide, his face a little flushed.

"Rune, dear, each of the gentleman has a song he'd like you to play,
and I have a request too, if you don't mind," Sapphire said softly, with
an angelic smile. "I know you must be ready for a break, but with five
more songs, I think dear Lerra might be ready to—you know."

Rune smiled back. "Anything for you ladies, Sapphire, and you know
it. I didn't get to play much out on the street today; my fingers aren't the
least tired."

That was a little lie, but five more songs weren't going to hurt them any.

"Thank you, dear," Sapphire breathed, her face aglow with gratitude.
That was one of the remarkable things about Sapphire; whatever she felt,
she felt *completely*, and never bothered to hide it. "All right, this is what
we'd like. 'Fair Maid of The Valley,' 'Four Sisters,' 'Silver Sandals,' 'The
Green Stone,' and 'The Dream of the Heart.' Can you do all those?"

"In my sleep," Rune told her, with a grin. Sapphire rewarded her with
another of her brilliant smiles, and started to turn to go—

But then she turned back a moment. "You know, I must have thought
this a thousand times, and I never told you. I am terribly envious of your
talent, Rune. You were good when you first arrived—you're quite good

now—and some day, people are going to praise your name from one end of this land to the other. I wish I had your gift."

"Well—" Rune said cautiously, "I don't know about that. I've a long way to go before I'm that good, and a hundred things could happen to prevent it. Besides—" she grinned. "It's one Guild Bard in a thousand that ever gets *that* much renown, and I doubt I'm going to be that one."

But Sapphire shook her head. "I tell you true, Rune. And I'll tell you something else; for all the money and the soft living and the rest of it, if I had a fraction of your talent, I'd never set foot upstairs. I'd stay in the common room and be an entertainer for the rest of my life. All four of us know how very hard you work, we admire you tremendously, and I want you to know that."

Then she turned and went back to her little gathering, leaving Rune flattered, and no little dumbfounded. *They* admired *her*? Beautiful, graceful, with everything they could ever want or need, and they admired *her*?

This was the first time she had ever been admired by anyone, and as she started the first of the songs Sapphire had requested, she felt a little warm current of real happiness rising from inside her and giving her fingers a new liveliness.

Even Jib thought I was a little bit daft for spending all my time with music, she thought, giving the tune a little extra flourish that made Sapphire half turn and wink at her from across the room. *Tonno keeps thinking about what I should be learning, Maddie doesn't understand how I feel about music, and even to Lady Amber I'm just another part of the common room. That's the very first time anyone has ever just thought that what I did was worth it, in and of itself.*

The warm feeling stayed with her, right till the end of the fifth song, when Sapphire laughingly drew one of the gentlemen to his feet and up the stairs after her.

She played one more song—and then she began to feel the twinges in her fingers that heralded trouble if she wasn't careful. Time for a break.

She threw the young gentleman a good-natured wink, which he returned, and set off to the kitchen for a bit of warm cider, since it was useless to ask Carly for anything.

They admire me. Who'd have thought it. . . .

Rune let her fingers prance their way across her lute-strings, forgetting that she was chilled in the spell of the music she was creating. Tonno listened to her play the piece she had first seen back in the summer, and thought impossible, with all its runs and triple-pickings, with his eyes closed and his finger marking steady time.

She played it gracefully, with relish for the complexities, with all the repeats and embellishments. She couldn't believe how easy it seemed—and how second-nature it was to read and play these little black notes on the page. She couldn't have conceived of this back in the summer, but one day everything had fallen into place, and she hadn't once faltered since. She came to the end, and waited, quietly, for her teacher to say something. When he didn't, when he didn't even open his eyes, she obeyed an impish impulse and put down the lute, picking up Lady Rose instead.

Then she started in on the piece again—this time playing it on the fiddle. Of course, it was a little different on the fiddle; she stumbled and faltered on a couple of passages where the fingering that was natural for the lute was anything but on the fiddle, but she got through it intact. Tonno's eyes had flown open in surprise at the first few bars; he stared at her all through the piece, clearly dumbfounded, right up until the moment that she ended with a flourish.

She put the fiddle and bow down, and waited for him to say something.

He took a deep breath. "Well," he said. "You've just made up my mind for me, dear. If ever I was desirous of a sign from God, that was it."

She wrinkled her brow, puzzled. "What's that supposed to mean?" she asked. "It was just that lute-piece, that's all."

"Just the lute-piece—which you proceeded to play through on an instrument it wasn't intended for." Tonno shook his head. "Rune, I've been debating this for the past two weeks, but I can't be selfish anymore. You're beyond me, on both your instruments. I can't teach you any more."

It was her turn to stare, licking suddenly dry lips, not sure of what to say. "But—but I—"

This was too sudden, too abrupt, she thought, her heart catching with something like fear. She wasn't ready for it all to end; at least, not yet. *I'm not ready to leave. There's still the whole winter yet, the Faire isn't until Midsummer—what am I supposed to do between now and then?*

"Don't look at me like that, girl," Tonno said, a little gruffly, rubbing his eyebrow with a hand encased in fingerless gloves. "Just because you're beyond my teaching, that doesn't mean you're ready for what you want to do."

"I'm—not?" she said dazedly, not certain whether to be relieved or disappointed.

"No," Tonno replied firmly. "You're beyond my ability to contribute to your teaching—*in music*—but you're not good enough to win one of the Bard apprenticeships. And I've heard some of your tunes, dear; you shouldn't settle for less than a Bardic position. Of all the positions offered at the Faire, only a handful are for Bardic teaching, and you are just not good enough to beat the ninety-nine other contenders for those positions."

Good news *and* bad, all in the same bite. "Will I ever be?" she asked doubtfully.

"Of course you will!" he snapped, as if he was annoyed at her doubt. "I have a damned good ear, and I can tell you when you will be ready. What we'll have to do is find some of my truly complicated music, the things I put away because they were beyond my meager capabilities to play. You'll practice them until your fingers are blue, and then you'll learn to transpose music from other instruments to yours and play *that* until your fingers are blue. Practice is what you need now, and practice, by all that's holy, is what you're going to get."

I guess it's not over yet. Not even close. She sighed, but he wasn't finished with his plans for her immediate future.

"Then there's the matter of your other lessons," he continued inexorably. "I've taught you how to read music; now I'll teach you how to write it as well—by ear, without playing it first on your instruments. I'll see that you learn as much as I know of other styles, and of the work of the Great Bards. And *then*, my dear, I'm going to drill you in reading, history in particular, until you think you've turned Scholar!"

"Oh, no—" she said involuntarily. While she was reading with more competence, it still wasn't something that came easily. Unlike music, she still had to work at understanding. History, in particular, was a great deal of hard work.

"Oh, yes," he told her, with a smile. "If you're going to become a Guild Bard, you're going to have to compete with boys who've been learning from Scholars all their lives. You're going to have to know plenty about the past—who's who, and more importantly, *why*, because if you inadvertently offend the wrong person—"

He sliced his finger dramatically across his neck.

She shuddered, reflexively, as a breath of cold that came out of nowhere touched the back of her neck.

"Now," he said, clearing the music away from the stand in front of her, and stacking it neatly in the drawer of the cabinet beside him. "Put your instruments back in their cases and come join me by the stove. I want you to know some hard truths, and what you're getting yourself into."

She cased the lute and Lady Rose obediently, and pulled her short cloak a little tighter around her shoulders. Tonno's stove didn't give off a lot of heat, partially because fuel was so expensive that he didn't stoke it as often as Amber fueled her fireplaces. Rune would have worried more about him in this cold, except that he obviously had a lot of ploys to keep himself warm, He spent a lot of time at Amber's in the winter, Maddie said; nursing a few drinks and keeping some of the waiting clients company with a game of pentangle or cards, and Amber smiled indulgently and let him stay.

I wonder what it is that he did for her, that they're such good friends?

Rune followed him to the back of the living-quarters, bringing her chair with her, and settled herself beside him as he huddled up to the metal stove.

He wrapped an old comforter around himself, and raised his bushy gray eyebrows at her. "Now, first of all, as far as I know, there are no girls in the Guild," he stated flatly. "So right from the beginning, you're going to have a problem."

She nodded; she'd begun to suspect something of the sort. She'd noticed that no one wearing the purple ribbon-knots was female—

And she'd discovered her first weeks out busking that every time she wore anything even vaguely feminine out on the street, she got propositions. Eventually, she figured out why.

There were plenty of free-lance whores out on the street, pretending to busk, with their permits stuck on their hats like anyone else. She found out why, when she'd asked the dancers that performed by the fountain every night. The permit for busking was cheaper by far than the fees to the Whore's Guild, so many whores, afraid of being caught and thrown into the workhouse for soliciting without a permit or Guild badge, bought busking permits. The Church, which didn't approve of either whores *or* musicians, ignored the deception; the city frowned, but looked the other way, so long as those on the street bought *some* sort of permit. Real musicians wore the ribbon knots on their sleeves, and whores didn't, but most folk hadn't caught on to that distinction. So, the result was undoubtedly that female musicians had a reputation in the Guild for being something else entirely.

But still—the auditions should weed out those with other professions. Shouldn't they? And why on Earth would a whore even *come* to the trials?

"The reason there aren't any females in the Guild," he continued, "is because they aren't allowed to audition at the Faire. Ever."

She stared at him, anger warming her cheek at the realization that he hadn't bothered to say anything to her about this little problem with her plans before this.

"I imagine you're wondering why I didn't tell you that in the first place." He raised an eyebrow, and she blushed that he could read her so easily. "It's simple enough. I didn't think it would be a problem as long as you were prepared for it. You've carried off the boy-disguise perfectly well; I've seen you do it, and fool anyone who just looks at the surface of things. I don't see any reason why you can't get your audition as a boy, and tell them the truth after you've won your place."

She flushed again, this time at her own stupidity. She should have figured that out for herself. "But won't they be angry?" she asked, a little doubtfully.

Tonno shrugged. "That, I can't tell you. I don't know. I do know that if you've been so outstanding that you've surprised each and every one of them, if they are any kind of musician at all, they'll overlook your sex. They might make you keep up the disguise while you're an apprentice, but once you're a master, you can do what you want and they can be hanged."

That seemed logical, and she could see the value of the notion. So long as she went along with their ideas of what was proper, they'd give her what she wanted—but once she had it, she would be free of any restraints. They weren't likely to take her title away; once you were a Master Bard, you were always a Master, no matter what you did. They hadn't even taken away the title from Master Marley, who had lulled his patron, Sire Jacoby, to sleep, and let in his enemies by the postern gate to kill him and all his family. They'd turned him over to the Church and the High King for justice, but they'd left him his title. Not that it had done much good in a dungeon.

"I intend you to leave here with enough knowledge crammed into that thick head of yours—and enough skill in those fingers—to give every boy at the trials a run for his money," Tonno said firmly. "I trust you don't plan to settle for less than an apprenticeship to a Guild Bard?" He raised one eyebrow.

She shook her head, stubbornly. Guild Minstrels only played music; Guild Bards created it. There were songs in her head dying to get out—

"Good." Tonno nodded with satisfaction "That's what I hoped you'd say. You're too good a musician to be wasted busking out in the street. You should have noble patrons, and the only way you're going to get that is through the Guild. That's the only way to rise in any profession; through the Guilds. Guildsmen keep standards high and craftsmanship important. And that's not all. If you're good enough, the Guild will make certain that you're rewarded, by backing you."

"Like what?" she asked, curiously, and tucked her hands under her knees to warm them.

"Oh, like Master Bard Gwydain," Tonno replied, his eyes focused somewhere past her head, as if he was remembering something. "I heard him play, once, you know. Amazing. He couldn't have been more than twenty, but he played like no one I've ever heard—and that was twenty years ago, before he was at the height of his powers. Ten years ago, the High King himself rewarded Master Gwydain—made him Laurel Sire Gwydain, and gave him lands and a royal pension. A great many of the songs I've been teaching you are his—'Spellbound Captive,' 'Dream of the Heart,' 'That Wild Ocean,' 'Black Rose,' oh, he must have written hundreds before he was through. Amazing."

He fell silent, as the light in the shop began to dim with the coming of evening. Soon Rune would have to leave, to return to Amber's, but curiosity got the better of her; after all, if Gwydain had been twenty or so, twenty years ago, he couldn't be more than forty now. Yet she had never heard anyone mention his name.

"What happened to him?" she asked, breaking into Tonno's reverie. He started a little, and wrinkled his brow. "You know, that's the odd part," he said slowly. "It's a mystery. No one I've talked to knows what happened to him; he seems to have dropped out of sight about five or ten years ago, and no one has seen nor heard of him since. There've been rumors, but that's all."

"What kind of rumors?" she persisted, feeling an urgent need to know, though she couldn't have told why.

"Right after he vanished, there was a rumor he'd died tragically, but no one knew how—right after that there was another that he'd taken vows, renounced the world, and gone into Holy Orders." Tonno shook his head. "I don't believe either one, if you want to know the truth. It seems to me that if he'd really died, there'd have been a fancy funeral and word of it all over the countryside. And if he'd taken Holy Orders, he'd be composing Church music. There's never been so much as a hint of scandal about him, so that can't be it. I just don't know."

Rune had the feeling that Tonno was very troubled by this disappearance—well, so was she. It left an untidy hole, a mystery that cried to be cleared up. "What if he gave up music for some reason?" she asked. "Then if he'd gone into the Church, he'd have just vanished."

"Give up music? Not likely," Tonno snorted. "You can't keep a Bard from making music. It's something they're born to do. No," he shook his head vehemently. "Something odd happened to him, and that's for sure—and the Guild is keeping it quiet. Maybe he had a brainstorm, and he can't play, or even speak clearly. Maybe he took wasting fever and he's too weak to do anything. Maybe he ran off to the end of the world, looking for new things. But something out of the ordinary happened to him, I would bet my last copper on it. It's a mystery."

He changed the subject then, back to quizzing Rune on the history she'd been reading, and they did not again return to the subject of Master Bard Gwydain. Eventually darkness fell, and it was time for her to leave.

She bundled herself up in her cloak, slung her instruments across her back underneath it to keep them from the cold, and let herself out of the shop, wanting to spare Tonno the trip up through the cold, darkened store. As she hurried along the street towards Amber's, the wind whipping around her ankles and crawling under her hood until she shivered with cold, she found herself thinking about the mystery.

She agreed with Tonno; unless *she* were at death's door, or otherwise crippled, she would not be able to stop making music. If Gwydain still lived, he must be plying his birthright, somewhere.

And if he was dead, someone should know about it. If he was dead, and the Guild was keeping it quiet, there must be a reason.

And I'll find it out, she decided, suddenly. *When I get into the Guild, I'll find it out. No matter what. They can't keep it a secret forever. . . .*

CHAPTER TEN

Rune fitted the key Tonno had given her into the old lock on the front door of the shop, and tried to turn it. Nothing happened.

Frozen again, she thought, and swore under her breath at the key, the ancient lock, and the damned weather. She pulled the key out and tucked it under her armpit to warm it, wincing as the cold metal chilled her through her heavy sweater, and flinching again as a gust of wind blew a swirl of snow down her neck. She glanced up and down the silent street; the only traffic was a pair of tradesmen muffled in cloaks much heavier than hers, probably hurrying to open their own shops, and a couple of apprentice-boys out on errands. Other than that, there was no one. The slate-colored sky overhead spilled thin skeins of flurries, and the wind sent them skating along the street like ghost-snakes.

Whatever could have been in God's mind when He invented winter? Thrice-forsaken season. . . .

It didn't *look* like a good day for trade—but Scholars made up half of Tonno's business, and days like today, she had learned, meant business from Scholars. They'd be inside all day, fussing over their libraries or collections of curiosities, and discover they had somehow neglected to buy that book or bone or odd bit of carving they'd looked at back in the summer. And now, of course, they simply *must* have it. So they'd wait until one of their students arrived for a special lesson, and the hapless youth would be sent out On Quest with a purchase-order and a purse, will-he, nill-he. Those sales made a big difference to Tonno, especially in winter, and made it worth keeping the shop open.

She pulled out the key and stuck it back into the lock quickly, before it had a chance to chill down again. This time, when she put pressure on it, the lock moved. Stiffly, but the door did unlock, and she hurriedly pushed it open and shoved it closed against another snow-bearing gust of wind.

"Tonno?" she called out. "I'm here!"

She flipped the little sign in the window from "Closed" to "Open," and made her way back to the counter, where she raised the hinged part and flipped it over. "Tonno?" she called again.

"I'm awake, Rune," he replied, his voice distant and a little weak. "I'm just not—out of bed yet."

She frowned; he didn't sound well. She'd better get back to him before he decided to be stubborn and open the shop himself. In weather like this, or so Amber told her, Tonno did better to stay in bed.

She pushed the curtain in the doorway aside and hurried over to his bedside. Before he had a chance to struggle out of the motley selection of comforters, quilts, and old blankets he had piled, one atop the other so that the holes and worn spots in each of them were compensated for by the sound spots in the others, she reached him and had taken his hand in both of hers, examining the joints with a critical eye. As she had expected, they were swollen, red, and painful to look at.

"You aren't going anywhere," she said firmly. "There's a storm out there, and it's mucking up your hands and every other bone you've got, I'd wager."

He frowned, but it was easy to see his heart wasn't in the protest. "But I didn't get up yesterday except—"

"So you don't get up today. what's the difference?" she asked, reasonably. "I can mind the shop. We'll probably get a customer or two, but not more. That's hardly work at all. And I'm *not* busking today; it's too damned cold and I'll not risk Lady Rose to weather like this. I might just as well mind the shop and give your lessons to—who is it today—Anny and Ket? I thought so. They're bare beginners. Easy. I could teach them half asleep. And their parents don't care if it's me or you who teaches them, so long as they get the lessons they've paid for."

"But you aren't benefiting by this—" Tonno said fretfully. "You should be out earning a few coppers—"

She shrugged. "There's no one out there to earn coppers from. I picked up a little in my hat at Amber's last night, enough for the tax and tithe. And I am benefiting—" She gave him a wide grin. "If I'm here, I'm not there, and I don't have to listen to Carly's bullying and whining."

"You haven't been tormenting her, have you?" Tonno asked sharply, with more force than she expected. She gave him a quizzical look, wondering what notion he'd gotten into his head. Surely Carly didn't deserve any sympathy from Tonno!

"Not unless you consider ignoring her to be tormenting her," she replied, straightening his bedcovers, then putting a kettle on the stove and a brick to heat beneath it. "I try not to let her bother me, but she does bully me every chance she gets, and she says nasty things about my playing to the customers. She'd probably say worse than that about me, but the only thing she can think of is that since I dress like a boy sometimes, I might be a poppet or an androgyn. That's hardly going to be an insult in a place like Amber's! It's just too bad for her that the clients all have ears of their own, and they don't agree with her. Maddie is the one who teases her."

Tonno relaxed. "Good. But be careful, Rune. I've been thinking about her, and wondering why Amber keeps her on, and I think now I know the reason. I think she's a spy for the Church."

"A *what*?" Rune turned from her work to gape at him. "Carly? Whatever for? What reason would the Church have to spy on a brothel?"

"I can think of several reasons," he said, his face and voice troubled. "The most obvious is to report on how many clients come and go, and how much money they tip in the common room, to make certain that all taxes and tithes have been paid for. That's fairly innocuous as things go, since we both know perfectly well that all the fees are paid at Amber's and on time, too. There's another reason, too, though; and it's one that would just suit the girl's sour spirit right down to the core."

"Oh?" she asked, a cold lump of worry starting in the pit of her stomach. "What's that?"

She couldn't imagine what interest the Church would find in a brothel—and if she couldn't imagine it, it must be something darkly sinister. She began wondering about all those rumors she'd heard of Church Priests being versed in dark magics, when his next words cleared her mind entirely. "Fornication," he said. "Fornication is a sin, Rune. Although the laws of the city say nothing about it, the only lawful congress by the Church's rule, is between man and woman who are wedded by Church ceremony. And, by Church rule, sins must be confessed and paid for, either by penance or donation."

Her first impulse had been to laugh, but second thought proved that Tonno's concern was real, though less sinister than *her* fears. She nodded, thoughtfully. "So if Carly keeps a list of who comes and goes, and gives it to the Church, the next time Guildsman Weaver shows up to confess and do penance, if he *doesn't* list his visit to Amber's—he's in trouble."

Tonno sighed, and reached eagerly for the mug of hot tea she handed to him. "And for the men of means who visit Amber's, the trouble will mean that the Priest will confront them with their omission, impress them with his 'supernatural' understanding, and assign additional penance—"

"Additional guilt-money, you mean," she finished cynically. "And meanwhile, no doubt, Carly's record-keeping is paying off *her* sins for working in a brothel in the first place." She sniffed, angrily. "Oh, that makes excellent sense, Tonno. And it explains a lot. Since Carly can't have a place at Amber's, she'll do her best to foul the bedding for everyone else. And *she'll* come out sanctimoniously lily-white."

She picked up the hot brick and tucked it into the foot the bed, replacing it under the stove with another. The heat did a great deal of good for Tonno; already there was a bit more color in his face, and some of the lines of pain around his eyes and mouth were easing.

He took another sip of tea, and nodded. "Do you see what I mean by suiting the girl's nature? Likely she's even convinced herself that this was why she came to work there in the first place, to keep an eye on the welfare of others' souls."

"No doubt," Rune said dryly. She stirred oatmeal into a pot of water, and set it on top of the stove beside the kettle to cook. "She'll always want the extreme of anything; if she can't be a highly paid whore, she'll be a saint. What I can't understand is why Amber lets her stay on—you pretty much implied that she knows what Carly's up to."

Tonno laughed, though the worry lines about his mouth had not eased any. "That's the cleverness of our Lady Amber, dear. As long as Carly is in place, she *knows* who the spy is. If there is truly someone whose reputation with the Church is so delicate that he *must not* be seen at Amber's, then all the lady needs to do is make certain Carly doesn't see him. And I suspect Lady Amber has whatever official Carly reports to quite completely bribed."

Wiser in the ways of bribery than she had been a scant six months ago, Rune nodded. "If she got rid of Carly, someone else might get *his* agent in, and she'd have to find out what *his* price was."

"But if she stopped bribing the old official, he'd report on what Carly had given him already." Tonno shrugged. "Amber knows what's going on, what's being reported, and saves money this way as well. And what does Carly cost her, really? Nothing she wouldn't be paying anyway. She'd have to bribe someone in the Church to be easy with the clients, no matter what."

Rune shook her head. "I guess I'll have to put up with it, and be grateful that I personally don't care that much about the state of my soul to worry about what working in a whorehouse is going to do to it. I'm probably damned anyway, for having the poor taste to be born on the wrong side of the blankets."

"That's the spirit!" Tonno laughed a little, and she cheered up herself, seeing that he was able to laugh without hurting himself. She gave the room a sketchy cleaning, and washed last night's supper dishes. By then the oatmeal was ready and she spooned out enough for both of them, sweetening it with honey. She ate a lot faster than he did; he wasn't even half finished with his portion when she'd cleaned her bowl of the last spoonful. She put the dish into the pan of soapsuds just as the bell to the front door tinkled.

He started to get up from sheer habit, but she glared at him until he sank back into the pillows, and hurried to the front of the shop.

As she'd anticipated, since it was too early for either of the children having music lessons to arrive, the person peering into the shop with a worried look on his face was one of the University Students. The red stripe on the shoulders of his cloak told her he was a Student of Philosophy. Good. They had money—and by extension, so did their teachers. Only a rich man could afford to let his son idle away his time on something like Philosophy. And rich men paid well for their sons' lessons.

"Can I help you, my lord?" she said into the silence of the shop, startling him. He jumped, then peered short-sightedly at her as she approached.

"Is this the shop of—" he consulted a strip of paper in his hand "—Tonno Alendor?"

"Yes it is, my lord," she said, and waited. He looked at her doubtfully.

"I was told to seek out this Tonno himself," he said. The set of his chin told her that he was of the kind of nature to be stubborn, but the faint quiver of doubt in his voice also told her he could be bullied. Another of Tonno's lessons: how to read people, and know how to deal with them.

"Master Tonno is ill. I am his niece," she lied smoothly. "He entrusts everything to me."

The soft, round chin firmed as the spoiled young man who was not used to being denied what he wanted emerged; in response to that warning, so did her voice. "If you *truly* wish to disturb him, if you feel you *must* pester a poor, sick old man, I can take you to his bedside"—*and I'll make you pay dearly for it in embarrassment,* her voice promised—"but he'll only tell you the same thing, young man."

Her tone, and the scolding "young man," she appended to her little speech, gave him the impression she was much older than he had thought. Nearsighted as he was, and in the darkness of the shop, he would probably believe it. And, as she had hoped, he must have a female relative somewhere that was accustomed to browbeating him into obedience; his resistance collapsed immediately.

"Scholar Mardake needs a book," he said meekly. "He looked at it last summer, and he was certain he had purchased it, but now he finds he hadn't, and he *has* to have it for his monograph, and—"

She let him rattle on for far too long about the monograph, the importance of it, and how it would enhance Scholar Mardake's already illustrious reputation. And, by extension, the reputations and status of all of Mardake's Students.

What a fool.

She tried not to yawn in his face, but it was difficult. Jib had more sense in his big toe than this puffed-up popinjay had in his entire body. And of all the things to be over-proud of—this endless debate over frothy nothings, like the question of what a "soul" truly consisted of, made her weary to the bone. If they would spend half the time on questions of a practical nature instead of this chop-logic drivel, the world would be better run. Finally he came to the point: the name of the book.

"By whom?" she asked, finally getting a word in. Of all of the Scholars, the Philosophers were by far and away the windiest.

"Athold Derelas," he replied, loftily, as if he expected that she had never heard of the great man.

"Ah, you're in luck," she replied immediately. "We have *two* copies. Does your master prefer the annotated version by Wasserman, or the simple translation by Bartol?"

He gaped at her. She stifled a giggle. In truth, she wouldn't have known the books were there if she hadn't replaced a volume of history by Lyam Derfan to its place beside them the day before. It was bad enough that she'd known of the book; but she'd offered two choices, and he didn't know how to react. He'd loftily assumed, no doubt, that she was the next thing to illiterate, and she'd just confounded him.

He'd have been less startled to hear a pig sing, or an ape recite poetry.

She decided to rub the humiliation in. "If your master is doing a monograph covering Derelas' work as a whole, he would probably want the annotated version," she continued blithely, "but if all he wants is Derelas' comments on specific subjects, he'd be better off with the Bartol translation."

Now the young man had to refer to the slip of paper in his hand. He looked from it, to her, and back again, and couldn't seem to come to a decision. His face took on a pinched look of miserable confusion.

"Perhaps he'd better have both," she suggested. "No knowledge is ever wasted, after all. The Wasserman is rare; he may find enough of interest in it for an entirely new monograph."

The Student brightened up considerably. "Yes, of course," he said happily, and Rune had no doubt that he would parrot her words back to his Scholar as if they were his own, and suggesting that the shop-girl hadn't known what a rarity the Wasserman was, so that he'd gotten the book at a bargain price.

Before he could change his mind—it was his master's money he was spending, after all, and not his own—she rolled the floor-to-ceiling ladder over to the "D" section, and scampered up it. The Student virtuously averted his eyes, blushing, lest he have an inadvertent glimpse of feminine flesh. As if there was anything to be seen under her double skirts, double leggings, and boots.

Besides being the most long-winded, Philosophers were also the most prudish of the Scholars—at least the ones that Rune had met. She much preferred the company of the Natural Scientists and the Mathematicians. The former were full of the wonders of the world, and eager to share the strange stories of birds and beasts; the latter tended to make up for the times when they lost themselves in the dry world of numbers with a vengeance. And both welcomed women into their ranks far oftener than the Philosophers.

Doubtless because women are too sensible to be distracted for long by maunderings about airy nothings.

She came down with both books clutched in her hand, eluding his grasp for them so easily he might not even have been standing there, and took them behind the counter. There she consulted the book where Tonno noted the prices of everything in the shop, by category. It was a little tedious, for things were listed in the order he had acquired them, and not in the alphabetical order in which they were ranked on the shelves. But finally she had the prices of both of them, and looked up, reaching beneath the counter for a piece of rough paper to wrap them in.

"The Wasserman, as I said, is rare," she said, deftly making a package and tying it with a bit of string. "Master Tonno has it listed at forty silver pieces."

His mouth gaped, and he was about to utter a gasp of outrage. She continued before he had a chance. "The other is more common as I said; it is only twenty. Now, as it is Master Tonno's policy to offer a discount to steady clients like your Scholar, I believe I can let you have both for fifty." She batted her eyelashes ingenuously at him. "After all, Master Tonno does trust me in all things, and it isn't often we have a fine young man like you in the shop."

The appeal to his vanity killed whatever protest he had been about to make. His mouth snapped shut, and he counted out the silver quickly, before she could change her mind. He knew very well—although he did not know that *she* knew—his Scholar was anything but a steady customer; he bought perhaps a book or two in a year. What he did not know—and since he was not a regular customer, neither would his Scholar—was that she had inflated the listed prices of both books by ten silver pieces each. She had heard other Scholars speaking when she had tended the shop before, chuckling over Tonno's prices. She heard a lot of things Tonno didn't. The Scholars tended to ignore her as insignificant.

So whenever she had sold a book lately, she had inflated the price. Scholars would never argue with her, assuming no woman would be so audacious as to cheat a Scholar; their Students never argued with her because she bullied and flattered them the same way she had treated this boy, and with the same effect. And when she added the nonsense about a "discount," they generally kept their mouths shut.

She handed him the parcel, and he hurried out into the cold. She dropped the taxes and tithes into the appropriate boxes, and pocketed the rest to take back to Tonno. Merchants with shops never went to a Church stall the way buskers and peddlers did; they kept separate tax and tithe boxes which were locked with keys only the Church Collectors had. The Collectors would come around once a week with a city constable to take what had accumulated in the boxes, noting the amounts in their books. Rune actually liked the Collector who serviced Tonno's shop; she hadn't expected to, but the first day he had appeared when she was on duty he had charmed her completely. Brother Bryan was a thin, energetic man with a marvelously dry sense of humor, and was, so far as she could tell, absolutely honest. Tonno seemed convinced of his honesty as well, and greeted him as a friend. And whenever she was here and Tonno was ill, he would make a point of coming to the back of the shop to see how the old man was faring, pass the time of day with him, and see if he could find some way to entertain Tonno a little before he continued on his rounds of the other shops.

She dipped a quill in a bit of ink and ran a delicate line through the titles of the two books to indicate they had been sold, and returned to Tonno.

He sat up with interest, and demanded to know what had happened. He shook his head over her duplicity with the spurious "discount," but she noted that he did not demand that she refund the extra ten silvers.

"You should update your prices," she said, scolding a little. "You haven't changed some of them from the time when your father ran this shop. I know you haven't, because I've seen the prices still in his handwriting."

He sighed. "But people come here for bargains, Rune," he replied plaintively. "Even when father had the shop, this district was changing over from shops to residences. Now—it's so out of the way that no one would ever come here at all if they didn't know they'd get a bargain."

"You can make them think you've given them a bargain and still not cheat yourself," she said, taking the empty bowl from the floor beside his bed and swishing it in the painfully cold wash-water until it was clean.

"I hope you put what was due in the tax box, and not what was in the book," he said suddenly.

She grimaced, but nodded. "Of course I did. Although I can't for the life of me see *why*. That Scholar isn't likely to tell anyone how much he paid, and you need every silver you can get. We may not have another sale for a week or more!" She put the bowl back on the shelf with a thud.

"Because it's our responsibility, Rune," he replied, patiently, as if she was a child. He said that every time she brought up the subject of taxes, and she was tired to death of hearing it. He never once explained what he meant, and she just couldn't see it. There were too many rich ones she suspected of diddling the tax rolls to get by with paying less than they should.

"*Why* is it our responsibility?" she asked fiercely. "And why *ours*? I don't see anyone else leaping forward to throw money in the tax and tithe boxes! You and Amber keep saying that, and I don't see any reason for it!"

He just looked at her, somberly, until she flushed. He made her feel as if she had said something incredibly irresponsible, and that made no sense. She didn't know why she should feel embarrassed by her outburst, but she did, and that made her angry as well.

"Rune," he said slowly, as if he had just figured out that she was serious. "There truly is a reason for it. Now do you really want to hear the reason, or do you want to be like all those empty-headed fools out there who grumble about taxes and cheat when they can, and never once think about who or what they're cheating?"

"Well, if there's a reason, I'd certainly like to hear it," she muttered, skeptically, and sat down in the chair beside his bed. "Nothing I've seen yet has given me a reason to think differently, and *you're* the one who taught me to trust my eyes and not just parrot what I've been told!"

"You've lived here for almost half a year," Tonno replied. "I know that there's a world of difference between Nolton and your little village; there are things we do here that no one would ever think of doing back in Westhaven." She made a face, but he continued. "I know I'm saying something obvious, but because it's obvious, you might not have thought about it. There are things that people take for granted after they've been here as long as you have; things that are invisible, but that we couldn't do without. Dung-sweepers, for instance. Who cleans up the droppings in Westhaven?"

"Well, no one," she admitted. "It gets kicked to one side or trodden into the mud, that's about it."

"But if we did that here, we'd be knee-deep in manure in a week," Tonno pointed out, and she nodded agreement. "Who do you think *pays* the dung-sweepers?"

"I never wondered about it," she admitted with surprise. "I thought the dung must be valuable to someone—for composting, or something—"

"It is, and they sell it to farmers, but that's not enough to compensate a man for going about with a barrow all day collecting it," Tonno pointed out. "The city pays them—right out of that tax box." She rubbed her hands together to warm them, about to say something, but he continued. "Who guards the streets of Westhaven by day or night from robbers, drunks, troublemakers and thieves?"

She laughed, because it was something else that would never have occurred to her old village to worry about. "No one. Nobody's abroad very late, and if they are, there's no one to trouble them. If a drunk falls on his face in the street, he can lie there until morning."

But she couldn't keep the laughter from turning uneasy. It might not have occurred to them, but it would have been a good thing if it had. A single constable could have prevented a lot of trouble in the past. If there'd been someone like the city guard or constables around, would those bullies have tried to molest her that day? Even one adult witness would likely have prevented the entire incident. How many times had something like that happened to someone who couldn't defend herself?

Was that how Stara had gotten into trouble in the first place, as a child too young to know better? Was that why she had gone on to trade her favors so cheaply?

If that incident with Jon and his friends hadn't occurred, would Rune have been quite so willing to seek a life out in the wider world?

"That will do for a little village, but what would we do here?" Tonno asked gently. "There are thousands of people living here; most are honest, but some are not. What's a shopkeeper to do, spend his nights waiting with a dagger in hand?"

"Couldn't people—well—band together, and just have one of them watch for all?" she asked, self-consciously, flushing; knowing it wasn't any kind of a real answer. "I suppose they could pay him for his troubles—" Then she shook her head. "That's basically what the constables are, aren't they? That's what you're trying to tell me. And they're paid from taxes too."

"Constables, dung-sweepers, the folk who repair and maintain the wells and the aqueducts, and a hundred more jobs you'd never think of and likely wouldn't see. Rat-catchers and street-tenders, gate-keepers and judges, gaolers and the men who make certain food sold in the market-place is what it's said to be." Tonno leaned forward, earnestly, and she saw that the light was fading.

"I suppose you're right." She lit a candle at the stove, but he wasn't going to be distracted from his point.

"That's what a government is all about, Rune," he said, more as if he was pleading with her than as if he was trying to win an argument. "Taking care of all the things that come up when a great many people live together. And yes, most of those things each of us could do for himself, taking care of his own protection, and his family's, and minding the immediate area around his home and shop—but that would take a great deal of time, and while the expenses would be less, they would come in lumps, and in the way of things, at the worst possible time." He laughed ruefully, and so did she. It hadn't been that long ago they'd had one of those lump expenses, when the roof sprang a leak and they'd had it patched.

She could see his point—but not his passion. And for something as cold and abstract as a government. "But you don't like paying taxes either," she said in protest, and he nodded.

"No, I don't. That's quite true. There are some specific taxes that I think are quite unfair. I pay a year-tax leavened against the shop simply because I own it, rather than renting, and when my father died, I paid a death-tax in order to inherit. I don't think those taxes are particularly fair. But"—he held up his hand to forestall her comments—"those are only two taxes, with a government that could leaven far more taxes than it does. I've heard of cities where they tax money earned, then tax the goods sold, then tax every stage a product goes through as it changes hands—"

She shook her head, baffled. "I don't understand—" she said. "How can they do that?"

He explained further. "Take a cow; it is taxed when it is sold as a weanling, taxed again when it is brought to market, the rawhide is taxed when it comes into the hands of the tanners, taxed again when it goes to the leather-broker, taxed when it is sold to the shoemaker, then taxed a final time when the shoes are sold."

Her head swam at the thought of all those taxes.

"That kind of taxation is abusive; when the time comes that the price of an object is doubled to pay the taxes on it, that is abusive. And governments of that nature are generally abusive of the people that live under them as well." Tonno leaned back into his pillows, and he looked like a man who was explaining something he cared about, deeply.

As deeply as I care about music, she thought in surprise. She had found his secret passion. And it was nothing like what she would have expected.

"Before you ask," he told her, carefully, as if he was weighing each word for its true value, "I can tell you that you'll get a different definition of an abusive government from nearly everyone who cares to think about such things. In general, though, I would say that when a government is more concerned with keeping itself in power, and keeping its officials in luxury, whether they were elected to the posts, appointed, or inherited the position, then that government is abusive as well. Government is what takes care of things beyond you. Good government cares for the well-being of the people it serves. Abusive government cares only for its own well-being. The fewer the people, the less government you need. Does that seem clear to you?"

She thought about it for a moment. She'd begun listening to this mostly because she respected Tonno, and this seemed to mean a great deal to him. But the more he'd said, the more she began to get a glimmering of a wider sphere than the one she was used to dealing with—and it intrigued her in the way the things the Mathematicians said intrigued her. And now she realized that Amber had said basically the same things, in cryptic little bits, over the past several months. Reluctantly, she had to agree that they were right.

Still—this was the real world she was living in, and not some Philosopher's book, where everyone did as he should, and everything was perfect. "But what about the stories I keep hearing?" she protested, taking one last shot at disproving his theories. "The things about the inspectors who take bribes, and the gaolers who turn people loose no matter what they've done, so long as they've got money enough? What about the clerics at the Church stalls, who'll take all your money as tax or tithe, then insist you owe as much over again for the one you didn't pay? I bet *they* pocket the difference!"

Tonno shrugged, then chuckled a little, though sadly. "You're dealing with people, Rune, and the real world, not a Philosopher's ideal sphere," he said, echoing her very thoughts. "People are corruptible, and any time you have money changing hands, someone is likely to give in to temptation. So I'll give you another definition: since there's always going to be corruption, a good government is one where you have a manageable level of corruption!"

He laughed at that one. She made a face, but laughed with him. "Right, I'll grant your stand on taxes, but what about tithes? What's the Church doing to earn all that money? They take in as much as the city, and *they* aren't hiring the rat-catchers!"

"What's the Church doing—or what is it *supposed* to be doing, rather?" he asked, his expression hardening. "What it's supposed to be doing is to care for those who can't care for themselves—to feed and clothe the impoverished, to heal the sick, to bring peace where there is war, to be family to the orphaned, find justice for those who have been denied it. The Priests are bound to make certain every child can read and write and cipher, so that it can grow up to find a place or earn a living without being cheated. That's what it's *supposed* to be doing. That, and give the time to God that few of us have the leisure for, so that, hopefully, God will know when we have need of His powers, having run out of solutions for ourselves."

She nodded. That was, indeed, what the village Priest was supposed to deal with—when he wasn't too busy with being holy, that is. He seemed to spend a great deal of time convincing the villagers that he was much more important than they were. . . .

Tonno took note of her abstracted nod. "And we all pay tithes to see that it gets done—because one day I may be too ill to care for myself, you may find yourself in a town on the brink of war, your friend's child may lose its parents, you might find yourself in the right—but up against the Sire himself, with no hope from his courts. And some of that is done."

"But?" she asked, a little more harshly than she intended. Nobody had seen that justice was done for her—or Jib. Had she been raped, would the Priest have lifted a finger to see that the bullies paid? Not a chance. More likely he'd have condemned her for leading them on.

"But not enough to account for the enormous amount of money the Church takes in," Tonno replied, his mouth a tight, grim line. "And I could be in very deep trouble if you were ever to repeat my words to a Church official other than, say, Brother Bryan. The Church is an example of an abusive government; it punishes according to whim, or according to who can afford to buy it off. Within Church ranks, dissenters must walk softly, and reform by infinitesimal degrees if at all. The Church is a dangerous enemy to have—and there's only one reason why it isn't more dangerous than it is. It is so involved in its own internal politics that it rarely moves to look outside its walls. And for that, I am profoundly grateful."

This last colloquy aroused intense feelings of disquiet in Rune's heart; she was glad when he fell silent. She'd never thought much about the Church—but the few glimpses she'd had from inside, in the hostels, only confirmed what Tonno had just told her. If the Church as a whole ever decided to move against something—

—say, for instance, the Church were to declare non-humans as unholy, anathema, as they had come very close to doing, several times, according to the history books she'd read—

She shivered, and not from the cold. Boony, Topaz—they were as "human" as she was. There was nothing demonic about them. And when would the Church end, once it had begun? Would exotics, like Pearl, also fall under the ban?

What if they decided to ban—certain professions? Whores, or even musicians, dancers, anyone who gave pleasure that was not tangible? That sort of pleasure *could* be construed as heretical, since it took attention away from God.

And what about all those rumors of dark sorceries that some priests practiced, using the mantle of the Church to give them protection?

She was glad to hear the shop bell, signaling the arrival of one of the two youngsters due for lessons today. Ket was due first; he was late, but that was all right. Her thoughts were all tangled up, and too troubled right now. It would be a relief to think about simpler things, like basic lute lessons.

She forgot about her uneasiness as she gave Ket his teaching, then drilled Anny in her scales. The children were easier to deal with than they normally were; this kind of weather didn't tempt anyone to want to play outside, not even a child. And Anny was home alone with her governess, a sour old dame who sucked all the joy out of learning and left only the withered husks; she was glad for a chance to get away and do something entirely different. The lute lessons and the sessions she had with her dancing teacher were her only respites from the heavy hand of the old governess.

So it wasn't until after they'd left that Tonno's words came back to trouble her—and by then she had convinced herself that she had fallen victim to the miserable weather. She made a determined effort to shake off her mood, and by the time she left Tonno curled up in his blankets with bread and toasted cheese beside him and a couple of favorite books to read, she was in as cheerful a mood as possible, given her long walk back to Amber's through the dark and blowing snow.

And by midnight, she'd forgotten it all entirely.

But her dreams were haunted by things she could not recall clearly in the morning. Only—the lingering odor of incense.

CHAPTER ELEVEN

Rune sailed in the door of Tonno's shop singing at the top of her lungs, with a smile as wide and sunny as the day outside, and a bulging belt-pouch.

"Well!" Tonno greeted her, answering her smile with one of his own. "What's all this?"

She leaned over the counter and kissed him soundly on the cheek. He actually blushed, but could only repeat, "Well! Welladay!"

She laughed, pulled her pouch off her belt, and spread her day's takings out on the countertop for him to see. "Look at that! Just *look* at it! Why, that's almost ten whole silver pennies, and a handful of copper! Can you believe it?"

"What did you do, rob someone?" Tonno asked, teasingly.

"No indeed," she said happily. "Do you remember that city ordinance that was passed at Spring Equinox session? The one that was basically about female buskers?"

He sobered, quickly. "I do, indeed," he replied. The ordinance had troubled him a great deal; he had fretted about it incessantly until it was passed, and he had warned Rune not to go out on the streets as a musician in female garb once it was passed. Not that she *ever* did, at least, not to busk. The ordinance had been aimed squarely at those females who were using busking to cover their other business; it licensed inspectors who were to watch street and tavern musicians to be certain that their income was derived entirely from music. A similar ordinance, aimed at dancers, had also passed. Rune, of course, had either not come under scrutiny—at least that she was aware of—because of her habit of taking on boy-disguise, or she had passed the scrutiny easily. For some reason it never occurred to the inspectors or to those who had passed the ordinance that males might be operating the same deceptions. But the ordinance had pretty much cleared the streets of those women who had bought cheaper busking licenses and were using them to cover their other activities. The ordinance directed that any such woman be made to tender up not one, but *two* years' dues in the Whore's Guild, and buy a free-lancer's license as well. The Whore's Guild and the Bardic Guild had backed it; the Whore's Guild since it obviously cut down on women who were practicing outside the rules and restrictions of the Guild, which set prices and ensured the health of its members. Amber hadn't said much, but Rune suspected that she both approved and worried.

She partially approved of it, obviously, because she felt the same way about those women who were abusing the busker's licenses as Rune felt about amateur musicians who thought they could set up with an instrument they hardly knew how to play and a repertoire of half a dozen songs and call themselves professionals. But Rune knew that Amber and Tonno both worried about this law because the Church had also been behind it—and they feared it might be the opening move in a campaign to end the Whore's Guild altogether, and make the Houses themselves illegal.

It had been hard for Rune to feel much concern about that, when the immediate result had been to free up half the corners in Nolton to *honest* musicians and dancers, and to send even more clients to Amber's than there had been before. Amber had been forced to add a fifth and sixth lady; both of whom had passed their trial periods with highest marks—which had made Carly even more sour than before. Carly now stalked the hall of the private wing with a copy of the Holy Book poking ostentatiously out of her pocket. And she spent most of her time off at the Church, at interminable "Women's Prayer Meetings." She had even tried to drag the boys off to a "Group Prayer Meeting," but both of them had told her to her face that they'd rather scrub chamber pots.

The two new ladies, Amethyst and Diamond, got along perfectly well with the other four; Rune liked them both very much, especially Diamond, who had the most abrasive and caustic sense of humor she'd ever encountered. It was Diamond who had suggested her current project.

Diamond was an incredibly slender woman with pure white hair—naturally white, claimed Maddie, who often helped Diamond with the elaborate, though revealing, costumes she favored. Diamond had been in the common room one night (dressed—so to speak—mostly in strings of tiny glass beads made into a semblance of a dress) when Rune had played a common song called "Two Fair Maids" at a client's request. Diamond had politely waited until that client had gone upstairs before she said anything, but *then* she had them all in stitches.

"Just once—" she'd said vehemently, "just *once* I'd like to hear a song about that situation that makes some sense!"

One of the gentlemen with her, who Rune had suspected for some time really *was* nobly born, had said, ingenuously, "What situation?" That had pretty much confirmed Rune's suspicions, since it would have been hard to be a commoner and not have heard "Two Fair Maids" often enough to know every word of every variant.

Diamond, however, had simply explained it to him without betraying that. "It's about two sisters in love with the same man," she told him. "He's been sleeping with the older one, who thinks he's going to have to marry her—but he proposes to the younger one, who accepts. When the older one finds out, she shoves the younger one in the river." She turned to Rune, then, and included her in the conversation. "Rune, what *are* all the various versions of it after that?"

"Well," Rune had answered, thinking, "There's three variations on how she dies. One, the older girl holds her under; two, she gets carried off by the current and pulled under the millrace; three, that the miller sees her, wants her gold ring, and drowns her. But in all of the versions, a wandering harpist-Bard finds her—or rather, what's *left* of her after the fish get done—and makes a harp of her bones and strings it with her long, gold hair."

"Dear God!" the gentleman exclaimed. "That's certainly gruesome!"

"And pretty stupid," Rune added, to Diamond's great delight. "I can't imagine why *any* musician would go making an instrument out of human bone when there are perfectly good pieces of wood around that are much better suited to the purpose! And I can't imagine why anyone would want to *play* such a thing!" She shivered. "I should think you'd drive customers into the next kingdom the first time they caught sight of it! But anyway, that's what this fool does, and he takes it to court and plays it for the Sire. And, *of course,* the moment the older sister shows up, the harp begins to play by itself, and sing about how the little idiot got herself drowned. And *of course,* the sister is burned, and the miller is hung, and the bastard that started it in the first place by seducing the first sister gets off free." She curled her lip a little. "In fact, in one of the versions he gets all kinds of sympathy from other stupid women because his syrupy little true love drowned."

"And that's what I mean by I wish that someone would write a sensible version," Diamond said, taking up where Rune left off. "I mean, if I was the wronged sister, I wouldn't blame my brainless sib, I'd go after the motherless wretch that betrayed me! And if I was the younger sister, if I found out about it, I'd *help* her!" She turned to Rune, then, with a mischievous look on her face that made her pale blue eyes sparkle like the stone she was named for. "You're a musician," she said, gleefully. "Why don't you do it?"

At first Rune could only think of all the reasons why it wouldn't work—that people were used to the old song and would hate the new version, that the Bardic Guild would hate it because their members had written a great many of the variants, and that it wasn't properly romantic.

But then she thought of all the reasons why, if she chose her audience properly, picking mostly young people who were in a mood to laugh, it *would* work. There were not a great many comic songs out in the world, and she could, if she managed this successfully, get quite a following for herself based on the fact that she had written one. In fact, there were a great many really stupid, sentimental ballads like "Two Fair Maids" in existence; if she wrote parodies of them, she could have an entire repertory of comic songs.

And songs like that were much more suited to the casual atmosphere of street-busking than the maudlin ones were.

She'd started on the project in late spring; she already had four. She'd moved to a new corner, vacated by one of the buskers-that-weren't, on a very busy crossroads. It wasn't a venue usually suited to busking, but she'd made a bargain with one of the Gypsy-dancers who had reappeared at the fountain in Flower Street with the spring birds. Rune would play the fiddle for her to dance from exactly midday until second bell and split the take, if the Gypsies would hold the corner for her to play from two hours before midday till the dancer showed up. No one wanted to argue with the Gypsies, who were known to have tempers and be very quick with their knives, so the corner was Rune's without dispute.

Now what she had planned to do, was to alternate lively fiddling with comic songs, to see how well they did, and if she could hold a rowdy crowd with them.

She had discovered this afternoon that not only could she hold the crowd, she now had a reputation for knowing the funny songs, and there were people coming to her corner at lunch just to hear them.

And furthermore, they were willing to *pay* to hear them. Every time she'd tried to go back to the fiddle today, someone had called out for one of her songs. And when she'd demurred, protesting that she'd already done it, or that people must be getting tired of it, at least three coins were tossed into her hat as an incentive. In the end, she had made as much during her stint alone as she and the dancer had together.

She explained all that to Tonno, who looked pleased at first, then troubled. "You didn't write anything—satiric, did you?" he asked, worriedly. "These were just silly parodies of common songs, am I understanding you correctly?"

She sighed, exasperated. He was beating around the bush again, rather than asking her directly what he wanted to know, and she was tired of it.

"Tonno, just what, exactly, are you asking me? Get to the point, will you? I'm not one of your Scholar customers, that you have to build a tower of logic for before you get a straight answer."

He blinked in surprise. "I suppose—did you make fun of anyone high-ranking enough to cause you trouble? Or did you sing *anything* satirical about the Church?"

"If anybody in one of those songs resembles someone in Nolton, *I* don't know about it," she told him in complete honesty. "And I must admit that I had considered doing something about a corrupt Priest, but I decided against it, after seeing Carly leaving my room. It would be just like her to take a copy to the Church with her, when she goes to one of her stupid Prayer Meetings, and find a way to get me in trouble."

Tonno let out a deep sigh of relief. "I'd advise you to keep to that decision," he said, passing his hand over his hair. "At least for now, when you have no one to protect you. Later, perhaps, when you have Guild status and protection, you can write whatever you choose." He smiled, weakly. "Who knows; with the force of a Guild Bard behind a satiric song, you might become an influence for good within the Church."

"What are you so worried about, really?" she asked, putting her instruments down on the counter. "Did Brother Bryan tell you something? Is the Church planning on backing more of those ordinances you don't like?"

He shook his head. "No—no, it's that I've been debating doing something for a while, and I've been putting it off because I didn't have the connections. Remember when I started sending you to other people for lessons this spring?"

She nodded. "Mandar Cray for lute, and Geor Baker for voice. You told me you weren't going to be useful for anything with me except for reading and writing." Mandar and Geor were two of the people she had considered as teachers when she first came to Nolton, as it turned out. Both of them were Guild musicians; both had very wealthy students. Had she approached them on her own, she probably would have gotten brushed off.

But both were clients and friends of both Tonno and Amber, and both had heard her sing and play. They were two very different men; Mandar tall and ascetic, Geor short and muscular; Mandar hardly every ate, at least at Amber's, and Geor ate everything in sight. Mandar fainted at the thought of bloodshed, let alone the sight of blood, and Geor was a champion swordsman. But they had one other thing in common besides being clients and friends of Amber and Tonno—they both adored music. For the opportunity to teach someone who loved it as much as they did, and had talent, as opposed to the rich, bored children who were enduring their lessons, both of them cut their lesson-rates to next-to-nothing.

They wouldn't teach her for free—for one thing, that could get them in trouble with the Guild—for another, they felt, like Tonno, that *paying* for something tended to make one pay attention to it. But they weren't charging her any more than Tonno had, and she was learning a great deal he simply could not show her.

"I've been wanting to find someone who could teach you composition,"

Tonno said, his expression still worried, "But the only Bards I knew of in the city were either in a Great Household, or—in the Church."

Rune's mouth formed a silent "O" of understanding. Now all of Tonno's fussing made some sense. If he'd wanted to find her a teacher and she'd gotten herself in trouble with the Church—

But he wasn't finished. "I didn't have the contacts to get you lessons with any of the Church Bards," he continued. "But last week Brother Bryan mentioned that he'd listened to you playing out on the street and that he thought you were amazing. He still thinks you're a boy, you understand—"

Rune nodded. Brother Bryan had never seen her in female garb; she and Tonno had judged that the best idea. Many Church *men* felt very uneasy around females for one thing—and it seemed no bad idea to have her female persona unknown to the Church, after all the ordinances and the snooping Carly was doing. They might not connect the "Rune" that busked with the "Rune" that played at Amber's. And even if they did, they might not know that Rune was really a girl, if Carly hadn't gone out of her way to tell them. Rune didn't think she had; she just reported the activities going on, but because *she* knew Rune's sex, she would probably assume the Church did, too.

"Well, Brother Bryan was very impressed by what he'd heard. He asked if you composed, then before I could say anything, he offered to see if he couldn't get Brother Pell to take you in his class." Tonno was clearly torn between being proud and being concerned at a Church Collector's interest in his pupil. "That's why I wanted to know what your comic songs were about; if you'd done anything to annoy the Church officials, going to that class could be walking you into a trap. The Church has no power outside the cloister, but once they had you inside, they could hold you for as long as they cared to, and the city couldn't send anyone to get you out. Assuming they'd even bother to try, which I doubt. The only people the constables and guards are likely to exert themselves for have more money than you and I put together."

Rune's mouth went dry at the bare thought of being held by the Church for questioning. She recalled the high walls around the cloister all too well—walls that shut out the world. And held in secrets? "They wouldn't—"

He saw her terrified expression, and laughed, easing her fear. "Oh, all they'd do, most likely, is try to frighten you; to bully you and make you promise never to write something like that again." He cocked his head sideways, for a moment, and his expression sobered. "But if they connected you with the musician at Amber's, they could threaten other punishments, and make you promise to spy at Amber's in return for being set free. I doubt Carly is terribly effective."

"I wouldn't do that!" she exclaimed, hotly.

"You might, if you were frightened enough," he admonished her. "I'm not saying you also wouldn't go straight to Amber afterwards and tell her what they'd gotten from you, but don't ever underestimate the power of a skilled Church interrogator. They could make you promise to do almost anything for them, and you'd weep with gratitude because they had for-given you for what you'd done to them. They are very skilled with words—with innuendo—with making threats they have no intention of carrying out. And they are a force unto themselves on their own ground."

"And maybe they're as skilled with magic as they are with words?" Rune frowned; those were some of the whispered rumors she'd heard. That the Church harbored Priests and Brothers who were powerful magi-cians, who could make people do what they wanted them to with a few chosen words and a spell to take over their will.

"Possibly," Tonno conceded wearily. "Possibly; I don't know. I've never seen a Church mage, and I don't know of anyone who has, but that doesn't mean anything, does it? Since you haven't angered them, and don't *intend* to, you're unlikely to see one either. Let's face it, Rune, you and I are just too small for them to take much notice of. It's not worth the time they'd spend."

"Something to be said for being insignificant," she commented sardonically.

He nodded. "At any rate, I'm quite confident that you'll be in no danger whatsoever, if you want to take these lessons. Brother Bryan told me that Brother Pell is—well, 'rather difficult to get along with,' is the way he put it. I pressed him for details, but he couldn't tell me much; I gather he has a bad temper and a sour disposition. He doesn't like much of anybody, and even someone as even-tempered as Bryan has a hard time finding good things to say about him."

"Sounds like taking lessons from Carly," she said, with a wry twist to her mouth.

"Perhaps," Tonno replied thoughtfully. "But there is this; Bryan said that by all reports, even of those who don't like him at all, Pell is the best composition teacher in all of Nolton."

"Huh," Rune said thoughtfully. "I'd be willing to take lessons even from Carly if she was that good. Am I supposed to be a boy or a girl?"

"Boy," Tonno told her firmly. "Women have very little power in the Church, at least here in Nolton, and I gather that Pell in particular despises the sex. Go as a girl, and he'll probably refuse to teach you on the grounds that you'll just go off and get married and waste his teaching." He gave her a long, level look, as he realized exactly what she'd said. "I take it that you want the lessons, then?"

"I said I'd even take lessons from Carly if she had anything worth learning," Rune replied firmly. "When can I start?"

She didn't feel quite so bold a few days later, as she meekly showed her pass to the Brother on watch at the cloister gate. In the year she'd been here, she'd never once been inside the huge cathedral in the center of Nolton, big enough to hold several thousand worshipers at once. In fact, she avoided it as much as possible. That wasn't too difficult, since there was no use in busking anywhere near it; the Priests and Brothers made a busker feel so uncomfortable by simply standing and staring with disapproval that it was easier to find somewhere else to play.

It was an imposing, forbidding edifice, carved of dark stone, with thousands of sculptures all over its surface; there wasn't a single square inch that didn't hold a carving of something. Down near the base, it was ordinary people doing Good Works, and the temptations of the Evil One trying to waylay them. Farther up, there were carvings of the lives of the saints and all the temptations that they had overcome. The next level held the bliss of Paradise. The uppermost level was carved with all the varied kinds of angels, from the finger-length Etherials, to the Archangels that were three times the height of a man.

There was a sky-piercing tower in the middle of it, carved with abstract water and cloud shapes, that held the bells that signaled the changes of the hours for everyone in the city. Inside, she had been told, it was different; not dark and foreboding at all, full of light and space—those carved walls held hundreds of tiny windows filled with glass, and most of the ones near the ground were of precious colored glass. Every saint's shrine, every statue inside had been gilded or silvered; places where the light couldn't reach were covered with banks of prayer candles. When the sun shone, or so Tonno claimed, the eye was dazzled. Even when it didn't, there were lights and reflective surfaces enough to make the interior bright as day in an open meadow.

She hadn't cared enough to want to see it, although it was quite an attraction for visitors just to come and gawk at. Behind the cathedral was the cloister; a complex of buildings including convents for men and for women, a school, and the Church administrative offices. All that was held behind a high wall pierced with tiny gates, each guarded day and night by a Brother. Rune had never been inside those walls, and didn't know anyone who had.

Plenty of people had been inside the cathedral though. The High Priest of Nolton was said to be a marvelous speaker, although, again, Rune couldn't have said one way or another. She hadn't cared to see *him*, either, though Carly went to the service he preached at as faithfully as the bells rang.

From the little she saw outside the walls, the cloister was twice as forbidding as the cathedral, because it had none of the cathedral's ornamentation. Now that she was *inside* the walls, it was worse, much worse. The place looked like a prison. The buildings were carved of the same dark stone, with tiny slits for windows. It looked as if it was a place designed to keep people from escaping; Rune hoped she'd never have occasion to discover that her impression was true.

The Brother at the gate, anonymous in his dark gray robe, directed her to go past the building immediately in front of her and take the first door she saw after that. She walked slowly across the silent, paved courtyard; nothing behind her but the wall with its small postern gate, nothing on either side of her or before her but tall, oblong buildings with tiny passages between them. Nothing green or growing anywhere, not even a weed springing up between the cobblestones. It seemed unnatural. A few robed figures crossed the courtyard ahead of her; none looked at her, no one spoke. In their dark, androgynous robes, she couldn't even tell if they were men or women.

Once past the first building, she felt even more hemmed in and confined. *How can anyone bear to live like this?* she wondered. No need to look for a reason why Brother Pell was so sour; if she had to live here, she'd be just as bitter as he was.

There was another Brother at the door of the building, sitting behind a tiny desk; once again, she showed her pass, and was directed to a second-floor room. She looked back over her shoulder for a moment as she climbed the stair; the Brother was watching her—to be certain she went where she was told? Possibly. That might be simple courtesy on the part of the Brothers. It might be something else. There was no point in speculating; she was just here for composition lessons, not anything sinister. She didn't want to stay here a moment longer than she had to. Let the Brother watch; he'd see only a young boy obeying, doing exactly what he was told.

She opened the designated doorway and went inside. There was no one there, and nothing but one large desk and six smaller ones. She discovered that she was the first to arrive of a class of six, including her. The classroom was a tiny cubicle, narrow, with enough space for their six desks arranged two by two, with Brother Pell's large desk facing them, and behind that, a wall covered in slate.

Brother Pell appeared last, a perfectly average man, balding slightly, with his hands tucked into the sleeves of his gray robe and a frown so firmly a part of his face that Rune could not imagine what he would look like if he ever smiled. If he had been anything other than a Brother, she would have guessed at Scholar or clerk; he had that kind of tight-lipped look.

There was a nagging sense of familiarity about him; after a moment, she knew what it was. She had seen this man often, out on the street, ever since the ordinance against pseudo-buskers had been passed. Presumably he was one of the inspectors. And now that she thought about it, she realized that there were a great many more Brothers and Sisters out on the street since the ordinance had been passed. Interesting; she had never thought of *them* as being inspectors, but it made sense. The inspectors were being paid very little, about the same as a lamp-lighter or a dung-sweeper. Unless you had no other job, it wasn't one you'd think of taking. A few of the real buskers had become inspectors by day, and did their busking at night. But Church clerics—well, it wouldn't matter to them how small the fee was. It was very probable that, since everyone in the Church took a vow to own nothing, their fees as inspectors went to the Church itself.

Very interesting, and not very comforting, that the Church who had backed the law should send its people out into the streets as an army of enforcers of that law. She'd have to tell Tonno about her suspicion and see what he said.

Brother Pell did not seem to recognize her, however, although she recognized him; his eyes flitted over her as they did the other five boys in the class without a flicker of recognition. He consulted a list in his hand.

"Terr Capston of Nolton," he said, and looked up. His voice, at least, was pleasant, although cold. A good, strong trained tenor.

"Here, sir," said a sturdy brown-haired boy, who looked back at the Brother quite fearlessly. Of all of them, he seemed the most used to being in the tutelage of Brothers.

"And why are you here, Terr Capston?" Brother Pell asked, without any expression at all.

Terr seemed to have been ready for this question. "Brother Rylan wants me to find out if I have Bardic material in me," the boy said. "I'm for the Church either way, but Brother wants to know if it will be as just a player or—"

"Stop right there, boy," Brother Pell said fiercely, and his cold face wore a forbidding frown. "There is no such thing as 'just' a player, and Brother Rylan is sadly to blame if that's the way he's taught you. Or is that *your* notion?"

The boy hung his head, and Brother Pell grimaced. "I thought so. I *should* send you back to him until you learn humility. Consider yourself on probation. Lenerd Cattlan of Nolton."

"Here—sir." The timid dark-haired boy right in front of Rune raised his hand.

"And why are you here?" the Brother asked, glaring at him with hawk-fierce eyes. The boy shrank into his seat and shook his head.

"You don't know?" Pell said, biting off each word. He cast his eyes upward. "Lord, give me patience. Rune of Westhaven."

"Sir," she said, nodding, and matching his stare with a stare of her own. *You don't frighten me one bit. And I'm not going to back down to you, either.*

She had expected the same question, but he surprised her. "No last name? Why not?"

That was rude at the very least—but she had a notion that Brother Pell was never terribly polite. She decided to see if she could startle or discomfort him with the truth. "I don't know who my father is," she replied levely. "And I judged it better than to claim something I have no right to."

One of the other boys snickered, and Pell turned a look on him that left Rune wondering if she scented scorched flesh in its wake. The boy shrank in his seat, and gulped. "You're an honest boy," he barked, turning back to Rune, "and there's no shame in being born a bastard. The shame is on your mother who had no moral sense, not on you. *You* did not ask to be born; that was God's will. You are doing well to repudiate your mother's weak morals with strong ones of your own. God favors the honest. Perhaps your mother will see your success one day, and repent of her ways."

If Rune hadn't agreed with him totally about her mother's lack of sense, moral or otherwise, she might have resented that remark. As it was, she nodded, cautiously.

"Why are you here, Rune?" *Now* came the question she expected.

"Because there is music in my head, and I don't know how to write it down the way I hear it," she replied promptly. "I can find harmonies and counter-melodies when I sing, but I don't know how to get *them* down, either, and sometimes I lose things before I even manage to work them out properly." He looked a little interested, so she continued. "Brother

Bryan heard me on the street and told my first teacher that he'd get me a recommendation into this class if I wanted it. I wanted it. I want to be more than a street busker, if it's in me. And if it's God's will," she added, circumspectly.

Pell barked a laugh. "Good answer. Axen Troud of Nolton."

Brother Pell continued the litany until he had covered all six of them, and Rune realized after she watched him listening to their answers that he had formed a fairly quick impression of each of them from both their words, and the way they answered. And as he began the first session and she bent all of her attention to his words and the things he was writing down on the slate behind him, she also realized that unlike Tonno, Brother Pell was not going to *help* anyone. He would never explain things twice. If you fell behind, that was too bad. You would keep up with *him* in this class, or you would not stay in it.

She had a fairly good idea that the timid boy would not be able to keep up. Nor would one of the boys who had answered after her; a stolid, unimaginative sort who was more interested in the mathematics of music than the music itself. And they might lose the first boy, who was plainly used to being cosseted by his teacher.

At the end of that first lesson, she felt as drained and exhausted as she had been at the end of her first lute lesson. If this had been the first time she'd ever felt that way, she likely would have given up right there—which was what the first boy looked ready to do.

But as she gathered up her notes under Pell's indifferent eye and filed out with the rest, she knew that if nothing else, she was going to get her money's worth out of this class. Pell *was* a good teacher.

And I've been hungry, cold, nearly penniless. I fiddled for the Skull Hill Ghost and won. If the Ghost didn't stop me, neither will Brother Pell.

No one will. Not ever.

CHAPTER TWELVE

Rune rang the bell outside the Church postern gate again, though she had no expectation of being answered this time, either. When after several minutes there was no sound of feet on stone, she beat her benumbed, mittened hands together and continued pacing up and down the little stretch of pavement outside the Gate. Her heart pounded in her chest at the audacity of what she was about to do, but she wasn't going to let fear stop her. Not now. Not when the stakes were this high.

She told her heart to be still, and the lump in her throat to go away. Neither obeyed her.

Tonno had taken a chill when he'd been caught between the market and his shop three weeks ago, on the day of the great blizzard, and it had taken him hours to stumble back home. The blizzard had piled some of the city streets so deeply with snow that people were coming and going from the second-floor windows of some places, although that was not the case with Amber's or with Tonno's shop. Rune had been busy with helping to shovel once the storm was over, and it had taken her two days to get to him. By then, the damage was done. He was sick, and getting sicker.

She had gone out every day to the Church since then, to the Priests who sent out Doctors to those who had none of their own. Each day she had been turned away by the Priest in charge, who had consulted a list, told her brusquely that there were those with more need than Tonno, and then ignored her further protests. Finally, today, one of the other women in line had explained this cryptic statement to her.

"Your master's old, boy," the woman had whispered. "He's old, he's never been one for making more than the tithe to the Church, no doubt, and he's got no kin to inherit. And likely, he's not rich enough to be worth much of a thanks-gift if a Doctor came out and made him well. They figure, if he dies, the Church gets at least half his goods, if not all— and if he lives, it's God's will."

That had infuriated and frightened her; it was obvious that she was never going to get any help for Tonno—and when she'd arrived today, he'd been half delirious with a fever. She'd sent a boy to get Maddie to come watch him while she went after a Doctor—again. And this time, by all that was holy, she was not going to return without one.

She had been in and out of the cloister enough to know who came and went by all the little gates; one lesson the Brothers had never expected her to learn, doubtless. She knew where the Doctors' Gate was, and she was going to wait by it until she spotted one of the physician-Brothers. They were easy enough to pick out, by the black robe they wore instead of gray, and by the box of medicines they always carried. When she saw a Doctor, or could get one to answer the bell, she was going to take him to Tonno—by force, if need be.

Her throat constricted again, and she fought a stinging in her eyes. Crying was not going to help him. Only a Doctor could do that, and a Doctor was what she was waiting for. She tried not to think about what he'd looked like when she left him; transparent, thin, and old—so frail, as if a thought would blow him away.

She stopped her pacing along enough to cough; like everyone else, it seemed, she'd picked up a cold in the past two weeks. She hadn't paid it much attention. Beside Tonno's illness, it was hardly more serious than a splinter. As she straightened up, she heard the sound of feet approaching; hard soles slapping wearily on the stonework. The *Church* certainly didn't lack hands to see that the streets about the cathedral and the cloisters were shoveled clean. . . .

She turned; approaching from a side street to her left was a man in the black robe of a Church Doctor, laden with one of those black-leather-covered boxes. He walked with his head down so that she couldn't see his face, watching his step on the icy cobbles.

She hurried to intercept him, her heart right up in her throat and pounding so loudly she could hardly hear herself speak.

"Excuse me, sir," she said, trotting along beside him, then putting herself squarely in his path when he wouldn't stop. She held out her empty, mittened hands to him, and tried to put all the terror and pleading she felt into her face and voice. "Excuse me—my master's sick, he's got a fever, a dry fever and a dry cough that won't stop, he's been sick ever since the blizzard and I've been here every day but the Priest won't send anybody, he says there's people with greater need, but my master's an old man and he's having hallucinations—" She was gabbling it all out as fast as she could, hoping to get him to listen to her before he brushed her aside. He frowned at her when she made him stop, and frowned even harder when she began to talk—he put out a hand to move her away from his path—

But then he blinked, as if what she had said had finally penetrated his preoccupation, and stayed his hand. "A fever? With visions, you say?" She nodded. "And a dry, racking cough that won't stop?" She nodded again, harder. If he recognized the symptoms, sure, surely he knew the cure!

He swore—and for the first time in months of living at Amber's, she was shocked. Not at the oath; she'd heard enough like it from the carters and other rough laborers who visited some of the other Houses on the street. That a Brother should utter a hair-scorching oath like that—*that* was what shocked her. But it seemed that this was no ordinary Brother.

His face hardened with anger, and his eyes grew black. "An old man with pneumonia, lying untreated for two weeks—and instead of taking care of him, they send me out to tend a brat with a bellyache from too many sweets—" He swore again, an oath stronger than the first. "Show me your master, lad, and be hanged to Father Genner. Bellyache my ass!"

Rune hurried down the street towards Tonno's with the Brother keeping pace beside her, despite the hindering skirts of his robe. "I'm Brother Anders," he said, trotting next to her and not even breathing hard. "Tell me more about your master's illness."

She did, everything she could recall, casting sideways glances at the Brother as she did so. He was a large man, black-bearded and black-haired; he made her think of a bear. But his eyes, now that he wasn't frowning, were kind. He listened carefully to everything she said, but his expression grew graver and graver with each symptom. And her heart sank every time his expression changed.

"He's not in good shape, lad," the Brother said at last. "I won't lie to you. If I'd seen him a week ago—or better, when he first fell ill—"

"I came then," she protested angrily, forcing away tears with the heat of her outrage. "I came every day! The Priest kept telling me that there were others with more need, and turning me away!" She wanted to tell him the rest, what the old woman had told her—but something stopped her. This was a Brother, after all, tied to the Church. If she maligned the Church, he might not help her.

"And I simply go where the Priests tell me," Brother Anders replied, as angry as she was. "Father Genner didn't see fit to mention *this* case to any of us! Well, there's going to be *someone* answering for this! I took my vows to tend to *all* the sick, not just fat merchants with deep pockets, and their spoiled children who have nothing wrong that a little less coddling and cosseting wouldn't cure!"

There didn't seem to be anything more to add to that, so Rune saved her breath for running, speeding up the pace, and hoping that, despite Brother Anders' words, things were not as grave as they seemed. But she was fighting back tears with every step. And the old woman's words kept echoing in her head. If the Church wanted Tonno to die, what hope did she have of saving him?

But this Brother seemed capable, and caring. He was angry that the Priests hadn't sent him to Tonno before this. He would do everything in his power to help, just for that reason alone, she was certain.

After all, many Doctors probably exaggerated the state of an illness, to seem more skilled when the patient recovered—didn't they?

She had left the door unlocked when she went out; it was still unlocked. She pushed it open and motioned to the Brother to follow her through the dark, cold, narrow shop.

Maddie looked up when Rune came through the curtain. "Rune, he's getting worse," she said worriedly. "He doesn't know who I am, he thinks it's summer and he keeps pushing off the blankets as fast as I put them back—" Then she saw the Brother, as he looked up, for his black robe had hidden him in the shadows. "Oh!" she exclaimed with relief. "You got a Doctor to come!"

"Aye, he did," the Brother rumbled, squinting through the darkness to the little island of light where Tonno lay. "And not a moment too soon, from the sound of it. You go on home, lass; this lad and I will tend to things now."

Maddie didn't wait for a second invitation; she snatched up her cloak and hurried out, pushing past them with a brief curtsy for the Doctor. Brother Anders hardly noticed her; all his attention was for the patient. Rune heard the door slam shut behind Maddie, then she ignored everything except Tonno and the Doctor.

"Get some heat in this place, lad," the Brother ordered gruffly, shoving his way past the crowded furnishings to Tonno's bedside. Rune didn't hesitate; she opened the stove door and piled on expensive wood and even more expensive coal. After all, what did it matter? Tonno's life was at stake here. She would buy him more when he was well.

And if he dies, the Church gets it all anyway, she thought bitterly, rubbing her sleeve across her eyes as they stung damply. *Why should I save it for them?*

Then she pushed the thought away. Tonno would *not* die, she told herself fiercely, around the lump of pain and fear that filled her. He would get better. This was a conscientious Doctor, and she sensed he'd fight as hard for Tonno as he would for his own kin. Tonno would get well—and she would use some of the money saved from last summer to buy him more wood and coal—yes, and chicken to make soup to make him strong, and medicine, and anything else he needed.

"Boil me some water, will you, lad?" the Doctor said as the temperature in the room rose. Tonno mumbled something and tried to push Brother Anders' hands away; the Doctor ignored him, peering into Tonno's eyes and opening his mouth to look at his throat, then leaning down to listen to his chest.

"There's some already, sir," she replied. He turned in surprise, to see her holding out the kettle. "I always had a fresh kettle going. I kept giving him willow-bark tea, sir. At first it helped with the fever, and even when it didn't, it let him sleep some—"

"Well done, lad." Brother Anders nodded with approval. "But he's going to need something stronger than that if he's to have any chance of pulling through. And do you think you can get me some steam in here? It'll make his breathing easier, and I have some herbs for his lungs that need steam."

She put the kettle back on the top of the stove, as he rummaged in his kit for herbs and a mortar and pestle to grind them. *Steam. How can I get steam over to the bed*— If she put a pan of water on the stove, the steam would never reach as far as the bed; if she brought a pan to boil and took it over beside the bed, it would stop steaming quickly, wasting the precious herbs.

Then she thought of the little nomads' brazier out in the shop; one of the curiosities that Tonno had accumulated over the years that had never sold. If she were to put a pan of water on that, and put the whole lot beside the bed—

Yes, that would work. She ran out into the shop to get it; it was up on one of the shelves, one near the floor since it was ceramic and very heavy. It was meant, Tonno had said, to use animal-droppings for fuel. If she took one of the burning lumps of coal out of the stove and dropped it into the combustion chamber, that should do. As an afterthought, she picked up the wooden stool she used to get things just out of her reach, and took that with her as well. There was a slab of marble in the living area that Tonno used to roll out dough on; if she put that on the stool, and the brazier on that, it would be just tall enough that she could fan steam directly onto Tonno's face. And the marble would keep the wooden stool from catching fire.

She set up the stool with the marble and brazier atop it, then carefully caught up a lump of bright red coal in the tongs and carried it over, dropping it into the bottom on the brazier to land on the little iron grate there. Then she got an ornamental copper bowl, put it atop the brazier, and filled it with water. She didn't look at Tonno; she couldn't. She couldn't bear to see him that way. When the water began to steam, and she started fanning it towards Tonno's face, the Doctor looked up in surprise and approval.

"Keep that up, lad," he said, and dropped a handful of crushed herbs into the water. The steam took on an astringent quality; refreshing and clean-smelling. It even seemed to make her breathing easier.

She tried not to listen to Tonno's. His breath rasped in his throat, and wheezed in his chest, and there was a gurgling sound at the end of each breath that sounded horrible. The Doctor didn't like it either; she could tell by the way his face looked. But he kept mixing medicines, steeping each new dose with a little hot water, and spooning them into Tonno's slack mouth between rattling breaths.

She lost track of time; when the water in the bowl got low, she renewed it. At the Doctor's direction, she heated bricks at the stove and kept them packed around Tonno's thin body. When she wasn't doing either of those things, she was fanning the aromatic steam over Tonno's face.

And despite all of it, each breath came harder; each breath was more of a struggle. Tonno showed no signs of waking—and the hectic fever-spots in his cheeks grew brighter as his face grew paler.

Finally, just before dawn, he took one shallow breath—the last.

Rune huddled in the chair beside the bed, silent tears coursing down her cheeks and freezing as they struck the blanket she'd wrapped herself in. The Doctor had gently given Tonno Final Rites, as he was authorized to do, then covered him, face and all, so that Rune didn't have to look at the body. He'd told her to go home, that there was nothing more to do, that the Priests would come and take care of everything—then he'd left.

But she couldn't leave. She couldn't bear the idea of Tonno being left alone here, with no one to watch to see that he wasn't disturbed.

She let the fire go out, though, after piling on the last of the wood and coal. There was no point in saving it for the damned Priests—

Let them buy their own, or work in the cold, she thought savagely. *I hope their fingers and toes fall off!*

But she just couldn't see the point of buying any more, either. After all, Tonno didn't need the warmth any more. . . .

It's all my fault, she told herself, as the tears continued to fall, *I should have gone after a Doctor before. I should never have gone to the Priests. I should have found Brother Bryan and had him help me. I should have seen if Brother Pell was any use. I should have told Amber that Tonno was sicker than I thought—*

But what could Amber have done? Oh, there were Herb-women attached to the Whore's Guild that kept the members of the Guild healthy and free of unwanted pregnancies, but did they know anything about pneumonia?

Probably not—but I should have tried! I should have gone to everyone I knew—

If she'd done that, Tonno would probably be alive now.

She'd spent hours talking to the empty air, begging Tonno's forgiveness, and promising him what she was going to do with the rest of her life because of what he'd taught her, and trying to say good-bye. She'd cursed the Priests with every curse she knew, three times over, but the essential blame lay with her. There was no getting around it. So she stayed, as the shop grew colder, the water in the pan beside the bed froze over, and the square of sun cast through the back window crept across the floor and up the wall. It wasn't much of a penance, but it was something.

She'd long ago talked herself hoarse. Now she could only address him in thought. Even if her voice hadn't been a mere croak, she couldn't have said anything aloud around the lump of grief that choked her.

I'm sorry, Tonno, she said silently to the still, sheet-shrouded form on the bed. *I'm sorry—I did everything I could think of. I just didn't think of things soon enough. I really tried, honestly I did. . . .*

And the tears kept falling, trickling down her cheeks, though they could not wash away the guilt, the pain, or the loss.

The Priests finally arrived near sunset, as another snowstorm was blowing up, when she was numb within and without, from cold and grieving both. A trio of hard-faced, vulturine men, they seemed both surprised and suspicious when they saw her beside Tonno's bed.

When they asked her what she was doing there, she stammered something hoarsely about Tonno being her master, but that wasn't enough for them. While two of them bundled the body in a shroud, the third questioned her closely as to whether she was bonded or free, and what her exact relationship to Tonno had been.

She answered his questions between fits of coughing. He was not pleased to discover that she was free—and less pleased to discover that Tonno was nothing more than her teacher. She had the feeling that this one had been counting on her to have been a bonded servant, and thus part of the legacy.

I'd rather die than work for you bastards, she thought angrily, though she held her tongue. *I can just imagine what the lives of your bonded servants are like!*

"I see no reason why you should have been here," the Priest finally said, acidly. "You did your duty long ago; you should have been gone when we arrived." He stared at her as if he expected that she had been up to something that would somehow threaten a single pin that the Church could expect out of Tonno's holdings. That was when she lost her temper entirely.

"I was his *friend,*" she snapped, croaking out her words like an asthmatic frog. "That's reason enough, sir—or have you forgotten the words of your own Holy Book? 'You stayed beside me when I was sick, you fed me when I was hungry, you guided me when I was troubled, and you asked no more than my love—blessed are they who love without reward, for they shall have love in abundance'? I was following the words of the Book, whether or not it was *prudent* to do so!"

The Priest started, taken aback by having the Holy Words flung in his face. It didn't look to her like he was at all familiar with that particular passage, either in abstract or in application.

She dashed angry tears away. "He gave me something more precious than everything in this shop—he gave me *learning.* I could never repay that! Why shouldn't I watch by him—" She would have said more, but a coughing fit overcame her; she bent over double, and by the time she had gotten control of herself again, the Priest who was questioning her had gone out into the shop itself. She looked outside at the snowstorm, dubiously, wondering if she should just try to stay the night here. It wouldn't have been the first time—in fact, she'd been sleeping on the couch, just to keep an eye on him these past two weeks. Then one of the other two Priests came back into the room and cleared his throat so that she'd look at him.

"You'll have to leave, boy," the Priest said coldly. "You can't stay here.

There'll be someone to come collect the body in a moment, but you'll have to leave now."

"In this snow?" she replied, without thinking. "Why? And what about thieves—"

"We'll be staying," the Priest said, his voice and eyes hard and unfriendly. "We'll be staying and making certain the contents of this place match the inventory. There might be a will, but there probably isn't, and if there isn't, everything goes to the Church anyway. That's the law."

What would I do if I didn't have anyplace else to go? she wondered— but it didn't look as though the Priest cared. He'd have turned anyone out in the snow, like as not—old woman or young child. Unless, of course, they were bonded. Then, no doubt, he'd have been gracious enough to let them sleep on the floor.

He stared at her, and she had the feeling that he expected her to have a fortune in goods hiding under her cloak. She took it off and shook it, slowly and with dignity, trying not to shiver, just to show them that there wasn't anything under it but one skinny "boy." Then she put it back on, stepped right up to him as if she was about to say something, and deliberately sneezed on him. He started back, with the most dumbfounded and offended look on his face she'd ever seen. If she hadn't been so near to tears, and so angry, she'd have laughed at him.

"Excuse me," she said, still wrapped in dignity. "I've been tending him for two weeks now. Out of charity. I must have caught a chill myself."

Then she pushed rudely past him, and past the other two, who were already out in the shop with Tonno's books, candles, and pens. She managed to cough on them, too, on her way out, and took grim pleasure in the fact that there wasn't a stick of fuel in the place. And at this time of night, there'd be no one to sell them any. Unless they sent one of their number back to the cloister to fetch some, which meant going out into the storm, they'd be spending a long, cold night. There wasn't any food left, either; she'd been buying soup for him from one of his neighbors.

I hope they freeze and starve.

She wrapped her cloak tighter around herself before stepping out of the door—which she left open behind her. One of the Priests shouted at her, but she ignored him. *Let him shut his own damn door,* she thought viciously. Then the wind whipped into her, driving snow into her face, and she didn't have a breath or a thought to spare for anything else but getting back to Amber's.

This wasn't as bad a storm as the one that had killed Tonno, but it was pure frozen hell to stagger through. She lost track of her feet first, then her hands, and finally her face. She was too cold to shiver, but under the cloak she was sweating like a lathered horse. It seemed to take forever to beat her way against the wind down the streets she usually traveled in a half hour or less. The wind cut into her lungs like knives; every breath hurt her chest horribly, and her throat was so raw she wept for the pain of it and tried not to swallow. She was horribly thirsty, but icicles and snow did nothing but increase the thirst. She wondered if she'd been the one that had died, and this was her punishment in the afterlife. If so, she couldn't imagine what it had been that she'd done that warranted anything *this* bad.

When she got to Flower Street, she couldn't bear to go around the back; she staggered to the front door instead. Amber would forgive her this once. She could clean up the snow later, or something, to make up for it. All she wanted was her bed, and something hot to drink . . . her head hurt, her body hurt, everything hurt.

She shoved open the front door, too frozen to think, and managed to get it slammed shut behind her.

She turned in the sudden silence and shelter from the wind to find herself the center of attention—and there wasn't a client in the place. All of the ladies were downstairs, gathered in the common room, around the fire, wearing casual lounging robes in their signature colors. And all seven sets of eyes—Amber's included—were riveted to her, in shocked surprise.

That was when the heat hit her, and she fainted dead away.

She came to immediately, but by then she was shivering despite the heat; her teeth chattering so hard she couldn't speak. She was flat on her back, in a kind of crumpled, twisted pile of melting snow and heavy cloak. Sapphire and Amber leaned over her, trying to get her cloak off, trying to pry her hands open so they could get her unwrapped from the half-frozen mass of snow-caked wool. Amber's hand brushed against her forehead, as Rune tried to get enough breath to say something—and the woman exclaimed in surprise.

"I-I-I'm s-s-s-sorry," Rune babbled, around her chattering teeth. "I-I-I'm j-j-just c-c-c-cold, that's all." She tried to sit up, but the room began to spin.

"Cold!" Amber said in surprise. "Cold? Child, you're burning up! You must have a fever—" She gestured at someone just out of sight, and Topaz slid into view. "Topaz, you're stronger than any of the boys, can you lift her and get her into bed?"

The strange, slit-pupiled eyes did not even blink. "Of course," Topaz replied gravely. "I should be glad to. Just get her out of the cloak, please? I cannot bear the touch of the snow."

"I'm all r-r-r-right, really," she protested. "Th-th-this is s-s-silly—"

Rune had forgotten the cloak; she let go of the edges and slid her arms out of it. Sapphire pulled it away, and before Rune could try again to get to a sitting position, Topaz had scooped her up as easily as if she weighed no more than a pillow, and was carrying her towards the stairs.

I didn't know she was so strong, Rune thought dazedly. *She must be stronger than most men. Or—maybe I've just gotten really light—* She felt that way, as if she would flutter off like a leaf on the slightest wind.

"No—" Amber forestalled her, as Topaz started for the staircase. "No, I don't think her room is going to be warm enough, and besides, I don't want her alone. We'll put her on the couch in my rooms."

"Ah," was all that Topaz said; Amber led the way into her office, then did—something—with the wall, or an ornament on the wall. Whatever, a panel in the wall opened, and Topaz carried her into a small parlor, like Rose had in the private quarters back at the Hungry Bear. But this was nothing like Rose's parlor—it was lit with many lanterns, the air was sweet with the smell of dried herbs, the honey-scent of beeswax, and a faint hint of incense.

But that was when things stopped making sense, for Topaz turned into Boony, and the couch she was put on was on the top of Skull Hill, and she was going to have to play for the Ghost, only Tonno was in the Ghost's robes—she tried to explain that she'd done her best to help him, but he only glared at her and motioned for her to play. She picked up her fiddle and tried to play for him, but her fingers wouldn't work, and she started to cry; the wind blew leaves into her face so she couldn't see, and she couldn't hear, either—

And she was so very, very cold.

She began to cry, and couldn't stop.

Someone was singing, very near at hand. She opened gritty, sore eyes in an aching head to see who it was, for the song was so strange, less like a song than a chant, and yet it held elements of both. It was nothing she recognized, and yet she thought she heard something familiar in the wailing cadences.

There was a tall, strong-looking old woman sitting beside her, a woman wearing what could only be a Gypsy costume, but far more elaborate than anything Rune had ever seen the Gypsies wear. Besides her voluminous, multicolored skirts and bright blouse, the woman had a shawl embroidered with figures that seemed to move and dance every time she breathed, and a vast set of necklaces loaded with charms carved of every conceivable substance. They all seemed to represent animals and birds; Rune saw mother-of-pearl sparrows, obsidian bears, carnelian fish, turquoise foxes, all strung on row after row of tiny shell beads. The woman looked down at her and nodded, but did not stop her chanting for a moment.

Everything hurt; head, joints, throat—she was alternately freezing and burning. She closed her eyes to rest them, and opened them again when she felt a cold hand on her forehead. Amber was looking down at her with an expression of deep concern on her face. She tried to say something, but she couldn't get her mouth to work, and the mere effort was exhausting. She closed her eyes again.

She felt herself floating, away from the pain, and she let it happen. When her aching body was just a distant memory, she opened her eyes, to find that she was somewhere up above her body, looking down at it.

Amber was gone, but the strange Gypsy woman was back again, sitting in the corner, chanting quietly. Rune realized then that she *felt* the chanting; the song wove a kind of net about her that kept her from floating off somewhere. As she watched, with an oddly dispassionate detachment, Pearl and Diamond entered the room; Pearl carrying a large bowl of something that steamed which she set down on the hearth, Diamond with a tray of food she set down beside the Gypsy.

Diamond kept glancing at the Gypsy out of the corner of her eye. "That's not one of the Guild Herb-women," she said finally to Pearl, as she moved a little away.

"No," Pearl confirmed. "No, this is someone Amber knows. How?"

Pearl shrugged expressively. "Amber has many friends. Often strange. Look at us!"

Diamond didn't echo Pearl's little chuckle. "Ruby says she's elf-touched," the young woman said with a shiver. "Ruby says she's a witch, and elf-touched."

Pearl shook her head. "She may be, for all I know. The Gypsies, the musicians, they know many strange creatures."

"Not like this," Diamond objected. "Not elf-touched! That's perilous close to heresy where I come from." She shuddered. "Have you ever seen what the Church does to heretics, and those who shelter them? I have. And I don't ever want to see it again."

Pearl cocked her head to one side, as if amused by Diamond's fear. "We—my people—we have old women and old men like her; they serve the villages in many ways, as healers of the sick, as speakers-to-the-Others, and as magicians to keep away the dark things that swim to the surface of the sea at the full moon. She deserves respect, I would say, but not fear."

"If you say so," Diamond said dubiously. "Is she—I mean, is Rune—" She cast a glance at the couch where Rune lay wrapped in a cocoon of blankets, her face as pale as the snow outside, with the same fever-spots of bright red that Tonno had on his cheeks.

"Yes," Pearl replied with absolute certainty. "She has told Amber that the girl will live, and if she makes such a pledge, she will keep it. Such as she is cannot lie—"

Rune would have liked to listen to more—in fact, she would have liked to see if she couldn't float off into another room and see what was going on there—but at that moment the old woman seemed to notice that she was up there. The tone of her chant took on a new sharpness, and the words changed, and Rune found herself being pulled back down into the body on the couch. She tried resisting, but it was no use.

Once back in her body, all she could think of was Tonno, and once again she began crying, feebly, for all the things she had not done.

Her head hurt, horribly, and her joints still ached, but she wasn't so awfully cold, and she didn't feel as if she was floating around anymore. She felt very solidly anchored inside her body, actually. She opened her eyes experimentally.

Maddie was sitting in the chair where the old woman had been sitting, working on her mending. Rune coughed; Maddie looked up, and grinned when she saw that Rune was awake.

"Well! Are you back with us again?" the girl said cheerfully.

Rune tested her throat, found it still sore, and just nodded.

"Hang on a moment," Maddie told her, and put her mending away. She went over to the hearth, where there was a kettle on the hob beside the steaming bowl of herbs—herbs that smelled very like the ones Brother Anders had used for Tonno. That—it seemed as if it had happened years ago—

Something had happened to her grief while she slept. It was still with her, but no longer so sharp.

Maddie picked up the kettle and poured a mug of something, bringing it over to the couch. Rune managed to free an arm from her wrappings to take it. Her hand shook, and the mug felt as if it weighed a thousand pounds, but she managed to drink the contents without spilling much.

It was some kind of herb tea, heavily dosed with honey, and it eased the soreness in her throat wonderfully.

"What happened?" she said, grateful beyond words to hear her voice come out as a whispered version of her own, and not a fever-scorched croak.

"Well," Maddie said, sitting herself down in the chair again. "You made a very dramatic entrance, that's for certain. Nighthawk said that she thinks you got pneumonia—Nighthawk's the Gypsy-witch Amber knows that treats us all for things the Guild Herb-women can't. Anyway, Nighthawk says you got pneumonia, but that your voice is going to be all right, so don't worry. It's just that you're going to be all winter recovering, so don't think you can go jumping out of bed to sing."

"Oh," Rune said vaguely. "What—what am I doing here?" She gestured at Amber's neat little parlor, in which she was the only discordant note.

"Amber says you're staying here where we can all keep an eye on you until you stop having fevers," Maddie said fiercely—and something in her voice told Rune that her recovery hadn't been nearly as matter-of-fact as Maddie made it out to be. "Then you can go back to your room, but you're going to stay in bed most of the time until spring. That's orders from Amber."

"But—" Rune began.

"That's orders from *Amber*," Maddie repeated. And the tone of her voice said that it was no use protesting or arguing. "And she says you're not to worry about what all this is costing. Or about the fact that you're not playing in the common room for your keep. You've been part of Amber's for more than a year, and Amber takes care of her people."

Rune nodded, meekly, but when Maddie finally left, she lay back among her pillows and tried to figure out exactly *why* Amber was doing all this for her. It wasn't as if this was the same set of circumstances as when she'd nursed Tonno—

—or was it?

She fell asleep trying to puzzle it all out, without much success.

She dreamed of Jib; dreamed of the Hungry Bear. Like her, he was two years older—but unlike her, he was still doing exactly the same things as he'd been two years ago. Still playing stable-hand and general dogsbody. His life hadn't altered in the slightest from when she'd left, and she was struck with the gloomy certainty that it never would, unless fate took an unexpected hand.

She woke again to near-darkness; the only light was from the banked fire. There was another full mug on a little table beside her, this time with doctored apple cider in it. She sipped it and stared into the coals for a long time, wondering how much of her dream was reality and how much was her fever-dreams.

What was going to happen to Jib? He'd been her friend, her only friend, and she'd run off without even a good-bye. She hadn't ever worried about what was going to happen to him with her gone. Was he all right? Had the bullies found something better to do, or were they still making his life a torment?

Was he satisfied? How *could* he be? How could anyone be satisfied in the position he held? It was all right for a boy, but no job for a man. But unless something changed for him, that was what he'd be all his life. Someone's flunky.

Now she remembered what he'd wanted to do, back in the long-ago days when they'd traded dreams. He'd wanted to be a horse-trader; a modest enough ambition, and one he could probably do well at if he stuck to the kind of horses he had experience with. Farm-stock, donkeys, rough cobs—sturdy beasts, not highly bred, but what farmers and simple traders needed. Jib knew beasts like that; could tell a good one from a bad one, a bargain from a doctored beast that was about to break down.

She tried to tell herself that what happened to him wasn't her responsibility, but if that was true, then it was also true that what happened to *her* was not Amber's responsibility. Yet Amber was caring for her.

Jib was old enough to take care of himself.

Well, that was true—but Jib had no way to get himself out of the rut he was in. He had no talent at all, except that of working well with animals. If he went somewhere else, he'd only be doing the same work in a different place. Would that be better or not? And would he even think of doing so? She knew from her own experience how hard it was to break ties and go, when things where you were at the moment were only uncomfortable, not unbearable. It was easy to tell yourself that they'd get better, eventually.

She fell asleep again, feeling vaguely bothered by yet more guilt. If only there was something she could have done to help him. . . .

Weak, early-spring sunshine reflected off the wall of the House across from her window, and she had the window open a crack just for the sake of the fresh air. She'd been allowed out of bed, finally, two weeks ago; she still spent a lot of time in her room, reading. Even a simple trip down to the common room tended to make her legs wobbly. But she persisted; whether she was ready or not, she would have to make Midsummer Faire this year, and the trials. For her own sake, and for the sake of Tonno's memory.

If only she didn't owe Amber so much. . . . Her indebtedness troubled her, as it did not seem to trouble Amber. But at the least, before she left, Rune had determined to walk the length and breadth of Nolton, listening to buskers and talking to them, to find Amber a replacement musician for the common room. That wouldn't cancel the debt, but it would ease it, a little.

"Rune?" Maddie tapped on the half-open door to her room; Rune looked up from the book she was reading. It was one of Tonno's, but she'd never seen fit to inform the Church that she had it, and no one had ever come asking after it. She had a number of books here that had been Tonno's, and she wasn't going to give them back until someone came for them. She reasoned that she could always use her illness as an excuse to cover why she had never done so.

She smiled at Maddie, who returned it a little nervously. "There's a visitor below," she said, and the tone of her voice made Rune sit up a little straighter. "It's a Priest. He wants to see you. He was with Amber for a while and she said it was all right for him to talk to you—but if you don't want to, Rune—"

She sighed, exasperated. "Oh, it's probably just about the books I have from the shop. The greedy pigs probably want them back." She tugged at her hair and brushed down her shabby breeches and shirt. "Do I look like a boy, or a girl?"

Maddie put her head to one side and considered. "More like a girl, actually."

"Damn. Oh well, it can't be helped. You might as well bring him up." She gritted her teeth together. He *would* show up now, when she was just getting strong enough to enjoy reading.

Maddie vanished, and a few moments later, heavy footsteps following her light ones up the kitchen stairs heralded the arrival of her visitor.

Rune came very near to chuckling at the disgruntled look on the Priest's face. Bad enough to have to come to a brothel to collect part of an estate—*worse* that he was taken up the back stairs to do so, like a servant.

That's one for you, Tonno, she thought, keeping the smile off her lips somehow. *A small one, but there it is.*

"Are you Rune of Westhaven?" the balding, thin Priest asked crossly. He was another sort like Brother Pell, but *he* didn't even have the Brother's love of music to leaven his bitterness. Rune nodded. She waited for him to demand the books; she was going to make him find them all, pick them up, and carry them out himself. Hopefully, down the back stairs again.

But his next words were a complete shock.

"Tonno Alendor left a will, filed as was proper, with the Church, and appointing Brother Bryan as executor of the estate," the Priest continued, as if every word hurt him. "In it, everything except the tithe of death-duties and death-taxes was left to you. The shop, the contents, everything."

He glared at her, as if he wanted badly to know what she had done to "make" the old man name her as his heir. For her part, she just stared at him, gaping in surprise, unable to speak. Finally the Priest continued in an aggrieved tone.

"Brother Bryan has found a buyer for the shop and contents, with the sole exception being a few books that Tonno mentions specifically that he wanted you to keep. Here's the list—"

He handed it to her with the tips of his fingers, as if touching her or it might somehow contaminate him. She took it, hands shaking as she opened it. As she had expected, they were all the books Tonno had insisted she keep here, at her room.

"If you have no objections," the Priest finished, his teeth gritted, "Brother Bryan will complete the purchase. The Church will receive ten percent as death-tithe. He, as executor, will receive another ten percent. City death-taxes are a remaining ten percent. You will receive the bulk of the moneys from the sale. It won't be much," he finished, taking an acid delight in imparting *that* bad news. "The shop is in a bad location, and the contents are a jumble of used merchandise, mostly curiosities, and hard to dispose of. But Brother Bryan will have your moneys delivered here at the conclusion of the sale, and take care of the death-duties himself. Unless you have something else from the shop you would like to keep as a memorial-piece." Again he pursed his lips sourly. "The value of that piece, will, of course, be pro-rated against your share."

She thought quickly, then shook her head. There was nothing *there* that she wanted. Everything in the shop would be forever tainted with the horrid memories of Tonno's sickness and unnecessary death. Let someone else take it, someone for whom the place would have no such memories. Not even the instruments would be of any use; she could only play fiddle and lute, and Tonno had sold the last of those months ago, during the height of summer.

The Priest took himself out, leaving her still dazed.

She didn't know what to think. How much money *was* "not very much"? Assuming that Brother Bryan only got a fraction of what the contents of the shop were worth—and she did not doubt that he would drive a very hard bargain indeed, both for her sake, and the Church's—that was still more money than she had ever had in her life. What was she to do with it? It beggared the pouch full of silver she'd gotten from the Ghost. . . .

She fell asleep, still trying to comprehend it.

This time, her dreams about Jib were troubled. He was plainly unhappy; scorned by the villagers, abused by Stara, ordered about by everyone. And yet, he had nowhere to go. He had no money saved, no prospects—

The village toughs still bullied him, and without Rune to protect him, he often sported bruises or a black eye. They laughed at him for being a coward, but what was he to do? If he fought them, they'd only hurt him further or complain that he had picked the fight, not they. They never came at him by ones or twos, only in a gang.

He'd had an offer from a horse-trader a month ago, an honest man who had been stopping at the Bear for as long as Jib could recall—if he had some money, the man would let him buy into the string and learn the business, eventually to take it over when the trader settled down to breeding. *That* was the answer to his prayers—but he had no money. The trader would keep the offer open as long as he could, but how long would he wait? A year? More? No matter how long he waited, Jib would still never have it. He got no pay; he'd *get* no pay for as long as Stara was holding the purse-strings. If he went elsewhere, he might earn pay in addition to his keep, but only if he could produce a good reference, and Stara would never let Jeoff give him one if he left.

He worked his endless round of chores with despair his constant companion. . . .

Rune woke with a start. And she knew at that moment exactly what she was going to do.

The days were warm now, and so were the nights—warm enough to sleep out, at any rate. Now was the time to leave; she'd be at the Faire when it opened if she left now.

But leaving meant good-byes. . . .

She hugged everyone, from Ruby to the new little kitchen-boy, with a lump in her throat. She'd been happier here than anyplace else in her life. If Tonno were still alive, she might have put this off another year.

Not now. It was go now, or give up the dream. Tonno's memory wouldn't let her do that.

"We're sorry to see you leave, Rune," Amber said with real regret, when Rune hugged her good-bye, her balance a little off from the unaccustomed weight of her packs. "But Tonno and I always knew this place wouldn't hold you longer than a year or two. We're glad you stayed this long."

Rune sighed. "I'm sorry too," she confessed. "But—I can't help it, Amber. This is something I *have* to do. At least I found you a replacement for me."

"And a good one," Diamond said, with a wink. "She'll do just fine. She's already giving Carly hives."

"*She* doesn't want to do anything else but work as a street-busker, so you'll have her for as long as you want her," Rune continued. "I was very careful about that."

"I know you were, dear," Amber said, and looked at the pouch of coin in her hand. "I wish you'd take this back. . . ."

Rune shook her head stubbornly. "Save it, if you won't use it. Save it for an emergency, or use it for bribes; it's not a lot, but it ought to keep the lower-level Church clerks happy. I know that's what Tonno would like, and it'd be a good way to honor his memory."

Half of the money she'd gotten from the sale of the shop she'd given to Amber, to repay her for all the expense she'd gone to in nursing Rune back to health. A quarter of it had been sent to Jib, via the Gypsies, with a verbal message—"Follow *your* dream." There were things the Gypsies were impeccably honest about, and one of them was in keeping pledges. They'd vowed on their mysterious gods to take the money to Jib without touching a penny. Once it had gone, she'd ceased to have nightmares about him.

The remaining quarter, minus the Gypsies' delivery-fee, and the things she'd needed for the trip, ought to be just enough to get her to the Midsummer Faire and the trials for the Bardic Guild. She had a new set of faded finery, a new pack full of books, and the strength that had taken so long to regain was finally back. She was ready.

Amber kissed her; the way a fond mother would. "You'd better go now, before I disgrace myself and cry," the Madam ordered sternly. "Imagine! Amber, in tears, on the steps of her own brothel—and over a silly little fiddler-girl!" She smiled brightly, but Rune saw the teardrops trembling at the corners of her eyes and threatening to spill over.

To prevent that, she started another round of hugs and kisses that included all of them. Except Carly, who was nowhere to be seen.

Probably telling the Church that I'm running away with my ill-gotten gains.

"Well, that's it," she said at last, as nonchalantly as if she was about to cross the town, not the country. "I'm off. Wish me luck!"

She turned and headed off down the street for the east gate, turning again to walk backwards and wave good-bye.

She thought she saw Amber surreptitiously wipe her eyes on the corner of her sleeve, before returning the wave brightly. Her own throat knotted up, and to cover it, she waved harder, until she was forced to round a corner that put them all out of sight.

Then she squared her shoulders beneath her pack, and started on her journey; destination, the Midsummer Faire.

And Tonno, she thought, as she passed below the gates and took to the road. *This one's for you, too. Always for you.*

CHAPTER THIRTEEN

All the world comes to the Midsummer Faire at Kingsford.

That's what they said, anyway—and it certainly seemed that way to Rune, as she traveled the final leg down from Nolton, the Trade Road that ran from the Holiforth Pass to Traen, and from there to Kingsford and the Faire Field across the Kanar River from the town. She wasn't walking on the dusty, hard-packed road itself; she'd likely have been trampled by the press of beasts, then run over by the carts into the bargain. Instead, she walked with the rest of the foot-travelers on the road's verge. It was no less dusty, what grass there had been had long since been trampled into powder by all the feet of the fairgoers, but at least a traveler was able to move along without risk of acquiring hoofprints on his anatomy.

Rune was close enough now to see the gates of the Faire set into the wooden palisade that surrounded it, and the guard beside them. This seemed like a good moment to separate herself from the rest of the throng, rest her tired feet, and plan her next moves before entering the grounds of the Faire.

She elbowed her way out of the line of people, some of whom complained and elbowed back, and moved away from the road to a little hillock under a forlorn sapling, where she had a good view of the Faire, a scrap of shade, and a rock to sit on. The sun beat down with enough heat to warm the top of her head through her soft leather hat. She plopped herself down on the rock and began massaging her tired feet while she looked the Faire over.

It was a bit overwhelming. Certainly it was much bigger than she'd imagined it would be. Nolton had been a shock; this was a bigger one. It was equally certain that there would be nothing dispensed for free behind those log palings, and the few coppers Rune had left would have to serve to feed her through the three days of trials for admission to the Bardic Guild. After that—

Well, after that, she should be an apprentice, and food and shelter would be for the Guild and her master to worry about. Or else, if she somehow failed—

She refused to admit the possibility of failing the trials. She couldn't— not after getting this far.

Tonno would never forgive me.

But for now, she needed somewhere to get herself cleaned of the road dust, and a place to sleep, both with no price tags attached. Right now, she was the same gray-brown as the road from head to toe, the darker brown of her hair completely camouflaged by the dust, or at least it felt that way. Even her eyes felt dusty.

She strolled down to the river, her lute thumping her hip softly on one side, her pack doing the same on the other. There were docks on both sides of the river; on this side, for the Faire, on the other, for Kingsford. Close to the docks the water was muddy and roiled; there was too much traffic on the river to make an undisturbed bath a viable possibility, and too many wharf-rats about to make leaving one's belongings unattended a wise move. She backtracked upstream a bit, while the noise of the Faire faded behind her. She crossed over a small stream that fed into the river, and penetrated into land that seemed unclaimed. It was probably Church land, since the Faire was held on Church property; she'd often seen Church land left to go back to wilderness if it was hard to farm. Since the Church owned the docks, and probably owned all fishing rights to this section of river, they weren't likely to permit any competition.

The bank of the river was wilder here, and overgrown, not like the carefully tended area by the Faire docks. Well, that would discourage fairegoers from augmenting their supplies with a little fishing from the bank, especially if they were townsfolk, afraid of bears and snakes under every bush. She pushed her way into the tangle and found a game-trail that ran along the riverbank, looking for a likely spot. Finally she found a place where the river had cut a tiny cove into the bank. It was secluded; trees overhung the water, their branches making a good thick screen that touched the water, the ground beneath them bare of growth, and hollows between some of the roots were just big enough to cradle her sleeping roll. Camp, bath, and clear water, all together, and within climbing distance on one of the trees she discovered a hollow big enough to hide her bedroll and those belongings she didn't want to carry into the Faire.

She waited until dusk fell before venturing into the river, and kept her eyes and ears open while she scrubbed herself down. She probably wasn't the only country-bred person to think of this ploy, and ruffians preferred places where they could hide. Once clean, she debated whether or not to change into the special clothing she'd brought tonight; it might be better to save it—then the thought of donning the sweat-soaked, dusty traveling gear became too distasteful, and she rejected it out of hand.

I've got shirts and under-things for three days. That'll do.

She felt strange, and altogether different once she'd put the new costume on. Part of that was due to the materials—except for when she'd tried the clothing on for fit, this was the first time in her life she'd ever worn silk and velvet. Granted, the materials were all old; bought from a second-hand vendor back in Nolton and cut down from much larger men's garments by Maddie. She'd had plenty of time on the road to sew them up. The velvet of the breeches wasn't *too* rubbed; the ribbons on the sleeves of the shirt and the embroidered trim she'd made when she was sick should cover the faded and frayed places, and the vest should cover the stains on the back panels of each shirt completely. That had been clever of Maddie; to reverse the shirts so that the wine-stained fronts became the backs. Her hat, once the dust was beaten out of it and the plumes she'd snatched from the tails of several disgruntled roosters along the way were tucked into the band, looked both brave and professional enough. Her boots, at least, were new, and when the dust was brushed from them, looked quite respectable. She tucked her remaining changes of clothing and her bedroll into her pack, hid the lot in the tree-hollow, and felt ready to face the Faire.

The guard at the gate, a Church cleric, of course, eyed her carefully. "Minstrel?" he asked suspiciously, looking at the lute and fiddle she carried in their cases, slung from her shoulders. "You'll need a permit to busk, if you plan to stay more than three days."

She shook her head. "Here for the trials, m'lord. Not planning on busking."

Which was the truth. She wasn't *planning* on busking. If something came up, or she was practicing and people chose to pay her—well, that wasn't planned, was it?

"Ah." He appeared satisfied. "You come in good time, boy. The trials begin tomorrow. The Guild has its tent pitched hard by the main gate of the Cathedral; you should have no trouble finding it."

She thanked him, but he had already turned his attention to the next in line. She passed inside the log walls and entered the Faire itself.

The first impressions she had were of noise and light; torches burned all along the aisle she traversed; the booths to either side were lit by lanterns, candles, or other, more expensive methods, like perfumed oil-lamps. The crowd was noisy; so were the merchants. Even by torchlight it was plain that these were the booths featuring shoddier goods; second-hand finery, brass jewelry, flash and tinsel. The entertainers here were— surprising. She averted her eyes from a set of dancers. It wasn't so much that they wore little but imagination, but the *way* they were dancing embarrassed even her; Amber had never permitted anything like *this* in her House. And the fellow with the dancers back at the Westhaven Faire hadn't had his girls doing anything like this, either.

Truth to tell, they tended to move as little as possible.

She kept a tight grip on her pouch and instruments, tried to ignore the crush, and let the flow of fairgoers carry her along.

Eventually the crowd thinned out a bit (though not before she'd felt a ghostly hand or two try for her pouch and give it up as a bad cause). She followed her nose then, looking for the row that held the cook-shop tents and the ale-sellers. She hadn't eaten since this morning, and her stomach was lying in uncomfortably close proximity to her spine.

She learned that the merchants of tavern-row were shrewd judges of clothing; hers wasn't fine enough to be offered a free taste, but she wasn't wearing garments poor enough that they felt she needed to be shooed away. Sternly admonishing her stomach to be less impatient, she strolled the length of the row twice, carefully comparing prices and quantities, before settling on a humble tent that offered meat pasties (best not ask what beast the meat came from, not at these prices) and fruit juice or milk as well as ale and wine. Best of all, it offered seating at rough trestle-tables as well. Her feet were complaining as much as her stomach.

Rune took her flaky pastry and her mug of juice and found a spot at any empty table where she could eat and watch the crowds passing by. No wine or ale for her; not even had she the coppers to spare for it. She dared not be the least muddle-headed, not with a secret to keep and the first round of competition in the morning. The pie was more crust than meat, but it was filling and well-made and fresh; that counted for a great deal.

She watched the other customers, and noted with amusement that there were two sorts of the clumsy, crude clay mugs. One sort, the kind they served the milk and juice in, was ugly and shapeless, too ugly to be worth stealing but was just as capacious as the exterior promised. No doubt, that was because children were often more observant than adults gave them credit for—and very much inclined to set up a howl if something didn't meet implied expectations. The other sort of mug, for wine and ale, was just the same ugly shape and size on the *outside*, though a different shade of toad-back green, but had a far thicker bottom, effectively reducing the interior capacity by at least a third. Which a thirsty adult probably wouldn't notice.

"Come for the trials, lad?" asked a quiet voice in her ear.

Rune jumped, nearly knocking her mug over, and snatching at it just in time to save the contents from drenching her shopworn finery. And however would she have gotten it clean again in time for tomorrow's competition? There hadn't been a sound or a hint of movement, or even the shifting of the bench to warn her, but now there was a man sitting beside her.

He was of middle years, red hair just going to gray a little at the temples, smile-wrinkles around his mouth and gray-green eyes, with a candid, triangular face. Well, that said nothing; Rune had known high-waymen with equally friendly and open faces. His costume was similar to her own, though; leather breeches instead of velvet, good linen instead of worn silk, a vest and a leather hat that could have been twin to hers. But the telling marks were the knots of ribbon on the sleeves of his shirt— and the neck of a lute peeking over his shoulder. A minstrel!

Of the Guild? Could it be possible that here at the Faire there'd be Guild musicians working the "streets"? Rune rechecked the ribbons on his sleeves, and was disappointed. Blue and scarlet and green, not the purple and silver of a Guild Minstrel, nor the purple and gold of a Guild Bard. This was only a common busker, a mere street-player. Still, he'd bespoken her kindly enough, and God knew not everyone with the music-passion had the skill or the talent to pass the trials—

Look at Tonno. He'd never even gotten as far as busking.

"Aye, sir," she replied politely. "I've hopes to pass; I think I've the talent, and others have said as much."

Including the sour Brother Pell. When she'd told him good-bye and the reason for leaving, he'd not only wished her well, he'd actually cracked a smile, and said that of all his pupils, *she* was the one he'd have chosen to send to the trials.

The stranger's eyes measured her keenly, and she had the disquieting feeling that her boy-ruse was fooling *him* not at all. "Ah well," he replied, "There's a-many before you have thought the same, and failed."

"That may be—" She answered the challenge in his eyes, stung into revealing what she'd kept quiet until now. "But I'd bet a copper penny that none of *them* fiddled for a murdering ghost, and not only came out by the grace of their skill but were rewarded by that same spirit for amusing him!"

"Oh, so?" A lifted eyebrow was all the indication he gave of being impressed, but somehow that lifted brow conveyed volumes. And he believed her; she read that, too. "You've made a song of it, surely?"

Should I sing it now? Well, why not? After the next couple of days, it wouldn't be a secret anymore. "Have I not! It's to be my entry for the third day of testing."

"Well, then . . ." he said no more than that, but his wordless attitude of waiting compelled Rune to unsling her fiddle case, extract her instrument, and tune it without further prompting.

"It's the fiddle that's my first instrument," she said, feeling as if she must apologize for singing with a fiddle rather than her lute, since the lute was clearly his instrument. "And since 'twas the fiddle that made the tale—"

"Never apologize for a song, child," he admonished, interrupting her. "Let it speak out for itself. Now let's hear this ghost tale."

It wasn't easy to sing while fiddling, but Rune had managed the trick of it some time ago. She closed her eyes a half-moment, fixing in her mind the necessary changes she'd made to the lyrics—for unchanged, the song would have given her sex away—and began.

"I sit here on a rock, and curse my stupid, bragging tongue,
And curse the pride that would not let me back down from a boast
And wonder where my wits went, when I took that challenge up
And swore that I would go and fiddle for the Skull Hill Ghost!"

Oh, that was a damn fool move, Rune. And you knew it when you did it. But if you hadn't taken their bet, you wouldn't be here now.

"It's midnight, and there's not a sound up here upon Skull Hill
Then comes a wind that chills my blood and makes the leaves blow wild—"

Not a good word choice, but a change that had to be made—that was one of the giveaway verses.

"And rising up in front of me, a thing like shrouded Death.
A voice says, 'Give me reason why I shouldn't kill you, child.'"

The next verse described Rune's answer to the spirit, and the fiddle wailed of fear and determination and things that didn't rightly belong on Earth. Then came the description of that night-long, lightless ordeal she'd passed through, and the fiddle shook with the weariness she'd felt, playing the whole night long.

Then the tune rose with dawning triumph when the thing not only didn't kill her outright, but began to warm to the music she'd made. Now she had an audience of more than one, though she was only half aware of the fact.

"At last the dawnlight strikes my eyes; I stop, and see the sun
The light begins to chase away the dark and midnight cold—
And then the light strikes something more—I stare in dumb surprise—
For where the ghost had stood there is a heap of shining gold!"

The fiddle laughed at Death cheated, thumbed its nose at spirits, and chortled over the revelation that even the angry dead could be impressed and forced to reward courage and talent.

Rune stopped, and shook back brown locks dark with sweat, and looked about her in astonishment at the applauding patrons of the cook-tent. She was even more astonished when they began to toss coppers in her open fiddle case, and the cook-tent's owner brought her over a full pitcher of juice and a second pie.

"I'd'a brought ye wine, laddie, but Master Talaysen there says ye go to trials and mustna be a-muddled," she whispered as she hurried back to her counter.

But this hadn't been a performance—at least, not for more than one! "I hadn't meant—"

"Surely this isn't the first time you've played for your supper, child?" The minstrel's eyes were full of amused irony.

She flushed. "Well, no, but—"

"So take your well-earned reward and don't go arguing with folk who have a bit of copper to fling at you, and who recognize the Gift when they hear it. No mistake, youngling, you *have* the Gift. And sit and eat; you've more bones than flesh. A good tale, that."

She peeked at the contents of the case before she answered him. *Not a single pin in the lot. Folks certainly do fling money about at this Faire.*

"Well," Rune said, and blushed, "I did exaggerate a bit at the end. 'Twasn't gold, it was silver, but silver won't rhyme. And it was that silver that got me here—bought me my second instrument, paid for lessoning, kept me fed while I was learning. I'd be just another tavern-musician, otherwise—" She broke off, realizing who and what she was talking to.

"Like me, you are too polite to say?" The minstrel smiled, then the smile faded. "There are worse things, child, than to be a free musician. I don't think there's much doubt your Gift will get you past the trials—but you might not find the Guild to be all you think it to be."

Rune shook her head stubbornly, taking a moment to wonder why she'd told this stranger so much, and why she so badly wanted his good opinion. Maybe it was just that he reminded her of a much younger Tonno. Maybe it was simply needing the admiration of a fellow musician. "Only a Guild Minstrel would be able to earn a place in a noble's train. Only a Guild Bard would have the chance to sing for royalty. I'm sorry to contradict you, sir, but I've had my taste of wandering, singing my songs out only to know they'll be forgotten in the next drink, wondering where my next meal is coming from. I'll never get a secure life except through the Guild, and I'll never see my songs live beyond me without their patronage."

He sighed. "I hope you never regret your decision, child. But if you should—or if you need help, ever, here at the Faire or elsewhere—well, just ask around the Gypsies or the musicians for Talaysen. Or for Master Wren; some call me that as well. I'll stand your friend."

With those surprising words, he rose soundlessly, as gracefully as a bird in flight, and slipped out of the tent. Just before he passed out of sight among the press of people, he pulled his lute around to the front, and struck a chord. She managed to hear the first few notes of a love song, the words rising golden and glorious from his throat, before the crowd hid him from view and the babble of voices obscured the music.

She strolled the Faire a bit more; bought herself a sweet-cake, and watched the teaser-shows outside some of the show-tents. She wished she wasn't in boy-guise; there were many good-looking young men here, and not all of them were going about with young women. Having learned more than a bit about preventing pregnancy at Amber's, she'd spent a little of her convalescence in losing her virginity with young Shawm. The defloration was mutual, as it turned out; she'd reflected after she left that it might have been better with a more experienced lover, but at least they'd been equals in ignorance. Towards the end they'd gotten better at it; she had at least as much pleasure out of love-play as he did. They'd parted as they'd begun—friends. And she had the feeling that Maddie was going to be his next and more serious target.

Well, at least I got him broken in for her!

But it was too bad that she was in disguise. Even downright plain girls seemed to be having no trouble finding company, and if after a day or two it turned into more than company—

Never mind. If they work me as hard as I think they will in the Guild, I won't have any time for dalliance. So I might as well get used to celibacy again.

But as the tent-lined streets of the Faire seemed to hold more and more couples, she decided it was time to leave. She needed the sleep, anyway.

Everything was still where she'd left it. Praying for a dry night, she lined her chosen root-hollow with bracken, and settled in for the night.

Rune was waiting impatiently outside the Guild tent the next morning, long before there was anyone there to take her name for the trials. The tent itself was, as the Faire guard had said, hard to miss; purple in the main, with pennons and edgings of silver and gilt. Almost—*too* much; it bordered on the gaudy. She was joined shortly by three more striplings, one well-dressed and confident, two sweating and nervous. More trickled in as the sun rose higher, until there was a line of twenty or thirty waiting when the Guild Registrar, an old and sour-looking Church cleric, raised the tent-flap to let them file inside. He wasn't wearing Guild colors, but rather a robe of dusty gray linen; she was a little taken aback since she hadn't been aware of a connection between the Guild and the Church before, other than the fact that there were many Guild musicians and Bards who had taken vows.

Would they have ways to check back to Nolton, and to Amber's? Could they find out she was a girl before the trials were over?

Then she laughed at her own fears. Even if they had some magic that could cross leagues of country in a single day and bring that knowledge back, *why would they bother*? There was nothing important about her. She was just another boy at the trials. And even if she passed, she'd only be another apprentice.

The clerk took his time, sharpening his quill until Rune was ready to scream with impatience, before looking her up and down and asking her name.

"Rune of Westhaven, and lately of Nolton." She held to her vow of not claiming a sire-name. "Mother is Stara of Westhaven."

He noted it, without a comment. "Primary instrument?"

"Fiddle."

Scratch, scratch, of quill on parchment. "Secondary?"

"Lute."

He raised an eyebrow; the usual order was lute, primary; fiddle, secondary. For that matter, fiddle wasn't all that common even as a secondary instrument.

"And you will perform—?"

"First day, primary, 'Lament Of The Maiden Esme.' Second day, secondary, 'The Unkind Lover.' Third day, original, 'The Skull Hill Ghost.' " An awful title, but she could hardly use the *real* name of "Fiddler Girl." "Accompanied on primary, fiddle."

He was no longer even marginally interested in her. "Take your place."

She sat on the backless wooden bench, trying to keep herself calm. Before her was the raised wooden platform on which they would all perform; to either side of it were the backless benches like the one she warmed, for the aspirants to the Guild. The back of the tent made the third side of the platform, and the fourth faced the row of well-padded chairs for the Guild judges. Although she was first here, it was inevitable that they would let others have the preferred first few slots; there would be those with fathers already in the Guild, or those who had coins for bribes who would play first, so that *they* were free to enjoy the Faire for the rest of the day, without having to wait long enough for their nerves to get the better of them. Still, she shouldn't have to wait too long—rising with the dawn would give her that much of an edge, at least.

She got to play by midmorning. The "Lament" was perfect for fiddle, the words were simple and few, and the wailing melody gave her lots of scope for improvisation. The style the judges had chosen, "florid style," encouraged such improvisation. The row of Guild judges, solemn in their tunics or robes of purple, white silk shirts trimmed with gold or silver ribbon depending on whether they were Minstrels or Bards, were a formidable audience. Their faces were much alike; well-fed and very conscious of their own importance; you could see it in their eyes. As they sat below the platform and took unobtrusive notes, they seemed at least mildly impressed with her performance. Even more heartening, several of the boys yet to perform looked satisfyingly worried when she'd finished.

She packed up her fiddle and betook herself briskly out—to find herself a corner of the cathedral wall to lean against as her knees sagged when the excitement that had sustained her wore off.

I never used to react that badly to an audience.

Maybe she hadn't recovered from her sickness as completely as she'd thought. Or maybe it was just that she'd never had an audience this important before. It was several long moments before she could get her legs to bear her weight and her hands to stop shaking. It was then that she realized that she hadn't eaten since the night before—and that she was suddenly ravenous. Before she'd played, the very thought of food had been revolting.

The same cook-shop tent as before seemed like a reasonable proposition. She paid for her breakfast with some of the windfall-coppers of the night before; this morning the tent was crowded and she was lucky to get a scant corner of a bench to herself. She ate hurriedly and joined the strollers through the Faire.

Once or twice she thought she glimpsed the red hair of Talaysen, but if it really was the minstrel, he was gone by the time she reached the spot where she had thought he'd been. There were plenty of other street-buskers, though. She thought wistfully of the harvest of coin she'd reaped the night before as she noted that none of them seemed to be lacking for patronage. And no one was tossing pins into the hat, either. It was all copper coins—and occasionally, even a silver one. But now that she was a duly registered entrant in the trials, it would be going against custom, if not the rules, to set herself up among them. That much she'd picked up, waiting for her turn. An odd sort of custom, but there it was; better that she didn't stand out as the only one defying it.

So instead she strolled, and listened, and made mental notes for further songs. There were plenty of things she saw or overheard that brought snatches of rhyme to mind. By early evening her head was crammed full—and it was time to see how the Guild had ranked the aspirants of the morning.

The list was posted outside the closed tent-flaps, and Rune wasn't the only one interested in the outcome of the first day's trials. It took a bit of time to work her way in to look, but when she did—

By God's saints! There she was, "Rune of Westhaven," listed *third*. She all but floated back to her riverside tree-roost.

The second day of the trials was worse than the first; the aspirants performed in order, lowest ranking to highest. That meant that Rune had to spend most of the day sitting on the hard wooden bench, clutching the neck of her lute in nervous fingers, listening to contestant after contestant and sure that each one was *much* better on his secondary instrument than she was. She'd only had a year of training on it, after all. Still, the song she'd chosen was picked deliberately to play up her voice and de-emphasize her lute-strumming. It was going to be pretty difficult for any of these others to match her high contralto (a truly cunning imitation of a boy's soprano), since most of them had passed puberty.

At long last her turn came. She swallowed her nervousness as best she could, took the platform, and began.

Privately she thought it was a pretty ridiculous song. Why on Earth any man would put up with the things that lady did to him, and all for the sake of a "kiss on her cold, quiet hand," was beyond her. She'd parodied the song, and nothing she wrote matched the intrinsic silliness of the original. Still, she put all the acting ability she had into it, and was rewarded by a murmur of approval when she'd finished.

"That voice—I've seldom heard one so pure at that late an age!" she overheard as she packed up her instrument. "If he passes the third day— you don't suppose he'd agree to being gelded, do you? I can think of half a dozen courts that would pay red gold to have a voice like his in service."

She smothered a smile—imagine their surprise to discover that it would *not* be necessary to eunuch her to preserve her voice!

She played drum for the next, then lingered to hear the last of the entrants. And unable to resist, she waited outside for the posting of the results.

She nearly fainted to discover that she'd moved up to second place.

"I told you," said a familiar voice behind her. "But are you still sure you want to go through with this?"

She whirled, to find the minstrel Talaysen standing in her shadow, the sunset brightening his hair and the warm light on his face making him appear scarcely older than she.

"I'm sure," she replied firmly. "One of the judges said today that he could think of half a dozen courts that would pay red gold to have my voice."

He raised an eyebrow. "Bought and sold like so much mutton? Where's the living in that? Caged behind high stone walls and never let out of the sight of m'lord's guards, lest you take a notion to sell your services elsewhere? Is *that* the life you want to lead?"

"Trudging down roads in the pouring cold rain, frightened half to death that you'll take sickness and ruin your voice—maybe for good? Singing with your stomach growling so loud it drowns out the song? Watching some idiot with half your talent being clad in silk and velvet and eating at the high table, while you try and please some brutes of guardsmen in the kitchen in hopes of a few scraps and a corner by the fire?" she countered. "No, thank you. I'll take my chances with the Guild. Besides, where else would I be able to *learn*? I've got no more silver to spend on instruments or teaching."

Tonno, you did your best, but I've seen the Guild musicians. I heard Guild musicians in the Church, at practice, back in Nolton. I have to become that good. I have to, if I'm to honor your memory.

"There are those who would teach you for the love of it—" he said, and her face hardened as she thought of Tonno, how he had taught her to the best of his ability. She was trying to keep from showing her grief. He must have misinterpreted her expression, for he sighed. "Welladay, you've made up your mind. As you will, child," he replied, but his eyes were sad as he turned away and vanished into the crowd again.

Once again she sat the hard bench for most of the day, while those of lesser ranking performed. This time it was a little easier to bear; it was obvious from a great many of these performances that few, if any, of the boys had the Gift to create. By the time it was Rune's turn to perform, she judged that, counting herself and the first-place holder, there could only be five real contestants for the three open Bardic apprentice slots. The rest would be suitable only as Minstrels; singing someone else's songs, unable to compose their own.

She took her place before the critical eyes of the judges, and began.

She realized with a surge of panic as she finished the first verse that they did *not* approve. While she improvised some fiddle bridges, she mentally reviewed the verse, trying to determine what it was that had set those slight frowns on the judicial faces.

Then she realized; she had said she had been *boasting*. Guild Bards simply did not admit to being boastful. Nor did they demean themselves by reacting to the taunts of lesser beings. Oh, God in heaven—

Quickly she improvised a verse on the folly of youth; of how, had she been older and wiser, she'd never have gotten herself into such a predicament. She heaved an invisible sigh of relief as the frowns disappeared.

By the last chorus, they were actually nodding and smiling, and one of them was tapping a finger in time to the tune. She finished with a flourish worthy of a Master, and waited, breathlessly.

And they *applauded*. Dropped their dignity and *applauded*.

The performance of the final contestant was an anticlimax.

None of them had left the tent since this last trial began. Instead of a list, the final results would be announced, and they waited in breathless anticipation to hear what they would be. Several of the boys had already approached Rune, offering smiling congratulations on her presumed first-place slot. A hush fell over them all as the chief of the judges took the platform, a list in his hand.

"First place, and first apprenticeship as Bard—Rune, son of Stara of Westhaven—"

"Pardon, my lord—" Rune called out clearly, bubbling over with happiness and unable to hold back the secret any longer. "But it's not son— it's *daughter*."

She had only a split second to take in the rage on their faces before the first staff descended on her head.

They flung her into the dust outside the tent, half-senseless, and her smashed instruments beside her. The passersby avoided even looking at her as she tried to get to her feet and fell three times. Her right arm dangled uselessly; it hurt so badly that she was certain that it must be broken, but it hadn't hurt half as badly when they'd cracked it as it had when they'd smashed her fiddle; that had broken her heart. All she wanted to do now was to get to the river and throw herself in. With any luck at all, she'd drown.

But she couldn't even manage to stand.

"Gently, lass," someone said, touching her good arm. She looked around, but her vision was full of stars and graying out on the edges. Strong hands reached under her shoulders and supported her on both sides. The voice sounded familiar, but she was too dazed to think who it was. "God be my witness, if ever I thought they'd have gone this far, I'd never have let you go through with this farce."

She turned her head as they got her standing, trying to see through tears of pain, both of heart and body, with eyes that had sparks dancing before them. The man supporting her on her left she didn't recognize, but the one on the right—

"T-Talaysen?" she faltered.

"I told you I'd help if you needed it, did I not?" He smiled, but there was no humor in it. "I think you have more than a little need at the moment—"

She couldn't help herself; she wept, like a little child, hopelessly. The fiddle, the gift of Rose—and the lute, picked out by Tonno—both gone forever. "Th-they broke my fiddle, Talaysen. And my lute. They broke them, then they beat me, and they broke my arm—"

"Oh, Rune, lass—" There were tears in *his* eyes, and yet he almost seemed to be laughing as well. "If *ever* I doubted you'd the makings of a Bard, you just dispelled those doubts. *First* the fiddle, *then* the lute—and only *then* do you think of your own hurts. Ah, come away lass, come where people can care for such a treasure as you—"

Stumbling through darkness, wracked with pain, carefully supported and guided on either side, Rune was in no position to judge where or how far they went. After some unknown interval however, she found herself in a many-colored tent, lit with dozens of lanterns, partitioned off with curtains hung on wires that criss-crossed the entire dwelling. Just now most of these were pushed back, and a mixed crowd of men and women greeted their entrance with cries of welcome that turned to dismay at the sight of her condition.

She was pushed down into an improvised bed of soft wool blankets and huge, fat pillows. A thin, dark girl dressed like a Gypsy bathed her cuts and bruises with something that stung, then numbed them, and a gray-bearded man tsk'd over her arm, prodded it once or twice, then, without warning, pulled it into alignment. When he did that, the pain was so incredible that Rune nearly fainted.

By the time the multicolored fire-flashing cleared from her eyes, he was binding her arm up tightly with bandages and thin strips of wood, while the girl was urging her to drink something that smelled of herbs and wine.

Where am I? Who are these people? What do they want?

Before she had a chance to panic, Talaysen reappeared as if conjured at her side.

"Where—"

He understood immediately what she was asking. "You're with the Free Bards—the *real* Bards, not those pompous puff-toads of the Guild," he said. "Dear child, I thought that all that would happen to you was that those inflated bladders of self-importance would give you a tongue-lashing and throw you out on your backside. If I'd had the slightest notion that they'd do *this* to you, I'd have kidnapped you away and had you drunk insensible 'till the trials were over. I may never forgive myself. Now, drink your medicine."

"But how—why—who *are* you?" Rune managed between gulps.

"'What are you?' I think might be the better place to start. Tell her, will you, Erdric?"

"We're the Free Bards," said the gray-bearded man, "as Master Talaysen told you. He's the one who banded us together, when he found that there were those who, like himself, had the Gift and the Talent but were disinclined to put up with the self-aggrandizement and politics and foolish slavishness to form that the Guild requires. We go where we wish and serve—or not serve—who we will, and sing as we damn well please and no foolishness about who'll be offended. We also keep a sharp eye out for youngsters like you, with the Gift, and with the spirit to fight the Guild. We've had our eye on you these—oh, it must be near a half-dozen years, now."

Six years? All this time, and I never knew? "You—but how? Who was watching me?"

"Myself, for one," said a new voice, and a bony fellow with hair that kept falling into his eyes joined the group around her. "You likely don't remember me, but I remember you—I heard you fiddle in your tavern when I was passing through Westhaven, and I passed the word."

"And I'm another." This one, standing near the back of the group, Rune recognized; she was the harpist with the Gypsies, the one called Nightingale. "Another of my people, the man you knew as Raven, was sent to be your main teacher until you were ready for another. We knew you'd find another good teacher for yourself, then, if you were a true musician."

"You see, we keep an eye out for all the likely lads and lasses we've marked, knowing that soon or late, they'd come to the trials. Usually, though, they're not so stubborn as you," Talaysen said, and smiled.

"I should hope to live!" the lanky fellow agreed. "They made the same remark my first day about wanting to have me stay a liltin' soprano the rest of me days. That was enough for me!"

"And they wouldn't even give *me* the same notice they'd have given a flea," the dark girl laughed. "Though I hadn't the wit to think of passing myself off as a boy for the trials."

"That was my teacher's idea," Rune admitted.

"It might even have worked," Talaysen told her, "if they weren't so fanatic about women. It's part of Guild teachings that women are lower than men, and can *never* have the true Gift of the Bards. You not only passed, you beat every other boy there. They couldn't have that. It went counter to all they stand for. If they admitted you could win, they'd have to admit that many other things they teach are untrue." He grinned. "Which they are, of course. That's why *we're* here."

"But—why are you—together?" Rune asked, bewildered. She was used to competition among musicians, not cooperation.

"For the same reason as the Guilds were formed in the first place. We band together to give each other help; a spot of silver to tide you over an empty month, a place to go when you're hurt or ill, someone to care for you when you're not as young as you used to be," the gray-haired man called Erdric said.

Nightingale spoke up from the rear. "To teach, and to learn as well. And we have more and better patronage than you, or even the Guild, suspects."

A big bear of a man laughed. "Not everyone finds the precious style of the Guild songsters to their taste, especially the farther you get from the large cities. Out in the countryside, away from the decadence of courts, they like their songs to be like their food. Substantial and heartening."

"But why does the Guild let you get away with this, if you're taking

patronage from them?" Rune couldn't help feeling apprehensive, despite
all their easy assurance.

"Bless you, child, they couldn't do without us!" Talaysen laughed. "No
matter what you think, there isn't a single creative Master among 'em!
Gwyna, my heart, sing her 'The Unkind Lover'—your version, I mean,
the real and original."

Gwyna, the dark girl who had tended Rune's bruises, flashed dazzling
white teeth in a vulpine grin, plucked a guitar from somewhere behind
her, and began.

Well, it was the same melody that Rune had sung, and some of the
words—the best phrases—were the same as well. But this was no ice-
cold princess taunting her poor chivalrous admirer with what he'd never
touch; no, this was a teasing shepherdess seeing how far she could harass
her cowherd lover, and the teasing was kindly meant. And what the cowherd claimed at the end was a good deal more than a "kiss on her cold,
quiet hand." In fact, you might say with justice that the proceedings got
downright heated!

It reminded her a bit of her private "good-bye" with Shawm, in fact. . . .

"That 'Lament' you did the first day's trial is another song they've
twisted and tormented; most of the popular ballads the Guild touts as
their own are ours," Talaysen told her with a grin.

"As you should know, seeing as you've written at least half of them!"
Gwyna snorted.

"But what would you have done if they had accepted me anyway?"
Rune wanted to know.

"Oh, you wouldn't have lasted long; can a caged lark sing? Soon or late,
you'd have done what I did—" Talaysen told her. "You'd have escaped
your gilded cage, and we'd have been waiting."

"Then, *you* were a Guild Bard?" Somehow she felt she'd known that
all along. "But I never hear of one called Talaysen, and if the 'Lament'
is yours—"

Talaysen coughed, and blushed. "Well, I changed my name when I
took my freedom. Likely though, you wouldn't recognize it—"

"Oh, she wouldn't, you think? Or are you playing mock-modest with us
again?" Gwyna shook back her abundant black hair. "I'll make it known
to you that you're having your bruises tended by Master Bard Gwydain,
himself."

"Gwydain?" Rune's eyes went wide as she stared at the man, who
coughed, deprecatingly. "But—but—I thought Master Gwydain was supposed to have gone into seclusion—or died—or took vows!"

"The Guild would hardly want it known that their pride had rejected
'em for a pack of Gypsy jonguelers, now would they?" the lanky fellow
pointed out.

"So, can I tempt you to join with us, Rune, lass?" the man she'd known
as Talaysen asked gently.

"I'd like—but I can't," she replied despairingly. "How could I keep
myself? It'll take weeks for my arm to heal. And—my instruments are
splinters, anyway." She shook her head, tears in her eyes. "They weren't
much, but they were all I had. They were—from friends."

Tonno, Rose, will you ever forgive me? I've not only failed, but I've managed to lose your legacy to me. . . .

"I don't have a choice; I'll have to go back to Nolton—or maybe they'll take me in a tavern in Kingsford. I can still turn a spit and fill a glass one-handed." Tears spilled down her cheeks as she thought of going back to the life she'd thought she'd left behind her.

"Ah lass, didn't you *hear* Erdric?" the old man asked. "There's nothing for you to worry about! You're one of us; you won't need to go running off to find a way to keep food in your mouth! We take care of each other—we'll care for you till you're whole again—"

She stared at them all, and every one of them nodded. The old man patted her shoulder, then hastily found her a rag when scanning their faces brought her belief—and more tears.

"As for the instruments—" Talaysen vanished and returned again as her sobs quieted. "I can't bring back your departed friends. 'They're splinters, and I loved them' can't be mended, nor can I give you back the memories of those who gave them to you. But if I can offer a poor substitute, what think you of these twain?"

The fiddle and lute he laid in her lap weren't new, nor were they the kind of gilded, carved and ornamented dainties Guild musicians boasted, but they held their own kind of quiet beauty, a beauty of mellow wood and clean lines. Rune plucked a string on each, experimentally, and burst into tears again. The tone was lovely, smooth and golden, and these were the kind of instruments she'd never dreamed of touching, much less owning.

When the tears had been soothed away, the various medicines been applied both internally and externally, and introductions made all around, Rune found herself once again alone with Talaysen—or Gwydain, though on reflection, she liked the name she'd first known him by better. The rest had drawn curtains on their wires close in about her little corner, making an alcove of privacy.

"If you're going to let me join you—" she said, shyly.

"Let!" He laughed, interrupting her. "Haven't we made it plain enough we've been trying to lure you like cony-catchers? Oh, you're one of us, Rune, lass. You've just been waiting to find us. You'll not escape us now!"

"Then—what am I supposed to do?"

"You heal," he said firmly. "That's the first thing. The second, well, we don't have formal apprenticeships amongst us. By the Lady, there's no few things you could serve as Master in, and no question about it! You could teach most of us a bit about fiddling, for one—"

"But—" She felt a surge of dismay. *Am I going to have to fumble along on my own now?* "One of the reasons I wanted to join the Guild was to *learn*! I can barely read or write music, not like a Master, anyway; there's so many instruments I can't play"—her voice rose to a soft wail—"how am I going to learn if a Master won't take me as an apprentice?"

"Enough! Enough! No more weeping and wailing, my heart's over-soft as it is!" he said hastily. "If you're going to insist on being an apprentice, I suppose there's nothing for it. Will I do as a Master to you?"

Rune was driven to speechlessness, and could only nod. *Me? Apprentice to Gwydain?* She felt dizzy; this was impossible, things like this only happened in songs—

—like winning prizes from a ghost.

"By the Lady, lass, you make a liar out of me, who swore never to take an apprentice! Wait a moment." He vanished around the curtain for a moment, then returned. "Here—"

He set down a tiny harp. "This can be played one-handed, and learning the ways of her will keep you too busy to bedew me with any more tears while your arm mends. Treat her gently—she's my own very first instrument, and she deserves respect."

Rune cradled the harp in her good arm, too awe-stricken to reply.

"We'll send someone in the morning for your things, wherever it is you've cached 'em. Lean back there—oh, it's a proper nursemaid I am—" He chattered, as if to cover discomfort, or to distract her, as he made her comfortable on her pillows, covering her with blankets and moving her two—no, three—new instruments to a place of safety, but still within sight. He seemed to understand how seeing them made her feel. "We'll find you clothing and the like as well. That sleepy-juice they gave you should have you nodding shortly. Just remember one thing before you doze off. I'm not going to be an easy Master to serve; you won't be spending your days lazing about, you know! Come morning, I'll set you your very first task. You'll teach *me*"—his eyes lighted with unfeigned eagerness—"that Ghost song!"

"Yes, Master Talaysen," she managed to say—and then she fell deeply and profoundly asleep.

CHAPTER FOURTEEN

The Faire ran for eight weeks; Rune had arrived the first day of the second week. Not everyone who was a participant arrived for the beginning of the Faire. There were major events occurring every week of the Faire, and minor ones every day. She had known, vaguely, that the trials and other Guild contests were the big event of the second week—the first week had been horse races, and next week would be livestock judging, a different breed of animal every day. None of this had made any difference to her at the time, but it might now. The final week of Faire was devoted to those seeking justice, and it was entirely possible that the Guild might decide to wreak further justice on her, in trials of another sort. She spent the night in pain-filled dreams of being brought up before the three Church Justices on charges of trying to defraud the Bardic Guild.

Each time she half-woke, someone would press a mug of medicinal tea into her hands, get her to drink it down, and take it away when she'd fallen asleep again. When she truly woke the next morning, the big tent was empty of everyone except Gwyna, the dark Gypsy girl, Erdric, and a young boy.

It was the boy's voice that woke her; singing in a breathy treble to a harp, a song in a language she didn't recognize. The harp-notes faltered a little, as he tried to play and sing at the same time.

She struggled to sit up, and in the process rattled the rings of the curtain next to her against the wire strung overhead. There was no sound of footsteps to warn her that anyone had heard her, but Gwyna peeked around the curtain and smiled when she saw that Rune was awake.

"Everybody's gone out busking," she said, "except us." She pulled back the curtain to show who "us" was. "It's our turn to mind the tent and make sure no one makes off with our belongings. What will you have for breakfast?"

"A new head," Rune moaned. Moving had made both head and arm ache horribly. Her head throbbed in both temples, and her arm echoed the throbbing a half heartbeat after her head. She also felt completely filthy, which didn't improve matters any.

"How about a bath, a visit to the privy, and a mug of something for the aches?" Gwyna asked. "Once you're up, it'll be easier to get around, but for the first couple of days Redbird has said you ought to stay pretty much in bed." Wondering who "Redbird" was, Rune nodded, wordlessly, and Gwyna helped her up. "I think you'll have to borrow some of my clothes until yours can be washed," the girl added, looking at Rune's stained, filthy clothing. "If you've no objection to wearing skirts."

"No—I mean, the whole purpose of looking like a boy was to get in the trials. . . ." Rune sighed. "I don't really care one way or another, and if you'd be willing to lend some clothing, I'd be grateful. I left some other stuff, my bedroll and all, up a tree, but most of the clothing in my pack was dirty too." She described where she'd left it, as the boy left his harp with the old man, and came close to listen.

"I'll go get it!" the child said eagerly, and was off before anyone could say a word, flying out the front of the tent, where the two flaps stood open to let in air. Erdric shrugged.

"Hard to keep them to lessons at that age," the old man said, not without sympathy. "I know how I was. He'll be all right, and he'll get your things without touching the pack, he's that honest. Though I should warn you, if you've got anything unusual, you'd better show it to him before he gets eaten up with curiosity, imagining all sorts of treasures. That's my grandson, Rune. His name's Alain, but we all call him Sparrow."

The name suited him. "Well, if he gets back before we're done, would you tell him I thank him most kindly?" Rune said with difficulty, through the pain in her skull. The ache made her squint against all the light, and it made her tense up her shoulder muscles as well, which didn't help any. "Right now, I can't think any too well."

"Not to worry," Gwyna chuckled. "We all know how you must be feeling; I think every one of us has fallen afoul of someone and has ended up with a cracked bone and an aching head. I mind me the time a bitch of a girl in Newcomb reckoned I was after her swain and took after me with a fry-pan. I swear, my head rang like a steeple full of bells on a Holy Day. Come on, Lady Lark. Let me get you to some warm water to soak the aches out, and we'll worry about the rest later."

Rune hadn't really hoped for *warm* water, and she wondered how tent-dwellers, who presumably hadn't brought anything more than what they could carry, were going to manage it. She soon found out.

The Free Bards were camped outside the Faire palings, alongside of another little stream that fed the great river, on much hillier, rockier ground than Rune had crossed in her explorations of the river. It was an ingenious campsite; the huge tent lay athwart the entrance to a little hollow beside the stream. That gave them their own little park, free from prying eyes, screened by thick underbrush and trees that grew right up to the very edge of the bank on the other side. This was a wilder water-course than the one Rune had crossed, upstream. It had a little waterfall at the top of the hollow, and was full of flat sheets of rock and water-smoothed boulders below the falls.

A hollow log carried water from the falls to a place where someone had cemented river-stones on the sides of a natural depression in one of those huge sheets of rock. There was a little board set into the rocks at the lower end like a dam, to let the water out again, and a fire on the flat part of the rock beside the rough bath-tub. The rock-built tub was already full.

"We've been coming here for years, and since we're here before anyone but the merchants, we always get this spot," Gwyna explained, as she shoveled rocks out of the heart of the fire, and dropped them into the waiting water with a sizzle. "We keep the tent in storage over in Kingsford during the year, with a merchant who sometimes lets it to other groups for outdoor revels. We've put in a few things that the wind and weather won't ruin over the years; this was one of the first. Do you know, those scurvy merchants over in the Faire charge a whole silver penny for a *bath?*" She bristled, as if she was personally offended. Rune smiled wanly. "You can't win," she continued. "You can get a bath for a copper in the public baths across the river in Kingsford, but you'd either get soaked going over the ford or pay four coppers coming and going on the ferry."

"That's a merchant for you," Rune agreed. "I suppose the Church has rules about bathing in the river."

"No, but no one would want to; up near the docks, it's half mud." She shook her head. "Well, when you're better, you'll have to do this for yourself, and remember, on your honor, you always leave the bath set up for the next person. He may be as sore and tired as you were when you needed it."

While she was talking, she was helping Rune get out of her clothing. Rune winced at the sight of all the bruises marking her body; it would be a long time before they all faded, and until then, it would be hard to find a comfortable position to sit or sleep in. And she'd have to wear long sleeves and long skirts, to keep people from seeing what had been done to her.

"In you go—" Gwyna said gaily, as if Rune didn't look like a patchwork of blue and black. "You soak for a while; I'll be back with soap."

Rune was quite content to lean back against the smooth rock, close her eyes, and soak in the warm water. It wasn't hot; that was too bad, because really hot water would have felt awfully good right now. But it was warmer than her own skin temperature, so it felt very comforting. A gap in the trees let sun pour down on her, and that continued to warm both the water and the rocks she rested on.

She must have dozed off, because the next thing she knew, Gwyna was shaking her shoulder, there was a box of soft soap on the rocks beside her. "Here, drink this. I'll do your hair," Gwyna said, matter-of-factly, placing a mug of that doctored wine in her good hand. "It's not fit to be seen."

"I can believe it," Rune replied. She took the mug, then sniffed the wine, wrinkled her nose, and drank it down in one gulp. As she had expected, it tasted vile. Gwyna laughed at her grimace, took the mug, and used it to dip out water to wet down her hair.

"We Gypsies only use the worst wine we can find for potions," Gwyna said cheerfully. "They taste so awful there's no use in ruining a good drink—and I'm told you need the spirits in wine to get the most out of some of the herbs." She took the box of soap, then, and began massaging it carefully into Rune's hair. Rune was glad she was being careful; there was an amazing number of knots on her skull, and Gwyna was finding them all. She closed her eyes, and waited for the aching to subside; about the third time Gwyna rinsed her hair, her head finally stopped throbbing.

She opened her eyes without wincing at the light, took the soap herself and began getting herself as clean as she could without wetting her splinted arm.

Finally they were both finished, and Rune rinsed herself off. "Can you stand a cold drench?" Gwyna asked then. "It'll probably clear your head a bit."

She considered it for a moment, then nodded; Gwyna let the water out by sliding out the board. Then she maneuvered the log over to its stand and let fresh, cold water run in; it swung easily, and Rune noted that it was set to pour water over the head of someone sitting beneath it in the tub. Rune rinsed quickly, getting the last of the soap off, and stuck her head under the water for as long as she could bear. Then she scrambled out, gasping, and Gwyna handed her a rough towel that might once have been part of a grain sack, and swung the log away again.

While Gwyna took the rocks out of the bottom of the pool, put them back beside the fire, then refilled the tub and built the fire back up, Rune dried herself off, wrapping her hair in the towel. There was clothing ready on the rocks in the sun; a bright skirt and bodice, and a minstrel's shirt with ribbons on the full sleeves, and some of her own under-things waiting for her. She got into them, and felt much the better; the medicine, the bath, and the clean clothing worked together to make her feel more like herself, especially after the worst of the bruises were covered. Even the ache in her head and arm receded to something bearable.

"Now what?" she asked Gwyna. "Where would you like me to go? I don't want to be in the way, and if there's anything I can do, I'd like to. I don't want to be a burden either."

The girl nodded towards the tent again.

"Back to bed with you," Gwyna said. "There's plenty you can do for us without being in the way. Erdric wants to hear some of those comic-songs Thrush said you did back in Nolton."

"Who?" she asked, astonished that anyone here knew about those songs. "How did you hear about those?"

"Thrush, I told you," Gwyna replied, a trifle impatiently. "You played for her to dance when her brothers were out busking the taverns at midday. The Gypsy, remember?"

"Oh," Rune said faintly. That was all the way back in Nolton! How on Earth had word of those songs gotten all the way here? How many of these Free Bards were there? And was there anything that they didn't know? "I didn't know—you all knew each other—" Then she burst out, impatiently, "Does *every* busker in the world belong to the Free Bards? Was I the only one who never heard of you before this?"

"Oh no—" Gwyna took one look at her angry, exasperated face, and burst out laughing. For some reason she found Rune's reaction incredibly funny. Rune wasn't as amused; in fact, she was getting a bit angry, but she told herself that there was no point in taking out her anger on Gwyna—

—even if she was being incredibly annoying.

Rune reined in her temper, and finally admitted to herself that she wouldn't be as exasperated if she wasn't still in pain. After all, what was she thinking—that the Free Bards had the same kind of information network as the Church? Now there was an absurdity!

"No, no, no," Gwyna finally said, when she'd gotten her laughter under control. "It's just the Gypsies. We're used to passing messages all over the Kingdoms. Anything that interests the Free Bards involves us, sooner or later."

"Why?" Rune asked, her brow furrowed. "You Gypsies are all related in one way or another, if I understand right, but what does *that* have to do with the Free Bards?"

"Quite a bit," Gwyna said, sobering. "You see, Master Wren came to *us* when he first ran away from the Guild, and it was being with us that gave him the idea for the Free Bards. He liked the kind of group we are. He says we're 'supportive without being restrictive,' whatever that means."

"All right, I can see that," Rune replied. "But I still don't understand what the Gypsies have to do with the Free Bards."

"For a start, it's probably fair to say that every Gypsy that's any kind of a musician is a Free Bard now. The Gift runs strong in us, when it runs at all. When anything calls us, music or dance, trading-craft, horse-craft, metal-craft, or mag—" She stopped herself, and Rune had the star-tling idea that she was about to say "magic." Magic? If it was not pro-scribed by the Church, it was at the least frowned upon. . . .

"Well, anything that calls us, calls us strongly, so when we do a thing, we do it well." Gwyna skipped lightly over the grass and held open the tent-flap for Rune. "So if we'd chosen the caged-life, every male of us could likely be in the Guild. That wasn't our way, though, and seeing that gave Master Wren the idea for the Free Bards. Of you *gejo*, I'd say maybe one of every ten musicians and street-buskers are Free Bards. No more.

The rest simply aren't good enough. You were good enough, so we watched you. We—that's Free Bards and Gypsies both."

Rune sighed. That, at least, made her feel a little less like a child that hasn't been let in on a secret. The Free Bards weren't everywhere; they didn't have a secret eye on everyone. Just the few who seemed to promise they'd fit in the Free Bard ranks.

"There weren't any Free Bards in Nolton. The Gypsies, though, we have eyes and ears everywhere because we go everywhere. And since we're always meeting each other, we're always passing news, so what one knows, within months all know. We're a good way for the Free Bards to keep track of each other and of those who will fit in when they're ready." Gwyna showed her back to her own corner of the tent, which now held her bedroll and the huge cushions, her pack, as well as the instruments Talaysen had given her.

"Food first?" the girl asked. Rune nodded; now that her head and arm didn't hurt quite so much, she was actually hungry. Not terribly, which was probably the result of the medicine, but she wasn't nauseated anymore.

Gwyna brought her bread and cheese, and more of the doctored wine, while Erdric's grandson came and flung himself down on the cushions with the bonelessness of the very young and watched her as if he expected she might break apart at any moment. And as if he thought it might be very entertaining when she did.

She finished half the food before she finally got tired of the big dark eyes on her and returned him stare for stare. "Yes?" she said finally. "Is there something you wanted to ask me?"

"Did it hurt?" he asked, bright-eyed, as innocent and callous as only a child could be.

"Yes, it did," she told him. "A lot. I was very stupid, though nobody knew how stupid I was being. Don't ever put yourself in the position where someone can beat you. Run away if you can, but don't ever be as stupid as I was."

"All right," he said brightly. "I won't."

"Thank you for getting my things," she said, when it occurred to her that she hadn't thanked him herself. "I really appreciate it. There isn't anything special in my pack, but it's all I've got."

"You're welcome," he told her, serious and proper. Then, as if her politeness opened up a floodgate, the questions came pouring out. "Are you staying with the Free Bards? Are you partnering with Master Wren? Are you going to be his lover? He needs a lover. Robin says so all the time. Do you want to be his lover? Lots of girls want to be his lover, and he won't be. Do you like him? He likes you, I can tell."

"Sparrow!" Gwyna said sharply. "That's private! Do we discuss private matters without permission?"

"If she's with us, it isn't private, is it?" he retorted. "If she's a Free Bard she's part of the *romgerry* and it isn't private matters to talk about—"

"Yes it *is*," Gwyna replied firmly. "Yes, she's staying, and yes, she's a Free Bard now, but the rest is private matters until Master Wren tells you different. You won't ask any more questions like that. Is that understood?"

For some reason that Rune didn't understand, Gwyna was blushing a brilliant scarlet. The boy seemed to sense he had pushed her as far as he dared. He jumped to his feet and scampered off. Gwyna averted her face until her blushes faded.

"What was that all about?" Rune asked, too surprised to be offended or embarrassed. After all, the boy meant no harm. She'd spent the night an arm's length away from Talaysen; it was perfectly natural for the child to start thinking in terms of other than "master and apprentice."

"We all worry about Master Wren," Gwyna said. "Some of us maybe worry a bit too much. Some of us think he spends too much time by himself, and well, there's always talk about how he ought to find someone who'd be good for him."

"And who is this 'Robin'?" she asked curiously.

"Me," Gwyna said, flushing again. "Gypsies don't like strangers knowing their real names, so we take names that anyone can use, names that say something about what our Craft is. A horse-tamer might be Roan, Tamer, or Cob, for instance. All musicians take bird-names, and the Free Bards have started doing the same, because it makes it harder for the Church and cities to keep track of us for taxes and tithes and—other things."

Yes, and I can imagine what those other things are. Trouble like I got myself into.

She turned a face back to Rune that might never have been flushed, once again the cheerful, careless girl she'd been a moment earlier. "Talaysen is Wren, Erdric is Owl, I'm Robin, Daran—that's the tall fellow that knew you—is Heron, Alain is Sparrow, Aysah is Nightingale. My cousin, the one who's making up your medicines, is Redbird. Reshan is Raven, you know him, too, the fellow who looks like a bandit. He's not here yet; we expect him in about a week." She tilted her head to one side, and surveyed Rune thoughtfully. "We need a name for you, although I think Wren tagged you with the one that will stick. Lark. Lady Lark."

Rune rolled the flavor of it around on her tongue, and decided she liked it. Not that she was likely to have much choice in the matter. . . . These folk tended to hit you like a wild wind, and like the wind, they took you where they wanted, without warning.

There's a song in that—

But she was not allowed to catch it; not yet. Erdric advanced across the tent-floor towards her, guitar in hand, and a look of determination on his face. She was a bit surprised at that; she hadn't thought there was anything anyone could want from her as badly as all that.

"My voice isn't what it was," Erdric said, as he sat down beside her. "It's going on the top and the bottom, and frankly, the best way I can coax money from listeners is with comedy. Now, I understand you have about a dozen comic songs that *no one else knows*. That's nothing short of a miracle, especially for me. You've no idea how hard it is to find comic songs."

"So the time's come to earn my bread, hmm?" she asked. He nodded.

"If you can't go out, you should share your songs with those that need them," Erdric replied. "I do a love song well enough, but I've no gift for satire. Besides, can you see a dried-up old stick like *me* a-singing a love ballad?" He snorted. "I'll give the love songs to you youngsters. You teach me your comedy. I promise you, I'll do justice to it."

"All right, that's only fair," she acknowledged. "Let's start with 'Two Fair Maids.' "

The Free Bards all came trickling back by ones and twos as the sun set, but only to eat and drink and rest a bit, and then they were off again. Mostly they didn't even stop to talk, although some of them did change into slightly richer clothing, and the dancers changed into much gaudier gear.

Erdric, his grandson, and Gwyna did quite a bit more than merely "watch the tent," she noticed. There was plain food and drink waiting for anyone who hadn't eaten at the Faire—though those were few, since it seemed a musician could usually coax at least a free meal out of a cook-tent owner by playing at his site. Still, there was fresh bread, cheese, and fresh raw vegetables waiting for any who needed it, and plenty of cold, clean water. And when darkness fell, it was Gwyna and Erdric who saw to it that the lanterns were lit, that there was a fire burning outside the tent entrance, and that torches were placed up the path leading to the Free Bard enclave to guide the wanderers home no matter how weary they might be.

Talaysen had not returned with the rest; he came in well after dark, and threw himself down on the cushions next to Rune with a sigh. He looked very tired, and just a trifle angry, though she couldn't think why that would be. Erdric brought him wine without his asking for it, and another dose of medicine for Rune, which she drank without thinking about it.

"A long day, Master Wren?" Erdric asked, sympathetically. "Anything we can do?"

"Very long," Talaysen replied. "Long enough that I shall go and steal the use of the bath before anyone else returns. And then, apprentice—" he cocked an eyebrow at Rune "—you'll teach me that Ghost song." He drained half the mug in a single gulp. "There's been a lot of rumor around the Faire about the boy—or girl, the rumors differ—who won the trials yesterday, and yet has vanished quite out of ken. No one is talking, and no one is telling the truth." His expression grew just a little angrier. "The Guild judges presented the winners today, and they had their exhibition— and they all looked so damned smug I wanted to break *their* instruments over their heads. I intend the Guild to know you're with us and if they touch you, there'll be equal retribution."

"Equal retribution?" Rune asked, swallowing a lump that had appeared in her throat when he'd mentioned broken instruments.

"When Master Wren came to us, the Guild didn't like it," Gwyna said, bringing Talaysen a slice of bread and cheese. " 'Twas at this very Faire that he first began to play with us in public. He wasn't calling himself Gwydain, but the Guildsmen knew him anyway. They set on him—they didn't break his arm, but they almost broke his head. We Gypsies went after every Guild Bard we caught alone the next day."

Talaysen shook his head. "It was all I could do to keep them from setting on the Guildsmen with knives instead of fists."

Erdric laughed, but it wasn't a laugh of humor. "If they'd hurt you more than bruises, you wouldn't have. They didn't dare walk the Faire without a guard—even when they wandered about in twos and threes, they're so soft 'twas no great task to beat them all black and blue. When we reckoned they'd gotten the point and when they started hiring great guards to go about with 'em, we left them alone. They haven't touched one of us since, any place there're are Gypsies about."

"But elsewhere?" Rune winced as her head throbbed. "Gypsies and Free Bards can't be everywhere."

"Quite true, but I doubt that's occurred to them," Talaysen said. "At any rate"—he flicked a drop of water at her from his mug—"there. You're Rune no more. Rune is gone; Lark stands—or rather, sits—in her place. The quarrel the Bardic Guild has is with Rune, and I don't know anyone by that name."

"As you say, Master," she replied, mock-meekly.

He saw through the seeming, and grinned. "I'm for a bath. Then the song; I'll see it sung all over the Faire tomorrow, and they'll know you're ours. When you come out with the rest of us in a week or two, they'll know better than to touch you."

"Come out? In two weeks?" she exclaimed. "But my arm—"

"Hasn't hurt your voice any," Talaysen replied. "You can come with me and sing the female parts; teach me the rest of your songs, and I'll play while you sing." He fixed her with a fierce glare. "You're a Free Bard, aren't you?"

She nodded, slowly.

"Then you stand up to the Guild, to the Faire, to everyone; you stand up to them, and you let them know that *nothing* keeps a Free Bard from her music!" He looked around at the rest of the Free Bards gathered in the tent; so did Rune, and she saw every head nodding in agreement.

"Yes, sir!" she replied, with more bravery than she felt. She *was* afraid of the Guild; of the bullies that the Guild could hire, of the connection the Guild seemed to have with the Church. And the Church was everywhere. If the Church took a mind to get involved, no silly renaming would make her safe.

She hadn't been so shaken since Westhaven, when those boys had tried to rape her.

Talaysen seemed to sense her fear. He reached forward and took her good hand in his. "Believe in us, Lady Lark," he said, his voice trembling with intensity. "Believe in us—and believe in yourself. Together we can do anything, so long as we believe it. I *know*. Trust me."

She looked into his green eyes, deep as the sea, and as restless, hiding as many things beneath their surface, and revealing some of them to her. There was passion there, that he probably didn't display very often. She found herself smiling, tremulously.

And nodded, because she couldn't speak.

He took that at face value; released her hand, and pulled himself up to his feet. "I'll be back," he said gravely, but with a twinkle. "And the apprentice had better be ready to teach when I return." He left the tent with a remarkably light step, and her eyes followed him.

When she pulled her eyes back to the rest, Rune didn't miss the significant glance that Erdric and Gwyna exchanged, but somehow she didn't resent it. Talaysen, though, might. She remembered all the questions that Sparrow had asked, and the tone of them, and decided to keep her observations to herself. It was more than enough that the greatest living Bard had taken her as his apprentice. Anything else would either happen or not happen.

A week later, it was Talaysen's turn to mind the tent, that duty shared by Rune's old friend Raven.

Raven had appeared the previous evening, to be greeted by all of his kin with loud and enthusiastic cries, and then underwent a series of kisses and backslapping greetings with each of the Free Bards.

Then he was brought to Rune's corner of the tent; she hadn't seen who had come in and had been dying of curiosity to see who it was. Raven was loudly pleased to see her, dismayed to see the fading marks of her beating, and angered by what had happened. It was all Talaysen and the others could do to keep him from charging out then and there, and beating up a few of the Guild Bards in retaliation. The judges in particular; he had the same notion as Talaysen, to break their instruments over *their* heads.

They managed to calm him, but after due thought, he judged that it was best he *not* go playing in the "streets" for a while, so he took his tent-duty early. He played mock-court to Rune, who blushed to think that she'd ever thought he might want to be her lover.

I didn't know anything *then,* she realized, as he bowed over her hand, but kept a sharp watch for Nightingale. She knew that once Nightingale appeared, he'd leave her side in a moment. She was not his type; not even in the Gypsy-garb she'd taken to wearing, finding skirts and loose blouses much more suited to handling one-handed than breeches and vests. All of his gallantry was in fun, and designed to keep her distracted and in good humor.

Oddly enough, Talaysen seemed to take Raven's mock-courtship seriously. He watched them with a faint frown on his face most of the morning. After lunch, he took the younger man aside and had a long talk with him. What they said, Rune had no idea, until Raven returned with a face full of suppressed merriment and his hands full of her lunch and her medicines.

"I've never in all me life had quite such a not-lecture," he whispered to her, when Talaysen had gone to see about something. "He takes being your Master right seriously, young Rune. I've just been warned that if I intend to break your heart by flirting with you, your Master there will be most unamused. He seems to think a broken heart would interfere more with your learning than yon broken arm. In fact, he offered to trade me a broken head for a broken heart."

Rune didn't know whether to gape or giggle; she finally did both. Talaysen found them both laughing, as Rune poked fun at Raven's gallantry, and Raven pretended to be crushed. Talaysen immediately relaxed.

But then he shooed Raven off and sat down beside her himself.

"It's time we had a real lesson," he said. "If you're going to insist I act like a Master, I'll give you a Master's lessoning." He then began a ruthless interrogation, having Rune go over every song she'd ever written. First he had her sing them until he'd picked them up, then he'd critique them, with more skill—and (which surprised her) he criticized them much harder even than Brother Pell had.

Of her comic songs, he said, "It's all very well to have a set of those for busking during the day, either in cities or at Faires, but there's more to music than parody, and you very well know it. If you're going to be a Bard, you have to live up to the title. You can't confine yourself to something as limited as one style; you can't even be *known* for just one style. You have to know all of them, and people must be aware that you're versed in all of them."

Of "Fiddler Girl," he approved of the tune, except that—"It's too limited. You need to expand your bridges into a whole new set of tunes. Make the listener feel what it was like to fiddle all night long, with Death waiting if you slipped! In fact, don't ever play it twice the same. Improvise! Match your fiddle-music to the crowd, play scraps of what you played then, so that they recognize you're recreating the experience, you're not just telling someone else's story."

And of the lyrics, he was a little kinder, but he felt that they were too difficult to sing for most people. "You and I and most of the Free Bards can manage them—*if* we're sober, *if* we aren't having a tongue-tied day—but what about the poor busker in the street? They look as if you just wrote them down with no notion of how hard they'd be to sing."

When she admitted that was exactly what she'd done, he shook his head at her. "At least *recite* them first. Nothing's ever carved in stone, Rune. Be willing to change."

The rest of her serious songs he dismissed as being "good for filling in between difficult numbers. Easy songs with ordinary lyrics." Those were the ones she'd composed according to Brother Pell's rules for his class, and while it hurt a bit to have them dismissed as "ordinary," it didn't hurt as much as it might have. She'd chafed more than a bit at those rules; to have the things she'd done right out of her head given *some* praise, and the ones she'd done according to the "rules" called "common" wasn't so bad. . . .

Or at least, it wasn't as bad as it could have been.

Then he set her a task: write him a song, something about elves. "They're always popular," he said. "Try something—where a ruler makes a bargain with an elf, then breaks it. Make the retribution something original. No thunder and lightning, being turned into a toad, or dragged off to hell. None of that nonsense; it's trite."

She nodded, and set to it as soon as he left. But she could see that he had not lied to her. He was not going to be an easy Master.

Talaysen left his instruments in the tent, and walked off into the Faire with nothing about him to identify who or what he was. He preferred to leave it that way, given that he was going to visit the cathedral—and that the Bardic Guild tent was pitched right up against the cathedral walls. Of course, there was always the chance that one of his old colleagues would recognize him, but now, at night, that chance was vanishingly slim. *They* would all be entertaining the high and the wealthy—either their own masters, or someone who had hired them for the night. The few that weren't would be huddled together in self-satisfied smugness—though perhaps that attitude might be marred a little, since he'd begun singing "Fiddler Girl" about the Faire. The real story of the contest was spreading, through the medium of the Free Bards and the gypsies. In another couple of weeks it should be safe enough for Rune to show her face at *this* Faire.

He was worried about his young charge, though, because *she* troubled him. So he was going to talk with an old friend, one who had known him for most of his life, to see if she could help him to sort his thoughts out.

He skirted the bounds of the Guild tent carefully, even though a confrontation was unlikely. His bones were much older than the last time he'd been beaten, and they didn't heal as quickly anymore. But the tent was dark; no one holding revels in there, not at the moment. Just as well, really.

He sought out a special gate in the cathedral wall, and opened it with a key he took from his belt-pouch, locking the gate behind him again once he'd entered. The well-oiled mechanism made hardly a sound, but something alerted the guardian of that gate, who came out of the building to see who had entered the little odd-shaped courtyard.

"I'd like to see Lady Ardis," Talaysen told the black-clad guard, who nodded soberly, but said nothing. "Could you see if she is available to a visitor?"

The guard turned and left, still without a word; Talaysen waited patiently in the tiny courtyard, thinking that a musician has many opportunities to learn patience in a lifetime. *It seems as if I am always waiting for something. . . .*

This was, at least, a pleasant place to wait. Unlike the courtyards of most Church buildings, this one, though paved, boasted greenery in the form of plants spilling from tiers of wooden boxes, and trees growing from huge ceramic pots. Lanterns hanging from the wall of the cloister provided soft yellow light. Against the wall of the courtyard, a tiny waterfall trickled down a set of stacked rocks, providing a breath of moisture and the restful sounds of falling water.

At least, it did when the Faire wasn't camped on the other side of the wall. Music, crowd-noise, and laughter spilled over the walls, ruffling the serenity of the place.

He caught movement out of the corner of his eye, and turned. A tall, scarlet-clad woman whose close-cropped blond hair held about the same amount of gray as his, held out her hands to him. "Gwydain!" she exclaimed. "I wondered when you'd get around to visiting me!"

He strode towards her, and clasped both her hands in his. "I was busy, and so were you, my dear cousin. I truly intended to pay my respects when the trials were over. Then my latest little songbird got herself into a brawl with the Guild, and I had to extract her from the mess my lack of foresight put her in."

"Her?" One winglike brow rose sharply, and Ardis showed her interest. "I heard something of that. Was she badly hurt?"

"Bruised all over, and a broken arm—" he began.

"Which is disaster for a musician," she completed. "Can you bring her here? I can certainly treat her. That *is* what you wanted, isn't it?"

"Well, yes," he admitted, with a smile. "If that won't bring you any problems."

She sniffed disdainfully. "The Church treats its Justiciars well. It treats its mages even better. Rank does bring privileges; if I wish to treat a ragtag street-singer's broken arm, no one will nay-say me. But there will be a price—" she continued, taking her hand away from his, and holding up a single finger in warning.

"Name it," Talaysen replied with relief. With the mage-healing Lady Ardis could work, Rune's arm would be healed in half the time it would normally take; well enough, certainly, to permit her to play by the end of the Faire. More importantly, well enough so that when he and she went on the road together, it wouldn't cause her problems.

"You shouldn't be so quick to answer my demands," the lady replied, but with a serious look instead of the smile Talaysen expected. "This could be dangerous."

"So?" He shrugged. "I won't belittle your perception of danger, and I won't pretend to be a hero, but if I'd been afraid of a little danger, I would still be with the Guild."

"So you would." She studied his face for a moment. "There's a dark-mage among the Brotherhood, and I don't know who it is. I only know it's a 'he,' since there are only two female mages, and I know it isn't a Justiciar."

Talaysen whistled between his teeth in surprise and consternation. "That's not welcome news. What is it you want me to do?"

She freed her other hand, and walked slowly over to one of the planters, rubbing her wrists as she walked. He followed, and she turned abruptly. "It isn't quite true that I don't know who it is. I have a guess. And if my guess is correct, he'll take advantage of the general licentiousness of the Faire to sate some of his desires. What I want is for *you* to watch and wait, and see if there are rumors of a Priest gone bad, one who uses methods outside the ordinary to enforce his will."

Talaysen nodded, slowly. "It's true that a Bard hears everything—"

She laughed, shortly. "And everyone tells a Bard everything they know. A Free Bard, anyway. If you hear anything, bring it to me. If you can somehow contrive to bring him *before* me in my official capacity, that would be even better. I can be certain that the other two Justiciars with me would be mages and uncorrupted."

"I'll try," he promised, and gestured for her to seat herself. She took the invitation, and perched on a bench between two pots of fragrant honeysuckle.

"So, what else do you need of me, cousin?" she asked, a look of shrewd speculation creeping over her even features. "It has to do with this little songster, doesn't it?"

"Not so little," he replied, with a bit of embarrassment. "She's quite old enough to be wedded with children, by country standards. She's very attractive, Ardis. And that's the problem. I promised to give her a Master's teaching to an apprentice, and I find her very attractive."

"So?" A lifted shoulder told him Ardis didn't think that was much of a problem.

"So that's not *ethical*, dammit!" he snapped. "This girl is my student; if I took advantage of that situation, I'd be—dishonorable. And besides, I'm twice her age, easily."

Ardis shook her head. "I can't advise you, Gwydain. I agree with you that pushing yourself on the girl would not be ethical, but what if she's attracted to you? If she's as old as you say, she's old enough to know her own mind."

"It's still not ethical," he replied stubbornly. "And I'm still twice her age."

"Very well," she sighed. "If it isn't ethical, then be the same noble sufferer you've always been and keep your attraction hidden behind a mask of fatherly regard. If you keep pushing her away, likely she'll grow tired of trying and take her affections elsewhere. The young are very short of patience for the most part." She stood, and smoothed down the skirt of her robes with her hand. "The fact that you're twice her age doesn't signify; you know very well I was betrothed to a man *three* times my age at twelve, and if my father hadn't found it more convenient to send me to the Church, I'd likely be married to him now."

He tightened his jaw; her light tone told him she was mocking him, and that wasn't the answer he'd wanted to hear, either. She wasn't providing him with an answer.

"I'm not going to give you an answer, Gwydain," she said, echoing his very thought, in that uncanny way she had. "I'm not going to give you an excuse to do something stupid again. How someone as clever as you are can be so dense when it comes to matters of the heart—"

She pursed her lips in exasperation. "Never mind. Bring your little bird here tomorrow afternoon; I'll heal up her arm for you. After that, what you do with each other is up to you."

He bowed over her hand, since the audience was obviously at an end, and took a polite leave of her—

He sensed that she was amused with him, and it rankled—but he also sensed that part of her tormenting him was on account of her little problem.

Little! he thought, locking the gate behind him and setting off back through the Faire. *A dark-mage in the Kingsford Brotherhood—that's not such a little thing. What is it about the Church that it spawns both the saint and the devil?*

Then he shrugged. It wasn't that the Church spawned either; it was that the Church held both, and permitted both to run free unless and until they were reined in by another hand. To his mind, the venial were the more numerous, but then, he had been a cynic for many years now.

One of his problems was solved, at least. Rune would be cared for. If one of the Gypsies like Nighthawk had been available, he'd have sent the girl to her rather than subject her to his cousin and her acidic wit, but none of those with the healing touch had put in an appearance yet, and he dared not wait much longer.

He had hoped that Ardis would confirm his own assertions; that the child was *much* too young, and that he had no business being attracted to her. Instead she'd implied that he was being over-sensitive.

Still one of the things she'd said had merit. If he continued acting in a fatherly manner, she would never guess how he felt, and in the way of the young, would turn to someone more suitable. Young Heron, for instance, or Swift.

He clamped a firm lid down on the uneasy feelings of—was it jealousy?—that thought caused. Better, much better, to suffer a little and save both of them no end of grief.

Yes, he told himself with determination, as he wound through the press of people around a dancers' tent. *Much, much better.*

Rune hardly knew what to say when Talaysen ordered her to her feet the next afternoon—she had been feeling rather sick, and had a pounding head, and she suspected it was from too much of the medicine she'd been taking. But if she *didn't* take it, she was still sick with pain, her head still ached, and so did her arm. She simply couldn't win.

"Master Wren," she pleaded, when he held out his hand to help her to her feet, "I really don't feel well—I—"

"That's precisely why I want you to come with me," he replied, with a brisk nod. "I want someone else to have a look at your arm and head. Come along now; it isn't far."

She gave in with a sigh; she was *not* up to the heat and the jostling crowds, even if most of the fairgoers would be at the trials-concert this afternoon. But Talaysen looked determined, and she had the sinking feeling that even if she protested that she couldn't walk, he'd conjure a dog cart or something to carry her.

She got clumsily to her feet and followed him out of the tent and down to the Faire. The sun beat down on her head like a hammer on an anvil, making her eyes water and her ears ring. She was paying so much attention to where she was putting her feet that she had no idea where he was leading her.

No idea until he stopped and she looked up, to find herself pinned between the Guild tent and the wall of the Kingsford Cathedral Cloister.

She froze in terror as he unlocked the door in the wall there; she would have bolted if he hadn't reached for her good hand and drawn her inside before she could do anything.

Her heart pounded with panic, and she looked around at the potted greenery, expecting it to sprout guards at any moment. This was it: the Church had found her out, and they were going—

"We're not going to do anything to you, child," said a scarlet-robed woman who stepped out from behind a trellis laden with rosevines. She had a cap of pale blond hair cut like any Priest's, candid gray eyes, and a pointed face that reminded her sharply of someone—

Then Talaysen turned around, and the familial resemblance was obvious. She relaxed a little. Not much, but a little.

"Rune, this is my cousin, Ardis. Ardis, this is the young lady who was too talented for her own good." Talaysen smiled, and Rune relaxed a little more.

Ardis tilted her head to one side, and her pale lips stretched in an amused smile. "So I see. Well, come here, Rune. I don't bite—or rather, I don't bite people who don't deserve to be bitten."

Rune ventured nearer, and Ardis waved at her to take a seat on a bench. The Priest—for so she must be, although Rune had never seen a scarlet-robed Priest before—seated herself on the same bench, as Talaysen stood beside them both. She glanced at him anxiously, and he gave her a wink of encouragement.

"I might as well be brief," Ardis said, after a moment of studying Rune's face. "I suppose you've heard rumors of Priests who also practice magic on behalf of the Church?"

She nodded, reluctantly, unsure what this had to do with her.

"The rumors are true, child," Ardis said, watching her face closely. "I'm one of them."

Rune's initial reaction was alarm—but simple logic calmed her before she did anything stupid. She trusted Talaysen; *he* trusted his cousin. There must be a reason for this revelation.

She waited for Ardis to reveal it.

"I have healing-spells," the Priest continued calmly, "and my cousin asked me to exercise one of them on your behalf. I agreed. But I cannot place the spell upon you without your consent. It wouldn't be ethical."

She smiled at Talaysen as she said that, a smile with just a hint of a sting in it. He chuckled and shook his head, but said nothing.

"Will it hurt?" Rune asked, the only thing she could think of to ask.

"A little," Ardis admitted. "But after a moment or two you'll begin feeling much better."

"Fine—I mean, please, I'd like you to do it, then," Rune stammered, a little confused by the Priest's clear, direct gaze. She sensed it would be difficult, if not impossible, to hide anything from this woman. "It can't hurt much worse than my head does right now."

The Priest's eyes widened for a moment, and she glanced up at Talaysen. "Belladonna?" she asked sharply. He nodded. "Then it's just as well you brought her here today. It's not good to take that for more than three days running."

"I didn't take any today," Rune said, plaintively. "I woke up with a horrid headache and sick, and it felt as if the medicine had something to do with the way I felt."

The Priest nodded. "Wise child. Wiser than some who are your elders. Now, hold still for a moment, think of a cloudless sky, and try not to move."

Obediently, Rune did as she was told, closing her eyes to concentrate better.

She felt the Priest lay her hand gently on the broken arm. Then there was a sudden, sharp pain, exactly like the moment when Erdric straightened the break. She bit back a cry—then slumped with relief, for the pain in both her head and her arm were gone!

No—not gone after all, but dulled to distant ghosts of what they had been. And best of all, she was no longer nauseous. She sighed in gratitude and opened her eyes, smiling into Ardis' intent face.

"You fixed it!" she said. "It hardly hurts at all, it's wonderful! How can I ever thank you?"

Ardis smiled lazily, and flexed her fingers. "My cousin has thanked me adequately already, child. Think of it as the Church's way of repairing the damage the Bardic Guild did."

"But—" Rune protested. Ardis waved her to silence.

"It was no trouble, dear," the Priest said, rising. "The bone-healing spells are something I rarely get to use; I'm grateful for the practice. You can take the splint off in about four weeks; that should give things sufficient time to mend."

She gave Talaysen a significant look of some kind; one that Rune couldn't read. He flushed just a little, though, as she bade him a decorous enough farewell and he turned to lead Rune out the tiny gate.

He seemed a little ill-at-ease, though she couldn't imagine why. To fill the silence between them, she asked the first thing that came into her head.

"Do all Priest-mages wear red robes?" she said. "I'd never seen that color before on a Priest."

He turned to her gratefully, and smiled. "No, actually, there's no one color for the mages. You can find them among any of the Church Brotherhoods. Red is the Justiciar's color—there *do* seem to be more mages among the Justiciars than any other Brotherhood, but that is probably coincidence."

He continued on about the various Brotherhoods in the Church, but she wasn't really listening. She had just realized as she looked at him out of the corner of her eye, what an extraordinarily handsome man he was. She hadn't thought of that until she'd seen his cousin, and noticed how striking *she* was.

How odd that she hadn't noticed it before.

. . . .*possibly because he was acting as if he was my father.* . . .

Well, never mind. There was time enough to sort out how things were going to be between them. Maybe he was just acting oddly because of all the people around him; as the founder of the Free Bards he must feel as if there were eyes on him all the time—and rightly, given Sparrow's chattering questions the other day.

But once the Faire was over and the Free Bards dispersed, there would be no one watching them to see what they did. Then, maybe, he would relax.

And once he did, well—

Her lips curved in a smile that was totally unconscious. And Talaysen chattered on, oblivious to her thoughts.

CHAPTER FIFTEEN

Rune caught a hint of movement in the crowd out of the corner of her eye. She kept singing, but she thought she recognized the bright red skirt and bodice, and the low-cut blouse the color of autumn leaves. . . .

A second glance told her she was right. It was Gwyna, all right, and dressed to be as troublesome as she could to male urges and Church sensibilities. Tiny as she was, she had to elbow her way to the front of the crowd so Rune could see her, and by the look in her eyes, she knew she was causing mischief.

Her abundant black hair was held out of her eyes by a scarf of scarlet tied as a head-band over her forehead; beneath it, huge brown eyes glinted with laughter. There was no law against showing—and none against looking—and she always dressed to catch the maximum number of masculine attentions. She garnered a goodly share of appreciative glances as she sauntered among the fair-goers, from men both high and lowly born. She preened beneath the admiration like the bright bird she so strongly resembled.

Rune and Talaysen were singing "Fiddler Girl," though without the fiddle; Rune's arm was only just out of its sling, and she wasn't doing anything terribly difficult with it yet. Instead, she was singing her own part, and Talaysen was singing the Ghost, and making it fair blood-chilling, too. Even Gwyna shivered visibly, listening to them, and she'd heard it so many times she probably could reproduce every note of it herself in *both* their styles.

They finished to a deafening round of applause, and copper and silver showered into the hat set in front of them. As Gwyna wormed her way to the center of the crowd, Rune caught sight of another of the brother-hood just coming along the street—Daran, called "Heron." Tall, gangling, and bony, he was easy to spot, as he towered a good head above the rest of the crowd. He looked nothing like a musician, but he was second only to Talaysen in the mastery of guitar, and that daft-looking, vacuous face with empty blue eyes hid one of the cleverest satiric minds in their company. His voice was a surprising tenor, silver to Talaysen's gold.

And no sooner had Rune spotted him than she recalled a bit of wick-edness the four of them had devised when she had first joined them out on the streets of the Faire, and her broken arm had prevented her from playing.

She whistled a snatch of the song—"My Lover's Eyes" it was, and as sickening and sticky-sweet a piece of doggerel as ever a Guild Bard could produce. She saw Talaysen's head snap up at the notes, saw his green eyes sparkle with merriment. He nodded, a grin wrapping itself around his head, then nodded at Gwyna to come join them. Daran had caught the whistle, too—he craned his absurdly long neck all about, blond fore-lock flopping into his eyes as usual, then sighted her and whistled back. That was all it took; while the crowd was still making up its collective mind about moving on, Gwyna and Daran edged in to take their places beside Talaysen and Rune, and the song was begun.

They sang it acappella, but all four of them had voices more than strong enough to carry over the crowd noise, and the harmony they formed—though they hadn't sung it since the fourth week of the Faire—was sweet and pure, and recaptured the fickle crowd's attention. The first verse of the ditty extolled the virtues of the singer's beloved, and the faithfulness of the singer-lover—Gwyna held Daran's hands clasped chin-high, and stared passionately into his eyes, as Rune and Talaysen echoed their pose.

So far, a normal sort of presentation, if more than a bit melodramatic. Ah—but the second verse was coming; and after all those promises of eternal fidelity, the partners suddenly dropped the hands they held and caught those of a new partner, and without missing a beat, sang the second verse just as passionately to a *new* "beloved."

Chuckles threaded the crowd. The audience waited expectantly for the next verse to see what the Bards would do.

They lowered their clasped hands, turning their heads away from their partners, as if in an agony of moon-struck shyness. At the end of the third verse, they dropped hands again, rolled their eyes heavenward as each lifted right hand to brow and the left to bosom, changed pose again (still without looking) and groped once again for the hands of the "beloved"—

Except that this time Talaysen got Daran's hands, and Gwyna got Rune's.

The crowd's chuckles turned into an appreciative roar of laughter when they turned their heads back to discover just whose hands they were clutching, and jumped back, pulling away as if they'd been burned.

The laughter all but drowned out the last notes of the song, sung to the eyes of their original partners.

As more coinage showered into the hat, one among the crowd turned away with a smothered oath, and a look of hatred. He wore the purple and gold ribbons of a Guild Bard.

"Well, here, my children—" Talaysen bent to catch up the laden hat. "Share and share alike. Feed your bodies that your voices not suffer; buy fairings to call the eyes of an audience, or other things—"

He poured a generous measure of the coinage into each of their hands. "Now off with you! We'll meet as usual, just at sundown, at the tent for dinner."

Gwyna slipped the money into her belt-pouch, and dropped Talaysen a mock-curtsy. "As you say, Master mine. Elsewhere, Tree-man, Master Heron, I'm minded to sing solos for a bit." Daran grinned and took himself off as ordered.

Rune noticed that his eyes had been following Gwyna for some time, and she reflected that *he* would be no bad company for the cheerful Gypsy. Gwyna had confided a great deal to Rune over the past few weeks; they'd become very good friends. Gwyna had said that she tended to take up with either Bards or Gypsies, but that she hadn't had a lover from amongst the Free Bards in four years.

Maybe she was thinking about it now.

As Gwyna strolled away, it seemed her thoughts were tending in that direction, for she pulled her guitar around in front of her and began a love song. Rune exchanged a glance full of irony with Talaysen, and they began her elf-ballad.

Gwyna didn't mind too carefully where she was wandering, until she noted that her steps had taken her away from the well-traveled ways and into the rows reserved for the finer goods. Here she was distinctly out of place, and besides, there were fewer fairgoers, and less of a chance for an audience. She turned to retrace her steps, only to find her path blocked.

He who blocked it was a darkly handsome man, as looks are commonly judged—but his gray eyes had a cruel glint to them that Gwyna did not in the least like, the smile on his thin, hard lips was a prurient one, and he wore the robes of a Church Priest. But they were wine-dark, and she thought she could see odd symbols woven into the hem of the robe, symbols which she found even less to her liking than the glint in his eyes.

"Your pardon, m'lord—" She made as if to step around him, but he moved like quicksilver, getting in front of her again.

"Stay, bright songbird—" He spoke softly, his voice pitched soft and low so as to sound enticing. "A word in your ear, if I may."

"I cannot prevent you, m'lord," Gwyna replied, becoming more uneasy by the heartbeat.

"You have no patron, else you would not be singing to the crowd—and I think you have, at present, no—'friend'—either." His knowing look gave another meaning entirely to the word "friend"; a prurient, lascivious meaning. "I offer myself in both capacities. I think we understand each other."

Although Gwyna was long past innocence, the blood rose to her cheeks in response to his words, and the evil, lascivious leer that lay thinly veiled behind them. Just listening to him made her feel used; and that made her angry as well as a little frightened.

"That I think we do *not,* 'my lord,' " she retorted, putting a good sharp sting in her reply. "Firstly, you are a Priest of the Church, and sworn to celibacy. If *you* will take no care for your vows, then I will! Secondly, I am a Free Bard, and I earn my way by song—naught else. I go where I will, I earn my way by *music,* and I do not sell myself to such as *you* for your caging. So you may take your 'patronage' and offer it among the dealers in swine and sheep—for I'm sure that *there* you'll find bed-mates to your liking in plenty!"

She pushed rudely past him, her flesh shrinking from the touch of his robes, and stalked off with her head held high and proud. She prayed that he could not tell by her carriage how much she longed to take to her heels and run.

She prayed that he wouldn't follow her; it seemed her prayers were answered, for she lost sight of him immediately. And as soon as he was out of sight, she forgot him.

◊   ◊   ◊

The Priest clenched his jaw in rage, and his saturnine face contorted with anger for one brief instant before settling into a mask of indifference. It was only a moment, but it was long enough for one other to see.

A plump, balding man, oily with good living, and wearing the gold and purple ribbons of a Guild Bard, stepped out from the shelter of a nearby awning and approached the dark-robed cleric.

"If you will forgive my impertinence, my lord," he began, "I cannot help but think we have an interest in common. . . ."

". . . so I told him to look for bedmates among the flocks," Gwyna finished, while Daran and Rune chuckled appreciatively. She took a hearty bite of her bread and cheese—no one among the brotherhood had had extraordinary good luck, so the fare was plain tonight—and grinned back at them. Neither Erdric nor Talaysen looked at all amused, however— Erdric was as sober as a stone, and Talaysen's green eyes were darkened with worry.

"That may not have been wise, Gypsy Robin," he said, sipping his well-watered wine. "It isn't wise to anger a Priest, and I would guess from your description that he is not among the lesser of his brethren. Granted, if you called him up before the justices this week, and you had witnesses, you could prove he meant to violate his vows—but even so, he is still powerful, and that is the worst sort of enemy to have made."

"So long as I stay within the Faire precincts, what can he do?" Gwyna countered, nettled at Talaysen's implied criticism of her behavior. "I *do* have witnesses if I care to call them, and if he dares to lay a hand on me—"

Her feral grin and a hand to the knife concealed in her skirts told the fate he could expect. Gwyna needed no man to guard *her* "honor"—such as it was.

"All right, Robin, I am rebuked. No one puts a tie on you, least of all me. Where away tonight?"

"A party—a most decorous party. Virtue, I tell you, will be my watch-word this eve. I am pledged to play and sing for the name-day feast of the daughter of the jewel-smith Marek, she being a ripe twelve on this night. I am to sing nothing but the most innocent of songs and tales, and the festivities will be over before midnight. I will be there and back again in my bed before the night is half spent."

She drooped her eyelids significantly at Daran, who looked first surprised, then pleased. Talaysen bit his lip to keep from chuckling; he knew that tacit invitation. Gwyna would not be spending the last nights of the Faire alone.

"Then may the Lady see to it that the jewel-smith Marek rewards you and your songs with their true value. As for the rest of us—the Faire awaits! And we grow no richer dallying here."

They finished the last bites of their dinners, and rose from their cushions nearly as one, each to seek an audience.

Gwyna's pouch was the heavier by three pieces of gold, and she was wearing it inside her skirts for safety, as she made her way down the aisle of closed and darkened stalls. One gold piece would go to Erdric, with instructions to purchase a roast pig and wine for the company, and keep the remainder for himself. The other two would go to Goldsmith Nosta in the morning, to be put with her other savings. Gwyna firmly believed in securing high ground against rainy days.

With her mind on these matters, she did not see the dark shadow that followed her, mingling with the other shadows cast by the moon. Her sharp ears might have warned her of danger, but there were no footfalls for her to hear. There was only a sudden wind of ice and fear that blew upon her from behind, and hard upon that, the darkness of oblivion.

She woke with an aching head, her vision blurred and oddly distorted, her sense of smell gone, to find herself looking out through the bars of a black iron cage. She scrambled to her feet with a frightened squawk, and a flurry of wings, shaking so hard with a sudden onset of terror that every feather trembled.

Feathers? *Wings?*

A dun-colored hanging in front of her moved; from behind it emerged the dark, bearded Priest she had so foolishly insulted. Beside him was a fat little man in Guild purple and gold. She had heard of Priests who practiced magic; now she knew the rumors to be true.

"And the foolish little bird takes the baited grain. Not so clever now, are we?" the Guild Bard chortled. "Marek's invitation was his own, but two of those gold pieces you so greedily bore away were mine, with m'lord Revaner's spell upon them."

"Is the vengeance sweet enough, Bestif?" The Priest's deep voice was full of amusement.

"It will be in a moment, m'lord." Bestif bent down so that his face filled Gwyna's field of vision. She shrunk back away from him, until the bars of the cage prevented her going farther. "You, my fine *feathered* friend, are now truly feathered indeed, and you will remain so. Look at yourself! Bird-brained you were, to make a mock of my masterpiece, and bird you have truly become, the property of m'lord, to sing at his will. You would not serve him freely, so now you shall find yourself serving from within one of those cages you have so despised, and whether you will or no."

"And do not think, little songbird, that you may ever fly away," the Priest continued, his eyes shining with cheerful sadism. "Magic must obey laws; you wear the semblance of a bird, but your weight is that of the woman you were, as is your approximate size. Your wings could never carry you to freedom, attractive though they may be."

Gwyna stretched out one arm—no, wing—involuntarily; her head swiveled on a long neck to regard it with mournful eyes. Indeed, it was quite brilliantly beautiful, and if the rest of her matched the graceful plumage, she must be the most striking and exotic "bird" ever seen. The colors of her garb, the golds and reds and warm oranges, were faithfully preserved in her feathers—transformed from clothing to plumes, she supposed despairingly. Circling one leg was a heavy gold ring—which could only be the gold pieces that had been the instrument of her downfall, cunningly transmuted.

Black, bleak despair filled her heart, for how ever would any of her friends guess what had become of her? Had she been woman still, she would have sunk to the floor of her cage and wept in hopelessness—

Here the most cruel jest of all was played on her. Her neck stretched out, her beak opened involuntarily, and glorious liquid song poured forth.

Her amazement broke the despair for a moment, and the music ceased to come from her. The Priest read her surprise correctly, and smiled a predatory smile.

"Did we not say you would serve me, whether you would or no? I was not minded to have a captive that drooped all day on her perch. No, the spell binding you is thus; the unhappier you are, the more you will sing. Well, Bard, are you satisfied?"

"Very, my lord. Very."

The Priest clapped his hands, summoning two hulking attendants in black uniform tunics. These hoisted her cage upon their shoulders, and carried her outside the tent, where the cage was fastened to a chain and hoisted to the top of a stout iron pole.

"Now all the Faire shall admire my treasure, and envy my possessing it," the Priest taunted her from below, "while you shall look upon the freedom of your former friends—and sing for my pleasure."

As dawn began to color the tips of the tents and roofs of the Faire, Gwyna beat with utter futility on the bars of her cage with her wings, while glorious music fell on the tents below her in the place of her tears.

By midmorning there was a crowd of curiosity-seekers below her cage, and Gwyna had ceased her useless attempts at escape. Now she simply sat, eyes half-closed in despair, and sang. She had learned that while she could not halt the flow of music from her beak, she could direct it; to the wonderment of the onlookers, she was singing every lament and dirge she could remember.

Once she saw Daran below her, and her voice shook with hopelessness. She was singing Talaysen's "Walls of Iron" at the time; it seemed appropriate. Daran stared at her intently as she sang it with the special interludes she had always played on her guitar. She longed to be able to speak, even to throw a fit of some kind to attract his attention, but the spell holding her would not allow that. She thought her heart would break into seven pieces when he walked away at the end of the song.

The Priest had her cage brought down at sunset and installed on a special stand in his tent. She was scrupulously fed the freshest of fruit, and the water in her little cup was renewed. Despite the warnings that she could not fly away, she watched avidly for an opportunity to escape, but the cage was cleaned and the provisioning made without the door ever being opened. Revaner evidently had planned a dinner party; he greeted visitors, placing them at a table well within clear sight of her cage. When all were assembled, he lit branching candles with a wave of his hand, the golden light falling clearly upon her. The guests sighed in wonder—her spirits sank to their lowest ebb—she opened her beak and sang and her music was at its most lovely. The celebrants congratulated the Priest on his latest acquisition. He preened visibly, casting a malicious glance from time to time back at the cage where Gwyna drooped on her perch. It was unbearable, yet she had no choice but to bear it. Torture of the body would have been far, far preferable to this utter misery of the spirit.

At last the long, bitter day was over. A cover was placed over her cage; in the darkness, bird-instincts took over entirely, and despite sorrow and despair, Gwyna slept.

Talaysen questioned everyone who knew the Free Bards, and especially those who knew Gwyna herself. Always the answer was "no." No one had seen her since the previous day; the last to see her was Marek, and she had left his tent well within the time she had promised to return.

It was bad enough that she had not appeared last night, but as the day wore on, it became more and more obvious that she wasn't just dallying with a new, chance-met lover. She was *missing*. And since it was Robin, who truly could defend herself, that could only mean foul play.

As Talaysen searched the Faire for some sign of her, he could only think about the incident she had reported the previous evening. The Priest who had approached her—he wasn't one that Talaysen knew, which meant he wasn't one of the Priests attached to Kingsford.

He ran a hand through his hair, distractedly, and another thought occurred to him—one which he did not in the least like. Ardis had asked him to be on the watch for a Priest who might violate his vows to please his own desires—a Priest who would use extraordinary means to get what he wanted.

Could this Priest and the one that threatened Gwyna be the same?

Given that she had quite vanished from the Faire, it was not only possible, it seemed likely. Ardis had said that she didn't know the exact identity of this Priest, which meant he wasn't one she ordinarily worked with as a mage. So he would be new to Kingsford, and probably camped in the Priests' tents with the other visiting clerics. If he had Gwyna, in any form of captivity, he would keep her there. He wouldn't dare bring her into the cloisters, not with Ardis on the watch for him.

Talaysen made up his mind, called his Free Bards together, and passed the word. *Look for anything that reminds you of Gwyna, anything at all. And look for it especially among the Priests' tents.*

The next day was like the first, save only that she was left outside the tent when the sun set. Evidently since he had no reason to display her, the Priest saw no reason to bring her inside. Or perhaps this was but another sadism on his part—for now she was witness to the Faire's night life, with its emphasis on entertainments. The cage was lowered, cleaned and stocked, then raised again. Gwyna watched the lights of the Faire appear, watched the strollers wander freely about, and sang until she was too weary to chirp another note.

She was far too worn to notice that someone had come to stand in the shadows below her, until the sound of a whisper carried up to her perch.

"Gwyna? Bird, are you Gwyna?"

She fluttered her wings in agitation, unable to answer, except for strangled squawks.

A second voice whispered to the first: "Daran, this seems very far-fetched to me—"

"Rune, I tell you it's Gwyna! *Nobody* performs 'Walls of Iron' the way she does—but this bird replicated every damn note! *Gwyna! Answer me!*"

As a cloud of helplessness descended on her and her beak began to open to pour forth melody, she suddenly shook as an idea occurred to her. No, she couldn't talk, but she could most assuredly *sing*!

She sang the chorus of "Elven Captive"—

A spell-bound captive here am I
Who will not live and cannot die.

A bitten-off exclamation greeted the song. Rune gasped. "Wait, that's—"

Daran interrupted her. "'Elven Captive'! No bird would pick that chorus just at this moment! It *is* Gwyna! Gypsy Robin, who did this to you?"

For answer Gwyna sang the first notes of "My Lover's Eyes" and the chorus of "The Scurvy Priest," a little ditty that was rarely, if ever, heard in Faires, but often in taverns of a particular clientele.

"Bestif and a Priest, probably the one she told us about. Oh hellfire, this is too deep for us to handle," Daran mumbled in a discouraged voice.

"Don't *ever* underestimate Talaysen, cloud-scraper." Rune sounded a bit more hopeful. "He's got resources you wouldn't guess—Gwyna, don't give up! We're going to leave you, but only to let Talaysen know what's happened. We'll be back, and with help! We'll get you back to us some-how, I swear it!"

There was a brief pattering of footsteps, and the space below her was empty again.

But the hope in her heart was company enough that night.

When dawn came, she looked long and hopefully for a sight of her friends among the swirling crowds, but there was no sign of them. As the day wore on, she lost hope again, and her songs rang out to the satisfaction of the Priest. When no one had appeared by sunset, the last of her hopes died. Talaysen must have decided that the idea of her transformation was too preposterous to consider—or that they simply were powerless to help her. She was so sunk in sadness that she did not notice the troupe of acrobats slowly making their way towards the Priest's dun-colored tent, tumbling and performing tricks as they came.

She only heard their noise and outcries when they actually formed up in the cleared space just in front of the tent and beneath her cage. Much to the displeasure of the Priest's chief servant, they began their routine right there, with a series of tumbles that ended with the formation of a human pyramid.

"Ho there—be off with you—away—!"

The major-domo was one to their many, and they simply ignored him, continuing with their act, much to the delight of the children that had followed them here. The pyramid collapsed into half-a-dozen somer-saulting bodies, and the air and ground seemed full of lithe, laughing human balls. The major-domo flapped his hands at them ineffectually as Gwyna watched, her unhappiness momentarily forgotten in the pleasure of seeing one of her captors discomfited.

This continued for several moments, until at last the Priest himself emerged to demand why his rest was being disturbed.

"Now!" cried a cloaked nonentity at the edge of the crowd—and Gwyna recognized Talaysen's voice with a start.

Everything seemed to happen at once—two of the acrobats flung a blanket over the Priest's head, enveloping him in its folds and effectively smothering his outcries. The rest jumped upon each other's shoulders, forming a tower of three men and a boy; the boy produced a lock-pick, and swiftly popped open the lock on Gwyna's cage. The door swung wide—

"Jump, Gwyna!" Talaysen and Daran held a second blanket stretched taut between them. She didn't pause to think, but obeyed. The ground rushed at her as she instinctively spread her wings in a futile hope of slowing her fall somewhat—

She landed in the blanket with one of her legs half-bent beneath her—it was painful, but it didn't hurt badly enough to have been broken. Before she could draw breath, Daran had scooped her up from the pocket of the blanket and bundled her under one arm like an oversized chicken; likely he was the only one of them big enough to carry her so. With Talaysen leading and the acrobats confusing the pursuit behind them, he set off at as hard a run as he could manage with the burden of Gwyna to carry. Gwyna craned her neck around in time to see the Priest free himself from the confines of the blanket, his face black with rage—then they were out of sight around a corner of one of the stalls.

They were hidden in the warm, near-stifling darkness of the back of a weaver's tent, in among bales of her work. Gwyna could hear Daran panting beside her, and clamped her bill tight on the first notes of a song. Her heart, high during the rescue, had fallen again. She was free, yes, but no nearer to being herself again than she had been in the cage.

There was a swish of material; Rune flung herself down beside them, breathing so hard she could hardly speak.

"Tal—Talaysen's gone to the cathedral, to the courts and the Justiciars—"

"Looking to the Church for help?" Daran whispered incredulously. "I thought the Wren cleverer than that! Why, all that bastard has to do is get there before him, lay a charge, and flaunt his robes—"

"There are Priests and Priests, Heron," Rune replied, invisible in the stuffy darkness. "And let me tell you, the Master's no fool. I thought the same as you, but he says he knows someone among the Justiciars today, and I think I know who it is. *He* knows who we can trust. He says to make a break and run as soon as we think it safe—I'm to get someone with the Gypsies, you're for the cathedral and the Court of Justice. The tumblers will do their best to scramble things again."

"All right—" Daran said doubtfully. "The Wren's never been wrong before, but—Lady bless, I hope he isn't now!"

All of them burst from the tent into the blinding sunlight—and behind them rose a clamor and noise; Gwyna looked back to see the Priest (how had he contrived to be so close to their hiding place?) in hot pursuit, followed by all of his servants and two of his helmeted and armed guards. If those caught them before they reached the goal Talaysen had in mind for them—

They burst into the Justice court of the cathedral itself, Revaner and his contingent hard on their heels; Talaysen was there already, gesturing to a robed man and woman and a younger man clad in the red robes of Church Justiciars.

"My lords—my lady—" he cried, waving at Daran and Gwyna. "Here is the one of whom I told you—"

"Justice!" thundered Revaner at the same time. "These thieves have stolen my pet—wrecked my tent—"

One of the guards seized Daran's arms. He responded by dropping Gwyna. She squawked in surprise at being dropped, then fled to the dubious safety of the feet of the three strangers before Revaner could grab more than one of her tail-feathers.

The lady reached down and petted Gwyna; comfort and reassurance passed from Priest to bird with her caress. Gwyna suddenly had far more confidence in Talaysen's scheme—this Priest was no ordinary, gold-grasping charlatan, but one with real power and a generous spirit!

The other two waited patiently for the clamor to die down to silence, quite plainly ready to wait all day if that was what it took.

At length even the yipping servants of the Priest ceased their noise.

"You claim, Bard Talaysen, that this bird is in fact one of your company, ensorceled into this shape," said the gray-haired man in Priest robes. "Yet what proof have you that this is so?"

"Mind-touch her, Lady Ardis—or have Lord Arran do so." Talaysen replied steadily. "Trust your *own* senses."

The man in red approached slowly, his hand held out as if to a shy animal. Gwyna needed no such reassurance. She ran limpingly to the young man's feet, chirping and squawking. She strove with all her might to project her *human* thoughts into the hireling's mind, spreading out the whole story as best she could.

Arran patted her feathers into smoothness, and from his touch came reassurance and comfort. More, words formed in Gwyna's mind, words as clear as speech.

Fear not, little singer; there is no doubt in my heart that you are wholly human.

The young man rose gracefully to his feet and faced the two mages. "This one is bespelled indeed; she *is* the Free Bard Gwyna—more than that, the evil being that has so enslaved her is *that* one"—he pointed an accusing finger at Revaner—"he who claims her as his property and pet. His accomplice in this evil was the Guild Bard Bestif."

At that, the Priest paled, and tried to flee, only to be held by the guards he had brought with him. At the same time, Gwyna felt the Lady-Priest's hand on her head, and some instinct told her to remain utterly still. She saw Talaysen take Rune's hand, his face harden with anxiety. Daran clutched his bony hands together, biting his lip.

"We shall need your help," the Lady-Priest said to Talaysen and Rune. "I think you have some small acquaintance with magic yourselves. And you know her."

She saw Rune start with surprise, saw Talaysen nod—

Then all was confusion. The courtyard spun around in front of Gwyna's eyes, moving faster and faster until it was nothing but a blur of light and shadow. The courtyard vanished altogether. Then light blazed up, nearly blinding her, and a dark *something* separated from her own substance, pulling away from her with a reluctant shudder. She could feel it wanting to stay, clinging with an avid hunger, but the light drove it forth despite its will. Suddenly she was overcome with an appalling pain, and crumbled beneath the onslaught of it. Her flesh felt as if it were melting, twisting, reshaping, and it hurt so much she cried out in sheer misery—

A cry that began as a bird's call, and ended as the anguished sob of a human in mortal agony.

The pain cut off abruptly; Gwyna blinked, finding herself slumped on the stone of the courtyard, her skirts in a puddle of red, gold, and scarlet about her, her dark hair falling into her eyes, and three gold coins on the stone before her.

She stared at one hand, then at the other—then at the faces of the three who stood above her; the Lady-Priest, Talaysen and Rune. Their brown, green, and hazel eyes mirrored her own relief and joy—

From the other side of the courtyard came an uncanny shriek—something like a raven's cry, something like the scream of a hawk. All four turned as one to see what had made the sound.

Crouching where the dark Priest had stood, was an ugly, evil-looking bird, like none Gwyna had ever seen before. Its plumage was a filthy black, its head and crooked neck naked red skin, like a vulture. It had a twisted yellow beak and small, black eyes. It stood nearly waist-high to the two guards beside it. As they watched, it made a swipe at one of them with that sharp beak, but the man was not nearly so ale-sotted as he seemed, and caught the thing by the neck just behind the head.

"Evil spells broken often return upon their caster," said young Arran, soberly. "As this one has. Balance is restored. Let him be exhibited at the gate as a warning to those who would pollute the Holy Church with unclean magic; but tend him carefully and gently. It may be that one day God will warm to forgiveness if he learns to repent. As for the Guild Bard Bestif, let him be fined twelve gold pieces and banned forever from the Faire. Let one half of that fine be given to the minstrels he wronged, and one half to those in need. That would be my judgment."

"So be it, so let it be done," said the older man, silent until now.

They made as if to leave; Gwyna scrambled to her feet, holding out one of the three gold coins. "My lords—lady—this for my thanks, an' you will?"

The older Priest took it gravely. "We are true Priests of the Church; we do not accept pay for the performance of our duty—but if you wish this to be given to the offerings for the poor?"

Gwyna nodded; he accepted the coin and the three vanished into the depths of the cathedral.

Gwyna took the others and tossed them to Talaysen, who caught them handily.

"For celebration?" he asked, holding it up. "Shall we feast tonight?"

"Have I not cause to celebrate? Only one thing—"

"Name it, Gypsy Robin."

"If you love me, Master Wren—buy nothing that once wore feathers!"

CHAPTER SIXTEEN

Rune shooed Talaysen away, so that she could apportion their belongings into packs. "This is apprentice-work," she told him sternly. "You go do what a Master does." Grinning, he left her to it.

She had acquired a bit more clothing here at the Faire, but her load was still much lighter than his, and she elected to take their common stores of food along with her own things. The tent was still full of people, or seemed to be, anyway. It was much smaller when all of them were packing up, with gear spread all over, and there was much complaining about how it had all magically multiplied during the sojourn at the Faire. Rune hadn't had that much to start with, and Talaysen did not carry one item more than he needed, but some of the others were not so wise.

When one stayed in one place for any length of time, Rune suspected, it was easy to forget how much one could carry. There had been this same moaning and groaning for the past two days, as the Free Bards departed in groups, by morning and afternoon.

The only folk not involved in the throes of packing were Erdric and his grandson. They lived here in Kingsford the year round; Erdric had a permanent place in the King's Blade tavern, and young Sparrow was learning the trade at the hands of his grandfather. They would see to it that the two men the Free Bards had hired to take down the great tent would do so without damaging it, and haul it off in their cart to the merchant it was kept with the rest of the year.

More than three-fourths of the Free Bards had already gone their way by this morning; Talaysen would be the last to depart, so that no one lacked for a personal good-bye from their leader.

That meant he and Rune wouldn't be able to cover a great deal of ground their first day, but Rune didn't much mind. She'd gotten a great deal to think about over the past several weeks, and most of it was unexpected.

The Free Bards, for instance—contrasted with the Guild Bards. Talaysen's group was a great deal more in the way of what she had *thought* the Guild Bards would be like. The Free Bards took care of each other; she had seen with her own eyes right here at the Faire how the Guild Bards squabbled and fought among themselves for the plum jobs. And if someone were unfortunate to lose one of those jobs due to accident, illness or the like, well, his fellow Guild members would commiserate in public but rejoice in private, and all scramble for the choice tidbit like so many quarreling dogs under the table.

And the Church—there had been a set of shocks, though she'd been prepared for some of them from the rumors she'd heard. That though it officially frowned upon magic, it held a cadre of mages—well, she'd learned that was true enough, though Lady Ardis had warned her not to confirm the rumor to anyone. And though there were plenty of venial Priests, there were some like Lady Ardis, who would aid anyone who needed it, and valued honor and ethics above gold.

Then there was Talaysen—an enigma if ever she saw one. A Guild Bard once, he could still claim his place any time he wanted to—and he refused. Even though that refusal cost him in patronage and wealth.

She wasn't certain how he felt about her. He didn't treat her as a child, though she was his apprentice. He watched her constantly when he thought she wasn't looking, and the eyes he followed her with were the eyes of a starving man. But when he spoke with her or taught her, he had another look entirely; he teased her as if he was her elder brother, and he never once gave a hint that his feelings ran any deeper than that.

Yet whenever someone else seemed to be playing the gallant with her, he'd find himself watched so closely that he would invariably give up the game as not worth it. After all, no one wanted to invoke Talaysen's displeasure.

And no one wants to interfere with anyone that Master Wren is finally taking an interest in, she thought, with heavy irony. *The only problem is, the Master doesn't seem to know he's taken that interest.*

Gwyna had at least told her that Talaysen had remained virtually celibate for the last several years, though no one knew why. There didn't seem to be any great, lost loves in his life, although Lady Ardis had hinted that he might at least have had a dalliance that *could* have become a love, if he had pursued it. For some reason, he hadn't.

Well, if there's no lost loves, there's no ghosts for me to fight. I've got that much in my favor.

Rune had decided in the last week of the Faire how *she* felt about Master Wren. And there was nothing celibate about what she wanted. She had never in all her life met with a man who so exactly suited her in every way. Of course, she'd never seen him out of company—out on the road, he might turn surly, hard to get along with. But she didn't think so. He had a great deal to teach, and she to learn, but in performance, at least, they were absolute partners, each making up for the other's weaknesses. She had every reason to think that the partnership would continue when they were on their own.

Now if I can just warm it up to something more than "partnership."

She finished the packs; Talaysen was making farewells and giving some last-minute directions, so she had elected to pack up, and not because she was the apprentice and he expected it—which he didn't. It was because he was doing what his duties required, and she had free hands. The accord had been reached without either of them saying a word.

She set the packs aside and waited for him to return. Out beyond the

Faire palings, the merchants were also breaking down and preparing to leave. The Midsummer Faire was over for another year.

She was surprised to feel an odd sense of loss, of uncertainty. For the past three weeks at least, ever since her splint had come off, she had known what every day would bring. Now it was completely new; she hadn't ever really traveled the roads for a living, and the idea was a little daunting.

Finally, as the sun crossed the zenith-line, he returned. "Well, are we ready?" he asked.

She nodded. "Packed and provisioned, Master Wren." She hefted her pack up and slung it over her back; her fiddle was safe inside, and her harp and lute were fastened securely on the outside. She wished briefly that Talaysen had a horse, or even a little donkey they could use to carry their supplies. With a beast their pace could be much faster, though it would be an added expense.

While you're wishing, Rune, why don't you wish for a pair of riding horses while you're at it?

Still, a donkey could eat almost anything; it wouldn't be that much of a burden unless they stayed in a town.

And a donkey makes you look more prosperous, and makes you a target for robbers.

Talaysen blinked in surprise, and hefted his own pack onto his back. "I hadn't expected you to be ready quite so soon," he said mildly. "I took you for town-bred, and not used to the road life."

She shrugged. "I walked from Westhaven to Nolton, from Nolton to here. I learned a bit."

"So I see." He shifted the pack into a comfortable position on his back. "Well, if you're ready, so am I."

So it was that simple, after all. They simply left the tent, with a farewell wave to Erdric as he gave the two hired men their instructions, and took their place in the steady stream of people leaving by the road to the north.

Talaysen seemed disinclined to talk, so she held her peace as they walked at a good pace along the verge. The press of people leaving was not as heavy as the one of those arriving had been, and most of them were driving heavily loaded wagons, not walking. *Their* pace was set by the pace of whoever was in the lead of this particular group of travelers. The other folk on foot, at least those that Rune saw, were limited to some small peddlers who had probably been vending impulse-goods from trays, and nondescript folk who could have been anything. The former toiled under packs that would have made a donkey blanch; the latter beneath burdens like their own. The pace that Talaysen set had them passing most other foot-travelers, and all the carts. The sun beat down on all of them, regardless of rank or station, and while there were frequent smiles and nods from those they passed, no one seemed inclined to talk. Halfway into the afternoon, though, they took the first turning to the right, a track so overgrown that she would never have picked it herself. It seemed no one else had chosen it either, at least not today. And no one followed them for as long as she could see the main road when she glanced behind them. She cast him a doubtful look that he never noticed, and followed along a step or two behind him, keeping a sharp watch for trouble.

Weeds grew ankle-high even in the ruts on the road itself, and were waist-high on the verge. Once under the shelter of overhanging trees, she was forced to revise her guess of how long it had been since the road had been used by other than foot traffic. From the look of the road—or rather, path—no one else had come this way since the beginning of the Faire at very best, unless they were foot-travelers like themselves. The weeds were not broken down the way they would be if cart wheels had rolled over them; she was, admittedly, no tracker, but it didn't seem to her that the weeds had been taken down by anything other than the passing of animals in days.

Trouble on a deserted way like this could come in several forms; least likely was in the form of humans, robbers who hunted up and down a seldom-traveled track precisely because they were unlikely to be caught on it and those they robbed were unlikely to be missed. Wild animals or farm animals run feral could give a traveler a bad time; particularly wild cattle and feral pigs. She didn't think that the larger predators would range this close to the Faire site and Kingsford, but that was a possibility that shouldn't be dismissed out of hand. There had once been a wild lion loose in the forest near Westhaven and there were always wolves about. But last of all, and most likely, was that it could be that the reason why this road was unused was the same reason the road through Skull Hill Pass was little used. Something really horrible could be on it. Something that had moved in recently, that Talaysen might not know about.

"Where are we going?" she asked Talaysen, not wanting to seem to question his judgment, but also not wanting to find herself facing something like the Ghost. The next uncanny creature might not be a music lover. And she was no hand at all with any kind of weapon.

"What's our next destination, do you mean?" he replied, "or where are we making for tonight?" He looked back over his shoulder at her to answer, and he didn't seem at all alarmed. Surely he knew about all the signs of danger on a road. . . . Surely he was better at it than her. . . .

"Both," she said shortly. The track widened a little, and she got up beside him so that he could talk to her without having to crane his neck around.

"Allendale Faire, ultimately," he told her. "That's about two weeks from now. The pickings there have been good for me in the past, and no one else wanted to take it this year, so I said we would. Tonight, there's a good camping spot I think we can make by moonrise; there's water, shelter, and high ground there. I've used it before. The track doesn't get any worse than this, so I don't see any problem with pressing on after sunset."

"After sunset?" she said doubtfully. "Master Wren, I don't think I'm up to struggling with tent poles in the dark."

"You won't have to," he said with a cheerful smile. "There won't be anyone there but us, and since the weather is fine, there's no need to worry about putting up a tent. With luck, the weather will hold until we reach Allendale in about two weeks."

Two weeks. That was a long time to walk through forest. She'd slept under the stars without a tent before, but never with company . . . still it wasn't that she was afraid something would happen, it was that she was afraid it *wouldn't*, without a little privacy to share. And she wasn't certain their provisions would hold out that long. "Is there anything on this road?" she asked.

"Quite a bit, after tonight. Small villages, a great deal like the one you came from, and about two days apart," he told her. "We ought to be able to pick up a few nights' worth of food and lodging for music on the way to Allendale Faire."

She frowned, not quite understanding why he was so certain of a welcome. "But they're so close to Kingsford—why would they bother to trade us for music so close to the city—and so close to Faire-time? In winter, now, I could see it—but now?"

He chuckled. "How often did the people in *your* village go even as far as the next one for anything? Maybe once or twice a year? The first village is close to a two-day walk from here, and most farmers can't afford to take that much time away from crops this time of the season. Not many people take this road, either, which is why I claimed it for the start of our journey."

"What if they've had a minstrel through here?" she asked. Then she remembered Westhaven, and shook her head. "Never mind, even if it was two days ago, we'll still be a novelty, won't we? Even if they have their own musicians. It was that way at the Hungry Bear in my village."

He laughed. "Well, with luck, we'll be the first musicians they've seen in a while. With none, they still won't have had a musician down this way for a few days, and what's more"—his grin grew cocky and self-assured—"he won't have been as good as we are, because he won't have been a Free Bard."

She chuckled and bent her head to keep her eye on her footing.

They walked on in silence; the grass grown over the track muffled their steps, and though their appearance frightened the birds right on the road into silence, farther off in the woods there were plenty of them chirping and singing sleepily in the heat. These woods had none of the brooding, ominous qualities of the ones around Skull Hill, and she began to relax a little. There was nothing at all uncanny that she could sense—and in fact, after all those weeks of throngs of people, and living with people at her elbow all the time, she found the solitude quite comforting.

She was glad of her hat, a wide-brimmed straw affair that she'd bought at the Faire; it was a lot cooler than her leather hat, and let a bit of breeze through to her head when there was any to be had. Though the trees shaded the road a bit, they also sheltered it from what little breeze there was, and the heat beneath the branches was oppressive. Insects buzzed in the knee-high weeds beside the road, a monotonous drone that made her very sleepy. Sweat trickled down her back and the back of her neck; she'd put her hair up under the hat, but she still felt her scalp and neck prickling with heat. At least she was wearing her light breeches; in skirts, even kilted up to her knees, she'd have been fighting her way through the weeds. Grasshoppers sprang away from their track, and an enterprising kestrel followed them for a while. He was quite 'a sight to see, hovering just ahead of them, then swooping down on a fat 'hopper that they frightened into bumbling flight. He would carry it on ahead and perch, neatly stripping wings and legs, then eating it like a child with a carrot, before coming back for another unfortunate enough to be a little too slow.

"Why Allendale Faire?" she asked, when the silence became too much to bear, and her ears rang from the constant drone of insects.

"It's a decently large local Faire in a town that has quite a few Sires and wealthy merchants living nearby," he replied absently. "We need to start thinking about a place to winter-up; I'm not in favor of making the rounds in winter, personally. And you never have; it's a hard life, although it can be very rewarding if you hit a place where the town prospered during the summer and the people all have real coin to spend."

She thought about trekking through woods like these with snow up to her knees instead of weeds, and shivered. "I'd rather not," she said honestly. "Like I told you when I met you, that isn't the kind of life I would lead by choice. That was one reason why I wanted to join the Guild."

"And your points were well made. So, one of those Sires or the local branches of the Merchants' Guild in or around Allendale might provide a place to spend our winter." He turned his head sideways, and smiled. "You see, most Sires can't afford a permanent House musician—at least the ones out here in the country can't. So they'll take on one that pleases their fancy for the winter months, and turn him loose in the spring. That way they have new entertainment every winter, when there are long, dark hours to while away, yet they don't have the expense of a House retainer and all the gifts necessary to make sure that he stays content and keeps up his repertory." The tone of his voice turned ironic. "The fact is that once a Guild Minstrel has a position, there's nothing requiring him to do anything more. It's his for life unless he chooses to move on, or does something illegal. If he's lazy, he never has to learn another new note; just keep playing the same old songs. So the people who have House Minstrels or Bards encourage them to stir themselves by giving them gifts of money and so forth when they've performed well."

"Gifts for doing the job they're supposed to do in the first place?" she replied, aghast.

"That's the Guild." He shrugged again. "I prefer our way. Honest money, honestly earned."

Still—*A place in a Sire's household, even for just the winter? How is that possible?* "I thought only Guild musicians could take positions with a House," she offered.

He laughed. "Well, that's the way it's supposed to work, but once you're away from the big cities, the fact is that the Sires don't give a fat damn about Guild membership or not. They just want to know if you can sing and play, and if you know some different songs from the last musician they had. And who's going to enforce it? The King? Their Duke? Not likely. The Bardic Guild? With what? There's nothing they can use to enforce the law; out here a Sire is frequently his own law."

"What about the other Guilds?" she asked. "Aren't they supposed to help enforce the law by refusing to deal with a Sire who breaks it?"

"That's true, but once again, you're out where the Sire is his own law, and the Guildmasters and Craftsmasters are few. If a Craftsman enforces the law by refusing to deal with the Sire, he's cutting his own throat, by refusing to deal with the one person with a significant amount of money in the area. The Sire can always find someone else willing to deal, but will the Craftsman find another market?" He sighed. "The truth is that the Guildmasters of other Crafts might be able to do something—but half the time they don't give a damn about the Bardic Guild. The fact is, the Bardic Guild isn't half as important out of the cities as they think they are. Their real line of enforcement is their connection with the Church, through the Sacred Musicians and Bards, and the Church is pragmatic about what happens outside the cities."

"Why is it that the Bardic Guild isn't important to the other Guilds?" she asked, hitching her pack a little higher on her back. There was an itchy spot right between her shoulderblades that she ached to be able to scratch. . . .

If she could keep him talking a while, she might get her mind off of the itch.

"Because most of the Crafts don't think of us as being Crafters," he said wryly. "Music isn't something you can eat, or wear, or hold in your hand, and they never think of the ability to play and compose as being nearly as difficult as their own disciplines." He sighed. "And it isn't something that people need, the way they need Smiths or Coopers or Potters. We aren't even rated as highly as a Limner or a Scribe—"

"Until it's the middle of winter, and people are growling at each other because the snow's kept them pent up for a week," she put in. "And even then they don't think of us as the ones who cheered everyone up. Never mind, Master Wren. I'm used to it. In the tavern back home they valued me more as a barmaid and a floor-scrubber than a musician, and they never once noticed how I kept people at their beer long past the time when they'd ordinarily have gone home. They never noticed how many more people started coming in of a night, even from as far away as Beeford. All they remembered was that I lost the one and only fiddling contest I ever had a chance to enter."

Silence. Then—"I would imagine they're noticing it now," he said, when the silence became too oppressive. "Yes, I expect they are. And they're probably wondering what it is they've done that's driving their custom away."

Were they? She wondered. Maybe they were. The one thing that Jeoff had always paid attention to was the state of the cashbox. Not even Stara would be able to get around him if there was less in it than there used to be.

But then again—habit died hard, and the villagers of Westhaven were in the habit of staying for more than a couple ales now; the villagers of Beeford were in the habit of coming over to the Bear for a drop in the long summer evenings. Maybe they weren't missing her at all. Surely they thought she was crazed to run off the way that she had. And the old women would be muttering about "bad blood," no doubt, and telling their daughters to pay close attention to the Priest and mind they kept to the stony path of Virtue. Not like that Rune; bastard child and troublemaker from the start. Likely off making more trouble for honest folk elsewhere. Up to no good, and she'd never make an honest woman of herself. Dreams of glory, thought she was better than all of them—

and she'd die like a dog in a ditch, or starve, or sell herself like her whore of a mother.

No doubt. . . .

Talaysen kept an ear out for the sound of a lumber-wagon behind them. The road they followed was cleared of weeds, if still little more than a path through the forest—but this *was* forested country; the towns were small, and the cleared fields few. Many of the villages hereabouts made their livings off the forest itself. Every other village boasted a sawmill, or a Cooper making barrels, or a craftsman hard at work on some object made of wood. The Carpenter's Guild had many members here, and there were plenty of craftsmen unallied with the Guild who traded in furniture and carvings.

Allendale was a half-day away, and Talaysen was both relieved and uneasy that their goal was so nearly in sight. The past two weeks had been something of a revelation for him. He'd been forced to look at himself closely, and he hardly recognized what he saw.

He glanced sideways at his apprentice, who had her hat off and was fanning herself with it. She didn't seem to notice his covert interest, which was just as well. In the first few weeks of the Midsummer Faire, when Rune's arm was still healing, he'd been sorry for her, protective of her, and had no trouble in thinking of her strictly as a student. He'd felt, in fact, rather paternal. She had been badly hurt, and badly frightened; she was terribly vulnerable, and between what she'd told him straight off, and what she'd babbled when she had a little too much belladonna, he had a shrewd idea of all the hurtful things that had been said or done to her as a child. Because of her helplessness, he'd had no difficulty in thinking of her *as* a child. And his heart had gone out to her; she was so like *him* as a child, differences in their backgrounds aside. One unwanted, superfluous child is very like another, when it all comes down to it. He had sought solace in music; so had she. It had been easy to see himself in her, and try to soothe her hurts as his father would never soothe his.

But once she stopped taking the medicines that fogged her thoughts; and even more, once her arm was out of the sling and she began playing again, all that changed. Drastically. Overnight, the child grew up.

He strode through the ankle-high weeds at the walking pace that was second-nature to him now, paying scant attention to the world about him except to listen for odd silences that might signal something or someone hidden beside the road ahead—and the steady clop-clopping of the hooves of draft-horses pulling timber-wagons; this was the right stretch of road for them, which was why the weeds were kept down along here.

Bandits wouldn't bother with a timber-wagon, but he and Rune would make a tempting target. Highwaymen knew the Faire schedule as well as he did, and would be setting up about now to try to take unwary travelers with their pouches of coin on the way to the Faire. They wouldn't be averse to plucking a couple of singing birds like himself and his apprentice if the opportunity presented itself.

And if Talaysen didn't anticipate them. He'd been accused of working magic, he was so adept at anticipating ambushes. Funny, really. Too bad he wasn't truly a mage; he could transform his wayward heart back to the way it had been. . . .

It was as hot today as it had been for the past two weeks, and the dog-days of summer showed no sign of breaking. Now was haying season for the farmers, which meant that every hot, sunny day was a boon to them. Same for the lumberjacks, harvesting and replanting trees in the forest. He was glad for them, for a good season meant more coin for them—and certainly it was easier traveling in weather like this—but a short storm to cool the air would have been welcome at this point.

A *short storm* . . . Summer thunderstorms were something he particularly enjoyed, even when he was caught out in the open by them. The way the air was fresh, brisk, and sharp with life afterwards—the way everything seemed clearer and brighter when the storm had passed. He wished there was a similar way to clear the miasma in his head about his apprentice.

He'd hoped that being on the road with her would put things back on the student-teacher basis; she didn't have real experience of life on the road, and for all that she was from the country, she'd never spent a night camped under the open sky before she ran away from home. This new way of life should have had her reverting to a kind of dependence that would have reawakened his protective self and pushed the other under for good and all.

But it didn't. She acted as if it had never occurred to her that she should be feeling helpless and out of her depth out here. Instead of submissively following his lead, she held her own with him, insisting on doing her share of everything, however difficult or dirty. When she didn't know how to do something, she didn't make a fuss about it, she simply asked him—then followed his directions, slowly but with confidence. She took to camping as if she was born to it, as if she had Gypsy blood somewhere in her. She never complained any more about the discomforts of the road than he did, and she was better at bartering with the farm-wives to augment their provisions than he was.

Then there was music, God help them both. She was a full partner there, though oddly that was the only place her confidence faltered. She was even challenging him in some areas, musically speaking; she wanted to know *why* some things worked and some didn't, and he was often unable to come up with an explanation. And her fiddling was improving day by day; both because she was getting regular practice and because she'd had a chance to hear some of the best fiddlers in the country at the Faire. Soon she'd be second to none in that area; he was as certain of that as he was of his own ability.

Not that he minded, not in the least! He enjoyed the novelty of having a full partner to the hilt. He liked the challenge of a student of her ability even more. No, that wasn't the problem at all.

This was all very exciting, but he couldn't help but notice that his feelings towards her were changing, more so every day. It was no longer that he was simply attracted to her—nor that he found her stimulating in other areas than the intellectual.

It was far worse than that. He'd noticed back at the last Faire that when they'd sung a love duet, he was putting more feeling into the words than he ever had before. It wasn't acting; it was real. And therein lay the problem.

When they camped after dark, he was pleased to settle the camp with her doing her half of the chores out there in the darkness, even if she didn't do things quite the way he would have. When he woke up in the middle of the night, he found himself looking over at the dark lump rolled in blankets across the fire, and smiled. When he traded sleepy quips over the morning fire, he found himself not only enjoying her company—he found himself unable to imagine life without her.

And that, frankly, frightened him. Frightened him more than anything he'd ever encountered, from bandits to Guild Bards.

He watched her matching him stride-for-stride out of the corner of his eye, and wanted to reach out to take her hand in his. They suited each other, there was no doubt of it; they had from the first moment they'd met. Even Ardis noticed it, and had said as much; she'd told him they were two of a kind, then had given him an odd sort of smile. She'd told him over and over, that his affair with Lyssandra wouldn't work, that they were too different, and she'd been right. By the time her father had broken off the engagement because he'd fled the Guild, they were both relieved that it was over. That little smile said without words that Ardis reckoned that *this* would be different.

Even the way they conversed was similar. Neither of them felt any great need to fill a silence with unnecessary talk, but when they *did* talk, it was always enjoyable, stimulating. He could, with no effort at all, see himself sharing the rest of his life with this young woman.

That frightened him even more.

How could he even *think* something like that? The very idea was appalling! She was younger than he was; *much* younger. He was not exaggerating when he had told Ardis that he was twice her age. He was, and a bit more; on the shady side of thirty-five, to her seventeen or eighteen. How many songs were there about young women cuckolding older lovers? Enough to make him look like a fool if he took up with her. Enough to make *her* look like a woman after only his fame and fortune if she took up with *him*. There was nothing romantic about an old man pairing with a young woman, and much that was the stuff of ribald comedy.

Furthermore, she was his apprentice. That alone should place her out of bounds. He was appalled at himself for even considering it in his all-too-vivid dreams.

He'd always had the greatest contempt for those teachers who took advantage of a youngster's eagerness to please, of their inexperience, to use them. There were plenty of ways to take advantage of an apprentice, from extracting gifts of money from a wealthy parent, to employing them as unpaid servants. But the worst was to take a child, sexually inexperienced but ripe and ready to learn, and twist that readiness and enthusiasm, that willingness to accommodate the Master in every way, and pervert it into the crude slaking of the Master's own desires with no regard for how the child felt, or what such a betrayal would do to it.

And he had seen that, more than once, even in the all-male Guild. If the Church thundered against the ways of a man and a maid, this was the sin the Priests did not even whisper aloud—but that didn't mean it didn't occur. Especially in the hothouse forcing-ground of the Guild. That was one of the many reasons why he'd left in a rage, so long ago. Not that men sought comfort in other men—while he did not share that attraction, he could at least understand it. The Church called a great many things "sins" that were nothing of the sort; this was just another example. No, what drove him into a red rage was that there were Masters who abused their charges in body and spirit, and were never, ever punished for it. The last straw was when two poor young boys had to be sent away to one of the Church healers in a state of hysterical half-madness after one of the most notorious lechers in the Guild seduced them both, then insisted both of them share his bed at the same time. The exact details of what he had asked them to do had been mercifully withheld—but the boys had been pitiful, and he would not blame either of them if they had chosen to seek the cloisters and live out their lives as hermits. In the space of six months, that evil man had changed two carefree, happy children into frightened, whimpering rabbits. He'd broken their music, and it was even odds that it could be mended.

Talaysen still boiled with rage. It was *wrong* to take advantage of the trust that a student put in a teacher he respected—it was worse when that violation of trust included a violation of their young bodies. He'd gone to the Master of the Guild when he'd learned of the incident, demanding that the offending teacher be thrown out of the Guild in disgrace. Insisting that he be turned over to the Justiciars. Quite ready to take a horsewhip to him and flay the skin from his body.

He'd been shaking, physically shaking, from the need to rein in his temper. And the Master of the Guild had simply looked down his nose at him and suggested he was overreacting to a minor incident. "After all," Master Jordain had said scornfully, "they were only unproven boys. Master Larant is a full Bard. His ability is a proven fact. The Guild can do without them; it cannot do without *him.* Besides, if they couldn't handle themselves in a minor situation like that, they probably would not have passed their Journeyman period; they were just too unstable. It's just as well Master Larant weeded them out early. Now his valuable time won't be wasted in teaching boys who would never reach full status."

He had restrained himself from climbing over the Master's desk and throttling him with his bare hands by the thinnest of margins. He still wasn't certain how he'd done it. He had stalked out of the office, headed straight to his own quarters, packed his things and left that afternoon, seeking shelter with some Gypsies he'd met as a young man and had kept contact with, renouncing the Guild and all that it meant, changing his name, and his entire way of life.

But there it was; he'd seen how pressure of that nature could ruin a young life. How could he put Rune in the untenable position those poor boys had been in? Especially if he'd been misreading her, and what he'd been thinking was flirtation was simple country friendliness.

And there was one other thing; the stigma associated with "female musicians." Rune didn't deserve that, and if they remained obviously student and teacher, all would be well. Or at least, as "well" as it could be if she wore skirts. But he wouldn't ever want her to bear that stigma, which she would, if she were ever associated with him as his lover. Assuming she was willing . . . which might be a major assumption on his part.

Oh, if he wasn't misreading her, if she *was* interested in him as a lover, he could wed her. He'd be only too happy to wed her. . . .

Dear gods, why would she *ever* want to actually wed him? Him, twice her age? She'd be nursing a frail old man while she was still in the prime of her life, bound to him, and cursing herself and him both.

Furthermore, there would always be the assumption by those who knew nothing about music that she'd become his apprentice only *because* she was his lover; that she was gaining her fame by borrowing the shine of his.

No, he told himself, every time his eyes strayed to her, and his thoughts wandered where they shouldn't. *No, and no, and no. It's impossible. I won't have it. It's wrong.*

But that didn't keep his eyes from straying.

Or—his heart.

Rain fell unceasingly down from a flat gray sky, plopping on her rain-cape, her hat, and into the puddles along the road. Rune wondered what on Earth was wrong with Talaysen. Besides the weather, of course. He'd been out of sorts about something from the moment they'd left the Allendale Faire. Not that he showed it—much. He didn't snap, rail about anything, or break into arguments over little nothings. No, he *brooded.* He answered questions civilly enough, but neither his heart nor his thoughts were involved in the answer.

It could be the weather; there *was* more than enough to brood over in the weather. After weeks of dry, sunny days, their streak of good luck had finally broken, drowning the Allendale Faire in three days of dripping, sullen rain.

But they'd gotten around that; they'd succeeded in finding a cook-tent big enough to give them a bit of performing room, and they'd done reasonably well, monetarily speaking, despite the weather.

The rain had kept away all the wealthy Guildmasters and the three Sires that lived within riding distance, however. Perhaps that was the problem. They'd made no progress towards finding a wintering-over spot, and she sensed that made Talaysen nervous. At the next several large Faires, he had told her soberly, they could expect to encounter Guild musicians, Journeymen looking for permanent places for themselves. And they could encounter toughs hired by the Guild, either to "teach them a lesson" or to keep them from taking hire with one of the Sires for the winter.

One thing was certain, and only one; *she* was just as out-of-sorts as he was, but her mood had nothing to do with the weather or the state of their combined purse. She knew precisely why she was restless and unhappy. Talaysen. If this was love, it was damned uncomfortable. It wasn't lust, or rather, it wasn't lust alone—she was quite familiar with the way *that* felt.

The problem was, Talaysen didn't seem inclined to do anything to relieve her problem, despite all the hints she'd thrown out. And she'd thrown plenty, too. The only thing she hadn't tried was to strip stark naked and creep into his bedroll after he fell asleep.

Drat the man, anyway! Was he made of marble?

She trudged along behind him, watching his back from under her dripping hat-brim. Why didn't he respond to her?

It must be me, she finally decided, her mood of frustration turning to one of depression, as the rain cooled her temper and she started thinking of all the logical reasons why he hadn't been responding. *Obviously, he could have anyone he wanted. Gwyna, for instance. And she's not like me; she's adorable. Me, I'm too tall, too bony, and I can still pass for a boy any time I choose. He just doesn't have any interest in me at all, and I guess I can't blame him.* She sighed. The clouds chose that moment to double the amount of rain they were dropping on the two Bards' heads, so that they were walking in their own road-sized waterfall.

She tallied up her numerous defects, and compared herself with the flower of the Free Bard feminine contingent, and came to the even more depressing conclusion that she not only wasn't in the running, she wasn't even in the race when it came to attracting her Master in any way other than intellectually. And even then—the Free Bards were anything but stupid. Any of the bright lovelies wearing the brotherhood's ribbons could match witticisms with Talaysen and hold her own.

I don't have a prayer. I might as well give up.

Depression turned to despondency; fueled by the miserable weather, she sank deep inside herself and took refuge in composing the lyrics to songs of unrequited love, each one worse and more trite than the one before it. Brother Pell would have had a fit.

She stayed uncharacteristically silent all morning; when they stopped for a brief, soggy lunch, she couldn't even raise her spirits enough to respond when he finally did venture a comment or two. He must have sensed that it would be better to leave her alone, for that was what he did, addressing her only when it was necessary to actually tell her something, and otherwise leaving her to her own version of brooding.

On the the fifteenth repeat of rhyming "death" with "breath," she noticed that Talaysen had slowed, and was looking about for something.

"What's the matter?" she asked dully.

"We're going to have to stop somewhere for the night," he said, the worry evident in his voice, although she couldn't see his expression under *his* dripping, drooping hat brim. "I'm trying to find some place with at least a little shelter—however small that may be."

"Oh." She took herself mentally by the scruff of the neck and shook herself. *Being really useful, Rune. Why don't you at least try to contribute something to this effort, hmm?* "What did you have in mind?" she asked.

He shrugged—at least, that was what she guessed the movement under his rain-cape and pack meant. "I'd like a cave, but that's asking for a bit much around here."

She had to agree with him there. This area was sandy and hilly, rather than rocky and hilly. Not a good area for caves—and if they found one,

say, under the roots of a tree, it would probably already have a tenant. She
was not interested in debating occupancy with bears, badgers or skunks.

"Let's just keep walking," she said, finally. "If we don't find anything
by the time the light starts to fade, maybe we can make a lean-to against
a fallen tree, or something. . . ."

"Good enough," he replied, sounding just as depressed as she was. "You
watch the right-hand side of the track, I'll watch the left."

They trudged on through the downpour without coming to anything
that had any promise for long enough that Rune was just about ready to
suggest that they *not* stop, that they continue on through the night. But
it would be easy to get off the track in weather like this, and once tangled
in the underbrush, they might not be able to find their way back to the
road until daylight. If there was anything worse than spending a night
huddled inside a drippy lean-to wrapped in a rain-cape, it was spending
it caught in a wild plum thicket while the rain beat down on you unhin-
dered even by leaves.

Meanwhile, her thoughts ran on in the same depressing circle. Talaysen
was tired of her; that was what it was. He was tired of his promise to
teach her, tired of her company, and he didn't know how to tell her. He
wanted to be rid of her. Not that she blamed him; it would be much
easier for him to find that wintering-over place with only himself to worry
about. And if that failed, it would be *very* much harder for him to make
the winter circuit with an inexperienced girl in tow.

He must be bored with her by now, too. She wasn't very entertaining,
she wasn't city-bred, she didn't know anything about the Courts that she
hadn't picked up from Tonno—and *that* was precious little.

And he must be disgusted with her as well. The way she'd been shamelessly throwing herself at him—he was used to *ladies*, not tavern-wenches.
Ill-mannered and coarse, a country peasant despite her learning. Too ugly
even to think about, too.

She felt a lump of self-pity rising in her throat and didn't even try to
swallow it down. Too ugly, too tall, too stupid—the litany ran around and
around in her thoughts, and made the lump expand until it filled her
entire throat and made it hard to swallow. It overflowed into her eyes,
and tears joined the rain that was leaking through her hat and running
down her face. Her eyes blurred, and she rubbed the back of her cold
hand across them. They blurred so much, in fact, that she almost missed
the little path and half-ruined gateposts leading away from the road.

Almost.

She sniffed and wiped her eyes again hastily. "Master Wren!" she
croaked around the lump in her throat. He stopped, turned. "There!" she
said, pointing, and hoping he didn't notice her tear-marred face. She was
under no illusions about what she looked like when she cried: awful.
Blotchy face and swollen eyes; red nose.

He looked where she pointed. "Huh," he said, sounding surprised. "I
don't remember that there before."

"It looks like there might have been a farmhouse there a while back,"
she said, inanely stating the obvious. "Maybe you didn't notice it because

the last time you were through here you weren't looking for a place to shelter in."

"If there's a single wall standing, it'll be better than what we have now," he replied, wearily. "If there's two, we can put something over them. If there's even a corner of roof, I'll send Ardis a donation for her charities the next time we reach a village with a Priest."

He set off towards the forlorn little gate; she followed. As overgrown as that path looked, there wasn't going to be enough room for them to walk in anything other than single file.

It was worse than it looked; the plants actually seemed to reach out to them, to tangle them, to send out snags to trip them up and thorns to rake across their eyes.

The deeper they went, the worse it got. Finally Rune pulled the knife from her belt, and started to hack at the vegetation with it.

To her surprise, the going improved after that; evidently there was point of bottleneck, and then the growth wasn't nearly so tangled. The bushes stopped reaching for them; the trees stopped fighting them. Within a few moments, they broke free of the undergrowth, into what was left of the clearing that had surrounded the little house.

There was actually something left of the house. More than they had hoped, certainly. Although vines crawled in and out of the windows, the door and shutters were gone entirely, and there was a tree growing right through the roof, there were still walls and a good portion of the roof remaining, perhaps because the back of it had been built into the hill behind it.

They crossed the clearing, stepped over a line of mushrooms ringing the house, and entered. There was enough light coming in for them to see—and hear—that the place was relatively dry, except in the area of the tree. Talaysen got out his tinderbox and made a light with a splinter of wood.

"Dirt floor—at least it isn't mud." Rune fumbled out a rushlight and handed it to him; he lit it at his splinter. In the brighter flare of illumination, she saw that the floor was covered with a litter of dead leaves and less identifiable objects, including a scattering of small, roundish objects and some white splatters. Talaysen leaned down to poke one, and came up with a mouse-skull.

He grinned back at Rune, teeth shining whitely from under his hat brim. "At least we won't have to worry about vermin. Provided you don't mind sharing your quarters with an owl."

"I'd share this place with worse than an owl if it's dry," she replied more sharply than she intended. Then she laughed, in a shaky attempt to cover it. "Let's see what we can do about putting together someplace to sleep. *Away* from where the owl is. I can do without getting decorated with castings and mutes."

"Why Rune, we could set a whole new fashion," Talaysen teased, his good humor evidently restored. He stuck the rushlight up on what was left of a rock shelf at the back of the house, and they set about clearing a space to bed down in.

CHAPTER SEVENTEEN

"There," Rune said, setting her makeshift broom of broken branches aside. "That's as clean as it's going to get." She made a face at the piled debris on the other side of the ash tree; there had been too much garbage to simply sweep out the door.

"That's clean enough," Talaysen told her, from where he knelt just under the window, striking his flint and steel together as he had been the entire time she'd been sweeping. He had a knack for fires that she didn't; making a fire from sparks was a lot harder than village-folk (or especially city-folk) realized. "Now if I can just—there!"

He blew frantically at the little pile of dry leaves and shavings in front of him, and was rewarded this time with a glow, and then with a tiny flame. Carefully sheltering it from an errant breeze, he fed it with tiny twigs, then branches, then finally built a real fire with wood scavenged from the cottage's interior about his core-blaze. Just as well, as it was definitely getting darker outside. Hopefully the smoke would go *out* the window, and not decide to fill the cottage. The chimney of this place was choked with birds' nests and other trash.

Rune took a look around, now that she had more light to see by. This hadn't been a big farmhouse; one room, with a tiny loft just under the roof for sleeping. But the inside looked very odd for a place gone to ruin, and she puzzled over it as Talaysen picked up wood, trying to figure it out.

Then she had it: the cottage had been abandoned in a hurry. Nothing had been taken, not even the smallest stool. The wood that Talaysen was collecting had come from wrecked furniture. The doors and windows had been forced—but forced *out*, not in, and the shutters over the windows had been smashed at about the same time. *Something got in here, then smashed its way out. But what could have been strong enough to do that—and nasty enough to keep the owner from coming back for his goods?* She felt a chill finger of fear trace a line down the back of her neck. . . .

But then she shrugged and turned her attention to setting up their "camp." Whatever had done this was long gone, and not likely to return; there was no sign that anything had been living here except the owl.

He handed their nesting cook-pot and kettle to her; she dug out the dried meat and vegetables and the canister of herb tea. It was Talaysen's turn to cook, while she spread out the sleeping rolls and went to get water.

Well, that wouldn't be hard. There was a lot of water available right now.

She stuck the kettle, then the pot, out the window, holding them under the stream of water coming off the eaves. After all the rain they'd been having, the roof was surely clean. As clean as most streams, anyway. The presence of the owl probably kept birds from perching on the roof by day, and there wasn't much else that would matter.

Already it was hard to see across the clearing. She was profoundly grateful that they'd found this bit of shelter when they had. Now they'd be able to have a hot meal, warm and dry their clothing by the fire, check their instruments, maybe even practice a little.

As if he had followed her thoughts, Talaysen looked up from his cooking. "Get my lute out, will you, Rune? I think it's warm and dry enough in here that it won't come to any harm."

She nodded, and took the instrument out of its oiled-leather case, inspecting it carefully for any signs that the rain or damp might have gotten to it. Satisfied that it was untouched, she laid it on his unrolled bedding and did the same with her fiddle.

Like any good musician, she made a detailed examination of both instruments. So detailed, in fact, that by the time she was finished, the food and tea were both ready. She dug into her own portion with a nod of thanks, a little surprised at how hungry she was. The food evaporated from her wooden bowl, and she mopped every last trace of juice up with a piece of tough traveler's bread. The bowl hardly needed to be washed after she was through, and Talaysen's was just as clean.

Once they had finished eating, Talaysen was not to give her any time to brood over the thoughts that had caused her depression today, either. Instead, he insisted that they rehearse a number of songs she was only vaguely familiar with.

Odd, she thought, after the first few. He seemed to have chosen them all for subject-matter rather than style—every single one of them was about young women who were married off to old men and disappointed in the result. In a great many of the songs, they cuckolded their husbands with younger lovers; in the rest, they mourned their fates, shackled for life to a man whose prowess was long in the past. Sometimes the songs were comic, sometimes tragic, but in all of them the women were unhappy.

After about the fifth or sixth of these, she wondered if he was trying to tell her something. After the fifteenth, she was certain of it. And despite the message, she grew more and more cheerful with every chorus.

He *had* noticed how she'd been flinging herself at him! And this wasn't the reaction she'd been thinking he'd had to her. Was the message in these ballads that he was attracted, but thought he was too old to make her happy? It surely seemed likely.

Where did he get an idea like that? He wasn't *that* much older than she was! Girls in Westhaven got married to men his age all the time— usually after they'd worn out their first wives with work and childbearing, and were ready for a pretty young thing to warm their beds at night. Oh, at thirty-mumble, if he had been a fat merchant, or an even fatter Guild Bard, maybe she'd have been repulsed . . . but it would have been the overstuffed condition of his body that would have come between them, not his age.

At first she was too startled by what she thought he was trying to tell her to act on it—then, after a moment of reflection, she decided she'd better not do anything until she'd had a chance to plan her course of attack. She held her peace, and played the dutiful apprentice, keeping her thoughts to herself until they were both too tired to play another note. By then, the fire was burning low, and she was glad to creep into her now-warmed blankets.

But although she intended to ponder all the possible meanings of the practice session, though she did her best to hold off sleep, it overtook her anyway.

There. I think I've gotten my message across. Talaysen put his lute back in its case with a feeling of weary, and slightly bitter, satisfaction. Hopefully now his young apprentice would think about what she was doing, and stop making calf's-eyes at him.

What he was going to do about the way he felt was another matter altogether.

Suffer, mostly.

Eventually, though, he figured that he would be able to convince himself that their relationship of friendship was enough. After all, it was enough with all the other Free Bard women he'd known.

Maybe he could have another brief fling with Nightingale to get the thought of Rune out of his head. Nightingale had yet to find the creature that would capture *her* heart, but she enjoyed an amorous romp as well as anyone.

At least he'd given Rune something to think about. And the next time they met up with one of the gypsy caravans or another gathering of Free Bards, she'd start looking around her for someone her age. That should solve the problem entirely. Once he saw her playing the young fool with all the other young fools, his heart would stop aching for her.

He looked down at her sleeping face for a moment, all soft shadows and fire-kissed angles. *Maybe I shouldn't have been so hard on Raven,* he thought, dispiritedly. *Maybe I should have encouraged him. He was one of her teachers before; he knows her better than I do. They might get on very well together. . . .*

But though the idea of Rune with another was all right in the abstract, once he gave the idea a face, it wrenched his heart so painfully that his breath caught.

Dear God, I am a fool.

He slipped inside his own bedroll, certain that he was going to toss and turn for the rest of the night—

Only to fall asleep so quickly he might have been taken with a spell of slumber.

It was the sound of a harp being played that woke him; he found himself, not lying in his bedroll in the tiny, earthen-floored cottage, but standing on his feet in the middle of a luxuriously green field. Overhead was not a sky filled with rain clouds—not even a sky at all—but a rocky vault studded with tiny, unwinking lights and a great silver globe that shone softly down on the gathering around him.

Before him, not a dozen yards away, was a gathering of bright-clad folk about a silver throne. After a moment of breathlessness and confusion, he concluded that the throne was *solid* silver; for the being that sat upon it was certainly not human. Nor were those gathered about him.

Eyes as amber as a cat's stared at him unblinking from under a pair of upswept brows. Hair the black of a raven's wing was confined about the wide, smooth, marble-pale brow by a band of the same silver as the throne. The band was centered by an emerald the size of Talaysen's thumb. The face was thin, with high, prominent cheekbones and a sensuous mouth, but it was as still and expressionless as a statue. Peeking through the long, straight hair were the pointed ears that told Talaysen his "host" could only be one of the elven races.

There were elvenkin who were friends and allies to humans. There were more who were not. At the moment, he had no idea which these were, though the odds on their being the latter got better with every passing moment.

The man was clothed in a tunic of emerald-green silk, with huge, flowing sleeves, confined about the waist with a wide silver belt and decorated with silver embroidery. His legs were encased in green trews of the same silk, and his feet in soft, green leather boots. His hands, resting quietly on the arms of his throne, were decorated with massive silver rings, wrought in the forms of beasts and birds.

A young man sat at his feet, clad identically, but without the coronet, and playing softly on a harp. Those about the throne were likewise garbed in silks, of fanciful cut and jewel-bright colors. Some wore so little as to be the next thing to naked; others were garbed in robes with such long trains and flowing sleeves that he wondered how they walked without tripping themselves. Their hairstyles differed as widely as their dress, from a short cap like a second skin of brilliant auburn, to tresses that flowed down the back in an elaborate arrangement of braids and tied locks, to puddle on the floor at the owner's feet, in a liquid fall of silver-white. All of them bore the elven-king's pointed ears and strange eyes, his pale flesh and upswept brows. Some of them were also decorated with tiny quasi-living creations of magic; dragon-belts that moved with the wearer, faerie-lights entwined in the hair.

Talaysen was no fool, and he knew very well that the elves' reputation for being touchy creatures was well-founded. And if these considered themselves to be the enemies of men, they would be all the touchier. Still—they hadn't killed him out of hand. They might want something from him. He went to one knee immediately, bowing his head. As he did so, he saw that his lute was lying on the turf beside him, still in its case.

"You ventured into our holding, mortal," said a clear, dispassionate tenor. He did not have to look up to know that it was the leader who addressed him. "King" was probably the best title to default to; most lords of elvenkin styled themselves "kings."

"Your pardon, Sire," he replied, just as dispassionately. "I pray you will forgive us."

When he said nothing else, the elven-king laughed. "What? No pleas for mercy, no assertions that you didn't *know*?"

"No, Sire," he replied carefully, choosing his words as he would choose weapons, for they were all the weapon that he had. "I admit that I saw the signs, and I admit that I was too careless to think about what they signified." And he had seen the signs; the vegetation that tried to prevent them from entering the clearing until Rune drew her Iron knife; the Fairie Ring of mushrooms encircling the house. The ash tree growing right through the middle, and the condition of the house itself. . . .

"The mortal who built his house at our very door was a fool, and an arrogant one," the elven-king replied to his thought, his words heavy with lazy menace. "He thought that his God and his Church would defend him against us; that his Iron weapons were all that he needed besides his faith. He knew this was our land, that he built his home against one of our doors. He thought to keep us penned that way. We destroyed him." A faint sigh of silk told him that the king had shifted his position slightly. He still did not look up. "But you were weary, and careless with cold and troubles," the king said. His tone changed, silken and sweet. "You had no real intention to trespass."

Now he looked up; the elf lounged in his throne in a pose of complete relaxation that did not fool Talaysen a bit. All the Bard need do would be to make a single move towards a weapon of any kind at all, and he would be dead before the motion had been completed. If the king didn't strike him down with magic, the courtiers would, with the weapons they doubtless had hidden on their persons. The softest and most languid of them were likely the warriors.

"No, Sire," he replied. "We had no intention of trespass, though we *were* careless. It was an honest mistake."

"Still—" The elf regarded him with half-closed eyes that did not hide a cold glitter. "Letting you go would set a bad example."

He felt his hands moving towards his instrument; he tried to stop them, but his body was no longer his to control. He picked up his lute, and stripped the case from it, then tuned it.

"I think we shall resolve your problems and ours with a single stroke," the elf said, sitting up on the throne and steepling his hands in front of his chin. "I think we shall keep you here, as our servant, to pay for your carelessness. We have minstrels, but we have no Bards. You will do nicely." He waved his hand languidly. "You may play for us now."

Rune awoke to a thrill of alarm, a feeling that there was something wrong. She sat straight up in her bed—and a faint scrape of movement made her look, not towards the door, but to the back of the cottage, where it was built into the hillside.

She was just in time to see the glitter of an amber eye, the flash of a pointed ear, and the soles of Talaysen's boots vanishing into the hillside as he stumbled through a crack in the rock wall at the rear of the cottage. Then the "door" in the hill snapped shut.

Leaving her alone, staring at the perfectly blank rock wall.

That broke her paralysis. She sprang to her feet and rushed the wall, screaming at the top of her lungs, kicking it, pounding it with hands and feet until she was exhausted and dropped to the ground, panting.

Elves. That was what she'd seen. Elves. And they had taken Talaysen.

She had seen the signs and she hadn't paid any attention. She should have known—

The mushrooms, the ash tree—the bushes that tried to keep us out—

They were all there; the Fairie-circle, the guardian ash, the tree-warriors—all of them in the songs she'd learned, all of them plain for any fool to see, if the fool happened to be thinking.

Too late to weep and wail about it now. There must be something she could do—

There had to be a way to open that door from this side. She felt all over the wall, pressing and turning every rocky projection in hopes of finding a catch to release it, or a trigger to make it open.

Nothing.

It must be a magic door.

She pulled out her knife, knowing the elves' legendary aversion to iron and steel, and picked at anything she found, hoping to force the door open the way she had forced the trees to let them by. But the magic in the stone was sterner stuff than the magic in the trees, and although the wall trembled once or twice beneath her hand, it still refused to yield.

Thinking that the ash tree might be something more than just a tree, she first threatened it with her dagger, then stabbed it. But the tree was just a tree, and nothing happened at all, other than a shower of droplets that rained down on her through the hole in the roof as the branches shook.

Elves . . . elves . . . what do I know about elves? God, there has to be a way to get at them, to get Talaysen out! What do I have to use against them?

Not much. And not a lot of information about them. Nothing more than was in a half-dozen songs or so. She paced the floor, her eyes stinging with tears that she scrubbed away, refusing to give in, trying to think. What did she know that could be used against them?

The Gypsies deal with them all the time—

How did the Gypsies manage to work with them? She'd heard the Gypsies spoken of as "elf-touched" time and time again . . . as if they had somehow won some of their abilities from the secretive race. What could the Gypsies have that gave them such power over the elvenkin?

Gypsies, elves—

She stopped, in mid-stride, balancing on one foot, as she realized the secret. It was in one of the songs the Gypsy called Nightingale had taught her.

Music. They can be ruled by music. They can't resist it. That's what the song implied, anyway.

She dashed to her packs and fumbled out her fiddle. Elves traditionally used the harp, but the fiddle was *her* instrument of choice, and she wasn't going to take a chance with anything other than her best weapon. She tuned the lovely instrument with fingers that shook; placed it under her chin, and stood up slowly to face the rock wall.

Then she began to play.

She played every Gypsy song she knew; improvised on the themes, then played them all over again. The wailing melodies sang out over the sound of the storm getting worse overhead. She ignored the distant growl of thunder, and the occasional flicker of lightning against the rock in front of her. She concentrated all of her being on the music, the hidden door, and how much she wanted that door to open.

Let me in. Let me in. *Let me in to be with him. Let me in so I can get him free!*

She narrowed her eyes to concentrate better. She thought she felt something—or rather, *heard* something, only it was as if she had an extra ear somewhere deep inside, that was listening to something echo her playing.

Echo? No, it wasn't an echo, this was a different melody. Not by much—but different enough that *she* noticed it. Was she somehow hearing the music-key to the spell holding the door closed, resonating to the tune she was playing?

She didn't stop to think about it; obeying her instinctive feelings, she left the melody-line she was playing and strove to follow the one she heard with that inner ear. She felt a tingle along her arms, the same tingle she had felt when Gwyna had been transformed back to her proper form.

Not quite a match . . . she tried harder, speeded up a little, trying to anticipate the next notes. Closer . . . closer . . .

As she suddenly snapped into synch with that ghostly melody, the door in the wall cracked open—then gaped wide.

She found herself in a tunnel that led deep into the hillside, a tunnel that was floored with darkness, and had walls and a ceiling of swirling, colored mist. If she had doubted before, this was the end of doubts; only elves would build something like this.

The door remained open behind her. She could only hope it would stay that way and not snap shut to block her exit.

If she got a chance to make one.

She clutched her fiddle in her hand and ran lightly down the tunnel; it twisted and turned like a rabbit's run, but at length she saw light at the end. More than that, she heard music, and with her ears, not whatever she'd used to listen before. Music she knew; Talaysen's lute. But not his voice; he was not singing, and that lack shouted wrongness at her. There was a stiffness to his playing as if he was being constrained by something, forced to play against his will.

She ran harder, and burst through a veil of bright-colored mist at the very end of the tunnel. She stumbled onto a field of grass as smooth and close-clipped as a carpet, under a sky of stone bejeweled with tiny, artificial stars and a featureless moon of silver. Small wonder the songs spoke of elven "halls"; for all that they aped the outdoors, this was an artifice and would never look like a real greensward.

The elves gathered beneath that artificial moon in the decorous figures of a pavane stopped and turned to stare in blank surprise at her. Talaysen stood between them and her—and his expression was of surprise warring with fear.

She knew she daren't give them a moment to get over their surprise;

if they did, they'd attack her, and if they attacked her, they'd kill her. The songs made *that* perfectly clear as well.

She grasped for the only weapon she had.

So you want to dance, do you?

She shoved the fiddle under her chin, set bow to strings, and played. A wild reel, a dance-tune that never failed to bring humans to their feet, and called the "Faerie Reel." She hoped there was more in the name than just the clever title—

There was. Or else the elves *were* as vulnerable to music as Gypsy legend suggested. They seized partners by the hands and began flinging themselves through the figures of the dance, just as wildly as she played, as if they couldn't help themselves.

She didn't give them a respite, either, when that tune had been played through three full sets; she moved smoothly from that piece into another, then another. Each piece was repeated for three sets; she had a guess from some of what the Gypsy songs said that "three" was a magic number for binding and unloosing, and she wanted to bind them to their dancing, keeping them occupied and unable to attack.

She played for them as fiercely as she had for the Ghost, *willing* them to dance, faster and faster, until their eyes grew blank, and their limbs faltered. Finally some of them actually began dropping from exhaustion, fainting in the figures of the dance, unable to get up again—

One dropped; then two, then a half dozen. The rest staggered in the steps, stumbling over the fallen ones as if they could not stop unless they were as unconscious as the ones on the ground seemed to be. Another pair fainted into each other's arms, and the elven-king whirled, his face set in a mask of un-thought.

Then she changed her tune. Literally.

She brought the tune home and paused, for just a heartbeat. The elves' eyes all turned toward her again, most of them blank with weariness or pleading for her to stop. The elven-king, stronger than the rest, staggered towards her a step or two. She set bow to the strings again, and saw the flicker of fear in *their* eyes—

And she launched into the Gypsy laments.

Before she had finished the first, the weariest of the elves were weeping. As she had suspected, the Gypsy songs in particular held some kind of strange power over the elves, a power they themselves had no defense against. By the time she had completed the last sorrowing lament that Nightingale had taught her, even the elf with the coronet was in tears, helpless, caught in the throes of grief that Rune didn't understand even though she had evoked it.

She took her bow from her strings. Now there was no sound but soft sobbing.

They're mine. No matter what they try, they're too tired and too wrought up to move fast. I can play them into the ground, if I have to. I think. Provided my arms hold out. . . .

Elves, she couldn't help but notice resentfully, looked beautiful even when weeping. Their eyes and cheeks didn't redden; their noses didn't swell up. They simply sobbed, musically, perfect crystal tears dropping from their clear amber eyes to trickle like raindrops down their cheeks.

She looked for the one with the coronet; he was climbing slowly to his feet, tears in his eyes, but his chin and mouth set with anger. She strode quickly across the greensward to get past Talaysen as the elven-king brought himself under control, and by the time he was able to look squarely at her, she was between him and her Master, with her bow poised over the strings again, and her face set in an expression of determination she hoped he could read.

"No!" he shouted, throwing out a hand, fear blazing from his eyes.

She removed her bow a scant inch from the strings, challenge in hers.

"No—" he said, in a calmer voice. "Please. Play no more. Your magic is too strong for us, mortal. We have no defense against it."

About him, his people were recovering; some of them, anyway. The ones who could control themselves, or who had not fainted with exhaustion earlier, were helping those who were still lying on the velvety green grass; trying to wake them from their faint, helping them to their feet.

Rune said nothing; she only watched the elven king steadily. He glanced at his courtiers and warriors, and his pale face grew paler still.

"You are powerful, for all that you are a green girl," he said bitterly, turning a face full of carefully suppressed anger back to her. "I knew that the man was powerful, and I confined him carefully, wrapping his music in bonds he could not break so that he could not work against us. But you! You, I had not expected. You have destroyed my defenses; you have brought my people to their knees. No!" he said again, as she inadvertently lowered her bow a trifle. "No, I—beg you. Do not play again! Elves do not weep readily; many more tears, and my people may go mad with grief!"

"All right," she replied steadily, speaking aloud for the first time in this encounter, controlling her voice as Talaysen had taught her, though her knees trembled with fear and her stomach was one ice-cold knot of panic. "Maybe I won't. If you give me what I want."

"What?" the elven-king replied swiftly. "Ask and you shall have it. Gold, jewels, the treasures of the Earth, objects of enchantment—"

"Him," she interrupted, before he could continue the litany, and perhaps distract her long enough to work against both of them. "I want my lover back again."

Then she bit her lip in vexation. *Damn. Damn, damn, damn.* She had *meant* to say "Master," but her heart and her nerves conspired to betray her.

"Lover?" the elven-king said, one eyebrow rising in disbelief as he looked from Talaysen to her and back to Talaysen. "Lover? You—and he? What falsehood is this?" But then he furrowed his brows, and peered at her, as if he was trying to look into her heart. "Lover, no—" he said slowly, "but beloved, yes. I had not thought of this, either. Small wonder your music had such power against me, with all the strength of your heart behind it."

"You can't keep him," she said swiftly, trying to regain the ground she had lost with her inadvertent slip of the tongue. "If you can see our thoughts, then you know I am not lying to you. If you cage a songbird, it won't sing; if you keep a falcon mewed up forever, it will die. Do the same to my Master, and he'll die just as surely as that falcon will. He gave up everything for freedom—take it from him, and you take away everything that makes him a Bard. He'll waste away, and leave you with nothing. And I will *never* forgive you. You'll have to kill me to rid yourself of me, and the cost will be higher than you may want to pay, believe me."

The elven-king's eyes narrowed. "There's truth in that," he said slowly. "Truth in everything you have said thus far. But you, mortal girl—you're made of sterner, more flexible stuff. *You* would not pine away like a linnet in a cage. Tell me, would you trade your freedom for his?"

"Yes," she said, just as Talaysen cried out behind her, "No!"

The elf considered them both for a moment longer, then shook his head. "No," he said, anger filling his voice. "No, it must be both of you or neither. Cage the one, and the other will come to free it. Keep you both, and you will have my kingdom in ruins within the span of a single moon. You are too powerful to hold, too dangerous to keep, both of you. Go!"

He flung his arm up, pointing at the tunnel behind her. But Rune wasn't finished yet; the treachery of elves was as legendary as their power and secretiveness. She dropped the bow to the strings and played a single, grief-filled phrase.

"Stop!" The elven-king cried over it, tears springing into his eyes, hands clapped futilely over his ears. "What more do you want of us?"

She lifted the bow from the strings. "Your pledge," she replied steadily. "Your pledge of our safety."

She saw the flash of rage that overcame him for a moment, and knew that she had been right. The elven-king *had* planned to ambush them as soon as their backs were turned, and probably kill them. He had lost a great deal of pride to her and her music; only destroying them would gain it back.

"Swear," she insisted.

"By the Moon our Mother, the blood of the stars, and the honor of the Clan," Talaysen whispered.

"Swear by the Moon our Mother, the blood of the stars, and the honor of the Clan that you will set us free, you will not hinder our leaving; you will not curse us, nor set magic nor weapons against us. Swear it!" she warned, as the rage the elven-king held in check built in his eyes and threatened to overwhelm his self-control. "Swear it, or I'll play till my arms fall off! I played all one night before, I can do it again!"

He repeated it between gritted teeth, word for word. She slowly lowered her arms, and tucked fiddle and bow under one of them, never betraying by a single wince how both arms hurt.

She turned just as slowly, and finally faced Talaysen, just as fearful of what she might see in his eyes as of all the power the elven-king could raise against them.

He smiled, weakly; his face a mask that covered warring emotions that flickered behind his eyes. But he picked up his lute and case, and offered her his arm, as if she was his lady. She took it gravely, and they strolled out of that place of danger as outwardly calm as if they strolled down the aisles of a Faire.

But once they reached the cottage, the rock door slammed shut right on their heels, and she began throwing gear into her pack, taking time only to wrap her fiddle in her bedding and stow it in the very bottom for safety. He joined her.

"Are you thinking what I'm thinking?" he said, over the steady *boom* of thunder from overhead. The fire was almost out, but they didn't need it to see; lightning flashing continuously gave them plenty of light to see by.

"I think so," she shouted, stuffing the last of her gear into her pack, with her tiny harp cushioned inside her clothing to keep *it* safe. "I don't trust him, no matter what he swore by. He'll find a way to get revenge on us. We'd better get out of here."

"This may *be* his revenge!" Talaysen said grimly, packing up his own things and slinging them on his back, throwing his rain-cape over all, then pointing to the storm outside the windows. "He didn't swear not to set the weather on us. As long as he doesn't touch us directly, he hasn't violated his pledge. A storm, lightning—those aren't strictly weapons."

She swore. "Elves," she spat. "They should be Churchmen. Or lawyers. Let's get out of here! A moving target is harder to hit!"

Talaysen was in perfect agreement with her, apparently; he strode right out into the teeth of the storm, and she was right behind him.

The trees didn't stop them this time; evidently the prohibition against using magic held the grasping branches off. But the storm was incredible; lightning striking continuously all about them. Rain lashed them, pounding them with hammers of water, sluicing over their rain-capes until they waded ankle-deep on the path. Talaysen insisted, shouting in her ear to be heard over the storm, that they walk down in the streambed next to the road; it was full of rushing water that soaked them to their knees, but with the rain lashing them from every angle it didn't much matter, they were wet anyway. And when lightning struck the roadway, not once, but repeatedly, she saw the sense of his orders. The streambed was deep enough that not even their heads were above the roadway. Lightning always sought the highest point; they had to make certain that point wasn't them.

But the streambed turned away from the roadway eventually, and ran back into the trees. Now the question was: follow the road, and take their chances with the lightning, or follow the streambed and hope it led somewhere besides into the wilderness?

Talaysen wavered; she made up his mind for him, pushing past him and following the streambed under the trees. People always built their homes beside water; with luck, they'd come across something in a day or two.

With no luck, at least they wouldn't be turned into Bard-shaped cinders. And they could retrace their path if they had to, until they met up with the road again.

The terrain was getting rockier; when she could see through the curtains of water, the streambed looked as if it had been carved through what looked like good, solid stone. And the banks were getting higher. If they couldn't find a house, maybe they could find a cave.

If they couldn't find either, maybe they could just walk out the storm.

It was awfully hard to think with rain beating her skull, and water tugging at her ankles, forcing her constantly off balance. She was so cold she couldn't remember being warm.

The thunder and lightning raged above their heads, but none of it was getting down to the ground anymore, not even the strikes that split whole trees in half. And the very worst of it seemed to be behind them, although the rain pounded them unabated. Her head was going to be sore when they were out of this. . . .

Maybe they were getting out of the elven-king's territory. How far could magic reach?

She found out, as there was a sudden slackening in the rain, a moment when the lightning and thunder stopped. Both she and Talaysen looked up as one, but Rune was not looking up with hope.

She felt only a shudder of fear. This did not have the feeling of a capitulation. It had the feeling of a summoning. The elven-king was bringing one final weapon to bear upon them.

That was when they saw the wall of wind and water rushing down on them, walking across the trees and bending them to the earth as it came. Not like a whirlwind—like a moving waterfall, a barrier of water too solid to see through.

Talaysen was nearer to shelter; he flung himself down in a gully carved into the side of the streambed. She looked about frantically for something big enough to hold her.

Too late.

The wind struck her, staggering her—she flailed her arms to keep her balance, then in a flash of lightning, saw what looked like half a tree heading straight for her—

Pain, and blackness.

Talaysen saw the tree limb, as thick around as he was, hit Rune and drop her like a stone into the water, pinning her in the stream beneath its weight.

He might have cried out; it didn't matter. In the next instant he had fought through the downpour and was clawing at the thing, trying to get it off her, as the wind screamed around him and battered him with other debris. She'd been knocked over a boulder, so at least her head was out of the water—but that was all that fortune had granted her. She was unconscious; she had a pulse, but it was weak and slow.

And he couldn't budge the limb.

Frantic now, he forced himself to calm, to think. Half-remembered hunter's lessons sprang to mind, and he recalled shifting a dead horse off another boy's leg with the help of a lever—

He searched until he found another piece of limb long and stout enough; wedged it under the one pinning Rune, and used another boulder for a fulcrum. There should have been two people doing this—he'd had the help of the huntsman before—

Heave. Kick a bit of flotsam under the limb to brace it. His arms screamed with pain. *Heave.* Another wedge of wood. His back joined the protest. *Heave*—

Finally, sweating and shaking, he had it balanced above her. It wouldn't hold for long; he'd have to be fast.

He let go of the lever, grabbed her ankle, and pulled.

He got her out from under the limb just as it came crunching back down, smashing to splinters one of the bits of wood he'd used to brace it up.

The wind died, and the rain was slackening, as if, with Rune's injury, the elven-king was satisfied. But the lightning continued, which now was a blessing; at least he had something to see by.

He bent down and heaved Rune, pack and all, over his shoulders, as if she was a sack of meal. Fear made a metallic taste in his mouth, but lent him strength he didn't know he had and mercifully blanked the pain of his over-burdened, aging body.

He looked about, frantically, for a bit of shelter, anything. Somehow he had to get her out of the rain, get her warm again. Her skin was as cold as the stones he'd pried her out of—if he couldn't get her warm, she might die—

Lightning flickered, just as his eyes passed over what he'd thought was a dark boulder.

Is that—

He staggered towards it, overbalanced by the burden he carried, and by the press of the rushing water against his legs. Lightning played across the sky overhead—he got another look at the dark blot in the stream wall. No, it wasn't a boulder. And it was bigger than he thought—

He climbed up onto the bank, peered at it in another flash of lightning—and nearly wept with relief. It was. It was a cave. A small one, but if it wasn't too shallow, it should hold them both with no difficulty. Pure luck had formed it from boulders caught in the roots of a tree so big two men couldn't have spanned the trunk with their arms.

And a pair of bright eyes looked out of it at him.

He didn't care. Whatever it was, it would have to share its shelter tonight. The eyes weren't far enough apart for a bear, and that was all he cared about.

Somehow he got himself up into the cave; somehow he dragged Rune up with him. Erratic lightning showed him what it was in the cave with him; an entire family of otters. They stared at him fearlessly, but made no aggressive moves towards him. He ignored them and began pawing through the packs for something warm and dry to put on her.

He encountered the instruments first. His lute—intact. Hers was cracked, but might be repaired later. Her penny-whistle was intact, and the tiny harp he'd given her. The bodhran drum was punctured; his larger harp needed new strings—

All this in mental asides as he pawed through the packs, pulling out soaked clothing and discarding it to the side.

Finally he reached the bottom of the packs. And in the very bottom, their bedding; somehow dry. Her fiddle wrapped in the middle of it, safe.

There wasn't much time, and he didn't hesitate; every moment she stayed chilled was more of a threat. He stripped her skin-bare and bundled her into both sets of bedding. Then he stripped himself and eased in with her, wrapping her in his arms and willing the heat of his body into her.

For a long time, nothing happened. The storm died to the same dull rain they'd coped with for the length of the Faire; the lightning faded away, leaving them in the dark. Rune breathed, but shallowly, and her body didn't warm in the least. Her breathing didn't change. She wasn't waking; she wasn't falling into normal sleep. If he couldn't get her warm—

Lady of the Gypsies, help me! You are the queen of the forests and wilds—help us both!

Finally he heard faint snuffling sounds, and felt the pressure of tiny feet on his leg and knee.

The otters' curiosity had overcome their fear.

They sniffed around the bundle of humans and blankets, poking their noses into his ear and sneezing into his face once. It would have been funny if he hadn't been sick with worry for Rune. She wasn't warming. She was hardly breathing—

One of the otters yawned; another. Before he realized what was happening, they were curling up *on* him, on Rune, everywhere there was a hollow in the blankets, there was an otter curling up into a lithe—warm!—ball and flowing over the sides of the hollows.

As they settled, he began to warm up from the heat of their six bodies. And as he warmed, so, at last, did Rune. Her breathing eased, and finally she sighed, moved a little—the otters chittered sleepily in complaint—and settled into his arms, truly asleep.

He tried to stay awake, but in a few moments, exhaustion and warmth stole his consciousness away, and he joined her and their strange bed-companions in dreams.

He woke once, just after dawn, when the otters stirred out of sleep and left them. But by then, they were not only warm, they were a bit *too* warm, and he bade the beasts a sleepy, but thankful, good-bye. One of the adults—the female, he thought—looked back at him and made a friendly chitter as if she understood him. Then she, too, was gone, leaving the cave to the humans.

Rune woke with an ache in her head, a leg thrown over hers, and arms about her. Behind her, someone breathed into her ear.

What happened? She closed her eyes, trying to remember. They weren't in the cottage they'd found; that much was for certain. . . .

Then she remembered. The elves, her one-sided fight with music and magic, then the flight through the storm. After that was a blur, but she must have gotten hurt, somehow—

She wormed one arm out of the blankets, reached up to touch the place on her head that hurt worst, and found a lump too tender to bear any pressure at all, with a bit of a gash across the middle of it.

That was when she realized that she wasn't wearing so much as a stitch. And neither was Talaysen.

He murmured in his sleep, and held her closer. His hands moved in half-aware patterns, fitfully caressing her breasts, her stomach. . . .

And there was something quite warm and insistent poking her in the small of the back.

She held very still, afraid that if she moved, he'd stop. Despite the ache in her head, her body tingled all over, and she had to fight herself to keep from squirming around in his arms and—

Suddenly he froze, one hand on her breast, the other—somewhat lower. *He woke up. And now he's going to go all proper on me.*

"If you stop," she said conversationally, "I am going to be very angry with you. I thought you taught me to always finish a tune you've started."

Please, God. Please, whoever's listening. Don't let him go all formal now. . . .

"I—I—uh—" He seemed unable to form any kind of a reply.

"Besides," she continued, trying to think around the pain in her skull, "I've been trying to get you into this position for weeks."

"Rune!" he yelped. "I'm your *teacher*! I can't—"

"You can't what? What difference does being my Master make? You've only got one apprentice, you can't be accused of favoring me over anyone else. You haven't been trying to seduce *me*, I've been trying to waylay *you*. There's a difference." *There,* she thought with a certain satisfaction. *That takes care of that particular argument.* "It's not as if you're taking unfair advantage of your position."

"But—the pressure—my position—"

"I like the pressure," she replied thoughtfully, "though I'd prefer to change the position—" And she started to squirm around to face him. He choked.

"That's not what I meant!" he said, and then it was too late; they were face-to-face, cozily wound in blankets, and he couldn't pretend he didn't understand her. She could read his expression quite clearly from here. She smiled into his eyes; he blushed.

"I know that's not what you meant," she told him. "I just don't see any 'pressure' on me to drag you into my bed except the pressure of wanting you."

"But—"

"And if you're going to tell me something *stupid,* like you're too old for me, well you can just forget that entirely." She kissed his nose, and he blushed even redder. "I wouldn't drink wine that was a month old, I wouldn't play a brand new fiddle, and I wouldn't hope for fruit from a sapling tree."

"But—"

"I *also* wouldn't go to an apprentice in *any* Craft for anything important. I'd go to a Master."

"But—"

She blinked at him, willing the pain in her head to go away. "You're not going to try and tell me that you've been celibate all these years, are you? If you are, then Gwyna was lying. Or you are. And much as I'd hate to accuse my Master of telling falsehoods, I'd believe Gwyna on this subject more than I'd believe you."

His mouth moved, but no words emerged. She decided he looked silly, gasping like a fish, and saved his dignity by stopping it with a kiss.

He disengaged just long enough to say, "I yield to your superior logic—" And then the time for talk was over, and the time for a different sort of communication finally arrived.

CHAPTER EIGHTEEN

"You *are* going to marry me, aren't you?" Talaysen asked plaintively, picking his now-dry clothing off the rocks beside the stream and packing it away. There was no sign of last night's storm; even most of the debris had been washed downstream. And as if in apology, the day had turned bright and sunny around noon. Rune had caught a fish, using some of their soggy bread for bait; he'd managed to get a fire going, so they could cook it. The rest of the day they'd spent in laying out everything that had gotten wet to dry, and figuring out just how badly Rune had gotten hurt.

She'd gotten off fairly easily, as it turned out. She had gotten a bad knock on the head, but nothing a lot of valerian couldn't help. They were now a day behind, of course, but that was better than being lightning victims, or confined in the elven-king's hall.

Rune looked over at Talaysen's anxious face, and grinned wickedly, despite the black eye and bruises the tree limb had gifted her with. "Isn't it supposed to be *me* that's asking that?" she mocked. "You sound like one of the deflowered village maidens in a really awful Bardic Guild ballad."

He flushed. "I'm serious. I—you—we— We can't just go on like this. You're going to get harassed enough if we're legally wed! If we aren't—"

She looked at him with an expression of exasperation, and carefully folded one of her shirts before answering. "Is that the only reason? To make an 'honest woman' out of me? To protect me from disgrace?"

"No!" he blurted, and flushed again. "I mean—I—"

"Ah." She put the shirt back into her pack. "That's just as well, since protecting a nameless bastard from disgrace is pretty much like protecting a thief from temptation. Why don't you just tell me why you're so set on this, and let me think about your reasons."

For a moment, he sat back on his heels and stared at her helplessly. For all that he was a Bard, and supposed to be able to work magic with words, he felt suddenly bereft of any talent with his tongue whatsoever. How could he tell her—

She waited patiently, favoring her left side a little. He marshaled his thoughts. Tried to remember what he always told others when they were tongue-tied, when the gift seemed to desert them.

Begin at the beginning. . . .

So he did.

She listened. Once or twice, she nodded. It got easier as he went along; easier to find the words, though they didn't come out of his mouth with any less effort. He'd lived for so long without telling people how he felt— how he *really* felt, the deep feelings that it was generally better not to reveal—that each confession felt as if he was trying to lift another one of those trees. Only this time, the back he was lifting it from was his own. The logical reasons: why it was better not to give the Guild another target;

how being legally married would actually cut down on petty jealousy within the Bards; how it might keep petty officials of the Church not only from harassing *them,* but from harassing other Free Bard couples who chose to perform as a pair.

The reasons with no logic at all, and these were harder to get out: that he not only loved her, he needed her presence, that she made him feel more alive; his secret daydreams of spending the rest of his days with her; how she brought out the best in everything for him.

The reasons that hurt to confess: how he was afraid that without some form of formal tie binding them, one day she'd tire of him and leave him without warning; how he felt as if her refusal to formally wed him was a kind of rejection of *him,* as if she were saying she didn't feel he was worth the apparent sacrifice of her independence.

Finally he came to the end; he had long since finished his packing, and he sat with idle hands clenched on stones to either side of him.

She let out her breath in a sigh. "Have you thought about this?" she asked. "I mean, have you really thought it through? Things like—how are the other Free Bards going to react to a wife? You *think* that it will cut down on petty jealousy—why? I think it might just make things worse. A lover—that would be no problem, but a wife? Wouldn't they see me as some kind of interloper? I'm the newest Free Bard; how did I get you to wed me? Wouldn't they think I'm likely to try interfering with you and the rest of them?"

"I can't read minds," he said, slowly. "But I truly don't think there'd be any problem. I know every one of the Free Bards personally, and I just don't think the kinds of problems you're worried about would even occur. Marriage might make things easier, actually; I can't be everywhere at once, and sometimes I've wished there were two of me. And there are things the females haven't always felt comfortable in bringing to me— they tell Gwyna a lot of the time, but that really isn't the best solution. With you there—my legal partner—there's a partnership implied with marriage that there isn't with a lover. Stability; they aren't going to tell you something then discover the next time we met that there's someone else with me, and wonder what that means to their particular problem." He relaxed a little as she nodded.

"All right—I can see that. But we should try to anticipate problems and head them off before they *become* problems. For instance: divided authority. Someone trying to work us against each other. If you give me authority, it should be only as your other set of ears. All right?" She waited for his nod of agreement before continuing.

"What about children?" she said, surprising him completely.

"What about them?" he replied without thinking.

"I want them. Do you? Have you thought about what it would take to raise them as Free Bards?" She held up her hand to forestall his protest that it would not be fair to *her* to saddle her with children she might well have to raise alone. "*Don't* tell me that you're old, you'll die and leave me to raise them alone. I don't believe that for a minute, and neither do you."

He snapped his mouth shut on the words.

"Well?" she said, rubbing her head to relieve the ache in it. "Is there a way to have children and still be Free Bards?"

"We could settle somewhere, for a while," he suggested tentatively.

She shook her head, and winced. "No. No, I don't think that would work. You have to be visible, and that means traveling. If we lived in a big city, we'd have to leave the children alone while we busked—no matter how good we were, we would still be taking whatever jobs the Guild Minstrels didn't want, and that's pretty precarious living for a family. And the Guild would be only too happy to flaunt their riches in the face of your poverty—then come by and offer you your old position if you just gave all the Free Bard nonsense up."

She watched him shrewdly to see if he'd guess the rest of *that* story. "And of course, that would mean either giving you up, or persuading you to turn yourself into a good little Bard-wife and give up *your* music." He shook his head. "What a recipe for animosity! You know them better than I thought you did."

She snorted. "Just figured that if there was a way to make people jealous of each other, and drive a wedge between them, they'd know it. I imagine there's a lot of that going on in the Guild."

He pondered her original question for a moment, and emptied his mind, waiting to see if an answer would float into the emptiness. He watched the dance of the sunlight on the sparkling waters, flexing and stretching his fingers, and as always, waiting for the tell tale twinges of weather-soreness. His father had suffered terribly from it—

But then his father had also shamelessly overindulged himself in rich food and wine, and seldom stirred from his study and office. That might have had something to do with it.

"There's another way," he said suddenly, as the image of a Gypsy wagon did, indeed, float into his mind. "We could join a caravan of Gypsy families; get our own wagon, travel with them, and raise children with theirs. If there are older children, adolescents, they watch the younger ones, and if there aren't there's always someone with a task that can be done at the encampment that minds the children for everyone else."

She raised an eyebrow skeptically. "Mind you, this is all nasty tale-telling from evil-mouthed, small-minded villagers, but—I've never heard anything about Gypsy parents except that they were terrible. Selling their children, forcing them to work, maiming them and putting them out to beg—"

"Have you ever actually *seen* any of that with your own eyes?" he asked. She shook her head, carefully. "It's not true, any of it. They know how to prevent having children, so they never have more than they can feed— if something *does* happen to one or both parents, every family in the caravan is willing to take on an extra mouth. The children are tended carefully, the encampment is always guarded by dogs that would take on a wolf-pack for their sakes, and the children loved by everyone in the caravan. They grow up to be pretty wonderful adults. Well, look at Gwyna, Raven and Erdric."

She gave a dry chuckle. "Sounds too good to be true."

"Oh, there're exceptions," he admitted. "There are families other Gypsies refuse to travel with—there are families that are hard on their children and a general nuisance to the rest of the adults. Any child that doesn't learn how to get out of the way of a drunk or a serious situation is going to be on the receiving end of a cuff. You must admit, though, that can happen anywhere. Mostly, Gypsy children are the healthiest and happiest I've ever seen. The drawback is that they won't learn reading, writing, or the Holy Book—the Gypsies don't hold with any of the three."

"Reading and writing we can teach them ourselves," Rune countered. "And the Holy Book—they should read it when they're old enough to understand that what they're reading is as much what the Church wants you to believe as it is Holy Words." She thought that proposition over for a long moment. "That would work," she concluded, finally. "Having a wagon to live in eliminates one of the biggest *expenses* of living in a town or city, too."

"What, the rent?" He grinned. She'd already told him about her job at Amber's, and he knew very well they could always find something comparable if they ever cared to settle in one place for long.

"No," she countered. "The damned tithe and tax. If they can't catch you, they can't collect it. And if you leave before they catch you—"

"Point taken," he admitted. "Though, I'll warn you, I do pay tax; I've been paying both our shares. If you want decent government, you have to be prepared to pay for it."

He saw a shadow of something—some remembered pain—pass across her face. "Point taken," she said, quietly. "Tonno—felt the same way as you, and lectured me about it often enough. But the tithe serves no damned purpose at all. If it got into the hands of Priests like your cousin, that would be different. Most of the time, though, it ends up in the hands of men that are no better than thieves."

He snorted, and tried not to think too hard about most of his dealings with the Church—those that hadn't involved Ardis seeking out someone specific for him to speak to. "I've known thieves with more honor— and Ardis would be the first to agree with you. But we weren't talking about Ardis."

"No, we weren't." She leaned forward, intently. "Talaysen, what do you intend to *do* with the Free Bards?"

"Do?" Was she really asking what he thought she was asking? "What exactly do you mean?"

"What I said," she replied. "What are you going to *do* with them? Oh, it was enough to form them, to keep the Bardic Guild from getting rid of them when there were only a handful of you, I'm sure. But there are nearly fifty of you now—not counting the ones that didn't come to the Midsummer Faire. And there are more joining every year! They think of you not only as the founder, but as the leader—now what are you going to lead them to? Or is this just going to be a kind of Gypsy Clan with no other purpose than to live and play music?"

Of all of the Free Bards, Rune was the only one that had asked him that question, the question he had been asking himself for about three years.

"There are a lot of things I would like to do," he said, slowly, "but all of them involve having more power than we do now. That's why I've gotten the rest involved in trying to ingratiate ourselves with the Sires and Guildmasters outside the big cities."

"So that when you come to demand a change, there will be someone backing you." She nodded enthusiastically. "What's the change?"

"Mostly, we—I—want to see some of the privileges and monopolies taken away from the Bardic Guild," he replied. "I want them put on a completely equal footing with us. I don't want to set up the Free Bards in place of the Guild, but I want *any* musician to be free to take *any* place that's been offered him. I want the Sires able to hire and fire members of the Guild the same way they can hire and fire Free Bards and traveling minstrels. And there are some abuses of power within the Guild that I want looked into."

She sat back on her heels, and smiled. "That'll do," she replied. "That's enough for anyone's lifetime. Let your successor worry about the next step."

"Are you going to marry me now?" he asked, trying to sound plaintive, and actually sounding testy. She laughed.

"Since you ask me so romantically, I think so," she said, tossing a shirt at him that he had forgotten. "But don't think that you can go back to being aloof until the bonds are set." She bared her teeth at him, in a playful little snarl that was oddly erotic. He restrained himself from doing what he would have liked to do. For one thing, he wanted a more comfortable bed than the boulders of the stream-bank, sun-warmed though they were. . . .

"I don't know why I shouldn't," he replied provokingly. "After all, you've been hurt, your head probably aches and I'm sure you couldn't *possibly* be interested in—"

She pounced on him, and proved that she could, most *definitely* be interested in—

And he found that the rocks weren't as bad as he had thought.

Rune would have laughed at her lover, if she hadn't been so certain that she would badly hurt his feelings by doing so. Now that they were lovers, *she* was perfectly content. But *he* was heading them into Brughten, despite the fact that there was no Faire there and the pickings would be slim, because he wanted to find a Priest to marry them. Immediately. Incredible.

Well, there was a Priest and a Church, and the town was at least on the road. It wasn't the road they had left; this one they'd struck after following the stream for a couple of days rather than backtrack over the elven-king's territory. And they might be able to get lodging and food at one of the town's two inns. . . .

Talaysen left her at the marketplace in the center of the town, and she was grateful for a chance to find some fresh supplies. The storm had washed away or ruined most of their food, and they had been living off the land thanks to the fish in the stream and her scant knowledge of forest edibles. That had been mostly limited to the fact that cattail roots could be eaten raw, knowing what watercress looked like, and recognition of some bramble-bushes with fruit on them.

Their money hadn't washed away, but it was hard to get a squirrel to part with a load of nuts in exchange for a copper penny.

She had just about completed her final purchase, when she turned and caught sight of Talaysen striding towards her through the light crowd. Most people wouldn't have noticed, and he was being quite carefully courteous to the other shoppers as he made his way past and around them—but she saw the set jaw, and the stiff way that he held his head, and knew he was furious.

"What's wrong?" she whispered, as he reached her side. He shook his head.

"Not here," he said quietly, and she heard the anger in his voice. "Are you done?"

"Just a moment." She turned back to the old farm-wife and quickly counted out the money for another bag of traveler's bread without stopping to bargain any further. The old woman blinked in surprise, but took the coins—it wasn't *that* much in excess of what the real price should have been—and gave her the coarse string bag full of rounds of bread in exchange.

"All right," she said, tying the bread to her belt until she got a chance to put it in her pack. "Let's go."

He led her straight out of town, setting a pace that was so fast she had to really stretch her legs to keep up with him, until he finally slowed when they were well out of sight of the last of the buildings. She tugged at his arm, forcing him to slow still further. "All right!" she exclaimed, catching sight of the rage on his face, now that he was no longer having to wear a polite mask. "What happened?"

"I was told by the Priest," he said, tightly, "that we were vagabonds and tramps. He told me that trash such as you and I weren't fit to even set foot on sacred ground, much less participate in the sacrament of marriage. He further told me that if we didn't want him to call the Sire's watch to have us *both* pilloried, even though you weren't even there, that we'd better take ourselves out of town." He took a deep breath, and let it out in a long sigh. "There was a great deal more that he said, and I won't repeat it."

The look on his face alarmed her. "You didn't do anything to him—"

"Oh, I *wanted* to throw him into the duck pond on the green," Talaysen replied, and the rage slowly eased out of him. "But I didn't. I did something that was a lot worse." He began to smile, then, and the more he thought about whatever it was that he'd done, the more he smiled.

She had a horrified feeling that he had done something that really *would* get them pilloried, and her face must have reflected that, because he tossed back his head and laughed.

"Oh, don't worry. I didn't do anything *physical*. But it will be a very long time before he insults another traveling musician." He waited, the smile still on his face, for her to ask the obvious question.

"Well, what *did* you do?" she asked impatiently, obliging him.

"I informed him that he had just insulted Master Bard Gwydain—and

I proved who I was with this." He reached into his pocket and extracted the medallion of Guild membership that she had only seen on satin ribbons about the necks of the Guild Masters at the trials. This medallion was tarnished, and it no longer hung from a bright, purple satin ribbon, but there was no mistaking it for the genuine article.

A Master's medallion. The Priest must have been just about ready to have a cat.

He handed it to her; she turned it over, and there was his name engraved on it. She gave it back to him without a word.

"I don't think it ever occurred to him to question the fact that I had this," Talaysen continued, with satisfaction. "I mean, I *could* have stolen it—but the fact that I had puffed myself up like the proud, young, foolish peacock I used to be probably convinced him that it, and I, were genuine. He started gaping like a stranded fish. Then he went quite purple and tried to apologize."

"And?" she prompted.

"Well, I was so angry I didn't even want to be in the same town with him," Talaysen said, with a glance of apology to her. "I informed him that if he heard a song one day about a Priest so vain and so full of pride that he fell into a manure-pit because he wouldn't listen to a poor man's warning, he would be sure and recognize the description of the Priest if he looked into a mirror. Then I told him that I wouldn't be wedded by him or in his chapel if the High King himself commanded it, I shoved him away, and I left him on the floor, flapping his sleeves at me and still babbling some sort of incoherent nonsense."

"I wouldn't be wedded by a toad like that if it meant I'd *never* be wedded," she said firmly. "And if that's the attitude of their Priest, we'd better tell the rest of the Free Bards that Brughten is probably not a good place to stop. The Priest generally sets the tone for the whole village, and if this one hates minstrels, he could make a lot of trouble for our folk."

"I'm sorry, though—" he said, still looking guilty. "I never meant to deprive you of your wedding."

"Our wedding. And I really don't *care*, my love—" It gave her such a thrill to be able to say the words "my love," that she beamed at him, and he relaxed a bit. "I told you before. Amber showed me a lot of things; one of them was that there are plenty of people who have the 'proper' appearance who aren't fit to clean a stable, and more who that fat Priest would pillory, who have the best, truest hearts in the world." She touched his hand, and he caught hers in his. A delightful shiver ran down her back. "I don't care. You love me, I love you, and if a ceremony means that much to you, we'll get one of your Gypsy friends to wed us. It will be just as valid and binding, and *more* meaningful than anything *that* fat lout could have done."

She looked up at his green, green eyes, now shadowed, and started to say something more—when a dark cloud behind his head, just at the tree line, caught her eye. And instead of continuing her reassurance, she said, "What's more, we have a bit more to worry about than one stupid Priest. Look there—"

She freed her hand to point, and he turned. And swore. The cloud crept a little more into view.

"How long have we got until that storm hits us?" she asked, motioning to him to turn his back to her so she could free his rain-cape from the back of his pack, then doing the same so he could get hers and stow the bread away so *it* wouldn't get soaked.

"As quickly as that blew up?" He handed her the cape with a shake of his head. "I don't know. A couple of hours, perhaps? Would you rather turn back?"

"Not for a moment," she declared. "I'd rather have rain. I'd rather be *soaked* than take shelter in a place that has people in it like that Priest. Let's see how far we can get before it hits us. If we spot a place to take shelter along the way—"

"No deserted farmhouses!" he exclaimed.

She laughed. *After all, if it hadn't been for that farmhouse, he'd still be avoiding me like a skittish virgin mare!* "No," she promised. "No deserted farmhouses. Only ones with farmers, wives, and a dozen children to plague us and make us wish we were back with the elves!"

Just as the storm was close enough for them to feel the cold breath of it on their backs, Talaysen spotted a wooden shrine by the roadside. Those shrines usually marked the dwelling of a hedge-Priest or a hermit; a member of one of the religious Orders that called for a great deal of solitary meditation and prayer. Rune had seen it too, but after Talaysen's earlier experience, she hadn't been certain she ought to mention it.

But Talaysen headed right up the tiny path from the shrine into the deeper woods, and she followed. This time, at least, the trees weren't reaching out to snag them. In fact, the path was quite neatly kept, if relatively untraveled. Thunder growled—to their right, now, rather than behind them—and lightning flickered above and to the right of them as the woods darkened and the clouds rolled in overhead.

She caught a glimpse of the black, rain-swollen bellies of the clouds, and a breath of cold wind snaked through the trees. *This is going to be another bad one—*

Talaysen had gotten a bit ahead of her, but abruptly stopped. She just about ran into him; she peeked around him to see what had made him halt, and stared straight into the face of one of the biggest mastiffs she had ever seen in her life. The dog was absolutely enormous; a huge brindle, with a black mask and ears—and more teeth than she really wanted to see at such a close range.

She froze. Talaysen had already gone absolutely still.

There was another dog behind the first, this one tawny-and-black; if anything, it looked even bigger. The first dog sniffed Talaysen over carefully while the second stood guard; when it got to his boots, Rune quietly slipped his knife from the sheathe and pressed it into his hand, then drew her own. Knives weren't much against a dog the size of a small pony, but if the creature took it into its head to attack, knives were better than bare hands.

The dog raised its head, turned, and barked three times, as its companion watched them to make certain they didn't move. It waited a moment, then barked again, the same pattern, but this time there was no denying the impatience in its voice.

"All right, all right, I'm coming!" a voice from the path beyond the dogs called, sounding a little out of breath. "What on Earth can you two have— oh."

A brown-robed man, gray-brown hair cut in the bowl-shaped style favored by some of the Orders, and a few years older than Talaysen, came around the turning in the path that had blocked him from their view. He stared at them for a moment, as if he hadn't expected to see anything like them, and stopped at the second dog's rump. "You great loon!" he scolded affectionately, and the first mastiff lowered its head and wagged his tail. "It's just a couple of musicians! I would have thought you'd cornered an entire pack of bandits from all the noise you were making!"

The dog wagged its tail and panted, grinning. Talaysen relaxed, marginally.

"Oh, come *off*, you louts!" the robed man said, hauling at the second dog's tail until it turned around, and repeating the process with the first one. "Go on, be off with you! Back home! Idiots!"

The dogs whuffed and licked his hands, then obediently padded up the path out of sight. The robed man turned to them, and held out his hand (after first wiping it on his robe) to Talaysen. "I'm Father Bened," he said, vigorously shaking the hand that Talaysen offered in turn. "We'll save other introductions for the cottage—" He looked up as a particularly spectacular bolt of lightning arced over their heads. "If you'll just follow me, I think we might just out-race the rain!" Without any further ado, he picked up the skirts of his robes and ran in the same direction the dogs had taken without any regard for dignity. Talaysen wasn't far behind him, and Rune was right at Talaysen's heels. They all made the shelter of the cottage barely in time; just as they reached the door, the first, fat drops began falling. By the time Rune got inside and got her pack and gear off, the storm was sending down sheets of water and thumb-sized hailstones into the bargain. She pushed forward into the room so that the Priest could get at the door, but things seemed to be a confusion of firelight, shadows, and human and canine bodies.

"There!" Father Bened slammed the door shut on the storm outside and took Rune's pack away from her, stowing it in a little closet next to the door, beside Talaysen's. "Now, do come in, push those ill-mannered hounds over, and find yourself a bit of room. I'm afraid they take up most of the space until they lie down. Down, you overgrown curs!" The last was to the dogs, who paid no attention to him whatsoever, being much too interested in sniffing the newcomers over for a second time, in case they had missed some nuance on the first round of sniffs.

After a great deal of tugging on the dogs' collars and exasperated commands which the beasts largely ignored, Father Bened got the mastiffs lying down in what was evidently their proper place; curled up in the chimney corner on one side of the hearth. Together they took up about as much space as a bed, so it wasn't too surprising that the Father didn't have much in the way of furniture, at least in this room. Just three chairs and a table, and cupboards built into the wall.

Father Bened busied himself at one of those cupboards, bringing out a large cheese, half a loaf of bread, and a knife. He followed that with three plates and knives, and a basket of pears. Very plainly he was setting out supper for all three of them.

Talaysen coughed, and Father Bened looked over at him, startled. "Excuse, Father," the Bard said, "but you don't—"

"But I *do,* son," the Priest said, with a look of reproach. "Indeed I do! You've arrived on my doorstep, on the wings of a storm—what am I to do, sit here and eat my dinner and offer you nothing? I am not so poor a son of the Church as all that! Or so niggardly a host, either!"

While he was speaking, he was still bringing things down out of the cupboards; a couple of bottles of good cider, three mugs, and in a bowl, a beautiful comb of honey that was so rich and golden it made Rune's mouth water just to look at it.

"There!" he said in satisfaction. "Not at all bad, I don't think. The bread and honey are mine, the cheese is local—I trade honey for it. I can trade the honey for nearly everything that my local friends don't give me. Here, let me toast you some cheese—there is only one toasting-fork. I fear. I'm not much used to getting visitors—"

There didn't seem to be anything they could do to stop him, so Rune made herself useful by pouring cider, while Talaysen cut the bread and cheese. The dogs looked up hopefully at the proceedings, and Rune finally asked if they needed to be fed as well.

"The greedy louts would gladly eat anything that hits the floor, and look for more," Father Bened said, as he laid a second slab of toasted cheese, just beginning to melt, on a slice of bread. "I've fed them, but they'll try to convince you otherwise. I could feed them a dozen times a day, until their eyes were popping out, and they'd still try to tell you they were starving."

"What on Earth do you feed them?" Talaysen asked, staring at the dogs as if fascinated. "And where did you get them? They're stag-hounds, aren't they? I thought only Sires raised stag-hounds."

Father Bened ducked his head a little, and looked guilty. "Well—the truth is, they aren't mine, really. They belong to a—ah—a friend. I—ah—keep them for him. He comes by every few days with meat and bones for them; the rest of the time I feed them fish or whatever rabbits I can—ah—that happen to die."

Rune began to get a glimmering of what was going on. It was a good thing no one had ever questioned the good Father; he was a terrible liar. "And if the meat your friend brings them is deer, it's just really lucky that he found the dead carcass before it was too gone to be of use, hmm?" she said. Father Bened flushed even redder.

"Father Bened," she said with amusement, "I do believe that you're a poacher! And so is this 'friend' of yours!"

"A poacher? Well, now I wouldn't go that far—" he said indignantly. "Sire Thessalay claims more forest land hereabouts than he has any right to! I've petitioned the Sires and the barons through the Church I don't know how many times to have someone come out and have a look, but no one ever seems to read my letters. My friend and I are simply—doing the work of the Church. Feeding the hungry, clothing the naked—"

"With venison, cony, and buckskin and fur," Talaysen supplied. "I take it that a lot of the small-holders out here go hungry in the winter, else?"

The Father nodded soberly. "When the Sire claimed the forest lands, he also laid claim to lands that had been used for grazing and for pig-herding. Many of the small-holders lost half their means of support. You're Free Bards, aren't you?" At Talaysen's nod, he continued. "I thought you might be. A year ago last winter one of your lot stayed with me for a bit. A good man; called himself 'Starling' if I mind me right. I told him a little about our problem; he went out with my friend a few times to augment food supplies."

"I know him," Talaysen replied. "From a small-holder family himself."

"I thought as much." Father Bened shrugged, and laid out the third slice of cheese, then wasted no time in digging into his portion. Rune picked up the bread and nibbled gingerly; the cheese was still quite hot, and would burn her mouth if she wasn't careful. It tasted like goat-cheese; it was easier to raise goats on marginal land than cattle, especially if your grazing lands had been taken from you.

"I'm city-bred, myself," the Father continued. "When I was a youngster, the Church was very special to me, and I grew up with this vision of what it must be like—full of men and women who'd gotten rid of what was bad in them, and had their hearts set on God. Always felt as if the Church was calling me; went straight into Orders as soon as I could."

He sighed. Talaysen nodded sympathetically. "I think the same thing happened to you that happened to my cousin Ardis."

"If she had a crisis of conscience, yes," Father Bened replied sadly. "That was when I found out that the Church was just like anyplace else; just as many bad folk as good, and plenty that were indifferent. Since I hadn't declared for an Order yet, I traveled a little to see if it was simply that I'd encountered an unusual situation. I came to the conclusion that I hadn't, and I almost left the Church."

"Ardis decided to fight from within," Talaysen told him. "She got assigned to the Justiciars."

"I decided the same, but to work from below, not above," Father Bened replied. "There were more of the bad and indifferent kind when you were in the city, in the big cloisters attached to the cathedrals, or so it seemed to me. So I got myself assigned to the Order of Saint Clive; it's a mendi-cant order that tends to wayside shrines. I thought that once I was out in the country, I'd be able to do more good."

"Why?" Rune asked. "It seems to me if you were city-bred you'd have a hard time of it out in the wilds. You must have spent all your time trying to keep yourself fed and out of the weather—"

"I didn't think of that," he admitted, and laughed. "And it was a good thing for me that God takes care of innocent fools. My Prior took pity on me and assigned me here; this cottage was already built, and my predeces-sor had been well taken care of by the locals. I simply settled in and took up where he'd left off."

"What do you think of the Priest in Brughten?" Talaysen asked carefully. Father Bened's face darkened.

"Father Bened can only say that his Brother in the Church could be a little more charitable," he replied carefully. "But I am told that there is a poacher of rabbits who roams these woods that has called him a thief who preys on widows and orphans, a liar, and a toady to anyone with a title or a fat purse. And the poacher has heard that he goes so far as to deny the sacraments to those he feels are too lowly to afford much of an offering."

"I'd say the poacher is very perceptive," Talaysen replied, then described his encounter with the Brughten Priest, though not the part where he revealed himself to be Gwydain. Father Bened listened sympathetically, and shook his head at the end.

"I can only say that such behavior is what I have come to expect of him," the Priest said. "But at least I can offer a remedy to your problem. Friends, if all you wanted was to be wed—well, I have the authority. I don't have even a chapel, but if this room will suit you—"

"A marsh would suit me better than a cathedral right now," Rune said firmly. "And that fat fool in Brughten may have joy of his. This room will be fine."

Father Bened beamed at her, at Talaysen, and even at the dogs, who thumped their tails on the floor, looked hopefully for a morsel of cheese, and panted.

"Wonderful!" he exclaimed. "Do you know, you'll be my first wedding? How exciting! Here, finish your dinner, and let me hunt up my book of offices—" He crammed the last of his bread and cheese into his mouth, and jumped up from his chair to rummage through one of the cupboards until he came to a little leather-covered book. "I should have some contracts in here, too, if the beetles haven't gotten to them—" he mumbled, mostly to himself, it seemed. "Ah! Here they are!"

He emerged with a handful of papers, looked them over, and found the one he wanted. It had been nibbled around the edges, but was otherwise intact. He placed it on the table next to the cider, and leafed through the book.

"Here it is. Wedding." He looked up. "I'm supposed to give you a great long lecture at this point about the sanctity of marriage, and the commitment it means to each of you, but you both strike me as very sensible people. I don't think you need a lecture from *me,* who doesn't know a *thing* about women. And I don't expect you're doing this because you don't have anything else to do tonight. So, we'll skip the lecture, shall we, and go right into the business?"

"Certainly," Talaysen said, and took Rune's hand. She nodded and smiled at Father Bened, who smiled back, and began.

"Well, did that suit you?" Talaysen asked, as they spread their blankets in Father Bened's hardly used spare room. There was no furniture, the light was from one of their own candles, and the only sounds were the snores of Father Bened's mastiffs in the other room and the spattering of rain on the roof.

"Practical, short, to the point, and yes, it suited me," Rune replied, carefully spreading their blankets to make one larger bed. It practically filled the entire room. "There's a duly signed sheet of parchment in your pack that says we're married, and the next town we go through, we'll drop the Church copy off at the clerk's office." She stood up and surveyed her work. "Now, are *you* happy?"

Talaysen sighed. "If I told you how happy I was, you probably wouldn't believe it—"

Rune turned, smiled, and moved closer to him, until there was less than the width of a hair between them. "So why don't you show me?" she breathed.

He did.

It was a long time before they slept.

CHAPTER NINETEEN

"I cannot *believe* this!" Talaysen fumed, testing the bonds about his wrists and giving the effort up after a few moments. A good thing, too; since they were roped together at the wrists, his efforts had been wrenching Rune's shoulders out of their sockets. "First the damn Guild gets all free-lance musicians barred from the last three Faires—and now *this*—"

Rune didn't say anything, which was just as well. There wasn't much she could say—and certainly none of it would have made their guards vanish, eased his temper, or gotten them free of their bonds.

There were three major Faires up here in the north of the kingdom, all within a week of each other: the Wool Faire at Naneford, the Cattle Faire at Overton, and the Faire of Saint Jewel at Hyne's Crossing. Talaysen had planned to make all of them, for all three of them were good places to make contacts for wintering-over.

All three were held within the cathedral grounds inside each city—and at all three, when Talaysen and Rune had tried to gain entrance, they had been turned back by guards at the gates. Church guards, even though the Faires were supposed to be secular undertakings.

Each guard looked down his nose at them as he explained why they had been barred. There were to be no musicians allowed within except those with Guild badges. That was the beginning and the end of it. The Guild had petitioned the City Council and the Church, and they had so ruled; the Council on the grounds that licensing money was being lost, the Church on the grounds that musicians encouraged revelry and revelry encouraged licentiousness. If Rune and Talaysen wished to play in the streets of the city, or within one of the inns, they could purchase a busking permit and do so, but only Guild musicians and their apprentices would be playing inside the Faire. They found out later that there was *no* "free" entertainment in the Faires this year; anyone who wished to hear music could pay up a copper to listen to apprentices perform within a Guild tent, or a silver to hear Journeymen. That was the entertainment by day— anyone who sought music after dark could part with *three* silvers to listen to a single Master at night. There were no dancers in the "streets" or otherwise. In fact, there was nothing within the Faire grounds but commerce and Church rituals. Rune would not have been overly surprised to learn that the Guild had even succeeded in banning shepherds from playing to their herds within the Faire bounds.

It was Rune's private opinion that there would be so many complaints that this particular experiment would be doomed after this year, and Talaysen agreed—but that didn't help them now.

Talaysen had been angry at the first Faire, furious at the second, and incoherent with rage at the third. Rune had actually thought that he might brain the third gate-guard—who besides his Church-hireling uniform had worn Guild colors and had been particularly nasty—with his own two hands. But he had managed to get control of his temper, and had walked away without doing the man any damage.

But by then, of course, their coin-reserve was seriously low, and their efforts to find an inn that did not already have a resident musician had been completely without result. So rather than risk a worse depletion of their reserves, they headed out into the countryside, where, with judicious use of fish-hook and rabbit snare, they could at least extend their supplies.

In a few days they had gotten as far as Sire Brador Jofferey's lands. And that was where they ran into a trouble they had never anticipated.

Sire Brador, it seemed, was involved in a border dispute with his neighbor, Sire Harlan Dettol. By the time they entered Sire Brador's lands, the dispute had devolved into warfare. Under the circumstances, strangers were automatically suspect. A company of Sire Brador's men-at-arms had surrounded them as they camped—and Rune thanked God that they had not put out any rabbit snares!—and took them prisoner with hardly more than a dozen words exchanged.

A thin and nervous-looking man guarded them now, as they sat, wrists bound behind their backs and feet hobbled, in the shade of an enormous oak. *At least they gave us that much,* Rune thought wearily; they could have been left in the full sun easily enough. The Sire's men were not very happy about the way things were going; she had picked that up from listening to some of the conversations going on around them. Exchanging of insults and stealing or wrecking anything on the disputed land was one thing—but so far six men had been killed in this little enterprise, and the common soldiers were, Rune thought, justifiably upset. They had signed on with the Sire to be guards and deal with bandits—and to harass their neighboring Sire now and again. No one had told them they were going to go to war over a silly piece of land.

Another man-at-arms approached on heavy feet, walking towards them like a clumsy young bull, and the nervous fellow perked up. Rune reckoned that their captivity was at an end—or that, at least, they were going somewhere else.

Good. There's pebbles digging into my behind.

"The cap'n 'll see the prisoners now," the burly fellow told their guard, who heaved a visible sigh of relief and wandered off without any warning at all. That left the burly man to stare at them doubtfully, as if he wasn't quite certain what to do with them.

"You got t' get t'yer feet," he said, tentatively. "You got t' come with me."

Talaysen heaved a sigh of pure exasperation. "That's going to be a bit difficult on both counts," he replied angrily. "We can't *get* to our feet, because you've got us tied back to back. And we can't *walk* because you've got us hobbled like a couple of horses. Now unless you're going to do something about that, we're going to be sitting right here until Harvest."

The man scratched his beard and looked even more uncertain. "I don't got no authority to do nothin' about that," he said. "I just was told I gotta bring you t' the cap'n. So you gotta get t'yer feet."

Talaysen groaned. Rune sighed. This would be funny if it weren't so stupid. And if they weren't trussed up like a couple pigs on the way to market. It might get distinctly *unfunny*, if their guard decided that the application of his boot to their bodies would get them standing up . . . she contemplated her knees, rather than antagonize him by staring at him.

She looked up at the sound of footsteps approaching; yet another man-at-arms neared, this one in a tunic and breeches that were of slightly better quality and showing less wear than the other man's.

"Never mind, Hollis," said the newcomer. "I decided to come have a look at them myself." He surveyed them with an air of vacant boredom. "Well, what do you spies have to say for yourselves?"

"*Spies?*" Talaysen barked in sheer outrage. "Spies? Where in God's Sacred Name did you get *that* idea?"

Rune fixed the "captain," if that was what he was, with an icy glare. "Since when do spies camp openly beside a road, and carry musical instruments?" she growled. "Dear God, the only weapons we have are a couple of dull knives! What were we supposed to do with *those*, dig our way into your castle? *That* would only take ten or twenty years, I'm sure!"

The captain looked surprised, as if he hadn't expected either of them to talk back to him. *If all he's caught so far are poor, frightened farmers, I suppose no one has.*

He blinked at them doubtfully. "Well," he said at last, "if you aren't spies, then you're conscripts." As Talaysen stared at him in complete silence, he continued, looking them over as if they were a pair of sheep. "You—with the gray hair—you're a bit long in the tooth, but the boy there—"

"I'm not a boy," Rune replied crisply. "I'm a woman, and I'm *his* wife. And you can go ahead and conscript me, if you want, but having me around isn't going to make your men any easier to handle. And they're going to be even harder to handle after I castrate the first man who lays a hand on me."

The captain blanched, but recovered. "Well, if you're in disguise as a boy, then you're obviously a spy after all—"

"It's not a disguise," Talaysen said between clenched teeth. "It's simply easier for *my wife* to travel in breeches. It's not her fault you can't tell a woman in breeches from a boy. I'm sure you'll find half the women in this area working the fields in breeches. Are you going to arrest them for spying, too?" The captain bit his lip. "You must be spies," he continued stubbornly. "Otherwise why were you out there on the road? You're not peddlers, and the Faires are over. Nobody travels that road this time of year."

"We're *musicians*," Rune said, as if she was speaking to a very simple child. "We are carrying *musical instruments.* We *play and sing.* We were going to Kardown Faire and your road was the only way to get there—"

"How do I know you're really musicians?" he said, suspiciously. "Spies could be carrying musical instruments, too." He smiled at his own cleverness.

Talaysen cursed under his breath; Rune caught several references to the fact that brothers and sisters should not marry, and more to the inadvisability of intercourse with sheep, for this man was surely the lamentable offspring of such an encounter.

"Why don't you untie us and give us our instruments, and we'll *prove* we're musicians?" she said. "Spies wouldn't know how to play, now, would they?"

"I—suppose not," the captain replied, obviously groping after an objection to her logic, and unable to find one. "But I don't know—"

Obviously, she thought; but she smiled charmingly. "Just think, you'll get a free show, as well. We're really quite good. We've played before Dukes and Barons. If you don't trust both of us, just cut *me* loose and let me play."

Not quite a lie. I'm sure there were plenty of Dukes and Barons who were passing by at Kingsford when we were playing.

"What are you up to?" Talaysen hissed, as she continued to keep her mouth stretched in that ingenuous smile.

"I have an idea," she muttered back out of the corner of her mouth. And as the captain continued to ponder, she laughed. "Oh come now, you aren't afraid of one little woman, are you?"

That did it. He drew his dagger and cut first the hobbles at her ankles, then the bonds at her wrists. She got up slowly, her backside aching, her shoulders screaming, her hands tingling with unpleasant pins-and-needles sensations.

She *did* have an idea. If she could work some of the same magic on this stupid lout that she'd worked on the elves, she *might* be able to get him to turn them loose. She'd noticed lately that when they really *needed* money, she'd been able to coax it from normally unresponsive crowds—as long as she followed that strange little inner melody she'd heard when she had played for the elven-king. It was always a variation on whatever she happened to be playing; one just a little different from the original. The moment she matched with it, whatever she needed to have happen would occur. She was slowly evolving a theory about it; how it wasn't so much that the melody itself was important, it was that the melody was how she "heard" and controlled magic. Somehow she was tapping magic through music.

But she couldn't explain that to Talaysen. Or rather, she couldn't explain it right now. Later, maybe. If this really worked.

The captain poked their packs with his toe as she stood there rubbing her wrists. "Which one is yours?" he asked, without any real interest.

"That one, there," she told him. "Why don't you hand me that fiddle—that's right, that one. A spy would *never* be able to learn to play this, it takes years—"

"A spy could learn to play a couple of tunes on it," the captain said, in a sudden burst of completely unexpected thought. "That's all a spy would need."

He looked at her triumphantly. She sighed, took the instrument from him before he dropped it, and took it out of its case to tune it. "A spy could learn a couple of tunes," she agreed. "But a spy wouldn't know them all. Pick one. Pick anything. I couldn't possibly know what you were going to pick to learn to play it in advance, so if I know it, then I'm not a spy. All right?"

She saw Talaysen wince out of the corner of her eye, and she didn't blame him. No fiddler could know every tune; she was taking a terrible risk with this—

But it was a calculated risk, taken out of experience. If he'd been a bright man, she wouldn't have tried this; he might purposefully pick something really obscure, hoping to baffle her.

But he wasn't bright; he was, in fact, the very opposite. So he did what any stupid man would do; he blurted the first thing that came into his mind. Which was, as she had gambled, "Shepherd's Hey"; one of the half-dozen fiddle-tunes every fiddler wishes he would never have to play again, and which someone in every audience asks for.

She played it, thinking very hard about getting him to release them, and listening with that inner ear for the first notes of the magic. . . .

He started tapping his toe halfway through the first repetition; a good sign, but not quite what she was looking for. But his eyes unfocused a bit, which meant she might be getting through to him—

Or that he was so dense he could be entranced, like a sheep, by perfectly ordinary music.

Three times through. Three times was what had worked with the elves; three times had coaxed pennies from otherwise tight fists.

Two repetitions—into the third—and—

There. Just an echo, a faint sigh of melody, but it was there. She was afraid to play the tune again, though; repeating it a fourth time might break the magic.

"Pick something else," she called out to him, breaking into his reverie.

He stared at her with his mouth hanging open for a moment, then stammered, " 'Foxhunter.' "

Another one of the tunes she had learned to hate while she was still at the Hungry Bear. She sighed; if her feelings got in the way of the music, this might turn out to be a bad idea instead of a good one. But the magic was still with her, and stronger as she brought the "Hey" around into the first notes of "Foxhunter." His eyes glazed over again, and she began to get the sense of the inner melody, stronger, and just a little off the variant she played. She strove to bring them closer, but hadn't quite—not before she'd played "Foxhunter" three times as well.

But this was a subtle, slippery magic that she was trying to work. She had to get inside him somehow, and control the way he thought about them; this called for something quieter. Maybe that was why she hadn't quite managed to touch the magic-tune yet. . . .

This time she didn't ask him to pick something. She slowed the final bars of "Foxhunter," dragged them out and sent the tune into a minor key, and turned the lively jig into something else entirely different; a mournful rendition of "Captive Heart."

That did it! The hidden melody strengthened suddenly; grew so clear, in fact, that she glanced at Talaysen and was unsurprised to see a look of concentration on his face, as if he could hear it too.

Once, twice—and on the third repetition, something dropped into place, and her tune and the magic one united, just as the sun touched the horizon.

She played it to the end, then took her bow from the strings and waited to see what, if anything, the result of her playing was going to be.

The captain shook himself, as if he was waking from a long sleep. "I must—how—I think—" He shook himself again, then drew his knife and cut Talaysen's bonds, offering him a hand to pull the Master to his feet. "I don't know what I was thinking of," the captain said, vaguely. "Thinking two minstrels like you were spies. Stupid, of course. These past couple of weeks, they've been hard on us. We're looking for spies behind every bush, it seems."

"No harm done, captain," Talaysen said heartily, as Rune put up her fiddle as quickly as she could, and slung her pack on her back. She dragged his over to his feet, and he followed her example, still talking. "No harm done at all. Good thinking, really, after all, how could you know? I'm sure your Sire is very pleased to have a captain like you."

When Talaysen stopped for a moment to get his pack in place, Rune took over, pulling on his elbow to get him moving towards the edge of camp and the road. "Of course, how could you know? But we obviously *are* musicians and you don't need to detain us, now, do you? Of course not. We'll just be on our way. Thank you. No, you needn't send anyone after us, we'll be fine—we know exactly where we need to go, we'll be off your Sire's land before you know it—"

She got Talaysen moving and waved good-bye; Talaysen let her take the lead and wisely kept quiet. The other men-at-arms, seeing that their captain was letting the former captives go, were content to leave things the way they were. One or two of them even waved back as Rune and Talaysen made all the speed they could without (hopefully) seeming to do so.

It wasn't until they were on the open road again that Rune heaved a sigh of relief, and slowed her pace.

"All right, confess," Talaysen said, moving up beside her and speaking quietly out of the corner of his mouth. "I saw what happened, and I *thought* I heard something—"

"How much do you know about magic?" Rune asked, interrupting him, and gazing anxiously at the darkening sky.

"Not much, only the little Ardis tells me, and what's in songs, of course." He hitched his pack a little higher on his shoulders. "You're telling me that you're a mage?"

She shook her head slightly, then realized he might not be able to see the gesture in the gathering gloom. "I'm not—I mean, I don't know if I am or not. I know what happened with the elves, but I thought that was just because the elves were easier to affect with music than humans.

Now—I don't know. I hear something when I'm doing—whatever it is. And this time I think you heard it too."

"Ardis told me every mage has his own way of sensing magic," Talaysen said thoughtfully. "Some see it as a web of light, some as color-patterns, some feel it, some taste or smell it. Maybe a mage who was also a musician would hear it as music—"

He faltered, and she added what she thought he was going to say. "But you heard it too. Didn't you? You heard what I was trying to follow."

"I heard something," he replied, carefully. "Whether it was the same thing you heard or not, I don't know."

"Well, whatever is going on—when I really need something to happen, I think about it, *hard,* and listen inside for a melody at the same time. When I find it, I try to match it, but since it's a variation on what I've playing, it takes a little bit of time to do that, to figure out what the pattern is going to be. And it seems like I have to play things in repeats of three to get it to work. It's the moment that I match with that variation that I seem to be able to influence people."

"But what about with the elves?" he asked. "You weren't doing any variations then—"

"I don't know, I'm only guessing," she replied, looking to the west through the trees, and wondering how long they had before the sun set. "But what I was playing was all Gypsy music or music already associated with the elves, like the 'Faerie Reel.' Maybe they're more susceptible to music, or maybe the music itself was already the right tune to be magic. Next Midsummer Faire we are going to have to talk to your cousin about all this—I don't like doing things and not knowing how or why they work. Or what they might do if they don't work the way I think they will."

She was looking at him now, peering through the blue twilight, and not at the road, so she missed spotting the trouble ahead. Her first inkling of a problem was when Talaysen's head snapped up, and he cursed under his breath.

"We'll do that. If we're not languishing in a dungeon," Talaysen groaned. "If this isn't the worst run of luck I've ever had—if I hadn't already been expecting the worst—"

She turned her head—and echoed his groan of disgust. Just ahead of them was a roadblock. Manned by armed soldiers with a banner flapping above them in Sire Harlan's black-and-white stripes.

"Well, there's no point in trying to avoid them; they'll only chase us," Talaysen sighed, as the soldiers stirred, proving that they'd been sighted too. "God help us. Here we go again."

"This time, let's see if we can't get them to let us prove we're minstrels right off," Rune said, thinking quickly. "I'll try and work magic on them again. And since you heard what I was trying to follow, *you* join me on this one. Maybe with both of us working on them, we can do better than just get them to let us go."

"All right," Talaysen replied quietly, for they were just close enough to the barricade that a sharp-eared man might hear what they were saying. "Follow my lead."

He raised his arm and waved, smiling. "Ho there!" he called. "We are certainly glad to see *you*!"

Looks of astonishment on every face told Rune that he'd certainly managed to confuse them.

"You—sir, are you the captain?" he continued, pointing at one of the men who seemed to be in charge. At the other's wary nod, Talaysen's smile broadened. "Thank goodness! We have a lot to tell you about. . . ."

"Ten pennies and quite a little stock of provisions, *and* an escort to the border," Talaysen said in satisfaction, patting the pouch at his belt. "Not bad, for what started out a disaster. Maybe our luck is turning."

"Maybe we're turning it ourselves," Rune countered, but lazily. She was not going to argue about results, however they came about.

A good night's sleep in the Sire's camp had helped matters. They'd done so well that they'd become honored guests by the time they were through playing, instead of captives. And while Sire Harlan was not interested in taking on a musician until his little feud with his neighbor had been settled, he *did* know about the banning of non-Guild minstrels from the previous three Faires. When they had played for him personally, he spent quite some time talking with them afterwards, over a cup of wine. He had assured them that a similar attempt at Kardown had been blocked.

"Did you hear the rest of the story about the Faires?" Talaysen asked. "I asked Captain Nours about it, and got an earful."

She shook her head. "No, I wasn't close enough to listen, and that terribly earnest cousin of the Sire was pouring his life-story into my ear."

"That's what you get for being sympathetic," he chuckled, and kicked at a rock to keep from stepping on it. "It wasn't just the Bardic Guild. *All* the Guilds got together and barred non-Guild participants. Sire Harlan's captain is also a wood-carver, and he's heard that if they try the same again next year, the non-Guild crafts-people have threatened to hold their own Faires—*outside* the gates, and just off the road. Which means no Church tax or city tax on sellers, as well as an open Faire."

She widened her eyes. "Can they do that?" she asked.

"I don't know why not," he replied. "One of the farmers has agreed to let them use his fallow fields for free for the first year. That may be how the Kingsford Faire started; I seem to recall something like that—the Church putting a ban on entertainment or levying an extra use-tax. I can tell you that most common folk would rather go to an open Faire, given a choice. Anyway, he asked me to spread that bit of news as well, so that the small crafters are ready, come next year."

She nodded, stowing the information away in her memory. That was another thing the Free Bards did that she hadn't known; they passed news wherever they went. Often it was news that those in power would prefer others didn't know. Ordinary minstrels might or might not impart news as the whim and the generosity of their audience moved them; Bardic Guild musicians never did.

So in a way we are spies, she reflected. *Only not in a way that sheep-brained captain would ever recognize.*

"Aren't we going to meet Gwyna at Kardown?" she asked, suddenly, squinting into the sunlight, and taking off her hat to fan herself with it.

"That was the plan," he replied. "Why?"

"Oh, nothing—" she replied vaguely. She hadn't thought about the coming encounter, until the association of "news" brought it to mind.

She and Talaysen *were* news, so far as the Free Bards were concerned. When they had parted from the Free Bards, she and Talaysen had been Master and Apprentice. Now their relationship was something altogether different. Gwyna planned a course of travel that put her in and out of contact with a good half of the Free Bards over the year, not to mention all the gypsy Clans. *She* would be the one telling everyone she met of Master Wren's change of status, and if she didn't approve . . .

Rune realized then that she wanted not only Gwyna to approve, but all the rest of the Free Bards, including people she didn't even know yet. And not just for her own sake. If there was divisiveness in the Free Bards, trouble with Talaysen's leadership, the things she and Talaysen had talked about would never come to pass. The group might even fall apart.

We will never make a difference if that happens, she thought worriedly, and then realized with a start that for the first time in her life she was thinking of herself as a part of a group. Worrying about "we," where "we" meant people she'd never met as well as those she knew and liked.

It was a curious feeling, having been a loner most of her life, to suddenly find herself a part of something.

If Gwyna didn't approve of what had happened between her and Talaysen—

Then she mentally took herself by the scruff of the neck and shook herself. *Of course she'll approve,* she scolded. *She was practically throwing us into bed together before we all broke up. I'm running from shadows that aren't even there. The fact that we're married shouldn't make any kind of a difference to her. She told me herself that Talaysen spent too much time alone.*

She noticed that Talaysen was watching her with a concerned frown, and smiled at him. "It's all right, no disasters. Just thinking things through," she said cheerfully. "Tell me something, do you think we were working magic last night, or not?"

He hesitated a moment, taking the time to wipe some of the dust from his face with his scarf. "I never thought of myself as a mage, or anything like one," he said, finally. "Even though everything I've ever *really* wanted I've gotten. Now that I think about it, that is rather odd; I don't know of anyone who always gets what he wants or needs. I always thought it was plain fool luck, but maybe it wasn't just extraordinary good luck. Maybe it was magic all along."

"Your cousin's a mage," she pointed out. "I'd always been told that sort of thing runs in families. That's the way it is in ballads, anyway."

"That might explain it." He paused a moment, and Rune had an idea that he was gathering his thoughts. "Last night I told you that I heard the melody you were trying to match the first time we were caught. You wanted me to see if I could actually match it myself when we were wooing Sire Harlan's men, and I said I'd try, and we didn't have a chance to talk about what I did in private. Well, I heard the melody, just like before, and I tried to match it. Easier on a lute than a fiddle, by the way."

She nodded. "And you did it; I felt you snap into the melody at the end of the first time through, and the tune got stronger as we played it. Which was probably why they asked us to stay and play for them, why the men gave us supplies, and why the Sire gave us money and an escort."

"I think it's also why the Sire talked to us personally," he said. She raised an eyebrow in surprise, and he nodded. "When we played for his men, he was listening just beyond the fire. I didn't *see* him, but somehow I knew he was there, and I knew we needed his goodwill. I saw you were doing all right with the men, so I turned my attention to him. I hoped I could get him to help us out; the captain was pretty reluctant to exceed his authority." He frowned, as if thinking of something unpleasant.

"I'd say it worked," she replied, wondering why he was frowning.

"That's the trouble, it *did,* and too well." His frown deepened, and he tucked his scarf around his neck again. "He talked to us very like equals, he gave us money and an escort. He shouldn't have done any of those things, it's just not in the character of most Sires to welcome strangers into their camps and treat them like old friends. What I did somehow made him act completely differently—"

"Maybe not," she countered. "He was camped out there with his men, after all, and he's obviously liked as well as respected. Maybe he would have done all that anyway. Maybe he's used to treating underlings well; maybe he just likes music."

"Maybe, but it's not likely." He shook his head. "But that's not the point. The problem here isn't what he did, it's that *I made him do it.* I made him do those things just as surely as if I'd held a knife to his throat and ordered him to tell us the same things. Even though it kept us out of trouble, I don't like the implications. Being able to change the way people think and react is—well, it's frightening."

She started to object, then shut her mouth, thinking about it. It *was* frightening, and she found many reasons why what she was doing was wrong. "Can Ardis do that?" she asked.

He nodded. "That, and other things. Healing, for one. Mostly she doesn't use her magic. I think she told me that she uses it only when— after very careful consideration—she thinks it's just and fair to do so, and not simply convenient."

How would I feel about somebody coming in and changing my thinking around? she wondered. "Was it just and fair of us to keep those men-at-arms from throwing us in a dungeon, or conscripting us?" she countered. "I certainly think it was! They wouldn't listen to reason or logic, and I was running out of patience."

He grinned. "I'd have to say yes and you know it," he mocked. "That's a cheating question."

"Would it have been just and fair to get that Priest to marry us?" she continued.

"Now that is a good question." He mulled that over for a bit. "I would have to say no. Even though he was being an officious, uncharitable, vain and foolish man."

"Why not?" she asked, wanting to hear his reasoning.

"It would not have been just and fair to change his mind, because we were only inconvenienced. On the other hand, if those men-at-arms had jailed or conscripted us, we would undoubtedly have been harmed." He smiled feebly. "I don't do well in damp dungeons. And I wouldn't know one end of a sword from the other. In the former, I'd probably become ill rather quickly, and as a conscript I'd probably become *dead* just as quickly."

"Obviously the same goes for the elven-king," she replied, thoughtfully.

He nodded. "Elves aren't predictable. He might have kept us a while, or killed us when he tired of us. Now, whether or not we should have used this power of ours to change the minds of people at those Faires to let us in—I don't know."

"It's not worth debating," she told him, as a jay overhead called raucous agreement. "We couldn't have done anything to help ourselves or others at the last three Faires because the people we needed to influence directly were not going to come out to listen to us."

"True, but we could have started a riot," he said, so soberly that she knew he was not joking. "All we'd have needed to do would be stand outside the Church gates and sing rabble-rousing songs with that power behind them. People were annoyed enough already, especially the ones being turned away. We could quite easily have started a riot without anyone suspecting we were to blame."

The morning seemed suddenly cold, and she shivered. She'd never seen a riot. She didn't want to see one. People could be killed in riots; children often were trampled and either killed outright or maimed for life. "We don't do that," she said forcefully. "We don't *ever* do that."

"I agree," he replied, just as forcefully. "It would have to be something worlds away more serious than what we encountered to make starting a riot justified."

She paused to collect her thoughts. "You do realize that we're talking about this as if it's real, and not the product of some really good luck and our imaginations, don't you?"

"I don't have any doubt that it's real," he told her. "We've managed to change things three times with this—whatever it is. When something happens three times, it's not a coincidence, it's real."

It's more times than that, she thought wryly, remembering how she had coaxed money from unresponsive audiences. And then she sobered, thinking about what she'd done in a new light.

Had that been "fair and just"? After all, she hadn't done anything important to them, had she? They wouldn't have parted with their coins if they hadn't had them to spend. Would they?

Yes, but— She had still changed their thoughts, the most private thing a person could have. The poorest person in the world, the man accused of heresy and thrown into the Church's dungeons, a cripple who couldn't move arms or legs—they could still claim their thoughts as their own, and in that much they were wealthy and free.

But what she and Talaysen did could change that. Not in any large way, but it was still a change. And for what? Convenience, again. The convenience, perhaps, of not working quite so hard. . . .

Never mind that finding that elusive thread of magic-song and matching
it was harder work than simply playing well. She had to assume that one
day it might become easy. What then? Wouldn't it be a temptation to
simply sit back and play indifferently, knowing that she would be well-
paid no matter how she played?

She thought of all the cold days in the winter, busking on a corner in
Nolton, and had to admit that it would have been more than a temptation.
If she'd known about this, she'd have done it. And she'd have probably
teased her audiences into buying hot cider and sausage rolls from her
vendor friends as well, whether the listeners were hungry or not.

No. That was wrong. Absolutely wrong. It was a cheat, and it made her
music into a lie.

"We don't use it to make audiences like us, either," she said into the
silence, with more force than she intended. "They either appreciate us
on their own or not at all."

He raised an eyebrow at her outburst but agreed immediately. "What
do we have, then? Not for the sake of convenience, not when there are
other ways to deal with a situation, only when it's fair and just?"

She nodded and sighed. "You know, I hate to admit this, but it sounds
as if we're saying we can't use it to help ourselves at all."

He laughed. "Oh, partially. We can't use it unless we're really being
threatened, shall we say? Or it's for something that truly needs to be
done."

"That sounds good." She glanced at him, and couldn't help grinning.
"Now, does threat of *hunger* count?"

"I don't—"

"Or how about if I wait until you're hungry to ask that question?" she
said, and chuckled.

He only shook his head. "Women," he said, as if that explained everything, and then changed the subject.

Just like a man, she thought with amusement, and let him.

CHAPTER TWENTY

The Kardown Faire lasted only three days; it wasn't a very large Faire,
but because it was a wool-market Faire, it tended to be a wealthy one.
They found Gwyna waiting for them at the bare excuse for a gate in the
sketchy fence surrounding the Faire on the town common; she had already
found a good camping site, screened on three sides by bushes and trees,
and claimed it for all three of them. Rune was happy to see her; a real
friendly face, a known face, was a luxury she'd missed without realizing it.

Three days were just enough time for them to recoup some of their
losses—and barely time for Gwyna to finish telling them the news of her
adventures, and those of the other Free Bards she'd met with. Rune
noticed something a little odd about Gwyna's behavior from the first,

though it was nothing having to do with either her or Talaysen. Gwyna would keep glancing about nervously when she thought she was alone, and no longer bantered with strangers. And whenever she saw someone in a long robe, she became very, very quiet.

They had stayed together as a trio during the entire Faire; Gwyna had been delighted to hear of the wedding (much to Rune's relief). But that wasn't why they stayed as a group; their primary consideration was that Gwyna no longer seemed quite so fearlessly self-reliant, which accounted for the odd behavior Rune had noticed. Her misadventure with the mage-Priest had shaken her more than she would admit to anyone, even Rune. But Rune saw it in the way she constantly looked over her shoulder for trouble, even when there was no reason to, and in her troubled dreams at night. Gypsy Robin had gotten a bad shock, and she hadn't recovered from it yet.

She'd parted with Master Stork about a week after the Midsummer Faire, and it looked to Rune as if she hadn't had a steady night of sleep since. Talaysen told her he thought Gwyna must be sleeping with one eye open, and Rune figured he was probably right.

Gwyna played at being lighthearted, still, but her jesting often fell flat, her spirits were dampened, and she seemed to be certain that there was danger lurking just out of sight, especially at night. Not that Rune blamed her. But she was carrying more knives now, and openly; something that had the potential for serious problems if she felt herself threatened. If someone propositioned her in a way she thought was dangerous, in her state of heightened nerves, she might well draw on him—and use what she drew.

At the end of the third day, Gwyna went off to bring back water for their little camp, leaving Rune cleaning vegetables and Talaysen setting the fire, alone together for the first time that day. She decided to broach what had been on her mind since she'd seen the state Gwyna was in.

"Is it going to be any harder to find a wintering-over spot for a trio than it is for a duet?" she asked.

He looked up from the fire. "No, I don't think so," he said. "Are you thinking what I'm thinking?"

Rune nodded. "We can't let her go out there by herself until she gets over her nerves. She'll either wear herself out, or hurt someone."

"Or herself." He sat back on his heels. "I hadn't wanted to ask you, because it means—well—" He blushed. "We won't have our privacy."

"Lecher," she said, and grinned. "Oh, we can have our privacy. We just ask her to take a long walk. Seriously, though, we ought to invite her."

"You ought to invite her to what?" Gwyna asked lightly, as she rounded the corner of the half-shelter they'd erected, coming into their little protective circle of trees.

"We thought you ought to come with us for a while," Talaysen said. "We'd like your company. We've missed you."

"And?" Gwyna replied, setting down the canvas bucket in the hole they'd dug to hold it. "You're not inviting me because of my sparkling conversation, and you two have got quite enough companionship on your own, thanks."

"You look awful," Rune said frankly. "I told Wren that I thought it was because you're trying to stay up all night on guard. And we could use a third to split the watches with. It's hard enough sleeping at night with two; you never get a full night's sleep going watch-on-watch, and if you both fall asleep, well, you take your chances. Three can keep watches and still have time for a decent night's sleep."

"True," Gwyna replied thoughtfully, twining a strand of her hair around one finger. "There's a lot of unrest out in the countryside. I know there's been more feuds lately. They say it's because the High King is getting old and he's not keeping the Twenty Kings in line."

"What difference does that—" Rune began, then made the connection herself. "Oh. The Twenty Kings are busy trying to compete to be High King and ignoring the Barons and Dukes. And they're playing their own power games, and ignoring the Sires."

"Who are now free to take up their feuds again," Talaysen finished. "It all comes down to the bottom, eventually. That means us, who end up having to deal with bandits on the road; bandits who are there because the Sires aren't hunting them down." He grimaced. "The Church *should* be taking a hand here, but they won't."

"Other things come down to the common folk, too," Gwyna said. "I haven't seen any more bandits, but that's because I don't travel the main roads. Some of the others have run into trouble, though, and it seems to me to be more this year than last." She sat in thought for a while, her skirts spread in a colorful puddle around her. "I'll tell you what; I'll stick with you until the first snow. If you haven't found a wintering-up place for all three of us by then, we'll go thirds on a wagon and join one of my Family caravans. Will that suit you?"

Talaysen nodded and Rune heaved a silent sigh of relief. Gwyna could be so touchy when she thought someone was trying to protect her, but this time she *needed* protection. She was a lot younger than she looked, sounded, or acted. Gypsy children tended to grow up very quickly, but that didn't mean she was as mature as she appeared. A shock like she'd gotten could unseat the reason of someone Talaysen's age. Gwyna needed time to find her balance again.

"That solves our problem pretty neatly," Rune offered with absolute truth. "After getting shut out of three Faires, we were wondering if we were going to have even a chance at finding a winter position. So, if we don't"—she shrugged—"then we don't and we've got an alternate plan."

"Well good, then," Gwyna replied, relaxing. "Glad to be able to help. And don't worry about my getting underfoot too much. I'll find lots of reasons to take long walks, and some of them may even be genuine!" She winked, and Rune blushed, glad that the sunset color hid the red flush of her cheeks. "Are we leaving tomorrow morning early or late?"

"Late," Talaysen said. "All the heavy wagons and the herds are moving out at dawn, and I'd rather wait until they're well on their way. It's easier for us to pass them on the road than it is to get around the tangle when they leave." He grimaced. "And the drivers are a little less—"

The unusual sound of the clopping of hooves coming towards their campsite made him look up from his fire. "Who or what could that be?"

Rune shrugged, and looked over to Gwyna, who also shrugged. *Odd. It's plainly someone with beasts. What can he want with us?*

A weathered old man, a horse-trader by the harness-bits attached to his jacket, came around the corner of the half-shelter. He led a pair of sturdy pony-mules of the kind that the Gypsies used to pull their wagons and carry their goods, and stopped just as he reached conversational distance. The beasts stopped obediently behind him, and one nuzzled him and blew into his hair.

"Be you a minstrel called Rune?" he asked, looking directly at her.

Rune nodded in surprise.

"Can ye name me yer ma and yer village?" the old man continued.

"My mother is Stara, who last worked in the Hungry Bear Inn; that's in my old village of Westhaven," she replied politely. This had the sound of someone trying to identify her for some reason. Possibly a letter from Amber? But why send it via a horse-trader?

"An' who would ye say's yer best friend there?" the man persisted, though just as politely as she.

"That's an easy one," she said. "I only had one good friend when I left: Jib, the horse-boy."

"Then ye be the Rune I be lookin' fer." The man doffed his hat, and grinned. "Yon Jib's the lad I took on as m'partner this spring, an' damn if he ain't done better nor any on' us had reason t' think. He sen's ye these liddle lads, by way'o thanks, he says." He proffered the lead-reins, and Rune rose to take them, stunned with surprise. "He says ye's a right 'nuff lass, an' ye know how t' take care of a beast—I mind ye got a gyppo there by ye, though—" he nodded towards Gwyna, who nodded back. "There ain't none born can take care 'f a horse like a gyppo, so's ye make sure'n lissen t' the lady, eh?"

"I'll do that," Rune promised solemnly, too stunned to say anything else. "These are Vargians, right?"

"Aye," the man replied. "An' good lads, too. I wouldna let 'em go t' none but a gyppo or a friend or friend a'the lad. He's a good lad, Jib is."

"That he is," Rune replied faintly. This was a little too much to take in all at once. "One of the best in the world."

"Aye, well, I seen ye an' yer man an' yer fren' here at Faire, an' ye got all th' right friends," the man told her, so serious in his frankness that she couldn't even think of him as being rude. "Free Bards, eh? Free Bards an' gyppos, ye're the best folks on th' road. So, I'll tell Jib I caught up wi' ye, an' give his presents, an' I'll tell 'im ye're doin' right well. He'll be happy fer ye."

He turned to go, and Rune stopped him for a moment with one hand on his leather sleeve. "How is he, really?" she asked anxiously. "Is he all right? Is he happy?"

The man smiled, slowly, like the sun coming out from behind a cloud. "I reckon," he chuckled. "Oh, I reckon he'd say he's all right, though since he's set on weddin' m' girl an' I know her temper, I dunno how all right he'll stay! Still—they'll be settlin' down, I 'spect. Her mam had same temper, an' we never kilt each other enough so's ye'd notice. Like as not ye'll catch 'em both at Midsummer next year."

And with that, he put his hat carefully back on his head, and walked back down the road in the darkness, leaving Rune staring after him with the mules' reins still in her hands.

"Well, that solves one big problem," Gwyna said, breaking the silence. "And I know where we can get a wagon cheap, if you're willing to stay over a day while we get it refitted. I know I've got a third share's worth of coin. How about you two?"

"Oh, we have it," Talaysen replied, as Rune broke out of her stunned state, and came over to the fire for a couple pieces of wood for tethers and some rope for hobbles. "And draft beasts are always the expensive part of fitting up a wagon, am I right?"

Gwyna nodded, then rose and came over to look at the new acquisitions. She patted them down expertly, running her hands over their legs, checking their feet, then opening their mouths to have as good a look as she could with only firelight to aid her.

"A little old for a horse-mule, but middle-aged for ones out of a pony," she said, giving them both a final pat, and turning to help Rune stake them out to graze. "Especially for this breed; just like Rune said, they're Vargians. They'll live thirty useful years and probably die in harness, and they can eat very nearly anything a goat can eat. Hard to tell without pushing them, but their wind seems sound; I know their legs are, and he hasn't been doctoring them to make them look good." The same one that had blown into the old man's hair nuzzled her. "They're gentle enough even for you to handle, Master Wren!" She laughed, as if at some private joke, and Talaysen flushed.

"Here, let me see what they're called." She nudged the mule's head around so she could read the letters stamped on his halter in the flickering firelight. "This lad is Socks, evidently. And"—she squinted at the second halter—"the other is Tam. Good, short names, easy to yell." She left the mules, who applied themselves to grass with stolid single-mindedness. "I like your choice of friends, Lady Lark," she concluded. "It's nice to have friends who know when you might need a mule!"

The mules were a gift that impinged perilously on "too good to be true," and Talaysen pummeled his brain ceaselessly to reassure himself that neither he nor Rune had worked any of their "magic" to get them.

Finally, he slept, conscience appeased. They had not been anywhere near the animal-sellers. There had been no way that the old man could have heard them sing and been inadvertently magicked into giving them a pair of beasts. The mules were, therefore, exactly what they appeared to be: repayment of Rune's generosity to her old friend. When Rune had explained what she'd done, Gwyna had questioned her about the amount of money she'd sent the boy, and Gwyna had nodded knowingly.

"That's the right-size return on a gift like that," she had pronounced, when Rune worried aloud that she had bankrupted the boy. "Truly. He didn't send you horses, nor young mules; he didn't include any harness but the halters. If his year's been as good as the old man says, that's about right, and he'll still have profit."

Rune had been even more concerned how the old man had found

them, since there was no way—she had thought—for Jib to find out where she was. She'd been afraid the gift might have been some machination of the Guild in disguise. But Gwyna and Talaysen had both been able to put her mind at ease on that score.

It was the Gypsies, of course. Rune had sent her gift with them; they, in turn, knew all the news of the Free Bards and would have known as soon as Rune had joined them. When Jib wanted to find her, he would likely have turned to the Gypsies who had brought him the money in the first place. Sooner or later he would have found someone who'd been at Midsummer, and who would have known the general direction of the Free Bards' travels, and by extension, what Faires Rune and Talaysen were planning on going to. Then it was just a matter for the old man of planning *his* selling trip to try intercepting them at one or more of those Faires.

With everyone's fears eased, all three of them slept soundly. In fact, it was the rattle of the mules' halters the next morning that awoke them, as the beasts tried in vain to reach grass outside the circles they'd eaten bare.

Rune took them down to the well to water them, while Talaysen and Gwyna set off in search of a wagon.

Many Gypsies settled in Kardown, for it was on the edge of the treeless, rolling plains of the Arden Downs. The soil was thin and rocky; too hard to farm, but it made excellent pasturage, and most of the folk hereabouts depended on the sheep that were grazed out there. Most households had a little flock, and the most prosperous had herds of several hundred. There was always work for someone good with animals, and when Gypsies chose to settle, they often became hired shepherds. Such a life enabled them to assuage their urge to wander in the summer, but gave them a snug little home to retire to when the winter winds roared and the sheep were brought back into the fold.

Because of that, there were often Gypsy wagons for sale here. Gwyna, obviously a Gypsy and fluent in their secret language, was able to make contact with one of the resident families as soon as they reached the marketplace.

From there it was a matter of tracking down who had wagons for sale, who had wagons they were keeping but might be induced to part with, and where they were.

They had looked at three, so far. The first two were much too small; fit only for two, or one and a fair amount of trade goods. The third was a little too old and rickety; Gwyna clucked her tongue over it and told its owner that he'd waited a bit long to sell it; he'd have to spend a lot of time fixing it up now, before it was road-worthy again. The owner agreed, and said with a sigh that he'd not been truly certain he wanted to settle until this summer. . . .

They traded road stories for a bit, then moved on to the fourth and last.

"This lad will take a bit of persuading, I think," Gwyna said as they approached the cottage. "He came off the road because his wife wanted to settle a bit, though he didn't. That means the wife will be on our side; if she can get him to part with the wagon, it means she'll not have to fret about him taking the bit in his teeth, packing them all up, and rolling out without so much as a 'do you think we should,' or a word of warning."

Thus armed, Talaysen set about charming the lady of the house while Gwyna tackled the man. He was very young to have come off the road; a half-dozen children playing in the yard told Talaysen why the wife had wanted to settle. Two children in a wagon weren't bad, but a mob like this would strain the seams of even the largest wagons he'd seen.

He couldn't hear what Gwyna was telling the man, a very handsome Gypsy with long, immaculately kept black locks and a drooping mustache of which he seemed very proud. He didn't make much of an effort to overhear, either. She was giving the young man some advice from a woman's point of view, he thought. The Gypsies believed in the right of a woman to make her own decisions, and she was probably telling him that if he decided to pack up and take to the road again, he might well find himself doing so alone.

Whatever it was she told him, it had the desired effect. He agreed—reluctantly, but agreed—to show them the wagon and sell it if it was what they wanted.

He kept it in a shed in the rear of his cottage, and unlike the wagon that had been kept out in the garden, it was easy to see that the owner of *this* rig had been serious about his desire to return to the road one day. The bright red and yellow paint was fresh and shiny; every bit of bright-work, from the twin lamps at the front to the single lamp over the window at the rear, was polished until it gleamed like gold. The leather of the seat had been kept oiled, and the wheels were in perfect repair, not a spoke missing.

Right away, Talaysen knew that it was the *kind* of wagon they needed; this was a two-beast rig, and provided the pony-mules could pull it, they would have the strength of both at their service. With a one-beast rig, the mule not in harness would have to be tethered to the rear. It was possible to switch them off to keep them fresh, but a dreadful nuisance to harness and unharness in the middle of the day.

But when the young man pushed the rig out, Talaysen knew that without a shadow of a doubt—if the mules were up to it—this was exactly what they'd been looking for.

It slept four; two in one bed at the rear, and two in narrow single bunks along the sides that doubled as seating. There was ample storage for twice what they carried; the harness was coiled neatly in the box built beneath the right-hand bunk. There was even a tiny "kitchen" arrangement that could be used in foul weather, and a charcoal stove to keep it warm in the winter.

"Can the little mules pull it?" he asked Gwyna and her fellow Gypsy. She looked over at the man. "Vargians," she said.

He nodded. "No problem. It's built light, lighter than it looks." He showed them, by pushing it forward by himself. "I had Vargians. The harness is already rigged for them." Then he sighed and made mournful eyes at his wife, who did her best to hide her smile of triumph. "Looks like the Lady meant this rig for you. I'd best resign myself to being off the road till the little ones are marriage-high."

Gwyna then began some spirited bargaining, that ended with them shaking hands and most of Talaysen's money joining hers. The wife looked even happier at that, which made him guess that *she* had some plans for the unexpected windfall.

"Bring the mules here, and I'll harness her and you can drive her over," the man said, looking less resigned and more content by the moment. That eased Talaysen's mind quite a bit; he would never have willingly deprived someone of a cherished dream, however impractical it was.

They returned to camp and Gwyna took charge of the mules, leaving Talaysen and Rune to divide the chores of breaking camp. There wasn't much to do, since they'd be reloading everything into the wagon; and shortly after they were finished, burying the little garbage they'd produced in the fire-pit, covering it with the ashes, and putting the frame of the half-shelter over it all, Gwyna appeared, driving the wagon up the road, with the mules moving briskly and looking altogether content to be in harness.

It was a matter of moments to load the wagon and stow everything. Talaysen was amazed at how pleased and proprietary he felt. "Now what?" he asked Gwyna.

"Now we drive back to town, leave the wagon at a stable for safe-keeping, and go up to the market to buy what we need. Oil for cooking, oil for the lamps, harness-mending kit, salt and fodder for the mules—" She looked over at Rune.

"Hmm. Flour, salt, honey; some vegetables that keep well. Spices. A couple of pots and a frying pan." Rune's brow wrinkled as she thought. "Featherbeds, if we're going to winter over in there. Charcoal for the stove. A bit of milk. Cider. Oh, a fresh-water keg, there doesn't seem to be one. Currycomb, brush and hoof-pick. I think that's it."

"That sounds about right," Gwyna agreed. "If I can get some eggs, I'd like to."

Talaysen grinned, completely at sea in this barrage of domesticity, and perfectly content—

"A chicken," he said, suddenly. "Bacon. The bacon will keep fairly well. Sausage and cheese." He tried to remember what the family horses had needed. "Oh, blankets for both mules; they'll need them in the winter."

"Good." Gwyna nodded. "Now, the big question; have we enough money for all that?"

They put their heads and their resources together, and decided that they did—if they skipped the bacon and chicken, and bargained well.

"Split up?" Rune asked.

Gwyna shook her head. "Better stay together. Master Wren, try and look pinch-pursed and disapproving, as if everything we're buying is a luxury."

He set his face obediently in a scowl, and she chuckled. "That'll do. Rune, we'll take turns. When we get into a sticky spot, the other one will jump in and say 'He's cheating you,' or something like that."

"Good, and look like the vendor's a thief."

"Exactly." Gwyna surveyed the marketplace. "Well, shall we attack?"

The market wasn't as large as some, but it was held every day, rather than just one day a week. Talaysen found his part altogether easy, and watched the women bargain with the stall-keepers like a couple of seasoned housewives. At the vegetable stall, Rune leaned over and pointed out the discolored places caused by insects that might hide soft-spots or larvae, and gave the poor man a glare as if he'd put them there himself. He capitulated immediately. The cheese-maker was a fellow Gypsy, and so came in only for some good-natured bantering. The miller was condescending, and the women bent their entire attention on him, and to both his and Talaysen's amazement, actually *caught* him cheating, with sacks with gravel weighting the bottom. When they threatened to expose him there and then, he *gave* them their flour. They then went back to the cheese-maker and betrayed his secret. Gwyna grinned nastily as they went on to the charcoal-maker.

"He won't be able to get away with that anymore," she said. "I suspect the only reason he's gotten by this long is because he only pulls that trick on strangers. But short measure's against the law, and he knows it. He could be pilloried for that." She looked well content. "Once we get the charcoal, we'll have everything we need, I think."

It was at just that moment that Talaysen felt ghostly fingers on his pouch. He reached back, quick as a striking snake, and caught a wrist. A bony wrist; he pulled on it, hauling the owner forward before he could bolt.

The owner made not a sound as Talaysen dragged him—for it was a "he"—around to the front of them.

"What—?" Rune said in surprise, then nodded. "So. Someone who didn't do well at the Faire, hmm?"

"Caught a light-fingers?" Gwyna asked mildly. She crossed her arms and stared at the boy, who dropped his gaze to his bare, dirty feet. "You should know better than to try that game with a Gypsy, sirrah. We *invented* that game."

The thief was a lot older than Talaysen had expected; roughly Rune's or Gwyna's age. Undersized, though, for his age; he didn't top Gwyna by more than an inch. The bones under Talaysen's hand were sharp; the bones of the face prominent. Three-quarters starved and filthy, with an expression of sullen resignation, he made no effort whatsoever to escape.

Talaysen shook him a little. "Have you anything to say for yourself before I turn you over to the constables?" he asked. There was a flash of fear in the boy's face as he looked up, but then he dropped his eyes again and simply shook his head.

"He doesn't look much like a thief, does he?" Rune mused. "At least, not a good thief. I thought they tended to look a bit more prosperous."

Gwyna tilted her head to one side, and considered the boy. "You're right, he doesn't. He looks to me like someone who's desperate enough to try anything, including picking a pocket, but he doesn't look much like a real thief."

Talaysen thought privately that what the boy looked like was *bad*—blood and bone. But he held his peace; though no stranger would know it, Gwyna had already warmed to this rag-man.

"I don't think you should turn him over to anyone," Rune continued.

The boy looked up, quickly, surprise then apprehension flashing over his face, before he dropped his eyes again. Talaysen sighed.

"I don't think we should turn him over to anyone, either," Gwyna put in. She reached over and shook the boy's shoulder. "Here, you—if we feed you and give you a chance to clean up, will you promise not to run off until we've talked to you?"

He looked up again, and the expression of bewildered gratitude made Talaysen abruptly revise his opinion. That was not the expression of a bad youngster—it was more along the lines of a beaten dog who has just been patted instead of whipped. Maybe there was something worth looking into with this boy after all.

The boy nodded violently, and Talaysen released the hold he had on the boy's wrist. The youngster rubbed it a little, but made no move to escape, even though he probably could have gotten away in the crowd.

"Here," Gwyna said, shoving her load of packages at him. He took them, automatically, his eyes widening with surprise as he staggered beneath the weight. "Make yourself useful and carry these for me. Come along."

The boy followed her with complete docility. Or perhaps he was just stunned. If he was about Gwyna's age, he might not be too eager to run away at this point. Older men than he had been stunned by Gwyna on a fairly regular basis.

Talaysen smiled a little; there was a method to Gwyna's seeming foolishness. With that much burdening him, he couldn't run—unless he dropped the entire load, he was effectively hobbled. And if he dropped the packages, they'd know he was going to run.

They finished their purchases and returned to the wagon. The youngster handed his packages up to Rune to be stowed away, and looked—longingly, Talaysen thought—at the pony-mules.

Gwyna looked the boy up and down, critically. "You'll never fit Master Wren's clothes, nor mine," she said. "Rune, do you have a pair of breeches and a shirt I can borrow? His clothing won't be fit to wear without a lot of cleaning, and maybe not then."

"If you don't mind that they're not that far from the rag-bin themselves," Rune replied, doubtfully.

Gwyna snorted. "It's better than what he's wearing now."

Talaysen thought he detected a flush—of embarrassment?—under the layer of dirt coating the young man's face.

He still hasn't spoken a word . . . I wonder why?

With clean clothes in one hand and the boy in the other, Gwyna marched him off to the stream that had been serving for their bathing pool. He'd either bathe, or Gwyna would hold him down and wash him herself. Talaysen knew that look. He wouldn't have bet on the Master of the Bardic Guild against Gwyna when she wore that look.

And maybe this young man will give her something to think about besides her fear. For a little while, anyway.

Despite Gwyna's determination, Talaysen wasn't entirely certain that they'd see the lad again. On the other hand, he hadn't been acting as if he was going to run off. So Talaysen led the horses and wagon to their

old campsite and waited for Gwyna to reappear, with her charge, or
without him.

She returned with him—and cleaned up, he looked a great deal better
than Talaysen had expected. Some of the sullenness proved to be nothing
more than dirt.

"Here, lad," the Bard said. "We've got time to eat before we go, I
think." He cut the boy a chunk of bread and cheese, and poured him a
mug of water, presenting him with both as soon as the pair reached
the wagon.

The boy didn't snatch at the food as Talaysen would have expected
from his starved appearance. Instead he took it politely, with a little bow,
and ate it slowly and carefully rather than bolting it. Which was something
of a relief; in Talaysen's experience, food bolted by someone in the boy's
condition tended to come right back up again.

"All right," Talaysen said, as the young man finished the last crumb of
his meal. "The ladies here seem to have taken a liking to you. I suspect
they want me to invite you to come along with us for a bit. On the
other hand, you did try to lift my purse. So what do you have to say
for yourself?"

"I'm s-s-s-sorry, s-s-s-sir," the young man stammered. "I was s-s-s-starv-
ing. I d-d-d-didn't kn-kn-know wh-wh-what else t-t-t-to d-d-do."

The stutter, severe as it was, seemed to be something habitual rather
than feigned or out of fear. The youngster was obviously forcing the words
out, and having a hard time of it. He was red with effort and embarrassment by the time he'd completed the simple sentence.

Talaysen wanted to ask him more, but he was at a loss of how to get
any information from the youngster without a similar struggle. Then he
noticed that the lad's attention wasn't on him, but on something in the
wagon.

He turned to see what it was—but the only thing in sight was Gwyna's
three-octave harp, the one she could only play while seated. She rarely
took it out unless they were somewhere that it wouldn't be moved much.
She'd been about to cover it for the trip in its oiled-canvas case, but
during the packing it had been wedged between the side bunk and their
packs for safekeeping.

"Do you play, lad?" Talaysen asked. The young man nodded vigorously.
Without prompting, Gwyna climbed up into the wagon and handed the
harp down.

He sat right down on a stone with it cradled in his arms; placed it
reverently on the ground, and began to play.

Talaysen had heard many Masters play in his time, but this young man
was as good on the harp as Rune was on her fiddle. And this was an
original composition; it had to be. Talaysen knew most of the harp repertory, and this piece wasn't in it.

So, the boy could compose as well as play. . . .

The young man's face relaxed as he lost himself in the music, and his
expression took on the other-worldly quality seen in statues of angels. In
repose he was as gently attractive as he had been sullenly unattractive
when Talaysen caught him.

Talaysen felt something else, as well; the undercurrent of melody he associated with magic. The young man made no effort to match it, but it harmonized with what he was playing, and Talaysen found himself being lulled into a meditative trance. *Perhaps he hasn't learned to match it because he doesn't know he can—but the power is there, and so is the heart.*

Oh yes, the power was there indeed. He shook off the lulling effect of the music to glance over at Rune—just in time to intercept *her* glance at him. He inclined his head toward the young man; she nodded.

She hears it too.

Insofar as music went, this boy was a Bard in everything but name.

Now who is he, where is he from, and how in heaven's name did he get that way?

CHAPTER TWENTY-ONE

Talaysen reflected that it was a good thing that the wagon slept four. They looked to have acquired a second "apprentice."

After hearing the young man play, there was no way that Talaysen was going to let him wander off on his own again. Even if he hadn't been determined in that direction, the ladies were. So they packed everything down for travel, and he and the boy went into the back while Gwyna handled the reins and Rune watched and learned.

"Remember, speak slowly," he told the lad—no, not "the lad." The youngster had a name. Jonny Brede. He was going to have to remember that. A personable lad; thin and wiry, with a heart-shaped face and an unruly tangle of wavy brown hair. His eyes were the most attractive feature he had, probably because he tried to do most of his speaking with them rather than expose himself to ridicule. That stutter—the youngster must have gotten a lot of cruel teasing over it. "Speak very slowly. Take your time. I'm in no hurry, and neither are you, so take all the time you need."

Strange, lying here at ease on a bed, instead of trudging down the dusty road. Very strange, but obviously much more comfortable. Though he knew why he hadn't done this long ago, and it had nothing to do with money. He knew very little about the care of horses and nothing about harnessing or driving—all of his knowledge was of riding and hunting. That didn't serve to tell him what to do with these stout little draft-beasts. How often should they be rested, for instance? And how on Earth did one manage two sets of reins? What did one do if they didn't *want* to get between the shafts of the wagon?

Rune and Gwyna took up the bench seat in front, with their backs to the interior, although they could hear everything he and Jonny said. Rune evidently knew enough about mules from her days at the inn that she was a logical candidate for secondary driver. He and Jonny took their ease back in the wagon itself.

"Tell me the earliest thing you remember," he said, staring at the bottom of a cupboard just over his head. Like the rest of the interior of the wagon, it was of brown wood polished to a high gloss.

Jonny shook his head, his hands knotting and un-knotting in his lap.

"Don't you remember being very small?" Talaysen prompted. "Do you recall schoolmates? Siblings? Tutors or Priests? A birthday party, perhaps?"

Jonny shook his head even harder. "N-n-no," he replied. "N-n-nothing like that. Jus—just being sick, for a long, l-long time, and m-m-my M-M-Master."

"Start with that, then," Talaysen told him. "Slowly. Don't force the words out. Think of speech as a song; you wouldn't rush the cadence."

"I was r-r-real sick," Jonny said thoughtfully. "Fever; I w-w-was hot all the time. I was seeing things t-t-too. Men f-f-f-fighting, buildings b-b-burning. P-p-people yelling." He bit his lip. "Th-th-then I was at K-K-Kingsford, and M-M-Master was taking care of me."

"Master who?"

"M-M-Master D-D-Darian," the young man replied promptly.

Interesting. That was a name Talaysen knew, largely because Master Darian's arrival had caused such a fuss. *Master Darian wasn't rightly at Kingsford at all; he was from the Guild in Birnam. He should have gone there to retire, not to our kingdom.* Talaysen remembered the minor stir that had caused; Master Darian, half-senile, demanding to be allowed to lodge in the great Guildhall at Kingsford, claiming outrageous things. That his life was in danger, that there were assassins looking for him. How had that ended up? There had been something about a usurper—

Yes, he had it now. There had been a palace uprising, with the King of Birnam deposed by his brother, and a lot of the usual civil unrest that followed such a coup. Darian had been one of the King's Bards—a position that did not normally make one a target for assassins. The Guild had decided that old Master Darian might have seen a thing a two that had proved too much for his mind, and voted to permit him to stay instead of forcing him back to a place where he was afraid to go.

Had there been a boy with him, an apprentice? Talaysen couldn't remember—

Wait, there had been, and the boy had been sick with a marsh-fever. That was it. And that was another reason why the Guild had decided to let the Master stay. By the time they'd reached Kingsford, the boy had been in a bad way. It seemed too cruel even to the normally callous Guild Bards to turn them out for the boy to die on the road.

Hmm. If he'd been at Kingsford, one of the mages might have healed him of it. Ardis would know.

He made a mental note to write to her and ask.

"So, you were ill, and when you finally got well, you were in Kingsford. What then?"

"M-M-Master Darian took care of m-m-me, and when he got sick, I t-t-took care of him." The chin came up, and the big brown eyes looked defiantly into his. "Th-th-they said he was m-m-mad. He w-w-wasn't. He j-j-just had trouble remembering."

Yes, and that was why they had permitted him to keep the "apprentice" even though the boy probably wasn't learning anything from the old man. He took care of his Master, and that had freed up a servant to run attendance on other Masters. As long as he didn't get in the way, the rest of the members of the Guild ignored him. Talaysen recalled now thinking that he ought to do something about the boy himself; teach him, perhaps. But then other things had gotten in the way, and he'd forgotten all about it by the time he left the Guild in a rage.

"Th-th-they left us alone until M-M-Master died. Th-th-then they said I had t-t-t-to l-l-l-leave." The stutter got worse as he grew more distressed.

"Why?" Talaysen asked.

"B-b-because I d-d-didn't have a M-M-Master any- m-m-more," he said, his eyes dark with anguish. "And th-th-they s-s-s-said it w-w-wasn't w-w-worth w-w-wasting t-t-time on a ha-ha-halfwit."

Talaysen's fists clenched and he forced himself to relax them. *The bastards. The lazy bastards. A stutter is curable—and even if it wasn't, most people don't stutter when they sing, and they knew it! But this poor child had no one to speak for him, and he was a foreigner. So out he went.*

"Jonny, you are *not* a halfwit," he said quietly, but forcefully. "Whoever told you that was an idiot. The Guild Masters were too lazy to train you, and too foolish to see your worth, so they got rid of you and told you that to keep you from trying to get your rights." He thought quickly about all he knew of Guild law. "You came to Kingsford as an acknowledged apprentice. You had a right to another Master when yours died. You could have gone to any other Guild in Kingsford and gotten help to enforce that right—but the Bardic Guild Masters told you that you were a halfwit to prevent you from claiming that right."

"Th-th-they did?" Jonny's eyes cleared a little.

"I would bet fair coin on it. It's *just* the kind of thing they would do." He kept a tight hold on his temper; this was all in the past. Nothing could be done about it now—except to rectify what the Guild had done himself.

"B-b-but they s-s-said I c-c-couldn't s-s-sing, or wr-wr-write m-m-music—" he objected. "And I *c-c-c-can't.*"

"Jonny, when did anyone ever *teach* you to do those things?" Talaysen asked gently. "Those are skills, not things that you absorb just by being around Bards. Ask Rune; she'll tell you."

"Two years," Rune replied, leaning back into the wagon so she could be heard. "It took me two years to learn those things, and several different Masters."

"You see?" Talaysen's lips tightened. "Now if you really want to know what I think was going on—it's simple. The Bardic Guild is full of lazy, self-centered fools. They saw you had no Master, you weren't important to anyone, and in fact, no one in this country even knew you were here. So they decided you were too much trouble and sent you out the door."

Jonny nodded, slowly, his own hands clenched at his sides, knotted into tight little white-knuckled fists.

"Then what did you do?" Talaysen prompted. "After you left?"

"I w-w-worked. At wh-wh-whatever I c-c-could. Wh-wh-when the Faire came, I w-w-worked the Faire. Animals, m-m-mostly. Animals l-l-like me."

Talaysen could well imagine how the inarticulate lad had sought refuge in caring for creatures who didn't demand speech of him.

"How did you get from Kingsford to the Kardown Faire?" he asked.

"H-h-hiring fairs," the lad said simply. "G-g-got j-jobs all over. Had a j-j-job with a herder b-b-brought me here, b-b-but he sold his g-g-goats, and he d-d-didn't need me, and the m-m-man that b-b-bought them had his own h-h-h-herders."

Hiring fairs. That made sense. Hiring fairs were held in the spring and the fall, mostly for the benefit of farmers looking for hands or servants. Sometimes other folk would come looking for skilled or unskilled laborers—and Talaysen had heard of fairs that even had mercenaries for hire. The problem was, the unskilled labor jobs seldom lasted more than a season, as Jonny had undoubtedly learned. "So, that got you to the Downs. When?"

"Ab-b-b-bout two w-w-weeks ag-g-go," he said, sighing heavily. "Was all right d-d-during Faire, b-b-but there wasn't nothing f-f-for me after."

Gwyna laughed without humor. "True, when the Kardown Faire is over, the town pretty much dries up, unless you're an experienced hand with sheep. Shepherd's classed as skilled labor, not unskilled, and the only person that might be trusted to come on without experience is a Gypsy."

"And I take it you've always applied as unskilled?" Talaysen asked the young man. "And you've never learned a trade?"

He shook his head dumbly.

"G-g-got n-n-no one," he whispered. "And n-n-nothing. N-n-no g-g-good for anything. I w-w-was h-h-hungry, and I s-s-saw you b-b-buying th-th-things. I th-th-thought you w-w-wouldn't m-m-miss a c-c-copper or t-t-two."

"You play the harp the way you just did, and you say *that*?" Talaysen replied indignantly. The young man's mouth opened and closed as he tried to say something; Talaysen held up a hand, silencing him.

"You listen to me," he said fiercely. "You're among friends now. The Guild Bards may be fools, but the Free Bards aren't. I don't ever want to hear you say that you aren't good for anything. Not ever again. Is that understood?"

The young man had scooted back on the bunk as far as the limited space would permit when Talaysen began the tirade. With wide eyes, he nodded his agreement.

Both Gwyna and Rune had turned around, and their eyes carried a message to him that was child's play to read. Not that he minded, since he'd already made his decision about this young man.

"All right," Talaysen said, as much to them as to Jonny. "You're a Free Bard now. We'll undertake to do for you what the Guild *should* have. You, in turn, will have to abide by our rules. No theft, no troublemaking, no law-breaking. Treat us the way you would treat your family. When we play together, it's share and share alike, no holding anything back for yourself. Abide by those and we'll teach you everything we know, take you with us, with chores and profits shared alike. Will that do?"

For a moment, Talaysen feared the young man might burst into tears. But instead, he pulled himself up, looked each of them straight in the eyes, and said, with only a trace of a stammer, "Y-yes, sir. That w-will do. Y-you have my w-word on it."

"He'll need an instrument," Gwyna said from the front bench, her attention seeming to be entirely on the team. "He can use my harp until we get him his own—unless I find one I like better."

This time Talaysen distinctly saw him blink away tears before replying. "Th-thank you," he said. "Very much."

"I'll teach you lute, since we have two," Talaysen continued. "In fact, if it won't bother the drivers, I can begin now."

"It won't bother the drivers," Rune assured him. "And we're making splendid time. We'll be just outside Abbeydown at sunset; that's about two hours from now, which is more than enough time for a first lute lesson." She turned and grinned, and wriggled her fingers. "As I should know. Go ahead and use mine."

The young man looked completely overwhelmed, and paralyzed with indecision, unable to think of what to say or do next. Talaysen solved his problem for him, stripping Rune's lute of its case and putting it into his hands.

"Now," he said, positioning Jonny's fingers. "This is an A-major chord. . . ."

Three more days brought them to Ralenvale, and the Saint Brisa Faire. Technically, this was the first of the Harvest Faires that took place during the autumn months, since it featured all of the traditional Harvest Faire activities. There were competitions in vegetables, livestock and farm activities like tossing hay; contests in baking, preserving and handicrafts. There were races for anything that ran, from humans to ungelded stallions. Most of the trade here dealt with farm livestock, from chickens to enormous draft horses. The nobly born Sires—unless they thought of themselves as "gentlemen farmers"—seldom attended Saint Brisa's, but their stewards and seneschals did. It was barely possible that the quartet could find their wintering-over position through them.

Since this was the end of summer, few people wished to call it a "Harvest Faire." Winter was too close now, and no one wanted to be reminded of that. To reinforce that, there was a tradition that if anyone had the poor taste to refer to Saint Brisa's as a Harvest Faire, winter would arrive six weeks early.

Talaysen had no idea if that was true or not; *he* was looking forward to it as a chance to meet up with some of Gwyna's kin. Most especially he wanted to speak with Peregrine, a Gypsy horse-trader who had a reputation as a mage, and was reputed to deal regularly with elves.

Because they were here every year in such numbers, the Gypsies had their own traditional camp for this Faire; outside the Faire palisade, and on one side of a spring-fed pool. The other side was where most folk watered their beasts, but it was said that the spring was haunted—some said by the spirit of a jilted shepherd—and no one would camp there except the Gypsies and their Free Bard friends.

There was already a substantial group in place when they drove their new wagon up the trail towards the camp. Enthusiastic greetings met them when their identity was established, and Gypsies swarmed towards them.

But when Gwyna stood up on the wagon-seat, and announced to the entire camp that Rune and Talaysen were *vanderie*—in the Gypsy tongue, wedded—the greetings turned into an impromptu wedding celebration. In fact, for one moment Talaysen was afraid they'd all demand that the pair wed *again,* just so the entire gathering could witness it.

Talaysen was just glad that they no longer had to worry about setting up a camp, for they would have had no chance to do so. A swirl of adolescents descended on the surprised pony-mules, and had them unharnessed, rubbed down, and picketed with the rest of the camp-beasts before the poor mules knew what had happened. The wagon was parked in the outermost circle, pulled there by a dozen Gypsy men amid the cheers of the rest. And the entire party was carried off to the great fire in the center of the camp, where food and drink of every description was pressed upon them. As soon as they settled into seats around the fire, more Gypsies broke out instruments and struck up a dancing tune.

Even Jonny found himself seized upon and greeted with the same wild enthusiasm as the others, for all that he was a stranger to them. Talaysen was afraid at first that he might bolt for the wagon to hide, or even worse, just run away. But he didn't; he stayed, and even though Talaysen saw his eyes were wide with surprise tinged with apprehension, he managed a tremulous smile.

The Gypsies—particularly the girls—were chattering at him like so many magpies; half in their own language, and half in the common tongue, most of it completely unintelligible. Talaysen thought about interfering, then hung back, waiting to see how Jonny would handle it. The young man was going to have to learn to deal with crowds of strangers some time; far better that it be a friendly crowd.

Jonny let the group carry him along; let them press food and drink into his hands, and sat where they put him, still with that shy little smile that was slowly, slowly warming. He didn't speak—not surprising, since he was still painfully embarrassed by his stutter—but he let his eyes speak for him, and for the Gypsies, that was enough.

He'll do, Talaysen decided, and turned his attention to his own greeting-party, as they tried to press enough food and drink on him for five men.

Later, when the party had quieted down, Talaysen excused himself from the circle of musicians that had claimed him, and went wandering over the camp. Peregrine *was* here; he'd found out that much. But he hadn't appeared at the fire or at the dancing as darkness fell. Then again, Talaysen hadn't expected him; although he was a superb dancer, Peregrine seldom displayed his talent to such a large circle.

There was no point in *looking* for Peregrine; he'd learned long ago that Peregrine would permit himself to be found when Peregrine was ready. So it didn't much surprise him to find the Gypsy appear discretely at his elbow as he exchanged greetings with the clan chief.

"How goes your journeying, my brother?" Peregrine asked, when the amenities had been attended to and he turned to greet the Gypsy who some claimed was a mage. The Gypsy looked much the same as always; ageless, lean face, muscular body of a born fighter or dancer, bright black eyes, and long, flowing black hair without a single strand of gray.

Talaysen raised an eyebrow. *Something is going on here. Peregrine has never called me "brother" before—only "old friend."* "Strangely," he supplied.

"How, strangely?" the Gypsy asked, leading him to a pair of stools in the relative privacy of the shadow of his wagon. He took one; Talaysen settled on the other. From here they could see most of the camp, but because of the shadow, most of the camp could not see them.

"I have heard a new music," he replied, following the Gypsy way of circling around a subject for a while before plunging in. No Gypsy ever came straight to the point on any serious subject. If he had come out and asked Peregrine about magic, the Gypsy would assume he wanted to talk about something else entirely. Small wonder those who did not know them found the Gypsies infuriating to speak to.

"Music of what sort?" Peregrine returned, patient as a falcon waiting-on, as they moved their stools to get a better view of the camp.

"Music that is not heard by the ears," Talaysen stated calmly. "Music that sings to the thoughts, unheard, and sometimes unnoticed. Music that follows its own melody, and not that of the musician."

Peregrine was very quiet for a moment. "Music that causes things to happen, perhaps. Or so it seems. Music that the musician must match his own song to."

"Yes." Talaysen offered only that one word answer. Peregrine sat in silence again; in silence offering bread and sausage, in silence pouring wine. It was Talaysen's turn to be patient. While the offering of food and drink was a kind of ritual of hospitality with most Gypsies, he sensed that this time it represented something more. An offering of fellowship, perhaps. . . .

"I have waited for you to come into your power, my brother," he said, when the food was accepted and eaten, and the wine drunk. "That was the meaning of my greeting. I have long known that you and a handful of others among the Free Bards were among the *drukkera-rejek*—the mages of music—as I am. The sign of the power is without mistaking to one trained—as is the sign that a mage has come into his power. And now—there is much that I must tell you, and little time to do it in."

Talaysen's pulse quickened.

"So this *is* magic that I have touched—" Talaysen would have said more, but Peregrine hushed him, and the Bard subsided into silence.

"It is magic, indeed; it is the magic that the Bards and the elves both use. And there is one here who would speak to you." Peregrine waved his hand in an unobtrusive signal, and a shrouded shadow detached itself from the back of the wagon to approach them, and resolve itself into a two-legged creature enveloped from head to toe in a hooded cape. Talaysen had not seen anyone there, nor had he noticed anyone move there while he and Peregrine were speaking. He restrained himself from starting with surprise only with great effort.

The figure pulled back the hood of its cape to show that it was male—and elven.

Now Talaysen started, his hand going briefly to the hilt of his knife before dropping away.

He trusted Peregrine; the Gypsy had apparently invited the elf here. And besides, if the elf truly wanted Talaysen dead, the knife would be of little use against him. Striking him down where he sat would be child's play for an elven mage.

"Stars light your path," he said, instead. The solemn elven mouth lifted in a slight smile, and the elf moved a few steps closer.

"I see you have courtesy when you choose, mortal." The elf came within arm's length of them, then examined Talaysen as if the darkness and dim firelight was more than enough for him to see by.

Maybe it is. Elves were popularly supposed to have enhanced senses of hearing and sight.

"I have courtesy when I am not constrained against my will, and when I am an invited guest instead of being considered a superior type of pet," he replied boldly. "We mortals have a saying 'like begets like.' That holds true with manners as well as livestock." Peregrine bit off a bark of a laugh, and the elf nodded, his smile now ironic.

"I warned you not to match wits with a full Bard," the Gypsy mocked. "And this one most of all. Not just because of his training as a Bard, which makes of words a weapon. Talaysen dares to speak only the truth—which makes his speech bite all the sharper when he chooses to make it so." Peregrine's feral smile gleamed whitely in the darkness. "He has fangs, this one."

"I would not care to match either wits or magic against this one, new and raw as he is to his power," the elf replied, with complete seriousness not at all affected by the gypsy's derisive speech. Then he turned back to Talaysen. "Listen, for I bear word for you from *our* High King. He knows what occurred, and you need not anticipate reprisals. To Master Wren, he says, 'Think not to be caged, for that has been forbidden.' To Lady Lark, he says, 'Courage is rewarded.' And he sends these tokens—"

The elf held out a pair of slender silver bracelets that gleamed in the firelight, with a liquid sheen, so perfect it looked like the still surface of a pond. "Place these upon your wrists; they shall close, never to be removed, but fear not. They are meant to mark you as mortals with the High King's favor." Now the elf smiled, a wry smile that mimicked Peregrine's. "There shall be no more dances with lightning."

Peregrine laughed at that, in a way that made Talaysen think that he'd heard at least part of the story. The elf raised an eyebrow at him, knowingly.

Talaysen reached out gingerly and took the cool silver bracelets, sliding one over his hand. And as promised, once around his wrist it shrank to fit comfortably, the metal band becoming just a fraction thicker in the process. His stomach felt a little queasy, watching it—this was the first time he'd ever seen magic close at hand, magic that affected the material world. There would be no removing this "token" without first removing his hand.

"Thank you," he said to the elf, and meant it. "We have enemies enough without angering the Fair Ones."

"Oh, you angered only a greedy hothead with no thought but his own pleasure," the elf replied off-handedly. "He got his own desert, and that speedily. That it was delivered by a mere mortal simply humiliated him beyond bearing. There were those in his own court who thought he had gone too far when he took you, and were certain of it when he set the storm upon you. The High King has cooled his temper, I promise you."

"Still, I thank you," Talaysen replied. Then added with a rueful grin, "Is it now safe to cross a Faerie Ring, even by accident?"

The elf laughed aloud. "Safe enough, e'en by accident," he said. "With polite invitations tendered to you once you are within it to play for a brief evening. Your fame has traveled from Hill to Hill, and I think you should expect such invitations in the future. There will be many who wish to see the mortal Bards that could subdue King Meraiel. And more who will wish to hear your side of the tale."

And with no warning and only those parting words, he swirled his cloak about his shoulders and stepped into the shadows, to melt into them and vanish completely. As Talaysen had not seen him arrive, so he had no idea how the elf left—although he *thought* he heard a faint whisper of music as the shadows swallowed him.

Peregrine sighed, and shook his head. "Melodramatic, as ever," he commented. "Trust an elf to make a great show of simple leave-taking."

Talaysen chuckled, and relaxed a bit more. "Was that what you wished to show me and speak to me about?" he asked. "I must admit, that alone was worth being here for." He glanced over his shoulder at the now-empty shadows at the tail of the wagon. "I haven't said anything to the others, but the fact is, I've been uneasy about camping outside of settled lands ever since that particular incident occurred. This little trinket"—he tapped the bracelet—"takes a tremendous load off my mind."

Peregrine sobered. "In part, but only in part. I must speak to you of magic; of the usage and taming. Some of what I tell you, you may not understand for years—but it is all important, and I must ask you to pay close attention and grave it deeply in your excellent memory. If all goes as we wish, I may be able to continue to teach you for years to come. But if Fate rules against us, this may be all the instruction you will ever receive. I would give you as much as you can hold, planning for that."

Talaysen nodded, and quickly put himself into the little half-trance he used when he memorized lyrics in a foreign tongue. Everything he heard would be remembered, regardless of whether or not he understood it.

"Good." Peregrine took a deep breath, and held his hands out. A soft blue glow played over them, and Talaysen heard a faint, flute-like song, somewhere deep inside of him. "This is the way of the inner path, the hidden power. The way of magic. And now—it begins. . . ."

Rune watched Gwyna out of the corner of her eye, and grinned. There was *no* doubt about it; Gypsy Robin was well and truly smitten with their new charge, even though she might not know it yet.

She didn't act a great deal differently; in fact, it wasn't likely that anyone else noticed. But she paid no attention to anyone else in the camp, and when over the course of the evening several young men came up to her and whispered invitations in her ear, she declined them all with a shake of the head. That was not normal. Gwyna had a reputation as a lusty lover that rivaled any of the male Free Bards, and Rune had never heard of her declining all invitations for dalliance before. And especially not when several of those she declined had been her lovers in the past.

But she didn't leave the firelit circle with anyone, not even for an hour. And she stayed with Jonny, who smiled much and said little.

He was doing very well, now that he had begun to relax. The Gypsies paid no heed to his stutter, which was putting him at ease. He had begun to laugh at the jokes, and look up from his knees occasionally.

Gwyna was praising his melodic ability just now, which made him blush. Over the past two days, he had set melodies to several of Robin's lyrics that were easily the equal of any of the younger Free Bards' efforts. "Oh, but it's true," she said, to his mumbled disclaimer. "The words come easily to me, but melody? Never. You have the hardest part, Jonny."

"B-but I c-cannot find w-words," he replied earnestly. "I am j-just n-not cle-cle-cle-cle—cle-cle-cle—cle—oh d-d-*damn*!" His face twisted up, and Rune started to get to her feet, afraid that such a blatant exposure of his stutter would send him fleeing to solitude.

But he stayed, as the silence deepened, and the Gypsies held their breaths, sensing how precarious his moment of courage was. He stared at his fists which were balled up on his knees, and Rune hoped that it was not because he was about to go silent again.

Finally he looked up from his clenched fists, and managed a feeble smile. "D-d-damn it," he repeated. "S-s-stupid s-s-stutter. Cle-cle-cle—I s-s-sound l-l-like a *k-k-kestrel*."

A relieved laugh answered his feeble joke, and Giorgio, one of the largest of the clan, slapped him lightly on the back, with a care to his thin body and small stature. "Then you have named yourself, my friend!" he boomed. "'Master Kestrel' you shall be! And never disparage the kestrel, for he is bolder for his size than even the goshawk, brave enough to take on enemies that would make a meal of him if they could, brave enough even to attack the human who comes too near his nest!"

Giorgio raised his mug of wine. "To Master Kestrel!" he shouted.

The rest followed his lead. "To Master Kestrel!" they replied, Rune shouting just as loudly as the rest. And when she had drained her mug in the toast, and looked again, Jonny's eyes were shining, and he no longer stared at his hands.

Later, Gwyna even coaxed him out of his seat to dance with her. By then, Gwyna's other suitors had noticed her interest in the young musician, and had turned their attentions elsewhere. Rune couldn't help wondering at that point if Gwyna herself realized what had happened to her. She finally decided that the Gypsy probably hadn't recognized the symptoms of a condition she had caused so often in others. Gwyna had been heart-whole until now, enjoying her companions the way she enjoyed a round of good music or a dance. The oldest game of man and maid had been a sport to her, and nothing more.

I don't think it's a sport anymore, Rune thought, with amusement. *I wonder how long it's going to take her to notice that her outlook's changed in the past few days.*

The music, dance, and tale-spinning continued on long into the night, until the stars had swung halfway around in their nightly dance, and the moon had set. At moonset, the Gypsies and Free Bards began to trickle away to tents and wagons; singly, in pairs, and in family groups with sleeping children draped like sacks over their parents' backs. Just as Rune started to yawn and wonder where Talaysen was, he appeared at her side and sat down beside her.

"Where have you been?" she asked—curiously, rather than with any hint of accusation. "You said you were going to talk to Peregrine, and then no one knew where you were. I thought the Earth had swallowed you up."

"It almost did," he replied, rubbing his temple with one hand, as if his head ached.

She saw a gleam of silver in the firelight, and caught at the wrist of that hand. He was wearing a silver bracelet that fit so closely to his wrist that it might have been fitted to him, yet which had no visible catch. "Where did you get that? From Peregrine?" she asked, fascinated by the trinket. "It's really lovely—but I thought you didn't wear jewelry."

"I usually don't. Here." He slipped an identical bracelet over her hand before she could pull away, and she muffled an exclamation as it shrank before her eyes to fit her wrist just as tightly as Talaysen's fit his.

He put his lips to her ear. "A gift from the High King of the Elves. His messenger says that it marks us as under his protection."

She blinked, as a thousand possible meanings for "protection" occurred to her. "Is that good, or bad?" she whispered back. "I don't think I'm interested in another visit under a Hill like the last one."

"According to the messenger, these are supposed to keep visits like that within polite boundaries. By invitation, and of reasonable duration." She lifted an eyebrow at Talaysen, and he shrugged. "Peregrine said that the messenger's word was good, and he's been dealing with elves for longer than we have. I'd be inclined to trust his judgment."

"All right," she replied, still dubious, but willing to take his word for it. "So what else have you been doing, besides collecting bits of jewelry that are likely to get us condemned by the Church as elf-loving heretics?"

He chuckled, and put his arms around her, drawing her close to him so that her back nestled against his chest and they could both watch the dancing. "Nothing much, really. Just learning things that would get us condemned by the Church as renegade mages."

She restrained herself from jumping to her feet with a startled exclamation. "I hope you're going to explain that," she said carefully. "Since I assume it has something to do with that music we've both been playing with."

"Peregrine is a mage. It seems that we are, too. He told me that he'd identified the fact that we've 'come into our power' by something he saw when we showed up at camp. Then he gave me a very quick course in the Bardic use of magic, most of which I haven't sorted out yet." He sighed and his breath stirred her hair. "It's all in my head, though. I expect we'll get it figured out a bit at a time."

"I think I'm relieved," she replied, after a moment to ponder it all and turn the implications over in her mind. "I don't think it's a good idea to go wandering all over the countryside, playing about with magic without even knowing the first thing about it."

"That's almost exactly what Peregrine said, word for word," Talaysen chuckled. "He gave me quite a little lecture on—"

The bracelet tightened painfully around Rune's wrist, and she gasped. Her first thought was that the elven-made object was trying to cut her hand off—but then, it released the pressure on her wrist just as quickly as it had clamped down.

And Talaysen released *her.* He sat up quickly, and scanned the area outside the fire.

"There's someone out there, someone using offensive magic," he said, in a low, urgent voice. "Peregrine told me that these bracelets, being magic, would react to magic."

"Offensive magic?" she repeated. "But what is it? I don't see anything going on—how do we know it's being used against us, or even against the camp?"

He hushed her, absently. "We don't," he said unhelpfully. "But Peregrine will know. We might not be seeing anything because whoever it is may be using something to watch us, or to try and identify someone. Peregrine has all kinds of tricks and traps around this camp—and whoever it is will trip one of them sooner or—"

A cry of anguish from behind them interrupted him, and Rune turned just in time to see a pillar of flame, twice the height of a man, rise up from the shore of the pond.

A moment later she realized that it wasn't a pillar of flame—it was a man, standing bolt upright, transfixed in agony, burning like a pitch-covered torch.

She turned away, her stomach heaving, just in time to hear Peregrine shouting in the Gypsy tongue, of which she only knew a few words.

She couldn't make out what he was saying, but the warning was clear enough. She flattened herself to the ground, instinctively. And just in time, for an arrow sang out of the darkness, buzzing wasp-like past her ear, and *thock*ing into the wood of a wagon just where Jonny had been sitting a moment before. Two more followed it, both obviously aimed at Jonny, before the Gypsies got over their shock and counterattacked.

She had no weapons to hand, and no idea of where the enemy was, so Rune stayed right where she was, as angry Gypsies, men and women both, boiled out of the camp. They headed for the place where the arrows had come from, ignoring the man who was still burning.

He had fallen and was no longer moving; the Gypsies parted about the grisly bonfire as if his presence was inconsequential. They spread out over the area around the pond with torches in one hand and knives at the ready.

But after an agonizingly long time, it still didn't look as if they were finding anything. Rune got slowly to her feet, and made her way over to where Jonny and Gwyna had taken shelter behind a log-seat.

"Are you all right?" she asked Jonny, who nodded, his eyes wide and blank with fear.

"How about you?" she said to Gwyna.

The Gypsy sat up slowly, her mouth set in a grim line. "I've been better, but I'm not hurt," she replied. "What in the name of the Lady was that?"

"I don't know," Rune told her—as movement caught her eye and she saw Peregrine striding towards her, something shiny clutched in one hand, and a long knife in the other. "But I have the feeling we're about to find out. And that we won't like it when we do."

Peregrine sat back against the wooden wall of the wagon, his face impassive. "This was no accident."

Rune snorted, and gave Peregrine one of her most effective glares. "Why heavens, Peregrine, I thought assassins with magic amulets *always* hung around outside of farm Faires, looking for random targets!"

The Gypsy met her look with one of unruffled calm.

"All right," Gwyna said irritably. "We know it wasn't an accident. And I don't think anyone's going to doubt that Jonny was the target. Now *why*? Who's behind this, and why are they picking on a simple musician, a lad with a stutter, who wasn't even a good thief?"

Talaysen shook his head and sighed. All five of them were huddled inside Peregrine's wagon, one of the largest Rune had ever seen, so big it had to be pulled by a team of four horses. The windows had been blocked with wooden shutters, and the only way at them was through the door at the front, guarded by Peregrine's fierce lurcher-hounds.

And still Rune kept feeling her neck crawl, as if there was someone creeping up behind her.

Jonny shivered inside one of Peregrine's blankets, a glass of hot brandy inside of him, his eyes telling them what his tongue couldn't. That he was frightened—that was easy to understand. They were *all* frightened. But Jonny was terrified, so petrified with fear that he balanced on a very thin rope of sanity, with an abyss on either side of him.

Peregrine watched Jonny with an unfathomable expression, and the rest of them watched Peregrine, as the silence thickened. Finally the Gypsy cleared his throat, making them all jump nervously.

"The secret to all of this is—him," he said, stabbing a finger at Jonny. "This is not the first such attack, is it, boy?"

Jonny started, and shrank back—but as Peregrine stared at him, he shook his head, slowly.

"And it will not be the last. Two of the men got away. They will return." Rune didn't know why Peregrine was so certain of that, but it didn't seem wise to argue with him.

"So—young Kestrel. It comes down to you. *You* are the target of men who are very expensive to hire. And you say that you do not know the reason." Peregrine rubbed his upper lip thoughtfully. "Yet there must be one, and before we can decide what to do about this, we must discover it."

Gwyna obviously could stand no more of this. "Well?" she demanded, waspishly. "Are you going to stop playing the great mage and *tell* us how we're going to do this?"

Peregrine turned his luminous black eyes on her, and she shrank back. "I am," he said slowly. "But it is a path that will require courage and cooperation from one who has no reason to trust me."

He turned his gaze back to Jonny. "That one is you," he said. "Are you willing to place your mind and soul in my hands? Tell me, Kestrel, are you as brave as your namesake? Are you willing to face your past—a past so fearful that you no longer remember it?"

Jonny stared at him, and Rune wondered if Peregrine had snapped that last link he had with a sane world.

CHAPTER TWENTY-TWO

Talaysen touched Jonny's forehead, and his closed eyelids didn't even flutter. He held the young man's wrist for a moment, and found a pulse; slow, but steady. He had seen Ardis work this spell before, but never for this effect; for her, the sleep-trance was an end, not a means. He wondered if Ardis knew of this application: to search the patient's memory, even finding things he had forced himself to forget. "I think he's ready," he said to Peregrine. "As ready as he's ever likely to be."

"Oh, he is ready," the Gypsy replied. "What he may not be prepared for is his own fear. I hope in the days you have been with him that you have taught him trust to go with that fear, else all is lost." Peregrine leaned forward and tapped the young man's forehead three times, right between the eyes. "Kestrel," he rumbled, "do you hear me?"

"I hear you," Jonny whispered—without so much as a hint of a stammer. Out of the corner of his eye, Talaysen saw both Gwyna and Rune start with surprise.

"You will answer my questions. The one you know as Master Wren will also ask you questions, and you must answer him, as well. Do you trust him?" Peregrine's brow furrowed as he waited for an answer.

"I do," Jonny said, his voice a bit stronger.

"Good. You have placed your trust well. He and I will not do anything to harm you; and we will keep you *safe* from harm. We will be with you, even though you cannot see us. You will believe this."

"I believe this," Jonny affirmed.

Peregrine gestured curtly. "Ask," he said. "You know more of this than I, and you know more of the world that spawns those who hire assassins than any gypsy. I would not know what questions are meaningful and what without meaning."

Talaysen leaned into the tiny circle of light cast on Jonny's face by the lantern Peregrine had used to place him in a trance. "Jonny—Kestrel—do you hear me?"

"Yes," the young man sighed.

"I want you to remember the first day you came to Kingsford, to the Guild Hall. Can you remember that?"

"Yes." Jonny's forehead wrinkled, and his voice took on the petulant quality of a sick child. "I'm cold. My head hurts. My eyes hurt. Master Darian says I'm going to get better but I don't, and I feel awful—"

"He relives this," Peregrine said with a bit of surprise. "This is useful, but it can be dangerous, if he believes himself trapped in his past. Have a care, Master Wren."

Talaysen swallowed, and wet his dry lips. "Jonny, can you remember farther back? Go back in time, go back to before you entered Kingsford. Can you remember before you were sick?"

Abruptly the young man began to scream.

Peregrine moved as quickly as a ferret, clamping his right hand over the young man's forehead, and his left on Jonny's wrist. The screaming stopped, as if cut off.

"Who are you?" Peregrine said, with no inflection in his voice whatsoever.

Who are you? Talaysen thought, bewildered. *What kind of a question is that?*

"I—I *can't*—" Jonny bucked and twisted in Peregrine's grip; the mage held fast, and repeated the question, with more force. The young musician wept in terror—Talaysen had heard that sort of weeping before, from the boys that had been ruined by their Guild Masters. . . .

Peregrine had no more pity than they had, but his harshness was for a far better cause. "*Who are you?*"

"Ah—" Jonny panted, like a frightened bird. "I—I—ah—Sional! I'm Sional! I have to run, please, let me go! Master Darian! Master Darian! They're killing my father! Help me! *Ahhhhhhhhh—*"

"Sleep—" Peregrine snapped, and abruptly the young man went limp. The mage sat back on the bunk, and wiped sweat from his brow. He looked to Talaysen as if he had been running for a league. He was silent for a moment, staring at the young musician as if he had never seen him before.

"So." Peregrine took a sip of water from the mug safely stored in a holder mounted on the wall just above him. "So, we know this 'Jonny Brede' is nothing of the kind, and that his true name is Sional, and that someone wished his father dead. Do you know of any Sionals? Especially ones who would have run to a Guild Bard for help?"

Talaysen shook his head. Rune and Gwyna both shrugged. Peregrine scratched his head and his eyes unfocused for a moment. "Well, whoever he is, he is important—and long ago, someone killed his father. I think we must find out who and what this father was."

"Are you going to hurt him?" Gwyna asked in a small voice.

Peregrine shook his head. "I can promise nothing. I can only say I will try not to hurt him. The alternative is to find out nothing—and one day there will be nothing to warn him of the assassin in the dark. I think this the lesser of two bad choices."

Gwyna nodded, unhappily. Peregrine touched Jonny's—Sional's—forehead again. "Sional, do you hear me?"

"I—hear you," said a small, young, and very frightened voice. It sounded nothing like Jonny; it sounded like a young child of about twelve.

"How old was he, when he came to you at the Guild?" Peregrine asked Talaysen. The Bard furrowed his brow and tried to remember what the nondescript child had looked like on the few occasions he had seen the boy. The memory was fuzzy, at best, and the child had been quite ordinary.

"Twelve? Thirteen?" He shook his head. "He can't have been much younger than that, or I'd have noticed. Thirteen is just about as young as apprentices are allowed to be in Bardic Guild. Children younger than that are just that—children. They aren't ready for the kind of intensive study we give them. Their bodies and minds aren't suited for sitting in one place for hours at a time."

"Good. That gives me a safer place to start." He raised his voice again. "Sional—you are ten years old. It is your birthday. You are waking up in the morning."

Abruptly all the tenseness poured out of Sional's body, and a happy smile transformed his face.

"Good, a safe time, and a happy one," Peregrine muttered. "Sional, what is to happen today?"

"Today I get my first horse!" Sional's voice really *did* sound like a ten-year-old's, and Talaysen started in surprise. "It's my birthday present from father, a *real* horse, not a pony! Victor and I get to go to the Palace stables and pick it out, too! Victor's going to teach me trick riding! Then Master Darian will give me the present from mother that he's been saving for me; it's a harp, a big harp, with lots more strings than my little harp!"

"Why isn't your mother giving it to you?" Peregrine asked, curiosity creeping into his voice.

"She's dead," Sional said, matter-of-factly. "She died when we moved to this place. That was a long time ago, though. I hardly remember her at all. Just the way she sang—" His voice faltered a moment. "She was a wonderful musician and Master Darian says that if she hadn't been a woman and a princess she'd have been a Bard and—"

"Stop." Peregrine glanced over at Talaysen, with one eyebrow raised. Talaysen didn't have to ask what he was thinking.

A princess? Is that real—or just a child's fantasy and an old teacher's flattery?

"Sional, who is your father?" Peregrine asked, slowly and carefully.

"The King." Once again, the voice was completely matter-of-fact. "I have to call him My Lord Father; Master Darian calls him Your Majesty. Everybody else has to call him Your Royal Highness. But I don't see him very often."

"Stop." Peregrine was sweating again. "Sional, where do you live?"

"In the Dowager's Palace."

"No, I mean what land do you live in?"

"Oh, that. Birnam. It's the red place on the map. The green one next to it is Leband, the blue one is Falwane, the yellow one is—"

"Stop." Now Talaysen was sweating.

"Do realize what we have here?" he whispered. "This is the Crown Prince of Birnam—no—the *King* of Birnam!" He groped for Rune's hand and held it.

"Tell me!" the Gypsy demanded. "Tell me what you know of this!"

"I have to think," Talaysen replied, shivering despite the heat of the wagon. Dear God, what a cockatrice they had hatched! Their foundling was the rightful King of Birnam—and small wonder there were assassins seeking him. The current King was not likely to tolerate any rivals to his power.

"About six years ago, I think it was, the King of Birnam was overthrown by his brother. Mind you, the only reason *I* know about this is was because I was on the Guild Council at the time, and we were dealing with that entire business of Master Darian. The old man came to us with a boy he called his apprentice, claiming sanctuary with our branch of the Guild because he was supposedly in danger as a supporter of the former King."

"So your understanding is likely to be accurate, if sketchy?" Peregrine asked.

He nodded. "We did do some checking with the Guild in Birnam. The way I heard it, the brother slipped his men into the palace by night, murdered the King and all his supporters, and by dawn there was a new King on the throne and all the bloodstains had been politely cleaned away."

Peregrine snorted. "How—tidy of them."

Talaysen shrugged. "At that point, I imagine that there was nothing anyone could do. Darian swore to the Guild that he'd escaped death at the hands of the assassins as one of the old King's retainers—and he swore that both the King and his only child were dead. Obviously *that* wasn't true."

"Obviously," Peregrine said, with heavy irony. "Well, our Kestrel has turned into a most peculiar cuckoo. What are we to do with him? It is plain that his uncle knows that he is alive, and where he is, or we would not have killers at our wagons."

"Can't we hide him?" Gwyna asked, but her voice betrayed her own doubt.

Peregrine confirmed that doubt with a shake of his head. "Not possible," he said. "The amulet I found upon the man my trap took was one of seeking. No matter how or where we hid him in this land, they could find him with another such. He himself has confirmed that there have been attempts to slay him before this."

Talaysen remained silent, as Gwyna and Peregrine discussed other possibilities; concealing the young man with magic, or even asking the elves to take him under one of their Hills. *That* was chancy; what the elves took, they might not want to give back, once they'd heard young Sional play. He had the glimmering of an idea then—

It had occurred to him that there was too much they didn't know, and the only place to learn that information was in Birnam. So why not go *there*?

After all, why would the current King ever look for Sional in his own kingdom? The assassins could comb all of Rayden, from border to border—but if the object of their search was in the last place they expected him—

"We don't know nearly enough," he said, into an opportune silence. "We don't know if this is an idea of the King's, or if it's something one of his advisors thought was best. We don't even know if this is something set in motion long ago and forgotten. This King may be a tyrant—there may already be a movement in place to topple him that only lacks a focus. It seems to me that Jonny—I mean, Sional—ought at least to find these things out. Until he does, no matter where he goes or how he runs, he'll be running away from something, not *to* something."

Peregrine raised his eyebrows thoughtfully. "A good point, my brother," he acknowledged. "And there are things about the young man now that the assassins cannot know. Unless I miss my guess, they have associated him with you, but only at a distance, and as a chance-met set of friends. They would be looking for a group of three men and a woman—not two couples. Rune has been in breeches most of the time, yes?"

Rune shrugged. "It's habit mostly," she said, "But yes. And most men don't look twice at me in breeches, they assume I'm a boy."

"So now you wear skirts, and become most extravagantly feminine. Master Wren, we shall dye your hair as black as mine, but with magery, so that the dye neither grows out, nor washes out." Peregrine grinned. "And if I ever wished to be a rich man, I would sell the working of *that* spell, eh? It is a pity it only is effective on one who is already a mage."

"So we'll have two *young* gypsy couples traveling together. Good." Talaysen played that over in his head, and found no flaw with it. "Most wagons look alike to outsiders. Once we're on the road, there'll be no telling us from dozens of others without one of those amulets. Those have to be expensive; I'm sure not every hired killer has one."

"And if you leave by darkness tomorrow, we can make certain you are not followed," Peregrine told him. "Now, what of the Kestrel? Do I wake him with his memories, or no?"

"With them," Gwyna put in quickly. Peregrine turned to stare at her. "If I was in his place, that's what I would want," she said defensively. "While he still thinks he's Jonny Brede, he doesn't know why these people want to kill him. As Sional, he *will*. It seems to me that makes them less frightening."

Talaysen nodded. "I agree with her. Fear is worse when you don't know what it is you're afraid of. Right now these people are simply faceless, irrational attackers from a nightmare. Once he has his memories and identity as Sional back, they aren't faceless anymore, and they have a reason for what they're doing."

Peregrine nodded slowly. "Very well. Let me see if I *can* do this. He has built him a very stout wall between himself and those memories. It may take some doing to breech it."

When they showed no sign of moving, he coughed delicately. "I have no need of you now, and this were better done in private."

They took the hint, and left, crawling over the driver's seat and the lurcher-hounds draped over and on top of it, and down to the ground again.

"Now what?" Gwyna asked.

"We go back to our wagon and sleep," Talaysen told her and Rune both. Rune nodded; Gwyna looked rebellious. "Look, we can't help Peregrine and we're all tired. We *need* sleep. We already know the worst, and nothing we do or don't do in the next few hours is going to change it. So?"

"So we sleep," Gwyna sighed. "Though personally, I don't think I'm going to be able to do anything but stare into the dark."

Gwyna had been wrong, of course; despite their tension, all three of them fell deeply asleep once they reached the safety of their beds. And thanks to their Gypsy friends, their beds were as safe as possible in an open camp. The wagon had been moved from the outer to the inner circle, and a half-dozen fierce lurchers had been tied about it to keep away intruders. The wagon itself was stoutly built enough to withstand a siege once the doors and shutters were closed. Talaysen thought it a pity to shut out the cool night air, but better stuffy air than unexpected knives and arrows.

When he woke, it was near noon by the sun coming through the little smoke-hole over the charcoal stove, and the fourth bunk had a clothed and wakeful occupant.

It was Kestrel—and yet it wasn't Jonny Brede. Talaysen couldn't put his finger on the differences, but they were there; in the way the young man held himself, in the direct way he met Talaysen's gaze.

"Sional?" he said, tentatively.

The young man nodded, solemnly. "B-better stick to K-Kestrel, though," he replied, his stammer improved, but still very much a part of his speech. "Th-that's not a n-name we ought to b-be using much."

"Point taken." He sat up and scrutinized the young man carefully. He looked much older in an indefinable way—*now* he looked his real age; when he had been "Jonny," he had looked several years younger. Interesting.

"P-Peregrine t-told me what you want to d-do," the young man continued. "I th-think you're r-right; I th-think w-we ought to at l-least f-find out wh-what my uncle th-thinks he's d-doing. Th-there's j-just one thing— he s-said y-you w-were maybe th-thinking of f-finding a r-r-rebellion. W-well m-maybe I'm a p-prince, b-but I don't kn-know anything ab-bout b-being a K-King."

Talaysen's estimation of the young man rose several notches. Whatever Master Darian had taught him—whatever he had learned himself in his years of rootless wandering—this was the wisest conclusion he could possibly have come to. "That's very astute of you, Kestrel," he said. "I'm not being patronizing; you're very right. If there is a movement afoot to depose your uncle, we are going to have to investigate it very carefully. They may only be interested in putting a puppet on the throne."

"And r-right now th-that's all I'd b-be," Kestrel replied without bitterness. "Th-there's some other th-things you should kn-know. My f-father. He w-wasn't a n-nice man. He p-put m-me and m-mother away in the D-Dowager P-Palace, and j-just tr-trotted us out on s-special oc-casions. Th-that's why she d-d-died. Sh-she c-caught s-something, and he d-didn't bother sending a d-doctor until it was t-too l-late."

"So—what are you getting at?" Talaysen asked.

"I d-don't kn-know, really," Kestrel said frankly. "J-just that I d-don't f-feel like g-going after my uncle f-for r-revenge, I g-guess. I hardly ever s-saw my f-father. I m-mean, I kn-knew who h-he w-was, and he g-gave m-me p-presents wh-when it s-suited him, b-but th-that was all. I s-saw him d-die by accident. B-but it w-was j-just s-someone I kn-knew d-dying, n-not m-my *father.* R-revenge w-would b-be p-pretty s-stupid."

He shrugged, and Talaysen read in that gesture that the young man was confused on any number of subjects, but that on this one he was certain: he was not interested in heroic vendettas.

"Most young men your age with your background would be champing at the bit, hardly able to wait to get their uncle at the point of a sword and give the big speech about 'You, scum, killed my noble, sainted Father! Now you die by the son's blade!' I was all ready to try and calm you down—"

"M-most p-princes h-haven't s-spent th-the last f-four y-years s-sweeping f-floors and t-tending g-goats," Kestrel interrupted, with that disarming matter-of-factness. "I d-don't know, I'm p-pretty c-confused. I j-just w-want t-to s-see what's g-g-going on. And I *really* w-want p-people t-to *stop* t-trying t-to *k-kill* me!"

"Fine," Talaysen replied. "We'll take it from there, and see where it leads."

"Good," Kestrel replied, nodding vigorously.

The young man's reaction gave Talaysen a great deal of food for thought, as they waited for darkness to fall so that they could sneak away. That reaction was, as he had told Sional, not what he had expected. It was a great deal more practical than he had anticipated.

It *might* be wise to see if there was a rebellion brewing; the rebels might be able to protect Sional better than they could. But then again— they might already have their figurehead for revolt, and they might not welcome the intrusion of the "rightful King" into their plans.

There was a possibility that they could stage Sional's "death" convincingly, enough to get the hounds called off. That was another plan to be discussed and plotted out.

Gwyna slowly coaxed a few more of his memories out of him over the course of the day. Talaysen slowly built a picture up in his mind of the boy Sional had been, some eight years ago.

A lonely boy; packed away in what was apparently a drafty, damp "palace" in constant need of repair, with a single, half-deaf servant and his tutor, Master Darian. That surprised him; Guild Bards—and Darian *had* been a Guild Bard, his credentials were impeccable—were not normally employed as tutors for boys, not even when they were princes. Although he could not be certain, Talaysen framed the notion that Master Darian had been a great friend and admirer of the unhappy Queen, and had volunteered his services in the capacity of tutor when the lady died.

The obvious romantic notion—that Darian was really Sional's father, and that Queen and prince had been mewed up out of sight because of the scandal—Talaysen discarded after only a few moments of consideration. *If* it had been true, the King would have gotten rid of the erring spouse and unfortunate offspring—either directly, or discreetly. There were a dozen routes he could have taken, and a dozen princesses who would have brought a great deal of advantage to Birnam as new brides. No, it seemed that Master Darian's relationship with the Queen was the same as Tonno's with Rune: friend and mentor.

So why had the Queen been put away?

Most likely was that the King disliked her intensely, but that she was too circumspect to give him a reason to be rid of her.

But then, why had the prince been discarded with her? In the hopes that he, too, would die, and leave his father free to seek a spouse more to his taste, with the urgency of the succession giving him a reason to urge the wife he *wanted* on his Councilors?

It wouldn't have been the first time that particular ploy had been used, particularly not when the first wife was one chosen for the King by his own father.

Sional, as he had said, had seen very little of his father. He had been in the Crown Palace completely by accident the night that his father had been murdered.

It would have been comic if the circumstances had not been so dire. He had discovered on a previous visit that there was a greenhouse full of fruit-trees that were forced to bloom and bear out of season. He got very little in the way of luxurious food; it seemed that he, Darian, and the servant were brought whatever was left from meals at the Crown Palace after the servants had taken their shares. He *never* saw out-of-season fruit, and boy-like, had decided to filch himself a treat. The greenhouse was just under the King's private chambers, and the way into it—if you were an adventurous child—was through the air vents in the glassed-over roof.

Not only had it been a marvelous adventure, it had been an unrivaled opportunity to spy on his mysterious and aloof father. Double the guilty pleasure for a single act.

Even better had been to discover that his father was not alone. Master Darian had described the goings-on between men and women in a singularly detached fashion that had left him wondering why anyone bothered. *Now* he saw why they bothered—and he stayed and stayed—

So he had been looking in the windows when the assassins surprised his father—and the lady—in bed, just about ready to finish their evening's exertions. The men sent to kill the King had not been expert, and in a panic at the lady's screams, they had also butchered her.

Terror-stricken, sick, and in shock, he had run straight to Master Darian, his only friend and protector.

Poor old man, Talaysen thought pityingly. *No wonder we thought him half-mad. How did he do it? How did he smuggle a child out of a place crawling with killers, get the boy away, and smuggle him out of the country? He was no hero—he wasn't even young. He was an old, tired man with his best days behind him. One day I am going to have to write a song about him. Bravery and intelligence like that are all too rare . . . and we never even recognized them while he was alive.*

Sional must have been in shock for some time, shock that made him terribly vulnerable to illness. Small wonder he took marsh fever crossing the fens at the Birnam-Rayden border. But that must have been a blessing to Master Darian, for during the boy's illness, he managed to convince him that he was someone else entirely—the boy named "Jonny Brede." And that made it easier to hide him.

The rest, Talaysen knew—except for one small detail. The reason *why* Jonny Brede had been unable to hold a job, anywhere.

The killers, the mysterious murderers, who would appear out of nowhere and try to take his life.

They'd made their first attempt right after Master Darian had died. He'd had three close calls, not counting the attempt last night, and on numerous occasions he had learned they were looking for him just in time to flee. Small wonder he'd been starving. The place Talaysen had offered must have seemed God-given—for surely if he moved about every few days, no mysterious killer was going to be able to find him!

Talaysen could hardly imagine the hellish life the boy must have endured. Having no friends for more than a few months, constantly hungry, cold, lonely—with people out of a nightmare one step behind him, and never knowing the reason why.

Now he knew one difference in Kestrel's demeanor: relief. Now Sional *knew* why the killers were after him. There was a logical reason. He no longer lived in an irrational nightmare.

Now he lives in a rational one.

Somehow, that made him angrier than anything else. Talaysen made himself a small promise. If and when they found Sional's uncle in a position of vulnerability, *he* was going to give the man a little taste of what he'd been dealing out to Sional all these years. Just a little.

But it would be a very sharp taste. . . .

They moved out by night, with Gypsies spread all over the downs on either side of the road to make sure they weren't spied upon, in company with three other wagons of the same general shape and size. The other three turned back at moonrise; Gwyna kept the ponies moving on, to the north. Across the downs and past the fens on the other side was the border with Birnam. It could be crossed two ways—by the causeway, or, if you were desperate, through the fens on paths only the march-dwellers knew. Talaysen guessed that the latter was the way Master Darian and Sional must have arrived. *They* would take the causeway. There was no reason not to—and every reason to be as open as possible.

Birnam itself could cause them any number of problems. None of them, other than Sional, had ever been there. The few Gypsies who had could give no real details about the place, and in any event, they hadn't been much past the border area. The fens were too tedious to cross, and in bad seasons, the causeway flooded. Once you crossed the fens, Birnam had no large faires; most commerce took place at weekly Markets instead. Goods moved through the auspices of the Trader's Guild. The Free Bards were not yet numerous enough to expand outside this kingdom, so Talaysen had no idea of what the lot of the traveling musician was like within Birnam.

Not terribly helpful, he thought sleepily, taking his turn at the reins while Gwyna dozed inside. Somehow young Kestrel was sound asleep—

but perhaps, like a soldier, the young man had learned to take sleep when and where he could get it.

He and Rune were to drive while the moon was up, giving the mules light enough to see the road. Since it was a straight track across the downs, bounded on either side by hedgerows, there was small chance they'd get lost. The worst that could happen would be that the mules would stop, pull the wagon over to the side of the road, and proceed to gorge themselves or sleep in their harness until someone woke up and got them back on the job.

Even if something frightened them, they likely wouldn't bolt—or so Gwyna claimed, saying that was the reason the Gypsies preferred mules over horses as draft animals. She claimed that when startled, they would probably stand stock still and wait for whatever it was that frightened them to show itself to be either aggressive and dangerous, or not a threat after all.

"And if they *do* bolt," she'd told him, "Let them have their heads. If they run, they've either been hurt badly by something you can't see, or they've seen something they already know is dangerous. They probably have a better idea of what's safe to do when there's real danger than you do. Let them follow their instincts."

As if he could do anything else! If they took it into their stolid heads to run off, he wasn't even sure he'd be able to hang onto the reins.

Rune climbed out of the back to sit beside him on the driver's bench. After a moment, she began massaging his shoulders, and he sighed with pleasure.

"I've been thinking," she said. "About magic."

"So have I," he replied. "I know we don't know everything. I know *Peregrine* doesn't know everything, however much he likes to pretend that he does."

"Exactly." She nodded her head vigorously. He glanced out of the corner of his eye at her, and smiled.

"Can I say something gauche and male?" he asked. "I think you look wonderful. The dress, your hair down, no leather hat hiding your face—"

"Oh, that's gauche and male, all right," she grinned. "But I like the compliment. I have to admit, sometimes I get a little tired of breeches and loose tunics. A pretty dress—well—Gwyna will probably tell you I was preening like a popinjay when we were going through the outfits the other women offered me and picking out the new clothing."

He cautiously took his attention from the road for a moment to steal a kiss. She stole one back.

"Now, about magic—" she said. He sighed.

There was no getting her mind off business when she was determined. "All right. About magic."

"For every offense in *everything* else, there's always a defense. I can't believe that there's no defenses against this seeking-talisman those killers are using." She braced herself against the swaying of the wagon over an uneven stretch of road, and waited for his response.

"I've been thinking the same thing," he said. "That was why I managed to talk Peregrine out of the one he took from the dead man. I was hoping we could find a way to fool it if we studied it long enough."

He transferred the reins cautiously to his left hand, and fished the talisman out of his breeches pocket. "Here," he said, handing it to her, and taking proper control of the reins again.

She examined it as best she could by the illumination of the three-quarter moon. It wasn't very impressive by either sun or moonlight; there wasn't much there but a small copper disk with a thin lens of glass cemented over it, suspended from a copper chain. She peered at it.

"Is there something under that glass?" she asked.

She had better eyes than he did. "Peregrine says it's a single strand of hair. He says that places where magic is used more openly tend to be very careful about things like nail-clippings and hair. We'd probably better assume that Birnam is one of those places. They'd probably been keeping every strand of hair he lost since he was a baby, and when they knew he was alive, they started making talismans to find him."

Talaysen had no idea how the thing had been made, but the fact that it had survived the fire intact was remarkable enough. It didn't look at all damaged, in spite of the fact that it had been the actual focus of Peregrine's defenses, the point from which the fire sprang. A distinct disadvantage of having a magical object; unless you also had a magical defense—which Peregrine called a Shield—your object could actually call an offensive spell to it, simply by existing.

Once they'd figured out how to outwit this thing, Talaysen planned to sink it in a deep well.

"Does it still work?" she asked.

"Try it for yourself," he told her. "Hold it in your hand and tell yourself that you want to find Sional."

She obeyed—and frowned. "It still works, all right. Nasty thing." She rubbed the hand that had been holding it against her skirt, although there was nothing physically there to rub off. Talaysen had done exactly the same thing after Peregrine had shown him the trick of working it.

"I haven't been able to figure out *how* it works," he confessed. "Though I have to admit, I haven't done as much with it as I might have if it didn't feel so—slimy."

She agreed, grimacing distastefully. "Still—I grew up working in an inn. I emptied chamber pots, cleaned up after sick drunks, mucked out the stables. It won't be the first time I've had to do something nasty, and so far, this doesn't make me feel any worse than one of those jobs. I'll see what I can do with it."

She was quiet for a very long time, her brow furrowed, her eyes half-closed. After a while he began to "hear," with that strange inner ear, little snatches of melody and dissonance.

When she finally spoke, he wasn't ready for it, and he jumped, startled.

"Sorry," she apologized. "I guess I should have moved or something first."

"It's all right," he assured her. "I was sort of dozing anyway, and I shouldn't have been. Have you gotten anything figured out?"

"Well, I think I know why Peregrine said nothing could be done about it," she replied thoughtfully. "This doesn't work like *our* magic—in fact, I'd be willing to believe that it wasn't made by a *human* at all."

"Huh." That made sense. Especially if you were doing something that you didn't want countered. There were pockets of strange races scattered all over the Twenty Kingdoms; it wouldn't be unheard of to find other races that worked magic. And unless you found another mage of the same race, your odds against countering what had been done might be high.

"That could be why it feels—and sounds—so unpleasant," he offered. "It's not operating by laws of melody that we understand, or even feel comfortable with. I've been told that there are some things living off by themselves in the swamps in the south that can make you sick by humming at you."

She nodded vigorously. "You know, that's really what's going on here; it isn't that it really feels *bad*, it's that it makes *you* feel bad. I had a chance to talk to a Mintak about music once; he said he couldn't stand human sopranos and a lot of human instruments because they were too shrill for him. And I couldn't hear half of the notes of a Mintak folk-song he sang for me."

He bent his head down so he could scratch the bridge of his nose. One of the mules looked back at him, annoyed at getting a rein-signal it didn't understand.

"Maybe what we need to do is figure out the logic, the pattern in it— then try and disrupt or block that pattern with something we can stand?" he offered.

"I don't know," she replied, dubiously. "That could be like trying to catch a Mintak with a minnow-net. Or a minnow in a snare. But I suppose that's the best we can do right now. You want to try?"

He took the charm with distaste. "I don't *want* to, but I will. Besides, maybe some of this stuff Peregrine stuck in my head will help."

"Maybe," she replied. "It couldn't hurt, anyway, as long as you remember we aren't playing by human rules anymore."

"I don't think I could forget," he said, and bent with grim determination to his task.

CHAPTER TWENTY-THREE

Rune's stomach heaved. "You know," she said conversationally to Kestrel, as they neared the border-post at the edge of the fens, "if I didn't like you so much, I think I'd have left you back in the mud with that copper charm and saved myself this."

Heat pressed her down and humidity made her head ache. The ever-present reek of the marsh permeated everything. Gnats and midges buzzed in annoying clouds around her head, but thanks to the thick, sticky herb-juice the Gypsies had given them, neither landed nor bit. But the juice itself had a bitter, unpleasant smell, and that added to her misery. The sun glared down through a thick heat-haze, making the road shimmer and dance.

After much trial and error, she and Talaysen had worked out the counter to the magic of the talisman. Comprised of notes they felt more than heard, it only made them *slightly* ill to work. Just enough that Rune refused to eat anything this morning, since they were going to have to cross the border before noon. She hadn't wanted anything in her stomach, and right now she was chewing a sprig of mint in the vain hope that it would settle her rebellious insides.

Sional grimaced. "I'd d-do it m-myself, but I'm not g-good enough yet." He held out his hands and shrugged. "I w-wish I w-was."

"Oh, don't worry about it," she replied, closing her eyes to subdue another surge of nausea. "Besides, if I'd dumped you in the mud, Robin would have gone back after you, and then we'd have gotten to smell fen-stink until we cleaned you up."

As she opened her eyes, she saw him flush and turn away, and smiled in spite of her roiling stomach. Robin was in love with Kestrel, and he was returning her feelings with interest. How long it would last, she had no idea.

Nor did she know whether it would survive the kinds of pressures put on a would-be King. . . .

Worry about that if we get there, she told herself firmly. *We have enough trouble to handle right now.*

One problem they did not have to worry about was whether Sional would be recognized from a physical description. Anyone looking for Jonny Brede as he had last appeared would never see him in this young man. Regular meals and hauling the wagon out of soft spots in the road through the fens had put a lot of muscle on him, and the sun had tanned him as dark as any Gypsy. In clothing given by some of the younger men and his long hair tied back in a tail, he didn't look much like Jonny Brede, and even less like a prince.

The border-station grew from a dot at the end of the long, straight causeway, to a tiny blob of brown, to a doll's house with doll-guards, to something her eyes would accept as a building. This flat expanse of fen was disorienting to someone used to forested hills. There were no trees, no points of reference—just an endless sea of man-high grass stretching in either direction. Forever, as far as eyes could determine.

The border-guards had plenty of time to see them coming and take up their stations in a leisurely manner. No surprise inspections at *this* post, assuming anyone ever bothered inspecting at all. And if there should ever be hostilities between Rayden and Birnam, it was improbable that anyone would ever try to bring an army along this way.

She would not have been at all surprised to see that the guards were slack and slovenly, but in fact, they were the very opposite. Brisk, business-like, they did a brief inspection of the wagon and the occupants and sent them on their way. In fact, there were only two jarring notes.

The first was that they were plainly looking for someone. The serjeant in charge consulted a piece of paper and kept glancing from it to them, as if comparing them with a set of notes.

The second was that one of the men did not come out at all. Rune caught a glimpse of him in the doorway; he was not wearing a uniform of Birnam's soldiers, and she thought she saw a glimpse of copper in his hand—and that was when she thought she heard a bit of that unsettling drone that came from the seeking-charm. She increased the humming that rattled her teeth unpleasantly and made her stomach churn, and concentrated very hard on creating a barrier between Kestrel and the rest of the world.

Finally the inspection was over, and the man she'd seen moved to the door again, just long enough to shake his head at the serjeant. She didn't get a good look at him, but she thought he had a face that was so ordinary that the fact in itself was remarkable. And it occurred to her that if *she* was creating a disguise, that was precisely how she would go about doing so.

It wasn't until after they were out of sight of the guard-house that she stopped her humming and dropped her magical defenses. By then, they were nearing the end of the causeway, and in the distance there was a haze of green that marked the blessed presence of trees.

Gwyna fanned herself with her hat, her hair curling from the heat and damp. "Blessed Lady, no wonder no one comes this way," she said faintly. "It's *fall*, for heaven's sake! Doesn't it ever cool off in there?"

"All that shallow water holds heat very well, Robin," Talaysen said from his place on the driver's bench. "The damp air makes it seem worse than it is. Just be glad we had that juice Vixen made up to rub on us, or we'd have been eaten alive by insects, and the mules with us."

"I want a bath," Rune said, sick to death of feeling sticky and hot. "I want a bath, and fresh food, and I *don't* want to have to hum that Shielding spell again. Or at least, not for a while."

Kestrel, silent until now, roused at that. "D-did you s-see the s-s-sorcerer? The one in the guardhouse?"

"I did," she replied grimly. "And he was looking for you. For us. He didn't catch that we were what he was looking for, though."

"We hope," Talaysen replied pessimistically.

Kestrel shook his head. "He d-didn't. Th-they w-wouldn't have l-let us by. Th-they'd have k-killed us."

"True, oh doubting Wren," Gwyna said. "They haven't hesitated for a moment, before this, even when Kestrel was nothing more than a harmless boy. They would have had no reason to hesitate now, and *every* reason to cut all four of us down. After all, who'd miss a few Gypsies?"

Talaysen's shoulders relaxed. "You're right," he admitted. "I probably worry too much. I think of all the sneaking things I might try, then assume someone else would do the same things I would. But there's no reason for them to let us into Birnam to kill us, when they could kill us with impunity anywhere."

"Well, the first hurdle is passed," Rune told him. "We're in Birnam. Now what?"

"Now we find a good place to camp and people who are willing to talk, in that order," Talaysen told them all, turning for a moment to meet their eyes, each in turn. "And remember: this is the enemy's home ground. We have to be much cleverer than he is. Quiet, elusive, and completely harmless as far as anyone can tell. We have to keep the enemy's eyes sliding right past us."

"And m-most of all," Kestrel added unexpectedly. "W-we have t-to find out wh-what he's up to. And *why.*"

"Exactly," Rune said. "Exactly. And maybe the why is more important than the what."

Kestrel met her eyes, and nodded.

But a week later they were no nearer to the answer to either question. They camped for the night in the shelter of an arm of a greater forest that stretched the length of Birnam, and set up a camp complete with a very welcome fire. Now that they were out of the marsh, it got cold at night, and the days of frost weren't far off. Rune sat and stared at the flames beside Talaysen, waiting for Kestrel and Robin to settle down too.

"If I were looking for a place to foment rebellion, I'd throw up my hands in despair," Talaysen said, as he leaned back against the tree trunk behind him. "These people are so contented it sounds like a tale. I find it all very hard to believe, except that the evidence is right before my eyes. The King can't have paid *everyone* off to pretend to contentment!"

Sional nodded, reluctantly. Rune held her peace. Both of the men had done their level best to find trouble; they had found nothing at all. No trouble, no discontent, just a placid, contented countryside. This was grazing land, full of sheep and dairy cattle, though it was not the hilly, stony ground of the downs they had left in Rayden. These hills were rich, covered with a lush grass that cattle thrived on; not only cattle, but every other grazing animal. And the people were as fat and contented as their cattle.

"I wish we could find someone to talk to that we knew we could trust," Talaysen said fretfully. "I don't like it. These people are like sheep; they're so happy with King Rolend that it makes no sense. *Everyone* has at least a little grievance against those in power!"

Rune fingered the elven-bracelet on her arm, then stopped and stared at it as an idea slowly formed in her mind. "Maybe we can find someone— at least, someone who's neutral. That is, if you're willing to trust the word of an elf."

Talaysen sat straight up, his laziness vanishing. "An *elf?* Where would we find an elf?"

"We call one," she told him, staring into his eyes from across the fire. "All four of us, together. I think that if we work as a group we're strong enough to manage it."

Talaysen licked his lips nervously; the other two watched her with speculation. "Wh-what did you have in m-mind?" Sional asked.

"There's a song we do, with the name of 'Elf-Call,' and now that I know about this magic we can do with music, I wonder just how close to the truth the title is," she said speculatively. "Especially since that friend of Peregrine's gave us these—"

She held up her wrist. Was it her imagination, or did the silver seem to shine with an especially brilliant gleam?

"So what do you intend us to do?" Talaysen asked, with one eyebrow raised.

"Well, we're in a forest, and there might be a Hill of elves around here," she replied, thinking as she spoke. "If we sang 'Elf-Call,' and thought about how we'd like someone to come talk to us—well, maybe someone would."

"We'd better hedge that in," Talaysen said grimly. "Put conditions around it, before we get ourselves in trouble. We'd better limit our 'wish' to elves nearby, and to elves who don't have anything particular they want to do tonight. I *don't* want to get another King angry with me!"

"Uhm—right." Neither did she, actually, One such experience was enough for a lifetime. "All right, how many conditions do we have?"

"Four, one for each of us," Gwyna supplied. "An elf who actually *knows* the answers to the questions we have, one who is willing to talk to humans, one who is nearby, and who would probably be amused by our ingenuity and audacity." She stood up. "Shall I get the instruments?"

Rune nodded. "Do that. I'll help."

"I'll ready the circle," Talaysen offered. "Kestrel, would you make sure we have enough wood for the fire? And food; we're all going to be hungry after this."

Sional nodded without speaking; while his stammer was much better, and improving daily, he preferred not to speak, if he could avoid it. Rune couldn't help wondering what that would do to his effectiveness as a leader.

Well, maybe they'll think he's just very wise, too wise to waste words.

She and Gwyna brought out the harp, Talaysen's round-drum, Gwyna's lute and Rune's fiddle. "Elf-Call" required a strong, hypnotic rhythm pattern, quite as complex as any of the instrumental parts. Talaysen was by far and away the best drummer of the four of them.

While Sional piled wood between his place in the circle and Gwyna's, she and Robin set up the instruments and tuned them. Talaysen positioned their cushions so that they would all be comfortable enough to concentrate, and so that each of them was precisely at a compass point. Talaysen had north; Rune east. Robin was in the south and Kestrel beside her in the west. Male faced female across the fire. This, they had worked out, was the best way to perform Bardic magic in a group. Much of what they were doing now was in the nature of experiment; in some things they had completely outstripped everything Peregrine had taught Master Wren, and in others, they had barely scratched the surface of those teachings.

They settled into their places, each taking up his instrument as if it was a weapon—

At least, that was the way Rune felt.

"I'll take the condition of 'friendly,' " she said. "That may be the hardest to find."

"Ah, 'nearby' for me," Gwyna decided. "I'm not as good as the rest of you are at this. That's going to be the easiest to concentrate on."

" 'Knowledge.' " Kestrel chose with as few words as possible.

"That leaves me with 'willing,' the compliment to 'friendly,' and probably just as difficult a condition to fill," Talaysen finished. "All right are we ready? In tune? One run-through to get the fingers working and the mind set, then we start concentrating. Remember, *listen* for the under-song, and match it. And on four—"

"*Mortals. So ponderous.*"

The voice behind Rune was full of humor and amusement, but it startled her heart right out of her body; she jumped a good foot, and dragged her bow across her strings with a most unmusical squawk.

With a full-throated laugh, their visitor stepped between her and Talaysen into the circle of firelight, stole a cushion from the pile behind her back and dropped gracefully down onto it. If all she had seen was his costume, she'd have known him for elven; no human could have stitched those fanciful silken feathers of scarlet and gold, a tunic in the likeness of a phoenix. But the sharply pointed ears gave his race away as well, and the distinctly unhuman cast of his features as he turned to smile at her.

"You really should have learned by now that you've trained your *wills,*" he scolded gently. "For creatures sensitive to magic, you need only be thinking about your needs and channeling the magic with the *thought* of the music. For mortals, perhaps, as earth-bound as you are, you will need a formal ceremony, or the music sung aloud. But not for us. Now, what is it that I can answer for you? In return, of course, you will come to the Hill to play for our dancing tonight."

"Of course," Talaysen said with grave courtesy. Rune couldn't speak; she was still trying to get her heart to take its proper place in her chest. "Thank you for responding to us."

"Oh, how could I not?" the elf laughed. "You are legend, after all! The mortals favored by the High King—you do realize, don't you, that one day you'll have to perform for *him?* And the favor he will ask for his protection might be a weighty one. Or—not. He has his whims, does the High King."

His smile was a bit malicious, but Talaysen simply shrugged. "Nothing comes without a price," he said philosophically. "But what we would ask of you is so little that you may consider it inconsequential."

"And that is?" The elf crossed his legs tailor-fashion, propped one elbow on his knee, and rested his chin on his hand.

"We want to know what the people of this land think of their King—and what they thought of the last one—"

"What, this lad's father?" At Kestrel's start, he laughed again. "Don't trouble your head, child, your secret is safe with us. While King Rolend has the wisdom to welcome us and leave us in peace, we never meddle in mortal politics. So, you wish the tale of King Rolend and his wicked brother, King Charlis, hmm?"

"Wicked brother?" Talaysen raised an eyebrow. "Is that an elven judgment, or the judgment of history as written by the victor?"

The fire popped and crackled, flaring up briefly, and reflecting from their visitor's eyes. "Both, actually." The elf sobered. "I hope the boy there has no great illusions about the quality of his parent—"

Kestrel shook his head. "H-hardly knew him."

"Good. Your father should never have been given power, and that is *our* judgment. He was ill-suited to it, being spoiled and accustomed to having his will in all things. I take it you have been asking discreet questions of the fat herds out there?" The elf nodded towards the road and the dairy farms beyond. "And they have been full of praise for King Rolend? They are right to be. Under his brother, they and their lands groaned beneath taxes so ruinous that their children went to bed hungry one night out of three—and that *here*, in the richest land in the Kingdom. And what did the wicked King Charlis spend their money on?"

He looked at Rune, who shrugged. "Armies?" she hazarded, shifting her position a little.

"They might have forgiven armies. No, he spent it on his own amusement. On exotic pleasure-slaves, on foods from far beyond his borders; on magical toys and rare beasts for his menagerie. On extravagant entertainments for himself and his court—caging the gardens under a great tent and heating it until the trees bloomed in midwinter, flooding the walled court with water and staging a battle of ships." The elf shook his head, and his long hair rippled with the motion. "He neglected his Queen, who did not share his exotic tastes, and his son, who was an inconvenience. That neglect killed his Queen, and cost him the regard of that son. Oh, a few loved him. The Bardic Guild, whom he showered with gifts and gold. The men of the Church, whom he gave license to pursue anything not human as unholy and anathema—which meant ourselves, of course. The select courtiers he favored, and the Dukes and Sires, who he left to themselves, so that they could feud and rule their lands and people as they chose, and make riot of the countryside. But no one else."

"But King R-Rolend?" Kestrel asked. As far as Rune could tell, he wasn't the least upset by the unflattering description of his father.

"Ah, now that is interesting." The elf taped the bridge of his nose with a long, graceful finger. "He is mixed, like most mortals; some bad, but most good. He remitted many of the taxes when he stole the throne, and spent what was left in the treasury restoring the lands. The *honest* Churchmen, whom he raised up after casting a-down the corrupt and proud, favor him and his policy of tolerance to those not human. His people love him, and love his son, who is so like the father that one must look for gray hairs to determine which is which." The elf smiled sardonically, and cast a glance at the bracelets Rune and Talaysen wore. "He has received certain—considerations—from my people. The courtiers no longer receiving rich gifts do not favor him. The corrupt men of the Church curse his name and lineage. The Sires, who must now bend to the laws of the land, grumble among themselves. And the Bardic Guild is—very quiet, lest he recall where so much of the kingdom's coin vanished. From time to time men gather and speak of a 'rightful King,' and talk of rebellion, but nothing comes of it."

"No one is as perfect as you claim King Rolend is," Talaysen said dryly.

"Did I say he was perfect?" The elf shrugged, and his wing-like eyebrows flew up towards his scalp. "He is mortal. No mortal is perfect. He hears the rumors of a 'rightful King,' and he fears, of course. He has had men put to death for simply whispering such words. With every year, he grows less flexible, less forgiving, harder. Power brings him temptations, and he does not always withstand them. But as Kings go, there have been worse, and these people give praise to their Sacrificed God daily for the one they have."

He stood up from his cushion, so smoothly Rune hardly knew he was doing so until he was looking down at them. "Have I given you all that you desire?"

Talaysen looked over at Kestrel, who nodded, slowly.

"Well, then. I have answered your invitation, now you must answer mine."

"Willingly," Talaysen said, getting to his feet. Rune and the others did the same, gathering up their instruments. She cast a nervous glance at the wagon and mules; the elf followed her glance and thoughts with the lightning-quick understanding of his kind.

"Never fear for your goods and beasts," he said—he didn't *quite* mock. "They will be guarded. The fire will be tended. Now, to the Hill, and the feast, and the dancing!"

Certainly. And allow me to get my little dig in at you and yours, my friend. "Gladly," she said sweetly, as they followed him into the forest. "And we promise to *stop* when you are weary."

His teeth gleaming back at her in a vulpine smile were all the answer he gave.

The King's private study seemed full of lurking shadows tonight, not all of them born of firelight. Some of them were born of unpleasant memory. *Why did I ever take the throne?*

Rolend's temple throbbed, and nothing the Healer-Priests did for him would make the pain stop. One of them had the audacity to tell him that he was doing it to himself. He slumped over his desk and buried his head in his hands.

He was doing it to himself. Whatever the hell that was supposed to mean.

The question of why he had taken the crown was rhetorical, of course; he'd usurped the throne to keep his brother from looting the country to the point where the people would rise up and slaughter anyone with a drop of noble blood in his veins. And *that* had been nearer than anyone but he and a few choice advisors even guessed.

Shadows danced on the wall, shadows that mimed the conflict of men and their dreams. He had hoped to capture Prince Sional; the boy had been young, young enough, he had hoped, to be trained. Young enough even to come to understand what his uncle had done, and why, and forgive him one day?

Perhaps. Perhaps not. It didn't matter. The boy's tutor had taken him and fled. For years he had forgotten the child—had hoped, when he thought of him at all, that the boy had died. But then the rumors had started—that the old man had fled to the Bardic Guild in Rayden, that he had the boy with him. There was no telling what hate-filled lies he'd brought the child up on; the Bardic Guild hated him because there were no more rich plums falling into their laps from the Crown. Doubtless the Guild in Rayden had seen to it that the boy learned only to hate and fear his uncle, and to dream of the day when *he* would take back the throne. Doubtless they had filled his head with idle ballads of foul usurpers and the noble heroes who threw them down.

Doubtless they had made him grateful to them for sheltering him—

encouraged him to trust in *their* word, and the words of those who waited for his return.

Doubtless he was now a handsome young puppet for their playing; everything a King should *look* like, but nothing of substance. And certainly no more in his head but the insubstantial sugar-fluff of vanity and dreams.

The Bardic Guild was very, very good at creating the semblance of dreams. Those Churchmen he trusted had warned him of this. When he heard their prophecies fulfilled, he acted. He dared be nothing less than ruthless, so he called upon the wizened, unhuman folk of the fens, the ones his people termed "goblins," and gave them Sional's hair, bidding them make him seeking-charms. And when the charms came back, wrapped in leaves, he gave them to his agents and told them to kill. His conscience had troubled him, but he had soothed it with visions of *who* would use the boy for their own ends, if they found him. He would not give them that focus.

He had slept better, then, except for the times when he agonized about ordering the death of a mere child—he had been sure, despite the three times that the boy had escaped, that eventually they would find him and dispose of him. He had been utterly certain of that—until tonight.

Tonight the last of his agents had sent him word. One of their number was dead, killed by magic. The boy was gone. No one knew where, or how. The entire area had been combed and recombed, and not a trace of him could be found. The Gypsies he had last been with professed to know nothing of him, and had closed ranks against King Rolend's agents. There were forty or more of *them,* and only three of the agents; the men had wisely deemed it time to retreat.

My hold on the throne is shaky enough. Once my enemies find out the boy lives—and they will—they'll track him down. He may even come to them. Even if he's still innocent—even if by some miracle the Guild did not fill him full of hate for me, they will when they find him. And they'll use him. A boy of eighteen has no chance against them.

He groaned aloud, and then looked up as footsteps from the royal suite warned him of someone's approach from the private rooms. He had no fear that it might be an enemy; his guards were loyal and alert, and the only way into the suite besides this door was through a window. But he hoped that it wasn't his wife; she was as dear to him as his right hand, but he did not want to be soothed at the moment.

"Father?" His son hesitated on the threshold, just within the reach of the firelight, and Rolend sighed with relief. Victor was welcome; he wouldn't try to pretend that troubles would just go away if he ignored them. And he wouldn't try to *soothe* his father. "Father, I heard you—ah—"

"It's my head again, Victor," he replied. "It doesn't matter; I was going to call for you anyway."

"Ah." The young man—twenty, and mature for his age—walked on cat-quiet feet into his father's study, then settled into a chair beside Rolend's desk. Looking into his son's face was like looking into a time-reversing mirror. The same frank brown eyes under heavy brows, now knitted with concern—the same long nose, the same thin lips and rounded jaw. "Bad news, I take it?"

"They've lost him." No further explanation was needed; Rolend had kept his son advised of everything from the day he'd taken the crown. That accounted for his maturity, perhaps. Sometimes Rolend felt a pang of guilt for having robbed the boy of a carefree childhood, but at least if something happened to *him,* Victor would have the knowledge, the wits, and the skill to keep himself and his mother alive.

"Oh." Victor's expression darkened with unhappiness. "Father—"

"Speak your piece." Victor was about to say something he thought Rolend wouldn't like, but the King had never forbidden his son to speak his mind before and he wasn't about to start now.

"Father, I can't be sorry. I think you were wrong to try and—" The young man hesitated, choosing his words with care. "To try to—get rid of him—in the first place. He has never done anything to give you a moment of lost sleep—never even tried to come home! Why should he try to conspire against you now?"

Rolend sighed, and tried once more to make the boy see the whole truth of the situation. He didn't blame Victor for the way he felt; the boy remembered his cousin quite clearly, and when Victor thought of the assassins his father had sent out to Rayden, he probably pictured himself in Sional's place. "Even if he were as innocent as a babe, son, he's still a danger to me. As long as he lives, he can be used against me. And the hard fact is, he's not the cousin who you taught to ride and the one you gave your old pony to. He's probably been fed hate and bitter words with every meal, and he's probably looking forward to spitting you like a skewered capon, right beside me."

Victor shook his head stubbornly. "I can't believe that, father. Master Darian loved Queen Felice, and he *hated* Uncle Charlis for what he did to her. *He's* the one that took Sion, and he took him into *Rayden,* not to the Guild here! You *know* that no branch of the Guild really gives a clipped coin for what happens to another, so long as nothing happens to them! I can't believe that Master Darian would bring Sion up to be as twisted as you think."

"It doesn't matter, son," Rolend sighed. "It really doesn't matter. Once the Church and the Guild here find out he's alive, they'll have him. And once the Church mages have him—the dark ones, anyway—they'll strip his mind bare and put what *they* want in there."

Now Victor fell silent, and nodded. Reluctantly, but in agreement. He'd seen at first hand what a dark mage could do to someone's mind, when they'd taken back what had once been a faithful guard from those who had captured him. No matter what had been in there before, when the dark mage was done, there was nothing left of the original but the shell.

"I don't like it," he said, finally. "But I can't think what else you could do."

"Do you think *I* like it?" Rolend burst out. He lurched up out of his chair and began to pace in front of the fire. "I've ordered a murder—I ordered the murder of a *child.* I sent those agents out when the boy was fourteen—perhaps fifteen! But what else am I to do?" He sat down again, heavily; buried his face in his hands, and confessed to his son what he would not have told another living man, not even his Priest. "I hate what

I've done, and I hate myself for ordering it. And sometimes I think that perhaps this is my punishment from God for trying to murder a child. Maybe I deserve to find myself facing Sional across a blade. But what else could I have done?"

"I don't know, Father," Victor whispered. "I don't know."

Rune took her turn at the reins, with everyone else closeted inside the wagon. The capital city of Kingstone loomed ahead of them, a huge place that had long ago spilled out past its walls. She wondered what was going on in Kestrel's mind right now. They were near the end of their goal, and still he had not decided what he wanted to do—

Well, if he has, he hasn't told us.

The elf hadn't lied, or even exaggerated. The people of Birnam were content with King Rolend on the throne, and were secure in the belief that his son would be just as good a ruler as his father.

Nor had the elf made any mistake in the quality of King Rolend's enemies. He had them, but they were all too often the kind of men—and a few women—who made Rune's skin crawl. Selfish, greedy, venial, power-hungry . . . there were some honest folk among them, people who felt that the "rightful King" should be on the throne. Frequently they voiced a legitimate concern: could a man who had ordered the murder of his own brother, for whatever reason, however good, remain uncorrupted himself? How long would it be before he found other reasons to order the deaths of those who opposed him—and how long would it be before merely disagreeing with him became "opposing" him?

Power corrupted; power made it easy to see what you wanted as something that was morally "right." Power made it easy to find excuses. Had King Rolend already fallen victim to the seductive magic that Power sang?

Those who voiced those questions hoped for the "lost prince" to return as someone who had not yet fallen victim to that seductive song. Rune couldn't help noticing that they used the same words in describing this mythical Sional as the Priests used in describing the Sacrificed God. . . .

But behind all these well-meaning and earnest folk, these dreamers and mystics, there were always the others. The powerful who had lost the power they craved, the Priests who had been toppled from thrones of their own, the pampered and indulged who had fallen from grace.

If they found Sional they'd make him over into *exactly* the image the others craved. The pure innocent.

The pure innocent fool, who'll say whatever they tell him to say. . . .

But there was one possible way that Sional could win back his throne without becoming a puppet. To take it the same way that his uncle had. Except that instead of soldiers, he'd have Bardic magic on his side. Magic that might even make it possible to avoid killing King Rolend and the cousin he vaguely remembered.

And if that was what he truly wanted—well, Rune would back him, and she suspected that Talaysen would, too. They'd had some long, late-night discussions about good government, about the seduction of power. Discussions that reminded her poignantly of the ones she'd had with Tonno.

They'd slipped into more than a dozen meetings of these purported enemies of the King, most of which were held on Church grounds, which somehow hadn't surprised her much. She and Talaysen had gotten fairly adept at rooting out who the malcontents were, convincing them to reveal what they knew with a focused thought and a few hummed phrases of music. They were even more adept at going to the meeting-places cloaked, and persuading the guards with their magic that they were trusted conspirators. Once or twice, they'd even put guards to sleep that way. This magic, though it left them weary, still represented a lot of power, and it was very tempting to use it for more than defense. And it was in one of those discussions of power that Rune had realized with a little shock how easy it was to just *use* it. Power was as seductive as anything else, and now she could see why others had succumbed to the lure of it, even in the Church. How close had she and the others come to that kind of attitude, where the end was more important than the means, and all that mattered was that the end be *theirs*?

That was when they'd had other discussions, about the kind of people who were behind the uneasy stirrings of unrest. Unspoken agreement had been reached about the use of magic, then, and the late-night sorties into the camps of the conspirators ended.

She knew that Talaysen was worried. However well-meaning Sion was, how could he stay out of the hands of those people for long once he revealed who and what he was? And if he somehow managed to, against all odds, how long would he be able to *hold* his throne? How long could he play their game without getting caught at it?

She sighed, and the mules flicked back their ears at the sound.

They'd turn against him eventually—unless he managed to play the Church against the nobles, and vice versa—and use the Guild to keep both sides stirred up.

She shook her head, and rubbed her temple. Her head ached from all the unresolved problems. A man as old as Rolend, and as experienced, could probably do just that. In fact, there were some signs that he had begun to play that very game, now that his country was stable and prosperous. Several of the little cabals they had visited had been very suspicious of outsiders, and not as agents from the King, but as agents from one of the *other* groups. That must surely be Rolend's work, at least in part.

But could Sional play that kind of game?

I don't know. Talaysen could—but Sional—he's no older than I am. And I don't think I could, not for long.

And there was one final concern—insignificant so far as the fate of a kingdom was concerned, but one that was tearing her heart in two.

Gwyna.

Gypsy Robin had fallen in love with Kestrel, and he with her. And now, the nearer they came to the palace and the throne, the more Gwyna looked at Kestrel and saw Prince Sional.

Prince Sional, who could not possibly marry even with a commoner, much less with a Gypsy.

Gwyna grieved—characteristically, in silence, hiding her grief behind a smile and a quick wit. But she mourned Kestrel's loss already. Rune felt it, and she could do nothing, for there was nothing she *could* do. Their worlds could not be reconciled. If Prince Sional took his throne, Kestrel died.

If Prince Sional failed in his attempt to take his throne, Kestrel died.

But if Kestrel was to live, *something* must be done about the assassins. And what *that* solution was, Rune had no idea.

It wasn't possible that the King would believe that Sional didn't want the throne. And even if he did, he must know that the moment his enemies discovered Sional's existence, they'd try to use him.

So even if Prince Sional gave up his throne, sooner or later, Kestrel would die.

If Talaysen had any plans on that score, he hadn't confided them to her.

So they had their answers now—but they weren't any help. And Rune couldn't keep herself from feeling that she was driving their little wagon into a maze with no escape.

CHAPTER TWENTY-FOUR

The wagon seemed the safest place to stay, all things considered. Rune found a travelers' inn that would let them pull their wagon in behind the stable for a fee. It was clean, shaded and secluded back there; evidently there were often travelers staying in their own conveyances, and the inn had set up this little yard for them. A little more money produced fodder and water for the mules, and gave them use of the inn bathhouse. While the others got their baths, she fetched some hot food from the inn's kitchen; they were all tired of their own limited cooking abilities. They returned about the same time she did, and she went for her wash.

By the time she got back, it was obvious from the tense atmosphere in the wagon that Kestrel was about to make a decision, and had been waiting for her to return. He and Gwyna sat on one bunk, not touching, and Talaysen sat facing them. The food was hardly touched, Gwyna was sitting very still and her face had no color at all, and Talaysen had not bothered to light the lamps.

Rune climbed into the wagon, lit the lamp beside the door herself and shut the door behind her. Kestrel cleared his throat self-consciously, and Gwyna jumped.

"I—I d-d-don't want the d-d-d-d-damn th-throne," he said, thickly. "I w-wouldn't b-be ha-ha-half the K-King m-my uncle is. I'm a g-g-good m-musician. I'd be a *ho-horrible* K-King!"

Gwyna made a curious little sound, half laugh, half sob. Talaysen let out the breath he'd been holding in, and Rune sat down on the bunk with a *thud.*

"I can't tell you how glad I am that you've decided that," Talaysen said, wiping his brow with the back of his hand. "I agree with you. But that just gives us another problem. How the hell are we going to keep you alive?" He reached for his mug of cider and took a long drink. Rune picked up a barely warm meat pie to nibble on. Their problems weren't over yet; in fact, as Talaysen had pointed out, they'd just begun.

"C-can't we k-keep d-doing what w-we have b-been?" Kestrel asked, after a moment of forlorn hesitation.

Rune and Talaysen both shook their heads, and Rune spoke first. "Sooner or later he's going to find another kind of seeking-charm, and give the *new* ones to his agents. We won't know how to counter them, and they'll find you again. And while we're waiting for that to happen, some of these other lunatics we've seen are going to realize you really are alive, and come looking for you themselves. Then what?"

She put the pie down; her appetite was entirely gone.

Sional set his mouth stubbornly and raised his chin. "I t-tell them t-to g-go t-to hell."

"And when they find a mage to change your mind for you?" Talaysen asked, gently. "Oh, don't shake your head, Kestrel. They've got mages, especially Church mages. And ask Gwyna how powerful some of them are. She spent several days as a bird—a real bird, with feathers—and for anyone who can turn a woman into a bird, taking over your mind would be a mere exercise." He closed his eyes for a moment. "What we've begun to learn—it's nothing compared to what happened to Gwyna. I think that one day, we *will* be powerful enough to protect you from all of them. Rune, especially; I've never heard of anyone facing down elves the way she did. But we aren't that strong yet."

"I—I d-d-d—" He paused, and flushed. "I h-have to t-talk t-to my uncle," he said, his eyes meeting first Rune's, then Gwyna's. "I d-don't kn-know what else t-t-to s-say. H-he w-wasn't always l-like th-this. M-m-maybe if I t-talk t-to him, he'll und-d-derstand. And l-leave m-me al-l-lone. Th-that's th-the only th-thing I c-can th-think of." His face twisted up, and he looked about to cry. "R-Robin, I l-l-l-"

She caught his hands in hers. "I know that," she replied. "I do, I know that. I love you. And if there's *any* way I can make you safe—"

"How are we going to get you to him?" Rune asked. "That's the first question—"

"I c-c-an remember th-the p-palace, g-g-good enough to d-draw a m-map," he said. "If Master Wr-wren c-can d-do what P-P-Peregrine d-did to m-make m-me remember—"

"I can," Talaysen said slowly. "Then what?"

"I f-find a w-way to t-talk t-to my uncle alone," Sion repeated. "In h-his b-bedroom, m-maybe. If I c-can t-talk t-to him alone, h-he'll *have* to believe me!"

"First problem," Rune pointed out. "Getting into the palace."

"You can leave that to me," Talaysen told her. "I've slipped into a fair number of buildings in my time. The easiest way in is as a servant, openly, since servants are invisible to those they serve."

"Next problem—what if your uncle won't believe you?" Gwyna was still pale, and she didn't look as if she liked this plan at all.

"Magic," Rune said. "At least we can keep him convinced long enough for us to get out of here and somewhere safer. After that—well, our influence is going to wear off after a while."

"I say we can fake Kestrel's death once we're well away," Talaysen said unexpectedly. "I faked my own, I ought to be able to do his!"

Slowly Gwyna's color came back, and she nodded. "That should work," she said, and grinned a little—a feeble grin, but it was there, and real. "If it makes him safe from his uncle and those greedy fools, that's the best solution of all."

Rune sighed with relief. *Good sense to the rescue,* she thought. "The only question I can see is, the fake won't hold forever—it didn't for Master Wren. Then what? We're right back at the beginning!"

Talaysen chuckled, much to her surprise, and evidently to Kestrel and Robin's as well, from the incredulous looks they gave him.

"Kestrel wasn't a famous Bardic Guild Master who refused to quit making music," he said. "That was my own fault. If I'd had the sense to become a carpenter or something, they'd never have found me again. Kestrel, on the other hand, is *not* going to go find himself another position as a prince, and no one but us knows he really *is* a Bard."

"All right," Rune said. "I can accept that. So now the question is—how do we get into the palace? Everything we want to do hinges on that. If we can't get in and convince Rolend long enough to give us that breathing space to fake a death, we can't make all this work."

"I've been thinking for the past week or so," Talaysen said slowly. "Trying to come up with a plan that would work whether Kestrel wanted the crown or not—and I think I've got one."

He couldn't possibly have said anything that would have had a better chance of capturing their attention. As one, they leaned forward to listen.

Talaysen nodded, as if he was satisfied. "Remember what I said about servants being invisible? Think about that—then remember what Rune and I can do to fog peoples' thoughts and confuse them. Combine those two factors, and I think we can get in ourselves, find a way into the private quarters, for all of us, and once we have that, we have everything. Now—here is what we do, to start. Or rather, what Rune and I do. . . ."

Rune scrubbed pots with a will, her hands deep in lukewarm, soapy water, and kept her head down with her hair straggling into her eyes.

She hummed as she worked, concentrating on *not being noticed.* The girl whose clothes she had stolen was her same height and general build, but she looked *nothing* like the Bard—and while she could use magic to keep people from looking too closely at her, if she worked too hard at bespelling people now, she'd have no energy reserves for dealing with King Rolend later. The kitchen suffered from lack of light, though, which was to her advantage. Talaysen and the other two looked a great deal more like their own counterparts, but she was the weakest link here; there simply weren't too many women with Rune's inches.

Too bad she didn't have another job, Rune thought, with an idle corner of her mind, as she chipped away at some burnt-on porridge that had been left there since this morning. *When I left the Bear, I thought I'd left this behind me too. Ick. I hate pot-scrubbing.*

The stone-walled kitchen, too small for the number of people crowded into it, was ill-lit, with only two lanterns for the whole room, cramped and hot; in the inevitable confusion of dinner preparation it had been fairly simple for them to slip into the root-cellar to hide, then to lure individuals away and knock them out with a song of sleep. Their victims would be found in the cellar some-time tomorrow, but the chances of their being discovered before then was fairly remote—Talaysen had waited until the last foray after roots and onions was over before sending them to dreams. There was no reason for anyone to go down there now, and raw roots weren't high on anyone's list of edibles to steal. King Rolend's expert handling of his people extended to his kitchens and servants—they were all well-fed, and if they stole anything to munch on, it would be a bit of meat or a pastry, not a raw onion.

The pot-scrubbers ate first, even before the courtiers and high servants that the meal had been prepared for, so the only time anyone said anything to Rune and her fellow cleaners, it was about the dirty dishes. Other than that, they were left alone.

She freed a hand long enough to wipe sweat from her forehead and the back of her neck. The other three had taken the place of other cleaners and sweepers. Gwyna was two stations over, in charge of pewter mugs and utensils; Talaysen and Sional had been in charge of carrying garbage out to the compost-heaps. Now they waited, brooms in hand, for the signal that the nobles were finished eating. That was when they and the other cleaners would trot up the steps into the dining-hall—

That is, that's what they would do if they really *were* sweepers.

The lowest of the low, the invisibles. Dull-witted, just bright enough to clean up after others, not bright enough to be any danger to anyone. That was the kind of servant Talaysen had been looking for to impersonate. Someone no one in his right mind would ever suspect.

It wouldn't be long now. The great ovens were closed; the last of the pastry courses had been sent out. Servants were trickling out of the kitchen, in the opposite direction of the stair *they* were going to take; heading for the barn-like servants' hall and their own dinner. A gong sounded above, as Rune watched them out of the corner of her eye. That was the signal that dinner was over, and no one was lingering over food or wanted something else. The cooks gathered up the last of their utensils and dropped them in the nearest dishtub. The cleaners could now begin their job—

The chief cook and all her helpers swept out of the room, chattering and complaining, which left no one to oversee the kitchen itself. The drudges on dishwashing duty were normally half-wits at best, like Maeve; dull creatures that would do anything they'd been set at until the last dish was washed, or until they were stopped and set on something new. They wouldn't notice when Gwyna and Rune left.

Talaysen and Sional hung back from the rest of the sweepers; like the drudges, the sweepers weren't the brightest of folk. Probably no one would notice that they were missing until noses were counted—and then it would be assumed that the missing men were either off drinking filched wine, or tupping the missing drudges. When servants were missing, their superiors generally assumed "improper conduct" rather than anything sinister, and the lowlier the servant, the more likely that was. That was why

Talaysen had chosen the ones he had; the ones thought to be shiftless, ne'er-do-wells. When he and Rune had made their earlier foray into the kitchens, there'd been trouble with those two men over laziness and slacking. For the kitchen steward, it would simply seem a repetition of the same, with the tall simpleton drawn into the group to make up a foursome.

Gwyna and Rune dropped what they'd been working on back into the dishtubs and joined the men. As they had figured, the other drudges didn't even look up from their work.

"Follow me," Talaysen whispered, propping his broom in an out-of-the-way corner full of shadows where it might not be seen for a while. Kestrel did the same. Rune wiped her hands on her apron, grateful that the King's concern for his servants extended to keeping them bathed and clean. Some of the drudges she'd seen in inn kitchens would have given them away by the reek of their stolen clothing, and there weren't any fleas to torment the conspirators with unexpected biting at precisely the wrong moment.

They followed Talaysen up a back stair—not quietly, but yawning and letting their feet scuff against the stairsteps, talking among themselves as if they had just finished dinner and were heading for bed. Talaysen first, followed by Kestrel—then Robin and Rune together, as if they were two best friends, whispering and giggling behind Kestrel's back. This part of the staircase was well and brightly lit, and it would have been impossible to slip past the guard posted at the entrance to the second floor—so they weren't even going to try. Instead, they were going to be as obvious as possible.

The guard on the landing of the second floor—the floor with the royal suite on it—nodded to each of the men, and winked slyly at the women. Rune giggled and hid her face behind her hand as if she was shy. Robin gave him a saucy wink right back, and wrinkled her nose at him.

He gave her a pinch as she went by; she squealed and slapped playfully at his hand—but once again, the King's care for choosing his servants came to the fore. He made no effort to follow them, and no effort to back up his flirtation except a verbal one.

"Saucy wench like you needs a man t' keep her warm o'nights," the guard said, with a grin, but without leaving his post. "Tell ye what, ye be tired of an empty bed, or cold around about midnight, ye come lookin' for Lerson, eh? By then I be off."

"I might," Gwyna replied smartly, not betraying by so much as a blink that the guard had just told them something they hadn't known—when the change of guard was. "Then again, I might *not!*"

"Ah," Lerson growled playfully, faking a swat at her with his halberd. "Get along with ye!"

She scampered up the stairs behind Rune, who'd waited for her. They giggled together all the way up to the next landing—which was unguarded—where they opened and closed the door twice, to make it seem as if they'd gone to their quarters.

But instead of leaving the stairs at the servants' floor, they continued quietly, carefully, to the top, and the seldom-used storage rooms for old furniture.

Talaysen had been here before them, in the guise of a dim-witted fellow
assigned to carrying up barrels of summer clothing, and he had made
certain that the door at the top of the stairs was well-oiled. Nevertheless,
Rune held her breath as he opened it, they all filed through it, and he
closed it behind them without a betraying creak.

The darkness in this hall was total, and the air was thick with dust. She
suppressed a sneeze.

This part of the plan was pivotal. She waited as Talaysen felt his way
past them; then took Gwyna's hand at his whispered command. Gwyna
held Kestrel's hand, and Kestrel had hold of Talaysen. Careful questioning
of palace servants on Talaysen's last visit had told him of the existence of
a spiral stairway that went straight from the Royal Suite to the attics, with
no doorways out onto any other floors. It was guarded—but by only one
man. It came out in a linen closet at the end of the hall, and had been
built so that bedding and furniture could be lowered down the hollow
center of the stairs by means of a block and tackle. That had been
Talaysen's second job here—lowering *down* the boxes of warming-pans
and featherbeds for winter. With no landings in between, the stairs could
be made as narrow as feasible and still be used by men to guide the
burden up or down. There was, however, no railing. And the stairs were
bound to be just as dark as these attics.

Talaysen found the door and opened it, a little at a time. It *did* creak,
and Rune just hoped that the guard at the bottom would attribute the
tiny squeaks as Talaysen moved it, bit by bit, to mice.

She tried not to think of the drop that awaited her if she missed her
step, and waited until it was her turn to follow Gwyna into the stairway.
She felt her way along the wall, and inched her foot over the doorframe.

There. Her hand encountered the rough brickwork of the inside of the
staircase, and her foot found the first step. And the abyss beyond it.

She pulled her foot back, and began the agonizingly slow progress down.

There was no way of telling time in the thick, stuffy darkness. She
thought she heard Gwyna breathing just ahead of her, and the occasional
scuff of a toe against the stone of the stair, but that was all. She couldn't
have seen her hand if it was right in front of her face, rather than feeling
the wall. She counted twenty steps—thirty—began to wonder if there was
going to be an end to them. Maybe this was all a dream—or worse yet,
maybe they were all really dead, killed protecting Kestrel, and this was
their own private little hell, to descend this staircase forever and ever and
never come to the bottom of it—

But before she managed to give herself a case of the horrors, her
questing foot found only a flat surface, and she bumped into Gwyna.

Talaysen held his breath for a moment, and pressed his ear against the
crack that marked the door into the linen closet. He heard nothing.

Good.

The King never expected any serious threat from above—so the guard
on this stair was really one of the guards that patrolled the hallway beyond.
And if what he had been told—under the influence of a "trust me" spell
on another of the guards—was true, the guard stationed here was more

in case someone broke in through one of the windows. He never checked in with anyone, from the moment he went on station, to the moment he turned his watch over to the next guard.

Talaysen eased the door open, slowly—*this* one, thank God, had been better taken care of than the one above. It opened with scarcely a squeak.

Now there was light; outlining the door at the other end of the closet. He motioned to the others to stay where they were, and eased himself up to kneel beside it, pressing his ear against the gap between door and frame.

There—there were the steps, slow, and steady, of the guard. He began to hum under his breath, timing his magic so that the guard would begin to feel sleepy just about when he reached the door to the linen closet.

The footsteps receded—then neared, and began to falter a little. He heard a yawn, quickly stifled, then another.

He hummed a little louder, concentrating with all his might. He would have to overcome the will of a stubborn, trained man—one who *knew* his duty was to stay awake, and would fight the magic, although he didn't know what he was fighting.

Another yawn; a stumble. A gasp—

The sound of a heavy body falling against the wall beside the door, and sliding to the floor.

He flung open the door, quickly, squinting against light that was painful after the darkness of the stairway. A man in guard-uniform sprawled untidily on the dark wooden floor, his brow creased as if he was still trying to fight off the effects of the spell. With a quick gesture, Talaysen summoned Kestrel, and together they pulled the guard into the closet.

In a few moments, as the women sent him deeper into sleep, they had stripped him of weapons, bound and gagged him, and muffled him in a pile of sheets and comforters. Talaysen took his sword; while he wasn't an expert, he knew the use of one. Kestrel, who hadn't held a sword since childhood, seized the knife. With a quick glance up and down the hall to be certain they were unobserved, they stole out and headed for the King's private study at the end of the suite—the one place they knew they had a chance of catching the King alone. That had been the last bit of information they'd gotten on their scouting foray. No one entered that room without Rolend's express permission, not even servants—and Rolend always went there directly after dinner.

It was a rather ordinary room, when they finally found it. Talaysen had been expecting something much grander; this place looked to have been a kind of heated storage closet before Rolend had taken it over. A single lantern burned on the desk; the rest of the light came from a cheerful blaze in the tiny fireplace. There were no windows; the walls were lined with bookshelves, and the only furniture was a scratched and dented desk, and three comfortable-looking chairs. It was an odd-shaped room as well, with a little niche behind the door, just large enough for all four of them to squeeze into without having the door hit them in the faces when it opened. Which was exactly what they did.

Rune tapped his shoulder once they were in place, with Kestrel, as the

youngest and most agile, at the front of the group. He leaned over so
that she could put her lips right up against his ear and whisper.

"It would be just our luck that he decided to go straight to bed,
wouldn't it?" she said.

Silently he begged God and the Gypsy's Lady that Rune wouldn't prove
to be a prophet.

They huddled there long enough for him, at least, to start feeling stiff
and cramped, and more than long enough for him to begin to think about
all the possible things that could go wrong with the plan. . . .

Footsteps.

They stiffened as one, and he held his breath, listening. Someone *was*
coming this way; someone with the slow, heavy gait of the middle-aged—
someone wearing men's boots—

Someone who saw no need to carry a candle; someone who knew there
would be light and a fire waiting in here.

The door opened; closed again. Before them was the back of a large,
powerful man. Kestrel struck, like his falcon-namesake.

Sheer youth and desperation gave him the reflexes to overwhelm a man
who had fought for most of his life; he had a knife across his uncle's
throat in a heartbeat, and Talaysen was right behind him. As the older
man whirled, his first instinct to throw his attacker off, he found himself
facing the point of one of his guard's swords in the hands of someone he
didn't recognize.

"I wouldn't shout if I were you," Talaysen whispered quietly. "Between
us, Sional and I can take out your throat before you could utter a single
sound."

The man's eyes widened at Sional's name, and the blood drained from
his face, leaving it pasty and white. His eyes went dead, and Talaysen
sensed that he expected to die in the next few moments.

That, and the family resemblance to Sional, convinced him that they
had the right man. That had been a possibility he hadn't mentioned to
anyone—that someone else might be caught in their little trap.

"So, King Rolend, what have you got to say for yourself?" he continued,
cruelly—*knowing* that he was being cruel, but with the memory of Kestrel's own frightened face in the back of his mind. "And what do you
have to say to your nephew?"

The man was brave, he had to give him that much. As Sional relaxed
his grip a little, and Talaysen transferred the tip of his sword to the base
of Rolend's throat and backed him up against the desk so that Sional
could come to stand beside him, Rolend didn't beg, didn't plead. His eyes
went to Sional, then back to Talaysen.

"Who are you with?" he said, harshly. "Whose pay are you in?"

Talaysen shook his head slightly. "That wasn't what I expected to hear,"
he chided. "You've been sending killers after this young man for years.
Don't you think an explanation is in order?"

"Before I die, you mean?" Rolend drew himself up with as much dignity
as a man with a sword at his throat could muster. "I did what I thought
I had to do for the good of the country."

"For the good of the country—or for your own good?" Rune asked, challengingly, coming up behind Talaysen, her own knife in her hand. "They're not the same, and don't try to pretend they are."

The King's eyes widened in surprise, and he opened his mouth, as if to shout—

But nothing came out, and Talaysen heard Gwyna humming behind him. "Robin's got him silenced," Rune said, not taking her eyes off Rolend. She raised her chin with that defiant look Talaysen recognized from the past. "You can whisper if you want, King, but it won't do you any good to call for help."

His eyes were now as round as coins, and his lips formed a single word. "Magic—"

"Y-y-you ought to kn-know, Uncle," Kestrel said bitterly. "Y-you s-set it on m-m-me enough!"

He moved closer, and strangely, Talaysen saw tears in his eyes.

"Wh-why, uncle?" he whispered in anguish. "Wh-why? I n-n-never d-d-did anything t-to you! V-V-Victor w-w-was th-the only f-f-friend I h-had, b-besides M-Master D-Darian!"

The young man's obvious anguish got through to Rolend as nothing else had. "I thought—I thought—you'd hate me—"

Rune was humming, and Talaysen recognized the "trust me" spell. So far the plan they'd made had fallen in place—to find Rolend alone, and somehow convince him, with the aid of magic if need be—to leave Kestrel in peace. But would it work? He sensed the King fighting the spell—and a man with a strong will could get himself clear of it.

Then a gleam of silver on the King's wrist suddenly caught his attention, and he remembered that the elf they had spoken with had mentioned something about the non-humans of Birnam now being under a sort of royal protection.

He held up his wrist to show the elven bracelet there, and once again, the King's eyes went round in surprise. The surprise at seeing the elven token made his resistance falter. "You asked me whose pay I was in," he said fiercely. "No—*not* the elves. And not the Church's, nor the Bardic Guild, nor the men you cast down out of power. And Sional is *not* here as my puppet! We—*we* are here beside him because he is our friend, for no more reason than that."

"We are under the protection of the High King of the elves," Rune said, breaking off her humming, and showing her own elven token. "Think on that a moment—think what that might mean if you harmed us—and *listen* to your nephew."

"I d-d-don't want th-the d-d-damned th-throne!" Sional hissed. "I d-d-don't w-want the c-c-crown! M-my F-Father w-w-was a d-d-damned f-f-*fool*, and y-y-you're a h-h-hundred *times* th-th-the King he w-w-was! W-w-will you c-c-call off y-your hounds? I j-just w-w-want t-t-to b-be left *alone*!"

"I can't do that—" the King faltered. "You know I can't. I can't let you go free—the moment someone discovers that you're alive—"

He's weakening. We have him off-balance, and he's weakening.

"Wait—" Talaysen said, and held up the bracelet again. "Remember this. Remember that we are mages. We could have killed you; we didn't.

If we say we know of a way to take Sional out of the game completely, will you believe us and at least listen?"

The King nodded, slowly, and Talaysen took a chance and lowered the sword. Rolend sagged back against his desk, then made his way to the chair behind it, and collapsed into its embrace.

"L-listen to me, Uncle," Sional said. "I'm n-not a r-ruler. D-d-do you th-think for a m-minute that p-people w-would r-r-respect a m-man wh-who s-sounds l-like I d-d-do?" He laughed, a sound with no humor in it. "N-not even a Ch-church m-mage c-could m-make p-people b-believe I'm anyth-thing other th-than a s-s-simpleton!"

"Well—" Rolend looked uncertain.

"I've b-b-been a b-beggar, a th-thief, a sh-shit-s-s-sweeper. Th-think *those* are g-g-good qu-qualific-c-cations f-f-for a K-King?"

"I—"

Rune was humming again; since Kestrel seemed to have the situation well in hand, stutter and all, Talaysen joined her. The King had stopped resisting the spell—now if they could just get it to take—

"B-but I've s-s-seen wh-what y-you've d-d-done. I've b-b-been one of th-the p-p-people. Th-they'd r-rather a g-g-good ruler th-than a fool. T-tomorrow m-morning, y-you and I c-c-can g-g-go stand on F-Father's d-d-damned b-balcony and I'll r-r-renounce th-the throne." He took a deep breath. "As I am. S-s-stutter and all. S-s-so p-p-people c-can s-see I'm n-n-not s-s-some g-g-gilded p-prince out of a b-b-b-ballad."

The King was capitulating; Talaysen felt it. So did Sional. "L-let me g-g-go g-get V-V-Victor," he urged. "We c-c-can *all* t-t-talk about it. Even Aunt Fe-Fe-Fe—"

"No—please," Rolend said, closing his eyes and putting his hand to his head. "Not your Aunt Felice. She'll raise half the palace, and then she'll take you off and have you married to one of her ladies-in-waiting before the sun rose. Go get Victor; he's in the Rose Room." He looked each of the Bards in the eyes, in turn. "You're right. We should talk. Perhaps—"

Talaysen saw hope dawning in the King's eyes slowly, and the relief of seeing the end of a burden in sight.

"—perhaps we can make this work—"

Talaysen watched from the steps of the balcony over the Audience Square, standing with the other servants from the King's retinue, with one arm around Rune and one at Gwyna's waist. Sional was doing very well, though he doubted that anyone else was under that impression. The abdication ceremony took three times as long as expected, because of Sional's stutter. Enough witnesses were found to swear that this *was* the lost Prince to have convinced most people—and one of Rolend's mages clinched it by casting a spell over the young man that proved that hair known to have been Sional's had been his. As he had promised, he never changed from his rough working-man's garments, and if anyone had any notions of a romantic hero, he managed to crush them all.

Surely before he was through, a good portion of the people watching—and criers had gone through the city at dawn to ensure that the square was full—were going to be convinced he was a halfwit.

But how long will Rolend believe that he's no danger? That was the one doubt that kept nagging at him. While they remained, all would be well—but the spell they'd worked would fade in time—and then what? How long could they hope to keep Sional safe? Despite his earlier assurances, it was not easy to fake a death; would they have time to set up Kestrel's demise convincingly enough?

There were few cheers as Sional completed the ceremony, swearing on the holiest relics that could be found that neither he nor any of his progeny would ever return to claim the throne from Rolend and his heirs. But as Rolend and the Priest in charge of the ceremony turned to lead the way off the balcony, he stopped those few cheers with an upraised hand.

This wasn't in the plan! What was the boy up to?

"I kn-know that th-there are s-still p-people who w-won't believe m-my sw-sworn w-word," he said clearly, now looking down on the folk below, suddenly transformed from the bumpkin to something else entirely, despite the stutter. "S-s-so I'm g-going to m-make c-certain that n-no one c-can ever use m-me or m-mine ag-gainst my uncle."

He turned, ran down the stairs to the assembled servants, caught Gwyna's hand, and drew her up the stairs to the front of the balcony where everyone could see her. She looked around in confusion, not certain what he had in mind.

Rune squeezed Talaysen's hand in excitement, and he hugged her back. Was the boy about to do what she *thought*?

There were gasps from the people below, as they saw her in all her Gypsy finery. Gasps of outrage, mostly. Bad enough to have this bumpkin-prince on the royal balcony, but a Gypsy?

They were about to get an even bigger shock.

"G-Gwyna Kravelen, Free B-Bard, will you m-marry me?" he asked, his voice carrying clearly to the edge of the square.

The silence could have been cut and eaten.

"I—oh—I—" she stammered just as badly as *he* had, and Rune giggled.

"I'll t-take that for a yes," he said, and looked over her head at the Priest who had conducted the abdication ceremony. "Y-you've w-w-witnessed it, Father," he continued, and kissed her.

At that, Victor could no longer restrain himself. He was already half delirious at having his cousin back—and discovering that Sional *didn't* hate them. Now he lost every shred of dignity.

He gave a wild whoop of joy, threw his hat into the air, where it sailed up and landed on the roof—and threw his arms around the both of them.

Then the cheers began.

CHAPTER TWENTY-FIVE

"So, who's the happiest man in Birnam today?" Rune asked Talaysen, as they showered the mob of mixed Gypsy and servant children under the balcony with candy to keep them out of mischief.

"Kestrel?" Talaysen hazarded. She shook her head, and pitched sweets to some of the littlest who weren't getting any.

"Almost, but not quite," she told him. "He will be when he gets Robin out of here, but the celebrating is wearing thin. Weddings are really for women, anyway." She giggled. "I think the happiest *person*, not only in Birnam but in all of Alanda, is the Queen. She not only got to plan an entire wedding, she got to play mother to the groom *and* the bride!"

"The King?" Talaysen guessed. "No—probably not. When he offered to host this wedding he never guessed that every Gypsy within three kingdoms was going to descend on him." They both laughed, though Rune couldn't help but think he deserved at least that much anxiety, after all those years of pain that he'd given Kestrel. But there would be bills coming to the Palace for pilfered goods and stolen livestock for the next month at least. And stodgy little Birnam would never be the same again. They'd been invaded by an army of folk who had no ties but to the road, no responsibilities but to each other, and they had been set on their ears by the experience.

"It isn't me," the Bard said, after a moment.

"Really?" She raised an eyebrow at him. "You got what *you* wanted. Free Bards have exactly the same privileges as Guild Bards in Birnam—"

He nodded, and sighed. "But to get that, I had to agree to be Laurel Bard to the throne."

That had been to keep the Bardic Guild out of making mischief with the King's enemies. Now there would be an information network everywhere—the Free Bards and the Gypsies who remained—that the Church, the Guild, and the disgruntled Sires couldn't touch or even trace.

She *tsked* at him, and threw another handful of candy. "Poor Master Wren. Property, the title of Sire—I know people who'd kill for that—"

"I had that all and gave it up," he reminded her. "Never mind. We can go scandalize Birnam some more, and build a Free Bard school in the manor—how does that sound?"

"Good," she told him contentedly. "But you still haven't answered my question."

"I give up," he said, and popped a candy in her mouth.

"Victor," she said, tucking it into her cheek.

"Why Victor?" That answer had clearly surprised him.

"First—he got his cousin back. Second—his mother got to have a wedding, and *he* didn't have to get married. She'll probably leave him alone for a few more months. Third—the King isn't a child-killing ogre anymore, and I don't think he's in any danger of making that grave a moral decision again—and last, but by no means least—Prince Victor has been *very* popular with our Gypsy friends." She laughed at the look on his face. "He's their favorite *gejo* at the moment. He has gotten *quite* an education, I promise you! Frankly, I'm surprised he can walk of a morning!"

"So that's why he's—" Talaysen broke off what he was going to say, much to her disappointment. "Look—here comes the wagon!"

A brand new and beautifully painted wagon, the King's wedding gift to the happy couple, driven by Raven and drawn by two glossy black mares, clattered across the cobblestones of the courtyard. Nightingale balanced on the top, scattering coppers to all sides, which had the effect of sending the children out of harm's way, shrieking with delight.

Raven pulled them up smartly, and just below the balcony, the great doors flew open. Kestrel and Robin, dressed head-to-toe in the Gypsy finery in which—to the utter scandal of the court—they had been wedded, ran hand-in-hand out onto the cobblestones. Raven jumped down off the driver's bench as Nightingale slid from the top. Raven handed Gwyna up, holding her long enough for a hearty kiss, then turned the reins over to Kestrel.

Kestrel jumped up onto the driver's bench and took his place beside Gwyna. He had proved to be a good driver, with Raven to tutor him, and the mares responded to his touch on the reins promptly. As he got the spirited mares turned, the thunder of hooves rang out from the entrance to the courtyard.

A flood of of Gypsy riders poured in, each one trying to outdo the other in stunt-riding.

They swirled around the wagon, and as Kestrel cracked the whip above the horses' heads, they surrounded it, whooping at the tops of their lungs.

And just as the entire equipage started to pull out, escort and all, another rider appeared at the far side of the courtyard, from the direction of the royal stables.

He let out a wild war-cry that caught even the Gypsies' attention, and plunged towards them.

"Is that—*Victor*?" Talaysen said, incredulously.

It was. Dressed—not quite in wild Gypsy regalia, but certainly in the brightest gear his closet had to offer. He spurred his horse towards the wedding cortege with another wild cry, circled the group three times, and cried, "Come *on*! The road won't wait forever!"

He pounded off towards the courtyard gate, the clear leader of the pack, with the rest of the mob streaming along behind him, wagon in their midst.

The stunned silence that filled the courtyard was more eloquent than words. Finally Talaysen shook his head.

"Poor Birnam," he sighed. "Poor, stiff-necked Birnam. We've unmade their King, turned their Princes into Gypsies, their lands into a haven for ne'er-do-well vagabonds, elves, and Free Bards, and stolen the power from their Bardic Guild. What's left?"

"Oh," she said, thinking of a little secret she had just shared with

Gwyna. *He'll find out about it in a month or two. I think he'll like being a father.* "I'll think of something. Trust me."

"And you'll probably manage to surprise me as much as we've surprised Birnam," he chuckled.

She just smiled, and waved to the vanishing Gypsies.

Book II
~The~
Robin and
the Kestrel

Dedicated to
Dr. Paul Welch, and the other
avian veterinarians who keep
the namesakes of our Free Bards
wild and tame, alive and well.

CHAPTER ONE

Jonny Brede—aka "Free Bard Kestrel"—shook mud and cold, cold water out of his eyes. He grunted as he heaved another shovelful of soft mud from beneath the wheel of their foundered travel-wagon. And the hole immediately filled up with water. This was *not* how a honeymoon was supposed to be conducted. Not in a blinding downpour, with more mud on him than even this flood of rain could wash away. Not with their wagon stuck in a pothole the size of Birnam. What happened to "and they lived happily ever after?"

It's stuck at the end of tales in stupid Guild ballads, that's what happened to it. Real people get stuck in potholes, not platitudes.

Jonny Brede grinned at that, in spite of the miserable situation; it had a good ring to it. A nice turn of phrase. He'd have to tell Robin; she could store it away in her capacious memory and put it in a song some time. She was the one with a talent for lyrics, not he. They hadn't been out of Birnam for more than a week when she'd already crafted a song about the two of them, "The Gypsy Prince." "If I don't, someone else will," she reasoned, "and if it isn't Rune or Talaysen, they'll probably get it all wrong. Never trust your story to someone else."

Well, she had a point. Though he simply could not think of himself as "Sional," much less as "Prince Sional"—not anymore.

Not when the "Prince" was in command of no more than himself, two mares, and a shovel. Better "Jonny," or better yet, "Free Bard Kestrel."

He shoveled a little more muddy gravel under the wheel of their caravan-wagon and took a cautious peek at his bride of a few scant weeks through a curtain of rain. The last time he'd looked at her, she'd been giving the wagon a glare as black as the thunderclouds overhead. She'd been standing to one side of their patient, sturdy, ebony mares, fists on her hips, gaudy clothing pasted to her body by the rain, with her ebony hair flattened down on her head and her lips moving silently. He did not think she was praying. The look on her face had boded ill for the King's road crew, if she ever discovered who had permitted this enormous pothole to form and fill with soft, sucking mud.

Her temper did not seem to have improved in the past few moments. She held the bridles of their two well-muscled horses and murmured encouraging things into their ears, but the scowl on her face belied her soft words. Hopefully her temper would cool before she actually needed to find a target for her anger other than the storm itself. Robin had a formidable temper when it was aroused.

Kestrel sighed, and stamped down on the gravel to make it sink into the mud and hopefully pack down. *He* was happy, despite being soaked to the skin, cold and muddy. Their horses had shied at a lightning strike, running off onto the verge of the road and now their wagon was mired at the side of the road. So what? It was not an insurmountable problem. The wagon had not been hit, their horses had not broken legs, neither of *them* were hurt. It was just a matter of hauling the thing out themselves, or waiting until someone came along who could help them.

So what? He wasn't going to let a little accident upset his cheerful mood. In fact, he thought he had never been so happy before in all his life. Certainly not during his best-forgotten childhood.

He shoveled in another load of gravel, which splashed into the yellow mud and sank. *Prince Sional, huh. Oh, it's a great thing to be a Prince, when your father sticks you in a so-called palace that's half derelict, with one servant to care for a child, an invalid Queen to do all the char work, and deal with leaky roofs and cracks in the walls. It's a great thing to be royal, when your kingly father trots you out only for special occasions when a live son is useful. It's a fine thing to be a Prince, when you've got snow on your satin bedspread in the winter, leaks onto your head in the summer, and the servants at the Crown Palace eat better than you do. When your only friend is a Guild Bard who should have retired a hundred years ago . . .*

He'd been ignored by his wastrel father, who was too busy debauching himself to pay attention to his son *or* his land, and willfully neglected by his father's underlings. The only thing good in that childhood had been his mother and tutor, a Guild Bard of Birnam, one Master Darian, who had been father, mother, and mentor to him. Master Darian had taught him about honor and about care. And within his own specialty, first the love of music, then the means of making it.

Kestrel's eyes misted over and a tear or two joined the rain on his cheeks. *Darian, my good Darian, faithful one. Oh, Master, I wish you could see me now. I think you'd be pleased. You always said it was the music that should be important, and the skill of those who played it. I think you'd like Robin. I know you'd like Talaysen.*

King Charlis' royal chickens had come home to roost with a vengeance. When he had wrung his land near-dry to support his self-indulgence, some of his subjects could bear no more. One, Charlis' own brother, was willing to act on their desperation. He staged an uprising; flooded the palace with his own men, and killed his brother, taking the throne for himself.

Now, at long last, Kestrel knew why his uncle had taken those drastic steps. And he knew now what neither he nor Darian had known then; that Rolend had no intention of harming his nephew, and that the orders that night had been to stay away from the Dowager Palace. Then in the morning, after the situation had been resolved, Rolend had planned to bring Sional to the Crown Palace to be installed with his cousin and his cousin's tutors.

Whether he would have given me preference for the throne over Victor—well, that hardly matters. He wasn't going to kill a child.

But Sional had been snooping, as a young boy would, in places he shouldn't have been; he had seen his father's assassination and the beginning of the uprising, and had run to his tutor in terror. Old Darian, not knowing any of the plans afoot, had assumed the worst, and had smuggled them both out of the palace, out of the city, and out of Birnam through the terrible fens between Birnam and Rayden.

As a Guild Bard from Birnam the old man was given a certain respect, even though he had been in the scant train of the Queen until she died, then had chosen to live in obscurity as Sional's tutor for her sake. But the Guild in Rayden was not minded to see any prize places go to some outsider, and Jonny and his ailing mentor had been shuffled off to the Guild Hall at Kingsford and left to rot.

Kestrel wiped away a couple more tears; of anger this time, at the arrogant bastards who'd politely jeered at the brave old man, and had accounted his stories of revolt and assassins to be a senile fool's meanderings. They had never questioned the boy that Darian called "Jonny Brede."

I was sick with marsh-fever. And they wouldn't have believed me, anyway. The marsh-fever had taken his memory and left him thinking he was no more than a peasant boy that Darian had chosen for his apprentice despite the "obvious unsuitability" of the boy; either the fever or the trauma of flight had also left him with a stutter he still suffered.

He scrubbed the back of his hand across his mouth and tasted grime and dilute salt. *Damn them. Darian should have been covered with honors, and what did they do? They stuck him in the worst room in the Guild Hall, a room they wouldn't even put a servant in, and left him to die. If it hadn't been for me, he would have died within a week. He was too old and too tired to flee across two countries with a sick boy.*

He had to keep reminding himself that it was all in the past. Otherwise he'd get too angry about things he couldn't change. That was what Master Wren kept telling him, and he was right.

He shoveled in another load of gravel, packing it down savagely. Oh, that was what everyone told him, but *forgetting,* now—that was the hard part.

The Guild had a lot to answer for. When Master Darian died, it was their own law that he be found a new Master. He was, after all, a full apprentice, and had anyone been watching out for his rights, he would have gotten that new Master. But no one wanted to be bothered with a stuttering apprentice—and one who was a "legacy," chosen by a Bard from another kingdom, at that. There would be no grateful parents sending gifts as there would have been if he had been born well-off. There would be no gifts from the boy to the Master who had discovered him, if and when he achieved fame, for that Master was Darian. There was no one to insist that the boy's rights be observed, for that troublemaker, Master Talaysen, had vanished after tossing all his honors into the face of the Guild Master.

In short, there was no profit in taking the boy, and it would mean a great deal of wasted time trying to train him out of the stutter.

So the Guild Master and his chosen cronies told him he was feeble-minded, a half-wit; told the same tale to anyone who looked the least bit curious. Then they had thrown him out into the street with only the clothes on his back and those few personal possessions he still had, denied his rights to a new Master, denied even the old harp his Master had left when he died.

Something Talaysen had said made him smile in spite of his anger. "The irony is, they trained *plenty* of half-wits in there, and they are still doing so. It doesn't take wits to play without any sense of the music. Half-wits are conscious only of form and style, not content—and form and style are all the Guild cares about."

If I'd had that harp, I could at least have made some kind of living as a street-busker. That had been the worst of it; he had no skills, and he was too old to find another Apprenticeship in a trade. *If I'd had the harp, I would have found the Free Bards earlier—or they would have found me, the way they found Rune. They'd have told me I wasn't worthless. . . .*

Still, there was no point in dwelling on *that.*

No, he certainly had no pleasure in looking back at *those* years. Nor at the ones that followed; with no harp to play to make a living, and no way of ever getting one, he had been forced to look for whatever work he could find as an unskilled laborer. He worked himself to the bone in the worst of conditions, stealing when there was no work.

That was when his life had truly fallen to pieces. His uncle, King Rolend, had gotten wind of the fact that he was still alive. The King's own grasp on the throne was as shaky as his predecessor's had been; he could not afford a pretender to it, however young. And a young boy, had anyone *known* what he was, would have been easy to manipulate. There were plenty of people in Birnam who would have been very pleased to get their hands on a figurehead for a counter-rebellion.

So King Rolend had made the cruelest decision of his life. To have seeking-talismans made, and send out hired killers bearing them, to find Sional, now only fifteen or sixteen, and kill him.

Since Sional had no inkling of who and what he was, this was even crueler than it seemed. He was now caught in the heart of a senseless nightmare. Hired killers were after him, and he had no notion *why.* Their mere existence made it impossible for him to accept a permanent job even when one was offered, for he dared not stay in one place for too long.

He shook rainwater out of his eyes, and glanced over to his beloved Robin again. She had that knack for dealing with animals that all Gypsies seemed to have; the mares were listening to her and had calmed considerably.

Flickering light overhead made him cock his head to look at the sky. An area of clouds just above him lightened again, and a distant mumble of thunder followed the light.

Good. All the lightning was up in the clouds. *May it stay there.* This was a bad place to be caught by lightning, here in an area of road lined by oaks. Oak trees seemed to attract lightning, for some reason, and several of the huge trunks nearby bore mute testament to that.

He had done all he could for this wheel. He moved to the other, and started in again, his thoughts returning to the past. *If anyone wanted to devise a hell for someone,* he thought, packing the gravel as far in under the wheel as he could, *it would surely have been a life like mine!* Able to find only the most menial of work, watching over one's shoulder for the mysterious killers—and not knowing why they pursued, much less how to get rid of them!

He had taken a job as a goat-driver, a job that brought him to the edge of the Downs and the little town of Karsdown. What he had not known

was that this late in the season, there would be no further work in Karsdown for an unskilled laborer. He found himself trapped in a tiny sheep-
herding town with no work in it, without enough money to buy himself
provisions to get to someplace else, and without the woods-knowledge
needed to live off the land. He had been desperate; desperate enough to
try to pick the pocket of a tall man with graying red hair, who appeared
to have enough coin that he would not miss a copper or two. His target
was a man he had not then known was a Bard, since he was not carrying
an instrument, nor wearing the Guild colors of purple and silver or gold.
He had tried to pick the pocket of one known both as "Master Wren"
and—by a chosen few—as the great Free Bard Master Talaysen. Wren
was the same man who had fled acclaim and soft living to form the loose
organization known as the "Free Bards"—but before he had done that,
he had won Guild Mastery as well, under the far-famed name of Master
Gwydain. The songs and music of Gwydain were famed in every kingdom—though the songs and music of Free Bard Talaysen bid fair to
eclipse that fame.

Funny—Wren outshines even himself!

All *he* had known at the time was that the man was accompanied by
two young and attractive women, and to Jonny's eyes was spending a great
deal of money. He had assumed that the man was—well—their "honey-
papa," as the shepherds would say, an older man who bought young ladies
nice things and received most particular and personal attentions from
them in return.

That he had been mistaken was his good fortune rather than his bad,
for that was when his streak of horrible luck finally broke. Talaysen had
caught him, but had not sought to punish, but to *help* him. The young
women had been his wife, the Free Bard Rune, and a Gypsy Free Bard
named Gwyna, but far more often referred to as "Robin."

Kestrel grinned at *that* memory. Robin had first loaded him down with
all her packages to carry, without so much as a "by-your-leave," and then
had marched him off to get a bath in the stream and had made it very
clear that either *he* would bathe, or *she* would bathe him. And her expression had told him wordlessly that if she did the bathing, it would be
thorough, but not pleasant. He opted to scrub himself down, and change
into some old clothing of Rune's rather than his own rags.

*Amazing how much better being clean for the first time in months can
make you feel. And* she *certainly thought I cleaned up well enough.*

He stole another glance at her, and it seemed to him as if she looked
a trifle less angry. Perhaps talking to the horses had calmed her. He hoped
so; there was no reason to be angry, after all. Even though the pothole
seemed to be the size of Birnam, the wagon that was stuck in it was *theirs,*
the horses that drew it were *theirs,* and it all was a gift of his uncle—

The same uncle who had tried to kill him, true, but King Rolend wasn't
trying to kill him anymore.

He grinned again. Poor Uncle Rolend! He had been no match for the
wits of Talaysen, the magic of the Gypsies, and the determination of his
three new friends to see him *out* of the mess!

One of the Elves who'd come to his wedding, one of those who were allies of both Talaysen and King Rolend, had told him that it was no accident, his being in Karsdown at the same time as the other three. "Your Bardic magery was awakening," the Elf had said, with lofty off-handedness. "It called to them, as theirs called to you. If you had not met then, you would have met soon."

He rubbed his nose, uneasily. He wasn't altogether certain about this "Bardic Magic" business. It was easy enough for Wren to be blithe about it; *he* was a Master twice over, in the Guild Bards and the Free Bards, and a nobleman to boot. *He* was used to power of all sorts. Kestrel was far from comfortable with the idea that he could influence people and events just by thinking and singing. . . .

Well, right now that hardly mattered. No magic, Bardic or otherwise, was going to get this wagon out of the muck. It was going to take nothing more esoteric than muscle of man and beast.

But was that really why Talaysen had so readily "adopted" him? Master Wren said not, no matter what the Elf said. "All it took was to hear you play," the Bard had said, simply. "I knew you were one of us, and that we had an obligation to help you."

He grinned, through the rain dripping down his back, and in spite of the aches in his muscles. To hear that, from the one he admired most in the world—

I wouldn't have blamed him if he'd gotten rid of me that night in Ralenvale when the killers caught up with me. . . .

Though no one had been hurt except the killers themselves, it had been a terror-filled night, both for Kestrel, who had hoped to escape his pursuers, and the Gypsies they had camped with.

But before that, he had been having the time of his life, for the Gypsies treated him as one of their own, and made him feel at home with them. That was when Jonny had earned his Bardic nickname of "Kestrel" from the Gypsies; he had said, in disgust, that his stutter made him sound like a kestrel. The Gypsies had seized upon that and promptly dubbed him "Free Bard Kestrel." They'd included him in their music, their dancing— and never once teased him about the way he sounded when he talked.

Then the attack had come. One of the assassins had died, challenging a magical trap set by the Gypsy mage, Peregrine. The rest had fled when their weapons missed their target.

I thought for certain when they realized how much trouble I was bringing to them that they would tell me to make my own way. But instead, Wren had decreed his lost past must be plumbed—to find out why he was the target of such attacks, so that something could be done to prevent or evade them.

Peregrine had performed the magic that unlocked Kestrel's lost memories, and *then* "Jonny Brede" learned who and what he really was. It had been a shock to all of them, but it had been Talaysen who decreed they must go to the source of those memories, to discover the truth of the matter, and what, if anything, they should do about that truth.

From the first, *he* had never really entertained fantasies of being the "lost Prince" returned to reclaim his throne—or not for long, anyway. He wasn't certain what the others had in their minds. But the further into

Birnam they got, and the more questions they had asked, the more the truth about the current and past King emerged, although they had more questions on the whole than they had answers. So, at last, they had taken the risky chance of summoning Elves to answer what had become a series of vital questions.

And the answers the Elf gave them had not been in keeping with any fantasy of "lost Princes." Kestrel's father Charlis had indeed, even by Elven standards, been a terrible King; he had wasted the resources of his land on his own pleasure, and had taken no thought to truly governing it. King Rolend had acted in part to keep his brother from destroying his own lands and people with his greed. Rolend was the very opposite of his brother, and had, through sacrifice and hard work, brought Birnam back into prosperity.

The obvious question then was why had such an apparently good and honorable man been sending killers to rid himself of a child?

The Elves had an answer to that as well, for they were privy to Rolend's counsels and many of his secrets; Rolend believed that the King's concern lay with all the peoples of his realm, and not just those who were human.

Rolend, they said, had learned that the Prince had survived his flight into Rayden and had become more and more nervous, as the boy grew older, that one day someone might use the Prince as a front in an attempt to regain the throne. He was, after all, the "rightful" heir to his father. And there were plenty of folk who had profited when Charlis sat the throne, who now were not profiting in the reign of his honest brother. These folk, a mixture of dishonest Priests of the Church, discontented Dukes and Sires who had enjoyed considerable autonomy in their own holdings under Charlis, and the Birnam Bardic Guild who had lined their pockets with Birnam's gold, would have been overjoyed to have a figurehead to use for a counter-rebellion, particularly one as romantic as a "lost Prince." *Most* particularly, one who could be manipulated, as a young, and presumably naive, child could be.

So King Rolend had gritted his teeth and sent assassins, armed with tokens that would lead them to the Prince.

He would never feel safe until "Prince Sional" had been taken out of the picture, permanently.

Intellectually—well, I could understand that. Kestrel stood for a moment to ease his cramping shoulders, then went back to his work. *And now that I've met with Uncle—all I can say is, I'm glad things worked out this way. The trouble with Uncle Rolend is that he is very good at convincing himself that he is doing something for the best possible reason. It's awfully easy for someone like that to think that the end justifies the means.*

Kestrel did not *want* the throne; he knew, deep in his heart, that he was a good musician, but would make a terrible King. He knew nothing of governance outside of the little gleaned from a few ballads, which was hardly the best source of information.

Oh, Rune would have made a better King than me!

The only way to stop the assassins, short of dying or taking the throne, was to find a way to renounce his heritage. So, with the help of Talaysen,

Rune, and the Gypsy named Robin whom he had come to love, he had taken himself out of the picture. Permanently.

A midnight incursion into the palace was in order; they held Rolend "hostage" briefly while they explained themselves and worked a little Bardic magic to make him *believe* what they were saying. That was followed by a sunrise abdication—a very public abdication—on Kestrel's part.

And then Kestrel sealed his "unsuitability" by publicly proposing marriage to a Gypsy . . . and being accepted.

The corners of his mouth turned up in a smile he could not repress. The look on her face when he had proposed!

It probably matched the look on mine when she accepted.

No King could ever wed a commoner; the Dukes, Barons, and Sires would never permit it. No nobleman could *ever* wed a Gypsy; by doing so he had rendered not only himself, but all his future offspring, completely ineligible for the throne of Birnam. By that single action he had ensured his safety and that of those with him, no matter how suspicious his uncle might become.

So here they were, riding off to make their way in the world as "mere" Free Bards in a gypsy caravan complete to the last detail and as luxurious in its appointments as it could be and not attract robbers and brigands—

Well, we were "riding" up to an hour ago, anyway.

—the wagon itself a gift of his uncle, who had been only too obviously relieved to see the last of him.

With Talaysen and Rune now safely installed as Rolend's court Bards, and Talaysen actually appointed Laurel Bard to the throne, hopefully Rolend's fears would *stay* safely buried.

But Kestrel had always preferred to hedge his hopes with defenses. *A man who fears shadows can sometimes manufacture enemies, as Gwyna's people say.*

Besides, there had been no point in courting trouble or giving King Rolend any cause for more sleepless nights. The best way to show him that "Prince Sional" was dead and *not* lamented, was to keep as far from Birnam as possible.

Not exactly a hardship, to keep his distance from one little pocket-kingdom when he had all the wonders of Alanda to roam in. He had always been fascinated, even as a very tiny child, by the stories about all the myriad races and cultures of this strange and patchwork world. Now he had the chance to see them firsthand. *All* of them, or at least as many as he could in a single lifetime.

I am far more likely to thank my uncle than hold a grudge against him. This time he didn't bother to hold back the grin. *He is stuck on that stupid block of a throne for the rest of his life, and he will never move more than twenty leagues from his own castle. He will never see the Mintaks and their step-pyramids, the canal-streets of the Loo'oo'alains, the walled fortress-city of the Deliambrens! Why, he probably won't even go under the Elven Hills with the Elves in his own little kingdom!*

Birnam had never been a home to him; in fact, he had never really known a home, nor did he have a clear recollection of a time when he had owned more than he could carry in a thin rucksack on his back. A luxurious wagon was home enough for him! And the road was all the country he needed. Besides, now he need no longer watch his back for the mysterious men who had kept trying to murder him.

His grin widened. Altogether, this was a *wonderful* life, mud, stuck wagon, and all!

"What *are* you grinning about?"

Robin came around the side of the wagon, and scraped a draggle of wet hair out of her eyes as she spoke. Jonny seized her wrist and pulled her over to him, giving her a muddy hug and a passionate kiss, both of which she returned with such interest that he began to think he might steam himself dry in her arms. He let go with reluctance.

"I'm g-g-grinning at th-this!" he said, waving his hand at the wagon, the horses, themselves. "I m-m-mean, think ab-b-bout it! We may be s-s-stuck, but we c-c-can just unhitch th-th-the horses and g-g-get inside if w-w-we want! Th-th-there's nothing s-s-stopping us, if w-w-we d-decide to g-g-give up for a little. It's *ours*. Y-y-you s-s-see?"

She nodded, finally, and a ghost of a smile appeared as her frown of worry faded. "You know, you're right. We don't have to be anywhere. We've got anything a Gypsy could ever want, we *can* get out of the wet if we get tired of trying to fish this thing out of the mud, and the horses will survive a soaking."

He nodded vigorously. "You s-s-see? We aren't even b-b-blocking the r-r-road! W-w-we can w-w-wait unt-t-til someone c-c-comes along who c-c-can give us a h-h-hand! And if anything is b-b-broken, w-we have the m-money to f-f-fix it! Th-th-that's m-m-more than I've ever been able to say b-b-before!" He lowered his eyelids suggestively. "Th-th-there's lots of w-w-ways to get w-w-warm."

Now she grinned right along with him, and tossed her head to get her wet hair out of her eyes. "True," she agreed. "But I would like to think I'd at least tried to get this thing out of the muck before we give up and go inside. The horses are ready any time you are." Her smile turned wistful. "I don't think either of us thought we'd be spending part of our honeymoon trying to boost a wagon out of a pothole."

"A m-m-muddy p-p-pothole," he said, ruefully, looking at the state of his clothing. Impossible now to tell what color it had been, as mud-soaked as it was.

She shrugged, and put her shoulder to the other wheel. "Still, I'll keep telling myself that it is our wagon. We have options I never had before. A year ago I'd have been huddling under a rock overhang if I was lucky, or trying to stay warm under a fallen log if I was not."

He bent to his wheel and she whistled to the horses, who strained forward in their harnesses while the two of them pushed the wagon from behind.

Indeed. This was *their* beautiful, if mud-splashed, wagon. They were safely in Rayden again, and on their way out, after which dear Uncle would have no clue as to where they might have gone. And shoving away at his side was the loveliest—if muddiest—lady he had ever known in all his life. And she had picked *him*.

All right, I'm prejudiced, he admitted, as the wagon rocked a little in place, but otherwise refused to move. *But I'm also not blind, and I think I've seen enough lovely ladies to know true beauty when I spot it!*

After several attempts, the wagon was not budging, the horses were straining, and the rain showed no signs of abating. Robin panted, bending over with her hands braced against her knees, her wet hair dangling down. Kestrel massaged his hands and again tried to see if anything was obviously wrong.

He was beginning to think that there might be something broken or jammed; this wagon had axles built into the body to protect them. A good idea, but it made it difficult to judge what might have gone wrong without the tedious business of taking off the bottom plate.

He sighed, and Robin turned her head and caught his eye.

"Are you s-s-sorry you d-d-didn't get the K-K-King of B-B-Birnam after all?" he asked, ruefully. "You w-w-wouldn't be standing in the m-m-mud if you had."

But Robin only grinned, her good nature restored by the exertion. "Powers forfend!" she replied. "The King of Birnam would be fair useless getting this blasted wheel out of the mud! Let's try that notion of yours, of heaving up and trying to shore up the wheel while it's up."

It had been a faint hope more than an idea, but if Robin wanted to try it he was game.

"You d-d-do the c-c-counting," he said, with a self-deprecating laugh. "If I d-d-do, we'll b-b-be here all d-d-day!"

CHAPTER TWO

Gwyna shoved little bits of wood under the wheel, using a larger piece to protect her hands in case the wagon slipped back. *Damn the rain. Always comes at the worse possible time.* A rain-soaked lock of hair fell down across her nose in a tangled curl again, and she didn't have the hand to spare to push it out of the way. It tickled, and it got in the way of her vision.

It was hard to stay cheerful when you were dripping wet, your hair was snarled and soaked, and there was mud everywhere the rain didn't wash it away. But there was Kestrel, laboring manfully beside her, for all his slight build, and *he* wasn't complaining. Poor thing, he wasn't much taller than she, nor much more muscled, though regular feeding had put a *little* more weight on him. He still inspired women to want to take him home and feed him pastries and milk.

And then feed him something else entirely, girl, she told herself, and grinned, in spite of the cold rain dripping down her back and the certain knowledge that at the moment she looked more like a drowned kitten than a seductress. Well, he was *hers*. The others would simply have to look and wish.

Even soaking wet and muddied to his ears, he was a handsome piece, though he hadn't a clue that he was, bless his heart. Long, dark hair, as dark as a Gypsy's, now plastered to his head, but luxuriant and wavy when it was dry, set off his thin, gentle face with its huge, innocent dark eyes and prominent cheekbones—definitely a face to set maidens' hearts a-flutter. And when you added in the promise in the sensual mouth and clever hands, well, it set the hearts of no-longer-maidens aflutter, too. And he looked fine, very fine, in the flamboyant colors and garments favored by the Gypsies. He did most of his "speaking," when he could, with eloquent gestures and with his eyes. Right now, they held a cheer that not even their dismal situation could quench. And relief that once again, she had affirmed that she would rather have Kestrel the Free Bard than all the Kings in the Twenty Kingdoms.

And what would I do with a King, if I had one? Thank you, no. She was nothing if not practical. *A King has all of his duties, and little time for pleasure, if he is a good King. I should see him for perhaps an hour or two in the day. I have my Kestrel with me as much as I like.*

The horses stamped restively; she went up to the front of the wagon to reassure them. Thank the Lady that King Rolend had the sense to fling gold at Gypsy Raven with which to outfit a wagon and buy horses for it, rather than trusting such a task to his own stablemen. Not that the King's stablemen were unfit to choose horses, but a pair of pampered highbloods would be ill-suited for tramping the roads in all weathers. No, these mares were as sturdy as they were lovely; two generations out of the wild horses of the Long Downs, and crossbred to Kelpan warmbloods for looks and stamina. Truly a wedding present fit for a Prince, for all that he was Prince no more. A Prince of the road, then.

Why would she ever trade a life bound to one place for her free life on the road, anyway? She'd had a dislike for being tied to one spot *before* her unfortunate encounter with the dark-mage Priest, an encounter that left her with a horror of cages and being caged; now she was positively phobic about the notion.

Kestrel did not know about that, beyond the bare bones, that a renegade Priest-mage had turned her into a bird and caged her. He did not know how she had refused the Priest's demand she be his mistress, and that he had not only turned her into a bird, he had turned her into a bird too heavy to fly! He'd put her in a cage just barely large enough to hold her, and had displayed her by day for all the Kingsford Faire to see as his possession, and by night to the guests at his dinners.

Only the intervention of Rune and Talaysen had freed her; only Talaysen's acquaintance with a decent mage-Priest had enabled them to break the spell making her a bird. It had then rebounded upon its caster, who was still, for all *she* knew, languishing in the same cage he had built for her, in the guise of the ugliest and biggest black bird she had ever seen.

But ever since, the thought of staying in one place for too long brought up images of bars and cages. . . .

No, thank you. No Kings for me! No matter how luxurious, a cage is still a cage.

The horses calmed, she went back to her task of shoving wood wedges under the wheel. Trying to, at any rate. It was awfully hard to tell if she was getting anywhere at all; the mud was only getting worse, not better, as the rain continued to pound them.

" 'Ware!" Kestrel warned her with a single word; he could usually manage single words without stuttering. She snatched her hands and board out of the way, called to the horses, and the wagon settled as Kestrel and the mares let it down.

He closed his eyes and sagged against the back of the wagon. She appraised him carefully, trying to measure with her eyes just how exhausted he was, how strained his muscles. *We can't manage too many more of these attempts,* she decided. *He hasn't got them in him, and neither do I.*

She thanked her Lady that he was *not,* like so many men she knew, inclined to overextend himself in the hope of somehow impressing her. That sort of behavior didn't impress her and it inevitably led to the man in question hurting himself and *then* pretending he was not hurt!

Kestrel, on the other hand, was naive enough about women to take what she said at face value—and bright enough not to do something stupid just for the sake of impressing her.

And I am just contrary enough to say precisely what I mean, so all is well. She had to shake her head at herself as she admitted that. *I would not have him change for the world and all that is in it. I am no easy creature to live with. He would not change me, either. So he says, and so I believe.*

She leaned against the wagon, and tried to knot her wet hair at the nape of her neck, but little strands kept escaping and straggling into her eyes. She gave it up as a hopeless cause.

This naivete of his was something to be cherished—if that was precisely the right thing to call it. Perhaps it was simply that he had no one to teach him that women were anything other than *persons.* Truly, he had no one to teach him that women were *anything*!

After all, his childhood was spent with that old Master of his, and not even a female servant about—and the rest of his time was spent trying to earn enough to keep fed and running to save his life.

For whatever reason, he was one of the few men she knew, Free Bards and Gypsies included, who simply *assumed* that she was his partner—his equal in most things, his superior in some, his inferior in others. She had met a few men who were *willing to accept* her as a partner, but Kestrel was only one of three who simply *assumed* the status, and the other two were Raven and Peregrine. There was a difference, subtle, but very real to her, between that *acceptance* and *assumption.* It was a distinction that made a world of difference to her.

He never asked her to prove anything; he simply assumed that if she claimed she could do something, it was true. When she said she could not, he worked with her to find a way around the problem. When he knew how to do something, he asked her opinion before he simply *did* it—and she gave him the same courtesy.

Like this situation that they found themselves in now; neither of them knew a great deal about wagons, at least of this type, and neither of them were large and muscular. Without any arguing, they had each tried the other's suggestions, and when things didn't work, they simply went on to try something else.

Oh, they had arguments; everyone did. But when it counted, they were partners. Arguments were for times of leisure!

In a peculiar way, even standing in the pouring rain, wet and miserable, cold and besmeared with muck, was a wonderful and rare experience. It proved something to her that she had hoped for all along; that she was his friend, companion, the person he trusted, as well as his lover. She could count the number of couples who could say that on one hand, and have fingers left over.

"Ready?" she asked, when it looked as if he had recovered as much as he was going to. He nodded tiredly.

"C-c-can't d-d-do this m-m-much l-longer," he said, simply. "I'm ab-b-bout gone."

"So am I," she admitted. "And so are the mares. But let's give it what we have, yes?"

He nodded. She counted. On *four*, she shouted to the horses, and they all strained to the limit.

Nothing happened. Just as nothing had really happened all the times before, no matter what they had tried.

"'Ware!" she shouted, and they both let go as the horses slacked the harness. The wagon did not even move a great deal as it settled back.

Her good temper finally broke under the strain. She clenched fists and jaw, and glared at the wagon, the pothole, the mud that now reached halfway to the wheel-hub. "Damn," she swore under her breath, as she backed off and stared at the cursed thing. "Stupid, stubborn, blasted, demon-possessed pile of *junk*!" It was pretty obvious that there was nothing they were able to do alone that was going to free the wheels. They were *not* going to get it out, and everything they did now that it *was* obvious was a wasted effort.

She muttered a few Gypsy curses at the wheels under her breath for good measure. Kestrel just pulled the hair out of his eyes and leaned back so that the rain washed the mud from his face. After a few moments with his mouth open, drinking the fresh rain, he lowered his head and looked at her apologetically, as if he thought that *he* was somehow responsible for the situation.

"It's really s-s-stuck, isn't it?"

She nodded and, in a burst of fading annoyance, kicked the wheel.

As she had *known* it would, this accomplished nothing except to hurt her toe a little.

"Damn," she swore again, but with no real vehemence; she was too tired. Then she sighed. "It's really, really stuck. Or else something is broken. Let's get the horses under whatever cover we can, and try and dry off before we catch something."

As if to underscore the triumph of nature over the hand of man, the skies *truly* opened up, sluicing them with rain that seemed somehow *much* colder than the downpour that had already drenched them.

◊   ◊   ◊

The horses cooperated, but their harness didn't; stiff leather, soaked with water and heavy, met cold stiff fingers. It took so long to unharness the mares that Robin's temper was well on the way to boiling by the time they had the two sodden beasts hobbled under the scant shelter of a low tree, wrapped in woolen horse-blankets.

They did *not* tether the team under an oak. And they did spread a canopy of canvas over the branches above, giving each beast a nose bag of grain to make up for their sad excuse for stabling.

Robin and Kestrel finally took shelter in the wagon, involuntarily bringing at least four or five buckets of rain in with them through the open door. By then, they were so cold that Robin despaired of ever feeling warm again. The charcoal stove in the wagon took time to heat up; that made it safer in a wooden wagon, but it meant it took a while to make any difference. In the meantime, they huddled in blankets that didn't seem to help very much even though they were dry.

Robin stared at the tiny stove, willing it to get warmer. The rain showed absolutely no sign of stopping; she'd had a forlorn hope that once *they* gave up, the rain might, too. She'd even seen a patch of blue to the east, but it had closed up again before it had ever fulfilled its promise.

She and Jonny were too far from any village to walk to shelter, even assuming they would be willing to leave the horses, the wagon and everything in it. Neither of them were, of course. She didn't know if the mares were broken to saddle; if they weren't, trying to ride them would probably end in someone getting dumped on his head.

Besides, only a fool would walk or ride off and leave everything he owned unprotected. She pulled the blanket closer around her shoulders, and shivered. Rain pounded the wooden roof, making it very hard to hear anyone who wasn't shouting.

If I can just get warm again, this could be pleasant. . . .

Oh, the frustration that a little prosperity could bring! And the unexpected discomforts!

The more you have, the more you have to lose, and the less willing you are to let go of it.

Back when she was on her own, traveling afoot, burdened only by her pack and her instruments, she would never have found herself in such a fix. It seemed so long ago that she had been so footloose, and yet it was no more than a few months ago! Hard to believe that this was the first really *bad* rain of late fall—and she had begun journeying with Lark and Wren at the very end of summer. They didn't even meet Jonny until the first of the Harvest Faires.

If I was still alone, I would be sitting beside a warm fire right now—

Her conscience, which had a better memory than the part of her that controlled wishful thinking, sneered at her and her pretensions. A warm fire? Maybe. *If* she had been clever enough to read the weather signs and *if* she had been lucky enough to get a place at an inn. And even *if* she met both those conditions, there was no guarantee that the fire would be a warm one, and she would probably not be sitting right beside it, but rather off to one side. The paying customers got the flame; more often than not, the entertainers had to make do with the crackle.

Anyway, it would be under a solid roof—

Solid? Maybe. Maybe not. Her conscience called up a long litany of leaking roofs, inns without shutters, stinking little hovels without *windows,* dirt-floored, bug-infested places with only a hole in the center of the roof to let the smoke from the fire in the middle of the room escape. Which it mostly didn't. . . .

Maybe, if she hadn't even found that kind of scant shelter, not a roof at all.

In fact, if she hadn't been clever or lucky, she *could* be shivering in the so-called "protection" of her travel-tent right now, a lot colder and wetter than she was, or even be huddled under a bush somewhere. The wagon was solid, the fire was their own, and they were entitled to the flame and the crackle, once the stove warmed up.

If it ever does.

But memory did supply some honest memories of sitting on the clean hearth of a good, clear fire, in a good quality inn; sipping a mug of spiced cider or even wine, listening to the rain drum on the roof while she tuned her lute. In fact, she had spent whole seasons in such venues, the valued fixture of the tap room who brought in custom from all around.

Will this stove never heat up?

"Th-they s-say a w-w-watched p-pot never b-boils," Kestrel said, his voice muffled under his blanket. "D-do w-watched s-s-stoves n-never heat?"

"I'm beginning to think so," she replied. "I—"

"Hello the wagon! Having trouble?"

The clear tenor voice from outside carried right over the drumming of the rain on the roof. She was out of her blanket and had poked her head out of the door at the rear of the wagon before Kestrel could even uncurl from his "nest." That voice was more than welcome, it sounded familiar!

Another vehicle had pulled up on the road beside them, a wagon much, much larger than theirs. So large, in fact, that it probably had to keep to the major roads entirely, for the minor ones would not be wide enough for it. As it was, there was just barely room for a farm-cart to pass alongside of it. Anything larger would have to go off to the side of the road and wait.

It had tall sides, as tall as a house, and rather than wood, it was made of gray, matte-finished metal. It had glass windows, *real glass,* covered on the inside by shutters. Below the windows were hatches, perhaps leading to storage boxes. It was drawn by four huge horses, the like of which Robin had only seen when the Sires held one of their silly tournaments and encased themselves in metal shells to bash each other senseless.

As if they weren't already senseless to begin with.

The huge beasts stood with heads patiently bowed to the wind and weather, rich red coats turned to a dull brown by the rain, white socks splattered with mud, "feathers" matted. They were beautiful beasts, but she did not envy their driver, for they would eat hugely and be horribly expensive to keep. That was why only the Sires could afford such beasts, although their great strength would be very useful to any farmer. Then again, anyone who could afford a rig like *this* would have no trouble affording the feed for these four huge horses.

Their little Gypsy caravan would easily fit inside this colossus, with room for two or three more.

The driver sat in sheltered comfort inside a porch-like affair on the front, enclosed on the left and right, roofed and floored. He leaned out around the side, just as she tried to make out who or what he was—and as soon as he saw her, his face was lit by a mixture of surprise and delight.

"Old Owl!" she exclaimed, jumping from the back of the wagon to the ground. "By our Lady, I can't think of anyone I'd rather see more!"

Kestrel poked his head out of the door of the wagon just in time to hear Robin address the driver of an utterly amazing vehicle as "Old Owl."

Both made his eyes widen. The wagon was like *nothing* he had ever seen before in his life. It seemed as alien to this road and forest as a coronet on a rabbit. The driver was as astonishing as his wagon, and he certainly saw why Robin—and presumably the other Free Bards—would call him by that name.

He looked *quite* owllike, although he was more human than a Mintak or a Gazner—but much less so than an Elf. While Kestrel stared, the driver grinned down at them both, perfectly protected from the rain by the roof over the driver's box. Kestrel simply gaped at him, unashamed, since he didn't seem to mind.

"Welladay, I can think of places and times I'd *rather* see you in, other than mired in a morass, Gypsy Robin," the driver replied cheerfully, cocking his head to one side. "I suppose now I shall *have* to get you out. If I don't, you'll write some kind of nasty little ditty about me and I shall never be able to show my face in polite company again."

"I?" Robin made innocent eyes at him, and pretended shock. "Why should I do anything like that?"

"Because you are the Gypsy Robin, and no male, human or not, escapes your charm without regretting it." The strange being bowed from the waist, and winked at Kestrel. "Give me a moment to change and I will be down beside you."

Robin snorted, and shook her head. To Kestrel's bemusement, Gwyna was now as cheerful as if their wagon was safely on the road and the sun was shining overhead. What magic did this man have to make her suddenly so certain he would be able to fix all their problems? "Still a clothes-horse, now as ever! Your wardrobe, no doubt, is the reason for the size of your wagon!"

"How not?" he countered. "Why not?" and disappeared inside.

Kestrel blinked. "Old Owl"—whoever and whatever he was, had been one of the oddest attractive creatures he had ever seen. His face and body—what Kestrel had seen of the body, anyway—had been fairly human. But that was where the similarity ended. He had long, flowing, pale hair growing along his cheekbones, giving his face the masklike appearance of an ancient owl. These were not whiskers or a beard; this was hair, as fine and silky as the shoulder-length hair on his head, and it blended into that hair on either side of his face. To complete the image of an owl-mask, his eyebrows were enormous, as long as Kestrel's thumb, and wing-shaped.

The hair on his head had been cut in some way that made parts of it stand straight up, while parts of it lay flat, all of it forming a fountainlike shape. It gave the man's head a fantastical appearance, and his clothing—

Well, what Kestrel had seen of it, left him dazzled and astonished, and quite, quite speechless. It had certainly rivaled anything he'd seen on any Gypsy; not only was it brightly and brilliantly colored and cut in fantastic folds and draperies with flowing sleeves and a capelike arrangement at the shoulders, but parts of it gleamed with a distinctly metallic sheen, and some had the look of water, and still other parts were as iridescent as an insect wing.

No wonder he had not wanted the mud to spoil it!

First and foremost—who *was* this person, this "Old Owl"? And what was he to Robin? "Wh-wh—" Jonny began.

"Who is that?" Robin asked, turning around to give him a lopsided grin. She waded back to the wagon through ankle-deep mud. "Well, we call him 'Lord' Harperus, or 'Old Owl' since he is something of an honorary Free Bard, he's pulled so many of us out of fixes like this one. No one knows if he's really entitled to the 'Lord' part, but he has piles and piles of money, as much as any Sire, so everyone calls him 'Lord.' He's a Deliambren."

A Deliambren! Kestrel blinked, and his interest sharpened considerably. The Deliambrens were top of the list of beings Kestrel had always wanted to see. They were reputed to be wizardly mechanics, building clockwork creations that could do almost any task. You found their constructions in the homes of the wealthiest of the Barons and Dukes, and the palaces of Kings. Very few Sires could afford the handiwork of Deliambrens, and very few merchants, even Guild Masters. Those who *could* afford them boasted about it.

The Deliambrens knew how to make magical lights that illuminated without creating heat or needing any oil to fuel them. They created boxes that produced music, melody after melody, fifty tunes or more without repetition, boxes no bigger than a wine cask. It was even said they could build wagons that did not need horses to pull them, and conveyances that could fly!

They lived, so Kestrel had been told by his tutor, in a place called "Bendjin." It was a "Free Republic," whatever the hell *that* was; there were no Kings, Sires, Dukes, or anything else there, he'd been told. How they were governed, he had no notion; it sounded completely chaotic to him.

And that was all he knew of them, other than the fact that they had something so complicated it was akin to magic that they used to create their toys. And the toys answered to anyone, mage or not.

"I've n-n-never s-s-seen a D-Deliamb-b-bren," he managed to get out. "D-d-do they all l-l-look l-like th-that?"

Robin laughed, and reached up and hugged him. "Old Owl is not the only one you'll see on the road, and that is just about the only place you ever will see them," she told him, all her good cheer back, now that the stranger had offered his help. "Unless you earn an invitation to Bendjin, that is. They don't make very many of those, so don't get your hopes up. I don't know if they all look *quite* like that, but they are all pretty flamboyant. We call him *Old* Owl because Erdric back at Kingsford is an Owl too, but Harperus is his senior by a century or so."

Kestrel tried not to goggle at that. "*How* old is he?"

She shook her head, as the rain slacked off a little. "I don't exactly know," she replied, after a moment of thought. "Wren said he was at least a hundred years old, and guessed from records and stories that he might be as old as two hundred. That was the best guess he had, but Wren said he couldn't be sure."

He hopped down off the back of the wagon to join her; she gave him a flirtatious kiss. "We'd better get things ready so when he comes out, all he has to do is use our chains to pull us out." Kestrel nodded, and waded through the mud beside her. They were already so wet and mired that a little more wouldn't matter.

"I've been inside Bendjin," she offered, as they got the tow-chains out of the box on the back of the wagon where they were kept safe from rusting in an oiled bag. "Once, when I was very small. They brought in my Clan to entertain for a festival of some kind. I don't think they let anyone but Free Bards and Gypsies inside the walls; I don't think they trust anyone else." She chuckled. "I suppose they know we have no reason to covet their powers, since no Gypsy would ever own anything he couldn't repair himself in a pinch, and no Free Bard would care about anything other than making music."

"W-was it l-like they s-say?" he asked, fascinated by the mere idea of being inside the Deliambrens' mysterious fortress-city.

Robin took her end of the chains and fastened them carefully to the loops built into the frame of the wagon before she answered. "I wasn't very old, but it was rather amazing, even to a child. It was quite dazzling, that's all I can tell you," she said reminiscently, as he copied her movements with the chains on his side. "Lights; that's what I mostly remember. Lights everywhere. Not candles or lamps or anything of that sort. They have lights outside that glow when darkness falls, and little light-globes inside that light up and grow dark again at the touch of a finger. All the colors of lights that you can possibly imagine. They do have wagons that move by themselves, without horses. And they have boat-shaped things that fly. I only saw the little ones; Old Owl told me there were bigger ones that they use for their special trading missions outside Bendjin, and some even bigger ones that they only use once in a while, because they kind of break down a lot."

Kestrel grimaced. He couldn't imagine anything involving a Deliambren *breaking down*—

"I wish I could describe what I saw for you," she concluded, with a little shrug of apology, "but I was only five or six years old. I don't remember much more than that. Oh, I do recall one other thing; they had some pet birds that were just as flamboyant as their costumes, birds that sat on your shoulder and talked! I played with one for hours, and I really wanted one, but Old Owl told me that they just couldn't stand cold, and it would die in the first winter."

"I'll f-f-find you one th-that w-w-won't," Kestrel promised, and was rewarded with a smile. A warm and lovely smile, that said, *You understand.* And he did. He truly did.

Besides, it was not all that difficult a promise to fulfill. With all of the creatures of Alanda, surely there was a bird like that somewhere. . . .

"Well!" said Harperus, popping his head out of the door of his vehicle. "Are you ready?"

"I think so, unless you want to come down here and look things over first," Robin called up to him.

He nodded; that amazing hair was all tucked under a shiny hood, the hood of a coat made of the same shiny blue material. Water slid right off it without soaking in, as if it were made of bright metal like the wagon itself. "Good idea. I probably know a bit more about wagons than you do, little one. Unless you've studied them since I saw you last, or this young man is an expert—?"

Kestrel shook his head, not trusting his voice. He would surely stutter, and look a fool.

Robin laughed. "This 'young man' is my *vanderlan,* Old Curiosity."

"You? *Vanderie?*" Harperus seemed as delighted as he was surprised, which was something of a relief to Kestrel. "It must be a true-love match then, for *you* would never settle for less! My felicitations and blessings, my children! Not that you need either, from me, or anyone else—"

He leapt down to the ground with remarkable agility for someone who was a hundred years old—

Or maybe two hundred!

He held out his hand to Kestrel, who took it and shook it gingerly. Then Harperus kissed Gwyna chastely on one cheek. "And that is all you shall get from me, you young minx!" he said, when she pouted. "Forget your flirtations, please! I have no wish to make your young man jealous or he will begin to look daggers at me!"

When Kestrel grinned shyly, and managed, "R-R-Robin c-can t-t-take c-c-care of hers-s-self," the Deliambren laughed with pure delight.

"I see you have yourself a wise partner, pretty bird," Harperus said with approval. "Now, let me have a look at this bit of a predicament—"

He continued talking as he peered under the wagon, then extracted an object from his coat and did *something* around the axle. Flashes of light came from beneath, and Kestrel wondered what he could be doing under there. . . .

"Are you new to the Free Bards, youngster?" he asked Kestrel, his voice emerging from beneath the wagon as if from the bottom of a well. "I don't recall anyone mentioning someone of your description before—"

Now Kestrel was in a quandary; he wanted desperately to talk to this man—but he was afraid that his stutter would make him sound like a fool.

But then Harperus cocked his head just enough so that he could look out and Kestrel could see one intelligent eye peering up at him. The color of that eye was odd—not quite brown, not quite yellow. A metallic gold, perhaps, with the soft patina of very old metal. "Take it slowly, lad, and take your time in answering. I'm in no great hurry, and you mustn't be ashamed if you have a trifle of trouble speaking. Plenty of intelligent people do; it is often because they are so intelligent that their thoughts run far ahead of their mouths. Simply work with one word at a time, as if you were composing a lyric aloud."

Kestrel was momentarily speechless, but this time with gratitude. "I— have only b-been w-w-with the F-F-Free B-Bards since f-first H-Harvest F-F-Faire."

"We found him, Wren and Lark and I, I mean," Gwyna put in. She gave Kestrel an inquiring glance; he nodded vigorously, much relieved that she wished to tell their story. Better she tell the tale. If he tried, they'd be here all day.

She summed up the entire mad story in a few succinct sentences. Harperus made exclamations from time to time, sounds that were muffled by the fact that he was halfway under the wagon by now. Finally he emerged, amazingly mud-free and dry.

"Fascinating," he said, eying Jonny as if he meant it. "Absolutely fascinating. I must hear more of this, and in detail! I must have a record of all this—it could be very significant in the next few years."

Robin laughed at him. "You and your *datas*," she mock-scolded. "That's all you people are interested in!"

"*Data*," he corrected mildly. "The singular is the same as the plural. It is *data*."

"Whatever," she replied. "You Deliambrens are the worst old maids I ever saw! You can't ever hear a story without wanting *every single detail* of it! Like sharp-nosed old biddies with nothing more on your minds than gossip!"

To Kestrel's surprise, Harperus did not take any offense at Gwyna's words. "It is all information, my dear child," he told her. "And information is yet another thing that we collect, analyze, and sell. Somewhere, sometime, there will be someone who will want to know about this story, for there will be all manner of rumors and wild versions of it before the winter is over. And we will tell him, for a price. And he will trust *our* version, for he will know it to be composed of nothing but the facts. Facts are what we sell, among other things."

"Just so long as you don't sell him who we are and *where* we are," Robin replied sharply, suddenly suspicious. "Those same people could be more interested in using Jonny than in *facts*, my friend. You people—"

"You know better than that," he said, with immense dignity. "Now, however, is not the time to discuss the ethics of information-selling. Firstly, it is very wet—"

"Tell me something I *don't* know!" Robin exclaimed, tossing her sodden hair impatiently.

"—and secondly, I have some bad news concerning your wagon. I fear you have cracked the axle." He *tsk*ed, and shook his head as Robin winced and Jonny bit off a groan. That was something they could not fix themselves; not without help, at any rate. "It is just as well that you could not budge it. You might have caused more damage. If you had attempted to drive on it, that would break it, within a league." He nodded, as Gwyna grimaced. "You must go somewhere there is a cartwright; I do not have the equipment to fix a vehicle such as yours."

"I know where there's a cartwright, and it isn't that far from here but—" Robin began, biting her lip anxiously.

He brightened. "Ah! Well, then in that case, there is no true problem. I can get you out without further damage, and I can tow your wagon without breaking the axle."

Kestrel gaped at him. "How?" he gasped.

Harperus laughed. "Watch!" he said. "And see! Am I not a Deliambren? There will be wonders! Or at least"—he amended, with a sheepish smile—"there will be *winches.*"

CHAPTER THREE

There were, indeed, winches; just as Harperus promised. Or *a* winch, with a hook on the end of a cable, a winch that swung out from the back of Harperus' vehicle. Once Gwyna had an idea of what he intended, she made him wait while she extinguished the fire in the charcoal stove; there was no point in risking coals spilling and setting fire to the entire wagon. It was quite a powerful winch, although not at all magical, simply very well made. Harperus maneuvered his huge wagon so that the winch was as close to the back of their wagon as possible without the wheels of his vehicle leaving the firm roadbed. Then he unwound the cable, fastened the hook of his winch to the chains they already had in place, and enlisted the help of both Bards with the business-end of the winch.

It required hand-cranking; if there were any of the magical machines legend painted anywhere in or on the wagon, they were not in evidence. As the two Bards helped Harperus turn the capstan, the cable and chains slowly tightened; then, the rear rose with a wide and amusing variety of odd noises as the mud fought against releasing the wheels.

The mud was no match for Harperus' winch. Jonny was relieved at how relatively easy it was to crank it up by hand. He knew a little, a very little, about machinery. This winch must have some clever gearing to make it so easy to use.

As the wagon creaked and groaned, the wheels pulled free with a sucking sound, and rose above the muck. Blobs of thick mud plopped back into their parent pothole.

They didn't stop there. Harperus continued to winch the wagon higher, until the damaged rear was well above the roadbed. Jonny hoped that everything was stowed away properly in there. If it wasn't—well, there was no hope for it. It was going to be a mess inside, with things tumbled everywhere.

A small price to pay for getting out without losing the axle while moving. *That* would have caused more than a mess; they might have lost the whole wagon. They surely would have been injured, perhaps seriously, depending on how fast they would have been going when the axle broke.

The rain finally slacked off, and by the time Harperus was ready to actually haul their wagon up onto the road, it had thinned to a mere drizzle.

They fastened the halters of the mares to the front—now the rear—of their wagon, stowed the harness away in the exterior storage boxes under the driver's seat, but left the blankets on them, and put away the tarpaulin and nose bags. The mares didn't look unhappy about moving; they couldn't have been very comfortable in the rain and chill wind. Before too very long, everything was ready.

Harperus checked and double-checked everything, from the set of the hook to the lock on the winch, before he had convinced himself that all was as it should be. Then, with a self-satisfied grin, he handed them both up to the driver's bench on his wagon. Jonny admired the arrangement as he took his place; there was a clever set of steps built into the front of the wagon, and the front panel had a door set into it. Harperus took his place beside them, handling the reins of all four horses with the confidence of long practice.

He clucked to them and shook the reins. The four huge horses leaned forward into their harnesses, pulling with a will.

The wagon crawled forward; the wheels creaked and squealed, and more creaks and groans came from the Gypsy wagon behind them as Harperus sought to pull it free.

Sucking mud made obscene sounds that sent Robin into giggles. Kestrel leaned around the side of the driver's box and gazed anxiously back at their precious wagon.

But Harperus knew what he was doing. The wagon was fine; protesting, but fine. Inch by inch, bit by bit, Harperus pulled it free of the mud that had held them trapped for most of the day. As the front wheels rolled up onto the roadbed with a rumble and a crunch of gravel, Kestrel let out a sigh of relief, and pulled his head back in under the shelter of the roof.

Harperus regarded him with faint disappointment. "You doubted me!" he accused.

"N-not y-you," Kestrel protested. "I w-w-wasn't sure ab-b-bout *our* w-w-w-wagon!"

"Ah." Harperus beamed with the pleasure of accomplishment, then his expression changed to one of concern. "Oh, you two look near-frozen. And you're certainly soaked. There are blankets under the bench; wrap yourselves up in them before you catch something."

Kestrel was a little disappointed; he wanted, badly, to have a look inside the fascinating vehicle, and it would have been nice if Harperus had invited them to go inside to warm up. He sighed as he fished around under his seat with one hand until he encountered something soft that felt like cloth.

He pulled it out; it was a blanket, with no discernible weave, of a tan color nearly the same as all the mud. It seemed awfully light and thin to do any good, but it was better than nothing. Or so he thought, until he actually wrapped it around his shoulders and head.

Suddenly he was warmer; *much* warmer. And—was he getting drier, as well? It seemed so! He stared at Harperus in surprise; the Deliambren returned his look blandly.

Maybe all the wonders weren't inside the wagon after all!

He began examining the "driver's box" covertly, while pretending to watch the horses.

They were under as much shelter as most porches on a house provided. The driver's seat was well-padded and quite soft, covered with something that looked superficially like leather, but didn't feel quite like leather. And now that they were moving, there was a gentle stream of warm air coming from underneath it, drying his feet.

The box itself was quite spacious, with a great deal of room behind the driver's bench, more than had been apparent from the ground. There was quite enough room for all three of them on the bench, side-by-side, and there was enough room for a second bench behind the first. Maybe Harperus intended to put one in some day, for passengers who would rather not ride inside the wagon. . . .

Then he noticed something else; now that they were on the move, the horses did not seem to be leaning into their harness at all. In fact, on a closer look, he would have said, if he were asked, that they were guiding the wagon rather than pulling it. They certainly weren't straining in the least.

Could it be that the wagon propelled itself, and their presence was a deception?

It was certainly a very good possibility—

But his curiosity would have to go unappeased; he had no way of checking his supposition, and if Harperus did not want them to know something, then that was his business.

Still, that didn't help assuage his curiosity in the least.

The Deliambren was the first nonhuman being Kestrel had ever seen up close, with the exception of the Elves who had attended the wedding. There had been both a Mintak and a Gazner at King Rolend's palace, but they were ambassadors of some kind, and he had not wanted to approach them.

That had been more caution on his part; he could not have gone near them without causing new suspicions in his uncle's mind just when it had been settled.

He had been very, very careful how he looked and acted around Rolend's court. Why would he be talking to a foreign ambassador after he had renounced his title? Rolend would have immediately suspected he was intriguing. Perhaps plotting with nonhumans, looking for a way to get power again. Surely, that is how Rolend would have thought of it.

He had told himself that he had the rest of his life to talk to anyone he wanted. What would have been the point of creating trouble when eventually he would find other nonhumans to talk to freely?

He wanted to ask Lord Harperus thousands of questions. Harperus seemed amazingly approachable, and quite affable. Gwyna had closed her eyes and was settling back for a nap, so he wouldn't be interrupting anything *she* had planned. "Wh-what are y-y-you d-doing out here, L-L-Lord?" he asked, trying to frame each word carefully. Gwyna snuggled into his shoulder, and gave him a little smile and a nudge of encouragement.

"What is my reason for being on the road, do you mean?" Harperus replied, and chuckled, as Robin grimaced a little. "Collecting information. As your dear lady will tell you, we Deliambrens do an inordinate amount of that. This *is* a much more elaborate vehicle than I am wont to use, however, as I assume our Gypsy Robin has noted. I am also acting as an advance scout, of a kind, this time. My people will be embarking on a most ambitious project shortly, and I am establishing contacts for them, so that they will never lack for allies on the ground in the initial part of the journey."

"Ambitious project?" Robin said. "Just what do you mean by that?" She sounded suspicious again, and her eyes opened, but narrowed thoughtfully. "Are you planning something we Gypsies ought to know about?"

"Nothing sinister, my dear," Harperus replied soothingly. "In fact, it is something that your people will find useful, I think. We intend to make maps—maps of all of Alanda, eventually, and those, like the Gypsies, who assist us will get maps for their efforts. Road maps, terrain maps, population maps, resource maps—we intend to build something we call a 'data base,' so that if someone has an abundance of corn or copper, coal or pre-Cataclysm artifacts, we will be able to find a buyer for him."

"Which information you will no doubt give him for a price," Robin said dryly. But despite her heavy irony, she had relaxed again, and was braiding her hair.

"And, if he does not have the means to transport his product, or fears being cheated, we can act as broker," Harperus replied, just as blandly. "Why not? We also have an *honorable* intent, though you might not believe it, Gypsy Robin," he added. "We intend to see to it that those with superior forces do not take those resources that do not belong to them. I mean this," he finished, his voice suddenly without any hint of humor. "I am quite, quite serious about this. Before the Cataclysm, my people acted as a policing force among the stars. Presumably, the rest of them still do, somewhere. Now that we have stabilized our position and regained our mobility, our mission can be resumed, albeit on a smaller scale. It is, after all, in our interest to see that no culture is exploited. They are all potential customers, when all is said and done."

"Huh," Gwyna replied. "So now you're looking for more allies than just the Gypsies?"

"Allies on the ground, yes," Harperus replied. "We cannot do everything. We will need folk we can trust in or near every land we travel through, in case there are things we need, or repairs we need to make."

Allies on the ground? An interesting choice of words. Did they imply that this "project" would involve people traveling through the air? Were they going to bring one of those air-wagons Robin had described out into Alanda?

How much dared he ask, without becoming impolite?

Or worse; perceived as dangerous? Harperus had power, money, and resources he could not even dream of. It would be very foolish to make Harperus think he might be a threat of any kind.

"H-h-how long h-h-have you kn-known R-Robin?" he asked, instead of the questions he *wanted* to ask. Perhaps, after feeling the Deliambren out, he could ask them later.

"Oh, since she was very young," Harperus told him, turning to wink at him. The skin around the Deliambren's eyes crinkled when he smiled, and he pulled back the hood of his coat and shook his hair free. "I first met her when her Clan came to perform at the Four Worlds Festival. She was always getting into places she was not supposed to, and I was detailed to keep an eye on her."

"Me?" Gwyna exclaimed. "I never—" Then she began to cough, as if she had not intended to say anything.

"Most adventuresome was her foray into the upper reaches of the butterfly conservatory; I had no notion that a five-year-old could climb so high," Harperus continued as if he had not heard her protest. "Most interesting was when she decided that the fountain in Hazewood Square required fish, and began transporting them, in her bare hands, one at a time, from the view-ponds in the Aquarium nearby. Amazingly, they all survived the trip! It was quite a surprise to the fountain-keepers, however."

He turned to Gwyna, who was blushing furiously. "How *did* you catch them, anyway? I have never been able to figure that out."

"I tickled them," she said, in a small, choked voice.

"You tickled them." Harperus shook his head, and peered ahead through the curtain of rain. "Some sort of obscure Gypsy secret, I suppose." He turned back to Kestrel. "At any rate, I have been the 'adopted uncle' for any number of Gypsy youngsters, and she is one of them. Although I must admit that our dear Robin is one of my favorites."

Kestrel relaxed a trifle; if Robin had known him *that* long ago, then certainly he was not one of the odd creatures you heard about from time to time whose behavior was so bizarre you never knew whether they considered themselves your dearest friend or your worst enemy. "D-d-do you d-d-do m-much tr-traveling?" he asked.

"I would say that I am probably on the road for about half of the year," Harperus said, after a moment of thought. The wagon swayed slightly beneath them; nothing like the rough jouncing of their own little caravan. "Some of us enjoy traveling, trading, and gathering information, and those of us who do spend as much time out and about as we may. Usually we travel in wagons about the size of yours, and there is very little to distinguish it from a Gypsy caravan. Frankly, dear boy, I would *not* have taken this vehicle if it were not for two things, and one of them is that it can defend itself from an unpleasant visitor. It is far too conspicuous for my liking."

A little shiver ran down Kestrel's back at that. *It can defend itself. . . .* He could not even begin to imagine what that could imply. He did not want to find out at first hand. And he was very glad that Harperus did not consider them "unpleasant visitors."

"Have you made any good bargains lately?" Gwyna asked casually.

Harperus brightened at that, and began rattling off a number of trades that he considered to be something of a coup. A "laser imaging system" ("still functional, if you can believe it!") for a small glass-smelting furnace; a "complete cache of memory crystals" for an equal number of precious stones. Or rather, Kestrel assumed they were precious; Harperus referred to them as "cultured" pearls, rubies, and sapphires. Kestrel was not certain just what "cultured" meant. Perhaps they were better educated than other gems. Something else Harperus said made him feel a little better.

"You know, value lies in rarity, really," the Deliambren told Gwyna, when she raised her eyebrow and asked who had gotten the *real* bargain. "They were using the memory crystals for jewelry, and valued them no more than quartz. We simply gave them something better suited to display—and tripled *our* library. To us, memory crystals are rare. To them, our cultured stones are. Everyone benefits, and no one feels cheated. That is the essence of a good bargain."

Gwyna laughed and told him he would never make a horse-trader, and then settled back for a *real* nap against Kestrel's shoulder as the rain changed to a dismal drizzle. He held her with an arm around her shoulders, supporting her so that she could nap, as the unknown source of warmth beneath their seats dried them all and made her drowsy.

Harperus patiently waited through Kestrel's stuttering, and answered all of his questions, though Jonny could not tell just how much of what he said was evasion. Finally he turned the tables on the Free Bard and began his own series of questions.

Mostly, he concentrated on Kestrel's own story, and seemed particularly fascinated by the intervention of Rune and Talaysen and the latter's discovery of the power of Bardic Magic.

"I have often suspected something of the sort existed among you humans," Harperus said thoughtfully. "Particularly in light of some things I have seen Gypsy Bards do—calming crowds that were in an ugly mood, or charming coins out of the previously unwilling. Fascinating. And you have this power?"

"Wren s-s-says s-s-so," Kestrel replied, but with uncertainty. "And he says G-G-Gwyna does too. I th-think he's r-r-right. B-but I d-d-don't know if I w-w-w-want t-t-to use it s-s-since it c-can c-cause as m-much t-trouble as it s-solves."

Harperus nodded, his face very still and sober. "I can understand that— but you may be forced to. You should at least master this power before it masters you. Not learning to use it could be more hazardous than mastering it."

Jonny shook his head.

"If you do not learn how to control this 'magic,' it may act without your knowledge or control," Harperus amended. "Let me give you an example. Some peoples we have encountered have the power to read the thoughts of others—and if they do not learn how to do this at their will, it happens without control, and they can be overwhelmed by intruding thoughts so that they do not know who, where, or even *what* they are. Do you understand now?"

Kestrel nodded, then. And Harperus was right; if he did not learn how it "felt" to invoke this magic, he might use it when he didn't want to, and that could have some unfortunate consequences. Especially if he was using it on someone who had the ability to *tell* when magic was being used, and had a reason to resent it being used on him!

"If I may bring up a possibly delicate subject?" Harperus said, carefully. "Your—ah—difficulty in speaking?"

Kestrel flushed. "Wren th-thinks it's b-because of the f-f-fever I c-c-caught when w-w-we esc-c-caped B-B-Birnam."

Harperus shook his head. "I would think not. From all that I know, such a problem is more because of some kind of extreme upset in the past. Your escape, I would say, is itself to blame, and the fear and stress you went through. Not the fever. My people have been known to treat such things, and they are usually successful. May I offer some advice?"

Jonny nodded eagerly. Wren had some advice to give, but he had been no expert, and admitted it. No one else had anything to say on the subject. Robin didn't seem to care—but it would have been so wonderful to tell her all the things she deserved to hear without falling all over the words!

"As I said, this is sometimes the case of your mind running ahead of your words. First, you must learn to relax, and think about the *words*, not about what your listener is going to think when he hears you." Harperus smiled as he saw Jonny's eyes widen with surprise. "You see, some of this is also from tension. You wish to make a good impression, so you tense up. Your mind runs on ahead, and ceases to control your speech, so the tension makes you stammer. You stutter—you fear you are making a bad impression—you grow tenser—and you stutter more. You try to speak faster, to get your words out through the stuttering, and this makes you more tense, which makes it worse yet. If you relax, and take things at their own, slow pace, you will find your problem easing. Think of each word as a note in a melody, and pronounce it with the care you have in singing, and *do not think* about your listener. When you sing, what are you thinking of? The audience, or the song?"

"The s-s-song!" Kestrel replied in surprise. "I alw-w-ways r-relax when I s-sing!"

"And you do not stutter, I wager." Harperus shrugged. "This is how I would begin to overcome the difficulty. The rest is much, much patience. It will take a very long time, and you must not be discouraged. It took, perhaps, ten years to establish this pattern in you. It cannot be unlearned in a day, or a week, or even a year, necessarily. But you will improve, a very little, every time you speak, and people who have not heard you for some time will be astonished at what you think is no progress at all."

Kestrel bit his lip and stared at the ears of the nearest horse. He *wanted* a magical cure; for Harperus to touch his lips with a machine, and make the stutter go away.

But something that could take the stutter away might not keep it away. And understanding it might. . . .

He raised his eyes and stared at the road ahead, misty in the steadily falling rain, and followed the Deliambren's advice, concentrating on each word.

"Thank you, L-Lord Harperus," he managed, with a minimal stammer. "I will t-try your adv-vice."

"I hope that it works," Harperus replied earnestly. "And try to keep this in mind, every time you are tempted to hurry your words. It will take *longer* to get them out if you stammer than if you took your time with them. You are a good young man, and a bright one. You do not speak without much thought. A wise man will be willing to wait to hear your words, and you need not waste them on a fool."

He might have said more, except that at that moment there was a polite tap on the wall of the driving box behind them.

Kestrel's head snapped around, as the back of the box slid open. So *that* was how Harperus had gotten in and out of his wagon! And evidently Harperus was not alone on this "collecting" mission of his—

"Harperus," said a deep, resonant voice from the darkness beyond the open door, "I wonder if I might join you and your guests?" The opening was shrouded in shadow, and all Jonny saw was a vague, hump-backed shape in the darkness. But the voice sent a thrill of pleasure down his spine. It was a pure delight simply to hear it; a deep bass rich with controlled vibrato.

"Certainly, T'fyrr," the Deliambren replied immediately. "There are no xenophobes here. I'm sure my friends would welcome meeting you and your company."

"I am pleased to hear it," the voice replied, and the shapeless figure, who was shrouded in fabric, or an all-enveloping cloak, ducked its head and came out into the light.

It was *not* wearing a cloak.

As it carefully closed the door at the rear of the box behind it with one taloned hand, and folded down a hitherto-invisible seat from the side of the box, the "shrouding cloak" proved to be a set of wings, and the hood, head-feathers. Gwyna woke from her half sleep to glance at, and then stare at, Harperus' road companion; T'fyrr was nothing more or less than a *true* nonhuman, an enormous bird-man.

As the being arranged himself on the seat with a care to those folded wings and a tail that must have made most chairs impossible for him, Harperus made introductions. "T'fyrr, this is Gwyna, who is also called Robin. She is a Gypsy and a Free Bard, and I believe I have mentioned her before. This is her husband, Jonny, who is called Kestrel; he is also a Free Bard. As you know, T'fyrr, all Free Bards have trade-names, so that the Bardic Guild will never know precisely who they truly are. In public, you must call them 'Robin' and 'Kestrel.' My friends, this is T'fyrr."

The huge beak—quite obviously that of a raptor—gaped open in what was very likely T'fyrr's attempt at a smile. "I see from your expressions that you have never met one of my kind before this. You should not be surprised, since the Haspur do not travel much outside their own land, and few wish to venture into it. My land is very mountainous, and since we fly, we have not made such niceties as *roads* and *bridges*. This makes it difficult for the wingless—and thus, the harder to invade."

"So you keep it that way." Robin had recovered enough to show her sense of humor. "As a Gypsy, I approve. Our way to keep from being hunted and hounded is never to stay in one place for more than a day or two. The best defense is to let something besides yourself provide the 'weapons' and barriers."

"So we say. Much talk of weapons and dangers, but our world is not a kind one," T'fyrr said towards Harperus in what must have been a private joke. The avian had very little difficulty with human speech, despite his lack of lips, and Jonny was completely fascinated. How could something with that huge, stiff beak manage human words?

He watched closely as T'fyrr spoke. "Your t-t-tongue!" he blurted aloud, without thinking.

T'fyrr intuited what he meant with no difficulty, and laughed, a low, odd sort of caw. "It is very mobile, yes. A kind of finger, almost. This is a good thing, for I, like the two of you, am a singer of songs, and I am thus not limited to those of my own people."

"You're a Bard?" Gwyna exclaimed. "Do they have such things among your folk?"

"A kind of Bard, indeed, though I am far more like the Free Bards; we do not have anything like this 'Guild' Harperus has told me of." He made a clicking sound that expressed very real disapproval. "They seek to cage music, or so it would seem. I like them not. It is a pursuit for fools; a waste of intellect."

Gwyna grimaced. "We don't like them either. Free Bards don't believe in caging anything, music, people, or thoughts."

Within moments, the two of them were immersed in a deep discussion of freedom, thought, the politics of both, and other philosophical considerations, much to Harperus' amusement. Jonny was completely content with the situation, since it gave him the opportunity to study T'fyrr to his heart's content.

The only thing at all human about the bird-man was his voice and his stance; upright on two legs. He had just told them that the wings he bore on his back were entirely functional, and Jonny would have given a great deal to see him in flight. As large as he was, his wingspan must be very impressive.

He was as completely feathered as any bird Jonny had ever seen, from the top of his head to his "knees." His "hands" were modifications of his "feet"; both had sharp talons on fingers and toes, and scaled skin stretched over bone, with prominent thin, strong muscles beneath the skin. Those feet and hands were formidable weapons, Kestrel was quite certain—and he was just as certain that, in a pinch, T'fyrr would not hesitate to use his strong, sharp beak as a weapon as well.

T'fyrr's chest was very deep, much deeper than the chest of a human, and probably accounted for the resonance of his voice. In color he was a gray-brown, with touches of scarlet on the very edges of his wings and tail.

He wore "clothing" of a sort; a close-tailored wrapping that covered his torso without impeding the movement of any limbs or his wings and tail. It did not look very warm, and Jonny did not blame T'fyrr for staying in the shelter of the wagon until now. An odd, spicy scent came from his feathers—or perhaps, from his clothing—when he moved, very pleasant and aromatic.

But it was his voice that interested Jonny—as a musician. There were over- and under-tones to his speaking voice that made Jonny sure his singing voice would be incredibly rich. It would surely sound as if it were three people singing in close harmony rather than one.

"I am a folklorist," he said at last, when the discussion of philosophy ended in mutual agreement. "I am collecting songs, most particularly songs of what my people refer to as the 'outreach era,' when we first ventured outside of our borders after the Cataclysm. We have long known of the Deliambrens and in fact have traded with them for certain rarities. When it became obvious that to complete my quest for certain knowledge, I would have to go outside the Skytouching Mountains and the aeries of my people, I knew whom I must recruit to my efforts."

He nodded at Harperus, who chuckled and bowed. "I think it was a matter of mutual recruitment," Harperus said modestly. "After all, there are things even Deliambrens cannot do, and that is to fly without a machine. We are trading in skills. He originally pledged to aid me in return for Deliambren aid. When I asked if he would aid me now, he agreed. He is to scout by air for me; I am to help him continue his musical quest—"

"He and his people have a way of capturing music and sound and holding it. We had this ability before the Cataclysm, but we have lost the skill of making the devices, as well as the tooling," T'fyrr said, before Harperus could finish his sentence. "So there you have it. We aid each other, and we each have skills the other does not. I had been learning the songs I did not know from Harperus' collection; at about the time I had learned all that he had, he decided to go out on this collecting venture and asked if I would pay my debt by accompanying him. When I learned he would be visiting some of the lands where my songs originated, I agreed, of course."

Jonny was completely fascinated, and a bit dazzled. After years of *hearing* about exotic creatures and never meeting one, he had just encountered, not one, but *two* in the same day!

So, while Gwyna engaged both Harperus and T'fyrr in yet another discussion, this time concerning politics, he simply sat quietly and watched and listened with every nerve.

Gwyna was charmed by Kestrel's open fascination with both Lord Harperus and T'fyrr, although she did not share it—or at least, not to the same extent. She had been around nonhumans all of her life, after all. Her Clan had often been asked to perform by Harperus, and there were any number of talented linguists in her family, so they were often requested as translators wherever they went. While she had never seen a bird-man before, and she was intrigued by the sheer novelty of such a creature, the novelty wore off fairly quickly. She was far more interested in what Harperus and his companion had seen and heard so far on this trip.

And in the philosophies of an avian race, which to her seemed very complimentary to the Gypsy way of life.

Harperus' wagon astounded and intrigued her far more than either Harperus or his friend. She didn't often lust after anything material, but she had the feeling that the more she saw of this wonderful conveyance, the more she would want it.

For one thing, it was quite obvious to anyone who knew horses that this thing was propelling itself. The horses were only there for guidance. And she had not missed the fact that Harperus had disconnected some esoteric device *before* he had asked for their help in winding up the winch. If she and Kestrel had not been present, he probably would not have used that capstan at all. Doors appeared in walls that seemed solid, seats could be folded down out of nowhere. The wagon itself had glass windows, with metal sides that obviously required neither painting nor maintenance. What a time-saver that would be! There was none of the jouncing around associated with their vehicle, and she rather doubted that Harperus would ever suffer the inconvenience of a broken wheel or a cracked axle. The heated air coming up beneath their seat must be coming from somewhere, and only gave a hint of how comfortable the interior of this vehicle must be. She already knew about the Deliambrens' "magical" heating and lighting, and she could not imagine Harperus doing without either.

And Harperus' little dropped comment about how the wagon could "defend itself"—

There must be wonder upon wonder inside this vehicle, and she wanted to see the inside, badly.

And yet, if she did—she would *have* to try to calculate just how much it would take to get the Deliambrens to part with enough of their precious "technology" to give her something like the luxurious appointments in this thing. And she had the horrible suspicion that it would require selling herself, Jonny, and any children unto the ninth generation into virtual slavery to acquire it.

But wouldn't they thank you for it every time they woke in warmth or cool comfort?

Maybe if she saved Harperus' life, or something . . .

Even as part of her was thinking these thoughts, the rest was aghast. How could she *want* anything that badly? Wasn't she a Gypsy and a Free Bard? How could she even think about becoming tied down to anything or anyone for the sake of a mere possession?

But—! that interior voice of greed wailed.

To get her mind off that greedy little inner self, she turned the subject to politics. The Deliambrens always wanted to hear about politics, for politics affected trade, and trade was a large part of their life.

And there were serious changes occurring, changes that seemed minor and subtle, but could build to devastating results.

"It isn't just the Bardic Guild, though it's the worst of the lot. What Talaysen thinks is that the Guilds are trying to get as much power as the Dukes," she said, after describing some of the troubles the Bardic Guild had been causing for the Free Bards. "And the High King seems to be letting them get away with it."

Harperus looked troubled. "I fear that is because the High King has lost interest in governing the lesser Kings," he said, after a moment. "There is much unrest among the Twenty Kings, and more still among the nobles. Many of them have gone back to feuding, quarrels which would have been strictly squashed a few years ago. There is something amiss in the High King's court."

"What is worse, to my mind, is that the Guild and the Church seem to be working together to cause problems for anyone who does not agree to the rules of the Guild and Church," Gwyna said. "And the High King is letting them get away with this."

"But the twenty human Kingdoms are but a small part of Alanda," T'fyrr objected, flipping his wings impatiently. "They are insignificant in scale! Surely, Harperus, you concern yourself too much with them—"

"They are a small part, it is true, but they are strategically placed," Harperus pointed out. "If there is war among them, as there was in the days before the High King, they can effectively cut us off from many things that we need."

"And as you have often pointed out to me, humans breed like rabbits," Gwyna interjected with some sarcasm. "They may only be the Twenty Kingdoms, but they have spread out to occupy a great deal more territory than they held originally. We aren't a peaceful species, Harperus. And I don't care *how* superior your weapons are, my friend, enough bodies with spears and swords can take over that precious Fortress City of yours, either by treachery or by siege. While they may not have the stomach for losses that great, they can certainly lock you inside that Fortress for ever and aye."

"That had not escaped our notice," was all Harperus said. But though his tone of voice was mild, she detected an edge to it. "This is the other of the reasons why I was willing to take this particular vehicle. I can leave small devices now that can collect more information without the need for human agents. I fear that we will have need of such information."

Gwyna sighed. "Are we heading for the Waymeet between Westhaven and Carthell Abbey?" she asked. "If we are, that would be a good place to talk to people and to leave one of your little 'collectors,' both. I'm certain that the Waymeet family will give you no difficulty over leaving such a thing."

At Harperus' nod, T'fyrr asked with puzzlement, "What is a Waymeet? You have not told me of this."

"I did not tell you because we were not going there until we encountered our two young friends," Harperus replied. "But Robin tells me that there is a cartwright there, and a cartwright is what they most urgently need at the moment."

"The Gypsies created the Waymeets," Gwyna told the Haspur. "We created them, and we continue to run them, even though now there are a number of non-Gypsies who know about them and use them." She thought for a moment; she had lived with the knowledge of Waymeets all her life, and had never needed to describe them to anyone before. "You find them just off the major trade roads," she continued, finally. "They're a special, permanent camping-place, with a caretaker, certain things like bathhouses and laundries, a small market, and a population of craftsmen. One thing is pretty important: they're all on land that doesn't *belong* to anyone, not Duke nor Sire, not Guild nor Church. And another: no one stays there more than a few days at a time, except when bad weather really bogs things down. I know there will be a cartwright there, which solves *our* problem, and there will be people for Harperus to talk to with fresher news than ours."

T'fyrr nodded as he followed her words. "And the caretaker charges a certain amount for the amenities?" he hazarded. "Such things would make camping there more attractive than camping in the wilderness. Civilized."

"Exactly so," she said, nodding. "They're also, as the Old Owl here well knows, excellent places to pick up information, gossip, or both. People speak more freely there—and if *I* pass the word," she added, a little arrogantly, "they will speak very freely to him."

Harperus smiled. "I am certain of that, Gypsy Robin. For all of us, this Waymeet will be most productive."

CHAPTER FOUR

Stillwater Waymeet lay just off the main trade road, down a lane of its own that was—currently, at least—in better repair than the trade road. The Sire had not been keeping up his road repairs lately; another sign that the King of Rayden had become lax in seeing that his nobles attended to their duties. Probably the road would remain in poor repair until a Guild Master or a high Churchman had to pass this way. Ruts were the least of the problems along the trade road; much worse were the potholes at the edge of the road that gradually crept into the right-of-way and formed an actual hazard to traffic. By contrast the Waymeet lane was smooth, graded gravel, well-tended, and potholes had not been permitted to form on the edge.

There was a single sign at the joining of the lane and the road, a sign that said *Stillwater Waymeet* and had little carvings of a bucket of water, a caravan, and an ear of wheat, signifying that water, camping, and food were available. As large as it was, Harperus' wagon negotiated the turn easily, although the wagon filled the entire lane and the wheels were a scant finger length from the edge of the gravel.

Robin yawned discreetly; it had been a very long day, and trying to get their wagon out of the mud had pretty much done her in. As thick as the clouds were, there had been no real "sunset," only a gradual thickening of the darkness. It *was* dusk now, though; a thick, blue dusk with darker blue shadows under the trees, and she was going to be very glad to stop, get something hot to eat, and get to sleep.

"How long is it to the Waymeet itself?" Harperus asked, probably puzzled by the fact that the long tunnel of trees arching over the lane gave the illusion that it went on without any end. Most of the leaves had fallen from the seasonal trees, but there was a healthy percentage of evergreens along here that kept the lights of the Waymeet from showing. Despite the constant rain, the bitter scent of dead leaves hung in the air along the lane, and the gravel was covered with a carpet of fallen leaves that muffled the steady clopping of the horses' hooves.

"Not far," Robin assured him. "There's a slight, S-shaped bend up ahead that you can't see from here; it keeps this from being a straight line to the road. Keeps people from driving up like maniacs and running someone over."

The Gypsies were responsible for the creation of the Waymeets, building them up from a series of regular camping grounds along the roads. When a camping site always seemed to hold at least two Gypsy families and never was completely unoccupied, people would naturally begin to improve it. After a while, permanent, if crude, amenities (protected fire pits, stocks of wood, bathing and laundry areas, wells) were built at such places, slightly more elaborate than similar arrangements at large Fairesites. With people always at a site, there was little chance that such amenities would be vandalized, and incentive to take care of them. Then the next logical extension was for someone to decide he was tired of living on the road, but did not want to live in a town—

That unknown Gypsy had settled instead at one of those camping grounds, and had built not only living quarters for himself and his family, but a bathhouse, a laundry, and a trading post, and had begun selling odds and ends to the others who came to camp. This had the result of bringing in more campers; after all, why take the possibly dangerous step of camping alone when you could go somewhere, not only safe, but which boasted some small luxuries? From that moment, it was only a matter of time before others who wished to retire in the same manner found other such sites and did the same thing.

Then someone had the bright notion to open the sites up to *anyone* who traveled the trade-roads, for a fee.

The results of these enterprises were varied. Some Waymeets wound up resembling an inn, but without a building to house travelers. Some turned out, as was the case with Stillwater, rather along the lines of a village, without the insularity.

Robin had been to Stillwater many times. The camping grounds were laid out in sections for wagons and for tents, and patrolled by the proprietor's two tall sons and three of his cousins, to discourage theft and misbehavior. There was clean water in both a stream and a well. It also boasted a bathhouse and laundry, a cartwright, a blacksmith, and a carpenter. A small store sold the kinds of things people who traveled often broke, lost, or forgot; it served as a trading post for those who had goods to trade or sell. The fee to camp was minimal, the fees charged for the other services reasonable. Virtually all of the permanent residents were Gypsies, since generally any Gypsy who wished to retire from the road but still wanted the excitement of life on the road looked for a Waymeet that needed another hand about the place. At a Waymeet it was possible to have most of the excitement and change of traveling without ever leaving your home.

Waymeets were well known, and their locations clearly marked on most maps, since most experienced travelers with their own wagons used them—often in preference to the Church hostels set up for similar purposes. Most merchants would rather pay the higher fees of the Waymeets than endure the lodging-with-sermons one got at the hostels. Only in truly vicious winter weather were the hostels more popular than the Waymeets.

The result was a peculiar village where the entire population changed over the course of a week—more often than that in summer, when travel was easier.

As they rounded the first curve, the lights of the Waymeet began to glimmer through the screening of trees. As they rounded the second, the Waymeet lay spread out before them.

Right on the lane at the entrance, surrounded by lanterns on posts, was the building housing the laundry, bathhouse, store, and proprietor's quarters. A tall, handsome young Gypsy was already waiting for them beside the lane as Harperus pulled up. He wore a cape of oiled canvas against the rain, but he had pulled the hood back, and mist-beads glistened in the lantern light as they collected on his midnight-black hair.

"Not full, are you?" Harperus asked anxiously, as the young man strolled over to the driver's box after appraising the horses with an admiring eye.

"Fullish, Old Owl, but not full-up," the young man replied. "It's about the last chance of the season for traders, an' we got folk comin' home from Harvest Faires. Ye don't recognize me, I reckon, but I'm Jackdaw, Guitan Clan. I mind I met you when I was knee-high—"

"You're the lad with the knack with penny-whistles!" Harperus exclaimed, to the young man's delighted smile that the Deliambren had remembered him. "Dear heavens, has it been *that* long since I saw you last? How did you come here? I thought you and your family were somewhere near Shackleford!"

"Sister went *vanderei* with Blackfox, he got Stillwater from his nuncle, reckoned he could use some hands an' tough heads." Jackdaw shrugged, and grinned, his teeth gleaming whitely in the gathering dusk. "Not much call for a penny-whistle carver, and never could carve naught else. Fee's ten copper pennies for th' two wagons, indefinite stay, you bein' Free Bard an' all—"

He peered through the gloom, and Robin spoke up to save his eyes. "Robin of Kadash Clan, *vanderei* with Free Bard Kestrel. I hope the cartwright isn't full-up, we've got a cracked axle, or so Old Owl says. The road has gone all to pieces since I was here last."

"Nay, nay, nothin' he can't put aside, anyway, since he's a cousin." Jackdaw looked the pair of wagons over with an expert eye. "Kin come afore *gajo*. I'll tell him t' come look you over as soon as this blasted rain clears. Right about the road, though, an' the Sire ain't done nothin' about it. Prob'ly won't, 'till he breaks his own axle. Tell you what, there's two sites all the way at the end of the last row left; pull both rigs into the first site, drop the little wagon, then pull the big 'un up into the second site. You'll both be right an' tight t' pull straight out when y' please."

Robin had already pulled out her purse and passed the ten coppers over to Jackdaw before Harperus had a chance to protest or pay the lad himself. "You pulled us out and towed us here, so let me discharge the debt and cover your fee," she said firmly. Harperus had known Gypsies more than long enough to understand the intricate dance of "discharging debt," so he did not argue; he simply followed Jackdaw's instructions and drove the horses to the next-to-last path on the left, then all the way down to the end. The lanes were also marked clearly with lantern poles, with another set of poles halfway down, and large white stones marking the place to pull into each site.

Parking the wagons was as simple as Jackdaw had stated, which was a relief; Robin had known far too many Gypsies who would try to wedge a wagon into a space meant for a one-man tent-shelter. The camping sites were on firm, level grass, with trees and bushes between each adjoining site, and a rock-rimmed, sand-lined fire pit for each site as well. Robin didn't get a chance to see much of the Waymeet, however, for by the time they were parked and the horses unhitched, night had fallen, and a thick darkness made more impenetrable by the mist that had taken over the area.

Kestrel took all six horses to the common corral and stable area; shelter was provided, and water, but food must either be bought or supplied from their own stores. Just as he left, the mist thickened, and then the rain resumed, pouring down just as hard as it had during the day.

Robin cursed under her breath, and Harperus looked annoyed. "T'fyrr, you stay in the wagon," he ordered. "There is nothing worse than the smell of wet feathers, and I don't want to chance you catching something in this cold. Robin and I can deal with unhitching her caravan and pushing it back."

He did *something* at the side of the driver's box, and soft, white lights came on at the rear and the front of his wagon. Robin's eyes widened, but she said nothing. The lights looked exactly like oil lamps, and if you had not seen them spring to life so suddenly and magically, you might have thought that was what they really were. A flamelike construction flickered inside frosted glass in a very realistic manner.

But the "flames" were just a little too regular in their "flickering;" there was certainly a pattern there. And besides, oil lamps required someone or something to light them, they simply didn't light themselves.

Then she shrugged, mentally. If Harperus wanted to make things look as if he was driving a perfectly normal—if rather large—wagon, that was his privilege. If he wanted to pretend that he had no Deliambren secrets in there, that was his problem. No one who had ever seen Deliambren "magic" was going to be fooled for a second. The glass in the windows was enough to show this was no ordinary wagon, and the smooth metal sides were too unlike a wooden caravan to ever deceive anyone.

Together they cranked the winched-up caravan down; it was no problem for only two to handle, even in the downpour, since it was always easier to get something *down* than it was to get it *up*. And it was not as hard as she had thought it would be, to push the caravan back a few paces from the rear of Harperus' wagon. The wheels moved easily on the wet grass. Harperus climbed under the damaged rear end again and poked and prodded, and created his mysterious little flashes of light, then finally emerged and shook water and bits of leaves off his hands.

"That axle will hold your weight, I think," he said, as Robin's nose turned cold and she shivered in the light breeze. "I wouldn't worry about sleeping or moving around in the wagon. I wouldn't trust it to take the abuse of the road, but sitting here on grass there should be no problems."

She had no idea how Harperus could tell all of this just by looking at the axle—or what little could be seen of the axle inside its enclosure—but she was quite confident that he was right. Deliambrens were seldom, if ever, wrong about something that was physical or structural.

"Thank you, Old Owl," she said with gratitude. "I don't know how we'd have managed if you hadn't come along—"

He cut short her speech of gratitude with a wave of his hand. "You are freezing, little one, and all this can wait until morning. I will go and see to our horses while you get something warm to eat and some sleep. Think of it as trade for the rumors you are going to track for me. You can thank me in the morning. All right?"

She nodded, with a tired sigh. Deliambrens as a whole were not very good at judging the strength of human emotions, nor the strength of the actions that emotions were likely to induce, but this time Harperus had gauged her remaining reserves quite accurately. "Right," she said, without any argument. "Talk to me in the morning and let me know what you want me to listen for tomorrow, what you want me to say to the others."

Harperus nodded and turned back to his own wagon, hurrying through the rain to the front, which was the only place on the vehicle with an entrance. The exterior lights went out as abruptly as they had come on as soon as she reached the door of her own little caravan. No matter; she knew where everything was, and lit the four *real* oil lamps by feel, filling the interior of the wagon with a mellow, golden light, and very grateful for the stock of sulfur-matches that had come with the wagon. They were precious and hard to come by; she only used one, then lit the rest of the lamps from a splinter she kindled at the first lamp.

Once again she lit the tiny charcoal stove, and waited for the place to warm up. The interior of the caravan was well-planned as far as usable space went. Their bed was in the front, just behind the driver's seat, and the door there slid sideways rather than swinging open, so that someone could lie on the bed and talk to the driver while the wagon moved down the road. And on warm nights, a curtain could be pulled across the opened door, giving privacy and fresh air. A second curtain could be pulled across the other side of the bed, giving privacy from the rest of the wagon. It *was* possible to sleep four, in a pinch; an ingenious table and bench arrangement on the right-hand wall under the side window could be made into a bed just wide enough for two. But the arrangement would not be good for long periods, unless the people in that bed were children.

There was storage for their clothing under the bed, more storage above it. The stove was bolted away from the wall in the rear beside the rear door, and had a cooking surface on the top of it. Storage for food was nearby and their pans and utensils hung from the ceiling above it. There were small windows surrounded by shallow storage cabinets on either wall, where they kept everything else they needed, from instruments to harness-repair kits. The table and benches, bolted to the wall and floor, were beneath the right-hand window, and a built-in basin above a huge jar for fresh water with a spigot on the bottom, were beneath the left-hand window. The basin could be removed from its holder, to be emptied out the window or filled from the jar.

Harperus' suggestion of hot food was a good one. How long had it been since they'd eaten? Certainly not since noon.

Still shivering, she made the simplest possible hot meal, toasting thick slices of bread and melting cheese over the top of them—and putting a kettle for tea on top of the stove. The activity kept her from feeling *too* cold, and by the time Kestrel returned, the wagon had begun to warm.

"I—got the h-horses—put up," Kestrel told her, as she stripped his sodden clothing from him and wrapped him in a thick robe made from the same material as their blankets. "And f-fed."

"Good—here, eat this, you'll feel better." She put a slice of toast-and-cheese in his left hand and a mug of tea well-sweetened with honey in his right. With a smile of gratitude, he started on both. "And next time, I can put the horses up and you can make dinner."

"D-done," he agreed, as he joined her on the bed.

"Thank goodness Harperus came along," she sighed. "We'd still be out there if he hadn't."

Jonny nodded. "I've n-never seen a D-Deliambren before. Are th-they all like h-him? So c-courteous?"

"Most of them." She sipped her tea, carefully; it was not that far from being scalding. "All of them would stop to help someone they knew, and most would stop to help a stranger. They can afford to. With their magic, there aren't too many people who would be a threat to them."

"Ah." He shifted a little more, and tucked his feet in under his robe. "I w-was w-wondering if they all are so—so—d-d-detached."

"As if Harperus is always observing the rest of the world without really being part of it?" she asked in reply, and at his nod, she pursed her lips. "They really are pretty much all like that," she told him. "All the Deliambrens I've met, anyway. They just don't understand our emotions, but they're completely fascinated by them. I think that's why they enjoy being around the Free Bards and the Gypsies. They like to hear the songs that we sing that are full of very powerful emotions, and they like to watch the emotional reactions of our listeners. It seems to be a never-ending source of entertainment for them."

Kestrel made a face of distaste. "L-like we're s-some kind of b-bug."

"No, not at all," she hastened to tell him. "No, it's something like the fascination I have for watching someone blow glass. I can't do it, I don't understand it, but I love to watch. This fascination of theirs gets them in trouble too—they are *very* apt to go running off into a bad situation just because it looks interesting. Wren had to pull Harperus out of a mob once, for instance, and another Deliambren we know nearly got disemboweled for asking one too many questions about a particular Sire's lady." She hoped Harperus had more sense than that. "It's not that they don't feel things, they just don't express them the way we do. Harperus has a very good sense of humor and tells excellent jokes—but he can't always tell when things have turned serious, and he can't always anticipate when serious things have turned deadly. They seem on the surface to be very shallow people, and I've heard some Churchmen call them 'soul-less' because of that."

Kestrel's expression grew thoughtful. "Th-the things the Church is s-saying, about th-the n-nonhumans? H-having no souls? And b-being d-damned?"

"Could be very, very dangerous for the Deliambrens," she said, catching his meaning. "And they don't even realize it. They have no idea how very emotional people can be when it comes to religion, and how irrational that can make them."

Kestrel finished his bread, took the last sip of his tea, and put the mug down on one of the little shelves built above the foot of the bed. "M-maybe. And m-maybe he d-d-does. He asked *you* t-to listen for r-rumors."

She licked her lips thoughtfully, then nodded, as a sudden flash of lightning illuminated the cracks around the doors and the shutters. The thunder followed immediately, deafening them both for a moment.

"You might be right," she admitted. "If so, it may be the *first* time he's been able to figure out when he's treading on dangerous emotional ground! But—"

"It c-can wait unt-til tomorrow," Kestrel said firmly, and took her mug away from her. He put it down beside his own, and then took her in his arms. "I m-may be t-tired, b-but I h-have other p-plans."

And he proceeded to show her what those plans were.

Afterwards, they were so exhausted that not even the pounding rain, the thunder, or the brilliant lightning could keep them awake.

Jonny woke first, as usual; he poked his nose out from under the blankets and took an experimental sniff of the chill air.

Clear, clean air, but one without a lot of moisture in it. Maybe the rain had cleared off?

He opened up one eye, and pulled back the curtain over the door by the bed. Sunlight poured through the crack, and as he freed his head from the bedclothes, he heard a bird singing madly. Probably a foolish jay, with no notion that it should have gone south by now. He smiled, let the curtain fall, and closed his eyes again.

In a few more minutes, Robin stirred, right on schedule. She cracked her eye open, muttered something unintelligible about the birds, and slowly, painfully, opened her eyes completely. Jonny grinned and stretched. Another day had begun.

He crawled past Robin, who muttered and curled up in the blankets. She was never able to wake up properly, so he was the one who made breakfast; he got the stove going and made sausage, tea, and batter-cakes, while she slowly unwound from the blankets. He ate first, then cleaned himself and the tiny kitchen up while she ate. And about the time her breakfast was finished, Robin was capable of speaking coherently. About the time she finished her second mug of tea, the cartwright arrived.

Kestrel left her to clean herself up, and joined the cartwright in the clear and rain-washed morning.

There was no sign of life in Harperus' wagon, but it was entirely possible that the Deliambren and his guest were up and about long ago; there was enough room in there for six or eight people to set up full-time housekeeping. Certainly it was possible for Harperus to be doing anything up to and including carpentry in that behemoth without any trace of activity to an outside watcher.

The cartwright was a taciturn individual, although not sullen; he seemed simply to be unwilling to part with too many words. Clearly another Gypsy by his dark hair and olive skin, his scarlet shirt and leather breeches, he nodded a friendly greeting as Jonny waved to him. "Free Bard Kestrel?" he asked, then crawled under the wagon without anything more than waiting for Kestrel's affirmative reply. He had brought a number of small tools with him; he took off the protective enclosure on the offending axle while Kestrel watched with interest. He studied the situation, with no comment or expression on his dark face, then replaced the cover and crawled back out.

"Right," he said then. "Cracked axle. Not bad. Start now, done by nightfall. Fifty silver; good axle is thirty, ten each for me and Grackle."

Robin poked her head out of the wagon as he finished, and Kestrel blanched at the price of the repair. They *had* it; had it, and a nice nest-egg to spare, but all the years of abject poverty made Kestrel extremely reluctant to part with *any* money, much less this much. He looked to Robin for advice. Was this fair, or was the man gouging them?

Robin shrugged. "It's a fair price," she said. "An axle has to be made of lathe-turned, kiln-dried oronwood, and the nearest oronwood stand that *I* know of is on the other side of Kingsford."

The cartwright (whose name Kestrel *still* did not know) nodded, respect in his eyes, presumably that Robin was so well-informed. Kestrel sighed, but only to himself. There would be no bargaining here.

"G-go ahead," he said, trying not to let the words choke him.

The cartwright nodded and strode briskly off down the lane towards the cluster of buildings at the front of the Waymeet, presumably to get his partner, tools, and the new axle.

"D-do we s-stay here?" he asked Robin. "Are w-we s-supposed to help?"

"Not at that price," she replied, jumping down out of the wagon. "I heard him out here, so I locked everything up, figuring if he could start immediately, we could go wander around the Waymeet for a while, and see if there's anyone I know here. We can't do anything in the wagon while he has it up on blocks, changing out the axle."

She reached up and locked the back door, then slipped the key in her pocket. The bird in the tree above them, who had been silent while the cartwright was prodding the wagon, burst into song, and she looked up and smiled at it.

That smile lit up his heart and brought a smile to his lips. He reached for her hand, and she slipped it into his. "Th-there's lots of n-news t-to tell, and m-more t-to hear. L-let's at least g-go tell Gypsies and F-Free B-Bards ab-bout Wren and L-L-Lark. And th-the w-welcome to Free B-Bards in B-Birnam. Th-that's g-good news."

"Surely," she agreed. "And we'll see if there's anything of interest to us in what the other folk here have to tell us in the way of news."

To Robin's delight, the first people they encountered, cooking up a breakfast of sausage around their fire, were people she knew very well.

It was a trio of Free Bards: Linnet, Gannet, and Blackbird. Blackbird jumped up, nearly stepping into the fire, when he spotted Robin, and rushed to hug her.

Linnet was a tiny thing, with long, coppery-brown hair that reached almost to her ankles when she let it down. Gannet's hair was as red as flame, his milky face speckled with freckles; Blackbird's red-gold hair was lighter and wavy rather than curly, like Gannet's. All three had sparkling green eyes, and slight builds. They made a striking group, whether they were dressed for the road or in their performance costumes.

She made the introductions hastily; none of the trio had ever seen Jonny or even heard of him, so far as she knew.

"Linnet is flute, Gannet is drum, and Blackbird is a mandolin player," she told him, concluding the introduction. "Kestrel is a harpist, and he's learning lute—"

"Well, if Master Wren declared he's one of us, that's good enough for me," Blackbird declared. "No other qualifications needed. Now, we heard there was some kind of to-do over in Birnam—but how did you end up mixed in it, and *how* did you end up wedded?"

She glanced over at Kestrel, who shrugged, and settled down on one of the logs arranged as seats around the open fire. "Finish your meal and we'll see if we can't get it all sorted out for you," she said, following his example. "We've already eaten, so go right ahead."

Jonny didn't say a great deal, but he did interject a word or phrase now and again; enough that it didn't look as if she was doing all the talking. Linnet and her two partners kept mostly quiet, although by their eyes, they were intensely excited by the whole story. They passed sausages and bread to each other, and filled tea-mugs, without their gazes ever leaving the faces of the two tale-tellers.

"—and then, well, it was just a matter of getting wedded," Robin concluded.

Kestrel grinned wryly. "And s-so p-p-publicly that K-King R-Rolend c-couldn't th-think I w-was g-going to b-back out of my p-p-pledge. S-s-so here w-we are."

"Lark and Wren are still in Birnam, and King Rolend made Wren his Bard Laurel, so he said to pass the word that Free Bards are welcome in *any* place in Birnam," Robin added. "That's the biggest news, really. Apparently the Bardic Guild in Birnam was one of the biggest benefactors of the old King's spendthrift ways, and they are *not* happy with Rolend."

"And th-the f-f-feeling is m-mutual," Jonny pointed out. "Th-things th-that Wren w-wants, he's h-happy t-to g-give. P-politely th-thumbing his n-nose at the G-G-Guild."

"Like the right for any musician to work anywhere, and take anyone's pay, at least in Birnam." Gwyna made no secret of her satisfaction, and the other three looked so satisfied that Robin wondered if they had been having trouble finding a wintering-over spot.

"Well, that's the best news I've had since the Kingsford Faire!" Linnet exclaimed. She glanced over at her two partners, who nodded. "I think the situation in Birnam is well worth crossing those damned fens, even at this late in the year. We haven't found a *single* wintering-over job, and we've been looking since the first Harvest Faire."

Robin blinked in surprise at that, as Gannet carefully poured the last of the tea-water over the fire, putting it out. Steam hissed up from the coals and blew away in the light breeze. "That's odd," she said carefully.

"Odd? It's a disaster!" Blackbird never had been one to mince words. "No one will take us. There's Guild musicians in every one of the taverns we've wintered over in before. The innkeepers just shrug and wish us well—elsewhere. They won't tell us why they hired Guild when they couldn't afford Guild before, and they won't tell us why they *don't* want us, when the Guild musicians aren't as good as we are."

But Gannet looked up with shadows in his dark eyes. "Got a guess," he offered. "Just now put it together—been a lot of Priests around, preaching on morality. We're a trio."

Robin shook her head, baffled, but Linnet put her hand to her mouth. "Oh!" she exclaimed, looking stricken. "I never thought of that! We're—" she blushed, a startling crimson. "We've always shared a room, you see—"

Robin grimaced. "If the Church Priests are going around the inns, threatening to cause trouble if there are 'immoral people' there, you three would be right at the top of their list, wouldn't you?"

"I never thought it necessary to announce that we're siblings every time we ask for a job," Blackbird said, with icy anger. "It doesn't exactly have anything to do with *music*."

"Well, maybe it does now," Gannet said, his jaw clenched. "Church's poking its nose into *our* lives, time we went on the defensive, maybe—"

"Or time we went into Birnam, where we don't have to make excuses, just music," Linnet said firmly. "No, *I* don't like running away any more than anyone else, but the Church scares me. It's too big to fight, and too big to hide from."

She stood up and shook out her skirts decisively. "If they decide not to believe that we're siblings, we have no way of proving that we *are*!" she continued. "And for that matter, a nasty-minded Churchman can make nasty assumptions even if they accept our word! Call me a coward, but there it is."

Gannet rose, nodding, as Robin and Kestrel got to their feet, leaving only Blackbird sitting. He stared up at them, stubbornly, for a long moment. Then he finally sighed and rose to his feet as well.

"We're too good a trio to break up," he said, with an unhappy shake of his head. "I think you're overreacting, but if it makes the two of you happy to head for Birnam, then that's where we'll go."

Robin let out the breath she had been holding. "I think you're being wise," she said. "It's just a feeling I have, but—well, incest is punishable, too, and the punishments are pretty horrible. It might be worse for Church Priests to know you *are* related, and sharing a room."

"Better to be safe," Linnet said, with a twitch of her skirts that told Robin that she was not just nervous, she was actually a little *afraid*, and had been the moment that Gannet mentioned the Church.

And that was not like Linnet.

Not at all.

Something had frightened her, something she hadn't even told her brothers. Threats from some representative of the Church?

Or some Priest deciding he liked her looks and promising trouble if she wouldn't become his mistress. It had happened to Robin, and the trouble had come. Small wonder Linnet would rather leave the country than come under Church scrutiny again. Robin would make the same choice, in her place.

She and Kestrel found several more Gypsies, and two more Free Bards, besides a round dozen wandering players who were not associated with either the Guild or the Free Bards. To all of them she passed the news that any musician was welcome to play wherever he could find work in the Kingdom of Birnam. Some of the ordinary musicians were interested, most were not—but they were folk who had a regular circuit of tiny inns, local dances and festivals, and very small Faires. They had places to play that no Guild musician would touch with a barge-pole, and while the living that they eked out was bare by her standards, it was enough for them.

The Free Bards were, like Linnet, *very* interested in her news, and had similar tales of finding Guild musicians—or, at least, musicians in Guild badges—playing in the venues where no Guildsman had ever played before.

But it was not until they found another musician who was both a Gypsy and a Free Bard that they had anything like an answer to the question of *why* this was happening.

The ethereal strains of a harp drew Kestrel across the clearing and into the deeper forest beyond the immediate confines of the Waymeet. Dead leaves crackled underfoot, and the scent of tannin rose at his every step. This was no simple song; this was the kind of wild, strange, dream-haunted melody that some of the Gypsies played—though Robin never would, claiming she had no talent for what she called *adastera* music. She said it was as much magic as music, and told him it was reputed to have the power to control spirits and souls, to raise ghosts and set them to rest again.

Robin followed him under the deep shadows of the trees, as the bare branches above gave way to thick, long-needled evergreens, a voice joined the harp, singing without words, the two creating harmonies that made the hair on the back of his neck stand on end. This was music powerful enough to make even Harperus weep! The harpist must be a Gypsy, but who was the singer? It did not sound like any human voice. . . .

The path they followed seemed to lead beside the stream that watered the Waymeet; it led through deep undergrowth, along the bottom of a rock-sided ravine that slowly grew steeper with every twist and turn of the path. The stream wound its way through a tangle of rounded boulders, but its gurgle did not sound at all cheerful, although it was very musical. It held a note of melancholy that was a match for the sadness in the music floating on the breeze ahead of them.

"Nightingale," Robin muttered. "She's the *only* person I can think of who plays like that! But who is the singer?"

They had their answer a moment later, as the stream and path brought them to a tiny clearing made by the toppling of a single tree that bridged the water. There, beside the tree, was the harpist, seated on a rock with her harp braced on her lap. And standing beside her was T'fyrr.

Not even the birds were foolish enough to make any sound that might disturb these two. The Haspur stood like a statue of gray granite in the twilight shadows of the forest, only his chest moving to show that he was alive, with his eyes closed and his beak open just enough to permit his voice to issue forth. Nightingale's eyes were closed as well, but most of her face was hidden in the curtain of her hair, as she bent over her harp, all of her concentration centered on her hands and the melodies she coaxed from the delicate strings.

Both of them were too deeply engrossed in the music to notice their audience—and Robin and Kestrel stopped dead to keep from breaking their concentration.

The song came to its natural end, a single harp-note that hung in the air like a crystal raindrop; a sigh from T'fyrr that answered it.

For a long, long moment, only silence held sway beneath the branches. Then, finally, a bell-bird sang out its three-note call, and the two musicians sighed and opened their eyes.

T'fyrr caught sight of them first, and clapped his beak shut with a snap.

"T-T'fyrr—" Kestrel said, softly, "th-that was w-w-wonderful."

The bird-man bowed, graciously. "It was an experiment—" he offered. "It was not meant to be heard."

"But since it was . . ." The Gypsy that Robin had identified as "Nightingale" cocked her head to one side.

Robin evidently knew her well enough to answer the unspoken question. "As critique from two fellow harpists—you've found the best match to your harp and your music I've ever heard," Robin replied. "I know Kestrel agrees with me, and he's a better harpist than I am. That was nothing short of magical."

Nightingale's mouth twitched a little, as if she found Robin's choice of words amusing. "Well, we had agreed, T'fyrr and I, that this song would be the last of our experiments this morning. And while my heart may regret that you found us and are about to make us cleave to that agreement, my hands are not going to argue." She began flexing them, and massaging each of the palms in turn. "A forest in autumn is not the best venue for a performance. It is very damp here, and a rock makes a chilly, and none-too-soft cushion." Her eyes met Kestrel's, sharp and penetrating, and just a little strange and other-worldly. "T'fyrr said that you would turn up eventually, and that you had some news?"

Once again, the two of them passed on their own news, with the added tales from Linnet's trio and some of the other musicians. "We started out with only good news," Robin concluded, ruefully, "but we seem to have acquired news of a more sober flavor. I feel like a bird who just finished the last song of summer, and sees the first storm of winter coming—"

Nightingale nodded. "And now you will hear why *I* am here, and not in my usual winter haunt. And I think I may have the answer you have been looking for, as to why there are fewer places for Free Bards, and Guild musicians crowding into our old venues."

As Robin took a place on the fallen tree, and Kestrel planted himself beside her, Nightingale glanced up at T'fyrr. "I think that some of what I have to say will affect you, my new friend," she said. "But—listen, and judge for yourself."

When Nightingale had found her usual winter position as the chief instrumentalist at a fine ladies' tea-shop closed to her, taken by a barely tolerable Guild violist, she did more than simply look for work, she began looking for the cause. And just as Gannet had, *she* had found clerics from the Church posted on street-corners, preaching against "immorality." But unlike Gannet, she had *listened* to the sermons.

"Time after time, I heard sermons specifically against *music*," she said. "And not just any music—but the music performed by what these street preachers referred to as 'wild and undisciplined street players.' They *always* went on to further identify these 'street players' as people no Guild would permit into its ranks, because of their lack of respect for authority, their immorality, and their 'dangerous ways.'"

"Us, in other words," Robin said grimly. "Free Bards. Just what were the complaints against us, anyway?"

Nightingale's mouth had compressed into a tight line, and Kestrel sensed a very deep anger within her. "According to what they *said*, directly, our music is seductive and incites lust, our lyrics licentious and advocate lust, and we destroy pure thinking and lead youths to rebel against proper authority. To hear them talk, the Free Bards are responsible for every girl that ever had a child out of wedlock, every boy that ever defied his parents, and every fool who sought strong drink and drugs and ruined his mind and body. But it wasn't only what they said directly, it was what they implied."

"Which w-was?" Kestrel prompted, quickly.

"That we're using magic," she said flatly. "That we're somehow controlling the minds of those who listen to us, to make them do things they never would ordinarily. He was full of examples—boys that had been lured into demon-worship by a song, girls that had run off with young brigands because of a song, folk who had supposedly been incited to a life of crime or had committed suicide, all because of the 'magic spells' we Free Bards had cast on them through our music. They even had the titles of the songs on their tongues, to prove their lies—'Demon-Lover,' 'Follow Come Follow,' 'Free Fly the Fair,' 'The Highwayman's Lady.' As if simply by knowing the title of a song, that proved there was evil magic behind the singing of it. *That* is why there are no jobs for Free Bards. Not because we're 'immoral'—but because no one wants to risk a charge that some patron did something wrong because the musician at the hearth somehow cast a sinister spell upon him and took control of his mind. Most especially they do not want to risk an accusation that such a spell had been cast against a minor child."

Kestrel felt cold. That was too close to the truth, as Wren had uncovered it. *Some* Free Bards *could* influence the thoughts of others. Not to any sinister purpose, but—

"And the Guild, in its infinite wisdom and compassion, has been offering an option to the owners of the better taverns and those citizens of modest wealth who may hire a musician or two," Nightingale continued, her voice dripping with sarcasm. "They have been recruiting what they call 'Guild-licensed' musicians—players who are not good enough to pass the Guild trials, but who may be barely competent musicians on one or two instruments. These people are certified *by the Church* and licensed by the Guild as being capable of entertaining without corrupting anyone. They wear Guild colors and double-tithe to the Church, plus pass back a commission to the Guild."

"Brilliant," Robin muttered, bitterly.

"This, of course, does leave us the street corners, the very poor inns and taverns, the common eating-shops, and the patronage of younger people who usually don't have a great deal of money," Nightingale concluded. "And, of course, the country-folk, who haven't gotten the word of our immorality and possible corrupting magic-use yet."

T'fyrr, who had remained silent through all of this, finally spoke. "I like this not, lady," he said, his voice echoing oddly through the trees.

"No more do any of us, friend," Robin answered for all of them.

They finished making their rounds of the other, non-musical "residents" of the Waymeet at just about the time that the cartwright (who they now knew was called "Oakhart") and his helper were taking the wagon down off the blocks. "She'll hold now," Oakhart said, with satisfaction. They shook hands on it, and the cartwright departed with his promised fifty pieces of silver. Kestrel let Robin pay the man; it gave him pain to see that much money leaving their hands.

Harperus appeared just as Oakhart was leaving, and invited them to dinner and a conference around the fire he had just built. He had quite a civilized little arrangement there; folding chairs, a stack of baskets, each containing a different, warmed dainty, and plates to eat from. "T'fyrr told me what your Gypsy-harpist friend said," the Deliambren told them, as they accepted plates full of food that obviously had never been prepared over a fire, tasty little bits of vegetables and meats, each with different sauces or crisp coatings, or sprinklings of cheese. "This is some of what I had heard, the rumors that I wanted you to track for me, but not the whole of it."

Gwyna picked up a bit of fried something, and bit into it with a glum expression. "I don't know how we're going to fight the Church, Old Owl. I don't know how anyone could."

"I h-heard some other things," Kestrel added casually, after popping a sausagelike thing into his mouth. "I d-don't kn-know if it m-means anyth-thing. Or if th-the Ch-Church has anyth-thing t-to d-do with this. N-no one else s-s-seems t-to think it m-means anyth-thing. J-just—th-that n-nonhumans are h-having a h-harder t-time of it, just I-like the F-Free B-Bards. All of a s-sudden it's all r-right t-to s-say y-you d-don't t-trust 'em, th-they're th-thieves, or sh-shifty, or l-lazy. Th-that it's h-harder for 'em t-to g-get any k-kind of p-position, any k-kind of j-job, and even t-traders are f-finding it h-harder t-to g-get c-clients, unless th-they've g-got some-thing ex-exclusive. And th-there are s-signs showing up, at inns and t-taverns and l-lodgings."

"What kind of signs?" Harperus asked, sharply.

"Ones th-that s-say 'Hu-humans only.'" He shrugged. "N-not a l-lot of them, th-they s-say, b-but I've n-never heard of th-that b-before."

"Nor have I." Harperus was giving him a particularly penetrating look. "You seem to think this is nothing terribly important, certainly nowhere near as important as these preachers and the apparent backing of the Bardic Guild by the Church."

Kestrel shrugged again. "It's j-just a c-couple of b-bigots," he said. "Wh-what h-harm c-can they do?"

"Could they express their bigotry so openly if they did *not* have some sanction?" Harperus countered sharply. "And if there are signs reading 'Humans only' *now*, how long will it be, think you, before there are signs that say, 'Citizens only,' 'Guild Members only,' or even 'No one permitted in the gates without Church papers and permissions'?"

Kestrel blinked, and his level of concern rose markedly. "D-do you th-think the Ch-Church is behind this, too?"

Harperus stroked his cheek-decorations with a thoughtful finger. "I find it peculiar that a Church whose scriptures speak of love and tolerance should suddenly have words of hate and intolerance in its collective mouth," he said. "I find it disturbing that it is effectively sanctioning things that should be repugnant to any thinking being. And I do not think that it is any accident that this should be happening to the two main groups who escape the Church's authority—the nonhumans, who do not share this human religion of the Sacrificed God, and the Free Bards and Gypsies, who have no address and cannot be followed, controlled, or intimidated."

"I find it significant too, my friend," boomed T'fyrr out of the darkness. "What is more, I have been speaking in greater depth with Nightingale, who tells me that the Church has never before preached against the use of magic—but now finds reasons to condemn even such beneficial magic as healing, if they are not performed by a Priest. And I wonder, how long before use of magic is declared a crime—and how long before anyone that the authorities wish to be rid of is called a magician?"

"A very good question, T'fyrr." Robin's face was grim, and Kestrel felt a cold and empty place in his stomach that the excellent food did nothing to fill. "A very good question. And I am beginning to wonder if the answer to your question can be measured in months."

"That," Harperus said, "is precisely what I am afraid of."

CHAPTER FIVE

Kestrel thought about the revelations of the day long into the night, and in the morning, while Gwyna took their mud-stained garments to the laundry to try to scrub them clean again, he waited for Harperus to make his appearance.

It was another clear, cold day, with a bite in the air that warned that winter was not far off. Kestrel's thin fingers chilled quickly, and he stuffed his hands into the pockets of his coat to warm them. The Deliambren came out of his wagon from the door at the front, looked around, and greeted Kestrel with some surprise. "I didn't expect to find you here, still," Harperus told him. "I expected that you and Robin would be on your way as soon as the sun rose. Have some breakfast?"

He had his hands full of something, and offered Jonny a very odd object indeed; a thin pancake folded around a brightly colored filling. Strange-looking, but Kestrel already knew that Harperus' odd-looking food was very good, and he accepted his second breakfast of the day with alacrity. There had been too many days in the past that he had had no breakfast, no lunch, and no dinner. Old habits said, "Eat when you can," so he did.

"W-we have ch-chores," Kestrel offered, after first trying a bite and discovering that it was as good as dinner had been last night. "Th-things w-we didn't g-get to. L-laundry, a l-little cl-cleaning. Re-s-stocking. And w-we hadn't d-decided where w-we w-were g-going, yet. S-South, that w-was all w-we knew. W-we needed t-to look at s-some m-maps."

There was still hot tea left in their wagon; he turned and got mugs well-sweetened with honey for both of them. Harperus accepted his with a nod of thanks. The warm mug felt very good in Kestrel's cold fingers.

"So. You'll be going out of Rayden, I take it, given the word you gathered yesterday?" Harperus regarded Kestrel shrewdly over a mug of steaming tea. "Obviously, you can't go back to Birnam, so where are you thinking of heading?"

"D-don't know." He finished Harperus' offering, and dusted off his hands. "Th-this b-business w-with the Ch-Church; I g-got the f-f-feeling you'd heard m-more than you t-told us l-last night."

"And if I have?" the Deliambren asked levelly.

Kestrel studied the odd, inhuman face. It was very handsome, the more so as he became accustomed to it; the swaths of silky hair only added to the attraction. There was no sign of aging at all; certainly no sign of the years Robin had claimed for the Deliambren. And there was no sign of any emotion that Kestrel recognized. Harperus' odd-colored eyes studied his, seeming more coppery this morning than yellow.

"Y-you've b-been w-watching th-things for a l-l-long t-time," he said, finally. "C-collecting inform-m-mation. S-so maybe you kn-know. H-how c-can wh-what the Church is d-doing b-be j-j-justified?"

"One of the characteristics of organized religion is that no action it takes has to be justified from outside, if it is justified by the religion itself, Kestrel," Harperus said, patiently. "That is a truism for nonhuman as well as human religions. No matter how irrational an action is, if it is done in the name of the religion, that alone serves the organizers."

Jonny shook his head. "I d-don't understand," he said, plaintively.

Harperus sighed. "Neither do I. But then, I have never claimed to be religious."

Both of them wore coats against the chill in the air, and once again, Jonny shoved one of his hands into his pocket and wished that he were somewhere warm that had never heard of the Church. "Wh-when I asked the tr-traders wh-why these th-things were happening, th-they d-didn't know either. And th-they didn't s-seem worried." He tried to make his glance at Harperus an inquiring one, and evidently Harperus read it that way.

"That seems to be the prevailing attitude." Harperus looked up at the sky, broodingly. "The only human folk who are worried are the Free Bards and the traveling musicians—and they seem concerned only with the immediate effect these sanctions are having on their livelihood. No one seems at all concerned about what could happen next, or the sanctions against nonhumans. To be honest with you, Kestrel, those worry me the most. And not because I am Deliambren, either."

Jonny had formed some ideas of his own last night, and he wanted to see how they matched with the Deliambren's. "Why?" he asked.

Harperus smiled thinly. "You pack many questions into a single word, youngster." He leaned back against the side of his vehicle. "I am not concerned for myself and my race, because there is no one in the Twenty Kingdoms who can effectively threaten us, my earlier protestations notwithstanding. We can simply *outlive* human regimes. We have the capability of closing up the Fortress and outliving this current generation. We have done so before, and are always prepared to do so again. It is simply not our policy to boast of that ability."

Jonny's eyebrows rose. He had not expected Harperus to be so frank. . . .

"However, the reason that these little, petty annoyances worry me is that they seem to have been formulated, by accident or deliberately, to undermine a great deal of the progress that has been made here in the last few centuries. Progress in cooperation, that is." The Deliambren's expression was a brooding one. "Each little action seems designed to strike in such a way that the group that is acted against is *quite* certain that the actions against them are far more important than the petty annoyances of other groups." He leaned towards Kestrel, his mouth set in a thin, tight line. "Look at you—the Gypsies think there is no problem at all, because it is only happening in the settled places, and they pay very little heed to anything done in towns. They assume that if trouble spreads, they can simply drive away from it. The Free Bards are more concerned with the restriction on their ability to make a living, and not on the reputation they may be getting thanks to the tales spread by Churchmen—"

"N-not N-Nightingale," Kestrel protested.

"True. Not the Nightingale. But she is unique among all the Free Bards and Gypsies I have spoken to." He shook his head. "None of them are at all thinking about what is happening to the nonhumans, because they think their own problems are much greater. I have not heard from the nonhumans themselves—and that alarms me. Are they being harassed? Are they being arrested and taken off into oblivion? Are they being deported? Or is there nothing happening at all? I have heard nothing, and when I hear nothing, I worry more than when I hear rumors. I only *know* that the few nonhuman traders I know have simply turned over their routes in Rayden to human partners. The human traders frankly see this in terms of less competition and more profit. The nonhumans are gone, and I cannot question them."

Kestrel blinked. He had not considered the possibility that there might actually be bad things happening to the nonhumans. "Do you th-th-think—"

"That any of that has happened?" Harperus' grim expression lightened a little. "Not yet, Kestrel," he said gently. "But I greatly fear it *may*."

"M-m-me t-t-too." Jonny was serious about that; he had seen too many "insignificant" things turn out to be dangerous, had things that should have been no more than annoyances turn out to be life-threatening.

"There is a last 'why' that I have not answered," Harperus continued. "That is because I do not know. Why is this happening? I honestly have no idea, partly because my people do not think like yours. It would seem to me that the Church is doing very well without all this nonsense. Or it is, if you take the Church's primary goal as being the saving of souls and directing people to act in a moral and responsible manner. But if the Church's goal has changed to something else—"

"Th-then th-that m-may b-be the *why*." Jonny licked his dry lips, nervously, and ventured his thought on the matter. "M-maybe it isn't j-just a wh-why. M-maybe it's also a *who*."

Now it was Harperus' turn to raise his eyebrows. "This might be the work of one person? Perhaps a person in a position of power within the Church? Or—someone who wishes to use these changes as a means of gaining more power for himself?" At Jonny's nod, he pursed his lips, thoughtfully. "An interesting speculation. I will look into this."

Harperus handed Jonny his mug, then shoved away from the side of the wagon, turned on his heel, and headed back to the door, vanishing inside. Jonny turned and went back to his vehicle, walking slowly and thoughtfully.

He was not offended by Harperus' abrupt departure; he knew better than to expect human behavior or even what a human would think of as "politeness" out of a nonhuman. In fact, he was rather gratified; it meant that the Deliambren took him and his speculations seriously.

But Harperus was not the only person who now had that particular speculation to "look into." Jonny had decided last night that if the Deliambren thought enough of his idea to take it seriously, *he* would see what he could do to track down the center of all these troubles.

As he had told Harperus, there often was a *who* in the middle of something like this, and if you could find him and deal with him, before he had become so protected that it was impossible to get near him, you could actually do something. In fact, you could effectively stop the movement before it had gained its own momentum and had, not one, but many people devoted to keeping it alive. It was like extracting the root of a noxious plant, before it spread so far and had sent up so many shoots it was impossible to eradicate.

He had learned a great deal about politics in the short time he had been in Birnam, watching the way the people opposed to his uncle's rule had operated. He had probably learned more than anyone else had ever guessed.

Ordinary people, he had noticed, tended to do what they were told, as long as they were given orders by someone who was a recognized authority. Or, as long as the orders did not affect their own lives very much, they would support the orders through simple inaction. If you made changes gradual, and made them seem reasonable, no one really cared about them.

And the changes mounted, imperceptibly, until one day people who had been "good neighbors"—which basically meant that they had not disturbed each other and had no serious quarrels with each other—were now deadly enemies. And it all seemed perfectly reasonable by then.

As long as nothing bad happens to them, people they know, or anyone who agrees with them— "Atrocities" only happened to your own kind. "Just retribution" was what happened to other people. A cult or a myth was someone else's religion. Your religion was the right and moral way.

Or as the Free Bards put it, "One man's music is another man's noise." As long as people were able to listen to what they called music, they didn't care if "noise" was banned. . . .

Well, this all might be something the Free Bards could do something about, at least if it was at a controllable stage. Maybe that was another "why"—why the Free Bards had come in for the greater share of trouble so far. They poked fun at pompous authority; they made the strange into the familiar. It was very difficult for a person who had heard Linnet's "Pearls and Posies" to think of Gazners as "cold-blooded" for instance—or Wren's own "Spell-bound Captive" to believe that Elves truly had no souls. The Free Bards opened up the world, just a little, to those who had never been beyond their own village boundaries. Jonny knew that Master Wren had wider ideas for the Free Bards than most of them dreamed at the moment. Wren saw his creation as a means to spread information that others would rather not have public—and perhaps he might even have a greater goal than that. But that was enough for Jonny, at least at the moment.

So, this whole situation just might be a state of affairs that Free Bards could do something about. It definitely was something they should know about if it turned out there was a single person behind the persecution!

So—the first thing to do would be to see if he and Robin could track the sermons to their source.

He thought about that for a moment. There were only two of them, and they could only go in one direction. There was Harperus, who would be "looking into things" as well. But what about asking Nightingale as well? She was the one who had stopped to listen to the preachers in the street. She was the one who had given them the most information. She was already observing. If she was willing to expand that a little—

He locked up the wagon, and went in search of Nightingale. He would find out what direction she planned to go when she left the Waymeet. They would go in the opposite direction. Perhaps this little group of Free Bards would be able to find some answers to all their questions. And—dare he hope—solutions as well?

Kestrel sighed, and took up the reins as the first fat drop of rain plopped down on the gravel lane in front of the horses. "An-nother b-beautiful d-day," he said sardonically.

"It could be worse," Robin replied, and patted his knee. "At least the rain held off long enough for our laundry to dry."

"And w-we d-did get that n-nice h-hot b-bath," he admitted. Although it had been something more than a mere "bath"—the bathhouse proved to be the kind that had several small rooms, each furnished with a huge tub, fully large enough for two. It had been well worth the money, all things considered.

"We did. We are clean, the wagon is clean, all our clothing is clean— we just might be presentable enough that they won't throw us out of Westhaven," Robin said, cheerfully.

The horses stamped, showing their impatience, but Kestrel was not going to let them move out just yet. Not until—

A sharp whistle behind him told him that Harperus was about to pull out. The Haspur had once again vanished into the depths of the wagon; Kestrel doubted that more than a handful of people had even glimpsed him during the three days they all camped here. It had been T'fyrr who had spoken to Nightingale and obtained her agreement to reverse her planned course and return to Kingsford, to see if the strange Church activities originated there, or elsewhere. "But then I am going to Birnam," she had said firmly. "I must eat, and I cannot eat if I cannot play."

Kestrel got the feeling that if it hadn't been for T'fyrr, she wouldn't even have agreed to that much.

Harperus' huge vehicle moved slowly into the lane parallel to theirs. Once they reached the trade road, Kestrel planned to follow him for the short period when they would both be going in the same direction. A few leagues up the road, a minor, seldom-used trade-road branched off this one. This was the road to Westhaven, which just happened to be Rune's old home, and that was the direction he and Robin were going, while Harperus and T'fyrr took the main road.

It was Robin's notion to spy on Rune's mother, if she was still there. She wanted to be able to tell Rune *something* about what was going on in her old haunts; she had told Jonny that she thought Rune would feel less guilty over leaving if she knew her mother was all right.

Personally, Jonny hadn't detected any concern for her mother on Rune's part, but he wasn't a female. There might have been things the two of them said to each other that made Robin think Lady Lark felt guilt over leaving her mother to fend for herself. And one road was as good as another, really—at least, when the road led eventually to Gradford. *That* particular city had a High Bishop in residence, which made it another logical candidate for information about the Church.

What was more, so far as he was concerned, there was an abbey, Carthell Abbey, lying on that little-used road that linked Westhaven and Gradford. Priests and the like who lived in isolated abbeys liked to talk to visitors; they might say something to give Kestrel a place to start.

How Harperus maneuvered that huge wagon so easily, Kestrel had no notion—but he brought it around smartly and was already on the lane leading to the trade-road by the time Kestrel got his mares in motion. The rear of the wagon was a blank wall; peculiar sort of construction.

Wagons were dark enough that most people cut windows everywhere they could.

The new axle performed exactly as Oakhart had promised; they jounced along in Harperus' wake, but thanks to the Deliambren, their course wasn't as bumpy as it could have been. Harperus' wagon was much, much heavier than theirs, and his wheels much broader, although the distance between his left and right wheels was about the same as between theirs. That was why Jonny was letting him lead; as long as he kept their wheels in the ruts left by the Deliambren's wagon, their ride was relatively smooth.

At about noon, they all stopped at the crossroads for a meal; Harperus supplying more of his odd, but tasty food, and Robin offering fresh honey-cakes she had bought at Waymeet.

"Be careful out there," Robin said, as they made their farewells. "If we see you at Gradford, I *don't* want to see you in trouble!"

"I?" The Deliambren arched an eyebrow at her. "I am a well-known and respectable trader. You, on the other hand, are a disreputable Gypsy, and a Free Bard to boot! I am far more like to see *you* in a gaol of one sort or another!"

Jonny shivered; after the things that Nightingale had told them, that was no longer very funny. "D-d-don't even j-j-joke about th-that," he said. "L-let's j-just s-say w-w-we'll s-s-see y-you b-b-before M-M-Midw-w-winter."

"So we shall. May your road be easy, friends," Harperus responded, gravely. "Now—if you are to make Westhaven before nightfall—"

"We had better be off." Robin swung herself up into the driver's seat, leaving Jonny to accept Harperus' clap on the shoulder and T'fyrr's handclasp—

—or clawclasp. Or whatever.

Then they parted company; Harperus to take his wagon onward, and Robin to turn theirs down a much smaller road, one covered with wet, fallen leaves and shaded by sadly drooping branches, with undergrowth so thick that once they were on the lane, it was no longer possible to hear or see the larger vehicle. In moments, they could have been the only people in the entire world. There was no sign of any human, nothing but the forest, the occasional birdcall, and the steady drip of water from the bare branches.

Kestrel sighed. In some ways, he was glad that the two of them were alone again, but he had enjoyed Harperus' company, and he wished he could have heard T'fyrr sing a few more times.

But most of all, he liked the feeling of security he'd had, being around the Deliambren and his formidable wagon. No one was likely to give Harperus any trouble, and if anyone did, against all common sense, he was probably going to regret doing so.

He only wished that the same could be said for them.

They reached the village of Westhaven quite a bit before nightfall. The fact that the road was considerably less traveled meant that it was, conversely, smoother than the main road. Less traffic during all this bad weather had made for fewer ruts, though there were erosion cuts to rattle

across. The mares made much better time that he or Robin had any right
to expect.

"If I recall, the inn is on the other side of the village," Robin said.
There wasn't much there, really; a few buildings around a square, although
there did seem to be a farmer's market going on. This was the kind of
village that Jonny Brede would have passed by, if he'd had the choice.
There was no room for an outsider here, everyone knew everyone else.
Still, though strangers might not be welcome, their coin was, and spending
money usually brought some form of speech out of even the most taciturn
of villagers.

"W-we should g-get some bread," he said. "M-maybe ch-cheese. S-S-
Stillwater d-d-didn't have either."

Robin glanced at him out of the corner of her eye, and smiled. "So we
can find things out without asking questions, hmm?" she replied. "Oh, I
can think of a few more things we could use. Roots, for one; and more
feed for the horses. Even at the 'good price' they gave me for being a
Gypsy, the price for grain at Stillwater was outrageous."

By that time, they were actually *in* the village; virtually everyone in the
square or the stalls along one side stared at them as they drove in. Robin
pulled the horses up to the single hitching post with ostentatious care,
then jumped down and tied the mares up to it. Kestrel climbed down on
his side, trying to look as formidable as possible.

The village square was centered around a well. No great surprise there,
most small villages were. There were four buildings on three sides of the
square, with two larger buildings, one clearly a small Church and the
other a Guild Hall, on the fourth side. A joint Guild Hall from the look
of it; there were boards with the signs for the Millers', the Joiners', the
Smiths' and the Tanners' Guilds up above the door. No Bardic Guild
harp, though, which was a relief.

The stalls had been set up along this side, and Kestrel followed Robin
as she opened the back of the wagon, got a basket, and made her way
directly towards them. It looked as if the rain that had plagued their travel
so far had scarcely touched Westhaven; the dust of the street was damped
down, but had not turned to mud, and beneath the dust, the street itself
was packed dirt that must surely turn into a morass every time it rained
heavily.

Now I remember why I like cities, Kestrel thought. Paved streets, and
regular collection of refuse, were two very good reasons.

As Robin approached the first stall, looking determinedly cheerful, he
decided he did not like the faintly hostile way the woman minding it and
the two loitering in front of it were staring at her. He steeled himself
for trouble.

But it never came. At least, not in the form of outright "trouble."

Instead, the thin, disagreeable-looking wench, who had a face like a
hen with indigestion and hair the color and texture of old straw, completely ignored them. She began chattering away at her two cronies at
such a high volume and rate of speech that it would have been impossible
for anyone to "get her attention" without interrupting her forcibly and
rudely.

But Kestrel knew that Robin had no intention of doing anything that would give the stallkeeper an excuse for further rudeness. And if the wench thought she was going to outmaneuver a Gypsy—

Instead, Robin silently surveyed the contents of the stall with a superior eye, counterfeiting perfectly the airs of a high-born nobleman. She raised one supercilious eyebrow, then sniffed as if she found the selection of baked goods *vastly* inferior to what she was expecting, and sailed on without a single word to any of the three.

At the sound of a smothered giggle from just ahead of them, Robin smiled, and exchanged a quick glance with Kestrel. He nodded slightly in the direction of the giggler, an older woman in the next stall, one with a plain but merry face, who was selling eggs, sausage, and bacon.

Although none of these things had been on their tentative shopping list, Robin headed straight for her, and engaged her in a spirited bargaining session. As Robin put her purchases in her basket, she cocked her head to one side, and paused for a moment.

"Is there any place here in Westhaven where I can get *fresh* bread?" she asked, loudly enough that the women at the first stall could hear her clearly. "Properly made bread?" The disagreeable hen-woman flushed, and the egg-seller's mouth tightened as she held back another giggle.

"Well, Mother Tolley isn't a baker, precisely, but she sells the *freshest* bread on market-days," the egg-seller said, with a slightly malicious sparkle to her eyes that told Kestrel there was a petty feud, probably of long standing, between her and the hen-woman. "It's from an old family recipe, and her own yeast, and I buy it myself. She's got the last stall in the row."

"Thank you *so* much," Robin replied, with a warm smile. "I really appreciate *your* courtesy."

She made her way past the next four stalls, still smiling, and paying no outward attention to the varied expressions of shock, amusement, and hostility the women there displayed. Interesting that there were only women in the market today. Perhaps the harvest was late.

Or perhaps the men did not consider market-day to be within their purview.

Now, Kestrel was no stranger to small villages or the behavior people who lived in them exhibited, particularly to outsiders, but the feeling here was—odd. By their clothing, by the condition of the buildings, and by the unused state of the road leading to Westhaven, this village was not exactly prospering. The women with stalls here *should* have been falling all over each other to attract the money Robin was so willingly spending.

But they weren't. The first woman had been actively hostile, and only the woman with the sausages seemed at all friendly—and that was simply because of the quarrel she had with the first stall-keeper. What was going on here?

The last stall held something they could actually use; some nice, freshly dug root-vegetables and two round, golden loaves of bread—obviously the last of a large baking, by the blank places on the cloth where they sat. "Mother Tolley" behaved in the way Kestrel had expected—she was obviously pleased to see them and their coins, and was only too happy to sell them whatever they wanted. Robin chatted with her about the weather, the terrible state of the roads, revealed the fact that they had come from Birnam by way of Kingsford and that they were on their way to Gradford.

"My, how you've traveled! And you've been through Kingsford! Oh, I wish I could see it some day," Mother Tolley said, brightly. "I hear the Kingsford Faire is something to behold!"

"It is, indeed," Robin replied, nodding. "I have been there as a performer every year since I was a child of ten."

"Truly?" Mother Tolley's eyes widened. "What is it like? Is it as great as they say?"

Robin spread her hands wide. "Absolutely hundreds of people attend the Faire, from Dukes to Guild Masters to every manner of peddler you can imagine. If there is anything in the world that can be sold, you'll find it at Kingsford Faire. All the best performers in the world come there, and the Holy Services at noon on Midsummer Day are beyond description."

"All the world comes to Kingsford Faire." Mother Tolley repeated the old cliché as solemnly as if she had made it up on the spot. "Well, say, since you are so well-traveled, and a musician and all—" she hesitated a moment, then, with a sly glance at the other women, continued on "—there was someone I knew once who had a hankering to go to the Kingsford Faire. It was a local child, with so many dreams—well, there aren't too many folk who believe in dreams, especially not here. I don't suppose you've ever heard tell of a fiddler girl named Rune?"

By now, Kestrel would have had to be a blind man not to notice how *all* the women, even those who were feigning indifference or displaying open hostility, were stretching their ears to hear Robin's reply to that question. And by the look in her eyes and the set of her jaw, Robin was about to give them more than they bargained for.

"Rune? Lady Lark?" she said brightly. "Why, of course I have! Everyone in all of Rayden and Birnam knows all about Free Bard Rune! Why, she's the most famous Free Bard in two kingdoms except for Master Wren!"

Mother Tolley blinked. Apparently that was not precisely the response she had expected. Kestrel figured she had hoped to hear something good about Rune, but not this. "Rune! Famous!" she said, blankly. "Why, fancy that—"

But Robin wasn't finished, not by half. "Oh, of course!" she continued, raising her voice just a little, to make certain everyone in the market got a good chance to hear. "First there was her song about how she bested the Skull Hill Ghost—I don't think there's a musician in Rayden that hasn't learned it by now."

"She—actually—" Mother Tolley was still trying to cope with the notion that Rune was famous.

"Oh, indeed! And she still has the Ghost's ancient gold coins to prove it!" Now Robin was getting beyond the truth and embroidering . . . and that made Kestrel nervous.

"Gold? The Ghost has gold?" That was one of the other women, her voice sharp with agitation.

"He did, but he gave it all to Rune, for her fiddling," Robin said brightly. "But that was just the beginning. Then she became an ally of the High King of the Elves for getting the better of one of the Elven Sires."

"Elves?" said another, in a choked voice. "She—"

Robin ran right over the top of her words. "But of course, what *really* made her famous was that she won the hand of Master Bard Talaysen himself with her talent and her musical skill—in fact, *she* was the one who saved him from that Elven Sire she bested. He wedded her, and now the two of them are the Laurel Bards to the King of Birnam, King Rolend, not just Laurel Bards but his personal advisors—"

Mother Tolley's face had gone so completely blank from astonishment that Kestrel couldn't tell what her feelings were. He guessed she would have been pleased to learn that Rune was doing well—but that this was something she wasn't prepared to cope with.

"I was at the ceremony, myself," Robin rattled on, in a confidential tone, as if she was a name-dropping scatterbrain. "As one of Lady Lark— that's what we call her, Lady Lark—one of Lady Lark's personal friends, of course. My! Even a Duke's daughter would envy her! She has twelve servants, all her very own—*three* of them just to tend to her wardrobe!"

Kestrel elbowed her sharply; she'd already gone too far three lies ago. She ignored him.

"The King himself gave her so much gold and gems that she couldn't possibly spend it all, and the weight of her jewelry would drown her if she ever fell into a river wearing it!" Robin gave him a warning look when he moved to elbow her again. "She wears silk every day, and she has three carriages to ride, and she bathes in wine, they say—" Robin simpered. Kestrel did his best not to laugh at her expression, despite his unease. He hadn't known she could *simper*. She was a better actress than he'd thought. "Our wagon and the horses and all—that was her present to me. You know, she gave wagons and horses to all her Gypsy friends who came to the ceremony. *So* sweet of her, don't you think?"

Mother Tolley had gone beyond astonished. "Yes," she said faintly. "Yes, very sweet. Of course."

Calling *Rune* one of King Rolend's Laurel Bards and a personal advisor was not exactly the truth—and the picture Robin had painted of Rune and Talaysen wallowing in luxury and wealth was not even *close* to being true. But Kestrel watched the faces of those who had been so eager to hear some terrible scandal about their prodigal runaway, and their puckered expressions told him that some of the good citizens of Westhaven were less than thrilled to hear that she was doing well. And the more sour those expressions became, the more Robin embroidered on her deceptions. He didn't think he had ever seen her look quite so smug before.

But while this was all very amusing to her, he was beginning to worry more than a little that she might be digging a hole they both were about to fall into.

"W-we must g-go," he said, firmly and loudly, before she could make up any more stories, this time out of whole cloth—either about Rune or about their supposed importance to her. Or worse yet, told the whole truth about *him*! He didn't know what was worse—to have these women believe Robin's tales, or to have them think her a liar.

"Ah," Robin said blankly as he completely threw her off her course for a moment with his interruption; then she regained her mental balance, and blinked, as if she had suddenly figured out that she might have gone a little too far. "Of course, you're right! We have a long way to go before we stop tonight."

She tucked her purchases carefully in her basket and allowed Kestrel to hurry her off.

"What w-were you th-thinking of?" he hissed, as they followed the sausage-woman's stammered directions to the mill.

"I'm not sure," she said weakly. "I got kind of carried away."

He refrained from stating the obvious.

"It was just—those sanctimonious prigs! You saw how they wanted to hear that I had never heard of Rune, that she was a nothing and a failure! I wanted to *smack* their self-satisfied faces!"

"Y-you d-did that all r-right," he replied, a little grimly, as they arrived at the mill.

The miller himself was busy, but one of his apprentices handled their purchase of grain for the horses. It took a while; the boy was determined that he was going to give them exact measure. By the time they returned to the wagon, the stalls were deserted, and the women gone from the marketplace.

Kestrel's stomach told him that there was no sinister reason for the empty market—it was suppertime, and these women had to return home to feed their families.

But the silence of the place unnerved him, and for once even Robin didn't have much to say. She unlocked the back of the caravan quickly and stowed her purchases inside; he went to one of the storage bins outside to put the grain away. Suddenly he wanted very much to be out of Westhaven and on the road.

Quickly. He felt eyes on his back; unfriendly eyes. The women might be gone, but they were still watching, from their homes and their kitchens. The sooner he and Robin had Westhaven behind them, the better.

He had put the last of the bags of grain away in the bin and locked the door, when he heard footsteps behind him.

"Hey!" said a nasal, obnoxious male voice. "What kinda thieves do we have here?"

CHAPTER SIX

He turned, but slowly, as if he had no idea that there was anyone at all there, pretending he had not heard the voice or the not-so-veiled insult. They weren't in any trouble—yet. An official, even in a tiny, provincial village like this one, would not be as young as the voice had sounded.

Obnoxious, surely. Officious, of course. But not young. So this must be some stupid troublemaker, a village bully and his friends.

He knew as soon as he turned that he had been right, for the young men wore no badges of authority. There were three of them, none of them any older than he. All three were heavily muscled, and two of them had teeth missing. All three were taller than Kestrel. He looked up at them, measuring them warily. Definitely bullies, else why have three against two?

Don't do anything. Maybe they'll get bored and go away.

"So, Gyppo, what'd ye steal?" one asked, rubbing his nose across the back of his hand. It was a very dirty hand, and the nose wasn't exactly clean either. Dirty hair, pimpled face, a sneer that would have been more appropriate on the lips of a bratty little six-year-old.

Then again, I doubt his mind's grown much beyond six.

Kestrel ignored them, and moved to the front of the wagon. Robin was already there, untying the horses from the hitching post. Bad luck there; they would have to lead the horses around to turn the wagon, and the three bullies were purposefully blocking the way. The horses were well-trained, but it would be easy enough to spook them.

"He's a Gyppo, he *had* ta steal sumthin'," said the second. The trouble-makers moved in a little closer, blocking any escape—unless they left the wagon and horses and fled on foot. And they were trapped between the wagon and the blank wall of the Guild Hall. Even *if* anyone here might be inclined to help, there would be no way to see what was going on. "Mebbe he stole th' wagon."

"Mebbe he stole the horses," said the third. "They's too good a horse fer a Gyppo."

"So's the wagon," replied the first. "Mebbe he stole both. Hey, Gyppo! Ye steal yer rig? Thas more likely than that tale yer slut spun, 'bout Rune given it to ye!"

Something about the bully's tone warned Kestrel that Robin's stories about Rune had brought them the trouble he feared. This fool had been no friend to Rune while she'd lived here—and he held a long-standing grudge against her, like the hen-faced woman.

"Yah," said the third, sniffing loudly and grinning. "*We* know all 'bout Rune! Her mam's a slut, she's a slut, an' I reckon her friends'r all sluts, too." He stared at Kestrel, waiting for an answer, and became angry when he didn't get one. "How 'bout it?" he growled. "Ain't ye gonna say nothin'?"

Kestrel had been watching them carefully, assessing them, and had concluded that while they were very likely strong, and probably the town bullies, they also didn't have a brain to share among them. They were slow, and moved with the clumsy ponderousness of a man used to getting his way through sheer bulk and not through skill. And the way they held themselves told him they were not used to having any real opposition. They wanted to goad him into anger, into rushing them like an enraged child. They would not be prepared for someone who struck back with agility and control.

Still, if they could get away without a physical confrontation—

He simply stood his ground, and stared at them, hoping to unnerve them with his silence.

Stalemate. They stared at him, not sure what to do since he wasn't reacting to their taunts in the way they were used to. He stared at them, not daring them to start anything, but not backing down either.

Robin made a movement toward the slit in her skirt that concealed her knife. He put his hand on her wrist to stop her.

Unfortunately, that movement broke the tenuous stalemate.

"Yah, Rune's a slut an' her friends'r sluts!" said the first one, loudly. "Right, Hill, Warren?" He grinned as the other two nodded. "Hey, boys, I gotta idea! We got our fill'a her—so how 'bout we get a taste'f her friend, eh? They say Gyppo women is real hot—"

And he made the mistake of grabbing for Robin—who had fended off more bullies in her time than there were people in this village. As she launched herself at her would-be molester, Kestrel sprang at the one grabbing for him.

Fighting off assassins for most of your life tends to make you a survivor; it also teaches you every dirty trick anyone ever invented. Kestrel turned into a whirlwind of fists and feet, and Robin was putting her own set of street-fighting skills into action. He hadn't wanted this to turn into a physical confrontation, but the bullies had forced it on him, and now they were going to find out that the odds of three large men against a tiny man and woman *had* been very uneven—but not in *their* favor.

He kicked the legs out from beneath the one nearest him by slamming his foot into the fool's knee before the man had a notion that he had even moved. The bully went down on his face and started to scramble up, putting his rear in perfect target-range. Kestrel followed his kick in the rump with one to the privates so hard that the bully could not even scream, only gasp and double up into a ball. Robin had already done the same to the fool who had grabbed her, except that she hadn't bothered to knock his legs out from under him first. And she hadn't hit him with the knee, either; he was expecting that. He had backed out of knee range, laughing. She had snap-kicked him as she had intended all along, and the laugh turned into a gasp as she put her full weight behind the kick. She had followed up *her* foot to the groin with a backhanded blow in his face with the hilt of her dagger that put him to the ground with a bleeding nose and a few less teeth.

They both converged on the third bully, the one who seemed to be the leader, slamming him up against the side of the wagon before he had quite comprehended the fact that his two friends were no longer standing.

They knocked the breath out of him, and Robin had her dagger across his throat before he could blink. Kestrel grabbed his wrists and twisted his arms back while he was still stunned, holding him so that no matter how he moved, it would *hurt*. And the more he moved, the more it would hurt.

"Now," breathed Robin, as the bully's eyes bulged with fear and the edge of her blade made a thin, painful cut across his throat, "I think you owe us an apology. Don't you?"

Kestrel jerked the bully's arms so that they wrenched upwards in their sockets. He gasped, and nodded, his eyes filling with tears of pain. Now the very fact that nothing of this confrontation could be seen from the square or the houses around it worked in *their* favor. So long as no one missed these fools and came looking for them, if things went well.

Then again—they probably won't come looking for someone who might be beating the pulp out of two strangers. No one wants to know what these three are doing, I'll bet.

"I *also* think it would be very wise of you to make that apology, like a gentleman, and say nothing more about this," she continued. *"Don't you?"*

Frantically, he nodded, his eyes never leaving her face. The bloodthirsty expression there would have terrified a denser man than he.

"Just a few things I want you to think about, before you make that apology," she said harshly. "You might have what you *think* is a clever idea, about claiming how we attacked you, after we drive off." She shook her head, as he broke out in a cold sweat. "That would be a very, very stupid idea. First of all, you'd end up looking like a fool. Why, look how *small* we are! We weigh less than you do, the two of us put together! Think how *brave* you'd look, saying that two *tiny* people attacked you and beat you up, and one of them a girl! You would wind up looking like a weakling as well as a fool, and everyone from here to Kingsford would be laughing at you. What's more, they'd say you can't be any kind of a man if you let a girl beat you up. They'd say you're fey. And they'd start beating *you* up, any time you left home."

The sick look in his eyes told Kestrel that her words had hit home, but she wasn't finished with him.

"There's another reason why that would be a very, very stupid idea," she continued. "We're Gypsies. Do you know just what that means?"

He shook his head, very slightly.

"That means that we have all *kinds* of ways to find out what you've been doing, even when we aren't around. It means we have even *more* ways of getting at you afterwards—and all of them will come when you aren't expecting them." Her eyes widened, and her voice took on a singing quality—

And Kestrel sensed the undercurrent of music in the mind, music that could not be detected by the ears, the music he only heard when someone was using Bardic Magic.

Robin's voice matched that music, turning her sing-song into a real spell, a spell meant to convince this fool that every word she said was nothing less than absolute truth. "We'll come in the night, when you're all alone—catch you on a path and send monsters to chase you until your heart bursts! We'll send invisible things, night-hags, and vampires to your bed, to sit on your chest and *squeeze* the breath from your lungs while you try to scream in pain and can't! We'll come at you from the full moon, and set a fire in your brain, until you run mad, howling like a dog!"

The bully was shaking so hard he could hardly stand now.

"Or—we'll wait—and one night, when you're sitting at your ease—"

Her eyes widened further, and he stared at them, unable to look away.

"—watching the fire—all alone—no one around to help you, or save you—"

He was sweating so hard now that his shirt was soaked.

"—suddenly the fire will *flare!* It will grow! You'll be unable to move as it swells and takes on a form, the form of a two-legged beast with fangs as long as your arm and talons like razors! You'll scream and scream, but no one will hear you! You'll try to escape, but you'll be frozen to your chair! You'll watch the *demon* tear out your heart, watch as it eats your heart still beating, and howl as it takes you down to hell!"

At the word "hell," a burst of flame appeared under his nose, cupped in the hand that was not holding the dagger.

A slow, spreading stain on the front of his pants and a distinctive smell betrayed just how frightened he was. The bully had wet his breeches with fear.

Kestrel let him go in disgust, and the man dropped to the ground, gibbering incoherently. Robin stepped back and smiled at him sweetly.

"Now," she said, "do you apologize for calling me a slut?"

He nodded frantically.

"Do you apologize for calling Rune a slut?"

His head bobbed so hard it practically came off his shoulders.

"Are you going to keep your filthy tongue off Rune and any other Free Bard? Are you going to take your two playmates and go away, and never say *anything* about this again?" She smiled, but it was not sweetly. "Are you going to pretend all this never happened?"

"Yes!" the bully blubbered, through his tears. "Yes! Oh, please—"

"You may go," Robin said, coolly, sheathing her dagger so quickly it must have looked to the man as if she had made it vanish into thin air. He fled.

The other two were just getting to their feet, but they had heard and seen everything Robin had said and done. And they had been affected by her Bardic spell too, just not as profoundly or immediately as the first bully. The one Kestrel had kicked helped the one with the bloodied face to his feet, and the two of them supported each other, getting out of sight as quickly as possible.

Which was precisely what Kestrel had in mind, as well—getting away before some other variety of trouble found them! He jumped into the driver's seat and picked up the reins, giving Robin just enough time to scramble into the passenger's side before turning the mares, and heading out of the village at a brisk trot, thanking whatever deity might be listening for the thickening dusk that hid both them and their erstwhile attackers, and for the emptiness of the village square.

"Wh-why d-did you *d-d-d-do* that?" he asked, as Robin arranged her skirts with a self-satisfied little smile.

"What?" she asked, as if he had astonished her by asking the question. "Why did I use the Bardic Magic? I wanted him to believe me! If I hadn't, he'd have gotten another dozen of his friends and come after us!"

"N-not using th-the B-Bardic M-Magic!" he scolded, guiding the mares around a tricky turn. "M-making th-them th-think w-we w-were evil m-m-mages! R-remember wh-what the Ch-church has b-b-been saying ab-b-bout m-mages?"

"Oh, that," she replied, indifferently. "What difference does it make?

He won't tell anyone *anything* now. He'll be sure that the moment he opens his mouth, a demon will come after him."

"N-now," Kestrel retorted. "You kn-know the m-magic w-wears off! H-how l-long b-before he t-tells a P-p-p-priest?"

"So what? We're never coming back." She had something cradled in her skirts; a moment later, he heard the distinctive clink of coins. "Hah!" she said, in the next moment, as the wagon jounced a little. "We actually came out ahead!"

"Wh-*what?*" he yelped. He knew exactly what *that* meant; she'd not only beaten and terrified those bullies, she'd *picked their pockets.* "Y-you d-d-d-didn't!"

"Of course I did," she said, calmly, taking the coins and pouring them into her belt-pouch. "Why not? They deserved worse than that! Didn't you hear them? I'll bet those louts absolutely terrified Rune while she lived here! They should be grateful that I was in a good mood! I almost made the three of them eunuchs while I was at it!"

"B-but—" he protested. "Th-that m-makes us n-no b-better th-than th-they are!"

"I don't think so." She folded her arms stubbornly across her chest. "I think we were simply the instrument of proper justice."

"B-but—" He gave up. She would never admit she was wrong, even if he managed to convince her of it—and even if he did, she would only think he was worried about the possible consequences. That wasn't what made him so upset, but how could he make her understand that she had just acted in as immoral and irresponsible a manner as the *Church* claimed Free Bards were?

How could they honestly refute the claims of the street preachers when they actually *did* what the street preachers said they did? Even though they had been provoked—

Never mind. Right now, the best thing he could do was drive. Maybe this would sort itself out later.

He hoped.

Darkness had fallen by the time they reached the next building on the road. The Hungry Bear inn—distinguished as such by the sign over the door, a crudely painted caricature of an animal that *could* have been a bear—or a brown pig—or a tree-stump with teeth. The sign was much in need of paint. The *inn* was much in need of repair.

Even in the fading twilight and the feeble flame of a torch beside the door, that much was all too obvious. It was clean, superficially at least, but so shabby that Gwyna would have passed it by without a second thought if they were really looking for a night's work.

But they weren't, so when Kestrel pulled the horses to a halt outside the front door—which didn't even have a lantern, only that crude pitch-and-straw torch—she hopped down to see if she could find the innkeeper.

She had barely one foot on the ground before a round blob of a woman dressed in clothing more suited to a coquettish girl came hurrying out to see if they might be customers.

As she came out of the darkness of the tap room and into the flickering light from the torch, Gwyna felt her eyes widen in surprise. Was *this* Rune's mother?

She must be—certainly the lavish use of cosmetics, and the straw-blond hair, the low-cut blouse and the kilted-up skirt matched Rune's descriptions. But if this was Rune's mother—either Rune's memory was horribly at fault, or the woman had doubled, or even tripled her weight, since Rune had left!

"Welcome to the Hungry Bear," the woman said, her eyes taking in their equippage, and probably evaluating it to the last penny. "My name is Stara, and I am the innkeeper's wife—how may I serve you?"

Well, that certainly clinched it. This *was* Rune's mother, and she had evidently managed to wheedle, connive, or blackmail her way into more than Jeoff's bed.

Well, Rune was right about that much. And since I don't see any other helpers around, I suspect they either can't afford more help anymore, or no one will work for them. So Rune was right there, too, in thinking Stara would have turned her into an unpaid drudge, given half a chance. If Rune had stayed, she'd have found herself shackled to this shoddy inn for the rest of her life, with music taking second place to whatever her mother wanted her to do.

"We are musicians, Innkeeper," Robin said, in a carefully neutral voice. "We hadn't really expected to find an inn here, but we usually offer our services in return for a room and a meal—"

Not that I'd sleep in any bed you had anything to do with. You probably haven't washed the sheets in months.

The balding and middle-aged innkeeper himself appeared at the door as Robin finished her little speech, but he held back, diffidently saying nothing, quite obviously very much the henpecked husband. Stara looked them over critically, and her eyes sharpened with mingled envy and greed at their prosperity. No one who drove a rig like theirs, new, and well-made, would be an inferior musician or poor. . . .

And given the general air of abandonment, when Rune ran off, most of the business went somewhere else. There should be at least a handful of customers in there, and the tap room is empty. I don't smell anything cooking, either, which means they don't get enough customers of an evening to have a regular supper ready.

So, if they stayed, there'd be an empty tap room, a poor meal and a cold and musty bed. And given what had just happened back in the village—

It probably wouldn't be a good idea to stop here. No matter what else I could find out about Stara. I think I've seen enough to tell Rune all she needs to hear. Enough to make her glad that she got out while she could.

"Uh—Stara—" the innkeeper said, timidly. "We don't know these people. We don't know anything about them. Remember what the Priest has been preaching? These people aren't wearing Guild colors. So many of these free musicians sing that licentious music, that music that makes people do sinful things—"

Stara started to wave him to silence, but it appeared that on this subject, at least, he would not be henpecked. He raised his chin and his voice stubbornly. "You know very well how sinful we were when that daughter of yours was playing her music here! And every night the tap room was full of people dancing, singing, taking no thought of their souls—"

"I know," Stara muttered resentfully, no doubt thinking how full the cashbox had been back then.

"Well, what if these people are the same kind?" he asked her, his voice rising with a touch of hysteria. "I'm sure the Sacrificed God has been punishing us for our sin of letting people like that play here while that daughter of yours was here. Worse than that, what if they're magicians? I don't think we should let anyone play here who hasn't been approved by the Church!"

Harperus' words rang at her out of memory. *"How long before the signs say, 'No one permitted without a Church license'?"*

She grimaced, her expression hidden in the shadows of the wagon. *Not that I'd want to play here, with or without a license.*

"I would not want to make anyone uncomfortable, much less give them the impression that they were sinning by simply listening to music," Robin said, smoothly. "I personally have never heard of any such nonsense as musicians who were magicians, but since your Priest evidently has, I will take his word that such things exist. And since obviously you don't want us, and no one can prove he *isn't* a mage, we'll just be on our way. We would never want to play where we were under suspicion, or where our music wasn't wanted." She raised her voice a little more, and pitched it to make certain that it carried. "We are really in no great need of lodging, as you can clearly see, so do not concern yourselves for us on that score."

Not that you would care, but it's a nice little dig, isn't it?

Stara looked disgusted and stormed back into the tap room. The inn-keeper followed, wearing a look that mingled triumph and apprehension in equal measure. Triumph that he had his way, no doubt—and apprehension for the way that Stara was going to make him pay for getting his way. The door shut behind them.

Kestrel looked over at her, holding the reins quietly. "Interesting," he said.

She nodded. "I really think we ought to try camping somewhere down the road. Between the bullies and Priests with tales of music that leads you into sin, I'd sooner trust myself to wolves than to Westhaven."

"But would ye trust yerselves to ghosts, young friends?" asked a hoarse voice from the shadows of the rear door, across the inn-yard from the sorry excuse for a stable. "An ye would not, turn back 'round and take the long road—or follow th' right-hand fork o' this one."

A stolid woman with a round, red face moved out of the shadows and into the uncertain light of the torch. "*She* wouldna tell ye, an' *he* would be just's pleased t'see a sinner come t'grief, but yon's the road over Skull Hill. There be a Ghost there, a murderin' Ghost. It's taken a priest in it's time, no less, so it don't care a tot fer holiness. Yer safe enough by day, but by night, ain't nobbut safe on Skull Hill."

Kestrel nodded, gravely. "Th-thank you, l-lady."

The cook looked pleased at being called "lady." "Tush. Tain't nothin' no *decent* person wouldna pass warnin' 'bout."

Robin looked closely at the woman; they knew all about the Ghost from

Rune, of course, but Rune had described someone very like this woman—
one of her few supporters after the innkeeper's first wife had died. The
cook—

"Are you Annie Cook?" Robin asked. The woman stared at her, and
nodded, slowly, her expression turning to one of apprehension.

"How d'ye know—" Annie began, clearly suspecting Robin of an
uncanny, unnatural method of learning her name.

"Rune told me about you," Robin replied quickly, not sure how long
it would be before Stara or Jeoff came to chase them off. "She said you
were a good friend to her while she was here."

The uneasy expression turned again to one of pleasure. "Rune! I hope
th' child's well! She did aright t' run off from here."

Impulsively, Robin decided to tell Annie a more edited—and truthful—
version of what she had told the villagers. "Rune is doing wonderfully;
she is a Master Free Bard herself, she's wedded Master Bard Talaysen,
and they are both in the service of the King of Birnam. She is *very* happy,
and she and Talaysen are expecting their first child in the summer."

Annie gaped at her, then the gape turned into a smile. "Ye *don't* say!
Welladay!" The smile widened. "Why good for the girl! If ever there was
a child deserved a bit'a luck, it was that 'un!" She glared at the closed
door of the inn. "Not like 'er mother. That bit can't get nothin' without
it bein' through some man's bed. An' had Rune stayed here, she'd'a been
slavin' away i' that tap room while her mam sat on 'er fat rump an' held
th' cashbox."

"*Annie?*" the voice from within was muffled, but clearly Stara's. Annie
rolled her eyes, waved a friendly, but silent farewell, and retreated to
her kitchen.

Dark as it was, the road was smooth enough to permit them to travel
by night, at least for a while. Kestrel held the horses to a walk. It wasn't
as if they had to fear pursuit from the village. It wasn't likely that, even
if by some miracle the three bullies got over their fright, any of them
would come pursuing the Gypsies in the dark. "S-so that w-was S-Stara,"
he said. "N-n-nasty, p-petty piece."

"I'd have run off long before Rune did," Robin said thoughtfully. "Long,
long before Rune did. That woman can't see past the end of her nose,
and if she ever had a generous bone in her, it's long since gone."

Kestrel chuckled. "S-sunk in f-fat."

It was still barely warm enough for crickets, which sang a melancholy
tune in the grasses beside the road. Overhead, thin clouds obscured the
stars; the overcast was blowing off, but the moon was not yet out. No
way to see past the dim lanterns on the front of the wagon, but the
underbrush was so thick on either side of the road that there was no
chance of the horses wandering off. And this road, according to the maps,
went straight to Carthell Abbey without forking.

By way of Skull Hill.

That was according to the map; according to Rune and Annie Cook,
the road forked a little way ahead, and while the old road still went over

Skull Hill, the locals had cut another, cruder path around the dangerous place. Passable, she had said.

"I th-think, that c-compared to S-Stara, the Gh-Ghost m-must have been a p-pleasant audience," he said, trying to make a small joke.

Robin chuckled. "Certainly more appreciative. And the Ghost *rewarded* talent instead of stifling it."

"T-true." The horses clopped on, through the thick darkness, carefully feeling their way. Kestrel had been watching for roadside clearings, but there didn't seem to be any. He was beginning to wonder if they ought to stop and camp along here, even if they had to camp in the center of the road. After all, it wasn't as if it got very much use—they were hardly likely to block anyone's travel! By the old tracks they had seen, they might have been the only wagon along here in the past week.

"Th-that p-place where the r-road f-forks should b-be around here s-soon," he said. "What if w-we—"

"What if we go up Skull Hill?" Robin asked, suddenly.

For a moment he wasn't certain he had heard her right. "Wh-what?" he blurted.

"What if we go up Skull Hill?" she repeated. "Confront the Ghost, just like Rune did?"

He *had* heard her correctly. "Are you c-c-c-crazy?" he spluttered. "Why?"

She laughed; she didn't *sound* crazy. She did sound rather determined, however. "Why not?" she replied. "Rune did, and she wasn't even fully trained! We already know it likes music, and it might have another silver hoard or something equally interesting to swap for our music. We might be able to get him to grant unmolested passage to Gypsies and Free Bards, and that would be worth a night of playing, alone—we might need a road some day that no one will take."

He chewed on his lip, fiercely, and thought about it. She had a point. She had a very real point. The old road ran this way for a reason; it was a shorter route than the one that Harperus and T'fyrr were taking. If Gypsies and Free Bards knew it was safe for them to use, it could take a couple of days off their trips in this part of the world.

And if no one else would use the road for fear of the Ghost—it made a very neat escape route in case of trouble. From here to Stillwater was no great distance, and Stillwater could be held against even armed men if necessary.

"Let me get a lantern and walk ahead of the horses, so I can spot the place where the road forks," she said, while he was still thinking about it.

He pulled the horses to a halt; she wriggled back over the bed, and popped out the back with a lit lantern in her hand. She trotted up to take the halter of the right-hand horse, and held the lantern over her head to keep from getting glare in her eyes.

Well, that was all very well for her, but nothing saved him from the lantern-glare! He squinted, but he couldn't quite make out the road. He let the reins go slack; she was the one who could see where they were going—

And he realized a few moments later that she was leading them down the left-hand fork of the road. The overgrown, but obviously older, fork of the road.

"Robin!" he yelped. "Wh-what are you *d-d-doing?*"

She stopped the horses, and looked back at him, a little defiantly.

"I told you!" she said. "I want to climb Skull Hill to meet this Ghost face to—whatever!"

Robin left the mares and brought her lantern back to Kestrel, placing it at his feet. She looked up into his face, carefully gauging his expression. "I don't think there's any real danger," she said, calmly and reasonably, watching his eyes. "Honestly, or I wouldn't even consider this."

He didn't seem frightened. Of course, he could be hiding his fear. "N-no d-d-danger," he repeat-ed sarcastically. "Wh-when wh-who kn-kn-knows *how* m-m-many p-p-p-people have d-d-died up th-there!"

She took a very deep breath and got a firm grip on her temper. He wasn't saying she was stupid—wasn't even implying it. "When have I ever done anything really reckless?" she asked him.

He looked as if he was about to say something—but thought better of it, and closed his mouth again. "G-go on," he said grimly. "I'm l-l-listening. If y-you have a r-r-real argument, b-b-besides c-curiosity, I w-want to h-hear it."

"I've known something about magic for a long time," she told him. "At least, about some of the tinier magics. Not Bardic Magic, but little things Gypsies take for granted; healing, animal-charming, that kind of thing. And I think I know how this Ghost kills. I am pretty sure that his only real *weapon* is fear, and he can't do anything unless you're already afraid of him."

Kestrel looked skeptical, but a little less grim. "S-so?"

She licked her lips, and stared at the lamp flame for a moment. "If you're afraid of him, he can turn that fear against you—he can make it so overwhelming that—that it becomes something the human body just can't deal with. The heart races until it just gives up, he chases you until you drop dead of exhaustion, that kind of thing. Maybe some people don't die—maybe *most* of them don't die, they just run mad in this wilderness until they die of thirst or starve, or wild beasts get them."

"Th-that's v-v-very c-c-comforting," he said with heavy irony.

"But the point is that if you *aren't* afraid of him, he can't hurt you," she insisted. "Or if you interest him, he won't use that weapon of his! Rune wasn't completely terrified of him—and she interested him. So she was able to stand up to him. I don't know why we can't!"

Kestrel shook his head. "Wh-who s-s-said w-we aren't af-f-fraid of h-him?" he muttered. "N-n-not m-m-me."

She chuckled, as if he had made a joke. "Jonny, do you think I would have suggested this if you weren't a Master Bard in your own right? Think a minute! Rune managed to entertain this Ghost before she was even *trained*—when she was just a little better than a common traveling musician like all those people back in the Waymeet. Just think for a moment what we might be able to find out from him! Jonny, you're going to be the best thing he's heard in—well, since he got stuck up there!"

The only thing he was vain about was his talent and his ability as a musician. He began to soften as she appealed to that vanity.

"I think we can do this with no danger," she said, persuasively. "I think *you* could do this all alone, but with two of us there, we can keep from getting too exhausted."

Finally, the stubborn line of his jaw softened, and he sighed. "You r-r-really want t-t-to d-do th-this, d-don't you?"

"Yes," she replied, firmly. "I do. Call it—a sort of test. I want to measure myself against the same standards as the best musicians I know. This is one of them."

He shook his head. "All r-r-right," he replied. "Th-this m-makes m-more s-sense than wh-what you d-did back in W-Westhaven, anyw-w-way."

And as she led the horses up to the top of Skull Hill, she was left to wonder—

What in heaven's name did he mean by *that*?

CHAPTER SEVEN

Gwyna was just as glad that Jonny was not as familiar with Rune's history as she was. It had not been easy to convince him to go along with her scheme, but her appeal to his only point of pride had turned the trick. If he had known as much about the Ghost as she did—he might not have agreed even under a threat to their lives.

Robin knew she had a distinct advantage over Kestrel; she had heard Rune tell the story of the Skull Hill Ghost in detail, several times. Jonny had only heard the song. She knew pretty much what to expect, and when to expect it; she knew all there was that Rune had been able to put into words about the *effect* the Ghost had on people. She had paid very close attention to that story each time Rune had told it, because even before she had ever met Jonny or had learned that she, too, had the gift of Bardic Magic at her disposal, she had intended to come to Skull Hill one day.

Not just because she was determined to prove—if only to herself—that what Rune could do, she could duplicate. No, that was the easy answer, the one she thought Jonny would best understand.

Robin had spent her life in the pursuit of answers for the questions that plagued her. The story of the Ghost had created more questions for her than answers, and had powerfully aroused her curiosity. What *was* this spirit, anyway? The impression she'd gotten from Rune was that it was not, and never had been, human. So what was it? Was it really a spirit at all, or something more like an Elf, except that it was both more limited and more powerful? If it was a spirit, then why was a spirit bound to Skull Hill? And if it was the spirit of some creature that had not been human when alive, then what had brought a nonhuman creature *here*, to the heart of a human kingdom, and what had bound its spirit here after death?

And why was it killing people with fear? Rune's story made it very clear

that the Ghost was deliberately *trying* to murder his victims; the deaths
that had occurred were as a result of the Ghost's deliberate use of his
powers to kill. By that definition it was a murderer.

But the fact that he—it—had also let Rune "buy" her way free with
her music implied that the Ghost could spare people when it chose to do
so. The things it had said implied that it was not free to leave. Those
implications only opened up a horde of questions so far as Robin was
concerned.

Before she had ever met Jonny, curiosity had driven her to do things
and go places when nothing else would have. Questions would burn inside
her until they found an answer. Talaysen often said it was her greatest
strength and her greatest weakness, and she didn't see any reason to
disagree. But her curiosity had gotten her information that might never
have come into the hands of the Free Bards or the Gypsies otherwise,
and many times, that information had been important to their survival.

This time both intuition and curiosity had combined forces. *This is
important,* that was the message she was getting from both. She didn't
get many "hunches," and she tried hard to follow them whenever she did;
they were right more often than they were wrong.

She kept the lantern over her head to keep her eyes from becoming
dazzled by the light, and led the horses up the untidy, long-neglected
track. It wasn't as overgrown as she would have expected, though; no
bushes or trees, only weeds, and those looked sickly and were no taller
than her calf, even after a summer's worth of growth. She knew what *that*
meant; there was a road underneath this track, one of the Old Roads, the
ones no one knew how to build anymore. If she got out a shovel and dug,
she knew she would hit the hard surface of one of the roadways that
dated back to the Cataclysm; it would be a lightless black substance, like
stone but yielding, like tar but much harder. Nothing could grow through
it; that was why there was nothing growing on this track but short weeds.
The earth and loam that had covered this road couldn't be more than an
inch or so thick; just enough for grass and weeds to take root in. There
would be no cracks or imperfections in it, unless she came to a place
where an earthquake had split it, or the edge of a Cataclysm-boundary,
where it would be cut off as if by a giant knife.

The Old Roads usually connected two or more important places—or at
least, places that *had* been important before the Cataclysm. There were
often ruins along them. The Deliambrens always wanted to know about
Old Roads, so the Gypsies kept track of the ones they ran across. Did
Harperus know this one was here?

Probably not. Whatever this segment had connected before, it certainly
connected nothing of any import now. Gradford was a very minor city-
state despite its pretentions otherwise, and what was Westhaven? Nothing,
full of nobodies. A dead-end, dying, and not even aware it was in its
death-throes. Too stupid to know that its days were numbered.

The only thing that makes it important is that Rune came from there,
Gwyna thought cynically, thinking of the women in the marketplace and
the three bullies they had left damaged. Of course, she had—she hoped—
inflicted some emotional damage on the women who deserved it, with

her descriptions of Rune's fame and prosperity. *I hope that hen-faced bitch is so envious of Rune that she chokes on her dinner. I bet she's the one that set those bullies on us. I hope she nags her husband about silk gowns and carriages until he beats her senseless. I hope that fool I scared into incontinence is her husband, and I scared him into impotence as well!* She kept her feral snarl to herself. *Vindictive? Oh, a tad.*

She knew better than to say any of this out loud. Jonny, bless his sweet little heart, was *not* vindictive. He believed that concentrating on revenge simply reduced you to the level of your persecutors. Gwyna believed in an old Gypsy proverb; *Get your revenge in early and often. You might not have another chance.*

Maybe that was why the Ghost fascinated her so. Was he somehow working out some bizarre scheme for revenge? If so, on who, and why? Was he choosing to let *some* people by, people they never even heard of because they were unaware that they had been in any danger at all?

Or was he a strange revenant from the distant past, from the time when this Old Road had been in use? Could something have called him up out of that past to haunt this stretch of roadway? Could his reasons and motives, or need for revenge, be buried so far in the past they no longer had any relevance?

Or if this creature was strange enough, could they even understand his reasons, much less his motives?

An owl called up above her, and she sighed. No point in following that line of speculation. He had to be understandable; there was no point in this, otherwise.

Well, he's enough like us to enjoy our music.

The track grew steeper, and she felt the strain in her calf muscles. Too bad she couldn't ride, but if she let the horses try to pick their own way, they might get hurt. She glanced back at Jonny; he was watching all around them, nervously expecting the Ghost to pop up at any moment.

She didn't think that was likely; the Ghost and things like him often picked specific times to appear. Sunset, midnight, moonrise, or moonset seemed to be the most often chosen. Since people had been caught out on this track by the spirit after dark, not knowing that it was there, and since Rune had climbed Skull Hill without seeing the Ghost and had to actually wait for it to appear, Robin guessed that it probably appeared at midnight or moonrise. Tonight the two would be almost simultaneous; midnight and moonrise within moments of each other.

And they would be at the top long before either. There would be plenty of time to rest her aching legs and eat a little. Time enough to park the wagon and ready the instruments. Time to think about what they were going to play, what they were going to say. Everything needed to be perfect for this performance.

After all, it was going to be the performance of a lifetime . . . and it had better be the best performance of their lives. She had the feeling that the Ghost would not accept anything less.

"You might as well eat something," Robin observed, biting into her bread-and-cheese with appreciation. Mother Tolley did, indeed, make very good bread; firm and sweet, with a chewy crust. *About the only thing good in that whole town,* she decided. *Unless Annie Cook's skills match Rune's memory.* The tasty bread settled into her stomach comfortably, and she took another bite.

"C-c-can't," Jonny replied, nervously fingering the tuning-pegs on his harp as he watched the shadows for any sign of the Ghost. There was nothing, and had been nothing since they had parked the wagon here. And if Rune's story was accurate, there would be plenty of warning when the Ghost *did* arrive; it was not going to sneak up on them when they weren't looking. *Likes to make an impressive entrance. I wonder if it was an actor once?*

They were at the very top of the hill, with the slash of the road going right across the clearing at the very peak. As overcast as it was, even with the lamp burning, you couldn't see a thing beyond the darker forms of trees and shrubbery against the slightly lighter sky. A cool breeze blew across the clearing, but it held no hint of moisture, and no otherworldly scent of brimstone or the fetor of the grave, either.

Robin shrugged as she caught Jonny's eye. "This would steady your stomach," she suggested. "It's going to be a long time until dawn. You're going to need a little sustenance before the night is over."

"I g-guess s-so," he said, after another long moment. But he groped after her hand, then seized the slice of bread-and-cheese she handed him without looking at it, and wolfed it down without tasting it, his eyes never leaving the clearing in front of their wagon.

With the help of the lantern, Gwyna thought she'd identified Rune's rock—that is, the one Rune had been sitting on when the Ghost appeared to her. They had parked the wagon with the tail of it facing that rock and the clearing in front of it. She figured it was the most likely place for the Ghost to manifest. Now it was just a matter of waiting.

Jonny was not taking the waiting well. He was as tight as a harp strung an octave too high, and if she hadn't *seen* him in crisis situations and *known* that he handled them well and settled once the crisis was upon them, she'd have been very worried about his steadiness.

Her stomach was fluttery—hence the bread-and-cheese—and her shoulders were tight. But her senses seemed a hundred times sharper than usual, and everything happened with preternatural slowness. She heard every cricket clearly and knew exactly where it was; she knew where the owls were hooting, and about how far away they were. She felt the breeze across her skin like a caress; she tasted the bitter tannin of dead leaves, the promise of frost in the air. All of it was very immediate, and very vivid.

She *wanted* this to happen; she had not felt so alive for weeks. That was what performance nerves did to her; she'd felt exactly like this when they'd gone in to confront Jonny's uncle, King Rolend. Afterwards, she might shake and berate herself for doing something so risky—but now, there was only the chill tingle of anticipation and—

And the moon was rising!

She caught the barest hint of it, a mere sliver of silver at the horizon, before it was covered by the clouds. But that was enough—and enough to tell her that the chill tingle she felt along her nerves was *not* anticipation. It was something else entirely.

Magic? The crickets!

The crickets stopped chirping abruptly, with no warning. They had not faded away; no, they had stopped entirely, leaving behind a hollow and empty silence that seemed louder than a shout. The breeze dropped into a dead calm.

Then, in the very next moment, a wind howled up out of nowhere, just as Rune had described, a wind carrying the chill of a midwinter ice-storm. It flattened their clothing to their bodies and if Robin had not taken the precaution of binding her hair up for travel, it would have blinded her with her own tresses. This was not a screaming wind—no, this wind *moaned.* It sounded alive, somehow, and in dire, deadly, despairing pain. A hopeless wind, a wind that was in torment and not permitted to die. A tortured wind, that carried the instruments of its own torture as lances of ice in its bowels.

It whirled around them for a moment, mocking their living warmth with deathly cold, as they huddled instinctively close together on the wagon-tail. There was more than physical *cold* in this wind; the hair on her arms rose as she realized that this wind also carried *power.* Not a power she recognized, but akin to it. The antithesis of healing-power . . . malignant, bitterly envious, and full of hate. The horses were utterly silent, and when she looked back at them, she saw them shaking, sides slick with the sweat of fear, and the whites of their eyes showing all around.

She didn't blame them. *Now,* now that it was far too late, she realized what an incredibly stupid thing she had done. Whatever had made her think she could bargain with this thing? This wasn't a spirit—it was a force that was a law unto itself. She shook with more than cold, she trembled with more than fear. She had walked wide-eyed into a trap. Her own confidence had betrayed her. Her guts clenched, and her throat was too tight to swallow; her mouth dry as dust and her heart pounding.

The wind spun out and away from them; in the blink of an eye it swirled out into the clearing, gathering up every dead leaf and bit of dust with it. In a moment it had formed into a column, a miniature tornado, swaying snakelike in the middle of the clearing.

There were eyes in that whirlwind; not visible eyes, but something in there watched her. She felt those eyes on her skin, felt them studying her and searching for weaknesses, hating her, hating Jonny, hating even the inoffensive horses. Hating every living thing, because *they* were alive and it was not.

She couldn't take her eyes off the whirlwind, and Rune's description quite vanished from her mind. All she could think of were the words of the song:

> . . . then comes a wind that chills my blood
> And makes the dead leaves whirl. . . .

But the song had said nothing about how the leaves glowed with a light of their own. Nor about the closing in of malignant power as it surrounded her and increased until it choked her.

Each leaf glowed in a distinctive shade of greenish-white, the veins a brighter white against the shape of the leaf, somehow calling to mind things rotting, things unhealthy. The leaves pulled together within the center of the whirlwind, forming a solid, irregular shape in the middle of the whirling wind and dust, a shape that was thicker at the bottom than the top, with a suggestion of a cowl crowning it all.

The shape grew more distinct by the moment as the wind whipped faster and faster until the individual leaves vanished into a glowing blur. Then the odd shape at the top of the column *was* a cowl, and the entire form was that of a hooded and robed figure, somehow proportioned in such a way that there was never any doubt that this *thing* was not, and had never been, human.

Exactly as Rune had described.

> . . . *rising up in front of me, a thing like shrouded*
> *Death.* . . .

Oh, it looked like Death in his shroud, all right—worse, it *felt* like Death. The wind died; it had, after all, done its work and was no longer needed. Robin had never felt so cold, or so frightened. Her heart seemed lodged somewhere in her throat, and her fingers were frozen to her instrument—

It's doing this, not you! The thought came sluggishly, up through a thick syrup of fear. *This thing is making you afraid! Didn't you feel the power? Fight it! Fight it, or you won't be able to speak! And if you can't speak, you can't bargain, and you certainly can't sing!*

With the thought came determination; with the determination and the sheer, stubborn will came the realization that the fear *was* coming from outside her! She clenched her jaw as momentary anger overcame the fear—

—and broke it!

It was gone, all in that instant, and once broken, the spell of fear did not return. She sat up straighter; she was free! Her stomach unknotted; her heart slowed. Her throat cleared, and she was able to breathe again.

The last of the leaves settled around the base of the robe. The figure within that robe was thin and dreadfully attenuated; if it had been human, it would have been nothing but bone, but bone that had been softened and stretched until the skeleton was half again the height of the average human male. *Elongated.* That was the description she was searching for. And yet, there was nothing fragile about this thing. The cowl turned towards them, slowly and deliberately, and there was a suggestion of glowing eyes within the dark shadows of the hood.

The voice, when the thing spoke, came as something of a surprise. Robin had expected a hollow, booming voice, like the tolling of a death-bell. Instead, an icy, spidery whisper floated out of the darkness around them, as if all the shadows were speaking, and not the creature before them.

"How is it"—it whispered—"that you come here? Not one, but two musicians? Have you not heard of me, of what I am, of what I will do to you?"

Robin felt the pressure of *magic* all around her, as the Ghost tried to fill her with fear and make her flee. But the fear failed to touch her; she sensed only the power, and not the emotion the Ghost sought to use against her. So it did not know she had broken its spell!

Time to enlighten it.

"Of course we have heard of you!" she said, clearly and calmly. "The whole world has heard of you! Listen—"

Her fingers picked out the introduction to "The Skull Hill Ghost." And she began to sing.

> *I sit here on a rock, and curse my stupid, brag-*
> *ging tongue,*
> *And curse my pride that would not let me back*
> *down from a boast*
> *And wonder where my wits went, when I took*
> *that challenge up*
> *And swore that I would go and fiddle for the*
> *Skull Hill Ghost!*

As she sang, she exerted a little magic of her own; warm and loving magic, Bardic Magic and Gypsy magic and the magic of one true lover for another. She sent it, not at the Ghost, but at Kestrel, all of it aimed at breaking the spell of fear that held Jonny imprisoned in his icy silence as she had been imprisoned a moment before.

The warmth must have reached him, for as she reached the chorus, he shook himself, and suddenly his harp joined the jaunty chords of her gittern as his voice joined hers in harmony.

> *I'll play you high, I'll play you low*
> *For I'm a wizard with my bow*
> *For music is my weapon and my art—*
> *And every note I fling will strike your heart!*

That was a change from the original wording of Rune's contest-song; more of a metaphor for the life-and-death battle she had waged to save herself from the Ghost *and* a life of grim poverty than the original chorus had been.

Robin continued in the "Rune" persona, with Kestrel coming in with the Ghost's first line—in a cunning imitation of the Ghost's own voice.

> *"Give me reason why I shouldn't kill you, girl!"*

She watched her audience of one as closely as she had ever watched *any* audience; had she seen the spirit start with surprise at hearing his own words?

She responded as Rune.

"I've come to fiddle for you, sir—"

Kestrel came in—and again, his voice was not a booming and spectral one, as Wren usually sang the part, but in that deliberate imitation of the Ghost's true disembodied whisper.

"—Oh have you so? Then fiddle, girl, and pray
you fiddle well.
For if I like your music, then I'll let you live to
play—
But if you do not please my ears I'll take you
down to Hell!"

The cowl nodded, ever so slightly. And the pressure of *magic* eased off. Now Robin concentrated on the music, and not the Ghost. She had his attention. Now she must keep it.

The song was a relatively short one, meant for a Faire audience that might not linger to hear an extended ballad. The last verse came up quickly.

At last the dawnlight strikes my eyes, I stop and
see the sun—
The light begins to chase away the dark and mid-
night cold—
And then the light strikes something more, I stare
in dumb surprise—
For where the Ghost once stood there is a heap of
shining gold!

Then she and Kestrel swung into a double repeat of the last chorus, laughing and triumphant.

I'll play you high, I'll play you low
For I'm a wizard with my bow
And music is my lifeblood and my art
And every note I sing will tame your heart!

They finished with a flourish worthy of Master Wren himself. The Ghost regarded them from under his hood with a speculation and surprise that Robin *felt*, just as she had felt the fear he had tried to force on her.

"Well," it whispered, the voice now coming from beneath that cowl and not from every shade and shadow in the clearing. "So, the little fiddler girl survived. Did she thrive as well as survive?"

There was more than a little interest in that question. And not a hint of indifference. He remembered Rune, and he wanted to know about her.

"She continues to thrive, sir," Robin said boldly. "Your silver bought her lessons and instruments, and brought her to the Kingsford Faire and the Free Bards. She got a Master from the Free Bards, and then more than a Master, for she wedded him and earned her title of Master and of Elf-Friend as well. They sing for a King now, and wander no more."

"A good King, I am sure," came the return whisper. "She would settle for naught else, the bold child who dared my hill." Then amazingly, something that *sounded* like a hint of chuckle emerged from beneath the cowl. "It is, I trow, hard to find a rhyme for 'silver'—and that *'heap of shining gold'* tells me why, on a sudden, a fool or two a year has come to dig holes in my hill when they never did before."

"And they f-f-find?" Jonny asked, boldly.

"Rocks. And, sometimes, me." Again the chuckle, but this time it chilled and had no humor in it. Once again, she sensed the power coiled serpentlike behind him, a power that quickened to anger at very little provocation. So before he had time to be angered at the song, at them, she spoke.

"Sir, we came to ask a bargain of our own. Not gold or silver or even gems—"

She was the entire focus of the Ghost's gaze now; the antithesis of the tropical sun, it fell upon her and froze her in a silence of centuries. Or tried. It was at that moment the Ghost must have realized she was not caught in his web of terror, for the spirit straightened a little in what looked very like surprise. "What—bargain?" it said at last.

"We will tell you anything you care to ask, in as much detail as you wish, if we know the answers," she said, faintly, from beneath the weight of that gaze. "We will sing and play for you until dawn, as Rune did. Information and entertainment, and in return—"

The frigid pressure of his regard deepened. "In return—what? Besides your lives, of course. You have not—yet—earned those."

She tried to answer, and could not. For a moment she struggled in panic, knowing that if she did not answer, he could and would use that as the only "excuse" he needed to take her, Kestrel—

"F-free p-passage f-for G-G-G-Gypsies and F-F-Free B-B-B-Bards," Kestrel stammered, forcing the words out for her, fighting his stutter as she fought the Ghost's compulsion. The Ghost's cowl moved marginally as his gaze transferred to Kestrel and the pressure holding her snapped.

"Exactly," she said, quickly, into the ominous silence. "Free and unmolested passage across your Pass at any time of the day or night for Gypsies and Free Bards. Including us, of course. That's all." She remembered now something else that Rune had said—that the Ghost had heard her tale of being harassed and plagued, and then had said that he and she might have more in common than she guessed. "We're something less than popular with the Church right now," she added, and had the reward of seeing the cowl snap back to point at her. "And with the Bardic Guild. We sing a little too much of the truth, and we don't hide what we know for the sake of convenience. We might need—"

"An escape route?" the Ghost hissed, and nodded. "Yes. I can see that."

He stood wrapped in weighty, chilling silence for a long time. She studied him, trying to determine what his race was—or had been. He matched nothing she had ever seen or heard of. Too tall for a Deliambren,

a Gazner, or a Prilchard. No place under that robe for the wings of
a Haspur—

"I am—astonished," the Ghost whispered at last. "To dare me and my
power simply to assure your friends of an escape route in case of danger—
to dare *me!*" He did not breathe, but he paused for as long as it would
take someone to take a deep breath. "Yes. I will make that bargain. With
a single exception."

Exceptions? Why would he have to have exceptions? Her eyes narrowed
with speculation and suspicion.

The Ghost returned her gaze, but this time without the pressure of his
magic behind it. "I must have the exception," he said, simply. "I am—
bound to a task, as I am bound to this place."

Now she sensed the full scope of the terrible power of his anger; once,
long ago, she had been in the presence of a dreadful weapon of what the
Deliambrens called *interstellar* warfare. This *interstellar* thing was something they could not explain to her, but she had sensed, nevertheless, the
shattering potential for destruction encased within the metal pod-skin of
the object they showed her. The Ghost's anger felt like that; like the
moment before the storm is about to break, when the earthquake is about
to strike, when some force too large for a mere human to comprehend is
about to be unleashed.

And yet, it was not directed at *her.*

*No—no, his anger is for those who have bound him here. May their
gods help them if he ever does get free!*

"If your Gypsies and Free Bards are not *sent* here from Carthell Abbey,
they may pass," he continued, in his ice-rimed whisper. "But if they are
sent, I have no choice. I—am bound to slay anyone who is sent from the
Abbey. Any other, I shall let pass, freely. This is the bargain; take it, or
not. Fear not for yourselves; I shall let you pass without your music if
you choose not to take it."

She looked at Kestrel out of the corner of her eye; he nodded slightly.
It was the best they were likely to get; the Ghost was giving a pledge
within the limits of his ability to fulfill it. Kestrel sensed that as well as
she did.

"Done," she said. "I won't hold you to something you can't promise."

The Ghost nodded, ever so slightly, but the atmosphere suddenly
warmed considerably, physically as well as emotionally. Although he did
not "sit," she felt a relaxation about him, and the chill breeze that had
swept through the clearing vanished, to be replaced by a breeze as comfortable as any of early fall, with a hint in it of false summer.

"I should have given this small comfort to the fiddler girl, had I recognized her bravery and honesty," the Ghost whispered, as Jonny took her
hand for a brief, congratulatory squeeze. "But she was the first I had ever
seen who deserved that consideration, so perhaps it is not surprising I did
not recognize this until after she was gone. So—tell me first of her, in
more detail. And of her song. . . ."

She almost smiled at that, and caught herself just in time. *So, he likes
being famous as well as any living being! Well, I think I can oblige him.*

She told him Rune's history, or at least as much of it as she knew, from the moment that Rune had left Skull Hill. How she had put his money to proper use, investing it in instruments and lessons, how she had gone to Kingsford Faire to take part in the trials for the Bardic Guild—

How her song of the "Skull Hill Ghost" had won her acclaim and the highest points in the trials—

How the Guild had treated her when they learned she was a girl and not a boy.

That made him angry again; interesting how she could sense his moods now, as if he had let down some sort of wall, or she had become more sensitive. She pitied the next Guildsman, Bard or Minstrel, that might pass this way by accident! He would take out his anger at what they had done to "his" fiddler girl on any of the Guild that came into his hands.

She went hastily on to describe how the Free Bards had rescued her, and what had happened to her then. He asked her detailed questions about Talaysen, Master Wren—and about King Rolend and her position in Birnam. She sensed his satisfaction in the rewarming of the emotional atmosphere.

"Good," he whispered at last. "Very good. I am pleased. Despite her enemies, she has triumphed. Despite fools, she has prospered." He nodded, and the crickets began to sing again, down the hill at first, then up around the clearing. He turned his cowl towards Kestrel. "Now music," he continued. "You, harper. Something with life in it. Warmth. The sun."

Kestrel nodded without speaking, and set his hands to the strings of his harp. As always, he was lost in his music within the first few bars, and as always, he invoked Bardic Magic without any appearance of effort. Robin wondered if he realized what he was doing; the Magic that he called was mild, harmless, and did nothing more than invoke a mood. In this case, in performing a sweet child's song about a mountain meadow, he enhanced it with a mood of sunny innocence.

The Ghost either did not notice, or else since it was not threatening, he simply ignored it. Probably the latter; Robin had the feeling he noticed *everything*.

As Jonny played, she paid careful attention to the flow and flux of powers about them all. About halfway through the song, she knew that there was a pattern to those flows . . . and near the end, she knew what it was.

She had a suspicion when he agreed to the bargain that the Ghost would take power from them, through the music, through the Bardic Magic he hoped they would invoke. And it looked as if she was half right; but only half. He was not *stealing* their power, nor pulling it in. It was as if they were campfires, and he was basking in the warmth they produced. *Taking* nothing, only enjoying what flowed to him naturally.

But she sensed something else as well. This benign enjoyment was the reverse side of something much, much darker. *That* was the side that his victims saw, the icy chill to the warmth . . . as he stole their life-force along with their life.

He chose a Gypsy love song from Robin next; she hid a grin, because she had the feeling he was hoping she'd sing something at and for Kestrel. Well, he would get that—but not just yet. Instead, she sang a song of a night of celebration and tangled lovers who could not make up their minds over who was going to pair off with who, until in the end, everyone ended up sleeping alone, for that night at least! She got the definite impression that her audacity pleased him, and that the song itself amused him.

"Tell me what this quarrel is that the Church has with your kind," he whispered, as soon as she had finished. "How did you come to this conclusion, and what are you doing to remedy it? All that you know, tell."

She found herself recounting what Nightingale had told them, what she and Kestrel had seen, and Harperus' speculations. He listened silently to all of this, not prompting her by so much as a single word, as she concluded with what she and Jonny were doing—heading to Gradford on the chance that the source of the problem lay in that direction, while Nightingale went in the opposite direction. The anger was back again, but this time she could not imagine what had invoked it. She was only glad that it hadn't been any of their doing.

"I think"—the Ghost began, after a cricket-filled silence—"your searches are like to bear more fruit than hers."

But before she could follow up that astonishing bit of information with a question of her own, he had already demanded a ballad "with free wind in it" from Kestrel.

He obliged with one of the Gypsy horse-trainers' racing songs, and by the time he had finished she knew without asking that question—*how* he knew that Gradford was the direction they must go—that the Ghost would only give them what he chose to in the way of information. It would be enigmatic, they would probably only understand what he meant after they discovered answers for themselves. And he was much too dangerous to play games with, verbal or otherwise.

So when he asked her again for a love song, this time she played one of her own, made for Jonny, and put her whole heart into it.

"I think," the Ghost said, tilting his cowl up towards the eastern sky, "that it is not long until dawn."

Gwyna shook soreness out of her weary arms; this had taken a lot more energy than she had ever suspected, and if *she* felt this way with Kestrel and talk to spell her, how had poor Rune ever survived her night of playing?

"I did not lend my strength to you as I did to the fiddler girl," the Ghost said, matter-of-factly, as if he had just read her mind. Perhaps he had; she would not place anything beyond him at this point, and she was very glad that they had both chosen to tell him only the strict and complete truth when he had asked his questions about the outside world. His interrogation had been fascinating to experience; things he had wanted to know, he wanted to know in depth, and things she had assumed he would be curious about, he cared nothing for.

But those things he wished to know—his questioning left her feeling like a rag that had been used to soak up something, then wrung dry. He not only extracted information from her, but as the night went on, he became more and more adept at extracting her feelings about something from her. She was not certain of his motives. It might only be that he had wished to *feel* things, if only vicariously. It might be he extracted some nourishment from emotions, which might also explain why he killed through terror. It might also be that for some reason he needed to understand if she felt strongly about something, and why.

"You did not need that strength," he continued. "There were two of you, and you did not play continuously. So. Dawn approaches. Your bargain is complete. You have given as you pledged, and fully. I shall pledge likewise. From this moment, all Gypsies and Free Bards that are not sent from Carthell Abbey may pass this way freely." He cocked his head a little sideways. "I may appear, and request a song—but it shall be a *request*."

Kestrel blew on his fingers to cool them, and echoed the Ghost's headpose. "I th-think s-such a req-q-quest would b-be honored," he said dryly.

There was a whispered chuckle from the Ghost. "You need not give them identifying marks," the spirit continued—which was something that had been in Gwyna's mind. "Such things can be stolen or counterfeited. I shall know them from their thoughts."

She didn't bother to hide her start of surprise. So he *could* read thoughts!

"On occasion," he whispered, and there *was* a hint of humor in his voice. And perhaps, a touch of smugness. "You have been generous in your bargain. I shall be as generous. Spend the morn in safety here, if you wish, or go on. Nothing shall molest you or disturb you while you sleep. My choice of manifestation is my own, for their compulsions were limited in nature—and if I choose to expend myself, the daylight need not hinder my powers—"

And with that final astonishing pronouncement, he disappeared—just as the first light of the dawn-red sun touched the precise spot on which he had been standing just the moment before.

The sunlight glinted on something metallic.

It was Kestrel who climbed down from the tail of the wagon, placed his harp carefully on the floor of the wagon, and walked stiffly across the sun-gilded weeds to the spot that shone with such bright and promising glints.

"Well," he said, carefully, looking down at the small mound. "It's s-s-silver. J-just l-like R-R-Rune's."

She let out the breath she had been holding, and rubbed her tired eyes. "He said he was going to be generous."

Kestrel tilted his head to one side, and dropped down to sit on his heels beside the pile of coins. "S-so l-let's s-see how g-g-generous, shall w-we?"

She yawned hugely, and blinked at the morning sun. "I can't think of any better way to relax before a good long sleep. Can you?"

He shook his head, and stole a kiss from her as soon as she joined him. Then the two of them knelt down beside the pile of coins that the Ghost had left as their personal reward. They counted with one hand each; their other two hands were clasped together lovingly.

CHAPTER EIGHT

Robin woke to the sounds of birdsong and the soft whistling of a human. She knew by the absence of a warm body next to her that she was alone in the bed; but since the whistling was nearby, she was not alone in the wagon. After a moment, the sound of creaking and tapping told her what was going on.

Kestrel was caching the silver coins in little hiding places all over the wagon. All Gypsy wagons had a few hidden caches for valuables, but none had so many as this one; while it was being built he'd been with the wagonwrights every day, planning hiding places everywhere it was possible to cache even a single tiny copper-piece. Robin knew where some of the caches were, but she hadn't a clue where he hid most of the money they had.

I think he does it so I can't spend it or give it all away, she thought with amusement. *Probably not a bad idea; sometimes I get a little too generous, I suppose. And I know I get a little too spendthrift when I know we have the money.*

Those days when he had not had even regular meals made him more cautious about money and lean times than even old Erdric, so she could hardly blame him. It was just something she was going to have to learn to live with.

She stretched, enjoying the rare luxury of having the bed to herself for a moment, and opened her eyes to stare up at the intricate carving on the underside of the cupboard over the bed. A nice touch, that. It was a sinuous form called "The Endless Knot" that was supposed to aid in concentration and relaxation if you followed it with your eyes long enough.

The encounter with the Ghost had given her more than she had hoped. They had the monetary reward, completely unexpected—and they had the safe-route across these hills for their people and theirs alone. Provided, of course, that none of their people managed to have themselves sent here from Carthell Abbey.

Therein lay the puzzle that kept her lying abed. *Carthell Abbey? Now what in the name of all that is holy could Carthell Abbey have to do with a murderous Ghost?* The Church had never dealt with ghosts at all, except to exorcise them; at least not that she had ever heard.

Well, the obvious answer was a simple one. The Church officials knew that the Ghost had been bound up on the Hill, and they used him, rather callously, as their convenient executioner. The Church was supposed to remand criminals to the civil authorities for trial and punishment, but everyone knew that a criminal Priest was dealt with within the Church itself. And in using the Ghost as their executioner, the Church kept its

382

hands officially clean of blood. Cynical, yes, but the Church was full of cynics.

An obvious answer, except for a few problems. The first was that the minions of the Church *should* have been under spiritual obligation to exorcise the Ghost once they learned he was here—not use him! Especially since he had managed to kill one perfectly innocent Priest already, at least according to Annie Cook.

Well, maybe they did try to exorcise him and that was how the Priest was killed. Maybe they figured since they couldn't be rid of him, they might as well use him. The Church employs other executioners, after all— this would just be one rather strange executioner.

Maybe. But if the Church was using this spirit, they were *definitely* under moral obligation to warn travelers about his existence! Yet there were no warning signs, and nothing telling a traveler that this was a dangerous road. There was no guard on the way up Skull Hill. What few warnings there were, at least on the Westhaven side, were haphazard at best. If the people of Westhaven had been charged with warning travelers, they were doing a damn poor job of it.

That brought everything back to the same question. Why would the Church have *anything* to do with a spirit like the Ghost? They should do any number of things that they had not; and should not be doing any number of things that they were.

She rolled over and poked her nose through the curtains on the wagon-side of the bed. Jonny was fitting a small pile of silver coins—the last, from the look of things—into the hem of the curtain above the sink. That was one of the caches she already knew about, and as he caught the sound of the bed creaking, he turned and grinned at her.

"All hidden?" she asked. He nodded.

"It's ab-bout noon," he told her. "If w-we move out n-now, w-we should b-be at the Abbey b-by sunset."

She nodded, and swung her legs down over the side of the bed, pushing the bed-curtains back to either side. "And you think we should go there. You think that we might find something out about this vendetta the Church seems to have with us?" she asked, as her bare feet hit the wooden floor with a dull thump.

He handed her a wooden comb, and cut bread and cheese while she washed her face and dealt with the tangle of her hair. "Th-the Gh-ghost made a p-point of m-mentioning it," he said, thoughtfully. "L-like he c-couldn't t-talk about s-something, b-but w-was trying t-to g-give us a c-clue."

"Hmm." She accepted bread-and-cheese with a nod of thanks. "There is something very strange going on here," she observed. "Do you remember, when I was describing how Nightingale went off towards Kingsford and I said we were looking towards Gradford, he said that we were likelier to find the source of our troubles than she was?"

" 'M-more l-likely to b-bear fruit,' he said," Kestrel agreed. "I d-don't know whether he m-meant the Abbey or G-Gradford, b-but I th-think we n-need to s-stop at the Abbey."

"It's a start," Gwyna replied, popping the last of her breakfast into her mouth, and licking a crumb of cheese from her thumb. "You know the proverb. 'Soonest begun, is soonest done.' Right?"

Kestrel kissed her nose, and gave her a playful shove in the direction of the driver's seat. As she crawled over the bed, she saw that he had already harnessed the horses, and turned the wagon so that it faced down the hill.

"Right" he agreed. "And *y-you* d-drive! I w-was up early, and I n-need a n-n-nap!"

Jonny had learned long ago the art of sleeping in odd places and under adverse conditions. A swaying, jostling wagon was no impediment to his drifting off to sleep. He had expected nightmares, or at the least, dreams troubled by the Ghost, but he slept deeply and soundly, and there was nothing to trouble his sleep. He woke shortly before suppertime.

He exchanged places with Gwyna, driving while she rummaged around in their stores for something for them both to eat that was *not* bread-and-cheese. While he recalled only too well the days when he would have been happy to eat bread-and-cheese for a month running, those days were in the past, and if he had a choice, well, the same food for three meals in a row was not going to be his choice.

This was true wilderness, except for the occasional sheep-farm, and by the rocky condition of the hillsides, he wasn't too surprised. Soil here was too thin to farm or graze; basically the only growing things keeping these hillsides from being completely barren were specialized plants suited to driving their roots into rock and holding tight. Two or three kinds of trees, wiregrass, lichen, moss, and some tough bushes; that was about it. Small wonder there were no people out here—the Ghost was hardly to blame for the condition of the land.

Funny, he thought. *Somehow, though, this looks like land that's been worn out, as if people* were *here a long time ago, but exhausted the soil so much that it couldn't support anything but this wilderness again.*

Well, that could be. Alanda was a strange world, and there were places in it like this, side-by-side with rich and virgin land, or a place like the stronghold of the Deliambrens. Maybe there had been people here, just after the Cataclysm—and maybe they had depended heavily on things coming from far outside *because* they had depleted their own land so much. And after the Cataclysm, when "outside" wasn't there anymore— they had died off, or gone elsewhere, leaving behind the land to recover on its own.

He shook himself out of his reverie as Gwyna reappeared with dinner for both of them. Speculation about the past was all very well, but at the moment he was perfectly willing to put such thoughts aside to concentrate on driving and dinner.

It was to be bread again, but this time with sausage, and an apple apiece. They thriftily saved out the seeds to be given to the owner of the next Waymeet; every Waymeet had some sort of orchard, planted from the seeds the Gypsies brought with them. So you might find apple trees growing side-by-side with Deliambren *pares,* Mintak *tiers,* and Likonian *severins.* Quite often fruits thought to be delicate turned out to thrive in unlikely climates, at least under the careful tending of the Gypsies.

"That's the last of the loaf," Robin told him, as she handed him his dinner through the hatchway. "At least we ate it before it went dry. How's the road?"

"Interesting," he replied, taking a bite. "W-well k-kept."

It was, too; one of the reasons why Gwyna hadn't been tossed all over the wagon while he negotiated potholes and pits. The road had been very carefully patched and graded, and that recently.

She poked her head out, then clambered over the ledge into her seat. "You're right!" she exclaimed. "Now why keep up a road that only leads to a dangerous pass and a nothing little village?"

Kestrel shrugged. "D-don't r-read t-t-too much into it," he cautioned her. "C-could j-just b-be the S-Sire d-doing his r-r-road d-duty r-right. After all, w-we w-were j-just c-complaining that th-the last S-Sire wasn't d-doing his d-duty on the r-roads. So n-no p-point in r-reading something into it wh-when th-the S-Sire's a g-good one."

"It could be, you're right." She settled beside him with her arm around his waist, and smiled up at him. He smiled back and caught her hand in his; a small hand, but very strong, with callouses on the fingers where only a musician would have them. A proper hand, to match the proper lady. Just being with her made him feel so warm—needed and wanted.

Being best friends is the only way to be lovers, he decided, as she rested her head against his shoulder. *Staying best friends is the only way to be married.*

"I th-think the Abbey isn't t-too far," he said, as shadows deepened under the trees, and the skies above the branches turned crimson and gold. "The n-next v-valley, m-maybe."

His guess was correct; as they topped the hill and looked down into the shallow valley stretching below them, it was obvious that they were back in some vestige of civilization. The leafless trees of an orchard lined both sides of the road, immaculately tended. And as the horses stretched their necks out with interest, the sound of bells ringing for evening services drifted clearly up the road.

He flicked the reins to get the horses moving again, for at the sound of the bells they stopped, their ears flicking forward nervously. Long shadows already filled the valley, and as they moved down the hill and went from the last light into evening's mist and blue dusk, the temperature dropped perceptibly. Gwyna huddled against him for warmth as well as companionship, and he shivered as a chill breeze cut through his shirt.

Once they were beneath the trees, they saw the lights of the Abbey shining up ahead of them, at the side of the road. There didn't appear to be any activity at all around it, which was a little odd.

Well, their harvest is obviously over. There's no real reason for anyone to be moving around at sunset, not when they just rang the bells for evening prayers.

The Abbey was fairly small, a complex of two or three buildings surrounded by a stone wall with a heavy wooden gate in the front. Trees grew right up against it, however, and Kestrel could only look at them wryly and remember a certain small boy who had found walls to be no hindrance as long as there were trees nearby. Presumably many generations of novices here had discovered the same truth.

He pulled the wagon up to the gate, handed the reins to Gwyna, and jumped down to knock for admission.

It opened immediately; there was a lantern just outside, and the light fell on a sour-faced Brother in a dull gray robe, who scowled at him as if Kestrel was personally responsible for everything that was wrong with the world. The man had the soft, ink-stained hands of a scholar, and a squint that suggested many hours spent in a library bending over half-legible manuscripts. His mouth was framed with frown lines, and his jowls quivered when he spoke.

"What do you want?" His voice was not pleasant: a harsh and untrained croak. Kestrel smiled encouragingly, and shyly. He tried a ploy that had worked with other officious, self-important men in the past; to look as harmless and humble as possible. This was the one time his stutter might be useful.

He bobbed his head, submissively. "W-we are t-t-travelers, sir, and w-we are s-seeking sh-shelter f-from the c-c-creatures of the n-night w-within the w-walls of the—"

The Brother did not even give him a chance to finish his sentence. "Be off with you!" he growled. "This is no hostel, and we do not take in any ne'er-do-well who comes requesting shelter! This is a holy order of recluses. We have chosen to leave the world and all the sin within it. We sought to leave such as you in our past, not to open our gates to you!"

"B-b-but—" Kestrel began; shocked as well as puzzled by the Gatekeeper's vehemence. He hadn't said or done anything to warrant such a reaction. The man acted as if they were dressed in rags and covered in filth, yet the wagon was quite clearly visible from the gate, and it was just as clear that they were not penniless wanderers. He had never yet met a Churchman who could resist the possibility of a donation.

Except that it seemed this Brother-Gatekeeper most certainly could and would. "Be off!" he repeated, raising his voice. "No one is allowed within these walls but the Brothers. No one! Find yourself some other shelter—vagabonds and mountebanks are not welcome here!"

And before Kestrel could get another word out, the Gatekeeper slammed the gate shut, right in his face.

He turned, slowly, and walked the few steps back to the wagon, to join Gwyna, who was just as surprised as he was. "What was that all about?" she asked, a little dazed. "What on *earth* made him say those things? Was he quite mad?"

He shrugged. "At l-least he d-d-didn't f-forbid us to c-c-camp up against the w-w-walls," he pointed out. "Th-there m-might b-be a w-w-well or a s-stream where w-we c-can g-get w-w-water."

He took the halter of the horse nearest him and led it off the road, onto the grassy area surrounding the walls of the Abbey, and beyond the circle of light cast into the blue dusk by the lantern beside the gate. Gwyna sat on the seat of the wagon, shaking her head. "I have no idea what could have set him off like that," she observed, dispassionately. "You

were the essence of politeness—*he* was the one who was rude. And every
single Abbey I have ever seen or heard of has always been willing to
take in a traveler or two, especially in the wilderness like this. This is
very strange."

He noticed that she was pitching her voice to carry, as if she was
speaking to an audience, and he grinned to himself. If Gwyna had her
way, her voice would drift right over the walls and just might reach the
ears of someone who cared a little more than the Gatekeeper what a
couple of "vagabonds and mountebanks" thought of this Abbey.

On the back side of the walls, he found the rear gate, and the path the
Brothers took to the orchards and to a small vegetable garden. There was
a well beside the garden, as he had hoped there would be; he picketed
the horses a little way away from it, in an area where there was some
grazing, and left them water and grain to augment the grass.

As he worked, he took in what he could of the area around the walls.
The place was unnervingly *ordered*, especially in comparison with the
country they had just passed through. The garden had been thoroughly
plowed up for winter, leaving not a trace of whatever vegetables had been
growing there. He had no clue what variety of tree grew in this orchard
of theirs; the thrifty monks had left not so much as a windfall fruit underneath them, and without leaves it was impossible to make any accurate
guess as to what they were growing here. While he took care of the
horses, Gwyna bustled about the wagon, preparing dinner, heating water
for washing, setting up a picture-perfect campsite. . . .

Too perfect, he realized after a moment. This was not like the Gypsy
Robin he knew! And he grinned again as he saw what she was up to. She
was acting in every way like a proper little wife, a well-trained trader's
wife who was a good Church-going woman and a lady who knew her
proper place. There was nothing to show that they were Gypsies and Free
Bards, and not ordinary, middle-class traders. And if the Free Bards were
in disfavor with the Church, the traveling traders were not.

So, they would look like traders; industrious, God-worshiping traders,
eh? He silently congratulated Gwyna on her cleverness, and did his best
to emulate her, right down to shoving their instruments into hiding when
he returned to the wagon. Just in case whoever showed up next from the
Abbey happened to look inside the wagon.

There *would* be someone; Gwyna had made certain of that, not only
by her words, but by the busy clatter she made with her pots and pans.

But they were left in peace to wash up and eat that hot dinner she
had prepared so carefully, and he began to wonder if this Abbey was
inhabited by nobody but a single, mad old man. But just as full darkness
fell, the expected visitor arrived.

They didn't even notice him, he moved so quietly, with hardly even a
swish of his robe against the grass. There were no twigs beneath the
branches of these trees to betray him by snapping unexpectedly underfoot;
the ground had been swept as clean as the floor in a house. In fact, when
the man cleared his throat to announce his presence, he succeeded in
startling both of them.

They looked up, to see him standing just within the light of their fire, a thin, diffident man with a pleasant expression and shy eyes. "Oh!" the Brother said, immediately apologetic, and hurrying forward into the light of their fire. "I'm so sorry, I certainly didn't mean to frighten you! I thought you knew I was there! Please, forgive me!"

Kestrel had been sitting beside the fire; he stood immediately, and went to meet the Brother, holding out his hand, which the man took in a firm and friendly clasp. "N-no offense. J-just d-didn't notice you. M-my n-name is J-J-Jonny B-Brede, good s-sir," he said, concentrating on speaking slowly and rhythmically as Harperus had instructed him. "M-my w-wife G-Gwyna and I are t-traders."

"And not vagabonds and mountebanks, I know," the Brother said, pulling back the cowl of his gray robe so that they could better see his ascetic, but friendly face and his apologetic smile. "I hope you will find it in your heart to forgive Brother Pierce; he is old, often ill, and altogether very unhappy. Life has not treated him well. Most of the Brothers here are not like him."

Kestrel returned his smile. "Well, I c-c-can s-see th-that *you* aren't, at any r-rate . . . B-Brother . . . ?"

"Oh! Ah! Brother Reymond, Trader Brede," the Brother replied, his smile widening when Jonny did not meet his friendly overture with a rejection. "I am the Abbey Librarian, and I wanted to apologize for the fact that we simply have no room for you and your wife. That is why Brother Pierce has been instructed to tell travelers we can take no one in. Every cell is occupied, we have no guest rooms, and since our order has taken a vow to use no beast of burden, we have not even a stable you might shelter in. I also wished to be certain that you were warned about the dangers hereabouts."

"Dangers?" Jonny looked around, nonplused. This certainly didn't look like a very dangerous area—

But on the other hand, this Abbey *was* a small island in the middle of the wilderness. They had been lucky so far; there was no telling what wandered under the branches of these trees once darkness fell.

"I fear so—" Brother Reymond had the grace to look guilty. "Of course, to experienced travelers like you and your wife, these things are likely to be no more than an inconvenience."

"Why don't you tell us what they are, first, before we decide," Gwyna said dryly from her place beside the fire. "Perhaps we ought to move on, after all."

"Oh no!" the Brother said, paling. "No, you *don't* want to do that! There's a Beguiler about, perhaps more than one! What if it found you on the road?"

Jonny shrugged; that was not a threat he took seriously, since they had a wagon to sleep in. Beguilers couldn't get into a closed wagon. "Then I s-suppose we'd d-drown," he replied lightly.

Beguilers were creatures that hypnotized their victims, then lured them into swamps to fall into deep water. Once their victims were safely dead, they feasted on the remains. They cast their "spell" with a combination of sound and light; if you saw them but did not hear them, you were safe enough, and if you heard but did not see them, it was possible to remain in control of yourself. Most often they caught unwary travelers who mistook the light for the lantern of a house or wagon, and were then lulled by the Beguiler's humming to their death. It was not too difficult to evade them, if you knew they were around."

"Oh, don't say that!" Brother Reymond seemed genuinely distressed. "Why, only last week—one of the farm boys hereabouts—not strong in his mind, but still—"

Jonny shook his head apologetically. "I b-beg your p-pardon, B-Brother," he said as quickly as he could. "I d-didn't mean t-to m-make a j-joke of it."

"I know you didn't; how could you have known?" Brother Reymond sighed, and signed himself. "May the poor lad rest in peace. But there are also treekies, an entire flock of them, out in the forest beyond the orchard. I hope you have nets for your horses? If you don't, the Abbey can loan them to you. In that much, at least, we can do our charitable duty."

"With, or without Brother Pierce's permission?" Gwyna asked lightly, and chuckled at Brother Reymond's blush. "No matter, Brother, we do have nets and fitted blankets for the horses, and good shutters on the wagon. We should be safe enough, if that is all we need to worry about." She patted the stool next to her. "Can we invite you to stay for a while? The treekies certainly won't come while the lanterns and the fire are burning, and the Beguiler may not come at all tonight. Even if it does, I see no reason why we can't avoid it."

"I would—yes, I would like to speak with you, if you do not mind," Brother Reymond said, shyly. He settled down onto the stool placed between Gwyna's and Jonny's, and accepted a mug of tea, but waved away a bowl of stew. "Thank you, dear lady, but I *have* supped, and I am not in the least hungered. While your stew smells delicious, our Order regards greed very seriously." He cradled the mug in both hands and smiled at both of them. "I am the Archivist, you see, and I have so little opportunity to speak with outsiders! I try to collect as much information as I can, but—" He shrugged. "My opportunities are few. We do not see many travelers on this road. I can't think why. It is a much shorter route to Gradford than the main trade road, and the Sire tends it well, at least within his lands."

Jonny kept his expression completely under control, but with difficulty. Either this Reymond was the finest actor in the world, or he was completely unaware of the Skull Hill Ghost less than half a day away from here!

"I had heard there was a legend about a haunted hill on this road," Gwyna said casually. "We didn't see anything, of course—but we also traveled between here and Westhaven by daylight. I don't suppose that could have anything to do with the scarcity of travelers?"

Brother Reymond blinked at her in surprise. "I suppose it might," he replied, clearly taken aback. "I should think. But this is the first time I have ever heard anything about a haunted hill!" His expression grew doubtful. "Perhaps the villagers in Westhaven were making a jest at your expense?"

"It c-could b-be," Jonny said, easily. "You kn-know h-how s-s-some of th-these v-v-village f-folk are ab-bout someone w-with an af-f-fliction. I d-do s-stutter. Th-they m-may have th-thought I w-was f-feeble-minded as w-w-well, and ch-chose t-to m-make a f-fool of m-me."

Brother Reymond flushed, averted his eyes in embarrassment, and murmured something appropriate and apologetic. Jonny watched him carefully and became convinced that the Brother was no actor. He really *didn't* know about the Skull Hill Ghost!

"I d-don't s-suppose th-there m-might b-be s-something in your a-archives?" he added. "I'm c-curious now. It w-would b-be n-nice t-to kn-know if I w-was b-being m-made a g-game of."

"Certainly," Brother Reymond said, after a moment of awkward silence. "I can look, of course. I don't remember anything, but that doesn't mean a great deal." He chuckled with self-deprecation. "My memory is not very good. I make a fine Archivist precisely because of that, you know, for I have to index and cross-index everything, or I would never be able to find a single reference."

Jonny laughed, and refilled the Brother's mug. They continued to chat about some of the things he and Gwyna had seen on the road, and inserted a question now and again about the internal affairs of the Church and the Abbey. They continued to talk for some time—or rather, he gradually turned the conversation so that Gwyna was doing most of the talking, and he could simply listen and look wise. The Brother was certainly a guileless sort, and quite transparently enthusiastic about any new knowledge—but he had no notion of any kind about the internal politics and policies of the Church of the present day. Politics and policies of the Church a hundred years ago, now, he knew quite well, but nothing current. It was fairly obvious why he was here; he was so innocent he would never have survived in one of the larger Church installations. The best and safest place for him was out of the way. In some other Abbey, he was far too likely to overhear something he shouldn't, and repeat it to anyone who cared to ask him about it.

Three mugs of tea later, he finally took his leave with obvious regret. Here in the lee of the Abbey walls, there was very little wind, but from the nip in the air, it had gotten much colder while they talked.

Brother Reymond stood, and sniffed the air. "There will be frost by morning," he said, and sighed. "This seems like such a sad time of year to me—and yet, it is such a pleasant season for the farm-folk! Well, so it is—one man's pleasure is another man's melancholy."

Jonny saw Gwyna raise her eyebrow at this unconscious echoing of a Gypsy proverb by a sober scion of the Church, and smiled just a little. "Quite true, Brother Reymond," she said smoothly, accepting the mug he returned to her. "But I can't conceive of anyone finding *your* conversation unpleasant. Thank you very much for coming out, and proving to us that your fellow Brother is the exception within your walls."

Brother Reymond colored up with pleasure, and murmured a shy disclaimer. Jonny had decided after the first mug of tea that he liked the Archivist, as much for his modesty as his eagerness to share knowledge. *And if there were more men like him,* he thought, as Brother Reymond thanked Gwyna for her hospitality and her tea, *the world would be a much better place than it is.*

"Don't forget about the treekies," Brother Reymond reminded them over his shoulder, as he hurried away towards the Abbey. "And the Beguiler!"

"We won't!" Gwyna promised. And as soon as Brother Reymond was out of sight, she exchanged a chuckle and a hug with Jonny.

"I like him," she declared. He nodded agreement.

"I d-do, too," he told her. "He's honest."

She didn't answer immediately; instead, she went to one of the storage bins that contained more of the horse-tack, and opened it, taking out carefully constructed horse blankets that covered everything except the ears and legs, then shook out a pair of nets made of wire-wrapped cord. Treekies, the little nocturnal flying beasts that Brother Reymond had warned them about, were more of a pest than anything else, although their attentions could prove fatal to the unwary. Light kept them away, and any material made of mesh too small for their mouths foiled and frustrated them. But if the bloodsuckers caught an animal out, unprotected, or an unwary human, there would be no next generation. They could drain a poor creature of blood completely, without the victim ever waking up.

They were usually creatures of much milder climes than this; it was the first time that Kestrel had ever heard of them being this far north.

"I trust him, Jonny," Gwyna said, as they fitted the horses with their thick, protective blankets, then hung the nets over them to keep the little monsters off the mares' legs and ears. "I really do. I don't think he's ever told more than a handful of lies in his life, and every time he did, I'd bet he gave himself away. He's never heard of the Ghost."

Kestrel nodded, and shrugged. "I c-can't explain it. M-mind, I d-doubt th-the B-B-Brothers are ever allowed out of th-the Abbey. S-so if th-they aren't f-from around here, th-they w-won't kn-know about l-local st-stories. B-but st-still!"

"Still, he should have heard something." She arranged the net over the patient mare's head. "I can't imagine why he wouldn't have. Unless—"

She paused and Kestrel waited.

"—unless the Abbot was keeping the existence of the Ghost a secret from the Brothers." She raised an eyebrow at Kestrel who had already come to that same conclusion.

"It c-could b-be innocent," he reminded her. "If th-they kn-knew about a Gh-ghost s-so n-near, the d-devout and th-the amb-bitious w-would b-both r-rush t-to t-try t-to ex—ex—g-get r-rid of it."

"Good point," she replied, as they both turned to go back to the shelter of the wagon. "We already know what fate *they* would have. And those who were neither devout nor ambitious would probably flee in terror. That's quite a reasonable explanation. There's only one problem with it. Remember what the Ghost said? About people being *sent* from here?"

He did. Only too well. "It st-still st-stands as an explanation," he replied. "J-just n-not as innocent."

"Hmm." She gave him a long look from under her eyelashes, as they climbed into the wagon to fasten down all the shutters. "You aren't as guileless as you look, Jonny Brede."

He grinned. "N-neither are you."

Their night passed with no real disturbance; they heard the Beguiler humming off in the far distance, but it never came anywhere near the Abbey. Eventually they fell asleep without ever hearing anything more sinister than a distant hum, out there in the darkness. Kestrel could not help but be glad that they were *not* afoot on this journey, however. They might have escaped the Beguiler—or they might not. If it had floated up to their camping spot in the middle of the night and begun singing right over their heads, they might have awakened and been trapped by it before they realized what it was.

No, it was a very good thing that they were traveling by wagon. And if the Beguiler was an example of the kinds of dangers lurking in this wilderness area—well, perhaps they didn't have to look for sinister reasons for the abandonment of this trade-road. Who would want to camp in woods where there were Beguilers and treekies?

But the Abbey should *be acting as a traveler's haven and shelter against things like that,* came the logical response, just as he drifted off to sleep. *Why isn't it? And why did the Ghost say that people were* sent *from here?*

And that brought up yet another question—for Brother Reymond had said that this Abbey was full. Why send so many Brothers to such a remote location? Surely there weren't that many men seeking the solitude of the wilderness, and the purity of a woman-less existence!

Kestrel loitered over their morning preparations, hoping that Brother Reymond would be able to get away and speak with them before they left, but it was not to be. Instead, they packed up and took to the road without any sign from within the Abbey walls that there was anything or anyone alive within them. Even the bells ringing for morning services could have been coming from somewhere else.

By mid-morning they had passed out of the true wilderness and had struck the same trade-road that they had left after the Waymeet. The road was broader and better tended here than it had been when they left it; there was quite enough room for two vehicles the size of Harperus' monster to pass on this section of the road, and it was very obvious that the local Sire took his road-tending duties very, very seriously. There was scarcely an uneven place in the roadway, much less one the size of the pothole that had brought their wagon to grief.

Gradford had no Sire; it was a political entity unto itself, although it owed allegiance to the King of Rayden. The inhabitants referred to it as a "city-state," or a "Free Trade City," and it was very nearly the equal of Kingsford in size and importance.

Located deep in the hills, it commanded an impressive number of resources; water, mines, and an advantageous position on a trade-road. The sole disadvantage to its location was the terrain; the hills grew steeper and rockier with every passing hour, and they often got out of the wagon and walked alongside it to spare the horses. These steep grades were very hard on them; going down, holding back the weight of the wagon, was very nearly as wearing for them as climbing.

They were so caught up with watching the mares for strain that it was almost nightfall before Robin noticed a peculiar lack of traffic on the road, and mentioned it to Kestrel.

He furrowed his brow for a moment, and shook his head slightly, but he waited until they took a breather for the horses before he spoke.

"It's f-fall," he pointed out, but with uncertainty. "It's the off-s-season f-for t-trade."

But she shook her head vigorously. "No it isn't!" she contradicted him sharply. "Not for the variety of trade that Gradford does! Oh, maybe the Faires are over for the year, but there should be a lot of people on this road, and there's no one! We haven't seen anyone all day!"

"W-we might not," he told her. "Th-they c-could be r-right ahead of us, and w-we'd n-never s-see them. N-not with all th-these h-hills."

By the look in her eyes, she clearly did not believe him, or his explanation. "W-we'll s-stop at an inn," he promised. "I w-want a r-real m-meal and a b-bath, if w-we c-can g-get one. Y-you'll s-see."

But when they did find an inn—fortuitously, just over the top of the next hill, for the mares needed a real rest—she was not the one who found her notions contradicted.

Robin finished ordering supper, and went hunting her husband. She found Kestrel out in the stable, making certain that the mares were getting all the care he had paid for. She dragged him away from his interrogation of a hapless stable-boy, and into the common room of the inn. Their supper was waiting, but that was not why she had brought him in here.

The dark but cozy common room was half empty, and from the forlorn expressions on the faces of the barkeeper and the serving girls, this was not an anticipated situation. They had been the last travelers to seek shelter here tonight, and most of the few patrons had already had their dinner and sought their rooms or wagons—but she had managed to find one man, at least, who was willing to delay his rest and talk to them in return for a pitcher of beer. The quiet of the common room, holding nothing more than the vague murmur of talk and the crackle of the fire in the fireplace at their end of the room, was relaxing and prompted confidences.

"Kestrel," she said, tugging him towards the table she had taken, in the corner, and away from any other where they might be overheard as they talked. "This is Rodrick Cunart. Rod, this is Kestrel." She did not bother to introduce Jonny as her husband; Rod was a pack-trader, a man whose entire life during trading-season was contained in a single pack carried by a donkey. He knew the road and the life on it; if a Gypsy with a bird-name was wandering the roads with another with a bird-name, it was safe to assume they were "together." And *not* safe to take liberties.

"Rod trades in books in the north, and ribbons and laces in the south," she continued, as Jonny took his place beside her, and gave Rod a nod of greeting. "And he's going up to Gradford, because of some news he got." She was pleased to see Jonny's interest perk up at that. "I asked him to tell us what's going on up there."

Kestrel settled down to his dinner of shepherd's pie without a word, but his eyes never left Rodrick's. The pack-trader poured himself a mug of his beer and took a long pull of it before beginning.

"It's a good thing yer lady found me," he said, slowly, his accent marking him as coming from one of the Southern Kingdoms. "You bein' Free Bards an' all. It could be bad for ye in Gradford. They've gone religious, they have, an' they don't look well on musickers, 'less they be outa the Church itself. Even Guild is lookin' a bit thin there, these days. Not much trade in anythin' but Church music, an' even the Guild musickers get mortal weary of that. As for us"—he shook his head—"thas' why ye see nobbut on road. 'Tis dead to trade, is Gradford."

Even Robin, who had been expecting some sort of bad news, had not been prepared for so bald a statement. "What happened?" she asked, incredulously, the hearty meal before her entirely forgotten for the moment.

Rodrick finished his first mug of beer before replying. "It's all on account of one Priest," he told them, his eyes thoughtful, as if he was putting things together for himself right there on the spot. "*Very* persuasive. They say the birds come down offa the trees t' hear his sermons. He *was* a Count, Count-Presumptive, that is. Count Padrik he woulda been, if he'd waited till his papa died 'fore he joined the Church. But—likely he made the better choice, if ye read him as a man with a bita ambition. He's been a-risin' in the Church like a lark in the mornin'. Fact is, he can't be no older'n me, an' already he's been made High Bishop of Gradford."

Kestrel's brow furrowed. "Isn't th-that a p-p-post th-that g-goes t-to a g-g-graybeard usually?"

Rodrick nodded. "Never heard it go to a man under the age of fifty, that's sure. Well, now he's High Bishop, and seems like all Gradford's gone mad for his notions. Inns—they're closing, 'cause they got no business. Trade in fancy-goods is way down. People are act'lly taking *vows,* an' doin' it like they thought the Second Cataclysm was this Midwinter! Only one trade's doin' any good, an' that's the trade in religious stuffs."

He nodded to himself with smug satisfaction, and Robin took a few bites of her neglected dinner while he basked in his own cleverness.

"I took m'self home, gathered up ev'ry book on the Church list, an' I've got 'em all loaded down on m'poor little donkey. Havna been able t' unload the half of 'em all these years—if Gradford's gonna come down with a plague'a piety, I'm gonna use the chance t' be rid'a this stuff!"

He beamed at them, and Robin chuckled. "Good for you, Rod, and thank you for telling us about this. It may not make us change our travel plans, but we're going to have to change our trades, I can see that."

Rod drank the last of the beer in his pitcher, and stood up to leave. "So long as it be religious, Gypsy Robin, ye'll profit," he said with a nod. "An' on that note, I'll be takin' m'leave."

"And a good night and fair profit to you." She returned the traditional trader's greeting. "And once again, thanks."

"Glad t' be of service," Rod replied, and took himself off, up the stairs to the sleeping quarters used by those who had no wagons to sleep in.

"Well," Robin said, turning to Kestrel as soon as Rod had taken the stairs out of sight and hearing. "Now what do we do?"

CHAPTER NINE

Jonny glanced around, quickly, to make certain there was no one near enough to overhear their conversation. He needn't have bothered; they were the only two patrons left in the common room, and since Robin had already paid for their meal, the serving girls were gone. The barkeeper polished the top of the counter and put clean mugs up on the shelf, obviously there only in the hope that they might order a drink.

If this common room was typical of the rest of the inn, it was one of the better such places Jonny had seen in all of his travels.

Then again, my pocket wasn't up to bearing the price of inns when I was on my own, he thought wryly.

But this was a good, solid place. Immaculately clean, the simple wood furniture was scarred by use and dark with age and many years of cleaning, but sturdily made; the floors were covered with clean rushes, and the smoke-blackened beams above were free of cobwebs. A few lanterns burned along the walls, but most of the light came from the fireplace. There were more lanterns along the walls, but they were not lit, perhaps in the hope of saving a little money on lamp oil.

"Eat," Robin advised him. "No one is going to hear us, or care what we say. They've heard everything in a place like this. They know we're Gypsies and Free Bards, and I rather doubt that the innkeeper is very fond of the Church and the High Bishop of Gradford. Right now, they're more concerned that their custom has dropped off than in anything we might say or do. We're just ordinary musicians, remember? What possible damage could two musicians do to anyone?"

He shook his head, and followed her advice. There was no point in wasting a perfectly good meal, especially not one as tasty as this; the cook had a good hand with pastry, and the tender, flaky crust covered a meat pie rich with brown gravy. But his stomach was a trifle uneasy and it took concentrated effort to calm it; Rodrick's information frankly disturbed him.

It appeared that the Ghost might have been right; certainly this High Bishop was an excellent candidate for the source of the sentiment against Free Bards. An ambitious man—as Padrik clearly was—could look for no better and quicker road to power than through the Church, and no quicker way to rise in the Church than to find *something* to get people upset about on religious grounds.

There aren't too many things that can get people aroused the way religion can, he observed, *and with this outbreak of "piety," sooner or later someone is going to find a "cause" to expend all their energy on. Unless Padrik is a fool, he'll be that someone; it will be the only way he can continue to control his followers. And if the "cause" turns out to be the control of music and musicians by the Church, it's going to be a bad day for the Free Bards.*

There his thoughts might have ended, if he hadn't spoken with Harp-erus and T'fyrr, but those conversations had opened his eyes to the fact that an attempt to control would not end with music. Control had to begin somewhere, and the best target for the initial stages of control would ideally be someone who was very obviously different, someone who was in the minority. An obvious set of targets for that method of control were the nonhuman citizens of the Twenty Kingdoms.

"So," Gwyna said, as he finished his dinner and pushed the wooden plate away. "We obviously need to go to Gradford even more now than before. What are we going to do? We can't go in as musicians. I have the feeling that we'd better have an obvious reason for being there, or we might find ourselves the center of some unwelcome attention."

"B-but we c-can g-go in as t-traders," Jonny replied. "Even th-the Gh-Ghost's silver won't l-last f-forever. W-we n-need t-to support ourselves s-s-somehow. Th-the only q-question is, wh-what do we s-s-sell?"

She toyed with a bit of bread, and a stray lock of hair slipped over her eye, curling in a most distracting and charming manner. "Religious goods. That would be the most obvious reason to be there. And it would be the safest, really. I don't think anyone is going to accuse a peddler of religious goods of impiety." She tucked the flyaway lock of hair behind her ear, and dropped the bread on the plate. "The quickest and easiest things for us to come up with on short notice are jewelry and display pieces; God-Stars are very easy to make, they're just tedious. And they're the kind of thing that only common, country folk display, so very few craftsmen ever bother with them. If no one in Gradford has thought of selling them, we'll have a temporary monopoly."

Jonny nodded; he had never seen God-Stars until he had arrived in Rayden as a child, for no one of noble blood would ever be caught wearing or displaying one. As wall-decorations, they were simply four-armed crosses, with colored yarn woven about the arms to form a solid square. The colors used varied with the prayers of the owner. Red, yellow, and white, for instance, meant the Star was a prayer for prosperity. Blue, green, and white meant a prayer for health, while blue, green, and *brown* was a plea for good harvests. He had never heard of anyone making God-Star jewelry, however.

"How d-do you make S-Stars as j-jewelry?" he asked.

"It isn't often done, because real jewelers and silversmiths can't be bothered," she replied, with a wry twitch to her mouth. "You can make them of embroidery thread and twigs, or metal and wire. With the wire ones, you have to be very careful so the wire doesn't break—but you use iron, copper, brass, and silver wire, and two nails for the Sacrificed God as the cross-pieces. Easy enough, and they make rather pretty little pendants."

He brightened. "Th-that would w-work. B-but where c-can w-we g-get materials?"

She thought for a moment, sipping at her mug of beer. "Well, Grad-ford's a center for metals and gems; I'd bet that we can find someone making wire outside the town and buy up a stock. Nails are easy. It shouldn't be too hard to find a weekly market to get dyed wool yarn, and linen embroidery thread, and sticks are under every tree."

"Wh-why not ask th-the innkeeper?" he asked, with a sudden inspiration. "W-wouldn't he know the b-best p-places t-to find things around here?"

She licked her lips, and nodded. "He would, and if he's like any other innkeeper I've ever met, he'll probably have a relative only too pleased to sell to us. That's fine; we'll make him happy and get our stock with a minimum of effort. The amount of money we'll save looking around for ourselves won't be worth the time we'll waste."

She shoved her stool away from the table, and trotted across the common room to consult with the barkeeper. After an exchange of a very few words, the barkeeper went off, and returned with the man Jonny had seen supervising the stable hands. Gwyna spoke with him for a little, and returned to her seat beaming.

"There!" she said. "It's taken care of. I told him part of the truth, that we were headed for Gradford and just heard we wouldn't be welcome there as musicians, so we need to continue our journey in another of our trades, peddlers selling handcrafted holy objects, since we couldn't afford the loss that going back would mean. He snorted, said, 'Religious trinkets, you mean,' and I knew he'd be willing to help us. He has a brother-in-law who can supply us with wire, and a cousin who can bring us the wool yarn and linen thread. He'll sell us horseshoe nails himself. So we're set."

Jonny shared her grin, and took her hand for a congratulatory squeeze. "S-so far," he replied, "s-so g-good. It's a g-good s-start, anyway!"

Four days later, thanks in no small part to the Ghost's gift, they left the inn with a full stock of God-Stars in several forms. They had bought all of the supplies that the innkeeper's relatives had brought, and still had some of the Ghost's silver left when they were done with their bargaining. There were several trays'-worth of the tiny Stars Robin had made up as pendants, from the cheapest Stars of linen thread and tiny twigs, to inexpensive copper Stars through Stars of mixed metals, to ones made entirely of silver wire and thin silver bars. Jonny had learned the knack of turning out wall-hanging Stars at a goodly clip, and he had used up all their yarn at about the same time Gwyna had run out of wire.

He was glad to pick up the reins and drive for a change; they had worked for as long as daylight lasted all during those four days, and his hands and wrists were sore from twisting yarn around sticks in movements he was not accustomed to making. He knew that Gwyna's hands hurt just as much; working with the wire was enough to try the patience beyond bearing, for it broke when flexed too often, and then it was impossible to mend without the mend showing. She'd been pierced with the sharp ends of nails and wire so often that her finger-ends looked like pincushions, and it was just as well that they were not going to be playing their instruments for a while, for her fingers needed to heal before she picked up her gittern or harp again.

They drove off into the dawn, with a friendly farewell from the helpful innkeeper (who had, without a doubt, skimmed off a commission from his relatives). The road was going to take them through a series of steep hills, and if they were going to get to Gradford before the gates closed at sunset, they needed to get this early start.

For a price, the cook had provided them not only with fresh rolls dripping with melted butter for their breakfast, but a packet of meat-pies for lunch on the road. With so little traffic about, Kestrel was able to eat with one hand and drive with the other. He enjoyed the fresh, hot bread, but Robin was in heaven over it, sensuously licking the dripping butter from her fingers until he warned her that if she continued in that fashion, they were going to have to make an unscheduled stop!

She laughed, and pouted at him, tossing her long hair over one shoulder in a flirting manner, and he growled at her playfully.

"Ah, well," she sighed. She popped the last bite into her mouth, and wiped her fingers carefully on a bit of rag. "I suppose we'd better behave. If we make an unscheduled stop, we *won't* get to Gradford before the gates close."

"P-precisely," he said, with mock-sternness. "*One* of us h-has t-to have s-some s-self-control!"

She laughed, and folded her hands modestly in her lap under the protective warmth of her coat, looking about with interest. It was a breathtakingly beautiful day, in a stark, monochromatic fashion, but there was no doubt that winter was only a breath or two away. Frost was so thick on the branches and dead, dry grasses that they looked as if they had grown white coats of fur; the cloudless blue sky held a sun that gave very little besides light. As the road wove its way onward, they passed streams that had rims of ice at the edges, and their breath and the mares' puffed out in white clouds whenever they talked or breathed. Crows called occasionally, off in the distance. The hills themselves were covered with forests of hardwood trees that had long since lost their leaves, and made a mist-like haze on the hillsides with the interweaving of their gray-barked, barren branches.

"If it looks like we can pass as 'Church-approved,' we *might* actually be able to play some music," she remarked, when the inn had receded from sight.

"I th-thought about th-that." While they had been hard at work on the God-Stars, in order to get themselves into the proper mood, they had polished up all the ballads about heroes of the Church that either of them knew. If nothing else, those songs were often used as teaching aids by the Priests, and singing them made a painless refresher course in theology and accepted doctrine, not to mention providing a good source of pious quotations to sprinkle over their conversation. "P-purely instrumental m-music ought t-to b-be safe, if it isn't a d-dance t-tune. And even d-d-dance t-tunes c-can b-be *made* s-safe."

"How?" she asked, full of immediate interest. "Oh! Of course! If we slow the tempo so it isn't a *dance* tune anymore, likely no one will recognize it!"

"And add l-liturgical ch-chord sequences, th-the k-kind you hear in h-h-hymns." He was very pleased with that idea; he'd already tried it out in his head, and it made even the liveliest toe-tapper sound as if it came straight from Holy Services.

She nodded, her face full of pleasure at his cleverness. Then her eyes grew thoughtful; he let her sit in silence, knowing that she was trying to work a sudden thought to its conclusion. He listened instead to the steady clopping of the mares' hooves, and the jingle of their harness in the clear, cold air. Finally, she spoke.

"Music isn't going to be forbidden everywhere," she said, slowly. "In fact, the one way to give brothels and pleasure-houses more business than they can handle is to try to forbid pleasure itself. And a pleasure-house is going to be a *very* good place to learn what's going on in Gradford—really going on, that is, and not just what the officials are telling people, or what street-gossip says. Musicians are probably going to be welcome there, if all the places haven't already been taken by Gradford natives."

"B-but it c-could be d-dangerous," Kestrel finished for her. "If Church officials d-decide t-to l-look for s-someone t-to use as an example. S-someone w-with n-no importance. Still. P-perhaps if w-we d-do what Rune d-did, and have t-two personae, one f-for the s-street and one f-for th-the b-b-brothel."

"It's worth thinking about when we get there," she agreed. "I have to admit I didn't think this was going to be all that important even after listening to Harperus and Nightingale—I thought this was just another bout of petty harassment, the kind we had when we first formed the Free Bards. Something's up though, something is different this time. I don't like what I've been hearing, and I want to do something about protecting our people before it's too late."

Jonny nodded, but did not add what he was thinking.

I only hope it's not already too late.

Their sturdy mares were in fine fettle after four days of rest and good feeding, and made much better time than either of them had expected. The walls of Gradford appeared in the distance in mid-afternoon, and they had plenty of time to study the city-state during their approach.

It had been built on the top of an enormous hill (or very small mountain) and was supposed to be the oldest complex continuously inhabited by humans in the Twenty Kingdoms. The city had expanded several times, and each time it had, a new set of walls had been built to accommodate the expansion. The original structure looked to have been either a military fortress or fortified castle; probably the original Duke of Gradford's holding. Its strange, blocky, angular architecture was at violent odds with the rest of the city, and it was easily the tallest structure either of them had ever seen in their lives. It must have been at least a full twenty stories tall, and Jonny could not imagine anyone climbing all those staircases to get to the top on a regular basis. The building itself, taken over by the Duke, was supposedly a structure that had made it through the Cataclysm intact. But the Duke's line had died out, and no relative could be found to claim the holding before the Mayor of the city below his fortress had claimed independence, supported by the High Bishop.

That had been in the early days, when no one really wanted the remote city, even though it was on a major trade road. Gradford's heyday had come when enterprising souls roaming the hills had discovered rich veins

of silver and copper beneath them to the east, and iron-ore and coal to
the west. To the south were finds of semiprecious and precious gems;
garnet, beryl, amethyst, topaz, peridot, citrine, tourmaline, moonstone,
and fine, clear quartz of all kinds.

Suddenly Gradford had something to trade. And by this time, it had
the blessing of the High Bishop, a strong Lord Mayor and a Council
comprised of Guild Masters from every major trade. The Council immediately let it be known that they were hiring the best mercenaries money
could buy, and there were no more rumors of war.

Gradford prospered and grew, but apparently the Mayor and Council
never forgot that there were nobles out there who lusted for its wealth.
Every building was neatly tucked inside that last wall, and all of the walls
sported sentries and guards, tiny as gnats at this distance, but clearly
vigilant and visible.

The road did not actually lead through the city, but rather went past
the base of the hill it was built upon. Long ago the hill had been cleared
of trees, to keep any hostile forces from creeping up under cover of the
branches. What remained was rock; rock, and very thin soil covered with
tough, wiry grass. The dead brown grass matched the sandy brown rock,
the same rock that had been quarried to form the city walls, so that the
city rose out of the hillside as if it had grown from the rocks themselves.

A switchback road cut out of the hillside and reinforced with more of
the same sandy-brown stone led up to the city gates, which stood wide
open at this hour. Hardly surprising, Jonny reflected. The guards on the
walls would see enemies coming long before they were any threat, and
by the time an enemy force was within striking distance, the gates would
already be closed and barred.

The road was wide and even, and so well-maintained that the mares
were not even sweating by the time they brought their wagon in under
the enormous gates, which had clearly been built to handle vehicles much
larger than theirs. There was not one gate, but several, although Jonny
suspected that only the outer, wooden gates, banded and reinforced with
iron straps, were ever closed at night. Behind the wooden gates was a
portcullis of iron bars that dropped down from above. Behind that was
another portcullis of thick stakes of wood, woven with iron straps. And
behind *that* was a second set of wooden gates, this pair sheathed with
iron plates on the inner side. Jonny suspected that there were murder-
holes in the floor of the walkway topping the gates, and that anyone who
got through the first set of gates would find molten lead, stones, or boiling
oil or water rained down on him from above. A truly cruel trick would
be to let an enemy pass the first set of gates, then drop the outer portcullis, trapping him between the inner gates and the outermost portcullis,
and destroy him at leisure.

They were stopped at the inner gates by a guard; a very brisk and
efficient middle-aged man, in chain-mail and a tunic with a badge embla-
zoned on the front. The badge was not one that Jonny recognized; it was
not the five coins of Gradford, but a single coin with a four-armed cross
superimposed upon it. This guard wanted to know their names, their
trade, and where they had come from before he would let them pass.

Gwyna spoke up for them both, although this made the guard frown slightly; evidently women were not supposed to be so forward in Gradford these days as to dare to speak for a man. But neither of them wanted someone as marked by a distinguishing characteristic as Jonny's stutter to be on a guard's list. Gwyna could dye or cut her hair, change her clothes— Jonny could not open his mouth without betraying himself.

So he feigned being mute when the guard made a hushing motion at Robin and ordered *him* to speak up. He hoped that Robin would pick up on his cues; they hadn't had time to rehearse *this* subterfuge! He shook his head as the guard frowned and raised his voice.

"Sorry, sir," Robin said, falling into the part of a woman forced into the role of 'caretaker.' "Me husband's mute, sir. Been so since the storm a year agone—" She sniffed, and the guard's expression turned from one of disapproval to sympathy. "Struck by lightning, he was. Mind is as sharp as ever, but he can't speak a word."

Jonny nodded vigorously, and spread his hands in a gesture of help-lessness, thanking whatever god might be listening for Gwyna's quick mind. The guard's expression softened further.

"Then give us the names and all, lass," he said, condescendingly, as if she were just a little feeble-minded. Kestrel clenched his jaw a little, and hoped she wouldn't react to that tone.

She didn't; she kept her temper, and smiled at the guard sweetly. "Jonny Brede and Jina Brede. We're traders in religious keepsakes, God-Stars. We came from Kingsford in Birnam when we heard of the work of your great High Bishop, and how Gradford had turned to pious ways."

Jonny let out his breath in a silent sigh of relief. Evidently Gwyna decided her name sounded a bit too much like she might be a Gypsy— they had taken the precaution this morning of dressing soberly, rather than in their Gypsy or Free Bard finery. Or else she was afraid someone might know the name "Gwyna," even though she called herself Robin in public. She could hardly use *that* name with the guard without branding herself a Free Bard! And she had wisely chosen a city far enough away that no one was likely to send to find out if they *had* been there recently.

"God-Stars?" the guard said, with interest. Gwyna dimpled, and brought out the samples they had stowed under the driver's seat.

"Little ones, for pendants, like, and the big ones, of course." She preened with pride as the guard examined both and praised the work. She started to offer him both, but to Jonny's surprise, he refused.

"That'd be bribery, dear, and we're honest men here in Gradford," he replied. "No, and I thank you, but you keep those in your pretty hands. Best of luck to you. Go right on in; there's no one in Gradford selling God-Stars like these, so you're no competition to a local trader, and that means you can set up in the market whenever you like. There's no tax on religious goods, other than the usual tithe."

Gwyna thanked him, and did not argue; if the guard was too silly to understand that a customer who bought a God-Star would probably *not* buy something else, it was not her problem. Kestrel shook the reins to send the horses forward.

And as soon as they cleared the gates, it was only too obvious that

Rodrick had been right. Although this was clearly the start of the market-district, there was not a single busker anywhere. No jugglers, no street-dancers, no musicians. The streets seemed to have plenty of people on them, until you realized that this *should* have been the busiest part of the city. Then it slowly became obvious that there was barely a third of the people here that there should have been.

The undercurrent of music to the chaotic crowd-noises was something that both of them had taken for granted. Now that it was gone, the lack made Jonny, at least, feel oddly off-balance, straining his ears, listening for something that simply wasn't there.

They passed several inns—it was never wise to take the first set of accommodations offered, for such places were invariably overpriced. They shared their side of the street with a number of other vehicles, but none of them were traders' wagons. So Rodrick had been right about that as well; the traders appeared to have deserted the city entirely.

There's no rain that doesn't water someone's garden, Jonny thought. *At least there'll be no shortage of rooms. And probably good prices.* Gwyna had told him that in most large cities it was against the law to sleep in wagons; anyone who wished to camp in his wagon had to do so outside the city walls.

He still wasn't certain which inn to patronize, and when he finally saw *the* sign, he knew instinctively he had found the right place for them. The signboard sported a bird, beak wide open and pointed to the sky, obviously singing for all it was worth. It also, unlike many others, had the name of the inn written under the painted bird.

The Singing Bird. The name seemed a good omen, and Jonny turned the horses into the arched gateway that led into the inn's court.

The lean and balding innkeeper was frantically happy to see them, and a glance at his stable showed them why. No more than a third of the stalls were occupied, and if that was an indication of the number of customers inside, it was no wonder that he was glad to see them and their cash.

He was *not* a Gypsy, somewhat to Jonny's disappointment, but his stables were good, and he saw to their needs personally.

"We'll need to be able to take the wagon out during the day," Gwyna told him. "We'll be using it as our stall in the marketplace."

That stopped him cold, just as he directed the stableboys to put their mares in two spacious loose-boxes. "I hope you aren't selling anything—like luxury goods?" he said, hesitantly, the bald spot on the top of his head growing red with anxiety. "There's not much call for such things in Gradford these days."

Jonny mentally gave him the accolade for his honesty. He could have gotten one night's lodging out of them before they found out the hard truth for themselves. Instead, he warned them.

Then again, if we were selling something proscribed, maybe he'd get arrested or fined for giving us lodging. It was a possibility. Given the lack of buskers and all that implied, Jonny was not taking anything for granted.

But Gwyna laughed, lightly. "God-Stars," she said, simply. "As jewelry and as wall decorations."

The innkeeper heaved a very audible sigh of relief, and mopped the top of his head with his apron. "There's no problem then. I'll have the boys ready your wagon and horses at the bell for Sunrise Service from the Cathedral; you come down for breakfast at Calling Bell for Prime Service and you'll find them harnessed and waiting when you finish. Best place for you will be in the market-square in front of the Cathedral, and to get there you just follow this street until it comes out at the square."

They locked up the wagon and took their bags from under the driver's seat, following their host across the yard to the inn itself. It was a sturdy, three-storied affair, substantial and built of dark timbers with whitewashed stone between. "I'm sorry I can't offer you any entertainment," he said apologetically. "But music's not allowed, unless it's from a Church-licensed musician."

His expression said what he would not say aloud. *And those are so bad I'd rather have no music than theirs.*

"Gradford has changed since last I was here," Gwyna replied casually. "There were no restrictions then, on what music could be played and what a peddler could sell."

The innkeeper shrugged, and once again his expression of faint distaste told Jonny that he did not care for the current state of things. But then, what innkeeper would? His custom had been cut down to a third of what it had been; *he* certainly was not prospering.

"I can't sell you strong liquor, either," he continued. "Only beer and ale, and hard cider." By his wary expression, some of his customers had found a great deal to object to in this particular edict, but Jonny only laughed.

"N-never d-drink anything s-stronger," he said, shortly, with a grin that made the innkeeper smile in return.

At that point, they entered the inn, and that was when Jonny realized just how bad things had gotten for the innkeepers of Gradford. Not that the place was ill-kempt, quite the contrary. The common room, with polished wooden tables and real chairs, with hangings on the walls and lanterns or candles on every table, with not one, but *two* fireplaces, was clearly a quality of hostelry they would not have been able to afford in the days of Gradford's prosperity. Or—perhaps, if their music pleased the innkeeper, they *might* have graced this room, but only as paid performers, and then only if a Guild musician didn't want the job. Or if the innkeeper didn't want the Guild musician. . . .

"I'll have a table ready for you as soon as you like," the innkeeper was saying as he hurried them across the waxed and polished stone floor of the common room and towards the staircase at the other side. "It's a good ham tonight, and sweetroots, or chicken and dumplings with carrots, and a nice stew of apples for after. Your room is up here—"

The room, up on the third floor, was obviously not the best in the inn, but it was finer than they *should* have gotten for their coin. It shared a bath with three other rooms; there were good rag rugs on the varnished wooden floor, a plain, but handsome wardrobe, matching tables on either side of the bed, and the bed boasted heavy bedcurtains, a feather mattress and feather comforter. No fireplace, of course, but it did have a small coal-fired stove, and presumably a certain amount of heat came up from the common room below. There were sturdy shutters to shut out the wind, and cheap, thick glass in the windows, full of bubbles and wavy—but in the class of inn they generally frequented, they were lucky to have shutters, much less glazed windows.

They ordered a bath for after dinner, put their gear away, and took the stairs back down to the common room. The ham, as promised, was good, and the room no more than a third full. Small wonder there were only two choices for a meal; with so few customers, this innkeeper could not afford to have several dishes prepared so that a patron had a wider choice.

"You know, we have a few hours of daylight left," Gwyna observed, as they lingered over their stewed apples and spiced tea. "We ought to walk around and see what's to be seen."

Jonny raised an inquiring eyebrow over that remark. Had she seen something he hadn't? He *had* been too busy driving to pay a great deal of attention to anything else.

"There seem to be a lot of street preachers," she said in answer to his unspoken question. "In fact, it looks almost as if the street preachers have taken over from the buskers."

"Ah," he replied, enlightened. "W-we should s-see what th-they're s-saying."

"Exactly." She sighed, and put aside her empty bowl and the spoon. "Much as I hate to ruin such a nice meal with a sour stomach. I think we really need to get a feel for things before we go out tomorrow."

"Right." He rose, and offered her his arm. "W-would m-my lady c-care t-take a s-stroll?"

"Why, yes, I think she would." She dimpled, and took the proffered arm. "The company, at least, will be pleasant."

"Even if th-the s-stroll isn't?" he replied.

She didn't answer him; she only shook her head with a warning look as they walked out into the inn-yard, and joined the thin stream of people leaving their work and going home.

CHAPTER TEN

There were plenty of street preachers, one for every corner, sometimes shouting so loudly that their speeches overlapped, and some of them were unintentionally funny. The trouble was, no one else seemed to see anything humorous in what they were saying.

A chilly wind whipped up the street, tossing skirts and cloaks, and numbing Kestrel's nose. It was a wind remarkably free of the usual stinks of a large city, and the gutters were empty of anything but a trace of water. Perhaps this place was like Nolton, with laws regarding the disposal of garbage, and crews to clean the streets. In a city like this one, with so many people crowded into so small an area and no river to cleanse it, that was not just a good idea, it was a necessity.

Buildings on both sides of the street loomed at least three stories in height, built of stone with tiny windows in the upper stories. Roofs were of a brownish slate, or of sandy tile. There wasn't a great deal of color, even in the dress of the passersby. Only the brilliantly blue sky above gave any relief to the unrelenting gray and brown. Nothing delineated the changes in Gradford quite so clearly as that; elsewhere, people reacted to the coming of winter by bringing out as much color in their clothing as they could afford. Presumably the people of Gradford had once done the same, but no more. The city *looked* sober, as if it already hosted nothing but Brothers and Sisters of various ascetic Orders.

They walked about a quarter mile towards the Cathedral, which loomed over the smaller buildings just as the Duke's Palace loomed over the city itself. They both paid careful attention to each preacher for at least a few minutes at a time; usually a few minutes were enough to get the gist of what each was saying.

Gradually Kestrel began to get a sense that there were three kinds of preachers, and each set shared a common style and a set of messages.

The first kind were the wild-eyed, unkempt street preachers he was used to seeing in every city or town he had ever found himself in. Dressed in strange assortments of tattered and layered garments, they exhorted the crowds passing with wildly waving arms and hoarsely shouted diatribes. They were fairly incoherent, contradicting themselves from sentence to sentence, and full of dire prophecies about the "Second Cataclysm." He'd always thought they were a little mad, and he didn't see any reason to change that opinion now. Interestingly, these men had only the same sort of audiences they got in other cities; people as mad as they were, gawkers, and adolescents who got a great deal of amusement out of making a mockery of them.

But the adolescents making mock were uniformly ruffians, rather than the mix of ne'er-do-wells and ordinary youngsters that usually tried to give these poor old men a difficult time. And the authorities, in the form of the City Constables, ran the youngsters off with warnings, and not the preachers, who would elsewhere have been considered nuisances.

So these days in Gradford, even the lunatics come in for a smattering of respect. Kestrel wouldn't have believed it if he hadn't seen it himself.

The second variety of street sermonizers was a type he normally saw only during Faires: country-fellows who were not ordained Priests and supported themselves through what they could collect on their own. These were men who would say, if questioned, that they felt "called by The Sacrificed God" to preach the Truth as they, and not the Church, saw it. They generally leapt at the chance to preach restraint to a crowd bent on celebration. Their motives were simple enough; perhaps move some of their listeners to moderation, or at least, through a bit of passing guilt, charm a pin or a coin out of their pockets and into the collection plate. Kestrel thought of them as a different form of busker, for they used the same venue as buskers. Their messages were along the line of "repent of your sins and be purified," and "do not waste your lives on short-term pleasures when your energy could better be spent in contemplating God." They urged sacrifice, with the veiled hint that a sacrifice tossed in their direction would find favor with God. More often than not—at a Faire at least—this kind of preacher would manage to "save" some fellow who'd been a chronic drunk all his life and had just hit bottom; having "saved" the fool, the preacher would parade him about like a hunter's prize. And the former drunk, having found a new addiction that made him the center of attention, would perform obligingly.

There were at least two with reformed drunks in tow on this street. And although these men were normally ignored by Faire-goers, who often parted around them like the water in a swift-moving stream avoiding a rock, here their message was falling on more appreciative ears. More than one listener looked both attentive and impressed. Interesting, but not unexpected.

Then there was the third class of preacher—a type that Kestrel had *never* seen preaching in the street before; real Priests, in immaculate robes, who clearly did not need to be out here and in fact had no collection plates at their feet. These men—they were always men, even though women could aspire to the Priesthood as readily as men—were clean, erudite, and well-spoken, pitching their trained, modulated voices to carry their words over the heads of the crowds.

It was this third type of preacher that had the messages that were very disturbing.

"—come from God are alone pure and righteous," the first of these was saying, as they came within hearing distance. He had a very well-trained and sonorous voice, and he already had a crowd three deep around him. He was brown of beard and hair and eye; his well-kept robe was a dark brown, and he should have blended in with his surroundings. But he didn't—he stood out from them, as if he was a heroic statue, the focus for all eyes. "No matter what the ignorant and unholy will tell you, *all* things called 'magic' are inherently evil. Magic can only be the tool of demons and false gods; there is no truth in it, and none in those who practice it."

He looked around at his audience; Kestrel was very careful to school his features into a semblance of sober interest. This man was no fool; any show of resistance to his words would cause him to single that person out for special attentions and special messages. The onlookers would notice. Things could become very awkward, very quickly.

"Perhaps you have heard somewhere that there are mages within the Church itself, but I tell you that this is *not* true. Whoever has told you this has lied to you," he said, lying gracefully and believably. "Magic is *deception;* magic only counterfeits the real and holy powers granted only to Priests by God. Those powers practiced within the Church come directly by grace and blessing of the Sacrificed God, and they are *nothing* like magic! And only those within the Church, *within the ranks of the ordained* will be blessed with those powers. Those who claim to achieve the same ends through their magic are false, deceptive, and evil. They seek to mislead you, seduce you to muddled thinking and questioning, and then to lead you astray down the paths of darkness."

Neat, Jonny thought, admiring the Priest's command of rhetoric, though not his words. *Redefine magic as anything that is not performed by a Priest, and then you can condemn it without condemning the Priests.*

"Not only is the magic itself inherently and by its very deceptive nature evil," the Priest continued, warming to his subject, "but anyone, *anyone* who uses it *or allows himself to be touched by it* is evil! Magic is a mockery of God's powers! God will not be mocked! He will not permit his servants to be mocked! The day is coming when all those evil ones who practice magic will perish, and those who permitted them to work their magic will perish with them! Those who live by magic will die by the hand of the righteous!"

There was more in this vein, although Jonny noticed that the Priest was very careful not to say *who* would be dealing out this punishment to the "evil magicians." Given the tales that had been spreading of musicians using magic to manipulate their listeners, it was easy to see where *this* was going. He might not have brought up the "evil musicians" yet, but it was only a matter of time.

Nightingale had been only too right, and so had Harperus.

He felt a sudden sickness in the pit of his stomach, and it didn't take any effort at all on his part to persuade Gwyna away and get out of hearing range. The Priest was still going strong when they left, and as far as Jonny could tell, it was more of the same. No mention, as yet, of musicians. But given the fact that there were no musicians anywhere in sight, perhaps he saw no need to mention them, in his condemnation of every other person who ever made use of magic and mages.

About the only encouraging note in this was that the Priest was losing listeners at a fairly steady rate—perhaps people who had used the services of a Healer, or those who had employed a mage for some minor work in finding a lost object, locating water, or taming a beast that would not respond to normal efforts. It would take more persuasive means than simply *saying* that magic was evil to convince most folk that it was bad.

After all, most people in their lives saw many instances of the use of magic, all of it hired and completely matter-of-fact. How could any of this be evil? Mages created amusing illusions for parties, rid homes of polter-geists and kobolds—they didn't do anything that a Priest couldn't do. And they generally didn't ask as much in return. Priests were often greedy in their demands when someone turned to them for help; a simple mage could only ask the usual rate, and did not care *what* god you followed or whether you were up to date on your tithing.

That was what Kestrel read in the faces of those who turned away from the preacher. But there were some who stayed, nodding in agreement. . . .

A very bad sign.

The sun had turned the sky above the city to a glorious crimson as they came into the "circle" of another of the real Priests out on the street. This man had a much larger gathering of listeners, and fewer of them were leaving with looks of stubborn disbelief on their faces. Jonny steeled himself to hear something unpleasant. This one also wore a brown robe, but he was a much older man, the kind that people would instinctively turn to for advice; clean-shaven with snow-white hair. But there was some-thing subtly cruel and hard about his eyes, and the set of his mouth indicated a man who would never accept any opinion but his own.

"If a soul is the image of God, and God created humankind in His image, how can any creature that does not wear that image have a soul?" the Priest asked, his voice rational and reasonable. "It is there in the Holy Writ, for all to read. *For God then created them, male and female, in His Own image.* Male and female, and human. *The soul is the reflection of God, and is in the image of God.* Human, entirely and wholly. No creature that is not fully human could possibly be in possession of a soul. The implications of this are obvious to anyone who takes the time to study the Holy Book and *think*. A creature that does not have a soul cannot be saved by the grace of the Church; it is that simple, and that profound. Only humans can be saved. Only humans have souls."

This Priest had an interesting demeanor; unlike the last one, who clearly preached *at* his audience, this man kept his voice calm and steady, his tone ingratiating, his expression persuasive. His manner invited his listeners to discover truth for themselves, not just to be told what the truth was and was not. In a village, this man would be the one most would go to for the settling of disputes.

"But there is a much more serious—yes, and frightening—side to this, and one that is not as obvious," he continued, his expression turning to one of warning. "A creature that does not have a soul and cannot be saved by the Church must *by definition* be evil! Oh, do not shake your heads; only think about it. To be evil is to act against the interests of God. But a creature that is soulless cannot know the interests of God, so how can he act in accord with them? They cannot be anything but evil by their very natures. Nothing can change that, not all the good intentions in the world, for it is bred into them, blood and bone, by their very differences. They are the damned and the doomed, and they will always be the enemies of the Church, for their inmost nature will cause them to resist the guidance of the Church." His expression hardened, and yet became sorrowful at the same time. "Surely you, who are thinking men, can see the result of this. The Church's charge is the safety, spiritual and actual, of humanity. The enemies of the Church must become, sooner or later, the enemies of all humankind, and the enemies of humankind will inevitably seek to destroy humanity."

Kestrel had no trouble anticipating the next statement.

"Those who would seek to destroy humankind *must* be destroyed first!" the Priest said fiercely. "There can be no sin in this; it is not murder, for they have no souls! It is self-defense and no more; ridding humanity of their cursed presence is no worse than ridding the city of rats! And *who* is it that has these unnatural magics, that you have been warned against? More often than not, it is these unhuman monsters!"

This time it was Robin who pulled him away, but he was not reluctant to leave; he had certainly heard enough to nauseate him. "God is l-love, l-love is b-blind, I am b-b-blind, therefore I am G-G-God," Kestrel muttered under his breath; something that had become a very unfunny joke. Horrid how the rules of logic could be twisted to make the illogical, irrational, and idiotic sound reasonable. . . .

Robin shushed him, and they crossed over to the other side of the street to return to their inn. The last light of the sun died away overhead; the little canyons between the buildings were already full of shadows, and lamplighters made their way along the street, pausing at each of the street corners. There were not too many people out at this point; those that were did not seem to be in any great hurry to get anywhere. Kestrel noted with thankfulness that the preachers had taken the coming of nightfall as a signal to leave their posts and find some other venue for their speeches. He'd had a bellyful of them, and he was not in the mood for any more.

But he was to get one more dose of Holy Word before they reached the relative safety of their room.

The last preacher of the night was hard to classify; he had the collection plate and the common clothing of an ordinary street preacher, but the trained voice and command of rhetoric of a full Priest. They could not get by, for his listeners had temporarily blocked the street, so they had no choice but to listen for a moment.

And for a moment, it seemed as if his message was no more insidious than any of the other lunatics out here this afternoon. "—idle time, time that is not spent in work or in contemplation, is time spent in evilness," he was saying. Kestrel could not see his face in the shadows; he kept his voice deliberately soft, so that anyone really listening had to lean forward to hear his words. The combination of the darkness, the soft words, the persuasive voice, worked in a hypnotic fashion before a listener was really aware of it.

Unless you were a musician, and had used similar tricks yourself, to create a mood of quiet persuasion in the middle of a crowded tavern.

"Because of this, anything done purely for pleasure or for simple enjoyment is also evil because these are things done in idleness. The only fit occupation for a true man is work; either the work of his hands and mind, or the work of God and the Church. Those temptations of hollow pleasure must be eliminated, and those who will not give them up must be taught the error of their ways. Gently, if possible, but if not"—he concluded, darkly—"then by whatever means necessary."

At that point the blockage cleared, and Robin and Kestrel hurried on, quickly, until they were well out of range of sight and sound of the final preacher.

"Now I'm glad we were warned," Robin sighed. "If we had come into town the way we usually enter a city—"

"P-playing and s-singing 'The S-saucy P-p-priest'?" Kestrel finished. "I th-think our w-welcome m-might have b-been w-warmer th-than w-we'd l-like."

"That, at least." Robin held his arm, tightly, as much for comfort as for appearances, as they entered the inn courtyard. It opened up like a haven of sanity after the speeches of the past hour. As they opened the door to the common room, one of the serving girls spotted them and hurried over to them.

"Would you like your baths now?" she asked. "The water is hot and ready, and no one has bespoken the room until later."

"Please," Robin said, and lowered her voice a little. "We were just taking a walk outside, and we couldn't help wondering—is every night like tonight? I've never seen so many preachers in one place before. Is there something special about tonight, or this street?"

The girl sighed, and rolled her eyes a little. "Nothing special about tonight, but they do seem to pick this street t' be doing their ranting. P'rhaps it's 'cause most visitors lodge here, or p'rhaps it's 'cause the Cathedral's so near. There's laws, thank heavens; they can't be preachin' long after dark, to disturb folks' rest, or we'd not get any. No offense—" she added hastily.

Kestrel managed a wan chuckle. "N-none t-taken," he said. "We're here t-to p-peddle our c-crafts, and if it's G-god-Stars th-these p-people w-want, th-that's what th-they'll g-get!"

The girl smiled warmly. "I shouldn't've said what I did, but I didn't think you was lunatic religious," she replied. "F'r one thing, they don't bathe near often enough!" And she wrinkled her nose. "Be glad it's 'bout winter! I tell you, some 'f them 'd choke a goat in hot weather!"

Robin shrugged. "We're traders," she said. "We were warned what had happened, and we changed our trade goods for something that would sell under the circumstances. Perhaps it may sound cynical, but if they'd all gone mad for—for some actor who fancied feather masks, for some reason, we'd be peddling those instead of God-Stars."

"But actors don't get y' pilloried—or worse," the girl muttered, then shook herself. "Well, sir an' lady, take y'rselves upstairs, whilst I call th' upstairs wench, an' by the time y' reach the bathing room, the baths'll be ready."

She was as good as her word. The bathing room had two tubs, side by side, and both were full and steaming, as promised, by the time they arrived at the bathroom door. They sank into the hot water with gratitude.

Jonny simply let his mind empty; he did not want to think about what he had just heard. He wanted to relax, just for a moment, and pretend that none of this was happening.

Church bells woke them; not uncommon in a large city, but they seemed unusually loud until Kestrel remembered the Cathedral was not far away. And they were *very* loud. He hadn't heard bells like this since—since—

Since I was a child, and living in the Guild Hall with my Master. The Cathedral was across the street, and every morning the first bells would wake us, no matter how tired we were, or how late we had been up the night before.

The remembrance was tainted with a little less bitterness now. It helped to know that his beloved Master had not been a crazed and half-witted old man, but a very brave and very frightened one. It helped to know that the Guild had been wrong about both of them.

Robin groaned as Kestrel got out of bed and pulled back the thick, dark curtains. He actually felt rather good, even after those wretched street sermons of the night before—and even though his dreams had been haunted by Priests leading fanatic mobs in chasing him. One thing about being in a city obsessed with religion—there was little or nothing to do after sunset, so going to bed was the only option.

I'll bet they have a population explosion around here in a few months— depending on how long this has been going on, he thought, pulling open the shutters to let the sunlight in. Robin groaned again. *I wonder if the herbs that protect against conception have been put on the proscribed list too?* That would be a logical move, if the Church really was interested in restricting people's interests. If a girl had a real chance of getting pregnant, she might be a bit warier about distributing her favors. And if a wife was burdened with one baby after another, she wouldn't have a great deal of leisure for anything else.

Like thinking for herself. . . .

Robin sat up, her curly hair tousled and a lock dangling over one eye, yawning hugely. "Gods," she moaned, squinting. "Sunlight."

Sun poured through the thick glass and pooled on the floor, catching the reds and blues in the rag rug there and making them glow. Kestrel grabbed clean clothing, while Robin watched, blinking sleepily from her nest of bedclothes. Sober clothing; muted browns and dark grays for him, browns and sand-tones for Robin. No Gypsy reds and yellows here; if he'd had any doubt as to the wisdom of such "disguises," last night in the street had convinced him.

"T-time t-to get to w-work," he reminded her. "W-we're p-peddlers, remember? W-we have t-to be out f-first th-thing when th-the m-markets open."

"I remember," she said, around another yawn. "Well, last night we heard the poison, now we need to find out what the source is. And *why* all these people are suddenly so full of maniacal religious fervor! A lot of the changes here required some changes in the *laws,* Jonny, and that doesn't happen overnight. You have to convince very powerful people to make changes that may not be to their advantage."

"You're v-very articulate this m-morning," he observed, with a bit of a smile, then lost the smile as something occurred to him. "One of th-the p-powerful p-people who s-supported Gradford f-from the b-beginning was th-the High B-Bishop. W-wouldn't he b-be on th-the C-Council? D-did you th-think about th-that?"

"Hmm. I think I was thinking about it even in my sleep." She climbed out of bed to join him in dressing, pulling on linen petticoats, wool stockings and boots, a sober brown wool skirt and sand-colored linen shirt, lacing her brown leather vest over both. "Someone has gotten the ears of anyone important, and has convinced the merchants who are losing money right now that they are better off not complaining about their problems. We should keep our ears open in the marketplace. There are probably some merchants out there that are just as cynical as Rodrick, and we might get them to tell us something. There's a piece missing to this puzzle."

As promised, a breakfast was laid ready for the inn's patrons, a buffet-style breakfast where they could help themselves to oatmeal, sliced bread and butter, honey, fruit, last night's ham, and pastries. And as promised, when they were finished and went out into the court, the wagon was standing ready with several others, mares in harness and stamping impatiently.

They swung themselves up onto the driver's bench, and took the wagon out into the street. All traffic, foot and wagon, was going in one direction this morning; towards the Cathedral. Robin had the reins, and she simply let the press of people carry them along at foot-pace.

"I'm c-curious," Kestrel said, as the Cathedral loomed at the end of the street. "H-how *d-did* you d-do that b-business w-with th-the f-fire in y-your h-hand in W-Westhaven?"

Robin chuckled. "Gypsy trick," she said, lightly. "Meant to fool the stupid. Special paper that burns very quickly, so quickly there isn't any heat to speak of, and it ignites with just a spark. A little misdirection, flint-and-steel and a bit of paper in your hand, and agile fingers, and there you are. I always carry some, and powder of the same sort, good for throwing into a fire to create a big flash."

Jonny watched the faces of the foot travelers around them. They were uniformly eager, clearly anticipating something. "C-can all of you d-do that?"

She nodded. "Useful skill to have, when you need to make someone think that you're more powerful than you really are. We pledge never to teach outsiders, though, so I'm afraid I can't even teach you."

"D-don't n-need it," he assured her. "G-got enough to worry about."

By that time they reached the place where the street emptied out into the square in front of Gradford Cathedral. For the first time they saw the Cathedral as something other than bits of towers and roof, and in spite of himself, Jonny was impressed and moved.

You couldn't get a sense of the Cathedral simply from the bits you glimpsed over the rooftops and at the end of the street. He had no idea how anyone could construct something like this building without it toppling straight over; it looked as fragile and delicate as any confectioner's masterpiece, and just as ephemeral.

He guessed that the four round steeples, one at each corner, must have been at least fifteen stories tall, maybe more. They spiraled up like the shells of some sea-beasts he had seen, coming to a point at their peaks. They were pierced by a fretwork of windows, and looked as delicate as lace. There were no sharp angles in these towers, nothing but curves; curved arches, round windows, spiraling, ramplike exterior ledges that ran from the bottom all the way to the top. The towers were covered with a network of carvings as well, cut in shallow relief into the pristine marble and alabaster. None of the towers were carved alike. The tower to his right was encrusted with waving kelp and seaweed, sinuous eels, spiny urchins, undulating waves, and delicate fish. The one to his left bore clouds in every form, from wisps to towering thunderheads, and among them sported all the creatures of the air, from birds to butterflies. Rainbows arched from cloud to cloud, and the delicate seeds of thistle and dandelion wafted among the flying insects on the lower level.

The other two towers were harder to see since they were on the opposite side of the Cathedral, but on one, Jonny thought he made out sensuous and abstract depictions of flames, salamanders, and the legendary phoenix, and on the other, carvings of plants and animals crept, climbed, and sported on the curves.

On the top of each tower was a single statue of an angel; they spread

wide wings and empty hands over the square below, as if bestowing blessings from on high. Unlike many carved angels Jonny had seen, the expressions on the faces of the two facing him were full of childlike wonder
and joy—and there were no weapons in those hands. These angels beckoned the beholder to share in their exultation, neither warning dourly of
punishment for sins, nor offering a fatuous and simpering "there, there"
in lieu of real comfort.

Within the pinnacle of each tower hung the bells, half hidden in the
shadows, but gleaming with polished bronze whenever the sun struck
them.

With those four towers to gape at, it was hard to imagine how the
Cathedral itself could be any more impressive than the towers were. But
somehow, it was, and it left him gaping.

Though by necessity it had to be square in form with a peaked roof, it
had been ornamented in the same sinuous style as the towers. The carvings all over the facade depicted the life of the Sacrificed God, and the
lives of the saints and heroes of the Church. Somehow, even those who
had died grisly deaths seemed not to be contorted with suffering, but
rather dancing to their deaths. Arrows and nooses, torture devices and
instruments of punishment seemed idle accessories to the dance—wounds
mere decorations.

And among the carvings were the windows.

Rather than making pictures with glass, the builders of the Cathedral
had chosen to make the windows a backdrop for the carvings, so instead
of complicated scenes and designs, there were flowing abstractions—more
curves, of course—of four or five pieces of glass in harmonious colors.
Some echoed the blue and white of a sky full of clouds, the dark blue
and scarlet of a sunset, the crimson and orange of flames, the greens of
ocean waves, the golds and browns of a field in harvest colors. The result
was breathtaking, and the Cathedral sparkled in the sun like a giant box
of jewels.

Jonny found himself thinking only one thing. *How, faced every day
with this, can these Priests be preaching things that are so small-minded
and petty?* For the Cathedral as a whole was a song, an expression in
stone of the wholeness of man and the world, however that world was
put together. There was no room in this structure for pettiness and prejudice. It had clearly been designed, built, and ornamented by men who
loved all of creation, and felt at one with the world.

It took a conscious effort for him to turn his attention back to the
mundane. But the Cathedral would be here for longer than they would,
and there was business to attend to.

There were many more wagons and stalls here in the cobblestone
square, all of them in a row ringing the Cathedral, some of the stalls still
untenanted, some with traders setting up. The buildings facing the square
were not shops, as he had assumed they would be. Rather, they were
private residences; very expensive private residences. The owners of the
stalls and wagons had courteously faced their businesses away from these
homes, and towards the Cathedral. While waiting for Prime to begin, the
first Service of the day that would be open to the public, the crowds

gathering here perused the contents of the wagons and stalls with varying
degrees of eagerness. Some were plainly killing time; others were in a
holiday mood and prepared to buy.

Robin tucked their wagon into a good corner, across from a private
home, and beneath a lamppost. No sooner had they tethered the horses,
than a City Constable came hurrying over, carrying a board to which
several papers were attached.

Jonny let Robin deal with him, keeping up his pretense of being a
mute, and set up their display on the side of the wagon facing the Cathedral, following the example of the rest of the merchants. The wall-Stars
he hung on the side of the wagon itself, where they caught the sun and
made a cheerful display of color against the brown wood. For the trays
of jewelry, he propped open the lids to two of the storage compartments
and laid two trays each on them; two of the inexpensive thread-and-twig
Stars, one of the lesser metals, and one of the solid silver and mixed
silver, copper, and bronze.

The Constable went away, and Robin carefully attached the paper he
had given her to the side of the wagon. Jonny took a look at it as soon
as he was done with his preparations.

It described both of them, their goods, their wagon and horses, and
declared that they were "certified" by the authority of High Bishop Padrik.

Clearly, since it described them so minutely, it would do an "uncerti-
fied" merchant no good to steal the certification of another. He had to
admit, grudgingly, that it was a good idea.

"The tithe here is fifteen percent, not ten," Robin told him in a low
voice, as she straightened the Stars in their tray. "It's because of the
location; he was nice enough to tell me that if we moved to the rear of
the Cathedral, it was the usual ten—"

"If w-we m-move, w-we w-won't see what w-we c-came to see." That
seemed obvious enough. "As l-long as w-we c-come out even—"

But already the first of their potential customers was hurrying over,
attracted by the brilliant Stars in the sunlight, and within a short time it
was clear they were not going to come out "even," they were probably
going to run out of Stars before two days were over, if they continued to
sell at this rate.

No matter. They could make more. It would be a good excuse to linger
around the inn, walk about the town, and *not* go to the market for a day
or more.

The jewelry proved unexpectedly popular; somewhat to Robin's obvious
surprise, the metal Stars sold as well if not better than the cheaper Stars
of thread. Jonny saw why, once he realized what it was that had been
bothering him about the wealthier women and their clothing.

The very drabness of it fooled him into concentrating on the color,
but as he watched customer after customer *immediately* don her Star,
stringing it on her own chain or using the ribbon Robin provided, he saw
faces transformed with delight. And he knew that these women had given
up *jewelry,* and missed it. After all, Gradford was famous for gemcraft
and metals, and it was known across the Twenty Kingdoms that Gradford

women all had dowries of lovely jewelry, some of it very ancient, passed down from generation to generation.

The current austere state of things dictated they must give up such adornments. They *missed* their jewelry, and here was a perfectly pious way to get it back.

There had been a number of women and men in finer materials than those coming to the wagon, who had spent some time studying the God-Stars from a distance. *Silversmiths,* he decided, after a while. *Goldsmiths and jewelers. There will be work into the night, tonight, and fine silver and gold Stars by morning. Poor apprentices. . . .*

Then again, considering that the apprentices had probably been doing and learning nothing of late, one long night wasn't going to hurt them. And, inadvertently, he and Robin had breathed new life into a dying business!

With that in mind, he sidled over to her in his first free moment, whispered his suspicions into Robin's ear, and added a suggestion. She nodded, and he went back to hanging up yarn God-Stars to replace the ones sold, confident that his idea was in good hands.

A few moments later, she left the wagon to hurry to the side of a gray-haired man in gray velveteen, who had a young, clever-faced woman at his side. The girl bore a remarkable resemblance to him; most probably his daughter, and possibly his apprentice as well.

Robin spoke to them in a low voice for a few minutes, then waved, inviting them to come to the wagon. They took her up on her invitation, and as they watched, she took apart one of the copper Stars, then remade it so they could see how it was done. The transformation in them was remarkable; they went from interested to animated in a few short moments, finally ending up laughing as she placed the copper Star into the girl's hands.

Jonny saw all this in between sales of smaller and larger Stars; by the time he was finished with the last customer, the two were gone. By this time, all of the wagons and stalls were losing their custom as the crowds left *en masse* and flowed in the direction of the Cathedral. Prime was about to begin, evidently, and no one wanted a place in the rear.

"Well?" he asked, as she sidled up to him and gave him a quick squeeze around the waist.

"Master Tomas and his daughter will be very happy to supply us with base-metal and silver-alloy wire and thin bar-stock at a very reasonable price in return for my instruction just now," she said with the intense satisfaction of any Gypsy who has made a good bargain. "I made some suggestions about chains made of very tiny Stars, and suspending Stars from some of the more elaborate chains they already had made up and couldn't sell. In return, *they* suggested ornamenting the ends of the posts with beads, putting a semiprecious stone or glass bead at the center join, and stringing the Stars on necklaces of beads. Everyone is very happy, me included." She grinned happily. "I could wish we were here just for the profit; we're doing *very* well, even after the fifteen-percent tithe."

She had been the one doing all the talking to the customers and the other traders who had come to see what they were offering that was doing so well;

he had played mute, and evidently the customers had assumed that meant he was deaf as well. "Wh-what d-did you find out s-so f-far?" he asked, as the crowds gathered tightly about the front of the Cathedral, and acolytes brought out a portable altar. Evidently, in spite of the cold, High Bishop Padrik was going to hold Prime outside, presumably because there was not enough room in the Cathedral itself for everyone waiting. Jonny wondered how on earth the man expected anyone to hear him. Most Churches were built to magnify the voice; he wouldn't have that advantage out here.

Or would he?

The magnificence of the Cathedral had made him ignore the *structure,* and the two wings of Church buildings on either side of it, inside a walled compound. They weren't on the square, they were *slanted,* like a funnel, with the front of the Cathedral the bottom of the funnel. And the elaborately carved front was in the shape of a shell—

Hadn't he heard of something like this, in an outdoor theater?

It should be just as effective in amplifying a speaker's voice as the interior.

"Well, I'm not sure I believe it," she said slowly, shaking him out of his study of the Cathedral, "but I've heard it from so many different people—" Her voice faltered. "They say Padrik works miracles."

He stared at her, startled. She nodded.

"That's what they say," she told him. "Padrik works miracles. Not just simple Healing, but really impossible things, like straightening limbs that have been malformed from birth, healing people born blind or deaf. Even the most skeptical are really awed by him. *That* is why everyone in Gradford has been overcome with religious fever. Because they're sure the High Bishop is a modern saint."

She was about to say more, when the bells rang out, drowning her voice in their clangor, and the doors of the Cathedral opened. The sun struck something inside, setting up a reflective glitter that made Kestrel's eyes water. An invisible choir saluted the crowd with music that made the heart stop with its pure, measured beauty. And a single figure clad in white Priest-robes and glittering with gold strode confidently out in front of the Cathedral, and raised his hands.

They were about to discover if the stories were true. High Bishop Padrik had begun the Prime Service.

CHAPTER ELEVEN

Padrik's voice, as beautiful a speaking voice as any Kestrel had ever heard, rang out over the crowd as clearly as one of the bells. It was such an incredible voice that Jonny wished he could hear Padrik sing, and listened closely for any signs that the High Bishop had Bardic training. Padrik was the single most impressive speaker Jonny had ever heard in his life, surpassing even the Bardic Guild Masters and the Wren himself.

Then came the moment in the Holy Services when the sermon was given. If he had not been braced to be skeptical and critical, he might have found himself convinced of the truth of the High Bishop's words, for in comparison with Padrik's superb command of rhetoric and argument, the street preachers of last night were as clumsy as toddlers arguing over a toy.

Padrik's sermon was a combination of all three of the "dangerous" ideas Jonny and Gwyna had heard last night. *Magic is deception and only the miracles of the Church are the truth and therefore magic is evil. Nonhumans are without souls, and therefore the enemies of the Church and humankind. Things done purely for pleasure are evil because they take time away from the work of God and the Church.*

But Padrik made them all seem logical, sane, and part of a whole. Part of a conspiracy, in fact, of nonhumans "and their friends, the betrayers of humanity," to destroy mankind, after first weakening it with magic, and to enslave the survivors. Only the vigilance of the Church stood between the faithful and these "perfidious servants of demons," who sought to bring on the Second Cataclysm and make all humankind the helpless prey of demons. How they were actually going to do that was not specified. But then, most people had no notion how or why the original Cataclysm had occurred.

Padrik completed his sermon with a glorious depiction of the triumph of humanity and a presumably all-human world, dedicated to the glory of God and the Church.

Kestrel shook off Padrik's spell with a shudder, and the cold wind whipping across the square was no match for the chill of fear in his heart. How long had *this* been going on? Long enough, evidently, that now no one openly objected to his ideas. Kestrel had not seen any nonhumans in Gradford, and now he was certain he wouldn't see any.

If they'd had brains worth speaking of, they'd have packed up as soon as the first rumblings of this nonsense started. Probably back when the nonhumans were only "without souls" and had not yet graduated to being the "enemies of mankind." Prejudice could be as damaging as persecution, and there had been outbreaks of nonhuman prejudice before this to act as an example.

The trouble was, they *hadn't* stayed to hear what simple prejudice had become; a call for a crusade against them. If they had, there would be alarms raised all through the Twenty Kingdoms and beyond, to all of the nonhumans across Alanda.

In fact, since only rumors of this had percolated to the outside world as a growing prejudice against nonhumans, it appeared that whoever stayed here long enough was co-opted into Padrik's ranks. Or else—they were gotten rid of somehow, before they managed to bring warning to the nonhumans.

Oh, *that* was a comforting thought!

But before he got too panicked, he took a moment to think the situation through. Traders looking to buy and sell metals and gems would probably find business mostly as usual, with only a few annoyances—the prohibition against the sale of strong drink, for instance. They would arrive, do their business, and leave, probably without even listening to a street preacher, much less Padrik himself. Most other people didn't travel much in the late fall and winter, not even Gypsies and Free Bards. The Gypsies tended to hole up in Waymeets for the winter; the Free Bards found wintering-over stops, in inns and the courts of minor nobles all over the Kingdoms. Those intending to winter-over in Gradford would have gotten the message last summer that non-Guild musicians were not welcome in the city-state. Why go where you weren't welcome? So one of the best sources of information in all the world was shut out of Gradford *before* all this escalated into madness. As for other visitors—how many would stay in a city that had gone mad for religion? The only people coming here would be those coming specifically to hear Padrik, and would be pulled into his followers immediately.

And as for the citizens themselves—nothing had really happened yet to show them that this was anything other than talk. Oh, the nonhumans were gone, but they'd gone off on their own, surely—and they were taking jobs and custom that could have gone to humans instead, so where was the harm?

Nothing to alarm anyone in that.

The Prime Service wound to its dignified end. And if only Padrik's words had not left such a bad taste in Jonny's mouth, he could have enjoyed it. The music was glorious, and Padrik quite the most impressive clergyman Kestrel had ever seen. As a show alone, it was fabulous.

The trouble was, this "show" was like a tasty candy with poison at the center, a slow-acting poison, one whose effects were so subtle that the poor fool who'd eaten it had no notion of what was happening until it was too late.

Padrik vanished into the Cathedral, and a secondary Priest stepped forward onto the platform. *This* was not a usual part of Prime Services—

"Let the sick be gathered, and the poor be brought," the Priest cried out, for all the world like a Sire's Herald announcing the start of a feast. "Let all those in need come forward into God's own House, for the High Bishop's prayers and God's blessing!"

The entire crowd surged towards the door. Kestrel and Robin exchanged a single look, and in a heartbeat had packed up all their remaining God-Stars, locked up the wagon, and were joining the tail of the crowd as it squeezed in through the wide-open doors of the Cathedral.

The building was as impressive on the inside as on the outside, with the same sinuous, sensuous carvings everywhere, and sunlight shining through the brilliant colored glass of the windows, staining the pristine marble with splashes of crimson and gold, azure and emerald. They were not there to sightsee, however, or to gawk at the statues and glass. What they wanted lay at the front of the Cathedral, where the altar stood—

Their experience in Faire crowds stood them in good stead here; they were able to wiggle and squirm their way up the side along the wall, until they were near enough the altar to hear every word and to see Padrik clearly.

And it seemed that no one was too terribly concerned either about damage to the carvings or to their dignity; people in the rear climbed up onto the pedestals of the carved saints and clung there, hanging onto their alabaster robes like so many children clinging to their mothers' skirts. Robin found footholds for two in the carving of Saint Hypatia the Librarian, and Kestrel joined her there, both of them clinging to the saint's arms, while the alabaster lips smiled down at them as if Hypatia was enjoying their company on her tiny pedestal.

They tried to compose their faces into the appropriate expressions of piety, but only Saint Hypatia was paying any attention. All eyes were riveted to the altar, Padrik, and the young man who had been brought to him on a sedan-chair.

The man seeking Padrik's blessing was in his twenties or thereabouts, dressed in an expensive silk and velvet tunic and shirt of a dark blue that seemed too big for his thin body. Unlike virtually everyone else they'd seen so far in the city, he wore heavy gold chains about his neck, massive gold rings, and matching gold wrist-cuffs. There was a velvet and fur robe covering his legs.

Padrik was young for one with such a high position in the Church; Kestrel judged him to be in his middle thirties, at most. There was no gray in his golden hair, no wrinkle marred the perfection of his face. In fact, he was just as handsome as any of the alabaster carvings in here, a face that matched the glorious voice. In his pristine white robes he was the very ideal Priest, the image of a modern Saint. The white surcoat over his white robes gleamed with gold embroidery, and Kestrel was willing to bet every copper penny they'd made that day that the embroidery had been done with *real* gold bullion.

"What brings you to me for the Church's blessing, my son?" he asked the young man, who was not *that* much younger than he.

The young man's voice quavered when he spoke. "It is my leg, My Lord Bishop. All of my life my left leg has been shorter than my right, and twisted—I cannot walk on it. No one has been able to heal it, and many have tried—"

Padrik's voice grew stern. "Are you saying you have sought the services of the Deceivers, the Unbelievers, those who dare to work that blasphemy they call *magic?*"

The young man did not answer; instead, he broke into tears, sobbing his plea for forgiveness. Padrik's voice softened immediately, and he laid a comforting hand on the young man's shoulder. "God is not mocked, but neither is he unforgiving," he said, his voice taking on the same tones of his sermon. "You have come to God for His blessing and forgiveness, and He shall be generous to you."

He raised his voice. "Let all who see, believe, and let all who believe, rejoice!"

As the crowd held its collective breath, he pulled the lap robe off and laid his hands on the young man's legs. It was very clear that one *was* shorter than the other, although if it was twisted, Kestrel couldn't tell, for the young man wore loose velvet trews with open bottoms instead of breeches or hose, and expensive leather boots. Still, every Healer would be the first to sigh and admit that those born with defective limbs were doomed to live with them; there was nothing any Healer could do to Heal those born with an ailment.

Nothing any Healer could do. Except, it seemed, this one—

As silence held sway over the crowd, Padrik slowly *stretched* the young man's bad leg, straightening it and pulling on it until it was exactly even with the good one!

And as the Cathedral rang with cheers, the young man leapt up from his sedan-chair and ran to the altar, to strip off his gold jewelry and place it there in thanksgiving.

There was more of the same, much more. Padrik healed several more people; one blind, one deaf, and one palsied, plus at least three cripples and a leper. Then as the secondary Priests brought forward a group of raggedly clothed folk, Padrik produced a shower of silver and copper coins out of the air as alms for the poor. Finally he singled out one young Priest for a "blessing of the Hand of God." A beam of golden light came from Padrik's upraised hands and bathed the Priest in momentary glory. The young man fell to the ground, chanting in some foreign tongue, while another Priest translated what sounded like prophecies, and messages from "the blessed Spirits and Angels" about members of the congregation. *Those* were all suitably vague enough they could have come from the head of any common fortune-teller at the Faire, but the rest of it impressed and even frightened Jonny.

But Padrik was saving the best for the last.

A shout came from the back of the Cathedral—a cry of "demon!" and "possession!" and shortly several Cathedral guards came forward, dragging a filthy, disheveled, struggling man with them. The man's eyes rolled wildly, and he shouted a string of blasphemies and insults that had Jonny flushing red within a few moments. As they threw the man down in front of Padrik, knocking over one of the many-branched candelabra at the front of the altar, he howled like a beast and spat fire at the Priest, setting fire to his robe.

Someone in the crowd screamed; the crowd surged back a pace. The guards seized him again at that, as one of the secondary Priests beat the flames out with his bare hands. Through it all, Padrik remained where he was, his face serene, his hands spread wide in blessing.

The High Bishop looked down upon the writhing man, whose face was contorted into an inhuman mask, and began to pray, alternately exhorting God to help the sinner, and ordering the demon to release its victim.

The man spat fire again, this time touching nothing, then vomited a rain of pins all over the carpet in front of the altar. Then he howled one final time and lay still.

Padrik directed one of the Priests to sprinkle the man with holy water; presumably as a test to see if he was still demon-haunted.

Evidently he was, for the holy water sizzled when it touched him, and left behind red, blistered places. There were gasps from the crowd, and a few moans.

Finally the High Bishop himself knelt down beside the man and laid his hands upon the man's forehead.

There was a tremendous puff of smoke from the man's chest, and an agonizing screech rang through the Cathedral, a terrible sound that could never have come from a human throat, unless it was a human being disemboweled alive. The man went limp, and Padrik sprinkled him with holy water again. This time it did not burn him, and Padrik declared him free of the demon that had possessed him, gently directing the other Priests to take him to the Cathedral complex to recover.

That, it seemed was the end of the show, for as Padrik stood, he suddenly swayed with exhaustion, and one of the Priests hurried forward to support him. He leaned heavily against the man, and immediately all of the others but one gathered around both of them, taking the High Bishop off through a door behind the altar. That one Priest announced— unnecessarily—that the High Bishop was exhausted by his ordeal, and there would be no more healing until the morrow.

He did not use the word "miracle," but everyone else in the Cathedral was already shouting the word aloud, praising God and the High Bishop in the same breath. Spontaneous hymn-singing broke out, three different songs at once. Most of the crowd headed for the door, but some flung themselves full-length in front of the altar to pray at the tops of their lungs.

Jonny clung to the arm of Saint Hypatia, feeling dazed and dazzled. In the face of all of that—

Surely Padrik *was* a Saint! And if he was a Saint, how could what he had been preaching be wrong?

All of his earlier convictions went flying off like scattered birds; and if Robin had not pulled him down off his perch and dragged him out, he probably would have remained there, clinging to the alabaster Saint, and wondering if he should prostrate himself as so many others were doing, and pray for forgiveness for his doubts.

He did not really take in Robin's expression until they got outside. Then he got one of the great shocks of his life, for her eyes burned with anger, fiery and certain, and her face was a cold mask donned to hide her true feelings.

She pulled him along until they reached their wagon, then shoved him roughly at the rear door as a hint to unlock it. He did so, hands shaking, and they both climbed in. Once they were inside, and not before, she finally spoke.

"Convinced, were you?" she said, her words hot with rage, although she whispered to keep her voice from carrying outside the wooden walls. "Just like all those other fools out there. *You* saw Padrik perform real miracles, didn't you? With your own eyes! *Damn* the man! May *real* demons come and snatch his soul and carry it down to the worst of his nightmare hells!"

"B-b-b-b-but—" Jonny couldn't get any more than that out.

"Produces alms from thin air, does he? Well so can I!" And before he could say or do anything, she showered him with coins that came from out of nowhere. "I can heal the blind and the deaf, too, if they were never blind nor deaf in the first place!"

"B-but the l-leper—" he managed.

She snorted. "Flour and water paste make the open sores, paint makes the skin pale, and you can wash it all right off. It's an old beggar's trick. Remember how he passed his hands over the 'leper's' limbs? He was wiping them with a damp sponge hidden in the big sleeves of that robe."

"The c-c-c-cripples—"

Her eyes narrowed. "Think a minute. The only one you actually saw 'healed' of anything was the first one. The rest simply showed up on crutches and danced off without them. Here—"

She sat down on the bed and did something with her boots, spreading her skirts over her legs to hide them as the first cripple's trews had hid his. And as soon as she sat down, sure enough, *one of her legs was longer than the other.* The right was longer by far than the left, by a good two inches.

Kestrel felt his eyes goggling. "H-h-how—"

"You'll see in a second. Take my feet in your hands the way Padrik did." He followed her instructions, taking her feet, one in each hand. "Now, *pretend* to pull on the left one, but *push* slowly on the right one."

He did so; as soon as he began he realized what she had done. She had pulled her right boot down, and as he pushed on the right foot, he pushed her foot back into place within the boot.

The skirts hid most of what was going on; distance would take care of the rest. And because attention had been focused on the *short* leg, it would appear that the shorter leg was being straightened, not the other being shortened. "You see?" she said, jumping down onto the floor of the wagon again, and stamping to get her feet back into the boots properly. "You see what he's doing? Tricks and chicanery, and probably every one of the people his miracles cure is someone from the Abbey here! The light that struck the Priest came from a mirror he had hidden in his palm; I saw him get into position to catch a gold-colored sunbeam coming through the stained-glass windows. Remember how he held his hands over his head when he prayed? He must have the location of every sunbeam in the Cathedral charted and timed!"

"Th-the p-prophecies w-were p-pretty vague," Kestrel said, feeling his confidence and conviction returning with a rush of relief.

"And if you get a big enough crowd of people in a place, *someone* is going to match the 'widow who lost a sum of money' and the 'trades-man searching for the son that ran away.' Gypsy fortune-tellers work that way all the time, when they don't have the true gift of sighting the future." Her expression was still angry, however. Whatever had put her in a rage, it was *not* that she had temporarily been convinced of Padrik's genuineness.

"B-but the d-d-d-demon—" he ventured, wondering at the truly grim set to her mouth.

"*That* is what got me so *mad!*" she said, gritting her teeth in anger. "Someone has been teaching Padrik Gypsy magic! Everything else is the brand of chicanery that professional beggars and false preachers have been doing for hundreds of years, but he could *not* have simulated that posses-sion without the help of Gypsy magic! Spitting fire—that's done with a mouth full of a special liquid in a bladder you keep in your cheek—remember how close the man was to the candles? He even knocked one over, and that was the one that he used to light the liquid as he spit it out. Vomiting pins is something only we know how to do. The first batch of holy water had a secret dye in it that only turns red after it touches another dye, which you paint on the skin; the water droplets left behind looked like blisters because you expected blisters to be there. The 'sizzle' came from someone dropping real holy water into one of the incense burners while everyone was watching the show; I watched him and I saw the steam. And the smoke when the 'demon' left the body is another one of our tricks! The howl came from someone frightening a peafowl up in one of the towers—either that, or they've trained it to cry on command." She spread her hands wide, some of the hot rage gone from her expression, replaced by determination and a colder fury. "Some of that Padrik could learn to do on his own, but most of it was done with accomplices. That means that not only is someone teaching him, someone is *helping* him! And I am going to find out who it is!"

Kestrel nodded, remembering she had told him that the Gypsies swore never to reveal their tricks to outsiders. This was an even greater betrayal of that oath than teaching Gypsy magic to *him* would be, by an order of magnitude. He was, after all, a Gypsy by marriage, and he suspected that if he really needed to learn the tricks, Gwyna could get permission from the head of her Clan to teach him. But to teach them to a complete outsider—worse, to one who was using those tricks to promote an agenda that would ultimately be very bad for other Gypsies—that was the worst of betrayals.

"N-not only wh-who," he told her, "but *why*. P-Padrik is already hurting n-nonhumans and F-Free B-Bards; h-how long b-before he s-starts on G-Gypsies?"

"Good point." She straightened her skirts. "We've done enough business already that no one will question our packing up early—in fact, if I drop the right remarks as I pay our tithe as we leave, we might even be considered very pious for not making too much of a profit from the faithful."

"S-so wh-what are we d-doing?" he asked, opening the back of the wagon again, to let them both out modestly, through the door, rather than crawling out the window over the bed.

"We're hunting information," she told him, as he took the reins of the mares, and she counted out the tithe from the bag of coins she'd hidden under her skirt. "Who and what and why."

When they paid the reckoning for the next week in advance, the innkeeper was positively faint with gratitude. Kestrel felt very sorry for him; apparently he'd lost two more patrons who had simply not been able to conduct the business they needed. The nonhuman gem-carvers these men wished to patronize had left in the summer, and the quality of the gems that the humans who had bought their business produced was apparently inferior to the original work.

So the innkeeper was only too happy to learn that *their* business was prospering and that they were prepared to stay some time. But then Robin took him aside for a long discussion in hushed whispers, and the man looked so alarmed that Kestrel wondered what on earth she could be telling him. When she returned, she had a set of written directions in her hand and a smug expression on her face.

"I thought with a name like 'The Singing Bird' this place had to have some sort of connection to the Free Bards or the Gypsies or both," she said, as she took his arm and led him from the inn into the street. "I said as much and frightened him half to death until he realized I was both a Free Bard and a Gypsy and not some sort of informer or blackmailer. Then he was frightened because he thought I was going to demand something unreasonable from him." Her tone grew a little bleaker. "I'm afraid that there are already some musicians in gaol here on the charge of 'perverting public morals,' and I think he expected me to ask for help in getting them out."

"Are th-they F-Free B-B-Bards?" Kestrel asked nervously, keeping a discreet eye out for anyone who might be following or listening to them.

"No, they can't be," she told him. "They've been in gaol since early fall, and we would have heard something if they were Free Bards. Someone would have missed them and passed the word. No, I'm afraid they're just ordinary musicians with bad luck. Or else they simply didn't pay enough attention to what was going on with the High Bishop. Wylie says they were arrested for singing 'The Saucy Priest' right at one of the street preachers."

Kestrel shook his head sympathetically. *They* had performed the same song any number of times, and quite often when there was a clergyman who clearly deserved to hear it nearby. Bad luck, bad timing, and worse ability to observe the situation around them, that was all it was.

"Wh-what's the c-connection t-to the Free B-Bards?" he asked, out of sheer curiosity.

Gwyna chuckled. "Dear old Master Wren again. When Wylie tried to start this inn, he was in a bad case, bills piling up and no customers coming in. Wren offered to play for room and board alone all one winter if he always gave Free Bards the best venue thereafter. He filled the inn every night within the first week and kept it filled all winter. So Wylie renamed his place 'The Singing bird' in Talaysen's honor, and he's always kept the bargain."

It was a little past midday, and the street preachers were already out in force. But there were none of the 'dangerous' type, the trained clerics. That confirmed Kestrel's notion that they *were* real Priests; or at least it did in his own mind. Real Priests would have duties during the day that they could not avoid; teaching, performing holy offices, attending to the business of the Church. Only after the workday was done would they be free to come down to the street to pretend to be one of the common folk, and spread Padrik's word to those who might not come to the Cathedral to hear it.

"S-so what d-did you ask him f-for?" Kestrel asked, grateful that everyone on the street at the moment apparently had somewhere to go. The street preachers were pouring their exhortations out to the empty air. None of them had an audience, except perhaps a few idle children with nothing else to do at the moment.

"Directions. Turn here." She nodded at a sidestreet that cut away from the main street.

He followed her direction, obediently. "D-directions to wh-where?"

"Well, I asked him for directions to a place where I could buy information, and just let it go at that," she told him. "I told him I had a former friend who'd been in the Whore's Guild here and I wanted to find out where she was. *He* was the one who told me what I really wanted. Directions to the worst part of town."

"The—what?" He felt his eyes boggling again.

"The worst part of town." She patted his hand reassuringly. "Dearest, it's broad daylight, and once people there know I'm a Gypsy they'll leave us alone, unless we're really, really stupid. That's where you find things out; and that's where the Whore's Guild moved, after Padrik shut down the Houses. That's where we'll find out who's helping him, if there's anyone in this town who knows outside of the Cathedral."

He felt sweat start up along his back, in spite of the chilly wind that cut right through his coat. Why did she do things like this?

But it was too late to back out now.

Robin knew that Jonny was nervous; all the signs were there for anyone to read, from the way he clutched her hand to the utter lack of expression on his face. And she didn't really blame him; despite her cavalier attitude, she was not particularly comfortable here either.

This district, tucked away between the tanners' and the dyers' quarters, was called "the Warren." It merited the name, for it was a maze of narrow streets too small for any size of cart to travel along, with buildings that leaned over the streets until they nearly touched, blocking out the sun. They hadn't been built that way, either; the Warren had been built over ground that had once been a refuse dump, and was now in the process of collapsing, and as it sank, the buildings leaned, coming closer and closer to falling down with every passing year. Constables never ventured in here; there were not enough of them. It would take a small army to clean out the Warren, and no one wanted to bother.

Sound echoed in here, and it was impossible to tell where a particular sound came from. This early in the afternoon, though, it was very quiet in the Warren. Somewhere there were children playing a counting game, a man coughed and could not seem to stop, babies wailed, and there were two people having a screaming argument. That was nothing compared with the noise and clamor in the inn district. The streets here were always damp, and slimy with things Robin didn't care to think about. The stench was not quite appalling; the horrible odors from both the tanner's and the dyer's district overwhelmed the local effluvia. A few undernourished, wiry children played in the streets—not the source of the childish voices, for these children were playing an odd and utterly silent game involving stones and chalk. But they were the exception here; most children in the Warren were hard at work—at a variety of jobs, some legal, most not. As soon as a child was able to hold something and take directions, it was generally put to work in a district like this one.

She was looking for a particular tavern; one of the few "reputable" establishments down here, and probably the only one boasting a sign. This was where—so Wylie had told her—musicians were wise to come, and where he would have sent them if they had come to Gradford as Free Bards and not as traders.

Finally she spotted what passed for a sign; an empty barrel suspended over a tiny door. It looked nothing like a tavern on the outside, but when they opened the unlatched door and stood at the top of a short set of stone stairs, it was clear they had come to the right place.

Although the enormous room—a converted cellar—was very dark, it was also clean. A few good lanterns placed high on the wall where they would not be broken in a fight gave a reasonable amount of light. The furniture was simple, massive seats and tables built into the walls or bolted to the floor, so that *they* would not be broken up in a fight, or used as weapons. A huge fireplace in one wall with ovens built to either side— an ancient stone structure as old as the building—betrayed that this had once been a bakery.

Wylie's directions included a name—"Donnar"—and when the bold-eyed, short-skirted serving wench sauntered up to them with hips swaying, that was who Robin asked for.

Fortunately they had chosen the middle of the day for this little visit, for "Donnar," a remarkably well-spoken and entirely ordinary-looking man with nothing villainous about him, proved to be the owner of the Empty Keg.

"If ye'd come past supper, I'd'a given ye short words," he said, as he sat down at their table and wiped his hands on his apron. "An' those'd been curses, I well reckon. So, m'friend Wylie sent ye?"

Robin nodded. Kestrel looked as if he felt a little more secure, with a wall to his back, and a fellow who could have been a perfectly ordinary citizen sitting across from them. Come to think of it, she felt a lot more relaxed, herself. "We're Free Bards," she said shortly.

Donnar raised an eyebrow. "Thas more dangerous these days than bein' anythin' but a Buggie," he said, using the rude term for a nonhuman. It came from the term "Bug-eyed Monster," notwithstanding the fact that most nonhumans were neither bug-eyed nor monsters.

"W-we're here as t-t-traders," Kestrel said softly, "in G-God-S-Stars. B-but w-we n-need t-to know what's b-been happening—why-why has G-Gradford g-gone crazy?"

"Ah." Donnar nodded wisely. "Good choice of trade-goods. So, ye want the short an' sorry tale'a what's been goin' on, eh? What happ'ned with Our Padrik, the miracle-worker?"

Robin sighed with relief. "That, and other things. What's it going to cost us?"

Donnar considered this for a moment. "The tale's on th' house, if ye buy some'a m'beer at m'high prices. The rest—we'll see, eh? Depends on what ye want."

Robin and Jonny listened attentively as Donnar described what had been happening, and the measures people had taken to get around the new rules. Virtually all forms of public entertainment and pleasure had been forbidden. No plays, no public performance of music, no Faire-type gatherings. Taverns and inns were not permitted to serve anything stronger than small beer. Extravagance and ornamentation in dress were frowned upon. The brothels had been closed, and the Whore's Guild officially disbanded.

So the Guild and every other form of entertainment organization had moved to the Warren, and the houses had taken on other guises.

"Ye go off t' Shawna Tailor's, fer instance," Donnar said, "an' ye ask fer th' 'personal fittings,' and personal is what ye get! Or there's 'bout a half dozen bathhouses where ye ask fer th' 'special massage.' But it costs more, it all costs more, eh. Outside the Warren, ye gotta pay off th' Constables an' the Church Guards; ye gotta bribe th' right people."

Even the Guild musicians had moved on to other cities, with the exception of the few who had steady employment with wealthy or noble families, or in the better class of inn. The few independent musicians still in the city now played only at "private parties," or, predictably, in one of the Houses. Taverns did not *sell* hard liquor; they sold the use of a mug or glass, and for a little more than the old price of a drink, one could go to a stall located conveniently near the tavern and purchase hard liquor in tiny, single-drink bottles. The glass-blowers were the only ones prospering at the moment; these were the same kinds of bottles that had been used for perfumes and colognes. If you wanted to drink with your cronies in the tavern, you bought your evening's drinks outside, and brought them into the tavern to drink them.

"Takes deep pockets, though," Donnar sighed. "It all takes mortal deep pockets. Bribes ev'rwhere ye turn. An' I tell ye, there's a mort'a folks who just canna understand why 'tis that last year they was good tax-payin' tithe-makin' citizens, an' this year they're criminals. Hellfires, I'm one'f 'em! Had me a tavern an' didn' have the means t' build me a liquor shop. Moved in here."

He sighed, and looked so depressed that Robin reached out to pat his hand comfortingly. He looked startled, but smiled wanly.

"Well," he continued, "advantage is I started out with rules here. Don' care who ye be, nor what ye do—in *here* we got peace. Got th' whole buildin'. Rented out th' upstairs t' the head'a th' Whore's Guild; her girls work as m' wenches when they ain't on duty. An' 'f they decide t' go on duty wi' a customer, 'tis all right w' me, eh?"

"Padrik—the High Bishop," Robin said, after a moment. "With all the thieves and professional beggars in the Warren, you *have* to know those miracles of his are faked!"

"'Course we know!" Donnar said in disgust. "Trouble is, we can't figger out how he does half of 'em, so what's the good of tryin' t' expose 'im, eh? It ain't no good fer *us* t'do anythin' unless we c'n show ever'thin' is faked! Otherwise, nobody's gonna believe us."

Robin sighed, and agreed that he was right. *She* was going to have to wrestle with her conscience over this one, and she wished desperately for a way to contact the Chief of her Clan. There was no way that she could expose Padrik as a fake without revealing how his "miracles" were performed, which was in direct violation of her oath.

"Does anyone know who's helping him?" she asked, hoping someone did. If she could discover who the Gypsy was that had given away the secrets, she might be able to force him to confess publicly that he had helped Padrik perform his "miracles." That would take care of the problem without revealing any Gypsy secrets.

But Donnar disappointed her, shaking his head. "Not a clue," he replied. "Wish we did. We figger it's got to be somebody in the Priests. Mebbe they found summat in some book somewheres that tells 'em how t' do all that stuff."

That was a possibility she had not even considered! And if anything, that made her quandary worse. If there was no one to blame for revealing secrets, if the Gypsy "secrets" turned out to be something that had already been put in print somewhere, did that make her oath invalid?

She shook her head. This situation was confusing enough without making it more complicated than it already was.

"Well, the last thing we need is something you can do for us better than anyone else," she said. "We need more information than we have, particularly on the Priests, and the best way to get that—"

She paused significantly, and Donnar grinned. "Is t' go workin' inna House, a'course!" he finished the sentence for her. "I 'spect ye mean as musicians; I tell ye what, I'll get ye an audition at th' place I reckon'll suit ye best. Rest is up t' you." He thought for a moment. "Ye come by in two days, same time as t'day, 'less I send ye a message at th' Bird. I'll have it set up fer ye. A good House; I'd say here, 'cept I already gotta feller who ain't bad, an' he's old. Th' girls spoil 'im rotten."

Robin returned his grin. "So now what do we owe you?" she asked.

He named a price she considered quite reasonable; she slid the coins over to him, and he pocketed them neatly. "That includes safe-passage through th' Warren," he said, as an afterthought. "It'll be 'rranged 'fore ye reach th' door. That means most won't mess with ye. Some will, but th' rest'll leave ye be, 'cause if they mess w' ye, an' I find out 'bout it, well, I got friends in here now." He looked about his establishment, and sighed pensively. "Got so used to it, when time comes I can go back t' runnin' a real tavern again—well, I might not."

And on that odd note, they left him, and made their way back through the Warren's noisome streets completely unmolested. As promised.

CHAPTER TWELVE

There was one truism that Kestrel had always found held up, no matter what happened. Crisis might come and go, war, tempest, disaster—but people still needed to eat and sleep, and somehow, business continued as usual.

And if they were to go on with their ruse, no matter how they felt about the situation, they had to act as if they were exactly what they appeared to be; simple traders. The next day was a repetition of the first; getting up with the dawn in time to be in the square before Prime, selling

God-Stars, listening to another of Padrik's sermons, and trailing into the Cathedral to watch more of Padrik's fake miracles.

This time, with Robin's demonstrations firmly in mind, Jonny was able to catch some of the trickery. He *also* noticed that many of the same people showed up to be "healed" today as had yesterday—only today they were suffering from entirely new ailments! He had quite some time to study them as they lined up for their "miracles." There was definitely a similarity of features among them, as if they were all related.

Or are members of the same Gypsy Clan?

There were no demon-possessions today; evidently Padrik saved his more spectacular tricks to ensure that they didn't lose their impact, and didn't perform them every day. He did produce alms, and heal three cripples, two blind men, a deaf woman, five cases of gout, a woman with palsy, a man with "a withered arm," and a man with running sores on his leg. Today evidently was the big day for "miraculous messages" from angels; he "struck" three different Priests with rays of light, one red, one gold, and one white. They took turns relating messages from departed relatives to the grieving survivors. The one thing these people all had in common were tales of misfortune and woe, and they came seeking answers from those who presumably now had access to all of the wisdom of God.

Kestrel should not have been surprised at the answers, but he was. A great many of these spurious messages claimed that the misfortune that had brought the relatives here to consult with Padrik was due to inheriting "tainted money" and urged the survivors to take what they had inherited and donate it to the Church. Padrik took the occasion to preach an extemporaneous sermon on the subject of the evil magic practiced by nonhumans, and how it tainted even the lives and the goods of those who dealt with them.

"Only by giving selflessly can the taint be washed away," he told the hushed congregation. "Only the Church has the power to cleanse and heal."

And although a scant handful of those who had come to Padrik seeking an answer frowned or looked bewildered and walked away, several dozen more began to weep with hysteria and rushed forward to the waiting Priests. Presumably the Priests were quite prepared to help them with the arrangements for transferring their inheritance into the hands of the Church. . . .

This time the angelic messages were very detailed, relating the circumstances of the person's life and death. Enough detail was included to bring gasps from those grieving relatives they were directed to, people the Priests identified by name. But Jonny had been watching and listening to what was going on in the crowd waiting for Prime Service while he had sold their Stars. His feigned muteness had fooled Padrik's corps of Priests into thinking he was deaf and probably feeble-minded; they had been out among the customers, questioning those who had bought the red and blue Stars for "help in adversity." They had worn ordinary clothing rather than the robes of their order, but something about the way they had spoken had alerted Jonny to the fact that these were no common folk. He had made note of faces—and lo! Here they were, in white robes like Padrik's, though not as elaborate.

So it was no word from "angels" that gave the three Priests "touched by the Hand of God" such detailed information on postulants—it was clever work beforetime by their fellow clergymen.

It was quite enough to make him sick, to see all these innocent people defrauded. And how could a man who was *supposed* to be protecting their souls, who was *supposed* to be giving them good counsel, be preying on them this way?

He left the Cathedral as disturbed as Robin had been angry the previous day. They returned to their wagon in silence; while she went back to her sales, he took refuge from his confused feelings by taking inventory of the Stars they had left, both the wall-Stars and the miniatures.

He knew they had been doing well, but when he opened the boxes and trays they were storing the Stars in, he was shocked. It didn't take a mathematical genius to figure out that they had been doing much better than he had thought. There simply wasn't that much left to count! There was no question in his mind; if they were to continue their mission here and maintain their guise as traders, they would have to take a day or two off and make more Stars. For that, they would need more materials.

Fortunately, just as the noon bells rang, they got a break. The ringing of the bells triggered hunger in the stomachs of those still in the square. Their customers finished their purchases and hurried towards the stalls selling hot pies and drinks, sausages, bread and cheese.

"W-we n-need supplies," he told Robin in a soft voice, as soon as he was certain they were not being watched. "W-we've got enough f-for t-today, and th-that's all."

She ran her hand through her hair, looking tired and distracted. "Already? Well, at least it will give us a break. Do you realize that even after our expenses we've doubled what the Ghost gave us? We could make a fortune here!"

"Unt-t-til someone else s-starts making S-Stars and undercutting our p-p-prices," he said sharply, annoyed that she was thinking only how much money they were making and not what was happening to the poor people Padrik was defrauding.

Or the people who are the sacrificial victims to bring him to power.

But Robin only shrugged. "Then we'd better make money while we can," she said, philosophically. "You know what we need, so go get our supplies. You'll find the jeweler I made our bargain with easily enough, it's Master Tomas and his daughter Juli at the sign of the Three Hearts in Silver Street, and they know what you look like. They can tell you where to go to get the yarn and things. I *have* to stay here, you're supposed to be mute, and it's going to look odd if you start telling people prices and bargaining with them."

She turned back to her task of hanging yarn Stars on the side of the wagon, leaving him to extract some coins from one of the little hoards in the wagon, and get off on his errand.

He wasn't sure how to handle Robin's attitude toward all this. She seemed so callous and indifferent. The only thing that really upset her, so far as he could see, was the fact that Gypsies had imparted some of their secrets to an outsider—and *not* what the outsider was doing with those secrets. He simply couldn't reconcile that with the Gwyna he thought he knew.

Silver Street, the street on which all jewelers and goldsmiths had their businesses and workshops, was not that far from the Cathedral. He met with the jeweler's daughter Juli, currently in charge of the shop, who did, in fact, remember him, and also remembered her father's promise.

"Business has been wonderful," she said, smiling. Her smile had already erased some of the little lines of worry he'd noticed on her forehead yesterday. "And it's thanks to your lady. The other smiths haven't figured out how to make proper God-Stars yet; they've been casting them, and they just don't look the same. You might as well try to make lace by cutting holes in cloth. We stayed up all night working, father, me, and his two 'prentices, and this morning, the *first thing* that happened was that our best patron came to ask if we had any Star Pendants! We sold him one for every member of his family, and he commissioned a chain of them for his wife!"

It was nice to see *someone* happy, for a change. And their silver and gold Stars certainly were beautifully made and impressive. The silver Stars they made were easily four times the size of the little ones that Robin turned out—but then, no one showing up at their stall would ever be able to afford a Star that size. Master Tomas' workers made the silver Stars of three different colors of silver wire, created by alloying the pure silver with different metals. The gold Stars were also made of three colors of wire—red gold, yellow gold, and white gold. Really quite beautiful enough to stay in fashion long after Padrik was gone.

The young woman surprised him then; she and her father were so pleased with the way things had gone this morning, that she had gone out and obtained base-metal wire for Robin as well as the silver that they had promised. And she named him a price for all that was so low he saw no need to bargain. "This is at our cost," she told him, as he carefully pocketed the rolls of wire. "And I dare say that since father and I are well known here, we got you a better bargain on the base-metal than you would have on your own."

"I m-must agree," Jonny replied; she had, especially compared to the price they'd paid for the same stuff back at that inn in the hills. "Th-thank you v-very much."

She dimpled at him, and sent him on his way again with directions to the weavers' and lace makers' street, where he could expect to get his thread and yarn.

While business did seem to be picking up in Silver Street, it was still not what he would call prosperous; and once he got to the area where the seamstresses, hat makers, lace makers and weavers were, the real impact of the new vogue for asceticism was only too obvious. Shops were closed, the windows empty, the doors themselves boarded up. Those remaining showed only the most sober of materials in their windows, and even so, there did not seem to be many folk here buying anything.

Following his directions, he came to a shop—still thankfully in business—which sold not only yarn and thread, but glass beads and crystals. The woman there looked at him askance when he asked for bright colors and beads, but took him into her storeroom and told him to pick out what he wanted.

The room was lined on all four sides with drawers; in sizes from the size of his shoe, to the size of a breadbox. One section contained embroidery thread in silk, raime, linen and wool; one contained sewing thread on spools instead of in hanks like the embroidery thread, and one contained wool yarn of varying thicknesses. A tall chest of smaller drawers contained beads, and the rest of the room was filled with racks of fabric.

Fortunately he was limited by what he could carry, because the temptations in that back room were tremendous—especially a scarlet linen he could easily picture Robin wearing. . . .

Obviously the woman who owned the shop could not imagine what he was going to do with all those proscribed colors of embroidery thread, the sparkling beads, or the bright yarns, but she was too polite—or too politic—to ask.

He paid her, and saw her eyes brighten a little as she put the coins in her cashbox. If only there was a way to help the whole city—

But there wasn't; not short of revealing Padrik for the fraud he was. And they were certainly working on that.

He headed back to the wagon, wondering how Robin was faring.

The moment that Kestrel left, the vultures descended, circling in on her when they realized she was alone.

At least, that was how Robin thought of them. Street preachers began to congregate in the vicinity of *her* wagon (and no one else's) when it appeared that she was alone. It was then that she noticed that of all the stall-keepers and wagon-vendors within *her* field of view, she was the only single female.

And evidently single women were fair game, although they wouldn't trifle with a woman with a male in evidence.

Some of the preachers confined themselves to looking down their noses at her, or giving her very superior looks, particularly when she made a sale. But the others were not so polite as that. They took it in turn to set up impromptu pulpits and preach, not only at the crowds coming to patronize her stall, but at her specifically.

Now she heard a fourth theme to the sermonizing, a new one so far as she was concerned and one that was so clearly calculated to make her angry that she held her temper just to spite them.

Women, according to these so-wise philosophers, were by their very nature "primitive, lascivious, and lewd." This was as God had intended, they said. Their function as childbearers made them prone to look no further than the acts that resulted in children; after all, that was what God had created for them to do. Women's bodies were created for one glorious purpose: childbearing. Women were inferior to men in all other counts; in morals, in intelligence, in the ability to reason—just as their smaller, weaker bodies made them inferior physically.

Women were nearer to the state of the animal than the angel, said the preachers. And again, that was as it should be, God had created them to be dependent on their partners for the things they lacked. It was up to *men*, with their superior intellect and power of reason, to rule women, to keep their essentially corrupt natures from overcoming them.

Men should make all decisions for a woman, the preachers proclaimed, pitching their voices to be certain that she heard every word. Men should control their every action. Women were not fit to govern themselves, and would be seduced by any creature with a soft word and a clever tongue.

They think I'm alone, she decided, as she continued to smile, thank those who purchased, wish them well with their prayers, and outwardly ignore the preachers. *They didn't do this when Kestrel was here. That's why there aren't any other women out here alone. I know what happens when one shows up. They ring her and start preaching at her before she can even turn around.*

Her blatant and blithe disregard of their words only made them redouble their efforts. And although she continued to ignore them outwardly, she was becoming very nervous.

How long, I wonder, will it be before those words become law here? How long before women in Gradford are forbidden to practice trades, hold property, or do anything at all without the consent and guidance of a man? What had happened to the nonhumans could only too readily happen to women, and to increasingly broader types of men.

It was happening to musicians; it had happened to mages. Once one group was eliminated, Padrik would need another group to focus on as the cause of all troubles. Why not women? There were few enough of them in power, most of whom could be eliminated easily enough.

Why not, indeed. There was no doubt in her mind whatsoever that although Padrik had said *nothing* like this in his sermons, these words were his, in the mouths of the street preachers. *One step at a time, that's how you get people. First you bombard them with the word from a lower source, until they come to think that it might possibly have a little merit. Then you put it in the mouth of a lower authority, so people become persuaded. Then, last of all, you put it in the mouth of the ultimate authority, and their resistance crumbles.*

In fact, some of her customers were beginning to look at her askance, as the meaning of the background hum of exhortation penetrated. She simply put on her most guileless and innocent smile, and hoped she could convince them that she had no idea that the street preachers meant their sermons for *her.*

When Kestrel finally showed up, she greeted him with such enthusiasm that the customers were startled, flying to embrace him, and take some of his burdens from him.

And as she greeted him with the words, "Husband! You're back! I don't know how I managed without you!" the preacher who had been spewing forth a particularly vehement and vituperative version of the corruption and folly of women who attempted to manage themselves alone, choked off his sermon in mid-word, coughed violently, and vanished into the crowd.

Well, she thought with satisfaction, as Kestrel returned her enthusiastic kiss with one rather startled, but just as enthusiastic. *They won't make that mistake again. I just made them look like fools.*

And they would probably hold that against her, too.

She dealt with the remaining customers, then, before any new ones could arrive, she put the rest of the Stars away and closed up the wagon, waving off any potential customers with a smile and a cry of "come back tomorrow!" Jonny was already inside, unloading his packages, and she joined him there with a sigh of relief, closing the door behind her and lighting one lantern to relieve the gloom of the interior. The inside of the wagon was warm compared with the wind-swept square.

Her feet throbbed with pain, and she had been more nervous beneath the steady barrage of the street preachers than she had realized. Her shoulders ached with tension, the corners of her mouth hurt from smiling so much, and she had a headache. Right now all she wanted was a hot bath, a good meal, and bed, the last with Jonny in it.

Jonny greeted her with a smile and a hug, and went back to his work. She took the materials for the miniature Stars from him, and put them neatly away in the trays they'd used to hold the finished products. He'd managed to get turned dowel-rods for the larger Stars, and toothpicks and thin brass rods for the miniatures. After they stowed the contents of his various packages away in the wagon, they took another accounting of their stock.

"We don't have enough for tomorrow," she said, reluctantly. "Good gods, and I thought we'd made enough Stars for a week!"

"B-by t-tomorrow there'll b-be others out here with S-Stars," Jonny pointed out. "P-probably not the j-jewelry ones, though."

"Which is why you concentrated on jewelry supplies; that was a good idea," she told him, standing on tiptoe to kiss his nose. "Well, I guess we're going to have to make some more stock, which means we take tomorrow off."

"Except f-for g-going to s-see about that j-j-job," he reminded her, a slight frown on his face. "I'm n-not sure I l-like th-the idea of w-working in a H-House."

Just what I needed. Being brought up in the Guild Hall must have made him a prude. She was exasperated, but she knew that her temper was probably more than a bit short. She decided not to say anything rather than retorting with a sarcastic comment. Which was rather a new thing for her—

But after her brief stint as a bird, *caused* by flinging insults at a lascivious Priest, she had kept a closer curb on her tongue than she had even done before. It only took one painful experience for *her* to learn her lessons!

Instead, she told him all about the street preachers who had surrounded her as soon as he'd left, and what they'd had to say.

"S-sounds to m-me as if th-the next t-targets are w-women," he said when she had finished, quickly coming to the same conclusion she had.

She nodded. "That was what I thought. And—I'm torn. The money we are making here is amazing. On the other hand, we've already learned *almost* everything we need—and certainly enough to warn Harperus of what's happened. If we return to him, we can warn the Free Bards and he can warn the other nonhumans. You heard what he said; I really think that given enough warning to get out, the Deliambrens can protect all the other nonhumans who care to accept that protection *and* themselves. I'm not sure we need to stay here. . . ." She shivered, as the shrill rants of one of the street preachers penetrated the wooden walls of the wagon, and a chill went up her back in reaction. "I don't like it here, love," she said in a small voice. "It was a Priest that caused me all that trouble before. Padrik has all of the Church and the Bishopric here behind him. There's just the two of us. Shouldn't we leave?"

Kestrel looked down at her, his eyes brooding in the half-light of the wagon. "Y-you w-were th-the one who w-wanted t-to find out wh-what Gypsies were helping him," he reminded her. "W-we still don't kn-know *wh-why* Padrik is d-doing all this—and I d-don't th-think he's even b-begun t-to fulfill his p-plans. And wh-what about th-those Gypsies? Sh-shouldn't *th-they* b-be dealt w-with?"

We have responsibilities, whether you like them or not, his eyes said to her. *We have to live up to those responsibilities.*

As soon as he mentioned the presumed renegades, the heat of anger began to chase away the chill of fear. And while she didn't have much use for people who were not Free Bards or Gypsies—well, this affected both those groups, intimately. She flushed, and nodded. "They should," she said, firmly. "In fact, they *have* to be. First, I can't just report a supposition to the Gypsy Clan Leaders; I have to have proof that I'm not just speculating. And I do have to find out exactly who they are before I can bring punishment down on them. Or rather, before the Clan Leaders do. That's for them to order, not me."

"Punishment?" Kestrel eyed her inquisitively. "Wh-what kind?"

"I can't tell you that," she said, with real regret. "But—it'll be appropriate. Peregrine will probably be the one to handle it. He's done it before."

She saw by the widening of his eyes that she had said enough. Kestrel was only too aware that Peregrine was a mage, possibly the most powerful magician they knew; he was an Elf-Friend, and he might be the ally of many more magical creatures. So any "punishment" would be magical in nature.

"At any rate, we can't do anything about it all now," she continued, and sighed. "I guess we should be trying to stay focused on the things we *can* do, and not worry about the things we have no control over. I'm going to take things as lightly as I can. Otherwise I'd fret myself to pieces in this town."

She sensed his sudden relaxation, as if she had answered some question in his mind that he hadn't even articulated. Well, whatever it was, there were enough mysteries to solve without trying to figure out what was going on in *his* mind!

"I want a hot bath, a good meal, and a little time alone with you before we start in on making more Stars," she said firmly, as she opened the rear door of the wagon and blew out the lantern. "Which I guess," she added, acidly, "makes me just as 'primitive, lascivious, and lewd' as these preachers claim!"

"I can o-only h-hope," he laughed, and followed her down the stairs, closing and locking the door after her. And wisely, very wisely, he said nothing else.

Practice made perfect, and that was as true with handicrafts as it was with music. They were much faster making this new batch of Stars than they had been with the first batch. Gluing bright glass beads to the ends of the crossbars of the miniature Stars was a good idea; it made them look more like jewelry. Stringing them on chains of matching beads was another wonderful notion.

And the best part—so far as Robin was concerned—was that no one else would have anything like them in the market. Once again, they would have a monopoly of sorts. While they were not here to make money, no Gypsy worth the name would ever have turned down such a golden opportunity.

And if any of the street preachers questioned the presence of the beads, she could blithely point out that there were no *colors* in the miniature Stars to indicate what the owner's intention-prayer was. The beads served that function, of course.

If they can use their twisted logic to prove that nonhumans are demon-inspired, I can use the same rules to my advantage, she thought, making the final wrapping on a miniature Star of copper with red and gold beads. *Let the rooster crow all he wants; it's the hen that lays the eggs, not him.*

They had gotten up early perforce, awakened by the morning bells, but they'd put the time between breakfast and lunch to good use. And when they came down to lunch, the innkeeper himself sauntered over to their table with a note in his hand.

He looked only mildly curious. "This's from m' old friend Donnar," he said. "It come this mornin'. He doin' well?"

"As well as can be expected," Robin replied, opening the sealed note. She noticed with amusement that Donnar had sealed it with a blob of candle wax and the impression of a coin. A rather unusual coin. It was, in fact, one of the silver coins she'd given him in exchange for his information and help, an ancient piece bearing a strange bird with two tails.

"Sometimes I wish I'd'a followed his advice," Wylie said wistfully, without elaborating on what the advice had been; then he shrugged, and took himself off.

The note said simply, "Go to Threadneedle Street, to the shop of Ardana Bodkin. Say, 'I've come to order an alabaster alb and an ivory altar cloth.' Don't bring instruments. It's been taken care of." There was no signature, which was wise on Donnar's part.

Robin memorized the code-phrase, and burned the note in the candle at their table. "Are you tired of making Stars?" she asked. "Could you use a break?"

Kestrel nodded.

"Good. So could I." She stood up, and brushed her skirts off. "Let's go for a walk."

He took her arm and paid their reckoning, and they walked out into the street. "Are w-we g-going where I th-think w-we're g-going?" he asked cautiously.

"Well, probably; since you got to see Threadneedle Street yesterday and I didn't, I thought it would make a nice walk," she replied. "There might be something down there I could use that you didn't notice."

"Ah." Jonny made no other comment, but his hand tightened on her arm. But he looked a little relieved; evidently he felt a bit better about visiting a House if it *wasn't* in the Warren.

Well, so did she! Donnar's protection notwithstanding, she did not want to visit that place after dark. There really was no such thing as "honor among thieves," and she did not trust anyone in that place once darkness fell.

Ardana Bodkin was the only seamstress prospering at all—the shop front was swept and newly painted, the windows filled with color, silk and satin, and two young women stitching away at crimson velvet inside. But that was only natural—since from the window display, Ardana Bodkin specialized in ecclesiastical robes.

The place was a feast for the eye after the browns and grays of the drab clothing outside. The crimson satin robes of a Justiciar sparkled with rich gold bullion embroidery; the vivid blue silk robes of an Intercessor boasted cutwork of impossible intricacy. Next to that, the emerald green robes for the Service of Vernal Equinox shone with lacework dyed to match. And there were, of course, dozens of the white robes favored by High Bishop Padrik and his Order, all brilliant with embroidery, lace, cutwork, and gems.

"May we help you?" asked one of the young ladies, a plain-faced blonde, as Robin gazed with hungry eyes on all the vivid, soul-satisfying color. She had not realized how much she missed her Gypsy finery.

"I've come to order an alabaster alb and an ivory altar cloth," she said carefully—and a little regretfully. A pity to have to leave all this color. . . .

But the young woman smiled, and said, "Please follow me," then led them both through the back room where a single woman stitched gold bullion to white satin, to a small door hidden behind a swath of velvet. She knocked twice, paused, and three times; the door swung open, and she motioned for Robin and Kestrel to go inside.

The moment they did, Robin swallowed; somehow, Donnar had made a horrible mistake! They were in the receiving room of a convent!

The room held about five or six lovely young women dressed in the robes of the Sisters and Novices of a religious Order; she didn't recognize the pearl gray and white of their habits, but they were clearly religious robes. The room itself was as stark as any in a convent; a few benches, plain white walls, a single bookcase full of books. The young ladies all turned to stare at the intruders.

"I—" she gasped. "Excuse us, we—"

The woman who closed the door behind them laughed. She too wore the robes of the Order, whatever it was, but her chestnut hair was left to stream unbound down her back, like a maiden's, confined only by a headband.

"You think you made a mistake, yes?" she said, in a rich contralto. "But you are Robin, and you, Kestrel; you play the harp, both, and you come from Donnar, yes?"

At Robin's dumb nod, she laughed again. "You have made no mistake. This is the House of the Penitents, and I am Madam—ah, rather, I am *Sister-Mother* Ardana."

Robin blinked—and then she took a second, closer look at the "habits" of the putative Sisters. They were cut to fit like second skins down the line of the torso. The robes left nothing and everything to the imagination, and were certainly teasingly erotic.

"But—why all this?" she asked, as Ardana led them across the room to the door on the other side.

"Well, it is very convenient, for one thing," she replied, tossing her rich brown hair over her shoulder as she opened the second door. "If the authorities were ever to come to this part of the shop, they would find that all of the ladies here are seamstresses—or, at least, they can sew enough to convince a fool Constable of the fact! We have everything in place to make it at least *look* like a convent, so long as we have time to clean the private rooms. There are many convents in Gradford these days, many women establishing their own charitable Orders which support themselves by a trade or a craft, since the miracles began. I have heard that one or two are even genuine."

The door she led them to opened onto a corridor, as austere as the receiving room, with doors on both sides. "Why so many new Orders?" Robin asked, puzzled. "I thought you had to get the permission of the Church to establish an Order."

Ardana laughed again, a good-natured chuckle. "Oh, my dear, no. The Church is indifferent—so long as the Orders find some means of supporting themselves. If they do not attempt to appoint or ordain Priests, collect alms, or usurp any of the privileges of the Church, the Church permits them to do what they will. So many single women in various trades have discovered it is a good thing to form an Order. They need not find convenient men to 'help' them with their businesses, if they do not choose to do so."

Robin exchanged a knowing look with Kestrel. So, it seemed that single women were already under a great deal of pressure here, as she had suspected might happen. And at least some of them had realized that it might not be too long before they lost the right to practice trades or crafts, or to run a business without a man—

—*or without the blessing of the Church. Very clever.*

"My last set of musicians was arrested for street-busking and sent out of the city," Ardana said, as she opened another door, this time to a nicely appointed office, furnished well, and comfortably, and decorated in a modest rose-pink. There were two small harps standing in the corner, beside two chairs. "Donnar said you were looking for a way to pick up information about Padrik; well, many of my clients are either in his employ or in his Order. If any of them are likely to let information slip, it will be here."

She gestured to the two harps. "Consider this your audition," she told them. "If I like what I hear, I will hire you for a few hours in the evening to play in the 'chapel'; you may keep your ears as wide open as you like, and I will tell my ladies to let you know if they hear anything."

She sat down behind her desk, as serene as the statue of Saint Hypatia in the Cathedral, and with that same hint of an amused smile on her lips. Robin passed one harp to Kestrel; she plucked a set of strings experimentally, but someone had done a good job of keeping them in tune. She looked over at him, and somehow, in spite of the tension, they both grinned.

" 'Th-the S-saucy P-Priest?' " he suggested.

Ardana laughed.

Kestrel had been very uncomfortable from the beginning about this; when they passed their audition, and Ardana hired them on the spot, he didn't lose any of that discomfort. In fact, it got worse.

It was worse still when Ardana led them to what she referred to as "the chapel," a room furnished with soft couches and cushions in jewel-bright satins and velvets, and tiny marble tables, where the "Sisters" lounged about in semi-transparent or very abbreviated versions of their "habits." This was where customers came when they wished some entertainment before or after the—main event.

Kestrel had never been in a House before, and he frankly did not know where to look. Or not look. And the ladies obviously noticed; they whispered to each other behind their hands, and cast measuring glances at him that made him flush uncomfortably.

He tried to confine his attentions to the harp that Ardana had loaned him—

Clever of her to know that carrying an instrument openly through the street would get us in trouble, he thought, staring at the ornamental bird-head carved into the support-post of the instrument, as he and Robin put the two harps into perfect tune with each other. *Forethought to the rescue again.*

By mutual consent they had decided to play only instrumentals; voice might give their identities away. And they would try to avoid speaking if they could. Ardana had given them robes that matched the ones the ladies in the receiving room wore, though not so tight across the body; those robes were very effective disguises. Kestrel was so small and clean-shaven he might even pass as a very plain, flat-chested girl.

Which is only fair, since Rune disguised herself as a boy to play. . . .

When the harps were in tune, Kestrel started a tranquil, calming piece; "Fortune, My Foe." Robin joined in on the second verse, playing a lovely descant. He relaxed against the back of his chair and let himself forget his surroundings in the music.

So effective was his effort that he woke from his self-induced trance with a start, as one of the "Sisters" touched his elbow and offered him a silver-plated goblet of fruit juice. He accepted it, but could not help the blush that burned across his face at the sight of her.

She chuckled, and he burned an even deeper and more painful red. But then she put one hand on his arm, and he raised his eyes to her face, to see that her expression was one of sympathy and not mockery.

"We assumed that this is the first time you've ever been in a House, Kestrel," she said, using his Free Bard name. "It's perfectly fine to feel out-of-place, embarrassed, in fact. I did, the first time I came here. We would *much* rather see a charming blush than a knowing smirk. *You* assume the best of us, and you blush for our sakes as much as your own. The man with the smirk assumes the worst of us, and can't wait to prove it."

Robin grinned at her, and she grinned back, a surprisingly gaminlike grin, full of mischief. "Both of you, consider yourselves as one of us; we're glad to have you," she finished. "I'm Sister Tera; if I can help you in any way, please let me know."

And with that, she delivered the second water-beaded goblet of fruit juice to Robin and took herself out of the room entirely.

The rest of the ladies were clearly "with" someone; offering them bits to eat, filling goblets, entertaining them with conversation. Somehow they had all come in without Kestrel even noticing.

"Don't worry," Robin whispered to him. "You were off in your usual trance, but I've been listening. You wouldn't believe how many of these men are associated with the High Bishop or the Cathedral!"

He gave the clients a second look; they were a well-fed lot, and wore self-satisfaction as if it were a garment. While that particular expression was not exclusive to the clergy, it seemed the exclusive property of the clergy in Gradford.

"I g-guess we've d-done the right th-thing," he whispered back, finishing off his juice and setting the goblet down beside his chair.

"I am very *relieved* to hear you say that," Robin replied with a sigh. "I was afraid you'd think I'd gotten us involved with something really repugnant."

He shrugged. "I'm always w-willing t-to l-learn," he told her philosophically. "Now. L-let's p-play."

"Promise *not* to go off into one of your trances again," she countered. "We're both supposed to be keeping our ears open, remember?"

He plucked the first few notes of "My Lady Spy" by way of an answer, and grinned. She returned it, picked up the tune within the first bar, and they were off again.

CHAPTER THIRTEEN

Their next several days settled into an odd routine; a routine Robin even felt marginally comfortable with. So long as she didn't listen too closely to the High Bishop's sermons, that is, and avoided street preachers entirely. They played in the "chapel" by night, and sold their trinkets in the market square by day. Early in the week, Robin took note of the fact that Kestrel had a shrewd business sense. She would not have expected that from someone who had grown up in the Bardic Guild Hall and had been born a Prince. His estimation that they would soon find others duplicating their God-Stars for a lower cost was right. They sold off all their wall-Stars at the same price that the new folks had set and did not bother to make any more. Instead, they concentrated on the miniatures; few people had a delicate touch with the fragile wire, and of those few, no one made them with beads or crystals hanging from the webs or mounted as end-caps on the crossbars.

They began to see the more expensive versions of the Stars on the breasts of wealthy folk in the Cathedral. They even began to see those same expensive Stars coming into Ardana's "chapel" at night. Many of them stayed with Ardana's ladies, gifts from grateful clients.

They were able to gather quite a bit of information about Padrik and his "special healing services" simply by listening. The most important bit of information came by accident—when one of the people Robin suspected was a Priest let it slip that Padrik had some "special helpers" who were the only ones permitted to assist him in planning the "healing services."

After that, they attended every one of the "healing services" until they began to be able to recognize certain faces, despite disguises. They were even able to put a name or two to those faces, by waiting at the entrance and listening carefully while these "postulants" talked among themselves.

That was when Robin realized that the man who specialized in "being possessed by demons" was a regular client at Ardana's!

She was certain enough that she was willing to put it to a test, the fourth night that they played Ardana's chapel, but she waited until that morning so that she could confirm it with Kestrel.

Robin figured that they were due for another "demon possession" at the healing service—probably today—and she was not disappointed. As they brought the man up to the front, spitting and sweating and breathing fire, she nudged Kestrel in the ribs. "Wasn't he the one with Sister Krystal last night?" she whispered.

Kestrel narrowed his eyes with concentration, and finally nodded. "I think so," he whispered back, "but wait until I get a better look at his face."

It wasn't until "the demon had been cast out" that they both got a really clear look at the man, but the smirk he wore as he was "helped" out of the Cathedral only made the identification surer. He had worn that same smirk last night.

The chapel was empty of clients; a good time to consult the statuesque Sister Krystal. "The client last night?" Sister Krystal wrinkled her aristo-cratic nose with distaste. "His name is Robere Patsono. Is he one of Padrik's 'special helpers' you were looking for?" At Robin's nod, she gri-maced. "I wouldn't be the least surprised to find out he was involved with Padrik's 'miracles.' He's always hinting about how important he is to the High Bishop, but he gets very coy about it when one of us tries to find out exactly what it is he does."

"If his name is Patsono, then he *is* one of the ones setting up the miracles," Robin replied grimly.

Someone lit a sweet-scented candle, and the smell of roses filled the chapel. Krystal tossed her long, ash-blond hair over one shoulder, and pursed her lips with speculation. "Do you think you might be able to—well—put a spike in Padrik's wheels?" she asked, hopefully. "Things were better when the Houses and the Guild were legal."

"Things?" Kestrel asked. He looked puzzled, although Robin had a notion what Krystal was talking about.

Krystal's reply confirmed her guesses. She sighed, and closed her gray eyes for a moment. "Now—well, things can happen to a lady, and the only recourse we have is for Ardana to ban them from the House. She can't always do that, even, because if the client is important enough, he could threaten to turn us over to the Cathedral Constables."

"The Guards of Public Morality?" Robin said, with heavy irony. "Very nice. As if they weren't violating the laws themselves. I've seen plenty of *them* in here too."

Krystal shook her head, and toyed with the silken folds of her robe. "Of course you have. But that wouldn't stop them from arresting us if they were ordered to. They don't care; why should they? We aren't important to them. *They* can always find another House."

"Wh-whereas you w-would w-wind up in g-gaol," Kestrel said for her.

"Or the work-house, where they make 'honest women' out of people like me." Krystal tossed her hair, but this time angrily.

That was new. "What's a work-house?" Robin asked.

Sister Jasmine chimed in. "It's a place where they're putting women convicted of something called 'immoral idleness.' Basically, it's if they don't have a husband or father supporting them, or work at a trade or a job. They do plain sewing and laundry for the Cathedral and the Abbey here."

"And get paid what?" Robin wanted to know.

"Nothing!" Jasmine said bitterly. "Their so-called 'wages' are confiscated to pay their fines and room and board."

"I've heard other stories, too, about that so-called 'work-house.'" Krystal's eyes flashed with anger. "It seems the Priests visit there. Very often. I've heard they have all of the advantages of a House, one reserved for the privileged few, but they don't have to pay for any of them. And not only that, but the laundry and sewing get done for nothing too!"

"Th-that's s-slavery!" Kestrel said, after a moment of appalled silence.

Krystal shrugged, and her hair slipped coquettishly over one eye. "That's the privilege of power," she replied. "And it's why so few of us have actually been *caught* in a raid. We don't want to end up in the work-house, so we all have ways to escape. If we have to—" she faltered, then continued. "—well, one way to make certain Padrik wouldn't want you is to make certain you aren't pretty anymore."

She might have said more, but Ardana appeared with a client in tow, a rather ordinary and dumpy little man, dressed like a middle-class merchant, with merry eyes. There was nothing about him to fire the imagination, and Robin could not for a moment imagine why Krystal's face lit up with a truly welcoming smile when she saw him. But the lady rose immediately and hurried over, leaving Robin and Kestrel to pick up their instruments and resume playing.

But Robin had everything she needed; anything else Krystal could have told her was of secondary importance, and minimal value. Most of it Robin had already deduced.

It made perfect sense to find the Patsono Clan mired up to their necks in this sordid business. They specialized in being involved in sordid undertakings.

It had never been anything on this scale, though; mostly petty trickery and fraud.

Even among the Gypsies a Patsono was watched carefully, and valuables kept out of easy filching reach. All Gypsies tended to cheat ordinary house-bound folk—who they called *gajo,* or in the Outsider tongues, "rootfeet" from their habit of never leaving a place for as long as they lived. It was not considered cheating so much as a combination of good bargaining and education . . . if the rootfeet learned to be careful, to watch their purse strings or to examine what they bargained for, then they got a cheap lesson in the ways of real life. Sometimes that cheating extended to a bit of outright theft, if the mark appeared to deserve such attentions. Robin had picked a pocket or two in her time. She considered it justice, not thievery; those whose purses she lightened were either far too wealthy for their own good, or they had been particularly noxious, like the bullies in Westhaven.

But Gypsies, as a rule, never made fellow Gypsies or Free Bards the targets of such thievery and trickery. The Patsono Clan had fleeced or robbed both quite as often as they'd victimized rootfeet.

The only question in Robin's mind was—why? Why were they doing this? What were they getting out of it? Why had they suddenly decided to throw in with a rootfoot—and not just any rootfoot, but a High Bishop? The Gypsies had no shared interests with Churchmen, not even a common religion.

She had personal experience with a Patsono or two; if there was one trait besides dishonesty they all had in common, it was a distinct aversion to cooperate with *anyone.*

There was only one way to find out that "why," and that was to do so in person.

Kestrel isn't going to like this, Robin, she told herself, as she devoted half her attention to her playing, while the other half was wrapped up in thinking up a way to get her into the black heart of the Patsono Clan. *So while you're at finding a way into Patsono, maybe you'd better find a way to talk him into accepting this. . . .*

Kestrel didn't like it. Not at all.

"You're *what?*" Anger had completely obliterated Jonny's stutter. He had listened to her careful explanation in relative calm, but the moment she had told him that she was going into the Clan enclave, he had exploded.

"I'm going to pretend I'm a distant cousin of one of the Patsono's," she explained again, patiently. "That's not at all hard; unless you go through a formal handfasting, there are plenty of Gypsies who don't bother with formalizing relationships, not even when there are children. There usually aren't when there's no handfasting, unless the woman is wealthy in her own right and wants a child. Gypsy women are all taught how to prevent conception."

"So how would you be some kind of relation then?" he shot back, eyes wide with emotion, although she could not tell whether it was anger or something more complicated.

"Because sometimes a woman can choose to have a child, and not care who the father is so long as he isn't a rootfoot," she said, trying not to show her exasperation at having to state the obvious. "And sometimes women are just stupid or careless. It doesn't matter! All I have to do is claim my father is one of the Patsonos, name some city I know the Patsonos were in, and give a vague description of the man. Patsonos have no imagination to speak of; of the entire Clan, at least a quarter of the men are named Robere, another quarter are called Tammio, and the rest are a mix of Berto, Albere, and Tombere. If I say my father's name was Robere and I *don't* try to claim any special privileges or demand one of the Roberes recognize me as his offspring, there shouldn't be any problems or questions. Among the Clans it's basically up to you and maybe the Clan Chiefs to keep track of who you're related to."

If she'd thought that would mollify him, she was proven wrong. "*Shouldn't,*" he scoffed, lip curling in mockery. "Shouldn't cause any problems or questions. Oh, grand. What if it does?"

"It won't as long as you aren't with me," she retorted, her own temper fraying. "Which you won't be. You couldn't pass for a Gypsy no matter how hard you tried, and by now I'm sure there are plenty of Clans who've heard of Robin and her *gajin vanderei.* But when I go in alone, there won't be any reason to connect me with—"

"*What?*" he yelped again. "You're doing no such—"

Her frayed temper snapped. "How *dare* you? You are *not* my master, you do *not* tell me what I will or will not do!" she hissed. "*I* rule my own actions!"

And with that, she whirled, yanked the door to their room open, and stalked away, down the hall, down the stairs, and out into the courtyard, walking as quickly as she could and still preserve her dignity. Once she reached the courtyard, she sprinted across it, and dove into the street beyond.

Evidently her angry defiance caught Kestrel off-guard; if he tried to follow her, he was too late about it, for she quickly lost herself in the early-evening crowds. She wrapped her warm woolen shawl around her shoulders and her head, and slipped through the slower-moving strollers with the agility of an otter in a stream. She knew exactly where she was going now, thanks to those evenings at Ardana's. According to the clients, Padrik's "special helpers" had a little enclave of their own on Church property. There was a walled courtyard on the opposite side of the Cathedral from the market-square, a courtyard that had a guest-house meant for groups of visitors. That was where the "special helpers" and their wagons were, so that was where Robin would go.

Moving at a brisk walk, she kept herself warm, and covered the distance between the inn and the Cathedral in very short order. She actually made better time than she had expected to, emerging into the deserted market-square before she realized that the crowds had thinned to nothing.

She looked up, and could not suppress a gasp; she stopped dead in her tracks to stare.

She had never seen the Cathedral at night; its impact was as great as the first view by daylight had been. The carvings were darker shadows, silhouettes against the colored glass of the windows, and every window shone with its own light. The colors gave the illusion of floating in the darkness of the Cathedral, and now she saw what she had missed before—that the windows themselves, framed as they were by the carvings, formed the simple shapes of stylized flowers and leaves. The Cathedral was a huge bouquet of flowers, made of light. . . .

A cold breeze whipped around her ankles, then blew up her skirt, and woke her to her self-appointed mission. She shook herself out of her trance and hurried across the cobble-stoned square. The windows of the houses surrounding the square were also alight, but this was familiar, homey light, and she concentrated on them rather than on the seductive and hypnotic beauty of the Cathedral. As they had peddled their God-Stars she had amused herself by imagining what lay beyond those windows; now, at least in part, she was able to see how the wealthy of Gradford spent that wealth.

It was often lovely, certainly expensive, but after spending time in the Royal Palace in Birnam, no longer impressive. In fact, the taste in this town tended towards the overblown, over-ornamented. Many of those who had decorated the interiors of these houses seemed determined, not to echo, but to outdo the Cathedral. Where one of the carvings of the sea-tower boasted a single strand of kelp, the gilded ceiling-moldings featured a dozen intertwined strands in a fraction of the space, and fish peeking through the kelp to boot. Where there was a pair of ribbon-tails in mating-flight on the air-tower, the frame of an enormous mirror had three dozen, all getting in one another's way, and looking less like a mating-flight than an absurd crashing bird-orgy. It would surely have embarrassed T'fyrr. Wallpaper or painted murals featured the same carvings as the towers, but painted in lifelike color—which did not improve the composition any, and made the paintings look overcrowded.

She sighed and shook her head. Sad, that so much money should be squandered on such bad taste. Perhaps this new trend towards austerity would creep over into the furnishings and decorations in these homes . . . if it did, for once Padrik's influence would be of excellent benefit.

The wall around the buildings to either side and to the rear of the Cathedral was an impressive one, and quite blank—which was, in itself, interesting. No carvings, which implied that the wall was new—and no entrances. So, the only way into the compound—unless there were gates in the wall on the other side—was through the single gate she had been told about, and through the Cathedral itself.

Well, if I wanted to keep an eye on the comings and goings of my underlings, that's how I would do it, she thought to herself. *In the robes that most of these fellows wear, climbing the wall would be a difficult proposition.*

Getting in was going to be a difficult proposition as well, unless the Patsonos left the gate open . . . and unless they were so incredibly stupid that they didn't bother to put a guard on it.

Then again, it's the Patsonos. They may be crooked, but they're also idiots.

Still, even idiots could have a moment or two of shrewdness. Plenty of smart people became dead smart people because they forgot that.

But as she rounded the corner, she was able to breathe easier. The gate stood open wide, with yellow light from the courtyard beyond spilling through it out onto the cobbles.

There wasn't even a token guard at the gate. Not even a child, watching to see who came in.

Oh, aye. It's the Patsonos all right.

She simply sauntered through, and once inside, re-arranged her shawl as a Gypsy would wear it, tucked into her belt. She loosened the strings of her blouse a little, and turned her businesslike stride into a slow, deliberately provocative walk.

She saw to her concealed relief that there were plenty of women here— and that, like her, while they might have adopted the mouse-browns and dust-grays of the townsfolk, they still *wore* their clothing like Gypsies. The wagons were arranged around the wall, with a communal fire in a great iron dish in the center of the courtyard. The building formed the rear of the courtyard; by the lights it was occupied, and by the size, there was nowhere near enough room in there for every Patsono here. It must be reserved for the elite of the Clan then, the Chief, his family, his advisors, and their families. There were a fair number of people loitering about; in all ways but the lack of color, music, and dancing, this looked like a fairly typical Gypsy camp situation.

Most of those loitering were young, and by their demeanor and lack of gold jewelry, of fairly low ranking in the Clan. It looked as if she had guessed correctly; the higher-ranked members were granted the greater comfort of the building, while the underlings made do with their wagons. On the whole, this lot was cleaner and better kempt than the majority of the Patsonos Robin had ever been forced to deal with. That made her job of fitting in a little easier.

If I don't stay around the younger and unimportant Clan members, I could get in trouble. The Clan Chief might be smart enough to ask about my "father," and I would get tripped up by a Chief. Unless I happened by pure accident to pick someone for my "father" who is dead, or simply isn't here.

She strolled over to a loose gathering beside the fire; someone passed a skin of wine in her direction and she squirted it deftly into her mouth, thus passing the informal "test" that showed she was a Gypsy. No *gajin* had ever mastered the Gypsy wineskins unless they were particularly deft Free Bards.

She let the fire warm her and tried to examine the faces nearby without really looking at them. Light enough came from the fire to see features clearly. Many seemed familiar; they were, perhaps, the people who were "healed" without any outward evidence of being sick or crippled, other than the canes and crutches. Those were simple deceptions that even a child could perform, and in fact, some children *had* performed them.

"So who's on duty tomorrow?" asked a young woman with a remarkably large nose and slender build. "Not me, I know that much." It sounded like the resumption of a conversation her arrival had interrupted.

"Little Robere, Bald Robere, Blind Robere, Tammio Blackbeard, Mindy, and Berto Lightfingers, that's all I know of," another voice said, from the other side of the fire. "There's a special demon-possession up; Padrik has a point he wants to make and a woman he wants to get back at, and people are getting bored with invisible demons anyway. Should be a good show, and it's going to be an impressive enough thing we don't need a big parade of victims."

"Oh, good," the large-nosed girl said with a grin. "That means I'm off. They keep making me play blind, and my legs are black and blue from stumbling into things."

"The bruises make it look good, dearie," said an old woman, with a cackle. "Now I remember when *I* played blind—"

"*Oh* yes, we know all about that, granny," a young man interrupted rudely. "We've heard it all a hundred times, how you broke a leg just to prove you couldn't see a thing. If I hear it again, I'm going to choke."

The grandmother looked mortally offended, and drew herself up with immense, if flawed, dignity. "Well!" she exclaimed. "If me wisdom and experience are going to fall on deaf ears, I will just go elsewhere, that I will!"

She limped off into the darkness, muttering to herself. The thump of her cane on the cobblestones punctuated her grumblings. Several of the younger Gypsies around the fire snickered.

One of the young men looked at Robin curiously for a moment, and she was certain that he was going to ask her who she was. But he only passed her the wineskin, and after she took her mouthful of rather good wine (from the High Bishop's cellars, no doubt), she realized why he hadn't confronted her with a demand for her identity.

"Who's special duty?" he asked instead. "Any magic tricks tomorrow besides the new demon?"

"Only the Chief and that Priest he works with. No one else, not even the peacock," the nose-girl said. Robin laughed a little, with a rueful grimace, and he grinned and winced. She passed the skin back to him.

He *had* seen her—in the Cathedral. And since he was seeing her now, here, he simply assumed that she was one of the other "special helpers." Perhaps there were Patsonos coming and going all the time—Patsono was a small Clan, but she had no idea of the true numbers. Perhaps there was not enough room for all of them here. Perhaps they were still collecting far-flung members as word spread they were needed.

For whatever the reason, she was accepted without question or qualm, and she took instant advantage of the fact, feeling a little smug. Kestrel had overreacted, of course. It was going to be satisfying to point out just how badly he had overreacted. . . .

"Bishop's got good wine," remarked someone, as the skin came around to him. The boy nearest Robin laughed drunkenly.

"Better'n I've ever had, anyway," the tipsy one said. slurring his words a bit. "Good food, good wine, an' trickin' the rootfeet! This's th' best!"

The girl with the nose laughed, just as someone threw another log on the fire, making it flare and casting a ruddy light on her face that made her seem diabolical. She had the most unpleasant laugh it had ever been Robin's misfortune to hear; it wasn't quite a scream, and it wasn't quite a bray, it was a combination of the two.

She sounded rather like the peacock. *Maybe they ought to use her and get rid of the bird.*

"What *I* love," she announced to one and all, "is that it's usin' their own religion to part 'em from everything they got! You seen those sheep when them Priests tell 'em they got cursed money? They can't throw it at us fast enough!"

She got a round of laughter at that. "Like that old goat t'day," the fellow on the other side of the fire said. "Had a bad minute with him, I thought when the priest told him 'bout the curse that he was gonna fall over with a brain-storm. Went purple, he did."

That unleashed another flood of anecdotes, with the nose-girl lamenting that she wasn't a little child anymore, since the children who were "healed" were often showered with gifts from the onlookers.

"Witnesses, Padrik calls 'em." The nose-girl sniggered. "Right. Tell 'em what they're gonna see, an' they sure do see it!"

"I hear that the Chief Robere's working on a really big illusion," the across-the-fire-voice offered. "It'll make the demon look—like a Faire-trick, so they say. Padrik asked him, says he wants a way to get the rootfeet to think they got to come up with the money for a hospice. An angel as big's the Cathedral, with, like, a big hospice in its hands. That'll make 'em cough up the silver."

"Gold too, for an angel," the nose-girl mused, the light of greed in her eyes. "How much of that do we get, you reckon? That'd be something."

Whatever else she was going to say was interrupted by the arrival of a much older, gray-haired man with a aura of self-important authority. "Meeting's running long," he said without preamble. "We're gettin' hungry and thirsty, an' we don't want the Bishop's servants carrying tales—"

"So you're lookin' for volunteers t' keep the cups an' plates filled, huh?" the nose-girl sighed. "Gray Tombere, I swear you think that's all we were born t' do for you Chiefs. You'd think we was servants."

He gave her a sharp look. "Maybe that's all you're good for, Rosa," he replied sharply. "I don't see *you* exertin' yourself for the Clan. Are you coming in, or not?"

She stretched ostentatiously, and yawned. "I guess. Just as good as bein' out here, an' it's warmer in there."

Robin waited until two more had volunteered before offering herself. Once again, no one gave her more than a second glance, not even the secondary chief who'd come for the volunteers. A moment later she was inside the "guest-house," in a large room heated to semitropic temperatures by an enormous fire in the fireplace. That was the only source of light; either the Clan Chiefs enjoyed this attempt to get the "feel" of an outdoor meeting, or else the Bishop did not trust them around candles and the resulting wax-drips on his furniture and paneling.

If so, he was wise, at least so far as Robin could tell. The carpet had been treated as if it was a dirt floor; the table was crusted with spills that had never been cleaned up, and the sideboard was in the same shape. The Bishop's furniture would never look as good as it once did, and he might have to replace it all after this.

There were platters of food waiting on the sideboard, and tall bottles of wine. In the dim light it was difficult to tell just what the food was, other than in the general sense of "meat," "bread," and "maybe cheese." She took the nearest open bottle, and turned towards the table, pouring it in any goblets that were less than full. Rosa took up a platter of meat slices and dropped them on plates with little regard for splattering sauces. The other volunteers picked up platters at random and did the same.

But the owners of the plates didn't seem to care, either. They picked up whatever was on their plates in their fingers, rolled it up, and stuffed the rolls in their mouths without paying any attention to the food itself. Instead, they leaned forward intently, and only a few brushed briefly at the spills on their clothing before bringing their attention back to the words of their Chief.

He was describing exactly the illusion that the boy outside had mentioned, of the Cathedral-tall angel with a hospice in its hands. With additions; the angel was supposed to be real to the touch, in case someone was brave enough to try, and it was to exude an aroma of incense. It was supposed to smile and nod, as a disembodied voice described the hospice Padrik was supposed to build.

"So what does the Clan get out of this one?" the gray-haired man asked as he sat down. "The demon f'tomorrow was hard enough! Has he got any idea what he's asking for? That scale of illusion isn't going to be an easy one to build or hold in place."

"We get a quarter of the take," the Chief replied. And as a storm of protest erupted, he held up his hand. "Let me finish, will you? Padrik expects more than you realize out of this one. Our cut is a quarter of the take, *or three thousand silver*, whichever comes out the biggest. *He* thinks we're likelier to wind up with three thousand in gold, not silver. Especially if he combines this with a big sermon about giving up adornments for the sake of God. He thinks that the jewelry is going to fill the collection plates, once the angel appears. In fact, his guess is that within two days, there won't be a piece of jewelry left to anybody with any claim to piety. There may not be a piece left in the city that isn't some sort of heirloom."

There was some grumbling, but finally grudging agreement; after the agreement, there was a pause while the participants resorted to their wine. Robin made three circuits of the table, emptying four bottles, before they got back to business.

They emptied their platters, too, stuffing food in their mouths as if they did not expect to eat ever again, and wiping greasy hands on their shirts and tunics. She kept herself from wrinkling her nose in distaste. It was just a good thing that the current vogue was for brown and gray; dark colors that didn't show stains and grease as badly as the usual Gypsy colors did.

Then again, it looked—and smelled—as if their clothing had been clean before they sat down to this meeting. Maybe the High Bishop's servants were discreetly taking away their soiled clothing and replacing it with clean while they slept, so that their appearance would not arouse suspicion that they did not belong here.

"Now, Gray Tombere, how's the House doing?" the Chief asked. "What's new out there?"

The old man grinned. "Better, since the Guards closed down Lady Silk's and the Snow Maiden. Sale of drink's been real good; new gambling tables are doing well. If we could just get a couple more Houses closed down, we'd be making as much money as the miracles."

But the Chief shook his head. "Don't try to force the Luck," he cautioned. "Most of the Houses are down in the Warren now; you push the local talent down there, and they may come out after us. We can't afford that yet; not until Padrik's got more than Gradford dancing to his tunes."

Robin listened and poured, poured and listened. There was more of the same, rather as she had expected. The Patsonos had basically moved into Gradford and set up their own little network of linked activities. They smuggled in drugs, strong liquor, and anything that had been deemed illegal; they dispensed these things at the House the Chief had spoken of—and Robin had a shrewd notion that if she were to trace the location of this House, she would discover it was one and the same with the "work-house" Krystal had described. They separated the gullible from their money at the gambling tables in the House, and they used their knowledge of who the clients were to extort yet more money from those same clients on occasion.

They had abandoned the usual schemes of fortune-telling and petty pickpocketing. They weren't even involved in horse theft; not here, and not now. They had tied the Clan's fortunes to High Bishop Padrik and his schemes—for just as the Patsonos got their share of the donations resulting from Padrik's "miracles," the High Bishop was taking his share of their income from the House.

And they were completely content with all of this. It apparently had never once occurred to any of them that Padrik and his Priests were observant and clever, and that once they figured out how to reproduce the "miracles"—or managed to find a mage they could coerce into doing the same—they would no longer need the Patsonos. With all the illegal activities the Clan had gotten involved with, it would be child's play to be rid of them.

No one would ever believe that the saintly High Bishop was involved with running a House—and it was doubtful that anyone had anything likely to prove the case. That assumed that the Patsonos would ever make it to a trial, of course. . . .

And with the example of *this* Gypsy Clan to inspire them, how long would it be before the High Bishop persuaded the King himself to legislate against Gypsies and Free Bards?

"*Hey!*" someone said suddenly, breaking into her reverie.

And even as she turned away from the table, wine bottle forgotten in her hand, one of the men behind her grabbed her wrist and wrenched her around. "What're you doin'?" he demanded. "You been *listening*! Who are you?"

"Reba," she said, quickly forcing an expression of vacant stupidity on her face. "Reba, Chief. Gray Tombere, he said come pour wine. Rosa, she say it's warm inside. So I come pour wine. Hey?"

The man examined her for a moment, closely. "Don't I know you from somewhere?"

She shrugged, tasting the sour bile of fear but trying to keep any expression at all from showing. Hadn't she heard of a Patsono that was hung for horse theft when she was a child? Could she remember his name? She made a quick, desperate guess. "Born on road, outside Kingsford. Mam's Clan don' like me, much. Pappy was Long Robere—"

"Ah, she must be that brat Long Robere got on the Ladras woman before they hung him," one of the others exclaimed, and laughed. "That's why you think you know her, old man—she's got that look of his."

As Robin nodded vigorously, the man pulled her a little closer, peered into her face as he exhaled wine fumes into her nose, then let go of her, nodding with grudging satisfaction. Of course, this was probably a fellow who did everything grudgingly. . . .

Robin breathed a small sigh of relief as he motioned to her to refill his goblet. "Yah, that's it, girl. You got your pappy's look about you. Long Robere allus was better looking than he was smart."

"Yah, well I heard that he didn't get his name from bein' *tall*," guffawed another of the men, and as the off-color jokes and comments followed swiftly, Robin turned to get another bottle of wine, too limp with relief to even think straight.

As she turned back to the table, though, the Chief looked directly at her. "You, Reba girl—" he said. "You just get here tonight?"

She didn't know what else to do besides nod. Presumably the Patsonos *had* put it about that their Clan was mustering here. She had better pretend that she answered that call.

"Then you don't know the rules. No hobnobbing with the rootfeet for girls, 'specially not with the Priests. You get your tail down the hall to the girls' room when we're done here," he said sternly. "No Patsono wench runs around loose where *gajin* can find her. Some of these Priests think our women are here for *them*. You get yourself a bed where it's safe—you, Rosa, you show her where, show her where the clothes is, that kinda thing."

Rosa nodded, and Robin's heart sank. But there was no help for it. Until she could get away, she was a Patsono.

Kestrel would be frantic.

And he'd say, "I told you so."

The meeting broke up shortly after that, and Rosa took her firmly by the elbow and led her down a long hallway to a huge room, lit by a bare four lanterns, and filled with cots. Most of them held young women and girls just past puberty; obviously this was a dormitory. The windows were small; too small to climb through.

"Chief wasn't joking," Rosa told her in a whisper, not unkindly. "These Priests, they seem to think we're just like the girls in their own special House. You just got what's on your back?"

At Robin's nod, she made a *tsk*ing sound. "Not the first time other Clan's have turned Patsono get out on the road with nothing," Rosa said. "Well, no matter. There's clothes in the closet there we all share; ugly, but nice make. Servants here take away dirty ones, we never have t'do no wash. You gotta take a bath every three days, though, that's a rule."

"Why all the rules?" Robin asked, in a whine. "Why the ugly clothes, hey?"

"T'make us fit in. Can't look like Gypsy, or the High Bishop might get in trouble." Rosa shrugged. "It's worth it; we're getting real money for makin' him look like a saint. Once you start helping with the services, you'll start getting the money, too."

She led Robin to a cot on the far side of the room—too far to get to the door without waking someone up. There were blankets there already, and a pillow. She patted the cot, and Robin obediently sank down onto it, trying not to show her dismay.

"I'll take you to services in the morning," Rosa said, full of self-importance. "You'll see what we do. Trust me, you'll like it! Even with the rules. This is the *best*!"

"Oh, yes," Robin mumbled, as Rosa went off to her own cot, unaware of Robin's irony. "This is really the best. . . ."

CHAPTER FOURTEEN

Jonny's anger evaporated the moment Robin flung the door open and vanished down the hall, but his indignation remained. He hadn't thought she'd storm off like that! But he stayed where he was, at least in part because he was just as stubborn as she was, and was *not* going to humiliate himself by running after her. He was certain that she would be back in a moment; in two, at most.

She knew he was right; she wasn't stupid. Once she got over being mad about the way he'd ordered her not to go, she'd realize he was right. The idea of trying to pose as some relative of these people was the height of insanity. Surely, if the Clan was as small as she claimed, they knew every single member. Just because she was a Gypsy, that wouldn't make her a believable Patsono!

She would come back. He would apologize for trying to order her around. That was *his* mistake, and he should have known better. Once he got a chance, he could explain that he was only worried about her, that he was afraid that her bravery (better not call it "foolhardiness") would be stronger than her fear, and she would end up in trouble—

No, that doesn't sound right—better say that she would be so intent on finding truth that she might find herself in some situation she hadn't expected.

He didn't even sit down; he stayed where he was, standing with his arms crossed over his chest, waiting for her to come back. Waiting to hear her footsteps, returning. Waiting for her to appear in the open doorway.

And kept waiting, staring at the wood of the hallway outside the door.

When it finally dawned on him that she really wasn't coming back, it was too late, of course. She was long out of reach; he had no idea where this Gypsy enclave was, so he didn't even have a clear idea of where she was heading.

His initial reaction was a resumption of his anger. He stormed over to the doorway, slammed the door and threw himself down onto the bed. And there he waited, certain she would not be able to get into this Gypsy enclave—

She has no sense of responsibility, dammit! The only people she thinks are important are Free Bards and Gypsies—she doesn't care about anyone else. She's as bad as Padrik! He thinks nonhumans are nonpersons, and she thinks the same of anyone outside her little circle. . . .

Hours passed; the anger burned itself out. Fear replaced it, turning him sick with anxiety for her. By the time the bells tolled for midnight, he was certain something terrible had happened to her. Maybe the Gypsies had turned her over to the Cathedral Guards; maybe they had taken matters into their own hands. Maybe she had been arrested for being out on the street after midnight. Maybe a common thief had knocked her unconscious, or even killed her!

Maybe someone had attacked her and she had used magic to defend herself, and now she was facing a judge for *that.*

He sat on the bed until the candle burned out. He was sleepless with tension, waiting to see if dawn would bring her back. His throat ached; his stomach twisted and churned, sending bile into the back of his throat. His skull throbbed with headache, and his eyes burned with fatigue. And above it all was helplessness—the knowledge that she was in a situation he couldn't discover, with people he didn't understand, and that his damnable stuttering speech would keep him from even asking a stranger about her.

When dawn came without her, his heart plummeted further, and he flung himself off the bed to stare at the rising sun with weary, aching eyes. There had to be *something* he could do!

Too restless with anxiety to stay in the room any longer, he tried to think where the best place might be to hear any news. Ardana's? No, she wouldn't be open for business yet. The Warren? Maybe; but he didn't want to venture in there unless he absolutely had to.

Finally he could only arrive at one answer; the Cathedral. Criminals were often displayed near there, in the stocks—though what she could possibly do to get herself arrested as a common criminal—

She could manage. Just by not going along with a Constable if he stopped her to question her, I suppose—

There was always gossip, the circulation of rumors among the merchants. By now he and Robin were a familiar sight, and many of the other merchants were friendly with the two of them. Maybe one of them would have heard something.

But I am supposed to remain "mute". . . .

He changed, splashed some water on his haggard face, and hurried down to the stable to get the wagon. The sooner he got to the square, the better.

The sun was barely above the level of the rooftops; the courtyard was still in shadow, and frost covered the cobblestones. He was too early for the stable hands and had to wait, pacing, in the frigid courtyard. He could have gone back to the common room to eat while he waited, but he could not even bear the thought of food at the moment. His stomach was so knotted up he was nauseous.

He took the reins of the horses and mounted to the driver's seat as soon as they brought up the wagon. It took all of his self-control to keep from galloping the horses down the street, to the market-square; he wanted to be there so badly that it seemed to take hours for the horses to walk the short distance to the market, and every momentary halt made him want to scream at those blocking the street. It took as much control to set up when he got there, as if everything was as usual; to smile and mime prices and sell the God-Stars as if nothing was wrong.

And there were no rumors, no gossip. Not even about a strange Gypsy being arrested for vagrancy or resisting arrest. Nothing. The other merchants seemed to think that Robin was ill, or resting—several of them took the time to come up and tell him to give his wife their best wishes, or to ask if anything was seriously wrong with her.

The only difference between today and all the previous days they had been here was the number of street preachers in the square itself. They were multiplying like rats this morning.

And this morning their sermons all focused on the same subject; the perfidy of women.

They were not preaching *at* Kestrel, not the way they'd preached at Robin the afternoon she had been alone; the description of him on their license said that he was deaf as well as mute, and most of them read the description and gave him a bored glance before beginning their harangues. Usually the street preachers ignored him entirely. But perhaps because the sun was concentrated here all morning, making this little corner of the square marginally warmer than the rest, there was never a moment between sunrise and Prime Service that there wasn't a preacher delivering a speech within earshot; sometimes there were two or even three, their speeches overlapping and creating aural chaos from Kestrel's point of view.

What was very different this morning, was that their speeches were so similar that they could have been reading from the same pre-written script.

Women are easily corrupted, and spread their corruption gladly. Women are by nature treacherous and scheming. Women are weak, and cannot resist temptation of any sort. Women have no grasp of true faith. Women are inferior, and nearer to the nature of animals than of angels. . . .

Kestrel wondered why none of the women listening seemed disturbed, or even insulted. If it had been *him*—

—or Robin—

—he would *not* have been standing there, listening to some fool claim he was some breed of lesser creature and needed a keeper to prevent him from doing wrong!

Why were they listening to this abuse, and saying, doing nothing? Did they believe it? And why was all this poison specifically directed against women pouring out *now*? What had happened to trigger it?

His anxiety mounted for a moment, if that was possible, as he wondered if Robin could have done something to cause this outburst of venom.

But no; why would they need to prepare people for the punishment of someone they had already *caught* in dubious activity? They wouldn't; more than that, with someone as unimportant as Robin, they'd simply fling her into a gaol-cell, and walk away.

So it couldn't be Robin; it must be that something else had happened, involving some woman of standing and importance. Or was there something *about* to happen?

As the sun rose and the square filled, his questions remained unanswered. And he began to wonder about something else. Could he have underestimated Robin? Could she have gotten herself into the Patsono Clan after all—and had she learned something that had made her stay there with them?

The more he thought about that—well, the more likely it seemed. Robin could well have been angry enough at him to punish him by not sending any word. Or she could have found herself in a position where she was unable to get away. Surely, surely, if she'd been caught, she'd have been paraded like any other common criminal!

But he could not convince himself of that, and he certainly could not convince his gut.

Out of habit, and for lack of anything constructive to do, he closed up the wagon and trailed off with the rest to the Healing Service, hoping that Robin would come to their usual place under the statue of Saint Hypatia. But Hypatia's pedestal was empty, and as the usual show played out in its usual mockery, he was tempted to leave—

Then came a cry that rang over the murmur of the crowd and brought the healing service to a complete halt.

"Demon!"

His head, and everyone else's, snapped around at the cry from the back of the Cathedral. No matter how often Padrik staged these "demonic possessions," they always gave him a shock. Four Cathedral Guards struggled forward with Robere Patsono—who this morning sported clothing that made him look several pounds heavier than he truly was, and a false moustache.

Kestrel sighed with frustration. The way the tension had been building, he had thought for certain Padrik was going to come up with some new revelation before the Healing Service was over. But just as they reached the altar, the expected scenario took an abrupt turn into something completely *unexpected.*

Robere suddenly gave a great cry, convulsed, and went limp in the arms of the Guards. His head sagged, chin against his chest, eyes closed, mouth hung slackly open.

And a thin stream of blue-gray smoke issued from his open mouth.

But it didn't act the way smoke was supposed to. Instead of rising, it snaked down his chest, eeled towards the space between him and Padrik, and pooled there.

He stared, along with every other person in the Cathedral. *If only Robin were here, she could tell me how they're doing this*— It looked real, *very* real. So real that the hair on the back of his neck crawled, and gooseflesh rose on his arms. The Cathedral was so silent that he wondered if anyone was even breathing. The Guards holding the man were white-faced and trembling; *they* certainly hadn't expected this to happen. Only Padrik was unmoved; he watched, face stern, one hand raised in a warding gesture, the other grasping his staff of office.

Then as more and more of the smoke gathered, a vague shape rose up out of the pool of mist—

And Kestrel heard a faint, discordant music. But not with his ears.

Music like, but unlike, the music he always heard when Rune or Talaysen worked real Bardic magic; the music he followed on the rare occasions that he had done the same. Someone was working magic, *real* magic, in the Cathedral!

And if it's not to produce this demon, I'll eat every God-Star I've made!

The shape shivered, thickened, grew opaque—and took on a clear, defined form. Then more than a form.

It became a demon; a real, three-dimensional being, that looked exactly as the demons portrayed in so many Church paintings and carvings. Pale gray, the color of stone. Manlike, but clearly not a man. Naked, except for a loincloth, clawed feet and hands, huge bat-wings, horns, a raptor's beak where a mouth should be—

—strangely similar to T'fyrr—

People nearest the demon screamed as it snarled at them, then turned its attention towards the altar, and hissed. But before Kestrel had any chance to wonder about that resemblance to T'fyrr, Padrik spread both his arms wide and over his head, his staff of office held between them. A white-gold glow surrounded the staff and the hands that held it.

"Begone, foul fiend!" he thundered, his voice filling the Cathedral and drowning the cries of panic from the crowd. "Begone, be banished, and trouble us no more!"

The fiend laughed, and Kestrel felt his knees turning to water with fear. He couldn't have moved; like everyone else in the building he was paralyzed with fright. He shivered with cold, drenched in an icy sweat; he shook as if he was trembling with fever, and started to sink to the floor in abject terror—

When he suddenly felt the internal music intensify, and a new melody join it, and realized that the fear he felt was not coming from within him, but from the music!

Once he knew that, he was able to shunt the music away, and fear vanished, exactly like a soap bubble popping. With it went the paralysis that had held him helpless.

He remained on his knees, however; if he had stood, he would have been terribly conspicuous amid all the rest of the grovelers. Padrik was the only man standing now, for even the Guards had dropped to their knees, leaving their "prisoner" to lie on the floor like a dead thing. The High Bishop glowed with hazy, golden light—light that was no more divine than the demon, Kestrel suspected.

"In the name of God and His Angels, begone!" Padrik cried again, his voice rising over the demonic laughter. "Begone, lest the wrath of God be unleashed upon you!"

The demon's only answer was to leap upon the High Bishop, claw-hands reaching for his throat.

Padrik brought down his staff just in time; the demon's hands closed upon it rather than flesh. The moment that it touched the wooden staff, however, the real show began.

The two combatants lurched in a bizarre circle-dance, linked by the High Bishop's staff, never once leaving the clear space before the altar. Coruscating lightnings of eye-searing yellow and blood-red lanced from the demon, grounding everywhere except on Padrik, whose golden glow had hardened to a visible shield about him. The demon's shrieks of rage echoed through the Cathedral, further terrifying the congregation. Now that Kestrel was no longer in the thrall of the artificially induced terror, he was able to admire the artistry, and wonder who among the Priests or the Gypsies was responsible. As a show, it was the best he'd ever seen; a truly professional illusion on the mage's part, and a truly fine acting perfor-mance on Padrik's. It really *looked* as if he was fighting something!

At first, the struggle appeared to be completely even, but gradually the tide turned in Padrik's favor. The High Bishop was back in his former position, where he'd started when the fight began. His back was to the altar, with his face to the congregation, and the demon's back to them. There he stopped and held his ground.

The demon cried out, and for the first time there was something like fear in its voice.

His face shining with well-simulated righteous wrath, Padrik forced the demon to its knees, and with a tremendous shout, wrestled the staff out of its hands and struck it across the head! A soundless explosion of light covered the lack of any sound of impact. It collapsed at his feet, and he planted the tip of his staff firmly in the middle of its back.

It groveled on the marble before him, whimpering.

A collective sigh passed through the crowd at the successful conclusion to the "struggle." Kestrel was impressed, Robin's disappearance momen-tarily forgotten; this was going to enhance Padrik's reputation no end! It was one thing to "banish" a "demon" no one could see—it was quite another to actually defeat such a creature in a battle anyone could see with his own eyes!

Even if it is as phony as glass diamonds.

But surely now the show was over. He expected the High Bishop to "banish" the creature as he always had before, though probably in a much more spectacular manner.

But once again the little play took an entirely different turn.

"Who sent you?" Padrik demanded, his voice booming and echoing in the silent Cathedral. "Who sent you to possess this man, and to attack me? What vile magician is it that you serve, creature of darkness? Answer! Or you will feel the might of the weapon of God once again!"

He raised his staff in threat, and the demon groveled and wept and whimpered so convincingly that Kestrel almost felt sorry for it.

"Lady Orlina Woolwright," the demon hissed, its voice harsh and hoarse. *"That isss my missstresss, the lady I sssserve—"*

Kestrel started with surprise, and he was not the only one to do so. *Orlina Woolwright?* He knew that name—and so did every native of Gradford, and every merchant who had been here more than a day or two.

She was one of the Mayor's Councilors, appointed by her Guild, for the Mayor surely would never have appointed anyone as outspoken as she was on his own. A few days ago, she had made a public speech or two of her own in the Cathedral square from the vantage of her own balcony, concerning the rights of tradesmen, with carefully veiled references to all the restrictions that Padrik had been attempting to have signed into law. She was beautiful, wealthy, a Master in the Weaver's Guild in her own right, and perhaps not so coincidentally, the only person on the Mayor's Council with a sense of humor. She'd certainly been able to make a mockery of some of Padrik's more outrageous statements in those speeches of hers. She had—unwisely now, it seemed—been flaunting the new wave of piety, by dressing as a woman of refinement and fashion, rather than a woman of the "new" Gradford.

She had been too prominent a target for Padrik to attack in the Council or in any other conventional, secular venue. That was what the other merchants had said, anyway. She held too many debts, knew too many secrets.

So has he chosen this way to bring her down?

"Orlina Woolwright? So be it!" Padrik raised his staff above his head, and gazed out over the heads of the crowd. "You have all heard it! You have heard the testament of the witch's own creature, sent to slay me! I now denounce Orlina Woolwright as a sorcerer, mage, and witch of the blackest and darkest! I declare her Anathema in the sight of all good Churchmen! Let no man aid her, let no man succor her, for the wrath of God is now against her!"

A bolt of lightning lanced down out of the ceiling of the Cathedral, and struck Padrik's staff with a *crack*. He pointed the staff down at the demon, and another bolt crackled down to strike it—

This one was so bright it brought tears to Kestrel's eyes, and when he blinked them clear again, gasping, all sign of the demon was gone. Padrik stood triumphantly before the altar, alone.

Was he the only one to notice that there was no sign *literally* of the demon—not even a blackened spot where the "bolt of lightning" just hit?

Silence for a moment, then a single voice rang out over the crowd, as a single, discordant chord of jarring music rang through his head.

"Get the witch!"

Before Kestrel could blink, the crowd had turned to a mob, a raging, maddened mob. He tried to stay where he was, tried to cling to the statue, but the press of people surging towards the exit was too great, and his grip was torn loose as the mob carried him away. It was all he could do to stay on his feet and not be trampled!

Now he was afraid, really afraid; frightened that he would stumble and fall, frightened that the mob's anger *might* turn against him for no reason at all. The brief glances he took at the faces of those around him only frightened him more. There was no sense in those dilated eyes, no sanity in the twisted mouths that spouted shouts of hatred.

He could only hold to one thought. *If I try to leave now, they'll turn on me and tear me to shreds along with whatever they do to Orlina Woolwright.*

Orlina Woolwright's home was one of the many fine houses on the square facing the Cathedral; the mob did not have far to go for their victim.

Two burly men at the front of the crowd sprinted ahead and broke in the door just as the main body of people got there. The house could never hold them all; and only part of the mob surged inside; the rest waited, shouting, for the first group to find their prey. Jonny could only watch helplessly as one poor servant who tried to stop them was beaten half to death and left beside the splintered remains of the door. Other servants ran for their lives; some crawled away with the marks of more blows upon their faces and bodies.

Within moments, glass shattered as something was thrown out of a window—a beautiful silver candelabra. A woman snatched it out of the air, and screamed, *"Take the witch's wealth! Strip her as naked as she was born!"*

That was the signal for all-out looting. Windows shattered as goods came tumbling out of them. The mob surged forward and people snatched at anything that the righteous looters inside pitched out a window— lengths of fabric, paintings, furniture, clothing and jewelry—a fork, a glass paperweight, an ornamental letter-opener—

People snatched their prizes and ran, and no one did anything to stop them. The City Guard had vanished; there wasn't even a Cathedral Guard to be seen. Jonny was quite certain that there was nothing left but the bare walls by the time Orlina appeared, herself bundled up like so much loot, bound and gagged and carried in the ungentle hands of the two men who had first broken down her door. And now the mob parted to let them through, then surged along behind them as they carried her off to Padrik. Strangely, they had not stripped her literally; that seemed odd in the light of their lack of restraint so far—she remained clothed in her fine gown of mulberry-colored wool; not even the badge of Master on its chain around her neck had been taken from her.

Once again, the mob surged forward; somehow, this time, Jonny managed to get to the edge near the front. If he got a chance to bolt for the wagon, he was going to take it!

The High Bishop met them at the foot of the staircase in front of the Cathedral doors, his face the very essence of a grieving saint. The two men tumbled the woman at his feet and forced her to kneel before him. Jonny could not see her face, but her back told him that if she had one hand free and so much as a letter-opener in it, Padrik would have been eviscerated before anyone could blink.

"You are a witch, Orlina Woolwright," Padrik thundered, as the mob quieted. "You are a dark mage, and a foul demon-lover. Your own acts condemn you, as should I. And yet"—his face softened, and his tone took on new sweetness—"and yet I cannot do other than forgive you."

Gasps came from everywhere, and one woman began to weep. Jonny had been nauseated before, but now his gorge rose, and he fought down a wave of sickness.

"Yes, I can forgive you, for you are only a woman, and by your very nature you are weak and need to be led in the proper path," Padrik continued, magnanimously. "And I, as man and as your spiritual leader, failed to give you that guidance. I shall remedy that lack now."

He took a pendant from around his neck, a peculiar piece of jewelry that Kestrel did *not* remember him wearing before. It was made of iron, black wrought-iron, in a lacy filigree design in the form of a double circle or an orb. That was all Kestrel could see of it—but something about it made his stomach twist, and he suddenly did *not* want to look any closer.

Padrik put the pendant around Orlina's neck, removing the chain that held her Master's badge—and that rigid, unyielding back went limp; she sagged forward in her bonds, bowing her head before him.

Padrik's smug smile of triumph made the hair on the back of Jonny's neck rise, and he forced back a snarl. "Here then, is your only sentence. You must make a pilgrimage, alone and unaided, on your own two feet, without benefit of carriage or beast. You must go to Carthell Abbey, place this token of your obedience on the altar with your own two hands. Only then can you return, and resume the proper duties of a true woman and a daughter of the Church."

He expected the woman to fight—or at least to defy the High Bishop. So Orlina's submissive nod made Kestrel's mouth fall open with surprise.

The mob, however, was not going to give her any opportunity to display that submission on her own.

The same two men hauled her to her feet and half-dragged, half-carried her along the street of the inns to the city gates. Once again, Jonny was forced by the press of bodies to go along, and so it was that he saw the end of the incident.

Once the mob reached the city gates, the two men who had carried her all this way cut her bonds and set her free, shoving her out of the gates and onto the road leading downward.

She stood up, shook off the bits of rope, and brushed her hands absent-mindedly across her hair. And without so much as a glance behind her, as if she was setting off on a stroll across the street, she strode down the road that led eventually to Carthell Abbey.

Robin's stance, not in the least submissive, gave her away, even though she wore the same drab clothing as every other woman in the square. When Jonny saw that familiar figure waiting for him beside the wagon, he was torn between giddy relief and wanting to strangle her with his bare hands.

Relief won easily. He shoved his way through the crowd towards her.

At the very last moment, though, he remembered that Robin was "supposed" to have been a little ill, not missing, and kept himself from running towards her and flinging his arms around her as if she had been gone since last night.

That did not, however, stop *her* from doing the same.

"I'm sorry, I'm sorry, you were right, I shouldn't have—" she babbled—and before she could say anything that might betray them to listeners, he stopped her the only way he could think of. With a kiss, and a hug that squeezed the breath out of her.

"Inside," he whispered into her ear, quickly. "Preachers."

She started, and took a quick glance around, her eyes widening at the sight of all the street preachers around. She nodded, and followed him inside the wagon.

She waited until he closed the door before finishing her sentence. "I'm so sorry"—she babbled, as they threw their arms around each other and hung on as if they would never let go again—"I'll never be that stupid again, I was an idiot, you were right—"

"But n-not r-right to act as if I c-could order y-you about," he interrupted, caressing her hair in the soft semidarkness. "Y-you w-were r-right, t-too. I'm s-s-sorry."

"Not half as much as I am," she replied, ruefully, calming down and chuckling a little. "I was a little *too* convincing. They thought I was a real Patsono, all right—and they put me up in the dormitory for their unattached women! I couldn't get out all night, and in the morning I had a self-appointed guide that glued herself to my elbow right up until that mob broke loose to go after that poor Woolwright woman!"

He shuddered; he couldn't help himself. He could all too easily imagine the same thing happening to himself, or any of the Free Bards. "I s-s-saw it all," he said, locking both his arms around her to stop her sudden shivering. "Th-the d-demon and everything. S-s-someone w-was using m-magic in th-there, of c-course. How d-did you g-get away?"

She put her head against his shoulder, until her shaking died down. "The girl who was watching me couldn't resist a chance at the loot, and she left me as soon as those brutes broke down the door," Robin told him, after a moment. She put her head back a little, so that she could see his face. "I didn't get any good looks at the demon-show—"

He smiled, wanly. "W-well, I d-did," he said, and proceeded to describe everything he had seen and heard, in as much detail as he could remember. She shook her head in disbelief several times, and her lips and chin tightened in anger long before he was done with his narrative.

She hugged him hard, then pushed him away gently when he had finished. "That's it," she said firmly. "That's all of this I can take. I don't know about you, but I've seen everything I need to; I can tell the Gypsy Chiefs who is betraying our secrets, we can warn the Free Bards, the nonhumans, and the Gypsies about what is starting here. Now I want *out* of here, before they do something like that to one of us!"

Kestrel nodded. "There's n-nothing back in our r-room at the inn th-that c-can't b-be replaced," he told her. "W-we k-kept everything important in th-the w-wagon. How ab-bout right n-now?"

Her face lit with a smile of relief. "That's the best idea I've heard in a long time!" she exclaimed. But then her face fell.

"What about Orlina Woolwright?" she said, hesitantly. "She's innocent—and we know that, and we didn't do anything to stop them—"

Jonny paused for a moment, hand reaching for the door, then turned. "W-we g-go after her," he replied. And wondered if Robin was going to argue with him. "W-we c-can take her t-to one of the J-Justiciars. Wren kn-knows one—"

He expected Robin to object, but she nodded with enthusiasm—a change in her that made *his* spirits rise. "I know her too!" she exclaimed. "And I doubt she'll have forgotten me! That is the perfect solution— surely what Padrik is doing can't be legal, even by Church standards. And—well, the Justiciar we both know is impartial enough that she has made judgments against Priests before this."

"All r-right, then," Kestrel agreed, opening the door. "Th-then let's g-get out of h-here b-before s-something else happens!"

CHAPTER FIFTEEN

Getting out was easier said than done.

Robin noticed that the square was filling up with people as they readied the horses and headed for the street of the inns; and that was odd, because at this hour, things were usually winding down and people were going home. But the moment they maneuvered the wagon out of the Cathedral market square and onto the street itself, it seemed that everyone in the city was determined to go *towards* the Cathedral while they struggled to move *away*. One or two folk struggled against the growing flow-tide of Gradford citizens, but most were trying to get to the very place she and Kestrel wanted to leave.

A pity that they weren't real merchants; they'd have sold everything they owned with a crowd this big!

I'd be doing my best to stay out of the street in this part of town, if I lived here, Robin thought grimly, a headache starting to form in both temples, *I'd lock my door and not open it until morning. It must be that they've heard about the demon and all the rest of it, and maybe they're trying to stream in to show their piety. Come to evening services and prove that you aren't a sorcerer! What a clever way to make certain no one ever decides to oppose your will! Surely every Councilor by now has seen the proverbial handwriting on the wall. Get in Padrik's way and he'll see that you wind up being accused of demon-summoning!*

And there would be no proper court of law for those who were so accused. Padrik had just set a precedent; *he* was judge and jury for those he accused—and his mobs would see that punishment was dealt out with a heavy hand.

Their wagon was forced to the far side of the street and kept there by the press of bodies. A blind cripple would have been able to walk faster than the horses could, and every time there was an intersection, there was a City Constable there, stopping traffic to let another stream of people onto Inn Street.

In the end, it was full dark long before they reached the city gates, and they had actually been able to retrieve their belongings from The Singing Bird after all. Robin simply hopped out and shoved and elbowed her way through the crowd when they were two buildings away; by the time the wagon reached the opening to the courtyard, she had gathered everything up and was waiting for him. It had been easy, and she hadn't even needed to give a parting explanation to the innkeeper, for The Singing Bird was so full of people she couldn't even see him. Not that she thought he'd be the loser in this; he was going to have the money they'd paid in advance for their next week. She was glad of that; it made leaving a little less distasteful. In fact, the only thing she regretted was leaving Ardana without entertainers, with no notice whatsoever. But if Ardana had heard what had happened tonight—well, she would probably understand.

She might even be thinking about a swift relocation herself right about now. What was the cost and difficulty of packing up and leaving, when compared to waking up to find yourself accused and convicted of dark sorcery?

Robin tossed the bags of their personal things up beside Kestrel and climbed onto the driver's bench, pushing open the doorway over the bed and shoving the bags in there quickly.

A good thing I went back, too, she reflected, as they inched along, both of them trying very hard to look relaxed and completely unconcerned about the press of traffic. *If Padrik or someone in his train is working magic, and he gets an inkling that we were something other than what we appeared to be, any mage can use our belongings to find us. Or to send things after us! I don't want to have to test Bardic Magic against that!*

She took mental stock of what provisions were still in the wagon; not a lot, unfortunately. They hadn't been planning on running. And she had no notion what they were going to do when they finally got out of Gradford; camp at the bottom of the hill and hope that the area was safe, probably.

Poor planning. Next time they did this, they'd have to make certain they were *ready* in case they had to make a run for it.

Next time! she thought, suppressing an hysterical giggle. *If there's a next time like this, I'm becoming a washerwoman!*

They reached the gates just before they were about to close for the night. There was no one else waiting to get out, and a thin stream of people coming in at the last minute. The Guards there looked at them a bit askance; usually people wanted to get into a walled city before the gates closed, not out of the place. But now that they were leaving, Robin didn't particularly care what they thought; she didn't bother to offer any excuses or make up any explanatory story. If luck was with her, she'd never have to visit Gradford again in her life!

Well, luck was with them enough that there was a high, full moon tonight. The switchback road down to the bottom of the hill stretched out before them, clear and pale gray in the bright moonlight. The horses were able to make their way down the road to the bottom of the hill with very little difficulty, and only a stumble or two over a rock or a hole.

Once at the bottom, though, it was clear that it would not be possible to go any further tonight. The valleys were deep in shadow, and anything could be hiding there. The horses could easily break legs over unseen obstructions. So they made camp; not a very satisfactory camp, as Robin had foreseen.

The provisions still in the wagon left a lot to be desired. The horses had grain and water, but not as much of the former as they wanted. There wasn't much to eat for the humans, either, no lamp oil, and only enough charcoal for the stove to warm the wagon and cook a scanty meal, not enough to keep the wagon warm all night. So Robin made unleavened griddle-cakes, two each, and generously loaded them with honey. Not enough to do more than tantalize. Then they went to bed still hungry, with only the blankets and each other to keep them warm through the night. That wasn't as bad as it could have been, though; they both had belated apologies to make to each other and a quarrel to mend. It was an argument that had proven to bring misery to both of them—but the reconciliation made up for the horrible night before.

Roosters high in the hills woke them at false-dawn, stiff with cold and muscles aching. There was nothing to eat, and only work to warm them. But they set off again as soon as the sun rose, with Jonny catching up on his missed sleep, and Gwyna driving, knowing they would easily reach the wayside inn by noon. The horses knew this road, now, and they remembered there was an inn on it, which meant a real stable, hay, and grain; they made very good time with no need for urging on Robin's part, setting off at a brisk walk when she gave them the signal.

Robin kept her eyes sharp for foot travelers. She expected at any moment to see Orlina Woolwright, limping along the side of the road. The woman was wealthy and not used to walking, after all; she was afoot, and they were in a wagon. Granted, the advantage of the wagon was somewhat negated by the fact that they were in hill country, and a man walking could make roughly the same time as any beast pulling a vehicle; only a person riding would outpace either. But as the hours passed, and Orlina did not appear, Robin began to wonder just what had happened to the woman. The only foot travelers she saw were a couple of shepherds and a farmer or two.

"Where can she *be*?" she wondered aloud, as the inn appeared on a hilltop in the distance, and there was still no sign of Orlina's mulberry-colored dress. Surely the woman hadn't just dropped out of sight! Robin hadn't heard of any robbers on this road; the local Sire kept it as well-patrolled as it was tended. And if she had fallen over from exhaustion, she should still be on the grassy verge. . . .

But Jonny didn't answer her; he was still asleep. She swallowed, and glanced back at the closed door behind her, feeling rather guilty. His red-rimmed eyes had told her more than he himself had about how *he* had spent the previous night. Well, she hadn't exactly enjoyed herself, but she had known where he was, and that he was safe enough in their room in the inn. He'd had no idea where she was, or what had happened to her—and likely, if they both hadn't been mistrustful of anything that passed for an authority in Gradford, he'd have had her name and description up with the Constables before sunrise.

That bewildered her a little, and touched her a great deal—and made her feel horribly guilty for making him so miserable. She wasn't used to having someone *worry* over where she was and where she had gone. Or at least, not since she was old enough to leave the family wagon and go out on her own. And to have someone worry himself sleepless over her . . .

But if it had been the other way around—hmm. I think I'd have done the same. If I hadn't known he would stay where he was, I still might have fretted myself into a lather—

She shook her head and gave up on it. She had promised she would never be that stupid again, and she meant to keep that promise. Too much going on, and not enough time to think about it all, that was the problem. Too many things happening too fast, and they had completely neglected to make plans together. Next time they'd do better. Weren't they partners? That was one meaning of *vanderei:* "partners on the road." Partners didn't leave one another in the dark. *He* never forgot that; it was time she started remembering.

And where on earth was that Woolwright woman? Surely no wealthy rootfoot could have *walked* this far—surely she wouldn't have walked all night!

But that assumed she was walking of her own will. She might not be; hadn't Jonny said something about how the woman had looked after Padrik put that curious "token" around her neck? Yes, he had; he'd been adamant about it.

Spell-struck, that was what he said. As if something had just thrown a spell over her, and had taken over her body, mind, and will.

If Padrik really didn't *care* if she returned or not, casting a spell on her mind to make her keep walking until she reached Carthell Abbey would be no great problem. What would it matter if she walked herself into exhaustion and collapse? What would it matter to him if she walked over a cliff? Why should he care? Any misfortune that befell her would clearly be the will of God.

So the least he had done, probably, was to make certain she *would* walk straight to the Abbey with no pause for rest. For a moment, Robin felt guilty again—they hadn't done anything to stop Padrik, and they could probably have used Bardic Magic to cancel the spell on that token. Had they stood by and condemned an old woman to death-by-exhaustion?

Maybe not; when she made that speech, she didn't look very frail to me. She's a Master in the Weaver's Guild; that's a lot of hauling, walking, lifting . . . even for a Master with a shop full of apprentices. She could be more fit than I had thought.

She could, in fact, have the reserves to walk a full day and a night without collapsing. And if that was the case—she would be a full day ahead of them by now!

Robin sighed with resignation, her guilt lost in a moment of self-pity. Last night had not been very comfortable, and she had been hoping to intercept the woman and enjoy a good rest at the inn. But this meant no warm bed in the inn tonight, and no supper cooked by someone else. Only a brief stop to properly reprovision the wagon—

At inn prices. She winced. While she was hardly parsimonious, a Gypsy was never happy without a bargain. There were few bargains to be had at inns as remote as this one.

So. It had to be done. Once they had restocked, they could go on, and hope to catch Orlina before she actually reached the Abbey.

And try to figure out what sort of spell they have on her, and how to break it, she realized, as the horses mounted the final hill and quickened their pace, with the inn in clear sight. *They* knew what was up there! *Otherwise, if we don't break it, she's going to keep right on walking to the Abbey, no matter what we do.*

The innkeeper was very happy to see them again; as she pulled the horses into the dusty yard in front of the door, he came out himself, beaming a cheerful greeting in the thin winter sunlight. "Well, my travelers!" he called out. "You return! And did you prosper in Gradford?"

"Ai," Robin said, sadly, and made a long face, as she halted the horses. "Everywhere one turns, there are hard times, and everyone is a thief. How can any honest craftsman prosper in times like these?"

"How, indeed." The innkeeper wiped his hands on his apron, and made a mock-sober face himself. "The times are hard. But you have come to stay, surely—"

His face truly fell when she shook her head; with custom already thin along here, the coming of winter must be hitting him hard. "No," she replied regretfully, "but we will have to reprovision here. We will need everything: horse-feed, oil, charcoal, food—we are down to nothing but a handful of meal and a few cups of oats. And I don't suppose your cook has any of those little meat pies that keep so well—?"

His expression regained its former look of cheer. "Why, he made a batch this very morning! And for you, of course, my prices on provisions will be so tiny, I shall make no profit at all!"

"I'm sure," she told him dryly, then settled down for a serious bargaining session.

Jonny slept all through the stop; he didn't even wake up when she entered the wagon to store everything she had bought, nor when the innkeeper's workhands clambered atop the wagon to store waterproofed sacks of charcoal up on the roof. The horses might not have gotten their warm stable, but she did see that they each got a good feed of grain, and bought more to store under the wagon. Their profits for their God-Stars paid for all of it; would, in fact, have paid for it all three times over. But she wept and wailed and claimed that the innkeeper was cheating her; he blustered and moaned, and swore she was robbing him, and in the end, they both smiled and shook hands, satisfied.

He had been able to unload some stocks that he clearly wasn't going to need this winter, and she was at least as satisfied as she was ever likely to get, buying provisions at an inn set out in the middle of nowhere.

The innkeeper hadn't seen anyone even remotely resembling the description of Orlina Woolwright, neither walking nor riding. None of his stablehands and servants had, either, and Robin wondered then if they had gone off chasing a phantom. Still, she reminded herself that their main reason for leaving hadn't been to run off to her rescue—it had been to escape while *they* still could! If they couldn't find her, they couldn't help her, and there was no getting around it.

But as Robin set the horses on the road again, reins in one hand, meat-pie in the other, that rationalization felt rather flat.

The woman isn't a Gypsy or a Free Bard, she told her uneasy conscience. *We don't owe her anything. We're doing our best for her, but how can we do anything until and unless we find her? We can't; and that's it.*

Except that both she and Jonny *knew* Padrik's demon was a fraud, his accusations completely groundless. They'd had the proof at the time, and they hadn't done anything to stop him. Robin had been in an even better position to do so than Jonny; she had, after all, been among the Patsonos. She could have done something to disrupt the illusion, or drugged the chief participants' wine, or—

Or something. I probably would have gotten caught, but I could have done something. She bit into the flaky crust of the pie, pensively, licking a bit of gravy from her fingers, as the horses plodded up the slope of yet another hill. The fleeting, fragile beauty these hills had held only a few short weeks ago was gone now; the trees were bare, gray skeletons in the thin sunlight; the grasses sere and brown. Only the evergreens provided a spot of color, and even their greens seemed washed-over with a thin film of gray dust. She wore her coat and a thick knitted sweater, woolen mittens, and a knitted hood, and still she was cold. She wondered how Harperus was faring, and T'fyrr. The winged Haspur hadn't seemed equipped to take the cold.

Then again, neither do hawks and falcons, and they do all right. Unless the hard weather came early, there wouldn't be any real snow yet for weeks, but by the time it came, the ground would be as unyielding as stone, and the ponds frozen over. She made soothing sounds at the horses, and longed for summer. Or at least, a good, weathertight room somewhere, with a big, cozy bed and a fireplace.

And hot meat-pies and wine. Or a great roast of beef, nicely rare, and fresh bread. Or a roast goose with stuffing, or better still, a duck, and yams. And while she was wishing, why not servants to wait upon her, and comfits and cream, and—

She shook her head at her own folly.

Uphill, and down; uphill and down. The horses plodded onward in resignation while the sun westered, and the trees cast ever-lengthening blue shadows across the road. The air grew perceptibly chillier.

Finally the little door behind her slid back, and Kestrel poked his tousled head out. He blinked at the light. "Are w-we th-there yet? Or c-close? How l-long d-did I s-sleep?" he asked, yawning.

"We've been there and gone. It's late afternoon," she told him. "I got supplies at the inn, but you were so tired you slept right through it all. We're on the road to Carthell Abbey, and I expect to get there about

sunset at the rate the horses are going. There's no sign of Orlina Woolwright, though, and no one at the inn saw her."

Kestrel frowned. "Th-there might n-not b-be," he said, "if sh-she's
b-bespelled, sh-she m-might n-not s-stop for anything. If sh-she p-passed
the inn at n-night—"

"Of course!" Gwyna replied, disgusted with herself. "She would have
passed the inn last night, about midnight, if she just kept walking."

"N-no reason n-not to," Jonny pointed out. "If sh-she's under a s-spell,
she w-won't b-be able t-to s-stop, even if she f-feels t-tired, and l-last
n-night was a f-full m-moon. Plenty of l-light t-to walk by. N-not likely
she'd f-fall off the r-road."

He crawled out over the sill, and into the seat beside her. He'd fallen
asleep coat and all, and looked rumpled head to toe.

"How l-long t-till s-sunset?" he asked.

She squinted at the sun. "Three hours," she said. "Roughly. Want a
pie?"

She pulled a pie out of the sack under her seat; it was cold now, and
not as tasty as it had been when it was warm, but the pies were still good
even cold, and far, far better than the bannocks they'd eaten last night.
And he must be ravenous.

Jonny took it with a nod of thanks, not *quite* snatching it, and devoured
it in a few moments. She handed him another, and took one herself.

*So, this time we make a plan first, and stick to it. A plan we can both
agree on.* "How are we going to approach the Abbey?" she wanted to
know. "The last time they weren't very friendly to us, and I don't think
that's going to change. But if that's where Padrik sent Orlina Woolwright,
she'll probably be inside. Or at least they should know where she is."

"I've b-been th-thinking about th-that," Kestrel replied, around a
mouthful of pie. "I have a p-p-plan. If y-you l-like it t-too, that is."

She grinned; they must have been thinking identical thoughts. "Just so
it's better than one of *my* plans!" she teased. "Going in there in disguise
as a Brother, for instance, is probably not a good idea. The last thing I
need to do is have to rescue you from an Abbot who thinks you're one
of his novices—or have him discover that I'm *not* a boy!"

"I'd th-thought of th-that," he admitted. "It w-would s-serve you r-right,
after all, t-to b-be on the other s-side of th-the w-w-worry!"

She slapped his knee with the ends of her reins by way of an answer.
"So what's the real plan?" she asked.

He finished the last of his pie, and licked his fingers. "Th-there *is* a
d-disguise, b-but n-not a d-dangerous one—"

It seemed to take forever to reach their destination, though perhaps
that was anxiety and not reality. Finally the road dove down into the valley
that contained Carthell Abbey; it was just before sunset, and the sky above
the western hills glowed flame-streaked and glorious. Too bad the valley
did not match the view—bare trees on either side of the road stretched
riblike limbs toward them; a clammy, spectral mist rose from stagnant
pools of water as they passed through the Beguilers' swamp. It was very
cold and damp here, and the deep shadows of the surrounding hills made

it colder still. But at least by now the treekies and the Beguilers would have gone into hibernation for the winter.

Now just so that there aren't any gellens or varks in this valley as well, Robin thought. Kestrel must have felt the same way, urging the horses to a faster pace. *Be just our luck that there are nocturnal winter monsters here as well as the ones that hibernate.*

Kestrel had taken over the reins shortly after he awoke; he stopped the horses well out of sight of the Abbey, and Robin climbed down off of the passenger's seat. She was dressed in her warmest and drabbest, and she only hoped that Brother Pierce, the surly Gatekeeper, hadn't gotten a good look at her the last time they were here. Right now, she looked like a very respectable young woman straight out of Gradford, and that was what she wanted him to think she was.

A very respectable, very wealthy, and very assertive young woman. The kind Brother Pierce would *have* to answer, whether he liked it or not.

They unhitched one of the horses, and threw a blanket over it, hoping that in the semidarkness, it would look like a saddle. She trotted up the road to the Abbey afoot, leading the horse, for she did not know if it had ever been broken to ride, and now was not the time to find out! The brisk pace warmed her thoroughly, her breath puffing out in front of her in clouds of white. There was going to be a hard frost here tonight, and perhaps a light sprinkling of freezing rain . . . not ideal weather for camping. There wouldn't be a choice, however; not tonight. Far safer to camp than trust to the safety of any shelter offered by the Church. Assuming they *would* offer it.

Not bloody likely.

The Abbey loomed up around a bend in the road, lanterns beckoning with a promise of warmth that she already knew would not be kept. She hurried her pace a little; the horse tugged on the rein in her hand, and whickered. Poor thing; it thought she was taking it to a stable. If there *were* varks out here, she wanted to get back to the wagon as fast as she could!

She stopped, a few paces away from the door, to compose herself. The horse pawed the ground with impatience. When she had caught her breath, she rang the bell with an imperious hand, hoping to sound like the sort of person who was not used to being kept waiting.

When Brother Pierce did make his appearance, he gave no sign of recognizing her as anything other than a female, and thus, a major intrusion into his life. He frowned at her, his face taking on all the look of someone who had bitten into an unripe plum.

"What do *you* want?" he asked, rudely. "Be off! We don't house vagabonds—"

"I'm no vagabond, you insolent knave!" Robin said, with shrill indignation. "If this were Gradford, I'd have my servants horsewhip you to teach you manners!" She had heard enough of the wealthy women of Gradford and the way they spoke to underlings who offended them to enable her to produce a pretty fair imitation of their mannerisms. She drew herself up tall and proud, as he gaped at her, clearly taken aback by her rude response. "I am Rowen Woolwright, sister to Master Orlina Woolwright of Gradford, and I demand to know what you have done with my sister! That cur of a High Bishop sent her here on some fool's errand and—"

Brother Pierce's wizened face flushed as she began her harangue, but a sly smile crept over his features when he heard who it was Robin claimed to be. He made an abrupt gesture, startling the horse, and cutting off her torrent of words.

"Shut your mouth, woman, before it condemns you to a fate like hers!" he snapped, interrupting her. Now it was her turn to stare at him in simulated surprise that he should even *dare* to interrupt her. "We'll have no truck with the agents of darkness here, nor heretics, either! She's not here, the sorcerous bawd! She conjured a demon and sent it to destroy the Holy High Bishop, but he was stronger than her dark magic, and the Hand of the Sacrificed God protected him. He defeated the demon, as a hundred witnesses can attest, and the demon itself betrayed its mistress."

Robin hoped that she looked appropriately stunned. Evidently she did, for Brother Pierce smiled nastily.

"High Bishop Padrik had every right to condemn her, but he forgave her and sent her on a pilgrimage of penance to this Abbey," he said, his voice full of glee. "She's been sent to a holy shrine in the hills by our Abbot, as is his right and duty. She was unrepentant when she came, and he has sent her on to be judged. The Sacrificed God himself will be her judge once she reaches the holy shrine of the hills; if she returns from the shrine, well and good, she will be restored to her former position by the High Bishop himself."

"And if she doesn't?" Robin asked, sharply, "What then? How will you protect her—"

He smiled, displaying large, yellowing, crooked teeth. "God will protect her, if she is innocent. If she doesn't return, well, then she is clearly a witch, guilty of the charge the blessed High Bishop laid upon her, and the God has sent her where she belongs. Her property will be confiscated, since all witches are traitors, and it will be turned over to the Cathedral and Carthell Abbey."

She did not have to feign the shock she felt. No wonder Padrik was a wealthy man, able to give an entire clan of Gypsies silver and even gold! If he was getting monies this way, as well as from the gifts of the faithful—

"The shrine—" she said, gasping out the words. "Where is this shrine?"

Brother Pierce grinned again, overjoyed to see her so discomfited, and obliged with a description.

"Ye follow this road *here*—" he said, pointing to the Old Road that led on to Westhaven. "Not the newer route, but this 'un. Ye take it into the hills, till ye come to a bare-topped hill. If ye get to a village called Westhaven, ye've gone too far. On top of the hill, that's the shrine. But I wouldn't go there—" he added, as she turned to go.

"Why not?" she asked, belligerently.

He laughed, the first time she had heard him do so. It sounded like an old goose, honking. "Because, woman, if you go there, ye'll be judged too! And be sure, if you don't return to your home and the duties of a proper woman, it'll be because demons have taken you like your sister!"

She turned away from him as he slammed the gate shut, feeling chilled, and not by the wind. The Old Road—a bare-topped hill? Between here and Westhaven? There was only one place he could possibly mean.

Skull Hill.

She ran back to the wagon as fast as her legs would carry her, the horse running alongside, but looking back over its shoulder with longing; there was a painful stitch in her side before she got there. "They sent her to Skull Hill," she said, panting, as she harnessed the horse up again, and flung herself into her seat. "I don't think she's very far ahead, not if they wanted to time her arrival for midnight—"

"R-right." Kestrel didn't waste any words; he simply slapped the reins against the horses' backs to get them moving again.

It was terrible. They wanted to gallop the horses and knew they didn't dare. It only took a single hole in the road to send both horses down— and at a gallop, that would mean broken legs and dead horses for certain, and if the wagon overturned as well, *they* could wind up dead.

It took a few moments for the pain in her side to leave; she breathed the cold air in carefully, holding her side, and waited, before the pain eased enough that she could speak again. "Now we know what the Ghost meant," she pointed out. "About people being sent from here."

"Y-yes," Jonny replied, urging the horses to a faster pace than a walk, until they were moving as fast as even Gwyna considered safe. "P-put one of th-those p-pendants on an enemy, it m-makes them c-come here. And it identifies th-them t-to th-the Ghost."

"He'll kill her, of course," Robin replied off-handedly. "He won't even hesitate. He told us that himself."

But Jonny only turned and flashed her a feral grin, teeth gleaming whitely in the moonlight.

"N-not if w-we f-find her f-first!" he said. Robin returned his grin, but uncertainly, then peered through the darkness ahead of them. She was hoping to spot Orlina Woolwright quickly, for at this pace, they could defeat their own purpose by accidentally running her down.

Through the valley of Carthell Abbey they raced, and out the other side into the hills; Robin could hardly believe that a woman on foot had come so far, so quickly. It seemed impossible—but the road was wet and muddy here, and they kept coming across the tracks of a human, pressed into the mud and visible even at a distance. They both knew how seldom anyone used this road, so who else could it be?

They were deep in the hills again before Robin realized it. And now she had the answer to another question—why tend this road so well if no one used it?

To make it as easy as possible for your victims to reach the place of ambush, she thought grimly. *It isn't the Sire who tends this road; it's the Abbey, I'd bet the Ghost's silver on it.*

But they were very, very near Skull Hill now; one more hill, and Orlina would be within the Ghost's grasp.

"There she is!" Kestrel exclaimed, his stutter gone in the tension and excitement. He slapped the reins over the startled horses' backs; they jerked into a canter, and she finally saw what he had seen. A fast-moving shadow ahead of them, a shadow that fluttered near the ground, with a flurry of skirts. It was Orlina, indeed, and she paid no attention whatsoever to the horses bearing down on her. Kestrel cracked the whip, startling the horses into a dangerous gallop; the wagon lurched as the horses bolted.

A few yards more, and it would be too late!

Heedless of her own danger, Robin launched herself from the seat of the wagon as Kestrel pulled the horses to a halt; the wagon slewed sideways with a rasping screech of twisting wood and grinding stone, blocking Orlina's way. Robin flew through the air and tackled the woman, knocking her to the ground. The song of the pendant rasped like an angry wasp in her mind as soon as she touched Orlina's flesh. They tumbled together into the underbrush; the thick and springy bushes alone saved them from broken limbs. Together they tumbled back into the road, and Robin yelped with pain as her shins and elbows hit rock.

She didn't even think, she simply grabbed the pendant, and jerked, breaking the chain, before the woman could get to her feet again. If Orlina ran, they might not be able to catch her before the Ghost took her.

The song in Robin's head whined—then faded. Orlina Woolwright sat up slowly, blinking, as if she had been suddenly awakened from a deep sleep. Moonlight poured down upon her as she frowned, looked quickly and alertly about her, and focused on Robin, who was sprawled in the dirt of the road beside her.

"What am I doing here?" she demanded, in a strong, deep voice. "What has been happening?"

Jonny came around the front of the wagon, first pausing long enough to soothe the bewildered mares. He reached down his hand, with a courteous grace Robin had seldom seen in him—except when he had been in his uncle's Palace. In one heartbeat, he had gone from the vagabond, to the Prince in disguise.

A useful ability. Orlina Woolwright recognized that grace for what it was, and took his hand. He helped her to rise; she accepted that aid, and when she next spoke, her voice was softer, less demanding.

"I last remember being hauled before that dog of a High Bishop," she said, her words clipped and precise. "What happened?"

"It's a l-long s-story, my l-lady," Jonny said, carefully. He helped Robin up; she moved carefully, but although she felt bruised all over, and had her share of scratches, there was nothing seriously damaged. Jonny gave her a quick hug, then led Orlina over to the back of the wagon, and opened the door for her. She got in as gravely as if it had been a fine carriage. "W-we'll t-tell you all, if y-you have the t-time."

As he lit the lantern inside and Robin climbed up the rear steps, she saw Orlina Woolwright smile as she took a seat upon their bed. It was not a condescending smile, and she took her place in their wagon as if they were both royal and she was honored to be there.

"High Bishop Padrik has left me little but time, young sir," she replied. "And I think he tried to take that, too." She gestured for the two of them to join her. "I would be very pleased if you would tell me the whole of it."

CHAPTER SIXTEEN

Robin was glad they had reprovisioned; with the stove going, the wagon seemed a cozy island of safety in all the darkness. She made hot tea for all of them, served up the last of the meat-pies, and tended to her own scratches and bruises—or at least the ones that she could get to without disrobing. Orlina did not seem to notice hers; perhaps some of the numbness of the spell that had been on her still lingered—or perhaps she was tougher than even Robin had thought. She was certainly younger than Robin had assumed, given her rank—in early middle age at most. It was the lady's leanness that had fooled her into thinking Orlina was older; there was not even a single strand of gray in her hair, and the muscles beneath the dress had been as strong as an acrobat's. But she ate like one who had been starving for a day, and drank so much tea Robin had to make a second pot. The tale was a long time in the telling, and it was well past moonrise before they finished it. They had a great deal of explaining to do; the lady believed them, but Robin had the feeling that if she had not found herself on a road in the middle of nowhere, with no memory of how she got there, she would not have.

She examined the pendant with interest, but did not touch it. "A nasty thing, that," she said, then looked thoughtful. "Guild lore has it that silk will insulate magic—"

"Gypsy lore too," Robin told her. "I'd like to wrap it up, but we don't have any."

"Allow me," Orlina said, and pulled a silk handkerchief out of her sleeve like a magician. Robin accepted it with gratitude, and quickly shrouded the pendant in its folds. At last the annoying mental whine of the pendant's "music" stopped.

Only one thing Orlina had no trouble believing; that the High Bishop had such a convenient way for disposing of those who caused him trouble.

"I've long suspected something of the sort," Orlina said grimly; there were dark circles under her eyes, and a bruise on one prominent cheekbone but she showed no other outward signs of weariness or damage. Except, of course, for her dress, which was as muddy and brush-torn as Robin's, and her disheveled hair. "He rose to power in the Church with amazing speed, and those who opposed him or were simply in his way found reasons to take themselves away from Gradford." Her lips compressed to a thin, angry line.

"Straight to the Skull Hill Ghost, I would guess," Robin replied. "But the immediate question is, what of you? Have you anywhere you can go?"

"Th-the Abbey isn't s-safe," Kestrel told her, quickly. "Th-the Abbot's in th-this."

"He's probably waiting for a messenger from Gradford to tell him what his share of the loot will be," Gwyna added. "If you go back there, he'll just find another way to be rid of you, and blame it on the Beguilers or the treekies."

Orlina looked down at her hands. "Other than my office of Master Weaver, I have nothing," she said softly; but she did not sound vulnerable, she sounded detached. "Padrik took it all from me, with a few moments of lies and some shoddy magic tricks." She looked up again, and there was fire in her eyes. "I should go back there and confront the dog! I—"

"Do that, and another mob will get you," Robin said firmly. "You haven't a chance against him."

"And you do, I suppose." She lifted one ironic eyebrow.

Kestrel shrugged. "S-some c-contacts. P-people wh-who w-will b-be interested in hearing th-the t-truth."

Orlina looked as if she was about to give them an argument, then looked down at her hands again. They were shaking with the fear she would not show, and this outward sign of her weakness must have convinced her, for she abruptly collapsed in on herself. "I have nowhere to go," she said, a new hesitancy in her voice. "A few relatives that I haven't seen in years, decades—"

"Then go to them," Robin urged. "Petition the King for justice from a position of safety."

"Or m-move t-to another K-Kingdom," Kestrel added, flatly. "If w-we c-can't d-do s-something about the s-situation in G-Gradford s-soon, th-that's wh-what w-we're d-doing. It w-won't b-be safe here for anybody."

Well, that was news to Robin, but it was news she agreed with. *He who flees, lives. Better a live fox than a dead lion.*

"You're still a Master of the Weavers, lady," Robin continued, as another idea occurred to her. "He didn't take *that* away from you, because he can't. Your Guild isn't one of the ones supporting him in Gradford; it should give you shelter that you're entitled to. You *earned* it, by your own work."

Some of her color returned; some of her pride as well. "That's true, young lady," she said after a moment, the fire returning to her hazel eyes. "And the Guild does take care of its own." She sat in thought for a moment. "I think I have enough gold and jewelry on my person to purchase transportation to the nearest Guild Hall." She smiled slyly. "And what that fool doesn't know is that the Master's *pendant* does not identify the Master, at least in our Guild. The ring does, made for the Master's hand."

She held out one of her trembling hands to display a ring, gold, with an inlaid carbuncle featuring the Weaver's shuttle. "Anyone who sees this will know me, and the Guild will protect me."

"Good, we can do that," Robin affirmed, as Jonny nodded.

"I'll t-turn the h-horses," he added. "W-we've a l-long r-road ahead of us."

Fortunately, the lady didn't ask him to elaborate.

◊ ◊ ◊

They left her at the door of a shepherd's home—one which providentially housed a member of her own Guild, as designated by the shuttle burned into the wood of the door. The family welcomed her with sleepy enthusiasm and some hearty curses for anyone who would dare damage a Guild Master.

They left the entire group listening to Orlina's tale, after first making certain that these people had no great love for the Abbot of Carthell Abbey.

"Greedy and grasping, I call it," the weaver said with a snort. "A bargain's one thing, but he cheats with short measures. Got so we make special trips up the road to trade, rather than trade with *him*. And that Padrik was no better when he was at Carthell Abbey."

They offered a good place to camp, and Jonny headed back in the direction they indicated.

"Are you thinking what I think you're thinking?" she asked, after the silence became unbearable.

"S-something h-has t-to be d-done," he said, flatly. "I'll bet th-there's s-something at the Abbey th-that'll t-tell us h-how t-to g-get rid of th-the Gh-ghost."

"Are you planning on breaking into the Abbey?" she asked softly.

He gave her a sideways look. "G-got a b-better idea?"

"Not at the moment." They drove on in silence for a while longer, the horses' weary hoofbeats clopping dully along the dusty road. "The worst that can happen is we can pretend to be looking for holy books. That we've been overcome with a terrible case of religion."

His sudden bark of laughter released the tension in both of them.

"Tomorrow night," she replied. "Not tomorrow during the day. We're both tired, and so are the horses. We can sleep as much as we need to, get rested, and get into the Abbey tomorrow night." She tilted her head toward him, coaxingly. "Hmm?"

For answer, he turned the horses off the road as soon as they reached the camping spot that the weavers had offered; just beyond a small bridge over a stream. The mares were more than glad to stop, and so was Robin.

"N-not afraid of t-treekies?" he teased, as she jumped down to unharness them and get them hobbled for the night.

"Not treekies, nor Beguilers, nor varks," she replied, her hands full of leather straps. "But I *am* afraid of your food, and it's your turn to fix dinner."

"S-so it is." He laughed, and went around to open up the back of the wagon. Presently she smelled lamp oil and bacon. By the time she finished with the horses and came around to the door, he'd warmed the wagon completely, and had hot tea, with sausages wrapped in bacon slices waiting for her.

And something else as well; which left her too weary to ask him anything more about his new plan before she drifted off to sleep.

Jonny had moved the wagon to a point just outside Church lands, and hidden it in a thicket off the road. They were still within easy walking distance of the Abbey—and more importantly, from here they could hear the bells as they rang for the various Holy Services of the day.

"It isn't m-much of a p-plan," Jonny told her the next day, as they waited, rested and fed, for the sun to sink. "B-but I used t-to b-break into Ch-Church b-buildings all the t-time when I w-was on my own. Only p-places they g-guard are th-the T-Treasury and th-the k-kitchen. I w-was l-looking f-for s-safe p-places to s-sleep. N-nobody g-guards the L-Library."

Robin took up the mass of her hair to braid it so that she could bind it around her head, out of the way. She gave him a puzzled look. "The treasury I understand," she replied, "but why the kitchen?"

"B-Brothers are always h-hungry," he told her. "N-novices are always *s-starving.*"

They were both wearing dark breeches, close-fitting sweaters, and soft boots; all clothing they had gotten for Gradford, so all of it a drab charcoal gray. Gray was better than black for hiding in shadows, as Jonny well knew.

They waited after the sun set until the bell for Sixte, the last of the day's Holy Services rang; then they waited another hour or so for the Abbey to settle.

Just before they left, Jonny impulsively picked up the silk-wrapped pendant; he had the feeling it might be useful, although he wasn't certain how.

He recalled noting certain trees beside the Abbey, easy to climb, with boughs overhanging the wall; they were just as easy for the two of them to climb as he had thought. The Abbey itself was dark, with not even the single lantern at the gate alight. That was both inhospitable and unusual; but he reflected, as he inched along the bough he had chosen, that he already knew that Carthell Abbey was both. With luck, they could come and go and never leave a sign that they had been here.

They took their time; no point in hurrying and possibly giving themselves away with an unusual sound, or worse still, a fall. Kestrel straddled the bough he had chosen, lying on his stomach, and pulling himself along with both hands, while both legs remained wrapped around it. If he lost his grip, he would still be held by his legs. Gwyna was behind him; he hoped she had chosen a similarly safe way to cross. Excitement warmed him; now they were finally *doing* something. It felt good, after all this time of simply sitting back and watching things happen.

The bulwark of the wall lay below him—then behind him. If this had been summer, this would have been a bad place to come in, for the soft ground would have betrayed him by holding his footprints. But the ground was rock-hard, and any tracks he left in the frost would be gone with the first morning light.

Bits of bark caught in his sweater, and the bough sank towards the ground. Good! That meant less of a drop.

But now he would have to carefully gauge the strength of the tree-limb he was on. If he went too far, he was in danger of snapping it.

The limb creaked a little as it bent—then it came to rest on the top of the wall. Enough. It wasn't going to get any better than this.

He clung with his hands, and slowly lowered his legs until he was hanging from the limb; then let go, flexing his knees for the fall.

He landed on turned earth; a tumble of frozen clods that made footing uncertain and gave him a bad moment as his ankle started to twist. But he managed to save himself by flailing his arms for balance, and a moment later Gwyna landed beside him.

He tapped her on the shoulder; she followed him to the building, where they crouched in shadow for a moment, listening intently.

Nothing. All was silent.

There were some advantages, he reflected, to trying to break into a building in a place where there were treekies at night. No such place would ever have guard dogs or sentinel geese; the treekies would happily make a meal of them.

This was probably the kitchen garden; the rear door into the kitchen itself would be to his right. But he didn't want that door—for as he had told Gwyna, the kitchen might well have a guard on it. *He* wanted a side door, preferably one that led into a meditation garden.

He went to the left, with Robin following. He left one hand on the wall to guide him and tried to feel how the ground changed under his feet. Here in the kitchen-garden, it would be gravel between the plots and the building; once he reached the meditation gardens, the gravel should give way to grassy lawn.

From time to time his hand encountered the frame of a window; when that happened, he warned Robin, and crouched down below the level of the sill, crawling on hands and knees to get past it. All it would take would be one sleepless Brother staring out at the stars, and seeing a man-shaped shadow pass between him and them, and it would all be over.

Finally, his foot encountered grass; thick, well-tended grass, by the feel of it. In the summer it must be like a plush carpet. Very difficult to achieve and maintain that effect; now he knew what the poor novices here spent their disciplinary time doing.

Praying and weeding; praying the weeds don't come back. He smiled a little, but it was a smile without humor. What need had an Abbey for a lawn like that? He wondered if the surly Brother Pierce was permitted to walk in this garden; such a lawn would make a barefoot "penance" into a sensual pleasure.

Two more windows—then his hand encountered a frame that did not mark a window, but a doorway. Exactly the place he wanted!

The door was unlocked, and swung open at a touch, without the creaking that the kitchen door would likely have emitted. A tiny vigil-lamp burned beside it on the inside wall. He slipped inside, Robin followed, and they closed the door lest a draft give them away.

This doorway gave out on a short hall; they followed it to the end, where it intersected with a much larger hall. He thought for a moment, trying out the pattern of most Abbeys in his mind.

The Library was always next to the Scriptorium, where the manuscripts and books were copied. The Scriptorium needed very *good* light, which generally meant a southern exposure; the Library demanded much less, lest

the manuscripts fade. He thought that the wall they had come in on faced
south—

There were two doors to the left; none to the right. He went left, and
opened the one to the room that had an outside wall.

The smell told him it was the Scriptorium; wet ink and paint drying.
So the room across the hallway should be the Library.

He tried the door; it was locked. He smiled to himself in great satisfaction. He knew from all his other clandestine forays that if the Library was
locked, it would definitely not be not guarded or watched. Locked,
because every Library had *some* "forbidden" work in it that the novices
spent their entire novitiate trying to get at to read. But it would not be
guarded, because, of course, novices would not dare to remove the treasured tome, lest they be caught with it in their possession.

But the locks of Libraries, as he had reason to know, were built to
impress, not for efficiency.

Gwyna might be skilled at picking pockets, but he was a Master of
Library Locks.

It was a matter of heartbeats with the help of a long, slender wire and
a bit of wood. The lock fell open, and the door swung inward.

To his relief, there were more of those tiny vigil-lamps burning here;
they would not have to work blind. As Gwyna closed the door behind
him, softly, he studied the bookshelves, and suddenly realized with dismay
that he had no idea where in all of this to start!

There were *hundreds* of books in here, not the mere two or three
dozen he had expected! Bookshelves filled the room, reaching from floor
to ceiling, and all of the shelves were full. If they were cataloged in any
way, *he* didn't know what it was. The key to all this probably resided in
the Librarian's head—

As he gazed at the wealth of books in an agony of despair, he shoved
his hands down into the pockets of his breeches—and encountered a
small, hard lump wrapped in silk.

The pendant!

In a heartbeat, Talaysen's lessons on the laws of magic flashed into his
mind. *What once was one is always connected. Things that are related
are connected. Things that are similar are connected.*—

It was the second law that he needed to use now. Things that were
related were connected, and under the proper circumstances, they would
attract or resonate with each other. Since the pendant had something to
do with the Ghost, it followed that the pendant could lead him to something else that related to the Ghost.

He hoped.

As Gwyna watched him curiously, he took the pendant out of its silk
wrapping, wincing a little at the discordant "music," and held it in his
hands, tuning his mind to find more of the same "music."

There was music of various sorts all around him; many, many of these
volumes had something to do with magic. Some of it was pleasant; some
absolutely entrancing, the kind he could get lost inside for hours.

But he didn't have hours, and he wasn't looking for anything pleasant.
Then he heard it; a thin, evil trickle that could not by any stretch of

the imagination be called a melody. A discordance of which the pendant was only a small part.

He turned and followed it; it led him to a panel on the back wall, to one side of one of the enormous bookcases. It was a panel like many others in the room, but when he tapped it slightly, he thought it sounded hollow.

The only trouble was, he couldn't open it.

He tried everything he could think of; pressed anything that looked like it might be a release, and all to no avail. Gwyna took her turn at it, but her skill was not in this, and she was no more successful than he was.

He was about to make another attempt, this time at forcing the panel open, when he felt a presence behind him.

He turned; Gwyna whirled at the same instant.

Brother Reymond stared at them in dumb shock, his mouth agape with surprise.

Robin didn't wait to see what he'd do; she muffled his mouth with both hands, as Kestrel grabbed his arms. Together they wrestled him around and stuffed him in a corner.

He looked at her; she looked back at him. "Now what?" she mouthed at him.

He shrugged. "We t-try to convince him," he whispered back, then looked into the frightened eyes of the Brother.

Robin only rolled her eyes skyward, and tightened her hold on Brother Reymond's mouth.

Afterwards, Jonny wasn't certain how long it took him to convince Reymond simply to stay quiet until he had heard them out. It felt like forever, and he was certain that Robin's arms were aching with strain by the time Reymond nodded a frightened agreement.

Things went a little faster, after that. She told him in detail about the Skull Hill Ghost, and the curious exception he had insisted on making to his promise. Then Kestrel told him about Padrik and his Healing Services.

Reymond's eyes grew larger and larger, the more they spoke, but his mouth betrayed, not fear, but dismay. When Robin related her little stay with the Patsonos, his brows drew together in anger—but when Kestrel finally told him about the demon-summoning, and the fate of Orlina Woolwright, he could hardly contain his agitation.

"Dear and gracious God!" he exclaimed in a hoarse whisper when they were done. "I never thought—I didn't want to think—but this explains all those visitors to the Abbot, the ones who seem to be in a trance, and who disappear, never to be seen again! They *all* wear pendants like that one"—he indicated the wrought-iron pendant in Kestrel's hand—"and that alone would convince me that you are telling the truth! But I have learned other things since you were last here. . . ."

"Like what?" Robin asked harshly, as his voice trailed off. He flushed with shame.

"About your Ghost," he said, unhappily. "I have found manuscripts that told me he was bound there by the first Abbot, some fifty years ago or so. I also learned that there are other manuscripts that would tell me more, much more, if only we could find them."

"What do you mean?" Robin asked, her face puzzled. "Are they lost? Were they taken away?"

He shook his head, growing more and more distracted with every word. "No, they were hidden, somewhere in this Library, but I cannot for the life of me find them, and I have been trying—"

Jonny cleared his throat, very delicately, and Brother Reymond started. "C-could they b-be b-behind this p-panel?" he asked, touching the offending bit of wood.

Brother Reymond looked at the panel curiously—then suddenly lost all his color. He reached out with trembling fingers, and did something complicated among the carvings.

The panel swung open. Behind it was a deep recess; in the recess was a bound manuscript.

They all reached for it at the same time, but Brother Reymond's reach was longer and he got it first. He removed it from the recess, hands shaking—but he did not hold it as if it was something precious, but as if it was something vile that he did not wish to contaminate them with.

He took it to a reading stand and lit the lamp from one of the vigil-lights. As the steady flame illuminated his face, he began to read, scanning the contents quickly.

"This is what I was looking for," he whispered. "This is the journal of the first Abbot of Carthell. He was a mage as well as Abbot, but he had been rejected as a Justiciar, and the rejection made him an angry and bitter man. He saw this appointment as an exile—I have read his first journals, and they are full of bile in the guise of piety."

He turned away; Robin moved belatedly to stop him, but he was only relocking the door. "Now we will not be disturbed," he said. "There may be some other restless souls abroad tonight."

He returned to the manuscript and scanned a little further. "Ah, here it is. *I have uncovered a new spell, one that will bind the spirit of a being to a particular place, and make it to do the will of the binder.* There, that's what we were looking for. *I must have a living being for this, for the spell will not work on the dead, not even the newly dead.* Dear and blessed God, he is contemplating murder here! *There are many travelers upon this road who are not human. I mean to use one of those. It would indeed be a grave and mortal sin to kill a human, but these monsters and monstrosities are beyond the Church pale and law, and therefore, it is no murder to do one to death.*"

Reymond was so white that Kestrel feared he might faint at any moment, but his voice was strong enough as he turned the pages.

"Here is the spell itself—no, I shall *not* read it, I had rather burn it! Here he selects his victim—*I have succeeded! My spell has worked beyond the wildest of my dreams! I drugged the creature's food, and carried him out to Bare Hill upon my own donkey; there I wrought the spell which slew and bound him all at once—and the spirit arose a hundred times more powerful and deadly than the monster had been alive!*"

Reymond's eyes flickered across the pages, as his voice filled with agony. "Here he tells how the Ghost he created killed at his command, destroying 'sinners' he sent to it for penance . . . here he tells how it also began to kill anyone who dared to cross its Hill after sundown. Look, here is the list of victims that the Abbot sent—and here the list of those who died 'accidentally'! One of them is the Priest of Westhaven who tried to banish the poor creature! And he says—oh, monstrous! Horrible, horrible—"

Now his voice broke, and he buried his face in his hands for a moment. Kestrel dared to place a hand on his shoulder, trying to offer some sort of wordless comfort. Reymond's shoulders shook, and when he removed his hands, his face was wet with tears.

But his voice was strong again. "This *fiend* wrote here, in his own hand, that he told the Priest only 'some things were better left to the hand of God,' and the Priest ignored his warning. His *warning*! That was no warning—that was not even an attempt at a warning! This man was a monster, a demon in human guise—"

He shook his head, violently. "And to not only leave that abomination in place, but to continue to *use* it! This is *not* the Church I joined; these are *not* the deeds of a good and God-loving man! This man was a monster of the basest sort, and the current Abbot is no better, cloaking his crimes, using what the other created!"

Robin broke the silence that followed his outburst. "Was Padrik educated here?" she asked, quietly.

Reymond nodded. "We thought it a matter of pride, that he should rise to be High Bishop," he whispered brokenly. "And now I find it to be not a cause for pride and rejoicing, but for shame. . . ."

"My people have a proverb, that two bad grapes don't mean all grapes are bad—but two spoiled grapes contaminate the whole bunch," Robin told him. "He and the Abbot together are doing terrible things in Gradford—"

"And if they are not stopped, those terrible things will spread." Reymond's back straightened, and his expression went from horrified to determined. "We must put this right, the three of us," he said, finally, and firmly. "I am not a mage, myself, but I have studied magic in the course of my work for some time. I may be able to free this poor spirit—I must study the binding spell, vile as it is. If there is a physical link, I need only break it to break the binding spell. If the spell can be broken at all, I can do so within the next two days. I can wait here for those who Padrik may send, and free them once they reach the Hill, by taking their pendants as you took Orlina's. And if I can, I will go with further victims to the Justiciars at Kingsford, lay this before them, and ask them to deal with Padrik."

Kestrel silently applauded the man's courage—he *knew* that the Ghost had killed dozens of people, and yet he was willing to dare its anger to free it! And then, not content with that alone, he would go petition the Justiciars as well, a long and uncomfortable journey in the heart of winter. His regard for Reymond rose, and he tried to put his admiration into his eyes, for he knew that his words alone would not convey it, poor and limping as they were. Now, *this* was a man of the Church who could restore his faith in the Church's honor!

"Y-you are a *g-good* man, B-brother R-Reymond," he said, warmly. "As g-good—as the f-first Abbot was evil."

Reymond blushed, and smiled shyly. "Thank you for those kind, but inaccurate words," he said softly. "I don't know if anyone could be good enough to counteract this evil."

"D-don't ever b-believe that, please. E-ever."

Robin had gone into the Scriptorium for pen and paper when Reymond made his declaration; she had been scribbling furiously ever since. Now she blew on the ink to dry it, folded the note, and handed it to Brother Reymond. "Give this to the first Gypsy you see on the road and tell him it *has* to get to a Gypsy named Peregrine, immediately," she told him. "I've left notes in other places for him, but you may be my fastest courier. When he reads it, he'll deal with the Clan that is helping Padrik with his frauds."

Reymond nodded gravely, and put the note carefully inside the pouch hanging on his belt beside the keys to the Library. "And what of you?" he asked, faltering just a little. He clearly wanted to hear them say they intended to *do* something, but he also was obviously afraid that they weren't going to.

Robin smiled, a smile that dazzled the poor man. "We're going to do the obvious," she said, simply, an abrupt turnaround from her earlier attitude that took Kestrel completely by surprise, and left him open-mouthed with amazement. "We're going back to Gradford, to see if we can't expose him as a fraud without getting ourselves thrown in gaol or hung. If you can free the Ghost, that's the least we can do."

Reymond blinked, and well he might. That was a tall task for anyone— "Can you do that?" he asked.

Robin shrugged. "We can try," she replied.

Jonny grinned, with a combination of relief and approval that made him want to cheer. "One th-thing w-we c-can do," he said, "is m-make sure as m-many p-people as p-possible learn P-Padrik is p-playing t-tricks. And w-we c-can p-prove it by s-showing that anyone can d-do them."

"Oh, now that is an excellent idea!" Brother Reymond applauded.

"That's probably one reason why he's forbidden public entertainment," Robin mused. "If some sleight-of-hand artist duplicates one of his 'miracles,' people are going to start wondering out loud." She frowned at that. "It's a pity we couldn't arrange a show."

"H-he m-may have f-forbidden p-public entertainment," Kestrel said slowly, "b-but he *can't* s-stop p-people from d-doing a t-trick or two t-to amuse th-their f-friends in p-public!"

Robin visibly brightened, and snapped her fingers. "Now *there* is an idea! And by the time any Constable gets there, well, the party has broken up and there's no one to arrest! I can think of a *lot* of people who would like to be in on that plan!"

So can I, Jonny thought, remembering Ardana's girls, and wondering if any of the unofficial Houses would welcome a trickster as entertainment instead of a musician. For that matter, a party made up of a few of the young ladies and their favorites could well wander the inns every couple of nights . . . or better yet, every couple of afternoons, so the ladies would not be losing any income.

With all the lovely ladies in such a party, eyes would naturally be drawn to it. And when someone offered to do a trick for the amusement of the group—

Oh, yes, that would work very well indeed. *Very* well.

He was so lost in his own musings that he missed part of what Robin was saying.

"We'll leave at dawn, and we should reach Gradford in a few days," she was saying to Reymond. "I know where we can leave the wagon, so we aren't recognized, coming in a second time."

"And I will do my part as soon as I believe I have mastered the binding spell," Reymond said, solemnly. "That will be two days, at the most. I *will* work this release by daylight; I am not brave enough to face your deadly spirit by night." Then he blinked. "You are braver than I, friends. The only foe I face is one who will likely help me if he can, when he learns my task. You face an entire city."

I wouldn't place any money on the odds of the Ghost helping you, Kestrel thought, and shrugged. "Th-that m-many p-people c-can work against each other," he only observed.

"May it be so," Brother Reymond said, making the words into a bene-diction. "Go with the blessing of God, my friends. I shall see you to the kitchen gate; no one will question *my* walking about so late."

"Thank you, Brother Reymond," Robin said, then grinned. "From a good heart, the blessing of your God is worth a thousand from anyone else—and I have the uneasy feeling we're going to need all the blessings we can get!"

CHAPTER SEVENTEEN

"This place is worse than it was when we left," Robin muttered under her breath, as they waited in line at the city gate for a Constable to get to them. "And I didn't think that was possible."

There was one advantage to returning to a city you knew something about; you also knew where things were, and the best way to disguise yourself as harmless. They had entered this time with a crowd of farm-folk, carrying simple packs. The wagon and horses had been left at the inn, along with most of their possessions. It had been a long time, nearly six months, since Robin had been forced to walk to get where she wanted to go, and she'd forgotten what a luxury it was to ride. . . .

Now her legs and back ached, and so did her arms; the last part of the journey, taking the switchback road up to the gates of Gradford, had nearly done her in.

But the shock of seeing the changes in the city they had left only a few days ago was enough to make her forget her aching legs.

It started at the gates; they were informed as they entered that their packs were going to be searched for unspecified "contraband." Robin suspected that "contraband" included money, and was very glad that she and Kestrel had hidden the horde of coins they had brought with them in the hems of her drab skirts and petticoats. That was where they had hidden the silk-wrapped pendant as well. It was a good thing they had taken that precaution, as it turned out. Even the clothing in their packs underwent an examination; one woman was found to have a pair of breeches in her bag, and was informed that "decent women are to be clothed decently in Gradford." The Guard gave her a long lecture on what a "decent" woman was and was not—and that if she were found "dressing against her sex" she would be thrown in the stocks for it.

The poor woman was in tears before he had finished with her. She was a simple farm-wife, here to see the great High Bishop and visit a sister who had just given birth, and it had never occurred to her that the wearing of breeches to do the heavy chores could possibly be considered "immoral" by anyone's standards.

Well, she wasn't alone; it hadn't occurred to Robin, either. Now she was very glad that she had left her breeches in the wagon. She was even gladder that they had left the wagon—nearby, a simple farm-cart had been stripped down to the bed in a search for "contraband," and she did not even want to think what kind of inspection their wagon would have gone through.

But these Guards were oddly reticent about touching women, although that reticence did not extend to their baggage. They never even laid a finger to her sleeve; they shied away from her as if simple contact might contaminate them.

Fortunately this very prudery concerning women kept them from searching Robin as they did Kestrel; he submitted to the humiliating search with a bored look on his face, and they found nothing more incriminating than a handful of Mintak copper coins, which were confiscated for bearing the images of nonhumans upon them. "Portraits of unbelievers," they were called.

To be fair, they did give him a chit for the supposed "value" of the coins, which could be redeemed at the Cathedral. Which they did not intend to do, for the Guard made it very clear that only those whose piety was in doubt would do such a thing; the rest would consider their lost coins a donation to the Church.

So much for the "honest men of Gradford." Robin wondered how that particular Guard, the one who had refused a gift of a God-Star, was doing now. Did actions like these bother him—or had he been persuaded like the rest of them?

As they waited for the endless questions and inspections to be over, Robin watched the street of the inns beyond this Guardpost. There were Guards and Constables everywhere. One was posted at the entrance to every inn, taking down the names of everyone who came to stay there. The street preachers had real podiums now, erected beneath the street lamps, from which to harangue the passersby.

There were rules now, endless rules. So many they made Robin's head swim, then ache. Things that could not be worn, eaten, drunk, said, or done. And they were informed that there was something called a "curfew," that once the bell had rung from the Cathedral signaling that Sixte was over, they had one hour to get inside. After that, only folk with emergencies or official passes had leave to be on the streets.

Public gatherings were prohibited. Public parties were prohibited. Gathering in an inn for the purpose of "idleness" was forbidden. Only those living in an inn were permitted to eat and drink in the inn. Strong drink was prohibited, as were gambling and music.

Except in that special House that Padrik owns . . .

And women must not be "forward," must always be "modest and unassuming," in word, deed—*and thought.* There were more rules about the proper conduct for a woman; Robin let them all wash over her without really noting them. If she did take note, she knew she would become so enraged she would give herself away.

Forewarned by the lecture to that poor, hapless farm woman, Robin let Jonny do all the talking, which he did in very slow monosyllables, constantly pulling on his forelock, and mumbling "yessir" and "nossir." Their story was as simple as his words. He was "Jon Brede," she was "Jen Brede." They "farmed." Their purpose in coming to Gradford—

"Same as them," Jonny said, nodding at the rest of the group. "Visit the Cathedral."

Not a lie, not at all; only a tiny part of the truth.

There was another new innovation—a little piece of pasteboard with their name, occupation, reason for visit, date of entry, and description written on it.

She and Jonny made no pretense of being able to read or write, and made a pair of marks—a scythe for him, a flower for her—where they were required to sign these "papers." Besides the physical description, Robin's said she was "meek and wifely." Jonny's described him as "simpleton." It was not very difficult to keep her face straight; she was so knotted with tension she could not have smiled if she wanted to.

Probably they would have to present these "papers" anytime anyone demanded to see them. People in authority would know where they stayed, where they ate, what they did.

Had it only been a week since they left? What could have happened in the interim?

They made their way down the street of the inns, but Robin had absolutely no intention of staying here. Not with Guards at every door—and if they were only farmers, there would be questions about where they had gotten the money to stay in a good inn. There couldn't be Guards *everywhere;* that wouldn't be feasible. Only people with good money would come here—poorer folk went elsewhere, and Padrik would have no real interest in poorer folk.

This was where the knowledge gleaned from their previous visit was invaluable. They did *not* have to search for lodging; they knew where to go. "Elsewhere" was all the way across the city, in a section not far from the Warren, a place Robin had noted against future need. Inns there sold sleeping space on the floor of the common room; they would have two or three large chambers above, where people would sleep in rows of cots, and perhaps four or six tiny chambers, hardly larger than closets, for those who wished a little more privacy. Their coins would go a long way in this section of Gradford.

All things considered, though, it was a good thing that their silver all bore the stamp of the King and not of any nonhumans. Otherwise, those coins would go straight to the coffers of the Church. Robin rather doubted that anyone in this town would accept a coin with the nonhuman stamp.

Her stomach was already in knots, and she had the feeling that things were going to get a lot worse.

They had to cross the Cathedral square in order to get there; it appeared that Padrik had decided that business was too good for the small merchants who *had* been setting up there. There were small stalls set up facing the Cathedral, selling the same merchandise as before, but they were all manned by young men in Novices' robes. There was even a stall selling God-Stars, both the pendants and the wall-decorations! But Robin noted that the workmanship was distinctly inferior, and from what she could see, so were the materials. A small victory, and a petty one, but this was the only bright spot so far.

"I guess the licenses weren't enough for him," she said in a low voice, after a quick glance around showed no one close enough to overhear a careful conversation.

"Aye," Kestrel replied sardonically. "L-look at the h-houses, th-though—"

Something about the square had struck her as odd, though she couldn't put a finger on just what was different about it. But once he said *that,* she took a closer look at the fine mansions that faced the Cathedral—

The outsides looked the same as before—but the windows were black and empty. It was getting dark, and there should have been lights in those windows, curtains across them. There was nothing, and there was no sign of life about them. Only bare, blank windows, like the empty eyes of a madman, staring at the Cathedral.

"They're deserted!" she exclaimed, keeping her voice to a surprised whisper.

"My g-guess," Jonny confirmed.

She could only wonder why. Had their wealthy owners decided that what had happened to Orlina could all too easily happen to them and cut down on their households and visibility—or had they decided that Gradford itself was no longer a healthy place for them and gone off elsewhere?

Or had Padrik decided that where Orlina had gone, others could follow? Were the prisons full of other "heretics," waiting to receive their own pendants?

If so, Padrik was going to get a big surprise eventually, when all of them surfaced to testify against him in Kingsford.

Always providing, of course, that the Justiciars at Kingsford did not consider High Bishop Padrik too dangerous a man to cross . . .

Robin was glad to be out of sight of the Cathedral, and away from a place where so many Guards and Constables were patrolling. The far shabbier quarter where they found themselves had fewer figures of authority in it—and even the street preachers were the kind they were familiar with; the disheveled, ill-kempt, near-lunatics. They found the class of inn they were looking for, as full night descended and the lamplighters made their rounds, giving the street preachers light to see and be seen by. It was small, nondescript, with the barrel that signified an "inn" hanging over the door, in a building flanked by a shop and a laundry. Both of those were, for a miracle, still open.

Robin stopped in the shop long enough to buy candles, sausage, cheese and bread, and despite Jonny's obvious nervousness and impatience, went to the laundry as well, for a spirited bargaining session. It was nice to do something as normal as bargain; for a moment she was able to forget her tension, and stop watching over her shoulder for Church Guards. When she came out, she had several old, but clean, blankets folded over her arm, and it was obvious from Jonny's expression that he did not understand why she had bought them.

"If they give us any bedding in here, it's not going to be much, and it'll be full of fleas," she said, very quietly. "This is stuff that was sent to be cleaned but never picked up. We can get clothing that way, too. That's why I wasn't worried when we didn't have much appropriate clothing. We'll be able to buy things that already look worn, not new." His eyebrows rose, and he nodded shortly.

They went in; the common room had a bare earthen floor, pounded hard and covered with rushes, with the only light coming from the fireplace at one end. That fireplace evidently served as the rude "kitchen" as well, since there was a large pot of something hanging over it that smelled strongly of cabbage, and a stack of bowls over the mantle. Furnished with crude trestle-tables and benches that had seen a great deal of hard use, it held two or three dozen people who looked to be the same class of farming folk that Gwyna and Jonny pretended to be. As Robin had expected, there were no Guards at the door here, but the innkeeper perused their "papers," reading slowly and painfully, with his finger under each line and his mouth moving as he spelled out the words. Then he required them to make their "marks" in a book, copying their names beside the marks, before he would rent them their room.

A scrawny boy, summoned from his station beside the fireplace, led them to it. It lay on the third floor, at the top of a steep and rickety stairway, in a narrow corridor with seven other rooms, and was lit with a single lamp. The lamp did not give off much light, which was probably just as well; Robin wasn't certain she wanted to see just how derelict the place was. They were allotted one tiny stump of a candle for light, given to them by the boy, who flung open the door and vanished after shoving the candle end at Kestrel.

The room was barely large enough for the bed; as Robin had expected, it was nothing more than a thin mattress on a wooden platform. Jonny lit the candle stub at the lamp in the hall, and stuck it on top of a smear of waxy drips, on a small shelf by the door. Robin closed the door, and looked around.

In the better light from the candle, it seemed that her worst fears had been groundless; the place was clean. The thin pallet held no fleas or bedbugs. The floor wasn't dirty, just so worn that there wasn't even a hint of wax or varnish, and gray with age and use.

There was one window, large enough to climb out of; that was good, if they ever had to make an unconventional exit. She dropped her pile of blankets on the bed, and opened the shutters—there was, of course, no glass in the window itself. The window overlooked a roof, and a bit of the alley in back of the inn; a rain-gutter ran beside it up to the roof, and the roof of the laundry was just below.

She smiled tautly in satisfaction. Curfew or no curfew, *here* was a way to come and go at night without being seen.

She closed the shutters again, and turned back to Jonny. "It isn't The Singing Bird," she said, apologetically.

"It's also n-not th-the g-gaol, or a d-dry s-spot under a b-bridge," he replied. "And it s-seems c-clean."

"Very true." She bent down for the blankets, but he beat her to them, unfolding them deftly and helping her make up the bed. "We'll have to take everything with us whenever we go out openly," she told him, "or it likely won't be here when we come back."

He turned to pull the latch-string in, barring the door to anyone who wasn't willing to break it down. "I t-take it w-we w-won't b-be d-doing a l-lot of th-that?"

"Probably not." She spread out her purchases on the bed. "The food here is going to be pretty dreadful, that's why I bought all this; since neither of us can afford to be laid up with a flux and cramps, we'd better buy our dinners elsewhere. They tend to buy rather dubious foodstuffs for these places—well, look at the candle, they buy these stubs in lots from the Cathedral and the homes of the rich, who won't burn a candle down to the end. The food'll be like that. There won't be any facilities here other than a privy in the alley. The laundry has a bathing room we can rent." She sliced up bread while Jonny dealt with the cheese and sausage. "One of us should stay in the room when the other leaves officially. That probably ought to be you."

He nodded. "B-between th-this st-stutter and th-the f-fact th-that you m-might n-not b-be s-safe here alone, I th-think you're r-right. J-just d-don't let any P-Patsonos s-spot you."

She winced, but he had a perfect right to remind her of that. *And a few weeks ago—I would have been angry that he had. Now it simply seems practical.* . . . "Right. Well, it looks as if our plans just got thrown right out. We can't take pleasure parties around to the inns doing magic tricks . . . and I'm not sure that any of the Houses are still in operation, except in the Warren itself." She frowned with thought. "I'll have to go in the Warren and start spreading the word about how Padrik actually works his 'miracles.' Maybe the people in there can do something. I'll start with Donnar, and see if there's anywhere I can go from there."

He ate several bites before replying—and as their candle-stub threatened to flicker out, took one of the new candles and lit it from the last flame of the old, pushing the unlit end down into the melted wax from the stub. "I d-don't l-like you g-going in th-there alone. B-but th-there's n-no ch-choice." Then he smiled shyly. "B-besides, you're p-probably more c-competent in there th-than m-me."

She glowed briefly with pleasure at his words, but then sighed, and ate a piece of cheese, pensively. "I only hope we aren't too late to do anything at all."

Donnar was willing to see her, but as she shared a jug and a plate of fried dough-bits with him, he listened to her brief explanation and shook his head.

"Ye're too late," Donnar said, flatly. "There's not a thing ye can do, now."

She glanced around his establishment, which was only half-full. The customers drank with one eye on their liquor, and one on the door. The Guards and Constables had not yet "cleaned up" the Warren, but rumor had it that they were getting ready to do so, and those rumors had every petty thief and freelance whore jumping at shadows. No one had molested Robin in any way on her way in; no one had any time to worry about one small, drab female, when there was so much more threat from other sources.

"What happened?" she asked, feeling desperation creeping into her voice. "Has everyone here gone mad?"

Donnar shook his head. "Ye'd think so," he sighed. "Padrik's got the Mayor an' the whole damn Council in 'is pocket. Couple three days ago, all of a sudden, like, comes all these new rules—an' all these new Guards an' Constables t'enforce 'em, an' the Mayor an' Council just back 'em right up. Padrik must'a been plannin' on this fer a while; most'a these clods ain't from Gradford. I heard they been in trainin' since summer, off on Church land somewheres. But whether that's true—" He shrugged. "I dunno where th' copper came t'hire 'em, but I'd bet it's from Church coffers, an' not the town's."

"So even if I could tell you, not only how Padrik does all his 'miracles,' but *who* showed him how, it wouldn't do any good?" she asked, tension and fear putting an edge to her words. How could this have happened? Never for a moment had she thought that there would be *nothing* they could do!

Donnar stared at her for a moment, then said, slowly, "Evr'one in th' Warren is a lawbreaker; either he started out like that, or th' Church an' th' law forced 'im into it. Who's gonna listen to *us*?"

He had a point, and she stared at her mug, utterly deflated, and all in a single moment. "No one," she replied, dully.

He nodded. "Tha's 'bout the size of it. He's got ev'thing but th' Warren, an' now there's rumors he's gonna take it, too. I dunno if Padrik's really gonna clean up th' Warren or not. Thing is, I kin think 'f one way he could do it, if he didn' give a fat damn what happened t'nobody, an' didn' have th' men t' do th' job."

She stared across the table at him. "How?" she whispered, rather certain that she was not going to care for the answer.

She didn't.

"Burn it down," he replied, succinctly, and a chill left her frozen in her place. "An' thas' why I'm leavin', soon's I can. Tomorrow, mebbe next day, at th' latest. Out through the Back Door, what I tol' you about."

The Back Door was a way out of the city via the sewers. Only the desperate took it, but it did avoid the Guards at the gates, who were stopping not only those going into Gradford, but those trying to leave. If

things had gotten bad enough that Donnar was going to take the Back
Door out, then they were bad indeed.

*And the average citizen is probably pleased with all the new Constables
to guard him and his property—so pleased, he doesn't realize he's been
locked into a prison he can't escape.*

She thanked him, in a daze, and went back out into the street. She still
had a few errands to run; things to buy—

Like a couple of sets of lock picks. She hadn't wanted to bring any into
the city; there was only so much she could fit into the hems of her
clothing. But there was certainly a locksmith here in the Warren, and in
the Warren, he wouldn't be selling just locks, he'd be selling the means
to open them.

It took her a while to find the man she wanted, but for once in Gradford, her sex worked *for* her in convincing him that she was not an agent
of the Guard or Constables. Apparently, no woman would ever be considered by Padrik's people for any important job.

The lock picks were expensive, but some of the finest she had ever
seen—and if it turned out that they *needed* them, they would have been
worth any price.

Those she hid under more prosaic purchases of food and drink—as she
had expected, the food in the inn *was* dreadful, and the beer was worse,
awful beer to start with, now gone flat and stale.

While she walked back to their inn, Donnar's last words kept coming back
to haunt her. He was right. If Padrik didn't care about how much damage was
wrought, or how many people died, that *would* be the easiest, perhaps the only
way, to "cleanse" the Warren. All he had to do would be to set Guards in the
streets to arrest anyone boiling out of the district, then set fire to buildings in a
ring around it. With real mages working with him, the fire could probably
be confined to the Warren and perhaps a few buildings nearby.

Padrik could even have the fire set "accidentally" and the Guards stationed there "coincidentally." Or, for that matter, he could have one of
the mages create that Cathedral-tall angel, and this time, give it a sword
of flame, and make it appear that the Sacrificed God Himself had set the
blaze going.

*And the average citizen would think him a hero, for clearing out all
the "criminals." It won't occur to the people that the same weapon could
be used to threaten his home, his family, if he ever opposes Padrik.*

She shivered inside her shabby, warm coat. Padrik had already proved,
many times over, that he cared for nothing except the path to power. She
could only hope this scheme had not yet occurred to him; that he was
whipping up a state of panic in the Warren by spreading rumors with no
substance behind them.

And meanwhile, now that their best plan for uncovering the High Bishop's fraud had gone awry, she and Jonny would have to think of something else. . . .

There had to be something, some solution. There was *always* something
else that you could do.

Wasn't there?

◊   ◊   ◊

In the next several days, they spent most of their time in their room, trying to think of that "something else." In the meantime, the rumors of the cleansing of the Warren had not yet come true—

But the Cathedral-tall angel put in his appearance, right on schedule.

Neither of them was there to see it, but while the vision had many people who had seen it speaking of it in awe, there were some who were just a trifle less than enthusiastic.

This was the first time that Robin had ever heard Padrik's devotees speak of him and his works with a little less than full enthusiasm and belief. Evidently Padrik had overstepped himself this time, for the angel only called to mind other illusions that these folk had seen, put on for the purposes of spectacle at festivals and other city-wide celebrations.

And when they were asked to describe what it had looked like, they told the tale in just those terms.

"Kinda like that red an' green dragon th' Mayor had conjured up fer the Midwinter Faire ten, fifteen years ago," one grizzled oldster said in answer to Gwyna's questions. "Yah, that's what it was like. Like that big ol' dragon. Ye could see through it, ye know, an' *it* didn' seem t' see anythin'—just smiled an' waved its wings, lazy-like."

Contributions to the hospice-fund were reported to be disappointing, although attendance at the Healing Services remained high. But Gwyna took a little more heart; if people would only start to *think* instead of simply following along like so many sheep—

There was no sign of whether or not Brother Reymond had managed to free the Ghost; but then, there probably wouldn't be. The spirit had no interest in staying around, after all. In all probability, the only interest it had was in getting rid of the men who had kept it bound all this time; the Abbot and Padrik—the former was within reach, but how would the Ghost know how to reach the latter? If Robin had learned anything on Skull Hill that night, it was that the spirit bound there was a great believer in expediency as well as revenge.

By now, he's gone, she thought more than once, but with only a feeling of relief. For even if Padrik was sending poor victims outbound with spell-laden pendants, Reymond was waiting at the other end of the road to free them.

She decided that it was time that the two of them started attending the Healing Services again. Perhaps, if they studied what was going on, they could get some notion of how to disrupt one of the services. Hopefully without getting arrested afterwards—they wouldn't do any good stuck in a cell, after all.

Jonny agreed.

"I'm g-getting t-tired of sitting around h-here, d-doing n-nothing," he told her. "At l-least, if w-we g-go w-watch, w-we'll b-be *t-trying*."

So they tucked all their belongings into their packs, wearing what wouldn't fit, and rolled up the blankets and tied them atop the whole. The Cathedral was not heated—it would have cost more than even the Church had to heat such a huge stone barn in the dead of winter. They would be glad of the extra clothing before the Service was over.

Gwyna put the lock picks where she could get at them quickly, just in case—in a pocket in the side of one of her boots. Jonny slipped the silk-wrapped pendant into his own pocket.

They set off for the Cathedral, joining a growing stream of people who trickled out of the inns and hostels along this street with their belongings on their backs. But they had the advantage of knowing the way, and knowing where to go when they got there; they beat most of the crowd to the Cathedral itself, and wormed their way very near the front, by working along the side wall.

Coincidentally enough, they found themselves in their old places, beneath the benevolent eye of Saint Hypatia. Gwyna took that for a good omen; Jonny had told her that Hypatia was the patron saint of knowledge and of truth-seekers.

Maybe she'd look kindly on their current task.

We can certainly use any blessings we can get, she recalled, uneasily, as she and Jonny took their places on either side of the saint's pedestal. Although they didn't plan on doing anything tonight, she was still nervous and distinctly jumpy. She kept looking out of the corner of her eye at their neighbors. Were there Patsonos who could recognize her nearby? Or Guards that would take exception to the way they acted?

There was a large, draped object on the platform near the altar; very bulky, and covered with a heavy dark cloth. Robin wondered what it was. Some new construction, perhaps? A new pulpit for Padrik to speak from? It was bigger than the old one; perhaps the old one wasn't grand enough anymore.

Finally, after every last bit of space had been filled by an eager observer, Padrik made his usual dramatic appearance from behind the altar, resplendent in his white robes, with an even bigger train of Priests following along behind than he'd had before.

And even though it was *not* appropriate for a Holy Service, the assembled crowd began cheering and applauding as soon as he appeared. They behaved more as if he was some sort of popular entertainer; perhaps, deep down inside, some of them *did* realize that was all he really was. A showman.

A fraud.

He smiled graciously, nodding his thanks—and *long* past the time when he should have tried to quell the outburst, he finally raised his hands for silence.

He got it; the cheers cut off immediately, leaving only the echoes of voices playing among the spires.

"My friends," he said, his beautiful voice making a melody of his words. "My children in God—I can see that there are no doubters among you *this* day!"

Which only proves he's not infallible, Robin thought wryly. *And that he can't read minds, no matter what other magic he's using. Didn't find us, and we're doubters for sure.* That was something of a relief, anyway.

Padrik's smile faded, replaced by an expression of deep sorrow. "I have heard rumors, though—terrible rumors. There are stories in the town that the vision of the Hospice Angel was no vision at all—and that if the angel is an illusion, then so are all the rest of the miracles you have witnessed here. This grieves me deeply, more deeply than I can express."

Robin kept her face stony-still, but she was astonished that he would have brought the subject up at all, much less addressed it so directly.

The crowd began to murmur uneasily, and with the same surprise as Robin. Padrik continued to look out at them, gently, benevolently.

"Oh, do not deny that you have heard those rumors—and perhaps, have been tempted to believe them! But I say unto you, that not only are those tales the basest of lies, but the temptation to believe them was *indeed* a *temptation,* a snare set by dark forces to lead you into disbelief! There are those out there among the unbelievers who only wish to spread dissension and lies, so that the truth will be obscured! There are those who would wish you to think that what is truth is a lie, and lies are truth!" His voice rose, just a little. "And today, I have the means to show you the agent of those rumors!"

He gave no sign that Robin could see, but suddenly the heavy drapery fell away from the construction near the altar—and it was not a new bit of building at all.

It was a cage.

A hanging-cage, to be precise; with a loop on the peak of its domed top, clearly meant to receive a hook. Spaced around the cage were iron loops, where bindings could easily be attached, and manacles and closed-hooks already hung from them.

There was something inside the cage, huddled on the floor. One of the guards prodded it to stand with the butt of his spear, and as it did so, both Gwyna and Jonny stifled gasps of recognition.

It was T'fyrr!

Robin's heart stopped, and Kestrel went completely white. Never in their worst nightmares could they have imagined this!

"This vile creature, this half-demon, was sent to spy upon the godly people of Gradford, and to lead them astray with false tales and rumors," Padrik proclaimed, as T'fyrr pulled himself up to his full height and glared at him through the bars of the cage. His beak had been clamped shut with some iron and leather contraption; he looked half-starved. "He was sent by the evil and decadent Deliambrens, who seek to destroy us and all humankind, to make us into their pets and slaves for their lusts and their amusements—and here is the proof!"

One of the Guards brought out a couple of bewildered-looking rustics, who twisted their hats in their hands, and said, yes, that they had seen this bird-man with a Deliambren. Oh, they knew it was a Deliambren; they'd seen the fellow before, and besides, only a Deliambren would have such a mucking great wagon, with all manner of strange things hung on it. They'd seen the two talking—and then the bird-man had flown off—

Padrik nodded wisely, and cut the last one short. The Priests hustled the puzzled men out, discreetly, as Padrik turned back to his audience.

"So you see!" he called, in stentorian tones. "Those honest toilers of the earth would not lie—nor would they produce such things out of their fantasies. But this creature is not only a half-demon himself, *he* is a mage, a mage of dark and terrible evil and—"

"Look!" cried someone in the audience, pointing at T'fyrr's cage.

A demon appeared in a puff of black smoke, a demon that looked a *great* deal like T'fyrr. It shot a bolt of red lightning at the lock on the cage door, as if trying to free the Haspur—though why it would do so *now*, in full view of hundreds of people, did not make any logical sense. But then, these people were not thinking logically. T'fyrr didn't move, didn't flinch; Robin wondered if perhaps *he* couldn't see the illusion, if it was meant for the eyes of those in the congregation alone.

But the demon only got off the one shot; Padrik whirled in an artistic swirl of white robes that made part of his costume stand away from him for a moment, like a pair of great white wings unfurled. He raised his staff of office over his head, and a beam of light shot from the top of it to strike the demon, who vanished without even a "pop."

The cheapest illusion there is! Done with mirrors, for heaven's sake! You don't even need any magic to pull it off! Only good for a few seconds—the type of illusion that anyone with any experience has seen at a dozen big Faires—but this lot is eating it up!

"You see!" Padrik exclaimed. "You see how he summons his evil minions to aid him! But they are not proof against the power of the Sacrificed God—"

There were shouts now, of "Kill him!" and "Destroy the beast!" Robin went cold with fear. They *had* to get to T'fyrr to free him—but how could they get past a mob in a killing mood?

But Padrik held up his hands, and the crowd calmed instantly. "*We* are not animals, *we* are not monsters, to tear apart our enemies in the heat of anger," he proclaimed, as Robin added nausea to her fear. "The power of God is sufficient to hold this evil, vile creature in his bonds. Nor shall we permit him to disrupt the work we are truly here for, God's own work of healing! We brought him here only that you might see the true face of your enemies, and know them for what they are."

"G-give me one of your p-pick-sets," Kestrel whispered, under cover of the speech. "I th-think I can g-get th-them t-to him."

And then what? she thought—but she handed him the set of lock picks anyway. He slipped off into the crowd, and if she hadn't seen him vanish, she wouldn't have known he was even there in the first place.

While Padrik continued to pummel the congregation with examples of *his* benevolence and the nonhumans' perfidy, she kept a watch on T'fyrr's cage. And in a moment, she "heard" that little thread of "melody" that meant someone was using magic. This was familiar enough—magic meant to rivet the attention to the speaker, and make his words seem the acme of truth. She was ready for it, and she was not caught like the rest. Padrik's sermon had mesmerized his audience to the point that no one, not even the guards, was watching T'fyrr.

And Jonny had taken advantage of that.

He'd taken advantage of something else, too.

There was another thin thread of mental "music," weaving with Padrik's siren song. Free Bard Kestrel was invoking Bardic Magic.

Don't look at me, the song ordered. *Don't see me. I'm not here. Ignore me. . . .*

And since it not only didn't interfere with Padrik's spell, it actually worked *with* the High Bishop's magic, no one noticed it except her.

She added her power to his, humming under her breath, following that "melody" in her mind with a real melody meant to reinforce the magic.

Once again, if she hadn't been watching, she would never have seen that shadow slipping among the statues of the saints, the movement down near the floor as something was tossed into the bottom of the cage, and T'fyrr's quick bend to retrieve what had been thrown in.

As Padrik wound down, Kestrel reappeared on the pedestal of Saint Hypatia, looking as calm as if he had never been gone. But he was breathing carefully, hiding the fact that he had been exerting himself, and he looked very, very tired.

Just about as tired as she felt. He flashed her a quick glance and a hidden gesture of approval; she gave him a strained and nervous smile in return.

Well, now T'fyrr had lock picks, hidden in his feathers. Whether or not he could use them was another story entirely. Whether he would get an opportunity to—

But Padrik's Priests were assembling those in the crowd who felt in need of healing—and with a quick glance and a nod, they both slid down from the pedestal to crowd up a little further to the front.

She bit her lip as her mind accelerated through plan after plan, shuffling bits of foolhardiness with honest fear. Wasn't there something they could do?

Suddenly Jonny grabbed her hand, and whistled a soft phrase of melody—that of "The Skull Hill Ghost."

She stared at him in puzzlement for a moment, completely baffled, as he shook her hand with impatience, and whistled the chorus. Then, as if dawn had suddenly broken over her, she *knew* what he was trying to tell her.

If the Ghost was free—oh, surely it was by now!—it would be only too happy to see Padrik again. And if it was free, well, couldn't they *call* it? They'd called an Elf before, just by thinking about Bardic music and magic and wanting to have an Elf answer them.

How could it hurt to try?

She nodded frantically, and began to hum Rune's tune under her breath, concentrating very, very hard on how *much* she wanted the Ghost of Skull Hill to appear right now—

Faintly, she heard Kestrel do the same. And as his melody joined hers, the internal music that sang of the power of Bardic Magic took on life and strength.

The line to the altar was long, but the two of them were so short that the Priests might have mistaken them for children; somehow they found themselves in the first rank when Padrik began the first "healing." Robin's teeth chattered unexpectedly and the melody she hummed broke for a moment. They hadn't expected to be up *here*—

Oh no—what am I supposed to be sick of? she thought in a panic, T'fyrr momentarily forgotten. *What can I fake? Infertility, maybe*—

Padrik had his hands on the head of a "cripple," one of the Patsonos, of course, who stared up at him in carefully simulated admiration while the High Bishop prayed. And just as Robin decided that infertility was probably a good choice—

Every light in the Cathedral suddenly blew out.

Then the windows darkened abruptly as well, plunging the interior of the Cathedral into thick gloom.

There were screams from outside, as Padrik stopped in mid-sentence, and looked up at the windows, a most unsaintly expression of annoyance on his face.

"What is going—" he began.

But before he could complete his sentence, his final word was obliterated, as a bolt of lightning struck the roof of the Cathedral directly over his head.

The thunder that accompanied it flattened everyone to the floor. Glass shattered and showered the people with tiny slivers and specks; Robin's eyes swam with tears of pain from the burst of light, and she tried to blink away the spots obscuring her vision. Now there were people screaming inside the Cathedral as well as outside, but only the loudest could be heard above the ringing in everyone's ears the thunderclap had caused. The crowd surged towards the exit; she stayed where she was. Trying to move in any direction at all could get them trampled.

Something made her look up, as soon as she was able to see anything at all. The lightning had torn an enormous hole in the roof; she glanced at Padrik, only to see that he was just as surprised as everyone else.

So this isn't *one of his miracles? Is this—could this be the Ghost?*

She hardly had time to do more than frame the thought. In the next heartbeat, a terrible, chilling wind rushed in through the hole in the roof, a wind that chilled the soul as well as the body, and howled like all the nightmares that had ever walked herded together. It formed into a whirlwind in front of the altar, picking up bits of everything from within the Cathedral and sucking them up into itself. The debris began to glow with a spectral, greenish-white light, and the whirlwind spun tighter, faster, forming a column—

Oh dear gods. I've seen this before!

—and then into a manlike shape, a shape that wore a deeply cowled robe, a robe that had never contained anything like a human form.

But this time the shape was five times the height of a man. And the posture of the Ghost of Skull Hill said without any need for words that he was *not* happy.

And that he saw, and recognized, his enemy.

Padrik made a hasty motion, and a ring of fire sprang up around the Ghost, confining it, momentarily at least. Robin couldn't hear anything above the screams, but she saw Padrik's lips moving, and she didn't think he was praying.

So he is *a mage!*

The Ghost looked down at the ring of flames surrounding him, and moved towards them, but the bottom of his robes flared and flickered as he advanced. The barrier held against him. Padrik's expression brightened for a moment—but in the next instant, the Ghost made a gesture of his own, and the whirlwind formed around him.

The wind whipped the flames, and the flames thinned, threatening to die away altogether.

Padrik gestured again, shouting now, words and incantations that Robin didn't understand, but which hummed in the back of her head like a hive of poisonous wasps. The flames rose up again with renewed strength.

The Ghost spun his whirlwind faster still, staring at Padrik across the barrier of fire and wind, his hatred a thing so real and palpable that it, too, was a weapon.

Behind the more dramatic action, T'fyrr worked frantically at the lock of his cage with the lock picks Kestrel had passed him. Robin noticed him—at the same time as the only one of Padrik's guards to remain standing fast.

The guard's mouth opened in a shout that simply could not be heard over the howling of the Ghost's eldritch winds. He ran towards the cage with the keys in his hands—

T'fyrr looked up at the movement, and froze, dropping the picks. Before Robin had blinked twice, the guard had reached the cage—

And had put himself into T'fyrr's reach.

T'fyrr's taloned hand shot through the bars, and grabbed the hapless guard by the throat, plucking the keys from his hand and tossing him aside like a discarded doll.

In a moment, the Haspur had the cage unlocked and kicked open the door. But the guard was not giving up on his responsibilities so lightly.

The guard rose to his feet, drew a sword, and charged the open cage door; the Haspur didn't even pause. His eyes were red with hunger-madness and he was quicker than she would ever have believed. He slashed out with his clawed hands, using them as his weapons, before the man could even bring his blade up to guard position.

He caught the Guard across the throat, tearing it open with a single blow.

Robin turned away, sickened, as blood sprayed across the white altar-cloth, and the man collapsed with a gurgling cry.

There was a thunder of wings, and when she looked again, it was to catch sight of T'fyrr in flight, vanishing up through the hole in the roof, fighting the magic-brought winds. A moment later, and he was gone.

Movement at her side caught her attention, and she glanced back over at Jonny just in time to see him fumble at his belt and drop the pendant he had carried out of his pocket, along with a few coins. It fell out of its silk handkerchief and onto the floor, although there was so much noise that the sound it made hitting the marble was completely lost.

He snatched it up, cocked his arm back, and flung it with all of his might, hitting Padrik square in the chest.

It struck hard enough to distract Padrik, and broke the High Bishop's concentration—and it caught in all the gold embroidery decorating his robe, becoming entangled there. Padrik froze in mid-gesture, staring open-mouthed down at his chest.

The ring of flames vanished, blown out as easily as a candle—

And the Ghost reached forward with a howl of triumph, and seized Padrik in both clawlike hands.

The sound of the Ghost's laughter did not—quite—drown out Padrik's screams.

Blackness as thick as a moonless night descended on the Cathedral, and the crowd went utterly mad. Gwyna and Jonny simply huddled on the floor for a moment, then slowly crawled towards the altar, hoping in that way to avoid being trampled. But before they reached that haven, light returned, pouring through the shattered windows. Padrik was nowhere to be seen.

The screams died, and Robin looked up.

"Witches!" someone cried out in despair. "*That evil creature slew the High Bishop!*"

She saw the face of a nightmare, a crowd ready to tear anything and anyone apart in sheer, unadulterated panic. In a moment, they might very well remember seeing Jonny fling that pendant at the High Bishop—

They'd kill him, and her—and then do exactly what Donnar had feared; run wild through the streets looking for evil mages, killing, and burning. They'd certainly run rampant through the Warren—and if they found T'fyrr, they'd tear him to pieces, too.

They weren't going to listen to *her*—

"You're a man!" she shouted at Kestrel. "They'll listen to you! Say something! *Stop them!*"

Jonny knew the face of the mob when he saw it; he'd already had a taste of what they could do. They were poised to act—and someone had to give them direction, or it would turn into hate, fear, and destruction. Someone had to say or do something before one of them pointed *him* out as the one who'd broken Padrik's defenses and let the Ghost through.

But *him*? He could hardly say two words without stuttering!

Fear held him paralyzed for a moment. Then, in his mind, he heard Harperus. "*You can't say it? So sing it.*"

He did not even waste a moment on consideration; he leapt to the top of the altar, and held up both his hands.

And gathered, reached, desperately, for the melody he needed. For the Magic . . .

"*Stop!*" he cried/sang, his voice ringing out like a trumpet.

The mob obeyed.

People froze in place, staring at him, mouths agape with astonishment.

Words poured from him as if from some supernatural source; he told them everything, as their faces gazed up at him, expressions dumbfounded. How Padrik was a fraud, working his "miracles" with the help of criminals. How he had truly used their donations—the House he ran, the luxuries he enjoyed. And before anyone could challenge him, he signaled to Robin, who began to reproduce some of those "miracles."

She started with bursts of flash powder, and then "magical appearances" of the altar-decorations by sleight of hand. She worked her way around the altar and made a couple of quick movements; Kestrel heard a muffled thump. She then found the mirror-rig, and used it to reproduce the "demon"—a puppet hanging slackly among the sculptures of angels up above the altar, out of sight of the congregation.

He told how Padrik had bound the spirit of a poor nonhuman, murdered by an evil Abbot of Carthell, to become the High Bishop's own personal executioner.

He stretched the truth a little, describing Reymond as a "holy mage of the Church," who had discovered this and had freed the Ghost, sending it to take its own revenge on Padrik.

He poured his heart into his words, falling into the same kind of trance he invoked when playing his music. Behind his words, he heard another strand of melody, as Robin wove her magics in with his. She was singing an accompaniment to his rhapsody, steadying his lips, giving him strength beyond his own. As if the words came from someone else, he heard himself eloquently describing how Padrik had taken over all the trade in the Cathedral market—how Padrik confiscated the goods of those he sent off to be slain by the Ghost—how he had been collecting more and more money, and doing less and less for the poor, the sick, those to whom it was supposed to go.

Somewhere in the back of his mind, part of him gave an astonished cheer as the crowd began to pay more and more attention to him—and as their mood, staring at Padrik's chosen Priests, turned uglier and uglier.

"Go!" he heard himself urge, as his voice rang out in a triumphal call-to-arms. "Go and look in his quarters! See what luxuries he has hidden there! See the place where those vagabonds he consorted with are living, how they eat from silver and drink from crystal! These things were bought with your money, and with blood-money! He has been living off of you and off the stolen goods of the innocents he has sent to their deaths, and all falsely in the name of God!"

A long silence filled the Cathedral for a moment.

It was broken by a single whisper of sound; the rustle of robes as one of the Priests tried to edge his way out of the Cathedral, ducking behind the statue of Saint Tolemy—

"They're running away! Get them!" someone shouted.

The false Priests broke and ran, holding up the skirts of their robes in order to run faster, fleeing into the Church buildings behind the Cathedral.

Robin plastered herself up against the altar as the mob flooded past her, storming after the fleeing Priests, brushing aside the guards. Kestrel just watched them go, sinking wearily to the surface of the altar. Padrik's quarters were in there, somewhere, and he had no doubt that they were as luxurious as he had described. The mob was going to have something to vent its rage on, after all.

When they had all gone, their shouts fading as they passed into other parts of the complex, he looked over at Robin and held out his hand. She smiled, exhausted, walked over to him, and took it.

Sunlight poured down through the hole in the roof to pool around the altar. Kestrel saw that there was someone lying behind the pulpit, quite unconscious, next to an obviously broken and jammed trapdoor. The back, and the clothing of the figure seemed oddly familiar.

Robin grinned, and turned the body over.

"Who is it?" he asked.

She straightened. "The Clan Chief of the Patsonos," she replied, her voice filled with glee. "Come give me a hand with him—"

She had grabbed one arm and tugged him, none-too-gently, across the marble floor.

"Why?" he asked, taking the other arm, and blinking in bafflement. "What do you want to do with him?"

They hauled the Gypsy up the altar stairs, as she panted out her answer. "Someone—ought to be here—to answer questions," she said, her voice and face brimming with malicious enjoyment. "And we have—a nice big cage here—to make sure *he* is the one to answer them."

"And not us," Kestrel supplied, in complete understanding and agreement. "Good idea!"

They locked the Gypsy in the cage that had held T'fyrr, first making sure that the Haspur had not left his lock picks behind, that the Patsono Chief did not have a set of picks on his person, and—with a judicious thump on the head with the pommel of Kestrel's dagger—that he would probably not wake up until after there was someone here to deal with him.

"That should do it!" Robin said, as they slammed the door shut on him. "Prey for Peregrine." She looked around the ruined Cathedral, thoughtfully.

"You know, things are going to get very interesting here for a while," she said, nibbling her lower lip. "And they just might be looking for more people to blame. . . ."

"I've always wanted to see Trevandia," Kestrel declared, even though he had no such longing until just that moment. But Trevandia was the farthest place *he* knew of from Gradford that still had welcomed Gypsies and Free Bards.

"Why, so have I!" Robin exclaimed. "You know, another kingdom seems like a very good place to be right now!"

They looked at each other for a long moment—then broke into only *slightly* hysterical laughter.

"Trevandia it is!" Kestrel said, when they could catch their breath. "As soon as we get the wagon."

There was a growling sound in the distance—growing nearer. It was that of an angry crowd returning.

"How about now?" Robin asked, innocently.

He did not bother to reply; only seized her hand. Together they ran out into the square, and did not stop running until they were past the gates of Gradford—and they did not once look back.

Book III
~The~
Eagle and
the Nightingales

Dedicated to
Gail Gallano,
Mother of all Tulsa wildlife rehabbers!

CHAPTER ONE

All the world comes to Kingsford Faire, the Midsummer Faire of Kings. . . .

A Gypsy known only as Nightingale sat on a riverside rock on the edge of the Faire grounds, with the tune of "Faire of the Kings" running through her head. Not that she liked that particular piece of doggerel, but it did have one of those annoying tunes that would stick in one's mind for hours or days.

A light mist hung over the Kanar River, and a meadowlark nearby added his song to the growing chorus of birds singing from every tree and bush along the riverbank. The morning air was still, cool, and smelled of river water with a faint addition of smoke. Sunlight touched the pounded earth that lately had held a small city made of tents and temporary booths, then gilded the gray stone of the Cathedral and Cloister walls behind the area that had been home to the Kingsford Faire for the past several weeks. Nightingale didn't particularly admire the fortress-like cloister, but examining it was better than looking across the river. She kept her eyes purposefully averted from the ruins of Kingsford on the opposite bank, although she was still painfully aware of the devastation that ended only where the river itself began. There was no avoiding the fact that Kingsford, as she had known it, was no more. That inescapable fact had lent a heaviness to her heart that was equally inescapable.

This had been a peculiar year for the annual Kingsford Faire, with something like half of the city of Kingsford itself in ruins and the rest heavily damaged by fire.

I am glad that I was not here, but the suffering lingers.

Perhaps other people could forget the suffering of those who had been robbed of homes, livings and loved ones by that fire, but Nightingale couldn't, not even with the wooden palisade surrounding the Faire and row after row of tents between her and the wreckage on the other side of the river. The pain called out to her, even in the midst of each brightly dawning midsummer day; it had permeated everything she did since she had arrived and crept into her dreams at night. She would never have used the Sight here, even if she had needed to—she knew she would only see far too many unquiet ghosts, with no means at her disposal to settle them.

She had dreams of the fire that had swept through the city last fall, although she had no way of knowing if her dreams were a true vision of the past or only nightmares reflective of the stories she heard. She'd had one last night, in fact, a dream of waking to find herself surrounded by flames that reached for her with a lifelike hunger.

Such a complete disaster as the fire could not be erased over the course of weeks or months. Even now, with the fire a year past, there were blackened chimneys and beams standing starkly in the midst of ashes, and a taint of smoke still hung in the air.

The Faire *had* been profitable for just about everyone who came this year, herself included. Knowing that the folk of Kingsford would be needing every possible article of daily living, even so many months after the fire, merchants had flocked to the Faire-site across the river with their wagons piled high, their pack-beasts loaded to the groaning point. They had prospered, and they had been generous to those who came to entertain. The Bardic Guild, bane and scourge of the Free Bards for as long as that loosely organized group had existed, had been remarkable for its reticence during the Faire.

Her polite encounters with Guild Bards had been odd enough that they still stuck in her mind. Time after time, she had gotten a distant nod of acknowledgement from Bard and Guild hireling alike, and not the harassment and insults of previous years. *One might had thought that the Guild did not particularly want attention drawn to it,* she mused. The Guild simply held its auditions and performances quietly and gave no opposition to anything that the Free Bards did. There were rumors, never verified, that the Bardic Guild had a hand in the burning of Kingsford, and that the Church, in the person of a Justiciar Mage and Priest called Ardis, as a consequence had its eye on them. Nightingale discarded both rumors; there was no reason to believe the former, and the Church and the Guild had always operated hand-in-glove in the past and it was unlikely that situation would change any time in the future. Never mind that Ardis was reputedly the cousin of the head of the Free Bards, Talaysen, also called Master Wren; there was only so much a single Priest could do. And one could not change attitudes by fiat.

The meadowlark flitted off, his yellow breast with the black "V" at his throat vivid in the morning sun. *Well, I endured; nightmares, sorrow hanging like a heavy mist over the Faire, and all. It will take more than old sorrows and nightmares to keep me from my music.* Nightingale had suffered too many lean seasons in her short life to allow personal discomfort to get in the way of her performances. She was, after all, a professional, however much the poseurs of the Guild might deny that. So she, too, had passed a profitable term at the Faire, and now at the close of it found herself prosperous enough to afford a donkey to carry her burdens for her for the first time in her life as a musician. Heretofore when she traveled she had been forced to rely on the kindness of fellow Free Bards or Gypsies, who would grant her a corner of their wagons to stow her goods in. And while the company was welcome, this arrangement forced her to depend on others, and constrained her to whatever itinerary they chose and not one of her own choosing. When given the option, she preferred to avoid cities, towns, even larger villages altogether. Unfortunately, such destinations were usually where her traveling companions preferred to go.

She closed her eyes and pressed her hands against her temples for a moment; not because she had a headache, but to remind herself to stay

calm and bulwarked against the outside world. She could not help but
wish she had chosen not to come to the Faire this year, but to stay in
one of the lands held by those who were not human, or even pass a
season or two in the halls of an Elven king, perilous as that was for
mortals. The Faire had posed a trial for her ability to keep herself isolated
from her own kind, and more than once she had been tempted to give
over her ambitions for a wider reputation as a musician and simply walk
away.

But all that was in the past now; there was a sweet-tempered little
donkey tethered beside her, his panniers loaded with her gear and her
two harps strapped over the top of it all. She had a tent as well, if a small
one, and with the donkey she could carry provisions to see her through
to better lodgings instead of being at the mercy of greedy or stingy
innkeepers.

She was all packed up and ready to go, and eager to be on the road
and away from the all-pervasive aura of tragedy that hovered over the city
across the river. Only one thing kept her here, an appointment that she
had made last night, and she wished *he* would just show up so that—

"Thank you for waiting, my friend." Talaysen's speaking voice was as
pleasant as his singing voice, and Nightingale gratefully turned her back
to the river and the Church's stronghold to catch his hands in hers in the
traditional greeting between Gypsies of the same clan. Talaysen smiled at
her, his gray-green eyes warming, and gave her hands a firm squeeze
before releasing them. Free Bard Talaysen looked prosperous, too, in his
fine leather jerkin, good linen trews, and silk shirt with the knots of many-
colored ribbons on the sleeves that denoted a Free Bard. *He* did not owe
his prosperity to the Faire, however. Talaysen shared the post of Laurel
Bard to the King of Birnam with his wife, Bard Rune, and his clothing
reflected his importance. They were the only Free Bards with any kind
of position in all of the Twenty Kingdoms.

Not that he has ever let rank go to his head, Nightingale reflected,
allowing his pleasure at seeing her to ease the distant ache of Kingsford's
sorrow within her. *He has made Birnam a haven of freedom for all of us.*

"I would wait until the snow fell for your sake, Master Wren," she told
him truthfully, scanning his honest, triangular face for signs of stress and
his red hair for more strands of gray than there had been the last time
she saw him. She saw neither, and felt nothing untoward from him, which
eased her worries a little. He had been so adamant in asking her not to
leave after the Faire closed—at least until he had a chance to speak
with her—that she had been afraid there was something wrong with him
personally. They were old friends, though only once, briefly, had they ever
been lovers.

"Well, it is lucky for us both that you won't have to do that," he replied,
and his eye fell on her little donkey. "So, the rumors of your prosperity
were not exaggerated! Congratulations!"

She raised her eyebrow at that, for there was something more in his
voice than simple pleasure in her good fortune. There was some reason
why he was particularly pleased that she had done well, a reason that

had nothing to do with friendship or his unofficial rank as head of the Free Bards.

"This simplifies matters," he continued. "I have a request to make of you, but it would have been difficult if you had already arranged to travel with anyone else this winter."

A blackbird winged by, trilling to find them standing in his territory, so near to his nest. Her other eyebrow rose. "A request?" she said cautiously, a certain sense of foreboding coming to her. "Of what nature?"

Wren can charm birds out of the trees and honesty out of Elves, and I'd better remember that if he's asking favors of me. It was mortally hard to refuse Wren anything.

But I can hold my own with the Elves; it will take more than charm to win me.

Talaysen sighed, and shifted his weight from one foot to the other, like a naughty little boy who had been caught in the midst of a prank—which further hardened her suspicions. "There is something I would like for you to do for me—or rather, not for me, but for the Free Bards. Unfortunately, it will involve a rather longer journey than you normally make; I expect it will take you from now until the first Harvest Faires to reach your goal even if you travel without stopping on the way."

She pulled in a quick breath with surprise. "From now until Harvest Faire?" she repeated, incredulously. "Where in the world do you want me to go? Lyonarie?"

She had thrown out the name of the High King's capital quite by accident, it being the farthest place from here that *she* could think of, but the widening of his eyes showed her that her arrow had hit the mark out of all expectation.

A pocket of sudden stillness held them both, and it seemed to her that the air grew faintly colder around her.

"You want me to go to *Lyonarie?*" she asked, incredulously. "But—why? What possible business have the Free Bards there? And of all people, why me? I am no Court Bard, I know nothing of Lyonarie, and—"

And I hate cities, you know *that,* she thought, numbly. *And you know why!*

"Because we need information, not rumor. Because of all people, you are the one I know that is most likely to learn what we need to know without getting yourself into trouble over it—or inflaming half the city." He nodded at the ruins of Kingsford behind her, and she winced; there were also rumors that enemies of the Free Bards had set that fire and that it had gotten out of hand. "You're clever, you're discreet, and we both know that you are a master of Bardic and—other magics."

"Perhaps not a master," she demurred, "and my talents are as much a hazard as a benefit—" But he wasn't about to be deflected.

"I know I can trust you, and that I can trust you to be sensible," he continued. "Those are traits this task will need as much as mastery of magic."

"Which is why you are not entrusting this to Peregrine?" she asked. "You could trust him, but he is not always sensible, especially when he sees an injustice."

"He does not do well in cities, any more than you do," Talaysen pointed out. "And he won't abide in them unless he must under direct threat to himself or his clan."

And because I have a large sense of duty, I will endure them if I must, she thought with misgiving. *I had better have a very good reason—other than that Wren wants me to, however.*

"What could possibly be so pressing as to send me across half the Twenty Kingdoms?" she replied, favoring him with a frown. "And there, of all places. Peregrine may not like cities, but neither do I, and I have better reason than he to avoid them." Her frown deepened. "I'm not minded to risk another witch-hunt because I seem to know a little too much for someone's comfort—or just because I am a Gypsy."

"Not in Lyonarie—" he began, but she interrupted him.

"So you *say*, but no one had word of what was chancing in Gradford until Robin stirred the nest and the wasps cam flying out to sting," she retorted. Talaysen did not wince this time; instead he looked ever more determined. "And I ask again, what is so pressing as to send me there?"

Now Talaysen's changeable eyes grew troubled, and the signs of stress that had not been there before appeared, faintly etched into his brow and the corners of his generous mouth. "King Rolend is concerned, and as Laurel Bard and leader of the Free Bards he often asks me for *my* opinion. High King Theovere has been—neglectful."

Now Nightingale snorted. "This is hardly news; his neglect has been growing since before Lady Lark joined us. And so just what is that I am supposed to do? March up to the High King and charge him with neglecting his duty?"

Talaysen smiled, faintly. "Scarcely, though I suspect *you* could and would do just that if it suited you. No, what Rolend and I both want is the reason why Theovere has become this way. He wasn't always like this—he *was* a very good ruler and kept the power neatly balanced among the Twenty Kings, the Guilds and the Church. He's mature, but not all *that* old, and there has been no suggestion that he has become senile, and he hasn't been ill—and besides, his father lived thirty years more than he has already, and *he* was vigorous and alert to the last."

She shook her head, though, rather than agreeing to take on Talaysen's little wild-goose hunt with no more prompting than that. "I won't promise," she said, as the dim sense of foreboding only increased with Talaysen's explanations. "I will think about it, but I won't promise. All I *will* say is that I will take my travels in the direction of Lyonarie." As Master Wren's face reflected his disappointment, she hardened her heart. "I won't promise because I have no way of knowing if I can actually reach Lyonarie," she pointed out. "I'm afoot, remember? You and Rune came here in a fine wagon with a pair of horses to pull you and the baby—travel is harder when you walk, not ride. *You* ought to remember that. A hundred things could delay me, and I won't promise what I am not sure I can deliver."

"But if you reach Lyonarie?" Talaysen persisted, and she wondered at his insistence. Surely he—and the King of Birnam—had more and better sources of information than one lone Gypsy!

"If I decide to go that far and if I reach Lyonarie any time before the next Kingsford Faire, I will reconsider," she said at last. "I will see what I can do. More, I won't promise."

He wasn't satisfied, but he accepted that, she saw it in his face.

"You still haven't answered the other question," she continued, suspiciously. "Why choose me?"

His answer was not one calculated to quell her growing unease, nor warm the prickle of chill prescience that threaded her back.

"Much as I hate to admit this," said Talaysen, wielder of Bardic Magics and friend to the High King of the Elves, "I was warned that this situation was more hazardous than we knew, and told to send you and only you, in a dream."

Three weeks from the day she had left Talaysen beside the river, Nightingale guided her little donkey in among the sheltering branches of a black pine as twilight thickened and the crickets and frogs of early evening started up their songs. Black pines were often called "shelter-pines," for their trunks were bare to a height of many feet, and their huge, heavy branches bent down to touch the ground around them like the sides of a tent. The ground beneath those branches was bare except for a thick carpet of dead needles. Nightingale held a heavy, resin-scented branch aside with one hand, while she led the donkey beneath it; her hair was wet, for she had bathed in a stream earlier that afternoon, and the still, cool darkness beneath the branches made her shiver.

It wasn't just the cool air or the dark that made her shiver. Not all the warm sunlight on the road nor the cheerful greetings of her fellow travelers had been able to ease the chill Talaysen's words had placed within her heart.

He was warned to send me to Lyonarie in a dream, she thought, for the hundredth time that day, as she unloaded her donkey and placed the panniers and wrapped bundles on the ground beside him. *What kind of dream—and who else was in it? Wren can be the most maddening person in the world when it comes to magic—he hates to use it. and he hates to rely on it, and most of all he is the last person to ever depend on a dream to set a course for him. So why does he suddenly choose to follow the dictates of a dream now?*

There had been a great deal that Talaysen had not told her, she *knew* that, as well as she knew the fingerings of her harp or the lies of a faithless lover, but he had simply shut his secrets inside himself when she tried to ask him more. Perhaps if she had agreed to his scheme, he might have told her—or perhaps not. Talaysen was good at keeping his own counsel.

She went outside the barren circle of needle-strewn ground within the arms of the black pine and found a patch of long, sweet grass to pull up for the donkey. She hadn't named him yet; Talaysen had driven all thoughts of such trivial matters out of her head.

Infuriating man. She hadn't even been able to enjoy the feeling of freedom that picking and choosing her own road had given her.

Once the donkey had been fed and hobbled, she made a sketchy camp in the gloom of dusk with the economy of someone who has performed such tasks too many times to count. She scraped dead, dry needles away from a patch of bare earth, laid a tiny fire ready to light, rigged a tripod out of green branches over it, and hung her small kettle full of the sweet water she had drawn at the last stream from the apex of the tripod. She took the tent and her bedding out of one of the panniers and dropped them both nearest to the trunk of the tree. Then she lit the fire and laid her bedding out atop the still-folded tent. Her weather-sense gave her no hint of a storm tonight, so there was no point in putting the tent up, and screen mesh was not needed since this wasn't the territory for blood-suckers. She preferred to sleep out under the open sky when she could; she would sprinkle certain herbs over the smoldering remains of her fire to keep biting insects away as she slept. Sometimes the touch of the moon gave her dreams of her own, and it would be useful for one such to come to her tonight.

The water in the kettle was soon boiling, and she poured half of it over tea leaves in her mug. She threw a handful of meal and dried berries into what remained; porridge was a perfectly good dinner, and she had feasted every night of the Faire. It would do her no harm to dine frugally tonight, and there were honey-cakes to break her fast on in the morning, an indulgence she had not been able to resist when she passed through the last village this afternoon.

The moon rose, serene as always. Its silver light filtered through the branches of the tree she sheltered beneath. The donkey dozed, standing hip-shot with his head hanging, the firelight flickering over him but not waking him. Somewhere in the further distance, an owl called.

Nightingale strained her ears for the notes of her namesake bird, but there was no sweet, sad song wafting on the warm air tonight. It was the wrong season for a nightingale to be singing, but she never drifted off to sleep without listening for one, no matter where she was or what time of year it might be. Nearby crickets sang cheerfully enough that she didn't miss the absence of that song too much.

Although it was very lonely out here. . . .

Abruptly, a whistle joined the cricket chorus, and Nightingale sat bolt upright on her sleeping-pad. That was no night-bird song, that was the first few bars of "Lonely Road"! There was someone out there—someone near enough to see the light of her tiny fire, even through the masking branches!

"Might a friend come in to your fire, Bird of the Night?" asked a voice out of the darkness. It was a clear voice, a silvery tenor, a voice of a *kind* that a trained musician would recognize, although she did not recognize who the speaker was. It held that peculiar lack of passion that only Elves projected.

An Elf? First Master Wren, and now one of the Elvenkin? The chill that had threaded Nightingale's spine since her meeting with Master Wren deepened.

Elves did not often call themselves the "friend" of a mortal, not even a Gypsy. Though Nightingale could boast of such a distinction if she cared to, she was very far from the hills and halls of those few of the Elvenkin who normally called her "friend."

"Any friend is welcome to share my fire," she replied cautiously. "But an unfriend in the guise of a friend—"

"—should be aware that the fierce Horned Owl is as much a bird of the night as the Nightingale," the voice replied, with a hollow chuckle. "Your reputation as a hunter in the dark also precedes you." The branches parted, with no hand to part them, as if servants held two halves of a curtain apart, and the speaker stepped through them as into a hall of state.

It was, quite unmistakably, one of the Elven lords, though the circlet of silver he wore betokened him a lord only, and of no higher estate than that. Amber cat-eyes regarded her with a remote amusement from beneath a pair of upswept brows; the unadorned circlet confined hair as golden as the true metal, cut to fall precisely just below his shoulders. His thin face, pale as marble, was as lovely as a statue carved of marble and quite as expressionless. Prominent cheekbones, tapering chin, and thin lips all combined to enhance the impression of "not-human." The tips of his pointed ears, peeking through the liquid fall of his hair, only reinforced that impression.

He was ill-dressed for walking through a forest in the dead of night, though that never seemed to bother the Elvenkin much. He wore black, from his collar to the tips of his soft leather boots, black velvet with a pattern of silver spiderwebs, velvet as soft as a caress and fragile as the wings of a moth. Nightingale had worn cloth like that herself, when she spent time beneath the Hills.

"Call me a friend of a friend, Bird of the Night," the Elven lord continued, as the branches closed behind him without even snagging so much as a sleeve. Nightingale sighed; the Elves always made such a performance out of the simplest of things—but that was their nature. "And in token of this, I have been asked to gift you with another such as the gift you already bear, the maker of which sends his greetings—"

He held out his hand, and in it was a bracelet, a slender ring of silver hardly thicker than a thread.

It had a liquid sheen that no other such metal had—it was the true Elven-forged silver, silver that no mortal could duplicate, more valuable than gold.

She opened herself cautiously, and "touched" it with a purely mental hand. She *did* know that bracelet; she wore its twin on her right wrist. The maker could be trusted, insofar as any Elf could be trusted. She relaxed, just a trifle.

"In the name of friendship, then, I accept the gift and welcome the bearer," she replied, holding out her hand. The Elf dropped the silver bracelet into her open palm without a word; the bracelet *writhed* in a strange, half-alive fashion and slipped across her palm and ringed itself onto her hand, then moved over her hand and onto her wrist, joining to the one already there. As it did so, she heard a strange, wild melody— but only in her mind. This was the music of Magic, true Magic, the magic that the Gypsies, the Elves, and some few—very few—of the Free Bards shared.

If she had not already had this experience with the quasi-life of Elven silver more than once, she would probably have been petrified with fear—

but that first bracelet had been set on her wrist when she was scarcely more than a child, and too inexperienced to be frightened. She had not known then that Elves could be as cruel as they were beautiful and that very few of them were worthy of trust by human standards.

For a moment, a fleeting moment, she felt very tired, very much alone, and a little frightened.

When she pulled her hand back to examine her wrist, she could not tell where the first bracelet began and the second ended—only that the circle of silver on her wrist was now twice as wide as it had been. She did not try to remove it; she knew from past experience that it would not come off unless she sang it off.

The Elven lord dropped bonelessly and gracefully down on the other side of her fire, and caught her eyes in his amber gaze. "I come with a message, as well as a gift," he said abruptly, with that lack of inflection that gave her no clue to his intentions. "The message is this: *The High King of the mortals serves his people ill. The High King of those who dwell beneath the Hills would know the reason why, for when mortals are restless, the Hill-folk often suffer. If Nightingale can sing and learn, her friends would be grateful.*"

The chill spread to Nightingale's heart, and she shivered involuntarily at this echo of Master Wren's words.

First Talaysen speaking for one king, now an Elven messenger speaking for another—This was so unreal that if someone had written it as a story-song she would have laughed at it as being too ridiculous to be believed. *Why is this happening to me?*

"Is there no further word from my friend?" she asked, hoping for some kind of explanation.

But the Elf shook his head, his hair rippling with the movement. "No further word, only the message. Have you an answer?"

It wasn't a wise thing to anger the Elves; while their magic was strongest in their Hills, they could still reach out of their strongholds from time to time with powerful effect. Songs had been made about those times, and few of them had happy endings.

"I—I don't know," she said, finally, as silence grew between them, punctuated by the chirps of crickets. Firelight flickered on his face to be caught and held in those eyes. "I am not certain I *can* send him an answer. I am only one poor, limited mortal—"

But the Elven lord smiled thinly. "You are more than you think, mortal. You have the gift of making friends in strange places. This is why the High King asks this question of you, why the runestones spelled out your name when he asked them why the mortals grew more troublesome with every passing month, and who could remedy the wrongness."

Nightingale grew colder still. The Elves lived outside time as humans knew it, and as a consequence had a greater insight into past and future than humans did. Elven runestones where the medium through which they sought answers, and if the runestones really *had* named her—

But I have only his word for that, and the word of the one who sent him. Elves lie as readily as they speak the truth; it is in their nature.

"I will do what I can," she said finally, giving him a little more of a promise than she had given Talaysen. "I cannot pledge what is not in my power to give. The seat of the High King of the mortals is far from here, and I am alone and afoot."

She waited for his response, acutely aware of every breath of breeze, every rustling leaf, every cricket chirp. He *could* choose to take offense; that Elves were unpredictable was a truism.

The Elven messenger regarded her with one winglike eyebrow raised for a moment, then grudgingly acknowledged that she had a point. She breathed a little easier.

"I will take him your answer," he said as he rose fluidly to his feet. Before she had blinked twice, the branches of the tree she sheltered beneath had parted once again, and he was gone.

There was nothing else to do then but finish her porridge, strip off her leather bodice and skirt, and lie down in her bedding. But although she was weary, she stared up into the interlacing branches overhead, listening to the crickets and the breeze in the boughs, tense as an ill-strung harp. This was two: Wren and the Elves. Gypsy lore held that when something came in a repetition of three, it was magical, a geas, meant to bind a person to an unanticipated fate.

Whether or not that person wanted it.

It was a long time before she was able to sleep.

She made better time than she had thought she would; she had assumed she would be walking at the same pace unburdened as carrying her own packs, but she found that she could make a mile or two more every day than she had anticipated, with no difficulty whatsoever. She reached the crossroads and the small town of Highlevee three days sooner than she had expected to—

Which only increased the tension she felt. If she went south or north, she would be traveling out of the Kingdom of Rayden and away from the road that would take her to Lyonarie. If, however, she traveled eastward, she would soon strike the King's Highway, which led to Lyonarie, and there would be no turning back. She'd hoped to have more time to think the problem through.

Though the height of summer was past, the heat had not abated in the least. The sun burned down on her with a power she felt even through her wide-brimmed, pale straw hat; dust hung in the air as a haze, undisturbed by even a hint of breeze. The grasses of the verge were burned brown and lifeless, and would remain that way until the rains of autumn. She had kilted up her skirts to her knees and pushed her sleeves up over her elbows for coolness, but she still felt the heat as heavy as a pack of weights on her back.

Summer would linger in Lyonarie, long past the time when it would be gone here—or so she had heard. At the moment, that did not seem particularly pleasant.

As she led the donkey down the dusty main street of Highlevee, a little after noon, she found herself dragging her feet in the dust, as if by walking slower she could put off her decision longer.

It was with a decidedly sinking feeling that she spotted someone she knew sitting at a table outside the Royal Oak Tavern, just inside the bounds of the town. It wasn't just any acquaintance, either.

Omens come in threes. So do portents. And so do the bindings of a geas set by Fate and the Lady. If ever there was an omen, this must surely be it—for there was no reason, no reason at all, for *this* man to be here at *this* time.

Unless, rather than a geas, this is a conspiracy set up among my dear friends. . . .

For sitting at his ease, quite as if he belonged there, was a man called "Leverance" by those who knew him well. The trouble was, most of those who knew him well lived within the walls of the fabulous Fortress-City that the Deliambrens called home.

He should not have been here. He *should*, by all rights, have been back there, amid the wonders of Deliambren "technology," as they called it. Few of the odd half-human folk ever left those comforts—why should they? There they had lighting that did not depend on candles, as bright as the brightest sunlight on a dark winter night. They had heat in the winter and cool in the summer, and a thousand other comforts even the wealthiest human could only dream of. He should not have been sitting calmly at a wooden table, with a wooden mug in one hand, nibbling at a meat pasty and watching the road, his strange features shadowed by a wide hat of something that was *not* straw.

He should definitely not have been watching the road as if he was watching for *her*.

She knew that he was going to hail her as soon as she saw him; the scene had that feeling of inevitability about it. She thought about trying to ignore him—but what was the use? If Leverance was not the next person to request her to go to Lyonarie, someone else surely would be.

Omen or conspiracy, it seems that I am caught.

So she led her donkey toward him, feeling weary to the bone, and wondering if for once she might get a real answer to her question of, "why me?" After all, the Deliambrens didn't believe in portents and omens. Their faith was placed on machinery, on curiosity, on discovery, on something they called "science."

"Don't tell me," she said, before he could open his mouth even to greet her. "You want me to go to Lyonarie to find out why the High King has been neglecting his duties."

Deliambrens resembled humans for the most part, far more than did, say, a Mintak. Leverance wore ordinary enough human garb: a jerkin, trews and boots of leather, and a shirt of what appeared to be silk. She knew better than to assume that the garments were as ordinary as they seemed, however, for nothing about a Deliambren was ever ordinary. Like all Deliambrens, the long, pale hair growing along the line of his cheekbones was immaculately groomed and blended invisibly into the identical shoulder-length hair of his head. His eyebrows were similar to those of an Elf in the way they rose toward his temples, but were thicker and as long as a man's thumb. Leverance fancied himself as something of an adventurer, so his hair was simply cut off straight rather than being styled into some fantastic shape as many Deliambrens sported. Nightingale sighed, but only to herself, knowing that Leverance was certain he was "blending in" with his surroundings. It would be quite impossible to convince him otherwise.

He stared at her with a flash of surprise, quickly covered. "Whyever do you say that?" he asked innocently. Too innocently.

"Because every other person I know seems to want me to go there," she replied tartly, and sat down on the wooden bench across from him. The wood of the table was smooth and bleached to gray by sun and rain, and another time she would have been quite pleased for a chance to sit here in the shade on such a broiling day. She had lost what patience she had and decided it was time to show it. "You may order me something to eat and drink, and you may pay for it. If you are going to try to get me to go to Lyonarie, you might as well begin with a bribe." She kept the tone of her voice tart, to show him she was not going to tolerate any evasions, no matter how clever.

Both of Leverance's eyebrows twitched, but he summoned the serving girl with a single lifted finger and placed an order for wine, cheese, and sausage pastries. The serving girl, dressed far more neatly than Nightingale in her buff linen skirt, bodice, and white blouse, glanced covertly at the Gypsy, her contemptuous expression saying all too clearly that she could not imagine why this exotic Deliambren would be ordering luncheon for such a scruffy stranger, and a Gypsy to boot.

Nightingale straightened abruptly, gathering all her dignity about her, then caught the girl's glance and held it, just long enough that the girl flushed, then paled, then hurried off. Now, at least, there would be no more covert looks and poorly veiled contempt.

"I wish I knew how you did that," Leverance said with interest and admiration.

Nightingale shrugged. There was no explaining it to him; he simply wouldn't understand why spending most of her time with Elves and other nonhumans made Nightingale seem strange and fey to those of her own kind. Most people, if asked why they avoided her after one direct confrontation, would stammer something about her expression—how they were *sure* she saw things that "normal folk" couldn't, and wouldn't want to.

Well, and I do, but that is not why I unnerve them.

As long as the impression she left with them caused them to leave her alone, she planned to cultivate the effect. If she had reasons to be fonder of her own company, and of nonhumans, than of her own kind, it was none of their business.

"Well," Leverance said, when the girl returned with the food and vanished again with unseemly haste, "as it happens, I *was* sent to find you, and to ask you to go to Lyonarie."

He laid the food out before her; wine in a pottery bottle, beaded with moisture, a thick slice of cheese and crusty rolls, beautifully brown pastries, a small pottery firkin of butter. She took her time; selecting a roll and buttering it, then pouring herself a cup of wine.

"Why?" she asked, then amended her question. "No, never mind. Why *me*?" She bit into the roll; it might just as well have been straw, for she could not taste it.

Now I discover if this is simple mortal conspiracy, or something I cannot escape.

Leverance stroked the hair on his cheekbones thoughtfully. "Several reasons, actually, although you are not the only person being asked to go there. And you *can* refuse."

Not the only person? That's new. Or does he mean that it is only his people who are sending more than one person to gather their information?

She snorted delicately. "You still haven't answered the question."

He held up a finger. "You are very observant, and yet you are very adept at making yourself unobserved." He held up a second finger. "You have served as a willing collector of information for your people, for the Elves and for mine in the past." A third finger joined the other two. "For some reason that my people are unable to fathom, things happen around you, and you are able to influence things through no medium that *we* recognize, and which other people refer to as 'magic.' We don't believe in magic, but we do believe you have some kind of power that acts in a way we can't measure. We think that will help keep you safe and sane where other investigators have failed."

Other investigators? This was the first time Nightingale had heard about others—and the chill now filled her, body, soul and heart. She put down the roll, all appetite gone. The still, hot air could not reach that chill to warm her.

"How, failed?" she asked in a small voice.

He correctly interpreted her frozen expression. "Nothing serious—no one *died*, for Hadron's sake! They were just found out, somehow, and they were discredited in ways that forced them to leave the city. We think we failed by choosing someone too high in rank. *You* know to extract information of all kinds—Harperus says that you have the ability to sieve gold out of the gutters. That is why you." He scratched his head, then added, "Besides, the roads north and south of here are closed. North the bridge is out, and south Sire Yori has put up a roadblock and he's taking all beasts of burden as 'army-taxes.' You could only go on to the King's Highway or retrace your steps."

Nightingale flushed, and mentally levied a few choice Gypsy-curses on the Deliambren for choosing the precise words guaranteed to make her go on. Gypsy lore held that to retrace one's steps was to unmake part of one's life—and you had better be very sure that was something you wanted and needed to do before you tried it.

Leverance blinked benignly at her as she muttered imprecations, just as if he didn't know the implications of his words. "Well," he asked. "Can you go? Will you help?"

Signs and portents, omens and forebodings. I do not want to go, but it seems I have no choice.

But she was not going to *tell* him that. For one thing, if they had sent others on this path, others who had been found out, that argued for someone *knowing* in advance that they had been sent. She trusted those Deliambrens that she personally knew, but within very strict limits—just as she trusted, within limits, those Elves she knew. But there were Gypsies that she would *not* trust, so why should every Elf, every Deliambren, or even every Free Bard be entirely trustworthy?

Talaysen probably didn't know about the others. The Elves might not have thought it worth stooping to ask help of mere mortals until now. Only the Deliambrens know the whole of this; but if there was someone acting as an informant against their agents, there is no reason why it could not have been an Elf, a Deliambren, or even one of us. Everyone has a price; it is only that most honest folk have prices that could never be met.

"I will think about it," she temporized, giving him the same answer she had given Master Wren. "My road goes in that direction; I cannot promise that I will end up there."

If there is an informant, damned if I will give you the assurance that I will be the next one to play victim! It is too easy for a lone woman, Gypsy or no, to simply disappear.

She smiled sweetly and ate a bite of tasteless roll, as if she had not a care in the world. "I am alone and afoot, and who knows what could happen between here and there? I make no promises I cannot keep."

Leverance made a sour face. "You'll think about it, though?" he persisted. "At least keep the option open?"

She frowned; she really did not want to give him even that much, but— she had a certain debt to his people. "Did I not say that I would?"

Leverance only shrugged. "You hedge your promises as carefully as if you were dealing with Elves," he told her sourly, as she packed up the rest of the uneaten lunch in a napkin to take with her. "Don't you know by now that you can trust us?"

The sun's heat faded again, although no clouds passed before it, and she took in a sharp breath as she steadied herself, looking down at the rough wood of the table, gray and lifeless, unlike the silver of her bracelet.

Trust them. He wants me to trust them, the Elves want me to trust them, and Talaysen, damn his eyes, trusts me. There is too much asking and giving of trust in this.

Her right hand clenched on the knot of the napkin; her left made a sign against ill-wishing, hidden in her lap.

"I only pay heed to what my own eyes and ears tell me," she said lightly, forcing herself to ignore her chill. "You should know that by now, since it is probably one of the *other* reasons why you picked me. Thank you for the meal."

She rose from the bench and untied her donkey from the handrail beside the road without a backward glance for him.

"Are you sure you won't—" Leverance began plaintively.

Now she leveled a severe look at him, one that even he could read. "I gave you what I could promise, Deliambren. A nightingale cannot sing in a cage, or tethered by a foot to a perch. You would do well to remember that."

And with that, she led her donkey back out into the road. It was, after all, a long way to Lyonarie, and the road wasn't growing any shorter while she sat.

She only wished that she could feel happier about going there.

CHAPTER TWO

From the vantage of a low hill, at the top of the last crest of the King's Highway, Lyonarie was a city guaranteed to make a person feel very small, entirely insignificant.

That was Nightingale's first impression of the metropolis, anyway. There was no end to it from where she stood; seated in the midst of a wide valley, it sprawled across the entire valley and more.

It did not look inviting to her; like something carved of old, gray, sunbleached wood, or built out of dry, ancient bones, it seemed lifeless from here, and stifling. In a way, she wished that she could feel the same excitement that was reflected in the faces of the travelers walking beside her. Instead, her spirit was heavy; she hunched her shoulders against the blow to her heart coming from that gray blotch, and she wanted only to be away from the place. Heat-haze danced and shimmered, making distant buildings ripple unsettlingly. As she approached, one small traveler in a stream of hundreds of others, she had the strangest feeling that *they* were not going to the city, it was calling them in and devouring them.

It devours everything: life, dreams, hope. . . .

The great, hulking city-beast was unlike any other major population center she had ever been in. There were no walls, at least not around the entire city, though there were suggestions of walled enclaves in the middle distance. That was not unusual in itself; many cities spilled beyond their original walls. It would have been very difficult to maintain such walls in any kind of state of repair, much less to man them. The city simply *was*; it existed, just as any living, growing thing existed, imbued with a fierce life of its own that required it to swallow anyone that entered and make him part of it, never to escape again.

Was this the reason why I felt such foreboding? That was reason enough; for someone of Nightingale's nature, the possibility of losing her own identity, of being literally devoured, was always a real danger.

It was not just the heat that made her feel faint. *Thousands of silent voices, dunning into my mind—thousands of people needing a little piece of me—thousands of hearts crying out for the healing I have. . . .I could be lost in no time at all, here.* She would have to guard herself every moment, waking and sleeping, against that danger.

She took off her hat and wiped her forehead with her kerchief, wishing that she had never heard of Lyonarie.

The shaggy brown donkey walked beside her, his tiny hooves clicking on the hard roadbed, with no signs that the heavy traffic on the road bothered him. Traffic traveled away from the city as well as toward it, right-hand side going in, left-hand side leaving, with heavy vehicles taking the center, ridden horses and other beasts coming next, and foot traffic walking along the shoulder. The road was so hard that Nightingale's feet ached especially in the arches, and her boots felt much too tight.

She'd had a general description of the city last night from the innkeeper at the tavern she'd stayed in. From this direction, the King's Highway first brought a traveler through what was always the most crowded, noisy, and dirty section of any city, the quarter reserved for trade.

Oh, I am quite looking forward to that. Stench, heat, and angry people, what a lovely combination.

About six or seven leagues from the city itself, the road had changed from hard-packed gravel to black, cracked pavement, a change that had given both Nightingale and her beast relief from the dust, but which gave no kind of cushioning for the feet. She knew by the set of the donkey's ears that his feet hurt him, too. This gray-black stuff was worse than a dirt road for heat, on top of that; waves of heat radiated up from the pavement, and both she and the donkey were damp with sweat.

I do wish I'd worn something other than this heavy linen skirt—and I wish I'd left off the leather bodice. I should have chosen a lighter set of colors than dark-green and black. This is too much to suffer in the name of looking respectable. I think I could bake bread under this skirt! She dared not kilt it up, either, not and still look like an honest musician and not a lady whose virtue was negotiable.

The road up the valley toward Lyonarie led across flat fields, every inch cultivated and growing a variety of crops, until suddenly, with no warning, the fields were gone and buildings on small plots of land had taken their place.

As if they had grown there, as well, like some unsavory fungus.

These were small, mean houses, a short step up from the hovels of the very poor, crowded so closely together that a rat could not have passed between them. Made of wood with an occasional facing of brick or stone-work, they were all a uniform, grimy gray, patched with anything that came to hand, and the few plants that had been encouraged to take root in the excuses for yards had to struggle to stay alive under the trampling feet of those forced off the roadway by more important or more massive traffic.

The sight made her sick. *How can anyone live like this? Why would anyone want to? What could possibly tempt anyone to stay here who didn't have to? No amount of money would be worth living without trees, grass, space to breath!*

The houses gave way just as abruptly a few moments later to warehouses two and three stories tall, and this was where the true city began.

Those who ruled the city now showed their authority. A token gate across the road, a mere board painted in red and white stripes, was manned by a token guard in a stiff brown uniform. He paid no attention to her whatsoever as she passed beneath the bar of the gate. His attention was for anyone who brought more into the city than his own personal belongings. Those who drove carts waved a stiff piece of blue paper at him as they passed—or if they didn't have that piece of paper, pulled their wagons over to a paved area at the side of the road where one of a half-dozen clerks would march upon them with a grimly determined frown. No one cared about a single Gypsy with a donkey, assuming they recognized her as a Gypsy at all. She passed close by the guard, fanning herself with her hat in her free hand, as he lounged against the gatepost, picking his teeth with a splinter. She was near enough to smell the onions he had eaten for lunch and the beer he had washed them down with, and to see the bored indifference in his eyes.

She was just one of a hundred people much like her who would pass this man today, and she knew it. There was virtue and safety in anonymity right now, and suddenly she was glad of the sober colors of her clothing. Better to bake than to be memorable.

How could I have forgotten? I wanted to be sure that no one would remember me; there might be someone waiting and watching to see if I show up! It must be the heat, or all this emotion-babble. . . .

But the press of minds around her was a more oppressive burden than the heat. *This* was why she hated cities, and Lyonarie was everything she disliked most about a city, but constructed on a more massive scale than anything she had previously encountered. There were too many people here, all packed too closely together, all of them unconsciously suffering the effects of being so crowded. Most of them were unhappy and had no idea how to remedy their condition—other than pursuing wealth, which brought its own set of problems whether the pursuit succeeded or failed. Their strident emotions scratched at her nerves no matter how well she warded them out.

Never mind that. I'm here, so now I need a plan, however sketchy. She hadn't actually formulated a plan until now; she'd been hoping, perhaps, for some unavoidable reason *not* to go on to Lyonarie. Geas or fate—or not—here she was, and it was time to make some kind of a plan.

Something simple; the simpler, the less likely it will be that I'll have to change it.

Once past the guard, Nightingale pulled the donkey off to the side of the road, taking a moment to stand in the shade of one of the warehouses. She fanned herself with her hat, pretended to watch the traffic, and considered her next move on this little gameboard.

It is a game, too—and I can only hope I've made myself less of a pawn than I would have been if I'd jumped into it without care and thought.

People streamed by her as she stood on the baking pavement with her patient little beast; as she watched, she saw everything from farmers hauling wagonloads of cabbage to the carriages of prosperous merchants—from footsore travelers like herself to the occasional creature more alien than a Deliambren. They all apparently had places to go, and they were all in a dreadful hurry to get there. They paid no attention to her; their eyes were on the road and the traffic ahead of them.

The buildings on either side of the road trapped the rays of the sun; the pavement beneath absorbed the heat and radiated it up again. Sweat ran down her face and back, and not even the most vigorous fanning helped cool her even a little. She licked her lips and tasted salt, wishing for the cooler clothing she'd worn at Kingsford Faire—the light skirt made of hundreds of multicolored ribbons sewn together from knee to waist,

but left to flutter from knee to ankle, the wide laced belt of doeskin, the
shirt of fabric just this side of see-through, and the sandals. . . . The
leather of her bodice and boots was hot, stifling hot. The soles of her
boots were far too thin to cushion her feet in any way or deflect the heat
of the pavement.

What she really wanted right now was a cool place to sit, a cool drink,
and a moment in semi-darkness to build up her mental defenses.

*Well, the sooner I join in this game, the sooner I can leave. If I'm both
lucky and clever, I might even be able to get out of here before winter.
At least I didn't lose any time on the road.*

In fact, she had made such good time getting here that it was not quite
Harvest Faire season. She had met with no obstacles, and her earlier good
start had been typical of the whole journey. She'd been able to stop before
dark every night, and hadn't even been forced to spend much of her hard-
earned Faire money.

In fact, her purse was now a bit heavier than it had been when she
had left Kingsford. She had made such good time that it had been possible
to trade performances in the kind of small country inns she preferred in
return for food, a bed, and whatever came into her hat. If she had just
been making her rounds of the Faire-circuit, she would have been pleased
but not particularly surprised by this. She was a *good* harpist, a fine
musician, and there was no reason why innkeepers should turn her away.
Her hat usually had a few coppers in it at the end of the night, no matter
how poor the audience.

But the very smoothness of her travel had made her suspicious, or
rather, apprehensive. It felt as if someone or something was making quite
sure she would get to Lyonarie, and seeing to it that she would be ready
for just about anything when she arrived there.

A geas? The hand of God or the Gypsy's Lady of the Night?

Or just a string of unprecedented good luck? And did it matter?

Not really. What did matter was coming up with a course of immediate
action that would keep her inconspicuous. *If I were truly in the "service"
of any of my so-needful friends, what would I do first?* she asked herself.
The answer seemed obvious: find a tavern or an inn at the heart of the
city and take up lodging there. If she was expected to gather information,
that would be *all* that she would do; there would be no time for anything
like taking on a regular job as a musician. And that *would* make her
conspicuous—someone who carried musical instruments, yet did not try
to find a position; someone who spent money but did nothing to earn
more. It would be "logical" to devote all of her time and energy to
collecting information, but it would not be wise.

So, since that is what is predictable and logical, it is what I will not do.

She considered her options further as she also pondered the question
of High King Theovere. The two were inextricably linked. How to gain
information on the High and Exalted without venturing out of her persona
as Low and Insignificant?

At least, now that she wasn't moving, she didn't seem to be quite
as warm.

As Talaysen had pointed out, the King should have been overseeing the business of his twenty vassals—but they had been left, more and more, at loose ends, without a guide or an overseer. As often as not, though the King of Birnam was an exception, they had been making use of this laxness to enrich themselves, or simply to amuse themselves.

The King of Birnam thought more of his people and their lands than himself; he was a good ruler, and as a result, his kingdom prospered in good times and survived the bad in reasonable shape. But those lands whose rulers were not out of Rolend's mold were showing all the signs of a careless hand on the reins. The signs were everywhere, and touching everything. In Rayden, for instance, there was little or no upkeep on the public roads: bridges were out, roads were rutted and full of potholes, signs were missing or illegible. In some remoter parts of Rayden and in other lands, the neglect was far more serious, as rivalry between Sires and even Dukes had been permitted to escalate into armed feuding.

The High King was supposed to represent the central unifying power in the Twenty Kingdoms. Now the Church was well on the way to taking over that function.

As if her thought of the Church had summoned a further reminder of its power, the tolling of bells rang out over the rumble of cart wheels on pavement and the babble of thousands of voices. Nightingale lifted her eyes from the road to see the spire of the Chapel housing those bells rising above the warehouse roofs.

And that represented another interest in the dance. There were perhaps hundreds of Chapels in Lyonarie, ranging in size from a single room to huge Cathedrals. The Church was an all-pervasive presence here, and there was no way to escape it. The Church might also have an interest in keeping Theovere weak and ineffectual.

She swallowed in sour distaste. There was no love lost between herself and most representatives of the Church. Too often of late she had been the subject of attempts by Churchmen to lay the blame for perfectly ordinary accidents at her door, because she was a Gypsy, a Free Bard, and presumably a wielder of arcane and darksome powers. In some places, at least, it seemed that the Church was trying to incite people against Gypsies, nonconformists, nonhumans—indeed, against anything that did not obviously and directly benefit the Church itself as much as a flock of sheep would benefit the herdsman.

Well, one advantage of being in a large city was that there were too many people for the Church to play at the kinds of games some Churchmen were able to foment in less populous places. It was harder to find an individual to use as a target and a scapegoat—harder to incite people against a stranger in a town when so *many* people were strangers, and in fact, people living on the same street might not even know or recognize each other.

Still, it behooved her to find a venue that was not too near a Chapel, if she could. *Not near the prosperous, either; they have the leisure to notice things.* All things considered, although this was probably the worst part of town, *this* district would be a good one to try to find a tavern that might have need of a musician.

Another good thing about a city this large—not all the Guild Bards in the world could take all the positions available here. Really, most of them are going to be positions no Guild Bard in his right mind would ever want!

Now that she had gotten her mind moving, and had managed a little rest, she felt ready to rejoin the mob. She pulled the donkey into the stream of traffic again, and scanned the fronts of the buildings she passed for tavern signs. *I'll look for information from two sources,* she decided as she walked, letting the traffic carry her along rather than trying to force a faster pace. *Once I get established, I'll build myself a little army of street-children and pay them to go listen for me. No one ever pays attention to them, and they can get into the most amazing places. . . .*

This would not be the first time she had built herself such a network. Children were never regarded as threatening by adults, but street-brats were wise beyond their years and knew how to listen for anything that might be of value. The nice thing about children was that they tended to stay loyal to the person who hired them. They might be wise beyond their years, but they lacked the experience that taught them double-dealing. Children still believed, in their heart of hearts, in playing fair.

Servants, too—they're the other invisibles. I'll show up at the kitchen doors, clean but very shabby. I'll ask to play in return for food. The Courts of Kings might boast the cream of entertainers, but the servants never saw it, and any chance for a little entertainment of their own usually was snatched at. Kitchen gossip often reflected the doings of the great and powerful long before many of their masters knew about it. So long as she pretended not to notice, she would probably get an earful.

Raven never did learn that lesson, silly boy. He would always *start asking questions rather than letting servants babble to each other.*

She would be just as invisible as a servant or a street urchin; just another common tavern-musician. There weren't many Free Bards who traveled all the way to Lyonarie; it was a long way from Rayden, where the group first came to be organized, and Free Bards had their routines like anyone else. Likely no one would even recognize the knot of multicolored ribbons on her sleeves as anything other than decoration. Even if they did know her for what she was, well, the Guild had made it difficult for a Free Bard to work in Rayden, and the Church had done the same in Gradford, so it made sense for someone to come this far afield for work.

I look like a Gypsy and there is no disguising that, but that might work for me rather than against me. People like things that are a bit exotic; it gives them a taste of places they'll never see, a kind of life they'll never lead.

Gypsies didn't like cities much, which also might mean she would *not* be recognized as one. Ah, well. It was always a case of playing odds being a Gypsy.

And if she was recognized, and it caused her trouble—well, she would deal with that when she saw what cards were in her hand.

The donkey suddenly gave a frightened bray and reared back against the lead-rope, trying to dig all four hooves into the pavement. The rope scraped her palm and she tightened her grip automatically as she looked around for what danger might have alarmed him—but a sudden whiff of powerful odor told her that he had simply reacted to another aspect of a city that she hated. There was no mistaking that charnel reek as it wafted into her face: blood and feces, urine and fear.

She put her hat back on her head and soothed him with her free hand as she continued to pull his lead, gently but firmly, until he started walking again. His eyes rolled, but he obeyed her. She couldn't blame him for balking; she'd have done the same in his place. He might even have scented a relative in that reek.

Or rather, an ex-relative.

The warehouses gave place to something else, and now she knew why she had seen so many carts laden with smaller beasts on this road. This was the district of slaughterhouses and all that depended on them.

She held the donkey's halter firmly under his chin as he fought to escape, shivered and rolled his eyes. There wasn't anywhere he could go, and the press of traffic on all sides was enough to keep him moving. Nightingale wished she had taken thought to cover her mouth and nose with a neckcloth as so many around her were doing—she needed both hands to control the donkey, and her kerchief was in her pocket.

The reek of the slaughterhouses and holding pens was not all that came drifting by on the breeze. There were other, equally unsavory smells— the stench of the leather-workers' vats, the effluvium of the glue-makers' pots, the pong of garbage-and dung-collectors' heaps. Fortunately there was something of a real current of moving air here, and it ran crossways to the road; as soon as they were out of the immediate area, the worst of the smell faded, diluted by distance.

But now the slaughterhouse odor gave way to new odors, or rather, older ones. Nightingale winced and tried to barricade herself against a stench that was both physical and mental. Her stomach heaved, and she tasted bile in the back of her throat.

Mighty God. Even animals wouldn't live like this. Even flies wouldn't live like this! And why does the Church allow this? There is a question for you!

Only the poorest would live here, so near the slaughterhouses and the dreadful stench, the flies, and the disease—and the tenement houses lining the road bore ample testament to the poverty, both monetary and spiritual, of those living within. The houses themselves leaned against each other, dilapidated constructions that a good wind would surely send tumbling to the street. Drunken men and women both, wrapped in so many layers of rags and dirt it was hard to tell what sex they were, lay in the alleys and leaned against the houses. Filthy children crowded the front stoops, big bellies scarcely covered by the rags they wore, scrawny limbs showing that those bellies were the sign of malnourishment and not of overeating. They, too, lay about listlessly on the steps, or sat and watched the passing traffic, too tired from lack of food to play. The scream of hungry babies joined the sound of commerce on the road; Nightingale resolutely closed her ears to other sounds, of quarrels and blows, of weeping and hopelessness. *This* was new; poverty was always part of a city, but never starvation, not like this. It was one more evidence of King Theovere's neglect, even here, in the heart of his own land and city.

I can't do anything about this—at least, I can't do more than I'm already planning to do. I can recruit some of my children from these—I can feed as many as my purse will permit. She salved her conscience with that; there was too much here for even every Gypsy of every clan to correct.

She sighed with relief as more and sturdier buildings took the place of the tenements. More warehouses, mills for cloth, flour and lumber—and something that Nightingale had never seen at firsthand among humans before, although she was familiar enough with the Deliambren version, which they called "manufactories."

Here, in enormous buildings, people made things—but not in the way they were accustomed to make them in villages and towns elsewhere. People made things *together*; each person performed a single task in the many stages of building something, then passed the object on to the next person, who performed another task, and so on until the object was completed. Every example was like every other example; every chair looked like every other chair, for instance, and every pair of trews like every other pair of trews. The system worked very well for the Deliambrens, but Nightingale was of two minds about it. It *did* mean made-goods were much cheaper; no one needed to be an expert in everything, and almost anyone could afford well-made trews or chairs or tea-mugs. But it felt like there was no heart in such goods, and nothing to show that a tea-mug was special. . . .

Ah, what do I know? I am a crafter of music, not of mugs—and I am sure there is still a demand for trews and chairs and mugs made by individuals. The system did the Deliambrens no harm; they took as much pleasure in life and crafting as any other being. Still—

I would not like to work in such a place, but that does not mean that other folk would feel the same. Stop making judgments for others, Nightingale.

The donkey relaxed as they entered this district; she let go her tight hold on his lead-rope, and let him have his head again. The shape of this area was determined by the river that ran through it; there was scarcely a bit of bank that did not have a mill wheel on it to make use of the swiftly-flowing current. The buildings here were old—and Nightingale suspected that few of the people traveling beside her had any idea how *very* old they were. The mill wheels and millraces were recent additions to buildings that had been standing beside this river since before the Cataclysm.

The buildings were not pretty; they were simple, brute boxes with square window-holes where there might, once, have been glass. Now they were covered with whatever might let in light and exclude weather; glass in some places, oiled paper or sheets of parchment in others, but mostly sheets of white opaque stuff the Deliambrens used for packing crates and padding. The base color of these dull boxes was an equally dull gray; where in the past people had tried to apply paint, either to cover the entire buildings or as crude advertisements, the paint remained only in patches, as if the buildings had some kind of scabrous disease. But the irony was that these places were solid still; they had stood for centuries and likely would stand for centuries more. Nightingale had been inside the Deliambren Fortress-City; she had seen buildings like these being erected. One actually *poured* the walls, using wood to make the molds to give the walls their form, as if they were huge ceramics. Once the gray stuff set, it was stronger than granite and less likely to age due to weathering.

So the irony, lost to those beside the Gypsy, was that these buildings which seemed relatively new were actually much, much older than the tenements that had been falling down.

The road crossed the river on a bridge that also dated back to the Cataclysm; Nightingale privately doubted that anyone could bridge the Lyon River in these days—except, perhaps, Deliambrens. It was a narrow and fierce stream, with a current so swift and deep that "to swim the Lyon" was a common euphemism for suicide.

For a moment, there was relief from the heat; the waters of the Lyon were as cold as they were swift, and a second river flowed above it—a river of fresh, cool air. Nightingale moved as slowly on the bridge as she could, stretching out her moment of relief.

On the other side, the manufactories gave way again to housing, but fortunately for Nightingale's peace of mind the people here lived in better conditions that those near the slaughterhouses.

There were more of those pre-Cataclysm buildings, in fact, given over to living quarters rather than manufactories. These had more windows, and from the look of things, the ceilings were not as high, granting more levels in the same amount of space. In between these older buildings, newer ones rose, not quite as dilapidated as the tenements on the other side of the river, but by no means in excellent repair. These newer buildings huddled around the old as if for support, as if without those gray bulwarks they could not stand against wind and weather.

Nightingale tried to imagine what this area might have looked like before the wooden tenements were built, but had to give up. She just could not picture it in her mind. Why would people have put so much open space between the buildings, then build the buildings so very tall? Wouldn't it have made more sense to lay everything out flat, the way a small village was built? That way everyone could have his own separate dwelling, and one would not be forced to hear one's neighbors through walls that were never thick enough for privacy. . . .

Ask anyone who has ever spent the night in an inn with newlyweds in the next room.

Well, there was no telling what the ancestors had been thinking; their world was as alien to the Twenty Kingdoms now as that of any of the nonhumans. Nightingale certainly was not going to try to second-guess them.

However, this area would be a good one in which to start her search. However much she disliked the crowding, she could hide herself better in a crowd than in more exclusive surroundings.

At the first sign of a tiny cross street, she pulled the donkey out of the stream of traffic and into the valley between two buildings, looking for a child of about nine or ten, one who was not playing with others, but clearly looking for someone for whom he could run an errand. Such a child would know where every inn and tavern was in his neighborhood, and would probably know which ones needed an entertainer.

And people think that children know nothing. . . .

Nightingale kept her back quite still with indignation as she pulled her donkey away from the door of the Muleteer. Her guide—a girl-child with dirty hair that might have been blond if one could hold her under a stream of water long enough to find out—sighed with vexation. It was an unconscious imitation of Nightingale's own sigh, and was close enough to bring a reluctant smile to the Gypsy's lips.

"Honest, Mum, if I'd'a thunk he was gonna ast ye pony up more'n music, I'd'a not hev brung ye here," the girl said apologetically.

Nightingale patted the girl on one thin shoulder, and resolved to add the remains of her travel-rations to the child's copper penny. "You couldn't have known," she told the little girl, who only shook her head stubbornly and led Nightingale to a little alcove holding only a door that had been bricked up ages ago. There they paused out of the traffic, while the girl bit her lip and knitted her brows in thought.

"Ye set me a job, mum, an' I hevn't done it," the child replied, and Nightingale added another mental note—to make this girl the first of her recruits. Her thin face hardened with businesslike determination. "I'll find ye a place, I swear! Jest—was it only wee inns an taverns ye wanted?"

Something about the wistful hope in the girl's eyes made Nightingale wonder if she had phrased her own request poorly. "I thought that only small inns or taverns would want a singer like me," she told the girl. "I'm not a Guild musician, and the harp isn't a very loud instrument—"

"So ye don' mind playin' where there's others playin' too?" the girl persisted. "Ye don' mind sharin' th' take an' th' audience an' all?"

Well, that was an interesting question. She shook her head and waited to reply until after a rickety cart passed by. "Not at all. I'm used to 'sharing'; all of us do at Faires, for instance."

A huge smile crossed the child's face, showing a gap where her two front teeth were missing. "I thunk ye didn' like other players, mum, so I bin takin' ye places where they ain't got but one place. Oh, I got a tavern-place that's like a Faire, 'tis, an' they don' take to no Guildsmen neither. Ye foller me, mum, an' see if ye don' like this place!"

The child scampered off in the opposite direction in which they *had* been going, and Nightingale hauled the donkey along in her wake. The girl all but skipped, she was so pleased to have thought of this "tavern-place," whatever it was, and her enthusiasm was quite infectious. Nightingale found herself hoping that this *would* be a suitable venue, and not just because her feet hurt, she was wilting with the heat, and her shoulders ached from hauling the increasingly tired and stubborn donkey.

She also wanted to be able to reward this child, and not have to thread her way out of the neighborhood the little girl knew and hunt up a new guide. The streets were all in shadow now, although the heat hadn't abated; much longer and it would be twilight. She would *have* to find at least a safe place to spend the night, then; it wasn't wise for a stranger to be out in a neighborhood like this one after dark. In a smaller city she wouldn't have worried so much, but she had heard of the gangs who haunted the back streets of Lyonarie by night; she was a tough fighter, but she couldn't take on a dozen men with knives and clubs.

The child turned to make certain that she was still following, and waved at her to hurry. Nightingale wished powerfully then for that rapport with animals that Peregrine and Lark seemed to share; if only she could convince the donkey that it was in his best interest to pick up his feet a little!

But he was just as tired as she was, and surely he was far more confused. He'd never been inside a city at all, much less had to cope with this kind of foot-traffic, poor thing.

The child slipped back to her side, moving like an eel in the crowd. "Tisn't but three streets up, mum, just t'other side uv where ye met me," she said, looking up into Nightingale's face anxiously. "Oh, I swan, ye'll like the place!"

"I hope so," the Gypsy replied honestly. "I can promise you, at least I won't dislike it as much as I did the last!"

The little girl giggled. "La, mum, ye're furrin, and the Freehold, it's got more furriners than I ken! Got Mintaks, got Larads, got Kentars, got a couple 'a Ospers, even! Half the folk come there be furrin, too!"

Now that certainly made Nightingale stand up a bit straighter. "Why all the—" She sought for a polite word for the nonhumans.

"Why they got all the Fuzzballs?" the child asked innocently. "Well, 'cause other places, they don' like Fuzzballs, they don' like furriners, they even look at ye down the nose if ye got yeller skin or sompin. Not Freehold, no, they figger Fuzzball money spends as good nor better'n a Churcher. I *like* Freehold. I'd'a taken ye there fust, but I thunk ye wanted a place where ye wouldn'—ah—"

"Where I wouldn't have any competition?" Nightingale replied, laughing at the child's chagrin. "Oh, my girl, I promise you I am sure enough of my own songs that I don't have anything to fear from other musicians!"

The child grinned her gap-toothed grin again and shrugged. "Ye'll see," she only said. "Ye'll see if be takin' ye wrong. Freehold—it's a *fine* place! Look—'tis right there, crost the street!"

But the building the girl pointed to was not what Nightingale expected—

The Gypsy blinked, wondering if the child was afflicted with some sort of mental disorder. This wasn't a tavern or an inn building—it was a warehouse!

It was one of the old, pre-Cataclysm buildings, four tall stories high, with a flat roof and black metal stairs running up the side of it from the second story to the rooftop, and more black metal bridges linking it and the buildings nearest it from roof to roof. She narrowed her eyes and tried to see if someone had partitioned off a little corner of it at ground level as a tavern, but there was no sign of any partitioning whatsoever. Whoever owned this building owned the whole thing. Set into the blank face of the wall was a huge sliding door, and a smaller entry-door was inset in it. This was a warehouse!

But there *was* a sign above the entry door, and the sign did say THE FREEHOLD. . . .

The child scampered on ahead and pounded enthusiastically at the door. It opened, and she spoke quickly to someone Nightingale couldn't see. By the time she managed to coax her willfully lagging donkey to the doorway, whoever had been there was gone, and the child was dancing from one foot to the other with impatience.

"He's gone t' git the boss," the child told her. "Ye wait here wit me, an' the boss'll be here in a short bit."

Nightingale looked up at the sign above her head, just to be sure. It did say THE FREEHOLD, that much hadn't changed. But how could anyone ever make any kind of profit running a tavern in a place this size? The cost of fuel and candles alone would eat up all the profits!

She tried to make a quick estimate of just how much it *would* cost to heat this huge cavern of a place in the winter; just as she came to the conclusion that she didn't have the head for such a complicated calculation, the "boss" appeared in the door.

A human of middle years, average in every way from his hair to his clothing, looked her up and down in surprise. "You *are* a Gypsy, aren't you?" he said, before she could say anything to him. "And a Free Bard?"

She nodded cautiously, but he only smiled, showing the same gap at the front of his teeth that the child boasted. "Well! In that case, we might be able to do some business. Will you enter?"

"What about the beast?" she asked dubiously, keeping a tight hold on the donkey's halter. She was not about to leave him outside, not in this neighborhood.

"Bring him in; there's a stable just inside the door," the man replied readily enough. "If you have a big enough building, you can do anything you want, really, and the owner thought it would be nice if people didn't have to go out into the weather to get their riding-beasts."

"Oh." That was all she could say, really. It was all anyone could say. Who would have thought of having a stable *inside* your tavern?

"Trust a Deliambren to think of something like that," the man continued, as an afterthought. "He's almost never here, of course, but he's always coming up with clever notions for the place, and the hearth-gods know a Deliambren has the means to make anything work."

Ah. Now it makes sense! And now it made sense for a tavern to be situated in a warehouse, for only a Deliambren would have the means to heat the place—yes, and probably cool it in the summer, as well!—without going bankrupt.

She turned to the girl, and held out the promised penny, and with the other hand fumbled the bag of travel food off the back of the packs. "Here, take this, too," she said, holding it out as soon as the child accepted her penny with unconcealed glee and greed. "Can I find you in the same place if I need a guide again?"

The child accepted the bag without asking what was in it—hardly surprising, since almost anything she was given would be worth something to her. Even the bag itself. She clutched the bag to her chest and nodded vigorously. Yes, mum, ye jest ast fer Maddy, an' if I ain't there, I be there soon as I hear!" She grinned again, shyly this time. "I tol' ye that ye'd like this place, mum, didn' I jest?"

"You did, and I don't forget people who are clever enough to guess what I'd like, Maddy," Nightingale told her. "Thank you."

Before she could say anything more, the child bobbed an awkward curtsey and disappeared into the crowd. The "boss" of the tavern was still waiting patiently for her to conclude her business with Maddy.

"Don't you think you ought to look us over and see what we can offer before you make a decision?" the man asked her, although his amused expression and his feelings, as loud as a shout, told her he was certain she would want to stay here. This was quite unlike the proprietor of the Muleteer, whose feelings of lust had run over her body like a pair of oily hands.

She simply raised an eyebrow; he chuckled, and waved her inside.

The doorway opened into a room—or, more correctly, an anteroom—paved like the street outside, furnished with a few wooden benches, with a corridor going off to the right. A Mintak boy appeared in the entrance at the sound of the donkey's hooves on the pavement.

Nightingale had seen many Mintaks in the course of her travels, but never a youngster. Like all the others she had seen, this boy wore only a pair of breeches and an open vest; his hide, exactly like a horse's, was a fine, glossy brown. His head was shaped something like a cross between a horse and a dog, but the eyes were set to the front, so that he could see forward out of both of them, like a human, instead of only one at a time, like a horse. He had a ridge of hair—again, much like a horse's mane—that began between his ears and traveled down his neck, presumably to end between his shoulderblades.

Unlike the adults, who were muscular enough to give any five men pause, this boy was thin, gawky, awkward, exactly like a young colt. Although he had three-fingered hands that were otherwise identical to a human's, with nails that were much thicker and black, his feet presumably ended in hooves, for Nightingale heard them clopping on the pavement.

"This lady is a musician, and she'll be joining us, Kovey," the man said. "Take her little beast and—" He turned back to Nightingale. "I assume that room and board will be part of the arrangement?"

"That's the usual," she replied shortly, unable to be anything but amused herself at the way he had decided that she was going to stay.

"Right then, have her things taken up to the Gallery and put 'em in the first empty room. Then leave word at the desk which it is."

The Mintak boy nodded his hairy head and trotted over to them, extending his hand for the donkey's lead-rope. The donkey stepped up to him eagerly as Nightingale put the rope into his large, square hands. He smiled shyly, showing the blunt teeth of a true herbivore.

Interesting. If I did not have the abilities I do, I would be very suspicious at this point. They have parted me from my transportation and my belongings and gotten me inside a building with no clear escape route. Do they assume that I am naive, or do they assume that as a Gypsy I do have other senses at my command?

It could be either. Her clothing marked her as country folk; it could be presumed that she was not familiar with the ways of cities and the hazards therein. On the other hand, the man had not only recognized her as a Gypsy, but as a Free Bard.

Boy and donkey trotted off down the corridor, and Nightingale's escort ushered her past the second doorway and into the "tavern" proper.

The man waited for her reaction, but she was not the country cousin she looked, and she didn't give him the gasp of surprise that he had expected. She had assumed that the "tavern" took up a good portion of the building as estimated from outside, and she had not been mistaken. Maddy had not been mistaken in comparing this place to a Faire. The main portion of the tavern—she couldn't think of a better name for it— had a ceiling that was quite three stories above the rest, and pierced with the most amazing skylights she had ever seen. They were not clear, but made with colored glass, exactly like the windows in the larger Cathedrals. Below the skylights hung contrivances that Nightingale guessed were probably lights. Beneath these skylights was an open floor, all of wood, with a raised platform at one end and with benches around it, exactly like a dance floor and stage at a Faire, except that at a Faire the dancing-area would be floored in dirt.

This took up approximately half the floor space. The rest—well, it looked very much as if someone had taken all of the entertainment and eating places at a really huge Faire and proceeded to stack them inside this building.

All around the walls, from the ground floor to the ceiling, there were alcoves for eating and drinking, many with comfortable seating and a small stage for one to three performers. Many of the alcoves had recognizable bars in the back; some had doors that could be slid across the front, cutting them off from the main room. Some boasted braziers and what might be odd cooking implements as well. Some had nothing at all but the seating.

Not that this place was as elegant as the skylights indicated; in fact, the opposite was true. The building showed its heritage quite clearly; walls and the ceiling were roughly finished, huge metal beams were exposed, and ropes and wires hung everywhere.

Still it was a monumental undertaking, putting this place together at all, and Nightingale rather liked the unfinished atmosphere. That was the difference—outside, things looked unkempt. In here, they looked unfinished. Out there in the rest of the city, there was the feeling of decay and decline, but in here there was unfulfilled potential.

It was then that she realized that she was no longer hot, or even warm; that from the moment she had passed within the front door, she had been cooled by a dry, crisp breeze that came out of nowhere.

Ah, more Deliambren magic, of course. And how better to lure patrons to a place like this, down in a dubious quarter of the city, than to ensure that they will be invisibly cooled in summer and warmed in winter!

There was no one on the main platform, but about half the other small stages had performers on them; not just musicians, but a juggler, a contortionist, a mock-mage, and a storyteller who had his audience of ten in stitches. Savory—though unfamiliar—aromas drifted from three of the tiny kitchens. It was difficult to say precisely where every sound and scent came from in this cavernous place, but Nightingale had the impression that there were similar setups just off the second or third floor balconies. And as Maddy had claimed, a good half of those customers that Nightingale spotted were not human.

"The top floor's lodgings," her escort said diffidently. He waved his hand vaguely at the upper story. "Right side's for customers, left's for staff. You'll be staff, of course—"

"You're assuming I'm going to stay," Nightingale could not resist pointing out dryly. He turned to her with his mouth agape in surprise.

"You—why wouldn't you?" he managed, after a moment during which his mouth worked without any sound emerging.

"You might not want me, for one thing," she said with patient logic. "You don't know anything about me."

"You're a Free Bard, ain't you?" the man retorted. At her nod, he shrugged, as if that was the only answer he needed. "Tyladen—that's the boss, the owner—he's left orders. Free Bards show up looking for work, they got it. *He* says you're all good enough, that's enough for me. He's the one with the cashbox."

The man had a point—but there were still a few things she had to get clear. "Before I agree to anything, I want to know the terms I'll be working under here," she told him severely.

He nodded, his former surprise gone. "You pick the shift—except we got no openings on morning, so it's afternoon, supper to midnight, or midnight to dawn. You can double-shift if you want, but we don't really like it."

Thus far, sounds reasonable. "Go on," she told him, as the sound of a hurdy-gurdy brayed out on her right.

"Terms are pretty simple: room and board, and you pick what kitchen you want your meals out of. We don't go writin' up food, so if you want to stuff yourself sick, that's your problem. You hire on as a musician, that's what you do—no cookin', no waitin' tables, no bartending, no cleanup."

She sensed that he was about to add something else, then he took a look at her and left the words unsaid. She knew what they were, of course—that she was not to offer "extra services" to the customers.

"We don't argue if the customer brings a—a friend here, and wants a room to share for—oh, a couple of hours," he said finally, "but we don't offer him things like that here."

"Oh, please," she said, exasperated. "I've been on the road most of my life. You don't have whores, and you do have an arrangement with the Whores' Guild, I take it, so you don't allow your entertainers to freelance their sexual services?"

He looked just as startled as he had when she had suggested that she might not want to work here, but again, he nodded.

She suppressed a smile. *Well, occasionally clothing does make the person, it appears. I dress like a Churchgoing country girl, he assumes that's what I am! I wonder what he'll think when he sees some of my performing clothing? Perhaps that I am some mental chameleon!*

"That will be fine with me—" she began, but he held up his hand to forestall her.

"There's only one more rule," he told her. "That's the one you might not like. No puttin' out a hat."

She raised one eyebrow as high as it would go. "Just how am I supposed to make a living, may I ask?" she said, more than a bit arrogantly. "No one has *ever* made that part of my arrangements before."

He flushed and looked apologetic. "That's the rule. There's a charge at the door t' get in. You get a salary, an' it depends on how big a draw you are. Lowest is five coppers each shift, highest—well, we only had one person ever get highest, that was a half-royal."

A half-royal? The equivalent of *five gold pieces?* It was Nightingale's turn to stare at him with mouth agape. Very few *Guild* Bards were ever granted that kind of money, and no Free Bard the Nightingale had ever heard of—not even Talaysen, Laurel Bard to a King, was ever paid that much!

"So in other words, I'm on trial until you see what kind of an audience I can collect," she said, finally, after she had gotten over her astonishment. "And I have to take your word for what I'm worth."

He lifted his shoulders, apologetically. "That's the terms; that's what the boss set," he replied.

She considered it for a moment, leaving her own pride out of it. This wasn't entirely a bad thing. She could, if she decided it was worth it, exert herself only enough to pay for her army of children. She had shelter, food, and an excellent venue to hear a great deal. A place like this one would be very popular, not only with working-class folk, but with those with wealth and jaded appetites—or a taste for "uncommon" entertainment. If she had petitioned the Lady of the Night for the perfect place for her information-gathering, she could not have come up with anything better.

Most of all, she would only have to work six hours of every day; that left her at least six to make her own investigations, provided she cared to exert herself that much. She could make herself as conspicuous, or as *inconspicuous* here as she wanted.

In fact, that was not a bad idea. She could play the exotic Gypsy to the hilt here within these four walls—but her persona outside the tavern could be as plain as a little sparrow. No one would connect Nightingale with—whatever she called herself in here.

And if she did that—well, she might not find herself in the "half-royal" category, but she was fairly certain that the five coins she would earn each shift would be silver, not copper.

"I believe I can live with these terms," she said, without bothering to try and strike a better bargain. Not that there would be much point to trying—the price a Deliambren set was not subject to bargaining. One accepted, or one did without.

"Excellent!" The man positively beamed. "I saw that you had harps; we don't have any harp players right now. I can put you up in the Oak Grove, that's on the third floor, far enough away from the dancing that you shouldn't have any trouble with noise. What shift?"

"Supper to midnight," she replied immediately, and he beamed again.

"Perfect! Let's go check the front desk and find out what room you've got—ah—" He looked a little embarrassed. "I didn't catch your name—"

"That's because I didn't give it to you," she replied, softening the words with a faint smile, as she ran a list of possible alternative names in her mind. She would save "Nightingale" for now—just in case *this* Deliambren was already part of her friend's little plot. "My name is Lyrebird."

He nodded with approval. "The lyre's a harp right? Got a nice sound to it—I'm Kyran, by the way, Kyran Horat."

She held out her hand, and he shook it, in the way of Gypsies sealing a bargain. "Welcome to Freehold, Lyrebird," he said heartily. "I think you'll be happy here. You can lighten up now; the bargaining is over."

She chuckled, then looked away from him and out over the expanse of the building and all it contained. There would be enough people here every night that she—or rather, Lyrebird—as flamboyant as that persona would be, would simply be one more flamboyant entertainer among many. She would earn enough to not only get her covert quest done, but quite possibly turn a profit. This place was built by a Deliambren, so she could probably expect some luxuries in her quarters that Kyran hadn't even seen fit to mention—which was a far sight better than anything she'd find in an ordinary inn. All things considered, this had turned out to be luck of the sort that had eased her journey all the way here.

"I think you're right, Kyran," she replied as she suppressed the shiver *that* thought brought her. "Shall we find out about that room?"

Luck this good has to break sometime, she thought as she followed him. *I only pray that when it does, it does not turn as bad as it has been good.*

And if this was the result of that fate, geas, or whatever else had brought her here—well, that turn of good luck to bad, *very* bad, was all too likely.

CHAPTER THREE

Nightingale found nothing to complain about in the room that Kyran assigned to her, except the lack of windows—and on the whole, although it did make her feel a bit closed in, that might have been as much of a benefit as a lack. Certainly there was not going to be much of a view around here, and if the wind happened to come from the wrong direction—well, what traveled on the wind from the direction of the slaughter-houses was nothing she wanted to have to endure.

She surveyed what was likely to be her refuge for the next several weeks, if not months, and on the whole was pleased. There was one light overhead in the main room, a second in the bathroom, both controlled by plates on the wall that one touched—her escort had shown her how to use them, and she had not revealed that she already knew what they were. This was Deliambren light, of course, not an oil lamp or candle; it replicated natural sunlight at about an hour after sunrise; warm, clear, but not too bright. The overall effect with the four walls bare of decoration was of a white box, but that was not altogether bad—Deliambren taste in artwork was not always something she admired, and only the Lady knew

who or what had this room before she got it. The one thing this room
did boast that was quite out of the ordinary was its own tiny bathroom.

*It's out of the ordinary, unless you happen to be acquainted with Deli-
ambrens, that is. By their standards, this is all patched together, old and
rather tired, the bare minimum for civilization.* She considered the closer
examination she'd been able to make as she walked up the open staircases
and along the balcony to her room. All visible equipment was very shopworn by Deliambren standards—*their* equivalent of secondhand goods. It
was all too heavy and too bulky to steal, which made it safe to use here,
surrounded by humans who just might try to carry it off otherwise. And
those dangling wires and furlongs of conduit—those weren't just after-
thoughts, things they hadn't quite tucked out of sight. The equipment was
probably reliable, but, to Nightingale's eyes at least, was very clearly cobbled together from several other mismatched pieces of heavy equipment,
and likely there was no place else for those wires to go.

The bathroom, stuck off one corner of the main room, was in keeping
with the general feeling of "making do." A tiny box, tiled on all surfaces
with some shiny white substance that *might* be ceramic, it had a small
sink, one of the Deliambren-designed privies, and an oblong object in one
corner that she was certain must puzzle the life out of ordinary folk. *She*
had been inside the Fortress-City any number of times; the Deliambrens
used these things in places of bathtubs. At a touch, water cascaded from
the nozzle in the wall, and although one could not soak in this contrivance,
it was the best thing in all the world for washing hair. To her delight,
her employers provided soap and towels—probably, she thought cynically,
because so few of their new employees had more than a nodding acquaintance with either. That was fine with her; those were two more things
she was not going to have to provide.

*It isn't a tenth as luxurious as the baths in their guest quarters at home,
though,* she thought smugly. *And if you look closely, those tiles show some
chips and scratch marks, which means they have been reused. Probably
all of the fixtures are reused. They probably believe that these rooms are
as austere as a Church Cloister, and feel guilty over putting their employees through such hardship!*

A rectangular opening high on the wall with a screen over it allowed
warm air—or cool, as now—to flow into the main room, while another
on the opposite side removed it. There was a similar arrangement in
the bathroom.

All of the furnishings were built into the walls, meaning that they could
not be moved—which was a minor annoyance. There was a wardrobe on
the same wall as the bathroom, a chest which doubled as a seat, and a
bed that folded up into the wall if she needed more floor space. A tiny
shelf folded down, next to the bed. It was a very nice bed, though—and
typically Deliambren. It bore very little resemblance to the kind of beds
that she would find in other inns here. Wide enough for two, the bed
was a platform that dropped down on a hinge at the head of it to within
an inch or two of the floor and perched on a pair of tiny legs that popped
out of the foot. The mattress was made of some soft substance she simply
could not identify. The same followed for the sheets, towels and pillows.

They weren't woven; that was the only thing she could have said for certain. A single light, small but bright enough to read by, was built into the cavity at the head of the bed; it too was controlled by a palm-plate.

Other than that, the room itself was unremarkable, and as she knew quite well, unlike the kinds of quarters that Deliambrens reserved for their guests.

Oh, I imagine that my good host, knowing that the rooms for staff among humankind are very simple, opted for this as being "typical." Trust a Deliambren never to ask advice on something like this!

The fact was, by most human standards, between the heating and cooling and the bathroom, this place was palatial. Her panniers, covered with road dust and shabby with use as they were, looked as out of place here as a jackdaw's nest in a porcelain vase. Though this "vase" had a few cracks in it, there was no doubt what it was.

She put the bed back up into the wall in order to have more room to work, then set about unpacking her things and putting them away. The harps she left in their cases for the moment, but set beside the cushioned chest-seat. Her costumes were next, and she quietly blessed her instincts as she unpacked them, one by one, and shook them out thoroughly before putting them away in the wardrobe. She *had* been tempted to get rid of the more flamboyant of them, relics of her first days on the road and ill-suited to her current life. There were three of them, all made of ribbons and scarves sewn into skirts; seamed together from the waistband to the knee, then left to flutter in streamers from the knee to the ground. With them went patchwork bodices made to match the skirts, and shirts with a May-dance worth of rainbow-ribbons fluttering from each sleeve. One was made up in shades of green (from forest-green to the pale of new leaves), one in shades of red (a scarlet that was nearly black to a deep rose), and one in shades of blue (from the sky at midnight to the sky at noon).

I was so proud of being a Free Bard, then, that I thought every bit of clothing I owned should shout to the world what I was. They were my flags of defiance, I suppose, and fortunately, at the time, no one who might have taken exception actually recognized them for what they were! Now I hardly ever wear them except at Kingsford Faire.

She hung those at the front of the wardrobe; they would do very nicely for Lyrebird in a casual mood. The majority of her clothing, sensible enough skirts—three of them, of linen and wool—bodices to match of linen, leather and more wool, and six good shirts with only a modest knot of ribbon on each sleeve, she hung in the rear. They were clearly worn and had seen much travel, the wool skirt and bodice were carefully mended, and three of the shirts plainly showed their origin as secondhand clothing to the experienced eye. Those she would use on the street; she could even add a patch or two for effect. She had done so before.

Then came underthings and a nightshift, stockings and a pair of sandals, her winter cloak and a pair of shawls for weather too cold for shirtsleeves but not chill enough for the heavy cloak.

Then, at the bottom of the pannier, the other clothing that would—oh, most definitely!—be suited to the exotic Lyrebird. *These* costumes would virtually guarantee that she was seen and remembered.

The packet she removed from the bottom of the pannier was hardly larger than one of her sensible skirts folded into a square. She had never worn these garments in *human* company before—not that anyone had ever forbidden her to, but she had never felt safe in doing so. Some would have considered them to be a screaming invitation to the kind of activity the proprietor of the Muleteer assumed she would be open to. Others would have considered their mere possession to qualify her for burning at the stake.

She unfolded the outer covering of black, a square of that same, soft black velvet that the Elven messenger had worn, and shook out the garments, one by one.

And as always, she sighed; what woman born could *refrain* a sigh, presented with these dresses? They were Elven-make, of course, and not even the Deliambrens could replicate them. *Elven silk. Incredible stuff. Now* there *is magic!* The sleeves, the skirts, floated in the air like wisps of mist; they gave the impression that they were as transparent as a bit of cloud, and yet when she wore them, there was not a Cloistered Sister in the Twenty Kingdoms who was as modestly clad as she. There was so much fabric in them that if one took a dress apart and laid the pieces out, they would fully cover every inch of space on the dance floor below, yet each dress packed down into the size of her hand and emerged again unwrinkled, uncrumpled.

One dress was black, with a silver belt, otherwise unadorned, but with its multiple layers of sleeve and skirt cut and layered to resemble a bird's feathers. One was a true emerald-green, embroidered around the neckline, sleeves, and hem with a trailing vine in a deeper green; it had a belt of silk embroidered with the same motif. The third was the russet of a vixen's coat, and the sleeves and hem were dagged and decorated with cutwork embroidery as delicate as lace; the belt that went with this was of gold-embroidered leather.

They would suite Lyrebird very well—and because no one save the Elves had ever seen *Nightingale* in this finery, there was very little chance that anyone would recognize her from a description. She would certainly stand out—but no one would know her.

Nor would anyone recognize, in the plain, shabby little mouse who would go out into the streets, the flamboyant harpist of Freehold in her Elven silks.

And since most of my customers and the members of my audience are going to be nonhuman, Lyrebird is going to be perfectly safe from any untoward conduct, even in her Elven silks. Very few nonhumans were going to find her attractive or desirable, which was just fine so far as she was concerned.

She selected the russet for her first performance—what better place for a russet vixen that an Oak Grove?—and gratefully stripped out of her sweat-soaked clothing and headed for the bathroom.

The water-cascade worked just like the one she remembered, and to her great pleasure the soap was delicately scented with jessamine and left a fresh perfume in her hair. She luxuriated in the hot water pouring over her body, washing every last trace of the long journey away. This would be wonderful for easing the aches and strains of long playing, caused by sitting in one position for hours at a time.

She dried and styled her long, waist-length black hair in an arrangement very unlike Nightingale's simple braid; this was an elaborate coil and twist along the back of her head, with the remainder of her hair emerging as a tail from the center of the knot, or allowed to trail as a few delicate tendrils on either side of her face. She slipped the silken dress on over her clean body—it would have been a desecration and a sin to have put it on without a full bath—reveling in the sensuous feel of the silk caressing her hips and legs, slipping sleekly over her arms.

Now she took the cover off the larger of her two harps, the one she could only play while seated, and tuned it. She ignored her stomach as she did so—she could eat later, if need be, but at the moment she had to get the harp ready in good time before her performance. Kyran had told her that he would send one of the servers up to her room, to guide her to the Oak Grove when it was time for her to play—her performance would extend past midnight, just this once, because she would never have had time to bathe and change and ready herself before suppertime.

It was very hard, though, to ignore the savory aromas wafting up from below. Most of them were as strange as they were pleasant—not exactly a surprise, if most of the clientele were not human.

She was going to surprise Kyran, however. He probably expected her to perform human-made music only, but Lyrebird was a bird of a different feather altogether.

Hmm. Perhaps I ought to have worn the black!

She was going to sing and play the music of at least three nonhuman cultures, besides the Elves. Human music would comprise the smallest part of her performance.

And again, since very few people, even among the Gypsies and the Free Bards, knew that she collected the music of nonhumans, this would be utterly unlike Nightingale.

She retired to her room in a glow of triumph, harp cradled in her arms, two hours after midnight; entirely pleased with herself and her new surroundings. Her particular performance room—which was, indeed, decorated to resemble a grove of trees with moss-covered rocks for seats and tables "growing" up out of the floor—was far enough from the dance floor that her own quiet performance could go on undisturbed. She had begun with purely instrumental music, Elven tunes mostly, which attracted a small, mixed crowd. From there she ventured into more and more foreign realms, and before the night was over, there were folk standing in line, waiting for a seat in her alcove. Most of them were not human, which was precisely as she had hoped; word had spread quickly among the patrons of Freehold that there was a musician in the Oak Grove who could play anything and sing "almost" anything. Most of the nonhumans were hungry for songs from home—and most of the time she could oblige them with *something*, if not the exact song they requested.

As she climbed the stairs to her room, oblivious to the cacophony of mixed music and babbling talk, she hardly noticed how tired she was. She was confident now that her salary would be in the three-or four-silver area, if not five. That would be enough; it would purchase the help of quite a number of children at a copper apiece. Kyran had checked on her during one of the busier moments, which was gratifying—he'd had a chance to see with his own eyes how many people were lining the walls, waiting for seats. His eyes had gone wide and round when he'd seen her in costume, too.

He certainly didn't expect that *out of the drab little starling at the front door!*

Finally she reached the top of the stairs, the balcony overlooking the dance floor, and the hallway leading off of it. Though the hall muffled some of the echoing noise from below, she couldn't help but notice that her room was just not far enough from the balcony for it to do much good. She put the harp down to open her door; set it inside and turned on the light, then closed the door behind her. The din outside vanished, cut off completely once the door was closed. She sighed with relief; her one worry had been that she might be kept awake all night by the noise. Evidently the Deliambren had thought of that, as well.

She set the harp safely in the corner, and reached for the plate that released the bed. It swung down, gently as a falling feather, and she fell into it.

And got up immediately at a tapping at her door. She answered it, frowning; had someone followed her up here, expecting the kind of entertainment that Kyran had *sworn* she would not have to provide? If so, he was going to get a rude surprise. Nightingale did not need a knife or a club to defend herself; her Lyncana friends made a fine art of hand-to-hand combat, and while she was a mere novice by their standards, she was confident that there was not a *single* human, no matter how large and muscular, who could force himself up her. Many had tried in the past, and many had ended up permanently singing in higher keys.

But when she opened the door, there didn't seem to be anyone there—until she dropped her eyes.

"Evenin' snack for ye, mum," said a tow-headed urchin with a pair of ears that could have passed for handles, holding up a covered tray. He had to shout to be heard over the bellows and cheers from the dance floor below. "Boss figgered ye'd be hungered."

She wasn't about to argue; she took the tray from the boy with a smile, and before she could even thank him, he had scampered away down hall to the staircase, nimble as a squirrel and just as lively.

Hmm. My first reward for a job well done? That could be; she wasn't going to press the point. She *was* hungry despite a few bites taken here and there during the breaks in performing. After all, she hadn't eaten since noon, and that was a long time ago!

She took the tray over to her bed, set it down, lifted the cover, and nearly fainted with delight.

There was quite enough there, in that "snack," to have fed her for two days if she'd been husbanding rations. A tall, corked bottle of something cold—water beaded the sides and slid down the dark glass enticingly—stood beside a plate holding a generous portion of rare roast meat, sliced thin and still steaming. Three perfect, crusty rolls, already buttered, shared the plate with the meat. Very few humans would have recognized the next dish, which resembled nothing so much as a purple rose, but she knew a steamed *kanechei* when she saw it, and her mouth watered. To conclude the meal, there was a plate of three nut-studded honeycakes.

Her stomach growled, and she fell to without a second thought. When she finished, there was nothing left but a few crumbs and a blissful memory.

Following Deliambren tradition, she took the tray to the door and left it next to the wall, just outside. As she looked up and down the hallway, she saw another tray or two, which meant that she had done the right thing. The shouting from below had died down somewhat, but it sounded rather as if the drummer for the musical group was having some kind of rhythmic fit, and the audience was clapping and stamping their feet in time. She closed the door again quickly.

Why is it that the drunker people become, the more drumming they want? Maybe the alcohol blunts their ability to enjoy anything subtle— like a melody.

She had intended to read some of her own notebooks of nonhuman songs—but after that wonderful meal, and especially the light, sweet wine that had accompanied it, she could hardly keep her eyes open. So instead, she slipped out of her gown and hung it up with a care for the delicate cutwork; drew her nightshift on over her head, turned off the light and felt her way into bed. She hardly had time to settle herself comfortably, when sleep overtook her.

"Therefore, my friends and brothers," the young Priest said, earnestly, his brown eyes going from one face below him to the next, "Yes, and my sisters, too! You must surely see how all these things only prove the *unity* of everything in the Cosmos—how God has placed the warmth of His light in *every* heart, whether the outer form of that heart walk on two legs or four—be clad in skin, hide, scales, or feathers—whether the being call God by the Name that we know him, or by something else entirely! What matters is this, only: that a being, whatever form he wears, strive to shelter that Light, to make it shine the brighter, and not turn his face to the darkness!"

The homely young Priest signaled his musicians and stepped back with a painfully sincere smile. Nightingale slipped out of St. Brand's Chapel just as the tiny—and obviously musically handicapped—choir began another hymn-song, slipping a coin into the offering box as she passed it. She stepped out into the busy street and blended into the traffic, squinting against the bright noon light.

This was the fourth Chapel she had attended in as many days, and it had her sorely puzzled. In the other three—all of them impressive structures in "good" neighborhoods—she had heard only what she had expected to hear. That only humans had souls; that nonhumans, having no soul to save, had no reason to be "good." That if they had no reason to be good, they must, therefore, be evil.

This wasn't the first time such an argument had been used against nonhumans; obviously one of the things that the Church absolutely *needed* in order to galvanize its followers was an enemy. It was difficult to organize opposition to an abstract evil—and even more difficult to get people to admit that there was evil inside themselves. That meant that the ideal enemy would be something outside the Church and outside the members of the Church, and as unlike the human followers of the Sacrificed God as possible.

Easy enough to point the finger at someone and say, "he doesn't look like you, he doesn't believe in what you believe, he must be evil—and your natural enemy," she thought cynically, as she settled her hat on her head and let the crowd carry her along toward Freehold. She had *expected* this; if the Church was snatching secular power away from the High King, Lyonarie would be the place where it would show its truest hand—and that would be the place where the Church officials would take a stand showing who they had selected to be the "Great Enemy."

What she had not expected was that here the Church was openly divided against itself.

When her patrons first began telling her about this, in discussions she had started during the breaks between her sets, she had at first dismissed it as being a trick of some kind. After all, why in the world would Priests openly preach against what was, supposedly, Church canon? She couldn't come up with a reason behind such a trick, unless it might be to lull the nonhumans into complacency—but what other reason could there be?

She decided to take to the Chapels herself to find out.

Thus far, she had discovered a pattern, at least. Chapels in certain districts—aggressively human-only—*always* held Priests who followed the canonical path. But Chapels elsewhere might just as often harbor Priests like Brother Brion back there; Priests who preached the brotherhood of all beings, and stressed the similarities among the most various of beings rather than their differences. They *could* have been operating the kind of trick she suspected—but they could not hide the feelings behind their words, not to her, not when she chose to follow the music of their emotions.

And the music was of a sweeter harmony than that sadly under-talented choir back there. These Priests truly, deeply, *believed* in what they were saying. And if the stories her patrons told her were true, there were just as many Priests of this radical line as there were who followed cannon.

The crowd carried her up to the front door of Freehold, and she slipped out of the stream and onto the doorstep. One or two others followed her there, but she knew after a quick glance that these were patrons, not fellow staff, and she simply granted them a brief smile before opening the door and taking the *other* hallway to the right, the one that led to the back stairs rather than the stable. She really didn't want anyone to know that "Tanager"—her street-name—and "Lyrebird" were one and the same. Especially not customers.

But as she climbed the dimly lit back staircase to the top floor, she couldn't help thinking about the words of that so-earnest young Priest, and all the trouble those words must surely be causing him in certain circles.

And in her brief experience, Priests, no matter how well meaning and sincere, simply did *not* do or say things that would get them in trouble with their own superiors.

Except that here and now, they were.

What, in the name of the Gypsy Lady and the Sacrificed God, was going on here?

T'fyrr tried to concentrate on the music coming out of his friend Harperus' miraculous little machine, but it was of no real use. A black mood was on him today, a black mood that not even music could lift.

He finally waved at the little black cube, which shut itself off, obediently. He turned and stared out the windows of Harperus' self-propelled wagon at the human hive called Lyonarie. *Humans again. Why am I doing this? Surely I shall never interact with humans without something tragic occurring!*

He examined the scaled skin of his wrists, where the marks of his fetters were still faintly visible, at least to his eyes. The invisible fetters, the ones that bound his heart, hurt far more than the physical bonds had.

Why did I agree to come here? How is it that Harperus can charm me into actions I would never take on my own?

Months ago, he had agreed to help Harperus in yet another of his schemes: a partial survey of the human lands. All had been well, right up until the moment that he had been caught on the ground by humans who claimed that he was a demon, a creature of evil, and had fettered and imprisoned him, starving him until he was more than half mad. Their intent had been to kill him in some religious spectacle—

That was what Harperus said. I scarcely recall most of it.

Little had he known he had friends among the crowd assembled to see him die: a pair of Free Bards, who had provided him with a distraction, the means to his escape.

Unfortunately, not everyone had been distracted at the crucial moment. A single human guard had seen that he was about to flee and had tried to stop him.

To a fatal end. . . .

That was the reason for his black depression. It did not *matter* that he had killed in self-defense; the point was that he had *killed*. The man he had eviscerated in his pain and hunger-madness had only been doing his duty.

In fact, no matter what Harperus claims, since he was doing his duty, to the best of his ability, he was as "good" as I—perhaps my spiritual better. Certainly he is—was—not the one with blood on his conscience.

Could this mean, in the end, that the fanatics who had called him a demon, and evil, were actually *right?* The question haunted him, and Harperus, who had found him shivering in a field after his flight, had not helped. Harperus merely shrugged the entire question off, saying that the guard had followed the orders of a superior who was in the wrong. He further claimed that the man must at some point have *known* that his

superior was in the wrong, and that evened the scales between himself
and the man he had murdered.

*But Harperus is a Deliambren, and they are facile creatures. They can
make white into black and sun into midnight with their so-called logic.*
Harperus simply could not understand why this should torment him so;
after all, it was over and done with, and there was nothing more to be
said or done but to move on.

*Oh, yes. To move on, without a load of guilt upon my soul so heavy
that I cannot fly.*

T'fyrr sighed gustily, and turned away from the window, waving at the
machine again. It started right up obediently. Not that T'fyrr didn't know
this particular human song by heart, but he wanted to have every nuance
that Harperus had recorded. This was a love duet, sung by two of the
finest of the human musicians—at least in T'fyrr's estimation—that Harperus had ever captured in his little cubes.

*Lark and Wren. Why do so many of these humans bear the names of
birds, I wonder?*

Of course, part of the passion here was simply because the two who
sang this song of love *were* lovers, and they allowed their feelings free
voice. Still, T'fyrr had heard other humans who were their equals since
he had descended from the mountains of his homeland, and not all of
those were represented in Harperus' collection.

The one called Nightingale, for instance. . . .

A Haspur's memory was the equal of any Deliambren storage crystal,
and his meeting with Nightingale was fraught with such power and light
that for a moment it completely overwhelmed his terrible gloom.

He and Harperus had taken a place for the Deliambren's living-wagon
in a park, a place created by Gypsies for travelers to camp together. This
was enlightened altruism; they charged a fee for this, and the intent of
the place was to sell them services they might not otherwise have in the
wilderness between cities.

*Still, they erect and maintain such Waymeets; surely they deserve rec-
ompense. I cannot fault them for charging fees.*

T'fyrr had been restless, and Harperus had not seen any reason why
he should have to remain mewed up in the wagon—the Gypsies were
very assiduous about protecting the peace of their patrons. So he had
gone for a walk, out under the trees surrounding the camping-grounds,
and after an interval, he had heard a strange, wild music and followed it
to its source.

It had been a woman, a Gypsy, playing her harp beside a stream. He
had know enough about humans even then to recognize how unique she
was. Black-haired, dark-eyed, her featherless skin browned to a honey-
gold from many miles on the open road beneath the sun, she was as
slender and graceful as a female of his own race and as ethereal as one
of the beings that Harperus called "Elves." With her large, brooding eyes,
high cheekbones, pointed chin and thin lips, she would probably have
daunted him in other circumstances, since those features conspired to
give her an air of haughty aloofness. But her eyes had been closed with
concentration; her lips relaxed and slightly parted—and her music had

entwined itself around his heart and soul, and he could not have escaped if he had wanted to.

They had shared a magical afternoon of music, then, once she finished her piece and realized that he was standing there. She had been as eager to hear some of the music of his people as he had been to learn the music of hers. An unspoken, but not unfelt, accord had sprung up between them, and T'fyrr sometimes took that memory out and held it between himself and despair when his guilt and gloom grew too black to bear.

The wagon lurched, and T'fyrr caught himself with an outstretched hand-claw.

Deliambren chairs were not made for a Haspur; the backs were poorly positioned for anyone with wings. Harperus had compromised by having a stool mounted to the floor of the wagon, with a padded ring of leather-covered metal that T'fyrr could clutch with his foot-talons a few *krr* above the floor. It was only a compromise, and T'fyrr found himself jarred out of his memory of that golden afternoon with Nightingale as the wagon lurched and he had to clutch, not only the footring, but the table in front of him, to avoid being pitched to the floor.

Those stabilizer-things must be broken again. Much of the Deliambren's equipment had a tendency to break fairly often; Harperus spent as much time fixing the wagon as he did driving it. Most of the time the things that broke merely meant a little inconvenience; once or twice the Deliambren had actually needed to secure the wagon in a place that could be readily defended at need and call his people for someone to bring him a new part.

Still, this was a marvelous contraption. T'fyrr had, out of purest curiosity, poked his beak into the wagons of other travelers, and this behemoth was to those little horse-drawn rigs as he was to a scarcely fledged starling.

The wagon was divided into four parts: an eating and sitting part, where he was now; a sleeping part; a bathing and eliminating part; and a mysterious part that the Deliambren would allow no one into but himself. T'fyrr suspected that this final part was where the controls for the wagon were, and where Harperus kept some of the "technical" and "scientific" instruments that he used. Not that it mattered. T'fyrr was supremely incurious where all that nonsense was concerned.

The wagon could propel itself down a road without any outside pulling by horses or other draft-beasts. Right at the moment it was doing just that, although up until this point the Deliambren had taken exacting pains to keep humans from knowing it could move of itself. On the hottest days, it remained cool within—on the coldest, it was as warm as the Haspur could have wished. There were mystical compartments where fresh food was kept, remaining fresh until one wished to eat it. There was another kind of seat for elimination of bodily waste, and a tube wherein one could stand to be sluiced clean with fresh water. The whole of the wagon was most marvelously appointed: shiny beige wall and ceiling surfaces, leather-covered seating, rough, heavy rugs fastened down on the floor that one could dig one's talons into to avoid being flung about while the wagon was moving. Even the beds were acceptable, and it had been difficult for T'fyrr to find an acceptable bed—much less a comfortable one—since he had come down out of the mountains.

The very windows of this contrivance were remarkable. *He* could see out, but no one could see in. T'fyrr still did not understand how that was possible.

Unfortunately, the view displayed by those windows at the moment was hardly savory.

And Harperus claims that this is not the vilest part of this city! It is difficult to believe.

The Haspur lived among the tallest mountains on Alanda; while they were not very territorial by nature, they were also not colony-breeders. Each Haspur kept a respectable distance between his aerie and those of his neighbors. No enclave of Haspur ever numbered above a thousand—and there were at least that many humans just in the area visible from the window of the wagon!

They crammed themselves together in dwellings that were two and three stories tall, with the upper floors extending out over the street in such a way that very little sunlight penetrated to the street below. There must have been four or five families in each of the buildings, and each family seemed to have half a dozen children at absolute minimum. T'fyrr could not imagine what it must sound like with all of them meeping and crying at once. And how did their parents manage to feed them all? A young Haspur ate its own weight in food every day during the first six years of its growth; after that, he ate about half his own weight each day until he was full-grown. That was one reason why Haspur tended to limit their families to no more than two—T'fyrr could not even begin to imagine the amount of food consumed by *six* children!

This was not even a good place in which to raise young. In addition to the lack of sun, there was a profound lack of fresh air in this quarter. The buildings restricted breezes most cruelly. T'fyrr did not want to think about how hot it must be, out there in the street; why these people weren't running mad with the heat was a mystery. And the noise must be deafening, a jarring cacophony also likely to drive one mad.

Perhaps they are all mad; perhaps that is why they have so many offspring.

Haspur did not have a particularly good sense of smell, which he suspected was just as well, for he was certain that so many people crowded together—like starlings!—must create an environment as filthy as a starling roost.

The crowds seemed to be thinning, though, and the standard of construction in the residences rising the farther they went. He was not imagining it—there definitely was more room between the buildings; there were even spots of green, though the greenery was imprisoned away behind high walls, as if the owners of the property were disinclined to share even the sight of a tree or a flower with the unworthy.

There were fewer children in the street, too, and those few were not playing; they were with adults, supervised. Some even seemed to be working under adult supervision, sweeping the gutters, scrubbing walls, polishing gates.

They paused for a moment; T'fyrr couldn't see what was going on at the front of the coach, but a moment later they were on the move again and he saw why they had stopped. There was a simple wooden gate meant to bar the road, now pulled aside, and several armed guards to make certain no one passed it without authorization. They watched the coach pass by stoically enough, but T'fyrr noted that they did seem—impressed? puzzled?

Well, Harperus is Deliambren, and he was bent on displaying the Deliambren wonders to the court of the High King . . . I suppose he must have decided to begin with everyone in the city.

Harperus had insisted that here in Lyonarie it was of utmost importance to display as much power as one could, conveniently. Abstractly, T'fyrr understood this; the powerful were never impressed by anyone with *less* power than they, after all. But this business of going out of their way to look strange and different, including operating the coach without horses—

Looking different can be hazardous; I have had a crop full of what that hazard can be. Displaying too much power can incite as much envy as anything else, and the envious, when powerful, are often moved to try and help themselves to what has excited that envy, at whatever cost to the current owner.

Still, Harperus claimed that he had "connections" at the court of Theovere, and given the dangerous trends of the past two years, he and his people had felt it was time to employ those "connections."

Theovere was a music lover of the most fanatic vein; apparently this was what had been occupying the time he should have been spending doing his duty as High King. Originally, Harperus was going to offer Theovere one of the music machines and a set of memory-crystals as a blatant bribe for a little more influence in legislation, but since the time that original plan had been conceived, he had evolved a better one—

Better, not just because it means no dangerous "technology" will be in the hands of those who might somehow manage to find an unpleasant use for it, but because it will mean—or so he thinks—that he will have a direct influence instead of an indirect one.

T'fyrr sighed, flipped his wings to position them more comfortably, and drummed his talons on the table. He was not looking forward to this. Harperus' plan was to have T'fyrr appointed as an official Court Musician to the High King himself. Harperus was unshakably certain that once the High King heard T'fyrr sing, the Haspur would become a royal favorite. And once a nonhuman was a royal favorite, it would be much more difficult for other interests to get laws restricting the rights of nonhumans past the High King.

Interests such as the human Church, perhaps . . . though I am not particularly sanguine about one Haspur being able to overcome the interests of the Church, however optimistic Harperus may be. Religion rules the heart, and the heart is the most stubborn of adversaries. Rule the religion, and you rule the heart, and no one can oppose you—unless what you offer is better. Then, you must convince them that what you have is better, and people will die to hold on to what they already believe. . . .

T'fyrr twitched his tail irritably. Harperus was optimistic about a great many things—and T'fyrr did not share his optimism in most of them.

Even if we can get in to see this High King, there is no guarantee he will be impressed with my singing. Even if he is, there is no guarantee that he will actually do anything about it personally; and from what I have seen, if he leaves my disposition up to his underlings, they will find a way to "lose" me. No, Harperus is counting on a great deal of good luck, and good luck seems to have deserted me.

T'fyrr glanced out the windows again and was impressed, though in a negative fashion, by the homes he now passed. *These* dwellings—each a magnificent work of art, each set in its own small park and garden—were clearly owned by those of wealth and high rank. And the guards on that gate they had passed showed just how unlikely it would be for a commoner to get access to these lovely garden-spots.

So the low and poor must crowd together in squalor, while the wealthy and high live in splendor. If I were low and poor—I think I would go elsewhere to live. My home would still be poor, but at least I would have sunlight and fresh air, green things about me and a little peace.

But—perhaps these humans enjoyed living this way. Starlings certainly did. That made them even less understandable.

Not that he had come close to understanding them so far. The humans' own Sacrificed God spoke of fairness and justice and faith in the goodness of others. These things should prevent believers from doing harm to strangers. Why should an underling, clearly seeing his superiors doing vile things to another living being, believe that those things were justified? How could he be convinced that another being, who had done *no* harm, was a monster worth destroying? How could such a man be so convinced that those superiors were correct that he would spend his own life to carry out their will?

Perhaps those superiors *were* right; perhaps T'fyrr was as potentially evil as they claimed. After all, *he* was the one who had killed. Perhaps he misunderstood what the Sacrificed God was all about—after all, if the Deliambrens could make white into black, maybe the humans could, too.

I only hope that Harperus' plan works as well as he thinks it will, T'fyrr thought, depression settling over him again. *I might somehow redeem myself, if only I can be in a position where I can do some real good—or perhaps this helplessness to affect anything for the better is punishment for my evil. . . .*

T'fyrr was not as expert at reading human expressions as he would have liked, but there was no mistaking the look the Court official facing them wore on *his* refined visage.

Disdain.

Not all of Harperus' Deliambren charm *or* magic had been able to remove that look from the face of this so-called "Laurel Herald." He had taken in the splendor of Harperus' costume—a full and elaborate rig that made the Deliambren look to T'fyrr's eyes rather like one of those multitiered, flower-bedecked, overdecorated cakes that some races produced at weddings and other festivities. He had watched the coach drive itself off to a designated waiting place with a similarly lifted brow. Of course, he was probably used to seeing similar things every day, and his livery of scarlet and gold, embroidered on the breast with a winged creature so elaborately encrusted with gold bullion that it was impossible to tell what it was supposed to be, was just as ornate in its way as Harperus' costume. He sat behind a huge desk—a desk completely empty so far as T'fyrr could se—in the exact center of an otherwise barren, marble-walled and mosaic-floored chamber. The walls were covered with heroic paintings of stiff-faced humans engaged in conflicts, or stiff-faced humans posing in front of bizarre landscapes. There was a single bench behind the desk, where many young humans in similar livery sat quietly.

Now he waited for Harperus to declare himself, which Harperus was not at all loath to do. The Deliambren adored being able to make speeches.

"I am Harperus, the Deliambren Ambassador-at-large," he announced airily to the functionary. He went on at length, detailing the importance of his position, the number of dignitaries he had presented his credentials to and the exalted status of the Deliambren Parliament. Finally, he came to the point.

"I have a presentation to make to Theovere," he concluded.

Not "His Majesty High King Theovere," but the simple surname, as if he and the High King were of equal stature. T'fyrr was impressed, by Harperus' audacity if nothing else.

The title Harperus claimed was not precisely a fiction, although very little of what the Deliambren actually did on his extensive trips ever had anything to do with conventional diplomacy. And it was entirely possible he had presented his credentials to every one of the dignitaries he named—they were all wealthy enough to afford Deliambren goods, and Harperus often acted as a courier for such things. The official favored Harperus with a long moment of silence, during which the "Laurel Herald" scrutinized the Deliambren as carefully as an oldster examining her daughter-in-law's aerie for dirt in the corners, unpolished furniture, or a fraction less *klrrthn* than was proper.

Harperus simply stood there, radiating a cool aplomb. T'fyrr was grateful that no human here could possibly have enough experience with Haspur to read their expressions and body language, or he would have given it all away with his rigid nervousness. He stood as straight and as stiffly as a perching-pole, his wings clamped against his back. Probably the official didn't notice, or if he did, thought it was stiff formality and not nerves.

He didn't seem to notice the Haspur at all; in the simple silk bodywrap, T'fyrr probably looked like a slave.

Finally the "Laurel Herald" elected to take them at face value; he signaled to a boy he referred to as "Page," one of the dozen waiting quietly on the bench behind his desk, and gave them over into the boy's keeping.

"Take them to the Afternoon Court," the Herald said, shortly, and turned his attention to other business on his empty desk.

After an interminable walk down glass-walled corridors that passed through the middle of mathematically precise gardens, the boy led them toward—a structure. If the scale of the Palace had been anything T'fyrr considered normal, it would have been another wing of a central building. But since everything was on such a massive scale, this "wing" was the size of entire Palaces. It was certainly the size of the huge Cathedral in Gradford, which was one of the largest human buildings T'fyrr had ever seen.

"That's Court, my lords," the boy explained, enunciating carefully. "That's all that goes on in that Palace building, just Court. Morning and Afternoon Court, informal Court, formal Court, Judiciary, Allocation, City—"

The boy rattled on until T'fyrr shook his head in disbelief. How many ways could one entitle the simple function of hearing problems and meeting people? Evidently quite a few . . .

The bureaucracy here must be enough to stun a thinking being. I feel dizzy.

The doors at the end of the corridor swung open without a hand to open them as they approached; T'fyrr glanced sideways at Harperus, who smirked in smug recognition.

A Deliambren device, of course. Why am I not surprised?

The doors closed behind them, silently, and the Haspur noted larger versions of the Deliambren lighting that Harperus employed in his coach hanging from the ceiling, encased in ornate structures of glass and gold. There were probably hundreds more examples of Deliambren wonders here, but none of them would be of the type that could be taken apart without destroying them.

Well, no matter what the Church says about the "evil magic" of those who are not human, past High Kings have not scrupled to buy and use our devices. T'fyrr grimaced. *No matter what happens, I would place a high wager that they would* continue *to use such things, even in the face of a Church declaration of Anathema. The Church would either look the other way, or the High King would pay the fine and continue to have his lighting and his self-opening doors.*

The High King would be able to *afford* whatever fine the Church levied without even thinking about it; T'fyrr knew, after traveling so long with Harperus, just how much that lighting, those doors, probably cost. Nor was the display of wealth limited to the nonhuman devices so prominently displayed and used. Of course, the money came from somewhere, and T'fyrr's mind played out an image of the human hive they had come through.

They followed down a hallway paved in polished marble with matching marble paneling. Graceful designs had been incised into the marble of the walls and gold wire inlaid in the grooves. At intervals, along the wall and beneath the lighting, where they were displayed at their best advantage, were graceful sculptures of humans and animals, also of marble with details of gold inlay. Between the sculptures stood small marble tables, topped with vases made of semiprecious jade, malachite and carnelian. The vases were filled with bouquets, not of fresh flowers, but of flowers made of precious stones and gold and silver wire.

T'fyrr could not even begin to calculate the cost of all this. Surely just one of those flowers would keep a commoner out in Lyonarie fed and clothed for a year!

The page led them to a pair of gold-inlaid, bronze doors, each a work of art in itself, depicting more humans—though for once, these were not in conflict, but gathered for some purpose. The doors swung open, and the boy waved them in.

"They'll have brought your name to the Presiding Herald," the boy whispered as T'fyrr caught sight of a jewel-bedecked throng just inside the door. "He'll add you to the list; just listen for him to announce you, and then present yourself to His Majesty."

"Thank you," Harperus said gravely. The boy bobbed an abrupt little bow, and hurried off; Harperus strode between those open doors as if he had every right to be there, and T'fyrr moved in his wake, like a silent, winged shadow.

He had not donned all of the finery that Harperus had wanted him to put on—a huge, gemmed pectoral collar, ankle-bracelets, armbands and wristbands, a dusting of gold powder for his wings. Now he was glad that he had not. Not only had the wrist and armbands and bracelets felt *far* too much like fetters, but T'fyrr was certain that he would only have looked ridiculous in the borrowed gear, as if he was trying to ape these jeweled and painted humans, who were oh-so-carefully *not* staring at the nonhumans in their midst. There did not appear to be any other nonhuman creatures in this room, although it was difficult to be certain of that. They could have been crammed up against the white marble walls—that, evidently, was the place where those of little importance were relegated. The magic circle of ultimate status was just before the throne, within earshot of everything that went on upon the dais. Harperus strolled toward that hallowed ground quite as if he had a place reserved for him there, and to T'fyrr's amazement, the haughty courtiers gave way before him.

Perhaps they are frightened by his costume!

The nearer they got to the throne, the more annoyed and resentful the glances of those giving way for them became. Just at the point where T'fyrr was quite certain Harperus was about to be challenged, the Deliambren stopped, folded his arms, and stood his ground, his whole attitude one of genial *listening.* T'fyrr did his best to copy his friend.

Harperus was *truly* paying attention to what was going on around the throne, unlike many of the humans here. As T'fyrr watched and listened, following the Deliambren's example, he became aware that there was something very wrong. . . .

The High King—who did not look particularly old, though his short hair was an iron gray, and his face sported a few prominent lines and wrinkles—sat upon a huge, gilded and jeweled throne that was as dreadful an example of bad taste as anything Harperus had ever inflicted on an unsuspecting T'fyrr. The King's entire attitude, however, was not at all businesslike, but rather one of absolute boredom.

On both sides of the throne were richly dressed humans in floor-length ornate robes embroidered with large emblems, with enormous chains of office about their necks, like so many dressed up dogs with golden collars. But these dogs were not the ones obeying the command of their master— rather, the prey was in the other claw entirely.

Harperus had been right. Harperus had actually been right. The High

King virtually parroted everything these so-called advisors of his told him to say.

Now, T'fyrr was mortally certain that very few of the courtiers were aware of this, for the Advisors bent over their monarch in a most respectful and unctuous manner, and whispered in carefully modulated tones what it was they thought he should say. They were taking great care that it appear they were only advising, not giving him orders. But a Haspur's hearing was as sharp as that of any owl, and T'fyrr was positive from the bland expression on Harperus' face that the Deliambren had some device rigged up inside that bizarre head-and neck-piece he sported that gave him the same aural advantage.

During the brief time that they stood there, waiting their turn, King Theovere paid little or no attention to matters that T'fyrr thought important—given as little acquaintance as he had with governing. There were several petitions from Guildmasters, three or four ambassadors presenting formal communications from their Kings, a report on the progress of the rebuilding at Kingsford—

Well, those might easily be dismissed, as Theovere was doing, by handing them over to his Seneschal. There was nothing there that he really needed to act upon, although his barely hidden yawn was rather rude by T'fyrr's standards. But what of the rest?

There was an alarming number of requests from Dukes, Barons, and even a mere Sire or two from many of the Twenty Kingdoms, asking the High King's intervention with injustices perpetrated by *their* lords and rulers. Wasn't that precisely the kind of thing that the High King was *supposed* to handle? Wasn't he supposed to be the impartial authority to keep the abuse of power to a minimum? That was how T'fyrr understood the structure of things. The High King was the ultimate ruler, and his duty was not only to his own land but to see that all the others were well-governed—enforcing that, even to the point of placing a new King on a throne if need be.

But most of these petitions, like the rest of the work, he delegated to his poor, overburdened Seneschal—everything that he did not dismiss out of hand with a curt "take your petty grievances back to your homeland and address them properly to your own King."

The Seneschal, however overworked he already was, always looked pained when the King used *that* particular little speech, but he said nothing.

Perhaps there isn't a great deal that he can do, T'fyrr thought. The Seneschal's chain was the last gaudy of all the chains of office—perhaps that meant that, among the Advisors, he had the least power.

The rest of the Advisors however were not so reluctant to voice their opinions—which were universally positive. They actually congratulated the High King every time he dismissed a petition or passed it on to the Seneschal.

They were particularly effusive when he trotted out that little speech.

"A fine decision, Your Majesty," someone would say. Another would add, as predictably as rhyming "death" with "breath," "It is in the interest of your land and people that they see you delegate your authority, so that when you are truly needed, you will be free to grant a problem your full attention." And a third would pipe up with, "You must be firm with these people, otherwise every dirt-farming peasant who resents paying tax and tithe to his overlord and the Church will come whining to you for redress of his so-called wrongs."

And the High King smiled, and nodded, and suppressed another yawn.

T'fyrr flexed his talons silently, easing the tension in his feet by clamping them into fists until they trembled. How in the world did Harperus think he could help with *this* situation? The King was getting all of this bad advice from high-ranking humans who were probably very dangerous and hazardous to cross!

Memories of fetters weighing him down made him shiver with chill in that overly warm room. Hazardous to cross. . . .

But before he could say anything to Harperus, the Presiding Herald announced their names, and it was too late to stop the Deliambren from carrying out his plan.

"My Lord Harperus jin Lothir, Ambassador-at-large from the Deliambren's, and T'fyrr Redwing, envoy of the Haspur—"

A tiny portion of T'fyrr's mind noted the rich tones of the human's voice with admiration; the rest of him was engaged in trying to watch the reactions of anyone of any importance to the announcement.

The King's face lit up the moment Harperus stepped forward; as the Deliambren launched into a flowery speech lauding the greatness of King Theovere, and the vast impact of the High King's reputation across the face of Alanda, the Advisors waited and watched like an unkindness of ravens waiting for something to die. They didn't know what Harperus was up to—if, indeed, he was up to anything. That bothered them, but what clearly bothered them more was the fact that for the first time Theovere was showing some interest and no boredom.

Theovere might not be the man he once was, but he still knows where the "marvels" come from.

Now T'fyrr wondered if the trouble *was* with the King's age; there was a certain illness of the aged where one regressed into childhood. Theovere certainly betrayed some symptoms of childishness. . . .

T'fyrr followed the speech; he knew it by heart, and his cue was just coming up. Without pausing or skipping a beat, Harperus went from the speech to T'fyrr's introduction.

"—and I bring before you one who has heard of your generous patronage of the art of music, the envoy of goodwill from the Haspur of the Skytouching Mountains where no human of the Twenty Kingdoms has ever ventured, here to entertain you and your Court."

Harperus stepped back, and T'fyrr quickly stepped forward. One of the Advisors opened his mouth as if to protest; T'fyrr didn't give him a chance to actually say something.

He had already filled his lungs while he waited for his cue, and now he burst into full-chested song.

Although the Haspur had their own musical styles, they also had the ability to mimic anything so exactly that only another Haspur could tell the mimicry from the genuine sound. T'fyrr had chosen that lovely human duet to repeat—it was ideally suited to his voice, since it was antiphonal, and he could simulate the under- and overtones of an instrumental accompaniment with a minimum of concentration. He did improve on the original recording, however. While Master Wren was a golden tenor, Lady Lark's lovely contralto was not going to impress an audience this sophisticated—so T'fyrr transposed the female reply up into the coloratura range and added the appropriate trills, glissandos and flourishes.

The King sat perfectly still, his eyes actually bulging a little in a way that T'fyrr found personally flattering, though rather unattractive. With his superior peripheral vision, he could keep track of those courtiers nearest him, as well, and many of them were positively slack-jawed with amazement.

His hopes and his spirits began to rise at that point. Perhaps he *was* impressive to this jaded audience! Perhaps he *would* be able to accomplish something here!

The instant that he finished, the staid, etiquette-bound courtiers of High King Theovere broke into wild and completely spontaneous applause.

But the Advisors applauded only politely, their eyes narrowed in a way that T'fyrr did not at all like. They resembled ravens again; this time sizing up the opportunity a snatch a bite.

"So," Harperus muttered under his breath, as T'fyrr took a modest bow or two, "now do you think I'm crazy?"

"I know you are crazy," the Haspur replied in a similarly soft voice, "but you are also clever. That is a bad combination for your enemies."

The Deliambren only chuckled.

CHAPTER FOUR

Ah, T'fyrr thought with resignation, perched uncomfortably upon the tall stool that had been brought for him. *I do enjoy being talked about as if I was not present.*

This was not the first time he had found himself in that position. At least, in this case, the discussion concerned his life and prosperity, not his imminent and painful death.

And at least this time he was seated, and on a relatively appropriate stool—in deference to his wings and tail—rather than standing in an iron cage, fettered at every limb.

Harperus was not part of this discussion, this Council session; the Deliambren had not been invited. This was probably more of an oversight than a deliberate insult, since the subject of this meeting was T'fyrr and not Harperus. T'fyrr wished profoundly for his company, though; as the only nonhuman, as well as the object of discussion, he was alternately being ignored and glared at. It would have been less uncomfortable if Harperus had been there to share the "experience."

By the standards of the Palace so far, this was a modest room, paneled in carved wood, with wooden floors and boasting Deliambren lighting.

The Council members, all of the King's Advisors, sat at a rectangular marble-topped table with the King at the head and T'fyrr at the foot. *They* had carved wooden chairs that could have doubled as thrones in many kingdoms; the King had a simpler wooden replica of the monstrosity in the room in which he held Court, gilded as well as carved. Behind the King stood a circle of four silent bodyguards in scarlet and black livery, armed to the teeth, in enameled helms and breastplates, as blank-faced as any Elf.

If they projected the fact that they are dangerous any harder, there would be little puddles of "danger" on the floor around them. Look, it's "danger," don't step in it!

"I want him as my personal Court Musician," King Theovere said, with a glare across the table at his Seneschal. The King had convened this Council meeting as soon as Court was over—and he had cut Court embarrassingly short in order to arrange the time for the meeting. Evidently nothing could be done, not even the appointment of a single musician to the royal household, without at least one Council meeting. But it was obvious to T'fyrr that no matter what his Advisors thought, this meeting was going to go the King's way. He wondered if they realized that yet. . . .

Lord Marshal Lupene shrugged his massive shoulders. The Marshal was an old warrior, now gone to fat to an embarrassing extent, though from the way he carried himself it was likely he didn't realize it—or didn't want to. "Your Majesty might consider what the envoys both have to say about it. They might have other plans."

Theovere did not quite glower, but T'fyrr was as aware as Theovere that the Lord Marshal's implying that the King had not already consulted with T'fyrr and Harperus was cutting dangerously close to insubordination. This Lord Marshal must have been very sure of himself to chance such insolence.

"He is willing—even eager!" Theovere said angrily as T'fyrr nodded slightly, though no one paid any attention to him. "The Deliambren Ambassador says that he can manage without T'fyrr along, that he and T'fyrr were really no more than convenient traveling companions. I tell you, I want him in my employ starting from this moment—"

Lord Chamberlain Vidor, who had charge of the King's Court Musicians, pursed his thin lips. The Lord Chamberlain was as cadaverous and lean as the Lord Marshal was massive. "Your Majesty cannot have considered the impact this will have on his other musicians," Vidor intoned, keeping his disapproval thinly veiled. "Musicians are delicate creatures with regards to their sensibilities and morale—appointing this *Haspur* could wreak great damage among them. After all—he isn't even human, much less a Guild Bard!"

Theovere turned towards his Chamberlain and raised one bushy eyebrow. "The second follows upon the first, doesn't it?" he asked testily. "The Guild won't *accept* nonhumans, which makes it altogether impossible for T'fyrr to *be* one. I have, in fact, considered the impact of this appointment, and I think it will serve as an excellent example to my other musicians. Having T'fyrr in their in their midst will keep them on their mettle. They have been getting lazy; too much repetition and too little original work. They could use the competition." His tone grew silken as he glanced aside at Lord Guildmaster Koraen. "Perhaps it might give the Bardic Guild cause to reconsider their ban on nonhuman members, with so excellent a musician being barred from their ranks."

And from lending the Guild my prestige, my notoriety, T'fyrr added silently, seeing some of the same thoughts occurring to the Guildmaster. Koraen was good at hiding his feelings, but T'fyrr detected the sound of the bulky, balding man grinding his teeth in frustration. *The Guild has just lost a fair amount of prestige thanks to my performance, and might lose some royal preference if I continue to succeed here. This man is going to be my enemy.* He mentally shook his head. *What am I thinking? They are* all *going to be my enemies! The only question is how dangerous they consider me!*

"The Bardic Guild—" the Guildmaster began.

Theovere slammed his open palm down on the table. "The Bardic Guild had better learn some flexibility!" he all but shouted. "The Bardic Guild had better learn how to move with the times! The Bardic Guild had better come up with something better than elaborations on the same tired themes if they want to continue to enjoy my patronage!"

"But this sets a very bad precedent, Your Majesty," interjected another Council member, a thin and reedy little man who had not been introduced to T'fyrr. He wore a sour expression that seemed to be perpetually fixed on his face.

"My Lord Treasurer is correct," agreed the Lord Judiciar smoothly, an oily fellow of nondescript looks who had been among the first to congratulate the King every time he dismissed a petition. "It sets a very bad precedent indeed. You are the High King of the Twenty *Human* Kingdoms; what need have you to bring in outsiders to fill your household?"

Now, for the first time, T'fyrr saw signs of petulance on the King's face, a childish expression that looked, frankly, quite ridiculous on a man with gray hair. And the royal temper, held barely in check, now broke—but not into shouting.

"I want him in my household, and by God, I will *have* him in my household!" the King grated dangerously, glaring at them all. "In fact—" His expression suddenly grew sly. "I'll appoint him my *Chief* Court Musician! Yes, why not? I have a vacant place for a Chief Musician in my personal household; let T'fyrr fill it! That is a position solely under *my* control, subject to *my* discretion, and the Council can only advise me on it, as you know."

As the expressions of the Council members around the table changed from annoyed to alarmed, he chuckled, like a nasty little boy who has been picking the wings off flies.

"But—but Your Majesty—" the Lord Chamberlain spluttered, obviously blurting the first thing that came into his head. "That is impossible! The— the—Chief Court Musician must be a Knight! All of Your Majesty's household must be of the rank of Sire or better!"

"Oh, well, if that is all there is to it—" Before anyone could stop him, the King rose from his seat and walked to T'fyrr's, pulling out his ornamental short sword as he came. "I can certainly remedy that. I am a

Knight as well as a King, and according to the rules of chivalry, I can
make other Knights in either capacity as I choose. They need only be
worthy, and T'fyrr is certainly far more worthy of this post than any Bardic
Guild popinjay you've presented me with thus far!"

Oh, good heavens. He's lost his mind.

T'fyrr was not certain what he should do, so he did nothing, except to
rise, turn to face the King, and bow. This did not seem to bother Theovere
at all. The King tapped him on each shoulder in a perfunctory manner,
then resheathed the sword. The Council members sat numbly in their
places, struck dumb by the sudden and abrupt turn of events. Clearly the
King was not supposed to take so much initiative.

*Obviously they have never tried to balk him before. They have just
learned a lesson. I believe they thought the King too much in their control
to slip his leash like this.*

"There," the King said, casually. "Sire, T'fyrr, I now name thee a Knight
of the Court, whose duties shall be to serve as my Chief Minstrel in my
own Household. Do you accept those duties and swear to that service?"

"I do," T'fyrr rumbled, and *then* a storm of protests arose.

By the time it was all over, the Council had suffered complete defeat.
T'fyrr was still Sire T'fyrr—a title which was fundamentally an empty one,
since no gift of land went along with the honor. He was still the Chief
Court Musician. When the Lord Chamberlain swore that the other Court
Musicians would never share quarters with a nonhuman, the King gleefully
added a private suite in the royal wing to the rest of T'fyrr's benefits.
When the Lord Treasurer protested that the kingdom could not bear the
unknown living expenses of so—unusual—a creature, Theovere shrugged
and assigned his expenses to the Privy Purse. The only real objection that
anyone could make that Theovere could not immediately counter was the
objection that "the people will not understand."

Finally Theovere simply glared them all to silence. "The people will
learn to understand," he said in a threatening tone that brooked no argument. "It is about time that the people became a little more flexible, just
as it is about time that the Bardic Guild and members of my Court and
Council became a little more flexible, and the example can be set here
and now, in my own household!" He glared once more around the table.
"I *am* the King, and I have spoken! *You* work for *me*. Is that understood?"

T'fyrr then saw something he had not expected, as the faces of the
Council members grew suddenly pale, and they shut their lips on any
further objections.

What? he thought with interest. *What is this? And why? They have
been treating him like a child until this moment—now, why do they suddenly act as if they had a lion in their midst? What was it about that
phrase, "I am the King and I have spoken," that has sudden changed the
entire complexion of this?*

Silence reigned around the table, and Theovere nodded with satisfaction. "Good!" he said. "Now, you may all go attend to your pressing
duties. I am sure you have many. You keep telling me that you do."

The Council members rose to a man in a rustling of expensive fabric, bowed, and filed silently out, leaving only T'fyrr and Theovere, and Theovere's ever-present bodyguards. The King chuckled.

"I am not certain, Your Majesty, that I deserve such preferential treatment," T'fyrr said at last, after a moment of thought. *I have had enemies made this day of nearly every important man in this Court. This appointment has just become a most comfortable and luxurious setting in which to be a target!* "Perhaps if you chose to return to your original plan?" he suggested gently. "I am only one poor musician, and there is no reason to make my position in your household into a source of such terrible contention."

Theovere shook his head. "I meant what I said," the High King replied. "They can learn to live with it. There has been too much talk of late about the superiority of humans—and you have just proven that talk to be so much manure, and you have done so in my open Court. It is time and more than time for people to learn better—you will serve as my primary example."

Thus making me a target for every malcontent in the city, if not in the Twenty Kingdoms! Thank you so much, Your Majesty!

"I will call a page to show you to your new quarters, and have your friend, the Deliambren, sent there to meet you," the King continued, rising to his feet. T'fyrr did likewise with some haste, bowing as the King smiled. One of the bodyguards reached for a bellpull, and as the King moved away from the table, a young, dark-haired, snub-nosed boy appeared in the still-open door, clad in the High King's livery of gold and scarlet.

The King acknowledged T'fyrr's bow with an indolent wave of his hand, and walked out of the Council room, trailing all but one of his bodyguards. The one left behind, the one who had summoned the page, gestured to the boy as T'fyrr rose from his bow.

"This gentleman is now the King's Chief Court Musician in his personal household," the bodyguard said to the boy in a voice lacking all expression. He kept his face at an absolute deadpan as well, and T'fyrr could only admire his acting ability. "His name is Sire T'fyrr. You will escort him to the royal wing, see that he is comfortably lodged in the Gryphon Suite, and from here on, see that his needs are attended to. For the immediate future, you will see to his special needs in furnishing his quarters, then, when Sire T'fyrr indicates, find the Deliambren Ambassador and escort him to Sire T'fyrr."

The child bobbed his head in wordless acknowledgement, and the bodyguard left, apparently satisfied that the King's orders had been correctly delivered.

As soon as he was gone, the boy glanced up at T'fyrr, and the Haspur did not have to be an expert in human children to see that the boy was frightened of him. His face was pale, and his fists clenched at his sides. If T'fyrr said or did anything alarming, the poor fledgling would probably faint—or forget his duty and bolt for someplace safe to hide!

"I am a Haspur, young friend," T'fyrr said gently, and chuckled. "We don't eat children. We do eat meat, but we prefer it to be cooked—and we would rather not have had a speaking acquaintance with it before it became our dinner."

The child relaxed marginally. "Would you follow me, Sire T'fyrr?" he said in a trembling soprano. "Do you have any baggage that you will need brought to you?"

"My friend Harperus will see to all that," T'fyrr told him, and added as an afterthought, "He is the Deliambren. You should have no trouble finding him; he is the only being in the Palace who is dressed to look like a saint's palanquin in a Holy Day Festival Parade."

That broke the ice, finally; the little boy giggled, and stifled the laugh behind both hands. But the eyes above the hands were merry, and when he turned a sober face back to T'fyrr, his eyes had a sparkle to them that they had lacked until that moment.

"If you would come with me, then, Sire?" the boy said, gesturing at the door.

T'fyrr nodded. "Certainly—ah, what is your name? It seems rude to call you 'boy,' or 'page.'"

"Regan, Sire," the boy said, skipping to keep up with T'fyrr as the Haspur strode down the hallway. "But my friends call me Nob."

T'fyrr coaxed his beak into something like a human smile. He had learned that the expression made humans feel better around him. "Very well, Nob," he said, projecting good humor and casualness into his voice. "Now, if you were in my place, granted a title and a new home, what would *you* do first?"

"You mean, about the suite and all, Sire?" Nob asked, looking up at T'fyrr with a crooked grin. "Well, I might have some ideas—"

"Then by all means," T'fyrr told him, "let me hear them!"

Harperus lounged at his ease on one of the damask-covered sofas in the reception room of the suite, watching T'fyrr try out the various pieces of furniture that Nob had suggested he order brought down from storage. Somehow, it all matched—or at least, it coordinated, as the main colors of the suite were warm golds and browns, with gryphons forming the main theme of the carvings. Padded stools proved surprisingly comfortable, as did an odd, backless couch that Nob particularly recommended. And to replace the bed—

When T'fyrr had sketched what a Haspur bed looked like, Nob had studied the sketch for a moment, and then snapped his fingers with a grin of glee. He hadn't said a word to T'fyrr, but he had called another servant—an oddly silent servant—and handed him with the sketch with a whispered explanation.

Six husky men appeared about an hour later, just as Harperus arrived with more servants bearing T'fyrr's baggage. The men took the bed out without a single word and returned with something that was the closest thing to a Haspur bed that T'fyrr had *ever* seen in these human realms. He stared at it, mouth agape, while Nob grinned from ear to ear.

He had a suspicion that there was more to this than met the eye, and his suspicion was confirmed when Harperus took one look and nearly choked.

"Very well," he said, mustering up as much dignity as he could. "Obviously this is not the Haspur bed that it appears to be. What *is* it?"

Nob clapped both hands over his mouth, stifling a laugh. "*You* tell him, my lord!" he said to Harperus, gasping. "I—nay, I can't do it!"

He turned around, growing scarlet in the face, obviously having a hard time containing himself. T'fyrr waited, curiosity vying with exasperation, while Harperus struggled to get himself under control.

"It's—it's something no well-bred boy should know about at Nob's tender age," Harperus managed finally. "Let's just say, it isn't meant for sleeping."

Enlightenment dawned. "Ah! A piece of mating furniture!" T'fyrr exclaimed brightly, and clicked his beak in further annoyance when both Nob and Harperus went off into paroxysms of smothered laughter.

I cannot, and never will, understand why the subject of mating should make these humans into sniggering idiots, he thought a little irritably. *It is just as natural as eating, and there are no whispers and giggles about enjoying one's breakfast! So that explains the ever-so-reticent servant that found the thing; in a place like this, there must be a servant in charge of romantic liaisons!*

By the winds, there was probably even a division of labor—one servant for discreet liaisons, one for *very* discreet liaisons, one for indiscreet liaisons, one for the exotic. . . .

Well, at least Nob hadn't been so bound up in this silly human propriety nonsense that he refused to have the object sent for! It might be a piece of mating equipment to these humans, but it made a perfectly *fine* nest-bed, and T'fyrr looked forward to having one of the first completely comfortable nights he'd had in a very long time.

Finally, after many false starts, the page got himself back under control, although he would not or could not look Harperus in the eye. "If you need me any more, Sire," he told T'fyrr with a decent imitation of a sober expression, "just ring for me."

"Ring for you?" T'fyrr asked, puzzled, and Nob walked over to the wood-paneled wall, pulled aside a brown damask curtain, and pointed to a line of gilded brass bellpulls.

"This is the guards—this is the kitchen, if I'm off running an errand—this is the bath servants, if I'm off running an errand—this is the maid, in case you need something cleaned. This is for me—I'm *your* page now, Sire. I'll be sleeping in that little room just next to the bathroom. Unless you want someone older, I'll be your body servant, too. That means I dress you." Nob eyed the simple wrapped garment that T'fyrr wore for the sake of modesty. "Doesn't look as if there's all that much work tending to your wardrobe."

"Not really," T'fyrr agreed. "Do *you* want to be assigned to me?"

"Oh yes, Sire!" Nob replied immediately, and his artless enthusiasm could not be doubted. "There's status in it; I'd be more than just a page—and you'll be a good master, Sire. I can tell," he finished confidently.

T'fyrr sighed. "I hope I can live up to that, young friend," he answered, as much to himself as to the boy. "Well, so what are all these other bells?"

When Nob finished his explanations, Harperus intervened. "I can show him the rest, young one," the Deliambren said easily. "My people built most of the complicated arrangements in this Palace. You go see to getting your own quarters set up."

"Yes, my lord," Nob said obediently, as T'fyrr nodded confirmation of Harperus' suggestion. "Thank you, my lord, I appreciate that—"

As the boy whisked out of the suite, Harperus turned to T'fyrr. "Well, now you're a Sire, and that lad is your entire retinue. The thing to remember is that Nob's duty is always to *you*, first. That means if you keep him doing things for you all the time, he has no right to eat, rest, or even sleep."

T'fyrr's beak fell open as he stared, aghast. Harperus just shrugged.

"It's the way these boys are brought up," he said philosophically. "Chances are, he was hired as a child of four or five, and he doesn't even live with his own family anymore—he probably doesn't see them more than twice or three times a year. His whole life is in Palace service. Just remember that, and if you want the boy to have any time to himself, you'll have to order him to take it."

"I'll keep that in mind," T'fyrr said absently. *Every time I think I have seen the last of subtle human cruelties, another pops up! Can it be that there are masters who would keep their servants so bound as to permit them no time to eat or sleep? Is that why he said he thought I would be a good master?*

"Well, come let me show you the bathing room, old bird," Harperus said, oblivious to T'fyrr's thoughts. "You'll probably like it better than the one in the wagon; since this is a royal suite, there should be a tub big enough for you to splash around the way you do when you find a pond." The Deliambren shook his head with amusement. "Honestly, you look like a wren in a birdbath when you do that!"

"I do *not*," T'fyrr responded automatically, but followed Harperus anyway. This room was bigger than the entire traveling wagon put together, tiled on the walls, floor and ceiling in beige and brown. The bathroom was all Deliambren in its luxury, every fixture sculpted into some strange floral shape, the floor heated, the rack for the towels heated as well. The sink was big enough to bathe an infant in, the tub fully large enough to have a proper Haspur bath, and the "convenience"—convenient, and discreetly placed behind its own little door. The "usual" Deliambren lighting could be made bright or dim as one chose. There was even one of the Deliambren waterfalls that Harperus called a "shower-stall," though it was much more luxurious than the one in the wagon. There were full-length mirrors everywhere, and T'fyrr kept meeting his own eyes wherever he looked. The Deliambren showed him the various controls, then ran water into the basin.

"There," he said under the sound of the running water, "if there's any spies listening, and I'm sure there are, this should cover our conversation."

"Ah." T'fyrr nodded cautiously and pretended to finger another fixture, as if he was asking questions. "Well? Did this proceed as you hoped?"

"I'm overjoyed. You could not have done better," Harperus told him gleefully. "You absolutely exceeded my wildest wishes."

"I didn't do anything—" T'fyrr objected, feeling uncomfortable about taking praise for something he'd had no hand in.

"You kept your beak shut and let the King have his way by not giving his Advisors anything to use against you; that was enough," Harperus said. "Now, I'll have to make my instructions very brief—there is one bag that isn't yours; there are some devices in it that you will recognize. I want you to place them around your rooms; tell Nob that they're statues from your home. Then talk to Nob about everything that happens to you that you think I should know. If there are spies listening, it won't matter; they won't be surprised that you're asking advice from a page, they'll think it shows how stupid you are, and they won't know what those 'statues' are."

T'fyrr made a caw of distaste. "If they are what I think they are—I've seen those little eavesdroppers of yours. They are hideous, and you will make Nob and those spies believe that my people have no artistic talent whatsoever."

Harperus grinned and went on. "You'll need to get directions eventually to a tavern called the Freehold. It's owned by a Deliambren, and he'll be your contact back to us if you need anything else." He correctly interpreted T'fyrr's dubious expression. "Don't worry, before the week is out, people will think it's odd if you *haven't* visited there at least once. It's the center of social activity for every nonhuman of every rank in Lyonarie—and a fair number of humans, as well. It's like Jenthan Square in the Fortress-City. You might even go there just to have a good time."

T'fyrr nodded, relieved, and Harperus reached over and turned the water off. "You may want to leave specific orders with Nob for baths," he said, as if he was continuing an existing conversation. "You know how the lights work, of course. Can you think of anything else?"

His eyebrows signalled a wider range to that question than was implied by the circumstance. T'fyrr only shook his head.

"Not really," he said truthfully, spreading his wings a little to indicate that he understood the question for what it was. "I only hope I can serve Theovere as well as you expect me to. I am, after all, less of an envoy and more of a messenger of good will."

Harperus raised his eyebrows with amusement at T'fyrr's circumspect reply. "In that case, I'll leave you to settle in by yourself," he said. "Once the boy finishes with his own gear, you should have him fetch a meal for the two of you. You'll be expected to eat in your own quarters, of course—people are likely to be uneasy dining around anyone sporting something like that meathook in the center of your face."

People will be offended if I dare to actually take my meals in public, with the rest of the courtiers and folk of rank. After all, I'm only a lowly nonhuman. I shouldn't allow myself any airs.

"Of course," T'fyrr agreed, allowing his irony to show. "I'm not at all surprised."

Harperus took his leave—and T'fyrr swallowed his own feeling of panic at being entirely alone in this situation and went to look for "his" servant. He found Nob putting away the last of his belongings in a snug little room just off the bathroom. When he suggested food, Nob was not only willing, he was eager, suggesting to T'fyrr that it was probably well past the boy's usual dinnertime.

Or else, that like small males of every species, he was always hungry.

But when Nob returned with servants bearing dinner, it was with *many* servants bearing dinner, and with three of the King's Advisors following behind. T'fyrr welcomed them, quickly covering his surprise, and invited them to take seats while the servants made one small table into a large table, set places for all of them, and vanished, leaving Nob to serve as their waiter.

"If you would arrange yourselves as is proper, my lords," he said finally, "I have no idea of precedence among you, except that you are all greatly above my rank. I would not care to offend any of you."

His three unexpected dinner guests all displayed various levels of amusement. Lord Seneschal Acreon actually chuckled; Lord Secretary Atrovel (a cocky little man who clearly possessed an enormous ego) smirked slightly. Lord Artificer Levan Pendleton only raised his eyebrows and smiled. The Seneschal, a graying man so utterly ordinary that the only things memorable about him were his silver-embroidered gray silk robes and chain of office, took charge of the situation.

"As our host, Sire T'fyrr, you must take the head of the table. As the lowest in rank, I must take the foot—"

Lord Levan and Lord Atrovel both made token protests, which the Seneschal dismissed, as they obviously expected him to.

"Lord Secretary, Lord Artificer, I leave it to you to choose left or right hand," the Seneschal concluded.

Atrovel, a short, wiry, dark-haired man robed in blue and gold, grinned. "Well, since no one has ever accused me of being *sinister*, I shall take the right," he punned. Levan Pendleton cast his eyes up to the ornately painted ceiling, but did not groan.

"Since I am often accused of just that, it does seem appropriate," he agreed, taking the seat at T'fyrr's left. "We are all here, Sire T'fyrr, in hopes of showing you that not everyone in the King's Council is—ah—distressed by your presence."

Acreon winced. "So blunt, Levan?" he chided. The Lord Artificer only shrugged.

"I can afford to be blunt, Acreon," the man replied, and turned again to T'fyrr. T'fyrr found him fascinating; the most birdlike human he had yet met. His head sported a thick crest of graying black hair; his face was sharp and his nose quite prominent. Perched on the nose was a pair of spectacles; they enlarged his eyes and made him look very owl-like. The rest of the man was hidden in his silvery-gray robe of state, but from the way it hung on him, T'fyrr suspected he was cadaverously thin.

"Why can you afford to be blunt, my lord?" T'fyrr asked, a bit boldly. The human laughed.

"Because I am in charge of those who make strange devices, Sire T'fyrr," he replied genially. "No one knows if they are magical or not, so no one cares to discover if I can accomplish more than I claim to be able to do. That is why folk think me sinister."

"That, and the delightful little exploding toys, and the cannon you have conjured," Atrovel said with a smirk. "No one wants to retire to his room only to find one of those waiting for him, either."

"Oh, piff," Levan said, waving a dismissive hand. "They're too easy to trace. If I were going to get rid of someone, I'd choose a much subtler weapon. Poison delivered in a completely unexpected manner, for instance. In the bathwater, or a bouquet of flowers. It would be a fascinating experiment, just to find out what kind of dosage would be fatal under those circumstances." And he turned toward Nob, who was offering a plate of sliced meat, his eyes wide as the plate. "Thank you, child—and I'll have some of that pudding, as well."

"There, you see?" Atrovel threw up his hands. "No wonder no one wants to dine with you! You'd poison us all just to see how we reacted!" He helped himself to the meat Nob brought him, and turned toward T'fyrr. "Levan would like to get on your good side because his worst rival is Lord Commerce Gorode; *he's* in charge of the Manufactory Guild, and they are always trying to purloin Artificers' designs without paying for them—and Lord Gorode already hates you just because you aren't human."

"Ah," T'fyrr said, nonplussed at this barrage of apparent honesty. He hoped that Harperus' little "devices" were hearing all of this.

"The Seneschal," Atrovel continued, pointing his fork at Acreon, who munched quietly on a plate of green things without saying a word, "is on your side because he actually thinks you're honest. Are you?"

"I try to be," T'fyrr managed, and both Levan and Atrovel broke into howls of laughter.

"By God, this *is* more entertaining than Court Dinner!" Levan spluttered. "T'fyrr, you must be honest, or you'd never have answered that way! What a change from all those oily, wily Guild Bards! Dare I actually ask if you are interested in *music* instead of advancing yourself?"

"Music is—is my life, my lord," T'fyrr said simply, expecting them both to break into laughter again. But they didn't; they both sobered, and the Seneschal nodded.

"You see?" Acreon said quietly. "Honest, and a true artist. Innocent as this boy, here—Sire T'fyrr, I thought you might need a friend, now I am certain of it. I hope you will consider me to be your friend, and call on me if you need something the boy cannot provide."

T'fyrr was at an utter loss of what to say, so he replied with the feeling that was uppermost at that moment. "Thank you, thank you very much, Lord Acreon," he said, as sincerely as he could. "I am not so innocent that I do not realize that my position here is extremely delicate. The King offended many of high estate today, but I am the safer target for their wrath, and they will probably try to vent it sooner or later."

"Innocent, but not stupid," Levan said, jabbing a fork into his meat with satisfaction. "I like that. So, Atrovel, why are *you* here, anyway?"

Atrovel waved his knife airily. "Because I enjoy seeing so many of our pompous windbags—ah, excuse me, *noble Council members*—discomfited. It is no secret that I dislike most of them, and am disliked in return. The King trusts me because I amuse him; they hate that. I enjoy causing them trouble. They are boring, they have no imagination, and they don't appreciate music. That is enough for me."

"And you appreciate music?" T'fyrr asked. Although none of them really watched him eating, they weren't going out of their way to avoid watching him swallow down neat, small bites of absolutely raw meat. That was interesting. Although he cold eat other things—and would dine on the cooked meat on one tray, soon—he'd deliberately chosen the raw steak as a kind of test.

Levan snorted and picked up his goblet to drink before answering. "Enjoy? Oh, my dear T'fyrr, *this* is the foremost musical critic of the Court! Or at least, *he* thinks so!"

"I know so," Atrovel replied casually, raising one eyebrow. "Your performance, by the way, was absolutely amazing. Were you simulating an instrumental accompaniment with your *voice?*"

So someone had noticed! "A very simple one," T'fyrr admitted. "A ground only. I could not have replicated a harp, for instance—"

"Oh, don't start!" Levan interrupted. "I like music as well as the next man, but having it dissected? Pah! You two wait until you're alone and let the rest of us just listen without having to know what it all breaks down to!"

"Fine words from one who spends his life breaking things into their components to find out how the universe runs," Acreon pointed out mildly. He had graduated from salad to some mild cheese and unspiced meats. T'fyrr suspected chronic indigestion; hardly surprising, considering how hard he worked.

"I prefer to leave some few things a mystery, and music is one of them," Levan replied with dignity. "However—are all your people so gifted? Or are you the equivalent of a Bard among them?"

T'fyrr passed an astonishingly pleasant hour with the three royal Advisors, and after the Seneschal and the Artificer pled work and left, spent two more equally pleasant hours discussing the technicalities of music with Lord Atrovel. The diminutive fellow was as much of a dandy as Harperus, and just as certain of the importance of his own opinions, but he was also scathingly witty, and his observations on some of the other Council members had T'fyrr doubled up in silent laughter more than once.

When Lord Atrovel finally left, T'fyrr sent Nob off to bed (over the boy's protests that he was *supposed* to help the Haspur undress), and unwrapped himself. He let the silk wrapping fall to the floor—consciously. No more picking up after himself; no more going to fetch things.

I have to give the boy something to do, or he'll think he isn't doing his job. This was not a situation he had anticipated, to say the least.

He had thought—when he actually let himself entertain the notion of success at all—that he might possibly end up as one of the King's private musicians. He had a notion what that meant; he would have been a glorified servant himself. That would have been fine—but this was out of all expectation.

He palmed the lights off, and stayed awake awhile, cushioned in his new bed, thinking.

I have a servant, a retainer—someone who depends on me to be a good

*master or a bad, and has no choice but to deal with what I tell him to
do. What kind of master will I make?* That was one worry on top of
everything else; could he, would he become abusive? He had a temper,
the winds knew; if he lost it with this boy, he could damage the child,
physically. On the practical side, he had no idea of the strength or the
endurance of a human fledgling; Harperus had said the boy was—what?
Something like twelve years of age. What could he do? What shouldn't
he do?

*Perhaps it will be safest to watch him, and send him to rest at the first
sign that he is tired. I wonder if he can read? If not, I shall see to it that
he learns. If so, I shall find out if he enjoys reading, and make that one
of his tasks.* It would be a safe way to make the boy rest, even if he didn't
think he should.

As for the task Harperus had assigned to *him*—

*I believe I have a far wider field of opportunity than either of us
thought.* He would have to give this a great deal of consideration. If he
was going to be the King's Chief Musician, that implied that he would
be performing solo, probably quite often, possibly even on a daily basis.
He would have plenty of opportunity to sing things that just might put
the King in mind of some of the duties he was neglecting.

*I wish that I had one of the Free Bards here; the ones that Harperus
says work magic,* he thought wistfully. *It would greatly help if I could
use magic to reinforce that reminder. . . . If only Nightingale were here!
She and I make such a good duo—and she is a powerful worker of magic,
I know she must be, even though Harperus didn't mention her by name.
And it would be so good to have a real friend, someone I could trust
completely, to be here with me.*

As well wish for Visyr and Syri to come help him; the Free Bards were
all very nearly as far away as the Fortress-City and his other two friends.

Well, it would be enough for the moment for him to keep the Deliambrens aware of developments by means of those ugly little "devices" of
theirs. They must surely have gotten an earful tonight, before the talk
turned to music!

And that brought him to something else he really should think about.

Lord Acreon, Lord Levan, and Lord Atrovel.

Out of all of the King's Advisors, three—admittedly three of limited
power, but still—had openly allied themselves with him. The question
was, why had they done so? The reasons were without a doubt as various
as the men themselves. And likely just as devious. T'fyrr was under no
illusions; each of these men had agendas of their own that allying themselves with him would further. The King would certainly notice that they
were openly his "friends," and that could hardly hurt them. Right now,
the King was not very happy with most of his Advisors, and while he
might forget that by tomorrow, he also might *remember.*

Whatever had been done to lull the King into the state he was in now,
for the moment, T'fyrr had cracked it, and with that crack, some of *their*
power had escaped.

Lord Acreon, the Seneschal. T'fyrr had the oddest feeling that the Seneschal had meant every word he had said; that he had sided with T'fyrr

because he thought that T'fyrr was honest, a real musician, and needed a friend who understood the quagmire this Court truly was. He wasn't entirely certain if Acreon actually *liked* him, but Acreon was going to help him.

Perhaps Acreon himself is not certain if he likes me. I doubt that he has had much commerce with anything other than humans. I wonder if I frighten him a little? He does not strike me as a particularly brave man, physically, although I think he is very strong in the spirit. I also think, perhaps, he does not know how strong he is.

Could Acreon be trusted? Probably. Of the three, he was the one with the least to lose and the most to gain if T'fyrr succeeded, out of all expectation, in making the King see where his duty lay. He was already overburdened and uncredited for most of the work he did; if the High King began acting like the ruler he was supposed to be, a great deal of that burden would be lifted from the Seneschal's shoulders.

He might even be able to enjoy spiced meat again, without suffering a burning belly.

He decided that he would make use of the Seneschal in the lightest way possible—by asking advice, not on difficult things, but on the subject that the Seneschal probably knew better than any other, his fellow Advisors. Acreon would probably tell him the truth, and if the truth were too dangerous, T'fyrr suspected he would be able to hint well enough for the Haspur to guess at the truth. Very well. Trust the Seneschal, as long as Acreon had nothing to lose by what T'fyrr was doing.

Levan Pendleton. The Lord Artificer was a puzzle. He liked music well enough. He was fascinated by the workings of things, and devoured facts the way a child devoured sweets. Those traits, T'fyrr was used to—the Deliambrens were rather like that.

He is also utterly amoral. He saw no difficulty in ridding himself of an enemy by murder; had even boasted tonight how he would do so. T'fyrr, adept at reading the nuance of voices if not of human expressions, sensed that he meant every word he said. *He might even have been warning me, obliquely. He all but said openly that he was for sale. He might have been telling me that someone might buy his services to use on me.*

There were only two things that Levan Pendleton valued—fact and truth. They were also the only things he cared about; he had said, more than once, that no matter what the cost, he would not conceal facts or distort the truth, as least when it came to his discoveries about the workings of the world. He had described, as if it were only an amusing anecdote, how his stand had already gotten him in serious conflict with the Church, and that only his rank and position had saved him from having to answer to Church authority.

T'fyrr could supply him with plenty of facts, anyway. He had traveled in lands that the Lord Artificer had never even heard of, and that meant he could enlarge Levan's knowledge of Alanda. As for things closer to home, the devices and machines that the Artificer so loved, if he could not explain the workings of Deliambren machinery, he could at least supply information on the workings of simpler things. The staged pumps that brought water up to the highest aeries, for one thing, or the odd, two-wheeled contrivance that the Velopids rode instead of horses.

I can probably entertain Levan for months, even years, and as long as I entertain him, I am too valuable for him to eliminate. I am also too valuable for him to permit anyone else to get rid of me. I can trust Levan Pendleton, but within strict limits.

And those limits would be determined mostly by what T'fyrr could or could not supply. An added benefit was T'fyrr's vast collection of music, much of it from strange cultures. Levan liked music, and to have someone who could not only perform it but explain the meaning or the story was something *he* had not anticipated. This could be a very good position to be in, so long as T'fyrr did not overestimate the limits of his entertainment value.

Levan Pendleton would be most useful simply as a patron. If people didn't like to go to dinner with him—they would also be disinclined to try to eliminate or disgrace one of his friends.

Lord Secretary Atrovel. Now there was a puzzle! He seemed completely shallow, a sparkling brook that was all babble and shine on the surface, but was nothing more than a lively skin of water, unable to support or hold anything of value. Yet the man was witty, and while it was possible to be witty *and* be stupid, it wasn't very likely.

Atrovel had access to everything the King did and said. That was his job. Now, it was probably not a bad idea to have a flippant fellow for a secretary, a man who really didn't care a great deal about the correspondence and documents he handled. But still—T'fyrr had the feeling that that sparkling surface was not all there was to Atrovel.

Perhaps, though, the deepest thing about him is his pride. He was certainly a man who had no doubts whatsoever about his own worth, and had no modesty about it, either. He would be the first to tell you just how important he was.

That might have been what T'fyrr sensed: beneath the flippant exterior was a man with a deep sense of pride in himself. If that was true, then the worst thing one could do to Lord Atrovel would be to harm his pride, to make *him* look foolish. He would never forgive that, and as Secretary he had access to the means to take revenge. Certain papers could fall into the hands of an enemy, perhaps . . . certain others vanish before they could be signed.

Lord Atrovel could be trusted—warily. And T'fyrr would have to be very careful of that touchy little man's feelings.

Oh, this is all too much to think about— Yet there remained one more human that T'fyrr sensed he must consider tonight, before he slept.

High King Theovere.

Now there—there was a puzzle and a question more complicated than that of Lord Atrovel.

For one thing, he is not *sane. He is not rational. He has mood changes that do not necessarily correspond to what is going on around him, and his ability to concentrate is not good. His priorities are skewed. His Advisors don't care, because his insanity gives them leeway to do anything they really want. The problem is, what caused that?* Theovere was *not* the man he once was. Harperus had been quite emphatic about that. High King Theovere had been well-respected, if not precisely beloved; he had kept every one of the Twenty Kingdoms under his careful scrutiny. So what happened? Why did he suddenly begin to lose interest in seeing things well-governed?

Was it a lack of interest? Was he ill, in some way that simply didn't show itself on the surface? There were certainly hints of that in the childishness, the petulance, the obsessive interest in music and other trivialities.

And yet—and yet there was still something of the old King there as well. King Theovere wanted T'fyrr the way a child wants a new toy, yes, but there was something else beneath that childish greed.

He is using me. Something in him is still vaguely aware that there is trouble in his Kingdoms, trouble involving nonhumans, and he is using me, he said so himself. I am to provide an example of excellence and tolerance. And I don't think the Advisors are truly aware that he is using me in that way, even though they heard him say *so. They don't believe he could still have that much interest outside his little world of Bards and Musicians.*

So, was there something there that T'fyrr could touch, perhaps even something he could awaken?

I think so. In spite of the childishness, the pettiness—there is something there. I believe that I like him, or rather, I like what he could be. There is a King inside that child, still, and the King wants out again.

At some point, King Theovere had been an admirable enough leader that his bodyguards were *still* inspired to a fanatic loyalty. A man simply did not inspire that kind of loyalty just because he happened to have a title.

I wish I could talk to one of the bodyguards, honestly, T'fyrr thought wistfully. It would never happen, though. They had absolutely no reason to trust *him*. For all they knew, he was just another toy, this one presented to the King by a foreigner instead of one of his Advisors, but a toy and a distraction, nevertheless.

I don't want to be a toy, and I especially don't want to be a distraction. I want to remind him of what he was.

Well, to that end, he had delved into Harperus' store of memory-crystals and come up with several songs *about* King Theovere. Most of them weren't very good, which didn't exactly come as a shock, since they had been composed by Guild Bards—but there were germs of good ideas in there, and decent, if not stellar, melodies. *I could improve the lyrics; even Nob could improve on some of those lyrics.* He could sing those, and literally remind the King of what he had been.

And there were other songs he had picked up himself on the way, songs that actually had some relevance to one of the situations the King had sloughed off into the Seneschal's hands.

I can certainly sing those songs that Raven and the rest wrote about Duke Arden of Kingsford—how he saved all those people during the fire, how he's beggaring himself to rebuild his city. That should get his attention where reports won't!

And if T'fyrr got his attention, he just might be moved to do something about the situation.

If I put a situation in front of him in music—ah, yes, that is a good idea. And who better to suggest such situations than the man who would otherwise have to take care of them—Lord Seneschal Acreon? Oh, now *there* was an idea calculated to make the Seneschal happier!

He'll help. This is exactly the kind of help that he has been looking for—I would willingly bet on it. The only problem is that if anyone besides Acreon figures out what I'm doing, they'll know I'm not just a blank-brained musician; they'll know I'm getting involved, and I might be dangerous. Which will make me even more of a target than I was already.

Well, that couldn't be helped. He had made a promise and a commitment, and it was time to see them through. *Now I have a plan. Now I have a real means to do what Harperus wants me to. And I have a chance to redeem myself in the process, to counter the evil I have already done.*

Suddenly the tension in his back and wing muscles relaxed, as it always did when he had worried through a problem and found at least the beginnings of a solution.

That was all he needed to be able to sleep; in the next instant, all the fatigue that he'd been holding off unconsciously descended on him.

Ah . . . I didn't realize I was so . . . tired.

He was already in the most comfortable nest he'd had in ages, and in the most comfortable sleeping position he'd had since he'd begun traveling with Harperus.

This nest is very good . . . very, very good. I don't think I want to move.

It was just as well that he was settled in, for as soon as he stopped fighting off sleep, it stooped down out of the darkness upon him, and carried him away—to dreams of falling, iron manacles and screams.

Midnight. You'd think the city would be quiet.

It wasn't though; the rumble of cartwheels on cobblestones persisted right up until dawn, and a deeper rumble of the machineries turned by the swiftly moving river water permeated even one's bones.

Nightingale perched like her namesake on the roof of Freehold, staring out into the darkness at the lights across the street. No Deliambren lights, these—though they were clever enough; she'd noticed them earlier this evening, just outside the building, where two of them stood like sentinels on either side of the door. Some kind of special air—a gas—was what these lights burned. One of her customers had told her that. It was piped into them from somewhere else, and burned with a flame much brighter than candles, without the flicker of a candle.

With lights like that, you wouldn't have to wait for daylight to do your work. . . .

No, you could work all night. Or, better still, you could have someone else work all night for you.

There were similar lights burning inside that huge building, but not as many as the owner would like. He would have been happier if the whole place was lit up as brightly as full day. Only a few folk worked inside that building at night, those who cleaned the place and serviced the machines.

Nightingale leaned on the brick of the low wall around the roof, rested her chin on her hands, and brooded over those lovely, clear, cursed lights and all they meant.

She had learned more in her brief time here than she had ever anticipated, and most of it was completely unexpected.

When she had arrived here, she had been working under the assumption that the Free Bards' and the nonhumans' chiefest enemies were going to be the Church and the Bardic Guild, that if anyone was behind the recent laws being passed it would be those two powers. It made sense that way—if the High King really *was* infatuated with music and musicians, it made sense for the most influential power in his Court to be the Bardic Guild, and the Bardic Guild and the Church worked hand-in-glove back in Rayden.

Well, they have gotten a completely unprecedented level of power, that much is true. But the Bardic Guild was by no means the most important power in the Court. They weren't even as important as they thought they were!

No, the most important power in this place is across the street. In those buildings, in the hands of the men who own them.

The merchants who owned and managed the various manufactories were individually as powerful and wealthy as many nobles. But they had not stopped there; no, seeing the power that an organization could wield, they had banded together to form something they called the "Manufactory Guild." It was no Guild at all in the accepted sense; there was no passing on of skills and trade secrets no fostering of apprentices, no protection of the old and infirm members. No, this was just a grouping of men with a single common interest.

Profit.

Not that I blame them there. Everyone wants to prosper. It's just that they don't seem to care how much misery they cause as long as they personally get their prosperity.

And the Manufactory Guild was now more powerful than the Bardic Guild and even many of the Trade Guilds. They even had their own Lord Advisor to the King!

Their agenda was pretty clear; they certainly didn't try to hide it. They tended to oppose free access to entertainment in general, simply because entertainment got in the way of working. They wanted to outlaw all public entertainment in the streets, whether it be by simple juggler, Free Bard or Guild Bard. They had laws up for consideration to do just that, too, and some very persuasive people arguing their case, pointing out how crowds around entertainers clogged the streets and disrupted traffic, how work would stop if an entertainer set up outside a manufactory, how people were always coming in late and leaving early in order to see a particular entertainer on his corner. There was just enough truth in all of it to make it seem plausible, logical, reasonable.

Oh, yes, very reasonable.

They had another law up for consideration, as well, a law that would allow the employers at these manufactories to set working hours around the clock, seven days a week. It seemed very reasonable again—and here was the example, right across the street. There was no reason why people couldn't be working all night, not with these wonderful, clear lights available. It would be no hardship to them, not the way working by candlelight or lamplight would be. It was the Church that opposed *this* law; it was the Church that decreed the hours during which it was permissible to work in the first place, and the conditions for working. Church law mandated that Sevenday be a day for rest and religious services. Church law forbade working after sundown, except in professions such as entertainment, on the grounds that God created the darkness in order to ensure that Man had peace in which to contemplate God and to sleep—or at least, rest from his labors, so he could contemplate God with his full attention.

The Manufactory Guild wanted a law that permitted them to hire children as young as nine, on a multitude of grounds—and Nightingale had heard them all.

So that children can be a benefit to their families, instead of a burden. So that families with many children can feed all of them instead of relying on charity. So that children can learn responsibility at an early age. To keep children out of the street and out of wickedness and idleness. Oh, it all sounds very plausible.

Except, of course, that one would not have to pay a child as much as an adult. A family desperate enough to force its nine-year-old child into work would be desperate enough to take whatever wage was offered. And that child, who supposedly was learning to read and write from his Chapel Priest, would be losing that precious chance at education. There *were* Church-sanctioned exceptions to the law—children were allowed to be hired as pages or messengers, and to help their parents in a business or a farm. But all of those exceptions were hedged about with a vast web of carefully tailored precepts that kept abuse of those exceptions to a relative minimum, and all those exceptions required that the child receive his minimum education.

You can't keep a child's parent's from working him to death, or from abusing him in other ways, but you can at least keep a stranger from doing so. That was basically the reasoning of the Church, which decreed the completely contradictory percepts that a child was sacred to God and that a child was the possession and property of his parents.

Then there's that lovely little item, the "job security law." That was a law that specifically forbade a worker in a manufactory from quitting one job to take another—effectively keeping him chained to the first job he ever took for the rest of his life, unless his employer chose otherwise, or got rid of him. That one had yet to be passed as well, but there was very little opposition, and the moment it was, it would mean the complete loss of freedom for anyone who went to work in a manufactory.

They say that retraining someone is costly and dangerous, since folk in a manufactory are generally operating some sort of machinery. Oh, surely. "Machinery" no more complicated than a spinning wheel! But I would think that to most people, who think a well-pump is very complicated machinery, they'd look at the manufactories and agree that having an inexperienced person "operating machinery" could be very dangerous. As if most of what I've been watching people actually do was any more complicated than digging potatoes.

But the Manufactory Guild wanted to keep that ignorance intact. And here the Church itself was divided; one group saw clearly the way this would take freedom away from anyone who worked in those places, leaving them virtual slaves to their jobs, but the other group was alarmed at the wild tales painted of accidents caused by "inexperience," and was in favor of the law.

She shifted her position, turning her back on the lights of the manufactory to stare up at the sky. You didn't see as many stars here as you could in the country; she didn't know why. Maybe it was all the smoke from the thousands of chimneys, getting in the way, like a perpetual layer of light clouds.

The nastiest piece of work she'd heard about was something that so far was only a rumor, but it was chilling enough to have been the sole topic of conversation tonight, all over Freehold.

This was—supposedly—a proposed law that had the support of not only some of the Church but the Manufactory Guild *and* the Trade Guilds as well.

They called it "the Law of Degree."

Nightingale shivered, a chill settling over her that the warm breeze could not chase away. Even the name sounded ominous.

It would set a standard, a list of characteristics, which would determine just how "human" someone could be considered, based on his appearance. But the "standard" was only the beginning of the madness, for it would mandate that those who were considered to be below a certain "degree" of humanity were nothing more than animals.

In other words, property. Bad enough that such things as being indentured are allowed everywhere, and that slavery is sanctioned in at least half the Twenty Kingdoms. The Church at least has laws that govern how slaves are treated, and an indentured servant has the hope of buying himself free. But this—this would be slavery with none of the protections! After all, it wouldn't be "reasonable" to have a law stating that a man couldn't beat his dog, so why have one saying he can't beat his Mintak?

Deliambrens, for instance, would be considered human under the law—but Mintaks and Haspur, with their hides of hair and feathers, their nonhuman hands and feet, their muzzles and beaks, would be animals.

Some people were arguing that as property, these nonhumans would actually have protection they did *not* have now—protection from persecution by the Church. "Animals" by Church cannon could not be evil, because they had no understanding of the difference between good and evil. It was also argued that some of the violence done to nonhumans in the past—the beatings and ambushes—would end if this law was passed, because since they would then be the property of a human, anyone harming one of them would have to pay heavy restitution to the owner.

Naturally all those nonhumans not falling within the proper degree of humanity would have their property confiscated—cattle can't own homes or business, of course—and both they and their property would be taken by the Crown. I'm sure that never entered the Lord Treasurer's consideration. And, of course, as soon as the ink was dry on the confiscation orders, the Crown would then have itself a nice little "animal" auction. More money in the King's coffers, and it wouldn't even be slavery, which is wicked and really not civilized.

Nasty, insidious, and very popular in some quarters. Yes, it would "protect" the nonhumans from the demon hunters, for a little while—until Church canon was changed to make it possible for animals to be considered possessed!

Which it would be; after all, it's in the Holy Writ. There were the demons possessing a human that were cast out, and then possessed a herd of pigs and made the pigs drown themselves.

Small wonder that the Manufactory Guild was also behind this one, at least according to the rumors. If it was passed, the owners of manufactories could neatly bypass all the Church laws on labor by acquiring a nightshift of "animals" to run the machines without wages. There was no Church law saying animals couldn't work all night—nor any Church law giving them a rest day. If it passed—

Well, most of the nonhumans would flee before they could be caught, I suspect, but there are always those who can't believe that something like that would happen to them. There would probably be just enough of those poor naive souls and their children in Lyonarie to make up a workforce large enough to work the manufactories at night.

There would be a business in hunters, too, springing up in the wake of this law. *Hunters? No, more like kidnappers.* They would be going out and trying to entrap nonhumans in whichever of the other human kingdoms existed that did *not* pass this law, and bringing them back here to sell.

Nightingale clutched her hands into fists and felt her nails biting into the palms of her hands. If she ever found out who the nasty piece of work was that first came up with this idea, she would throttle him herself.

With my bare hands. And dance on his corpse.

She told herself she had to relax; at the moment, it was no more than a rumor, and she had only heard about it *here.* No one had mentioned it in the High King's servants' kitchen this morning, nor even in the Chapels friendly to all species. It might be nothing. It might only be a distortion of one of the other laws being considered.

It might even be a rumor deliberately started by the Church in order to make some of the other things they were trying to have passed look less unappetizing.

Or to allow them to slip something else past while the nonhumans are agitating about the rumor.

She would wait until the morning, and see what was in the kitchens and on the street.

She took a deep breath—after a first, cautious sniff to make sure that the wind was not in the "wrong" direction. She let it out again, slowly, exhaling her tension with her breath. This was an old exercise, one that was second nature to her now. As always, it worked, as did her mental admonition that there was nothing she could do *now, this moment.* It would have to wait until tomorrow, so she might as well get the rest she needed to deal with it.

When she finally felt as if she *would* be able to sleep, she got to her feet and picked her way across the rooftop, avoiding the places where she knew that some of her fellow staff might be sheltering together, star-watching. Supposedly the Deliambren who owned this place was considering a rooftop dining area, but so far nothing had materialized, and the staff had it all to themselves.

And a good thing, too. The streets hereabouts aren't safe for star-watching or nighttime strolls before bed. When customers of wealth came here, they came armed, or they came with guards. Not only were there thieves in plenty, but there were people who hated those who were not human, who would sometimes lie in wait to attack customers coming in or out of Freehold. They seldom confined their beatings to nonhumans—they were just as happy to get their hands on a "Fuzzy-lover" and teach him a lesson about the drawbacks of tolerance.

Once or twice a week, some of the staff would turn the tables on them, but that was a dangerous game, for it was difficult to prove who was the attacker and who the victim in a case like that. If the night-watch happened to hear the commotion and come to break it up instead of running the other way as they often did, the Freehold staff often found themselves cooling their heels in gaol until someone came to pay their fines. The law was just as likely to punish Freehold staff as the members of the gang that had ambushed the customers.

Nightingale was still ambivalent about joining one of those expeditions; she *could* add a good margin of safety for the group if she used Bardic magic to make gang members utterly forget who their attackers had been. But if *she* was caught doing something like that, and fell into the hands of the Church—

Flame is not my best color, she thought, trying to drive away fear with flippancy.

She reached the roof door to the staircase going down, and turned to take one last look up at the stars. And she thought, oddly enough, of T'fyrr.

I am glad he is safe with Old Owl, the Deliambren, she thought soberly. *If any of the rumors are true, he would be in grave danger. At least, with Harperus, he has protection and a quick way out of any danger that should come.*

So at least one person she cared for was safe. And with that thought to comfort her, she took the stairs down to the staff quarters, and to her empty bed.

CHAPTER FIVE

Nightingale slipped out into the early morning mist by way of a back staircase. She had learned about it from one of the waiters, the second day of her arrival at Freehold. It was mostly in use by night, rather than by day; it locked behind you as you went out, but Nightingale had learned from the waiter that she already had a key. Every staff member had a ring of keys they got when they settled in; Nightingale didn't know even yet what half of them went to, but one of them locked the door to her room, and one unlocked this back staircase door.

She had visited the used-clothing market soon after setting up her network of children, and had acquired a wardrobe there that she really didn't want too many people in Freehold to know about. It was *not* in keeping with Lyrebird, or with the sober and dignified woman she had portrayed herself as when she arrived.

In fact, she rather doubted that she would have had a hearing if she'd shown up at the door in these patched and worn clothes. They *were* clean, scrupulously clean, but they did not betoken any great degree of prosperity. That was fine; she wasn't trying to look prosperous, she was trying to look like the kind of musician who would be happy to sing in the corner of a kitchen in exchange for a basket of leftovers.

She made one concession to city life that she hoped no one would notice, for it was quite out of keeping with her costume. She wore shoes. She had no stockings, and the shoes were as patched as her skirts, but she did have them, and no one as poor as she was supposed to be would own such a thing.

But I am not going out into a mucky street or traipse around on cobblestones all day without something to protect my feet, she thought stubbornly, as she crossed the street headed east, skipped over a puddle and skirted the edge of a heap of something best left unidentified. There was just so much she would do to protect her persona, and there was such a thing as carrying authenticity too far.

She did not carry a harp at all, only a pair of bones and a small handdrum, the only things a musician as poor as she would be able to afford.

The mist here beneath the overhanging upper stories of the buildings chilled the skin and left clothing damp and clammy, but in an hour or so it would be horribly hot, and the one advantage this costume had was that it was the coolest clothing she had to wear, other than the Elven silks. That was mostly because the fabric was so threadbare as to be transparent in places. It was all of a light beige, impossible to tell what the original color had been now. The skirt had probably once been a sturdy hempen canvas, but now was so worn and limp that it hung in soft folds like cheesecloth, and was as cool to wear as the most finely woven linen. She didn't have a bodice; no woman this poor would own one. Nor did she have a shirt. Only a shift, which if she really *was* this impoverished, would serve as shirt, petticoat, and nightclothes, all one. It was sleeveless, darned in so many places she wondered if any of the original fabric was left, and had at one time been gathered at the neck with a ribbon. Now it was gathered at the neck with a colorless string, tied in a limp little bow.

She hurried along the streets, sometimes following in the wake of one of the water-carts that was meant to clean the streets of debris and wash it all into the gutters. In the better parts of town, that was probably what it *did* do—but the street-cleaners were paid by the number of streets they covered, and every time they had to go back to the river filling-station to

get more water, they lost time. So in this neighborhood, the water sprinkling the street was the barest trickle, scarcely enough to dampen the
cobbles, and certainly not enough to wash anything into the gutters. Those
few businesses who *cared* about appearances, like Freehold, sent their
own people out to wash the street in front of the building. And there
were those who lived here who didn't particularly care for having garbage
festering at the front door, who did the same. But mostly she had to pick
her way carefully along the paths worn clean by carts and rag-pickers.

As the light strengthened and the mist thinned, she got into some better
neighborhoods, and now she took advantage of the directions her children
had given her, slipping along alleyways and between buildings, following
the paths that only the children knew completely. Even the finest of
estates had these little back ways, the means to get into the best homes,
so long as you came by the servants' entrance where no one who mattered
would see you.

*Even the Palace. They can put gates across the roads and guard the
streets all they like, but even the Palace has to have an alley. Even the
Palace has to have a way for people to come and go—people that the
lords and ladies don't want to know exist.*

Rat catchers. Peddlers. Rag-and-bone men. Dung collectors. Pot
scrubbers and floor scrubbers and the laundry women who did the lower
servants' clothing. Garbage collectors. There was a small army of people
coming and going through that back entrance every day, people who didn't
live *at* the Palace, despite the huge servants' quarters, but who lived *off*
the Palace. Even the garbage from the Palace was valuable, and there
was an entire system of bribes and kickbacks that determined who got to
carry away what. The Church actually got the best pickings of the edible
stuff, and sent the lowest of the novices to come fetch it every day. They
carried away baskets of leftovers from the royal kitchens that fed the lords
and ladies and the King himself. Allegedly those went to feed the poor;
Nightingale hadn't seen any evidence for or against that.

None of these people were "good enough" to warrant the expense of
clothing them in uniforms and housing them in the Palace; they got their
tiny wages and whatever they could purloin, and came and went every
day at dawn and dusk. They never saw a lord or a lady—the most exalted
person they would ever see would be a page in royal livery.

But, oh, they knew what was going on in that great hive, and better
than the lords and ladies who lived there! Each of them had a friend or
a relative who *did* rate quarters above, and each of them was a veritable
wellspring of information about just what was going on. Gossip was almost
their only form of entertainment, so gossip they did, till the kitchens and
lower halls buzzed like beehives with the sounds of chattering.

Very few of them ever got to hear even a street-singer; no one was out
in the morning when they would scamper in to work, and by the time
they went home in the evening, it was generally in a fog of exhaustion.
Sevenday was the day for Church services, and if one picked the right
Chapel and began at Morningsong and stayed piously on through Vespers,
the Priest would see that piety was rewarded with three stout meals. No
street-singer could compete with all the bean-bread, onions, and bacon

grease to spread on the bread that one could eat, and a cup of real ale
to wash it down. Sometimes on Holy Days, there were even treats of a
bit of cheese, cooked whole turnips, cabbage soup, or a sweet-cake . . .
all the more reason to come early and stay late. And if one happened to
doze off during the sermon, well, Sevenday *was* a day of rest, wasn't it?

So when a poor musician like Tanager showed up, looking for a corner
to sit in, asking nothing more than the leftovers that the kitchen staff
shared, she was generally welcomed. As long as she didn't get in the way
and didn't eat too much, her singing would help pass the time and make
the work seem lighter, and one just might be able to learn a song or two
to sing the little ones to sleep with.

So in the corner Tanager sat, drumming and singing, and between
songs listening to the gossip that automatically started up the moment
that silence began.

Now the alley was hemmed on both sides by high walls, walls with
tantalizing hints of trees and other greenery on the other side. Nightingale—or "Tanager"—joined the thin stream of other threadbare, tired-
looking people all making their way up this long, dark alley, some of them
rubbing their reddened eyes and yawning, all of them heading for their
jobs at the Palace.

There was nothing at the end of this corridor of brickwork, open to
the sky, but a gate that led to the Palace grounds.

By now, she was elbow-to-elbow with the Palace servants, none of
whom were distinguished by anything like a livery. No one ever saw these
people but other servants, after all. She slipped inside the back gate with
the others, completely ignored by the fat, bored guard there, whose only
real job was to keep things from *leaving* the Palace, not from entering it.

Now she saw the first real sunlight she'd seen this morning; the cobble-
stoned courtyard and kitchen garden was open to the sky. Here, the sun
had already burned away the mist, and she squinted against its glare as
she stared across the courtyard to the great stone bulk of the Palace, dark
against the blue sky, with the sun peeking over it.

She had no real idea just how big the Palace was; huge, that was all
she knew for certain—at least the size of several Freeholds. From all she
had been able to gather, this was only one building of several, all joined
by glazed galleries, and all as big as this one was. It made her head swim
just to think about it.

She paused just a moment to take in a breath of fresh air before she
headed for the back door to the servants' kitchen.

The servants, of course, were never fed out of the same kitchen that
conjured up the meals for the lords and ladies. In fact, there were *two*
kitchens that fed the servants: Upper and Lower. Upper Kitchen was the
one that fed the pages, the personal maids and valets, the Court Musicians,
nannies and nursemaids, tutors and governesses, all those who were not
quite "real" servants, but who were not gentry, either. Lower was for the
real servants: anyone who cleaned, cooked, sewed, polished, served food
and drink, washed, mended, or tended to animals or plants. Tanager would
never have dared intrude on the Upper Servants' Kitchen; Lower was
where she fit in, and Lower was where she went.

She needed that breath of fresh air when she got there; as usual, it was as hot as a Priest's Personal Hell in there, with all the ovens going, baking bread for afternoon and evening meals before it got too warm to keep the ovens stoked. Breakfast bread had been baking all night, of course, and Tanager's arrival was greeted right at the door by one of the undercooks, with enthusiasm and a warm roll that had a scraping of salted lard melting inside it. Tanager got out of the doorway and the ate the roll quickly, as would anyone for whom this would be a real breakfast. Then she hurried across the slate floor and took her seat out of the way, off in a corner of the kitchen that seemed to be an architectural accident; a bit of brickwork that *might* have served as a closet if it had been bigger, and *might* have served as a cupboard, if it had been smaller, and really wasn't right for either. Before she had come to sing, there had been a small table there. You could put a stack of towels there, or a few of the huge pans needed to cook the enormous meals they prepared here—or Tanager. There were other places for the towels and pans; now the wedge-shaped corner held a stool for her to sit on.

The kitchen was a huge, brick-walled room, lit by open windows and the fires of three enormous fireplaces, where soup and stew cooked in kettles as big around as a beer barrel. There were five big tables, and counters beneath the windows, where the cooks and their helpers worked. No fancy pastry cooks here; the fare dished out to the lower servants was the same, day in, day out: soup and stew made with meat left from yesterday, sent from the Upper Servants' Kitchen, bread, pease-porridge and oat-porridge. On special occasions, leftover sweets came over from the Upper Servants' Kitchen, as well—breakfast sweets came over at noon, lunch-sweets at dinner, and dinner-sweets appeared when all the cleaning up had been accomplished, by way of a treat and a reward for the extra hours. So far, Tanager hadn't seen any of those.

Tanager thought long and hard as she settled herself on her stool. This was the first time she had needed to hear about something specific. Something as odd as the "Law of Degree" was not going to come up in normal conversation.

And I'm not going to ask about it myself. That leaves only one option; I'll have to use Bardic Magic to coax it out of them.

Tanager was a simple girl; Nightingale was anything but. Easy in her power and comfortable with it, she had been using Bardic Magic for as long as she had been on her own, on the road. Often she had no choice. The use of Bardic Magic to influence the minds of those around her had sometimes been the only way she had gotten out of potentially dangerous situations. Living with the Elves had refined her techniques, since Bardic Magic was similar to one of their own magics. Now she scarcely had to think about tapping into the power; she simply stretched out her mind, and there it was.

I need a song as a vehicle; something that includes nonhumans. But nothing too jarring to start with; something they would enjoy listening to under ordinary circumstances. And it will have to be something with a strong beat as well, since I only have the drum to accompany me. Ah, I know; that song Raven wrote: "Good Duke Arden." It has several verses about Arden taking care of nonhumans in his train.

So she began with that, then moved on to other melodies, songs that dealt with nonhumans in a favorable light. And all the while she sang, she concentrated on one thing. *Talk about the nonhumans, what the lords and ladies are saying about them.*

She sat and sang and drummed until her wrist and voice tired; one of the pot scrubbers, with an empty dishpan and nothing better to do at the moment, brought her a cup of flat ale. Tanager pretended to drink it, but it really went down a crack at her feet. And while she drank, she listened.

There was nothing at all in the gossip about the "Law of Degree," but there *was* something that made her sit up straight in startlement.

"La, Delia, did ye see th' lad wi' all the snow-white hair, him an' his coach with no horses come in yestere'en?" asked one of the under-cooks. "Faith, 'tis all m'sister, her as is Chambermaid t' Lord Pelham's nannies, can talk about!"

Lad with all the hair? Coach with no horses? Dear Lady, that can't be—oh surely not—

"Coo, ye should'a seen what came w' him!" said another, one of the chief cooks. " 'Tis a great bird man, 'twas, w' wings an' all, an' a great evil beak like a hawk i' the middle'v his face! An' *claws!* I wouldn't want t' get on the wrong side uv him!"

Tanager sat frozen, her hands wrapped around her empty cup. It was! It was Harperus—and with him, T'fyrr! It must be! But why here, and why now?

"Ah, but ye haven't heard the best of it," said a third girl knowingly. "*My* second cousin is best friend t' Lord Atrovel's secretary's valet, an' this birdy-man like to set the whole Court on its ear!"

As Tanager sat in stunned silence, the girl gleefully told the entire story, while the rest of the kitchen worked and put in a word or two of commentary. According to the girl, a nonhuman who *had* be a Deliambren from the description, and another who was either T'fyrr or another of his race, had come in yesterday afternoon to Court. They had been announced as some kind of envoy, and at that point, for a reason that the girl either didn't know or couldn't explain, the bird-man broke into song. From there, her version differed slightly from the ones offered by a few others. The others claimed that the bird-man had challenged the King's Musicians to a contest and had won it; the girl maintained that he had simply begun singing, as a sample of what he could do.

At any rate, when it was all over, the King had appointed the bird-man to be his Chief Musician (the others claimed Laurel Bard), the rest of the Court Musicians were furious (no one differed on that), and most of the King's Advisors were beside themselves over the fact that the King had overruled them.

Ah, but if the first girl was to be believed, the King had not only appointed the Haspur—for it must be a Haspur, even if it wasn't T'fyrr— as his Chief Musician, he had appointed him directly to the Royal Household, made a Sire out of him, and installed him in a suite in the royal wing of the Palace!

I only hoped to hear something about the Law of Degree, Tanager thought dazedly, *not this—*

Could it be T'fyrr and Old Owl? She didn't know of any other Haspur and Deliambrens traveling together. But why would they come here?

Why am I here? Whoever these strangers are, it is for the same reason, surely.

Now she was grateful that she had been so careful to keep her real identity and purpose here a secret. With *two* sets of agents blundering about, it would have been appallingly easy for them to trip each other up.

Now I need only watch for them, and avoid getting entangled in whatever scheme they have going. Oh, yes, need only. If it is Harperus, that will be like trying to avoid the garbage in the streets! He's more clever than twenty Gypsies in his own way, and encompasses everyone he meets in his grand plots in some way or another. Ah, well, at least he doesn't know I'm here; I just hope he doesn't get T'fyrr in trouble. . . .

Somehow she managed to pull herself together and continue singing and playing for the rest of the morning. That was all the time she ever spent here—and that was reasonable, for Tanager. Mornings were fairly useless for a street-musician; the afternoon meant better pickings, and Tanager would now, presumably, go on to whatever street corner she had staked out as her own. There she could expect to earn "hard currency" for her work; pins, mostly, with a sprinkling of copper coins, and some food.

As usual, she spread out a threadbare napkin, and the chief cook filled it with her "pay"—mostly leftover bread, with a bit of bacon and a scrap of cheese, some of last night's roast from the Upper Servants' Kitchen that was too tough and stringy to even go into soup today. Tanager thanked her with a little bobbing curtsey, tied it all up into a bundle, and slipped out the door just in time to avoid the lunchtime rush.

She always hurried across the cobbles to the gate, but today she had more reason to half-run than usual. She wanted to find out if anyone in the city had heard anything about the bird-man, *or* the Law of Degree, and to that end, there were two places she needed to go. First, as Nightingale, the Chapel of Saint Gurd. Second, the square just down the street from Freehold where she generally met Maddy and the rest of her army of urchins just after lunch.

Surely, between them, Father Ruthvere or the children would have heard or seen something. And at the moment, she was not certain whether she wanted to hear more about the Law of Degree or—T'fyrr.

If that was who the feathered wonder was.

Nightingale slipped back into Freehold by the back door feeling quite frustrated. There had been nothing worth bothering about in the way of news at the Chapel; the Priest, Father Ruthvere, had heard nothing about a "Law of Degree," but he promised Nightingale fiercely that he would do his best to find out about it.

Father Ruthvere was something of an odd character, and Nightingale never would have trusted him with her true Bard-name if it had not been that *he* had recognized her Free Bard ribbons during one of her visits (not as Tanager) and had asked her how Master Wren and Lady Lark were faring. It turned out that he had some sort of connection to that cousin of Talaysen's who was also in the Church. He had been promoted to his own Chapel here, and he had promised Priest Justiciar Ardis when he was sent on to Lyonarie that he would keep an eye out for Free Bards and help them when he could.

That in itself was either an example of how small a world it truly was— or that there *was* something in the way of Fate dogging her footsteps.

The convoluted twists that this little mission of hers was taking were beginning to make her head spin.

For the meantime, however, Father Ruthvere was an ally she was only too glad to have found. He was one of the faction that followed the "we are all brothers" faith, and that made him doubly valuable to her, and vice versa. *He* knew what was going on, to a limited extent, within the Church—*she* had her information from the street and the Court. Together they found they could put together some interesting wholes out of bits and pieces.

Maddy and her crew hadn't come up with anything either, though as usual they were glad enough for her bag of leftovers and the pennies she gave them all. The only thing that one of the boys knew was that his brother had actually *seen* the horseless wagon on its way to the Palace. It had not been pulled or pushed by any beasts, and from the description, it could have been the wagon that Harperus used.

But then again, she thought to herself, as she scrambled up the staircase, *wouldn't any Deliambren wagon look like any other? I don't know for a fact that Harperus is the only one traveling about the countryside.*

But would any other Deliambren have a Haspur with him?

She slipped down the hall, making certain first that there was no one around to catch her in her Tanager disguise, then unlocked the door to her room and whisked inside.

"I don't even know that it's a Haspur," she told herself, thinking out loud. "There is more than one bird-race, and most of them would match the description that girl gave. It could be anyone. In fact, it's just not *likely* that it's Harperus and T'fyrr."

But as she changed out of her Tanager clothing and headed for the bathroom for a needed sluicing, she couldn't help but think that—given the way that things were going—the fact it wasn't likely was the very reason why it would turn out to be her friends.

She drifted down the stairs in one of her rainbow-skirts; the blue one this time. Today, Lyrebird was in a casual mood and had dressed accordingly.

Actually, today Lyrebird was ravenous and wanted to be able to eat without worrying about delicate dagging and fragile lace. She had missed her lunch in order to fit in a stop at Father Ruthvere's Chapel, and she'd given all those leftovers to the children without saving even a roll for herself.

Not that she had been hungry enough for stale rolls and stringy beef. Her stay here had spoiled her; there had been plenty of times when those leftovers would have been a feast.

Well, plenty of times in the long past, when she was between villages and her provisions had run out, maybe. Nightingale had *never* been so poor a musician that she'd *had* to sing for leftovers.

This hour was too late for lunch and a bit too early for dinner. Only a few of the eating nooks were open and operating, and all of those were on the ground floor. Lyrebird went to one of her favorites, where the cook was a merry little man with no use of his lower limbs because of an illness as a child. Not that he let it get in the way of his work; he *was* a cook, after all, and he didn't need to move much. He plied his trade very well from a stationary seat within a half-circle of round-bottomed pans, all heated on Deliambren braziers to the sizzling point. You picked out what you wanted from a series of bins of fresh vegetables, and strips of fowl, fish and meat in bowls sunk in ice, and brought it to him in your bowl; he would quick-fry it in a bit of oil, spice it according to your taste, and serve it all to you on a bed of rice, scooped out of the huge steamer behind him. If he wasn't busy, he was always happy to talk.

Nightingale was always happy to talk to him, and this time of day she was often his only customer.

"Well, Lyrebird, you're eating like a bird indeed today—twice your weight in food! You're eating like dear little Violetta!"

He winked at that; most of the staff found Violetta amusing. The name was female, and surely the little misfit dressed like a woman, but there wasn't a person on the staff who was fooled.

No matter. Freehold was full of misfits, and if "Violetta" wanted to dress in fantastic gowns and gossip like one of the serving-wenches, no one here would ever let "her" know that they had seen past the disguise.

"Skip your breakfast?" Derfan asked, eyeing the size of the bowl she had picked up at the start of the bins.

"And lunch," she confirmed, bringing him her selection and taking a seat on one of the stools nearby to watch him work. He had the most amazingly quick hands; *she* would have scorched everything, or herself, but Derfan never spoiled a meal that she had ever heard. And he never once burned himself, either.

He pursed his lips and shook his head at her. "That's very bad of you. You'll do yourself harm if you make that a habit. I should think you'd be ready to faint dead away. What was so important that you had to skip two meals?"

"That business with that new law people were so upset about last night," she replied casually. Since it had been the talk of Freehold, there was no reason why she should not have been out looking for confirmation. "I know a good Priest who keeps his ear to the ground and hears a great deal, but he's halfway across the city."

"And?" Derfan prompted, dashing in bits of seasoning and a spot of oil while he tossed her food deftly on the hot metal.

"He hadn't heard a thing," she told him. "I'm halfway convinced now that it was a rumor being spread so that our good leaders can slip something else into law while *we* are out chasing our tails over this."

"Could be, could be," Derfan agreed, nodding vigorously. "It wouldn't be the first time they've done things that way." The jovial man grinned infectiously as he ladled some juices here and there. "But we've got enough excitement right here in Freehold to keep everyone stirred up for the next few days, and never mind some maybe-so, maybe-no law out there."

She shook her head as he handed her the bowl full of rice and stir-fried morsels. "I haven't been here, remember?" she said, fanning the food to cool it, and daring a quick bite. It was too hot, and she quickly sucked in cool air to save her tongue.

"Our leader's shown up." Derfan raised both eyebrows at her.

She wrinkled her brow, unable to guess his meaning.

"Our real boss," Derfan elaborated. "The one Kyran works for." He sighed when she shook her head blankly. "Tyladen, the Deliambren, the owner of Freehold. He's here."

She stopped blowing on her food and looked up at him sharply. "No," she said. "I thought he never came here!"

Oh, this is too much! she thought as Derfan nodded and shrugged. *Not one, but* two *Deliambrens showing up in the space of a single day? What is this, a conspiracy? Is* everyone *around here involved in some kind of plot?*

"It isn't that he never comes here, it's just that he doesn't do it often," Derfan told her as she applied herself grimly to her food again. "Maybe he's decided he ought to, seeing as there's been all that law talk. Maybe it's about time he did, too—*he's* the one with all the money. Precious little you and me could do if the High King decides to make trouble for our friends, but Deliambrens have got the stuff that the high and mighty want, and that means they have money *and* a reason for the lords and ladies to listen to 'em. They've used that kind of influence before, I've heard."

"Well, if he wants to have any customers, he'd better get involved, I suppose," she agreed mildly.

Now what? What happens if he recognizes me? I didn't recognize his name, but that doesn't mean he doesn't know me. I've met a lot of Deliambrens, and I don't remember half of them. Damn! The last thing I want is some wealthy fuzzy-faced half-wit breathing down my neck right now, watching everything I do and wanting to know why I haven't found out more!

As if to confirm her worst fears, Derfan had even more news about Tyladen. "Word is," Derfan said in a confidential tone, "that Tyladen's going to make the rounds of the whole place tonight; look in on all the performers, the cooks and all, see how they're doing, see how many customers they're bringing in."

"Well, you have no worry on that score," Nightingale pointed out. Derfan blushed, but Nightingale spoke nothing but the truth. Derfan's little corner was always popular, since his customers always *knew* what was in the food he fixed for them. Some of them, like the Mintak, were herbivorous and could not digest meat. In addition, the food was ready quickly, and if you were very hungry, you didn't have to spend a lot of time waiting for someone to prepare your dinner, the way you did in some of the other little nooks.

"You don't either, from what I've heard," he countered. "You're very popular."

She shrugged. "Usually I would agree with you, but any musician can have a bad night. It would be my luck that tonight would be the one."

Derfan snorted. "I doubt it," he began. "A bad night for you is a terrific night for some other people around here and—" He interrupted himself. "Turn around! There he is, out on the dance floor, looking up at the light-rigs on the ceiling!"

She turned quickly and got a good view of the mysterious Tyladen as he stood with his hands on his hips, peering up at the ceiling four floors above. And to her initial relief, she didn't recognize him.

He was much younger than she had thought, although age was difficult to measure in a Deliambren; the skin of his face was completely smooth and unwrinkled, even at the corners of the eyes and mouth. He was dressed quite conservatively for a Deliambren, in a one-piece garment of something that looked like black leather but probably wasn't, with a design in contrasting colors appliqued from the right shoulder to the left hip and down the right leg. His hair was relatively short, no longer than the top of his shoulders, and so were his cheek-feathers, although she could have used his eyebrows for whisk brooms.

He dropped his eyes just as she took the last of this in, and she found herself staring right into them. For one frozen moment, she thought she saw a flash of recognition there.

But if she had, in the next instant it was gone again. He waved his hand slightly in acknowledgement of the fact that he knew they were both watching him and they were his employees, then went back to staring at the ceiling, ignoring them.

But now she was so keyed up, she even read *that* as evidence that he was going to try to interfere in her careful and cautious plans.

She finished her dinner quickly, thanked Derfan, and hurried up to the Oak Grove, certain that Tyladen was going to show up there and demand an explanation.

But as the evening wore on and nothing happened—other than Violetta showing up, as if Derfan's earlier mention of "her" had conjured "her"— she began to feel a bit annoyed. Granted, she really didn't *want* some Deliambren meddling in her affairs, but she wasn't sure she liked being ignored either!

When Tyladen finally did show up, it was during the busiest part of her evening and she was in the middle of a set. She didn't even realize he was there until she looked up in time to see him nod with satisfaction, turn, and walk out the door.

Just that. That was all there was to it.

Her shift came to an end without anything more happening, and none of her customers had any more information about either the Law of Degree or the mysterious bird-man at the High King's Court. Not even Violetta, who knew or at least pretended to know something about everything, had anything to say on either subject. On her way upstairs, she stopped at a little nook that sold prebaked goods and got a couple of meat rolls and an apple tart to take up to her room, half expecting to be intercepted between her room and the Oak Grove. No one materialized, though, and no one was waiting in her room.

She ate and cleaned up, and finally went to bed, feeling decidedly odd. She was just as happy that she wasn't going to be interfered with, but after getting herself all upset about the prospect to find that she was being ignored was a bit—annoying!

But that's a Deliambren for you, she decided, as she drifted off to sleep. *If they aren't annoying by doing something, they're bound to annoy you by not doing it!*

T'fyrr checked the tuning on his small flat-harp nervously for the fifth time. He had decided this morning what he was going to perform for this, his first private concert for the High King, and he was going to need more accompaniment than even *his* voice could produce. The flat-harp would be ideal, though, for the songs he had selected were all deceptively simple.

He had wanted to do something to remind the King of his duty; he had found, he thought, precisely the music that would. He had modified one of those songs about the King himself for his first piece—not changing any of the meaning, just perfecting the rhyme and rhythm, both of which were rather shaky. But from there, he would be singing about Duke Arden of Kingsford, a series of three songs written since the fire by a Free Bard called Raven. The first was the story of the fire itself, describing how the Duke had worked with his own bare hands in the streets, side by side with his people, to hold back the fire. While not the usual stuff of an epic, it was a story of epic proportions, and worthy of retelling.

Let him hear that, and perhaps it will remind him that a ruler's duty is to his people, and not the other way around.

If nothing else, it might remind the King of Duke Arden's straitened circumstances, better than a cold report would. *That* might pry the help out of him that the Duke had been pleading for.

That will make the Lord Seneschal happy, at any rate.

The second was a song about the first winter the city had endured, a saga as grueling, though not as dramatic, as the fire. It described the lengths to which Arden went to see that no one died of hunger or lack of shelter that season. The third and final song described not only Arden but his betrothed, the Lady Phenyx Asher, a love story wound in and around what the two of them were doing, with their own hands, to rebuild the city.

Actually, it is more about the lady than about the Duke; Raven truly admires her, and his words show it.

The next songs were all carefully chosen to do nothing more than entertain and show off T'fyrr's enormous range. A couple of them were not even from human composers at all.

And the last song was another designed to remind the King of his duties—for it had been written by another High King on his deathbed, and was called "The Burden of the Crown." Though sad, it was a hopeful song as well, for the author had clearly not found the Crown to be a burden that was intolerable, merely one that was a constant reminder of the people it represented.

If that doesn't do it, nothing will, T'fyrr thought, then sighed. *Well, I suppose I should not expect results instantly. I am not a Gypsy, with magic at my command. If he only listens to the words, it will be a start.*

He had been given nothing whatsoever to do except practice and wait for the King to send for him. He hadn't especially wanted to venture out of his suite, either; not until the King had heard him play at least once. He had spent all his time pacing, exercising his wings, and practicing. Nob had enjoyed the virtuoso vocalist's practice, but the pacing and wing-strokes clearly made him nervous. He had sought his room when T'fyrr suggested that he might want to go practice his reading and writing for his daily lessons with the pages' tutor.

Finally the summons had come this afternoon, and Nob brought T'fyrr to this little antechamber to the King's personal suite, a room with white satin walls, and furnished with a few chairs done in white satin and gilded wood. There he was to wait until the King called for him.

It seemed he had been waiting forever.

At last, when he was about to snap a string from testing them so often, the door opened and a liveried manservant beckoned. T'fyrr rose to his feet, harp under one arm, and followed him, the tension of waiting replaced by an entirely new set of worries.

As it happened, it was just as well that he had not set his expectations unrealistically high, for the King did not show that the songs affected him in any way—other than his delight and admiration in T'fyrr as a pure musician. He asked for several more songs when T'fyrr was through with his planned set, all of which T'fyrr fortunately knew. One of them gave him the opportunity to display his own scholarship, for he knew three variants, and asked which one Theovere preferred. That clearly delighted the King even further, and when at last the time came for Afternoon court, a duty even the King could not put off, Theovere sighed and dismissed the Haspur with every sign of disappointment that the performance was over.

"You will come the same time, every day," the stone-faced manservant said expressionlessly as he led T'fyrr to the door. "This is the High King's standing order."

T'fyrr bobbed his head in acknowledgement, and privately wondered how he was going to find his way back to his own quarters in this maze. He had *no* head for indoor directions, and more than a turn or two generally had him confused. It didn't help that all these corridors looked alike—all white marble and artwork, with no way of telling even what floor you were on if you didn't already know.

To his relief, Nob was waiting for him just outside the door, passing the time of day with the guard posted outside the King's suite. This was another of those dangerous looking bodyguards, but this one seemed a bit younger than the ones actually *with* the King, and hadn't lost all his humanity yet.

"Thought you might get lost," the boy said saucily, with a wink at the guard, whose lips twitched infinitesimally.

T'fyrr shrugged. "It is possible," he admitted. "Not likely, but possible, I suppose. This is a large building."

The guard actually snickered at that little understatement, and Nob took him in charge to lead him back to their quarters. "I admit I wasn't entirely certain I knew the way," T'fyrr told the boy quietly, once they were out of the guard's earshot. "The hallways seem to be the same."

"The art's different," Nob told him, gesturing widely at the statues. "This one, the statues are all of High Kings, see? We turn *here*, and the statues are wood-nymphs."

Nude human females sprouting twigs and leaves in their hair. So that is a wood-nymph! No wonder the shepherds in my songs are so surprised; I don't imagine that it is every day that a nude female prances up to the average shepherd and invites him to dance.

"We turn again here—" Nob continued, blissfully unaware of T'fyrr's thoughts, "and the statues are all shepherd couples."

Oh, indeed, if one expects shepherds to be flinging themselves after their sheep wearing a small fortune in embroidery and lace! This is as likely as nude women frolicking about among the thistles and thorns and biting insects, I suppose.

"Then this is our corridor, and the statues are historical women." Nob stopped in front of their door. "Here we are, between Lady Virgelis the Chaste, and the Maiden Moriah—"

Between someone so sour and dried up no one would ever want to mate with her, and someone who probably didn't deserve the title of "Maiden" much past her twelfth birthday, T'fyrr interpreted, looking at the grim-visaged old harridan on his left, who was muffled from head to toe in garments that did not disguise the fact she was mostly bone, and the ripely plump, sloe-eyed young wench on his right, who wasn't wearing much more than one of the wood-nymphs. He wondered if the juxtaposition was accidental.

Probably not. He had the feeling that very little in this palace was accidental.

"So," he said, as Nob opened the door and held it open for him, "to get to the King's suite, I go—right, through the ladies to the shepherds, left, through the shepherds to the wood-nymphs, left through the nymphs to the High Kings, and right through the Kings to where the guard is."

"Perfect," Nob lauded. "You have it exactly right." The page closed the door behind them, and T'fyrr decided that he might as well ask the next question regarding directions.

"Now," he said, "if I wanted to go into the city, how would I get out?"

One of the so-called "supervisors" in charge of expelling rowdy customers—who elsewhere would have been called "peace-keepers"—intercepted Nightingale on her way upstairs after her performance the second night after the Deliambren Tyladen arrived to take over management from Kyran.

"Tyladen wants to see you in his office," the burly Mintak said shortly, and Nightingale suppressed a start and a grimace of annoyance. "Tonight. Soon as you can."

"Right," she said shortly, and continued on up to her room to place her harp in safekeeping. *So, he recognized me after all, or someone warned him, or he got a message back to the Fortress-City with my description or even my image and they've told him I'm supposed to be doing some investigation for them*—She clenched her jaw tightly and closed the door of her room carefully behind her, making certain she heard the lock click shut. *I could deny it all, of course, and there is no way that he can* know *that I am Nightingale unless I admit it. Still, even if I deny it he'll be watching me, trying to see if I'm doing anything, likely getting underfoot or sending someone to follow me. Oh, bother! Why did I ever even consider this in the first place? I must have been mad. Every time I get involved with Deliambrens there's trouble.*

She fumed to herself all the way down the stairs, and even more as she wormed her way through the crowds on and surrounding the dance floor. That was no easy task; at this time of the night, the dance floor was a very popular place. Special lights suspended from the ceiling actually sent round, focused circles of light down on the dancers; the circles were of different colors and moved around to follow the better dancers, or pulsed in time to the music. Some folk came here just to watch the lights move in utter, bemused fascination. Many spectators watched from the balconies of the floors above. Nightingale was used to such things, but for most people, this was purest magic, and they could not for a moment imagine what was creating these "fairy lights." It was easy to see why Freehold was such a popular place; there wasn't its like outside the Fortress-City, and not one person in ten thousand of those here would ever see the fabulous Deliambren stronghold.

The lights made Nightingale's head ache, especially after a long, hard day, and she was less than amused at being summoned *now*. She wanted food, a bath, and bed in that order. She did *not* want to have to go through a long session of deception and counter-deception with some fool of a Deliambren.

Fortunately, she was tall for a woman, and hard to ignore. One or two human customers, more inebriated than most, attempted to stop her. All it took, usually, was a single long, cold stare directly into the eyes of even the most intoxicated, and they generally left her alone quickly. A touch of Bardic Magic, a hint of Elven coldness, delivered with an uncompromising glare—that was the recipe that said *leave me alone* in a way that transcended language.

She finally reached the other side of the dance floor with no sense of relief. The offices were down a short corridor between one of the eateries that catered to strict herbivores and a bar that specialized in exotic beers made from all manner of grains, from corn to rice. The corridor was brightly lit, which was the best way of ensuring that people who didn't belong there weren't tempted to investigate it. Somehow the adventurous never wanted to explore anything that was lit up like a village square at noon on midsummer day. It wasn't very inviting, anyway; just a plain, white-walled, white-tiled corridor with a couple of doors in it.

There were two doors on the corridor to be precise; the nearest was Kyran's office. She tapped once on the farthest and entered.

There wasn't much there except for a desk and a couple of chairs, although the Deliambren sitting at the desk quickly put something small, flat and dark into a desk drawer as she closed the door behind her. She guessed that whatever it was, she wasn't supposed to see it or know it existed. *More Deliambren devices, I suppose,* she thought sourly, *more Deliambren secrets. As if any of them would be useful to me!* But she schooled her face into a carefully neutral expression, and said shortly, "You wanted to see me, Tyladen?"

No "sir"; she was quite annoyed enough with him to omit any honorifics. But he didn't seem to notice the omission, or if he did, he didn't care. He smiled, nodded at the nearest chair, and put his hands back up on the empty wooden desktop.

"I did. Lyrebird, is it?" At her nod, he smiled again. "Good name. Appropriate for a musician. Quite. Well." He laughed, and she had to wonder if he was as foolish as he seemed at this moment. Probably not. "Seems you're very popular here at Freehold."

He waited for an answer, and again she nodded, cautiously, as she dropped gracefully into the chair. It didn't look comfortable, but to her surprise it was. "I'd like to think so," she added, making a bid for an appearance of modesty.

"Oh, you are, you are—one of our most popular musicians among the nonhumans, that's a fact." He continued to smile, and she waited with growing impatience for him to get to the point. What was he after? Did he want to know *why* she, a human musician, should be so popular among those who were not of her race? Was he going to challenge her and demand that she reveal her true identity?

He just waited, and finally she came up with another short answer for him. "That's what they tell me." She shrugged again, trying to appear modest.

"Well, they tell you true." He nodded like the child's toy they called a "head-bobber," still giving her that silly smile.

I know that Deliambrens have a hard time relating to humans and their emotions, but this is ridiculous. I can see why he has Kyran acting as manager here most of the time. He doesn't know the first thing about interacting with us. I know he can't be stupid, but he certainly projects himself as a prime silly ass.

Of course, he could be trying to soften her up for the confrontation. He could be hoping to make her think he was an idiot so that she would underestimate him and let something slip.

Well, if that was what he was waiting for, he'd be here until the building fell to pieces around him.

"Yes, they tell you true," he said, head still bobbing vigorously. "So I'm going to have to move you. Oak Grove isn't big enough, and some of the customers can't get up all those stairs, anyway. I want you down here, on the ground floor. Silas wants to join the dinner-to-midnight dance group, they want to have him, and that frees up the Rainbow, and that's where I want you."

The Rainbow? her mind babbled. *The biggest performance room in Freehold? Me? Take over from Silas? Me?*

As she sat there in stunned silence, he added, as if in afterthought, "Oh—and you'll be getting what Silas was, if that's all right. Two Royals a night?"

Two—two Royals? Me? Nightingale? Has he got the right person?

"Oh, that's quite fine," she replied in a daze, and he reached his hand across the desk. "Thank you. Thank you very much!" Without thinking, she leaned forward to take it as a token of her acceptance.

"Done then. We'll see you down here tomorrow night, then, Lyrebird." He took her hand, shook it once, awkwardly, and let it go. Then he waved his hands at her as she continued to sit there blinking, shooing her playfully out the door. "You need sleep, if you're going to open in the Rainbow tomorrow, my lady. Off with you."

She rose, opened the door in a daze, and walked back out into the noise and the music.

The Rainbow? It was the biggest performance room in Freehold! The only other venue larger was the dance floor itself. Silas was another human—or so he claimed—with an inhumanly beautiful face and body, a waist-length mane of golden curls, and a voice like strong bronze, powerful and compelling. Silas liked to display that body in clothing much like Tyladen had worn that first day, except that Silas' skintight garments *were* real leather. He was extremely popular with both male and female customers, and by reputation, distributed his favors equally between both sexes. She had heard rumors that he wanted to join the dance group, and she could certainly see why; he would be able to concentrate on singing, and choose the powerful and rhythmic music he preferred instead of the ballads that a performance room demanded. His guitar playing was the weakest part of his act; now he wouldn't need to worry about it, with an entire ensemble to back him.

And the dance floor will be more crowded than ever—Silas is bound to sing fast music, which will make people thirsty, which will sell a great many drinks. It is a good bargain all around, even at continuing to pay him his current salary or above. But—me? The Rainbow? Who am I? I'm not gorgeous, like Silas. I know I'm good, but I don't have a fraction of his charisma. I'm just a Gypsy street-player, a good one, but nothing more than that. How can I ever fill the Rainbow?

She found herself on the staircase, with no clear memory of how she had crossed the intervening floor. The Rainbow Room was easily three times the size of the Oak Grove. How could she ever justify being put there? Who would come?

All those people who wait for seats now, whispered an elated little voice in the back of her mind. *All those people who stand crowded into the back wall. And all those who want to hear you, but can't climb three flights of stairs. You know there are plenty of those. Derfan's said as much. Lady of the Night, now Derfan can even come listen to you!*

Well, that was true. Many of the folk who crowded into Freehold of a night were the human misfits of the city; those who, like Derfan, were *not* sound of body by everyday measure. Out there, they were cripples. In any other tavern in the city, they would still be cripples. Here, they were no stranger than anyone else, and their only limitations were how far up the staircases they could get—and there were plenty of nonhumans who couldn't manage that. Kyran and Tyladen spoke vaguely of putting in some sort of lifting system to accommodate them, but apparently there was some problem with getting it to work reliably. There *were* hoists for food and drink for the various tiny kitchens, but they were all powered by the muscles of Mintaks and other strong creatures and not really practical for hauling people up and down.

Besides, the worst that happened if a hoist failed was the loss of a little food and profit. The worst that could happen if a lift full of customers failed was not to be contemplated.

That was why the most popular acts were all on the first floor, where everyone could see them that wanted to.

Can I do it? she asked herself, and forced herself to think about it dispassionately. *Yes,* she decided, on sober contemplation. *I think that I can.*

But she had to stop on the way up and bespeak a pot of very hot water from one of the tea vendors. Mingled excitement, anticipation, and stage-fright were beginning to build inside her at the prospect of facing the largest audience at the greatest rate of pay she had ever, in her life, warranted. If she was going to be able to do anything tomorrow, she was going to need to get some sleep tonight, as Tyladen had pointed out. Fortunately, she had packed a number of herbal remedies in her panniers, and one of them was for sleeplessness.

And tonight she was going to need it.

The excitement was almost enough to drive her real reason for being here out of her mind.

Almost.

As she reached her room again, shut and locked the door behind her, and began to prepare for bed, her mind went back to what Tanager had heard at the Palace today. The Haspur—and if the mysterious new Court Musician wasn't a Haspur, he was of some race so like them that it made no difference—was the sensation of the Court and had inspired some of the most envious hatred in the King's musicians she had ever heard of. Some of them were threatening to pack up and leave the King's service; others swore they would "get rid of" the interloper. Nightingale was not particularly worried about the ability of the Court Musicians as individuals to "get rid of" their rival; they were Guild Bards after all, and as a group, Guild Bards were singularly ineffectual at doing anything of a practical nature. The trouble was that they all had been placed where they were by *someone*; they must have powerful allies, and those allies might decide to take an interest. Allies and patrons of that sort had access to all manner of unpleasant things, from simple thugs to sophisticated poisons. They might consider the new Court Musician to be too trivial a problem to bother with—but in a Court ruled by a High King with an obsession for musicians, that was not as likely as it would otherwise have been. In fact, the new musician might be considered as deadly a potential rival as any of the Grand Dukes and Court Barons—and one with fewer protections.

Did the Haspur know this?

I hope so, she thought, slipping into her nightshift and preparing her pot of soporific tea. *Oh, I hope so. I hope he is finding himself some equally powerful allies. Because if he doesn't—he's going to find himself wing-clipped and surrounded, and that lovely position he has earned himself will be no more than a beautifully gilded trap. . . .*

◊   ◊   ◊

Like most of the other performance rooms in Freehold, the Rainbow Room lived up to its name, but not in the way that anyone who had not seen it would have expected. It was not decorated in many colors, nor worse, festooned with painted rainbows like a child's nursery. The Rainbow Room was the plainest, simplest performance room in the building, its walls and ceiling painted a soft white, the floor and tables some seamless substance of a textured, matte black, the booths and chairs upholstered in black as well, something as soft and supple as black suede leather, although Nightingale was fairly certain that was not what it was. It would have cost a fortune to cover that much furniture in black leather, and not even a Deliambren had that much to spare on furnishings in a performance room.

No, it was when the lights were dimmed and the special performance lighting lit that the Rainbow Room lived up to its name.

For there were crystal prisms hidden everywhere: in the ceiling fixtures, in the pillars supporting the ceiling, set into the leaded glass windows that divided the room itself from the dance floor. When the performance lighting was illuminated, those prisms caught and refracted it into a hundred thousand tiny rainbows that flung themselves everywhere, and since many of the prisms were free to move with air currents, the rainbows moved as well in a gentle dance of color. With that as a backdrop, no performer needed anything else.

Silas had shown himself to advantage here, and Nightingale hoped to emulate him. To that end she had chosen her black Elven silks for this first performance in the new room.

And in fact, she was beginning to think farther ahead than just the next few days or even weeks. If she could sustain her popularity here—why go anywhere else? Why go back on the road, once she had collected the information that the Deliambrens, the Free Bards, and the Elves all wanted? She didn't particularly have a sense of wanderlust the way some Gypsies did; she simply had never found a place she wanted to stay for more than a few months at a time.

Why *not* stay here?

Granted, she hated cities, but she couldn't avoid them altogether, and if she was going to have to endure them, why not do so where she was guaranteed a level of comfort that she would *never* get anywhere else? Where else would she have her own room with her own bathroom, heated and cooled to perfection? Where else would she get her choice of foodstuffs, so that she could go all month and never eat the same meal twice? And where else would she find a performance venue like this one?

And to that end—if she stayed, she would need new costumes, many new costumes, all of the same quality as her silks. The Elves would owe her once she got their information back to them; she *could* send word back with her own messages that she needed new dresses, and ask for specific colors and designs. . . .

She shook herself out of her reverie as the doors of the room opened and people began to make their way in. *Concentrate on what's going on right now, foolish woman,* she scolded herself. *Deal with what you have*

*before you. Worry about far into the future when you know you will have
that kind of future.*

Outside on the dance floor, Silas and the other musicians were setting
up; she saw them clearly through the window. He must have sensed her
watching, for he turned toward the Rainbow Room and waved, grinning
broadly, then gave her the Gypsy sign for well-wishing. She smiled back
and did the same, knowing that he could see her as easily as she saw
him. He looked particularly wonderful and outrageous tonight, and his
tight leather costume would give most Church Priests heart failure. It was
cut out in unexpected patterns that allowed his golden-tan skin to show
through, and unless she was very much mistaken, he was wearing a leather
codpiece with a red leather rose appliqued on the front.

Showoff. But she smiled as she thought it. It was impossible not to like
Silas; he went out of his way to be kind to even the lowliest of the waiters
and cleaners and encouraging to the worst of his fellow entertainers. There
wasn't an unkind bone in Silas' body.

Unfortunately, there wasn't a chaste bone in there, either. "Promiscu-
ous" did not begin to describe him, and Nightingale feared he would
meet an early end, either torn to pieces among a dozen jealous lovers,
each of whom was sure he or she was Silas' only true love, or worn away
to nothing by the exertion of all his love affairs. Silas' one fault—and it
was a bad one—was that he had a habit of telling his lovers whatever
they wanted to hear. That had gotten him into trouble in the past, and
he had never learned better. Perhaps Silas unconsciously feared the same
early end that she suspected for him; he seemed to be trying to pack a
lifetime's worth of experience into months rather than years.

*But for now, at least, he's having a fine time as far as I can tell. Still,
it wouldn't be my choice to burn up like a falling star for the sake of a
single spectacular bout of fireworks. I would rather leave a carefully
crafted and large legacy of music behind me.*

This new venue was only going to give him more trouble in the popularity department; now he was free to move about the stage as he sang,
instead of being pinned to a stool behind a guitar. That was only going
to make him *more* attractive so far as his admirers were concerned. Up
until now they'd had no reason to suspect Silas danced as well as he sang.

Well, this wasn't the time to worry about Silas and his troubles; her
harps were in perfect tune, and the place was about as full as it was going
to get until and unless word spread tonight that her performances were
not to be missed. So—

*So it's time to start creating a performance that is not to be missed,
foolish wench!*

She ran her hands over her harp strings, and the quiet murmur of talk
died away as the lights above the stage brightened and the ones out in
the room dimmed slightly. She took a deep breath, mentally ran over all
of her options, and decided to begin with something she hoped would
impress even the most difficult critic. She chose an Elven piece, and
backed it with the appropriate Bardic Magic meant to enhance the moods
called up by the song.

After that, all of her attention was bound up in her music and the reactions of her audience. It seemed to her that the listeners were impressed; they were quiet when she wanted them to be, nodded or tapped along in time when she played or sang something lively, and responded to the subtle textures she added with the Bardic Magic she wove into the fabric of her songs. In this incarnation, the magic was only meant to enhance an experience, not to manipulate anyone's thoughts. That was how the Elves generally used it among themselves. The room continued to fill as she played, until at the end of her first set, there were not too many tables or booths empty. And this was at supper—once people were finished eating, the audiences should grow larger.

The lights came back up as she signaled the end of her set; she stepped off the stage and went into the back of the room, where a cleverly concealed door led into a small closet-like affair. This was where another of the nonhumans, a fellow whose race she didn't even know, sat doing arcane things with a board of sliding bits and buttons. Xarax was a likable fellow, though he didn't speak much to anyone; he looked as human as Nightingale until you got close to him and saw that his eyes were exactly like a goat's, with an odd, sideways, kidney-shaped pupil, and his skin was covered with tiny hexagonal scales. She didn't know if he was completely hairless, but his "eyebrows" were nothing more than a darker pattern of scales, he had no sign of a beard, and he always wore a shirt with a hood and kept the hood up. He was the one in charge of the lighting here; he worked this room for Nightingale now as he had worked it for Silas before.

"That was perfect," she told him warmly. "I couldn't have asked for anything better."

His thin, lipless mouth stretched in a smile. "Excellent," he replied, with no hiss at all to his words. "You are a more subtle performer than Silas; I hoped I would match that subtlety. The audience likes you. The exquisite Violetta actually came here to listen to you *before* she went off to the dance floor. That is a *good* omen and proves that the customers like you."

"They do?" she replied, knowing she sounded pathetically eager, as eager as any green child in her first appearance, and knowing it would not matter to Xarax. "Oh, I hope so—"

"Tyladen did not choose you wrongly to take Silas' place," the nonhuman assured her, even reaching out with one three-fingered hand to pat her on the shoulder in an awkward gesture of reassurance. "He was half minded to choose another exactly like Silas, but I told him that would be a mistake, for such a choice would only invite comparison and unwelcome rivalry. I said to him to choose someone as *unlike* Silas as possible; someone whose emphasis was on the music rather than the performer—and here you are, and you prove me right. And Tyladen, who chose you."

That was the longest speech she had *ever* heard out of Xarax, and he abruptly turned back to his buttons and boards, as if embarrassed by the outpouring of words. She knew better than to be offended at his abruptness; she thanked him again and left him alone with his beloved machinery.

When her break was over, most of the people from her first performance were still in the room, sipping drinks they had ordered from waiters during the interval, and many more had arrived to fill up the rest of the seats. As the lights dimmed again, she saw the dance group had ended its first performance, and the dance floor emptied. Silas and his group would be taking a longer break than she did—their work was physically more demanding. For a while, at least, the music in here would penetrate onto the open dance floor, and might attract more people here.

And even as she began her first song of the second set, she caught sight of someone who startled her so much that for a moment she faltered—

Then she recovered, so quickly that she doubted anyone in her audience noticed, or thought the break was more than a dramatic pause. But out there, striding across the empty dance floor, wings swept dramatically back behind his shoulders, was—

T'fyrr!

It *had* to be him! It was not just the wings, the feathered body, the raptorial head—it was the costume, the way that closely wrapped fabric fell in particular folds that she remembered, the color of the fabric itself. It was also the color of his feathers, a rich gray-brown with touches of scarlet on the edges of his primaries and tail feathers. Nightingale had a peculiarly good color memory; she was able to match even grays and beiges without having a swatch of the fabric in question with her. She knew, from all of her years as an observer of nature, that no two birds were *exactly* colored alike; there were subtle shadings of tone that enabled someone who watched them a great deal to tell them apart. Surely that was the same with the Haspur—

And yet he looked through the window of the Rainbow Room, straight into her eyes, and showed no sign of recognition. Her hands played on, a peculiar, haunting Gypsy song; it was one she was certain that T'fyrr could never have heard, and it had been a Gypsy melody that had brought him to her in their first meeting. Surely he could not have resisted a second such song—

But although he must have heard the music, he paid no attention to it or to her. He *was* looking for someone, however, and in a few moments, as Kyran brought Tyladen to him, it was obvious just who he was looking for. The two nonhumans strolled together in the direction of Tyladen's office and were soon out of sight, leaving Nightingale puzzled and a bit confused.

It can't have been T'fyrr. T'fyrr would never have gone past without at least greeting me. It must have been some other Haspur.

But how many Haspur were there? And how could another Haspur look so *exactly* like T'fyrr?

The lighting is odd out there. Maybe I mistook his coloring. I saw T'fyrr in shadowed daylight under trees; the light out on the dance floor is a lot dimmer than that, and there are all those colored lights to confuse things.

Maybe so—but in every other way, this Haspur looked enough like T'fyrr to have been his twin. . . .

And I only saw him for a day or two. I could be wrong. It feels *as if his image has been branded into my memory, but I could be wrong.*

All she really knew, if it came down to it, was this. There was a Haspur in this building who had come looking for a Deliambren. There was a

bird-man *with* a Deliambren who had arrived at the High King's Palace.
These two might even be the same as that pair. In a way, she hoped so.
This city was no place for someone like T'fyrr right now, and the position
that Haspur held at Court was no position for T'fyrr to be in. If there
had to be a Haspur in danger, she would really prefer it wasn't one she
knew, one she cared for.

So why, she asked herself, as she started on her next song, *am I still
so certain it is him—both here and there, and probably in danger in
both places?*

Nob's directions were exact to the last detail, and he had not been at
all surprised that T'fyrr wanted to visit the tavern called Freehold. "Pages
aren't allowed to go there," he said wistfully. "But as soon as I'm old
enough—"

"As soon as it is possible, I will take you there," T'fyrr promised, and
the boy's eyes lit up. "If it is as wondrous as I have heard, it would be a
crime not to let you see it."

And with that, armed only directions and a bit of money secreted in
his body-wrappings, he ventured into the city. He was not particularly
worried about being attacked; not in broad daylight, at any rate. He had
trodden the streets of worse neighborhoods than Freehold was in with
perfect safety. Most would-be attackers took one look at his foot-talons,
his hand-talons, and his beak, and realized that he was better armed than
the worst bravo. He wanted to reach Freehold now, before he *needed* to
go, so that he knew the way. If Nob's directions proved misleading or
erroneous in any way, he wanted to know now, when he had the leisure
to ask for better directions.

Still, there was always the chance that he would be followed—and he
really didn't want to walk the *entire* way.

So once he was out of the Palace and onto the grounds, he did the
obvious; he took to the air.

His shadow passed over the guards at the gate and they gaped up at
him as he flew overhead. They had heard of him by now, of course, but
hearing about him and seeing him in the air were obviously two different
things. His eyesight was good enough to see that their hands tightened
on their weapons as he passed them, but they did not make any kind of
threatening gesture. But—probably when he returned, he should come in
on foot and show them his proper safe-conduct from the King.

No point in giving them a target for arrow practice.

He was quite glad that he had decided to fly when he saw how crowded
the streets below him were. It would be hot down there, too; another
reason to put off landing until he had to.

*On the other hand, I'm not exactly inconspicuous. Anyone who wanted
to know where I'm going need only climb into the nearest Church tower
and watch me to see where I land.*

But if he was being followed—that might not occur to someone who
didn't himself fly.

*Well, what's done is done. No use closing the coop door after the pigeons
have flown.*

It wasn't at all difficult to follow Nob's directions from the air, and in a remarkably short period of time, he landed in a square next to a fountain about three blocks away from the building that housed Freehold. It took him longer to walk those three blocks than it had to fly the rest. Although foot traffic tended to part before him, the streets were still crowded, and there weren't too many places for other pedestrians to move in order to get out of his way.

He suspected that he was indeed being followed when he was two blocks from the place, and only then did it occur to him that it probably didn't matter if he flew or walked. This, as Harperus had pointed out, was a logical destination for him. All anyone had to do was to leave a watcher near the place, and sooner or later he was bound to show up.

If I'd had any sense, I would have sent a message to Tyladen that I was coming and would land on the roof, he told himself angrily. *But no, I have no more sense than an unfledged eyas. And this is all for no reason! I don't have anything at all to report!*

Other than to make T'fyrr the very visible symbol of his new policy of tolerance for nonhumans, the King literally had not done anything since T'fyrr's arrival. At least, he hadn't done anything that T'fyrr had witnessed. He left everything in the hands of his underlings, just as he had that very first day, and those underlings were making very certain that T'fyrr was given nothing whatsoever to do when the King wasn't requesting private performances. Other Court musicians regularly played for the humans gathered at various places during the day; not T'fyrr. Someone was being very careful to see that T'fyrr stayed out of sight. T'fyrr, on the other hand, was making very sure that he stayed visible, attending every open Court session that he could—but he really hadn't learned anything new.

Well, it was too late to do anything about followers now; he walked up to the front door of Freehold as if he hadn't a care in the world and presented himself to the doorkeeper with casual aplomb. He did enjoy the way the man's eyes widened at the sight of his wings and talons, but when he asked to see Tyladen, the man did not ask why or claim that the Deliambren was busy. Instead, he directed T'fyrr to go inside and said that he would tell Tyladen to come meet him.

T'fyrr followed the human's directions, but once inside the door, his senses were assaulted in a fashion that left him momentarily dazed by the barrage of light and sound. People—not only humans, but other peoples—were everywhere. Music pounded at his ears from the center of the room and echoed down off the high ceiling. A space in the middle of the room was full of creatures dancing to a wild reel; above the gyrating bodies was the group responsible for the high-volume, fast-paced music itself. *They* were all humans, but they played as if they were the demons that the Church claimed T'fyrr had represented.

A moment or two later, to his relief and gratitude, the music ended; the bronze-maned human singer threw back his hair, acknowledged the applause of the dancers, and indicated that he and the group were about to take a rest. T'fyrr sighed in gratitude; it would have been impossible to cross the rapidly emptying floor with it full of dancers, and he wasn't

certain he would have been able to maintain his equilibrium—literally!—
with that much music pounding into his ears.

As the dance floor cleared, T'fyrr started across it, sweeping his glance
across the many odd alcoves and glass-fronted rooms surrounding the
open space. Harperus and Nob had both described Freehold to the best
of their abilities, but both descriptions had come up rather short of reality.
If he had not been so concerned about those who had followed him, he
would have been happy to explore the place—

And then, as he glanced into a rainbow-laced room with a single performer upon the stage, his heart and footsteps faltered for an instant.

No.

But, yes. It was Nightingale. Not the Nightingale he remembered from
that single memorable afternoon, but a more elegant and exotic version
of the same woman. She wore a night-black gown that flowed about her
body like a second skin of feathers, and her hair had been left to flow
down her back in a single fall of darkest sable. But it was her—it was her.

And if he acknowledged her, whoever was following him and watching
him would want to know *why* he had done so—would want to know how
she had met him, and where, and what she was to him.

If those followers were from *any* of his enemies at Court, she would
not be safe, not even here. Her only safety lay in his pretending that she
was as much a stranger to him as anyone else here.

Yes, they would see him meeting with the Deliambren, Tyladen—but
the Deliambren could take care of himself. Beautiful, fragile Nightingale
could not.

So he allowed his eyes to brush across hers with feigned indifference
and pretended not to see the shock of recognition in *her* face. Instead,
he waited until he caught a glimpse of a Deliambren hurrying toward him
from a nearby corridor—who could only be Tyladen, the owner of this
place. He gave all of his attention to his host, and as Tyladen hurried him
into a back room, he did not even spare a second glance for the musician
in the room of rainbows—however much his heart yearned for a welcoming smile from her.

"I'm glad you came," the Deliambren said as he closed a reassuringly solid
door behind T'fyrr and turned a chair around so that the Haspur could lean
his arms on the back and have his tail and wings unencumbered. "I was
hoping to be able to catch you up on news from the Fortress-City before
things get to a point where they are critical. The listening devices are no
replacement for regular contact. We can *hear* you just fine, but unfortunately
we can't tell you what it is we'd like you to talk about."

"Something new?" T'fyrr asked.

The Deliambren shook his head. "Not exactly new—just that there is some
information we need to help us fill in some holes in our knowledge. You
know that we still want to map all of Alanda, of course. That hasn't changed."

"I didn't think it would," T'fyrr rumbled with a little reluctant amusement. "Once you people get a direction in your heads, you're as hard to
sway from it as a migrating goose."

Tyladen smiled. "We've run into some obstacles. There are some of the
human kingdoms that have decided they don't want any part of us, and

in order to carry out the expedition properly, we'll *have* to cross their lands. The High King can override their objections, so now we *need* his blanket permission in order to get the expedition underway."

T'fyrr blinked, as the conversations of several of the past few Court sessions he'd sat through played in his head. He had made a point of going to every single open Court that he knew about; not only to have something to do, but to make himself visible as an act of defiance against those Advisors who were trying to make him vanish. None of them seemed to realize just how good his hearing really was; he'd overheard a lot that he wasn't supposed to, both on the dais and among the courtiers. Once you knew the factions and who belonged to what, you knew where to listen.

In addition, he had been present at several private meetings between the King and his Advisors, in his capacity as the King's Personal Musician. He'd heard quite a bit there, too. He just hadn't realized that it meant anything.

"I believe I know what you need," he said. "There are several of the King's Advisors who are against the expedition, but they have not been showing their hands openly."

"Yes!" Tyladen exclaimed. "And we couldn't tell how the King himself really feels about it."

T'fyrr coughed. "Oh, the King—well, he is very enamored with your *technology*, though he refers to it as 'Deliambren magic.' He would like to have still more of your little wonders, and as long as he has that desire, he will be swayed in favor of letting you have anything you want, within reason. However—the Advisors are not the only problem you have to deal with."

"They aren't?" Tyladen looked puzzled.

"You forget," T'fyrr said, trying *not* to sound bitter, "how much these people are herded by the opinions of their religious leaders. There are several of them who are not happy with your 'magic' and are quietly lobbying the King against it. They are not necessarily the ones who are against nonhumans, by the way."

The Deliambren's eyebrows rose sharply. "Ah! I see! Yes, the religious leaders who hate and fear nonhumans are depressingly easy to recognize, but I had not realized that there were others who might be against technology."

T'fyrr snorted. "Think about it. Your ways have the potential to *prove* some of their assertions are a pile of mutes and castings, and that would be bad for their business. Of course they fear you! Now, since I know what it is that you need, let me name you some names."

He closed his eyes and brought up faces and attitudes in his mind's eye, then began to recite all that he knew. In the background, he was vaguely aware of a faint hum that was probably one of the recording-crystal devices at work, and of a steady tapping, which might mean that Tyladen was taking notes in some other way. He was rather surprised at the sheer volume of information he had, really. It wasn't only the King's Advisors who were important, it was also the factions with whom they were involved.

All of those factions were represented by people, and all of those people had names, descriptions, attitudes—weaknesses that could be exploited, perhaps—likes and dislikes.

He had to stop, rest and enjoy some cool water more than once in the course of his recitation. It all took a very long time, even for someone like him. His people relied on oral history before they met the Deliambrens, and as a consequence they were very good at organizing their memories. Still, it took *time* to get everything out, and when he was finished, he was well aware that it was very late.

"That was fabulous," Tyladen said with admiration as he tapped a few more things into some sort of device on his desk and slipped the device itself into a drawer. "You are going to prove to be a lot more useful than you thought, I'm sure of it. This is all information none of our human agents were high enough to obtain."

"I hope you are correct," T'fyrr told him sincerely. "I was not as sanguine about this position of mine as Harperus was; I simply did not see what a simple musician could learn that would make any difference to all of us."

It was the Deliambren's turn to snort. "Well, most 'simple musicians' can't hear a mouse squeak five hundred *sdaders* away, either. You're overhearing far more than anyone has any reason to believe. *Don't* let them know that, whatever you do."

"I won't!" T'fyrr hastened to assure him. "My safety lies in that, as I know all too well! Don't think for a moment that I am not aware of that."

"Good." Tyladen pushed himself away from his desk. "I need to go into the back and transmit all this home. Can you see yourself out? Oh— you can feel free to stay a while if you want. I left orders that whatever you ask for is no charge."

After all that—hmph. I should hope so. Then T'fyrr chided himself for the uncharitable thought and thanked his host. "Perhaps I will. Right now, I should like just a drink of something for my throat, and then I will look around a little, perhaps."

"Whatever." The Deliambren opened a door in an apparently blank wall. "Enjoy yourself." He slipped inside, and the door closed behind him, leaving, again, an apparently blank wall.

Evidently Tyladen *literally* meant for T'fyrr to show himself out. And evidently he trusted T'fyrr not to snoop around in the office, either.

Not that it was any kind of a temptation, no more than it had been a temptation to snoop in Harperus' exotic travel-wagon. If this had been a library full of music recordings, perhaps, but there was nothing likely to be in this office that would hold even a hint of interest for T'fyrr.

Not unless there is something on the personal records of the musicians here—

No. No, he would *not* try to look up Nightingale to see what had brought her here. That would be rude.

But he *could* go out and at least listen to her sing without revealing his presence. That wouldn't hurt anything or anyone.

Maybe, if the opportunity presented itself, he could find a way to contact her discreetly, privately. A note or a message, perhaps.

So with that thought in mind, he opened the door and walked out into the main room, which was once again crowded with dancers, preoccupied with the idea of seeing his friend again, and a little surprised at the pleasure that gave him.

CHAPTER SIX

It can't be T'fyrr. But how can it not be? It must be—but how can it be him? The thoughts circled one another in her head, mutually antagonistic. For a while, Nightingale was so taken aback by the appearance of a Haspur who could be T'fyrr's twin that she didn't pay a great deal of attention to the customers as people, only as her audience. That is, she reacted to them and paid attention to the way in which they reacted to her, but as a group, not as individuals.

And she also wasn't watching them for potential trouble. She *used* to keep a careful eye on every person in her audiences when she was on the road, because she never knew who or what was going to cause a problem for her. Sometimes trouble came from someone who just happened to be offended by the lyrics of a particular song; sometimes it came from a more obvious source, a drunk, or a person who had arrived with his own set of prejudices riding his shoulders like a pack. She had gotten out of the habit of looking for problems in her audience since she'd been here, and maybe that wasn't such a good thing. . . .

It wasn't until her second set was over that she shook herself out of her reverie and began that kind of "watching" that was normally second nature and due entirely to a Free Bard's healthy sense of self-preservation. Even when trouble erupted *around* a Free Bard, it generally came to *include* the Free Bard, even if it hadn't been intended to.

She scolded herself for neglecting that here in Freehold. Perhaps her instincts had been convinced that this was a kind of "safe" place, like a Waymeet or a Gypsy camp—after all, there *was* someone else watching out for trouble and troublemakers here. Many someone elses, actually, most of them Mintaks, or extremely large humans of the Faire-strongman variety. The "peace-keepers" generally kept the peace very effectively; their mere presence was enough to keep some types outside the doors.

But where the Haspur who was the King's Chief Musician was showing up—given that the possibility of *two* Haspur in the same city was vanishingly small—there might be someone following.

No. There would *be someone following. The only question would be if it was a friend or a foe.*

And the chances of the Freehold staff recognizing that sort of trouble if it walked in the door were remote. A "friend" would be fine—a guard assigned to protect the King's Musician discreetly. But a foe—well, anyone following the Haspur would be hired by someone attached to the Court, and he would not be the kind to catch the notice of one of the "peace-keepers." He would not be drunk, nor rowdy—in fact, he would take pains not to catch anyone's attention unless the Haspur showed up again.

But this was not the first time that Nightingale had needed to watch for *that* sort of trouble. Free Bards were always acquiring enemies among Bardic Guild musicians, for instance, and the Bardic Guild had plenty of coin to hire experienced ruffians. So as she took her break between sets, she got herself something to drink and began to stroll the floor, watching the customers, seeing who didn't quite fit in.

There was a general feeling about the customers at Freehold. No matter how well or poorly or oddly they dressed, they all acted pretty much the same. They were here to have a good time in a place where very few people were going to make any judgments about them; that engendered a certain relaxed air. Even those who were here for the first time generally succumbed to that all-pervasive mood after a while. This was especially true of the crowd around Silas and the dance-floor.

That was why the three men sitting at one of the tables near the entrance struck her watchful instincts immediately.

They were not here for a good time. They had drinks, and they watched the dancers, but there was nothing relaxed about them. They weren't even paying any attention to Silas, and that in itself was unusual. She let her barriers down just a trifle, and her immediate reading was confirmed by the state of alert, slightly nervous tension she read in them, the edginess showing they were prepared to do something physical, and soon. These men were here on some kind of dirty business, and they didn't want anyone to notice them.

She also had the feeling that she had seen them before, but not in this part of town. There was a nagging something about them; their clothing was wrong somehow. They didn't match the clothing; that was it. It was just a little too new, a trifle too expensive, and they were not comfortable in it.

Still, that edginess, the *waiting* feeling, could just mean they were here to meet a lady of negotiable virtue.

Or someone else's wives.

Just because they were here and on edge, and they weren't regulars, that really didn't mean much.

Maybe.

Then again . . . *They didn't show up until after the Haspur did, and they wouldn't have gotten through the door in time to see where he went. Now they're down here, near the entrance, just off the dance floor, in a spot where anyone arriving or leaving is going to have to pass them.*

She took her own drink to a table nearby, where she could see both the corridor leading to the offices and the table holding the three men. She watched them out of the corner of her eye, feeling rather put out; this was one of Silas' better performances, and she wasn't able to give it more than a fraction of her attention. Silas always needed one set to warm up, and by the fourth or fifth of the night he was beginning to tire, making his second and third sets perfect for someone who really appreciated seeing him at his best. And tonight was his first night with the dance group, making *him* doubly eager to do his finest. Nightingale would have liked to be able to sit back a little and enjoy it. Although Silas wasn't really her type, the sensuality he radiated tonight was enough to stir a corpse, and that skintight leather outfit of his made it very clear that however else Silas indulged himself, he did *not* neglect his physical health.

What was even more annoying was the simple fact that she couldn't sit here forever; *she* had her third set to do shortly, and she would have to leave. She was debating whether or not she should ask one of the peace-keepers to keep an eye on the three for her when the Haspur finally emerged from the office corridor, and one of the three men caught sight of him and sat straight up, as if someone had stuck a pin in him.

Then he quickly slumped back down, but not before Nightingale had seen his sudden interest. And not before she saw him lean over and say something quickly to his two companions.

No more than a heartbeat later, one of his companions calmly got to his feet and reached out onto the dance floor for one of the dancers.

He just seized whoever was nearest; it happened to be a human male, dressed, as many of Silas' followers did, in a carefully crafted imitation of one of Silas' outfits.

The dancer turned toward the man who had grabbed him in bewilder-ment—he started to say something, and the stranger calmly slung him around him around toward the tables and punched him in the face hard enough to knock him backward. He knocked over two tables as he fell and landed on a third, collapsing it. Those tables overturned, and their occupants scattered, more than a few of them getting to their feet and looking for the cause of the trouble with fire in their eyes.

Another heartbeat later, and that entire corner of the room was involved in a free-for-all—which quickly spread in the Haspur's direction.

Peace-keepers converged on the brawl from every part of Freehold; Nightingale spotted them making for the stairs and pushing their way through the dancers, most of whom were not yet aware that there was anything wrong.

But more violence erupted along a line between the strangers' table and the Haspur, with fighting breaking out spontaneously and spreading like wildfire.

Soon an entire quarter of the room was involved in the brawl, and fists were flying indiscriminately.

Fights were not all that usual here, especially not one of this magnitude. It was almost as if there was someone going through the crowd provoking more violence, instigating trouble and moving on before it could touch him—

Nightingale was still outside of the fighting, though many people around her had abandoned the dancing or their tables and were peering in the direction of the altercation. She jumped up onto her chair, then stood on her table and scanned the crowd as the fight converged on the openly startled Haspur and engulfed him.

Intuition and a feeling of danger warned her that the strangers must be in there, somewhere—and if the Haspur was their target, they would be moving in on him now.

Her flash of intuition solidified into certainty as she spotted them widely separated in the crowd. *There* they were, all right, converging on the

Haspur from three directions as he tried to extricate himself from the brawl without getting involved himself.

And as for the Haspur's identity—there was no glass between her and him now, and she had a good look at his head and face, at the way he moved. It *was* T'fyrr; it had to be. If it had been a stranger, she might have been tempted to let the peace-keepers handle it.

Well, it wasn't. *And damned if I am going to let these ruffians go after a friend!*

Her harp was safe in the Rainbow Room; she was no bar-brawler, but she hadn't been playing the roads for all these years without learning a few tricks. She jumped down off the table and began slithering through the crowd of struggling, fighting customers. As long as you knew what you were doing and what to watch out for, it was actually fairly easy to wade through a fight without getting involved—or at least, without suffering more than an occasional shove or stepped-on toe. She made her way to the spot in the milling mob where she'd last seen T'fyrr fairly quickly—but she actually got within sight of one of the men that were after him before she saw the Haspur.

That was when she *knew* that T'fyrr was in danger, real danger, and that these men weren't just planning on roughing him up. After all, if these people *weren't* after him, why would this one be carrying a net—why carry a net into a place like Freehold at all? Lyonarie was not a seaport—Freehold might offer a lot of entertainment, but fishing wasn't part of it—and this lad didn't look anything like a fisherman!

She looked around frantically for something to make his life difficult before he got a chance to use that net. If he caught T'fyrr in it, he could entangle the Haspur and—

No, best not to thing about that. Find a way to stop him!

There! She darted out of the fight long enough to seize a spiky piece of wrought-iron sculpture—or, at least, Tyladen alleged that it was a sculpture—from an alcove in the wall. It wasn't heavy, but it *was* just what she needed. She slid back into the crowd nearest the fellow with the net, just in time to see him back out of the crowd a little himself and spread the net out to toss it.

She heaved her bit of statuary into the half-open folds just as he started to throw it.

He lurched backward, unbalanced for the moment by the sudden weight of iron in the net. He was quick, though; he whipped around to see if someone had stepped on the net, and when saw how the spikes of the sculpture had tangled everything up, his mouth moved in what was probably a curse. He pulled the mess to him, since no one seemed to be paying any attention to him, and began to untangle it, moving out of the crowd completely for just a moment.

That was when Nightingale slipped up behind him and delivered an invitation to slumber with a wine bottle she'd purloined from an overturned table.

He dropped like a felled ox: net, statue, and all. Nightingale dropped the bottle beside him after giving him a second love-tap to ensure that he stayed out of the conflict for a while.

There was no longer a background of music to the brawl; Silas and the rest had probably deserted their stage before the fighting engulfed it.

She moved around the periphery of the fight, looking for T'fyrr, and finally spotted him again as his wings waved above the crowd momentarily. She worked her way in toward him.

But as she got within touching distance of him, she saw that another of the bully-boys was moving in on him, and the weapon *he* carried was like nothing Nightingale had ever seen before. In fact, she wouldn't have known he had a weapon at all if she hadn't see the "blade" glint briefly in the light. It was needlelike, probably very sharp—and poisoned? Dear Lady, who knew? It might very well be!

She was too far away to do anything!

She opened her mouth to shout a futile warning as the man lunged toward the Haspur.

But T'fyrr was not as helpless as he looked; somehow he spotted his attacker, coming from an angle where no human would have seen him moving. He grabbed a chair, whirled with the speed of a striking goshawk, and intercepted the weapon as the man brought it down toward the point where his back had been a heartbeat before. With all the noise, there was no sound as the man drove it into the chair-back, but he staggered as he hit the unyielding wood instead of the flesh and feathers he had been aiming for.

It must have embedded too deeply in the wood of the chair to pull free, for he abandoned the weapon and leapt back, looking around for help.

But there wasn't any help to be had. The third man had either seen Nightingale fell his partner, or simply had noticed that he was down. Instead of dealing with his part of the attack, the third man was helping the semiconscious net-wielder to his feet and dragging him out of the fight toward the door. There was no doorkeeper at this point, and he was not the only person helping an injured friend out.

They're going to get away, and I can't stop them, damn it!

The man with the stiletto took another look at T'fyrr, who had tossed the chair aside, and with wings mantling in rage, was advancing on him.

He gave up. Faster than Nightingale would have believed possible, he had eeled his way into the brawl and out of T'fyrr's sight and reach. While T'fyrr looked for him, futilely, Nightingale saw him reappear at the side of his two companions, taking the unconscious man's free arm, draping it over his shoulder, and hustling both of the others toward the entrance and out before she could alert anyone to stop them.

She cursed them with the vilest Gypsy curses she could think of—but she couldn't follow them with anything more potent than that.

With the peace-keepers converging on the fight wholesale, and no one around trying to keep it going, the battle ended shortly after that. Peace-keepers didn't even try to sort out who started what; they simply separated combatants and steered them toward the entrance, suggesting that if there was still a grievance after the cool air hit them, they could resume their discussions outside. There didn't seem to be anyone with injuries worse than a blackened eye, either, and a good three-fourths of the people involved had only been trying to keep themselves from getting hurt by the few folk actually fighting.

Nightingale had seen it all before; people who, either drunk or simply worked up over something, would take any excuse to fight with anyone who wanted to fight back. The three bravos must have known something like this would happen, too, and had counted on it.

Which, unfortunately, argued very strongly that they were professionals in the pay of someone with enough money to hire them.

While the peace-keepers dealt with the mess, Nightingale picked her way through the overturned tables and chairs toward T'fyrr. There was an uncanny silence beneath the dance lights—as she had thought, Silas and his crew had decided that discretion was better than foolhardiness and had abandoned their platform for the safety of one of the performance rooms. She saw them across the empty dance floor, with Silas in the lead, making their way cautiously back toward their stage.

But at the moment, she had someone else she wanted to talk to.

The Haspur stood so quietly that he might have been frozen in place—but there was a faint trembling of his wing feathers that told her he was locked in some kind of emotional overload.

Better break him out of it.

"Hello T'fyrr," she said calmly, touching his arm lightly, and projecting peace and a sense of security at him.

He jumped in startlement, and she saw, still floating in that strange, detached calm that exercising her power brought her, that he extended his talons for a moment before he recognized her. And he *did* recognize her; that tiny touch was all she needed to read the recognition and dismay flooding through his mind and heart.

He looked for one short moment as if he might still try to pretend that he didn't know her, but she kept her eyes fastened on his, and he finally shook his head.

"Hello, Nightingale," he replied in that deep, rumbling voice she knew so well. The tension in the arm beneath her hand told her he was still caught up in the fighting rage the attack had stirred up in him. But he spoke to her calmly enough to have fooled anyone but her, or someone like her. "I—I am sorry I did not greet you, but I was afraid that something like this might happen. I did not want anyone following me to know that I knew you."

She nodded; it would be time enough later to find out *why* he was being followed, and what in the world had brought him to Lyonarie—presumably with Old Owl, since that was the last Deliambren she had seen him with. Right now, there were other things she needed to do.

Bring him calm, for one thing, and help him convince himself that the danger is over for now.

"I saw them; there were three of them. One never got close to you, one had that stiletto knife, and one had a net."

He eyes widened at the mention of the word "net."

Well, that certainly touched a nerve.

"Whoever they are, they're gone now," she pointed out quickly. "I saw

them leave—unfortunately, I wasn't in a position where I   could get
someone to intercept them."

He took a deep breath. "I would rather that they escaped than you got
yourself involved in my troubles," he replied.

She only shook her head. "I have to start my next set," she said instead,
changing the subject completely. "Why don't you join me?"

He blinked at her slowly, as if he didn't quite understand what she had
just said. "Do you mean to listen," he asked, "or to participate?"

"Either," she told him. "Both. It will do you good to think about something else for a little until your thoughts get organized and you have a
chance to calm yourself down. I know how good your memory is; surely
we both know enough of the same music to fill a set. I also know how
good *you* are—and there is no one else I would rather share a stage with.
I would love to have you join me, unless you'd rather not."

But he took a deep breath and let it out slowly, as if her reply had
answered some need of his own. "There is nothing I would like better,"
he said, his voice now a bit more relaxed. "If you would care to lead the
way—?"

By the time the two of them reached her little stage, Nightingale
noticed that Xarax had altered the lighting to suit both of them. She gave
T'fyrr her stool and took a chair for herself; after a brief consultation to
determine some mutually acceptable music, they began.

The Rainbow Room had emptied as the brawl began, now it slowly
filled up again with customers who were shaken by what had just happened. While fights were not unheard of in Freehold, there had never
been one of this magnitude, and the regular customers were still asking
themselves how and why the violence of the outside world had intruded
on this place they had considered immune to it. Nightingale could have
told them, of course.

*When powerful people are determined that something will happen, no
place is safe that has not been warned and has not created specific defenses
against the weapons that they can bring to bear. Powerful people have
the means to* make *things happen, no matter what anyone else might want.*

But that was not what these people wanted to hear, and at the moment,
that was not what they needed to hear, either. They needed to be soothed,
and since that need matched T'fyrr's, that was what Nightingale gave
them all.

As she played and sang, and wove a web of magic to hold them all in
a feeling of safety and security, she opened herself cautiously to T'fyrr.
"Reading" a nonhuman was always a matter for uncertainty, but she
thought that she knew him well enough to have a solid chance at getting
a little beneath his surface.

*Do I? It is an intrusion. But he is in need—it's like the ache of an
unhealed wound. Could I see him wounded physically and not help? No,
this is something I must at least try to help with.*

She closed her eyes, set part of herself to the simple task of playing,
and the rest to weaving herself into the magic web, opening herself further
to him, letting herself slide into his heart.

There is fear; that is the surface. Singing seemed to ease him somewhat, but beneath the obvious concerns—anxiety over being followed, remnants of fear from the moment when he had seen an attacker targeting *him*, more fear for what the attack really meant—there was some very deep emotional wounding, something that went back much farther than the past few hours, or even weeks.

She sensed that, but she did not touch it. Not yet.

We are too much alike, more than I knew. If I go deeper—he will have me. She felt that old, unhealed ache of her own, the scars from all of those *others* that she had given herself to, who had in the end only seen that she knew them too well, and fled. *If I had known he would be another—*But she had not known.

She could pull herself back and *not* give what he needed to him. There was still time to retreat. *I cannot retreat. He is my friend. He was trying to protect me by pretending he did not know me; I owe him enough to venture deeper.*

So she did, slipping past the fear, the anger—

Ah. The fear and the anger are related. He fears the anger.

There was pain, dreadful pain both physical and spiritual; more fear, and with it a residue of self-hate, deep and abiding doubt, and a soul-wounding that called out to her. There was nothing to tell her *what* had caused all this, what had changed the confident, happy creature she had met in the Waymeet to the T'fyrr who doubted, even despised himself and sought some kind of redemption here in Lyonarie. She could only read the emotions, not what caused them.

But being Nightingale, now that she knew the hurt existed, now that it was a part of her, there was no choice for her, either. She had to find out what it was that troubled him, and why, and help him if she could.

The hurt was hers; the soul-pain was hers now, as she had known it would be. That was the curse that was also her gift. Once she read a person this deeply, she was committed to dealing with what she found—

Which was one of the reasons why she preferred to spend as much time in the company of those who were not human as possible. It was difficult to read nonhumans, harder still to read them to that extent; very seldom did she find those whose hearts called to hers for help. The concerns of the Elves were either only of the moment, or of the ages—she could help with neither. The Deliambrens were as shallow streams to her, for they simply did not understand human emotions. Other nonhumans either could not be read at all, or their needs were so alien to her that their pain slipped away from her and vanished into darkness before she could do more than grasp the fact that it was there.

Not so with T'fyrr. She braced herself against the pull of his needs and his hurts, but only to keep herself from being devoured by them. His aches were hers now, and would be until and unless she helped him to heal them. The bond between them might even last beyond that moment; it was too soon to tell.

And too late to call it back and say, "No, wait—"

She brought her awareness back to the here and now, her hands playing of their own will, despite the new hurts in her heart, the hurts that were not hers, and yet were now a part of her. She felt, as she always did on these occasions, as if the pain should somehow manifest itself physically, as if she should bear bleeding wounds on her hands and breast, as if she should look as bruised and broken outside as T'fyrr was within.

But, of course, there were no such signs, nor was it likely that T'fyrr had any notion what had just happened. He sang on, finding his momentary release in music, just as she herself often did.

Ah, Lady of the Night, we are more alike than I had thought!

With the readiness, if not the ease, of long practice, she walled as much away as she could inside herself and smoothed over the pain that she could not wall away. Eventually, it would all be dealt with. . . .

Or not. . . .

But for the moment, it was *this* moment that counted.

And there were more duties that she owed than this one. She had her duty as a musician as well as a healer, and it was as a musician that she was operating now. She sang and smiled, played and probed the needs of her audience, and answered those needs. And eventually, the set was over.

"Let's go somewhere quiet for the break," she said once they had taken their bows and left the stage. "We have a great deal of catching up to do." And as the skin around his eyes twitched, she added quickly, "Unless you have somewhere you need to go? I don't want to get in the way of anything that you are already committed to."

"No," he said after a moment's awkward silence. "No, I don't have anywhere to go, and no one is expecting me. I had hoped to get back before darkness fell, but—"

"Darkness had already fallen by the time you left Tyladen's office," she pointed out, and he sighed.

"I thought as much." He said it in a discouraged, but unsurprised tone. "I suppose I can fly in the darkness; there is enough light coming up from the streets—"

She interrupted him, feeling more than annoyed at Tyladen for not taking care of this himself. "It was Tyladen's fault that you were here longer than you wanted to be, and Tyladen's fault—or so I suspect—that you were caught here by those men. Tyladen can *damn* well arrange for you to be taken to—ah—wherever it is you need to go in some kind of protected conveyance! And I'll tell him so myself!"

She actually started in the direction of Tyladen's office, when T'fyrr, laughing self-consciously, intercepted her. "By the four winds, *now* I see the Nightingale defending the nestling!" he said, catching her arm gently. "So fierce a bird, no wonder nothing dares to steal her young! No, no, my friend, I *can* fly at night, I am not night blind like a poor hawk. And I will be far safer flying above your city at night than I will be in any kind of conveyance on the ground!"

She let herself be coaxed out of going to confront the owner of Freehold; he was right, after all. It would be difficult, if not impossible, for a marksman to make out a dark, moving shadow against the night sky. But that did not make her less wroth with Tyladen for his sake.

If I didn't dare let him know that I am working for the Deliambrens, I would give him a real piece of my mind! The wretched, stupid man! Oh, how I'd like to—

She forced herself to remain calm. Even Tyladen could not ignore this night's near-riot, and when she told him what she had seen—

Well, he just might decide to take a little better care of his agent!

She hesitated, then offered her invitation. "Then if you can stay—and want to stay—I have one more set. After it's over, we could go up on the roof; it's quiet up there, and no one will bother us. And no one will know if you leave from there if I don't tell them."

He pondered a moment, then agreed. But she sensed not only reluctance but resistance. He knew, somehow, that she was going to try to get him to talk about what had happened to him, and he was determined not to do so.

And being Nightingale, of course, this only ensured that she would be more persistent than his determination could withstand.

Just wait, my poor friend, she thought as they spoke of inconsequentials that he apparently hoped would throw her off the track. *Just wait. I have learned my patience from the Elves, who think in terms of centuries. If I am determined to prevail, you cannot hold against me.*

T'fyrr sat through Nightingale's last set as part of the audience, watching those who were absorbed in the beauty of her music and the power that she put into it. She held them captive, held them in the palm of her hand. There was no world for them outside this little room, and every story she told in melody and lyric came alive for them. He saw that much in their dreaming eyes, their relaxed posture, the concentration in their faces.

Was this that mysterious Bardic Magic at work? If so, he couldn't see any reason to find fault with it. She wasn't doing anything to hurt these people and *was* doing a great deal to help them. They listened to her and became caught up in her spell, losing most of the stress that they had carried when they entered the door of her performance room. How could there be anything wrong with that?

He only wished that he could join them. He was shaken by the fight, more than he wanted to admit. The entire incident was branded with extraordinary vividness and detail in his memory, and there was no getting rid of it. If he closed his eyes, he could still see the stiletto and the man holding it, the man with the cold eyes of someone who does not care what he does so long as he is paid for it.

The eyes of High Bishop Padrik. . . . Padrik had looked that way, the one time he had really *looked* at T'fyrr. He had weighted out T'fyrr's life in terms of what it would buy him and had coldly determined the precise way to extract the maximum advantage from killing the Haspur. T'fyrr had been nothing more to him than an object; and not even an object of particular value.

As much as by the memory of his attacker, he was shaken by the memory of his first instinctive reaction.

I lost all control. No one knows it but me, but I did. I could, easily, have murdered again. Granted, this time my victim would have been someone who was attacking me directly, without provocation, but it would still have been murder.

Rage had taken him over completely. A dreadful, killing rage had engulfed him, a senseless anger that urged him to lash out and disembowel the man. Only luck had saved the man, luck and the ability to get out of sight before T'fyrr could act.

Would he have felt that same rage a year or more ago? He didn't think so.

Singing with Nightingale calmed him; simply sitting here listening to her sing alone calmed him even more, but he was still shaking inside. That was as much the reason why he had decided to stay here for a bit as was his desire to talk to Nightingale.

Lyrebird. I must remember that she is called Lyrebird here. I wonder why?

In fact, paired with his desire to talk with her was his fear of resuming their interrupted friendship. *I cannot place her in jeopardy, and she will be in as much danger as I am from my enemies if they learn that we are friends. I am not certain that Tyladen will be willing to protect her even if I warn him; after all, she is nothing more than an employee to him.* And he knew, with deep certainty, that he *was* in danger from at least one enemy who was willing to hire bravos to come after him. He had known, even before Nightingale told him, that there were at least two people in that staged brawl who had been targeting him, and perhaps three or more. Being thwarted once would not stop them; they would only seek him somewhere else.

Or seek some other way to reach me than the direct route.

If he came and went via the sky, there would only be two places where they could ambush him: within the Palace grounds, or within Freehold. Both places had their own protections, and both had people who would protect him. But Nightingale had no wings; she could not travel except on the ground. He knew her kind, she was a Gypsy, and it was not natural for her to stay in one place for long; she *would* not stay here even if he warned her that it wasn't safe to leave. If his enemies knew that he valued her, they would not hesitate to use her against him.

He sighed and sipped at the iced herbal drink someone had brought him, while Nightingale sang and played one of her strange Gypsy songs. *I wish that I knew who my enemy was, and why he sent men after me. It could be one of the other Court musicians, who wishes to be rid of me. It could be one of the Advisors, or one of their allies, who thinks that I have too great an influence with the King.* He sighed. *If only I did! But that doesn't matter as long as someone believes that I do. If also could be someone who simply does not wish to see a nonhuman in a position of such importance and visibility. Or it could be for none of those reasons, for a cause I cannot even think of.*

It could also be that someone in this city, possibly with the Church, had recognized him as the "demon" who killed a Church Guard. Since that killing could not actually be *proved*, this might be their own way of seeing that justice was done.

All of those people would have ample reason to try to use Nightingale, even someone connected with the Church and High Bishop Padrik.

That might be worst of all for her. He had seen the shadowed fear in her eyes on the single occasion when they had spoken about the power of the Church—the idea of Nightingale in the hands of a sadist like Padrik left him cold and shaking.

He would not have been happy until he had forced her to confess to some awful crime, so that he could have her done away with in a way that brought him more power. He would have done it as casually as swatting an insect, and I know that there are more men like him in this human Church. I have seen them, watched them as they watch me in the Court, their eyes full of hot hatred, or worse, cold and calculating indifference. Like Padrik, others are important to them only as the means to power, or the taking of power from them.

He was so lost in his own bleak thoughts that he didn't realize Nightingale's last set was over until she came to his seat and tapped him on the shoulder. He started and stared up at her.

"Let's go up to the roof," she said, not commenting on how jumpy he was. "You'll feel better up there with open sky above you."

Now, how did she know that? Or was it simply logical deduction for a creature with wings?

Whatever the cause, it shows a sensitivity that I had not expected from a human.

He followed her up several flights of stairs, down a corridor on the fourth floor that she said was part of the staff's area, and up a short set of ladderlike stairs. She pushed open a hatchway and climbed up; he followed her to find himself once again under the open sky. But now it was quite dark, with stars winking through thin, high clouds.

She shut the hatch quietly. "There are probably a few more people up here," she said quite softly, "but they won't bother us, and I know where they are likely to be." She beckoned to him, and he followed her, a gracefully moving shadow, lightly frosted with silver from the half moon overhead. She took him to the very edge of the roof and patted the raised rim of knee-high poured stone that kept people from walking right off the edge.

"This makes a perfectly good bench if you aren't afraid of heights," she told him, laughing a little at the absurdity of the idea of a Haspur with no head for heights. He echoed her laugh—though it sounded a bit feeble to him—and joined her on the improvised seat. A warm thermal rose from the pavement below, still heated from the afternoon's sun.

"I come up here nearly every night except when I am very weary," she told him as she looked out over the city below, then up at the moon and stars above. "It's very peaceful. I'm sure Freehold is a wonderful place, but if you work here, you get very tired of it, especially if you aren't particularly used to cities. I don't like cities very much, myself. I prefer the countryside. I'd trade a hundred Freeholds for one good Faire at Kingsford."

He had more than his share of questions that he wanted to ask her about *that*. What in the world was she doing here, for one thing! Why here and why now? The last time he had seen her, she had been going in the opposite direction of Lyonarie! There were no Free Bards here, at least none that he knew of, and probably not many Gypsies, either. So what had possessed her to come here, and what had possessed her to take a position as an entertainer in *Freehold* of all places?

The trouble was, if he asked questions, she would be as free to ask questions of him. "I was rather surprised to find you working here," he said finally, trying to find a topic that would not lead back to the weeks he did not want to discuss.

Only a few weeks, really. Not very long at all to turn me into a rabid murderer.

"Not half as surprised as I was," she replied dryly. "I have been wondering if I should tell you this—but given what happened tonight, I think perhaps I'd better."

If she should tell him —She gave him no chance to collect his thoughts.

"Our mutual friends, the Deliambrens, wanted me to come here to ferret out information for them," she said, surprising him all over again.

Nightingale? Working as a Deliambren agent? But—

"Them, among others, that is," she added, and coughed. "I have many friends among the nonhumans, and they seem to have a high regard for my ability to observe things. They asked me to come here and try to discover what I could about—oh, I know this sounds ridiculous, but there are reasons—about the High King. He used to be a great leader, but now it seems that there are other people making all the decisions. I was besieged on all sides, when it came down to it; I had at least *three* different people ask me to come here and simply keep my eyes and ears open."

"Why you?" T'fyrr finally asked.

She tapped her fingers on the balustrade. "To be honest, I'm not certain. I *have* done similar things in the past, but—T'fyrr, it was never something like this. They have more faith in my limited abilities than I do, I suppose." She shook her head. "As it happens, they are all people to whom I owe something—loyalty, favors, respect. I did listen. I understood why they were asking me. I knew that there were, indeed, *some* things I could learn, even with my limited abilities. Much to their disappointment, I refused to promise anything, and I *hope* they are not even aware that I made it here."

He felt his beak gaping in shock at her words. Not just that the Deliambrens had tried to recruit her as an agent—but that she was going along with it *without* any of the help she would be getting if she had agreed to aid them!

"But why—why are you doing this alone?" he asked. "Isn't it more dangerous, uncertain?"

"One of my friends told me that they had already sent people in who had been uncovered and had to leave. It seemed to me," she continued, idly tapping out a rhythm on the stone, "that if even one person that I didn't *personally* know and could count on became aware that I was here and working as a Deliambren agent, that was one person who might betray me, either on purpose or inadvertently. "That's why I call myself 'Lyrebird' here—and I have yet another name out on the street. If I find anything of substance, I will tell those who wanted me to come here, but not before, and not until *I* am out of Lyonarie."

He reflected ruefully that it was too bad *he* could not have done the same. "It is a little more difficult to hide a pair of wings, a beak, and talons," he replied by way of acknowledgement that he was doing the same work as she.

"Ah." She listened for a moment, but he could not tell which of the street sounds or night sounds had caught her attention. "I take it that you *are* the new Court musician that everyone has been babbling about? And that our dear Deliambren friends talked you into promising what I wouldn't?"

He did not bother to ask how she knew; if the Deliambrens had tried to recruit her as an agent, she must have ways of gathering information that he had not even guessed. And here he had been under the impression that she was nothing more than a simple musician!

The more she revealed, the more mysterious she became, and the more attractive. And the more he was determined to protect her from the danger following him.

"It was Harperus' idea," he replied. "He seemed to think I might have some kind of influence for good on the High King. He was certain that I would at least be able to overhear things that would be useful."

"Hmm." He wished he could see her face so that he could tell what she was thinking. "And have you? Had influence on the High King, that is. I assume you would not have come here tonight if you hadn't already learned some things that were useful."

"Not that I have seen," he said honestly, then added, greatly daring, "but then, I have not got the magic that some of you Free Bards do. If I did, perhaps I could actually do something to influence King Theovere." *Now, let me see if that shakes loose an admission of magic from her!*

"Do we?" she retorted sharply. "Well, if I *had* magic, what do you think I would use it for, if I were in your position?"

"To get the High King to *listen* to what I am singing," he replied, feeling the pain and frustration he felt at seeing the King acting the fool building up in him yet again. "The King still has his moments when he does things that are not only wise but very, very clever. He was a good ruler, and not that long ago—yet now—"

"Now he delegates all his power to people who abuse it, and wastes his own time with musicians and Deliambren toys," she finished for him. "I know; I've heard all about it from the Palace kitchen. No one there knows why, though; or what caused the change. He hasn't been ill, he hasn't had an accident, and there's no record of this kind of—of loss of mental power running in his family. Is he being drugged, or has he simply been listening to the wrong people for so long that he no longer thinks clearly or pays heed to the warning signs about him?"

"I don't know either," he admitted, deflated. "And if anyone else knows, they haven't confided in me."

Nightingale turned toward him in the darkness and made a little sound—not quite a chuckle, but full of irony. "They wouldn't now, would they? After all, you are only a lowly musician. One of the very things that the King is frittering away his time with. Why should anyone who wants to restore Theovere to what he *was* trust you?"

He felt his talons scraping along the stone of the balustrade as he clenched his fist in frustration. He said nothing, though, and she did not press him.

"I heard—" she began again tentatively, and he sensed she was going to change the subject. "I heard that you had been traveling with Harperus all this time, that you were somewhere around Gradford last fall at around the time Robin and Kestrel were there, too."

Too near the bone! He shied away quickly. "I don't remember all the places we were," he lied, knowing the lie sounded clumsy. After all, given how precise his memory was, how *could* he forget where he had been? "Harperus' wagon travels faster than beasts can pull it, if he chooses to make it so. We have been too many places to count."

"I thought for certain I heard Harperus say the two of you were heading for Gradford when we parted company, though," she persisted, and he had the feeling that she *was* trying to probe for something. "Didn't you even tell me yourself that you were going to meet Robin and Kestrel there?"

He winced this time, and was glad that it was too dark for her to see it. "I don't recall," he lied again. "It's been a year, at least, after all."

"And a great deal has happened between then and now," she replied, but then she stopped pressing him. "Except, perhaps, to me. I didn't do very much in the time since you left me; I spent most of the time I passed among humans in very small villages where nothing much ever happens. My audiences are small, my recompense smaller, but it is enough to keep me. That is all the news that I have for you, I fear."

It took a moment for that statement to sink in, and when it did, he was astonished. *Why would she do that? Look how she fills rooms here, where there are all sorts of entertainers! Why would she choose places where they could never understand what a great musician she truly is?*

"But—" He fumbled for words that would not sound like an insult. "But you are a *superb* musician! You should be performing in places like Freehold all the time! Why do you spend your time, your talents, among people who can never appreciate them?"

"Never?" He heard the irony in her voice again. "But one of those people, not that long ago, was our own little Lady Lark. There are hidden treasures in those tiny villages, T'fyrr. Now and again I come upon one with the music-hunger in him, and I wake it up and show him that he does not have to remain where he is and let it starve to death. For that alone, it is worth the days and weeks among people who would not care how well I played, so long as I could play 'The Huntsman' twenty or thirty times running."

And from the tone of her voice, that was probably precisely what happened in those tiny villages she claimed to like so much. There must be other reasons—

"There are other reasons," she admitted, as if she had read his thoughts. "If some authority has a grudge against Free Bards or Gypsies, I generally know it the moment I set eyes on the people there, and I can keep moving. That is better than thinking that I am safe and suddenly finding an angry Mayor or Priest with a mob come to drive me out of town. And, at any rate, I try not to spend much time actually *in* those villages. There are other places where I am welcome."

Such as with the Elves, perhaps? Hadn't Harperus said something about that, at a time when he was trying to distract T'fyrr from his depression? He hadn't been paying as much attention as he wished he had now.

Something about Nightingale being considered odd, "fey," he said, even among her own people. That she spent more time among the Elves and other nonhumans than among her own kind. That sounds uncannily like— myself. Is there something that she is trying to avoid, I wonder, even as I? Is that why she spends much time among those who care little about her and much about her music? There was a great deal that she was not saying, and he found himself wondering what it was. She had her secrets too.

If that was the case, would she understand him and his guilt, as Harperus had not?

He was tempted to unburden himself, sorely tempted, but resisted the temptation. He really did not want to drag anyone else into his troubles or his dangers. And he did not want to burden her, of all people, with the knowledge of his guilt. She had enough to bear.

"I suppose I should go," he said finally, and glanced at her out of the corner of his eye. She nodded; reluctantly, he thought, but nodded.

"I have work tomorrow, and so do you," she said—then hesitated. "I don't suppose you might be free tomorrow afternoon, though, would you?"

"Normally the King does not need me in the afternoon," he said cautiously. "And at the moment, I believe I have learned all that I am likely to for a while from the Afternoon Court. Why?"

"Because I'd like to guide you in the city, to give you some idea what places are safe for you," she replied unexpectedly. "And there is someone I would like you to meet. Well, more than one person, actually, but there is one person I *particularly* want you to meet, someone I think will surprise you very pleasantly. I know he would like to meet you. If you'd like to come along with me, that is."

He struggled with his misgivings for some time before answering. He was so lonely—he hadn't realized just how lonely he was until tonight, but the few hours spent with Nightingale had forced him to see just how much he needed a real friend. Not someone like the Lord Seneschal, nor like Nob. The former was using him, and T'fyrr was using the Seneschal, and both were aware and comfortable with the arrangement. The latter was a child, and no real companion or equal. But Nightingale was different, even among all of the people he had met since leaving the mountains. She was comfortable with him; when he was with her, sometimes he turned to her and blinked to see that she did not have a beak and feathers. The only humans *that* comfortable among the Haspur were the ones who lived among them, sharing their mountaintop settlements and their lives. In a way, those people were as much Haspur as human.

"I—I think I would enjoy that," he said finally, letting his hunger for companionship overcome his misgivings. "Shall I meet you here, on the roof?"

"Perfect," she said. "Just after noon. Now, you'd better go, while the moon is still up."

He nodded—then, impulsively, reached out with a gentle talon and touched her cheek. She placed her own hand on the talon, and brushed her cheek and hair along the back of his hand in a caress of her own.

Then she released him—and afraid of doing or saying anything else that might release his pent-up emotions, he turned away from her abruptly.

Without stopping to make a more protracted farewell, he leapt to the top of the balustrade and flung himself over the edge of the roof, snapping his wings open and catching the rising current of warm air coming from the pavement below. In a moment, he was too far from Freehold to see if she was still there watching him.

But he sensed her, felt her eyes somehow finding him in the darkness, as he winged his way back to the Palace.

And he wished that he could turn and fly back to her.

In deference to Nightingale—

Tanager, he reminded himself. *On the street, she is Tanager.*

—in deference to Tanager they were afoot, but this section of the city was not as crowded as the streets around Freehold, and as before, crowds seemed to part before them, anyway. It was hot; he held his wings away from his body in a futile effort to cool himself, and his beak gaped a bit as he panted. Tanager looked comfortable enough, although there were beads of moisture on her brow and running down the back of her neck. She wasn't wearing much by human standards, although her costume revealed less than that of some of the humans he'd seen in the Palace.

Many of the people here were wearing similar clothing, anyway. Perhaps in deference to the heat, they had foregone some of that silly human body modesty. He would have been more comfortable doing without his body-wrapping, but Nob had advised against such a move.

"Where are we going?" he asked, dodging around a child playing in the middle of the walkway, oblivious to the foot traffic around her.

"I told you, I want you to meet someone, but first I want you to hear him speak," she said as she threaded her way along the narrow, stone-paved streets, slipping skillfully between pushcarts and around knots of playing children. "You'll understand why I want you to meet him once you've heard him."

At that moment, she darted across the street with him in tow and trotted up the worn steps of a fairly nondescript gray stone building. It wasn't until they were almost inside the door that he suddenly realized the building had a steeple—it was, in fact, a Church building, a Chapel, as they called them here.

He started to balk, but changed his mind just as abruptly as Tanager slipped inside the open door. *I have heard her express fear of Church Priests. I have seen the trouble that some of these men have caused her people as well as me. She would not bring me here if she did not have a very good reason.* Was *this* the place where she intended to have him meet that special person she had spoken of last night?

Could it—could it be her lover?

For some reason, his chest tightened at that thought, and he wanted, passionately, for that person to be anything, anyone, *but* a lover.

Be sensible. She said nothing about a lover. And why would she meet a lover in a Church building?

He followed her, noting with relief that it was much cooler inside the building than it was in the street. She seized his hand as they entered the sanctuary itself, gestured that he should be silent, and pulled him into a secluded nook at the rear of the sanctuary. They stood beneath the statue of a kind-faced, grieving man, out of the way, where his wings would be lost among the shadows.

The Chapel was relatively full for a mid-afternoon service, and the first thing that T'fyrr noticed was that not all of the people here were human. There were at least two Mintaks, and he noted a Felis, a Caniden, an entire family of Caprins—heads too oddly shaped to ever pass as human poked up among the caps, hoods and uncovered hair of the human attendees.

Nor did the humans seem to care!

He quickly turned his attention to the Priest presiding from the pulpit—for the Priest of such a congregation must be as remarkable as the congregation itself.

He was a middle-aged man, if T'fyrr was any judge. The hair of his head had thick strands of gray in it, and the hair of his beard boasted the same. He was neither short nor tall, and his build was not particularly memorable. His square face had the same kindly look to it as that of the statue they sheltered under, and his voice, though soft, was powerful, with pleasant resonances.

But it was his words that caught and held T'fyrr, just as they held everyone else here.

Perhaps not the words themselves, for it was evident that the Priest was no writer of superb speeches as Bishop Padrik had been. But the content of the sermon was something that T'fyrr had never expected to hear from the lips of a human Priest.

For this Priest, standing before humans, in a Chapel built by humans, was preaching the brotherhood of *all* beings, and citing examples of the "humanity" of nonhumans to prove his point.

T'fyrr's beak gaped open again, and not because he was overheated.

The more the Priest spoke, the more confused T'fyrr became. Bishop Padrik had used his Church's Holy Book to prove that any creature not wearing human form was evil. This Priest used the same Book—almost the same words!—to prove the very opposite.

He was sincere; T'fyrr could not doubt it. He was devout; there was no doubt of that, either. But he was saying, and clearly believed, the very opposite of what the High Bishop of Gradford swore was true.

How could this be?

He was still gaping in surprise when the Priest finished the service, and the congregation happily filed out, leaving the Chapel empty but for the Priest himself and the two of them. The Priest turned to the altar, putting away the implements of the service and cleaning it for the next service. Tanager remained where she was, and T'fyrr stayed with her.

"You can come out, now, Tanager," said the Priest over his shoulder as he folded and put away a spotless white altarcloth. "And your friend, too. I'm glad you came."

Tanager laughed—her laugh had a different sound than Nightingale's laugh; it was lighter, and somehow seemed to belong to a younger person. T'fyrr could only marvel at her ability to assume or discard a persona with a change of the costume.

"I persuaded my friend to come here to meet you, but he didn't know he was coming to a Church service, Father Ruthvere," she said banteringly. "I haven't had a chance to ask him if he was bored or not."

The Priest put the last of the implements away and turned, stepping off the dais and descending into the main body of the Chapel. "I hope he wasn't, my dear child," Father Ruthvere said, chuckling, "but I make no claims for my ability as a speaker. I never won any prizes in rhetoric."

As he moved forward, so did they; and as T'fyrr came out of the shadows, Father Ruthvere's eyes widened and then narrowed with speculation.

"There can't be more than one bird-man in this city," he began with hesitation in his voice. "But I have to wonder what this gentleman is doing *here*, rather than on the Palace grounds."

T'fyrr glanced down at Tanager, who nodded encouragingly.

"I am the only Haspur in all of this kingdom that I know of, sir," he replied gravely. "I am pleased to make your acquaintance, Father Ruthvere. I can assure you, you did not bore me."

"Coming from the High King's newly appointed Personal Musician, that is quite more praise than I deserve," Father Ruthvere responded just as gravely. "I hope you know that I meant every word, and I am not the only Priest in this city who feels this way." He held out his hand, and T'fyrr took it awkwardly. "I should be very pleased if you might consider me a friend, Sire T'fyrr," the Priest continued, then twinkled up at him. "I think, though, despite the message of my sermons, it might be a bit much for me to ask you to consider me as your brother!"

That surprised a laugh out of T'fyrr. "Perhaps," he agreed, and cocked his head to one side. He decided to try a joke. "If I were to present you as such, my people would be much distressed that you had feather-plucked yourself to such a dreadful extent."

Father Ruthvere laughed heartily. "That is a better joke than you know, Sire T'fyrr. I have a pet bird that unfortunately has that very bad habit—and my colleagues have been unkind enough to suggest that there is some resemblance between us!"

Tanager smiled; she was clearly quite pleased that T'fyrr and the Priest had hit it off so well. For that matter, so was T'fyrr.

They exchanged a few more pleasantries before T'fyrr and Tanager took their leave; the Priest hurried off to some unspecified duty, while they left the way they had arrived.

"Surprised?" Tanager asked when they reached the street again. "I was, the first time I heard him. And he's telling the truth; he's not the only Priest preaching the brotherhood of all beings. He's just the one with the Chapel nearest Freehold. It is a movement that *seems* to be gaining followers."

"I am trying to think of some ulterior motive for him, and I cannot," T'fyrr admitted. "Perhaps attendance falling off, perhaps a gain in prestige if he somehow converted nonhumans to your religion."

"Neither, and there're more problems associated with attracting nonhumans than there are rewards." Tanager told him. "As I told you, I was just as surprised, and I tried to think of some way that this could be a trick. I couldn't—and information I have assures me that Father Ruthvere truly, deeply and sincerely believes in what he was preaching."

T'fyrr picked his way carefully among the cobblestones and thought about the way that the Priest had met his own direct gaze. It was very difficult for humans to meet the eyes of a Haspur, for very long. Just as the gaze of a hawk, direct and penetrating, often seemed to startle people, the gaze of a Haspur with all the intelligence of a Haspur behind it, seemed to intimidate them. Father Ruthvere had no such troubles.

"No, I believe you," he said finally. "And I find him as disconcerting as you humans find me."

"He is one of my sources of information," she said as they turned into a street lined with vendors of various foods and drink. "We share what we've learned; he tells me what's going on inside the Church, and I tell him the rumors I've learned in Freehold and in the Palace kitchen."

T'fyrr nodded; she had already told him about her clever ploy that got her into the Lower Servants' Kitchen every day. "Well, I can add to that what I learn," he said, "though I am afraid it will be stale news to him."

She shrugged. "Maybe; maybe not. Oh—look down that street. That might be a good place for you to go if you're caught afoot and need to get into the air—"

She pointed down a dead-end street that culminated in a bulb-shaped courtyard. Unlike the rest of the street, there were no overhanging second stories there. He nodded and made a mental note of the place.

She continued to guide him through the narrow, twisting streets, pointing out flat roofs and protruding brickwork where he could land, then climb down to the street—finding places where he could get enough of a running start that he could take off again. And all the while she was showing him these things, she was also questioning him. . . .

She was so subtle and so good at it that he didn't really notice what she was doing until he found himself clamping his beak down on a confession of what had happened to him in Gradford. It was only the fact that he made a habit of reticence that saved him. The words tried to escape from him; he put a curb on his tongue, and still his heart wanted to unburden all of his troubles to her.

So he distracted both her and himself with a description of what the High King had done that day. Or, more accurately, what the High King had *not* done, and how troubled he was by it all.

"There is something fundamentally wrong with the way Theovere is acting," he said finally. "My people have no equivalent to his office, but— if you allow yourself to take advantage of great privilege and great power, should you not feel guilty if you do not also accept what obligations come with it? Should that not be *required*, in order to enjoy the privilege?"

Tanager sighed. "You'd think so, wouldn't you?" she replied. "I know that I would feel that way."

"The King's Advisors do not," he told her. "They continue to tell him that the most important thing that a King must learn is how to delegate responsibility. They praise him for shirking his most important tasks, for ignoring the pleas of those who have nowhere else to take their grievances and concerns. I do not understand."

Tanager looked very thoughtful at that—and more like Nightingale than she had since they had begun their tour of the streets. "I think that perhaps I do," she finally said. "Let's go back to Freehold. I want to talk about this somewhere I know is safe from extra ears."

That place—*somewhere safe from extra ears*—turned out to be her own room in Freehold, supplied as part of her wages. T'fyrr examined it while she took a change of outfit into the bathroom and turned from Tanager to Lyrebird.

There probably had not been much supplied with the room other than the furniture—and it was, unmistakably, the Deliambren notion of "spare." But Nightingale had put her own touches on the place: the bench and bed were covered with dozens of delicately embroidered and fringed shawls, and there were extra cushions on both. The walls had been draped with more shawls, and she had hung a small collection of jewelry on hooks fastened there, as well. Her harps sat in one corner, out of the way, and a hand-drum hung on the wall above them.

"I'd begun to wonder about something lately," Nightingale told him, her voice muffled a little by the closed door. "And what you just told me confirmed it."

She emerged, gowned in the dark green dress she had taken in with her, and settled herself on the chest, leaving the bed to him. "Humans are odd creatures," she said finally. "We often go out of our way to justify things that we *want* to do, and do it so successfully that we come to believe the justifications ourselves."

He nodded, waiting to hear more.

"Take King Theovere," she said after a pause. "He was working hard, *very* hard. He was certainly one of the best High Kings that Alanda has seen for awhile. And he solved four of the most terrible problems the Twenty Kingdoms have seen, all in a very short period of time." She held up a finger. "The Bayden-Anders border dispute." A second finger. "The Grain Smut and the resulting famine." A third finger. "The Kindgode incursion." And the fourth and final finger. "The Black Baron's Revolt. All four of those took place within a single decade. Any one of them would have been enough for a single High King to fail at or solve."

T'fyrr nodded, although he hadn't heard anything about three out of the four problems she mentioned—but then again, he had just begun to scrape the top of the Palace archives, and he didn't imagine there was much about a grain smut that would make a good ballad. "Your point?" he asked.

"Theovere would have every reason to be tired, *bone* tired, by the end of that time. And when his Advisors began to tell him that he had done enough, that he should rest, that he *deserved* to take a rest, he listened to them." She tilted her head to one side and stared up into his eyes, waiting for him to think about what she had said.

"But he did deserve to take a rest—" T'fyrr pointed out. "At least, he deserved *some* rest, if those problems were as weighty to solve as you say."

"Of course he did!" she exclaimed. "I'm not saying that he didn't—but the point wasn't that he didn't deserve to rest, the point is that he *couldn't* rest." She licked her lips, clearly searching for an explanation. "He is the High King; he *could* and probably *should* have reorganized his duties so that he had some time to recuperate, but he *could not* abandon his duties! Do you see what I'm saying?"

"I think so—" T'fyrr said hesitantly. "There really isn't anyone who can do what he can, who can be *the* ultimate authority. So when his Advisors started telling him to rest, to delegate important business to someone else—"

"They were telling him what he wanted to hear, but not the truth," she finished for him, when he groped for words. "He *could* arrange to take more time in solving those problems that won't get worse with time. He *can* ask for help from any of the Twenty Kings. He can look to his allies for some help. He *cannot* tell someone else to solve them for him."

T'fyrr shook his head. "It is easy to feel sorry for him," he said, thinking back to Theovere and realizing that he had seen signs of strain that he had not noticed at the time. Perhaps even those temper tantrums were a sign of that strain. "It seems like too much of a burden for one man. No one should be expected to bear that much."

Nightingale spread her hands in a gesture of bafflement. "There's no good answer," she admitted. "There is a reason why the High King has the privileges that he has; why he lives in a place that is second only to the Fortress-City in luxury, why virtually anything he wants is given to him. Since his duties can't be made easier, his life is made easier. But do you see what our answer might be?"

T'fyrr thought it all through before he answered. "Theovere was tired; his Advisors told him what he wanted to hear—that he needed to stop working so hard, he needed to rest, he needed to give over some of his responsibility to others. So he followed their advice and found that he liked the new life—and his Advisors only reinforced his feelings when they told him that he was doing the right thing. It probably began with very little things, but by now—by now it has built up to the point that Theovere is actually doing very little in the way of his duty, and the Advisors are still telling him what a wonderful leader he is."

Nightingale nodded emphatically as she put her hair up into a complicated twist. "Furthermore, since they are not letting anyone in to speak to him who is likely to tell him something that contradicts what they are saying, he believes that everything is exactly as it was when he was in his prime. He *wants* to believe that, and the sycophants are only too happy to tell him so."

T'fyrr fanned his wings a little in the breath of moving air from the ventilator grille. "It will be difficult to turn that trend around," he offered diffidently. "I have been trying—I have been inserting songs with a particular theme, that great power demands the acceptance of responsibility, into the performances that the King has asked me to give. But as I told you, I have not seen any evidence that he has paid any more attention to them than to the story ballads or the love songs."

Nightingale's hands stopped moving for a moment. Her eyes took on the expression of someone who is looking deep into her own spirit, and T'fyrr wondered what she was thinking.

Then, with an abrupt motion, as if she had suddenly made up her mind about something, she put the last twist into her hair and folded her hands on her lap. "T'fyrr, who told you that some of the Free Bards have— magic?" she asked.

"Harperus," he replied promptly. "Harperus told me that *you* have it, in fact. Well, not *magic*, as such—he told me that many of you have some sort of power that he and his people could not weigh or measure, but that observation would prove existed. He said that you could influence people's minds, among other things. He suspected that you could—well, see into the future. He said that some Deliambrens believe that you can influence events as well as minds, provided that the influence need only be very small. He has real evidence that you can heal people in ways that have nothing to do with medicine as he knows it."

She bit her lower lip and looked away from him for the first time. "I am not really supposed to admit to this," she said finally. "Especially not to someone connected with the Deliambrens." She looked back at him with a wan smile. "Harperus and his kind are driven mad by things they cannot measure, and if they knew we really *did* have abilities such as you describe, they would be plaguing us constantly to find out what it is we do and how we do it."

T'fyrr nodded but said nothing, only waited quietly for her to continue.

"There is—there is a power in music properly performed," she said after another long moment of silence, broken only by the sound of the air in the ventilators and the distant murmur of all the sounds of Freehold below them. "You might call it 'magic.' Certainly the Gypsies and the Elves do, and so does the Church, although the Churchmen have no idea how great or little that power really is. I'll put it to you briefly: some Bards are mages, and—among other things—we can influence the thoughts of others through our music. Some of us can do the other things you described as well, but it is that one particular power that pertains to our situation now. *Sometimes*, not often, we are powerful enough to make others act against their will. Most of us confine ourselves to very minor acts of—well, it *is* manipulation, and as such, it could be considered improper. Most of the time, all we do is enhance our audiences' ability to appreciate the music."

"But you can do more," T'fyrr stated. He had no doubt that she, personally, could do much more.

She nodded reluctantly. "This might be a case where doing more is justified. Would you care to add me, and my magic, to your performances for the King? All you need do is bring me in as your accompanist, and I can do the rest. Between the two of us, we may be able to reawaken his sleeping conscience and rouse his slumbering sense of duty. But I won't lie to you; this is interference in someone's mind, his thoughts. Before you take me up on this, you need to think about that—and if you would appreciate having something like this done to you, if your situation and his were reversed."

Now that she had put it baldly and *offered* her services, and now that she had admitted that this "magic" was as much a form of manipulation as the overt form that Theovere's Advisors were doing, the idea wasn't as attractive as it had been. In point of fact, the notion made him feel rather—shaken up inside.

Did he want to do this? If he were the King—if he were in Theovere's place—

If he were thinking clearly, thinking as his old self, he might. But doesn't this preclude his thinking clearly? Wouldn't we be clouding his mind as much as all that bad advice?

"It is a great power," Nightingale said softly. "This is why we so seldom use it. It is far too tempting to misuse it."

He took a deep breath. "It is also too great an issue to decide on impulse," he told her firmly. "I need to think about this at length."

And I wish there was someone, anyone, who I could ask for advice!

He was afraid that Nightingale would be annoyed with him for prevaricating after she had taken the great step of not only admitting she had this power, but offering to help him with it. But she only nodded, as if she had expected him to say something like that.

"You should see what you can do on your own," she told him. "You haven't been doing this for very long; you may be able to stir the King's conscience without any outside influence. That would be better—for him, and for you, I think."

She *did* understand. "I promise, I will think about this, the morality of it," he told her, and grimaced. "It may well be that the morality of manipulating one person's mind to rid him of bad influences is of less moment than the welfare of all the people, human and otherwise, in the Twenty Kingdoms."

"There is that," she agreed. "But I am not the one in the position to make the decision; you are. And I will not make your decisions for you."

"But what would you do if you were in my place?" he asked—no, begged.

She sighed and shook her head. "If I were in your place—I have traveled the roads of several of the kingdoms, and seen some of the worst places in this one. I can see what I think are unpleasant trends that are only going to continue if the High King remains neglectful. I am prejudiced; the people most immediately affected are friends of mine, my own people, and the Free Bards. There *are* other people who will prosper if things go as I believe they will, and they would certainly not thank us for interfering." She smiled a little. "This is a long explanation for a short answer, so that you can see why I feel the way I do. In your place, having weighed all the options and the outcomes, I would use the magic and see what happened. You may not come to the same conclusion. If you do not, I cannot and will not fault you for it."

Silence hung between them for a long time. She broke it first.

"It may be that by using the magic this way, we are making ourselves into worse monsters than even the Church believes us to be. The next time we are tempted, we might not resist. And the time after that, for something purely selfish? We might be able to justify it to ourselves as easily as the King justifies his current neglect. That is the danger."

He could see that. Oh, how easily he could see that! "I understand," he said very softly.

She rose. "And I must go, to the *legitimate* uses of my magic," she said, lightly, although he thought she was covering a heavy heart with her light tone. "You know the way to the roof?"

"I do," he replied, and then formed his beak into something like a human smile. "But I have time enough to let you work some of that magic on me, before I go."

He thought for a moment that he had startled her, but it might only have been a sudden shadow as she moved. In the next breath, she looked as serene as always.

"Well, then, shall we go down?" she asked. "I should be happy to include you in the spell."

"Perhaps one day, I shall ask you to weave a magic for me alone," he said playfully, opening the door for her as she picked up her harp to carry it down the stairs.

Once again, that startled look came over her face, but this time, when she turned to look at him, her expression was not as serene. There was a shadow there, and a hint of speculation.

"Perhaps you shall," was all she said. "And—perhaps I shall oblige you."

T'fyrr looked up from his reading as someone rapped on the door to the suite, but he did not rise to answer it. He knew better, now, after several sharp lectures from Nob about the propriety of the King's Chief Musician answering his own door. Nob answered the summons instead; he spoke briefly with someone there and came back to T'fyrr with a message in his hand.

"There's someone to see you, T'fyrr," he said with a grin. "That Deliambren who dresses like a tailor's worst nightmare." He handed the small piece of paper to T'fyrr, who found it was simply a note from Harperus asking if he was free. "Shall I tell the page to bring him up?"

"Certainly!" T'fyrr replied. "Absolutely!" At the moment he couldn't think of anyone he wanted to see more.

Except Nightingale, perhaps—

He shook the thought away. The one person he *dared* not think about was Nightingale, not now, not with Harperus around. While she hadn't exactly sworn him to secrecy about her magic, she had certainly told him in no uncertain terms that she did not want the Deliambrens to know she was in the city. If he thought about Nightingale, he might let that fact slip.

And she would be justifiably angry with me.

It was a pity, since Harperus, for all his faults, was the one person he wished he could discuss this "morality of magic" business with. But he couldn't do that without revealing who would actually be working the magic.

Well, I will just have to deal with this on my own.

It had occurred to him, more than once, that this just might be the chance he had hoped for, the act that would expiate his crime of murder.

The only question was—*which* act would be his redemption? The act of using the magic? Or the act of *not* using the magic?

The choice was almost as difficult to deal with as the aftermath of the crime. . . .

"T'fyrr!" Harperus exclaimed, breaking into T'fyrr's thoughts as Nob let him into the room. "You're looking well!"

"Let us say, the High King does not stint his servants," T'fyrr replied, rising to his feet and clasping Harperus' hand in his claws. "And you? What mischief have you been up to, Old Owl?"

"A great deal of mischief," Harperus replied, but soberly, and switched to Deliambren. "Actually, I am now, officially, and with absolute truth, the appointed Envoy to the High King from the Fortress-City. I am here with a direct request from the Deliambrens for Theovere; we absolutely need his blanket permission for the mapping expedition."

So the last attempt at local negotiations broke down. T'fyrr nodded and replied in the same language. "And you need from me?"

"Advice," Harperus told him. "We know more about the Advisors than we did—" he glanced at one of the "sculptures" to make his point "—but we still need to know the best time and place to approach Theovere on this."

T'fyrr closed his eyes and thought hard. Technically, this was *not* a problem that the King needed to call a Council about; he knew that much now, from all his listening. It was also not something that needed to be brought up at official Court. It was, in fact, in the nature of a personal favor, and well within the High King's purview.

If, of course, Theovere chose to see it that way.

"Everyone except the Seneschal is going in to Lyonarie in two days, in the afternoon," he said slowly, returning to the human tongue. "There is some sort of processional—religious, I think. It is apparently important for them to be seen attending, and many of them have made some elaborate arrangements for viewing stands and the distribution of alms and largesse."

"In the King's name, of course," Harperus said smoothly.

T'fyrr's nares twitched. "Of course," he agreed. "Theovere himself has been advised not to go—it is going to be very hot, and it would require standing in the direct sun for many hours. It has been deemed inadvisable for health reasons. So he, and the Seneschal, will remain at the Palace. I have been asked to perform for him then—but there will be an informal sort of Court at the same time."

Harperus' eyes narrowed. "What sort of Court?" he asked sharply.

T'fyrr shrugged with elaborate casualness. "Very minor. The presentation of some gifts, the requesting of personal favors, that sort of thing. I would not be performing if it were anything important, but it strikes me that you just might have a gift with you that you meant to present to Theovere."

"I just might." Harperus smiled and stroked the hair on his cheekbones. "I know how much he enjoys our little gifts."

Too much, T'fyrr thought a little sourly, but he didn't say that aloud. "He does indeed, and that would be a good time to give him such a gift, without disturbing those members of his Court who don't approve of Deliambren craftwork."

"True enough." Harperus suddenly stretched, and all of the tension ran

out of him like water from a broken jug. He glanced around, looking for
a piece of purely human furniture, and threw himself into a chair with
casual abandon.

"So, old bird," he said cheerfully. "What *have* you been up to?"

"More than you would guess," T'fyrr replied with perfect truth. "For
one thing, I have visited that fabulous Freehold place that you
recommended. . . ."

Two days later, T'fyrr was unsurprised to hear Harperus' name
announced during his performance at the informal Court. Theovere had
been playing a game of Sires and Barons with the Lord Seneschal, but
he readily abandoned it as Harperus came into the Lesser Throne Room,
holding a small package in his hand. T'fyrr brought the song he was
singing to a polite close, so that the King would not be distracted by
the music.

*And if Nightingale were here, we would be singing instead of staying
silent.*

"Harperus!" Theovere said. "What brings you back here so soon?" His
delight at seeing the Deliambren was obvious—in fact, T'fyrr didn't think
he even noticed that Harperus was carrying a package.

"Two things, Theovere," Harperus said genially. "This, for one." He
handed the package to one of the bodyguards to open. "One of my people
came up with a rather delightful little star-projector—ah, you simply put
it in a dark room, and it will mimic the patterns of the night stars on the
ceiling and walls. Very soothing to look at; orient it to the north and it
will follow the stars in all the changes of the seasons. Build a room shaped
like a dome, and it will mimic the sky perfectly."

"Really?" Theovere took the lumpy little device from the guard and
examined it with interest. "Why, you wouldn't have to go outside to cast
a horoscope, would you?"

Harperus had the grace not to wince; the Deliambrens were usually
very vocal in their scorn for astrology and astrologers. "No," he agreed.
"You wouldn't. The purpose is mainly entertainment, though."

"Well, it's a delightful gift," Theovere told him with a real smile. "Now,
what is the other reason? I have to assume that since you brought a gift,
you're going to ask a favor. Everyone else does it that way."

T'fyrr winced. That was a little too cynical, even for Theovere.

But Harperus only laughed. "Now who am I to go against the trend?
Yes, we do need a favor, but it's a minor one. It won't cost you or anyone
else a clipped copper, and it's mainly just to take care of some rather
stubborn folk who think we're demon-spawn."

Theovere sat back in his chair, wearing a widening grin. "Oh, I know
the type you're talking about. So what *is* this favor?"

"We need your blanket permission to cross the Twenty Kingdoms with
a rather large vehicle," Harperus told him. "We're going to map all of
this continent of Alanda. *Accurately*. We'll supply you and any other government with maps of your own territories, of course—they'll be detailed
down to the nearest furlong. We *can* do maps more detailed than that,
but they'd fill a room this size if we gave you maps of all of the kingdoms."

Theovere looked thoughtful at that. "We might need something that detailed," he said finally. "You ought to have some copies made up for the archives here if nothing else." Then he grinned again. "Oh, I know why those old goats don't want you crossing their kingdoms, and it has nothing to do with what you Deliambrens and your machines are or are not."

"It doesn't?" Harperus raised both his eyebrows in feigned surprise.

As if you didn't know the reason, too, Old Owl. It occurred to T'fyrr that Theovere's cynicism was contagious.

"Of course not!" Theovere glanced at his Seneschal for confirmation. "They know that once I have *accurate* maps, I'm likely to find out they've been adding to their territory an inch or two at a time for years! And, of course, once I have maps like that, I *have* to send my personal surveyors out to make certain that the borders are marked *correctly*. Don't I?"

The Lord Seneschal nodded, his lips compressed into a thin line, though whether from tension or because he was trying not to say something he shouldn't, T'fyrr wasn't certain.

"I believe you ought to give the Deliambrens that blanket permission, Your Majesty," the Lord Seneschal said, after a moment's pause. "You really don't have to call a council on it, any more than you *had* to call a Council to add Sire T'fyrr to your personal household. It *is* in the nature of a favor from you to Lord Harperus, after all."

T'fyrr held his tongue, though it was difficult. It was very clever of the Seneschal to have brought up the stormy Council session that ended with his own appointment to the King's personal household. Theovere was still steaming over that one—and the reminder of how recalcitrant most of his Advisors had been was exactly what Harperus needed.

Theovere would see this as a multiple opportunity now. He could do Harperus, who he liked, a favor. He could do the Deliambrens a favor that might earn him more little toys like the star-projector. He could thwart the Council, taking revenge for the way they had tried to block his appointment of T'fyrr.

He could obtain maps that would help him to solve disputes between the Kings, between the Barons, between the Sires. He could enforce decisions on the strength of those maps.

And he can prove that he is still the High King. Perhaps my music is working?

"This will harm no one, Your Majesty," the Seneschal urged. "And it will be of great benefit to many."

Theovere did not think it over for more than a heartbeat after that. "Fine," he said, and gestured to three of the Royal Scribes. "Consider it done." He leaned his head back for a moment and rattled off the appropriate language for the official document; the scribes took it all down as fast as Theovere recited.

Feeble-minded? I don't think so, T'fyrr remarked to himself. *Not when he can do that, without even blinking.*

When they finished, they presented all three copies to the Seneschal, who made certain that they were identical, then handed them on to Theovere to sign and seal.

One of the three he presented to Harperus on the spot. "There you are, Lord Harperus," he said with a smile. "Signed, sealed and official. No one will argue with your little expedition now." He turned to the Chief Scribe and handed him the remaining two copies. "See that the usual duplicates are made, and so," he told the man, "but—send them along to the councilors with, oh, the household documents. This certainly doesn't have any more importance than an inventory of linen."

The scribe bowed, face expressionless, and took himself out. The Lord Seneschal's mouth twitched. T'fyrr knew why.

They'll take those household accountings and give them to some flunky to file and never look at them. They'll never know about this declaration unless Harperus has to use it in some way that draws attention to it, and by then it will be too late, of course. Oh, clever! Feeble-minded? No, no, not Theovere.

"Now," the High King said, turning toward T'fyrr, who was *very* glad that he did not have a face that was as easy to read as a human's. "I'd really like you to hear more of your friend's magnificent singing, if you have the time for it."

Harperus smiled and took a seat when the King indicated he could. "I always have time for T'fyrr, Your Majesty," he said smoothly. "And I am glad that you have learned that my friend is far more talented than he seems."

T'fyrr only bowed without blinking an eye—but in subtle revenge, he began a Deliambren courting song, full of double and triple dealings, and such vivid descriptions of who did what to whom that a human Priest would have had it banned on the spot as the vilest of pornography.

And watching Harperus' face as he struggled to remain polite was revenge enough for all Harperus had thus far inflicted on him.

CHAPTER SEVEN

Nightingale waited for T'fyrr, perched on a metal balcony on the exterior of Freehold; streetlamps gave all the light she needed to see what lay below her, although it wasn't much cooler now than it had been this afternoon. T'fyrr had told her three nights ago that he wanted to arrive at Freehold openly tonight. She hadn't been all that sure it was a good idea, but apparently Harperus and Tyladen thought it was best if he were actually *seen* coming and going now and again.

But for him to be seen by the maximum number of people, he would have to arrive afoot just after sunset, and not come flying in to the roof long after dark.

No one has tried to attack him since the first attempt, she reminded herself. *No one has even dared to enter Freehold and so much as look at him crossly. We have walked the streets of Lyonarie during the day together, and no one has tried to ambush us. He believes the danger is over.*

So why did she still have misgivings? Why did she expect trouble, when there had been no sign of trouble?

She sighed, and rested her chin on her hand, peering between the bars of the railing. *Because I am always seeing danger,* she admitted to herself, *even where there might not be any danger. Isn't that why I am waiting here, above the street, watching for him? I'm gong to extremes because there* could *be trouble.*

At least she had the night off; those who were featured performers got one night in seven to rest. Silas was playing, though, and she was looking forward to listening to him with T'fyrr.

The exterior of Freehold was festooned in several places with metal balconies, staircases and walkways, some of which connected the building with others on the block, none of which could actually be reached from the ground outside, only from special window exits above the second floor, or from the roof itself. That made them good places to watch the street below. Many of the staff did just that in their off hours, especially in the balmier months.

This was not a balmy month; the heat rising from the street below was enough to bake bread on the balcony, and Nightingale's hair was damp with sweat. *I'm going to feel the right fool if nothing happens,* she thought ironically. *Getting baked for nothing but a stupid feeling that things have been too quiet. Ah well, it won't be the first time that I've made a fool of myself.*

At least there was no one here to see her, and from below, it was very difficult to tell that there was anyone at all on this second-floor walkway. She had made it even harder, since she was sitting cross-legged below the railing and had taken care to wear one of her nondescript "Tanager" outfits.

Nothing clever about that, though. I just didn't want to get anything nice all sweaty and dirty.

Freehold faced a much newer block of buildings across the narrow street; it was one of those blocks with second floors that overhung the street below. Just about everyone took shelter in the shadowed area under the overhang even at night. For one thing, people had a bad habit of tossing noxious things out of the second-floor windows at night, even though it was supposed to be against the law. For another, it was marginally cooler there; the pavement hadn't been baked all day long by the sun.

It wasn't hard to identify people, even from this walkway, and she amused herself by trying to recognize some of her regulars coming toward Freehold. Movement of something larger than a pedestrian coming up the street caught her eye, and she turned to see what was coming. *Odd. I haven't seen that many horsemen here in a long time. At least, not all together.* But she dismissed them from her mind as soon a she saw them, for she spotted T'fyrr turning the corner at the other end of the block, approaching Freehold from the shelter of the overhang like everyone else.

He looked relaxed; his wings were not held tightly to his body as they were whenever he was nervous. She smiled to see that tiny sign; something must have gone well for him today.

But her smile vanished—for the horsemen suddenly spurred their beasts into a lurching run, scattering the other pedestrians before them, and converged on him. The horses were quick, nimble-footed and used to the city streets, cutting T'fyrr off before he even knew they were there!

Her heart started up into her throat, and her chest constricted with sudden fear. There were seven of them; whoever his attackers were, they weren't taking any chances on him getting away.

They had closed in on him and surrounded him, trapping him under the overhang where he couldn't take to the air. His talons were of limited use in a situation like this one. No one was going to come to his aid, not in this neighborhood—there were a few of her army of children loitering about the street, but children could do nothing against horsemen, even unarmed horsemen. One of the boys rushed toward the door of Freehold and began to pound on it frantically, but there was no way that enough help would arrive in time from inside. In a few moments, they could subdue him, haul him onto a horse, and carry him away!

But she was a Gypsy, and a Gypsy is never unarmed.

She pulled the sash from around her waist and dove into her pocket for the pennies left over from her distribution of largesse to the children this afternoon. *Those aren't battle-trained cavalry beasts, those are only common riding horses*—Even as the first of the riders moved to pull something from his belt, she had fitted a penny into the pocket of her sash, whirled it three times over her head, and let it fly.

She had kept herself fed, many a time, with the sling. Her aim did not fail her this time, either, with a much larger target than the tiny head of a squirrel. Her penny hit the rump of the horse with a satisfying *smack*, and more satisfying was the horse's natural reaction to the stinging missile. It was, as she had hoped, *much* worse than the worst biting fly.

As the first horse reared and neighed wildly, completely unseating his rider, she lobbed another two pennies at two more of the hapless mounts. As the first man landed—badly—on the pavement, the next two horses reacted the same way the first one had. Only instead of simply throwing their riders and dancing around like beasts possessed, these two reared, bucking their riders off and bolted, lumbering into the rest of the horses, scattering them for the moment.

That was enough to give T'fyrr the opening he needed. He dashed into the gap left when the first horse ran off and launched himself into the air, wings beating powerfully, further panicking the horses.

The street was full of neighing, dancing horses, or so it seemed. Their riders had their hands full for the moment.

She didn't wait to see what would happen next; if anyone down there suspected that they had been attacked from one of the balconies and happened to look up, she could be in serious trouble. She ducked inside the nearest window exit, getting into hiding quickly, before any of T'fyrr's assailants had a chance to calm his beast, look up, and spot her.

Then she ran for the inside stairs, heading for the roof. That, surely, would be where he would go. Freehold meant the nearest point of safety, and the roof was the best place for him to land.

He'll be in a panic, and once he gets out of the streetlights, his eyes won't have time to adjust and he'll be flying half-blind. He may land hard—

She burst out onto the roof at the same time he landed as hard and clumsily as she had expected, and as he heard her footfall behind him, he whirled to face her, hands fanned, talons extended in an attack stance. His eyes were wild, black pupils fully dilated. His beak parted, and his tongue extended as he hissed at her.

"T'fyrr!" she cried, "It's me! It's all right, Joyee is getting the Freehold peace-keepers at the door—no one is going to get past them—"

She expected him to relax then, but he didn't so much relax as collapse, going to his knees, his wings drooping around him. One moment, he was ready to slash her to ribbons; the next, he was falling to pieces himself.

Dear Lady! She ran to him in alarm; he moved to reach for her feebly, and when she touched his arm, his emotional turmoil boiled up to engulf her, making her own breath come short and her throat fill with bile.

Quickly she shunted it away; helped him to his feet, and led him as quickly as she could to the staircase. *My room. I have to get him somewhere quiet. If he panics more—*

She didn't want to speculate. He was armed with five long talons on each hand, and four longer talons on each foot, not to mention that cruel beak. This collapse might only be momentary. If he thought he was in danger again, and lost control of himself—

Well, she had seen hawks in a panic; they could and did put talons right through a man's hand. T'fyrr was at least ten times the size of a hawk.

Somehow she got him into her room and shut the door; she lowered the bed and put him down on it, dimming the lights. He seemed to be in a state of shock now; he shook, every feather trembling, and he didn't seem to know she was there.

All right. I can work with that. I don't need him to notice me.

Of course not. All she needed was to touch him—and open up every shield she had on herself.

But there was no choice, and no hesitation. She sat down beside him, laid one hand on his arm, and released her shielding walls.

It was worse, much worse, than she had ever dreamed.

After a time, she realized that he was speaking, brokenly. Some of it was in her tongue, some in his own, but she finally pieced together what he was saying, aided by the flood of emotions that racked him. He could not weep, of course; it seemed horribly cruel to her that he did not have that release. If ever anyone needed to be able to weep, it was T'fyrr.

He *had* gone to Gradford, on behalf of Harperus, and he had been captured and held as a demon by agents of the Church. They had bound him, imprisoned him in a cage so small he could not even spread his wings, which had driven him half mad.

She tried to imagine it, and failed. Take all the worst nightmares, the most terrible of fears, then make them all come true. The Haspur needed

space, freedom, needed this things the way a human needed air and light.
Take those away—and *then* take away air, and light as well—

How did he endure it? Only by descent into madness. . . .

But that had not been enough for them. Then they had starved him—
which had sent him past madness altogether, turned him from a thinking
being into a being ruled only by fear, pain and instinct.

As familiar as she was with hawks, she knew only too well what they
were like when they hungered. Their entire being centered on finding
prey and eating it—and woe betide anything that got in the way. But
T'fyrr had never been so overwhelmed by his own instincts before; he
had not known such a thing could happen. He retained just enough of his
reasoning ability to take advantage of an opportunity to escape provided by
the Free Bards.

He did *not* have enough left to do more than react instinctively when
one of the Church Guards tried to stop him.

He did not realize what he had done until after—after he had killed
and eaten a sheep on the mountainside, and remembered, with a Haspur's
extraordinary memory, what had happened as he escaped. He could not
even soften the blow to himself by forgetting. . . .

*He killed. He had never killed, other than the animals that were his
food. Certainly he had never even hurt another thinking being before.* For
all their fearsome appearance, the Haspur were surprisingly gentle, and
they had not engaged in any kind of conflict for centuries. It was incon-
ceivable for the average Haspur to take a sentient life with his own talons.
Oh, there were Haspur who retained some of the savage nature of their
ancestors, enough that they served as guards to warn off would-be invad-
ers, or destroy them if they must. But the average Haspur looked on the
guards the same way the average farmer looked on the professional merce-
nary captain; with a touch of awe, a touch of queasiness, and the surety
that *he* could not do such a thing.

To discover that he could had undone T'fyrr.

To learn, twice now, that his battle-madness had been no momentary
aberration was just as devastating.

Gradually, he allowed her to hold him, as he shook and rocked back
and forth, his spirit in agony. He had come close, so close, to killing again
tonight, that the experience had reopened all his soul-wounds. The man
who had been nearest him had been reaching for a hand-crossbow at his
belt—and that was how he had been captured the first time, with a
drugged dart shot by a man who caught him on the ground. The horror
of that experience was such that he would rather die—

—or kill again—

—than endure it a second time.

And with her spirit open to his, she endured all the horror of it with
him, the horror of knowing that he could and would kill as well.

His throat ached and clenched; his breath came in hard-won gasps,
harsh and unmusical, and every muscle in his body was as tight as it could
be. If he had been a human, he would have been sobbing uncontrollably.

He could not—so she wept for him.

She *understood*, with every fiber of her spirit, just how his heart cried out with revulsion at the simple fact that he had taken a life, that if forced to he would do so again. There was no room in his vision of the world for *self-defense*, only for those who killed and those who did not. She *knew*, keep inside her bones, why he hated himself for it.

He had not stopped; had not tried to subdue rather than kill. Never mind that he was mad with fear, pain, hunger. Never mind that the man who had tried to stop his escape would probably have killed him to prevent it. The man himself was *not* his enemy; the man was only doing the job he'd been set. T'fyrr had not even paused for a heartbeat to consider what he was doing. He had struck to kill and fled with the man's heart-blood on his talons.

And she told him so, over and over, between her sobs of grief for him, just how and why she understood. She would have felt the same, precisely the same, even though there were plenty of people she considered her friends and Clansfolk who would never agree with her. Her personal rule—which she did not impose on anyone else—forbade killing. She knew that she *might* find herself in the position one day of having to kill or die herself. She did not know how she would meet that. She tried to make certain to avoid situations where that was the only way out.

Which was why, of course, she avoided cities. Death was cheap in cities; the more people, the cheaper it was. At least out in the countryside, life was held at a dearer cost than here, where there were people living just around the corner who would probably strangle their own children for a few coins.

All of that flitted through her thoughts as a background to T'fyrr's terrible pain, and to the tears that scalded her own cheeks. But there was a further cost to this ahead for her. She had thought that she had opened herself to him completely before; but now, as she held him and sensed that *this* would bring him little or no ease, she realized that she had still held something of herself in reserve. Nothing less than all of herself would do at this moment—because of what *he* was.

The Haspur had an odd, sometimes symbiotic relationship with the humans who shared their aeries and villages. Most of the time, it never went any deeper than simple friendship, the kind she herself shared with the Elves who had gifted her with the bracelets.

But sometimes, it went deeper, much deeper, than that.

She had always known, intellectually, that she was not the only human to have her peculiar gift—or curse—of feeling the needs and the emotions of others. She had never met anyone else with the gift to the extent that she had it, though. She had never encountered another human who found him- or herself pulled into another's soul by his pain or his joy; never found one who was in danger of losing himself when bombarded by the emotions of others.

But it seemed that there were many more of the humans who lived among the Haspur with that curse—or gift. Their gifts were—at least from what she gleaned from T'fyrr—as formidable as her own. And for those who bore that burden, a relationship with a Haspur could never be "simple" anything.

They felt, and felt deeply, but had no outlet for their extreme emotions.

At the ragged edge of pain, or sorrow, or that dreadful agony of the soul, the Haspur could only try to endure, dumbly, as their emotions tore them up from within, a raging beast that could not break free from the cage of their spirits.

But humans did have that outlet—at least, the humans he called "Spirit-Brothers" could provide it, by becoming unhesitatingly one, without reservations, with their friends, and sharing the pain.

Becoming one, without reservations. Giving all, and taking all, halving the pain by enduring it themselves.

She had one lover in all her life—one *real* lover, as opposed to friends who shared their bodies with her. She had not known; she was so young, she had not known that when she gave all of herself, the one she gave to might not be able to give in return—that he might not even realize what she had done. She had not thought she was the only one with this curse—or gift—and had supposed that her lover would surely feel all that she felt.

He didn't, of course. He hadn't a clue; he'd thought she was the same as all the other ladies he'd dallied with, and she lacked the words, the skill, the heart to tell him.

When Raven had left her the first time, it had felt as if something that was a part of her had been ripped away from her soul. She smiled and bled, and he smiled and sauntered off with a song on his lips.

And he had never understood. He still didn't; not to this day.

She had learned to accept that, and had forgiven him for not knowing and herself for her own ignorance. But she had vowed it would not happen again and had never opened herself to another creature that deeply, never under any other circumstances, until this moment. But nothing less would do now, but to give everything of herself, for nothing less would begin the healing T'fyrr needed so desperately.

She did not know, could not know, what would come of this. Perhaps an ending like the end of her love affair with Raven, and pain that would live in her forever, a place inside her spirit wounded and scarred and never the same again.

But she could bear the pain, and she could heal herself again, over time. She had done it once, and she could again. T'fyrr could not, not without her help, for he did not truly understand the emotions festering inside his soul.

Great power demands that the user consider the repercussions of actions. She had the power; she had long ago accepted the responsibility, or so she had thought.

I was fooling myself. I should have known that the Lady would put this on me.

But this was no time to have second thoughts; really, she had made all her choices long before she met T'fyrr, and this was only the ultimate test of those choices. What was it that Peregrine had said to her a few months ago? She had known at the time that he was trying to warn her of an ordeal to come—

You cannot speak truly of the path without walking it.

And she could not. Not without repudiating everything that she said, that she thought, that she was.

So she opened the last of her heart to him, opened her soul's arms to him and gathered him up inside the place where her own deepest secrets and darkest fears lay—she brought him inside, and she gave him all that she was, and all the comfort that she had.

T'fyrr did not know how he had gotten to Nightingale's room; he did not even realize that he was talking to her until he heard his own voice, hoarse and cracking, telling her things he had never intended to share with anyone.

Especially not with her.

She was too fragile, too gentle—how could she hear these horrible things and not hate him? He knew she was one of the kind who *felt* things; he had sensed that the first time he met her.

The same as the Spirit-Brothers, perhaps.

But not the same, not with the training or the knowledge, surely. The idea of *murder*—it would surely send her fleeing him in utter revulsion.

Only Harperus knew he had killed. Harperus had told him that it was an accident, something he could not have helped.

Harperus had not even begun to understand.

The Spirit-Brothers of the Haspur would have been able to help him bear the guilt, although it would have meant that he and the Brother who chose to help him would have been in debt to one another for all their lives, bonded in soul and perhaps in body as well. The latter happened, sometimes, though not often. But the Spirit-Brothers, male and female, were far away and out of reach, and he had no hope of reaching them for years, even decades. . . .

At some point in his babbling, it began to dawn on him that Nightingale not only understood, she *felt* as he felt. She wept for him as a Spirit-Brother would have wept, gave him her tears in an outpouring of release for both of them.

Something in him turned to her as a flower turns toward the sun, as a drowning creature seizes upon a floating branch. Something in her answered that need, granted him light, kept him afloat. He was beyond thinking at that point, or he would never have let her do what she did. It wasn't fair, it wasn't right, not for her! She was a Gypsy, a Free Bard, who should be as free as the bird that was her namesake, and not bound as a Spirit-Brother!

But it was already done, before thoughts even began to form in the back of his terror-clouded mind.

She stayed awake with him until his internal sense told him that the sun was rising, comforting and holding him, and even preening his feathers as another Haspur would—

—a Haspur, or a Spirit-Brother.

He did not understand how she knew to do this; he did not understand why he accepted it. He was beyond understanding now, beyond anything except feeling. It was feeling that held him here, weak as a newborn eyas, simply accepting the comfort and the understanding as an unthinking eyas would accept them.

Finally, he slept, exhausted.

◊   ◊   ◊

When he woke again, she was there beside him, stroking his wings with a hand so gentle it had not even disturbed his sleep, although he had felt it and it had soothed him out of the nightmares he had suffered for so long. He blinked up at her, astonished that she was still there.

Silence stretched between them; he felt as if he must be the one to break it. Finally, he said the only thing that was in his mind.

"You should hate me—" And he waited to see that hate and contempt in her eyes for what he had done.

Her expression did not change, not by the slightest bit.

"How could I hate you?" she asked, softly. "You hate yourself more than enough for both of us. I want to help you, T'fyrr. I hope you will let me."

He blinked at her again, and slowly sat up. She shook her hair back out of her face, and rubbed her eyes with her hand as she sat up too.

"I think that there is something that you believe you need to do, to make up for what you did," she said then. "I will help you, if that is what you want. I will come with you to the King, and stand beside you in your task. I will give you my music, and I will give you my magic; you can have one or both, they are freely given."

"And when the King sees again the things that he does not want to see?" T'fyrr asked, very slowly. "Will that—"

She nodded, deliberately. "I believe that will be what you need, as your duty and your penance. It will not be easy, and it will not be pleasant."

He sighed, and yet it was not because of a heaviness of spirit. Somehow, in truly accepting this burden, his spirit felt *lighter* rather than crushed further down. "No penance is," he replied somberly. Somehow, in the dark despair of last night, he had come to a decision—hopefully, it was one of wisdom and not of weakness and expediency. Theovere was too far down the road of irresponsibility to be recalled by ordinary means. "I will need your magic, if you will give it," he said, feeling as if he were making a formal request or performing a solemn ceremony with those simple words.

She nodded, and bowed her head a little. "Since you will have it, I will give it," she said, making her words a pledge as well as an answer.

Then she raised her lovely, weary eyes to his again and smiled tiredly. "And you should eat—for that matter, so should I. We can do nothing half-starved."

Those words, which would have made him wince away less than a day ago, only made him aware that he was ravenous. "And after we eat?" he asked. "Will you come with me to the Palace?"

"Yes." She brushed her hair back over her shoulders. "It is time I accepted my responsibilities as well, and stopped hiding in corners behind the name of 'Tanager.' But I will *not*," she added, with a warning look in her eyes, "be Nightingale. Not here, and not now. I do not trust Tyladen's friends, nor Harperus' associates. They speak too lightly and too often to too many people. They can afford to; they have many protections. I am only a Gypsy, and far from the wagons of my Clan. What few magics I have will not protect me if powerful men come hunting."

"As you are far from your people, I am far from the aeries of mine," he said impulsively, laying his hand over hers. "So perhaps we should fly our pattern together, from now on?"

"And we should begin now." She rose at that, and stretched, lithe and graceful. "Let me get clean, first, then. Lyrebird and T'fyrr will eat together, and he will take her to the Palace to present her as his accompanist. Or should you go and make some formal request for an accompanist? Should this be an official, perhaps a royal, appointment?"

He actually managed a smile at that. "It would be easiest simply to *do* so," he pointed out. "Just as Harperus did with me. If the King hears you once, he will see to it that the appointment simply happens. He is not about to put up with interference from his Council a second time over so 'trivial' a matter as his personal musicians. *They* believe it is trivial, and it is both unfortunate and our good luck that he does not. This one time, his obsession can work for us."

She paused for a moment, one hand on the door to the bathroom, then nodded. "I think I see that. It is a risk, but so is everything we are doing."

She closed the door behind her, and there came the sound of running water from beyond it. He lay back down on her bed, closing his eyes for a moment, intending to plan out the next few hours in detail. He would have to get her past the guards, first, of course. . . .

But his body had other ideas, and he dozed off, to awaken again with her hand on his arm. She was dressed in one of her most impressive costumes, and he had little doubt that the Ladies of the Court would attempt to emulate her dress before too long. He also had a shrewd notion that they would not succeed.

He got up, finding himself less stiff than he would have expected, given that he had spent the night in a human bed. She sent the bed back up into the wall with a touch of her hand; slipped the carrying case over her larger harp, and slung it across her back. It did not look as incongruous as he would have thought.

"Shall we?" she asked, gesturing to the door. He led the way; she locked the door after them both.

She disappeared into Tyladen's office for a moment, presumably to tell him where they were going and how long they expected to be gone. *She is one of their chief attractions; she owes her putative employer that much, I suppose.* After a hearty meal in the single eating nook open at this early hour, they went out into the street together. There was no sign of last night's altercation, but the moment they crossed the threshold of Freehold, his hackles went up, and he moved into the center of the street, away from dangerous overhangs.

It did not escape his notice that she made no objection to this, that, in fact, her eyes scanned the mostly-deserted street with as much wariness as his.

They stepped out together onto the cobblestones of the street, both of them dreadfully out of place in this part of the city. Between his appearance and her costume, anyone looking for them was likely to find them immediately.

Well, there was no help for it.

Nightingale walked beside him as serenely as if the previous night had never happened, as if she did not look like an invitation to theft. He tried to imitate her and actually succeeded to a certain extent.

But there was one thing, at least, that he *was* going to do. He had coins in his garment, plenty of them, and he was *not* going to appear at the gate to the Palace with her, walking afoot like a pair of vagabonds. As soon as they reached one of the more respectable sections of the city, he hailed a horse-drawn conveyance, an open carriage with two seats that faced each other, and gestured her up into it.

She raised an eyebrow at him, but said nothing. He took his place beside her, although it was dreadfully uncomfortable and he had to hold his wings and tail at odd angles to get them to fit inside.

Now, how am I going to get her inside the gate? The guards aren't going to want to let her pass, she hasn't a safe-conduct or an invitation. . . . He worried at the problem without coming to a satisfactory solution as the streets grew progressively busier, and stares more covert. This was not the only conveyance on the street, but many of the others were private vehicles, whose occupants gazed at them with surprise. He ignored them, trying to think what he could do with Nightingale. Perhaps he could leave her at the gate, go in, find the Seneschal and get a safe-conduct for her—

But that would leave her alone at the gate, and anyone who spotted her with me on the way here could—do whatever they wanted. She is with me, which makes her presumably valuable to me.

Would anyone dare to try anything under the noses of the guards?

Oh yes, they could and would. Especially if my unknown adversary is highly placed in the Court. A little thing like a kidnapping at the gate would hardly bother him. He could make it a private arrest, for instance.

There was reasonable foot traffic at this hour, and the conveyance made excellent time; not as good as he would have flying, of course, but still quite respectable. The two horses drawing it were able to trot most of the way.

They reached the gate long before he had come to any satisfactory solution to his problem. But, as it happened, the solution was waiting for him, standing beside the guards with a smaller and far more elaborate and elegant, gilded version of the conveyance waiting beside him. The Palace grounds were extensive enough that there was an entire fleet of conveyances and their drivers available for those who lived here, just to ferry them around within the walls.

Nob? What's he doing here?

"Is that someone you know?" Nightingale asked, as his eyes widened in surprise.

"Yes, it's my servant—but *how* did he know I was coming in this morning, and why did he order a conveyance?" T'fyrr asked, more as a rhetorical question than because he expected an answer.

But Nightingale shrugged. "I told Tyladen where I was going. Tyladen probably foresaw the difficulty of getting me inside without waiting around at the gate and sent word to Harperus. Old Owl must have exercised some of his diplomatic persuasion and got me an invitation or a safe-conduct. I expect that's why your lad is here; to bring the pass and to get us to the Palace in the manner suitable to your rank."

T'fyrr nodded; it made sense. But Nightingale added, "The one thing I *don't* want is to run into Harperus. He knows me on sight, and I don't want *any* of the Deliambrens aware that I'm here."

He grimaced; at this point, that was a very difficult request to satisfy. "I don't know how—"

But she interrupted him. "I can keep him from noticing me as long as I stay in the background. If Old Owl shows up at all, T'fyrr, *you* keep him busy, please? Don't let him think about talking to me. Tell him I'm shy, whatever it takes to get him to leave me alone. Make up something— or better yet, tell him about the attack last night. That should get his mind off me."

He wasn't at all sure he could do that, but he nodded again. "I can try," he said truthfully, and then the conveyance stopped in front of the gate, and it was too late to discuss anything more.

Nob had indeed brought "Lyrebird's" safe-conduct, although from here on she would have to come and go through a lesser gate elsewhere, she was only a lowly accompanist, after all, and not a Sire dubbed by the High King's own hand. Nob chattered excitedly at a high rate of speed, which kept T'fyrr from having to say much and Nightingale from having to say anything. The safe-conduct was from Theovere himself; Old Owl had gone straight to the highest authority available. He must have described Lyrebird in the most glowing terms; the King was most anxious to hear this remarkable player from the infamous Freehold.

"The Bardic Guild found out, too. I don't know how, but they had a Guildmaster protesting to the High King before I even got the safe-conduct," Nob continued, after describing how Harperus had come to get him early this morning. "They tried to get this lady banned from the Court because she's a Gypsy, then they tried to get her barred because she plays at Freehold and they have some kind of arrangement about the musicians at Freehold. The High King just ignored them. They were even going to make a fuss so you couldn't be heard, but Theovere got word of that before it ever happened and told them if they did *anything* he'd have them all discharged, so they gave up, I guess. The High King made her your Second, do you know what that means?"

T'fyrr shook his head. Nob was only too happy to explain. "She's more than a servant, like me, but she's not the High King's musician, she's yours. So nobody but you can discharge her, you see, not even Theovere if the Guild pressures the High King to do it, but she doesn't have the immunity you do if she offends somebody at Court. She can only be arrested by Theovere's personal guards, though, if she's accused of something."

"Then I'll just have to be certain I don't offend anyone," Nightingale said in a low, amused voice. Nob giggled.

"The Guild people are all pretty disgusted, but Harperus says not to worry, they can't do anything, and as long as you're real careful and never let any of them get you someplace without witnesses so they can claim you offended them, it'll be all right," Nob finished in a rush. He kept glancing over at Lyrebird with a certain awe and speculation in his eyes.

"When is Theovere expecting us to perform for him?" T'fyrr asked. That was the question of the most moment.

"As soon as you get there—I mean, after you get cleaned up and all," Nob replied, correcting himself with a blush. "You can't go before the King with dust on your feathers!"

Nightingale gave T'fyrr an amused look that he read only too easily— she had warned him something like this might happen, which was why *she* had made her own careful preparations before they left Freehold.

Nob hurried them both inside and, while Nightingale waited in the outer room, rushed him through his usual preparations.

Still harried by the energetic Nob, like a pair of hawks being chivvied on by a wren, they hurried up the hallways to the King's private quarters.

This time will be different. This time there will be magic. Elation and worry mingled in him in a confusing storm of emotion, leaving him feeling unbalanced. The least little things were unbalancing him, after last night. . . .

After last night. . . .

What exactly had happened? *Something* had passed between them, as ephemeral as a moon shadow and strong as spider silk. A whisper more potent than any shout, that was what it felt like; a stillness at the center of a whirlwind. As if every feather had been stripped from his body, leaving him bare to the winds.

Perhaps it was just as well that they had work to do immediately, so that he had no time to think about it. He did not want to think about it, not now, perhaps not ever.

But you will, his conscience told him. *You will have to, eventually.*

He didn't want to think about that, either.

Nightingale was too weary to be impressed by the Palace, the High King, or anything else for that matter. There wasn't much left of her this morning, except the magic and the music; she had saved enough of her energy for that, and had very little more. She felt as if she was so insubstantial she would blow away in a breeze, and so tired she could hardly walk.

It was not the physical weariness, although that was a part of it, certainly. She had stayed up to play for revels all night long and traveled with the dawn a thousand times. But this morning was very different.

But part of me dwells within him, now, and part of him in me. Strange and yet familiar, a breath of mountain air across her deep and secret forest; a hint of music strange and wild, a brush of feathers across her breast.

No time to think about it now; time only to enforce her *don't look at me* glamorie, spun with a touch of Bardic power and sealed with a hummed, near-inaudible tune. Time only to take her place behind T'fyrr in the King's chamber, set up her harp, tune it with swift fingers, and wait for his cues.

He would have to be the one to choose the tunes; she could only follow his lead, and try to set the magic to suit. They'd had no chance to discuss this, to pick specific songs. "If it is something you don't know, I'll sing the first verse alone," he whispered. "If we do that enough, it will seem done on purpose."

She nodded, and then they began.

With no time to set what they were to perform, with only their past performances together to use as patterns, he was not able to choose many songs suited to their intent. She was not particularly worried about that, not for this first attempt. She was far more concerned with setting so good an impression of her ability on the King that he would continue to support T'fyrr and, indirectly, her. It would take more than one session of magic to undo all the harm that had been wrought with years of clever advice and insidious whispers. It might be just as well that they were not too heavy-handed with the message for the first performance; better that they had more songs merely meant to entertain than to carry the extra burden. *She* must impress the King as well as convey the magic, after all.

She knew that she had done that much when the King ceased to play his game of Sires and Barons with one of his lords, and ignored everything else in the room, as well, closing his eyes and listening intently to the music they made. She knew that there was something more than herself at work when the bodyguards' faces took on an unexpected stillness, as if they, too, were caught up in the spell of harp and voice, when even the lord who had been playing at the game with the High King folded his hands in his lap and simply listened.

There is something of me in T'fyrr, as there is part of him in me. Has he learned to touch the magic through me? It could have been; Raven had his own touch of the magic, and she would never have noticed one way or another if he had acquired a little more of it from her after their bittersweet joining. So much of her soul was bound up in the magic, could she have ever spun it out to wrap T'fyrr's if the magic didn't come with it?

She sensed a terrible weariness in that second man, and as sensitive as she was this morning, she could not help but move to ease it. So when the music chosen did not particularly suit their purposes with the High King, she turned her attention and her magic to that weary lord, sending him such peace as she could. He was not a man who would ever feel much peace; his concerns were too deep, his worries never-ending. But what he would take in the way of ease, she would give him gladly. No one with such weariness on his heart could ever be one of the lot who were advising the King to neglect his duty. This could only be a man who was doing his best to make up for the King's neglect.

The King made no requests; T'fyrr simply picked songs as he thought of them, so far as Nightingale could tell. Finally, at some signal she could not see, he stopped, and it was a long, long moment before the King opened his eyes again and set his gaze on the two of them.

It was another long moment before he spoke.

"I do not ever wish to hear your musical judgment called into question again, T'fyrr," he said quietly, but with a certain deadly quality to his words. "You may bring whosoever you wish to accompany you from henceforth—but it will be my request that it be this gentle lady. Her safe-conduct to this Palace is extended for as long as she *wishes* to come."

The High King turned to the lord that had sat at play with him. "What think you of my Nightingales, Lord Seneschal?" he asked, but with a tone full of wry amusement, as if he expected some kind of noncommittal answer. Nightingale suppressed a smile at the unintended irony.

But the Lord Seneschal turned towards Theovere with an expression of vague surprise and a touch of wonder. "You know that I am not the expert in music that you are, Your Majesty," he said with no hint that he was trying to flatter. "I enjoy it, certainly, but it has never touched me— until today." He closed his eyes briefly, and opened them again, still wearing that expression of surprise. "But today, I felt such peace for a moment, that if I were a religious man, I would have suspected something supernatural . . . I thought of things that I had forgotten, of days long ago, of places and people. . . ."

Then he shook himself and lost that expression of wonderment. "Memories of—old times. At any rate, Your Majesty," he continued briskly, "if I were not so certain of the honor of the Guildmasters, I would have been tempted to say that they were opposed to this lady's performance because she would provide an unwelcome contrast to the performance of the Guild musicians."

Nightingale bowed her head to hide her smile. The Lord Seneschal's tone of irony was just enough to be clear, without being so blatant as to be an accusation against the Guild musicians. For all that the King had supported her against them, he had a long history of supporting them as well. At any moment, he could spring again to their defense, so it was wise of the Lord Seneschal to be subtle in his criticism.

Nor was that lost upon Theovere, who answered the sally with a lifted eyebrow.

"Let us discuss that, shall we," he said, and T'fyrr, taking that as the dismissal that it was, bowed them both out.

Nightingale parted company from him quickly after that, since Nob brought word that Harperus wanted to speak with him, and she most certainly did not want to be there when he showed up. She returned unaccompanied to Freehold, resolving to make her journeys hereafter in something less conspicuous in the way of a costume. The Elven silks would pack down readily enough, and she could change in T'fyrr's rooms, even if that would scandalize young Nob. With the safe-conduct in her hand, the quiet and respectable clothing would do very well for her to pass the gate reserved for those who were higher than servants but less than noble.

But she should think about spending some of her rapidly-accumulating monies on other clothing, as well. Granted, she could not lay her hands on more Elven silk, but there were perfectly good seamstresses in the city who would not scorn to sew to her design. She needed something appropriate but less flamboyant than Elven-made clothing. She was a commoner, an outsider, and it would not do to excite the jealousy of the ladies of the Court in the matter of dress. Every time she stepped onto the Palace grounds, she went completely out of her element, a songbird trying to swim like a fish. There was no point in making herself more problems than she already had.

She was uncomfortably aware of speculative eyes on her as she made her way to Freehold, and she was grateful that, although the hour tended toward noon, it was still too early for any of the more dangerous types to be wandering the streets. Pickpockets were easy enough to foil; she could leave broken fingers in her wake without seeming to do more than brush her hand across her belt-pouch. But in this particular outfit, she was fair game for ransom-kidnappers who could legitimately assume she had money or had family with money. And she was even more vulnerable to those looking to kidnap for other purposes.

So she set the *don't look at me* spell again, all too aware that it would only work on those near enough to hear the melody she hummed under her breath. If she were less tired, she could have included anyone within sight of her—

But she had just spent all night and part of the morning working the magics of music and the heart, and she had scant resources to spend on herself. She sighed with relief when Freehold loomed into view, and she had seldom been so glad to see a place as she was to see that deceptively plain door.

She took herself straight upstairs; fortunately, word had not yet spread of her Royal Command Performance, and she did not have to fend off any questioners. Only one of the Mintak peace-keepers appeared, silent as a shadow, to take her harp from her—and one of the little errand boys, with a tray of food and drink beside him. Neither asked any questions; they simply followed her to her room, put their burdens down, and left her.

She ate and drank quickly, without tasting any of it; she stripped off her gown and lay down in her bed, still rumpled and bearing the impression of her body and T'fyrr's, and the faint, spicy scent of his feathers. And then, she fell asleep, and slept like one dead until an hour before her first set of the evening.

She woke with the feeling that she had dreamed, but with no memory of what her dreams had been about. She woke, in fact, a little confused about where she was, until her mind began to function again. Then she lay staring up at the ceiling, trying to sort herself out.

There was a difference, a profound and yet subtle difference, in the way everything felt, but she had known that there would be.

Some of the magic—had not precisely left her, but it had changed. If she sang alone, she would still command the same power—but if she performed with T'fyrr, it was another story altogether. Together they would command more than the magic of two people; their abilities would work together as warp and weft, and the magic they wove would be stronger and firmer than anything she had ever dreamed of. *So T'fyrr shared the Bardic Magic now—or else, I have awakened the magic that was already there.* Not entirely unexpected, but certainly welcome, for as long as the two of them remained partnered.

She shoved that last niggling thought away, with a hint of desperation. She would not think of that. The pain would come soon enough, she did not need to worry at it until it *did* come, and T'fyrr went on his way again without her.

Or until she was forced by circumstance to leave him. The road traveled in both directions, after all.

The other changes within her were precisely as she had expected—except for the depth to which they ran. She did not particularly want to think about that, either.

But she wouldn't have to; there was a performance to give. T'fyrr would probably not be able to come—he could seldom manage two nights in a row. A brief stab of loneliness touched her, but she had expected it, and absorbed it.

I have been lonely for most of my life; I do not expect this to change. That was what she told herself, anyway. *Being lonely has never killed anyone yet, no matter what the foolish ballads say.*

And with that thought to fortify her, she finally rose from her bed and prepared to face another night of audiences.

She made her way across the city with far less of a stir this morning than she and T'fyrr had caused yesterday. No one would look twice at her, in fact, in her sober and honest clothing. The bundle at her back could be anything; unless you knew what a harp case looked like, there was no reason even to think she was a musician.

She presented herself and her safe-conduct at the Bronze Gate; the guard there scarcely glanced at it or her, except to note the size and shape of the bundle she carried and to order her to show what it was she had. When he saw it was only a musical instrument and a small bundle of cloth, he became bored again and passed her through.

She found a page to show her to T'fyrr's rooms, in plenty of time to use his bathroom and change into the gown she had brought with her. He was pacing the floor when she arrived, and turned to greet her with relief and disappointment.

Another sign of how we are bound, now; I know his feelings without needing to try to interpret his expression. The relief was because she was early; the disappointment he made clear enough.

"Theovere hasn't changed," he said as she asked him how they had been received yesterday. "He still hasn't done anything any differently. I don't understand—"

Before he could say anything any further, she seized his hand and drew him into the bedroom, away from the odd devices she recognized as Deliambren listening devices. She did *not* want the Deliambrens to know about the Bardic magic—at least, she did not want them to know that she was exercising it. They already knew there was something like it, of course, and they knew, from the results she got, that she used it. They might put "magic" and "harpist" together and come up with "Nightingale."

"Don't be impatient," she told him as his tail-feathers twitched a little from side to side and he shook his wings out. "Even with the magic, this is going to take *time*. For one thing, we didn't have the chance to select songs that would channel his mind in the direction we wanted it to go. For another, we are trying to change something that took several years to establish; we aren't going to do that overnight."

He opened his beak, then shut it abruptly, as if he had suddenly seen what she was talking about.

"Besides, you aren't in the special Council sessions," she continued.

"You have no access to the one place where he actually gets things done and issues real orders. You have no idea how he is speaking or acting within them. If I were the King—"

She let the nebulous thought take a more concrete form, then spoke. "If I were the King, and I began to take up the reins of my duty again—I would know that I would have to be careful about it. The Advisors aren't going to like the changes we're trying to bring about in him, and they are powerful people. He can oppose them in small things successfully, but—" She shook her head. "He was a very clever man, and I don't think that cleverness is gone. He was also a very observant man, and he must realize what has been going on. If I were the King, with my sense of duty reawakened, I would start working my will in very small things, taking back my power gradually, and hopefully by the time they realized what I was doing, it would be too late. And I would be very, very careful that I didn't *seem* to act any differently."

T'fyrr nodded then. "In a way, since he has let the power slip from his hands, Theovere has less power than any of them. Is that what you are saying?"

"More or less." She moved back into the other room with its insidious little listening devices. "Well, more to the point, what are we performing today? If you have anything that I don't know, I can probably pick it up with a little rehearsal."

"Which you have cleverly provided time for by arriving early." His beak opened in that Haspur equivalent of a smile, and she warmed with his pleasure in her company and *her* cleverness. "Well, here is the list I had thought we might perform."

He brought out a written list, which was thoughtful of him, and was what she would have done in his place. Armed with that, she was able to suggest alternatives to several of the songs she did not yet know, which left them enough time for her to pick up the melodies to the most important of the rest.

This time, she was no longer so tired that the white marble corridors blurred, one into the other, like the halls in a nightmare. She had a chance to make some mental notes as she walked beside him, his talons clicking oddly on the marble floor.

Did I have a nightmare involving these halls last night? Something about looking for T'fyrr in an endless series of corridors, all alike, all filled with strangers? Yes, and I kept finding single feathers, broken or pulled out at the roots—could you actually do that with feathers that long and strong? But I never found him, only rooms full of more strangers staring at me and saying nothing.

She didn't care much for the statuary, though. It all had a remarkable sameness to it, mannered and smug, beautifully carved and lifeless.

Rather like the Guild versions of our ballads, actually.

Was there a sculptor's version of a Bardic Guild? From the looks of these statues, she suspected there must be.

Theovere wasn't responsible for this, though; she had seen his suite and knew for a fact that he had better taste than to order anything like this statuary.

Huh. A Deliambren has better taste than this.

Some other High King—or more likely, some other servants of some other High King were responsible. The King had probably waved his hand and ordered that the austere corridors be decorated, and lo—

There were statues by the gross.

He might even had done it for the simplest of all reasons; to keep people from becoming lost. Certainly Nob and probably everyone else navigated the endless hallways by the statuary. If that was the case, the statues didn't need to be inspired, just all of the same theme. They could have been ordered like so many decorated cakes.

Let's see, we'll have a dozen each—High Kings, nymphs, shepherds, famous women, famous men, famous generals, famous warriors, famous animals, dancers, musicians, saints—what did they do when they ran out of obvious subjects? She amused herself, thinking that somewhere there was a corridor decked out in the theme of Famous Village Idiots, or Famous Swinekeepers.

*Each with his favorite piggy at his feet—*She smiled to herself, holding back a giggle, as they reached the door of the King's suite.

Well, once more into the fray. That was enough to sober her.

There was another potential problem, as if they did not have troubles enough. She had not told T'fyrr about a thought that had disturbed her own dreams last night. She did not *know* that there were people other than the Bards and Elves who could detect Bardic Magic at work, but there might be. After all, those who used Bardic Magic could detect other magics than their own. She did not know if the High King had someone with him or watching over him with the intention of catching anyone working magic on the King in the act. But it was a real possibility, and it was not likely that anyone would bother to ask *why* they were weaving spells if she and T'fyrr were caught at it.

As they waited for the guards to open the doors now, there was the chance that she had been detected yesterday, and that they were not going in to a performance but a trap.

But in all the years she had practiced her art, no one had ever accused her in a way that made her think they had proof she used magic. Nor had anyone else among the Gypsies. Churchmen, village heads, and Guildsmen told wild tales, but never with any foundation.

And never with any truth—that was the odd and interesting part. In all the times that Free Bards and Gypsies *had* worked magic, there had been no hint that anyone, even their worst enemies, had a notion that anything of the sort had been done. It was only the unbelievable stories that were spread, of how impressionable youngsters were turned to demon-worship, immorality, or suicide by one or another particular song. They accused the *song*, and not the singer, as if it were the song that held the power.

What nonsense. These are stories created by people who want to find something else to blame than themselves for their children's acts.

How could words and music, lifeless without the life given to them by the performer, ever influence anyone against his will or better judgment? Books could suggest new possibilities to an open mind, yes, so music could, too—but people were not mindless and they had their own wills, and it was the mind and the will that implemented decisions. The mind that made the decision was ultimately the responsible party.

She had to assume that would hold true now; had to, or she would be too apprehensive to perform the task she had sworn herself to.

She had sworn herself, knowing that this might take years, that it might cost her not only her freedom but her life if she were caught at it. She would not take back her pledge now.

T'fyrr sensed I was making a formal pledge, even though I didn't make a ceremony about it. Interesting.

The doors opened, and the King was waiting, and it was time to make good on that pledge; now, and for as many days as it took to bring the bud to flower. *If* it could be done.

T'fyrr watched Nightingale leaving the Palace from the balcony at the end of his corridor. It was a good vantage point, with the formal fore-gardens spread out beneath him in neat and geometric squares of color divided by walkways of white paving-stone, and was even better as a place from which to take to the air. He was at least four stories up—apparently, the higher you were in rank, the higher your rooms within the Palace. He could see all the way to the Bronze Gate from here, and he made a point of watching to see that Nightingale got that far. She always turned, just before she went through the Gate, and waved at him, knowing that he would see her clearly even though she was nearly a mile away.

She could not see him, though, so he didn't bother to wave back. Instead, he waited until that distant figure passed between the open leaves of the gate, then launched himself into the air, wings beating strongly, gaining altitude. The air above the Palace grounds was sweeter than that above the city, and cooler, yet another example of the difference between those who dwelled *here* and *there*.

They had been at this for two weeks now, and although he still had not seen any change in Theovere's behavior, his Advisors were increasingly unhappy with the High King. In Court, Theovere continued to act as if he were supremely bored with his duties, but the Lord Seneschal frowned a bit less these days, and the rest of the Advisors frowned a bit more, which argued that in private Theovere might be flexing his royal mus-cles discreetly.

Harperus showed no signs of disappearing the way he had right after he had gotten T'fyrr installed as Royal Musician. That *should* have been comforting, having at least one real ally with power and a great many tricks up his capacious and frothy sleeves, but it wasn't as comforting as it could have been. For one thing, the Deliambren clearly had his atten-tion and his mind on other things than T'fyrr. The Haspur actually saw the Lords Seneschal, Artificer, and Secretary more than he saw Harperus.

They often arrived to share T'fyrr's otherwise solitary dinners. The Lord Seneschal Acreon was more relaxed these days, though he was very disap-pointed to discover that Nightingale did not reside with T'fyrr in his rooms. She had impressed Acreon profoundly, it seemed.

I think she must have done something for him specifically with that magic of hers. I shall have to propose a special concert for him—perhaps a dinner concert on Nightingale's night off? We could do worse than have him on our side.

Lord Secretary Atrovel was his usual acerbic, witty, flippant self; whatever was going on in the private Council sessions didn't seem to be affecting him in the least. He continued to amuse T'fyrr with his imitations of the other Advisors, and his opinions on everything under the sun.

Lord Artificer Levan Pendleton came less often, as he was involved in some complicated project, but he was the only one of the three who actually *said* anything about changes in Theovere, and only a single comment. "He's up to mischief," the Lord Artificer had said briefly but with ironic approval, as if Theovere was a very clever, but very naughty, boy.

Atrovel was there last night with Pendleton, both of them flinging insults at each other and enjoying it tremendously. I wish Nightingale could have been there, too. I wish she would move into my suite. . . .

T'fyrr suppressed the rest of that thought and used his deepest wing-beats to get himself high into the sky, to a carefully calculated point where *he* would be able to make out Nightingale in the street below, but *she* would not see anything but a bird-form above if she looked up. He was worried about her. She told him not to worry, but he did anyway.

They tried to capture me, maybe even kill me. They haven't been successful, and it is going to cost them to find someone willing to make a third try. At least, that is the way Tyladen says things are done here. He thinks that makes me safe.

Well, maybe it made *him* safe, but it did nothing to protect Nightingale. An idiot could tell that he not only "hired" her, he cared for her. She was a single unarmed female; much easier to capture than a Haspur. She was, therefore, as much a target as he, and a much cheaper target at that.

She had to travel the dangerous streets between Freehold and the Palace twice a day, every day. *He* had volunteered to escort her, in spite of the fact that the crowds made him queasy and the streets brought on that fear of closed-in spaces all Haspur shared.

She had refused. He had offered to pay for a conveyance, and she had refused that, as well. Tyladen seemed unconcerned, saying only that "Gypsies can take care of themselves."

All very well and good, but there was only *one* Gypsy in this city, and she would have a difficult time standing up to six armed horsemen, for instance!

So he had started following her himself; not only from the air, but in the places where the streets were too narrow to make out where she was, by descending to use the metal walkways that connected buildings together above the second stories.

So far, nothing whatsoever had happened, but that did not make him less worried, it made him more worried. His unknown enemy could be waiting to see just how high a value T'fyrr placed on her before moving in to kidnap her. His enemy could also be trying to figure out just where she figured in Theovere's altering personality. Anyone who wanted to ask the bodyguards could find out what they were singing for the High King, and at least half of the songs were of a specific kind. You wouldn't even need magic to get a particular message across to Theovere, *if* he was listening. Their choice of music alone would alert that enemy to what they hoped to accomplish.

He looked down, spotting her from above by the misshapen bundle of the harp case on her back. She was out of the better districts and down into the lower-class areas of the city; the streets narrowed, and it was getting harder to watch her from this high. On the other hand, she was jostled along by the crowd, and it would be a bad idea for her to look up now that she was in this part of the city.

He descended. It wasn't time to take to a walkway, yet; just the point where he should skim just above the roof level. People doing their wash or tending their little potted gardens would gawk at him as he flew past, but he was used to that now. He moved fast enough that their interest didn't alert anyone in the street below.

And speaking of the street below—

He fanned his wings open, grabbing for a now-familiar roost. He came to rest on a steeple, clinging with all four sets of talons, and watched her as she turned the corner into another narrow street. He particularly didn't like this one. There were a dozen little covered alleys off it, places where you could hide people for an ambush. This was one of the worst districts she had to cross to get back to Freehold, too. There had been murders committed here in broad daylight with a dozen witnesses present, none of whom, of course, could identify the murderer.

She was nervous here, too; he sensed that as his neck hackles rose. His beak clenched tight, and the talons on his hands etched little lines into the shingles on the steeple. She felt that something was wrong—

And it was.

Three men stepped out of an alley in front of her just as three more stepped out of one behind her. They were armed with sticks and clubs— and as everyone else sandwiched in between their ranks fled the immediate area without being stopped, it was obvious who they were after.

One of them stepped forward and gestured with his club as Nightingale shrank away, putting her back up against a building.

T'fyrr shoved himself away from the steeple, plunging toward them in a closed-wing stoop.

Nightingale knew she was being followed; she'd known it the moment that her tailer picked her up just outside of Leather Street. He had been following her for the past five days, in fact, always picking up her trail at Leather Street and leaving it just before she got to Freehold. He was good, but not good enough to evade someone who could sense a tracker's nerves behind her.

That was why she had paid all of her army of street urchins an extra penny to follow her, as well, from the Palace gate to Freehold. They might be children, but they weren't helpless; you couldn't live in and on the street around here if you were helpless. They had their own weapons; tiny fists as hard as rocks, the stones of the street, slings like her own, even a knife or two. They had their orders: if someone tried to hurt Nightingale, they were to swarm him, give her a chance to escape, then run off themselves.

But she had not expected to be attacked by more than one or two at the most.

The three stepping out in front of her made her freeze in shock; the three closing in from behind brought a cold wave of fear rushing over her.

Quickly, as the normal denizens of the street vanished into their own little hiding places, she put her back to a wall and reached inside her skirt for her own knife. This was no time or place for magic—

Although a nice Elven lightning bolt would be welcome right now!

At that moment, the bolt from above *did* come in, wings half furled, talons outstretched, screaming like all the demons of the Church put together.

T'fyrr!

He raked the scalp of one with his foreclaws as he plunged in, striking to hurt and disable, not to kill. *That* man was down, blood pouring over his face so that he couldn't see; he screamed as loudly as T'fyrr. The pain of his wounds probably convinced him that T'fyrr had taken the top of his skull of and not just his scalp.

With a thunder of wings that sent debris flying, and a wind that whipped the ends of her hair into her face, he landed beside her and turned to face the rest of her enemies.

He didn't speak; he just opened his beak for another of those ear-shattering screams.

But any hope that he might simply frighten them into giving it up as a bad job died when three more appeared behind the five that remained standing.

Nightingale's fighting knife was out and ready in one hand, a nasty little bit of chain in the other. Good enough in the ordinary run of street fighting—

None of these men seemed at all impressed as they closed in.

She had never been in this kind of a fight before; she spent most of her time ducking, and the rest of it trying to fend off grasping hands with her knife. Fear choked her and made it hard to breathe; T'fyrr panted harshly through his open beak. Every fiber of her wanted to run, but there was nowhere to run to, no opening to seize. Bile rose in her throat; she tasted blood where she had bitten her lip. One of them kicked at her legs, expertly, trying to bring her down. She ducked head blows, but not always with complete success. Her breath burned in her throat, and sweat ran into her eyes and coldly down her back.

Nightingale fought like a cornered alleycat and T'fyrr like a grounded hawk, but neither of them were willing to strike to kill, and that actually worked against them. There were too many times when the only option open would have meant killing one of their assailants. . . .

A glancing blow to her shoulder made her drop her bit of chain as her arm and hand went numb; she slashed feverishly at the man who'd struck her, but he only stepped out of the way and came in again, swinging his lead-weighted club. With the chain, she might have been able to get the club away from him—

We're not going to get away— She swallowed bile again, and backed away from the man with the club, her stomach lurching with fear.

Suddenly, the street erupted in screams.

The children swarmed fearlessly into the fight, screaming their lungs out, kicking, biting, throwing stones, hitting, and most of all getting underfoot. They were too small and agile for the startled attackers to stop them, and there were too many of them to catch; when one of the bullies actually managed to grab an urchin, three or four more would mob him, kicking and biting, until he let go.

Nightingale spotted an opening at the same time T'fyrr did; they seized each other's hands, and T'fyrr charged through first, knocking one man aside with a wing, Nightingale hauled along in his wake.

They ran until their sides ached; ran until they could hardly breathe, ran until they were staggering blindly with exhaustion—and did not stop running until they came to Freehold.

CHAPTER EIGHT

"I can't believe you didn't break anything," Nightingale said as she carefully checked every bone in T'fyrr's fragile-appearing wings. She had already checked every inch of his body, from feet to sheath to keel, knowing from her experience with birds that the feathers could hide a number of serious to life-threatening injuries, and that seemingly insignificant tears in the skin could spread under sudden pressure to an unbelievable extent, especially across the breast muscles. Fortunately, his skin proved to be much tougher than the average bird's.

She ached, not only from her own injuries, but from his. *I know every bruise, every sprain, every torn muscle. I feel as if I am inside his body. This never happened with Raven!*

He sighed, and rubbed one elbow. Bruises didn't show on the scaly skin of his lower arms and legs, but there was so little muscle there that the bruises went to the bone. "It feels as if I have broken a hundred bones, but I know that I have not. It will be days before I can fly again."

He did not voice the fear that put into him; the fear of the winged creature left helpless on the ground. He did not have to voice that fear, for she felt it as well.

I was an idiot. I should have taken him seriously. I should have confronted Harperus and demanded some kind of damned Deliambren protection! I should have confronted Harperus and Tyladen and moved into the damned Palace. I was enjoying the anonymity that kept them from manipulating me, and enjoying my notoriety as Lyrebird too much. I was enjoying all the adulation and success I had here in Freehold, too. Now he's grounded and it's all my fault. Guilt made her avoid his eyes, but she could not avoid the emotions coming from him.

She sat back on the bed for a moment, once she had assured herself that she truly did not have any broken bones. She had injuries of her own, of course—a badly bruised shoulder, bruised shins, lumps on her head—

but his injuries were far more numerous than hers. He had shielded both of them with his wings, used the wings as weapons to buffet their attackers, and interposed himself between her and a blow she had not seen aimed at her any number of times.

Well, at least there is a solution to his injuries, if he'll take it. He might be grounded, but not for long.

"T'fyrr, I can—I can heal some of this, if you like," she offered tentatively. "It will still hurt, but I can sing it half-healed today, and do the rest tomorrow." Then she frowned. "I *think* I can," she amended. "I'm not sure if the magic will work on a Haspur, or if it will work the same. It should. I have not healed a nonhuman before, but my teacher Nighthawk has, and she never said anything about the magic working differently for them."

His feathers twitched, and she felt his relief at the idea that she *might* be able to give him enough freedom from pain and damage that he need not be caught on the ground. "Please!" he begged with voice and eyes and clenched talon-hands. "Half-healed will let me fly again!"

"You know how the magic works," she said, and smiled when he shook his head.

He'll find out in a moment.

"No, I don't—" he began, then his eyes widened in wonder. "Oh. Yes, I do. . . ." His voice trailed off, as his eyes sought hers, seeking answers.

They were answers she was not prepared to give him yet—perhaps never. Better that he should never know where that touch of magic and the knowledge of it came from, if there was to be nothing more between them than there had been between her and Raven. "Simply listen for the music and give yourself to it," she said, and placed both her hands atop his hard, sinewy talons. It no longer felt strange to reach for a hand and find something all bone and sinew and covered with the tough, scaly skin of a raptor's feet. Did it still seem strange for him to touch her, and find soft skin over muscle, with five stubby little scales instead of talons?

She gave him no chance to ask all the questions she felt bubbling up inside of him; she did not want to face those questions herself.

The answers, in all probability, would hurt far too much.

Instead, she plunged into the magic that Nighthawk had taught her—the combination of Bardic Magic and Gypsy healing, all bound up in the tonal chanting that suited Nighthawk's strong, harsh voice better than any song. But the Bardic song lay behind the chanting, and for Nightingale the chant turned into something far more musical than Nighthawk ever produced.

The results were the same, though; as she had when she had tried to ease T'fyrr's soul-wounds, she became one with him and his hurts and felt them as clearly as if they were hers. She came between him and the pain, in fact, shielding him from it as he had shielded her from the blows that had injured him.

If I had wings, and I could fly. . . . That was the refrain in many of the songs she and her kind sang to their audiences; now she spread wings of power rather than feathers and muscle, spread them over him and sheltered him beneath them, as he had sheltered her beneath his own. She was once again aware of the spicy scent of his feathers, and the bitter scent beneath it of sheer exhaustion.

With her song and the power in the song, she drove into each injury, speeding the healing that had already begun, strengthening the torn muscles, weaving reinforcement into the sprains, soothing the bruises. In the back of her mind, she reflected that it was too bad in a way that his skin was covered with feathers; nothing she had done would be visible. *On the other hand, injuries will not be obvious, either. He will appear up to full strength, which might mislead other would-be attackers.* She sensed him relaxing as the pain eased, sensed his surprise in the lessening of the pain, sensed him finding the song she chanted under her breath.

But then—

Instead of simply opening himself up to the song as she had asked, *he* began to sing, too.

And the power no longer flowed only from her to him, but came from his hands into hers, as if two great, rushing streams ran side by side, but in opposing directions.

Her shoulder stopped aching and throbbing, as he touched *her* with that brush of power as warm as the caress of a feather and as light. The many points of pain in her skull ebbed, as he brushed the power over them as well.

The quality of the chant changed a little, becoming more musical, with odd tonal qualities, but she was able to follow it effortlessly.

But she almost lost the thread of the chant in her own astonishment when she realized consciously what he had just done, and she felt his amusement and wonder—amusement at *her* surprise, and wonder at the thing that had been born between them.

In the past, anytime she had done this, when she had opened herself to someone, it had been entirely one-sided, as she had learned to her sorrow with handsome Raven. Even when she limited her openness to the minimum required to heal, she had still been open enough to feel the mental anguish that all to often came with injury, and always she had felt the pain itself. Never, ever, had someone *else* returned the gift. Never had someone joined her in the chant, to heal her.

And never had anyone ever opened himself to her heart as she had opened herself to his.

Until T'fyrr.

She *knew* that he read her soul as she had read his, felt the long loneliness, and the resignation deeper than despair and just as sorrowful. Her heart had no more secrets from his, for every wound, every scar, every bruise was laid bare to his raptorial eyes.

She was so surprised that she could not even react by closing herself off again.

She could not read thoughts—but she could read the feelings that came with the thoughts: feelings so mixed she could not have said where his wonder began and his own long loneliness ended. He began to speak aloud, giving her the images, the memories, that were calling up those feelings—and clearly he *knew* what she sensed.

"There are humans who live among the Haspur," he said, softly, as she continued to sing her healing chant, so lost in it now that she could not have stopped if she tried. He fitted the words to the music, and sang them to her as he sang healing into her body as well. "Most of them are as ordinary as bread, but some are granted a rare gift, that of seeing into the Spirit. That is why we call them Haspur Spirit-Brothers, for as often as they use that gift with their fellow humans they also use it with the Haspur, who are their friends and fellow-defenders. Mostly, they provide the simpler gifts: healing of the body as you are doing, ease of the heart in time of trouble. But sometimes, once in a very, very long time, there is need and a compatibility of spirits that binds healer and healed more closely than that. That is when the Spirit-Gift of the Haspur is awakened, and the two become a greater whole than two Spirit-Brothers are singly. They are—"

He sang a long, fluting whistle that somehow melded itself into the healing chant without disturbing it.

"There are no words in the human tongue for this. They are partner-healers, they are wisdom-keepers, they are two souls in two bodies still, but bound together in ways that neither time nor distance can change or sever. Sometimes they are lovers. They are the great treasures of the Haspur. I had not thought to find that potential in myself, though every Haspur at one time aspires to and dreams of such a thing. I would never have dreamed to have found it with you, O Bird of the Night, wild winged singer, dreamer of beauty and gentle healer of hearts—"

There was more, but half of it was in his own language, and at any rate, Nightingale would have lost half of it in her own daze at a single phrase. *Sometimes they are lovers.*

How could—well, she knew *how*, physically they were as compatible as many unlikely human pairings. Now that she had tended his hurts, she knew what was beneath that modesty-wrap he wore, and if he *said* that his people and humans sometimes became lovers, then of course it was possible. But how—

With care, of course, an impudent mental voice chided her. *Those talons could cause a bit of trouble, but on the other hand, you probably weigh more than he does, so—*

Oh, it was a very good thing that neither he nor she could read *thoughts*.

With her mind and body whirling, all unbalanced and giddy, she realized that the chant was nearing its end. She brought it to a close, rounding it in on itself, curling it into repose. And she opened her eyes to find herself curled in his arms, and he in hers, her head pillowed on the soft breast feathers, and his on her unbound hair.

Nor did either of them care to move, for a very long time.

The immediate effect of the healing chant was two-fold: both healer and healed were ravenous afterwards, and exhausted, so weary that even had she been ready to deal with the consequences of what had just happened between them, neither of them would have had the strength.

She had more strength than he for she had more experience at the healing than he. It was not the power itself that came from the healer, only the direction—but as riding a fractious, galloping horse takes strength, so did guiding the power. She had just enough reserves left to go down the stairs, leave a message for Tyladen saying that she was indisposed—which was *no* lie—and order some food brought up. He was asleep when she returned, and only came half-awake when the food arrived, just enough to eat and fall back into sleep. She was not in much better shape; she really didn't remember what she had ordered and hardly recognized it when it arrived. Her head spun in dizzy circles as she got up to put the tray outside the door; she lay back down again beside him and dimmed the light, and that was all she remembered.

But her dreams were wonderful, full of colors she had no names for, sensations of wind against her skin and a feeling of unbearable lightness and joy. She'd had dreams of flying before, every Free Bard did, it seemed, but never like this. This was real flight; the sensation of powerful chest muscles straining great wings against the air to gain height until the earth was little more than a tapestry of green and brown and gray below, then the plummeting dive with wind hard against the face and tearing at the close-folded wings, and the exaltation of the freedom, the freedom. . . .

She woke to find him already awake and watching her, a bemused expression in his eyes.

"Not now—" he said, before she could speak. "Not now. You have never known this was possible. You must think, you must meditate, or you will regret any decision you make in haste."

She nodded; he knew her as well as she knew herself.

Of course he does, said that little, amused voice. *And he knows that the outcome is perfectly certain. He can afford to wait, he knows what you will do, eventually, and he is patient enough to wait for that "eventually" however long it takes.*

"I want to talk to Tyladen," she said, finally. "This—I only have two choices that I can see, after this last attack. I either move to the Palace with you, or I reveal who I really am and get some of that protection these damn Deliambrens were so free in offering."

"My suggestion would be the latter," he replied. "As long as you are openly still Lyrebird, you have an ear in the city that I do not, that no one who is not human would have. You would not be able to discuss things with our friend Father Ruthvere, for instance. But it is your choice."

She nodded thoughtfully, agreeing with him. *He's right. We need that ear inside the Church that Father Ruthvere provides, and he needs the knowledge of the Court that we can give him. Church and Court are wound in an incestuous dance these days, and if anyone is to break the pattern, it will be Father Ruthvere and those who are with him. Moving into his suite would have forced me to make certain decisions anyway, and I'm not sure I want to even think about them much less make them.*

Things were already complicated enough.

It was something of a relief to close herself into the privacy of the bathroom and let the hot water from the wall nozzle run over her, washing away fatigue and letting her empty her mind, as well. She didn't have to guess that he might be feeling as uncertain as she; that was another complication to this situation. It was one thing to imagine finding someone for herself as she sang those love songs of longing and loneliness. It was quite another to find herself presented with a resolution.

And yet, hadn't she wanted someone exactly like this? Well, the old Gypsy proverb advised, "Be careful what you wish for, you might get it." She could not have designed a better partner than T'fyrr, for they were alike enough for joy and different enough for exploration.

And, oh, doesn't that open up a number of possibilities? One can just imagine. . . .

She fiercely shoved that little voice back into its corner. *One thing at a time,* she told it. *We'll take one thing at a time, and the most important comes first. We must deal with the High King and finish the task we have begun, assuming it can be finished.*

T'fyrr was all ready when she emerged, and he had cleaned up the room and put the bed into the wall, too. Perhaps he felt as uncomfortable with that particular piece of furniture so blatantly on display as she was.

Of course he is. He's feeling what I'm feeling, which will ensure that he feels the same! Oh, what a bother! No more polite and discreet lies just to salve his feelings! If we disagree on something, one of us will have to find a way to persuade the other, or the bad feelings will chafe between us until we are half-distracted!

They went downstairs together, to find that they were so early this morning that they were, by the standards of Freehold, still up late. The sun was just rising and the last-shift dance group performing its final number. So Tyladen would still be awake, not a bad thing, since she wanted first to speak with him. She was quite prepared to wake him, if she needed to.

Not that she was sure when he ever slept. The Deliambrens didn't seem to have the same sleep needs as humans did; she thought, perhaps, that he slept in the mid-morning hours, perhaps a little in the afternoon, but never for more than two or three hours at a time.

Of course they don't need to sleep the way we do. They don't have to sleep deeply enough for dreaming. They express their dreams and nightmares in their clothing.

Tyladen *was* still awake, but looked a bit surprised to have both of them strolling into his office together, and at that early hour. Nightingale shut the door firmly and put her back to it as T'fyrr leaned against the wall, giving him the advantage of looking *down* at the Deliambren.

"First of all, Lyrebird was attacked yesterday. She was hurt, and so was I, in trying to help her." His face was without expression, but Nightingale knew that every word was carefully chosen. "You might take note of the bruises, if you should happen to doubt my word."

Nightingale had sent word down at the same time that she had ordered the food that she was indisposed; presumably, Tyladen had found a substitute singer for last night. He just nodded, mobile face solemn for a change. Then again, there wasn't much he could respond to, yet.

And he didn't know that they were together, in more than one sense.

"We have reason to believe that the attack was more of an attempt to gain control over *me* than because she got in the way of some gang or other," T'fyrr continued. "In fact, we believe that the same person who was behind the other two attacks on me here was behind the one on her."

"That makes sense," Tyladen said cautiously, looking from Nightingale's face to T'fyrr's, as if he was trying to put a number of disparate bits of information together and not coming up with much. "Perhaps she ought to quit her position here, then, and move to the Palace? She doesn't precisely need to work here anymore, and surely you have—"

T'fyrr deliberately leaned over and placed both taloned hands on Tyladen's desk, scoring the surface. "Enough of the nonsense, Tyladen! We both know *why* I come here! It's not because I'm savoring the nightlife, nor because I happen to enjoy this lady's playing! We both know that I would *still* have to come here even if the lady moved into my suite at the Palace, so that I could continue to report to you! I'm your little Palace spy, Tyladen, an unpaid spy at that, and it's about time you and Harperus began giving me a bit more protection! And you might as well start offering that same protection—no, *more* protection—to Lyrebird!"

Tyladen didn't bat an eye; he simply put on a skeptical expression and said, "I can't see any good reason why—"

"Because," Nightingale interrupted him, "my name isn't Lyrebird. It's Nightingale—Nightingale of the Free Bards and the Getan Gypsies. And I've been working here on behalf of the Deliambrens *without* any support since I arrived."

For the first time in her life, Nightingale actually saw expressions of shock, dismay and surprise pass across a Deliambren face. And for the first time in her life, she saw one caught at a loss for words. Tyladen sat in his chair with his mouth half open; his lips twitched, but he couldn't seem to get any words out.

It would be funny, if the situation weren't so serious. He looked exactly like a stunned catfish.

Nightingale sat down gracefully. "Now," she said sweetly. "About that protection?"

T'fyrr smiled. "For both of us," he added, coming to stand behind her and putting both his taloned hands on her shoulders.

Tyladen just sat and stared at them both.

They returned to the Palace with a double Mintak guard; twins, or so it was said. They certainly looked like twins, insofar as a human could tell. Since this pair had been known to break up fights with their bare hands and now were armed with very impressive axes in their belts, Nightingale doubted that there would be any more ambushes today.

In fact, their path was remarkably clear of interference. Even peddlers found reasons to take their pushcarts out of the way.

As they walked steadily toward the Palace, her street-children slipped up to her one and two at a time, pretending to beg, but in actuality making certain that *she* was all right and gleefully recounting their own parts in the melee. It made her a little sick to realize that they had seen it as normal, quite in keeping with the life on the streets. Perhaps a bit more fun than most of the violent situations they witnessed or were a part of in the course of a month or so. She slipped each of them an extra couple of pennies for diligence and quick thinking; she would have given them more, but that would leave all of them open to robbery or worse.

No street-urchin dared carry more than a couple of pennies on his person, and very few of them had a safe place to cache money.

I can give them more, later. I can double their "wages." I can see to it that they can come to the kitchen door of Freehold and be fed, and have it taken out of my wages.

When they neared the Palace, T'fyrr took off into the air, much to the astonishment of the passers-by, leaving Nightingale to go on to the Bronze Gate with her double Mintak guard flanking her. Their presence raised an eyebrow from the gate guard, but one of the Mintaks grunted and said to him, "Been some trouble for Freeholders. People roughing up folks as works for us, callin' em Fuzzy-lovers. Boss wants his investment protected."

The gate guard nodded at that and waved her through; the inexplicable had been explained in terms he could understand. Nightingale passed inside and the two Mintaks went back across the street, took up a station in a nearby cafe that catered to the servants of those who came and went through the Bronze Gate, and set out a tiny portable Sires and Barons game between them. They would be there when she came out again, and *might* even hear or be told something useful while they were there.

Now all she had to worry about were the dangers *inside* the Palace. *About which I can do nothing. Hopefully, Tyladen or Harperus has something that can protect me.*

T'fyrr landed beside her in a flurry of wing feathers, as she traversed the stone-paved path between two regimented beds of fragrant flowers. With her practiced eye, she knew by his careful landing that he was still in some pain; his wingbeats were not as deep, and he landed on both feet, rather than one.

The flowers in these formal gardens weren't anything she recognized, but then, the High King's gardeners had access to flowers found nowhere else inside the Twenty Kingdoms, and their breeding programs could make even familiar blooms unrecognizable. She allowed herself to be distracted from her concerns for a moment by their beauty and their perfume, but she couldn't be distracted for long.

Among the major concerns, there were some minor ones. Nothing that really mattered in either the long or the short run, but somehow they nagged at her.

One was strictly personal, and a cause for some embarrassment. Would there be gossip about them? It was certainly possible. It would be the second time that T'fyrr had remained out of the Palace all night, and both times (if anyone was keeping track) he had been at Freehold, in her room. She found herself blushing at the notion of what people might be thinking, which rather surprised her. After all, hadn't she been willing to move into his suite and live there?

But that was different. . . .

Oh, certainly. With a preadolescent boy to act as chaperon, it was different. Indeed. She blushed even more.

This is ridiculous! I'm a Gypsy, a Free Bard; people have been saying things about me for as long as I've been alive, and I didn't care! I laughed at them!

She managed to get her blushes under control before they reached their goal, by dint of much self-scolding. Which, in itself, was ridiculous. . . .

But when they arrived at the Palace itself and entered the huge, self-opening doors, they found the place as chaotic as an overturned beehive.

The great hall at the main doors was full of courtiers and servants and everyone in between, all of them chattering, and all of them upset. People of all stations were standing together in tight little groups, rigid with apprehension, or rushing about—apparently with no clear destination in mind. Pages ran hither and yon on urgent errands, their eyes wide and faces pale. All that Nightingale could pick up was fear; fear and excitement, and all that those emotions engendered.

What's been happening? She and T'fyrr stood just inside the door, and no one noticed them, which in itself was nothing short of astonishing.

T'fyrr solved the entire question by reaching out and intercepting one of the page boys as he ran past. The boy felt the talons close on his shoulder and stopped dead, with a little squeak of surprise.

"*What* is going on here?" T'fyrr rumbled down at his captive. "What has happened since yesterday? Why is there all this commotion?"

The page stared at him with wide blue eyes and stuffed his fist into his mouth as he blinked up at them. He wasn't very old, no more than seven or eight—and very sheltered. One of Nightingale's street-urchins would have replied already and been well on his way. T'fyrr waited patiently. Finally the boy got up enough courage to speak.

"It's the D-deliambren, S-sire!" he stammered, then seemed to get stuck, staring up into the Haspur's raptorial eyes exactly like a mouse waiting for the hawk to strike.

"What about the Deliambren?" T'fyrr asked with a little less patience. "I haven't been here, I've just come in. What *about* the Deliambren?"

"H-he's—he's been attacked!" the boy blurted. "He's hurt, they say badly, they say someone tried to kill him!" Then as T'fyrr's grip loosened with shock, the page pulled away and ran off again.

T'fyrr's shock didn't last past that moment; he knew where Harperus' suite was, and may the Lady help anyone who got between him and his destination. He headed off in that direction with a purposeful stride that Nightingale had to match by running. Her mind flitted from thought to thought, infected a little by all the fear around her. *Attacked? By who? Is he really hurt badly? Is he—oh dear Lady, not dead, surely!* The idea of Old Owl dead—no, it was not to be thought of, surely not he, not with all of his Deliambren devices to protect him? He had outlived her grandfather with no sign of old age, how *could* he be dead?

But how could he have been attacked? How could anyone have gotten in to him, past his devices, to attack him?

They ran past rank after rank of statuary, taking the quickest path to the Deliambren suite. Past animals, past famous generals, past mermaids—up the stairs to the fourth floor and past guildsmen, past famous Bards, past farmers—*oh dear, there is one with his favorite piggy at his feet!* she thought distractedly—past the Allies of the Twenty Kingdoms—

And there was the door to Harperus' suite, *now* guarded by a pair of the King's personal bodyguards, who let T'fyrr and herself past without so much as a challenge. T'fyrr flung himself inside immediately. But she stopped at the door and caught the attention of one of the guards, one she thought she recognized from the King's suite. "What happened?" she asked shortly.

He looked down into her eyes, his own as flat and expressionless as blued steel. Finally he opened his thin, grim lips and answered.

"Someone broke in here last night while Envoy Harperus was with the High King. They—there was more than one—were ransacking the suite when the Envoy came in and found them still there. His devices had stunned and captured one of them, and the others were trying to get him free. When the Envoy surprised them, they clubbed him and fled. The Envoy is still unconscious. The High King has put his own personal servants in place here, since the Envoy's assigned servants have disappeared and might even have been in collusion with his attackers."

"We have the one the device caught in custody," the other guard said at last. "The envoy regained consciousness long enough to tell us what had happened, how to free the man, and to ask for Sire T'fyrr, and then collapsed again."

She might have thought she was imagining a faint tone of disapproval that T'fyrr had not been here when Harperus asked for him, except that she sensed the disapproval as well as heard it. She simply nodded with dignity, and said, "Sire T'fyrr and I were attacked by nine armed men in the city last night. We were some time in being tended to and unable to send word to the Palace. It seems that someone would like to harm the High King's foreign allies."

Then she passed on through the doors into the Deliambren suite, knowing that the bodyguards were far more than mere soldiers, and knowing that what she had just said would be recounted, with exact tone and inflection, to the High King's Spymaster. And whether that mysterious gentleman served Theovere only, or served some of the Advisors as well, there would be no doubt that she and T'fyrr were well aware of *what* their attackers were, if not who.

It was a risk to reveal that, but it was an equal risk to seem unaware of their situation. Perhaps this would make their enemy a bit more wary.

But for right now, she was grimly certain that Harperus had better have someone at his side who was his friend, guarding him. The King's bodyguards might help so long as whoever was after Harperus tried to pass the doors, but they wouldn't be of much help if an attacker were one of the King's servants, or came in by some other means.

The suite didn't look a great deal different from theirs, except in one small detail. Harperus had none of the "Deliambren sculptures" around the suite. That might explain why Tyladen didn't know about the attack. Yet.

Nightingale passed through the reception room and into Harperus' bedroom, where there were two more guards at the door. T'fyrr had already settled at Harperus' bedside, displacing a servant; Nightingale bit her lip, then reached out to touch the Deliambren's bruised brow and hummed a fragment of the healing chant under her breath.

But she emerged almost immediately from her brief trance with a feeling of profound relief. "He'll be all right," she told T'fyrr, whose tense shoulders and twitching tail signaled his own worry and fear. "He's healing himself; he doesn't even need me to do anything. That is why he went unconscious again. He has a concussion, but when he wakes it will have been taken care of. I'm going to your suite to get something; I'll be right back."

T'fyrr started up at that, and she knew what must be in his mind. "If anyone got into your suite last night, it won't matter," she pointed out. "Whoever was behind this was probably behind the attack on us, and he *knows* where we were. After Harperus was attacked, the King's men probably checked all the suites to make sure no one else was hurt, so even if the attackers got into yours, Nob is surely all right."

He sank back down on his stool, and nodded. "Nob is all that I care about," he said, a bit hoarsely. "Anything else can be replaced, and most of it is not mine, anyway. Things can be restored; people cannot."

She hurried out, running as soon as she reached the hallways, picking up her skirts like a child so that she could run the faster.

Despite what she had told him to reassure him—*thank the Lady we can't read thoughts!*—she was by no means sure that she would find either the suite or Nob intact. In the excitement, the guards might *not* have thought to check. Nob could be lying with his skull cracked in the bathroom of the suite or in his own room even now.

But as she pushed the door open, Nob came flying out of the bedroom with a cry of relief to see her, and the room seemed intact.

"T'fyrr is all right," she said, and gave him the short version of the attack in the streets—and then, for the benefit of Tyladen's listening devices, a short story of the attack on Harperus. Nob had known that there had been an attack on *someone*, for guards had come checking the other suites as she had suspected they might, but he had known nothing more than that one of the envoys had been hurt. He hadn't known which one, and he'd been afraid to leave the suite to find out. He hadn't known what to do; his training in etiquette hadn't covered this sort of situation, and he was afraid to act without orders.

But now that T'fyrr was back he had someone to give him orders, which put *his* world back in place again. Nightingale gave him the first of those orders, on behalf of his master.

"Have someone bring T'fyrr his breakfast in Harperus' suite," she said, "then you bring him fresh clothing. He'll want you to stand guard over Harperus while he uses the envoy's bathroom. He still hasn't had much of a chance to get completely clean after those bravos attacked us."

Nob nodded; his eyes were full of questions, but he was too well-trained to ask them. Nightingale was not going to say anything; it wasn't her place. Whatever T'fyrr wanted him to know, T'fyrr would tell him.

"I will perform for the High King, as usual," she told the boy. "We will hope he will find me a satisfactory substitute. I'll be going there as soon as I get my harp in tune."

As soon as Nob was out of the room, she locked the door and gave a much more detailed accounting of everything for the sake of the listening devices. "That is all we know now," she said. "I presume we will find out more when Harperus awakens. In the meantime—"

She stopped herself; after all, what could she suggest that was of any real value? "In the meantime, I will substitute for T'fyrr with the High King, unless I receive orders from the King to the contrary. I will not be back to Freehold for the next day or so."

As she took her harp in its case off her back—she was so used to the weight that she hadn't really noticed it, even when she'd run to the suite—she tried to calm herself. She would not be able to call the magic if she was too tense to hear its melody above her own.

The trouble was that this second attack pointed all too clearly to an enemy within the highest ranks, an enemy who had at least some inkling that she, Harperus, and T'fyrr were all working together, presumably to bring about changes in the King that this enemy did not want to see occur.

And depending on *how* high that enemy was—

We are already marked. We could be doomed.

And with that cheerful thought in mind, she passed out of the doors and into the hall, walking swiftly on her way to entertain the King.

She and T'fyrr sat beside Harperus turn and turn about; sometimes they practiced their music, softly, but without the addition of the magic. Their only connection to the world outside the suite was Nob. She worried, briefly, about the Mintaks she had left. Presumably someone from Freehold would send for the twins—

But in case Tyladen didn't think of it, she finally sent Nob down to the Bronze Gate with a note for them, letting them know what had happened and that she would not be coming out today. If they were thorough, they would probably wait to see if this was a ruse, and when she didn't show up, return to Freehold on their own. Tyladen could confirm her note to them then. At any rate, they would have passed a fairly pleasant morning and afternoon in congenial surroundings paid for by Tyladen.

There were other things she would *like* to see him pay for, but she was unlikely to see *that* happen in her lifetime.

Damned Deliambrens, interfering in our lives and playing at games with us, never thinking there might be any real danger involved—after all, we're all backward barbarians, and how could we be a danger to anyone. . . .

Then the two of them watched over their friend with care and concern, thinking no more of the outside world, until the outside world intruded on them, in the form of the King's Physician.

He did not deign to explain himself to them, nor did he pay any particular attention to them. He simply breezed past the guards and into Harperus' bedchamber, ignoring them both. While this was rude, it was not entirely unexpected, at least to Nightingale. While T'fyrr theoretically outranked a mere physician, it was only in theory, and there wasn't much T'fyrr could do if this man chose to ignore his rank and even his presence just because he was not human.

But the moment he ceased doing a simple physical examination and opened up the bag of instruments he brought, he found T'fyrr's talons clamped around his wrist.

He had reached out so quickly that Nightingale did not even see him move, only that his talons were suddenly locked around the physician's wrist.

He told me once that a Haspur can kill a deer with his hands, and a buffalo with his feet. I hope this physician cooperates. He will find it difficult to practice medicine with a broken wrist.

"What do you think you are doing?" the Haspur snarled, his beak parted in threat.

Startled, the human glanced around for help from the guards. But the guards were not disposed to interfere, at least not yet. T'fyrr hadn't done anything contrary to their orders, and Nightingale doubted that they had any idea just how much pressure those hand-claws could exert.

And if they did, they still might not interfere.

The man made an abortive move to free his wrist and discovered just how strong a Haspur's grip was. Nightingale stayed out of the way and in the background. The less she drew attention to herself, the better. Too many people already had her marked as it was; she didn't need to add the physician to the list.

Finally the man decided that answering was better than standing there with his wrist in the grip of a giant predator—although he tried to look as important as possible. That was a bit difficult, given that he was also wincing from the pain of T'fyrr's grip.

"I am going to wake him," the physician said arrogantly.

Oh, truly? Then he is more of a fool than I took him for! Nightingale thought in surprise. If Harperus' trance had not been self-induced, it *would* have been very serious indeed. It might have been dangerous to Harperus to wake him—and it might have been impossible.

And even though the trance *was* self-induced, and therefore it was unlikely the physician could break down the wall of Harperus' will, trying to wake him could easily interfere with the self-healing process.

"And just how much do you know about the Deliambrens?" T'fyrr all but purred, dangerously. "Have you studied Deliambren head injuries? Have you ever had a Deliambren patient before?"

"Well, no, but—" the man stuttered, surprised into telling the truth. He had probably never had anyone challenge his expertise before.

"Have you ever had *any* nonhuman as a patient?" T'fyrr persisted, his eyes narrowing, his voice dropping another half-octave so that the purr became a growl. "Have you even studied nonhuman injuries?"

The man blanched and tried to bluff. "No, but that hardly matters whe— *ouch!*" T'fyrr had tightened his talons on the man's wrist. Nightingale winced. Surely the bones were grinding together by now.

"Why then is it so imperative that Lord Harperus be wakened?" T'fyrr asked, "when you know that you know nothing of how his body functions, and in waking him you might kill him? Is this on the orders of the King?" He pulled the man a little closer to him, effortlessly, and looked down at him with his beak no more than a few inches from the physician's face.

"It—no—*ow!*—it's because of the escape, you fool!" The physician was dead-white now, with anger as much with fear, although fear was swiftly gaining the upper hand.

After all, there is a beak fully capable of biting through his spine less than a hand's-breadth from his nose.

T'fyrr shook the wrist he held, ever so slightly. "What escape?" he asked urgently, and Nightingale felt the hair on the back of her neck rise, both in reaction to his dangerously icy tone and in premonition. Her stomach knotted with T'fyrr's, both of them with chills of fear running down their backs.

"The man—the man who was caught here," the physician stammered, unable to look away from T'fyrr's eyes. "He escaped early this evening. We need to talk to the Envoy to discover if there was anyone he recognized among the rest of his attackers. We need to find more of the perpetrators before they have a chance to get away."

"*What?*" T'fyrr dropped the man's wrist; the physician did not even stop to gather up his instruments. He fled the suite, leaving only T'fyrr and the guards. T'fyrr turned toward the guard nearest him, who shrugged.

"I hadn't heard anything, Sire," the man said. "We've been here as long as you have. I can send to find out, though."

"Do that," T'fyrr ordered brusquely. "If the man really did escape, there are now at least three people who need to see that Lord Harperus does not get a chance to identify them, all loose in this Palace. Now we don't know who any of them are; they could be among the very servants sent here to serve Lord Harperus. You might consider that when you send your message."

The guard's grim face grew a bit grimmer, and he himself disappeared for a moment or two, leaving his fellow twice as vigilant. When he returned, it was with his own Captain striding by his side. Nightingale recognized the Captain from the High King's suite; he was one of the ones usually close at Theovere's side.

"I understand you have not heard the latest of our incidents, Sire T'fyrr," the Captain said with careful courtesy. "I can tell it to you in brief: the Palace does not normally hold prisoners. Normally we send them elsewhere, within the city, which has better gaols than we. This time, however, it was deemed better to keep the man here, in one of the storage rooms in the cellars, with a guard on his door. Not," he added, with a wry lift of an eyebrow, "one of *us*. This was merely a Palace guard, not one of the Elite."

T'fyrr nodded, and the Captain went on. "I am told that at about dinner time, according to the guard left on duty, a woman appeared with whom several of the guards were familiar, he among them. She is ostensibly a maid here, and yet no one will admit now to having her in their service. At any rate, there was supposedly a good reason for her to be in the storage area, and when she saw the guard who knew her, she flirted with him as she has often done in the past. He allowed his caution to slip; she was only a woman after all, and alone."

"She then incapacitated the guard and let the prisoner escape," T'fyrr concluded, seeing the obvious direction the tale was heading.

"She didn't bloody incapacitate him; she knocked him cold with a single punch!" the Captain corrected bitterly. "A single woman, no taller than his chin! It's unnatural! I've never seen nor heard of the like, for a woman half a man's size to take him down with one blow, even if he didn't expect it!"

Nightingale had, of course, but she kept her peace. There was no point in getting suspicion pointed in her own direction. The regular guards by now were smarting with the disgrace; they would be looking for an easy suspect, and she was in no mood to provide them with one. It would be all too easy for someone to claim that *she* had somehow slipped down to the cellar, perhaps during one of the brief times she had gone to fetch something for T'fyrr from his suite.

Especially since she *had* been seen in the Lower Kitchen and could have been mistaken for a maid, with a long stretch of the imagination. There were cooks and the like who would be perfectly able to identify her as "Tanager," and for a noble, there wasn't a great deal of difference between a "maid" and a "street-musician."

"So the man is gone, and we have no suspects whatsoever." T'fyrr clacked his beak with anger. "This is not cheerful news, Captain."

"Do tell," the man retorted heatedly. "At the moment our best hope is that Lord Harperus regains consciousness and can tell us what he saw. That is probably why the physician was sent—I expect it was by the Captain of the Watch." The Captain's tone turned condescending. "I'm afraid that he hasn't had much experience with injuries. I am certain he thought a head injury was no more serious than a drunken stupor and could be dealt with in much the same way."

His tone implied that the Watch Captain had no combat experience, which was probably true—and the scars on his own face and hands spoke volumes for *his* expertise.

"So your best hope is to keep him *safe*." T'fyrr turned the full force of his gaze on the Captain. "I am the nearest you have to an expert on Deliambren medicine—although, if you want a real expert, there is a Deliambren running a tavern in the city, a place called Freehold. His name is Tyladen. He probably has a great deal more knowledge than I."

"I know the place," the captain replied. "Many of my men have been there, now and again, and they speak highly of the place. I've been there myself."

For entertainment? Not primarily, I warrant. Probably to see if it was a hotbed of Fuzzy subversion. But it wasn't, and so he permits his men to visit it recreationally.

"Tyladen of Freehold might be persuaded to come attend to his fellow countryman's needs," T'fyrr said, and Nightingale sensed his fragment of ironic pleasure at the notion that Tyladen just might be forced to *do* something besides sit in his office like a spider in a web, collecting information at no cost or danger to himself. She was beginning to have a very poor opinion of Tyladen's courage, and she knew T'fyrr shared it. "Other than Tyladen, I am your nearest source, and I assure you, it would be *much* better to wait until Lord Harperus wakes of his own accord. It could be dangerous to try to bring him to consciousness at this point."

The Captain acknowledged T'fyrr's expertise with an unwilling nod. "I'll have that noted, Sire T'fyrr," he added politely. "Now, by your leave, I'll take mine."

T'fyrr bowed slightly, and the Captain walked out, at a slightly faster pace than he'd arrived. T'fyrr had impressed him with a level head and good sense, at any rate.

They both returned to their seats beside Harperus' bed. Nob had long since closed the curtains against the night and lit a lamp or two, turning them low. Most of the room was in shadow; the rest in half-light. Curtains pulled halfway around the bed to keep the light from disturbing the occupant left the bed itself in deep shadows, in which Harperus' white hair gleamed softly against the pillow.

The Haspur turned to Nightingale and touched her hand, as lightly as a puff of down, with the talon that had just come close to crushing the wrist of the interfering physician. She smiled tremulously at him.

"When do you think he'll wake?" he asked her in a tense whisper.

She closed her eyes and again dropped briefly into the healing spell with three key notes of the chant. The song Harperus wove about himself was coming to a close, winding in and around itself the way that all Deliambren music ended, in a reprise of the beginning, a serpent swallowing its own tail. "Soon, very soon," she said, opening her eyes again. "Within an hour or two at the very most, I suspect."

T'fyrr sighed with relief. "It cannot be too soon for me."

"Nor for me," she replied. "I still need to invoke healing on you again—"

"And I on you," he interrupted, and a gentle warmth washed over her as he touched the back of her hand again. "But we may be sitting here guarding Harperus until—"

"Until what?" came a weak voice from the shadows. "Until the moon turns blue? Until the Second Cataclysm?"

"Until you wake, old fool!" T'fyrr said, turning quickly toward the head of the bed. "By the winds, you had us worried!"

"Not half so much as I worried myself," Harperus replied with a groan and a sigh as he tried to sit up. "I'm too old to be practicing self-healing. It is a bad habit to get into, relying on self-healing too much."

"It is a worse habit to put yourself in situations where you *need* to practice it," Nightingale scolded. By now the guards just outside the bed-chamber had heard the third voice, and one had come to investigate. He had come in at least twice so far today, fooled by T'fyrr's mimicking ability while they were practicing their music.

"Lord Harperus is awake and ready to speak," T'fyrr told him, as the man opened his mouth to ask what was going on. "While you are notifying those in authority, you ought to send a servant to bring some food for Lord Harperus—"

"Light food," Nightingale interrupted. "Suitable for an invalid. *And make sure it is tested before you serve it to him.* Remember, we do not know who attacked him, or what positions his attackers hold. They *could* work in the kitchen."

"Oh, not tea and toast!" Harperus complained, but subsided at her glare, sinking into the shadows of the bed. "Well, all right. I suppose you know best, Nightingale, you *are* healer-trained. What *are* you doing here, anyway? I thought you wouldn't promise to come here!"

"I wouldn't," she said, tartly, in the Gypsy tongue. "And *this* is the reason why! I've been here all along; I'm T'fyrr's accompanist. I just didn't want you delightful people to endanger my safety by telling everyone on the planet that I was your agent. None of you Deliambrens have an ounce of sense among you when it comes to keeping secrets."

The Deliambren sighed and lifted a hand to rub his head. He replied to her in the same language. "For once, I have to agree that you were probably right. But in our own defense, Nightingale, we never thought that anyone would resort to a direct attack."

"A direct attack?" T'fyrr said sharply. "There have been *three* thus far, *old friend*, one on me alone and one on Nightingale yesterday that I became involved in! That is why we were not here last night!"

"What? What?" Harperus sat up abruptly—too abruptly, for he sank back down again, holding his hand to his head. "Does Tyladen—"

"Tyladen knows all about it, since we confronted him about it this morning," Nightingale replied glad that they had all switched to the Gypsy language, though she had not been aware that T'fyrr knew it. *Then again, with all the Gypsy songs he learned and has been learning, I suppose he would have had to. And I know Harperus has some sort of machine that puts languages into one's head.* "And since I spent the better part of an hour reciting what happened to *you* at those listening devices in T'fyrr's room, he knows about what happened to you, too."

"Whether or not he can be persuaded to come out of the safety of Freehold to do anything to help you is another question altogether," T'fyrr added, and clacked his beak. "And this open chattering is another reason why Nightingale and I have been reluctant to work with you—you may *hope* that there is no listening post in the walls, and that no one else here knows this language, but I would not hope for it very hard! This is the Palace after all, and I would wager that the King's Spymaster has a man in every room, and an expert in every tongue on Alanda!"

Oh, well said, my love! she applauded mentally. *It isn't likely that anyone within listening distance actually does know the Gypsy tongue, but they could very easily find someone to listen, now that they know we're likely to use it among ourselves. Since I am a Gypsy, it is logical to assume that we are using that language.*

Harperus shrank down into his pillows. "I am rebuked," he said in a small voice. "Justly rebuked. And I apologize for all that has happened so far."

"Cease apologizing and start thinking how you can protect us," Nightingale replied, switching back to the common tongue. "That will be apology enough."

At that moment, both Harperus' food and the Captain of the Elite Bodyguards arrived, and Nightingale and T'fyrr got out of the way.

"Do you think we need to spend the night here?" she asked him in an undertone.

He shook his head. "There is no point in trying to silence him now," the Haspur replied. "What would be the point? If he saw anyone he knows, he'll tell the Captain. I think we can return to the suite and get some rest of our own."

She licked her lips nervously. "I wonder," she said, tentatively, "if we might leave Nob here to take care of him? They've replaced all his servants, and I'd like someone here tonight we can trust."

He blinked at her, and she sensed his speculation and growing excitement as he realized that they would be alone in the suite if they left Nob here. He was probably wondering if she meant what he thought she did.

Well, I'm wondering if I really mean what I think I do. . . .

"I believe that would be a good idea," he replied. He beckoned to Nob, who was sitting in a chair in the corner, pretending to read.

"I'd like you to stay here with Lord Harperus tonight until we can bring him a body-servant that we know can be trusted tomorrow," T'fyrr told the boy soberly.

Nob glowed with the pleasure at the implied trust. "Yes, Sire!" he said eagerly. "I'd be happy to, Sire!"

"We're relying on you, Nob," T'fyrr added. "There isn't anyone else in the Palace I trust as much as you. We're leaving his safety in your hands. I must count on you to be clever and cautious. Test his food before he eats it—watch anyone who comes in that is not one of the Royal Elite Bodyguards. And if anything seems amiss, do *not* confront the person yourself, go get the Bodyguards."

The boy sobered, but continued to glow. "You can count on me, Sire T'fyrr," he replied fervently. "I won't fail your trust."

T'fyrr parted his beak in a smile. "Thank you, Nob." He waited until the Captain had finished questioning the Deliambren, then brought the boy over to Harperus' bedside.

"Well, that was a bit of bad news and good," Harperus said as the Captain left. The bed-curtains had been drawn back, and the bruise on Harperus' forehead stood out in vivid ugliness. "The bad news being that my prisoner escaped, the good that I knew one of the others by name—he was a common guard I'd had to complain about to his superior. He's likely still on duty, or at least in the Palace garrison; probably doesn't know I have a damned good memory for names and faces. They'll have him in a *real* gaol within the hour."

"We're leaving Nob with you for the night," T'fyrr told him, resting one hand on the boy's shoulder as Nob stood straight and tried desperately to look older than his years. "He's the only one we trust to see to you until we can get Tyladen to send someone from Freehold that we can rely on."

"Whatever you need, my lord, I'll take care of," the boy replied earnestly. "Just ask! I can do whatever you need to have done."

Harperus looked sharply from T'fyrr to Nightingale and back again, but said nothing except, "That will be welcome indeed; I know what a good body-servant Nob is. I have seen his work in your suite, T'fyrr. I appreciate it very much, both that you, T'fyrr, are willing to do without his service for one night, and that you, Nob, are willing to put in the extra hours and the effort to help me."

Now the boy blushed and dropped his gaze, nearly bursting with pride.

"We'll leave you for now," T'fyrr said gravely, his voice giving no hint of anything but weariness and concern for Harperus. "Don't overwork Nob, Old Owl."

Harperus smiled, winked, and waved them both off, then turned to Nob with instructions for drawing him a bath. T'fyrr took Nightingale's hand in his own, and the two of them left the suite together.

He didn't seem inclined to drop her hand when they entered the hall, and she didn't withdraw hers. In spite of worry, the reminders of yesterday's attack in the form of distant aches, and the deeply lurking fear the attack on Harperus had left with her, she was happier than she had been since she was a child.

In fact, the only other time she recalled being this happy was when she had first learned to invoke the Bardic Magic. *That was—oh, too many weary years ago, when the world was all new and shining, all music was a delight, and every day brought only new adventures. The world is new again, all music is pleasure, and there are more possibilities in each new day than I can count. . . .*

She knew what she was doing—

Oh, do I?

Well, she knew what she was doing, but the consequences? Did she know that as well? Could she even *guess* at the consequences?

They passed through the statue-lined hallways in silence and met no one. It was the dinner hour; most of those who lived on this floor were in the Great Hall dining in the presence of the High King and his Advisors. Perhaps by now the word that Harperus had identified another of his attackers had made its way to the Hall. Perhaps it had not. No one would know until tomorrow that she had stayed in T'fyrr's suite.

But once again, she blushed. She did not want his name and hers in the mouths of these idle courtiers, who would speculate and gossip maliciously just out of sheer boredom. Some would use the gossip to further damage their cause with the High King. Others would use it to create whatever damage they could elsewhere.

There were Church laws about the congress of humans and those who were not—based on Holy Writ forbidding the congress of humans and demons.

Only now was she recalling those strictures; only now that there was a moment of leisure was she able to think of them. Her earlier embarrassment had probably been because, in the back of her mind, she knew that there could be trouble over this.

Oh, it was just because I knew there would be gossip, hurtful gossip. And that someone in this vast hulk would use that gossip to cause trouble for us.

"I doubt that anyone will believe that you and I are partnering," he murmured quietly, for her ears alone. Once again, he had guessed what she was thinking from the emotions her thoughts engendered. "Most of these folk hawk for game in the game preserve, you know. Most have falcons and other raptors, and know something about them. How do you tell a male raptor from a female?"

"By the size, usually," she replied vaguely, unable to guess what his meaning was. Then it occurred to her, and she bit her lips to cover a giggle. "Oh—oh, of course! You *can't* tell a male from a female by sight, unless they have different feather-colorations. The don't have—what you have!"

"Precisely," T'fyrr said, dryly humorous. "Only Nob knows that I am not like a hawk in that respect, and he will take that secret to his grave if I ask it of him. The rest assume I am as externally sexless as a saint's statue. I have heard as much, through Nob. He is very good at listening and reporting what he has heard, and no one pays any attention to the pages."

So, he had discovered that for himself, had he? It was an echo of her own observation, that no one ever paid any attention to the children. Once again, their minds ran on parallel tracks!

She squeezed his hand by way of reply, and he squeezed hers in return, just as they reached the door of his suite—which now also had a pair of the Royal Bodyguards standing watch outside. T'fyrr bid them both a grave goodnight, and they returned his salutation.

When they closed the door of the suite behind them and locked it, T'fyrr paused and looked around the room. Someone had already been here, leaving the lamps lit and food in covered dishes on the sideboard. That was probably standing orders, since he had mentioned more than once that he was not welcome to dine in the Great Hall. She wondered for a moment what he was frowning at, until she saw his eyes resting on each of the "sculptures" in turn.

"Have you any idea how sensitive those are?" he asked her quietly. "Could they hear into the next room, do you think?"

She had to shake her head. "I haven't a clue," she admitted.

"Well, then since I do not believe that Tyladen is entitled to *any* vestige of my private life, and since I believe him to be as enthusiastic a voyeur as he is a coward, I think that for one night there will be *no* listening." He took each of the "sculptures" in turn and buried it under a pile of pillows and cushions thieved from the furniture.

"There," he said with satisfaction. "That should take care of that!"

He turned to her and held out his hand again. She took it, the dry, hard skin feeling warmer than usual beneath her hand. "I would like a bath," he said. "Would you?"

She nodded, unable to actually say anything.

"I do warn you," he continued, "I look altogether miserable when wet. If your romantic inclinations survive the sight of me with my feathers plastered to my skin, they will survive anything."

She smiled, suddenly shy. "I suspect they will survive," she said in a low voice. "Yours may not survive seeing me without a beautiful costume to make up for my otherwise—"

He put a talon across her lips and led her into the bathroom, where they discovered that romance survives a great many trials, and thrives on laughter.

CHAPTER NINE

Harperus was still bedridden, many days later; T'fyrr had come to make one of his morning visits.

He had not been the only visitor, but Harperus' second guest had come as the bearer of bad tidings.

The Captain of the Bodyguards left them after delivering his unwelcome news, and if a man's retreating back could signal chagrin, profound embarrassment, and disgust with a situation, his did.

It well should have.

"I cannot *believe* this!" T'fyrr exploded, once the Captain was out of the suite and out of earshot. Harperus shrugged, philosophically, from the shelter of his huge bed. The bruise on his forehead had faded to an unpleasant pale green and brown, and on the whole he was doing well. But the effects of the self-healing trance—and the exhaustion of handling what had probably been a cracked skull as well as a concussion—were longer-lasting than either of them had anticipated.

"I had actually expected something like this," the Deliambren said with a sigh. "I didn't want to say anything, lest I be seen to imply that Theovere's people are less than competent, but I was holding my breath over it. If a man can be spirited away from a locked and guarded room in the Palace, surely the city gaols are no more secure."

T'fyrr only snarled, and his talons scraped across the floor as he flexed his feet angrily.

No sooner had the man Harperus identified been arrested, taken into custody, and turned over to a city gaol, than he was free again. This time it was nothing so obvious as a guard being seduced. No, the man escaped from a locked and barred cell, and a lace handkerchief had been left in his place.

It seemed that their mysterious female adversary was not above taunting them.

Damn her. Whoever she is. She *had* to be someone either in high Court circles herself, or with connections there. There was no other way that she could have known that the man had been arrested, much less that he had been taken to a particular city gaol. There were *three* main gaols, after all, and a dozen lesser ones, never mind the many Church gaols; he could have been in any of them.

"And the King has not called for you once since my attack." Harperus pursed his lips unhappily. "He was displeased by Nightingale? Or is he displeased with your performances?"

"Not at all," T'fyrr replied bitterly. "He made a point of thanking her for coming the day after you were attacked. No, the reason is that he has a new toy to intrigue him; I am no longer a novelty. I have been subverted, it seems, by my good friend Lord Atrovel."

Harperus raised an eyebrow. "I had heard nothing of this," he said. "What new toy? And I thought Lord Atrovel liked you!"

T'fyrr sighed and flexed his feet again. "He does—but he cannot resist a challenge, and the head of the Manufactory Guild set him one. Do you recall that box of yours that plays music? The one that Theovere has hinted he would like?"

"The one that we will not give him because taking it apart would give these people too many secrets we do not want them to have?" Harperus responded. "Only too well. Why? What of it?"

"That is what Lord Atrovel was challenged to reproduce," T'fyrr told his friend sourly. "And he did it, too."

As Harperus' eyebrows shot toward his hairline, T'fyrr amended the statement. "It is *not* a recording device, nor is it small enough to sit on a table. It would fill—oh, a quarter of the room here. It is entirely mechanical, mostly of clockwork so far as I can tell, entirely human-made, and requires a page to push pedals with his feet, around and around, to power it." He brooded on his mechanical rival. "I suppose it is a kind of superior music-box. It has more than one instrument though, and three puppets to simulate playing them. There is an enameled bird—*much* prettier than I—that 'sings' the tunes, accompanied by a puppet harpist, flute player, and a puppet that plays an instrument made of tuned bells. It is all instrumental, of course—which means no awkward lyrics to remind Theovere of much of anything."

"You've seen it, then?" Harperus asked.

"How not? It was presented in open Court two days after your injury, with more ceremony than you made with me." T'fyrr stopped flexing his feet; he was cutting gouges in the floor. "It plays exactly one hundred of Theovere's favorite songs, which he can select at will."

Harperus looked impressed in spite of himself. "I had not thought they had that much ability."

T'fyrr only ground his beak. "It was pointedly said during the presentation that the device will always play exactly whatever song is desired, and play it in precisely the same way, every single time. This, I suppose, to contrast it with me, who may not cooperate in the choice of music, who sometimes sings things that make Theovere uncomfortable, and who never sings the same song in the same way twice in a row."

Harperus pondered the implications of that. "Theovere may be tiring of the novelty of working against his Advisors; he may be recalling that responsibility is work."

"And he may be weary of hearing me sing about those who take their responsibilities seriously," T'fyrr sighed. "I did not want to tell you about this, but since Theovere still seems enamored with his toy, I am afraid that I have been supplanted for the foreseeable future. I have not precisely been demoted from my rank, but I am no longer a novelty even with Nightingale to accompany me. I have not been called for in more than a week."

Harperus rubbed his temple for a moment, his face creased with worry.

"I am not certain that I care for the timing of all this. Within a day of the attacks on both of us, the Manufactory Guild presents Theovere with a new toy? Does that indicate anything rather nasty to you?"

"That they thought either one or both of us might be removed from play and had their own distraction ready?" T'fyrr countered. "Of course it occurred to me. It *could* simply be good timing on their part, however—or they could have been holding this toy back, waiting for the best opportunity to present it. There is no point in assuming a conspiracy—but there is no point in discounting one, either. I wish that *you* were in place to collect Court gossip. It would be nice to know one way or another."

Harperus picked fretfully at the comforter covering his body. "And here I am, incapacitated. Trust me, Tyladen is doing all he can; he has responsibilities you are not aware of. He is not a coward, he simply cannot do his job and mine as well."

"I will believe it if you say it," T'fyrr told him finally. "Though I doubt you would get Nightingale to believe it; she is not terribly fond of Tyladen and has called him a spider sitting snug in a safe web more than once. I am not sure she cares for Deliambrens at all, right now; Tyladen hasn't done much about the troubles in Lyonarie, either. I have more bad news from outside the Palace, I am afraid. There is more unrest in the city. The situation is deteriorating for nonhumans: more beatings, slogans written on the walls of nonhuman homes and businesses, vandalism, gang ambushes outside Freehold."

"More attacks?" Harperus started to get up, and fell back against his pillows again, turning a stark white. *"Damn!"* he swore, with uncharacteristic vehemence. "Why must I be confined to my bed at a time like this?"

T'fyrr only shook his head. "I have been spending more and more time in Freehold with Nightingale. We have been trying to do what we can with the tools at our disposal. At least there we can do some good; our music is heard, and the message in it."

"You are preaching to the choir," Harperus reminded him. "No one goes into Freehold that is not on the side of the nonhumans."

T'fyrr could not reply to that; he knew only too well that it was true. But the message he and Nightingale were placing in their music was a complicated one, and one he thought would have some effect on those who might otherwise not take a stand but would rather stand aside. He hoped, anyway. There were plenty of those, visitors to Freehold out of curiosity, or those who only came occasionally.

It may be that what they need is a leader, and one has not stepped forward thus far. I had hoped Tyladen would be that leader, but I fear he is a weak branch to land that eyas on. Harperus would, but he is not physically able. Which leaves—us. I could do with a better prospect.

"I must go," he said finally. "I'll probably be staying there tonight again. It's safer than flying back, even after dark. I'll tell Nob to come here and help you, as usual."

At least Nob would be safer with Harperus than alone in T'fyrr's suite, especially now that Harperus had raided his traveling-wagon for more protective devices. Tyladen had actually ventured out of Freehold to fetch the mechanisms and to set them up in Harperus' room—while Old Owl was well enough in mind and spirit after his ordeal, he needed someone to look after him. So Nob could be useful *and* protected by staying with the Deliambren. Right now, T'fyrr would be much happier if he were working alone—but since that was impossible, better to get those who were not flying the attack under cover of the trees.

"Thank you," Harperus said with real gratitude. "The boy is an endless help. I'm thinking of checking where he came from and offering to purchase his services if he hasn't any parents about. We can use young humans like him in the Fortress-City."

"What, in your—ah, what did you call it? The 'exchange program'?" T'fyrr asked, getting up from his stool. "He'd be good there; he has an open mind, and a clever one, and I have to keep restraining him from taking apart your devices to see how they work."

Harperus held up a hand just as T'fyrr began to walk toward the door. "Wait a moment, please. You and Nightingale—" he began.

What? Is he going to try to interfere there now? I think not!

T'fyrr shook his head and began an annoyed retort, but Harperus waved his hand before he could begin to form it.

"No, no, I don't mean to tell you to leave her alone—dear Stars, that's the last thing I'd want for either of you!" T'fyrr relaxed a little at that, and Harperus continued, with an expression of concern on his face. "I just want to know if—if you are weathering these stresses as a couple. I want to know that the two of you are still together and not being torn apart by the situation."

"Better than we would alone," T'fyrr said softly. "Much, much better than we would alone. She is the one unreservedly good thing that has happened to me since I came here. I tell her so, at least twice a day."

Harperus smiled, his odd eyes warming with the smile. "Good. Good. I feel rather paternal about both of you, you know. I have known her for most of her life—and if it were not for me, you would not be in the Twenty Kingdoms at all." He hesitated a moment, as if deciding whether or not to say something, then continued. "I want you to know that whatever I can do for both of you, I will. You have both been involved in situations you would never have had to deal with if it were not for me. I am very, very pleased that the two of you have found happiness in each other."

T'fyrr looked down on the Deliambren, sensing nothing there but sincerity. "I think I knew that," he said finally. "But thank you anyway." He shook himself, rousing all his feathers, and bits of fluff and feather sheath flew through the air. "Now I *must* go. Nightingale is waiting, and we have work in the city, even if I have none here."

Harperus nodded, and T'fyrr took himself out, via Harperus' balcony. It was safer that way; he no longer trusted even the corridors and hallways of the Palace.

He no longer made a target of himself by flying low over the city; he gained altitude while he was still over the Palace grounds, taking himself quickly out of the range of conventional weaponry. He would drop down out of the sky in a stoop, once he was directly over Freehold, landing on the roof, though never twice in exactly the same place. He hoped that this made him less of a target for projectiles from the other roofs, although a skilled hunter could probably track him in and hit him—

He tried not to think about that. He was no longer the only target in this city. He had not wanted to worry Harperus further by giving him details of the troubles in Lyonarie, but it was no longer safe for most nonhumans to walk alone in certain districts even by day—and by night, they must not only go in large groups, but they must go armed with such weapons as the laws permitted them. Some of them had gotten immensely clever with weighted clubs, tough leather jackets, and things that could legitimately be considered their "tools."

They were harassed and attacked by pairs and large gangs of bravos armed with clubs. There had been no deaths—yet—but at least a hundred males, two dozen females, and a handful of children of various nonhuman races had wound up with broken bones or concussions. That was not even detailing the beatings that left only bruises, or simple harassment or vandalism.

Nor was Harperus' attacker the only escapee from justice in the King's gaols; even when attackers and vandals were identified and brought to justice, they very next day they would no longer be in the gaol. Some were released "by accident," some released when other parties posted bonds, and some simply slipped away.

There were ugly rumors in the streets, making even ordinary folk look angry whenever nonhumans were mentioned. One of the rumors claimed that the Manufactory Guild planned to release all the human workers and import nonhumans, since they were not subject to the laws of the Church. As miserable as working conditions were inside those buildings, apparently having any job was better than being out of work, and the folk who filled those mills and tended the machinery were looking blackly at any nonhuman who crossed their paths.

Other rumors were wilder, less believable, yet some people believed them: that the nonhumans had a new religion that required each new initiate to sacrifice a human child and eat it; that they were spreading diseases deliberately among the humans to weaken or kill them, softening up Lyonarie for future conquest; that the Deliambrens were going to bring in a huge, invulnerable, flying ship and from it lay waste to the Twenty Kingdoms, turning each of the kingdoms over to a specific nonhuman race and making the humans into slaves.

As if we'd want humans as slaves. They'd make poor slaves; not as strong as a Mintak, not as versatile as a Jrrad, not as obedient as a Fenboi. They are too self-determined, strong-willed and clever to be slaves. The spirit that makes them poor slaves is what makes them good friends.

T'fyrr reached the top of his arc, turned, and plunged downward again, his goal a tiny speck among the rest of the rooftops below him. Wind rushed past his face, tore at his feathers, thundered in his ears; he brought the nictating membranes over his eyes to protect them. At this speed, striking a gnat or a speck of dust could bring much pain and temporary blindness.

That last rumor was interesting, since it had just enough truth to supply a seed for the falsehood. The Deliambrens *were* bringing in a huge flying ship; the platform from which they were doing their intensive survey. It wasn't armed, couldn't be armed, in fact, nor was it invulnerable. It leaked air like a sieve, and couldn't go much higher than treetop level. But it did exist, and to the ignorant, it must look frightening enough. It was certainly larger than most villages and many small towns, and the vast array of nonhumans swarming over it might be taken for an army. The strange surveying instruments often looked like weapons, and the engines that bore it up in the air did sometimes flatten things below. That was one of the reasons for getting the High King's blanket permission to mount the expedition; to keep people from panicking at the sight of it, thinking it was a military operation.

As for turning humans into nonhuman slaves, now *that* was a clever twisting of the truth, since that was precisely what some of the humans were trying to do to the nonhumans in their midst.

The Law of Degree would do that very nicely.

The rooftop of Freehold rushed up toward him, filling his vision; he flared his wings at the last possible moment, and the air wrenched them open as if they'd been grabbed by a giant and pulled apart. He flipped forward in midair, extending his legs toward the rooftop as he flared his tail as an additional brake. His feet touched the surface; he collapsed his wings and dropped down into a protective cruoch, glaring all around him for possible enemies.

As usual, there weren't any. As usual, he was not willing to take the chance that there might be some.

Neither was Nightingale. She slipped out of the shelter of one of the cowlings covering some of Freehold's enormous machines, but stayed within reach of other such machinery as she joined him.

But for one transcendent moment, all caution and fear was cast aside as they embraced.

As always.

Ah, my bright love, my singing bird, my winged heart— She could not hear the endearments he whispered to her in his mind, but he knew she certainly felt the emotion that came with them. Whatever happened, they had this between them—a joy he had never expected to find. If tomorrow a hunter's arrow found him, he would go to the winds with a prayer of thanks for having had this much.

"Anything new?" he asked into the sweet darkness of her hair.

"More of the same," she replied into his breast feathers. "I'll tell you inside."

They sprinted for the door of the roof, hand in hand, but ducking to remain out of the line of sight of possible snipers. Once they were safely on the staircase, she sighed and gave him the news.

"Outright sabotage, this time," she said. "Three incidents, all uncovered this morning. Someone burned down a Lashan-owned bakery; the printing presses at Kalian Bindery were smashed, the page proofs and manuscripts there were burned, and the type cases overturned all over the floor. And the furnaces at the new Ursi glassworks were—just blown up. They say that no more than two bricks out of every five will be salvageable."

"How?" T'fyrr asked astonished. "That doesn't sound like anything a human could do!"

She shrugged. "Tyladen has some theory about pouring water into the furnaces while they were hot; I don't know. But do you see a pattern there?"

He nodded; living at the Palace as he was, he would be the first to see it. "The glassworks was in the process of making a special telescope for Theovere as a presentation piece on behalf of the Deliambren expedition. Kalian Bindery was putting together a library of nonhuman songs in translation—as a presentation piece for Theovere. And the bakery makes those honey-spice cakes he likes so much, that his own cooks at the Palace can't seem to duplicate."

"All three, places with projects on behalf of Theovere or meant to impress him and gain his favor," she agreed as they wound their way down the stairs toward the ground floor, his talons clicking on the stair steps. "And only someone at court would now that, just as you have been saying."

He ground his beak, thinking. "The man Harperus identified escaped last night as well. And everyone who has escaped has done so from the *High King's* city prisons. Not the Church prisons, or the city gaols."

She turned to look at him with her eyes wide. "Why—that's right! The few criminals we *have* managed to hold onto were all in the city gaols!"

"That argues for more than an informant," he said, his eyes narrowing with concentration. "That argues for cooperation, at the very least, from an official. Probably a high official. Likely an Advisor."

She didn't groan, but he sensed her spirits plummeting. "How can we possibly counteract someone with that much power?" she asked in a small voice. He felt her fear; she was not used to opposition at so high a level. She had always been the one to run when opposition grew too intense. He understood that, and in the past it had made sense for her to do that. She was a Gypsy; she could go anywhere, so why remain someplace where an authority wanted to make trouble for her?

But she could not do that now—and more importantly, neither could all the nonhuman citizens, not only of Lyonarie, but of the Twenty Kingdoms.

If they were going to do what he had decided *must* be done—to give the nonhumans here the leader they so urgently, desperately, needed—he had to put some heart in her.

He stopped, seized her by the shoulders, and looked deeply into her eyes. "Think, Nightingale! Think of how much damage has been done in the past few days—as if our enemy was desperately trying to do as much damage as he can before he is caught or rendered ineffective! I think he *is* desperate, that although Theovere may be wrapped up in his new toy, the novelty of it can't last forever. Sooner or later he will grow tired of the same songs, played the same way, and look for us again. What is more, I think the magic we set in motion is still working, and Theovere is coming back to himself, whether or not he *likes* the fact. And I think our enemy knows that, too. I believe he *is* at the end of his resources, and he's hoping to overwhelm us now, before Theovere recovers."

"She," Nightingale said. "Our enemy may be a female. Remember the lace handkerchiefs left in cells, the woman who seduced the guard? A woman's been seen in other places as well, just before things happened."

"She, then. He or she, or they, it doesn't matter much. There may be two, working in collusion—whoever it is, I sense the desperation of a hunter-turned-hunted." He waited for Nightingale's reaction; it was slow in coming, but gradually the fear within her ebbed, and she nodded.

"Now, let's get down to the street, collect Tyladen's friends, and go about our business," T'fyrr continued, after first embracing her. "Father Ruthvere is waiting for us. It is time for us to act, instead of waiting for something to happen to us and reacting to that."

"What are you thinking of?" she asked sharply.

"We need to provide these people with more than a message," he told her slowly, thinking things out as he spoke. "We need to give them something more than words. Tyladen won't do it, and Harperus can't."

"You're saying they need a leader," she said, and to his relief she did not seem as upset at that as he had feared she would be. "I had a feeling you were finally going to decide that—and I was afraid you would decide it should be us." She shivered a little, then shook herself. "I'm also afraid that you're right. If no one has come forward yet, no one is going to. It will have to be us, or no one."

She looked up into his eyes, standing quite still; making no secret of the fact that she was afraid, but also making it very clear that she was with him.

He embraced her impulsively. "Great power—" he reminded her.

"Yes, is great responsibility." She sighed. "I think I would prefer being a simple musician—but on the other hand, this may be the payback for all those times I charmed my way out of trouble." She leaned into his breast feathers for a moment, then pushed herself gently away. "Well, if we are going to do it, let's get it over with."

He smiled, and took her hand. "Leadership, once assumed, cannot always be released. Are you willing to accept that as well, lover?

Nightingale nodded again, eyes suddenly clear of worry. "As readily as I accepted you into my heart and soul."

Three days later, T'fyrr stood in a most unfamiliar place—the pulpit of Father Ruthvere's Chapel—and surveyed the closely packed faces below him. There was no room to stand in the Chapel; people were crowded in right to the doors. Roughly half of those faces were not human, but it was the human faces among the rest that gave him hope that this might work.

He cleared his throat, and the quiet murmur of voices below him ceased. Behind him, Nightingale sent a wordless wave of encouragement to him, which held him in an embrace that did not need arms or wings. They were going to try something different today: Bardic magic without a melody, a spell of courage and hope, meant to reinforce his message and give them the strength to take advantage of the leadership he promised them. With luck, it would work.

With none, we will fall flat on our faces.

"I asked Father Ruthvere to call some of you here on my behalf," he said slowly, allowing his eyes to travel over the entire group assembled below. "Some of you are friends or patrons of Freehold. Some are simply merchants and workers; all of you are people of good will and open minds. I ask you all to open your minds a little further, for I have a message that may shock you. There is an enemy of *all* of us, human and nonhuman, working in this city, and he is working to enslave us."

He waited for a moment for them to take that in, then continued. "Our enemy is skilled, cunning and devious; our enemy's weapons are clever. The chief of them is fear. He spreads rumors to increase that fear and divide us, each rumor carefully calculated to prey upon the things that we all fear most."

He looked directly into the eyes of a clutch of human manufactory workers. "Fear of poverty," he said to them. "Fear of failure. Fear of a future full of uncertainty." And he knew that he had struck home when he saw their eyes widen.

He turned toward a group of families, human and not, who lived near the Chapel. "The terrible fears that all parents of whatever race have for their children." This bolt too struck the heart, as the hands of fathers tightened on their children's shoulders—mothers' arms closed protectively around their babies.

He swept his gaze over them all. "These fears divide us, each from the other," he told them. "They make us fear each other and keep us from talking to each other. Let me tell you who are human what rumors have been circulating among *our* homes and workplaces."

He told them about the Law of Degree, about the other rumors flying wildly among the nonhuman communities. He added some he had heard elsewhere—how a demon-worshiping *human* sect had sprung up, whose initiates must murder and eat a *nonhuman* child, and how the humans were planning to descend on the homes and workplaces of nonhumans on a particular night to burn and pillage them, killing adults and making children into pets and slaves. He added the rumors of drugs in the water supply that would kill or incapacitate nonhumans but were harmless to humans, and the stories that there were those within the Church who planned to declare all nonhumans to be demons or descended of demons.

He saw by the startled looks among the humans that they had heard nothing of these tales—and as he and Nightingale wove their web of courage and clarity, he saw that they were all beginning to *think*, comparing the rumors and finding them suspiciously similar.

"Do you see what is happening?" he asked them. "Can you see the hand of *one* source behind all of this? How could these tales be so similar, and yet so cleverly tailored to match our darkest nightmares? And how else could someone keep all of us from even speaking to one another, except by making us fear one another?" Then he challenged them. "Can you think *why* someone would do this? What would he have to gain? Ask yourself that—for there is gain to be had here, in making us fear each other, in keeping us hiding in the darkness of our homes and listening only to rumors and wild tales."

He chose his next words with care. "For all that I am strange to you who are human, I am a student of your history. I have seen this pattern

repeated before—in your history, and in our own, for we are not as
different from you as you may think. *We* have had our tyrants, our exploiters,
and our would-be dictators. Here is what I have seen, over and over again.
When people are divided against one another, there is *always* a third party
standing ready to profit when both sides have preyed so much upon each
other that they cannot withstand the third. Sometimes it is another land,
another people, but I do not think that is the case here." He took a deep
breath, and made the plunge. "I think that the third party here is a single
person; a person who would see both humans and nonhumans enslaved to
his purposes. First he drives fear enough into the humans that they grant
him the power he needs to make slaves of the nonhumans. *Then* he turns
that power upon those who gave it to him, and enslaves everyone."

There were a few nods out there; only a few, but that much was
encouraging. The rest would need time to think about what he was saying.

"Ponder this, if you will," he finished. "How soon would it be before
something like a Law of Degree was applied, not only to those who do
not look human, but to those who do not meet some other standard?
When have any of you ever seen a law that took away the freedom of
one group used *only* against that group? How about if our unknown
enemy convinced you all that it should be applied to the indigent—street
trash, beggars, and the like? It sounds reasonable, does it not? And who
would really choose to have beggars and slackards sleeping in doorways,
if they could be out doing useful work—and at least, as slaves, they would
not be drinking, robbing, causing trouble in the street. But how if, after
a delay of time to make it comfortable, it was then applied to those who—
say—do not own property? After all, if you do not own your home, are
you not indigent? What if it were applied to those who did not have a
business, were not in a Guild, or happened not to have a job at a particular
moment? After all, if you have lost your job, are you not indigent?"

Startled looks all around the room showed him that he had not only
caught their attention, he had brought up something they had never in
their wildest dreams thought of. Very probably the majority of the humans
here only rented their tiny living-quarters from someone else—and every
manufactory worker lived in fear of losing his job.

"Before you dismiss these truths as fantasy, remember that every one
of you who has been robbed, cheated or raped—or knows someone who
has, human or nonhuman—knows that there are those in our world who
are capable of such evils. Remember that it is *fear* that makes all this
possible," he concluded. "Fear which keeps us from organizing, from
questioning to find out the truth, which keeps us divided, human from
nonhuman, men from women, those who are prosperous from those who
are not. Remember that, go and think and talk and ask questions; and
then, if you will, come back to Father Ruthvere. He is a man of caring
and courage, and he has tasks that need doing to make certain that this
enemy does *not* take all our freedom away from us."

He stepped down from the pulpit then, in an aura of stunned silence,
and Father Ruthvere stepped back up into it.

Then the talk broke out, an avalanche of words, as those of the Chapel and those who were not cast questions up to Father Ruthvere, and he answered them as best he could.

His best was fairly accurate, since he, Nightingale and T'fyrr had been talking about this for the past three days, gathering all the information they could and putting this little meeting together. They had decided that Father Ruthvere, and not T'fyrr, should be the putative leader of this group; he was human and would be trusted by the humans—he was a man of the Church, and presumably honorable and above reproach. Not that the real leader would not be T'fyrr—

Or rather, the real target. I am the obvious target, leaving Father Ruthvere to do his work.

Fortunately, the Father *was* honorable and above reproach, and he was trained to be a leader of his flock. He had the skills T'fyrr did not; T'fyrr had the skills of rhetoric that he did not.

Perhaps, rather than the leader, I should style myself as a figurehead. Or perhaps an organizer? Oh, no, I believe I like Nightingale's term better: "rabble-rouser."

But standing behind the pulpit and filling the choir loft was another group that T'fyrr and Nightingale turned to face—as many of Father Ruthvere's fellow Churchmen as could be gathered together here at such short notice. T'fyrr had not had a chance to look them over before he stepped up to make his speech, but now he saw that among the gray, black, and brown robes, there were two men dressed in the red robes of Justiciars, two men and a woman in the deeper burgundy of Justiciar Mages, and one iron-faced individual in the white and purple robes of a Bishop.

His hackles rose for just a moment at that—but a heartbeat later, he smoothed them down. While the face of this man might be implacable, his eyes were warm and full of approval. He had heard T'fyrr out, and he seemed to like what he heard.

He knows the truth when he hears it. He is hard and cannot be shaken, but he is no fanatic. He knows reason; he does not let fear blind him. And he is no one's tool or fool.

It was this man who approached them first, while Nightingale swallowed and groped for T'fyrr's hand. He clasped it, reassuringly. The Bishop's eyes flickered down to their joined hands as the motion caught his attention, then they returned to T'fyrr's face with no less warmth in them than before.

And he sees nothing wrong with a human and one who is not being together. That alone shows more of an open mind than I had dared to hope for.

"You are a remarkable speaker, musician," the old man said in a surprisingly powerful and musical voice. "Your command of rhetoric is astounding."

T'fyrr bowed a little, acknowledging the compliment. "It is not just rhetoric, my Lord Bishop," he said in reply. "Every word I spoke was the truth, all of it information gathered not only across this city, but across the Twenty Kingdoms."

"That is what makes it astounding," the Bishop said with a hint of a smile. "Rhetoric and the truth seldom walk side-by-side, much less hand-in-hand. And that was what I wished to ask you, for some of those rumors I had not heard in this city. So the poison spreads elsewhere?"

T'fyrr nodded, and the Bishop pursed his lips thoughtfully. "That seems to match some things that I have observed within the Church," he mused. "And—I believe I agree with you and your friends. There is a force moving to destroy our freedoms, a secular force, but one with fingers into all aspects of life, including the Church. Would you not agree, Ardis?" he called over his shoulder.

The woman in the robes of the Justiciar Mages stepped forward, regarding T'fyrr with eyes that were remarkably like that of a Haspur—clear, direct and uncompromising. "I would agree, my Lord Bishop," she said in a challenging voice as remarkable as the Bishop's. "That, in fact, was why I was visiting my friend Ruthvere. His letters indicated to me that there were some of the same elements moving in Lyonarie as had been at work in Kingsford just before the fire that destroyed our city. I wanted to see if that was the case and do something to prevent a similar tragedy if I could."

A thread of excitement traced it way down T'fyrr's back, but it did not come from him but from Nightingale. She knew something about this woman—something important. He would have to ask her later—

But then the woman turned her eyes toward Nightingale and said, in a tone as gentle as her voice had been challenging before, "Please tell my good cousin Talaysen that I miss his company—and far more than his company, his wisdom and his gentle wit, and if his King can spare him for a month or two, I have need of both in Kingsford. It need not be soon, but it should be within a year or so."

Nightingale bowed her head in deepest respect—something T'fyrr had never seen her do before to anyone. "I shall, my Lady Priest," she replied. "I believe that I can send him word that will reach him before the month is out. I will tell him to direct his reply to you with all speed."

The Justiciar Mage smiled. "I had thought as much," she said, and turned back to the Bishop. "My noble lord, are you satisfied now that Ruthvere and I told you nothing less than the truth?"

"More than satisfied—I am in fact convinced that there is more amiss than even you guessed." He extended his hand to T'fyrr, who took it—a little confused, since he was not certain if he was supposed to shake it or bow over it. The Bishop solved his quandary by simply clasping it firmly, with no sign that the alien feel of the talon disturbed him. "Sire T'fyrr, I thank you for your courage and your integrity—and your dedication. Rest assured that there are enough men and women of God in the Church to take the reins of the situation there and bring it under control. I wish that I could promise you help in the secular world as well, but I fear it will be all our forces can muster to cleanse our own house. At least you need not look for attack on one front."

He let go of T'fyrr's hand then, and turned toward the rest of the Priests. "My brothers and sisters—it is now our task to go and do just that. Let us be off."

With that, he strode through the group, which parted before him and formed up behind him, and led the way to the Priest's door at the rear of the choir loft. They were remarkably well organized and regimented; within moments they were all gone, with no milling about or confusion.

He glanced over at Nightingale. "What was that business with the woman all about?" he asked.

Nightingale shivered, but not from any sense of fear, more of a sense of awe, a reaction he had not expected a Priest to invoke in her.

"Lady Ardis is Master Wren's cousin," she said quietly. "Talaysen trusts her more than anyone else in the world, I think. I knew she was a Priest, but I *didn't* know she was a Justiciar Mage! They may be the strongest mages in the Twenty Kingdoms—and I know that they are the best schooled. Could you hear the power in her?"

Now that he thought about it, there *had* been a deep and resonant melody about her, though not of the kind he associated with Bardic Magic. Not precisely droning—more like the kind of chant that he recalled from Nightingale's healing magic. But stronger, richer, with multiple voices. He nodded.

"I've never heard anyone like that," Nightingale continued. "Never! With power like that, she doesn't *need* rank; in fact, high rank would only get in her way." Exultation crept into her voice. "And she's on *our* side! Oh, T'fyrr, this is the best thing that could have happened to us!"

Father Ruthvere turned his head toward them for a moment. "Between Ardis and the Lord Bishop, we do not need to worry about the Church aiding our enemy, I think," he said, his voice sounding more relaxed and confident than in the past several days. "As the Bishop said, this means one less front to guard; it means that I have leave to do whatever I can to help you, including offering you the sanctuary of the Church if you need it."

"And it means one less ally for our enemy," T'fyrr added. But Father Ruthvere was not finished.

"I do have another concern that Lady Ardis' presence reminded me of. There is one other thing I believe you have not made accounting for," he said, and worry entered his voice again. "Magic. Our enemy has not been able to silence you by direct attack, or by indirect. That leaves magic. Ardis and her companions cannot stay for they will be needed in Kingsford, and there are no Justiciar Mages in Lyonarie who can devote themselves to your protection."

Magic! That *was* one thing he had not counted on! He had witnessed so little magic in his life, and most of it was of the subtler sort, the kind that Nightingale used. "But what can they do?" he asked, puzzled. "Surely anything magical can be countered."

But Nightingale's hand had tightened on his own spasmodically. "They can do quite a bit, T'fyrr," she said hesitantly, "if they have a powerful enough mage. I have seen real magic, the kind that the Deliambrens do not believe exists. If I told you some of what I have witnessed, you would not believe it either. I think perhaps I had better call in someone I had not intended to ask favors of—"

He shrugged, unconvinced. "If you will," he said. "You know more about this than I do. But in the meantime, I will not be stopped. We have momentum now, and we must keep it going! Any hesitation at this moment will bring everything to a standstill!"

Father Ruthvere nodded agreement, and turned his attention back to the assembled group below. The crowd had thinned somewhat, but those remaining were the leaders of their own little coteries. And all of them, human and nonhuman, seemed inspired to work together.

"We need to get back to Freehold," T'fyrr said in an aside to Nightingale, as the bells in the tower overhead chimed the hour. "We still have the meeting there this afternoon. *That* will be as much your meeting as mine."

She knew the folk of Freehold, the customers, the staff. She knew them the way he never could, for she had been reading their feelings for the past several weeks. He might be able to make a fine speech to rouse those who were unaware of what was going on around them, but for those of Freehold who knew only too well the rumors circulating, the harassment, and the sabotage, it would take another skill to rouse their courage and show them that they must work together—that they literally *dared* not stand aside at this moment.

She squeezed his hand. "I think Father Ruthvere has this end well in hand," she agreed. "Let's go."

Perhaps T'fyrr didn't realize it, but Nightingale knew only too well how much of a target he had made himself *He* was the obvious focal point of this new organization; *he* was the King's Personal Musician, the one who came and went from the Palace, who presumably had the King's ear at least part of the time. On his own, he had no more power or wealth than any of the denizens of the neighborhoods around Freehold, but *they* didn't know that. The folk of the streets saw only that here was a powerful courtier, a Sire, no less, who was urging them to stand up for their freedom and their rights against the nobles, the fearful or uneducated, and this unknown enemy.

And Ruthvere had been absolutely right. Their enemy had tried every other way to eliminate T'fyrr's influence, and that had been *before* he went on his campaign to organize the nonhumans and their human supporters and friends. Now he was not only an influence, he was a danger. He reminded them all that the Twenty Kings, the Court, and the High King himself ruled only as long as the people permitted it.

Those were frightening words to someone whose ultimate goal was surely more power.

If there was one thing that the powerful feared, it was that those they sought to rule discovered that ultimately the real power lay only in their own acquiescence to be ruled.

Lions can only be convinced that they are sheep as long as no one holds up a mirror to show them their true faces.

All attempts to silence T'fyrr, open and covert had failed. But their foe had not yet tried magic. If ever there was a time when he—

Or she, Nightingale reminded herself, yet again.

—or she, would use magic, it was now.

They had a little time before the Freehold meeting, and Nightingale used it.

T'fyrr was in the bathroom, and he was a most enthusiastic bather. He would be in there for some time, giving her a space all to herself.

She settled herself cross-legged on her bed as T'fyrr splashed water all over her bathroom, and laid her right wrist in her lap. The thin band of Elven silver gleamed beneath the lights of her room, a circlet of starlight or moonlight made solid.

She had been given a gift, she had thought; could it be that it was not a gift after all, but a promise? The Elves had a flexible view of time; sometimes their vision slipped ahead of human vision—seeing not what *would be*, but all of the possibilities of what *might* be. And sometimes, when one was markedly better than the rest, they would move to see that it came to pass.

No one with ambition for ruling all the Twenty could afford to let the Elves live in peace, she thought soberly. *They are too random an element: unpredictable and unreliable, and most of all, ungovernable. Whoever this person is, he cannot allow the Elves to remain within human borders. So perhaps that is why the second bracelet came to me.*

She laid her left hand over the warm circle of silver and closed her eyes. As she held her mind in stillness, listening, she caught the distant melody of Elven Magic, so utterly unlike any other music except that of the Gypsies.

She added her own to it, brought it in, and strengthened it. It must carry her message for her, and it had a long, long way to travel.

She sang to it, deep within her mind, weaving her words into the melody, to be read by every Elf that encountered it. The more that knew, the better.

First, her Name, which was more than just a name; it was the signature of her own power, her history, and her place among her Elven allies. *Bird of song, and bird of night,* she sang, *Healing Hands and Eyeless Sight. Bird of passage, Elven friend, walks the road without an end. Pass the wall that has no door, sail the sea that has no shore—*

No one but the Elves would know what three-fourths of that meant; it was all in riddles and allusions, and if there was anything that the Elves loved, it was the indirect. There was more of it, and she sang it all. One did not scant on ceremony with the Elves, especially not with *their* High King. He might have been her lover, once—but that had been a long time ago, before he became their High King. It had been nothing more than a moment's recreation for him, and scarcely more for her. He had been the ease after Raven—a physical release. She had been—amusement. Later she became more than that, once he learned of her power and heard her play; *that* was what had made her an Elven friend, not the idyll amid the pillows of his most private bower.

But that was part of her history with them, and she could not leave it out without insulting him.

When she came to the end of her Name, she began the message; first, a condensation of everything she had learned here, beginning with the fact that it was the Elves who had asked her to come here in the first place.

And lastly, her request, a simple one. It was couched in complicated rhyme, but the essence was not at all complicated. *I may need you and your magic, and if I do, my need will be a desperate one. You know me, you know that I would not ask this frivolously; if I call, will you come?*

She had not expected an answer immediately. She had no idea, after all, how far this message would have to travel, or how many times it would be debated in the Elven councils before a reply was vouchsafed her.

She had most definitely not expected a *simple* answer. She had never gotten a simple answer more than a handful of times in all the years she had known them.

So when she sent the message out, and sat for a moment with her mind empty and her hand still clasping her bracelet, it was not with any expectation of something more than a moment of respite before T'fyrr emerged from his bath.

But she got far more than she had reckoned on.

The spell of music and message she had sent out had been a delicate, braided band of silver and shadow. The reply caught her unawares and wrapped her in a rushing wind, spun her around in a dizzying spiral of steel-strong starlight, surrounded her with bared blades of ice and moonbeams, and sang serenely into her heart in a voice of trumpets and the pounding sea.

And all of it, a simple, single word.

YES.

When T'fyrr emerged from the bathroom, he found her still shaking with reaction and the certainty that if their reply had been so ready and so simple, there must be a reason. So she sat, and trembled, and she could not even tell him why. She could only smile and tell him it was nothing to worry about.

She moved through the day holding onto each moment, savoring every scrap of time with him—but trying her best to act as if nothing had changed between them. He knew there was something wrong, of course, but she was able to convince him that it was only her own fears getting the best of her. She told him that she would be all right; and she bound herself up in the rags of her courage and went on with all their plans.

But when the blow came, as she had known it would, it still came as a shock.

He had spent the night at the Palace, hoping for a summons from the High King, but not really expecting one. She was expecting him in mid-morning, as always; she sensed his wild surge of delight as he took to the air, and went to the roof to await his arrival.

She shaded her eyes with her hand and peered upwards into the blue and cloudless sky, even though she knew she would never see him up there. It would take the eyes of an eagle to pick out the tiny dot up there; if she'd had a hawk on her wrist, it *might* have looked up and hunched down on her fist, feathers slicked down in fear, all its instincts telling it that a huge eagle flew up there. Nothing less than a hawk's keen senses would find T'fyrr in the hot blue sky, until the moment he flattened out his dive into a landing.

But she always looked, anyway.

She was looking up when the blow struck her heart, and she collapsed onto the baked surface of the roof, breath caught in her throat, mouth opened in a soundless cry of anguish.

It was pain, the mingling of a hundred fears, a wash of dizziness and a wave of darkness. She could not breathe—could not see—

She blacked out for a moment, but fought herself free of the tangling shroud of unconsciousness, and dragged herself back to reality with the sure knowledge that her worst nightmare had come to pass.

They had taken T'fyrr, snatched him out of the sky by magic.

And there was nothing that anyone could have done to prevent it, for the sky was the one place where they had thought he was safe.

T'fyrr was gone.

"You're sure?" Tyladen said for the tenth time. She bit her lip, and said nothing. She'd already told him everything there was to say, at least three times over.

But Harperus, who had a listening device of his own, growled at both of them from his room in the Palace, his voice coming through a box on Tyladen's desk. "Of course she is sure, you fool! Didn't I just tell you he left here an hour ago? He went straight from my balcony—and he was going directly to Freehold! If Nightingale says he was kidnapped, then you can take it as fact!"

"B-but magic—" Tyladen stuttered. "How can you kidnap someone with something that doesn't—"

"These people believe that what we do is magic, child," Harperus interrupted. "If you must, assume it's a different technology; for all we know, that's exactly what it is! Just accept it and have done! Nightingale, what can we do, if anything?"

She had thought this out as best she could, given that her stomach was in knots, her throat sore from the sobs she would not give way to, and her heart ready to burst with grief and fear. "I don't know yet," she said honestly. "I'm not certain how you can combat magic. I have to do something myself—I was promised help from the Elves, and I'm going to get that help when I am through talking to you. I think that I can find T'fyrr myself, or at least find the general area where he's being held. After that—I may need some of your devices, if there are any that could find exactly where he is in a limited area." She had some vague notion there were devices that could probably do that, some Deliambren equivalent of a bloodhound, but that those devices probably had a limited range. They couldn't scour the whole city for her, but if she could give them a small area, they might be able to narrow down the search to a specific building. "I do need someone to watch the High King and the Advisors around him. Father Ruthvere will provide sanctuary if we are being hunted from the Palace, or by someone connected with the Palace, but I need to be warned if someone comes up with a charge against us. If you can think of anything—"

"I will take care of it," Harperus promised. "Now—you go do what you can."

"I will—" Then her voice did break on a sob as she told him the one thing she did know. "Old Owl, wherever he is, he's hurt. He's hurt badly. I don't know how badly, but all I can feel from him is pain—"

Harperus swore in his own language, a snarl of pure rage. She had never heard him so angry in her life.

"Go—" he urged. "This youngster and I will work together."

She rubbed at her burning eyes with the back of her hand, got up from her seat, pushed open the office door half-blinded with tears, and fled up the stairs to her room. She had not yet called in her promise from the Elves, and she needed to prepare the room before she could do that.

The Elves did not care for the human cities and did not like to walk among the artificial buildings, but it seemed that for her sake, they would put their dislikes aside. She put the bed up into the wall, and pushed all the furniture out of the way. She put her harps in the bathroom. She swept every vestige of dust and dirt from the floor so that it was as white and shiny as the day the surface was laid. Only then did she lay ready the circle with a thin trickle of blue sand on the white floor, inscribing a pattern that the Elven mage she had been pledged service from would be able to use as a target.

Then she stood outside the circle, clasped her hand around her bracelet, and let her heart cry out a wordless wail of anguish and a plea for help.

The air in her room vibrated with a single, deep tone, like the groaning of the earth in an earthquake; the floor sang a harmonic note to the air, the walls a second, the ceiling a third, the whole room humming with a four-part chord of dreadful power.

Then the blue sand exploded upward in a puff of displaced air.

She did not recognize the Elven mage who stood where the circle had been, blinking slowly at her with his amber eyes slitted against the light. His hair was as amber as his eyes; his clothing of deep black silk, a simple tunic and trews without ornamentation or embroidery of any kind. By that, she knew he was more powerful than any Elven mage she had ever yet met; only a mage of great power would be confident enough to do without the trappings of power.

"Tell me, Bird of Night," he said as calmly as if he had not appeared out of thin air in her room, so alien to his kind; as serenely as if he had not heard the tears of her heart calling. "Tell me what you need of me."

She told him in the same words that she had told Tyladen and Harperus, and it did not get any easier to bear for the retelling. He nodded and waited for her to answer his second question.

"From you, my lord, I need protection," she said. "Protection from the spells of human mages, for myself, and for the one who once wore this—"

She handed the Elf a feather, shed only yesterday from T'fyrr's wing. He took it and smoothed it between his fingers.

"A mage-musician, with wings in truth," he said, as his eyes took on the appearance of one who is gazing into the far distance. "But he is in a place that is dark to me; I cannot find him."

"I can find him," she said promptly. "But I cannot protect myself from the magics that stole him, nor can I protect him from the spells of our enemy, once I find him."

"I can," the Elven mage replied, with a lifted brow. "There is no mortal born who can set a spell that can break my protections, if those protections are set with consent."

She nodded, understanding his meaning. With consent, the mage was not limited to his own power in setting a protection; he could draw upon the strength of the spirit of the one he protected as well.

"You have mine," she promised him instantly, "and you will have his, once I reach him."

"Then I will be away," the mage replied, and as she widened her eyes in alarm, he smiled thinly. "Fear not, I do not desert you, nor do I travel far, but I must go to a place more congenial to my kind. Your walls and metals interfere with my working. I have his feather, you have your Silver. That will be enough. When you need the protections, clasp your hand about the band of Silver, and call me." He regarded her with an unwinking gaze, and then added, "I am Fioreth."

She bowed slightly, acknowledging the fact that he had given her part of his Name, enough to call him with. It was a tremendous act of trust on the part of an Elf. He bowed in return, then the room hummed a four-fold chord of power once more, and he was gone.

Now there was only one thing left to do.

Find him.

The pain in her heart had a direction: north, and a little east. She needed to follow that—"

Someone pounded at her door, and before she could answer it, the door flew open.

"Lady!" gasped one of the younger serving boys, panting with the effort of running up four flights of stairs. "Lady, there are guards at the door, and they want *you!* They say they have a warrant—"

"What colors are they wearing?" she asked instantly.

The boy blinked at her for a moment, obviously thinking that she was crazy. "Green and blue, but—"

"Then they *aren't* the High King's men; they're someone's private guards," she replied. "They can't have a warrant; they probably just have a piece of paper to wave, counting on the rest of us not to know it has to be signed and sealed. Since I'm T'fyrr's Second, they would *have* to have a warrant signed by Theovere directly, and he would have sent his own bodyguards. Tell Tyladen to demand the warrant and if it isn't signed and sealed with Theovere's seal, it isn't valid. That should delay them. And tell him to tell Harperus!"

Before the boy's scandalized eyes, she stripped off her skirts. "Give me your breeches!" she ordered.

"What?" he gasped.

"Your breeches! I can't climb in skirts! *Now!*" She put enough of the power in her order that he obeyed her, blushing to the roots of his hair, and she pulled his breeches on, leaving him to look frantically for something to cover himself with.

Which is ridiculous; he's wearing more now than some of the male dancers wear on stage.

"Go!" she snapped at him, running for the stairs to the roof. "Tell Tyladen what I just told you!"

She didn't wait to see how he solved his embarrassing quandary; time was not on her side.

The King can't know about this; that means that this arrest is on a trumped-up charge at worst. That means I won't have to dodge every guard in the city, only the ones in blue-and-green livery.

They would probably bully their way inside, and might even get as far as her room before Tyladen called in enough help to throw them out again.

And I left my harps!

But T'fyrr was worth all the harps in the world. The Elves could make her a new pair of harps; all the universe could not make her a new T'fyrr.

She scampered across the roof in a bent-over crouch, in case someone was watching from one of the other rooftops. When she got to the edge, she scanned the area for a lookout.

There was one, but he wasn't very good; she spotted him before he saw her, and commotion down on the street caught his attention long enough for her to get over the side away from him and down onto one of the walkways. She paused just long enough to coil up her hair and knot it on top of her head—then, from a distance, she was just a gangly boy, not a woman at all.

She stood up and shoved her hands in her pockets, and strolled in a leisurely manner along the walkway until she got to the building across the street. No shouts followed her, and she did not sense any eyes on her for more than a disinterested few heartbeats.

She took care not to seem to be in any hurry; she even stopped once to look down with interest at the milling knot of guards at the side door of Freehold. One or two of them looked up, then ignored her.

Then she reached the haven of the next building and threw her leg over the side of the roof there, climbing up onto it, rather than going down to street level. Just as if she had been sent on an errand over to Freehold and was returning.

When she was reasonably certain that no one was watching her, she sprinted across to the other side of the roof. There was another walkway down the side of the building there, and this one went all the way to the ground if you knew how to release the catch on the last staircase.

All Freeholders, of course, did.

She careened down the metal staircase, knocking painfully into the handrails and slipping on the steps in her hurry. She tumbled down to the drop-steps, hit the catch, and let her weight take the steps down into the noisome alley below.

Then, at last, she was in the street, and it would take a better tracker than a noble's guard to find her.

CHAPTER TEN

I had not known it was possible to hurt so much. T'fyrr had always thought that when you were injured, you lost track of the lesser pains in the face of the greater. *Evidently, I was mistaken,* he thought, far back in the fog of pain and background fear. Odd how it was possible to think rationally in the midst of the most irrational circumstances. Probably that ironic little mental voice would go right on commenting up until the moment he died, since it seemed more likely that he would die of his many wounds rather than maddening hunger.

So T'fyrr cataloged every pain, every injury, working inch by inch over his abused flesh in his mind. He had to; it was the only way he could keep himself sane. As long as he had something to concentrate on in the face of darkness, fear and the absolute certainty that not only did he not know where he was, no one else did either, he could stay marginally sane.

Whoever had plucked him out of the sky at the height of his climb had known exactly what they were doing. They were ready for him the moment he tumbled, sick and disoriented, onto the floor of the room they had brought him to. He had not been able to raise so much as a single talon in his own defense.

Magic. They caught me in a magic net and dragged me down to their hiding place. And to think I was laughing in my heart at Nightingale's "irrational" fear. Magic could do nothing to me, of course. It has no power over the physical world. I wonder if I will get a chance to apologize to her?

Before he could move, four burly men had swarmed over him, trussing him up like a dinner-fowl. But they had more surprises in store for him.

They hooded me. They hooded me like an unruly falcon! The hood *had* to have been made to order, as well; there were no hunting birds out there with heads as large as T'fyrr's. Maybe they were willing to kidnap him by magic, but they weren't counting on magic to keep him docile.

And someone, somewhere, made them a hood to fit a Haspur. Not them, I think. They do not strike me as the sort to be falconers, or they would know that hooding a raptor does not make him deaf or unconscious. So someone, somewhere, probably in this city, made them a hood. That someone will know who they are. If I can get free. If I can pursue justice against them. . . .

Then to add insult to injury, they had put some sort of contraption over his beak that kept him from opening or closing it completely. *A bit*, he thought, *combined with a muzzle.* It was somewhat difficult to be sure, since they had put it on him after they hooded him.

Padrik's people only starved and beat me. At least they didn't torture me like this. . . .

They had already pulled all of his primaries; the feather sockets ached any time he moved his wings. They were working on the secondaries. They'd clipped his talons until blood flowed in order to collect that as well. This in addition to bruises and aching bones.

Correction. They weren't exactly *torturing* him, technically, since that wasn't their intention.

Whoever they are.

In fact, he wasn't supposed to be alive at all. The mages hired to steal him from the sky had been ordered to kill him on the spot. They'd had a little argument about it while he lay there bound and hooded and helpless. One of them had been in favor of carrying out their orders as stated, but the rest had overruled him.

Thank the winds for temptation, and those unable to resist it.

He had heard them talking, every word; they might have been under the impression that he couldn't understand them, rather than thinking he was like a falcon and would "go to sleep" when deprived of light. It seemed he was very useful to these mages, and a source of much profit. *My blood and feathers—and the talon bits too, I suppose—are valuable, but only when taken from a living creature; and therefore I am more valuable alive than dead. I doubt their employer knows of this little trade on the side.*

Why bits of *him* should be useful to a mage, he had no notion—but then again, this situation was frighteningly similar to a rumor circulating about human mages who were capturing nonhumans and "sacrificing" them. What if there *were* human mages who were capturing nonhumans, but using bits of them for magic? The idea would have made him sick, if he'd had the leisure to be sick.

Do they do this to their own kind, I wonder? Or is this reserved for "lower creatures"? They were so indifferent to the amount of pain and damage they inflicted as they collected their trophies that he could well imagine they were not above kidnapping fellow humans and treating them the same way.

Which might account for the rumors of nonhumans who captured *humans* and sacrificed them . . . and would certainly account for the expertise with which he'd been trussed up.

Why was it that humans were inclined to spawn both the best "saints" and the worst villains among their numbers? Was it just that humans were inclined to the extreme?

His mind was wandering, ignoring his urgent need to find a way out of his bindings and escape, and meandering down philosophical paths that had nothing to do with what he wanted to think about.

How long have I been here? He wasn't certain. They never took off the hood, and although they hadn't been feeding him, he had "heard" the music of magic near him several times, as if they were nourishing him that way instead of by conventional means. He wasn't thirsty or hungry, at any rate, which was different from his captivity at the hands of Padrik's men.

But closed inside the hood, with his body racked with pain, there was no way of telling how much time had passed. It could have been hours . . . or days.

There was an escape open to him; a realm of illusion and hallucination that would at least take him out of his pain and current fear. All he had to do would be to give in to the beckoning, grinning specter of madness, as he had when the Church had held him, and—

I will not go mad. I will not lose heart.

Nightingale was out there, somewhere; he sensed her, a tugging in his soul that actually had a physical direction. She was as racked with grief for his loss as he was with pain, but she had not given up to despair. Yet. He could not tell what she was doing, but he knew that much at least.

She is trying to find me, trying to find a way to free me. I must believe that. She has those damned Deliambrens to help her, and maybe more help than that. She must come; she will *come.* But it was hard to hold on to hope when his strength drained away steadily.

I have made some difference in the world, he told himself defiantly. *I have redeemed myself—and I have had love. Even if I die—*

No, that was the way of despair! He shied away from the thought with violence. *I will not die!* he shouted against the darkness. *I will not! I will fight every step of the way, with everything at my command!*

Which at the moment was not a great deal. . . .

Voices, muffled by a wall, grew nearer. They were coming again. He waited, wild with rage at his own helplessness, as a door opened and two men entered, still talking.

"— probably another week or so," one was saying. "I don't know how these creatures replace blood loss, but we're draining him fairly quickly."

He felt hands fumbling at his restraints. This time they didn't seem to have brought any of their bravos with them. Could he—?

He tried to lash out at them as they freed his arms, tried to leap to his feet. *If I can injure one, the other will run off and I can hold the injured one and make him take off the hood—*

Visions of escape flashed across his mind.

He flung out his taloned hands with a strength only slightly less than that of an unfledged eyas; he got as far as his knees before he threw himself off balance and tumbled in an ungainly sprawl across some hard surface.

The men both laughed, as he sought for a reservoir of strength and found it empty. "I see what you mean," said the other. "Still—we can't keep him around for too long, or our client is going to hear about the new artifacts in the market and is going to wonder where all those vials of blood and feathers are coming from."

"He gave us permission to take what we would—" the first man argued.

"But you don't get fresh blood from a week-old corpse," the other reminded him.

Artifacts, T'fyrr thought miserably, as the two men threw him on his stomach, pinned his wing and arms effortlessly, and plucked another handful of secondary feathers. *I am nothing to them but an object, to be used at their pleasure. They harvest me as if I were a berry patch.*

Each feather, as if was pulled, invoked a stab of exquisite pain; he squawked involuntarily as his tormenters extracted them. Finally they left him alone.

They were only after feathers this time, not blood. Just as well, every talon ached where they had cut each one to the quick to collect blood. *Now I know how human victims must feel; why they deem having nails pulled out to be such a torment.* If he got free, he would not be able to walk comfortably for weeks. *And I will not fly for months until the feathers grow again.*

"Shall we truss it back up again?" the first man asked when they finally left him alone for a moment, and he decided that they were done with him for the nonce. "We'll be gone all evening, with no one here to watch him."

The second one prodded him with a toe, and all T'fyrr could do was groan. "I don't think so," he said. "He isn't going anywhere. All those bindings were breaking feathers anyway; we need to get as many prefect feathers from him as we can. Only the perfect feathers are any good, magically. Now that makes me wonder, though—we need to do some research and see if the down and body feathers could be used for anything."

The sounds of their feet receded. "Considering what we're getting for feathers and blood, can you imagine what the heart and bones will be worth?" the first one said, greed and awe in his voice. "Not to mention the skull and the talons?"

"We will be able to purchase mansions and titles, at the very least," the second chuckled over the sound of a door opening. "And as many—"

The door closed, cutting off the end of the sentence.

The heart. The skull. His people did not have much in the way of ceremony to mark one's passing, but the idea that he would be parceled out in bits to the highest bidder made him so sick to his stomach that he started to gag.

And that was when the despair he had been holding off finally swooped down on him and took him.

I am going to die here, alone, in the dark, half-mad and utterly forgotten! Nightingale will never find me; I will never see her again—

He couldn't sit up, he was too weak and dizzy; he could only curl into a shivering ball and clutch his legs to his chest, shaking with despair. No one would ever find him. There was no rescue at hand. Probably no one had even bothered to make the attempt.

No one cared.

No! I can feel her out there; I know she hasn't forgotten me! If no one else tries, she will! She will come to me by herself if she must!

But it was hopeless. How could one woman, however resourceful, find him hidden away in this hive of a city? How could anyone find him, even with all the resources of the King? Lyonarie was too big, too impersonal, for anyone to search successfully.

Even clever Nightingale. There were too many places even she could not go.

He could not weep, but his beak gaped as much as the muzzle would permit, and he keened his despair into the uncaring darkness.

Oh, I would rather that Tyladen were doing this.

The moon shone down on rooftops encrusted with ornamental false towers and crenellations, on chimney pots shaped like toadstools, flowers, trees, tiny castles—anything *but* a chimney-pot. Nightingale crouched in the lee of a chimney, bracing herself on the slanted slate roof, and took Harperus' device off her belt, holding it before her like a hand-crossbow. She braced herself a little more, then cupped her hand around it to shield it, as she would have shielded a lantern, and felt for the little raised bump near where her thumb fell.

Magical guards above and physical guards below. If this was *not* where T'fyrr was being held, then there was something very peculiar going on in the old mansion upon whose roof she now perched, less like the bird she was named for than a chimney swift.

A square area lit up inside her shielding hand, giving off a dim, red light. It represented a square space, twenty feet on a side, with herself in the middle.

The little bright dot that was supposed to represent T'fyrr was just a little to the left of center—a dot that had *not* appeared on this "screen" the other times she had used the device.

She smiled tightly; he *was* here. Getting him out—well, she would save the rejoicing for the moment that happened. She pressed the thumb-point again, and a set of numbers appeared.

Roughly fifteen feet below her; that would put him in the top floor, just below the attics. That made sense; they were probably thinking of him as a big bird. They wouldn't want to put him in a basement where he might catch a chill and die of shock. In these town mansions, unlike those in the country, the master and mistress had their private rooms at the top of the house, where you might get a breath of a breeze in the summer, and where all the heat rose in the winter. In a town mansion like this, the rooms at street level, next to the kitchens, were ovens themselves in the summer, and in winter, no amount of fuel kept them warm.

Her heart had led her here; it had once been a wealthy district, with huge homes showcasing the wealth of their owners. Now the area was shabby-genteel at best, and whoever lived here was usually out of favor, the tag-end of a once-prosperous family now running out of money, or the last of a long line dying out. As the homes were lost to their original owners, they were bought by other, less "genteel" folk. She knew of at least three brothels here, and more ominously, one of the houses was rumored to belong to a dealer in illegal goods—very illegal, because someone had to die in order for those particular "goods" to come on the market.

She had hoped she had the right district when she realized that mages tended to need buildings with a great deal of space to practice their art. She *knew* she had the right district when her street-urchins traced the blood and feathers showing up on the mage-market to this very area. People really *didn't* pay any attention to what children overheard.

If we survive this, perhaps I shall set up an information service and live off the results of that.

That was when she sent Maddy to Tyladen for one of the devices she had asked for. She herself had not gone back to Freehold since the guards arrived. Freehold would be watched—but she had a secure hiding place in Father Ruthvere's steeple, and others scattered elsewhere across the city. She had money sewn into the money belt she never took off except to sleep, and then kept beneath her pillow. She could look like whatever kind of woman she chose, and she was familiar with the "bad" parts of Lyonarie. No guard or militia from the Palace could find her here if she did not want to be found.

The child returned with this, a set of closely written instructions, and the other child that Nightingale had asked her to find.

That was all she had been waiting for. She had waited until dark, then

began scaling the walls and getting onto the rooftops of every likely building in the area—with help. She was *not* a thief, and she could not have
done this alone, but she had the help of someone who was more at home
on the rooftops of Lyonarie than beneath them. It was safer to operate
this thing from above than from below. There was less chance of being
seen, for one, and she really didn't want to be caught loitering out in the
street with *this* bizarre-looking thing in her hands.

I don't believe I can claim it is a musical instrument.

Thanks to the fact that even here there was very little space between
the buildings, and to the fact that her accomplice had some quite remarkable climbing and bridging devices at his disposal, she had mostly been
able to scramble from roof to roof. That further limited her time on the
ground; a good thing, even if it was hair-raisingly risky to pick her way
across strange rooftops in the middle of the night.

She put the device away, and considered her options.

*He is in the middle of the building, probably in a closet, as far as
possible from a window. Now, how do I tell what room that closet
belongs to?*

A scrabbling of tiny hands and feet across the slates signaled the arrival
of her partner in crime and guide across these heights. "'E 'ere?" whispered Tam, the chimney-sweep, a boy about thirteen years old, but as
thin as one of his brushes and with the stature of a nine-year-old.

"Right below me, just about," she whispered back. "I'm certain they're
keeping him in a closet, but how do I tell which room it's in?"

He chuckled. "Easy, mum. By chimbleys. This 'un like drops down
inter th' room ye want." He patted it fondly, the way a driver would pat
the neck of his horse. "These big ol' 'ouses, they got fireplaces fer ever'
room. Wants I should go look?"

Before she could stop him, he had clambered nimbly up the side of
the chimney, and slid down inside it.

She waited, numb with shock, expecting at any moment to hear the
commotion from below that meant he'd been spotted and seized.

Nothing.

Then, off to the side, a faint whistle, the song of a nightingale.

She eased her way over to the edge of the roof where the whistle had
come from, and looked cautiously down.

Tam's sooty face looked up at her impudently, his teeth and the whites
of his eyes startlingly bright in the moonlight. "Empty room, lots uv
scratches on the floor. Got a locked closet 'ere, mum. Be a mort uv them
scratches there, goes to 'tother side uv door. Mebbe some blood, too."

She didn't hesitate a moment longer; she lowered herself down over
the edge of the roof, feeling for the window ledge with her feet as her
arms screamed with outraged pain. Tam caught her ankles deftly and
guided her feet to secure places; she caught hold of decorative woodwork
and eased herself down to the window itself. She wanted to fling herself
inside, but she didn't dare make that much noise—but she nearly wept
with relief when she was safe on the floor inside.

I am not a thief. I am not a hero. I am only a musician; I am not supposed *to be crawling about on rooftops! And we are leaving this place by the* stairs, *and no other way!*

The room itself was completely empty; not even a single stick of furniture, just as Tam said. The moonlight coming in the windows revealed that there were traces of painted diagrams on the wooden floor, though, and she guessed that it was sometimes used for magical ceremonies.

All the more reason to get him out of here!

She went straight to the closet door that Tam pointed to, and saw that what he had mistaken for blood was nothing of the sort. It was only spilled paint. The scratches could have come from anything—dragging a heavy piece of furniture to the closet for storage.

For a moment, her heart sank; then she heard the faint scraping of talons beyond the door, and the whimpering keen of a bird of prey, exhausted and near death.

"I'm gone, mum," Tam declared, and slipped back up the chimney. That was fine; she'd already paid him for his help, and she had told him that she didn't want him around if things began to get dangerous. Since that had suited the boy just perfectly, the bargain had been easy to strike.

It had been much harder to persuade Maddy and her little army of partisans to stay behind. The loyalty of children ran deep, and somehow she had earned it. Only promising them that they could stand guard over the Chapel when she and T'fyrr were safely inside had kept most of them from following her and Tam over the rooftops.

She turned back toward the door, expecting a complicated lock—perhaps even a mage-made lock—and stained her senses for the music that magic-touched things held within them.

Silence.

Nor was their any other sign of a lock, complicated or otherwise.

In stunned surprise, she tried the doorknob automatically.

It turned easily, and swung open without so much as a creak.

There wasn't much light, but there was enough for her to see the crumpled, feather-covered figure lying on the floor of the closet, head enveloped in a giant, scuffed hood.

A surge of grief and rage enveloped her, and she flung herself down on her knees beside him, fearing she was too late.

The head turned blindly toward her as she reached for him. "I-ale?" came a whisper, a mangled version of her name as spoken from around the cruel device they had clamped on his beak. "I—a—oo?"

"It's me; I've come to get you out of here." The fastenings on the gag and the hood weren't even complicated; she had the former off and flung into a corner. The hood followed it, and she gathered him into her arms with her throat constricted with tears. He was so weak! He had no primaries at all, and few secondaries; he wouldn't have been able to fly out of here even if he'd had the strength.

I'll worry about how to get him out of here after I get him under protection. And to do that, she needed his permission. "T'fyrr," she said urgently, "I need to put barriers against any more magical attacks on you. May I?"

He wrapped his own arms weakly around her and nodded, too spent to even ask her what in the world she thought she was doing. She reached both arms around behind his back and clasped her silver bracelet with her free hand under cover of the embrace, and concentrated hard for a moment.

With a silvery glissando, the Elven protections she wore slithered over him as well, wrapping him in a cocoon of power, identical to hers.

Now, just let the mages try something! They'd waste their time trying to crack *this* shell, and if she knew Elves, that mage would take malicious pleasure in tracking the attack to its source and—dealing—with it.

Hopefully those same mages hadn't sensed the power she'd brought here. That *was* supposed to be one of the protections, but who knew? It was Elven-work, and chancy at best, constrained only by what this particular mage felt like doing at the time.

"Can you stand?" she asked in an urgent whisper, glad that she could not clearly see all the damage that had been done to him. "We have to get our of here, before—"

"The mages—are gone," he interrupted her, breathing as hard as if he had been flying for miles at top speed. "I heard them say—they were leaving—for the night."

Well! That put another complexion on it entirely! They were as secure here as they would be anywhere, and as likely to remain undisturbed. With only the guards below—who, with the absence of their masters, would be slackening their vigilance at the least, and with luck would be getting drunk on the masters' wine—there was no one to disturb them.

"I can heal you again, T'fyrr, enough to get us both out, over the rooftops. You can still climb, can't you?"

A feeble chuckle. "Only if you can heal my talon-tips, beloved. I would not be very silent, otherwise."

"I can do that," she replied, her heart swelling. *He said it! He called me "beloved"!* There had been times in the dark of the lonely nights, waiting for word of him, that she had been certain when he came to his senses, he would be revolted by her love for him. She could have misinterpreted what he'd said about the Spirit-Brothers; he could have mistranslated. But—

But he would not use those words so casually unless—

Unless they were so real to him that he *could* use them casually, as casually as flying.

"Then let me work the magic on you, beloved," she said, with a joy so great it eclipsed fear. "And this time—*don't* try and help me!"

He only chuckled again, a mere wheeze in the darkness, and let her work her will on him.

The trip back over the rooftops had been nightmarish, but not such a nightmare as trying to get out past the guards would have been. She had been able to give him strength enough to climb, and had been able to heal the tips of his talons so that they didn't bleed every time he moved a hand or a foot, but there hadn't been enough time to do more than that. Every time she thought she heard a door slam below, or footsteps in the hall, she had been jolted out of the trance.

The return trip was easier than it might have been—she didn't have to make side trips over every roof in the district to check her device for his presence. Some of those charming, ornamental rooftops had been the purest hell to get across the first time.

Why do people pitch their roofs that steeply? Doesn't it ever occur to them that someday, someone is going to have to climb all over it, replacing slates and cleaning chimneys?

Evidently not. Perhaps that was why this district had deteriorated; the charming manses were impossible to keep in repair.

She was able to pick out a path that, while not precisely *easy* or *gentle*, at least avoided the worst of the obstacles. But it was a long time before they came to one particular abandoned house at the edge of the district and were able to slip down through the holes in the roof that had let her and her accomplice have access to the roof-highway in the first place.

They felt their way along staircases that shook and groaned alarmingly with every step they took, and down halls that must have been ankle-deep in dust by the amount they kicked up. But they reached the street level without mishap, and just inside the front door, Nightingale stooped in the darkness and felt for the bundle she had left there.

It wasn't anything anyone would be likely to steal; this neighborhood hadn't deteriorated so far that a bundle of rags was worth anything: a tattered skirt for her, to go over her black trews and black shirt, a bedraggle cloak, and an equally tattered great-cloak for him, big enough to completely envelop him. It was as threadbare as the skirt and wouldn't have done a thing to protect him from the wind or weather, but that wasn't the point.

"Here," she said, and sneezed, handing him the cloak. She pulled the skirt on over her head and wiped the roof-soot from her face and hands with the tail of it. He fumbled the cloak on after a moment of hesitation.

"Won't I look just as odd in this?" he asked as he tied the two strings that held it closed at the throat.

"Yes and no," she told him. "There are plenty of people who go cloaked at night, even in the worst heat of summer—and anyone who does is probably so dangerous that most people deliberately avoid him. Someone who doesn't want you to notice him is someone you likely don't want to notice *you*."

She picked up the second, equally tattered cloak, flinging it on and pulling up the hood. Better to broil in this thing than to have her face seen—and she could not rely on her own magic to work properly inside this Elven protection.

And two people, together, cloaked in this heat—they are twice as unlikely to be bothered.

They waited until the street was empty of traffic, and stepped out as if they belonged in the house they had just left, on the chance that someone might be looking out a window. Thieves and escaped prisoners were not supposed to stroll out like a pair of down-at-the-heels gentry.

It was a long, weary walk to the Chapel, and they had to stop often, so that T'fyrr could rest. But when they got within a few blocks of the Chapel, they were swarmed.

But not by guards looking for them, nor by the mages' men, but by Nightingale's pack of children. Tam had taken word ahead, which Nightingale had *not* expected him to do, and the children must have been waiting, watching, along every possible route to the Chapel.

A wheelbarrow appeared as if conjured; the children coaxed the Haspur into it—he had no tail and very little in the way of wing feathers to get in the way of sitting, now—and a team of a dozen rushed him along the street faster than Nightingale could run. She caught up with them at the entrance to the Chapel, her side aching, but her heart lighter than she'd had any reason to expect when she had set out a few hours ago.

Father Ruthvere was waiting for them; he opened the door to the Chapel just enough to let them inside, and shut it again quickly.

"They've been here looking for you," he told Nightingale. "They have warrants for you and T'fyrr both."

His thin face was creased with worry and exhaustion, and her heart sank. Warrants? Already? How could they have gotten legal warrants past the King?

"A warrant for *T'fyrr?*" she said incredulously. "But he's in the King's household, how could they get a warrant out on him?"

"It's part of the original warrant for the men who attacked the Deliambren," the Priest told them, his mouth twisting into a grimace as he led them into the sanctuary. "The King already signed it; they've altered it to read 'humans or nonhumans' and they're claiming that T'fyrr set up the attack in the first place—that the Deliambren Envoy recognized him, and that was why he kept asking for T'fyrr."

When T'fyrr made a growl of disgust, Nightingale only shrugged fatalistically. *It figures. I shouldn't have been so surprised.* "It doesn't have to be *logical*," she pointed out, "it only has to be legal, and since the King has already signed it and probably initialed the change, it's legal. And me?"

"You're supposed to be the mysterious female who freed the attacker the Deliambren caught." Father Ruthvere sighed and shook his head. "I haven't a clue how they're managing to get past the fact that you'd have had to be two places at the same time—"

"If they have their way, it would never get to a trial where they'd have to produce proof," she pointed out bitterly, feeling a surge of anger at High King Theovere, who had probably just signed the warrants without ever *reading* them once he was told what they were—vaguely—about. "When criminals can escape from locked dungeons or walk away legally, it doesn't take any stretch of the imagination to see that two more 'criminals' could be murdered during an 'escape attempt.' And we don't have any friends in high places or awkward relatives who might ask questions."

T'fyrr drooped despondently. "I had hoped that we had awakened Theovere to his sense of duty enough that things like this, at least, could not happen. I thought he—"

She took his arm, hoping to give him comfort. To have gone through all he had, only to be hit with more bad news, seemed grossly unfair.

"Never mind," Father Ruthvere said firmly. "You have sanctuary here, for as long as you like, and no one can pry you out of it since the Bishop is behind you. You can stay until you're stronger, or your feathers have grown back, and fly out."

"But what about Nightingale?" T'fyrr asked instantly.

She actually had an answer to that one, although she wouldn't bring it up in front of Father Ruthvere. *Well, an Elf who can appear in my room and disappear as well, can certainly manage to take me with him.* She knew how he was doing it, of course; opening up Doors into Underhill wherever he chose. It took a tremendous amount of magical power, but—

But they might do it, just to tweak the noses of the human leaders and prove that the human mages are no match for them.

"I can find a way to safety, love, trust me," she said, and patted his arm reassuringly. "I found you, didn't I?"

T'fyrr still looked stricken, and she felt his despair enveloping him like a great black net. She tried to think of something, anything, to say—and swayed with sudden exhaustion, catching herself with one hand on a pillar just before she fell.

Father Ruthvere took over, his expression mirroring his relief at having something immediate he could do. "Never mind all that now," he said soothingly. "Tomorrow everything may change. Before anything can happen, you both need to rest, recover your strength." He made shooing motions with his hands in the direction of the belltower. "Go!" he said. "The Bishop will be sending his own guards to make sure you aren't taken from sanctuary by force. You won't need to stay awake to avoid arrest. All you need to do is get your strength back."

Nightingale sighed with relief and let down her guard. Weariness came over her then, so potent it left her dizzy.

Fortunately they were *not* supposed to go up to the top of the belltower—for one thing, when the bells rang they would have risked deafness or even death up there. No, there was a well-insulated tiring room at the base of the tower that they would be living in for the next few days at the very least. It had a staircase that led directly up to the top of the tower, so that once T'fyrr grew his feathers back—a matter of two or three weeks, at a guess—he would have free access to one of the better takeoff points in this district. If he had to fly out, and he left at night, no one would ever know.

The two of them staggered into the tiring room to find that Father Ruthvere had been there before them, laying out bedding, wash water and a basin, even food. *One* set of bedding.

But by the time they reached the doorway, they were so tired that all they cared about was the bedding. They literally collapsed into it, Nightingale only a fraction of a heartbeat behind T'fyrr, and curled up together in a comforting tangle of limbs. She pulled the blankets up over them both, as much to hide the sad state of his feathers as for warmth.

He was asleep first; she listened to his regular breathing and allowed herself to weep, very quietly, with relief and joy. Not many tears, but enough that she had to wipe her face with a corner of a blanket before she was through. That released the last of her tension; she had only two thoughts before slumber caught her.

We are as surely in prison here as in the gaol. We cannot leave without being taken by our enemies. We have been caged at last.

It doesn't matter as long as we are together.

T'fyrr would never have known how long he slept if Father Ruthvere hadn't told him.

"Three days?" he said incredulously. "Three *days?*"

The Priest nodded, and T'fyrr shook his head. "I believe you, but—"

"Well, you woke up long enough to eat and—ahem," Father Ruthvere said, blushing. "But other than that, you slept. Nightingale, too," he added as an afterthought. "Though she stayed awake a bit longer than you did."

Probably healing me. That would account for how well I feel and the memories of music in my dreams.

T'fyrr sighed and roused his feathers. "Well, what has been happening? Are we still under siege?" he asked. "Or are our enemies satisfied to have us bottled up and out of the way?"

Father Ruthvere played with his prayer beads. "The latter, I suspect," he said after a moment. "You obviously cannot press charges against your captors since you are a fugitive yourself, and as for Nightingale—" He shrugged. "The nonhumans are in an uproar, but there is no one to lead them and Theovere—"

"And Theovere is near death."

They all turned as one, T'fyrr feeling the blood draining from his skin and leaving him cold everywhere there were no feathers.

Harperus stood in the door to the tiring room, face drawn and as pale as his hair, his costume little more than a pair of plain trews and an embroidered shirt. "Thank the Stars you're awake at last," he said without preamble, as both Nightingale and T'fyrr stared at him, trying to make some sort of sense out of his first statement. "Theovere was attacked and is in a coma, his physicians are baffled—" He held up his hands as T'fyrr mantled what was left of his wings in anger. "Wait, let me tell this from the beginning."

T'fyrr subsided. "Make it short, Old Owl," he rumbled. "None of your damned Deliambren meanderings!"

Harperus nodded. "Shortly, then. The marvelous music box broke down completely this morning, and no amount of fiddling by Lord Levan would get it working again. The High King sent pages looking for you, and found me instead, and *I* gave him an earful."

The Deliambren crossed his arms over his chest, his dour expression reflecting a smoldering anger beneath the stoic surface. "I told him about your vanishing, the warrants that *he* had signed, the attacks and the kidnapping. I told him that now that the warrants had been signed, by his hand, neither you nor Nightingale had any protection *or rights* under the law. He was very—stunned."

T'fyrr only growled; he had lost all patience with the once-great High King about the time his captors had pulled out his third primary.

I am not entirely certain I even want to help him now. . . .

"I told him the Church had you in sanctuary," Harperus continued, "convinced that both of you were innocent of any wrongdoing. And I *showed* him how all those things that you had been hinting at were true, all the abuses of nonhumans, all the things that had been happening to human and nonhumans alike. I guessed that he might have been so thoroughly shaken up that he might actually *listen* instead of dismissing it all."

"Well, was he?" T'fyrr asked. *It would take a miracle—*

But evidently that miracle had occurred. "Enough to issue orders immediately revoking the warrants on you two, and to take the Seneschal and a gaggle of secretaries into a corner and start drafting interkingdom edicts granting basic rights to all peoples of all species," Harperus said with a note of triumph. But his triumph faded immediately. "That was when, according to the Seneschal, that mysterious woman struck. He called for breakfast; it arrived, and with it a lace handkerchief and a message. Theovere picked it up, opened it, and read it before any of the bodyguards even thought to look at it first—and he collapsed on the spot." Harperus shook his head. "I looked at him, and I'm baffled. There's no contact poison I know of that would work that way, and he shows no other signs of poisoning other than being in a coma no one can wake him from."

T'fyrr looked aghast at Nightingale, who only nodded, her lips compressed into a thin line. "If our enemy can hire mages to pluck T'fyrr from the sky, she can certainly hire a mage to write a note-spell to try to disable or kill Theovere. There was nothing on the note when they looked at it, right?"

"Right," Harperus replied, looking at Nightingale with respect and a little awe. "But it didn't kill him—"

"It doesn't have to," she pointed out. "If he is in a coma, he could stay that way indefinitely. The Advisors can reign as joint Regents on the pretense that someday he *might* wake up. This could go on for years. Come to think of it, that's better than killing him for their purposes. If a new High King was selected, they'd all be out of their positions."

"But what can we do?" T'fyrr asked, puzzlement overlaid with despair. *Now—we have no choice. Nightingale and I may have a day or so to escape while our enemies obtain new warrants for us, but what of all the nonhumans in the Twenty Kingdoms? What is there left for them but to gather what they can, and flee?* "We are not physicians, and even if we were, surely the King's own doctors know best what is good for him."

"The King's doctors are as baffled as I am," Harperus replied. "And *I* am baffled by the message I received less than an hour ago." He raised his eyebrows and looked straight at Nightingale as if he suspected her of some duplicity. "The messenger seemed human or Deliambren, but had—unusual eyes and ears. And he spoke in riddles."

The corner of Nightingale's mouth twitched. "Go on," she said. "That sounds like an Elf to me. I happen to know there's one—ah—in the area."

In answer, Harperus handed her a piece of paper. She took it, and read it aloud for the benefit of T'fyrr and Father Ruthvere.

"'Tell the Bird of Night and the Bird of the King that the High King can be sung back from the darkness in which he wanders, if the guard-dog is released to return to his home. Half of the futures hold Theovere high, half of them hold him fallen. If the two Birds should sing to him as one, hearts bound, wrongs remembered but not cherished, their enemies may be confounded. No Elf, nor human mage, nor brightly-conceited artificer can command the power to accomplish this, for this is the magic of the heart and the Sight.'"

"I'm not certain I care for that 'brightly conceited,' part," Harperus muttered under his breath. Nightingale must have heard him anyway, for she treated him to an upraised eyebrow.

"Does this mean that Nightingale and I have—the ability to *sing* him out of this?" T'fyrr said incredulously. "But how?"

"It was accomplished by magic," Nightingale pointed out. "It's possible that magic can undo it. There might even be a mage somewhere inside his mind, holding him unconscious; if that's the case, Bardic Magic could reach Theovere in a way no other magic could duplicate—or block."

T'fyrr thought about that for a moment, and nodded. "I believe that I see," he said, and roused what was left of his feathers with a hearty shake before straightening up and holding his head high. "Those in a coma are said to understand what happens around them. We must go, of course—"

"Wait a moment!" Harperus objected, blocking the door. "I haven't told you the rest of it. If you flee now, you'll be outrunning warrants that won't ever have a chance to catch up with you before you cross a nonhuman border. If you stay, try, and *don't* succeed —the Advisors are spreading the rumor that Nightingale is the female assassin and in the hire of T'fyrr. They're saying as proof of this that there was no trouble until T'fyrr arrived at Court. If Theovere dies, you'll die—and if he simply remains in a coma, you'll die anyway. *Someone* has decided that you two are the obstacles that need to be removed for the Advisors to have a free hand again."

Nightingale dropped the paper at her feet. "That doesn't matter," she said steadily, and glanced over at T'fyrr.

I was wrong to discount Theovere. He can be reached; he was nearly his old self before they struck him down. We must help him, for his own sake, and for the sake of all those who are depending on us.

His heart swelled with pride and love for her. "She is right," he agreed. "It does not matter. Our enemies are counting on our cowardice. We must teach them better. And—" He hesitated for a moment, as the last of his anger with Theovere washed away. "And the High King needs us," he concluded. "If we desert him—we are no better than they. Perhaps, we are worse. We will try, for nonhumans and humans alike."

Harperus wordlessly stood aside, and the two of them walked out of the tiring room, through the Chapel and out into the street.

High King Theovere needs us, and he is the Twenty Kingdoms, for better or worse. With luck on our side—

—perhaps we can make it, "for better."

Nightingale settled at the High King's side, next to T'fyrr. The Haspur looked very odd, with patches of down-feathers showing where coverts had been taken, with his wings denuded, with reddened, visible scars and with not even a stump of tail.

No one could deny his dignity, however, a dignity that transcended such imperfections.

That dignity had gotten them past the Bodyguards to Captain, and from there to the one person T'fyrr thought might still back them: the Seneschal. The Captain and the Lord Seneschal had been skeptical of their claims to be able to reach Theovere by music—but they were also no friends of the King's Physician. The Seneschal simply didn't trust someone who was often in and out of the suites of the other Advisors. The Captain just didn't trust him, period. It was his opinion that there had been too much talk of purgings and bleedings, and not enough of things that would strengthen rather than weaken a patient.

So the Captain of the King's Bodyguard chose a time when the Advisors were all huddled together in Council, threw out the Physician and smuggled them in.

"Now what?" T'fyrr asked her as she surveyed Theovere's bed. Theovere *was* in it, somewhere in the middle, hardly visible for all the pillows and feather comforters piled atop him, and lost in the vast expanse of it. The bed itself was big enough to sleep three Gypsy families and still have room for the dogs. "Do we need to have physical contact with him?"

"I don't think so," she replied as the Captain moved a little in silent protest to that suggestion. He might not trust the Physician, but he also made no bones about the fact that his trust for them was very limited. "No, there's nothing we can do with a physical contact that we can't do without it."

She turned to the Captain, then, as something occurred to her. "You were there when he collapsed, weren't you?"

The beefy man nodded, face red with chagrin and anger at himself. "And why I didn't think—"

"You're not at fault," she interrupted gently. "There should have been no way for a note to get to the King that hadn't been checked for problems first. Unless—"

He looked sharply at her. "Unless?"

"Unless that note was put on the tray by one of the King's Advisors and had the seal of the Council on it," she said, and got the satisfaction of seeing his eyes narrow with speculation. "Now, I know if *I* were an Advisor to the High King, knowing that the King wasn't getting any younger, and suspecting that a successor might be named soon who would want his own Advisors in place . . . " She let her voice trail off and raised an eyebrow significantly.

The Captain nodded, his face as impassive as a stone wall, but his eyes bright with anger. "I take your meaning, and it's one I hadn't thought of."

Nightingale shrugged, pleased that she had planted her seed in fertile ground. But the Captain was not yet finished.

"Lady, I—" She sensed his groping for words through a fog of grief, though there was no outward sign of that grief on his features. "I served Theovere all my life. I've seen him at his best, and at his worst, and—"

He stopped and shook his head, unable to articulate his own feelings. She held her hands tightly together in her lap, holding herself tightly braced against the wash of his emotions, as strong as the tide at its full.

Now she knew why every man in the Bodyguards was so fanatically devoted to the King.

He could inspire that devotion once. Lady grant we make it possible for him to do so again.

She caught his eyes and nodded gravely, once, then turned back to the enormous bed and its quiet occupant. "If we succeed, Captain, it will be for the good of all—and if we fail, then at least we will have been able to give Theovere a parting gift of the music he loved so much."

"Nightingale," T'fyrr said suddenly, in the Gypsy tongue, "didn't you tell me that there might be a—a spirit of some kind, holding Theovere away? *Look over there.*"

He pointed with his beak rather than draw the attention of the Captain, and Nightingale stared in the direction he pointed.

There is a shadow there, where a shadow has no business being!

It hovered just above Theovere's head, but it did not *feel* like Theovere. It felt hungry, cruel, petty—

What is it? Whatever it was, she knew at that moment that they would have to deal with it before they could bring Theovere back to himself.

"I think it's occupied," T'fyrr whispered, his voice shaking a little. "I think—I think it might be tormenting Theovere."

Odd. That sounded familiar. A little like—

Like the Ghost that Rune fiddled for, that Robin and Kestrel helped to free! It had been bound to a pass by a malicious magician, and had taken out its rage on those who tried to cross the pass by night. *If you had something like that—a lesser spirit, perhaps—and bound it to your service—*

Then you might have something that you could set on a man simply by sending him a note to which it had been attached—something that could drive the soul from his body and keep it there. You *would* have something that would become more and more bitter and malicious the longer it stayed bound.

Which meant it was half in this world and half in the next; and wasn't that the definition of those with the Sight? She had it—she just hadn't used it much, not when her greater power lay with the heart rather than the soul.

And the Elven message had clearly said, "this is magic of the heart and the Sight." Elves simply didn't get any clearer than that. *Well, the first thing to do is get its attention. I haven't invoked the Sight in a long time. . . .*

She put her hands on the strings of her harp, and began to play quietly, humming the melody under her breath as she slowly sharpened her focus out of this world and into the next. She sensed T'fyrr following her lead, and wondered if he would *share* her Sight, or if he had a touch of it himself.

The room grew gray and dim, and faded away at the edges as she moved her vision into that other world where shadows were solid and restless spirits dwelled. She could still see Theovere, but now—

Now there were two of him.

One was in the bed, the other standing at the foot of the bed, an expression of fear and frustration on his face. And hovering above the Theovere in the bed was—something.

It wasn't human, not precisely. There was a certain odd cast to the face, as if the structure of the skull was subtly different from a human's. The red eyes were slanted obliquely toward the temples. The fingers were too long and there were seven of them; the limbs looked oddly jointless. It had the pointed ears of an Elf, but It wasn't an Elf, either. At the moment, It was watching Theovere, and it was enjoying his plight.

"Can you See anything?" she whispered to T'fyrr, and she described what she Saw. Out of the corner of her eye she saw him shake his head.

"Only the shadow," he replied. "I will trust you to know what to do."

I only wish I did! she thought; but they were in it now, and there was no turning back. Whatever It was, It didn't seem to be paying any attention to her or her music. It also wasn't *doing* much—except to keep Theovere from reentering his own body. Which meant—what?

That It's probably not all that powerful. That I'm not reaching It. But I'm not really trying. Think, Nightingale! What do you do when you have to reach an audience and you don't know what they want?

You try something so beautiful they can't ignore it.

She heard It speaking now, faintly; It taunted Theovere with his plight and his helplessness, playing with the symbols of his power that It conjured up into Its own hands. It didn't have the *real* crown, rod, or sword, of course—but Theovere didn't know that.

Her hands moved of themselves on the strings, plucking out the first chords of "The Waterfall," one of the most transcendently beautiful songs she knew. She didn't do it often, because she didn't have the range to do it justice.

But T'fyrr did.

She poured her heart into the harping, and he his soul into the music— and It snapped Its narrow head around, affixing them with its poppy-red eyes, as the ephemeral Objects of State vanished into the nothingness from which they had been conjured.

It said nothing, though, until after they had finished the song.

"What are you doing here?" It asked in a voice like wet glue.

She started to answer—then stopped herself just in time. To answer It *might* put herself in Its power; Its primary ability must be to drive a spirit from the body, then keep that spirit from reentering. It might be able to do that to more than one person at a time. But the Laws of Magic were that It could not do so if It did not know her; It must have been fed what It needed to take Theovere, but she was a stranger to It. It needed a connection with her to find out what tormented *her.*

So instead, she started a new song hard on the heels of "The Waterfall," and followed that one with a third, and a fourth.

I have to make It go away, and I can't do that by driving *It away. It's already here by coercion.* The longer It stayed silent, listening to her, the more she sensed those shadow-bindings, deeper into the shadow-world than It was, that kept It blocking Theovere's return. But the bindings were light ones; It could break them if It chose.

So It was here because It liked being here. It enjoyed tormenting people.

Well, so had the Skull Hill Ghost, but Rune and then Robin had tamed the thing, showing it—what?

All the good things of the human spirit! All the things that give life joy instead of pain!

And her hands moved into the melody of "Theovere and the Forty-Four," one of the songs that she and T'fyrr had used to try and wake the High King up to his former self.

It was a moving tale of courage and selflessness, all the more moving this time because the Theovere-spirit listened, too, and wept with heartbreak for what he had been and no longer was. He was in a place and a position now where he could no longer lie to himself—and very likely, that was one of the things his captor had been tormenting him with. The truth, bare and unadorned, and equally inescapable.

He has looked into the mirror and seen a fool.

She sensed T'fyrr pouring his own high courage into the song, the courage that had sustained him while captive, the courage that made him go out and try to *do* something to remedy the ills he saw around him. And while she did not think that courage was particularly her strong suit, she added her own heart, twined around his.

She saw Its eyes widen; saw the maliciousness in them fade, just a little, and moved immediately to "Good Duke Arden." The Theovere-spirit continued to weep, bent over with its face in both its ephemeral hands, and the Shadow softened a little more.

But she sensed just a hint of impatience.

Change the mood. It's getting bored.

She moved through the entire gamut of human emotions: laughter, courage, self-sacrifice, simple kindness, sorrow and loss. Always she came back to two: love, and courage. And with each song they sang, she and T'fyrr, with their spirits so closely in harmony that they might have been a single person with two voices, It softened a little more, lost some of Its malicious evil, until finally there was nothing of evil in It anymore. Just a weariness, a lack of hope that was not *quite* despair, and a vast and empty loneliness.

That was when she thought she knew something of Its nature. It was a mirror that reflected whatever was before It—or a vessel, holding whatever was poured into It. It was as changeable as a chameleon, but deep inside It did have a mind and heart of Its own, and she seemed to be touching It.

Her hands were weary, and her voice had taken on that edge of hoarseness that warned her it was about to deteriorate. And under T'fyrr's brave front, she felt bone-tiredness.

If ever we can drive this thing away—no, lead it away!—it must be now!

So she changed the tune, right in the middle of "Aerie," to one of the simplest songs she had ever learned:

"The Briars of Home."

It was the lullaby of an exile to her child, singing of all the small things she missed, all of them in her garden. The smell of certain flowers in the spring; the way that the grass looked after the rain. The taste of herbs that would not grow where she was now. The leaves falling in autumn;

the snow covering the sleeping plants in winter. The songs of birds that would not fly in her new garden. The feel of the soil beneath her hands, and the joy of seeing the first sprouting plants. And the homesickness, the bittersweet knowledge that she would never experience any of those tiny pleasures again, for all that she was happy enough in the new land. And last of all—how she would give all of the wealth she possessed in the new place for one short walk in her own garden at home.

And as the last notes fell into silence, It spoke to her for the second and last time.

"I have a garden."

And with those four words, It snapped the coercions binding It, and vanished.

But Theovere did not return to his body; instead, he stood there staring at it, empty-eyed and hollow. He looked old, terribly old; he stood with hanging hands, stooped-over and defeated.

What's wrong? Why won't he wake?

She stretched out her already thin resources to him, trying to sense what was wrong. But she had nothing left; she could not touch him, and her own spirit cried out in frustration—

T'fyrr began to sing. Softly at first, a song she did not recognize initially, until she realized that he was singing it in a translation so that Theovere would understand it. It was not from any of the Twenty Kingdoms, and she doubted that anyone here had ever heard it but herself before this moment. It was a song T'fyrr had told her had been written by and for the Spirit-Brothers.

"What is courage?" its chorus asked—and the song answered, "It is to give when hope is gone, when there is no chance that men may call you a hero, when you have tried and failed and rise to try again." It asked the same of friendship, answering that "the friend stands beside you when you are right and all others despise you for it—and corrects you when you are wrong and all others praise you for it." There was more, much more, and the more T'fyrr sang, the more the Theovere-spirit took heart. In a strange way, these definitions, intended to guide the Spirit-Brothers of the Haspur as they endeavored to help their own kind and their adopted brothers, were equally applicable to—say—a High King.

With the words, came the *feelings*. Not only the ones called up by the definitions, but the pain-filled emotions, the things that both of them had endured over the past several years at the hands of those who hated and feared anything that did not fit their own narrow definitions of "appropriate." The Theovere-spirit took those in, too, wincing more than a little as he was forced to acknowledge that this was due to his own neglect, but accepting that as well.

He is looking into the mirror again—but this time, he is seeing not only what is, but what was, and what may be again!

She simply followed the music with her harpsong, as her heart, this time, followed his.

When it was over, the Theovere-spirit stood up straight and tall, looking many years younger than his true age, his eyes bright again with light and life. A sword appeared from nowhere in his hand; he swept it, silvery and bright, and used it to salute both of them.

And then he faded away into a bright mist.

Oh—NO!

Nightingale dropped back into the outer world with a violent shock.

She stared at the bed, certain that the figure in it was no longer alive. Her eyes blurred with exhaustion, as what seemed to be a hundred people suddenly poured into the room.

She shrank away, waiting for them to seize her, seize T'fyrr, haul them both off into the gaols never to be seen again.

And Theovere slowly sat up with a firm, determined smile set on his face.

The Bodyguards shoved the interlopers rudely away from the bed, and she realized that there weren't a hundred people; there weren't even twenty. Only the Advisors, and who had told *them* what was going on? Most of them seemed to be shouting at the Captain and the Seneschal, both of whom were shouting back.

Her eyes blurred again, and she slid a little sideways, into the comforting embrace of T'fyrr. "What happened?" she asked.

"I'm not sure." He held her closely, his own arms trembling with fatigue. "You did something, and made the shadow go away, then we sang Theovere back, like the Elves said to do—he woke up and spoke, and then all the Advisors began pouring in. I'm not sure how they found out that we were doing anything here."

"It's a good thing they didn't get in until we were done," she said, a bit grimly, as Theovere gained enough strength from somewhere to outshout all of them.

"*Silence!*" he bellowed. "*Enough!*"

The babble ceased, and he glared at all of them. "We have," he said, clearly and succinctly, his eyes shining with dangerous anger, "a traitor among us. The note that held the—call it a curse—that felled me was sealed with the Council Seal."

Out of the corner of her eye, Nightingale saw the Captain of the Bodyguards go momentarily limp with relief.

But she saw something else as well.

Heading up a contingent of his own private guards and standing at the back of the room was someone who looked oddly familiar to her.

"Who is that?" she whispered to T'fyrr, under the sound of the King's furious but controlled questioning of his guards and his Advisors. "He looks familiar somehow."

He glanced in the direction she was looking. "That's Lord Atrovel," he said. "But you can't have seen him before; he never leaves the Palace, and you never encountered any of the other Advisors except the Lord Seneschal."

Just at that moment, the odd little man moved into a wash of shadow that darkened his hair. She saved herself from gaping at him only by a strong effort of will.

She *had* seen this "Lord Atrovel" before—but not here.

In *Freehold.* And "he" had been—

Violetta. That's Violetta—one of the Great Lords of State—and the biggest gossip in Freehold. Someone who was in a position to know everything that was going on in the King's Chambers, in his private correspondence and in Freehold—

And who had the knowledge and the means to sabotage all of it.

And I'll bet he wasn't leading those guards here to protect us if we failed to bring back the King!

"T'fyrr—" she whispered, clutching his hand and turning her head into his feathers to make certain her voice didn't go any further. "Put long black hair on Lord Atrovel and tell me what you get."

She knew by the tension in his muscles that he had seen the same thing that she had. "Violetta—" he whispered.

Then he stood up abruptly, and she scrambled out of his way. She had never seen him like this before—but she *had* seen a hawk about to attack an enemy.

"Violetta!" he roared.

Lord Atrovel started—but so did all the other Great Lords. But none of the others had that look of panic in their eyes—and none of the others had been making his leisurely way toward the door as the King continued to question his Advisors.

T'fyrr launched himself at Lord Atrovel in a fury, and Nightingale was only a second or so behind him. Lord Atrovel's guards scattered, but the King's Bodyguards came pouring in from the room beyond, alerted by T'fyrr's scream of anger.

T'fyrr reached the traitor first.

He seized the little man in his talons and picked him up bodily. His beak was parted in fury, his eyes dilated, and all Nightingale felt from him was a flood of red rage—

Oh, Lady no—if he kills the man—

He'll never forgive himself.

No one moved; no one *could.*

T'fyrr held the man for a moment longer, then flexed the muscles of his arms—

And gently set Lord Atrovel down, right into the "welcoming" arms of the Elite Bodyguards.

"I believe that this is the man you have been looking for," T'fyrr said, so gently that he might have been soothing a child. "He frequented Freehold under the name and disguise of 'Violetta,' and likely other places as well. I believe he owns a house in the Firemare quarter, where you will find two or three mages in his employ who held me captive and maimed me—one of them probably set the spell that nearly slew His Majesty. Hunt through his private papers, his suite, and question his servants, and you will probably find a trail of sabotage and evil as vile as the man himself. And you will likely find lace handkerchiefs that match those left by the mysterious gaol-raider. As well as a—" he coughed "—remarkable selection of female garments made in his size, which should explain the missing 'maid' who freed that first captive."

The Captain took custody of Lord Atrovel himself and fired off a burst of orders as the rest of the Lord Advisors scattered like so many frightened quail. T'fyrr ignored them all, turning back to Nightingale.

The terrible rage inside him was gone.

She went weak-kneed with relief as she saw his face, and sensed the calm that now lay within him. *He doesn't need revenge—*

"I don't need revenge," he said softly, echoing her own thoughts, taking her hands in his. "I have you, and I have love. Vengeance is a waste of valuable time."

She smiled up at him tremulously. "It is, isn't it?"

He touched her cheek with one gentle talon. "I know that you don't like cities," he said wistfully, "but—could you consider making your home in one?"

"A home is where the people you care for are," she told him, impossible joy beginning to bubble up inside her. "And if the people I care for live in a city—or the High King's Palace—then that is where my home will be. I think I will survive living in this one."

He laughed, then, and gathered her to him for a long embrace. Together, they turned and walked back to the side of High King Theovere, who watched them with a truer smile than any he had worn in Nightingale's memory.

Theovere clasped the hand of the Captain of the Elite Bodyguards, and the stalwart soldier smiled as broadly as his King, with the glint of a tear in one eye.

"Welcome back, my King," was all he said, and then he turned to face T'fyrr and Nightingale. He nodded, still smiling. And as he walked away to tend to his duties, Nightingale heard with some surprise that he was whistling a Gypsy melody, of how all was right with the world.